Anonymous

A Handy Concordance of the Septuagint

giving various readings from codices Vaticanus, Alexandrinus, Sinaiticus, and

Ephraemi, with an appendix of words from Origen's hexapla, etc.

Anonymous

A Handy Concordance of the Septuagint
giving various readings from codices Vaticanus, Alexandrinus, Sinaiticus, and Ephraemi, with an appendix of words from Origen's hexapla, etc.

ISBN/EAN: 9783337235819

Printed in Europe, USA, Canada, Australia, Japan

Cover: Foto ©Andreas Hilbeck / pixelio.de

More available books at **www.hansebooks.com**

A

HANDY CONCORDANCE

OF THE

SEPTUAGINT,

GIVING

VARIOUS READINGS FROM CODICES VATICANUS, ALEXANDRINUS, SINAITICUS, AND EPHRAEMI;

WITH AN

APPENDIX

OF WORDS, FROM ORIGEN'S HEXAPLA, ETC., NOT FOUND IN THE ABOVE MANUSCRIPTS.

Εἰς τὸν αἰῶνα, κύριε, ὁ λόγος σου διαμένει ἐν τῷ οὐρανῷ.
PSALM CXVIII. 89.

LONDON:
S. BAGSTER AND SONS (LIMITED), PATERNOSTER ROW.

INTRODUCTION.

This Concordance of the Septuagint is founded upon the Vatican text as usually printed, but gives the variations where the manuscript itself differs from the printed editions.

Various Readings from the Codices Alexandrinus, Sinaiticus, and Ephraemi are also given.

It has been judged best to base the Concordance on the above uncial manuscripts, independent of the Complutensian and other printed editions, which are really no authority as to the genuineness of a reading.

As the modern printed editions of the Septuagint are not quite uniform, and vary a great deal in marking the chapters and verses, it was necessary to follow some *one* Edition: that of Tischendorf (in two vols. 8vo. Leipsic) has been adopted. The Sixth Edition, 1880, has been used.

In some places Tischendorf gives in his margin two different figures for the same verse—one large and the other small—the large figures are invariably followed. It will be found that the small figures often point out the corresponding place in the Hebrew text, which is a very useful addition.

In a few places the chapter or verse is placed in ( ), either where Tischendorf so marked them, or where some irregularity occurs in the succession of the figures.

In some places lines are added in the text without any verse being attached: these are referred to either as *post* the verse that precedes, as 1 Kings 3 *p* 14; or *ante* the verse that follows, as Hosea 14 *a* 1. At 1 Kings 12 *p* 24 a section of some length follows, without any division into verses: here the *line* is also noted, and the reference stands thus—1 Ki. 12 *p* 24 *l* 25.

The various hands which corrected the manuscripts are for the most part noted as Tischendorf and Dr. Nestle (in his useful Appendix to Tischendorf's Edition) give them: as S^1, S^2, &c. Where corrections are given in the margin, or where the particular hand is not known, or the reading is in any other respect doubtful, they are marked with a * as S*. Where references are given as $S^{3\ \text{contra}\ 8}$, the reading of S^3 only is recorded, or the variation omitted altogether.

It has not been attempted to give the various readings where the variation is an inflexion of the same root-word; the variations recorded are restricted to words belonging to different roots.

Variations are, with a few exceptions, recorded *twice:* once under the root of the word in the text, and once under the root introduced by the variation. Where the root-word occurs more than once in the verse, by referring to *both* entries it will be seen which word is altered.

A few readings are placed in ( ) where the word is doubtful.

Of some of the unimportant words and the numerals the various readings only are recorded. Pronouns, prepositions, &c., are omitted altogether.

The records of the various readings may, in many places, be regarded as an *index* to the alterations, rather than as giving the variation in full. Thus under σφάζω stands Exodus 29 : 11 – A; but the Alexandrian manuscript omits the whole verse (the omission is recorded under all the important words in the verse). Again, under σκηνή stands Exodus 30:27+B; but there is added in the Vatican *manuscript* καὶ τὴν σκηνὴν τοῦ μαρτυρίου (words which are not found in that verse in the Vatican text as commonly *printed,* and as given by Tischendorf): other words in the same verse are also transposed. In every case reference should be made to the text, to see the extent and precise nature of the variation.

An attempt was made to give the variations of the Proper Names, but these were found to be so very numerous, and so many of the variations unimportant, that this part of the work was abandoned.

An endeavour to refer the Greek words to the corresponding words in the Hebrew original, as is done in Tromm's Concordance, was also abandoned. It would have greatly confused the work, and the correspondence would often have been untrustworthy, as phrases could not have been given in so condensed a work. Hebrew Concordances are now easily available.

An attempt however, has been made to classify the words θεός and κύριος under the various Hebrew equivalents; but the various readings are recorded only under the word in the Greek text.

Transpositions have not been recorded, even where a sentence is left out in one verse and added in another. Thus in 1 Kings 10 the lines which follow verse 22 are omitted by Codex A, but are included in verses 15–25, which it adds in chapter 9.

All reference to the Apocrypha has been omitted; principally because it was judged that the Apocryphal books should never have a place with the Holy Scriptures. There was also the fact, that Tromm had not at all fully recorded the references to the Apocrypha. If given at all, they need to be dealt with entirely afresh, as we have done with the canonical books. If the present work is found to be useful, and the apocryphal parts are thought to be needed, any one so disposed can carry out that work.

An Appendix is added of words not found in the body of the work, giving readings from Origen's Hexapla and Uncial and Cursive Manuscripts: see page 266.

There are a few items of interest that need to be noted, which could not be inserted in the body of the work. For instance, the Alexandrian and Sinaitic Manuscripts give the Song of Songs divided, with the various speakers, &c. pointed out—additions which cannot be called various readings. Thus—

CH. 1: 2 *praemittit* ἡ νύμφη AS
3 *ante* διὰ τοῦτο *add* ὁ νυμφίος A
4 *ante* εἰσήνεγκε *add* ταῖς νεανίσιν ἡ νύμφη διηγεῖται τὰ περὶ τοῦ νυμφίου ἃ ἐχαρίσατο αὐτῇ S
4 *ante* ἀγαλλιασ. *add* τῆς νύμφης διηγησαμένης ταῖς νεανίσιν· αἶδε· εἶπαν S
4 *ante* εὐθύτης *add* αἱ νεανίδες τῷ νυμφίῳ βοῶσιν τὸ ὄνομα τῆς νύμφης εὐθύτης ἠγάπησέν σε S
5 *praem.* ἡ νύμφη AS
7 *praem.* πρὸς τὸν νυμφίον χριστόν S
8 *praem.* ὁ νυμφίος πρὸς τὴν νύμφην S
10 *praem.* αἱ νεανίδες πρὸς τὴν νύμφην S
12 *ante* νάρδος *add* ὁ νυμφίος A, ἡ νύμφη πρὸς ἑαυτὴν καὶ πρὸς τὸν νυμφίον S
15 *praem.* ὁ νυμφίος πρὸς τὴν νύμφην S
16 *praem.* ἡ νύμφη A, ἡ νύμφη· πρὸς τὸν νυμφίον S

CH. 2: 1 *praem.* ὁ νυμφίος πρὸς ἑαυτόν S
2 ,, καὶ πρὸς τὴν νύμφην S
3 ,, ἡ νύμφη· πρὸς τὸν νυμφίον S
4 ,, ταῖς νεανίσιν ἡ νύμφη φησίν S
6 ,, πρὸς τὸν νυμφίον· ἡ νύμφη S
7 ,, ταῖς νεανίσιν ἡ νύμφη S
8 ,, ἀκήκοεν τοῦ νυμφίου· ἡ νύμφη S
9 *ante* ἰδού *add* ἡ νύμφη πρὸς τὰς νεανίδας σημαινουσα αὐταῖς· τὸν νυμφίον S
10 *ante* ἀνάστα *add* ὁ νυμφίος A
15 *praem.* τοῖς νεανίαις ὁ νυμφίος· τάδε S
16 ,, ἡ νύμφη τάδε S
17 *ante* ἀπόστρεψον *add* ἡ νύμφη A

CH. 3: 3 *ante* μὴ ὃν *add* ἡ νύμφη τοῖς φυλάξιν εἶπεν S
4 *ante* ἐκράτησα *add* εὑροῦσα τὸν νυμφίον εἶπεν S
5 *praem.* τὰς νεανίδας ὁρκίζει ἡ νύμφη τοῦτο δεύτερον S
6 *praem.* ὁ νυμφίος A, ὁ νυμφίος πρὸς τὴν νύμφην S

CH. 4: 16 *praem.* ἡ νύμφη A

CH. 5: 1 *praem.* ἡ νύμφη αἰτεῖται τὸν πατέρα ἵνα καταβῇ ὁ νυμφίος αὐτοῦ S
1 *ante* εἰσῆλθον *add* ὁ νυμφίος A, ὁ νυμφίος πρὸς τὴν νύμφην S
1 *ante* φάγετε *add* τοῖς πλησίον ὁ νυμφίος S
2 *ante* φωνή *add* ἡ νύμφη ἴσθετε (*sic*) τὸν νυμφίον κρούοντα ἐπὶ τὴν θύραν S
2 *ante* ἄνοιξόν *add* 'ἡ νύμφη τάδε' ὁ νυμφίος S
3 *praem.* ἡ νύμφη A, ἡ νύμφη τάδε S
9 *praem.* αἱ θυγατέρες Ἰερουσαλὴμ καὶ οἱ φύλακες τῶν τιχέων πυνθάνονται τῆς νύμφης S
10 *praem.* ἡ νύμφη σημαίνι τὸν ἀδελφιδὸν ὁποῖος ἐστίν S
17 *praem.* πυνθάνονται τῆς νύμφης αἱ θυγατέρες Ἰερουσαλὴμ που ἀπῆλθεν ὁ ἀδελφιδὸς αὐτῆς S

CH. 6: 1 *praem.* ἡ δὲ νύμφη ἀποκρίνεται S
3 *praem.* ὁ νυμφίος A, ὁ νυμφίος πρὸς τὴν νύμφην S
9 *praem.* ἡ νύμφη A, θυγατέρες καὶ βασίλισσαι εἶδον τὴν νύμφην καὶ ἐμακάρισαν αὐτήν S
10 *praem.* ὁ νυμφίος πρὸς τὴν νύμφην S
10 *ante* ἐκεῖ *add* ἡ νύμφη τάδε πρὸς τον νυμφιον S
12 *praem.* ὁ νυμφίος πρὸς τὴν νύμφην S

CH. 7: 1 *praem.* ταῖς βασιλίσσαις καὶ ταῖς θυγατεράσιν ὁ νυμφίος τάδε S
9 *ante* πορευόμενος *add* ἡ νύμφη S

CH. 8: 5 *praem.* αἱ θυγατέρες καὶ αἱ βασίλισσαι καὶ οἱ τοῦ νυμφιου εἶπαν S
5 *ante* ὑπὸ μῆλον *add* ὁ νυμφίος A, ὁ νυμφίος τάδε πρὸς τὴν νύμφην S
10 *praem.* ἡ νύμφη παρρησιάζετε S

The above words added in the Codex Sinaiticus are all in red ink.

The following portions are wanting in the Alexandrian manuscript (A), and are *not* recorded as omissions under the respective words.

Genesis 14 : 14 to 17, perished.	Leviticus 6 : 19 to 23, omitted.
15 : 1 to 6, "	1 Samuel 12 : 17 to 14 : 9, wanting.
16 to 19, "	1 Kings 3 : post 46, omitted.
16 : 6 to 10, "	Psalm 69 : 19 to 79 : 10, wanting.

In some places, the Alexandrian Codex inserts verses which are omitted in the Vatican. These are marked thus, 1 Samuel 17 : 12 A.

The Vatican manuscript commences at πόλιν εἰς γῆν, Genesis 46 : 28 ; is wanting in Psalms 105 : 26 to 137 : 6 ; and omits—

1 Samuel 17 12 to 31.	1 Kings 11 : 23 to 25.
55 to 18 : 5.	14 : 1 to 20.
18 : 9 to 11 ; 17 to 19.	Nehemiah 12 : 14 to 21.
1 Kings 9 : 15 to 25.	

The Codex Sinaiticus, including the part formerly called Codex Frederico-Augustianus (S), contains the following portions of the Old Testament—

Genesis 23 : 19 to 24 : 46.	Proverbs.
Numbers 5 : 27 to 7 : 20.	Ecclesiastes.
1 Chronicles 9 : 27 to 19 : 17.	Canticles.
Ezra 9 : 9 to end.	Isaiah.
Nehemiah.	Jeremiah.
Esther.	Lamentations to 2 : 20.
Job.	The Minor Prophets except Hosea, Amos, and Micah.
Psalms.	

The Codex Ephraemi (C) contains the following, but with many parts imperfect—

Job 2 : 12 to 4 : 12 ; 5 : 27 to 7 : 7 ; 10 : 9 to 12 : 2 ; 13 : 18 to 18 : 9 ; 19 : 27 to 22 : 14 ; 24 : 7 to 30 : 1 ; 31 : 6 to 35 : 16 ; 37 : 5 to 38 : 17 ; 40 : 20 to 42 : 17.	Proverbs 18 : 11 to 19 : 26 ; 22 : 17 to 23 : 25 ; 24 : 23 to 56 ; 26 : 23 to 28 : 2 ; 29 : 30, 31.
Proverbs 1 : 1 to 2 : 8 ; 15 : 29 to 17 : 1 ;	Ecclesiastes 1 : 1 to 14 ; 2 : 18 to 12 : 24.
	Canticles 1 : 1 to 3 : 9.

A notice of any errors that may be discovered will be gladly received through the publisher, to be corrected should a second edition be called for.

It is hoped that all details have been sufficiently explained. The reader is again reminded that he must distinguish between the Vatican Codex as *printed* (on which the Concordance is based), and the *Manuscript* of the Codex, which, where it differs from the text as commonly printed, is marked herein as B.

Many thanks are given to those friends who have aided by their counsel and in other ways.

That the work, notwithstanding its condensed character, may, under Divine blessing, be useful in the study of the Holy Scriptures, is the hope of the compiler, and to God be all the praise and the glory.

G. M.

1887.

VARIATIONS IN THE ORDER OF THE CHAPTERS AND VERSES.

JEREMIAH.

SEPTUAGINT.		HEBREW AND ENGLISH.
Ch. 25 : 13 to 18	...	Ch. 49 : 34 to 39
26	...	46
27	...	50
28	...	51
29 : 1 to 7	...	47 : 1 to 7
8 to 23	...	49 : 7 to 22
30 : 1 to 5	...	49 : 1 to 5
6 to 11	...	28 to 33
12 to 16	...	23 to 27
31	...	48
32 : 1 to 24	...	25 : 15 to 38
33	...	26
34 : 1 to 21	...	27 : 2 to 22
35	...	28
36	...	29
37	...	30

SEPTUAGINT.		HEBREW AND ENGLISH.
Ch. 38	...	Ch. 31
39	...	32
40	...	33
41	...	34
42	...	35
43	...	36
44	...	37
45	...	38
46	...	39
47	...	40
48	...	41
49	...	42
50	...	43
51 : 1 to 30		44
31 to 35		45

THE PSALMS.

SEPTUAGINT.		HEBREW AND ENGLISH.
Ch. 9 : 1 to 21	..	Ch. 9
22 to 39	...	10 : 1 to 18
10	...	11
and so to		
146		147 : 1 to 11
147 : 1 to 9		147 : 12 to 20

A Alexandrian Manuscript.
B Vatican ,,
C Ephraem ,,
S Sinaitic ,,
+ An addition.
— or - An omission.
a ante, before.

p post, after.
l line.
ter, qtr, qnq, sex, sep. Three, four, five, six, or seven times in the same verse.
( ) Doubtful readings or errors.

CONCORDANCE TO THE SEPTUAGINT.

ἆ ἆ.

Jud. 6:22
Jud. 11:35[a]

[a] A οἴμμοι.

ἀβασίλευτος.

Proverbs 24:62

ἄβατος.

Lev. 16:22
Job 38:27
Psa. 62: 2
106:40
Jer. 2: 6
6: 8
12:10
28:43
29:14, 18
Jer. 30: 2, 11
31: 9
32: 4, 24
33:18[a]
39:43
41:22 A[b]
49:18[c]
51: 6, 22
Amos 5:24

[a] A ὀπωροφυλάκιον
[b] pro ἔρημος. [c] S[1] Αἴγυπτος.

ἀβατόω.

Jeremiah 29:21

ἀβιρά.

Nehemiah 1: 1

ἀβοήθητος.

Psalm 87: 5

ἀβουλία.

Pro. 11: 6 A[a]
Pro. 14:17

[a] pro ἀπώλεια.

ἄβρα.

Gen. 24:61
Exo. 2: 5, 5
Est. 2: 9
4: 4, 16

ἀβροχία.

Jer. 14: 1
Jer. 17: 8

ἄβρωτος.

Proverbs 24:23

ἄβυσσος.

Gen. 1: 2
7:11
8: 2
Deu. 8: 7
33:13
Job 28:14
36:16
38:16
41:22, 23
23
Psa. 32: 7
35: 7
41: 8, 8
70:20
21—S
76:17
Psa. 77:15
103: 6
105: 9
106, 26
134: 6
148: 7
Pro. 3:20
8:24
Isa. 44:27
51:10
63:13
Eze. 26:19
31: 4, 15
Amos 7: 4
Jon. 2: 6
Hab. 3:10

ἀγαθοποιέω.

Nu. 10:32
Jud. 17:13 A[a]
Zeph. 1:12

[a] pro ἀγαθύνω.

ἀγαθός.

Gen. 24:10
45:18, 20
23
50:20
Exo. 3: 8
18: 9
20:12
Nu. 10:32
Nu. 14: 7, 23
32:11
Deu. 1:25, 35
39
3:25, 25
4:22
6:11, 18
8: 1+A
7, 10
9: 4, 6
11:17
26:11
28:11, 12,
47
30: 9, 15
31:20, 21
Jos. 23:13, 15
Jud. 8:32+A
35[a]
9: 2[b]
11
10:15[c]
11:25—A
25—A
15: 2[d]
17: 6 A[e]
18: 9, 19[b]
19:24
Ruth 2:22
3:13
4.15
1 Sa. 1: 8, 23
2:24, 24
26
3:18
8:14, 16
9: 2, 2,
10
11:10
12:23
14:36, 40
15: 9, 9
22, 28
16:12, 12
16, 18
23
19: 4, 4
20:12
24: 5, 18
19, 20
20—A
25: 3, 3[f], 8
15, 21
30, 36
26:16
27: 1
29: 6, 6, 9
10
2 Sa. 2: 6
3:36+A
7:28
10:12
13:22
14:17, 32
15: 3, 26
16:12
17: 7, 14
14
18: 3, 27
27
19:27, 35
37, 38
24:22
1 Ki. 1:42
2:32
(3)38
42+A
3: 9
8:36, 56
1 Ki. 8:66, 66
10: 7
12: 7
14:15 A
20: 2
2 Ki. 2:19
3:19, 19
25, 25
5:12
8: 9
10: 3, 5
15: 3 A[e]
20: 3, 13
19
25:28
1 Ch. 4:40
13: 2
16:34
17:26
19:13
21:23
28: 8
29:19
2 Ch. 5:13
6:27, 41
7: 3, 10
10
10: 7, 7
12:12
18: 7, 12
12, 17
19: 3, 11
21:13
30:18, 22
Ezr. 3:11
5:17
7: 9, 28
8:18, 22
27
9:12, 12
Neh. 2: 5
5+S[3]
7, 8
16, 18
18
5: 9, 19
9:13, 20
25
36 ABS
Est. 5: 8+S[3]
7: 3+S[3]
9+S[3]
8: 5+S[3]
9:19
19+ABS
21, 22-S
22—A
Job 2:10
7: 7
17:15
20:20+A
21—A
21:13, 16
25
22:18, 21
30: 4, 26
36:11
42: 8+A
Psa. 4: 7
15: 2—B
24:13
26:13
33:11, 13
15
34:12 A[g]
35: 5
36:27
37:21
38: 3
Psa. 44: 2
52: 2, 4[h]
53: 8
64: 5
72: 1, 28
83:12
85:17
91: 2
102: 5
106: 9
108: 5
110:10
117: 1, 2, 3
4—AS
8, 9, 29
118:71, 72
122
121: 9—S[1]
124: 4
127: 5
134: 3
135: 1[i]
142:10[k]
146: 1
Pro. 1: 7
2: 9, 20
4: 2
5: 2
6:11, 12
8:21
9:10
11:10, 17
23, 27
27
12:14, 25
13: 2
12—S[j]
13, 15
15, 21
22
14:14, 19
22, 22
33
15: 3, 15
16: 1, 5
13 C[m]
17, 20
29
17: 1, 13
20
18:22 *ter*
19: 7, 8
22: 1, 21[n]
24: 7, 13
40+ACS[2]
41[o], 49
58
25:22, 25
28:10, 21
29:30
Ecc. 2: 1, 3
24, 24
26, 26
3:12, 12
Ecc. 3:13, 22
4: 3, 6, 9
9, 13
5: 4, 17
6: 3, 9
7:1, 2, 2, 3
3, 4, 6, 9
9, 11, 12
15[p], 19
21, 27
8:12, 13
15
9: 2, 2, 4
7, 16, 18
11: 6, 7
12:14
Cant. 1: 2
7: 9
Isa. 1:19
7:15
16
16—S[1]
39: 8
52: 7
55: 2, 2, 3
58:14
63: 7
Jer. 2: 7
5:25
6:16
8:15
10: 5
14:11, 19
15:11
17: 6
18:10, 20
20
21:10
24: 5, 6, 6
27:12
36:32
38:12, 14
39:39, 42
40: 9, 9
46:16
47: 5
49: 6
Lam. 3:17, 25
26, 27
37
4: 1
Eze. 34:14, 14
36:31
Dan. 1:15
Hos. 3: 5
8: 3
10: 1
14: 2
Amos 9: 4
Mic. 1:12
7: 3
Zec. 1:17
8:19
9:17

[a] A ἀγαθωσύνη. [b] A βελτίων.
[c] A ἀρίσκω. [d] A κρείσσων.
[e] pro εὐθὴς [f] A καλυς.
[g] pro καλός. [h] S[1] χρηστότης.
[i] AS[1] χρηστός. [k] ABS ἅγιος.
[j] A κακός. [m] pro ὀρθός.
[n] A ἀληθής.
[o] ACS[2] σοφός. [p] S[1] ἀγαθωσύνη.

ἀγαθόω.

1 Sa. 25:31, 31
Jer. 39:41
Jer. 51:27[a]

[a] A ἀγαθύνω.

ἀγαθύνω.

Jud. 16:25
17:13[a]
18:20
19: 6, 9, 22
Ruth 3: 7, 10
1 Sa. 2:32+A
2 Sa. 13:28
1 Ki. 1:47
2 Ki. 9:30
10:30
Ezra 7:18
Neh. 2: 5, 6
Psa. 35: 4
48:19
50:20
124: 4
Ecc. 7: 4
11: 9
Jer. 51:27 A[b]
Dan. 6:23

[a] A ἀγαθοποιέω. [b] pro ἀγαθόω.

ἀγαθῶς.

1 Sa. 20: 7
2 Ki. 11:18

ἀγαθωσύνη.

Jud. 8:35 A[a]
9:16—A
2 Ch. 24:16
Neh. 9:25, 35
13:31
Psa. 37:21 S[2 b]
51: 5
Ecc. 4: 8
5:10, 17
6: 3, 6
7:15
15 S[1 a]
9:18

[a] pro ἀγαθός. [b] pro δικαιοσύνη.

ἀγαλλίαμα.

Est. (9)16+S[3]
Psa. 31: 7
47: 3
118:111
Pr. 11:10+ABS[2]
Isa. 16:10
Isa. 22:13
35:10
51: 3, 11
11+A
60:15
61:11
65:18, 18

ἀγαλλίασις.

Job 8:21 A[a]
Psa. 29: 6
41: 5
44: 8, 16
46: 2
50:10, 14
62: 6
64:13
Psa. 99: 2
104:43
106:22
117:15
125: 2, 5, 6
131: 9+A
16
Isa. 51:11+S

[a] pro ἐξομολόγησις.

ἀγαλλιάω.

2 Sa. 1:20
1 Ch. 16:31
Psa. 2:11
5:12
9: 3, 15
12: 5, 6
13: 7
15: 9
18: 6
19: 6, 8 S[1 a]
20: 2
30: 8
31:11
32: 1
34: 9, 27
39:17
47:12
50:10, 16
52: 7
58:17
59: 8
62: 8
65: 5
67: 4
5—S[1]
69: 5
70:23
Psa. 74:10
80: 2
83: 3
88:13, 17
89:14
91: 5
94: 1
95:11, 12
96: 1, 8
97: 4, 8
117:24
118:162
131: 9, 16
144: 7[b]
149: 2, 5
Cant. 1: 4
Isa. 12: 6
25: 9
29:19
35: 1, 2
41:17
49:13
61:10
65:14, 19
Jer. 30: 4
Lam. 2:19
Hab. 3:18

[a] pro μεγαλύνω. [b] A ὑψόω.

ἄγαλμα.

Isa. 19: 3
Isa. 21: 9

ἀγαπάω.

Gen. 22: 2
24:67
25:28, 28
29.18
20—A
30, 32
34: 3
37: 3
44:20
Exo. 20: 6
21: 5
Lev. 19:18, 34
Deu. 4:37
5:10
6: 5
7: 8,9,13
10:12, 15
18, 19
11:1,13,22
13: 3
15:16
19: 9
21:15, 15
16
23: 5
30: 6, 16
20
32:15
33: 5, 12
26
Jos. 22: 5
23:11
Jud. 5:31
14:16
16: 4, 15
Ruth 4:15
1 Sa. 1: 5
16:21
18: 1A
3A
16, 20
22, 28
20:17+A
17, 17
2 Sa. 1:23
7:18
12.24
13: 1, 4
15, 21
19: 6, 6
1 Ki. 3: 3
5: 1
10: 9
11: 2
1 Ch. 17:16
29.17
2 Ch. 2:11
9: 8
11:21
18: 2
20: 7
Neh. 1: 5
13:26
Est. 6: 9
Job 19.19
Psa. 4: 3
5:12
10: 5,7
17: 2
25: 8
28: 6
30:24
32: 5
33:13
36:28
39:17
44: 8
46: 5
50: 8
51: 5, 6
68:37
69: 5

Psa. 77:36, 68
83:12
86: 2
93:19[a]
96:10
98: 4—S[1]
108: 4, 17
114: 1
118:47, 48
97, 113
119, 127
132, 140
159, 162
165, 166
167
121: 6
144:20
145: 8
Pro. 3:12
4: 3
8:17, 21
36
9: 8
12: 1, 1
13:25
15: 9[b], 12
16: 1, 13
17
19: 8
20:13
21:17
22:11, 14
24:50
28: 4, 13
17
Ecc. 5: 9, 9
9: 9
Cant. 1:3,4,4,7
3:1,2,3,4
Isa. 1:23
3:25
5: 1, 1, 7
41: 8
43: 4
44: 2
48:14
51: 2
56: 6
57: 8
60:10
61: 8
63: 9
66:10[c]
Jer. 2:25
5:31
8: 2
11:15
12: 7
14:10
20:14
38: 3
Lam. 1: 2
Eze. 16:37
Dan. 9:4
Hos. 2:23[d], 23[d]
3: 1 *ter*
4:18
8: 9, 11
12
9: 1, 10
15
10:11
11: 1
12: 7
14: 4
Amos 4: 5
5:15
Mic. 6: 8
Zec. 8:17, 19
10: 6
Mal. 1: 2 *ter*
2:11

[a] AS[2] εὐφραίνω. [b] S[1] ἀπατάω.
[c] A ἐνοικέω, S[2] κατοικέω.
[d] A ἐλεέω.

ἀγάπη.

2 Sa. 1:26A[a]
13:15
Ecc. 9: 1, 6[b]
Cant. 2: 4, 5, 7
3: 5, 10

Cant. 5: 8
7: 6
8: 4, 6, 7
7
Jer. 2: 2

[a] *pro* ἀγάπησις. [b] S ἀπάτη.

ἀγάπησις.

2 Sa. 1:26, 26[a]
Psa. 108: 5
Pro. 24:50
Jer. 2:33

Jer. 38: 3
Hos. 11: 4
Hab. 3: 4
Zeph. 3:17[b]

[a] A ἀγάπη. [b] S[1] εὐφροσύνη.

ἀγαπητός.

Gen. 22: 2, 12
16
Jud. 11:34+A
Psa. 44: 1
59: 7
67:13
13—S
83: 2
107: 7

Ps. 126: 2
Isa. 5: 1
26:17
Jer. 6:26
38:20
Amos 8:10
Zec. 12:10
13: 6

ἀγαυρίαμα.

Isa. 62:7ABS[1] [a]
Jer. 31: 2ABS[a]

[a] *pro* γαυρίαμα.

ἀγγεῖον.

Gen. 42:25
43:10
Lev. 11:34
14: 5
Nu. 4: 9[a]
5:17
1 Sa. 9: 7
10: 3
25:18

Pro. 5:15[b]
Isa. 30:14
Jer. 14: 3
18: 4, 4
31:11, 11
38
39:14
47:10
Lam. 4: 2

[a] A ἅγιος. [b] S[1] ἅγιος.

ἀγγελία.

1 Sa. 4:19
2 Sa. 4: 4
2 Ki. 10: 7
Pro. 12:25
25:25
26:16

Isa. 28: 9
37: 7
Jer. 31:34—S[1]
Eze. 7:26, 26
21: 7
Nah. 3:19

ἀγγέλλω.

2 Sa. 15:13 A[a]
18:11 A[b]

Jer. 4:15[c]

[a] *pro* ἀπαγγέλλω. [b] *pro* ἀναγγέλλω. [c] AS ἀναγγέλλω.

ἄγγελος.

Gen. 6: 2A[a]
16: 7, 8, 9
10, 11
19: 1, 15
16
21:17
22:11, 15
24: 7, 40
28:12
31:11
32: 1, 3, 6
48:16
Exo. 3: 2
4:24
14:19
23:20, 23
32:34
33: 2
Nu. 20:14, 16
22:10+A
22, 23
24, 25
26, 27
31, 32
34, 35
24:12
Deu. 32: 8, 43[b]

Deu. 32:43 AB[a]
33: 2
Jos. 7:22
Jud. 2: 1, 4
4: 8
5:16[c]
23
6:11, 12
14, 16
20, 21
21, 22
22, 35
35+A
7:24
9:31
11:12, 13
13+A
14, 17
19
13: 3, 6, 9
11, 13
15, 16
16, 17
18, 20
21, 21
1 Sa. 6:21
11: 3, 4, 7

1 Sa. 11: 9, 9
16:19
19:11, 14
16, 20
20, 21
21
23:27
25:14
29: 9+A
2 Sa. 2: 5
3:12, 14
26
5:11
11: 4
19, 22
22, 23
25
12:27
14:17, 20
19:27
24:16, 16
16, 17
1 Ki. 13:18
19: 2+A
7
21: 2+A
5, 9
22:13
2 Ki. 1: 2, 3, 3
5, 15
16—B
5:10
6:32, 32
33
7:15, 17
9:18
10: 8
14: 8
16: 7
17: 4
18:14
19: 9, 14
23, 35
1 Ch. 14: 1
19: 2, 16
21:12, 15
15, 15
16, 18
27, 30
2 Ch. 18:12
32:21
35:21
36:15, 16
Neh. 6: 3
Job 1: 6, 14
16, 17
18
2: 1

Job 4:18
5: 1
9: 7+BS
20:15
33:23
36:14
38: 7
40: 6, 14
41:24
Psa. 8: 6
33: 8
34: 5, 6
77:25, 49
90:11
96: 7
102:20
103: 4
137: 1
148: 2
150:p.6
Pro. 13:17
16:14
17:11
25:13
26: 6
Isa. 9: 6
18: 2
30: 4
33: 7
37: 9, 14
24, 36
44:26
63: 9
Jer. 29:15
34: 2
Eze. 17:15
23:16, 40
30: 9
Dan. 3:28
6:22
Hos. 12: 4
Hag. 1:13
13—AS[2]
Zec. 1: 9, 11
12, 13
14, 17
19
2: 3, 3
3: 1, 3, 5
6
4: 1, 4, 5
5: 5, 10
6: 4, 5
12: 8
Mal. 1: 1
2: 7
3: 1, 1

[a] *pro* υἱός. [b] AB υἱός.
[c] A ἐξεγείρω.

ἄγγιον.

Lev. 12: 4AB[a] [a] *pro* ἄγιος.

ἄγγος.

Deu. 24: 2
1 Ki. 17:10
Jer. 19:11

Eze. 4: 9
Amos 8: 1, 1

ἀγέλη.

1 Sa. 17:34
24: 4
Pro. 27:23
Cant. 1: 7

Cant. 4: 1, 2
6: 4, 5
Isa. 60: 6

ἁγιάζω.

Gen. 2: 3
Exo. 13: 2
12+A[2]
12
19:14, 22
23
20: 8, 11
28:34, 37
29: 1, 21
27, 33
33, 36
36—A[1]

Exo. 29:37, 37
43, 44
44
30:29, 29
30
31:13
40: 6—A
7, 9, 11
Lev. 6:18, 27
8:11 *ter*
12, 15
30-AB[1]

Lev. 10: 3
11:44
16: 4, 19
20: 3, 8
21: 8, 8
12, 15
23
22: 2, 3, 9
16, 32
32
25:10, 11
27:14, 15
16, 17
18, 19[a]
22
Nu. 3:13
5: 9, 10
6:11, 12
7: 1, 1
8:17
16:16, 37
38
18: 8, 9, 29
20:12, 13
27:14, 14
Deu. 5:12, 15
15:19
22: 9
32:51
33: 3
Jos. 7:13, 13
Jud. 13: 5+A
17: 3[b], 3
1 Sa. 7: 1[c], 16
16: 5, 5
21: 5
2 Sa. 8:11, 11
11: 4
1 Ki. 8: 8, 8, 64
9: 3, 7
2 Ki. 10:20
12:18
1 Ch. 18:11
23:13
26:26, 27
28

2 Ch. 2: 4
5:11
7: 7, 16
20
26:18
29:33
30: 8
31: 6, 18A[d]
35: 3
Ezr. 3: 5
Neh. 3: 1, 1
12:47, 47
13:22
Psa. 45: 5
Pro. 20:25
Isa. 8:13
10:17
13: 3+AB[e]S
29:23, 23
49: 7
Jer. 1: 5
17:22
24—S[1]
27
28:27
Eze. 20:12, 20
41
28:22, 25
36:23, 23
37:28
38:16, 23
39:27
44:19, 24
46:20
47:11 A[e]
48:11
Dan. 12: 7+A
10—B[1]
Joel 1:14
2:15, 16
3: 9
Amos 2:12
Zeph. 1: 7
Hag. 2:12

[a] B ἀγοράζω. [b] A ἁγιασμός.
[c] A ἀναγκάζω. [d] *pro* ἁγνίζω.
[e] *pro* ὑγιάζω.

ἁγίασμα.

Exo. 15:17
25: 7
28:32
29: 6, 34
30:32, 37
36:39
Lev. 16: 4 A[a]
25: 5
1 Ch. 22:19
28:10
2 Ch. 20: 8
26:18
30: 8
36:15, 17
Ezr. 9: 8
Psa. 77:54, 69
88:40
92: 5

Psa. 95: 6
113: 2
131: 8, 18
Isa. 8:14
63:18+A
Jer. 17:12
38:40
Lam. 1:10
2: 7, 20
Eze. 11:16
20:40
45: 2, 3A[a]
48:21
Dan. 9:17
11:31
Amos 7:13
Zec. 7: 3

[a] *pro* ἅγιος.

ἁγιασμός.

Jud. 17: 3 A[a]
Jer. 6:16 A[b]
Eze. 22: 8 B[c]

Eze. 45: 4
Amos 2:11

[a] *pro* ἁγιάζω. [b] *pro* ἁγνισμός.
[c] *pro* ἅγιος.

ἁγιαστήριον.

Lev. 12: 4
Psa. 72:17

Psa. 73: 7
82:13 AS[a]

[a] *pro* θυσιαστήριον.

ἅγιος, τὸ ἅγιον, etc.

Exo. 3: 5
12:16, 16
15:11, 13
16:23

Exo. 19: 6
22:31
23:22
26:33 *ter*

Exo. 26:34, 34
28: 2, 3, 3
4, 23
26, 31
34, 34
39
29:20, 30
31, 33
37, 37
30:10, 10
13, 24
25, 25
29, 29
31, 32
35, 36
36
31:11, 14
15
35: 2, 18
18+A
21
23+A
26 A[a]
35
36: 1, 3, 4
6, 8, 38
38:25
39: 1, 1, 2
13, 19
40: 7, 9, 9
11
Lev. 2: 3, 3
10, 10
4: 6, 17
5:15, 15
16
6:16, 17
17, 25
25, 26
27, 29
29, 30
31, 31
36 ter
8: 9, 31
10: 4, 10
12, 12
13, 14
17 ter
18, 18
11:44, 44
45, 45
12: 4[b]
14:13 ter
16: 2, 3
4[n]
16, 17
20, 23
24, 27
32, 33
33
18:21
19: 2, 2, 8
12−AB
24, 30
20: 3, 7, 7
26, 26
21: 6, 6, 7
8, 8, 12
12, 22
22, 22
23
22: 2, 2, 3
4, 6, 7
10, 10
12, 14
14, 15
16, 32
23: 2, 3, 4
7, 8, 20
21, 24
27, 35
36, 37
24: 9 ter
25:12
26: 2, 31
27: 3, 9
10, 14
21, 23
25, 28
28, 30

Lev. 27:32, 33
Num. 3:28, 31
32, 38
47, 50
4: 4, 4
9A[c], 12
15 ter
16, 19
19, 20
6: 5, 8
20
7: 9, 13
19, 25
31, 37
43, 49
55, 61
67, 73
79, 85
86+A[2]
8:19
10:21
15:40
16: 3, 5, 7
18: 1, 3, 5
9, 9
10 ter
16, 17
19, 32
19:20
28: 7, 18
25, 26
29: 1, 7, 12
31: 6
35:25
Deu. 7: 6
12:26
14: 2, 20
23:14
26:13, 15
19
28: 9
Jos. 5:15
6:19
24:15, 19
Jud. 13: 7[d]
16:17[d]
1 Sa. 2: 2, 2−A
10
6:20
21: 4
1 Ki. 6:16, 16
7:36, 36
37, 37
8: 4, 6, 6
7, 8, 10
2 Ki. 4: 9
12: 4, 18
18
19:22
1 Ch. 6:49, 40
9:29
16:10, 29
35
22:19
23:13, 13
28
32−AB
24: 5
26:26, 28
28:12
29: 3, 16
2 Ch. 3: 8, 8
10, 10
4:22, 22
5: 1, 5, 7
7, 9, 11
6: 2
8:11[e]
15:18, 18
20:21−A
23: 6
24: 7
29: 5, 7, 21
30:19, 24
27
31:14, 14
18
35: 3
6+A
7 B[f]

2 Ch. 35:13, 15
Ezr. 2:63, 63
8:28, 28
9: 2
Neh. 7:65, 65
8: 9, 10
11
9:14
10:31, 33
39
11: 1
17+S[3]
Job 5: 1
6:10
15:15
Psa. 2: 6
3: 5
5: 8
10: 4
14: 1
15: 3
17: 7
19: 3, 7
21: 4
23: 3
26: 4+A
27: 2
28: 2
32:21
33:10
42: 3
46: 9
47: 2
50:13
55: 1
59: 8
62: 3
64: 5
67: 6, 18
25
36 S[g]
70:22
73: 3
76:14
77:41
78: 1
82: 4
86: 1
88: 6, 8, 19
21, 36
95: 9
97: 1
98: 3, 5, 9
9
101:20
102: 1
104: 3, 42
105:16, 47
107: 8
109: 3
110: 9
133: 2
137: 2, 2
142:10 ABS[h]
144:21
150: 1
Pro. 5:15 S[1][c]
9:10
24:26[i]
Ecc. 8:10
Isa. 1: 4
4: 3
5:16, 19
24−A
6: 3 ter
10:20
11: 9
12: 6
14:27
17: 7
8+S
23:18
26:21
27: 1, 13
29:23
30:12, 15
19, 29
31: 1
33: 5
35: 8

Isa. 37:23
40:25
41:16, 20
43: 3, 14
15, 28
44:28
45:11
47: 4
48: 2, 17
49: 7
52: 1, 10
54:17 S[1][k]
55: 5
56: 7
57:13, 15
15, 15
58:13, 13
60: 9, 9
13, 14
62: 9, 12
63:10, 11
15, 18
64:10, 11,
65: 9, 11
25
66:20
Jer. 2: 2, 3
3:16, 21
4:11
11:15
27:29
28: 5, 51
32:16
38:23
Lam. 4: 1
Eze. 5:11
7:24
8: 6
9: 6
10: 6, 7
20:39, 40
21: 2
22: 8[l], 26
26
23:38, 39
24:21
25: 3
28:14
36:20
21, 22
23 A[m]
38
37:26, 28
39: 7 ter
25
41: 4, 4
21, 21
23, 25
42:13 ter
13−A
13−A
13
14 ter
20
43: 7, 8, 12
12, 21
44: 1, 5, 7
8+A
8, 9, 11
13 ter
15, 16
19, 23
27
45: 1, 1
3[n], 3
4+A
4, 6, 7
7, 18
46:19
47:12
48: 8
10, 10
12 A[o]
12, 12
14, 18
18, 20
21, 21
Dan. 4: 5, 6
10, 14
15, 20

Dan. 5:11+A
7:18, 21
22, 22
25, 27
8:11
13−A
13, 13
14, 24
9:16, 20
24 ter.
26
11:28, 30
30, 45
Hos. 11: 9, 12
Joel 2: 1
3:17, 17

Amos 4: 2
Obad. 16, 17
Jon. 2: 5, 8
Mic. 1: 2
Hab. 1:12
2:20
3: 3
Zeph. 3: 4−S[1]
11
Hag. 2:12
Zec. 2:12, 13
8: 3
9:16
14: 5, 20
21
Mal. 2:11

[a] pro αἴγειος. [b] AB ἄγγιον. [c] pro ἀγγεῖον. [d] A ναζειραῖος. [e] B ἀγρός. [f] pro αἴξ. [g] pro ὅσιος. [h] pro ἀγαθός. [i] A[2] ἄνθρωπος. [k] pro δίκαιος. [l] B ἁγιασμός. [m] pro μέγας. [n] A ἁγίασμα. [o] pro γῆ.

ἁγιωσύνη.

Psa. 29: 5
95: 6
Psa. 96:12
144: 5

ἀγκάλη.

1 Ki. 3:20
Pro. 5:20

ἀγκαλίς.

Job 24:19

ἄγκιστρον.

2 Ki. 19:28
Job 40:20
Isa. 19: 8
Eze. 32: 3
Hab. 1:15

ἀγκύλη.

Exo. 26: 4, 5, 5
10, 10
11
Exo. 37:15, 17
38:18, 20
39: 6

ἀγκών.

2 Ch. 9:18, 18
Job 31:22
Eze. 13:18

ἀγκωνίσκος.

Exodus 26:17

ἁγνεία.

Nu. 6: 2, 21
2 Ch. 30:19

ἁγνίζω.

Exo. 19:10
Nu. 6: 3
8:21
11:18
19:12
31:19, 23
Jos. 3: 5
1 Sa. 21: 5
1 Ch. 15:12, 14
2 Ch. 29: 5, 5
2 Ch. 29:15, 16
17, 17
18, 19
34, 34
30: 3, 15
17, 17
18
31:18[a]
Isa. 66:17
Jer. 12: 3

[a] A ἁγιάζω.

ἅγνισμα.

Numbers 19: 9

ἁγνισμός.

Nu. 6: 5
8: 7, 7
19:17
Nu. 31:23
Jer. 6:16[a]

[a] A ἁγιασμός.

ἀγνοέω.

Gen. 20: 4
Lev. 4:13
5:18
Nu. 12:11
1 Sa. 14:24
1 Sa. 26:21
2 Ch. 16: 9
Eze. 45:20+A
Hos. 4:15

ἀγνόημα.

Genesis 43:11

ἄγνοια.

Gen. 26:10
Lev. 5:18
22:14
1 Sa. 14:24
2 Ch. 28:13
Psa. 24: 7
Ecc. 5: 5
Eze. 40:39
42:13
44:29
46:20

ἄγνος.

Lev. 23:40
Job 10:17 AS[2][a]

[a] pro ἀγρός.

ἁγνός.

Psa. 11: 7
18:10
Pro. 15:26
Pro. 19:13
20: 9
21: 8

ἀγνωσία.

Job 35:16

ἄγξις.

Psa. 31: 9 A[a]

[a] pro ἄγχω.

ἄγονος.

Exo. 23:26
Deu. 7:14
Job 30: 3

ἀγορά.

Ecc. 12: 4, 5
Cant. 3: 2
Eze. 27:12, 14
Eze. 27:16, 19
22

ἀγοράζω.

Gen. 41:57
42: 5, 7
43: 3, 21
44:25
47:14
Lev. 27:19 B[a]
Deu. 2: 6
1 Ch. 21:24, 24
2 Ch. 1:16
34:11
Neh. 10:31
Isa. 24: 2
55: 1
Jer. 44:12

[a] pro ἁγιάζω.

ἀγορασμός.

Gen. 42:19, 33
Neh. 10:31
Pro. 23:20

ἀγρεύω.

Job 10:16
Pro. 5:22
Pro. 6:25, 26
Hos. 5: 2

ἀγριαίνω.

Daniel 11:11

ἀγριομυρίκη.

Jeremiah 17: 6

ἄγριος.

Exo. 23:11
Lev. 21:20
26:22
Deu. 7:22
28:27
Jos. 23: 5
2 Ki. 4:39−A
Job 5:22, 23
6: 5
Job 30: 7
39: 5
Psa. 79:14
Isa. 32:14
56: 9
Jer. 14: 6[a]
31: 6
Dan. 4: 9, 18
20, 22, 29

[a] S ὄναγρος.

ἄγροικος.

Gen. 16:12
Gen. 25:27

ἀγρός.

Gen. 2: 5, 5
19, 20
5:18
23: 9, 11
13, 17
17, 17
Gen. 23:19, 20
25: 9, 10
27:27
30:14, 16
33:19
39: 5

Gen. 49:29, 32
Exo. 8:13
20:17
22: 5qnq
23:16, 16
Lev. 19: 9
23:22
25: 3, 4, 5
31, 34
26:20
27:16, 17
18, 19
20, 20
21, 22
22, 24
28
Nu. 16:14
20:17
21:22
23:14
Deu. 5:21
11:15
14:21
20:19[a]
22:27
24:21, 21
28: 3, 16
32:13
Jos. 15:18
19: 6
21:12
24:32
Jud. 1:14
5: 4, 18
9:27, 32
42[b]
43—A
44
13: 9
19:16
20:31
Ruth 1: 1, 2, 6
6, 22
2:2,3,3,6
7, 8, 9
17, 22
4: 3, 3, 5
1 Sa. 4: 2
6: 1, 14
18
8:14
11: 5
13:17
14:15, 25
19: 3
20:11, 11
12, 24
35
22: 7
25:10
27: 5, 7[c]
11
30:11
11+AB
2 Sa. 1:21
2:18
9: 7
10: 8
11:11, 23
14: 6, 30
17: 8
19:29
20:12
21:10
23:11
1 Ki. 2:26
12: p 24
l 44
14:11 A
2 Ki. 4:39, 39
7:12

2 Ki. 8: 3, 5, 6
9:25, 37
14: 9
18:17
19:26
1 Ch. 11:13
16:32
27:25
2 Ch. 8:11 B[d]
25:18
31: 5
Neh. 5: 3[e],4,5
11, 16
11:25, 30
12:29
13:10
Job 5:23+A
23+A
25
24:5, 5+A
6—A
39:15
40:17[f]
Psa. 49:10 AS[2g]
11
102:15
103:11
106:37
Pro. 24:42
Ecc. 5: 8
Cant. 2: 7
3: 5
5: 8
7:11
8: 4
Isa. 5: 8, 8
7: 3
27: 4
32:12
33:12
36: 2
43:20
55:12
Jer. 4:17
5:17 S[2h]
6:12, 25
7:20
8: 7, 10
12: 4—A, 9
13:27
14: 5
33:18
34: 5
39: 7, 8, 9
15, 25
43, 44
42: 9
47: 7, 13
48: 8
Lam. 4: 9
Eze. 16: 7
17:24 A[i]
29: 5 A[k]
31:13
33:27
34: 5, 8 A[i]
36:30
39:17 A[i]
Dan. 2:38
Hos. 2:12, 18
4: 3
10: 4
12:11
13: 8
Joel 1:11, 12
19
Mic. 1: 6
2: 2, 4
3:12
Zec. 10: 1
Mal. 3:11

Job 21:32
Psa. 101: 8
120: 1

Pro. 8:34
Cant. 5: 2

[a] A δρυμός. [b] A πεδίον.
[c] B ὁδός. [d] pro ἅγιος.
[e] S[1] υἱός. [f] AS[2] ἁγνός.
[g] pro δρυμός. [h] pro ἄρτος.
[i] pro πεδίον. [k] pro γῆ.

ἀγρυπνέω.

2 Sa. 12:21
Ezra 8:29

ἄγρωστις.

Deu. 32: 2
Isa. 9:18
37:27

Hos. 10: 4
Mic. 5: 7

ἀγύναιος.

Job 24:21 ABS[1a] [a] pro γύναιον.

ἀγχιστεία.

Ruth 4: 6, 7
7, 8

Neh. 13:29

ἀγχιστεύομαι.

Ezra 2:62
Neh. 7:64

ἀγχιστεύς.

Ruth 3: 9, 12
12
4: 1[a]
3—A

Ruth 4: 6, 8, 14
2 Sa. 14:11
1 Ki. 16:11+A

[a] AB ἀγχιστευτής.

ἀγχιστευτής.

Ruth 4:1 AB[a] [a] pro ἀγχιστεύς.

ἀγχιστεύω.

Lev. 25:25, 26
Nu. 5: 8
35:12, 19
21:24
25, 27
27
36: 8, 8

Deu. 19: 6, 12
Jos. 20: 3, 5A, 9
Ruth 2:20
3:13 qtr
4: 4 qnq
6 ter
7—A

ἄγχω.

Psa. 31: 9[a] [a] A ἄγξεις.

ἄγω.

Gen. 2:19, 22
38:25
42:20[a], 34
37
43: 6, 8, 28
44:32
46: 7, 32
47:17
Exo. 3: 1
14:25
15:22
22:13
Lev. 13: 2
24:11
26:13
Nu. 5:15
11:16
14:13 B[b]
31:12
32:17
Deu. 8: 2, 15
29: 5
32:12
Jos. 15: 9[c]
24: 8
Jud. 1: 7
18: 3 A[d]
19: 6[e]
21:12 A[d]
1 Sa. 15:20
19:15
30:11
2 Sa. 3:13
23 AB[f]
6: 3
12:28 A[g]
14:10, 23
1 Ki. (3)40
14:10 A
2 Ki. 4:24
6:19[h]
9:20, 20
28—A

2 Ki. 17:24, 28
28 A[i]
19:25 A[g]
23:30
24:16
25: 6, 7
20[j]
1 Ch. 5:26
13: 7
20: 1
29:19
2 Ch. 2:16, 16[k]
16: 6 A[l]
22: 9
28: 5—B
33:11, 11
35:24
36:17
Neh. 5: 2 S[1m]
12:28 S[1g]
Est. 1:18 A[n]
2: 8
6:14+S[3]
9:17, 18
19
19+BS
21, 22
28[o]
Job 38:20, 32
40:20
Psa. 42: 3
44:16
77:52[p]
Pro. 1:20
7:22
11:12
13:12
18: 2, 6
24:11
Ecc. 3:22
8:10 C[q]
11: 9
12:14

Isa. 9: 6
11: 6
13: 3
3+B[r]S
16: 3[r]
20: 4
23: 1
31: 2
42:16
43: 5, 6, 6
9
46: 2, 11[s]
11
48:15, 21
49:10, 22
52: 4
53: 7
8 S[1t]
8
60: 9, 11
63:12, 13
14
66:20
Jer. 2: 7[u]
11:19
19: 1
20: 5
24: 1
25: 9
29: 9
38: 8
42: 2[v]
3 A[w]
47: 1[h]
48:12
50:10

Jer. 51: 2 S[x]
52: 9, 11
26
Lam. 1: 4
Eze. 7:24+A
8: 3
11: 1, 24
12:13
16:25 A[y]
40
17:12
20+A
19: 4
20:10, 35
22: 4
27:26
28:16
30:18 AB[t]
31: 4+A
4
32: 9
38:17 B[b]
40: 1, 19[v]
24[v]
43: 1
47: 6[h]
Dan. 3:13, 13
5: 3 A[d]
13
6:16, 24
9:24
11:13[z]
Amos 7:11, 17
Mic. 1:15
Nah. 2: 7
Zec. 3: 8[aa]

[a] A κατάγω. [b] pro ἀνάγω.
[c] A ἐξάγω. [d] pro φέρω.
[e] A ἄρχω. [f] pro ἔρχομαι.
[g] pro συνάγω. [h] A ἀπάγω.
[i] pro ἀποικίζω. [j] AB ἀπαγω.
[k] A συνάγω. [l] pro λαμβανω.
[m] pro φάγω. [n] pro λεγω.
[o] S[1] αἴρω. [p] S ἀναγω.
[q] pro εἰσάγω. [r] AB[2]S ἀπαρχή.
[s] S[1] ποιέω. [t] pro αἴρω.
[u] S εἰσαγω. [v] A εἰσάγω.
[w] pro ἐξάγω. [x] pro ἐπάγω.
[y] pro διαγω. [z] A ἔχω.
[aa] S[3] ἐπάγω.

ἀγωγή.

Est. 2:20
Est. 10: 3

ἀγών.

Isaiah 7:13, 13

ἀγωνίζομαι.

Daniel 6:14, 14

ἀδαμάντινος.

Amos 7: 7

ἀδάμας.

Amos 7: 7, 8, 8

ἀδάρ.

Ezra 6:15
Est. 2:16
3: 7, 13
8:12

Est. 9: 1, 15
16, 19
21, 22

ἄδειπνος.

Daniel 6:18

ἀδελφή.

Gen. 4:22
12:13, 19
20: 2, 5, 12
24:30, 30
59
60+A
60
25:20
26: 7, 9
28: 9

Gen. 29:13
30: 1, 8
14—A
34:13, 14
27, 31
36: 3, 22
46:17
Exo. 2: 4, 7
6:20, 23
15:20

Lev. 18: 9, 11
12
13—A
18
20:17, 17
19, 19
21: 3
Nu. 6: 7
25:18
26:59
Deu. 27:22
23—A
Jos. 2:13 A[a]
Jud. 15: 2
2 Sa. 13: 1, 2, 4
5, 6, 11
20, 22
32
17:25
1 Ki. 11:19, 19
20
12: p 24
l 18
2 Ki. 11: 2[b]
1 Ch. 1:39—B
2:16
3: 9, 19
4: 3, 19

1 Ch. 5: 7 B[c]
7:15, 18
30, 32
2 Ch. 22:11
Job 1: 4
17:14
42:11
Pro. 7: 4
Cant. 4: 9, 10
12
5: 1, 2
8: 8, 8
Eze. 16:45, 45
46, 46
48+A
49, 51
52, 52
55, 56
61
22:11 A[d]
11
23: 4, 11
11, 18
31, 32
33
44:25
Hos. 2: 1

[a] pro οἶκος. [b] A υἱός.
[c] pro ἀδελφός. [d] pro νύμφη.

ἀδελφιδέος.

Gen. 14:14[a], 16 [a] A ἀδελφός.

ἀδελφιδός.

Cant. 1:13
14—B
16
2: 3, 8, 9
10, 16
17
5: 1, 2, 4
5, 6, 6

Cant. 5: 8[a], 9
9, 9, 9
10, 10
17, 17
6: 1[b], 2, 2
7: 9, 10
11, 13
8: 1, 5, 14

[a] S[1] ἀδελφός. [b] B ἀδελφός.

ἀδελφός.

Gen. 4: 2, 8, 8
9, 9, 10
11, 21
9: 5, 22
25
10:21, 25
12: 5
13: 8, 11
14:12, 13
13, 14A[a]
16:12
19: 7
20: 5, 13
16
22:20, 21
23
24:15, 27
29, 48
53, 55
25:18, 26
27: 6, 11
23, 29
30, 35
37, 40
41, 42
43, 45
28: 2, 5
29: 1, 4, 10
10—A
10, 12
15
31:23, 25
32, 37
37, 46
54
32: 3, 6, 11
13, 17
33: 1, 3, 9
34:11, 14
25
35: 1, 7
36: 6

Gen. 37: 1, 4, 5
8, 9, 10
11, 12
13, 14
16, 17
19, 23
26:26
27, 27
30
38: 1, 8, 8
9, 9, 11
29, 30
42: 3, 4, 4
6, 7, 8
13, 15
16, 19
20, 21
21, 28
32, 33
34, 34
38
43: 2, 3, 4
4, 5, 6
6, 12
13, 15
28, 28
29, 32
44:14, 19
20, 23
26, 26
33
45: 1, 3
3+A[a]
3, 4—A
4, 12
14, 15
15, 16
17, 24
46:20, 31
31
47: 1, 2, 3
5, 6

Gen. 47:11, 12
48: 6, 19
22
49: 5,8,26
50: 8, 14
15, 22
24
Exo. 1: 6
2:11, 11
4:14, 18
6:20
7: 1, 2, 7
9, 19
8: 5
10:23
22:25[b]
28: 1,2,37
29: 5
32:27, 29
Lev. 10: 4, 4, 6
16: 2
18:14, 16
16
19:17
20:21, 21
21: 2, 10
25:25, 25
35, 35
36, 39
46, 46
47, 48
49, 49
26:37, 37
Nu. 1:49+A[a]
3: 9+A
6: 7
8:26
16:10
18: 2, 6
20: 3,8,14
25+A
25: 6
27: 4, 7, 9
10, 10
11, 13
32: 6
36: 2
Deu. 1:16, 16
28
2: 4, 8
3:18, 20
10: 9
13: 6
15: 2, 3, 7
7,9,11
12
17:15, 15
20
18: 2,7,15
18
19:18, 19[c]
20: 8
22: 1, 1, 2
2, 3, 4
23: 7, 19
20
24: 9, 16
25: 3, 5, 5
7, 7
7−A
7
9,9,11
28:54
32:50
33: 9, 16
24
Jos. 1:14, 15
2:13, 18
6:23
14: 8
15:17
17: 4, 4, 6
22: 3, 4, 7
8
Jud. 1: 3, 13
17
3: 9
5:14+A
8:19
9: 1, 3, 3

Jud. 9: 5, 18
21, 24
24, 26
31, 41
56
11: 3
14: 3
16:31
18: 8,8,14
19:23
20:13, 23
28
21: 6, 22
Ruth 4: 3, 10
1 Sa. 14: 3
16:13
17:17 A
17 A
18 A
22 A
28 A
20:29, 29
22: 1
26: 6
30:23+A
2 Sa. 1:26
2:23, 26
27
3: 8, 27
30, 30
4: 6, 9
6: 3, 4
10:10
13: 3,4,7,8
10, 12
20 *qtr*
20, 32
14: 6, 7, 7
15:20, 34
18: 2
19:12, 41
20: 9, 10
21:21
23:18, 24
1 Ki. 1: 9, 10
2: 7, 15
21, 22
9:13
12:24
p 21 *l* 80
13:30
16:22
21:32, 33
2 Ki. 1:18
18+A
7: 6
9: 2
10:13, 13
11: 2−AB
13:13 B[d]
23: 9
1 Ch. 1:19 A
2:25, 42
4: 8, 9
12, 27
5: 2, 7[e]
13
15−AB
6:39, 44
48
7: 5
16−B
22, 35
8:14, 31
32, 32
39
9: 6, 9
13, 17
19, 25
32, 37
38, 38
11:20, 26
38 A[f]
45
12: 2, 29
32, 39
13: 2, 7
15: 5, 6, 7
8,9,10
12, 16

1 Ch. 15:17, 17
18
16: 7, 37
38, 39
19:11, 15
20: 5, 7
23:22, 32
24:25, 31
31
25: 7, 9
9 *to* 31
26: 8,9,11
12, 20
22, 25
26, 28
30, 32
27: 7,7,18
28: 2
2 Ch. 5:12
11: 4, 22
19:10, 10
21: 2,4,13
22: 8
11+B
28: 8, 11
15
29:15, 34
30: 7, 9
31:12, 13
15
35: 5, 6, 9
14, 15
36:4, 10
Ezr. 3: 2, 2 B
8, 9, 9
6:20
7:18
8:17, 18
19, 24
10:18
Neh. 1: 2
3: 1, 18
4: 2, 14
19
5: 1, 5, 7
8,8,10
14
7: 2
10:10, 29
11:12
13−ABS[1]
14
17+S[3]
19
12: 7
8+S[3]
8, 12
24, 36
13:13
Est. 2: 7
15−S[1]
9: 7S[1] [g]
Job 1:13, 18

Job 19:13
22: 6
30:29
31: 1 S[1] [h]
41: 8
42:11, 15
Psa. 21:23
34:14
48: 8
49:20
68: 9
121: 8
132: 1
150: *p* 6 *bis*
Pro. 6:19
17: 2, 17
18:9,19,19
19: 7
27:10, 10
Ecc. 4: 8
Cant. 5: 1,8S[1] [i]
6: 1 B[i]
Isa. 3: 6
7: 3 A[f]
9:19
20+A
19: 2
41: 6
66: 5, 20
Jer. 7:15
9: 4, 4
12: 6
13:14
22:18
23:35
29:11
32:12
38:34 A[k]
34[c]
39: 7, 8, 9
12
41:14
17+AS[3]
42: 3
48: 8
Eze. 4:17
11:15
24:23
33:30
38:21
44:25
47:14
Hos. 2: 1
12: 3
13:15
Joel 2: 8
Amos 1: 9, 11
Obad. 10, 12
Mic. 5: 3
Hag. 2·22
Zec. 7: 9, 10
Mal. 1: 2
2:10

[a] *pro* ἀδελφιδοῦς. [b] A[1] λαός.
[c] A πλησίος. [d] *pro* βασιλεύς.
[e] B ἀδελφή. [f] *pro* υἱός.
[g] *pro* Δελφών. [h] *pro* ὀφθαλμός.
[i] *pro* ἀδελφιδός. [k] *pro* πολίτης.

ἄδηλος.

Psalm 50: 8

ᾅδης.

Gen. 37:35
42:38
44:29, 31
Nu. 16:30, 33
Deu. 32:22
1 Sa. 2: 6
1 Ki. 2: 6, 9
(3) *p* 1
Job 7: 9
11: 8
14:13
17:13, 16
21:13
26: 6
33:22
38:17

Psa. 6: 6
9:18
15:10
17: 6
29: 4
30:18
48:15, 15
16
54:16
85:13
87: 4
88:49
93:17
113:25
114: 3
138: 8

Ps. 140: 7
Pro. 1:12
2:18
5: 5
7:27
9:18
14:12
15:11, 24
16:25
24:51[a]
27:20
Ecc. 9:10
Cant. 8: 6
Isa. 5:14

Isa. 14: 9, 11
15, 19
28:15, 18
38:10, 18
18
57: 9
Jer. 41: 5
Eze. 31:15, 16
17
32:27
Hos. 13:14, 14
Amos 9: 2
Jon. 2: 3
Hab. 2: 5

[a] A[1] ἀρά.

ἀδιάκριτος.

Proverbs 25: 1

ἀδιάλυτος.

Exo. 36:31[a] [a] A διάλυτος.

ἀδικέω.

Gen. 16: 5
21:23
26:20
42:22
Exo. 2:13
5:16
Lev. 6: 2, 4
19:13
Deu. 28:29, 33
Jos. 2:20
1 Sa. 12: 4
2 Sa. 19:19
24:17
1 Ki. 8:47
2 Ch. 6:37
26:16
Ezra 10:13
Est. 1:16[a]
4: 1
Job 8: 3
10: 3[b]
Psa. 9:24
34: 1
43:18
61:10
70: 4
88:34

Ps. 102: 6
104:14
105: 6
118:121
145: 7
Pro. 1:32
17: 8 S[c]
24:44
Isa. 1:17
3:15
10:20
17: 8+S
21: 3
23:12
25: 3, 4
51:23
65:25
Jer. 3:21
9: 5
21:12
22: 3
44:18
Eze. 17:20+A
39:26
Dan. 9: 5
Hab. 1: 2

[a] A ἀτιμάζω. [b] A ἀσεβέω.
[c] *pro* εὐοδόω.

ἀδίκημα.

Gen. 31:36
Exo. 22: 9
Lev. 6: 4
16:16
1 Sa. 20: 1
26:18
2 Sa. 22:49
Pro. 17: 9

Isa. 56: 2 AS[a]
59:12
Jer. 16:17
22:17
Eze. 14:10, 10
28:15
Zeph. 3:15

[a] *pro* ἄδικος.

ἀδικία.

Gen. 6:11, 13
26:20
44:16
49: 5
50:17, 17
Exo. 34: 7
Lev. 16:21, 22
18:25
Nu. 14:18
Deu. 19:15
32: 4
Jud. 9:24
1 Sa. 3:13, 14
14:41
20: 8−A
25:24
28:10
2 Sa. 3: 8, 34
7:10, 14
14:32
21: 1
1 Ki. 2:32
8:50

1 Ki. 17:18
2 Ki. 17: 4
1 Ch. 17: 9
2 Ch. 19: 7
Job 11:14
15:16
33:17
17+A
34: 6, 32
36:10[a], 18
33
Psa. 7: 4, 15
17
10: 5
13: 4 B[b]
16: 3
26:12
27: 3[c]
41: 8 A[b]
51: 4, 5
54:12
57: 3
61:11

Psa. 63: 3
65:18
71:14
72: 6, 7, 8
74: 6
81: 2
88:33 AS[d]
91:16
93: 4
100: 8[e]
118:29, 69
104
163
139: 3
143: 8, 11
Pro. 8:13
11: 5−S[1]
15:29
21: 9
28:16
Isa. 33:15, 15
43:24
25+A
57: 1
58: 6
59: 3
60:18
61: 8
Jer. 2:22
3:13
11:10
13:22[f]
14: 6+A
10, 20
16:10
18 AS[g]
18:23
27:20
28: 5, 6
24 A[g]
37:14, 10[h]
38:34
40: 8
43: 3
Lam. 2:14
3:57 A[i]
4:13
22 A[b]
Eze. 3:18, 19
4: 4, 4, 5
5,6,17
7:16, 19
9: 9, 9
12: 2
14: 3, 4, 7

Eze. 14:10
17:20+A
18: 8, 17
17, 18
19, 20
20
22 A[k]
24, 30
21:23, 24
25, 27
27, 27
29
22: 7
25+A
29
24:23
28:18
33:13 A[b]
13
35: 5
39:26
44:10, 12
45: 9
Dan. 4:24
9:13, 16
24[m], 24
Hos. 4: 8
15+B[*a]
5: 5
7: 1
8:13
9: 7, 9
10: 9, 10
13
15−A
12: 7, 8
13:12
12 A[d]
14: 1, 2
Joel 3:19
Amos 3:10
Jon. 3: 8
Mic. 3:10
6:10
7:18 A[b]
19
Nah. 3: 1
Hab. 2:12
Zeph. 3: 5−A
5, 13
Zec. 3: 9
5: 6
Mal. 2: 6, 6
3: 7

[a] S[1] ἀκακία. [b] *pro* ἀνομία.
[c] S[1] ἀνομία. [d] *pro* ἁμαρτία.
[e] AS ἀνομία. [f] A κακία.
[g] *pro* κακία. [h] S δίκαιος.
[i] *pro* δίκη. [k] *pro* παράπτωμα.
[m] A ἀνομία. [n] A ἀδ. *pro* Ὦν.

ἄδικος.

Gen. 19: 8
Exo. 23: 1, 1, 7
Lev. 19:12, 15
35
Deu. 19:16, 18
18
25:16−A[1]
1 Sa. 25:21
2 Sa. 18:13
22: 3
2 Ki. 9:12
Job 5:16, 22
6:29, 30
9:35+
AS[2]
13: 4
16:11, 17
18:21
22:23[a]
24:20
27: 4
29:17
31: 3
36: 4
21 BS[1] [b]
23

Psa. 17:49
24:19
26:12
34:11
42: 1
62:12
100: 7
118:118
128
119: 2
138: 4−S[2]
139: 2,5,12
Pro. 4:24
6:17, 19
10:31
11:18
12:17, 19
21
13: 5, 23
14: 5
15:26
16:33[c]
17: 1, 15[d]
15
19: 6 A[e]
29:12, 27

Isa. 9:17; 29:21; 32: 7; 54:14; 56: 2[f]; 57:20; 58: 6; 59:13, 13; Jer. 5:31; 7: 9
Jer. 34:11, 12; 12, 13; 35:15; 36: 9, 31; Eze. 21: 3; 4—A; 33:15; Amos 8: 5; Zeph. 3: 5; Mal. 3:18 A[g]

[a] S^1 κακός. [b] pro ἄτοπος. [c] S^1 δίκαιος. [d] S δίκαιος. [e] pro ὄνειδος. [f] AS ἀδίκημα. [g] pro ἄνομος.

ἀδίκως.

Lev. 6: 3, 5; Job 20:15; 24:10, 11; 36: 4; Psa. 34:19 A[a]; 37:20; 68: 5; 118:78, 86
Pro. 1:11, 17; 11:21; 16: 5; 17:23; 19: 5, 24; Isa. 49:24; Eze. 13:22+A

[a] pro ματαίως.

ἀδόκιμος.

Pro. 25: 4
Isa. 1:22

ἀδολεσχέω.

Gen. 24:63; Psa. 68:13; 76: 4,7,13
Ps. 118:15, 23; 27, 48; 78

ἀδολεσχία.

1 Sa. 1:16; 1 Ki. 18:27; 2 Ki. 9:11
Psa. 54: 3; 118:85

ἀδοξέω.

Isaiah 52:14

ἁδρός.

2 Sa. 15:18—A; 1 Ki. 1: 9[a]; 2 Ki. 10: 6, 11; Job 29: 9
Job 34:19[a]; Isa. 34: 7; Jer. 5: 5

[a] A ἀνήρ.

ἁδρύνω.

Exo. 2:10; Jud. 11: 2; 13:24[a]; Ruth 1:13
2 Sa. 12: 3; 2 Ki. 4:18; Ps. 143:12 ABS[1b]

[a] A αὐξάνω. [b] pro ἱδρύω.

ἀδυναμία.

Amos 2: 2

ἀδυνατέω.

Gen. 18:14; Lev. 25:35; Deu. 17: 8; 2 Ch. 14:11[a]; Job 4: 4
Job 10:13; 42: 2; Isa. 8:15; Dan. 4: 6; Zec. 8: 6, 6

[a] A δυνατέω.

ἀδύνατος.

Job 5:15, 16; 20:19 ACS[2a]; 24: 4,6,22; 29:16; 30:25
Job 31:16,20,34; 34:20; 36:15, 19; Pro. 24:53; Joel 3:10[b]

[a] pro δυνατός. [b] S^1 δυνατός.

ἄδυτος.

2 Ch. 33:14+AB*

ᾄδω.

Exo. 15: 1,1,21; Nu. 21:17; Jud. 5: 1, 3; 2 Sa. 19:35, 35; 1 Ch. 6:31
1 Ch. 15:27; 16: 9, 23; 25: 7; 2 Ch. 23:13; 29:27, 28
Ezra 2:41, 65; 65[a], 70; 7: 7, 24; 8:17[b]; 10:24[c]; Neh. 7: 1, 44; 68, 68; 72; 10:28, 39; 11:22; 12:28, 29; 42, 45; 46, 47; 13: 5, 10; Psa. 7: 1; 12: 6; 20:14; 26: 6; 32: 3; 56: 8; 58:17
Psa. 67: 5, 33; 88: 2; 95: 1, 1, 2; 97: 1, 4; 100: 1; 103:33; 104: 2; 107: 2; 136: 3—S^1; 4; 137: 5; 143: 9; 149: 1; Ecc. 2: 8, 8; Isa. 5: 1; 23:16; 26: 1; Jer. 20:13; 37:19; Hos. 7: 2[d]

[a] B ᾠδή. [b] B ὁδούς. [c] S^3 ᾠδή. [d] A συνᾴδω.

ἀδωναΐ vide κύριος.

ἀδωρίμ.

Nehemiah 3: 5

ἀεί.

Jud. 16:20+A; Psa. 94:10
Isa. 42:14; 51:13

ἀέναος, ἀένναος.

Gen. 49:26; Deu. 33:15, 27
Job 19:25

ἀεργός.

Pro. 13: 4; 15:19
Pro. 19:15

ἀέρινος.

Esther (9)15+S^3

ἀετός.

Exo. 19: 4; Lev. 11:13; Deu. 14:12; 28:49; 32:11; 2 Sa. 1:23; Job 9:26; 39:27; Ps. 102: 5; Pro. 23: 5; 24:23; 52, 54
Isa. 40:31; Jer. 4:13; 29:17, 23; Lam. 4:19; Eze. 1:10; 10:14 A; 17: 3, 7; Dan. 7: 4; Hos. 8: 1; Obad. 4; Mic. 1:16; Hab. 1: 8

ἄζυμος.

Gen. 19: 3; Exo. 12: 8, 15; 18, 20; 39; 13: 6, 7; 23:15, 15; 29: 2; 2—A; 23; 34:18, 18; Lev. 2: 4, 4, 5; 6:16; 7: 2; 8: 2, 26; 10:12; 23: 6, 6; Nu. 6:15, 15
Nu. 6:17, 19; 19; 9:11; 28:17—A; Deu. 16: 3,8,16; Jos. 5:11; Jud. 6:19, 20; 21, 21; 1 Sa. 28:24; 2 Ki. 23: 9; 1 Ch. 23:29; 2 Ch. 8:13; 30:13, 21; 22; 35:17; Ezra 6:22; Eze. 45:21

ἀηδία.

Proverbs 23:29

ἀήρ.

2 Sa. 22:12
Psa. 17:12

ἀθανίν.

1 Kings 8: 2

ἀθαρείν.

Numbers 21: 1

ἀθερσασθά.

Nehemiah 7:65

ἀθεσία.

Jer. 3: 7 S[a]; 20: 8
Dan. 9: 7[b]

[a] pro ἀσυνθεσία. [b] A ἀθέτησις.

ἀθετέω.

Exo. 21: 8; Deu. 21:14; Jud. 9:23; 1 Sa. 2:17; 13: 3; 1 Ki. 8:50; 12:19; 2 Ki. 1: 1; 3: 5, 7; 8:20, 22; 22; 18: 7, 20; 24: 1, 20; 1 Ch. 2: 7; 5:25; 2 Ch. 10:19; 36:13, 14; Neh. 1: 8 S[1a]; Est. 2:15; Psa. 14: 4; 32:10; 10—S^1
Psa. 77:57 S[2a]; 88:35; 131:11; Pro. 11: 3 A; Isa. 1: 2; 21: 2, 2; 24:16, 16; 27: 4; 31: 2; 33: 1 *ter*; 48: 8, 8; 63: 8; Jer. 3:20, 20; 5:11, 11; 9: 2; 12: 1, 6; 15:16; Lam. 1: 2; Eze. 2: 3+A; 22:26; 39:23; Dan. 9: 7

[a] pro ἀσυνθετέω.

ἀθέτημα.

1 Ki. 8:50; 2 Ch. 36:14
Jer. 12: 1[a]

[a] A ἀθέτησις.

ἀθέτησις.

1 Sa. 24:12; Jer. 12: 1 A[a]
Dan. 9: 7 A[b]

[a] pro ἀθέτημα. [b] pro ἀθεσία.

ἀθροίζω.

Gen. 49: 2 A[a]; Nu. 20: 2[b]; 1 Sa. 7: 5; 2 Ki. 6:24
1 Ch. 16:35-ABS; Jer. 18:21; Eze. 36:24

[a] pro συνάγω. [b] A συναθροίζω.

ἀθυμέω.

Deu. 28:65 A[a]; 1 Sa. 1: 6, 7; 15:11; 2 Sa. 6: 8
1 Ch. 13:11; Isa. 25: 4; Jer. 30:12 S[1b]

[a] pro ἀπειθέω. [b] pro θυμόω.

ἀθυμία.

1 Sa. 1: 6; 16+A
Ps. 118:53

ἄθυτος.

Leviticus 19: 7

ἀθῷος.

Gen. 24:41, 41; Exo. 21:19, 28; 23: 7; Nu. 5:19, 28; 31; 32:22; Deu. 24: 7; 27:25; Jos. 2:17, 19; 20; Jud. 15: 3 A[a]; 1 Sa. 19: 5; 25:26, 31; 2 Sa. 3:28; 14: 9
1 Ki. 2: 5—B; 2 Ki. 21:16; 24: 4, 4; 2 Ch. 36: 5, 5; Job 9:28; 10:14; 12: 6; 22:30; Psa. 9:29; 14: 5; 17:26, 26; 23: 4; 25: 6; 72:13; 93:21
Ps. 105:38; Jer. 2:34, 35; 7: 6; 19: 4
Jer. 22: 3, 17; 26:28; 33:15; Nah. 1: 3

[a] pro ἀθῳόω.

ἀθῳόω.

Jud. 15: 3[a]; 1 Sa. 26: 9; 1 Ki. 2: 9; (3) p 1; Pro. 6:29; 16: 5; 17: 5
Jer. 15:15; 18:23; 26:28; 29:13, 13; Joel 3:21; Nah. 1: 3

[a] A ἀθῷος.

αἴγειος.

Exo. 25: 4; 35: 6, 26[a]
Nu. 31:20

[a] A ἅγιος.

αἰγιαλός.

Jud. 5:17 A[a]

[a] pro παραλία.

αἰγίδιον.

1 Samuel 10: 3

αἰδέομαι.

Proverbs 24:38—S

ἀΐδης vide ᾅδης.

αἰδοῖον.

Ezekiel 23:20, 20

αἰθάλη.

Exodus 9: 8, 10

αἰθῆ.

1 Ki. 1: 9[a]

[a] A λίθος.

αἰθρίζω.

Eze. 41:12 B[a]

[a] pro διορίζω.

αἴθριος.

Job 2: 9; Eze. 9: 3; 10: 4; 18+A
Eze. 40:14, 15; 15, 19; 19; 47: 1

αἴλ, αἰλεῦ.

Eze. 40:9,21,24; 26, 29; 31, 33
Eze. 40:34, 36; 37, 48; 41: 3

αἰλάμ.

1 Ki. 6: 7; 33—A; 7: 3, 7, 8; 43 *ter*; 44, 44; 45; 49+A; 2 Ch. 3: 4; Eze. 8:16; 40: 6, 7, 7; 9, 9; 9+A; 9, 10
Eze. 40:14, 15; 16, 16; 16—A; 25, 31; 40, 48; 48, 48; 49, 49; 41: 1, 2; 15, 25; 26; 44: 3; 46: 2, 8

αἰλαμμών.

Eze. 40:21, 22; 22, 24; 25, 26; 29, 29; 30 A
Eze. 40:33, 33; 34, 36; 36, 37; 38

αἷμα.

Gen. 4:10, 11; 9: 4, 5, 6; 6; 37:22, 26; 31
Gen. 42:22; 49:11; Exo. 4: 9, 25; 26—B; 7:17, 19

Exo. 7:19, 20
21
12: 7, 13
13, 22
22, 23
23:18
24: 6, 6, 8
8
29:12, 12
16, 20
21, 21
30:10
34:25
Lev. 1: 5, 5
11, 15
3: 2, 8
13, 17
4: 5, 6, 6
7, 7, 16
17, 18
18, 25
25, 30
30, 34
34
5: 9, 9
6:27, 30
32
7: 4, 16
17, 23
8:15, 15
19, 23
24, 24
30
9: 9 *ter*
12, 18
10:18
12: 4[a], 5, 7
14: 6, 11
17, 25
28, 51
52
15:19, 25
16:14, 14
15 *qtr*
18, 18
19, 27
17: 4, 4, 6
10, 10
11, 11
12, 12
13, 14
14, 14
19:16
20:18
Nu. 18:17
19: 4, 4, 5
23:24
35:12, 19
21, 24
25, 27
27, 33
33, 33
Deu. 12:16, 23
23
27 — B
15:23
17: 8, 8
19: 6, 10
10, 12
13
21: 7, 8, 8
9
27:25
32:14, 42
42 — B
43
Jos. 20: 3, 5 A
9
Jud. 9:24
1 Sa. 14:32, 33
34
19: 5
25:26, 31
33
26:20
2 Sa. 1:16, 22
3:27, 28
4:11
14:11
16: 7, 8, 8

2 Sa. 20:12
21: 1, 2 AB[b]
23:17
1 Ki. 2: 5, 5 — B
9, 31
32, 32
33
(3) *p* 1
37
18:28
20:19 *ter*
22:35, 35
38[e], 38
38
2 Ki. 3:22, 23
9: 7, 7, 26
26, 33
16:13, 15
15
21:16
24: 4, 4
1 Ch. 11:19
22: 8, 8
28: 3
2 Ch. 19:10 — A
10
24:25
29:22, 22
22 — B
24
30:16
35:11
36: 5, 5
Est. 7: 3 S[1d]
Job 6: 4
16:18
39:30
Psa. 5: 7
9:13
13: 3 — A
15: 4
25: 9
29:10
49:13
50:16
54:24
57:11
58: 3
67:24
77:44
78: 3, 10
93:21
104:29
105:38 *ter*
138:19
Pro. 1:11
16 AS[a]
6:17
21: 3
24:68
29:10
Ecc. 5: 5 A[1e]
Isa. 1:11, 15
4: 4
14:19
15: 9
26:21[f]
33:15
34: 3, 6
6 — AS
7
49:26
59: 3, 7
63: 3[c], 6
66: 3
Jer. 2:34
7: 6
19: 4
22: 3, 17
26:10
28, 35
31:10
33:15
Lam. 4:13, 14
Eze. 3:18, 20
5:17
14:19
16: 6, 6, 9
22, 36
38 + A

Eze. 16:38
38 + A
18:10, 13
21:32
22: 2, 3, 4
6, 9, 12
13, 27
23:37, 45
45
24: 6, 7, 8
9 + A
14, 17
28:23
32: 5
33: 2 + A
4, 5, 6, 8
25 A
25 A
35: 6, 6
36:18 + A
38:22

Eze. 39:17, 18
19
43:18, 20
44: 7, 15
24
45:19
Hos. 1: 4
4: 2, 2
12:14
Joel 2:30, 31
3:19, 21
Amos 2: 4 A[h]
Jon. 1:14 — S[1]
Mic. 3:10
7: 2
Nah. 3: 1
Hab. 2: 8, 12
17
Zeph. 1:17
Zec. 9: 7, 11
15 + AS[g]

[a] A ἱμάτιον. [b] *pro* ἔλλειμμα. [c] A ἅρμα. [d] *pro* αἴτημα. [e] *pro* στόμα. [f] A στόμα. [g] S[1] ἱμάτιον. [h] *pro* μάταιος.

αἱμορροοῦσα.

Leviticus 15:33

αἱμωδιάω.

Jer. 38:29, 30 Eze. 18: 4 + A

αἴνεσις.

Lev. 7: 2, 2, 3
5
1 Ch. 16:35
25: 3
2 Ch. 20:22
29:31
31 — A
33:16
Ezr. 10:11
Neh. 9: 5
12:31 — ABS[1]
38 S[3]
40 S[3]
46
Psa. 9:15
25: 7
32: 1
33: 2
47:11
49:14, 23
50:17
55:13
65: 2, 8
68:31

Psa. 70: 8, 14
72:28
77: 4
78:13
101:22
102: 2[a]
105: 2, 12
47
106:22
108: 1
110:10
115: 8
141: 1, 21
146: 1
149: 1
Isa. 12: 2
35:10
42:21
51: 3, 11
Jer. 17:26
40: 9
11 + A
Jon. 2:10
Hab. 3: 3

[a] A ἀνταπόδοσις, S ἀπόδοσις.

αἰνετός.

Lev. 19:24
2 Sa. 14:25
22: 4
1 Ch. 16:25

Psa. 47: 1
95: 4
112: 3[a]
144: 3

[a] S[1] αἰνέω.

αἰνέω.

Gen. 49: 8
Jud. 16:24 A[a]
1 Ch. 16: 4, 7
10 — S[1]
35, 36
41
23: 5, 5
30
29:13
2 Ch. 5, 13
6:26
7: 3
8:14
20:19, 21
21 — A
23:12
31: 2
Ezra 3:10, 11

Neh. 5:13
12:24, 36
37
Job 33:30
35:14
38: 7
Psa. 17: 4
21:24, 27
34:18
55:11, 11
62: 6
68:31, 35
73:21
83: 5
99: 4
101:19
105:12[b]
106:32

Ps. 108:30
112: 1, 1
3 S[1c]
113:25
116: 1
1 S[1d]
118:164
175
134: 1, 1, 3
144: 2
4 A[1d]
145: 1, 2
146: 1
147: 1
148: 1, 1, 2
2, 3, 3
4, 5, 7
13

Ps. 149: 3
150: 1, 1, 2
2, 3, 3
4, 4, 5
5, 6
Pro. 29:46, 48
49
Cant. 6: 8
Isa. 38:18
62: 9 — S[1]
Jer. 4: 2
20:13
38: 5, 7
Dan. 2:23
4:31, 34
5: 4, 23
Joel 2:26

[a] *pro* ὑμνέω. [b] S[3] εἰμί. [c] *pro* αἰνετός. [d] *pro* ἐπαινέω.

αἴνιγμα.

Nu. 12: 8
Deu. 28:37
1 Ki. 10: 1

2 Ch. 9: 1
Pro. 1: 6

αἰνιγματιστής.

Numbers 21:27

αἶνος.

2 Ch. 23:13
Ezra 3:11
Neh. 11:17 + S[3]

Job 15:27 + A
Psa. 92: 1
94: 1

αἴξ.

Gen. 15: 9
30:32, 33
35
31:10, 12
38
32:14
37:31
38:17, 20
Lev. 3:12
4:23, 28
5: 6
7:13
9: 3
16: 5
17: 3
22:19, 27
23:19
Nu. 7:16, 22
28, 34
40, 46
52, 58
64, 70
76, 82
87
15:11, 24
27
18:17

Nu. 28:15, 22
30
29: 5, 11
16, 19
22, 25
28, 31
34, 38
31:28 B[a]
Deu. 14: 4
Jud. 6:19
13:15, 19
14: 6 — B
15: 1
1 Sa. 16:20
19:13, 16
25: 2
1 Ki. 21:27
2 Ch. 29:21
31: 6
35: 7[b]
Ezra 6:17
Cant. 4: 1
6: 4
Eze. 43:22
45:23
Dan. 8: 5, 8, 21

[a] *pro* ὄνος. [b] B ἅγιος.

αἰπόλιον.

Proverbs 24:66

αἰπόλος.

Amos 7:14

αἵρεσις.

Leviticus 22:18, 21

αἱρετίζω.

Gen. 30:20
Nu. 14: 8[a]
Jud. 5: 8 A[b]
1 Ch. 28: 4, 6
10
29: 1
2 Ch. 29:11
Psa. 24:12
118:30

Ps. 118:173
131:13, 14
Eze. 20: 5
Hos. 4:18
Hag. 2:23
Zec. 1:17
2:12
Mal. 3:17, 17

[a] B ἐρεθίζω. [b] *pro* ἐκλέγω.

αἱρετώτερος.

Pro. 16:16, 16 Pro. 22: 1

αἱρέω.

Deu. 26:17, 18
Jos. 24:15 A[a]
2 Sa. 15:15[b]
1 Ch. 21:10[b]

Job 34: 4
Isa. 38:17
Jer. 8: 3
Eze. 26:16 A[ac]

[a] *pro* ἐκλέγω. [b] A ἐρῶ. [c] *pro* ἀφαιρέω.

αἴρω.

Gen. 35: 2
40:16
43:33
44: 1
45:23, 23
46: 5
47:30
Exo. 25:13, 26
27
27: 7
30: 4
38: 4, 10
24
Lev. 10: 4, 5
11:25, 28
40
15:10
Nu. 1:50
2:17
4:15, 15
24, 25
31, 32
47, 49
7: 9
10:17, 21
11:12
13:24
Deu. 10: 8
31: 9, 25
32:40
Jos. 3: 3, 6, 6
8, 13
14, 15
15, 17
4: 5, 9, 10
16, 18
6:12
13 A[a]
9: 6
Jud. 3:18 A[a]
8:28
9:48[b]
49 + A
54
19:17[c]
21: 2[d]
Ruth 2:18
1 Sa. 2:28
4: 4
6:13
10: 3 *ter*
11: 4
14: 1, 3, 6
7, 12
12, 13
13, 14
17
18 — A
15:25
16:21
17: 7, 41 A
18:11 A
22:18
24:17
25:28
30: 4
31: 4, 4, 5
6
2 Sa. 2:22, 32
3:32
4: 4
6: 3
3 + A
13
13:34

2 Sa. 15:24
18:15
19:42
23:37
24:12
1 Ki. 2:26
(3) *p* 1 — A
4:21
5: 9, 15
17 + A
6: 2
8: 3
31 B[e]
10: 2, 11
13:29 — A
14:28
15:22
18:12
2 Ki. 2:16[f]
4: 4, 10
20 — AB
5:23
7: 8
9:26
14:20
19:22
23:16
25:13
1 Ch. 5:18
10: 4, 4, 5
11:39
12: 8
15: 2
2 — BS
26, 27
23:26
2 Ch. 9: 1
14: 8
35: 3[d]
Neh. 4:17[g]
13:19
Est. 4: 1[h]
5: 2
9:29 S[1i]
Job 6: 2
15:25
21: 3[k]
Psa. 23: 7, 9
24: 1
27: 2
62: 5
82: 3
85: 4
90:12
92: 3 + AS[a]
95: 8
118:48
120: 1
122: 1
125: 6 AS[lm]
6
142: 8
150: *p* 6 *bis*
Pro. 1:12
Cant. 5: 7
Isa. 5:23, 26
8: 8
10:14, 15
11:12
13: 2
15: 9
16: 4, 10
17: 1
8 + S[1]
18: 3

Isa. 26:10, 14
30:14−S[1]
32:13
33: 8, 23
37:23
45:20
46: 1[n], 3
7
48:14
49:18, 22
22, 22
51: 6, 13[o]
53: 8[p], 8
57: 1, 1, 2
14
58:13
59:15
60: 4, 4
66:12
Jer. 3: 2
6: 1
10: 5, 5
5+S[1]
17:21, 27
28:12, 27

Jer. 28:27[q]
38:24
50:10
Lam. 2:19
19+A
3:27, 28
Eze. 12:12
20:28, 42
23:27
30:18[r]
36: 7
44:12
47:14
Dan. 7:18
8: 3, 13
9:27
10: 5
Jon. 1:12
Mic. 2: 1, 3
4: 3 A[s]
Zec. 1:18, 21
2: 1
5: 1, 9
6: 1

[a] *pro* φέρω. [b] A λαμβάνω. [c] A ἀναβλέπω. [d] A ἐπαίρω. [e] *pro* ἀράομαι. [f] B εὑρίσκω. [g] S διαίρω. [h] S[1] ἐρῶ. [i] *pro* ἄγω. [k] A βαστάζω. [m] *pro* βάλλω. [n] A ἴδομαι. [o] A ἀρίσκω. [p] S[1] ἄγω. [q] A ἀφορι θ. [r] AB ἄγω. [s] *pro* ἀνταίρω.

αἰσθάνομαι.

Job 23: 5
40:18
Pro. 17:10

Pro. 24:14
Isa. 33:11[a]
49:26

[a] AS[2] αἰσχύνω.

αἴσθησις.

Exo. 28: 3
Pro. 1: 4, 7
22
2: 3+AB[a]C[2]
10
3:20
5: 2
8:10+B[a]
10:14

Pro. 11: 9
12: 1, 23
14: 6, 7, 18
15: 7, 14
18:15
19:25
22:12
23:12
24: 4

αἰσθητήριον.

Jeremiah 4:19

αἰσθητικός.

Proverbs 14:10, 30

αἰσχρός.

Gen. 41: 3, 4, 19
19, 20

Gen. 41:21

αἰσχρῶς.

Proverbs 15:10

αἰσχύνη.

1 Sa. 20:30, 30
2 Sa. 23: 7
1 Ki. 18:19, 25
2 Ki. 8:11
2 Ch. 32:21
Ezra 9: 7
Job 6:20
8:22
Psa. 34:26
39:16
43:16
68:20
70:13
88:46
108:29
131:18
Pro. 9:13
19:13
26:11, 11

Isa. 3: 9
19: 9
20: 4
30: 3, 5
42:17
45:16
47: 3, 10
50: 6
54: 4
Jer. 2:26
3:24, 25
12:13+A
20:18
38:19
Eze. 7:18
16:36, 37
22:10
23:10[a]
18[a]

Eze. 23:29
Dan. 9: 7, 8
12: 2
Hos. 9:10

Obad. 10
Mic. 7:10
Nah. 3: 5[a]
Hab. 2:10

[a] A ἀσχημοσύνη.

αἰσχύνω.

Gen. 3: 1
Jud. 3:25
5:28[a]
1 Sa. 13: 4
27:12, 12
2 Sa. 16:21 A[b]
19: 3
2 Ki. 2:17
1 Ch. 19: 6
2 Ch. 12: 6
Ezra 8:22
9: 6
Job 6:19+A
19: 3
32:21
34:19 A[c]
Psa. 6:11, 11[d]
24: 3
30:18
34: 4, 26
68: 7
69: 3, 4
70:13, 24
82:18
83:17
96: 7
108:28
118: 6[e], 46
78, 80
128: 5
Pro. 1:22
13: 5
20: 4[f]
22:26
28:21
29:15, 25
Ecc. 10:17
Isa. 1:29[g]

Isa. 1:20[e]
20: 5
23: 4
24: 9
23+S[1]
26:11
29:22
30: 6+AS
33: 9
11 AS[2h]
41:11
42:17
44: 9
11−S[3]
45:16, 17
24
49:23
50: 7[i]
65:13
66: 5
Jer. 2:26
6:15 AS[b]
8: 9
12:13
14: 4
17:13 S[1b]
20:11
22:22
27:12
28:51
31: 1
39−S[1]
Eze. 16:52, 63
23:29[k]
36:32
Hos. 10: 6
Joel 1:12
Zec. 9: 5

[a] A ἐσχατίζω. [b] *pro* καταισχύνω. [c] *pro* ἐπαισχύνομαι. [d] AS[2] καταισχύνω. [e] AS[1] ἐπαισχύνομαι. [f] S καταισχύνω. [g] A καταισχ- [h] *pro* αἰσθάνομαι. [i] [illegible] καταισχύνω. [k] A ἀσχημονέω.

αἰτέω.

Exo. 3:22
11: 2
12:35
22:14
Deu. 10:12
18:16
Jos. 14:12
15:18
19:50
21:42
Jud. 1:14
5:25
8:24, 26
1 Sa. 1:17, 20
27
8:10
12:13+A
17
19
2 Sa. 3:13
12:20
1 Ki. 2:16, 20
20, 22
22
3: 5, 10
11 *qnq*
13
10:13
12:*p*24, *l*17

1 Ki. 19: 4
2 Ki. 2: 9, 10
4: 3, 28
1 Ch. 4:10
2 Ch. 1: 7, 11
11, 11
9:12
11:23
Ezra 6: 9
7:21
8:22
Neh. 13: 6
Job 6:22, 25
Psa. 2: 8
20: 5
26: 4
39: 7[a]
77:18
104:40
Pro. 24:30
Ecc. 2:10
Isa. 7:11, 12
58: 2
Lam. 4: 4
Dan. 2:49
6: 7, 12
13
Mic. 7: 3
Zec. 10: 1

[a] AS ζητέω.

αἴτημα.

Jud. 8:24[a]
1 Sa. 1:17, 27

1 Ki. 3: 5
12:*p*24 *l*17

Est. 5: 6+S[3]
7
8+S[3]
7: 2, 3[b]
Psa. 19: 6

Psa. 36: 4
105:15
Dan. 6: 7, 12
13

[a] A αἴτησις. [b] S[1] αἷμα.

αἴτησις.

Jud. 8:24 A[a]
1 Ki. 2:16, 20

Job 6: 8

[a] *pro* αἴτημα.

αἰτία.

Gen. 4:13
Job 18:14

Pro. 28:17

αἰτιάομαι.

Proverbs 18:22

αἴτιος.

1 Samuel 22:22

αἰχμαλωσία.

Nu. 21: 1
31:12, 19
26
Deu. 21:13
28:41
32:42
Jud. 5:12
2 Ki. 24:14
2 Ch. 6:37
28: 5, 11
13, 14
15, 17
29: 9
Ezra 2: 1
3: 8
5: 5
8:35
9: 7
Neh. 1: 2, 3
4: 5
7: 6
8:17
Psa. 13: 7
52: 7
67:19
77:48 S[1a]
61
84: 2
95: 1
125: 1, 5
Isa. 1:27
20: 4
45:13
Jer. 1: 3
15: 2, 2
20: 6

Jer. 22:22
25:18
26:27
37:18
38:19, 23
Lam. 1: 5, 18
2:14, 21
Eze. 1: 1, 2
3:11, 15
11:15, 24
25
12: 3, 4, 7
11
25: 3
29:14
30:17−A
32: 9
33:21
39:25
40: 1
Dan. 1: 3
2:25
5:13
6:13
8:11
11: 8, 33
Hos. 6:10
Joel 3: 1, 8
Amos 1: 6, 9, 15
4:10
9: 4, 14
Hab. 1: 9
Zeph. 2: 7
3:20
Zec. 6: 9
14: 2

[a] *pro* χάλαζα.

αἰχμαλωτεύω.

Gen. 14:14
34:29
Nu. 24:22
1 Sa. 30: 2+A
2, 3, 5
1 Ki. 8:50
2 Ki. 5: 2
6:22
1 Ch. 5:21
2 Ch. 6:36, 36
38
38−AB
28: 5, 8 A[a]
11, 17 A[a]
Est. 2: 6

Job 1:15, 16
17
Psa. 67:19
105:46[b]
136: 3
Isa. 14: 2
49:24, 25
Jer. 27:33
Eze. 6: 9
12: 3
39:23
Amos 1: 5[c], 6
5: 5, 5
Obad. 11
Mic. 1:16

[a] *pro* αἰχμαλωτίζω. [b] AS *ibid.* [c] A *ibid.*

αἰχμαλωτίζω.

Jud. 5:12
1 Ki. 8:46, 46
2 Ki. 24:14
2 Ch. 28: 8[a], 17[a]
30: 9
Psa. 70: 1

Ps. 105:46 AS[b]
Lam. 1: 1
Eze. 12: 3+A
30:17+A
Amos 1: 5 A[b]

[a] A αἰχμαλωτεύω. [b] *pro ibid.*

αἰχμαλωτίς.

Gen. 31:26

Exo. 12:29

αἰχμάλωτος.

Exo. 22:10
14−A[1]
Nu. 21:29
Est. 2: 6
Job 12:17, 19
41:23
Isa. 5:13
14: 2
23: 1

Isa. 46: 2
52: 2
61: 1
Eze. 12: 4
30:18
Amos 6: 7
7:11, 17
Nah. 3:10

αἰών.

Gen. 3:22
6: 3, 4
13:15, 17
Exo. 12:24
14:13
15:18, 18
19: 9
21: 6
29: 9
32:13
40:13
Lev. 3:17
25:46
Deu. 5:29
12:25+A
28
13:16
15:17
23: 3, 6
28:46
29:29
32: 7, 40
Jos. 4: 7
8:28
14: 9
Jud. 2: 1
1 Sa. 1:22
2:30
3:13, 14
13:13
20:15, 23
42
27:12
2 Sa. 3:28
7:13, 16
16, 24
25
25+A
26, 29
29
12:10
22:51
1 Ki. 1:31
2:33, 33
3:45
8:13 A
9: 3
3+B
5
10: 9
2 Ki. 5:27
21: 7
1 Ch. 15: 2
16:15, 34
36
36−BS
41
17:12, 14
14, 16
22, 23
24−ABS
27, 27
22:10
23:13, 13
25
28: 4, 7, 8
29:10, 10
18
2 Ch. 2: 4
5:13
6: 2
7: 3, 6, 16
9: 8

2 Ch. 13: 5
20: 7, 21
30: 8
33: 4, 7
Ezra 3:11
4:15, 19
9:12, 12
Neh. 2: 3
9: 5
5−A
13: 1
Est. 9:31
Job 1:21+A
3:18 AS[2a]
7:16
19:18, 23
Psa. 5:12
9: 6 *ter*
8, 19[b]
37 *ter*
11: 8
14: 5
17:51
18:10, 10
20: 5
5+B[a]S[1]
5
7+S[1]
7, 7
21:28, 28
24: 6
27: 9
28:10
29: 7, 13
30: 2
32:11
36:18, 27
27−S[1]
28, 29
29
40:13, 14
14
43:10
44: 3, 7, 7
18 *ter*
47: 9, 15
15, 15
15−B
48: 9, 12
20
51:10 *ter*
11
54:20, 23
60: 5, 8, 9
9−S[2]
65: 7
70: 1
71:17
19−S[1]
19−S[1]
19−S[1]
72:12, 26
73:12
74:10
76: 8
77:69
78:13
80:16
82:18, 18
83: 5, 5
84: 6
85:12

Psa. 88: 2, 3, 5
29, 30
30, 37
38, 53
89: 2, 2, 8
91: 8, 8, 9
92: 2
99: 5
101: 13, 29
102: 9, 17
17
103: 5, 5
31
104: 8
105: 1, 31
48, 48
106: 1
109: 4
110: 3, 3, 5
8, 8, 9
10, 10
111: 3, 3, 6
9, 9
112: 2
113: 26
116: 2
117: 1, 2, 3
4—S
29
118: 44 *ter*
52, 89
93, 98
111, 112
142, 144
152, 160
120: 8
124: 1, 2
130: 3
131: 12, 14
14
132: 3
134: 13
135: 1 *to* 26
23—S^1
137: 8
142: 3
144: 1 *ter*
2—B
2—B
2—B
13, 21
21, 21
145: 6, 10
148: 6 *ter*
Pro. 6:33
8:21, 23
9: 6—S^2
10:25, 30
19:21
27:23
Ecc. 1: 4, 10
2:16
3:11, 14
9: 6
12: 5
Isa. 9:6+AS^2, 7
13:20
14:20
17: 2
18: 7
19:20

Isa. 25: 2
26: 4
28:28
30: 8
32:14, 17
33:20
34:10, 17
40: 8
44: 7
45:17
46: 9
47: 7
48:12
51: 6, 8, 9
57:15
15+S
16
59:21
60:21
63: 9
64: 4
Jer. 2:20
3: 5, 12
7: 7, 7
17:25
20:11
25: 5, 5
27:13+A
39
28:26, 62
29:14
30:11
35: 8
38:40
40:11
42: 6
Lam. 3: 6, 30
5:19
Eze. 25:15 A[c]
26:20, 21
27:36
28:19
32:27
37:25+A
25, 26
28
43: 7, 9
Dan. 2: 4, 20
20, 44
44
3: 9
4:31
5: 4+AB^2
10
6: 6, 21
26
7:18, 18
12: 3, 7
Hos. 2:19
Joel 2: 2, 26
27
3:20
Amos 9:11
Obad. 10
Mic. 4: 5, 7
5: 2
7:14
Zeph. 2: 9
Zec. 1: 5
Mal. 1: 4
3: 4

[a] *pro* αἰώνιος. [b] AS^2 τέλος.
[c] *pro* εἰς.

αἰώνιος.

Gen. 9:12, 16
17: 7, 8, 13
19
21:33
48: 4
Exo. 3:15
12:14—A
17
24+A
27:21
28:39
29:28
30:21
31:16, 17

Lev. 6:18, 22
7:24, 26
10: 9
13+B
15
16:29, 31
34
17: 7
23:14, 21
31, 41
24: 3, 8, 9
25:34
Nu. 10: 8
15:15

Nu. 18: 8, 11
19, 19
23
19:10, 21
25:13
2 Sa. 23: 5
1 Ch. 16:17
Job 3:18[a]
10:21
21:11
22:15
33:12
34:17
40:23
Psa. 23: 7, 9
75: 5
76: 6
77:66
104:10
111: 6
138:24
Pro. 22:28
23:10
Isa. 24: 5
26: 4
33:14
35:10
40:28
45:17
51:11
54: 4, 8
55: 3, 13
56: 5

Isa. 58:12, 12
60:15, 19
20
61: 4
4 S^1[b]
7, 8
63:11, 12
65:15 S^1[c]
Jer. 5:22
6:16
18:15, 16
20:17
23:40, 40
25: 9, 12
27: 5
28:39—S^1
38: 3
39:40
Eze. 16:60
26:20
35: 5, 9
36: 2
37:26
46:14+A
Dan. 3:33
4:31
7:14, 27
9:24
12: 2, 2
Jon. 2: 7
Mic. 2: 9
Hab. 3: 6, 6

[a] AS^2 αἰών. [b] *pro* ἔρημος.
[c] *pro* καινός.

ἀκαθαρσία.

Lev. 5: 3, 3
7:10, 11
15: 3 *ter*
24, 25
26:30
31, 31
16:16, 16
19
18:19
19:23
20:21, 25
22: 3, 4, 5
Nu. 19:13
Jud. 13: 7 A[a]
2 Sa. 11: 4
2 Ch. 29: 5, 16
Ezra 6:21
9:11
Pro. 6:16

Pro. 24: 9
Jer. 19:13
39:34
Lam. 1: 9
Eze. 4:14
7:20
9: 9
22:10, 15
24:11
13+A
13+A
36:17+A
17, 17
25, 29
39:24
Hos. 2:10
Mic. 2:10
Nah. 3: 6[b]

[a] *pro* ἀκάθαρτος. [b] S^1 ἁμαρτία.

ἀκάθαρτος.

Lev. 5: 2 *qtr*
7: 9
11 *ter*
10:10
11: 4, 5, 6
7, 8
24, 25
26, 26
27, 27
28, 28
29, 31
31, 32
32, 33
34, 34
35 *ter*
36, 38
39, 40
40, 43
47
12: 2, 2, 4
5, 5
13:11, 15
36, 45
46, 46
51, 55
14:19+AB
36, 40
41, 44
45, 46

Lev. 14:47, 47
57
15: 2, 4, 4
5, 6, 7
8, 9, 10
10, 11
16, 17
18, 19
20, 20
21, 22
23, 24
24, 25
26, 27
27
17:15
20:25, 25
22: 5, 6
27:11, 27
Nu. 5: 2
9: 6, 7, 10
18:15
19: 7, 8, 10
11, 13
14, 15
16, 17
19:19
20, 21
22 *ter*
Deu. 12:15, 22

Deu. 14: 7, 8, 10
18
15:22
26:14
Jud. 13: 4, 7[a]
14
2 Ch. 23:19
Job 15:16
Pro. 3:32
16: 5
17:15
20:10
21:15
Ecc. 9: 2

Isa. 6: 5, 5
35: 8, 8
52: 1, 11
64: 6
Lam. 4:15
Eze. 4:13
22: 5, 26
24:14
44:23
Hos. 8:13
9: 3
Amos 7:17
Hag. 2:13—S^3
Zec. 13: 2

[a] A ἀκαθαρσία.

ἀκάθεκτος.

Job 31:11 A[a] [a] *pro* ἀκατάσχετος.

ἀκακία.

Job 2: 3
27: 5[a]
31: 6
36:10 S^1[b]
Psa. 7: 9
25: 1, 11

Psa. 36:37
40:13
77:72
83:12
100: 2

[a] S κακία. [b] *pro* ἀδικία.

ἄκακος.

Job 2: 3[a]
8:20
36: 5
Psa. 24:21
Pro. 1: 4, 22
2:21+AS^2
8: 5

Pro. 13: 6 A
14:15
15:10
21 S^2[b]
21:11
Jer. 11:19

[a] A δίκαιος. [b] *pro* κακός.

ἀκάλυπτος.

Lev. 13:45[a] [a] A ἀκατακάλυπτος.

ἄκαν.

2 Kings 14: 9, 9

ἄκανθα.

Gen. 3:18
Exo. 22: 6
Jud. 8: 7, 16
2 Sa. 23: 6
Psa. 31: 4
57:10
117:12
Pro. 15:19
26: 9
Ecc. 7: 7
Cant. 2: 2

Isa. 5: 2, 4, 6
7:23, 24
25
32:13
33:12
34:13 A[a]
Jer. 4: 3
12:13
Eze. 28:24
Hos. 9: 6
10: 8

[a] *pro* ἀκάνθινος.

ἀκάνθινος.

Isa. 34:13[a] [a] A ἄκανθα.

ἀκάρδιος.

Pro. 10:13
17:16

Jer. 5:21

ἀκαρπία.

Proverbs 9:12

ἄκαρπος.

Jeremiah 2: 6

ἀκατακάλυπτος.

Lev. 13:45 A[a] [a] *pro* ἀκάλυπτος.

ἀκαταπάτητος.

Job 20:18 A[a] [a] *pro* ἀκατάποτος.

ἀκατάποτος.

Job 20:18[a] [a] A ἀκαταπάτητος.

ἀκατασκεύαστος.

Genesis 1: 2

ἀκαταστασία.

Proverbs 26:28

ἀκατάστατος.

Isaiah 54:11

ἀκατάσχετος.

Job 31:11[a] [a] A ἀκάθεκτος.

ἀκατέργαστος.

Psalm 138:16

ἄκαυστος.

Job 20:26[a]
[a] AS^* ἄσβεστος, BS^1 ἀκουστός.

ἀκηδία.

Psa. 118:28
Isa. 61: 3

ἀκηδιάζω.

Psa. 60: 3
101: 1

Psa. 142: 4

ἀκηλίδωτος.

Pro. 25:18 AS^2[a] [a] *pro* ἀκιδωτός.

ἀκιδωτός.

Pro. 25:18[a] [a] AS^2 ἀκηλίδωτος.

ἀκίνητος.

Exo. 25:14
Job 39:26

ἀκίς.

Job 16:10

ἄκλητος.

Esther 4:11

ἄκμων.

Job 41:15

ἀκοή.

Exo. 15:26
19: 5
22:23
23: 1, 22
22—A
Deu. 11:13, 22
15: 5
28: 1, 2
1 Sa. 2:24, 24
15:22
2 Sa. 13:30
22:45
23:23
1 Ki. 2:28
10: 7
2 Ch. 9: 6
Job 37: 1
42: 5

Psa. 17:45
111: 7
Isa. 6: 9
52: 7
53: 1
Jer. 6:24
10:22
27:43
29:15
30:12
38:18
44: 5
Eze. 16:56
Dan. 11:44
Hos. 7:12
Obad. 1
Nah. 1:12
Hab. 3: 1

ἀκόλαστος.

Pro. 19:29
20: 1

Pro. 21:11

ἀκολουθέω.

Nu. 22:20
Ruth 1:14
1 Sa. 25:42
1 Ki. 16:22+A

1 Ki. 19:20
Isa. 45:14
Eze. 29:16
Hos. 2: 5 A[a]

[a] *pro* πορεύω.

ἀκονάω.

Psa. 44: 6
51: 4[a]
63: 4

Ps. 119: 4
139: 4
Pro. 5: 4

[a] BS^1 ἐξακονάω.

ἀκοντίζω.

1 Sa. 20:20, 36
36, 37

Psa. 75: 9 B^1[a]
[a] *pro* ἀκοντίζω.

ἀκοντιστής.

1 Samuel 31: 3

ἄκοσμος.

Proverbs 25:20

ἀκουσιάζομαι.

Nu. 15:28
Jud. 5: 2 B[a]
Ezra 7:10 B[a]

[a] pro ἑκουσιάζομαι.

ἀκούσιος.

Nu. 15:25, 25, 26
Ecc. 10: 5

ἀκουσίως.

Lev. 4: 2, 13, 22, 27; 5:15
Nu. 15:24, 27, 28, 29; 35:11, 15
Deu. 19: 4 A[a]
Jos. 20: 3, 9
Job 31:33

[a] pro εἰδέω.

ἀκουστής

Deu. 30:13[a]

[a] A ἀκούω.

ἀκουστός.

Gen. 45: 2
Exo. 28:31
Deu. 4:36
Jud. 13:23 A[a]
1 Sa. 9:27 A[b]
2 Ki. 7: 6
Job 20:26 BS[1][c]
Ps. 105: 2; 142: 8
Isa. 18: 3; 23: 5; 30:30; 45:21; 48: 3, 5, 6, 20, 20+S[1]; 52: 7; 62:11
Jer. 27: 2; 38: 7[d]

[a] pro ἀκουτίζω. [b] pro ἀκούω. [c] pro ἄκαυστος. [d] S ἀκούω.

ἀκουτίζω.

Jud. 13:23[a]
Psa. 50:10; 65: 8; 75: 9[b]
Cant. 2:14; 8:13
Jer. 30: 2

[a] A ἀκουστός. [b] S[1] ἀκοντίζω.

ἀκούω.

Gen. 3: 8, 10, 17; 4:23; 11: 7; 14:14; 18:10; 21: 6, 12, 26; 23: 6, 8, 10, 11, 13, 15, 16; 24:30, 52; 27: 5, 6, 8, 34, 43; 28: 7; 29:13, 33; 31: 1; 34: 5, 7; 35:22; 37: 6, 17, 21, 27; 39:15, 18, 19; 41:15, 15; 42: 2, 23; 43:25; 45: 2; 47: 5; 49: 2, 2, 2—A
Exo. 2:15; 3: 7; 15:14, 26; 18: 1, 19—A, 24; 19: 5, 8, 9; 23:13, 22, 22; 24: 3, 7; 32:17, 18; 33: 4
Lev. 5: 1; 10:20; 24:14
Nu. 7:89; 9: 8; 11: 1, 10; 12: 2, 6; 14:13, 14, 15, 27; 16: 4; 20:10; 21: 1; 22:36; 23:18; 24: 4, 16; 30: 5, 6, 8, 8, 9, 12, 13, 15, 16; 33:40
Deu. 1:17, 34; 2:25; 4: 1, 6, 10, 12, 28, 32—A, 33, 33, 36; 5: 1, 23, 24, 25, 26, 27, 27, 28, 28; 6: 3, 4; 7:12; 8:20; 9: 1, 2; 10:10 B[a]; 11:13[b], 22, 27, 28[c]; 12:28; 13: 3, 4, 11, 12, 18[c]; 17:13; 18:14, 15, 16, 19; 19: 9[c], 20; 20: 3; 21:20 A[d], 21; 27: 9; 28: 1[c], 2[c], 9[c], 13, 45 A[a], 49; 29: 4, 19; 30:12, 13 A[a]; 31:12, 12, 13; 32: 2
Jos. 1:17, 17, 18; 2:10, 11; 3: 9; 5: 1; 6:10, 20; 7: 9; 9: 1, 9, 15, 17—A, 22; 10: 1; 11: 1; 14:12; 22: 2, 11, 30; 24:24, 27
Jud. 3: 4; 5: 3, 16[c]; 7:11, 15; 9: 7, 7, 30, 46; 11:10, 17, 28[c]; 14:13; 18:25; 19:25 A[a]; 20: 3, 13 A[f], 13[c]
Ruth 1: 6; 2: 8
1 Sa. 1:13; 2:22, 23, 24, 24, 25; 3: 9, 10, 11; 4: 6, 14, 19; 7: 7, 7; 8: 7, 9, 19, 21, 22; 9:27[g]; 11: 6—A; 12: 1, 14, 15[c]; 13: 3, 4; 14:22, 27; 15: 1, 14, 19, 20, 22, 24; 16: 2; 17:11, 23 A, 28 A, 31 A; 19: 6; 22: 1, 6, 7, 12; 23:10, 10, 11, 25; 24:10; 25: 4, 7, 24, 35, 39; 26:19; 28:18, 21—A, 21, 22, 23; 31:11
2 Sa. 3:28; 4: 1; 5:17, 17, 24; 7:22; 8: 9; 10: 7; 11:26; 13:14, 16, 21; 14:16, 17; 15: 3, 10, 35, 36; 16:21; 17: 5, 9, 9; 18: 5—A; 19: 2, 35; 20:16, 16—A, 17, 17; 22:45[h]
1 Ki. 1:11, 41, 41, 45, (3) 42+A; 3: 9, 28; 4:30, 30; 5: 1+A, 7, 8; 6:11; 8:28, 41+A; 9: 3; 10: 1, 6, 7, 8, 24; 11:21, 43; 12:15, 16, 20, 24, p24, l14, ll 16, 82; 13: 4, 26; 14: 6 A; 15:20, 21; 16:16; 17:22+A; 19:13; 20:15, 16; 21: 8, 25, 36; 22:10, 28+A
2 Ki. 3:21; 5: 8; 6:30; 7: 1; 9:13, 30; 11:13; 14:11; 16: 9; 17:14, 40; 18:12, 12, 26, 28, 31, 32; 19: 1, 4, 6, 7, 8, 9, 11, 16, 16, 20, 25+A; 20: 5, 12, 16; 21: 9, 12; 22:11, 13, 18, 19, 19; 25:23
1 Ch. 10:11; 14: 8, 8, 15; 15:19; 17:20; 18: 9; 19: 8; 28: 2
2 Ch. 6:20, 21, 21, 35, 39; 7:12; 9: 1, 5, 6, 7, 23; 10: 2, 15, 16; 13: 4; 15: 2—8, 8; 16: 4, 5; 18:18, 27; 20: 9, 15, 20, 29; 23:12; 24:19, 19 A[d]; 25:20; 26:15; 28:11; 29: 5; 33:10 A[i]; 34:19, 21 B[a], 26, 27, 27; 35:22
Ezra 3:13; 4: 1; 9: 3
Neh. 1: 4, 6; 2:10, 19; 4: 1, 4, 7, 15[k], 20; 5: 6; 6: 1, 6, 16; 8: 2, 9; 9: 9, 16, 27, 29, 29; 12:42, 43; 13:3, 27
Est. 1:18, 20; 2: 8; 4: 4; 7: 8
Job 1:20+A; 2:11; 3:18; 4:16; 5:27; 13: 1, 6, 17 ter; 15: 8, 17; 16: 2; 20: 3; 21: 2, 2; 26:14; 27: 9 A[a]; 28:22; 29:10, 11, 21; 30:20[m]; 31:30, 35; 32:11, 11, 11+A; 33: 1, 8, 31+A, 31, 33; 34: 2, 10, 16, 34; 36:11, 31 B[n]; 37: 1, 3; 39: 7, 34; 42: 4, 5, 11
Psa. 6:10 AS[2][a]; 17: 7; 18: 4; 25: 7; 29:11; 30:14; 33:3, 12; 37:14, 15; 43: 2; 44:11; 47: 9; 48: 2; 49: 7; 58: 8; 61:12; 65:16; 77: 3, 21, 59; 80: 6, 9, 9, 12, 14; 84: 9; 91:12[a]; 93: 9; 94: 8; 96: 8; 101:21; 102:20; 113:14; 118:149; 131: 6; 134:17 A[p]; 137: 1—A, 4; 140: 6
Pro. 1: 5, 8, 33; 4: 1, 10; 5: 7, 13; 7:24; 8:32, 33 AS[2]; 16:21; 18:13; 19:20; 20:12; 22:17; 23:19, 22; 29:24
Ecc. 4:17; 7: 6, 6, 22; 9:16 ACS[a]; 9:17; 12:13
Cant. 2:12
Isa. 1: 2, 10; 5: 9; 6: 8, 9, 10, 10; 7:13; 15: 4; 16: 6; 21: 3, 10, 10, 10; 24:16; 28:12, 14, 19, 22, 23, 23; 29:18; 30: 9, 15, 21; 32: 3, 4, 9, 9 A[a]; 33:13, 15, 19, 19; 34: 1, 1; 35: 5; 36:11, 13, 16; 37: 1, 4, 6, 7, 8, 9, 11, 21, 26; 38: 5; 39: 1, 5; 40:21, 28; 41:26; 42: 2, 18, 20, 24; 43: 9—S[1]; 44: 1, 8—AS; 46: 3, 7 AS[1][a], 12; 47: 8; 48: 1, 6, 7, 12, 14, 16, 18; 49: 1; 50: 4, 10 A[d]; 51: 1, 4, 4, 7, 21; 52:15; 55: 2—B; 58: 4; 60:18; 64: 4; 65:19; 66: 4, 5, 8, 19
Jer. 2: 4, 31; 3:13 A[d], 21, 25 A[d]; 4: 5, 15, 19, 21, 31; 5:15, 20, 21, 21; 6: 7, 10 ABS[a], 10, 10+AS[2], 17, 17, 18, 19, 24; 7: 2, 13[q], 23, 24[r], 26 BS[o], 28; 8: 6, 16; 9:10, 13, 19, 20; 10: 1; 11: 2, 3, 4, 6, 10 A[a]; 13:11 AS[1][a], 15, 17; 17:20, 22, 23[c], 24 A[a], 27[r]; 18: 2, 10, 13, 18; 19: 3, 3; 20: 1, 10, 16; 21:11; 22: 2, 21—A, 21, 29; 23:16, 18, 22[q], 25; 25: 7[m]; 26:12; 27:43, 45, 46; 28:51; 29:15, 21, 22; 30:12; 31: 5, 20; 33: 3, 4, 5[m], 7, 10, 11, 12—S, 13, 21, 21; 34: 7, 13; 35: 7; 36: 8; 37: 5; 38: 7 S[a], 10, 15, 18; 39, 23, 33[t]; 40: 9, 10; 41: 4, 14, 17; 42: 8[c], 10, 13, 14[c], 15 AB[a], 16, 18; 43: 3, 11, 13, 16, 24, 31; 44: 2, 5, 14 AS[a]; 45: 1, 7, 15, 20, 25, 27; 47: 3[c], 7, 11; 48:11; 49: 4, 6, 6, 13, 14, 15:21[c]; 50: 4, 7; 51: 5, 16, 23, 24, 26
Lam. 1:18, 21, 21; 3:55—A, 60
Eze. 1:24; 2: 1, 2, 5, 7, 8; 3: 6, 10, 11, 12, 17, 27, 27; 6: 3; 9: 5; 10: 5, 13—A; 12: 2, 2; 13: 2; 16:35; 18:25; 19: 4, 9; 20:47; 25: 3; 26:13; 33: 4, 4, 5, 7, 30, 31, 32; 34: 7, 9+A; 35:12, 13; 36: 1, 4, 15; 37: 4; 40: 4; 44: 5
Dan. 3: 5, 7, 10, 15, 24; 4: 6; 5:14, 16, 23—A; 6:14; 8:13, 16; 9:11[c], 18, 19 A[a]; 10: 9, 9, 12; 12: 7, 8
Hos. 4: 1; 5: 1
Joel 1: 2
Amos 3: 1, 13; 4: 1; 5: 1, 23; 7:16; 8: 4, 11
Obad. 1
Jon. 2: 3
Mic. 1: 2; 3: 1, 9; 6: 1, 1, 2, 9
Nah. 2:13; 3:19
Zeph. 2: 8
Hag. 1:12
Zec. 3: 8; 8: 9, 23
Mal. 2: 2[a]

[a] pro εἰσακούω. [b] B εἰσακούω. [c] A εἰσακούω. [d] pro ὑπακούω. [e] pro ἀκουστής. [f] pro εὐδοκέω. [g] A ἀκουστός. [h] A ὑπακούω. [i] pro ἐπακούω. [k] A γινώσκω. [m] AS εἰσακούω. [n] pro ἰσχύω. [o] BS[1] εἰσακούω. [p] pro ἐνωτίζω. [q] S εἰσακούω. [r] ABS εἰσακούω. [s] pro ἀκουστός. [t] A θέλω.

ἄκρα.

Deu. 3:11
2 Sa. 5: 9
1 Ki. (3) p1 *bis*
10: *p* 22
1 Ki. 11:27
12: *p* 24, *l* 11
Isa. 22: 9

ἀκρατής.

Proverbs 27:20

ἄκρατος.

Psa. 74: 9
Jer. 32: 1

ἀκριβασμός.

Jud. 5:15 A[a]
1 Ki. 11:34+A
2 Ki. 17:15+A
Pro. 8:29+AS[2]

[a] *pro* ἐξικνέομαι.

ἀκρίβεια.

Daniel 7:16, 16

ἀκριβής.

Esther 4: 5—A

ἀκριβῶς.

Deu. 19:18
Eze. 39:14+A
Dan. 7:19

ἀκρίς.

Exo. 10: 4, 12
13, 14
19, 19
Lev. 11:22
Nu. 13:34
Deu. 28:38
Jud. 6: 5
7:12
2 Ch. 6:28
7:13
Psa. 77:46
104:34
Ps. 108:23
Pro. 24:62
Ecc. 12: 5
Isa. 33: 4
40:22
Jer. 26:23
28:14
27—S[1]
Joel 1: 4, 4
2:25
Amos 7: 1
Nah. 3:15, 17

ἀκρόαομαι.

Isaiah 21: 7

ἀκρόασις.

1 Ki. 18:26
2 Ki. 4:31
Ecc. 1: 8
Isa. 21: 7

ἀκροατής.

Isaiah 3: 3

ἀκροβυστία.

Gen. 17:11, 14
23, 24
25
34:14, 24
Exo. 4:25
Lev. 12: 3
Jos. 5: 3
1 Sa. 18:25, 27
2 Sa. 3:14
Jer. 9:25

ἀκρογωνιαῖος.

Isaiah 28:16

ἀκρόδρυα.

Cant. 4:13
5: 1
Cant. 7:13

ἄκρος.

Gen. 28:18
47:21, 21
31
Exo. 29:20 *qtr*
34: 2
36:27, 27
38: 7, 7, 16
16
Lev. 8:23, 23
24:24
14:14, 14
17, 17
25, 25
28, 28
Deu. 4:32, 32
13: 7, 7
Deu. 28:64, 64
30: 4, 4
33:17
Jos. 19:33 A[a]
Jud. 1: 6, 6, 7
7
6:21
1 Sa. 2:10
3:21, 21
14: 2, 27
43
1 Ki. 6:16
1 Ch. 14:15
2 Ch. 20:16
25:12, 12
Neh. 1: 9
Neh. 1: 9+S[3]
Psa. 18: 7, 7
71:16
Pro. 1:21
8: 2, 26
17:24
24:27
Isa. 2: 2
5:26
13: 5
17: 6
28: 4
Isa. 40:28
41: 5, 9
42:10, 11
43: 6
51:20
52:10
Jer. 12:12, 12
25:15
Eze. 17: 4
Mic. 5: 4
Hag. 2:12, 12

[a] *pro* Δωδάμ.

ἀκροτήριον, *vide* **ἀκρωτήριον.**

ἀκρότομος.

Deu. 8:15
Jos. 5: 2, 3
1 Ki. 6:11
Job 28: 9
40:15
Ps. 113: 8

ἀκρωτήριον.

Lev. 4:11
1 Sa. 14: 4+B
4 B[a]
Job 37: 8[b]
Eze. 25: 9

[a] *pro* ὀδός. [b] A ἀκροτήριον.

ἄκυρος.

Pro. 1:25
Pro. 5: 7[a]

[a] S[1] μακρύνω.

ἀκχούχ, ἀχούχ, ὀχόζ.

2 Ch. 25:18, 18

ἄκων.

Job 14:17

ἀλάβαστος.

2 Kings 21:13

ἀλαζονεύομαι.

Proverbs 25: 6

ἀλαζών.

Job 28: 8
Pro. 21:24
Hab. 2: 5

ἀλαιμώθ.

1 Chronicles 15:20

ἀλάλαγμα.

Psalm 43:13

ἀλαλαγμός.

Jos. 6:20
1 Sa. 4: 6+A
Psa. 26: 6
32: 3
46: 6
Psa. 88:16
150: 5
Jer. 20:16
32:22

ἀλαλάζω.

Jos. 6:20
Jud. 15:14
1 Sa. 17:20 A
52
Neh. 9:26 BS[2][a]
Psa. 46: 2
65: 1
80: 1
94: 1, 2
Psa. 97: 4, 6
99: 1
Isa. 41: 1 S[a]
Jer. 4: 8[b]
29: 2
30: 3
32:20
Eze. 27:30

[a] *pro* ἀλλάσσω. [b] A ἀλλάσσω.

ἄλαλος.

Psa. 30:19
Psa. 37:14

ἅλας.

Lev. 2:13, 13
Jud. 9:45
2 Ki. 2:21
Ezra 6: 9
Ezra 7:22
Eze. 43:24
47:11

ἀλγέω.

2 Sa. 1:26
Job 5:18
14:22
Job 16: 6
Psa. 68:30
Jer. 4:19

ἀλγηδών.

Psalm 37:18

ἄλγημα.

Psa. 38: 3
Ecc. 1:18
Ecc. 2:23

ἀλγηρός.

Jer. 10:19
Jer. 37:12, 13

ἄλγος.

Psa. 68:27
Lam. 1:12, 12
Lam. 1:18

ἀλέγω.

Isa. 40:15 S[1][a] [a] *pro* ἀλλ' ἐγώ.

ἄλειμμα.

Exo. 30:31
Isa. 61: 3
Dan. 10: 3

ἀλείφω.

Gen. 31:13
Exo. 40:13, 13
Nu. 3: 3
12 A[a]
Ruth 3: 3
2 Sa. 12:20
14: 2
2 Ki. 4: 2
2 Ch. 28:15
Est. 2:12
Eze. 13:10, 11
12, 14
15, 15
22:28
Dan. 10: 3
Mic. 6:15

[a] *pro* λαμβάνω.

ἀλέκτωρ.

Proverbs 24:66

ἄλευρον.

Nu. 5:15
Jud. 6:19
1 Sa. 28:24
2 Sa. 17:28
1 Ki. (3) *p* 46
4:22
1 Ki. 17:12, 14
16
2 Ki. 4:41
1 Ch. 12:40
Isa. 47: 2
Hos. 8: 7

ἀλέω.

Isaiah 47: 2

ἀλήθεια.

Gen. 24:27, 48
32:10
47:29
Exo. 28:26
Lev. 8: 8
Deu. 22, 20
33: 8
Jos. 2:14
Jud. 9:15, 16
19
1 Sa. 12:24
2 Sa. 2: 6
15:20
1 Ki. 2: 4
3: 6
22:16
2 Ki. 19:17
20: 3
19+A
1 Ch. 12:17
2 Ch. 18:15
19: 9
32: 1
Neh. 9:13, 33
Job 9: 2
19: 4
23: 7
36: 3
Psa. 5:10
11: 2
14: 2
Psa. 24: 5, 10
25: 3
29:10
30: 6, 24
35: 6
39:11, 11
12
42: 3
44: 5
50: 8
53: 7
56: 4, 11
60: 8
68:14
70:22
83:12
84:11, 12
85:11
87:12
88: 2, 3, 6
9, 15
25, 34
50
90: 4
91: 3
95:13
97: 3
99: 5
107: 5
110: 7, 8
113: 9
Ps. 116: 2
118:30, 43
75, 86
90, 138
142, 151
160
131:11
137: 2
142: 1
144:18
145: 6
Pro. 8: 7
11:18
14:22
20:28
22:21
26:28
28: 6—S[1]
29:14
Ecc. 12:10
Isa. 1:21+S[1]
10:20
11: 5
16: 5
Isa. 26: 2, 3, 10
37:18
38: 3
42: 3
45:19
46:13+S[1]
48: 1
59:14, 15
Jer. 4: 2
9: 5
14:13
23:28
33:15
Dan. 2: 8, 47
9:13
10:21
11: 2
Hos. 4: 1
Mic. 7:20
Zec. 8: 8, 16
16—A
19
Mal. 2: 6

ἀληθεύω.

Gen. 20:16
42:16
Pro. 21: 3
Isa. 44:26

ἀληθής.

Gen. 41:32
Deu. 13:14[a]
Neh. 7: 2
Est. 1:20+A
Job 5:12
17:10
42: 7
8—A
Pro. 1: 3
22:21
21 A[b]
Isa. 41:26
43: 9
65: 2 S[1][c]
Dan. 8:26 A[d]

[a] B ἀληθῶς. [b] *pro* ἀγαθής. [c] *pro* καλός. [d] *pro* ἀληθως.

ἀληθινός.

Exo. 34: 6
Nu. 14:18
24: 3 A[a]
Deu. 25:15:15
32: 4
2 Sa. 7:28
1 Ki. 10: 6
17:24
2 Ch. 9: 5
15: 3
Job 1: 1, 8
2: 3
4: 7, 12
6:25
8: 6, 21
17: 8
27:17
Psa. 18:10
85:15
102: 8+A[a]
Pro. 12:19
Isa. 25: 1
38: 3
57:18
59: 4
65: 2 AS[3][b]
16, 16
Jer. 2:21
Dan. 2:45
4:34
6:12
10: 1
Zec. 8: 3

[a] *pro* ἀληθινῶς. [b] *pro* καλός.

ἀληθινῶς.

Nu. 24: 3[a], 15 [a] A ἀληθινός.

ἀλήθω.

Nu. 11: 8
Jud. 16:21
Ecc. 12: 3, 4

ἀληθῶς.

Gen. 18:13
20:12
Exo. 33:16
Deu. 13:14 B[a]
17: 4
Jos. 7:20
Ruth 3:12
1 Sa. 22: 7
1 Ki. 8:27
18:39
2 Ch. 6:18
Psa. 57: 2
Jer. 28:13
35: 6
Dan. 3:14, 24
8:26[b]

[a] *pro* ἀληθής. [b] A ἀληθής.

ἁλιαίετος, ἁλίετος A

Lev. 11:13
Deu. 14:12

ἁλιεύς.

Job 40:26
Isa. 19: 8
Jer. 16:16
Eze. 47:10

ἁλιεύω.

Jeremiah 16:16

ἁλίζω.

Lev. 2:13
Eze. 16: 4

ἀλιμαζονεῖς.

2 Chronicles 22: 1

ἅλιμος.

Jeremiah 17: 6

ἄλιμος.

Job 30: 4, 4

ἀλισγέω.

Dan. 1: 8, 8
Mal. 1: 7, 7, 7[a]
Mal. 1:12

[a] S² ἐξουδενόω.

ἁλίσκομαι.

Exo. 22: 9
Deu. 24: 9
Pro. 6: 2, 30
31
11: 6
28:12
Isa. 8:15
13:15
14:10
22: 3
24:18
27: 3
28:13
30:13
Isa. 31: 9
33: 1
Jer. 2:26
8: 9—S¹
27: 2, 9
24
28:31, 41[a]
56
Eze. 17:20
21:24
33:21
40: 1
Zec. 14: 2

[a] S¹ λαλέω.

ἄλλαγμα.

Lev. 27:10, 33
Deu. 23:18
2 Sa. 24:24 AB[a]
1 Ki. 10:28
20: 2[b]
Job 28:17[c]
Isa. 43: 3
Lam. 5: 4
Amos 5:12[d]

[a] *pro* ἀνάλλαγμα. [b] A ἀντάλλαγμα. [c] C ἀντάλλαγμα. [d] B ἀντάλλαγμα.

ἀλλάσσω.

Gen. 31: 7
35: 2
41:14
45:22 A[a]
Exo. 13:13, 13
Lev. 27:10 *ter*
27, 33
33, 33
Jud. 14:13—A
2 Sa. 12:20
1 Ki. 5:14
21:25
2 Ki. 5: 5, 22
23
Ezra 6:11, 12
Neh. 9:26[b]
Est. 2:20 A[c]
Ps. 101:27 S¹[d]
27
105:20
Isa. 24: 5
40:31
41: 1[e]
Jer. 2:11, 11
4: 8 A[f]
13:23
52:33
Dan. 4:13, 22
29

[a] *pro* ἐξαλλάσσω. [b] BS² ἀλαλάζω. [c] *pro* μεταλλάσσω. [d] *pro* ἑλίσσω. [e] S ἀλαλάζω. [f] *pro* ἀλαλάζω.

ἀλληλούϊα.

Ps. 104: 1
105: 1
106: 1
110: 1
111: 1
112: 1
113: 1
114: 1
115: 1
116: 1
117: 1
Ps. 118: 1
134: 1
135: 1
145: 1
146: 1
147: 1
148: 1
149: 1
150: 1
6 + BS

ἀλλήλων.

Gen. 15:10
42:28
Exo. 4:27
14:20
18: 7
25:19
26: 3-A, 5
36:11
38:15
2 Ch. 20:23
25:21
Job 1: 4—S¹
Job 4:11
Pro. 22: 2
29:13
Isa. 34:15
Eze. 1:11
Dan. 7: 3
Amos 4: 3
Zec. 10: 9 A[a]

[a] *pro* λαός.

ἀλλογενής.

Gen. 17:27
Exo. 12:43
29:33
30:33
Lev. 22:10, 12
13, 25
Nu. 1:51
3:10, 38
16:40
18: 4, 7
Job 15:19
Job 19:15
Isa. 56: 3, 6
60:10
61: 5
Jer. 28:51
49:17
Eze. 44: 7, 9, 9
Joel 3:17
Obad. 11
Zec. 9: 6
Mal. 4: 1

ἀλλόγλωσσος.

Ezekiel 3: 6

ἄλλοθεν.

Esther 4:14

ἀλλοιόω.

1 Sa. 21:13
1 Ki. 14: 2 A
2 Ki. 25:29
Psa. 33: 1
41: 1—A
59: 1
68: 1
72:21
79: 1
80: 1 A[a]
Ps. 108:24
Lam. 4: 1
Dan. 2:21
3:19, 27
28
4:13, 20
5: 6, 9, 10
6: 8, 17
7:25, 28
Mal. 3: 6

[a] *pro* ληνός.

ἀλλοίωσις.

Psalm 76:11

ἅλλομαι.

Jud. 14: 6[a], 19[a]
15:14[a]
1 Sa. 10: 2, 10
Job 6:10
41:16
Isa. 35: 6

[a] A κατευθύνω.

ἄλλος.

Gen. 24: 4[a]
41: 6+A
Exo. 9:14—A
Deu. 4:35+A
1 Sa. 9:24[b]
2 Sa. 21:24—A
1 Ki. 18: 6+A
1 Ki. 21:37—A
Job 1:18[c]
31:10 A[d]
Ecc. 5:19 B¹[e]
Eze. 13:10 A[f]
Mal. 2:15 A[g]
&c., &c.

[a] AS ἀλλά. [b] A ἄνθρωπος. [c] S ἕτερος. [d] *pro* ἕτερος. [e] *pro* πολύς. [f] *pro* αὐτον. [g] *pro* καλός.

ἀλλότριος.

Gen. 17:12
31:15
35: 2, 4
Exo. 2:22
18: 3
21: 8
Lev. 10: 1
16: 1
Nu. 3: 4
16:37
26:61
Deu. 14:20
15: 3
17:15
23:20
29:22
31:16, 18
20
32:12, 16
Jos. 24:14
Jos. 24:20 A[a]
23
Jud. 10:16
19:12
1 Sa. 7: 3
2 Sa. 22:45, 46
1 Ki. 8:41, 43
9: 9[b]
11: 1, 4—A
7
2 Ki. 19:24
2 Ch. 6:32, 33
14: 3
28:25
33:15
34:25[b]
Ezra 10: 2, 10
11, 14
17
18—S¹
Ezra 10:44
Neh. 9: 2
13:26, 27
Job 17: 3
19:13
Psa. 17:45, 46
18:14
43:21
48:11
53: 5
80:10
108:11
136: 4
143: 7, 11
Pro. 2:16
5:10, 10
17, 20
6:24
7: 5
9:18
18+AS²
18, 18
11:24+S²
23:27, 27
33
26:17
27: 2, 13
Isa. 1: 7, 7
28:21
43:12
62: 8
Jer. 1:16
2:21, 25
3:13
5:19[b]
19—A
7: 6, 9, 18
8:19
11:10
13:10
16:11
19: 4, 13
22: 9
25: 6
37: 8
42:15 AS[a]
Lam. 5: 2
Eze. 7:21
11: 9
28: 7, 10
30:12
31:12
Dan. 11:39
Hos. 3: 1
5: 7
7: 9
8: 7, 12
Obad. 11, 12
Zeph. 1: 8
Mal. 2:11
3:15

[a] *pro* ἕτερος. [b] A ἕτερος.

ἀλλοτριόω.

Genesis 42: 7

ἀλλοτρίως.

Isaiah 28:21

ἀλλοτρίωσις.

Neh. 13:30
Jer. 17:17

ἀλλόφυλος.

Exo. 34:15+A²B
Jud. 8:10—A
10: 6 A[a]
7 A[a]
11 A[a]
13: 1 A[a]
5 A[a]
Jud. 14: 2 A[a]
1 Sa. 4: 9—B
7:11—A
2 Ki. 8:28
1 Ch. 14:12 ABS
Isa. 2: 6, 6
61: 5
&c., &c.

[a] *pro* Φυλιστιίμ.

ἀλλόφωνος.

Ezekiel 3: 6

ἄλλως.

Est. 1:19
9:27
Job 11:12
40: 3

ἅλμα.

Job 39:25

ἅλμη.

Psalm 106:34

ἁλμυρίς.

Job 39: 6

ἁλμυρός.

Jeremiah 17: 6

ἀλοάω.

Deu. 25: 4
Jud. 8: 7[a]
16[a]
1 Ch. 21:20
Isa. 41:15—S¹
Isa. 41:15
Jer. 5, 17
28:33
Mic. 4:13

[a] A καταξαίνω.

ἄλογος.

Exo. 6:12
Nu. 6:12
Job 11:12 A¹[a]

[a] *pro* λόγος.

ἀλόη.

Cant. 4:14 S[a]

[a] *pro* ἀλώθ.

ἀλοητός.

Lev. 26: 5[a]
Amos 9:13 A[b]

[a] AB ἀμητός. [b] *pro* ἀμητός.

ἀλοιφή.

Exo. 17:14
Job 33:24
Eze. 13:12
Mic. 7:11

ἅλς.

Gen. 14: 3
19:26
Lev. 2:13
24: 7
Nu. 18:19
Deu. 29:23
Jos. 3:16
12: 3
Jos. 18:19
2 Ki. 2:20
1 Ch. 18:12
2 Ch. 13: 5
25:11
Job 6: 6—S¹
Psa. 59: 2
Eze. 16: 4

ἄλσος.

Exo. 34:13—A
Deu. 7: 5
12: 3
16:21
Jud. 3: 7
6:25, 26
28, 30
1 Sa. 7: 3, 4
12:10
2 Sa. 5:24
1 Ki. 14:15 A, 23
15:13
16:33
18:19, 22
2 Ki. 13: 6
17:10
2 Ki. 17:16—A
18: 4
21: 3, 7
23: 4, 6, 7
14, 15
2 Ch. 14: 3
17: 6
19: 3
31: 1
33: 3, 19
34: 3, 4, 7
Isa. 17: 8 A[a]
Jer. 4:29
33:18
Mic. 3:12
5:14

[a] *pro* δένδρον.

ἀλσώδης.

2 Ki. 16: 4
17:10
2 Ch. 28: 4
Jer. 3: 6, 13
17: 8
Eze. 27: 6

ἁλυκός.

Gen. 14: 3, 8, 10
Nu. 34: 3, 12
Deu. 3:17
Jos. 15: 2, 5

ἁλυσιδωτός.

Exo. 28:22, 24
1 Sa. 17: 5

ἄλφιτον.

Ruth 2:14
1 Sa. 25:18
2 Sa. 17:28

ἀλφός.

Leviticus 13:39

ἀλώθ.

Cant. 4:14[a]

[a] S ἀλόη.

ἅλων, ἅλως.

Gen. 50:10, 11
Exo. 22: 6, 29
Nu. 15:20
18:27, 30
Deu. 16:13
Jud. 6:37
15: 5[a]
Ruth 3: 2, 3, 6
14
1 Sa. 19:22[b]
23: 1
2 Sa. 6: 6
24:16, 18
21, 24
1 Ki. 20: 1
2 Ki. 6:27
1 Ch. 13: 9
21:15, 18
21, 22
28
2 Ch. 3: 1
Job 5:26
39:12
Isa. 25:10
Jer. 28:33
Dan. 2:35
Hos. 9: 1, 2
13: 3
Joel 2:24
Mic. 4:12
Zeph. 2: 9
Hag. 2:19

[a] A στυβή=στοιβή. [b] A μέγας.

ἀλώπηξ.

Jud. 1:35
15: 4
1 Ki. 21:10
Neh. 4: 3
Psa. 62:11
Cant. 2:15
Lam. 5:18
Eze. 13: 4

ἅλως vide ἅλων.

ἅλωσις.

Jeremiah 27:46

ἅμα.

Gen. 22:19 — A
Jos. 6: 4 — A
2 Ki. 18:27 — A
Psa. 52: 4 — S[1]
Isa. 20: 4 + B

ἅμαξα.

Gen. 45:19, 21, 27; 46: 5
Nu. 7: 3, 3, 6, 7, 8
1 Sa. 6: 7, 7, 8, 10, 11; 14:14
2 Sa. 6: 3, 3
1 Ch. 13: 7, 7; 21:23 + A
Isa. 25:10; 28:27; 41:15
Amos 2:13

ἁμαρτάνω.

Gen. 4: 7; 20: 6, 9; 39: 9; 40: 1; 43: 8; 44:32
Exo. 9:27, 34; 10:16; 20:20; 23:33; 32:30, 31, 33
Lev. 4: 2, 3, 3, 3, 14, 22, 22, 23, 27, 28, 28, 35; 5: 1, 4, 5, 6, 6, 7, 10, 11, 13, 15, 16, 17; 6: 2, 3, 4; 19:22, 22
Nu. 5: 7 A[a]; 6:11; 12:11; 14:40; 15:27, 28; 16:22; 21: 7; 22:34; 32:23
Deu. 1:41; 9:16, 18; 19:15; 20:18; 32: 5
Jos. 7:11, 20
Jud. 10:10, 15; 11:27
1 Sa. 2:25 *ter*; 7: 6; 12:10, 23; 14:33, 34; 15:18, 24, 30; 19: 4, 4, 5; 20: 1; 22:17 AB[b]; 24:12; 26:18, 21
2 Sa. 12:13; 19:20; 24:10
1 Ki. 8:31, 33, 35, 46, 46, 47, 50; 14:16A, 22; 15:30 + A; 16:13 + A; 18: 9
2 Ki. 17: 7; 18:14; 21:17
1 Ch. 21: 8, 17
2 Ch. 6:22, 24, 26, 36, 36, 37, 39; 12: 2; 19:10, 10; 22: 3; 28:13
Neh. 1: 6, 6; 6:13; 9:29; 13:26
Job 1:22; 2:10; 5:24 + A, 24; 7:20; 8: 4; 10:14; 11: 6; 15:11; 31:33; 33: 9, 27; 34: 8; 35: 3ACS[a], 6; 42: 7
Psa. 4: 5; 24: 8; 35: 2; 38: 2; 40: 5; 50: 6; 74: 5; 77:17, 32; 105: 6; 118:11
Pro. 8:36; 11: 9 S[1 c]; 12:26; 13:21; 14:21; 20: 2; 28:24; 29: 6
Ecc. 2:26; 7:21, 27; 8:12; 9: 2, 18
Isa. 24: 6; 29:21; 42:24; 64: 5
Jer. 2:35; 3:25; 8:14; 14: 7, 20; 16:10; 27: 7; 40: 8, 8; 47: 3; 51:23
Lam. 1: 8; 3:41; 5: 7, 16
Eze. 3:21, 21; 14:13; 16:51; 18: 4, 20, 24; 28:16; 33:16[d]; 35: 6; 37:23 + A, 23
Dan. 9: 5,8,11, 15, 16
Hos. 4: 7; 10: 9; 12: 8; 13: 2
Mic. 7: 9

[a] *pro* ποιέω. [b] *pro* ἀπαντάω. [c] *pro* ἀσεβής. [d] A ποιέω.

ἁμάρτημα.

Gen. 31:36
Exo. 28:34
Lev. 4:29
Nu. 1:53; 18:23
Deu. 9:27; 19:15; 22:26
Jos. 22:17; 24:19
1 Sa. 15:25
2 Sa. 12:13
1 Ki. 5: 4[a]
Job 14:17 A[b]
Isa. 40: 2; 58: 1; 59: 2
Jer. 14:20
Lam. 1:22
Eze. 18:10
Hos. 10: 8, 13[c]

[a] A ἀπάντημα. [b] *pro* ἀνομία. [c] A ἅρμα.

ἁμαρτία.

Gen. 15:16; 18:20; 20: 9; 41: 9; 42:21; 50:17 — A
Exo. 10:17; 20: 5; 28:39; 29:14, 36; 30:10 + A; 32:21, 30, 30, 31, 32, 34; 34: 7, 7A[a], 9
Lev. 4: 3, 3, 8, 14, 14, 20, 20, 21, 23, 24, 25, 26, 28, 28, 29, 32, 33, 34, 35; 5: 1, 5, 6, 6, 6, 6, 7, 7, 8, 9, 9, 10, 11, 11, 12, 13, 17; 6:17, 25, 25, 30, 37; 7: 8, 27; 8: 2, 14, 14; 9: 2, 3, 7, 8, 10, 15, 22; 10:16, 17, 17, 19, 19; 12: 6, 8; 14:13, 13, 19, 19, 22, 31; 15:15, 30; 16: 3, 5, 6, 9, 11, 11, 15, 16, 21, 25, 27, 27, 30, 34; 19: 8, 17, 22, 22; 20:17, 19; 22: 9; 23:19; 24:15; 26:18, 21, 24, 28, 39, 39 — AB, 40, 40, 41
Nu. 5: 6,7,15, 31, 31; 6:11, 14, 16; 7:16, 22, 28, 34, 40, 46, 52, 58, 64, 70, 76, 82, 87; 8: 8, 12; 9:13; 12:11; 14:18, 18, 19, 34; 15:24, 25, 27, 31; 16:26[b]; 18: 1[c],1,9, 22, 32; 27: 3; 28:15, 22 — A, 30; 29: 5, 11, 11, 16, 19, 22, 25, 28, 31, 34, 38; 30:16; 32:23
Deu. 5: 9; 9:18, 21; 15: 9; 19:15; 21:22; 23:21, 22; 24:17, 18; 30: 3
Jos. 22:20
1 Sa. 2:17; 12:19; 14:38; 15:23
1 Ki. 8:34, 35, 36; 12:30; 13:34; 14:16A, 22; 15: 3, 26, 30 — A, 34; 16:13, 19, 19, 26, 31; 22:53
2 Ki. 1:18; 3: 3; 10:29, 31; 12:16; 13: 2,6,11; 14: 6, 24; 15: 9, 18, 24, 28; 17:21, 22; 21:16, 17; 24: 3
1 Ch. 21: 3
2 Ch. 6:25, 26, 27; 7:14; 25: 4; 28:13, 13; 29:21, 23, 24; 33:19; 36: 5
Ezra 6:17; 8:35; 9:13 + S[3]
Neh. 1: 6; 9: 2, 37; 10:33
Job 1: 5; 7:21; 10: 6; 13:23, 26; 14:16, 17 S[a]; 22: 5; 24:20; 31:33; 34:37; 42: 9, 10
Psa. 9:36; 18:14; 24: 7, 11, 18; 31: 1, 2, 5, 5 6[a]; 37: 4, 10; 39: 7; 40:21 + S[2]; 50: 4, 5, 7, 11; 58: 4, 13; 77:38; 78: 9; 84: 3; 88:33[d]; 102:10; 108: 7, 14 S[1 a], 14; 140: 4
Pro. 5:22; 10:16, 19; 12:11 S[1 e], 13; 13: 6 A, 9; 14:34; 15:27; 20: 9; 21: 4; 24: 9; 26:11, 11, 26; 28: 2; 29:16, 22
Ecc. 10: 4
Isa. 1: 4, 14, 18; 3: 9; 5:18; 6: 7; 13:11; 14:21; 21: 4 S[1 a]; 22:14; 27: 9; 30: 1,1,13; 33:24; 38:17; 40: 2; 43:24, 25 — AS; 44:22; 50: 1; 53: 4, 5, 6, 10, 11, 12, 12 A[a]; 55: 7; 57:17; 59: 2,3,12; 64: 7, 9; 65: 2, 7; 66: 4
Jer. 5:25; 14: 7, 7; 15:13[f]; 16:10, 18; 18:23; 27:20; 37:14, 16; 38:30, 34; 39:18; 40: 8; 43: 3
Lam. 1: 8; 3:38; 4:13
Eze. 3:20; 8: 6 A[a]; 16:51, 51 A[a], 52; 18:14, 24; 21:24; 23:49; 28:17, 18; 29:16 A[a]; 33:12 + A, 14, 16; 36:19[h]; 39:23; 40:39; 42:13; 43:10, 19, 21, 22, 25; 44:29; 45:17, 22, 23, 25; 46:20
Dan. 4:24; 8:12, 13, 23; 9, 20, 20, 24, 24
Hos. 4: 8; 8:11, 13; 9: 9; 13:12[i]
Amos 3: 2; 5:12
Mic. 1: 5,5,13; 3: 8; 6: 7, 13; 7:19
Nah. 3: 6 S[1 k]
Zec. 14:19, 19

[a] *pro* ἀνομία. [b] B ἀπαρτία. [c] B ἀπαρχή. [d] AS ἀδικία. [e] *pro* ἀτιμία. [f] A κακία. [g] A ἀσέβεια. [h] A ἀνομία. [i] A ἀδικία. [k] *pro* ἀκαθαρσία.

ἁμαρτωλός.

Gen. 13:13
Nu. 16:37; 32:14
Deu. 29:19
1 Ki. 1:21
2 Ch. 19: 2
Psa. 1: 1, 5; 3: 8; 7:10; 9:17, 18, 24, 25, 36; 10: 2, 6; 27: 3; 31:10; 33:22; 35:12; 36:10, 12, 14, 16, 17, 20, 21, 32, 34, 40; 38: 2; 49:16; 54: 4; 57: 4, 11; 67: 3; 70: 4; 72: 3, 12; 74: 9, 10; 81: 2, 4; 83:11; 90: 8; 91: 8; 93: 3,3,13; 96:10; 100: 8; 103:35; 105:18; 108: 2, 6; 111:10, 10; 118:53, 61, 95 — S[1], 110, 119, 155; 124: 3; 128: 3, 4; 138:19[a]; 139: 5, 9; 140: 5, 10; 144:20; 145: 9; 146: 6
Pro. 11: 9 S[2 b], 31; 12:13; 15: 8 S[b]; 23:17; 24:19
Isa. 1: 4, 28, 31; 13: 9; 14: 5; 65:20
Eze. 33: 8[c], 11 A[b], 19
Amos 9: 8, 10

[a] S[1] ἐξαμαρτωλός. [b] *pro* ἀσεβής, [c] A ἄνομος.

ἁμασενίθ.

1 Chronicles 15:21

ἁμάσητος.

Job 20:18

ἁματταρί.

1 Samuel 20:20

ἁμαυρός.

Lev. 13: 4, 6, 21, 26, 28, 56

ἁμαυρόω.

Deu. 34: 7
Lam. 4: 1

ἁμαφέθ.

1 Samuel 5: 4

ἁμάω.

Lev. 25:11
Deu. 24:21
Isa. 17: 5; 37:30
Mic. 6:15

ἀμβλύνω.

Genesis 27: 1

ἀμβλυωπέω.

1 Ki. 12: *p* 24, *l* 33, 1 Ki. 14: 4 A

ἀμέθυστος.

Exo. 28:19; 36:19
Eze. 28:13

ἀμείψις.

Psalm 118:112 S[1 a]

[a] *pro* ἀντάμειψις.

ἀμέλγω.

Job 10:10
Pro. 24:68

ἀμελέω.

Jer. 4:17
Jer. 38:32

ἄμελξις.

Job 20:17

ἀμελῶς.

Jeremiah 31:10

ἄμεμπτος.

Gen. 17: 1
Job 1: 1, 8
2: 3
4:17
9:20
11: 4
Job 12: 4
15:14
15 + A
22: 3, 19
25: 5 A[a]
33: 9

[a] pro καθαρός.

ἀμέτρητος.

Isaiah 22:18

ἀμήν.

1 Ch. 16:36
Neh. 5:13
Neh. 8: 6

ἀμητός.

Gen. 45: 6
Exo. 34:21
Lev. 26: 5 AB[a]
Deu. 16: 9
24: 1, 1, 21
Ruth 2:21
2 Ki. 19:29
Pro. 6: 8, 11
10: 5
20: 4
Pro. 25:13
26: 1
Isa. 9: 3
17: 5, 11
18: 4
23: 3
Jer. 8:20
28:33
Amos 9:13[b]
Mic. 7: 1

[a] pro ἀλοητός. [b] A ἀλοητός.

ἀμισθί.

Job 24: 6

ἀμμαδαρώθ.

Judges 5:22 + A

ἀμμαζειβί.

2 Kings 12: 9

ἄμμος.

Gen. 13:16, 16
22:17
28:14
32:12
41:49
Exo. 2:12
Jos. 11: 4
Jud. 7:12
1 Sa. 13: 5
2 Sa. 17:11
1 Ki. 2:35
(3)p 46
4(20) A
1 Ki. 4:25
Job 6: 3
Psa. 77:27
138:18
Pro. 27: 3
Isa. 10:22
48:19
Jer. 5:22
15: 8
26:22
Hos. 1:10
Hab. 1: 9

ἀμνάς.

Gen. 21:28, 29
30
31:41
Lev. 5: 6
Nu. 6:14
7:17, 23
29, 35
41, 47
Nu. 7:53, 59
65, 71
77, 83
88
Jos. 24:32
2 Sa. 12: 3, 4, 6
Job 42:11

ἀμνήστευτος.

Exodus 22:16

ἀμνός.

Gen. 30:40, 40
31: 7
33:19
Exo. 12: 5 A[a]
29:38, 39
39, 40
41
Lev. 9: 3
12: 6, 8
14:10, 12
Lev. 14:13, 21
24, 25
23:18, 19
20
Nu. 6:12, 14
7:15, 21
27, 33
39, 45
51, 57
63, 69
Nu. 7:75, 81
87
15: 5, 11
28: 3, 4, 4
7, 8, 9
11, 13
14, 19
21, 21
27, 29
29
29: 2, 4, 4
8, 10
10, 13
15, 15
17, 18
20, 21
23, 24
26, 27
29, 30
Nu. 29:32, 33
36, 37
Deu. 14: 4
2 Ch. 29:21
22 − B
32
35: 7, 8
Ezra 6: 9, 17
7:17
8:35
Job 31:20[b]
Isa. 34: 6 − AS
53: 7
Eze. 27:21 − A
46: 4, 5, 6
7, 11
13, 15
Hos. 4:16
Zec. 10: 3

[a] pro ἀρνός. [b] A ἀρνός.

ἀμορίτης.

1 Chronicles 16: 3

ἄμπελος.

Gen. 40: 9, 10
49:11
Lev. 25: 3, 4
Nu. 6: 4
20: 5
22:24[a]
Deu. 8: 8
32:32, 32
Jud. 9:12, 13
13:14
1 Ki. (3)p 46
4(25) A
2 Ki. 4:39
18:31
Psa. 77:47
79: 9, 15
104:33
127: 3
Cant. 2:13, 15
6:10
7: 8, 12
Isa. 5: 2
7:23
16: 8, 8, 9
Isa. 24: 7
32:12
34: 4
36, 16
Jer. 2:21, 21
6: 9
8:13
31:32
Lam. 2: 6
Eze. 15: 2, 6
17: 6, 6, 7
8
19:10
Hos. 2:12
10: 1
14: 7
Joel 1: 7, 12
2:22
Mic. 4: 4
Hab. 3:17
Hag. 2:19
Zec. 3:10
8:12
Mal. 3:11

[a] A ἀμπελών.

ἀμπελουργός.

2 Ki. 25:12
2 Ch. 26:10
Isa. 61: 5
Jer. 52:16

ἀμπελών.

Gen. 9:20
Exo. 22: 5, 5
23:11
Lev. 19:10, 10
19
Nu. 16:14
20:17
21:22
22:24 A[a]
Deu. 6:11
20: 6
22: 9, 9
24: 2, 23
28:30, 39
Jos. 24:13
Jud. 9:27
11:33 + A
14: 5
15: 5
21:20, 21
1 Sa. 8:14, 15
15: 9
22: 7
1 Ki. 20: 1, 2, 2
2, 6, 6
7, 15
16, 18
2 Ki. 5:26
18:32
19:29
Neh. 5: 3, 4, 5
11
Neh. 9:25
Job 24: 6
Ps. 106:37
Pro. 9:12
24:45
Ecc. 2: 4
Cant. 1: 6, 6, 14
2:15
7:12
8:11, 11
12
Isa. 1: 8
3:13
5: 1, 1, 3
4, 5, 6, 7
16:10, 10
27: 2
36:17
37:30
65:21
Jer. 5:17
12:10
38: 5
39:15
42: 7, 9
Eze. 28:26
Amos 4: 9
5:11
9:14
Mic. 1: 6
Zeph. 1:13

[a] pro ἄμπελος.

ἀμπλάκημα.

Daniel 6: 4[a] [a] AB[1] ἀμβλά-

ἀμύγδαλον.

Ecclesiastes 12: 5

ἀμύθητος.

Job 8: 7
36:28
Job 41:21

ἀμύνω.

Jos. 10:13
Est. 6:13
Ps. 117:10, 11
Ps. 117:12
Isa. 59:16

ἀμφιάζω.

Job 29:14
31:19
Job 40: 5

ἀμφίασις.

Job 22: 6
24: 7
Job 38: 9

ἀμφιβάλλω.

Habakkuk 1:17

ἀμφίβληστρον.

Ps. 140:10
Ecc. 9:12
Hab. 1:15, 16
17

ἀμφιβολεύς.

Isaiah 19: 8

ἀμφιέννυμι.

2 Kings 17: 9

ἀμφίταπος.

2 Sa. 17:28
Pro. 7:16

ἄμφοδον.

Jer. 17:27
Jer. 30.16

ἀμφοτεροδέξιος.

Jud. 3:15
Jud. 20:16

ἀμφότερος.

Gen. 21:27, 31
22: 8
33: 4
40: 5
41:11 − A
Exo. 12:22, 23
22: 9, 11
25:17
26:19, 19
21, 21
24, 25
28:24, 25
32:14
36:11, 13
24, 25, 28
38:14
Lev. 3:10, 15
8:16
20:11, 12
13, 18
27
Nu. 7:13, 19
25, 31
37, 43
49, 55
61, 67
73, 79
12: 5
25: 8
Deu. 22:22, 24
23:18
Jud. 19: 6 + A
8 + A
Ruth 1: 5, 19
4:11
1 Sa. 2:34
1 Sa. 3:11
4: 4, 11
17
5: 4, 4
14:11
17:10
20:11, 42
23:18
25:43
27: 3
30: 5, 18
2 Sa. 2: 2
9:13
14: 6
1 Ki. 3:18
6:23, 25
31
7: 9, 27
28 ter
11:29
18:21
2 Ki. 2: 6, 7, 8
11
21:12
Est. 5: 5
Job 9:33
Pro. 20:10, 12
22: 2
24:22
27: 3
29:13
Jer. 10: 3 + S[3]
26:12
Dan. 8: 7
11:27
Zec. 6:13

ἄμωμος.

Exo. 29: 1 + A
1, 38
Lev. 1: 3, 10
3: 1, 6, 9
4: 3, 14
23, 28
32
5:15, 18
6: 6
9: 2, 3
12: 6
14:10, 10
22:19, 21
23:12, 18
18
Nu. 6:14 ter
7:69 + A
88
15:24
19: 2
28: 3, 9, 11
19 − A
27, 31
29: 2, 8
13, 17
Nu. 29:20, 23
26, 29
32, 36
2 Sa. 22:24, 31
33
Psa. 14: 2
17:24, 31
33
18: 8, 14
36:18, 28[a]
63: 5
100: 2, 6
118: 1, 80
Pro. 11: 5, 20
20: 7
22:11
Ecc. 11: 9
Isa. 33:15 + S
Eze. 28:15
43:22, 23
23, 25
45:18, 23
46: 4, 4, 6
6, 13

[a] AS[2] ἄνομος.

ἀναβαθμίς.

Exodus 20:26

ἀναβαθμός.

1 Ki. 10:19, 20
2 Ki. 9:13
20: 9 A[a]
10 A[a]
10 − A
10 A[a]
11
11 + A
2 Ch. 9:18, 19
Ps. 119: 1
120: 1
121: 1
122: 1
Ps. 123: 1
124: 1
125: 1
126: 1
127: 1
128: 1
129: 1
130: 1
131: 1
132: 1
133: 1
Isa. 38: 8 qtr
Eze. 40: 6, 49

[a] pro βαθμός.

ἀναβαίνω.

Gen. 2: 6
13: 1
17:22
19:28, 30[a]
24:16
26:23
28:12
31:10, 12
32:26
35: 1, 3, 13
38:12, 13
41: 2, 3, 5
18, 19
22, 27
44:17, 24
33, 34
45: 9, 25
46:29, 31
49: 4, 4, 9
50: 5, 6, 7
Exo. 2:23
8: 3, 4
10:12
13:18
16:13
17:10
19: 3, 12
13, 18
20, 24
24
20:26
24: 1, 9, 12
13, 15
18
32:30
33: 1
34: 1, 2, 3
4, 24
40:30, 31
Exo. 40:31
Lev. 25: 5, 11
Nu. 9:17, 21
21 + A
10:11
13:18, 18
22, 23
31, 31
32, 32
14:40, 40
42, 44
16:12, 14
21:33
27:12
32: 7 A[b], 9
11
33:38
Deu. 1:21, 22
24, 26
28, 41
41, 42
43
3: 1, 27
5: 5
9: 9, 23
10: 1, 3
17: 8
25: 7
28:43
29:23
30:12
32:49, 50
34: 1
Jos. 2: 1, 8
4:19
6:20
7: 3 ter
4
8: 1, 3, 10

Jos. 8:11, 20
21—A
10: 4, 5, 6
7, 33
12: 7
14: 8[c]
15: 3,8,15
16: 1, 10
17:15
18:12
22:12, 33
Jud. 1: 1, 2, 3
4, 11[d]
16, 22
2: 1
4: 5, 10
10, 12
6: 3, 3A[e]
5, 21[f]
35
7: 9A[g]
8: 8, 11
9:48, 51
10:17
11:13[h],16[h]
12: 3
13: 5, 20
20
14: 2, 19
15: 6[i], 9
10, 10
16: 3[k], 5
17, 18
18, 31
18: 9
9+A
12, 17
19:25
20: 3,9,18
18, 18
23, 23
26, 28
30[m],31
31+A
40, 40
21: 5, 5, 8
19
Ruth 3: 3
4: 1
1 Sa. 1: 3,7,11
21. 22
22, 24
2:10, 14
19, 28
5:12
6:20
7: 7
9:11, 13
13, 14
14, 19
26
10: 3
11: 1
13:4,5,5,15
14: 9, 10
10, 12
12, 13
20[n], 21
46
15: 2,6,34
17:23 A
25 A
25 A
23:19
24:23
25: 5, 13
35
27: 8
28:13, 14
15
29:11
2 Sa. 2: 1 *ter*
2, 27
5:17, 19
19, 22
23
8: 7
11:20
15:24, 30
30—B

2 Sa. 15:30, 30
17:21
18:33
19:34
20: 2
22: 9
23: 9[o]
24:18, 19
1 Ki. 1:35+A
40, 45
2:34—B
(3) *p* 1
4:30—A
9:16 A
24 A
10:29
12:18, 24
p 24, *l* 49
l 73
l 76
l 80
27, 28
32, 33[p]
33
14:25
15:17, 19
16:17
18:29
36+A
41, 42
42
43+A
43, 44
21: 1, 1
22[q], 26
22: 4,6,12
15, 15
20, 29
2 Ki. 1: 4, 6, 6
7, 9
11+A
13+A
16
2:23 *qtr*
3: 7,8,20
21
21 A[r]
4:34, 35
6:24
8:21
9:17, 27
12: 4[s], 10
17, 17[d]
18
14:11
15:14, 19
16: 5, 7
9—A
12
17: 3, 5, 5
18: 9, 13
17, 25
25
19:14, 23
28
20: 5, 8
22: 4
23: 2, 9
29
24: 1, 10
1 Ch. 5: 1
11: 6
13: 6
14: 8, 10
10, 11
21:18[t], 19
2 Ch. 1:17 A[u]
10:18
11: 4
12: 2, 9
16: 1
18: 5, 11
14, 19
28
20:16
21:17
24:13, 23
25:21
29:20, 21
34:30

2 Ch. 35:20
36: 6, 16
23
Ezra 1: 3,5,11
2: 1, 59
3: 3
4:12
7: 1, 6, 7
28
8: 1
Neh. 2:15
4: 3,7,12
7: 5,6,61
12: 1, 37[v]
Job 7: 9
18: 5 A[w]
20: 6
36:20
Psa. 17: 9
23: 3
46: 6
67:19
73:23
77:21, 31
103: 8
105: 7
106:26
121: 4
131: 3
138: 8
Pro. 24:27
25: 7
Ecc. 3:21
10: 4
Cant. 3: 6
4: 2
6: 4 S[x], 5
9 A[1 y]
7: 8
8: 5
Isa. 2: 3
5: 6, 24
7: 1, 6
8: 7
11: 1
14: 8, 13
14
15: 2, 5
22: 1
32:13
34: 3, 10
35: 9
36: 1, 10
10—A
37: 1
14—AS[3]
24, 29
38: 8, 22
40: 9
55:13, 13
65:16
Jer. 3:16
4: 7, 13
29—S[1]
5:10
6: 4, 5[z]

Jer. 8:22
9:21
14: 2
22:20
26: 7, 8, 8
9, 11
27: 3, 44
28:42, 50
53
29: 2, 20
30: 6—S[1]
9
31: 5, 18
35, 44
33:10
38: 6
39:35
42:11
11 A[aa]
44: 5, 11
51:21
Lam. 1:14
Eze. 8:11
9: 3
11:23, 24
20:31
24: 8[bb]
26: 3
36: 3[cc]
37: 8
38: 9, 10
11, 16
18
40:22, 49
41: 7
47:12
Dan. 2:29
7: 3,8,20
8: 3, 8
11:23
Hos. 1:11
4:15
8: 9
10: 8
14: 3
Joel 1: 6
2: 7,9,20
20
3: 9, 12
Amos 5: 5 A[b]
8: 8
9: 2, 5
Obad. 21
Jon. 1: 2
3—S[1 dd]
2: 7
4: 6
Mic. 4: 2
Nah. 2: 2, 7
3: 3
Hab. 3:16
Hag. 1: 8
2:22 A[ee]
Zec. 14:16, 17
18, 18
19

[a] A ἐξέρχομαι. [b] *pro* διαβαίνω. [c] A συναναβαίνω. [d] A πορεύω. [e] *pro* συναναβαίνω. [f] A ἀνάπτω. [g] *pro* ἀνίστημι. [h] A ἀνάβασις. [i] A ἐμβαίνω. [k] A ἀναφέρω. [m] A τάσσω. [n] A ἀναβοάω. [o] AB ἀναβόαω. [p] A ἐπιβαίνω. [q] A ἄνειμι. [r] *pro* ἀναβόαω. [s] B λαμβάνω. [t] A[2] λαμβάνω. [u] *pro* ἐμβαίνω. [v] S[1] ἀναβοάω. [w] *pro* ἀποβαίνω. [x] *pro* ἀναφαίνω. [y] *pro* ἐκκύπτω. [z] A διαβαίνω. [aa] *pro* εἰσέρχομαι. [bb] A[1] καταβαίνω. [cc] A γίνομαι. [dd] ABS[2] ἐμβαίνω. [ee] *pro* καταβαίνω.

ἀναβάλλω.

1 Sa. 28:14
Psa. 77:21
88:39

Ps. 103: 2
Isa. 37:19[a]

[a] ABS ἐμβάλλω.

ἀνάβασις.

Nu. 34: 4
Jos. 10:10
18:17
Jud. 1:36[a]
8:13 A[b]
11:13 A[c]
16 A[c]
19:30
30+A
1 Sa. 9:11
2 Sa. 6: 2
15:30
1 Ki. 6:12
1 Ch. 26:16, 18

2 Ch. 9:11
20:16
32:33
Ezra 7: 9—AB
Neh. 3:19, 31[d]
32+AB
4:21
9: 4
12:37
Psa. 83: 6
Isa. 15: 5
Eze. 47:12
Hos. 2:15
Amos 9: 6

[a] A ἐπάνω. [b] *pro* παράταξις. [c] *pro* ἀναβαίνω. [d] B ἀνὰ μέσον.

ἀναβαστάζω.

Judges 16: 3

ἀναβάτης.

Exo. 14:23, 26
28
15: 1,4,19
21
Deu. 20: 1
Isa. 21: 7*ter*, 9
22: 6
30:16

Isa. 36: 8, 9
Jer. 28:21 A[a]
22
Eze. 38:15
39:20
Hag. 2:22, 22
Zec. 10: 5
12: 4

[a] *pro* ἐπιβάτης.

ἀναβιβάζω.

Gen. 37:28
41:43
46: 4
Exo. 3:17
4:20
8: 6
17: 3
32: 4, 6, 9
Lev. 2:12
Nu. 20:25, 27
22:41
23: 4, 14
Deu. 20: 1
32:13
Jos. 2: 6
9: 4
22:23
Jud. 2: 1
6: 8 A[a]

2 Sa. 2: 8
1 Ki. 8: 4+A
4+A
9:25 A
21:33
2 Ki. 10:15
2 Ch. 23:20 A[b]
35:24
Est. 6: 9
11—A
Isa. 57: 7
58:14
63:11
Jer. 28:27—S[1]
28
Lam. 2:10
Eze. 39: 2
Amos 8:10

[a] *pro* ἀνάγω. [b] *pro* ἐπιβιβάζω.

ἀναβλαστέω.

Job 5: 6

Job 8:19

ἀναβλέπω.

Gen. 13:14
15: 5
18: 2
22: 4, 13
24:63, 64
31:12
32: 1
33: 1, 5
37:24
43:28
Exo. 14:10
Deu. 3:27

Deu. 4:19
Jos. 5:13
Jud. 19:17 A[a]
1 Sa. 14:27
Job 22:26
35: 5
Isa. 8:21
40:26
42:18
Eze. 8: 5, 5
Joel 1:20
Zec. 5: 5

[a] *pro* αἴρω.

ἀνάβλεψις.

Isaiah 61: 1

ἀναβοάω.

Gen. 21:16
27:34
38—A
Exo. 2:23
11:10
Nu. 20:16
Deu. 26: 7

Jos. 6:10, 10
24: 7
1 Sa. 4:13
14:20 A[a]
17: 8
20:38—A
38[b]

1 Sa. 28:12
2 Sa. 18:25
23: 9 AB[a]
1 Ki. 17:20, 22
18:36
2 Ki. 3:21[c]
4:40
Neh. 9:27, 28[d]
12:37 S[1 e]

Isa. 36:13[e]
57:13
58: 1
Eze. 9: 8
11:13
Jon. 1: 5[b], 14
3: 8
Zec. 6: 8

[a] *pro* ἀναβαίνω. [b] A βοάω. [c] A ἀναβαίνω. [d] S βοάω. [e] AS βοάω.

ἀναβολή.

1 Ch. 19: 4
Neh. 5:13

Eze. 5: 3

ἀναβράσσω, —άζω.

Eze. 21:21

Nah. 3: 2

ἀναγγέλλω.

Gen. 3:11
9:22
21: 7
22:20
24:23, 28[a]
47
29:12 A[b]
31:20, 22
27
32: 5, 29
37:14
38:24[a]
43: 5
45:26
48: 1 A[b]
49: 1
Exo. 4:28
13: 8
14: 5
16:22
18: 6[a]
19: 3, 9
20:22
Lev. 14:35
Nu. 23: 3
Deu. 1:22[c]
4:13
5: 5
8: 3
13: 9, 9
17: 4,9,10
11
24:10
26: 3
30:18
32: 7
Jos. 4:10, 22
7:19
9:30[a]
Jud. 4:12
9: 7, 42[a]
47[a]
13:10[a]
14: 9[d]
16: 2[a], 6A[b]
10, 13[c]
17[a]
18 A[b]
18 A[b]
Ruth 2:19[a]
4: 4
1 Sa. 3:13[e]
15 A[b]
17:31 A
25:12
27: 4, 11
2 Sa. 1: 4 A[b]
20
10: 5 A[b]
17 AB[b]
11:10
12:18
14:33 A[b]
15:31
35 AB[b]
17:16[a], 17
17, 18[d]

2 Sa. 17:21 AB[b]
18:10, 11[f]
21
19: 1, 6, 8
24:13
1 Ki. 1:23, 51
14: 3 A
18:11
13 A[b]
19: 1
21:17 A[b]
2 Ki. 4: 2, 27
6:11, 12
13 AB[b]
7: 9, 10
11, 12
15
8: 7
9:36
18:37
1 Ch. 16:23
2 Ch. 9: 2
Ezra 2:59
Est. 4: 4
Job 8:10
11: 6
12: 7 A[b]
13:17
15:17, 17
18 A[g]
17: 5
21:31 C[b]
26: 4
27:11
32: 7, 11
33:23
36: 9, 33
38: 4A[b], 18
42: 3
Psa. 9:12
18: 2, 3
21:31, 32
29:10
37:19
43: 2
49: 6
50:17
51: 2
63:10
70:15 S[b]
17 S[b]
77: 6 S[b]
91: 3, 16
95: 3—A[1]
96: 6
101:22, 24
110: 6
150: *p* 6
Pro. 8:21
15: 2
29:24
Ecc. 8: 7
10:1[p]
Isa. 2: 3
3: 9
5: 5
7: 2

Isa. 12: 4, 5
19:12
21: 2,6,10
28: 9, 9
30:10, 10
33:14, 14
36:22[a]
38:16, 19
40:21
41: 1
22—S[1]
23, 26
28
42: 9, 9[k]
12
43: 9,9,12
44: 7—AS[i]
7
45: 8 B[m]
19, 21
21
46:10
47:13
48: 3,5,14
20, 20[o]
52:15
53: 2
58: 1
66:19
Jer. 4: 5
15 AS[a]
16
5:20
Jer. 9:12
16:10[i]
26:14
27: 2, 28
28:10, 31[n]
31, 31
31: 4, 20
38:10
40: 3 A[b]
43:13, 16
16, 18
20
45:15, 25
27
49: 3, 4
Eze. 23:36[a]
24:19[n], 26
37:18[a]
Dan. 2: 2, 4, 7
9[a], 9
11, 16[a]
24, 25
26, 27
3:32
5:12, 12
15
9:23
10:21
11: 2
Amos 3: 9[d]
4: 5[a]
Mic. 6: 8

[a] A ἀπαγγέλλω. [b] pro ibid. [c] B ἀπαγγέλλω. [d] AB ibid. [e] A ἀναφέρω. [f] A ἀγγέλλω. [g] pro ἐρῶ. [h] pro ἐξαγγέλλω. [i] AS ἀπαγγέλλω. [k] A ἀνατέλλω. [m] pro ἀνατέλλω. [n] pro ἀγγέλλω. [o] S[1] ἀπαγγέλλω.

ἀναγινώσκω.

Exo. 24 :7
Deu. 17:19
31:11
Jos. 9: 7, 8
2 Ki. 5: 7
19:14
22: 8, 10
16
23: 2
2 Ch. 34:18, 24
30
Ezra 4:23
Neh. 8: 3,8,18
9: 3
13: 1
Est. 6: 1
Job 6:17 C[a]
31:36
Isa. 29:11, 11
Isa. 29:12
37:14—AS[3]
Jer. 3:12
11: 6
19: 2
28:61, 63
36:29
39:11+AS
14
43: 6, 6, 8
10, 13
14, 15
15, 21
23
Dan. 5: 7,8,15
16, 17
Amos 4: 5
Hab. 2: 2

[a] pro ἐπιγινώσκω.

ἀναγκάζω.

1 Sa. 7: 1 A[a]
Pro. 6: 7

[a] pro ἁγιάζω.

ἀνάγκη.

1 Sa. 22: 2
Job 5:19
7:11
15:24
18:14
20:22
27: 9
30:25
36:19
Psa. 24:17
30: 8
106: 6, 13
19, 28
118:143
Pro. 17:17
Jer. 9:15
15: 4
Zeph. 1:15—A

ἀνάγλυφος.

1 Kings 6: (18) A

ἀναγνωρίζω.

Genesis 45: 1

ἀνάγνωσις.

Nehemiah 8: 8

ἀνάγω.

Gen. 42:37
50:24
Exo. 8: 3[a],6,7
10:14
33:12, 15
Lev. 11: 3, 4, 4
5, 6, 7
45
Nu. 14:13[b]
16:13
20: 4, 5
Deu. 14: 6, 7, 7
Jos. 7: 3, 24
24
24:17, 32
Jud. 6: 8[c],13[d]
15:13 A[e]
1 Sa. 2: 6
6:21
7: 1
8: 8
10:18
12: 6
28: 8, 11
11
2 Sa. 2: 3+A
6: 2, 12
15
17 A[e]
7: 6
1 Ki. 8:15
9: 9
10:p22
12:28
17:19 A[e]
18:44
2 Ki. 2: 1
10:24
17: 7, 36
23: 8
1 Ch. 13: 6, 6
1 Ch. 15:25, 28
17: 5
2 Ch. 6: 5
8: 8, 11
36: 6 A[f]
Psa. 29: 4
39: 3
70:20
21—S
77:52 S[g]
80:11
101:25
134: 7
Isa. 8: 7
Jer. 2: 6
7:22
10:13
11: 4
16:14, 15
23: 7[h]
28:16
37:17
38: 9
40: 6[i]
45:10, 13
Eze. 23:46
26: 3, 19
29: 4
32: 3
37: 6, 12
13
38:16, 17[b]
39: 2[a]
Hos 12: 9, 13
13: 4
Amos 2:10
3: 1
4:10
9: 7
Mic. 6: 4

[a] A συνάγω. [b] B ἄγω. [c] A ἀναβιβάζω. [d] A ἐξάγω. [e] pro ἀναφέρω. [f] pro ἀπάγω. [g] pro ἄγω. [h] S[1] συνάγω. [i] A ἐπάγω.

ἀναδείκνυμι.

Habakkuk 3: 2

ἀναδενδράς.

Psa. 79:11
Eze. 17: 6

ἀναζεύγνυμι.

Exo. 14:15
40:30, 31
Nu. 2: 9 A[a]
16 A[a]
Nu. 2:17 A[a]
24 A[a]
31 A[a]

[a] pro ἐξαίρω.

ἀναζέω.

Exo. 9: 9, 10
Job 41:22

ἀναζητέω.

Job 3: 4
Job 10: 6

ἀναζυγή.

Exodus 40:32

ἀναζώννυμι.

Jud. 18:16[a]
Pro. 29:35

[a] A περιζώννυμι.

ἀναζωπυρέω.

Genesis 45:27

ἀναθάλλω.

Psa. 27: 7
Eze. 17:24
Hos. 8: 9

ἀνάθεμα.

Lev. 27:28, 28
Nu. 21: 3
Deu. 20:17
Jos. 6:17, 18
18, 18
7: 1,1,11
12, 12
Deu. 7:26, 26
13:15, 17
Jos. 7:13, 13
22:20
Jud. 1:17[a]
1 Ch. 2: 7
Zec. 14:11

[a] A ἐξολόθρευσις.

ἀναθεματίζω.

Nu. 18:14
21: 2, 3
Deu. 13:15
20:17
Jos. 6:21
Jud. 1:17+A
Jud. 21:11
1 Sa. 15: 3
2 Ki. 19:11
1 Ch. 4:41
Ezra 10: 8
Dan. 11:44+A

ἀναιδής.

Deu. 28:50
1 Sa. 2:29
Pro. 7:13
25:23
Ecc. 8: 1
Isa. 56:11
Jer. 8: 5
Dan. 2:15
8:23

ἀναιδῶς.

Proverbs 21:29

ἀναίρεσις.

Nu. 11:15
Jud. 15:17

ἀναιρέω.

Gen. 4:15
Exo. 2: 5, 10
14, 14
15
15: 9
21:29
Nu. 16:37
31:19
35:31
Deu. 13:15, 15
Jos. 4: 3, 5
9:32
11:12, 17
12: 1, 7
Jud. 8:21 A[a]
9:45 A[a]
1 Sa. 15:18—A
2 Sa. 10:18
1 Ki. 2:25, 29
31
(3) 46
Job 5: 2
6: 9
20:16
Isa. 10: 4+AS[3]
11: 4
14:30, 30
26:21
27: 1, 7, 7
8
28: 6
37:36
65:15
Jer. 4:31
7:32
18:21
33:15, 19[b]
19, 24
45: 4, 25
48: 8, 8
Eze. 26: 6[c], 8
11
28: 9
Dan. 1:16
2:13, 14
5:19, 30
7:11

[a] pro ἀποκτείνω. [b] A ἀναίρω. [c] A πίπτω.

ἀναίρω.

Jeremiah 33:19 A[a]

[a] pro ἀναιρέω.

ἀναίτιος.

Deu. 19:10, 13
Deu. 21: 8, 9

ἀνακαινίζω.

2 Ch. 15: 8 B[a]
Psa. 38: 3
102: 5
Ps. 103:30
Lam. 5:21

[a] pro ἐγκαινίζω.

ἀνακαίω.

Eze. 5: 2
24:10[a]
Hos. 7: 6, 6

[a] A ἐκκαίω.

ἀνακαλέω.

Exo. 31: 2
35:30
Lev. 1: 1
Nu. 1:17
10: 2
Jos. 4: 4

ἀνακαλύπτω.

Deu. 22:30 A[a]
Job 12:22[b]
20:27
28:11
Job 33:16
41: 4 A[a]
Psa. 17:16
Isa. 3:17[b]
Isa. 20: 4[c]
22: 8, 9, 14
24: 1
26:21
Isa. 47: 2, 3
49: 9
Jer. 13:22
29:11

[a] pro ἀποκαλύπτω. [b] A ibid. [c] B ἅμα καλύπτω.

ἀνακάμπτω.

Exo. 32:27
Jud. 11:39 A[a]
2 Sa. 1:22
8:13
1 Ki. 12:20
1 Ch. 19: 5
Job 39: 4
Jer. 3: 1 ter
15: 5
22:11 S[b]
Eze. 1:14 A
7:13+A
Zec. 9: 8

[a] pro ἐπιστρέφω.
[b] pro ἀναστρέφω.

ἀνάκλισις.

Canticles 1:12

ἀνάκλιτος.

Canticles 3:10

ἀνακράζω.

Jos. 6: 4, 5
Jud. 7:20
1 Sa. 4: 5
1 Ki. 12: p24(0)
22:32
Eze. 9: 1
21:12
Joel 3:16—S[1]
Zec. 1:14, 17

ἀνακρίνω.

1 Samuel 20:12

ἀνακρούω.

Jud. 5:11
2 Sa. 6:14, 16
1 Ch. 25: 3, 5
Eze. 23:42

ἀνακύπτω.

Job 10:15

ἀναλαμβάνω.

Gen. 24:61
45:18[a], 19
27
46: 5, 6
48: 1
50:13
Exo. 4:20
10:13, 19
12:32, 34
19: 4
28:12
Nu. 14: 1
23: 7, 18
24: 3, 15
20, 21
23
Deu. 1:41
32:11
Jos. 4: 8[b]
Jud. 19:28 A[c]
2 Sa. 22:17 A[c]
2 Ki. 2: 9, 10
11
2 Ch. 23:28
Job 13:14
17: 9
21:12
22:22
27:21
36: 3
Job 40: 5
Psa. 49:16
71: 3
77:70
138: 9[d]
145: 9
146: 6
Isa. 40:24 AS[3] c
46: 4
63: 9
Jer. 4: 6
7:29
13:20
26: 3
Lam. 3:40
5:13
Eze. 2: 2
3:12, 14
8: 3, 3
10:19
11: 1, 24
12: 6, 7
16:61
43: 5
Dan. 4:31
Hos. 11: 3
Amos 5: 6 B[e]
26
7:15
Zec. 5: 9

[a] A παραλαμβάνω. [b] AB λαμβάνω. [c] pro λαμβάνω. [d] S[1] λαμβάνω. [e] pro ἀναλάμπω.

ἀναλάμπω.

Job 11:15
Isa. 42: 4
Amos 5: 6[a]

[a] B ἀναλαμβάνω.

ἀνάλγητος.

Proverbs 14:23

ἀναλέγω.

1 Sa. 20:38 | 1 Ki. 21:33

ἀνάλημμα.

2 Chronicles 32: 5

ἀναλημπτήρ.

2 Chronicles 4:16

ἀναλίσκω.

Gen. 41:30
Nu. 14:33
Pro. 23:28
24:23, 37
Isa. 32:10
66:17[a]
Jer. 27: 7–S[1 b]

Eze. 5:12
15: 4, 5
19:12
Joel 1:19
2: 3
Nah. 2: 1 S[3 c]

[a] A καταναλίσκω. [b] ABS[3] *ibid.* [c] *pro* ἐξαίρω.

ἀνάλλαγμα.

2 Sa. 24:24[a] [a] AB ἄλλαγμα.

ἀνάλωσις.

Deu. 29:20
Eze. 15: 4, 6

Eze. 16:20

ἀναμάρτητος.

Deuteronomy 29:19

ἀναμαρυκάομαι.

Lev. 11:26 A[a] | Deu. 14: 8 A[a]

[a] *pro* μηρυκάομαι.

ἀναμένω.

Job 2: 9–S[1]
7: 2

Isa. 59:11
Jer. 13:16

ἀναμίγνυμι.

Eze. 22:18, 18
46:14

Dan. 2:41, 43
43

ἀναμιμνήσκω.

Gen. 8: 1[a]
41: 9
Exo. 23:13
Nu. 5:15
10: 9
2 Sa. 18:18
20:24
1 Ki. (3) *p* 46
4: 3[b]
17:18

2 Ki. 18:18, 37
Neh. 9:17 BS[1 c]
Job 24:20[a]
Ps. 108:14
Jer. 4:16
Eze. 21:23, 24
24
23:19
29:16
33:13[a], 16[a]

[a] A μιμνήσκω. [b] B ὑπομιμνήσκω. [c] *pro* μιμνήσκω.

ἀνάμνησις.

Lev. 24: 7
Nu. 10:10

Psa. 37: 1
69: 1

ἀνάνευσις.

Psalm 72: 4

ἀνανεύω.

Exo. 22:17, 17
Nu. 30: 6 *ter*
9 *ter*

Nu. 30:12
Neh. 9:17
Job 33:24

ἀναντλέω.

Job 19:26[a] [a] S[1] ἀντλέω.

ἀναξηραίνω.

Jer. 27:27 | Hos. 13:15

ἀνάξιος.

Jer. 15:19[a] [a] ABS[1] ἄξιος.

ἀνάπαυμα.

Job 3:23[a] | Isa. 28: 2[b], 12

[a] ACS[2] ἀνάπαυσις [b] AS *ibid.*

ἀνάπαυσις.

Gen. 8: 9
49:15
Exo. 16:23
23:12[a]
31:15
35: 2[a]
Lev. 16:31
23: 3, 24
39, 39
25: 4, 5, 8
Nu. 10:34
Ruth 1: 9
3: 1
1 Ch. 22: 9
28: 2
Est. 9:17
Job 3:23ACS[2 b]
7:18
21:13

Psa. 22: 2
114: 7
131: 4, 8
Ecc. 4: 6
6: 5
9:17
Isa. 11:10
17: 2–S[1]
23:12
13+AS
25:10
28: 2 AS[b]
32:17
34:14
37:28
65:10
Jer. 51:33
Lam. 1: 3
Mic. 2:10

[a] A ἀναπαύω. [b] *pro* ἀνάπαυμα.

ἀναπαύω.

Gen. 29: 2
49:14
Exo. 23:12
12 A[a]
35: 2 A[a]
Lev. 25: 2
Nu. 24: 9
Deu. 5:14
28:65
33:20
Jud. 4:11 A[b]
1 Sa. 16:16
2 Sa. 7:11
1 Ki. 5: 4
13:30+A
1 Ch. 22: 9, 18
Neh. 9:28
Est. 9:16, 17
18, 22
Job 2: 9
3:13, 17
26
10:20
13:13
32:20
Pro. 14:33 S[2 c]
21:16, 20

Pro. 29:17
Ecc. 7:10
Isa. 7:19+AS
11: 2[d]
13:20, 21
21
14: 1, 3, 4
4, 6, 30
27:10
32:16, 18
34:14, 17
57:15, 20
Jer. 29: 6
30:12
31:11[e]
49:10
Lam. 1: 6+S[1]
5: 5
Eze. 16:42
17:23, 23
31:13
34:14, 15
Dan. 12:13
13+A
Mic. 4: 4
Hab. 3:16
Zec. 6: 8

[a] *pro* ἀνάπαυσις. [b] *pro* πλεονεκτέω. [c] *pro* ἀνήρ. [d] S ἐπαναπαύω. [e] S[1] παύω.

ἀναπείθω.

Jer. 36: 8, 8[a] [a] S πείθω.

ἀναπετάζω.

Job 39:26

ἀναπηδάω, –δύω.

1 Sa. 20:34[a]
25: 9

Pro. 18: 4
[a] A ἀποπηδάω.

ἀναπίπτω.

Genesis 49: 9

ἀναπληρόω.

Gen. 2:21
15:16
29:28
Exo. 7:25
23:26–AB
26

Lev. 12: 6
1 Ki. 7:37
Est. 1: 5
2:12, 12
15
Isa. 60:20

ἀναπλήρωσις.

Daniel 12:13

ἀναπνέω.

Job 9:18

ἀναποιέω.

Lev. 6:40
40–A
Nu. 6:15
7:13, 19
25, 31
37, 43
49, 55
61, 67
73, 79
8: 8

Lev. 7: 2
23:13
Nu. 15: 4?, 6[b]
9[b]
28: 5, 9, 12
12, 13
20, 28
29: 3, 9, 14
Isa. 30:24

[a] A φυράω. [b] A ἀναφυράω.

ἀναπτερόω.

Pro. 7:11 | Cant. 6: 4

ἀναπτύσσω.

Deu. 22:17
Jud. 8:25

2 Ki. 19:14
Eze. 41:16, 21

ἀνάπτω.

Jud. 5: 8+A
6:21 A[a]
2 Ch. 13:11
Psa. 17: 9
77:21
Jer. 9:12
11:16
17:27
21:12, 14
27:32

Jer. 31: 9 A[b]
Lam. 2: 3
4:11, 15
Eze. 20:47
Joel 1:19
2: 3
Amos 1:14
Mal. 1:10
4: 1

[a] *pro* ἀναβαίνω. [b] *pro* ἅπτω.

ἀναρίθμητος.

1 Ki. 8: 5
Job 21:33[a]
22: 5
31:25

Job 36:27 S[1 b]
Pro. 7:26
Joel 1: 6

[a] A ἀριθμητός. [b] *pro ibid.*

ἀναρπάζω.

Jud. 9:25 A[a] [a] *pro* διαρπάζω.

ἀναρρήγνυμι.

2 Ki. 2:24
8:12

2 Ki. 15:16

ἀνασκάπτω.

Psa. 7:16 | Psa. 79:17

ἀνασπάω.

Amos 9: 2 | Hab. 1:15

ἀνάστασις.

Psa. 65: 1–S
Lam. 3:62

Zeph. 3: 8

ἀναστέλλω.

Nah. 1: 5[a] [a] S[3] ἀνίστημι.

ἀναστενάζω.

Lamentations 1: 4

ἀνάστημα.

Gen. 7: 4, 23
1 Sa. 10: 5

Zeph. 2:14
Zec. 9: 8

ἀναστρέφω.

Gen. 8: 7[a], 9
11
14: 7
18:14
22: 5
32: 6
37:29
30 A[b]
49:22
Exo. 24:14
Deu. 24:21[c]
Jos. 2:16 A[d]
5: 5
7: 3
19:12, 29
29

Jud. 3:19 A[e]
7:13[f]
8:13 A[b]
18:26 A[b]
20:39+A
Ruth 1:15
1 Sa. 3: 5, 5, 6
9
6:16
9: 5 B[d]
14:21 B[b]
15:25, 26
30, 31
17:15 A
53[g]
23:28

1 Sa. 24: 2
25:12
26:25 B[d]
27: 9[h]
29: 7
2 Sa. 1: 1
2:26 B[d]
30[g]
3:16, 16
26
10:14
12:23
17:20
22:38
1 Ki. (3) 41[b], [i]
6: (12) A
11:22
12: 5, 12
24 A[d]
p 24 *l* 81
13:10
15:21
19:15, 20
21
21: 5
9 A[b]
22:17, 33[k]
2 Ki. 2:18–8[h]

2 Ki. 9:18, 20
1 Ch. 20: 3
2 Ch. 18:16
Job 10:21
Pro. 2:19
8:20
20: 7
26:11
Jer. 3: 7, 7
8: 4[m]
15:19, 19
22:10 A[b]
11[n]
26: 5, 16?
27
44: 8–S[1]
47: 5?
48:14
Eze. 3:15
19: 6
22: 7, 29
30
39:25 A[d]
46: 9
Dan. 11: 9
Jon. 3: 8 S[3 d]
Zec. 3: 7
7:14

[a] A ὑποστρέφω. [b] *pro* ἐπιστρέφω. [c] A ἐπαναστρέφω. [d] *pro* ἀποστρέφω. [e] *pro* ὑποστρέφω. [f] A καταστρέφω. [g] A ἀποστρέφω. [h] A ἐπιστρέφω. [i] B ἀποστρέφω. [k] AB ἀποστρέφω. [m] AS ἐπιστρέφω. [n] S ἀνακάμπτω.

ἀνασύρω.

Isaiah 47: 2

ἀνασχίζω.

Amos 1:13

ἀνασώζω.

Gen. 14:13
2 Ki. 19:31
2 Ch. 30: 6
Jer. 26: 6
27:28, 29
28: 6, 50
51:14
Lam. 2:22
Eze. 6: 8, 9

Eze. 7:16, 16
14:22
21:26, 27
33:21
Joel 2: 3, 32
Amos 9: 1
Obad. 14, 21[a]
Zec. 2: 7
8: 7 A[b]

[a] A σώζω. [b] *pro* σώζω.

ἀνατέλλω.

Gen. 2: 5
3:18
19:23
32:31
Exo. 22: 3
Lev. 13:37
14:43
Nu. 24:17
Deu. 29:23
Jud. 9:33
14:18[a]
16:22 A[b]
2 Sa. 10: 5
23: 4
2 Ki. 3:22
19:29
1 Ch. 19: 5
2 Ch. 26:19
Job 3: 9
9: 7+A
7
11:17
25: 5+A
5+A
Psa. 64:11
71: 7

Psa. 84:12
91: 8
96:11
103:22
Pro. 11:28
Ecc. 1: 5, 5
Isa. 13:10
14:12
42: 9 A[c]
43:19
44: 4, 26
45: 8, 8[d]
58: 8, 10
11+AS[3]
60: 1
61:11
66:14
Jer. 13: 6 B[e]
Eze. 16: 7
17: 6
29:21
Hos. 10: 4
Jon. 4: 8
Nah. 3:17
Zec. 6:12
Mal. 4: 2

[a] A δύνω. [b] *pro* βλαστάνω. [c] *pro* ἀναγγέλλω. [d] B ἀναγγέλλω. [e] *pro* ἐντέλλω.

ἀνατίθημι.

Lev. 27:28, 29
1 Sa. 31:10
2 Sa. 6:17
Mic. 4:13
7: 5

ἀνατιναγμός.

Nahum 2:10

ἀνατολή.

Gen. 2: 8
10:30
11: 2
12: 8, 8
13:11, 14
25: 6, 6
28:14
29: 1
Exo. 27:13 A[a]
37:11
Lev. 1:16
16:14
Nu. 2: 3
3:38
10: 5
21:11
23: 7
32:19
34: 3, 10
11, 11
15
35: 5
Deu. 3:17, 27
4:41, 47
49
Jos. 1:15
4:19
8:11
11: 3, 8
12: 1, 1, 3
3
13: 5,8,27
32
15: 5
16: 1, 5, 6
6
17:10
18: 7, 20
19:12, 13
27, 34
20: 8+A
Jud. 5:31 A[b]
6: 3, 33
7:12
8:10+A
11
11:18
20:43
21:19
1 Ki. 7:12, 25
17: 3
2 Ki. 10:33
13:17
1 Ch. 4:39
5: 9, 10
7:28
9:18, 24
12:15
26:14, 17
18
2 Ch. 4: 4, 10
5:12 A[c]
2 Ch. 29: 4
31:14
Neh. 3:26, 29
12:37+S[3]
Job 1: 3
Psa. 49: 1
67:34
102:12
106: 3
112: 3
Isa. 9:12
11:11, 14
27:13 A[d]
41: 2, 25
43: 5
45: 6
46:11
59:19
60:19
Jer. 23: 5
38:40
Eze. 8: 5
16+A
11: 1
16: 7
17:10
40: 6, 19
21, 22
23, 32
40, 40
42: 1,9,12
15, 16
20
43: 1, 2, 4
17
44: 1
45: 7, 7
46: 1, 12
47: 1, 1, 2
8, 18
18, 18
48: 1, 2, 3
4, 5, 6
7, 8, 8
16
17−A
18, 21
21 A[e]
23, 24
25, 26
27
28−AB
32
Dan. 8: 9+A
11:44
Amos 8:12
Zec. 3: 8
6:12
8: 7
14: 4−A
4
Mal. 1:11

[a] pro νότος. [b] pro ἔξοδος. [c] pro κατέναντι. [d] pro ἀπόλλυμι. [e] pro θάλασσα.

ἀνατρέπω.

Ps. 117:13
Pro. 10: 3
Pro. 21:14
Ecc. 12: 6

ἀνατροπή.

Habakkuk 2:15

ἀναφαίνω.

Job 11:18
13:18
24:18
Job 40: 3
Cant. 6: 4[a]

[a] S ἀναβαίνω.

ἀναφαιρέω.

2 Sa. 4: 7 B[a] [a] pro ἀφαιρέω.

ἀναφάλαντος.

Leviticus 13:41

ἀναφαλάντωμα.

Lev. 13:42, 42
Lev. 13:43 AB[a]

[a] pro φαλάντωμα.

ἀναφέρω.

Gen. 8:20
22: 2, 13
31:39 A[a]
40:10
Exo. 18:19, 22
26
19: 8
24: 5
29:18, 25
30: 9, 20
35:21 B[*b]
Lev. 2:16
3: 5, 11
14, 16
4:10[b], 19
26, 31
6:15, 26
35
7:21
8:16, 20
21, 27
28
9:10, 20
14:20[c]
16:25
17: 5
23:11, 11
Nu. 5:26
14:33
18:17
23: 2, 30
Deu. 1:17
12:13, 14
27−B
14:23
27: 6
Jud. 6:26, 28
11:31
13:16, 19
15:13[d]
16: 3 A[e], 8
18[f]
20:26, 38
21: 4
1 Sa. 2:19
3:13 A[g]
6:14, 15
15
7: 9, 10
10: 8
13: 9, 10
12
15:13
18:27[f]
20:13
2 Sa. 1:24
6:17[d]
21:13
24:22, 24
25
1 Ki. (3)p 1
3: 4
5:13
8: 1 A[a]
9:15 A
10: 5, p 22
12:27
17:19[d]
2 Ki. 3:27
4:21[f]
1 Ch. 15: 3, 12
14
16: 2, 40
21:24, 26
23:31
29:21
2 Ch. 1: 4, 6 A[a]
6 A[a]
2: 4
4:16
5: 2
5+A
5
8:12, 13
9: 4
16−B
23:18
24:14
29:21, 27
27, 29
31−A
32
35:14
Ezra 3: 2, 6
Neh. 10:38
12:31
Job 7:13
Psa. 50:21
65:15
158[2]S[2h]
Pro. 8: 6[i]
Isa. 18: 7
53:11, 12
57: 6
60: 7
66: 3, 20
Jer. 39:35
Eze. 36:15[f]
43:18, 24
Dan. 6:23, 23

[a] pro φέρω. [b] AB διαναφέρω. [c] A[2] φέρω. [d] A ἀνάγω. [e] pro ἀναβαίνω. [f] A φέρω. [g] pro ἀναγγέλλω. [h] pro ποιέω. [i] A ἀνοίγω.

ἀναφορά.

Nu. 4:19
Psa. 50:21

ἀναφορεύς.

Exo. 25:12, 13
14, 26
27
27: 6[a], 7[a]
7[a]
35:11
Nu. 4: 6, 8
Nu. 4:10, 11
12, 14
14
13:24
1 Ch. 15:15
2 Ch. 5: 8, 9, 9

[a] AB[1] φορεύς.

ἀναφράσσω.

Nehemiah 4: 7

ἀναφυράω.

Nu. 15: 6 A[a]
Nu. 15: 9 A[a]

[a] pro ἀναποιέω.

ἀναφύω.

Gen. 41: 6, 23
1 Sa. 5: 6
Isa. 34:13
Eze. 37: 8 A[a]

[a] pro φύω.

ἀναφωνέω.

1 Ch. 15:28
16: 4, 5
1 Ch. 16:42
2 Ch. 5:13

ἀναχωρέω.

Exo. 2:15
Nu. 16:24
Jos. 8:15
Jud. 4:17 A[a]
1 Sa. 19:10
25:10
2 Sa. 4: 4
Ps. 113: 5 S[1b]
Pro. 25: 9
Jer. 4:29
Hos. 12:12

[a] pro φεύγω. [b] pro στρέφω.

ἀνάψυξις.

Exodus 8:15

ἀναψυχή.

Psa. 65:12
Jer. 30: 9
Hos. 12: 8

ἀναψύχω.

Exo. 23:12
Jud. 15:19 A[a]
1 Sa. 16:23
2 Sa. 16:14
Psa. 38:14

[a] pro ζάω.

ἀνδραγαθία.

Esther 10: 2

ἀνδρεία.

Psa. 67: 7
Pro. 21:30
Ecc. 2:21
Ecc. 4: 4
5:10[a]

[a] S[1] ἀνήρ.

ἀνδρεῖος.

Pro. 10: 4
11:16
12: 4
13: 4
Pro. 15:19
28: 3
29:28

ἀνδρίζω.

Deu. 31: 6,7,23
Jos. 1: 6, 7, 9
18
10:25
2 Sa. 10:12
13:28
1 Ch. 19:13−BS
22:13
28:20
2 Ch. 32: 7
Psa. 26:14
30:25
Jer. 2:23
18:12
Dan. 10:19
Mic. 4:10
Nah. 2: 1

ἀνδρόγυνος.

Pro. 18: 8
Pro. 19:15

ἀνδρόομαι.

Job 27:14
Job 33:25

ἀνειλέω.

Ezekiel 2:10

ἄνειμι.

1 Ki. 21:22 A[a] [a] pro ἀναβαίνω.

ἀνελεημόνως.

Job 6:21
Job 30:21[a]

[a] A ἀνελεήμων.

ἀνελεήμων.

Job 19:13
30:21 A[a]
Pro. 5: 9
11:17
Pro. 12:10
17:11
Pro. 27: 4

[a] pro ἀνελεημόνως.

ἀνέλπιστος.

Isa. 18: 2, 7 S[a] [a] pro ἐλπίζω.

ἄνεμος.

Exo. 10:13−A
13, 19
14:21
2 Sa. 22:11
1 Ki. 14:15 A
1 Ch. 9:24
Job 13:25
15:30
21:18
28:25
Psa. 1: 4
17:11, 43
34: 5
82:14[a]
103: 3
134: 7
Pro. 8, 27
9:12
11:29
24:27
25:14, 23
27:16
Ecc. 5:15
Ecc. 11: 4
Isa. 17:13
41:16
57:13
64: 6
Jer. 5:13
13:24
14: 6
18:14, 17
22:22
25:15, 15
28: 1
Eze. 5:10, 12
12:14
17:10, 21
19:12
37: 9 A[b]
Dan. 7: 2
8: 8
11: 4
Hos. 13:15
Zec. 2: 6
6: 5

[a] S[1] πῦρ. [b] pro πνεῦμα.

ἀνεμοφθορία.

Deu. 28:22
2 Ch. 6:28
Hag. 2:17

ἀνεμόφθορος.

Gen. 41: 6,7,23
24, 27
Pro. 10: 5
Isa. 19: 7
Hos. 8: 7[a]

[a] A -ριος.

ἀνεξέλεγκτος.

Pro. 10:17
Pro. 25: 3

ἀνεξιχνίαστος.

Job 5: 9
9:10
Job 34:24

ἀνεπιείκεια.

Proverbs 12:26+A

ἀνέρχομαι

1 Ki. 13:12[a] [a] A ἀπέρχομαι.

ἄνεσις.

2 Ch. 23:15
Ezra 4:22

ἀνετάζω.

Jud. 6:29 A[a]
Est. 2:23 S[3b]

[a] pro ἐπιζητέω. [b] pro ἐτάζω.

ἄνευ.

Job 6: 6−S[1]
Job 39: 3 A[a]

[a] pro ἔξω.

ἀνέχω.

Gen. 45: 1
1 Ki. 12:p24/82
Job 6:11, 26
Isa. 1:13
42:14
Isa. 46: 4
63:15
64:12
Amos 4: 7
Hag. 1:10

ἀνεψιός.

Numbers 36:11

ἀνήκοος.

Nu. 17:10
Job 36:12
Pro. 13: 1
Jer. 5:23
6:28

ἀνήκω.

Jos. 23:14[a]
Jud. 8: 3 A[b]
1 Sa. 23:13
27: 8

[a] A ἥκω. [b] pro ἀνίημι.

ἀνήλατος.

Job 41:15

ἀνήρ.

Gen. 2:23
3: 6, 16
4:23
12:20
14:21, 24
16: 3
17:23, 27
18: 2, 16
22
19: 4, 5, 8
8,9,10
11, 12
20: 2, 3
24:16, 32
54
26: 7, 7
27:11, 11
29:19, 22
32, 34
30:15, 18
20
32: 6
33: 1
34: 7, 20
38:21
39: 1, 2
43:14, 17[a]
46:32, 32
34
47: 2, 5
49:15
Exo. 2:13
10:11
12:37
17: 9
18:21, 21
25
21:18, 22
22, 28
29
22:31
32:28
35:22, 29
36: 6
38:22
39: 2
Lev. 13:29, 38
15: 2,2,18
33
20:10, 18
27
21: 3, 7
22:12
Nu. 1: 5, 17
44[b], 44
52, 52
4:49, 49
5: 6, 10
12, 12
13, 19
20, 27
6: 2
9: 6, 7
11:16, 24
25, 26
13: 3, 3, 4
17, 33
14:22
15:32
16: 2, 2, 7
35
19:18
22:21 A[c]
30: 7, 8, 9
9, 11
12, 13
13, 14
14

Nu. 30:16—AB
17
31: 3, 21
32, 35
42, 49
50, 53
32: 2 A[c]
34:17, 19
Deu. 1:13, 15
16, 22
23, 23
35
2:14, 16
3:11
13:13
17: 2
21:20, 21
22: 5, 5
21 A[c]
22, 22
23
24: 4, 5, 5
6
25: 5, 5, 7
7, 11
28:30, 56
29:10, 18
31:12
33: 8
Jos. 2: 2, 3, 4
4, 5, 7
14, 17
3:12
4: 2
2+A
4
6:21
7: 2, 3, 3
4, 4, 5
5, 14
17
8: 1,3,21
25
9: 8
10: 2, 18
17: 1
18: 4, 8, 8
Jud. 1: 4, 24
25, 26
2: 6—A
21
3:15, 17
28, 29
29, 29
31
4: 6, 10
14
20—A
20, 22
5:30—A
6: 3 A[d], 8
16, 27
27, 28
29, 30
31
7: 6, 7, 7
8 *ter*
13, 14
16, 19
21[e], 22
23, 24
8: 1, 4, 5
8, 8, 9
10, 14
14, 15
16, 17
18, 21
22, 24

Jud. 8:25
9: 2 *ter*
3, 4, 5
6,7,9[a]
18, 18
20, 20
23, 23
24, 25
26, 28
36, 39
46, 47
49—A
49—A
49, 49
51, 55
55, 57
10: 1, 18
18
11: 3, 39
12: 1[f],2,4
4
5+A
5
6+A
13: 2, 6, 9
10, 10
11, 11
14:15, 18
19
15:10, 11
15, 16
16: 5, 19[g]
27, 27
17: 1, 5A[h]
6,8,11
18: 2, 7, 8
11, 14
16, 17
17+A
19, 22
25
19: 1
1+A
3, 6, 7
9, 10
15, 16
16, 16
17, 17
18, 20
22 *ter*
23 *to* 26
27 [i]
28+A
30+A
30+A
20 *passim*
20+A
38 A[d]
39 A[d]
42 A[d]
48 A[d]
21: 1A[d], 1
8,9,10
12, 21
22, 24
24, 25
Ruth 1: 1, 2, 3
5,9,11
12, 12
13
2: 1 *ter*
11, 19
20
3: 3,8,14
16, 18
4: 2, 7
1 Sa. 1: 8, 11
18, 22
23
2: 9, 15
16[a], 19
25, 25
33, 33
4: 2, 2, 9
9—B
10, 12
13, 16
17, 19
21
22+A

1 Sa. 5: 7, 9
6:15, 19
19, 19
20
7: 1
11—A
8: 4, 22
9: 1 *ter*
2, 16
21, 22
10: 2, 3, 6
21, 22
11: 1, 3
5—A[k]
7, 8, 8
9,9,10
12
12: 1+A
13: 2, 2, 6
15
14: 2,8,12
14, 20
22+A
23, 36
40, 52
52
15: 3
16:16, 17
18
18+A
18
17: 2, 4, 8
10, 12A
12A, 19A
23A, 24A
24A, 25A
25A, 25A
26A, 26A
27A, 28A
33, 40
41A, 52
53
18: 5A, 23[a]
27, 27
21:14
22: 2,6,18
19
23: 3, 5, 8
12A, 13
24, 25
26 *qtr*
24: 3, 3, 4
5, 7, 8
23
25:11, 13
13+A
13, 15
19, 20
26: 2, 15
27: 2, 3, 8
9, 11
28: 1, 4, 8
14
29: 2, 4, 4
11
30: 1, 2, 3
4,9,10
10, 11
13, 17
21, 22
22, 31
31: 1, 3
6+A
7,7,12
2 Sa. 1: 2, 11
13
2: 3, 4, 4
17, 29
30, 31
31, 32
3:15, 16
20, 20
39
4: 1,2,11
11
5: 6, 21
6:19
7:14
8: 4, 5
9: 3

2 Sa. 10: 5, 5, 6
6
11:16, 17
23, 26
26
12: 1, 4, 4
5, 5, 7
13: 3, 9, 9
20[c], 34
14: 5,7,16
25
15: 1, 2
2+A
4, 5, 6
11, 13
18—A
18, 30
16: 5, 7, 7
8, 13
15[m], 18
17: 1, 3, 3
8,8,12
13+A
14, 18
24—A
25
18: 7, 10
11, 12
17, 20
24, 26
26, 27
28
19: 7,8,14
14, 15
16, 17
22, 28
32, 32
41 *ter*
42, 42
43 *qtr*
20:1,1,2 B
2, 4, 7
11, 12
13, 21
22
21: 4, 5, 6
12, 17
20
22:26, 49
23: 1, 7, 9
17, 20
21, 21
24: 9 *ter*
15
1 Ki. 1: 5
9+A[l]
9 A[n]
42, 49
2: 2, 4, 9
26
(3) *p* 1
3:13—A
4:11+B
5: 6+A
13
7: 2
16+A
8: 2+A
25, 39
9: 5, 27
10: *p* 22
11:14, 17
18, 18
28
12: *p* 24,
l 69, *l* 76
13:25
18: 4, 13
13+A
22, 44
19:18
20:10
11—B
13—B
13+A
21: 8, 17
30, 33
39 *ter*
42
22: 6,8,10

2 Ki. 1: 6, 7, 8
2: 7, 16
17, 19
3:23, 25
26
4: 1,9,14
22, 26
29, 29
40, 42
43
5: 1, 1, 7
24, 26
6: 2, 19
32
7: 3, 3, 5
6,9,10
9:11, 16
21
10: 5, 6, 6
7, 14
14, 19
21, 24
24, 24
25
11: 8, 9, 9
11
12: 4+A
4, 4, 5
9, 15
13:21, 21
14:12
15:20, 25
17:30
30—A
30
18:21, 27
31, 31
20:14
22:15
23: 2,8,10
10, 17
18, 35
24:16
25: 4, 19
19, 19
23, 23
24, 25
1 Ch. 2: 3 A[o]
4:12, 22
42
5:18, 21
24, 24
7:21, 40
8:40
9: 9
10: 7—S
12
11: 4, 19
22, 23
23—S
12: 8, 19
30, 38
16: 3—S
3,3,21
18: 4,5,10
19: 5
20: 6
21: 5,5—B
14
22: 9
23: 3
26:31
2 Ch. 2: 2,7,13
14, 17
5: 3+A
6: 5, 16
22, 30
7:18
8: 9
9: 7, 14
10:17
13: 3,7,15
15, 17
15:13
17:13
18: 5,7,33
19:10
20:27
23: 7, 8
24:24

2 Ch. 28: 6, 15
31:19
31:12, 23
Ezra 1: 4
2: 1,2,27
28
3: 1
4:11, 21
5: 4, 10
6: 8
8:16+B
18
10: 1, 9
16—S[3]
17
Neh. 1: 2, 11
2:12
3: 2
7-ABS
22, 28
4:15, 18
19, 23
23
5: 7, 13
17
6:11
11+A
7: 2, 3, 3
6—S[1]
7, 28
29, 30
31, 32
33, 34
8: 1, 2, 3
16
11: 2, 3, 6
12:44
13:10, 25
30
Est. 1:18, 20
4:16+S[1]
9: 6, 12
15
Job 3:23
4:17
6:25+A
10: 5
12: 4
14:10
15:16
16:21
20:25 A[p]
22:15
24: 2+A
30:25
31: 9, 11
32: 5
33:20
31+A
34: 7,9,11
19 A[n]
19—C
23, 34
35: 8
36:24
38: 3, 26
40: 2
41: 8
Psa. 1: 1
5: 7
17:26, 40
25: 9
27: 3+S[1]
31: 2
33: 9
36:23 S[1q]
39: 5
54:24
58: 3
75: 6
79:18
91: 7
111: 1, 5
138:19
139: 1, 12
12
140:10
Pro. 1:10, 11
18
2:12

Pro. 3:31
5:21, 22
6: 2, 11A[r]
12, 26
34—S[1]
7:19
10: 4, 10
13, 23
32
11: 6—S[1]
7, 12
13, 16
17, 25
12: 2, 4, 4
8,9,14
16-ABS
23, 25
27
13: 8, 22
14: 7, 10
14, 17
29, 30
33[s]
15:18, 18
21
16: 1, 14
25, 26
27, 28
29, 32
32+
AC[2] S[3]
17:12, 18
20, 23
24, 26
27
18: 1,4,11
12, 14
14, 20
22
19: 6, 11
14, 19
21, 22
23, 25
20: 3, 5, 5
6, 6
24, 25
21:2,16,17
20, 26
28, 29
22: 8, 14
24, 29
29
23: 6
24: 1, 5, 9
24, 45
54, 58
25:18, 20
28
26:12, 21
27:17, 21
23
28: 2,5,11
14, 17
20, 21
22, 24
25
29: 1, 1, 2
3, 4, 6
8, 9, 9
10, 20
22, 22
23, 25
26, 27
27, 29
30, 39
40, 41
46, 49
Ecc. 1: 8
4: 4
5:10 S[1t]
6: 2, 2, 3
7: 6
9:14, 15
15
10:10
12: 3
Cant. 3: 8
8: 7,11-A
Isa. 2: 9
5:15

Isa. 14:30 AS[q]
22:17
28:14
31: 8
36: 6-ABS
11 A[q]
12 A[q]
41: 7
44:13
45:14
54: 1
55: 7
56: 2
57: 1
59:16
63: 3
Jer. 2: 6[n]
3: 1, 1
4: 3-A, 4
5:26
6:11
7: 5
10:23
11: 2, 9[v]
21
12:11
13:14
14: 9
15:10
17:25
18:11, 21
19: 3-A
10
20:10
22: 7, 19
30
30+A
23: 9[w]
27:30
28:22, 32
30:15
31:31
33:17, 22
36: 6
39:12-AS
32
41: 9, 18
42:19
45:22
47: 7, 7, 8
9
48: 1, 2, 5
5, 8, 16
50: 2, 6, 9
51:15, 19
52: 7, 25
25
Lam. 3: 1, 27
32, 34
38
Eze. 3:26
8: 2, 11
16
9: 2, 2, 3
4
6-A

Eze. 9:11
10: 2, 3, 6
11: 1, 2, 15
12:16
14: 1, 3, 14
16, 18
16:32, 45
45
18: 7 A[x], 8
20: 1
21:31
22: 9, 30
23:14, 40
42, 45
24:17, 22
27:10, 27
33:26 A
39:14, 20
40: 3, 4, 5
43: 6
44:25
47: 3
Dan. 2:25
3: 8, 12
12+A
20, 21
22+A
24, 25
27
5: 1+A
11
6:11, 15
24
8:15, 16
9: 7, 21
23
10: 5, 7, 11
19
12: 6, 7
Hos. 2: 2, 7, 16
3: 3
6: 9
Joel 1: 8
2: 7
3: 9
Amos 1: 5
6: 9-B
7: 7+A
Obad. 7, 7
21+A
Jon. 1:10, 10
13, 16
3: 5
Mic. 2: 2, 2
7: 6
Nah. 2: 4
Hab. 2: 5
Zeph. 1:12
3: 4
Zec. 1: 8, 10
2: 1
3: 8
6:12
7: 2
8:23, 23
13: 7

[a] A ἄνθρωπος. [b] A[2] ἄρχων. [c] pro ἄρχων. [d] pro υἱός. [e] A ἕκαστος. [f] A υἱος. [g] A κουρ. ὑς. [h] pro οἶκος. [i] A κύριος. [k] B υἱός. [m] A λαός. [n] pro ἀδρός. [o] pro "Ηρ[2]. [p] pro ἄστρον. [q] pro ἄνθρωπος. [r] pro δρομεύς. [s] S[2] ἀναπαύω. [t] pro ἀνδρεία. [u] ABS[1] om. [v] A πόλις. [w] A[2] ἄνθρωπος. [x] pro ἄρτος.

ἀνθέμιον.

Ecclesiastes 12: 6

ἀνθέω.

Lev. 13:12[a]
Job 14: 2
7 A[b], 9
20:20+A
21-A
Psa. 89: 6
91:13
Ecc. 12: 5
Cant. 6:10
10 A[c]
Cant. 7:12 ter
Isa. 17:11
18: 5 ABS[c]
Isa. 35:1
Eze. 7:10
Hos. 14: 5

[a] AB ἐξανθέω. [b] pro ἐπανθέω. [c] pro ἐξανθέω.

ἄνθινος.

Exodus 28:30

ἀνθίστημι.

Lev. 26:37
Nu. 10: 9
22:23, 31
34
Deu. 7:24
9: 2
11:25
19:18
25:18
28: 7
Jos. 1: 5
7:13
21:44[a]
23: 9
Jud. 2:14
2 Sa. 5: 6
2 Ch. 13: 7 A[b], 7
8
20: 6, 12
Est. 9: 2[c]
Job 9:19
41: 1, 2
Psa. 16: 7
75: 8
Isa. 3: 9
50: 8
59:12
Jer. 14: 7
27:24, 29
44
29:20
Hos. 14:a1
Obad. 7, 11
Mic. 2: 8[d]
Nah. 1: 6
Hab. 1: 9
Mal. 3:15

[a] AB ἀνίστημι. [b] pro ἀνίστημι. [c] S[3] ἀνίστημι. [d] A ἀντικαθίστημι.

ἀνθομολογέομαι.

Psalm 78:13

ἀνθομολόγησις.

Ezra 3:11

ἄνθος.

Exo. 28:14
30:23
Nu. 17: 8
Job 14: 2
15:30, 33
Ps. 102:15
Cant. 2: 1, 12
Isa. 5:24
Isa. 11: 1
18: 5, 5
28: 1, 4
40: 6, 7
61:11
Eze. 19:10
Dan. 11: 7
Zeph. 2: 2

ἀνθρακινός.

Est. 1: 7[a]

[a] S[1] ἀνθρακίος.

ἄνθραξ.

Gen. 2:12
Exo. 28:18
36:18
Lev. 16:12
2 Sa. 14: 7
22: 9, 13
Job 41:11, 12
Psa. 17: 9, 13
119: 4
139:11
Pro. 6:28
25:22
Pro. 26:21
Cant. 8: 6+S[3]
Isa. 5:24
6: 6
44:16-AS[1]
19
47:14
54:11, 16
Eze. 1:13
10: 2, 9
24:11
28:13

ἀνθρωπάρεσκος.

Psalm 52: 6

ἀνθρώπινος.

Nu. 5: 6
19:16[a], 18
Job 10: 5
Eze. 4:12, 16
37: 1

[a] A ἄνθρωπος.

ἄνθρωπος.

Gen. 1:26, 27
2: 5, 7, 7
8, 15
18, 24
4: 1
5: 1
6: 1, 2, 3, 4
4, 5, 6, 7
7, 9, 13
7:21, 23
Gen. 8:21, 21
9: 5, 5, 6
6, 20
11: 3, 5
13: 8, 13
16:12
20: 7, 8
24:21, 23
26, 29
30, 30
Gen. 24:32, 43
58, 61
65
25:27, 27
26:11, 13
31 A[a]
30:43
32:24, 28
34:14, 21
22
37:15, 15
17, 28
38: 1, 2, 22
25
41:33, 38
39
42:11, 30
33
43: 2, 4, 5
6, 10
12, 13
15, 15
16, 16
17 A[b]
18
22+A
27, 32
44: 1, 3, 4
10+A
15, 17
26
49: 6
Exo. 2:11, 19
20, 21
4:11
5: 9
8:16, 17
18
9: 9, 9, 10
19, 22
25
10: 7
11: 3, 7
12:12
13: 2, 13
15
19:13
21:19
22: 7
30:32
32: 1, 23
33:20
Lev. 1: 2
5: 3, 4
6: 3, 38
7:11
13: 2, 9, 44
14:11
15: 5, 16
16:17, 21
17: 3, 3, 4
8, 8, 9
10, 10
13, 13
18: 5, 6, 6
27
19:20
20: 3, 4, 5
9, 9, 10
21: 9, 17
18 to 20
22: 3, 4, 4
5, 12
13+A
14, 18
18, 21
24:10, 15
17, 17
20, 21
25:14, 17
27
27:14, 16
20, 24
28, 28
29, 31
Nu. 2: 2
3:13
5: 8, 15
30, 31
8:17
Nu. 9: 6, 7, 10
10, 10
13, 13
12: 3, 3
13:32
14:15, 36
37, 38
15:35
16:14, 22
26, 29
29, 30
32
17: 5
18:15, 15
19: 9, 11
13, 14
16 A[c]
20
21: 8, 9
22: 9, 20
35
23:19, 19
24: 3, 7, 15
17
25: 6, 8, 8
14
26:64
27: 8, 16
18
30: 3, 3
31:11, 26
28, 28
30, 35
40, 46
47
32:11, 14
Deu. 1:17, 31
4: 3, 28
32
5:24
8: 3, 3, 5
17: 5, 12
12, 15
18:19
19:11, 15
16, 17
20: 5, 5, 6
6, 7, 7
8, 19
21:15
22:16, 18
22, 23
24, 25
25+A
26, 29
30
23:10
24: 9, 13
14
25: 1, 7, 9
11, 11
27:15, 26
29:20
32:26
33: 1
Jos. 1: 5, 18
5:13
6:26
10:14
14: 6
Jud. 9: 9 A[b]
13
13: 6, 8
16: 7, 11
13, 17
18: 7[d], 28
1 Sa. 1: 1, 3
21
2:16 A[b]
20, 26
27
4:13, 14
18
9: 6, 6, 7
7, 8, 10
17
24 A[e]
13:14
14:24, 28
15:29
1 Sa. 16: 7, 7
17:12 A
18:23 A[b]
25: 2, 2, 3
3, 3, 25
29
26:19
2 Sa. 7:14, 19
23: 3
24:14
1 Ki. 2:32
4:26, 27
8:27, 38
39, 40
11:28
12:22
p 24 sep
13: 1, 2-A
4, 5, 6
6, 7, 8
11, 12
14, 14
21, 26
28
29-A
31
14: 3A, 4A
17:18, 24
21:28, 35
35
37-A
37
2 Ki. 1: 9, 10
11, 12
13
4: 7[f], 9
16+A
21, 22
25
25-AB
40, 42
5: 8+A
6: 6
7:10, 17
8: 4, 7, 8
11
13:19
19:18
23:14, 16
16, 17
20
1 Ch. 17:17
21:13
23:14
27:32
28: 3
29: 1
2 Ch. 6:18, 29
29, 30
36
8:14
11: 2
14:11
19: 6
24: 6
25: 7, 9, 9
30:11, 16
32:19
Ezra 3: 2
6:11
Neh. 2:10, 12
9:29
12:24, 36
Est. 1: 8
2: 5
4:11
6: 6, 7, 9
9, 11
7: 6
Job 1: 1, 1, 3
8+A
8
2: 3, 4
4:13
5: 7, 17
7: 1, 9, 17
20
9:32
10: 4
11:12
Job 12: 2, 10
14
14:12, 14
19
15: 7
16:21-S[2]
20: 4, 29
21: 4, 33
25: 4+A
6, 6
27:13
28:13, 21
28
32:14, 21
33:15, 16
17, 23
25, 26
27
34:11, 21
29, 30
35: 8
36:25
37: 6, 6, 19
23
38:26
Psa. 4: 3
8: 5, 5
9:20, 21
39
10: 4
11: 2, 9
13: 2
16: 4
20:11
21: 7, 7
24:12
30:20, 21
32:13
33:13
35: 7, 8
36: 7, 23[g]
37
37:15
38: 6, 7, 12
12
40, 10
42: 1
44: 3
48: 3, 8, 13
17, 21
51: 9
52: 3
54:14
55: 2, 12
56: 5
57: 1, 12
59:13
61: 4, 10
10
63: 7, 10
65: 5, 12
67:19
72: 5, 5
75:11
77:25, 60
79:16, 18
81: 7
83:13
86: 5, 5
87: 5
88:48, 49
89: 1, 8, 3
93:10, 11
12
102:15
103:14, 15
15, 23
104:14, 17
106: 8, 15
21, 31
107:13
108:16-S[1]
113:12, 24
115: 2
117: 6, 8
118:134
123: 2
126: 5+A
127: 4
134: 8, 15

Ps. 139: 1, 5
140: 4
143: 3, 3, 4
144:12
145: 3
146: 8–A
Pro. 3: 4, 13
30
8: 4,4,31
34
12: 3
14:12
15:11, 28
18:16
20: 6, 27
21:10
23:31
24:23, 23
25, 25
26 A[2 b]
37, 45
26:18
27: 8, 15
19, 20
28:12, 23
29:25
Ecc. 1: 3, 13
2: 3,8,12
18, 21
21, 22
24, 26
3:10, 11
13, 18
19, 19
21, 22
5:18
6: 1,7,10
7: 1, 1
1–C
3, 15
21, 29
30
8: 1, 6, 8
9,9,11
15, 17
17
9: 1,3,12
12, 15
10:14
11: 8
12: 5,9,13
Isa. 2: 9, 11
11, 17
17, 20
3: 2, 5, 5
5, 6
4: 1
5: 3,7,15
6: 5, 11
12
7:13, 21
8: 1, 2, 8
15
9:19, 20
13: 7, 12
14, 14
14:16, 18[i]
30[k]
17: 7, 11
19: 2, 2, 4
20
22: 6, 25
23:15
24: 6
25: 3, 4, 4
5, 5
29:11, 12
13, 19
21
31: 2, 3, 7
8
32: 2, 3
33: 8
36:11[m]
12[m]
37:19
38:11
39: 3
40: 6
41:12

Isa. 43: 4
44: 7, 11
13, 15
45:12
47: 3, 15
50: 2
51: 7, 12
12
52:14, 14
53: 3, 3, 6
56: 2
58: 5
66:24
Jer. 2: 6 S[a],6
4:25, 29
7:20
8: 6
9:10, 12
22
10:14, 23
11: 3
13:11
14: 9
16:20
17: 5, 5, 7
9, 16
20:15, 16
21: 6
22:30
23: 9 A[2 b]
9
24+A
34, 36
27: 3, 40
40
28:14, 17
43, 62
29: 2, 16
19, 19
30:11, 11
31:14, 36
36
33:11, 16
20
36:26, 26
32
37: 6
38:22, 27
39:19, 43
40: 5, 10
10, 12
42: 4, 13
43:19, 29
44:13
45: 4 *ter*
9, 10
11, 16
24
46:17
48: 4, 15
49:17
51: 7
52:25
Lam. 3:35, 38
Eze. 1: 5,8,10
26
2: 1, 3, 6
8, 10
3: 3,4,10
17, 25
4: 1, 16
17
5: 1
6: 2
7: 2, 13
8: 5, 6, 8
12, 15
17
10: 8
14 A
21
11: 2,4,15
12: 2, 3, 9
18, 22
27
13: 2, 17
14: 3, 4, 4
7, 7, 8
13, 13
17, 19

Eze. 14:21
15: 2
16: 2
17: 2, 12
18: 2, 5, 7
16
19: 1+A
3, 6
20: 3,4,11
13+A
13, 21
27, 46
21: 2, 6, 9
12, 14
19, 28
22: 2, 18
24–A[l]
23: 2, 36
42
24: 2, 16
25
25: 2, 13
26: 2
27: 2, 13
16
28: 2, 2, 9
12, 21
29: 2,8,11
18
30: 2, 21
31: 2, 14
32: 2, 13
18
33: 2, 2, 7
10
12+A
24, 30
30
34: 2
35: 2, 7
36: 1, 10
11, 12
13, 14
17, 37
38
37: 3,9,11
16
38: 2, 14
20, 21
39: 1, 15
17
40: 4
41:19

Eze. 43: 7, 10
18
44: 5, 25
47: 6
Dan. 2:10, 38
43
3:10
4:13, 14
14, 22
22, 29
29, 30
5: 5, 21
21
6: 7, 12
12
7: 4, 4, 3
13
8:17
10:16, 18
Hos. 6: 7
9: 7, 12
11: 4, 4, 9
13: 2
Joel 1:12
Amos 4:13
5:19
9:12
Obad. 9
Jon. 1:14–S[1]
3: 7, 8
4:11
Mic. 2:12
5: 5, 7
6: 8
7: 2
Nah. 2: 4
Hab. 1:14
2: 8, 17
Zeph. 1: 3, 17
Hag. 1:11
2:12
Zec. 2: 4
4: 1
8:10, 10
9: 1
11: 6
12: 1–A
13: 3, 5
5–A
Mal. 2:12
3: 8, 17
4: 5

[a] *pro* ἕκαστος. [b] *pro* ἀνήρ.
[c] *pro* ἀνθρώπινος. [d] A Συρία.
[e] *pro* ἄλγος. [f] A κυριος.
[g] S[1] ἀνήρ. [h] *pro* ἅγιος.
[i] A ἕκαστος. [k] AS ἀνήρ.
[m] A ἀνήρ. [n] *pro* οὐθείς.

ἀνθυφαιρέω.

Leviticus 27:18

ἀνίατος.

Deu. 32:21, 33
Job 24:20
Pro. 6:15
Isa. 13: 9
Isa. 14: 6
Jer. 8:18
Lam. 4: 3

ἀνίημι.

Gen. 18:24
49:21
Exo. 23:11
Deu. 31: 6, 8
Jos. 24:19
Jud. 8: 3[a]
1 Sa. 9: 5
11: 3
12:23
15:16
27: 1–B[b]
2 Sa. 21:16
1 Ch. 21:15
28:20
2 Ch. 10: 9
Neh. 10:31
Psa. 38:14
Isa. 1:14
2: 6, 9
3: 8
5: 6, 24
25:11
27:10
35: 3
37:27
42: 2
46: 4
62: 1
Jer. 15: 6
27: 7
Eze. 1:25+A
Mal. 4: 2

[a] A ἀνήκω. [b] A ἔρχομαι.

ἀνίπταμαι.

Isaiah 16: 2

ἀνίστημι.

Gen. 4: 8
9: 9
13:17
19: 1 A[a]
14, 15
33, 35
21:14, 18
32
22: 3,3,19
23: 3, 7
24:10, 54
61
25:34
26:31
27:19, 31
43
28: 2, 18
31:13, 17
35, 55
32:22
35: 1, 3
37: 7
38: 8, 19
43: 7, 12
14
44: 4
46: 5
Exo. 1: 8
2:17
10:23 A[a]
12:30, 31
24:13
26:30
32: 1, 6
Lev. 26: 1
Nu. 1:51
7: 1
11:32
16: 2, 25
22:13, 14
20, 21
22
23:18, 24
24: 9, 17
25
32:14
Deu. 2:13, 24
6: 7 A[b]
9:12
13: 1
17: 8
19:15, 18
22: 4, 4
25: 7
28: 9
29:22
31:16
32:38
33:11
34:10
Jos. 1: 2
6:12, 15
7:10, 13
8: 1, 3
18: 4, 8
21:44 AB[e]
24: 9
Jud. 2:10
3:21, 31
4: 9, 14
5: 7[d], 7
12[d]
7: 9[e], 15
24 A[f]
8:20, 21
21
9:32, 34
35, 43[g]
10: 1, 3
13:11
16: 3
18: 9
9+A
30 A[h]

Jud. 19: 3, 5, 7
9, 10
27, 28
28+A
20: 5,8,18
19, 33
Ruth 1: 6
2:15
3:14
4: 5, 10
1 Sa. 1: 9
2: 8, 35
3: 6+A
8
9: 3, 26
26
13:15
15:12
16:12, 13
17: 8 B[h]
48, 52
18:27
20:41, 43
21:10
23: 4, 13
16, 24
24: 1, 5, 8
8, 9
25: 1, 29
41, 42
26: 2–A, 5
27: 2
28:23, 25
31:12
2 Sa. 2:14, 14
15
3:10, 21
6: 2
7:12
11: 2
12:17, 20
21
13:15, 29
31
14:23, 31
15: 9, 14
17: 1, 21
22, 23
19: 7, 8
22:39
23: 1, 10
24:11
1 Ki. 1:50
(3)40
3: 4, 12
15, 20
21
8:20, 20
22[i], 54
9: 5
11:18, 40
12:*p*2 ‖20
‖ 20,31,33
14: 2A, 4A
12A, 14A
17 A
17: 9, 10
19: 3, 5, 6
7, 8, 21
20: 7, 15
16, 18
2 Ki. 1: 3, 15
3:24
4: 7A[k], 30
6:15
7: 5, 7
12[m]
8: 1, 2, 21
9: 2, 6
10:12
11:11 A[h]
12:20
13:21
21: 3[n]

2 Ki. 23: 3, 25
25:26
1 Ch. 17:11
22:16
2 Ch. 6:10, 41
7:18
10:15
13: 4, 6
6 B[o], 7[p]
20: 5, 19
23[q], 23
21: 4
23:18
24:13, 20
25: 5
28:12, 15
29:12
30:14, 27
34:31 A[h]
35:19
Ezra 1: 5
2:63
3: 2
5: 2
9: 5, 9
10: 3–S[3]
4, 5, 6
10
Neh. 2:12, 18
3: 1
4:14
7:65
9: 5
Est. 5: 9+S[3]
9: 2 S[3 c]
Job 1: 5, 20
4:16
7: 4
14:12
16: 8
19:18, 26
24:22
42:18, 18
Psa. 1: 5
3: 8
7: 7
9:20, 33
11: 6
16:13
19: 9
34: 2, 11
40: 9, 11
43:24, 27
67: 2
73:22
75:10
77: 5, 6
81: 8
87:11
93:16
101:14
131: 8
Pro. 24:16
29: 4, 33
46
Ecc. 4:15ACS[h]
12: 4
Cant. 2:10, 13
3: 2
5: 5
Isa. 2:10, 19
21

Isa. 11:10
14:21
21: 5
24:20
26:14, 19
28:21
32: 9
33:10
37:30[r]
38: 9
39: 1
43:17
49: 7
51:17
52: 2
54:17
Jer. 1:17
2:27, 28
6: 4, 5
8: 4
13: 4, 6
18: 2
23: 4, 5
20 S[3 h]
26:16
27:32
28:29 S[1 a]
64
29:15
30: 6, 9
32:13
33:17
37: 9, 12
38: 6
44:10
48: 2
Lam. 2:19
Eze. 3:22, 23
13: 5, 6
16:60, 62
26:20
34:23, 29
Dan. 2:39, 44
44
4:14
6:19
7: 5, 17
24, 24
8:22, 23
27
10:11
11: 2,3,7[s]
15, 20
31
12: 1
11+A
13
Hos. 6: 2 AB[a]
Amos 5: 2, 2
7: 2, 5, 9
8:14
9:11, 11
Obad. 1
Jon. 1: 2, 3, 6
3: 2, 3
Mic. 2:10
4:13
6: 1
7: 8
Nah. 1: 5 S[3 t]
Hab. 2: 7
Hag. 2: 9

[a] *pro* ἐξανίστημι. [b] *pro* διανίστημι. [c] *pro* ἀνθίστημι. [d] A ἐξανίστημι. [e] A ἀναβαίνω. [f] *pro* καταβαίνω. [g] A ἐπανίστημι. [h] *pro* ἵστημι. [i] A ἵστημι. [k] *pro* ἔρχομαι. [m] B ἵστημι. [n] A ἀποστρέφω. [o] *pro* ἀφίστημι. [p] A ἀνθίστημι. [q] B ἀφίστημι. [r] AS ἐξανίστημι. [s] B[1] ἵστημι. [t] *pro* ἀναστέλλω.

ἄνισχυς.

Isaiah 40:30

ἀνόητος.

Deu. 32:31
Psa. 48:13, 21
Pro. 15:21
17:28

ἄνοια.

Job 33:23[a]
Psa. 21: 3
Pro. 14: 8
Pro. 22:15
Ecc. 11:10

[a] CS[2] ἀνομία.

ἄνοιγμα.

1 Kings 14: 6 A

ἀνοίγω.

Gen. 7:11
8: 6
21:19
29:31
30:22
41:56
43:20
44:11
Exo. 2: 6
4:12, 15
21:33
Nu. 16:30, 32
19:15
22:28
26:10
Deu. 11. 6
15: 8,8,11
11
20:11
28:12
Jos. 8:17—A
10:22
Jud. 3:25, 25
4:19
11:35, 36
15:19 A[a]
19:27
1 Sa. 3:15
1 Ki. (3) p 46
7:21
8:29, 52
2 Ki. 4:35
6:20
9: 3, 10
13:17, 17
15:16
19:16
1 Ch. 9:27
17:25
2 Ch. 6:20, 40
7:15
29: 3
Neh. 1: 6
6: 5
7: 3
8: 5, 5
13:19
Job 3: 1
7:11
11: 5[b]
12:14
30:11
31:32[b]
32:20
33: 2
Job 35:16
38:17, 31
41: 5
Psa. 5:10
13: 3—A
21:14
37:14
38:10
48: 5
50:17
77: 2, 23
103:28
105:17
108: 2
117:19
118:131
144:16
Pro. 8: 6 A[c]
24:76, 77
29:15
Cant. 5: 2, 5, 6
Isa. 13: 2
22:22—B
22
24:18
26: 2
35: 5
37:14
17—AS
41:18
42: 7, 20
45: 1, 3
48: 8
50: 5
53: 7, 7
57: 4
60:11
64: 1
Jer. 13:19
27:25, 26
Eze. 1: 1
3:27
16:63
20:21
33:22, 22
37:12, 13
44: 2—A
46: 1,1,12
Dan. 6:10
7:10
9:18
10:16—A
Amos 8: 5
Nah. 3:13, 13
Mal. 3:10

[a] pro ῥήγνυμι. [b] C διανοίγω.
[c] pro ἀναφέρω.

ἀνοίκητος vide ἀοίκητος.

ἀνοικοδομέω.

Deu. 13:16
Ezra 4:13[a]
6:14[a]
Neh. 2: 5
Pro. 21:12
Isa. 58:12
Jer. 1:10—A
18: 9
Jer. 21: 6
Lam. 3: 5, 7, 9
Hos. 2: 6
Amos 9:11, 11
Mic. 1:10
Zec. 1:16
Mal. 1: 4
3:15

[a] B οἰκοδομέω.

ἀνομέω.

Exo. 32: 7
Nu. 32:15
Deu. 4:16
Deu. 4:23-AB[1]
25
9:12
Deu. 31:29
1 Ki. 8:32, 47
1 Ch. 10:13
2 Ch. 6:37
20:35
Job 33: 9
35: 6
Psa. 24: 3
105: 6
118:78
Isa. 21: 2, 2
Isa. 24: 5
29:20
43:27
Jer. 2:29
10:21 S[1] b
Eze. 16:52
22:11
Dan. 9: 5, 15
11:32
12:10
Amos 4: 4 A[c]

[b] pro νοέω.
[c] pro ἀσεβέω.

ἀνόμημα.

Lev. 17:16
20:14
14 A[a]
Deu. 15: 9
Jos. 7:15
24:19
1 Sa. 25:28
Psa. 50: 3
Isa. 58: 1 S[a]
Jer. 23:13
Lam. 5: 7
Eze. 16:49, 50[b]
39:24

[a] pro ἀνομία. [b] A ἄνομος.

ἀνομία.

Gen. 19:15
Exo. 34: 7,7[a],9
Lev. 16:21
19:29
20:14[b]
22:16
26:43
Nu. 14:18
Deu. 9: 5 A[c]
31:29
2 Sa. 14: 9
19:19
22: 5, 24
24:10
2 Ki. 7: 9
1 Ch. 9: 1
10:13
Ezra 9: 6,7,13
Neh. 4: 6
9: 2
Job 7:21
8: 4
10: 6, 14
15 A[d]
13:23
14:17[e]
20:27[f]
31: 3, 28
33:23 CS[2g]
34:37
Psa. 5: 5, 6
6: 9
7:15
13: 4[h]
17: 5, 24
25:10
27: 3 S[1i]
30:19
31: 1,5,5[k]
35: 3, 4, 5
13
36, 1
37: 5, 19
38: 9, 12
39:13
40: 7
44: 8[m]
48: 6
49:21[n]
50: 4, 5, 7
11
51: 3
52: 2, 5
54: 4, 10
11
56: 2
57: 3
58: 3, 4, 5
6
63: 7
68:28, 28
72:19
73:20
Psa. 78: 8
84: 3
88:23, 33
89: 8
91: 8, 10
93: 4, 16
20, 23
100: 8 AS[i]
102: 3, 10
12
105:43
106:17, 17
42
108:14[o]
118: 3, 133
150
124: 3, 5
128: 3
129: 3, 8
138:24
140: 4, 9
Pro. 13:11
Isa. 1: 5
3: 8
5: 7, 18
6: 7
9:18
21: 4[o]
24:20
27: 9
33:15
43:25, 26
44:22
50: 1
53: 5, 8, 9
12[a]
58: 1[p]
59: 3, 4, 6
12, 12
61: 6
Jer. 5:25
16:18
36:23
Lam. 4: 6,6,22
22[m]
Eze. 3:19
7:23
8: 6,6[a],9
13
15+A
17, 17
9: 4
11:18, 21
12:16
16: 2, 36
43, 47
51[a],51
58
18:12, 13
20, 21
24, 27
20: 4, 30
22: 2, 5
Eze. 23:21, 36
44
28:16
29:16[a]
32:27
33: 6, 8
9[c]
10, 12
12,13[m]
18, 19
36:19 A[q]
31, 33
Eze. 37:23
43: 8
44: 6, 7
Dan. 9:24 A[i]
Hos. 6: 9
Mic. 6:10 A[r]
7:18[m]
Zeph. 1: 9 A[c]
Zec. 3: 4
5: 8
Mal. 1: 4

[a] A ἁμαρτία. [b] A ἀνόμημα.
[c] pro ἀσέβεια. [d] pro ἀτιμία.
[e] A ἁμάρτημα, S ἁμαρτία.
[f] S[1] ῥομή. [g] pro ἄνοια.
[h] B ἀδικία. [i] pro ἀδικία.
[k] B ἁμαρτία. [m] A ἀδικία.
[n] S[1] ἄνομος. [o] S[1] ἁμαρτία.
[p] S ἀνόμημα. [q] pro ἁμαρτία.
[r] pro ἄνομος.

ἄνομος.

Lev. 5: 4
18:30 A[a]
1 Sa. 24:14
1 Ki. 8:32
2 Ch. 6:23
24: 7
Job 5:23
11:11, 14
12: 6
19:29
27: 4,7 S[b]
34: 8, 17
20 A[c]
22
35:14[d]
36:20+A
Psa. 36:28 AS[2e]
49:21 S[1f]
50:15
64: 4
72: 3
103:35
Pro. 1:19
10: 2
12: 3
14:16
21:18
27:21
28:10
29: 8g,27
Isa. 1: 4, 25
28, 31
3:11
9:15, 17
Isa. 10: 6
13:11
29:20
31: 6
32: 6, 7
33:14
48: 8
53:12
55: 7
57: 3, 4
66: 3
Jer. 6:13
Eze. 3:18 ter
19, 19
5: 6
7:11
13:22
16:50 A[h]
18:20, 21
23, 24
27
21: 3
4—A
25, 29
33: 8 A[i],8
12 A[k]
Dan. 12:10, 10
Mic. 6:10,10[m]
11
Hab. 3:13
Zeph. 1: 3
Mal. 3:15, 18[n]
4: 1, 3

[a] pro νόμιμος. [b] pro παράνομος.
[c] pro παρανόμως. [d] B ὄνομα.
[e] pro ἄμωμος. [f] pro ἀνομία.
[g] A λοιμός. [h] pro ἀνόμημα.
[i] pro ἁμαρτωλός. [k] pro ἀσεβής. [m] A ἀνομία. [n] A ἄδικος.

ἀνορθόω.

2 Sa. 7:13, 16
25+A
1 Ch. 17:12, 14
24
22:10
Psa. 17:36
19: 9
Ps. 144:14
145: 8
Pro. 24: 3
Jer. 10:12
40: 2
Eze. 16: 7

ἀνορύσσω.

Job 3:21
Job 39:21

ἀνόσιος.

Ezekiel 22: 9

ἄνους.

Psa. 48:11
Pro. 13:14
Hos. 7:11

ἀνταίρω.

2 Sa. 18:28 A[a]
Mic. 4: 3[b]

[a] pro ἐπαίρω. [b] A αἴρω.

ἀντακούω.

Job 11: 2

ἀντάλλαγμα.

Ruth 4: 7
1 Ki. 20: 2 A[a]
Job 28:15
17 C[a]
Psa. 54:20
88:52
Jer. 15:13
Amos 5:12 B[a]

[a] pro ἄλλαγμα.

ἀνταλλάσσω.

Job 37: 3
Pro. 6:35

ἀντάμειψις.

Ps. 118:112[a]
[a] S[1] ἀμείψις.

ἀνταναιρέω.

Psa. 9:26
45:10
50:13
57: 9
71: 7
Ps. 103:29
108:23
140: 8
Pro. 8:10 +A

ἀνταποδίδωμι.

Gen. 44: 4
50:15
Lev. 18:25
Deu. 32: 6, 35
41 A[a]
41, 43
43
Jud. 1: 7
16:28[b]
1 Sa. 24:18, 18
20 A[c]
25:21
2 Sa. 3:39 A[a]
19:36
22:21, 21
1 Ki. (3)44
2 Ki. 9:26
2 Ch. 32:25[d]
Job 21:19, 31
Psa. 7: 5, 5
17:21, 21[e]
25
25 +A
30:24
34:12
37:21
40:11
102·10
Ps. 115: 3, 3
118:17
130: 2
136: 8, 8
137: 8
141: 8
Pro. 19:17
25:22
Isa. 35: 4, 4
40:14+AS[1]
59:18
63: 7
65: 6+S
66: 4[f],6
Jer. 16:18
18:20
27:29
28: 6, 24
56
57—S[1]
Hos. 4: 9
12: 2 A[a]
14
14: 2
Joel 2:25
3: 4, 4, 7
Obad. 15
Zec. 9:12

[a] pro ἀποδίδωμι. [b] A ἐκδικέω.
[c] pro ἀποτίνω. [d] B ἀποδίδωμι.
[e] S[1] ἀποδίδωμι. [f] S ibid.

ἀνταπόδομα.

Gen. 50:15
Jud. 9:16 A[a]
14: 4 A[b]
2 Ch. 32:25
Psa. 27: 4
136: 8
Pro. 12:14
Isa. 1:23
Jer. 28: 6
Lam. 3:63
Joel 3: 4, 4, 7
Obad. 15

[a] pro ἀνταπόδοσις.
[b] pro ἐκδίκησις.

ἀνταπόδοσις.

Jud. 9:16[a]
16:28[b]
2 Sa. 19:36
Psa. 18:12
68:23
90: 8
93: 2
102: 2 A[c]
Isa. 34: 8
59:18
61: 2
63: 4
66: 6
Jer. 28:57+A
Hos. 9: 7

[a] A ἀνταπόδομα. [b] A ἐκδικήσια.
[c] pro αἴνεσις.

ἀνταποθνήσκω.

Exo. 22: 3[a]
[a] A ἀποθνήσκω.

ἀνταποκρίνομαι.

Jud. 5:29 A[a]
Job 16: 8
Job 32:12—S[1]
[a] pro ἀποκρίνω.

ἀνταπόκρισις.
Job 13:22[a]
Job 34:36[a]

[a] A ἀπόκρισις.

ἀνταποστέλλω.
1 Ki. 21:10A[a] [a] pro ἀποστέλλω.

ἀνταποτίνω.
1 Sa. 24:20 B[a] [a] pro ἀποτίνω.

ἀντεῖπον.
Gen. 24:50
Jos. 17:14
Est. 1:17
17−S[1]
8: 8
Job 9: 3
23:13[a]
32: 1
Isa. 10:14

[a] A ἀντερῶ, S[3] ἀντιπίπτω.

ἀντερῶ.
Gen. 44:16
Job 20: 2
Job 23:13 A[a]
Pro. 8:10+B

[a] A pro ἀντεῖπον.

ἀντέχω.
Deu. 32:41
Neh. 4:16
Job 33:24
Pro. 3:18
4: 6
Ecc. 7:19
Isa. 48: 2
Isa. 56: 2, 4, 6
57:13
Jer. 2: 8
8: 2
51:10
Dan. 10:21
Zeph. 1: 6

ἀντί.
Jud. 11:36+A
2 Sa. 17:25−A
18:33−A
1 Ki. 10:20−A
2 Ch. 30: 9 B[a]
[a] pro ἐναντι.

ἀντίγραφος.
Est. 3:14
4: 8
Est. 8:13, 13

ἀντιδίδωμι.
Ezekiel 27:15

ἀντιδικέω.
Jud. 6:31 A[a]
Jud. 12: 2 A[b]

[a] pro δικάζω. [b] pro μαχητής.

ἀντίδικος.
1 Sa. 2:10
Est. 8:11−A
Pro. 18:17
Isa. 41:11
Jer. 27:34
28:36
Hos. 5:11

ἀντίζηλος.
Leviticus 18:18

ἀντίθετος.
Job 32: 3

ἀντικαθίζω.
2 Kings 17:26

ἀντικαθίστημι.
Deu. 31:21
Jos. 5: 7
Mic. 2: 8 A[a]
[a] pro ἀνθίστημι

ἀντίκειμαι.
Exo. 23:22, 22
2 Sa. 8:10[a]
1 Ki. 11:25 A
Est. 8:11
9: 2
Job 13:25
Isa. 41:11
45:16
51:19
66: 6
Zec. 3: 1
[a] B κεῖμαι.

ἀντικρίνω.
Job 9:32
Job 11: 3

ἄντικρυς.
Nehemiah 12: 8+S[3]

ἀντιλαμβάνω.
Gen. 48:17
Lev. 25:35
1 Ki. 9: 9, 11
1 Ch. 22:17
2 Ch. 7:22
28:15, 15
23
29:34
Psa. 3: 6
17:36
19: 3
39:12
40:13
47: 4
62: 9
68:30
88:44
106:17
117:13
Ps. 118:116
138:13
Pro. 11:28
Isa. 9: 7
26: 3
41: 9
42: 1
49:26
51:18
59:16
63: 5
64: 7
Jer. 23:14
Eze. 12:14
16:49
20: 5, 6
Dan. 6:27
Mic. 6: 6

ἀντιλέγω.
Isa. 22:22−S[1]
50: 5
Isa. 65: 2
Hos. 4: 4

ἀντιλήπτωρ.
2 Sa. 22: 3
Psa. 3: 4
17: 3
41:10
45: 8, 12
53: 6
58:10, 17
Psa. 58 18
61: 3, 7
88:27
90: 2
108:12
118:114
143: 2

ἀντίληψις.
Psa. 21: 1, 20
82: 9
83: 6
Psa. 88:19
107: 9

ἀντιλογία.
Exo. 18:16
Nu. 20:13
27:14
Deu. 1:12
17: 8, 8
19:17
21: 5
25: 1
32:51
33: 8
2 Sa. 15: 4
Psa. 17:44
30:21
54:10
79: 7
80: 8
105:32
Pro. 17:11
18:18

ἀντίον.
2 Sa. 21:19
1 Ch. 11:23
1 Ch. 20: 5

ἀντιπίπτω.
Exo. 26: 5, 17
Nu. 27:14
Job 23:13 S[2][a]
[a] pro ἀντεῖπον.

ἀντιποιέω.
Lev. 24:19
Dan. 4:32

ἀντιπολεμέω.
Isaiah 41:12

ἀντιπρόσωπος.
Gen. 15:10
Exo. 26: 5
2 Sa. 10: 9
1 Ch. 19:10
Eze. 42: 3, 8

ἀντίρρησις.
Ecclesiastes 8:11

ἀντιστήριγμα.
Psa. 17:19
Eze. 30: 6

ἀντιστηρίζω.
Psa. 36:24
Isa. 48: 2
Isa. 50:10

ἀντιτάσσω.
1 Ki. 11:34
34+B
34
Est. 3: 4−A
Pro. 3:15, 34
Hos. 1: 6, 6

ἀντιτίθημι.
Leviticus 14:42

ἀντλέω.
Gen. 24:13, 20
43[a]
Exo. 2:16
17−A
Exo. 2:19
Job 19:26 S[1][b]
Pro. 9:12
Isa. 12: 3

[a] AS ὑδρεύω. [b] pro ἀναντλέω.

ἄντρον.
1 Kings 16:18

ἄνυδρος.
Deu. 32:10
Job 30: 3
Psa. 62: 2
77:17
40[a]
104:41
105:14
106: 4
35−S[1]
142: 6
Pro. 9:12
Isa. 35: 7
41:19
43:19, 20
44: 3
Jer. 2: 6
28:43
Eze. 19:13
Hos. 2: 3
Joel 2:20
Zeph. 2:13
[a] S[1] ἔρημος.

ἀνυπόδετος.
2 Sa. 15:30
Isa. 20: 2, 3, 4
Mic. 1: 8

ἀνυπομόνητος.
Exo. 18:18[a] [a] A[2] ἀνυπονόητος.

ἀνυπονόητος.
Exodus 18:18 A[2][a]
[a] pro ἀνυπομόνητος.

ἀνυπόστατος.
Psalm 123:5

ἀνυψόω.
1 Sa. 2: 7
Ezra 4:12
Psa. 112: 7

ἄνω.
Exo. 20: 4
Lev. 11:21
Deu. 4:39
5: 8
28:43, 43
29:18
30:12
Jos. 2:11
15:19
16: 5
21:22+A
Jud. 7:13
1 Ki. 8:23
10:p 22−A
12:p24l18
14:15 A
2 Ki. 18:17
19:30
1 Ch. 7:24
22: 5
2 Ch. 4: 4
8: 5
20: 6−A
26: 8
32:30
Neh. 3:25, 28
Psa. 49: 4
113:11+S[1]
Pro. 8:28
Ecc. 3:21
5: 1−AS
Isa. 5:30+S
7: 3
8:21
34:10
36: 2
37:31
Eze. 41: 7, 7
Joel 2:30+S[3]

ἄνωθεν.
Gen. 6:16
27:28+A
39
49:25
Exo. 25:20, 21
36:28−B
40
38: 5 A[a]
16, 19
Exo. 40:17
Nu. 4: 6, 25
7:89
Jos. 3:16
2 Sa. 11:21[b]
1 Ki. 7:17+A
40
Job 3: 4
31: 2
Isa. 45: 8
Jer. 4:28
Eze. 1:11−A[1]
Eze. 1:26
41: 7

[a] pro ἐπάνωθεν.
[b] A ἀπάνωθεν, B ἐπάνωθεν.

ἀνωφελής.
Pro. 28: 3
Isa. 44:10
Jer. 2: 8

ἀξίνη.
Deu. 10: 5
Jud. 9:48
1 Sa. 13:20, 21
Psa. 73: 5
Isa. 10:15
Jer. 26:22

ἀξιόπιστος.
Pro. 27: 6
Pro. 28:20

ἄξιος.
Gen. 23: 9
Deu. 25: 2
1 Ch. 21:22, 24
Est. 7: 4
Job 11: 6
30: 1
Job 33:27
Pro. 3:15
8:11
Jer. 15:19 ABS[1][a]
Mal. 2:13

[a] pro ἀνάξιος.

ἀξιόω.
Gen. 31:28
Nu. 22:16
Est. 4: 8
5: 6
7: 8
8: 3
9:12
Isa. 33: 7+AS[2]
Jer. 7:16
11:14
Dan. 1: 8
2:16, 23
3:30−B[1]
30+A
6:11

ἀξίωμα.
Exo. 21:22
Est. 5: 3
6+S[3]
7
Est. 5: 8+S[3]
7: 2, 3
Ps. 118:170

ἄξων.
Exo. 14:25
Pro. 2: 9, 18
Pro. 9:12

ἀοίκητος.
Deu. 13:16
Jos. 8:28
13: 3
Job 8:14
15:28
Job 18: 4[a]
38:27
Pro. 8:26
Hos. 13: 5
[a] C ἀνοίκητος.

ἄοκνος.
Proverbs 6:11

ἀορασία.
Gen. 19:11
Deu. 28:28
2 Ki. 6:18, 18

ἀόρατος.
Gen. 1: 2
Isa. 45: 3−A[1]

ἀπαγγελία.
Ruth 2:11

ἀπαγγέλλω.
Gen. 12:18
14:13
21:26
24:28 A[a]
49
26:32
27:42
29:12[b], 12
15
37: 5, 16
38:13
24 A[a]
41: 8, 24
42:29
43: 6
Gen. 44:24
45:13
46:31
47: 1
48: 1[b], 2
Exo. 18: 6 A[a]
Lev. 5: 1
Nu. 11:27
Deu. 1:22 B[1][a]
Jos. 2: 2
9:30 A[a]
10:17
Jud. 9:25
42 A[a]
47 A[a]

Jud. 13: 6
10 A[a]
14: 2, 6
9 AB[a]
12, 12
13, 14
15, 16
16, 16
17, 17
19
16: 2 A[a]
6[b]
13 B[a]
15
17 A[a]
18[b], 18[b]
Ruth 2:11
19 A[a]
3: 4
1 Sa. 3:15[b], 18
4:13, 14
8: 9
9: 6, 8, 18
19
10:15, 16
16, 16
11: 9
12: 7
13:23+B
14: 1, 9, 33
43, 43
15:12, 16
18:20, 24
26
19: 2, 3, 7
11, 18
19, 21
20: 9, 10
22:21−A
22, 22
23: 1, 7, 11
13, 25
24: 2, 19
25: 8, 14
19, 36
37
2 Sa. 1: 4[b], 5
6, 13
2: 4
3:23
4:10
6:12
7:11
10: 5[b], 17[c]
11: 5, 18
22, 22
13: 4, 34
14:33[b]
15:13[d], 28
35[e]
17:16 A[a]
18 AB[a]
21[c]
19:25
21:11
1 Ki. 1:20
23+B
2:29

1 Ki. (3)39, 41
10: 3, 3, 7
12: 6[e]
18:12
13[b], 16
21:17[b]
2 Ki. 1: 6−AB
4: 7, 31
5: 4
6:13[e]
9:12, 15
18, 20
10: 8
1 Ch. 19: 5, 17
2 Ch. 9: 2, 6
34:18
Neh. 2:12, 16
18
6: 7
7:61
Est. 1:15
2:10
4:12
6: 2
Job 1:15, 16
17, 19
12: 7[b]
21:31[f]
23: 5
38: 4[b]
Psa. 39: 6
54:18
70:17[g], 18
77: 4, 6[h]
88: 2
104: 1
141: 3
144: 4
147: 8
Pro. 12:17
Ecc. 7: 1−C
1+A
10:14 AS[a]
20
Cant. 1: 7
5: 8
Isa. 30: 7
36:22 A[a]
41: 8
48:20 AS[a]
57:12
Jer. 16:10 AS[a]
28:31 S[1 a]
40: 3[b]
Eze. 23:36 A[a]
24:19 A[a]
37:18 A[a]
Dan. 2: 6
9 A[a]
16 A[a]
Hos. 4:12
Amos 3: 9 AB[a]
4: 5 A[a]
13
Jon. 1: 8, 10
Mic. 3: 8
Nah. 1:14

[a] *pro* ἀναγγέλλω. [b] A *ibid.* [c] AB ἀναγγέλλω. [d] A ἀγγέλλω. [e] AB παραγγέλλω. [f] C ἀναγγέλλω. [g] B ἀναγγέλλω. [h] S *ibid.*

ἀπάγχω.

2 Samuel 17:23

ἀπάγω.

Gen. 31:18, 26
39:22
40: 3
42:16, 19
Deu. 28:36, 37
Jud. 4: 7 A[a]
19: 3+A
1 Sa. 6: 7
23: 5
30: 20, 22[b]
2 Sa. 12:31 A[c]

1 Ki. 1:38
2 Ki. 6:19 A[d]
19
11: 4
17:27[e]
24:15
25:20 AB[d]
2 Ch. 36: 6[f], 17
Job 21:30
24: 3
Psa. 59:11
Ps. 107:11
124: 5
136: 3
Pro. 16:29

Ecc. 11:10 S[1 g]
Jer. 17: 1 A[d]
Lam. 3: 2
Eze. 17: 6 A[d]

[a] *pro* ἐπάγω. [b] A ἐπάγω. [c] *pro* διάγω. [d] *pro* ἄγω. [e] A ἀπαίρω. [f] A ἀνάγω. [g] *pro* παράγω.

ἀπαγωγή.

Isa. 10: 4[a] [a] AS ἐπαγωγή.

ἀπαδικέω.

Deu. 24:16[a] [a] A ἀποστερέω.

ἀπαιδευσία.

Hosea 7:16

ἀπαίδευτος.

Pro. 5:23
8: 5
15:12, 14[a]
17:21

Pro. 24: 8
27:20
Isa. 26:11
Zeph. 2: 1

[a] S[1] ἀσεβής.

ἀπαίρω.

Gen. 12: 9
13:11
26:21, 22
33:12, 17
35:16
37:17
46: 1
Exo. 12:37
16: 1
17: 1
19: 2[a]
Nu. 9:17, 18
20[a], 21
21+A
22, 23
14:25
20:22
21: 4, 10
12, 13
22: 1
33: 3

Nu. 33:5 *to* 36
36, 37
41 *to* 48
Deu. 1: 7, 19
2: 1
13−A
24
10: 6, 7, 11
Jos. 3: 1, 3, 14
9:23
Jud. 5: 4
18:11
1 Ki. 21: 9
2 Ki. 3:27
17:27 A[b]
19: 8, 36
Psa. 77:26[c], 52
Isa. 37: 8−AS
Eze. 10: 4
Nah. 3:18

[a] A ἐξαίρω. [b] *pro* ἀπάγω. [c] B[1] ἐπαίρω.

ἀπαιτέω.

Deu. 15: 2, 3
2 Ch. 36: 4
Neh. 5: 7, 7
Isa. 3:12

Isa. 9: 4
14: 4
30:33

ἀπαίτησις.

Neh. 5:10
10:31

Zeph. 3: 5−A

ἀπαλείφω.

Gen. 6: 7
2 Ki. 21:13 *ter*

Isa. 44:22
Dan. 9:24

ἀπαλλάσσω.

Exo. 19:22
1 Sa. 14:29
22: 1 A[a]
Job 3:10
7:15
9:12, 34

Job 10:19[b]
27: 5
34: 5
Isa. 10: 7
Jer. 39:31

[a] *pro* ἀπέρχομαι. [b] A *ibid.*

ἀπαλλοτριόω.

Jos. 22:25
Job 21:29
Psa. 57: 4
68: 9

Jer. 19: 4
27: 8
Eze. 14: 5, 7
Hos. 9:10

ἀπαλλοτρίωσις.

Job 31: 3

Jer. 13:27

ἁπαλός

Gen. 18: 7
27: 9
33:13
Lev. 2:14+AB

Deu. 28:54, 56
1 Ch. 22: 5
29: 1
Isa. 47: 1

ἁπαλότης.

Deu. 28:56−B

Eze. 17: 4, 9

ἁπαλύνω.

2 Ki. 22:19
Job 33:25

Psa. 54:22

ἀπαμαυρόω.

Isaiah 44:18

ἀπαναίνομαι.

Job 5:17

Psa. 76: 3

ἀπαναισχυντέω.

Jeremiah 3: 3

ἀπαντάω.

Gen. 28:11
33: 8
49: 1
Jud. 8:21 A[a]
15:12 A[a]
18:25 A[a]
Ruth 1:16
2:22
1 Sa. 10: 5
15: 2
22:17[b], 18
25:20

1 Sa. 28:10
2 Sa. 1:15
1 Ki. 2:32, 34
Job 4:12[c]
21:15−C
36:32
Pro. 26:18
Jer. 13:22
34:15
Dan. 10:14
Hos. 13: 8

[a] *pro* συναντάω. [b] AB ἁμαρτάνω. [c] A συναντάω.

ἀπάντη.

Jud. 4:22 A[a] [a] *pro* συνάντησις. *vide* ἀπάντησις.

ἀπάντημα.

1 Ki. 5: 4 A[a]

Ecc. 9:11

[a] *pro* ἁμάρτημα.

ἀπάντησις.

Jud. 4:18 A[a]
6:35 A[a]
11:31 A[a]
34 A[b]
14: 5 A[a]
15:14+A
19: 3 A[a]
20:25 A[a]
31 A[a]
1 Sa. 4: 1
6:13
9:14
13:10, 15
15:12
16: 4
17:55 A
18: 6+A
21: 1
25:32, 34[c]
30:21, 21
2 Sa. 6:20
10: 5 A[d]
15:32 A[d]
16: 1 A[d]
19:15 A[d]
16 A[d]
24 A[d], 25

1 Ki. 2: 8 A[d]
19 A[d]
(3) *p* 1 A[d]
20:18 A[d]
21:27 A[d]
2 Ki. 4:26 A[d]
31 A[d]
5:21 A[d]
8: 8 A[d]
9 A[d]
9:18 A[d]
21 A[d]
10:15 A[d]
16:10 A[d]
23:29 A[d]
1 Ch. 12:17
14: 8[e]
19: 5
2 Ch. 12:11
15: 2
19: 2
20:17
28: 9
Jer. 28:31[e], 31
34: 2
48: 6
Zec. 2: 3 A[a]

[a] *pro* συνάντησις. [b] *pro* ὑπάντησις. [c] A ἀπάντη. [d] *pro ibid.* [e] A ὑπάντησις.

ἀπάνωθεν.

Jud. 16:20−A
2 Sa. 11:20
21 A[a]
24
20:21

1 Ki. 1:53
2 Ki. 2: 5 A[b]
10:31[c]
Amos 2: 9 A[b]

[a] *pro* ἀπὸ ἄνωθεν. [b] *pro* ἐπάνωθεν. [c] AB *ibid.*

ἅπαξ.

Gen. 18:32
Exo. 30:10
Lev. 16:34
Nu. 16:21, 45
Deu. 9:13
Jos. 10:42
Jud. 6:39, 39
15: 3
16:18, 20
20, 28
20:30, 30
31, 31
1 Sa. 3:10, 10

1 Sa. 17:39
20:25, 25
26: 8
2 Sa. 17: 7
1 Ch. 11:11
2 Ch. 9:21
Neh. 13:20
Job 33:14
39:35
Psa. 61:12
88:36
Isa. 66: 8
Hag. 2: 6

ἀπαρνέομαι.

Isaiah 31: 7

ἄπαρσις.

Nu. 33: 2[a] [a] A ἔπαρσις.

ἀπαρτία.

Exo. 40:30
Nu. 10:12
16:26 B[a]

Nu. 31:17, 18
Deu. 20:14
Eze. 25: 4

[a] *pro* ἁμαρτία.

ἀπαρτίζω.

1 Kings 9:25 A

ἀπαρχή.

Exo. 22:29
23:19
25: 2, 2, 3
35: 5
36: 6
39: 1
Lev. 2:12
22:12
23:10
Nu. 5: 9
15:20, 21
18: 1 B[a], 8
11, 12
12, 12
29, 30
32
31:29
Deu. 12: 6−B
11, 17
18: 4, 4
26: 2, 10
33:21
1 Sa. 2:29
10: 4

2 Sa. 1:21
2 Ch. 31: 5, 10
12, 14
Ezra 8:25
Neh. 10:37, 39
12:44
13: 5
Psa. 77:51
104:36
Isa. 16: 3 AB[a] S[b]
Eze. 20:31, 40
40
44:30, 30
45: 1, 6, 7
7, 13
16
48: 8, 9, 10
12, 12
12 A[c]
18, 18
20, 20[d]
21, 21
Mal. 3: 8[e]

[a] *pro* ἁμαρτία. [b] *pro* ἄγω. [c] *pro* ὅριον. [d] B ἀρχή. [e] S[1] ἀρχή.

ἀπάρχομαι.

2 Ch. 30:24, 24
35: 7, 8, 9

Pro. 3: 9

ἀπατάω.

Gen. 3:13
Exo. 8:29 A[a]
22:16
Jud. 14:15
16: 5
2 Sa. 3:25
1 Ki. 22:20, 21
22
2 Ki. 18:32
2 Ch. 18:19, 20
21

2 Ch. 32:11, 15
Job 31:27
Psa. 76: 3
Pro. 15: 9 S[1 b]
24:15
Isa. 36:14, 18
37:10
Jer. 4:10, 10
20: 7, 7, 10
29: 9
45:22

[a] *pro* ἐξαπατάω. [b] *pro* ἀγαπάω.

ἀπάτη.

Ecc. 9: 6 S[a] [a] *pro* ἀγάπη.

ἀπαυτομολέω.

Pro. 6:11[a] [a] A αὐτομολέω.

ἀπειθέω.

Exo. 23:21
Lev. 26:15
Nu. 11:20
14:43
Deu. 1:26
9: 7, 23
24
21:20
28:65[a]
32:51
Jos. 1:18
5: 6
2 Ki. 5:16
Neh. 9:29
Psa. 67:19
Pro. 1:25[b]
24:21
Isa. 1:23, 25
3: 8
7:16—S[1]
8:11
30:12
33: 2
36: 5
50: 5
59:13
63:10
65: 2
66:14
Jer. 13:25
Eze. 3:27, 27
Hos. 9:15
Zec. 7:11

[a] A ἀθυμέω. [b] AS προσέχω.

ἀπειθής.

Nu. 20:10
Deu. 21:18
Isa. 30: 9
Jer. 5:23
Zec. 7:12

ἀπειλέω.

Gen. 27:42
Nu. 23:19
Isa. 66:14
Nah. 1: 4

ἀπειλή.

Job 23: 6
Pro. 13: 8
17:10
19:12
20: 2
Isa. 50: 2+S[1a]
54: 9
Hab. 3:12
Zec. 9:14

[a] AS[3] pro ἐλεγμός.

ἄπειμι.

Exo. 33: 8
10+A
Job 6:13
Pro. 25:10
Hos. 5: 3 A[a]

[a] pro ἀφίστημι.

ἀπεῖπον.

1 Ki. 11: 2
Job 6:14
10: 3
Job 19:18 A[a]
Zec. 11:12

[a] pro ἀποποιέομαι.

ἄπειρος.

Nu. 14:23
Jer. 2: 6
Zec. 11:15

ἀπέκτασις.

Job 36:29[a] [a] AS[2] ἐπέκτασις.

ἀπελαύνω.

Ezekiel 34:12[a] [a] A συνάγω.

ἀπελέκητος.

1 Ki. 5:17+A
6: 2, 33
7:46+A
1 Ki. 7:48, 49
10:12 A[a]
12—A[b]

[a] pro πελεκητός. [b] B πελεκ-

ἀπελευθερόω.

Leviticus 19:20

ἀπελπίζω.

Isaiah 29:19

ἀπέναντι.

Gen. 3:24
21:16, 16
23:19
25: 9
49:30
Exo. 14: 2, 9
26:35
30: 6, 36
40:24
Lev. 6:14
9: 5
16:12, 18
Lev. 17: 4, 6
19:14
Nu. 7:10
18: 2
19: 4
20: 9, 10
25: 4 B[a]
32:29
33: 7, 7, 8
47
Deu. 26: 4
10—B[b]
Deu. 28:66
32:52
Jos. 3:16
7: 8, 13
9: 6
11: 2
15: 3, 7
18:17
24:1[f], 26
Jud. 19:10[c]
20:43[d]
2 Sa. 10:17[e]
12:12
1 Ki. 21:29
2 Ki. 16:14
19:26
1 Ch. 13:10
17:16[e]
2 Ch. 2: 4
8:12
Neh. 3:31
Neh. 7: 3
8: 3
11:11, 22
13:21
Psa. 13: 3—A
35: 2
Isa. 1:16
17:13
Jer. 16:17
38:39
Lam. 2:19
Eze. 1: 9[e]
8:16
10:19
11:23
26: 8—A
40: 2, 47
42: 7
Hos. 7: 2
Jon. 4: 5

[a] pro κατέναντι. [b] A ἔναντι. [c] A κατέναντι. [d] A ἐξεναντίας. [e] S ἀπεναντίον. [f] A ἐναντίον.

ἀπεναντίον.

Jos. 22:29 A[a]
1 Ch. 17:16 S[b]
Cant. 6: 4

[a] pro ἐναντίον. [b] pro ἀπέναντι.

ἀπενεόομαι.

Daniel 4:16

ἀπέραντος.

Job 36:26

ἀπερείδω.

Jud. 6:37 A[a]
1 Ki. 14:28
1 Ch. 10: 1
Eze. 24: 2
Amos 5:19

[a] pro τίθημι.

ἀπερικάθαρτος.

Leviticus 19:23

ἀπερίτμητος.

Gen. 17:14
Exo. 12:48
Lev. 26:41
Jos. 5: 4, 6, 7
Jud. 14: 3
15:18
1 Sa. 14: 6
17:26 A, 36
36, 37
31: 4
2 Sa. 1:20
1 Ch. 10: 4
2 Ch. 28: 3+A
Isa. 52: 1
Jer. 6:10
9:26, 26
Eze. 28:10
31:18
32:19+A
21, 24
26, 28
30, 32
44: 7, 7, 9
9

ἀπέρχομαι.

Gen. 3:19
11:11
15:15
18:33
19: 2
21:14, 16
24:51, 55
56, 61
26:16, 17
29: 7
30:25, 26
31:13 A[a]
13, 18
30, 55
32: 1
34:17
38:11, 19
42:26, 33
45:17
50: 5 B[b]
Exo. 3:21
4:19
26—B
5: 4, 18 A[c]
8:29
10:28
Exo. 12:21, 28
18:27
19:13
21: 2[d], 7
Lev. 11:34 A[e]
25:10, 10
27, 28
41
Nu. 11:30
12: 9, 10 A[f]
13:23[g]
22:26
24:25, 25
Deu. 16: 7 A[h]
17: 3 A[h]
24: 4
28:41
Jos. 1:15
2:16, 16
6:11, 14
10:29, 31
34, 36
22: 4, 8, 9
24:33
Jud. 1:26 A[c]
2: 6 A[h]
Jud. 4: 6
6:21 A[e]
9:55 A[e]
18:21
24 A[e]
19: 2, 5 A[e]
7 A[e]
8 A[e]
9 A[e]
9 A[e]
10
14 A[e]
27 A[e]
28 A[e]
28
20: 8[i]
21:21 A[e]
24 A[k]
1 Sa. 2:11, 20
6: 6, 8
10: 2, 3, 9
25, 26
13:15
14:46
15: 6, 27
34
16:13
17:13 A
20 A
19:12
20:13, 43
22: 1[k], 3
23:18
24:23
25: 5
26:11, 12
25
28, 25
29:11
30: 2
2 Sa. 2:29
3:22, 23
24 A[m]
24
4: 7
5: 6
6:19
12:15
16:17
17:21, 23
19:24
20:21
1 Ki. 1:49 A[h]
50
1 Ki. 8:66
11:22
12: 5, 5, 16
p 24 l 16
l 21, 39
l 46, 72
l 73
13:10
12 A[n]
23
18: 7 A[h]
12, 29
19: 3, 19
19[o]
21:36, 43
2 Ki. 4: 5
5:11, 12
19
6:22, 23
23+B
8:14
2 Ch. 10: 5
16: 3
24:25
25:10
Ezra 6: 5—B
Neh. 5: 9[p]
8:12
Job 1:21
5:26 A[h]
7:21
10:19 A[q]
21:33
27:21
34:15
Psa. 33: 1
38:14
Ecc. 2:12 S[2e]
5:15
Cant. 2:11
5: 6 S[a]
17
Isa. 23: 6, 12
24:11-ABS
37:37
38:12
Jer. 3: 1
5:23
9: 2
21: 2
28: 9
44: 9, 9
Dan. 6:18

[a] pro ἐξέρχομαι. [b] pro ἐπανέρχομαι. [c] pro πορεύω. [d] A ἐξαποστέλλω. [e] pro ἐπέρχομαι. [f] pro ἀφίστημι. [g] AB ἔρχομαι. [h] pro ἔρχομαι. [i] A εἰσέρχομαι. [k] A ἀπαλλάσσω. [m] pro εἰσέρχομαι. [n] pro ἀνέρχομαι. [o] B ἐπέρχομαι. [p] S ἐπέρχ- [q] pro ἀπαλλάσσω.

ἀπέχω.

Gen. 43:22
44: 4
Nu. 32:19
Deu. 12:21
18:22
Jud. 18: 9+A
1 Sa. 21: 5
Job 1: 1, 8
2: 3
13:21
28:28[a]
Ps. 102:12
Pro. 3:27
9:18
Pro. 15:29
22: 5
23: 4, 13
Isa. 29:13
54:14
55: 9, 9
Jer. 7:10
Eze. 8: 6
11:15
22: 5
Joel 1:13[b]
2: 8
3: 8
Mal. 3: 7

[a] C ἐπέχω. [b] S[1] ἐπέχω.

ἀπηλιώτης.

Exo. 27:11[a]
Jer. 32:12
Eze. 20:47
21: 4

[a] A (πορρᾶν) βορρᾶς.

ἄπιος.

1 Chronicles 14:14, 15

ἆπις.

Jeremiah 26:15

ἄπιστος.

Pro. 17: 6
28:25[a]
Isa. 17:10, 10

[a] A ἄπληστος.

ἄπλαστος.

Genesis 25:27

ἄπληστος.

Ps. 100: 5
Pro. 23: 2
Pro. 27:20
28:25 A[a]

[a] pro ἄπιστος.

ἁπλόος.

Proverbs 11:25

ἁπλοσύνη.

Job 21:23[a] [a] ACS[4] ἀφροσύνη.

ἁπλότης.

2 Sa. 15:11
1 Ch. 29:17

ἁπλόω.

Job 22: 3[a] [a] BS[1] ἀπωθέω.

ἁπλῶς.

Proverbs 10: 9

ἀποβαίνω.

Exo. 2: 4
Job 8:14
9:20
11: 6[a]
13: 5, 12
16
15:31, 35
17: 6[b]
Job 18: 5[c]
22:11
24: 5
27:18
30:21 A[d]
31
34:19
Pro. 9:12—S[1]

[a] A παραβαίνω. [b] B ἐπιβαίνω. [c] A ἀναβαίνω. [d] pro ἐπιβαίνω.

ἀποβάλλω.

Deu. 26: 5
Pro. 28:24[a]
Isa. 1:30

[a] A ἀποβιάζομαι

ἀποβιάζομαι.

Pro. 22:22
Pro. 28:24 A[a]

[a] pro ἀποβάλλω.

ἀποβλέπω.

Jud. 9:37+A
Psa. 9:29
10: 4
Pro. 24:47 BS[1a]
Cant. 5:17
Hos. 3: 1 A[a]
Mal. 3: 9, 9

[a] pro ἐπιβλέπω.

ἀπογαλακτίζω.

Gen. 21: 8, 8
1 Sa. 1:22, 23
23
24+A
Ps. 130: 2
Isa. 28: 9
Hos. 1: 8

ἀπογινώσκω.

Deu. 33: 9—A

ἀπόγονος.

2 Sa. 21:11, 22
1 Ch. 20: 6

ἀπογράφω.

Jud. 8:14 A[a]
Pro. 22:20

[a] pro γράφω.

ἀποδείκνυμι.

Est. 2: 9 AB[a]
Job 33:21

[a] pro ὑποδείκνυμι.

ἀποδεκατόω.

Gen. 28:22
Deu. 14:21
Deu. 26:12
1 Sa. 8:15, 16, 17

ἀποδεσμεύω.

Proverbs 26: 8

ἀπόδεσμος.

Canticles 1:13

ἀποδέω.

Jos. 9:10
Pro. 6:27

ἀποδημέω.

Eze. 19: 3 A[a] [a] pro ἀποπηδάω.

ἀποδιαιρέω.

Jos. 1: 6[a] [a] A ἀποδιαστέλλω.

ἀποδιαστέλλω.

Jos. 1: 6 A[a] [a] pro ἀποδιαιρέω.

ἀποδιδράσκω.

Gen. 16: 6, 8
27:43
28: 2
31:20, 21
22, 26
35: 1, 7
Jud. 9:21
11: 3 A[a]
1 Sa. 20: 1
2 Sa. 4: 3
13:34, 38
1 Ki. 2: 7
(3):39
11:17, 40
12:p24l13
2 Ki. 7: 7
Job 9:25
14: 2
Psa. 3: 1
56: 1
Isa. 35:10
51:11

[a] pro φεύγω.

ἀποδίδωμι.

Gen. 20: 7, 7, 14
25:31, 33
29:21 A[d]
30:26
37:22, 27
28, 36
42:25, 28
34
45: 3+A
4, 5
47:20, 22
Exo. 5:18
20: 5
21 ·7, 17, 35
22: 1, 26
30[a]
23: 4
Lev. 6· 4, 5
25:14, 15
16, 25
27, 27
28, 29
50, 51
52
26: 4, 26
27:20, 23
24, 28
Nu. 5: 7, 7, 8
8
8:13, 15
16, 19
21
14:18
18: 9
21:29
31: 3
36: 2
Deu. 2:28, 28
5: 9
7:10, 10
14:20, 24
22: 1—A[1]
2
23:21
24: 9, 15
17
28:31
32:30, 41[b]
Jud. 2:14
3: 8
4: 2, 9
10: 7
Jud. 17: 3, 3, 4
1 Sa. 6: 3, 3, 4
8, 17
7:14, 14
12: 3, 9
2 Sa. 3:14, 39[b]
22:25
1 Ki. 21:34
2 Ki. 4: 7
2 Ch. 6:23 ter
32:25 B[c]
34:16, 28
Neh. 5:12
10:31
Job 22:25, 27
24:20
31:37
33:26—S[1]
34:11
39:12
Psa. 17:21 S[1 e]
21:26
27: 4
43:13
49:14
50:14
54:21
55:13
60: 9
61:13
64: 2
65:13
75:12
78:12
93: 2, 23
115: 5—AS
9
Pro. 7:14
17:13
24:12
28:21
29:42
Ecc. 5: 3, 3, 4
Isa. 19:21
26:12
42:22
65: 6, 7
66: 4 S[e]
15
Jer. 22:13
39:18
19 A[d]
Lam. 3:63, 64
Eze. 18: 7, 12
30:12+A
33:15—A
34:27 A[d]
46:17
Dan. 6: 2
Hos. 12: 2[b]
Joel 3: 6, 7, 8
8
Amos 2: 6
Jon. 2:10
Nah. 1:14

[a] A δίδωμι. [b] A ἀνταποδίδωμι.
[c] pro ἀνταποδίδωμι.
[d] pro δίδωμι.

ἀποδιώκω.

Lamentations 3:42

ἀποδοκιμάζω.

Ps. 117:22
Jer. 6:30, 30
7:29
Jer. 8: 9
14:19, 19
38:37

ἀπόδομα.

Nu. 8:11, 13
16, 19
Nu. 8:21

ἀπόδοσις.

Deu. 24:15
Psa. 102: 2 S[a]

[a] pro αἴνεσις.

ἀποθερίζω.

Hosea 6: 5

ἀποθήκη.

Exo. 16:23, 32
Deu. 28: 5, 17
1 Ch. 28:11, 12
12, 13
20
1 Ch. 29: 8
Ezra 7:22 B[a]
Jer. 27:26
Eze. 28:13

[a] pro βάτος.

ἀποθλίβω.

Numbers 22:25

ἀποθνήσκω.

Gen. 2:17
3: 3, 4
5: 5, 8, 11
14, 17
20, 27
31
7:21, 22
9:11, 29
11:11, 13
13, 15
17, 19
21, 23
25, 28
32
19:19
20: 3, 7
23: 2
25: 8, 11
17
26: 9, 18
27: 4, 7, 10
33:13
35: 8, 18
19, 29
36:33, 34
35, 36
37, 38
39
38:11, 12
42: 2, 20
38
43: 7
44: 9, 20
22
45:28
46:12, 30
47:15, 19
19, 29
48: 7, 21
50:24
Exo. 10:28
12:33
14:12
16: 3
Exo. 20:19
21:12, 18
20, 28
22: 2, 3 A[a]
14
28:31, 39
30:20, 21
Lev. 8:35
10: 2, 6, 7
9
11:39
15:31
16: 2, 13
19:20
20:20, 21
22: 9
24:17, 18
21
25:41 A[b]
Nu. 1:51
3:10, 38
4:15, 19
20
6: 7, 9
14: 2, 2, 35
37
16:29
17:10, 13
13
18: 3, 7, 32
19:13, 14
20: 3[c], 26
28
21: 6
23:10
26:11, 15
61, 65
27: 3, 3, 8
33:38, 39
35:12, 17
17, 18
18
18 A[d]
20, 21
Nu. 35:23, 23
25, 28
28, 30
32
Deu. 2:14—A[1]
16
4:22
5:25, 25
10: 6
13: 5, 10
17: 6 ter
12
18:16, 20
19: 5
6+A
11, 12
20: 5, 6, 7
21:21, 22
22:21, 24
24: 5, 9, 18
18, 18
25: 5
32:50
33: 6
Jos. 1:18
10:11
20: 3, 6 A, 9
22:20
24:30, 33
Jud. 1: 7
2:19
3:11, 30
4: 1, 21
6:23, 30
31 A[d]
8:32, 33
9:49, 54
55
10: 2, 5
12: 7, 10
12, 15
13:22
15:18
16:16[e], 30
20: 5
21: 5 A[d]
Ruth 1: 3, 5, 17
17
2:11
1 Sa. 2:34
4:11, 18
20
5:12
11:13
12:19
14:39, 42
43, 44
45
19: 6
20: 2, 14
32
22:16
25: 1, 38
39+A
26:10
28: 3
31: 5, 6
2 Sa. 1: 1, 4
4+B
4, 15
2:23, 23
3:27, 33
6: 7, 23
10: 1, 18
11:15, 17
21, 21
22, 24
24, 26
12:13, 14
18, 21
13:32, 33
33, 39
14: 5, 14
17:23
18: 3, 20
19:10, 23
37
20:10
24:15
1 Ki. 2: 1, 25
1 Ki. 2:30
(3)37, 42
46+A
3:19
11:40
12:18 p 24
ll 14, 47
13:31
14:12 A
17 A
16:18
22—A
17:12
19: 4
20:10—B
13
15+A
22:35
2 Ki. 1: 1, 4, 6
16, 17
3: 5
4: 1, 20
7: 3, 4, 4
4, 17
20
8:10, 15
9:27
11: 1, 8, 15
16
12:21
13:14, 20
24
14: 6, 6, 6
17
18:32
20: 1
23:34
25:25
1 Ch. 1: 44 to 50
51+A
2:19, 24
30, 32
10: 5
5+A
6, 6, 7
13
13:10
19: 1
23:22
24: 2
28—A
2 Ch. 10:18
12:16
14: 1
15:13
18:34
21:19
22: 4
23: 7, 14
14
24:22, 25
25: 4 ter
25
35:24
36: 4
Job 9:29
10:18
14:14
18: 4
21:23
23:12+A
27: 5
36:14
Psa. 40: 6
48:11, 18
81: 7
117:17
Pro. 11: 4
23:13
24: 9, 30
Ecc. 2:16
3: 2
4: 2
7:18
8:12+S[2]
9: 5
Isa. 6: 1
14:28
22:13, 14
18
Isa. 38: 1, 18
50: 2
51: 6
59:10
60:12 A[f]
65:20
Jer. 11:21, 22[g]
14:15
16: 4
20: 6
21: 6, 9
22:12, 26
33: 8
35:16, 17
38:30
39: 5 A[h]
41: 5
44:20
45: 2, 10
24, 26
49:16
52:11, 34
Eze. 3:18, 19
20, 20
11:13
13:19
18: 4
13 A[d]
18, 20
21, 24
26, 26
28, 31
32
24:18+A
28: 8
33: 8, 9, 11
13, 15
18
Hos. 13: 1
Amos 2: 2
6: 9
Jon. 4: 3, 8
Hab. 1:12
Zec. 11: 9, 9

[a] pro ἀνταποθνήσκω.
[b] pro ἀποτρέχω. [c] A ἀπόλλυμι.
[d] pro θανατόω. [e] A θάνατος.
[f] pro ἀπόλλυμι. [g] A πίπτω.
[h] pro καθίημι.

ἀποικεσία.

2 Ki. 19:25[a]
24:15
Ezra 6:16, 19
Ezra 6:20, 21
9: 4 A[b]
10: 6 A[b]

[a] B ἀπὸ οἰκε- [b] pro ἀποικία.

ἀποικέω.

2 Ki. 17:11[a] [a] AB ἀποικίζω.

ἀποικία.

Jud. 18:30[a]
2 Ki. 25:27[a]
Ezra 1:11
2: 1
4: 1
9: 4[b]
10: 6[b]
7—ABS[1]
8, 16
Neh. 7: 6
Jer. 13:19
30: 3
31: 7
35: 4, 6
36: 1, 1, 4
22[c], 31
37: 3, 18
39:44
40: 7, 7, 11
47: 1

[a] A μετοικεσία. [b] A ἀποικεσία.
[c] S[1] ἀπόκρισις.

ἀποικίζω.

1 Sa. 4:22+A
22
2 Ki. 15:29
16: 9
17: 6
11 AB[a]
20 A[b]
23, 26
28[c], 33
18:11
24:14, 15
25:21
1 Ch. 9: 1[d]
2 Ch. 36:20
Ezra 2: 1
4:10
5:12
Neh. 7: 6
Jer. 13:19
24: 1, 5
34:17
36: 4, 7
47: 7 B[e]
50: 3, 12
52:31
Lam. 4:22

[a] pro ἀποικέω. [b] pro ἀπωθέω.
[c] A ἄγω. [d] B κατοικίζω.
[e] pro κατοικίζω.

ἀποικισμός.

Jer. 26:19
31:11
Jer. 50:11
11—S[1]

ἀποίχομαι.

Gen. 11:12
26:31
Gen. 28: 6 A[a]
Hos. 11: 2

[a] pro ἀποστέλλω.

ἀποκαθαίρω.

Job 7: 9
9:30
Pro. 15:27

ἀποκαθαρίζω.

Job 25: 4

ἀποκάθημαι.

Lev. 15:33
20:18
Isa. 30:22
64: 6
Lam. 1:17
Eze. 22:10
36:17[a]

[a] A ἄφεδρος.

ἀποκαθίστημι.

Gen. 23:16
29: 3
40:13, 21
41:13
Exo. 4: 7
14:26, 27
Lev. 13:16
Nu. 35:25
2 Sa. 9: 7
Job 5:18
8: 6
22:28
33:25
Psa. 15: 5
34:17
Isa. 23:16
Jer. 15:19
16:15
23: 8
24: 6
27:19
29: 6
Eze. 16:55
55+A
55
17:23
Hos. 2: 3
11:11
Amos 5:15
Mal. 4: 5

ἀποκακέω.

Jeremiah 15: 9

ἀποκάλυμμα.

Judges 5: 2—A

ἀποκαλύπτω.

Gen. 8: 2 A[a]
13
Exo. 20:26
Lev. 18: 6, 7, 7
8, 9, 10
11, 11
12
13—A
14, 15
15, 16
17, 17
18, 19
20:11, 17
18 ter
19, 19
20, 21
Nu. 5:18
22:31
24: 4, 16
Deu. 22:30[b]
27:20
Jos. 2:20
Jud. 5: 2—A
Ruth 3: 4, 7
4: 3
1 Sa. 2:27, 27
3: 7, 21
9:15
20: 2, 13
22: 8, 8, 17
2 Sa. 6:20 ter
22—A
7:27
22:16
Job 12:22 A[c]
41: 4[b]
Psa. 28: 9
36: 5
97: 2
118:18
Pro. 11:13
27: 5
Cant. 4: 1
Isa. 3:17 A[c]
47: 2
52:10
53: 1
56: 1
Jer. 11:20
13:26
20:12
Lam. 2:14
4:22
Eze. 13:14
16:36, 37
57
21:24
22:10
23:10, 18
18, 29
Dan. 2:19, 22
28, 29
30, 47
47
10: 1
11:35
Hos. 2:10
7: 1
Amos 3: 7
Mic. 1: 6
Nah. 2: 7
3: 5

[a] pro ἐπικαλύπτω. [b] A ἀνακαλύπτω. [c] pro ἀνακαλυπτω.

ἀποκάλυψις.

1 Samuel 20:30

ἀπόκειμαι.

Gen. 49:10 Job 38:23

ἀποκενόω.

Judges 3:24—A

ἀποκεντέω.

Nu. 25: 8
1 Sa. 31: 4, 4
Eze. 21:11
Zeph. 1:10

ἀποκέντησις.

Hosea 9:13

ἀποκεφαλίζω.

Psalm 150:p 6

ἀποκιδαρόω.

Lev. 10: 6 Lev. 21:10

ἀποκλαίω.

Pro. 26:24
Jer. 31:32
Jer. 38:15

ἀπόκλεισμα.

Jeremiah 36:26

ἀπόκλειστος.

1 Kings 6:19+A

ἀποκλείω.

Gen. 19:10
Jud. 3:22, 23
24 A[a]
9:51 A[b]
20:48 A[c]
1 Sa. 1: 5[d]
17:46
23: 7[e], 11
11
24:19
26: 8
2 Sa. 13:17, 18
18:28
2 Ki. 4: 4, 5, 21
33
6:32
2 Ch. 29: 7
Psa. 67:31[f]
Isa. 22:22—B
24:22
26:20

[a] pro σφηνόω. [b] pro κλείω. [c] pro ἐπιστρέφω. [d] A συναποκλείω. [e] A ἀποκλίνω. [f] S[1] ἐκκλείω.

ἀποκλίνω.

1 Sa. 23: 7 A[a]
2 Sa. 6:10
Job 12:14 A[b]

[a] pro ἀποκλείω. [b] pro κλείω.

ἀποκλύζω.

2 Chronicles 4: 6

ἀποκνίζω.

Lev. 1:15
5: 8
1 Sa. 9:24
2 Ki. 6: 6
Eze. 17: 4, 22

ἀποκομίζω.

Proverbs 26:16

ἀποκόπτω.

Deu. 23: 1
25:12
Jud. 1: 6, 7
5:22 A[a]
2 Sa. 10: 4
Psa. 76: 9—S[1]
Isa. 18: 5[b]

[a] pro ἐμποδίζω. [b] AS κατακόπτω.

ἀποκρίνω.

Gen. 18: 9, 27
23: 5, 10
14
24:50
27:37, 39
29:26[a]
31:14, 31
36, 43
34:13
40:18
41:16, 16
42:22
45: 3
Exo. 4: 1
19: 8, 19
21: 5
24: 3
Nu. 11:28
13:27
22: 8, 18
23:26
32:31
Deu. 1:14, 41
20:11
Deu. 21: 7
25: 9
26: 5
27:14, 15
Jos. 1:16
7:20
9:30
14: 7
22:21, 32
24:16
Jud. 5:29[b]
29 A[c]
7:14
8: 8, 8
18:14
19:28
20: 4
Ruth 2: 6, 11
1 Sa. 1:15, 17
4:17, 20
9: 8, 12
17, 19
21
10:12
1 Sa. 12: 3, 3
14:12, 28
37, 39
39, 41
16:18
17:30 A
20: 3, 7, 10
28, 32
21: 4, 5
22: 9, 14
23: 4
25:10
26: 6, 14
14—AB
22
28: 6
29: 9
30:22
2 Sa. 1:16
3:11
4: 9
13:32
14:18
15:21
19:21, 42
43
20:20
24:13
1 Ki. 1:28, 36
43
2: 1, 22
30
3:26, 27
12: 6, 9, 13
16
p 24, l 57
ll 59, 67
18:21, 24
21: 4, 11
12
2 Ki. 1:10, 12
3:11
4:29
7: 2, 13
19
18:36, 36
1 Ch. 10:13
21:12
2 Ch. 10: 6, 9, 13
16
29:31
34:15
Ezra 3:11
5:11
10: 2, 12
Neh. 8: 6
Est. 7: 3
Job 1: 7, 9
3: 2+A
16: 3
20: 3
Job 32: 3, 15
16
33:32
38: 3
39:31, 32[d]
40: 2
Psa. 87: 1
101:24
118:42
Pro. 15:28
16: 1
18:13
22:21
24:41
26: 4, 5
Cant. 2:10
Isa. 3: 7
14:10, 32
21: 9
36:21, 21
41:28
45:10—AS[2]
Jer. 7:13
11: 5
23:35
32:16
40: 3
49: 4
51:15, 20
Lam. 3:32
Eze. 9:11
14: 3, 3, 4
7
20: 3, 31
31
Dan. 2: 5, 7, 8
10, 14
26, 27
47
3:14, 16
16, 28
4:16+A
16, 27
5:10+A
17 A[c]
6:13
9:23
Joel 2:19
Amos 7:14
Mic. 3:11
6: 3, 5
Hab. 2: 1, 2
Zeph. 2: 3
Hag. 2:12, 13
14
Zec. 1: 6, 10
11, 12
13
3: 4
4: 5, 6, 11
6: 4, 5

[a] A εἶπον. [b] A ἀνταποκρίνομαι. [c] pro ἀποστρέφω. [d] S[1] ὑποκρίνω. [e] pro εἶπον.

ἀπόκρισις.

Deu. 1:22
Ezra 7:12
Job 13:22 A[a]
15: 2
31:14
32: 4, 5
Job 33: 5
34:36 A[a]
35: 4
39:34
Pro. 15: 1
Jer. 36:22 S[1 b]

[a] pro ἀνταπόκρισις.
[b] pro ἀποικία.

ἀποκρύπτω.

2 Ki. 4:27
Job 3:23+A
13:24 A[a]
24:15
Psa. 18: 7
37:10[b]
68: 6 S[2 a]
Ps. 118:19[c]
Pro. 27:12
29: 8 S[d]
Isa. 26:20
40:27
Jer. 39:17
Zeph. 3: 5—A

[a] pro κρύπτω. [b] ABS κρύπτω. [c] S[1] ἀποστρέφω. [d] pro ἀποστρέφω.

ἀποκρυφή.

2 Sa. 22:12
Job 22:14
Psa. 17:12

ἀπόκρυφος.

Deu. 27:15
Job 39:28
Psa. 9:29
30—A
16:12
26: 5
30:21
Psa. 63: 5
80: 8
Isa. 4: 6
45: 3
Dan. 2:22
11:43

ἀποκτείνω.

Gen. 4: 8, 14
15, 23
25
12:12
18:25
20: 2, 11
26: 7
27:41, 42
34:25, 26
37:18, 20
26
38: 7
42:37
49: 6
Exo. 1:16
4:23, 24
5:21
13:15
16: 3
17: 3
21:14
22:19, 24
23: 7
32:12, 27
Lev. 20: 4, 15
16
Nu. 11:15
16:13, 41
20: 4
21: 5
22:33
25: 5
31: 7, 8, 8
17, 17
35:19, 19
21[a]
Deu. 9:28
13: 9
22:22, 25
32:39
Jos. 7: 5
8:24
10:11, 26
41+A
11:11, 17
13:22
Jud. 7:25, 25
8:17, 18
19, 20
21[b]
9: 5, 18
24, 24
45[b], 54
56
15:12+A
16: 2 A[c]
20: 5 A[c]
1 Sa. 15: 3, 8
16: 2
17:46
24:11, 12
19
2 Sa. 4:10, 11
12
12: 9
14: 7
2 Sa. 23:21
1 Ki. 2: 5, 32
9:16 A
11:24 A
12:27
18:12, 13
14
19: 1, 10
14
2 Ki. 8:12
10: 9
11:18
17:25
1 Ch. 2: 3
7:21
10:14
11:23
19:18, 18
2 Ch. 21: 4, 13
22: 1, 8, 9
11
25: 4
28: 6[d], 7, 9
36:17
Neh. 9:26
Est. 2:21
9: 6—S[1]
10+AS[3]
15
Job 1:15[a], 17[e]
Psa. 9:29
58:12
77:31, 34
47
93: 6
100: 8
101:29
134:10 S[1 f]
10
135:18
138:19
Pro. 21:25
Ecc. 3: 3
Isa. 14:20
66: 3
Jer. 20:17
33:21
45: 9, 16
Lam. 2: 4, 20
21
3:42
Eze. 7:16
9: 6
13:19
23:10, 47
33:27
Dan. 2:13
3:22+A
Hos. 2: 3
6: 5
9:16
Amos 2: 3
4:10
9: 1, 4
Hab. 1:17

[a] A πατάσσω. [b] A ἀναιρέω. [c] pro φονεύω. [d] B ἀποστέλλω. [e] S[1] ἀπόλλυμι. [f] pro πατάσσω.

ἀποκυλίω.

Gen. 29: 3, 8, 10

ἀποκωλύω.

1 Sa. 6:10; 25: 7, 15; 33, 34
1 Ki. 1: 6; 21: 7
Ecc. 2:10

ἀποκωφόομαι.

Eze. 3:26; 24:27
Mic. 7:16

ἀπολακτίζω.

Deuteronomy 32:15

ἀπολαμβάνω.

Nu. 34:14
Isa. 5:17

ἀπολανθάνω.

Isa. 51:13 B[a]
Eze. 22:12 B[a]

[a] pro ἐπιλανθάνω.

ἀπολαύω.

Proverbs 7:18

ἀπολέγω.

Jonah 4: 8

ἀπολείπω.

Exo. 5:19; 12:10
Lev. 22:30
Jud. 9: 5A[a], 9[b]; 11[b], 13[b]
2 Ki. 10:21—A; 21—A
2 Ch. 10: 5
Job 11:20
Pro. 2:17; 9: 6, 12; 19: 9 S[1 c]; 27
Isa. 55: 7

[a] pro καταλείπω. [b] A ἀφίημι.
[c] pro ἀπόλλυμι.

ἀπολήνιον.

Zec. 14:10[a] [a] ABS ὑπολήνιον.

ἀπολιθόω.

Exodus 13:16

ἀπόλλυμι, —ύω.

Gen. 18:24, 28; 28, 29; 30, 31; 32; 19:13; 20: 4; 35: 4
Exo. 10: 7; 19:24; 30:38
Lev. 7:10, 11; 15, 17; 17:10; 20: 3, 5, 6; 23:30; 26: 6, 38; 41
Nu. 14:12; 16:33; 17:12; 20: 3 A[a]; 21:29, 30; 24:19, 20; 24; 32:39; 33:52, 52; 53, 55
Deu. 2:12, 21; 4:26; 7:23, 24; 8:19, 20; 20; 9: 3; 11: 4, 17; 12: 2, 3; 22: 3; 28:20, 22; 24, 45
Deu. 28:51; 30:18; 32:28; 33:27
Jos. 7: 7; 11:14; 15:63; 16:10; 23: 5, 13; 24:10
Jud. 5:31
1 Sa. 9: 3, 20
2 Sa. 1:27
2 Ki. 10:19; 11: 1; 13: 7; 19:18
2 Ch. 22:10
Est. 3: 7, 9; 4: 7, 8, 14; 16; 8: 5; 9: 2; 6+S[3]; 11, 12; 16; 24+AS[3 b]
Job 1:17 S[1 c]; 2: 3; 3: 3, 11; 4: 7, 7, 9; 20, 21; 5:11, 15; 6:18; 7: 6; 8:13[d]; 9:22; 23+A
Job 11:20 A[e]; 12:15, 23; 14:19; 18:17; 20: 7; 29:13; 30: 2; 31:12, 19; 42: 8
Psa. 1: 6; 2:12; 5: 7; 9: 4, 6, 7; 19, 37; 20:11; 30:13; 36:20; 40: 6; 48:11; 67: 3; 72:19, 27; 79:17; 82:18; 91:10; 101:27; 111:10; 118:92; 95—S[1]; 176; 141: 5; 142:12; 145: 4
Pro. 5:23; 10:28[f]; 11:23; 12: 4; 13:23; 15: 1, 6[g]; 6—S[1]; 17: 5; 19: 9[h], 16; 21:28; 23:28; 29: 3
Ecc. 3: 6; 5:13; 7: 8, 16; 9: 6, 18
Isa. 1:25; 11: 9, 12; 13; 13: 9, 11; 14:20, 22; 25; 15: 1, 1, 2; 16: 4; 17: 3+AS; 23: 1, 11; 14; 24:12; 25:11; 26:14; 27:13[i], 13; 29:14, 20; 30:25; 31: 3; 34: 2, 16; 37:11, 12; 19 AS[k]; 38:17
Isa. 41:11; 43:28; 46:12; 48:19; 49:20; 57: 1; 60:12[m]; 65: 8
Jer. 1:10 A[n]; 4: 9; 6:15, 21; 9:12; 10:11, 15; 14:21; 15: 7—S; 18: 7, 18; 23: 1; 25:10; 26: 8; 27: 6; 28:18, 55; 29: 4, 8; 31: 8, 35; 36, 42; 32:21; 34:12, 12; 47:15; 51:12[o]
Lam. 2: 9; 3:18
Eze. 7:26; 12:22; 19: 5; 25: 7, 16; 26: 2; 17+A; 28:10; 29: 8; 30:10, 11[p]; 12, 13; 14[p], 15; 16+A; 18; 31:17; 32:12, 13; 33:28; 34: 4, 16; 25 A[q]; 29; 35: 7; 37:11; 39: 3
Dan. 2:12, 18; 24, 24; 7:11, 26
Joel 1:11
Amos 1: 8; 2:14; 3:15
Obad. 8
Jon. 1: 6; 14—S[1]; 3: 9; 4:10
Mic. 4: 9; 5:10; 7: 2
Zeph. 2: 5, 13
Zec. 9: 5

[a] pro ἀποθνήσκω.
[b] pro ἀφανίζω. [c] pro ἀποκτείνω.
[d] A ὄλλυμι. [e] pro ἀπώλεια.
[f] AS ὄλλυμι. [g] AS[2] ὄλλυμι,
[h] S[1] ἀπολείπω. [i] A ἀνατολή.
[k] pro ἀπωθέω. [m] A ἀποθνήσκω.
[n] pro ἀπολύω. [o] S πολεμέω.
[p] A ἀφανίζω. [q] pro ἀφανίζω.

ἀπολογέομαι.

Jer. 12: 1
Jer. 38: 6

ἀπολόγημα.

Jeremiah 20:12

ἀπόλοιπος.

Eze. 41: 9, 11; 11, 12; 13, 14
Eze. 41:15, 15; 42: 1, 10

ἀπολούω.

Job 9:30

ἀπολυτρόω.

Exo. 21: 8
Zeph. 3: 1

ἀπολύω.

Gen. 15: 2
Exo. 33:11
Nu. 20:29
Psa. 16:14[a]; 33: 1
Jer. 1:10[b]

[a] AB*S ὀλίγος. [b] A ἀπόλλυμι.

ἀπομέμφομαι.

Job 33:27[a] [a] A ἀποπέμπω.

ἀπόμοιρα.

Ezekiel 45:20—A

ἀπονέμω.

Deuteronomy 4:19

ἀπονίπτω.

1 Ki. 22:38
Pro. 24:35, 55

ἀποξενόω.

1 Ki. 14: 5 A; 6 A
Pro. 27: 8

ἀποξέω.

Job 2: 8 A[a] [a] pro ξύω.

ἀποξηραίνω.

Jos. 4:23, 23; 5: 1
Psa. 36: 2
Jon. 4: 7

ἀποξύω.

Lev. 14:41; 41—AB
Lev. 14:42, 43

ἀποπειράομαι.

Proverbs 16:29

ἀποπεμπτόω.

Gen. 41:34
Gen. 47:26

ἀποπέμπω.

Job 33:27 A[a]

[a] pro ἀπομέμφομαι.

ἀποπηδάω.

1 Sa. 20:34 A[a]
Pro. 9:18
Eze. 19: 3[b]
Hos. 7:13

[a] pro ἀναπηδάω. [b] A ἀποδημέω.

ἀποπιάζω.

Jud. 6:38 A[a] [a] pro ἐκπιάζω.

ἀποπίπτω.

Lev. 19: 9; 23:22
Job 24:24; 29:24
Psa. 5:11; 7: 4; 36: 2; 89: 6

ἀποπλανάω.

2 Ch. 21:11
Pro. 7:21
Jer. 27: 6

ἀποπλάνησις.

Deuteronomy 29:19

ἀποπλύνω.

2 Sa. 19:24[a]
Jer. 2:22
Jer. 4:14
Eze. 16: 9

[a] A πλύνω.

ἀποπνίγω.

Nahum 2:12

ἀποποιέομαι.

Job 8:20; 14:15; 15: 4
Job 19:18[a]; 36: 5; 40: 3

[a] A ἀπεῖπον.

ἀποπομπαῖος.

Leviticus 16: 8, 10

ἀποπομπή.

Leviticus 16:10

ἀπόπτωμα.

Jud. 20: 6[a], 10[a] [a] A ἀφροσύνη.

ἀπορέω.

Gen. 32: 7
Lev. 25:47
Pro. 29:29
Isa. 8:22
Isa. 24:19; 51:20
Jer. 8:18
Hos. 13: 8

ἀπορία.

Lev. 26:16
Deu. 28:22
Pro. 28:27
Isa. 5:30
Isa. 8:22; 24:19
Jer. 8:21
Hag. 2:17 S[1 a]

[a] pro ἀφορία.

ἀπορρέω.

Jud. 6:38 A[a]
Job 36:34
Psa. 1: 3

[a] pro στάζω.

ἀπορρήγνυμι.

Lev. 13:56
Job 39: 4
Ecc. 4:12

ἀπορρίπτω.

Exo. 22:31
Jud. 2:19
2 Sa. 22:46
1 Ki. 9: 7
2 Ki. 13:23; 17:15+A; 20; 24:20
Job 27:22 A[a]; 30:22
Psa. 2: 3; 30:23; 50:13; 70: 9
Isa. 38:17
Jer. 7:15, 15; 29; 8:14, 14; 9:19
Jer. 16:13; 22:26[b]; 28: 6; 29: 5
Eze. 16: 5; 18:31; 20: 7, 8; 23:35; 38:11
Hos. 10: 7; 11: 1, 1
Amos 4: 3
Obad. 5
Jon. 2: 4
Mic. 2: 9; 7:19
Zec. 11:10, 14
Mal. 2: 9[c]

[a] pro ἐπιρρίπτω. [b] A παραδίδωμι. [c] S[3] παραρρίπτω.

ἀποσάττω.

Gen. 24:32[a] [a] A ἐπισάττω.

ἀποσβέννυμι.

Pro. 20:36
Isa. 10:18

ἀποσείω.

Isaiah 33:15

ἀποσιωπάω.

Jer. 45:27[a] [a] A σιωπάω.

ἀποσκαρίζω.

Judges 4:21+A

ἀποσκευάζω.

Leviticus 14:36

ἀποσκευή.

Gen. 14:12; 15:14; 31:18
Gen. 34:28; 43: 7; 46: 5

Exo. 10:10, 24 | 12:37 | 27:19 A[a] | 39:22[b]
Nu. 16:27 | 31: 9 | 32:16[c], 17, 24, 26
Nu. 32:30
Deu. 20:14
1 Ch. 5:21
2 Ch. 20:25 | 21:14, 17 | 32:29, 29
Ezra 1: 4, 6

[a] *pro* κατασκευή. [b] A παρασκευή. [c] A κατασκευή.

ἀποσκηνόω.

Genesis 13:18

ἀποσκληρύνω.

Job 39:16

ἀποσκοπεύω.

Lam. 4:17, 18 | Hab. 2: 1

ἀποσκοπέω.

Jud. 21: 9 A[a] | 1 Ch. 12:29

[a] *pro* ἐπισκέπτομαι.

ἀποσκορακίζω.

Psa. 26: 9S[2] S[2a] | Isa. 17:13

[a] *pro* ἐγκαταλείπω.

ἀποσκορακισμός.

Isaiah 66:15

ἀποσοβέω.

Deu. 28:26 A[a] | Jer. 7:33

[a] *pro* ἐκφοβέω.

ἀπόσπασμα.

Jer. 26:20 | Lam. 4: 7

ἀποσπάω.

Lev. 22:24
Jos. 8: 6[a]
Jud. 16: 9[b]
Job 41: 8[c]
Isa. 28: 9
Jer. 12:14
Eze. 19: 5 A[d]

[a] A ἀφίστημι. [b] A διασπάω. [c] S[1] πάσχω. [d] *pro* ἀπωθέω.

ἀποστάζω.

Pro. 5: 3 | 10:31, 32
Cant. 4:11

ἀποσταλάζω.

Joel 3:18 | Amos 9:13

ἀποστασία.

Jos. 22:22[a]
1 Ki. 20:13 + A
2 Ch. 29:19
2 Ch. 33:19 A[b]
Jer. 2:19

[a] A ἀπόστασις. [b] *pro ibid.*

ἀποστάσιον.

Deu. 24: 3, 5
Isa. 50: 1
Jer. 3: 8

ἀπόστασις.

Jos. 22:22 A[a]
2 Ch. 28:19
2 Ch. 33:19[b]
Ezra 4:19

[a] *pro* ἀποστασία. [b] A *ibid.*

ἀποστατέω.

Nu. 31:16
Neh. 2:19
Neh. 6: 6
Ps. 118:118

ἀποστάτης.

Nu. 14: 9
Jos. 22:16, 19
Job 26:13
Isa. 30: 1

ἀποστάτις.

Ezra 4:12, 15

ἀποστέλλω.

Gen. 8: 6, 8 | 19:13 | 20: 2 | 21:14 | 24: 7 | 40 S[a] | 26:27 A[a] | 27:45 | 28: 5, 6[b] | 30:25 | 31: 4 | 32: 3, 5, 18 | 26, 26 | 37:13, 14 | 32 | 38:17, 17 | 20, 23 | 25 | 41: 8, 14 | 42: 4, 16 | 43: 3, 4, 7 | 13 | 44: 3 | 45: 5, 7, 8 | 23, 27 | 46: 5, 28
Exo. 2: 5 | 3:10 | 12 A[a] | 13, 14 | 15 | 4:13, 28 | 5:22 | 7:16 | 8:28[c] | 9:15, 27 | 10:10 | 11: 1 A[a] | 15: 7, 10 | 23:20, 27 | 28
Lev. 16:10 | 25:21 | 26:22
Nu. 13: 3, 3 | 4 A[a] | 17, 18 | 28 | 14:36 | 16:12, 28 | 29 | 20:14, 16 | 21: 6, 21 | 32 | 22: 5, 10 | 15, 37 | 40 | 24:12 | 31: 4, 6 | 32: 8
Deu. 1:22 | 2:26 | 7:20 | 9:23 A[a] | 19:12 | 22: 7 | 28: 8, 20[c] | 29:22 | 32:24 B[d] | 34:11
Jos. 1:16 | 2: 1, 3 | 6:25 | 7: 2, 22 | 8: 3, 9 | 10: 3, 6 | 11: 1 | 14: 7, 11 | 22:13 | 23: 5 | 24: 9, 28[c]
Jud. 3:15 A[a] | 4: 6 | 5:15[c] | 6:35 B[a] | 7:24[c] | 9:31 | 11:12, 14
Jud. 11:17[c], 17 | 19, 28 | 38[c] | 13: 8 | 16:18 | 18: 2[c] | 19:29[c] | 20: 6 B[a] | 12[c] | 21:10, 13
1 Sa. 4: 4 | 5: 8 | 11 A[a] | 6: 2, 3 A[a] | 21 | 9:16 | 11: 3, 7 | 12: 8, 11 | 15: 1, 18 | 20 | 16: 1, 11 | 12, 19 | 19, 22 | 18: 5 A | 19:11, 14 | 15, 20 | 21, 21 | 20:12, 21 | 31 | 21: 2 | 22:11 | 25: 5, 14 | 25, 32 | 39, 40 | 26: 4 | 30:26 | 31: 9
2 Sa. 2: 5 | 3:12 | 14 A[a] | 15, 21 | 22, 23 | 26 | 5:11 | 8:10 | 9: 5 | 10: 2, 3, 3 | 5, 6, 7 | 16 | 11: 1, 3, 4 | 5, 6, 6 | 6, 14 | 18, 27 | 12: 1, 25 | 27 | 13: 7, 27 | 14: 2, 29 | 29, 29 | 32, 32 | 15:10, 12 | 36 | 17:16 | 18: 2, 29 | 19:11 − A | 14 | 22:15, 17 | 24:13
1 Ki. 1:44, 53 | 2:29, 29 | (3)36 + A | 42 | 5: 1, 2, 8 | 8[e], 9 | 14 | 7: 1 | 9:27 | 12: 3 + A | 18, 20 | p24 l60 | l162, 64 | 15:20 | 18:10, 19 | 20 | 19: 2 | 20: 8 | 11 − B | 11 − B | 14
1 Ki. 21: 2, 5[f], 6 | 7, 9 | 10[g], 17
2 Ki. 1: 2, 6, 9 | 11, 13 | 16[c] | 18 B[h] | 2: 2, 4, 6 | 16, 17 | 17 | 4:22 | 5: 6, 7, 8 | 10, 22 | 6: 9, 10 | 13, 14 | 23, 32 | 32 | 7:13, 14 | 8: 9 | 9:17, 19 | 10: 1, 5, 7 | 21 | 11: 4 | 12:18 | 14: 8, 9, 9 | 19 | 16: 7, 8, 10 | 11 | 17: 4, 13 | 25, 26 | 18:14 | 17 − A | 27 | 19: 2, 4, 9 | 16, 20 | 20:12 | 22: 3[c], 15 | 18 | 23: 1, 16 | 24: 2
1 Ch. 8: 8 | 10: 9 | 13: 2 | 14: 1 | 18:10 | 19: 2, 3, 4 | 5, 6, 8 | 16 | 21:12, 15
2 Ch. 2: 3, 3, 7 | 8, 11 | 13, 15 | 6:34 | 7:10, 13 | 8:18 | 10: 3, 18 | 16: 2, 3, 4 | 17: 7 | 24:19, 23 | 25:15 | 17 − B | 18, 18 | 27 | 28: 16[i], 16 | 30: 1 | 32: 9, 9, 21 | 31 | 34: 8 − B | 23, 26 | 29 | 35:21 | 36: 5, 10 | 15
Ezra 4:11, 17 | 18 | 5: 5, 6, 7 | 6:13 | 7:14 | 8:16
Neh. 2: 6, 9 | 6: 2, 3 | 4 − A | 4, 5, 8 | 12, 19[k] | 8:10, 12
Est. 1:22 | 3:13 | 4: 4, 5 | 5:10 + S[l] | 8: 5[m]
Est. 9:16 + S[3] | 19 | 20 A[n]
Job 1: 5, 11 | 2: 5 | 5:10 | 8: 4 | 38:35 | 40: 6
Psa. 58: 1 | 77:25 | 103:10 B[a] | 104:17[n] | 20[o] | 106:20 | 110: 9 | 147: 4, 7
Pro. 9: 3 | 21: 8 | 25:13 | 26: 6, 13
Ecc. 11: 1
Cant. 5: 4
Isa. 6: 6, 8, 8 | 9: 8 | 10: 6[p], 16 | 14:12 | 16: 1, 8 | 18: 2 | 19:20 | 20: 1 | 33: 7 | 36: 2, 12 | 37: 2, 4, 9[q] | 17, 21 | 39: 1 | 43:14 | 48:16 | 57: 9 | 58: 6 | 61: 1
Jer. 2:10 | 7:25 | 9:16 S[1d] | 17 | 14: 3[r], 14 | 15 | 16:16, 16 | 19:14 | 21: 1 | 23:21, 32 | 38 | 24:10 | 25: 4, 4, 9 | 29:15 | 31:12 | 32: 1, 2, 3 | 13 | 33: 5, 5, 12 | 15 | 34: 2, 12 | 14 | 35: 9, 15 | 36: 1, 3, 9 | 25, 28 | 28 ABS | 31, 31 | 41:10[s], 14 | 14 A[a] | 42:15 | 43:14, 21 | 44: 3, 7, 15 | 17 | 45:14 | 46:14 | 47: 1, 5, 14 | 49: 5, 6, 20 | 21 | 50: 1, 2, 10 | 51: 4, 4
Lam. 1:13
Eze. 2: 4 + A | 5:16[t] | 7: 3 | 13: 6 | 30:11 | 34:26 A[a] | 39: 6
Dan. 3: 2, 28 | 5:24 | 6:22 | 10:11
Hos. 5:13
Amos 1: 4[u]
Zec. 2: 8, 9 | 11 A[a] | 6:15
Mal. 4: 4

[a] *pro* ἐξαποστέλλω. [b] A ἀποιχομαι. [c] A ἐξαποστέλλω. [d] *pro* ἐπαποστέλλω. [e] A ἐπιστέλλω. [f] AB ἀποστρέφω. [g] A ἀνταποστέλλω. [h] *pro* ἀφίστημι. [i] *pro* ἀποκτείνω. [k] B ἐπιστέλλω. [m] AS[3] ἐξαποστ. [n] A[2] ἐξαποστέλλω. [o] BS[1] ἐξαποστέλλω. [p] S[1] ἀποστρέφω. [q] A ἀποστρέφω. [r] S[1] ἀφίστημι. [s] S ἐξαποστέλλω. [t] AB ἐξαποστ. [u] *pro* δίδωμι.

ἀποστέργω.

Deu. 15: 7[a]

[a] A ἀποστρέφω.

ἀποστερέω.

Exo. 21:10
Deu. 24:16 A[a]
Mal. 3: 5

[a] *pro* ἀπαδικέω.

ἀποστολή.

Deu. 22: 7
1 Ki. 4:30 − A | 9:16 A
Psa. 77:49
Ecc. 8: 8
Cant. 4:13
Jer. 39:36

ἀπόστολος.

1 Kings 14: 6 A

ἀποστρέφω.

Gen. 3:19 | 14:16, 16 | 15:16 | 16: 9 | 18:22, 33 | 22:19 | 24: 5, 6, 8 | 27:45 | 28:15, 21 | 31: 3, 55 | 33:16 | 38:22 | 42:24 | 43:11, 11 | 17, 20 | 44: 8 | 48:21 | 50:14 B[a]
Exo. 3: 6 | 4:18[b], 18 | 21 | 10: 8[b] | 13:17 | 14: 2 | 23: 4, 25 | 32:15
Nu. 13:26[b] | 14: 3, 4, 43 | 45 | 22:34 | 23: 6, 16 | 17, 20 | 24: 1, 25 | 25: 4 | 32:15, 18 | 22
Deu. 5:30 | 9: 3 | 13:17 | 15: 7 A[c] | 16: 7 | 17:16, 16 | 20: 5[b], 6[b] | 7[b], 8 | 22: 1 | 23:14 | 28:68 | 31:17, 18 | 18[b] | 32:20
Jos. 2:16[d] | 8:21 B[e] | 10:21[b], 38 | 11:10 B[e] | 22: 4, 16 | 18, 29[f] | 32 | 23:12
Jud. 2:19 | 5:29[g] | 7: 3 A[e] | 3 A[e] | 8:33 A[e] | 9:56 A[e] | 57 A[e] | 11:13 + A | 35[h] | 20:41 A[e] | 21:14 A[e] | 23 A[a]
Ruth 1: 6[b], 8 | 16, 21 | 2: 6
1 Sa. 5:10 | 6:21 | 9: 5[i] | 15:11 | 27 A[e] | 29 | 17:53 A[k] | 22:18 A[e] | 25:12, 39 | 26:25[i] | 29: 4, 4 − B | 30:22[b] | 31: 9
2 Sa. 1:22 | 2:23 A[e] | 26[b i] | 30 A[k] | 5:23 | 11: 4, 15 | 14:24, 24[b] | 15:25, 29 | 18:16 | 20:12, 22
1 Ki. 2:16, 17 | 20, 20 | 30 AB[e] | 32 AB[e] | 33 A[e] | (3)41 B[k] | 8:14 | 34 AB[e] | 35[b], 57 | 9: 6, 6

1 Ki. 10:13
11:21
12:24[1]
13:11 A[e]
17:22+A
18:43+B
44 B[e]
21: 5 AB[m]
22:26
33 AB[nx]
2 Ki. 9:15
13:25 A[e]
14:14
22 A[e]
15:20
16: 6 A[e]
17:13
18:14, 24
19: 7
8 A[a]
9 A[a]
28, 33
36
20: 2[n]
21: 3 A[e]
3 A[o]
22: 9[b]
23:26
1 Ch. 4:22
10:14 S[e]
12:23[h]
13:13
14:14
2 Ch. 6:25, 42
7:14, 19
20
9:12
10: 2
11: 4, 4
12:12
13:13, 14
18:25, 31
32
19: 1 B[ne]
21:17
25:13
28:11
29: 6, 10
30: 8, 9[b]
9
32:21
34: 7
36:19, 22
Ezra 9:14 A[e]
10:14
Neh. 1:11+S[3]
9:35[b]
Est. 8: 5
Job 9:12, 13
10: 9
15:22
33:17
39:22
Psa. 6:11 AS[e]
9: 4, 18
32
12: 2
17:38
21:25
26: 9
29: 8
34: 4, 13
39:15
43:11, 25
50:11
52: 7[p]
53: 7
68:18
69: 3, 4
73:11, 21
77:38, 57[q]
84: 2[b], 4, 5
87:15
88:44, 47
89: 3
101: 3
103: 9 B[e]
29
105:23
118:19 S[1 r]

Ps. 118:37
59 S[e]
128: 5
131:10
142: 7
Pro. 4:27
10:32[s]
15: 1
20: 3
22:14, 14
24:18[t], 65
27:11
28:27
29: 8[a]
Cant. 2:17
6: 4
Isa. 1:15
5:25
7: 6
8:17
9:12
13 AS[e]
17, 21
10: 4
6 S[1 m]
12: 1
13:14
14:27
22: 9
30:11, 15
35:10
36: 9
37: 7, 8, 9
9 A[m]
29, 34
37
38: 2, 8
42:17
43:13
44:25
45:23
50: 6
51:11
53: 3
54: 8
55:10, 11
57: 9+AS[3]
17
58:13
59: 2, 20
64: 7
Jer. 2:25, 35
3:10 A[e]
19
4: 8, 28
8: 4, 5
14: 3
15: 6
18:11, 20
22:27[b]
23:14, 20
22
25: 5, 18
26:16 A[k]
21 ABS[e]
27:16
30:13
33: 3
35: 3
36:10
37: 3, 3, 18
21, 21[b]
24
38: 8, 21
21−S[1]
22, 23
39:33[v], 40
44
40: 5, 7[w]
11[v]
42:15
43: 3, 7
44: 7, 20
45: 22
26[b v]
47: 5 A[k]
48:10, 16
16
50: 5
51: 5

Lam. 1: 8, 13
2: 3, 8 AS[e]
8[u v]
Eze. 3:18, 19
20
7:22, 24
12:23
13:22
22+A
14: 6
16:41, 53
53, 53
18: 8, 17
21, 23
24, 26
27, 28
30
21: 5, 30
23:27, 34
48
29:14
33: 9, 9, 11
11, 12

Eze. 33:14, 18
19
34: 4[b], 6
10, 16[x]
38: 8
39:23, 24
25[t], 27
29
Dan. 9:13, 16
Hos. 2:11
7:16
8: 3, 13
14: 4
Amos 1: 3, 6, 9
11, 13
2: 1, 4, 6
Jon. 3: 8[z], 9, 10
Mic. 2: 4
3: 4
Nah. 2: 3
Zeph. 2: 7[y]
Zec. 1: 4
10: 6

[a] *pro* ὑποστρέφω. [b] A ἐπιστρέφω. [c] *pro* ἀποστέργω. [d] A ἀναστρέφω. [e] *pro* ἐπιστρέφω. [f] A ἀφίστημι. [g] A ἀποκρινω. [h] B ἐπιστρέφω. [i] B ἀναστρέφω. [k] *pro* ἀναστ. [m] *pro* ἀποστέλλω. [n] AB ἐπιστρέφω. [o] *pro* ἀνίστημι. [p] B[2]S ἐπιστρεφω. [q] B[1]S ἐπιστ. [r] *pro* ἀποκρυπτω. [s] S[2] καταστρέφω. [t] S[1] ὑποστρέφω. [u] S ἀποκρύπτω. [v] S ἐπιστρέφω. [w] BS[3] ἐπιστρέφω. [x] AB[1] ἐπιστ. [y] S[1] ἐπιστ. [z] S[3] ἀναστ.

ἀποστροφή.

Gen. 3:16
4: 7
Deu. 22: 1
31:18
1 Sa. 7:17
Isa. 1:27+S[1]
Jer. 5: 6

Jer. 6:19
8: 5
18:12
Eze. 16:53 *qtr*
33:11
Mic. 2:12

ἀποσυμμίγνυμι.

Dan. 11:6 A[a] [a] *pro* συμμίγνυμι.

ἀποσυνάγω.

2 Ki. 5: 3, 6, 7 | 2 Ki. 5:11[a]
[a] A συνάγω.

ἀποσυρίζω.

Isaiah 30:14−S[1]

ἀποσφράγισμα.

Jer. 22:24 | Eze. 28:12

ἀποσχίζω.

Nu. 16:21, 26
2 Ch. 26:21

Dan. 2:34[a]
[a] A τέμνω.

ἀποτάσσω.

Ecc. 2:20 | Jer. 20: 2

ἀποτείνω.

Exodus 8:28

ἀποτεκνόομαι.

Gen. 27:45[a] [a] A ἀτεκνόω.

ἀποτέμνω.

Jud. 5:26 A[a] Jer. 43:23
[a] *pro* σφυροκοπέω.

ἀποτηγανίζω.

Jeremiah 36:22

ἀποτίθημι.

Exo. 16:33, 34
Lev. 16:23

Lev. 22:23 A[2a]
24:12

Nu. 15:34
17: 7, 10
19: 9
Jos. 4: 8

2 Ch. 18:26
Eze. 21:10[b]
Joel 1:18

[a] *pro* ποιέω. [b] AB ἀπωθέω.

ἀποτίναγμα.

Jud. 16: 9 A[a] [a] *pro* στυππίον.

ἀποτινάσσω.

Jud. 16:20 A[a]
1 Sa. 10: 2

Lam. 2: 7

[a] *pro* ἐκτινάσσω.

ἀποτιννύω.

Gen. 31:39 | Psa. 68: 5

ἀποτίνω, –τίω.

Exo. 21:19, 34
36
22: 1, 4, 5
5, 6, 7
9, 11
12, 13
14, 15
17
Lev. 5:16
6: 5
24:18
Ruth 2:12

1 Sa. 2:20
24:20[a]
2 Sa. 12: 6
15: 7
2 Ki. 4: 7
Job 34:33
Psa. 36:21
Pro. 6:31
22:27
Isa. 9: 5
Eze. 33:15

[a] A ἀνταποδίδωμι, B ἀνταποτίνω.

ἀποτομή.

Jud. 5:26 A[a] [a] *pro* σφύρα.

ἀποτρέχω.

Gen. 12:19
24:51
31:26
32: 9
Exo. 3:21
10:24
21: 5, 7
Lev. 25:41[a]
Nu. 22:13
24:14
Jos. 23:14
Jud. 7: 7 A[b]

Jud. 19:18 A[b]
1 Sa. 8:22
1 Ki. 2:26
12:16
21:36
22:36+A
2 Ch. 10:16+A
Est. 2:14
Jer. 41:21
44: 9
47: 5

[a] A ἀποθνήσκω. [b] *pro* πορεύω.

ἀποτρίβω.

Jud. 5:26 A[a]
Hos. 8: 5

Mic. 7:11[b]

[a] *pro* διηλόω. [b] A ἀπωθέω.

ἀποτροπιάζω.

Ezekiel 16:21

ἀποτρυγάω.

Amos 6: 1

ἀποτυγχάνω.

Job 31:16

ἀποτυφλόω.

Deu. 16:19[a] [a] A ἐκτυφλόω.

ἀποτύφλωσις.

Zechariah 12:4

ἀποφαίνω.

Job 27: 5 | Job 32: 2

ἀποφέρω.

Lev. 20:19
Nu. 16:46
2 Sa. 13:13
1 Ki. 14:26−A
2 Ch. 36: 7
Ezra 5: 5, 14
Job 3: 6−S[1]
15:28

Job 21:32
Psa. 44:15, 15
16
Ecc. 10:20
Isa. 57:13
Jer. 52:17
Eze. 32:30[a]
38:13

Hos. 10: 6
Mic. 7: 9 A[b]

Zec. 5:10

[a] A λαμβάνω. [b] *pro* ποιέω.

ἀποφθέγγομαι.

1 Ch. 25: 1
Psa. 58: 8
Eze. 13: 9, 19

Mic. 5:12
Zec. 10: 2

ἀπόφθεγμα.

Deu. 32: 2 | Eze. 13:19

ἀποφράσσω.

Pro. 8:33 AS[a] | Lam. 3: 8

ἀποφυσάω.

Hosea 13: 3

ἀποχέω.

1 Ki. 22:35
2 Ki. 4: 4

Lam. 4:21

ἀποχωρέω.

Jeremiah 26: 5

ἀποχώρησις.

Judges 3:24+A

ἀποχωρίζω.

Ezekiel 43:21

ἀπτόητος.

Jer. 26:28 | Jer. 27: 2

ἅπτω.

Gen. 3: 3
20: 4, 6
26:11
32:25, 32
Exo. 19:12, 13
29:37
30: 8 A[1a]
2 ?
Lev. 5: 2, 3, 3
6:18, 27
7: 9, 11
11: 8, 24
26, 27
31, 36
39
12: 4
15: 5, 7, 10
11, 12
19, 21
22, 23
27
22: 4, 5, 6
Nu. 3:10, 38[b]
4:15
16:26
17:13
19:11, 13
16, 18
21, 22
22
31:19
Deu. 14: 8
Jos. 9:25
Jud. 6:21
20:41 A[c]
Ruth 2: 9
1 Sa. 6: 9
10:26
2 Sa. 5: 8

2 Sa. 11:10
1 Ki. 6:25 *fer*
19: 5, 7
2 Ki. 13:21
15: 5
1 Ch. 16:22
2 Ch. 3:11, 11
12 A
12 A
Job 1:11, 12
19
2: 5
4: 5
5:19
19:21
20: 6
31: 7
Ps. 103:32
104:15
143: 5
Pro. 6:29
9:17
Isa. 6: 7, 7
52:11
Jer. 1: 9
4:10, 18
12:14
31: 9[d], 32
Lam. 4:14, 15
Eze. 17:10
41: 6
42:14, 14
Dan. 8: 5, 18
9:21
10:10, 16
18
Mic. 1: 9
Hag. 2:12, 13
Zec. 2: 8, 8

[a] *pro* ἐξάπτω. [b] A προσπορεύομαι. [c] *pro* συναντάω. [d] A ἀνάπτω.

ἄπυρος.

Isaiah 13:12

ἀπφουσιώθ.

2 Ki. 15: 5 | 2 Ch. 26:21

ἀπφώθ.

Jer. 52:19[a]

[a] S σαφφώθ.

ἀπωθέω.

Jud. 6:13 A[a]
1 Sa. 12:22
2 Ki. 4:27
17:20[b]
21:14
23:27
2 Ch. 35:19
Job 18:18
22: 3 BS[1 c]
34:33
Psa. 42: 2
43:10, 24
59: 3, 12
61: 5
73: 1
76: 8
77:60, 67
87: 6, 15
88:39
93:14
94: 4—AS
107:12
118:10
Pro. 1: 8
4:24
6:20
14:32
16: 1
19:26
Isa. 37:19[d]

Jer. 2:36
4:30
6:19
7:29
23: 2 A[e]
17
Lam. 2: 7
3:17, 30
44, 53
5:22, 22
Eze. 5: 6, 11
11:16
16:45, 45
19: 5[f]
20:13, 16
24
21:10 AB[g]
13
43: 9
Hos. 4: 6, 6
9:17
Amos 2: 4
5:21
Jon. 2: 5
Mic. 2: 6
4: 6 A[e], 6
7
7:11 A[h]
Zeph. 3:19

[a] pro ἐκρίπτω. [b] A ἀποικίζω.
[c] pro ἁπλόω. [d] AS ἀπόλλυμι.
[e] pro ἐξωθέω. [f] A ἀποσπάω.
[g] pro ἀποτίθημι.
[h] pro ἀποτρίβω.

ἀπώλεια.

Exo. 22: 9
Lev. 6: 3, 4
Nu. 20: 3
Deu. 4:26
7:23
8:19
12: 2
22: 3
30:18
32:35
1 Ch. 21:17
Est. 7: 4
8: 6
Job 11:20[a]
20: 5, 28
21:30
26: 6[b]
27: 7
28:22
30:12
31: 3
41:13
Psa. 87:12
Pro. 1:26
6:15, 32
10:11, 24
11: 4, 6[c]
10+
AB[b] S[2]
13: 1, 15

Pro. 15:11
16:26, 26
24:23
27:20
28:28
Isa. 14:23
22: 5
33: 2
34: 5[d], 12
47:11, 11
54:16
57: 4
Jer. 12:11, 17
18:17
26:21
30: 2, 7, 10
51:12
Eze. 25: 7
26:16, 21
27:36
28: 7, 19
29: 9, 10
12
31:11
32:15
Dan. 2: 5
3:29
8:25
Hos. 10:14
Obad. 12, 13

[a] A ἀπόλλυμι. [b] S[1] πτωχεία.
[c] A ἀβουλία, S[2] ἀσέβεια. [d] S[1] γῆ.

ἀπῶρυξ.

Ezekiel 17: 6

ἀπωσμός.

Lamentations 1: 7

ἆρα.

Gen. 18:13
26: 9
37:10

Neh. 4: 2, 2
Job 27: 8
&c., &c.

ἀρά.

Gen. 24:41
26:28
Nu. 5:21, 21
23, 27
Deu. 29:12, 14
19, 20
21, 27 A[a]
30: 7
1 Ki. 8:31
2 Ch. 6:22
Neh. 10:29
Psa. 9:28

Psa. 13: 3—A
58:13
Pro. 12:23
24:51 A[1 b]
26: 2
Isa. 24: 6
Jer. 49:18
51:22
Eze. 17:13, 16
Hos. 4: 2
Zec. 5: 3

[a] pro κατάρα. [b] pro ᾄδης.

ἄραβα.

Jeremiah 52: 7

ἀράομαι.

Nu. 22: 6[a], 11
23: 7, 8, 8[b]
Jos. 24: 9
Jud. 17: 2[c]

1 Sa. 14:24
1 Ki. 8:31[d]
2 Ch. 6:22, 22

[a] A καταράομαι. [b] B καταρ—
[c] A ἐξορκίζω. [d] B αἴρω.

ἀραρέθ.

Jer. 28:27 A[a]

[a] pro αἴρω.

ἀραφώθ.

2 Samuel 17:19

ἀράχνη.

Job 8:14
27:18
Psa. 38:12

Psa. 89: 9
Isa. 59: 5

ἀργέω.

Ezr. 4:24, 24
Ecc. 12: 3

ἀργία, —γεία.

Exo. 21:19
2 Ki. 2:24+A

Ecc. 10:18
Isa. 1:13

ἀργός.

1 Kings 6:11

ἀργύρεος, —οῦς.

Gen. 24:53
44: 2, 4
Exo. 3:22
11: 2
12:35
20:23
26:19, 21
25, 32
27:10, 17 A[a]
17
37: 4, 15
17
38:20, 20
Nu. 7:13, 13
19, 19
25, 25
31, 31
37, 37
43, 43
49, 49
55, 55
61, 61
67, 67
73, 73
79, 79
84
84—A
86+A[2]

Nu. 10: 2
2 Sa. 8:10
1 Ki. 10:25+A
15:15
2 Ki. 12:13, 13
25:15
1 Ch. 18:10
28:14, 16
17
2 Ch. 9:24
24:14
Ezra 1: 9, 10
11
5:14
6: 5
8:26
Neh. 7:71 S[3 a]
Est. 1: 6, 6, 7
Cant. 8: 9
Isa. 2:20
31: 7
Jer. 52:19, 19
Dan. 2:32
5: 2, 3, 4
23
Hos. 2: 8
Zec. 11:12, 13

[a] pro ἀργύριον.

ἀργύριον.

Gen. 13: 2
23: 9, 13
15, 16
16
24:35

Gen. 31:15
42:25, 27
28, 35
35
43:11, 11

Gen. 43:14, 17
20, 20
21, 21
22
44: 1, 8, 8
47:14, 14
15, 15
16, 18
Exo. 21:11, 21
32, 34
35
22: 7, 17
25
25: 3
27:11[a]
17[b]
30:16
31: 4
35: 5, 24
32
37:15, 15
17
17+AB
18—AB
39: 2, 4
Lev. 5:15, 18
22:11
25:37, 50
51
27: 3, 6, 7
15, 16
18, 19
Nu. 3:48, 49
50
7:85
22:18
24:13
31:22
Deu. 2: 6, 6, 28
28
7:25
8:13
14:24, 24
25
17:17
21:14
22:29
23:19
29:17
Jos. 6:19, 24
7:21, 21
22
22: 8
Jud. 5:19
9: 4
16: 5, 18
17: 2, 2, 3, 3
4, 4, 10
1 Sa. 2:36
9: 8
2 Sa. 8:11
18:11, 12
21: 4
24:24
1 Ki. 7:37
10:21, 22
27, 29
29—A
15:18, 19
16:24
20: 2, 6, 15
21: 3, 5, 7
39
2 Ki. 5: 5, 22
23
23—B
26
6:25, 25
7: 8
12: 4, 4
4—A
4, 7, 8
9, 10
10, 11
13, 15
16
16—A
18 A[c]
14:14
15:19, 20

2 Ki. 15:20+A
16: 8
18:14, 15
20:13
22: 4, 7, 9
23:33, 35
35, 35
1 Ch. 18:11
19: 6
21:22, 24
22:14, 16
29: 2, 3, 4
5—AB
5—AB
7
2 Ch. 1:15, 17
17—A
2: 7, 14
5: 1
9:14, 20
21, 27
15:18
16: 2, 3
17:11
21: 3
24: 5, 11
11, 14
25: 6, 24
27: 5
32:27
34: 9, 14
16, 17
36: 3, 4
4—A
4
Ezra 1: 4, 6
2:69
3: 7
7:15, 16
18, 22
8:17, 17
25, 26
28, 30
33
Neh. 5: 4, 10
11, 15
7:71
71—AB[d]
Est. 3: 9, 11
4: 7+S[3]
Job 3:15
22:25
27:16
28: 1, 15
Psa. 11: 7
14: 5
65:10
67:31
104:37
113:12
118:72
134:15
Pro. 2: 4
3:14
7:20
8:10
10+A
19
16:16
22: 1
25: 4
26:23
27:21[e]
Ecc. 2: 8
5: 9, 9
7:13
10:19[f]
12: 6
Cant. 1:11
3:10
8:11—A
Isa. 1:22
2: 7
13:17
39: 2
43:24
46: 6
48:10
52: 3
55: 1, 1, 2

Isa. 60:17
Jer. 6:30
10: 4, 9, 9
39: 9, 10
25, 44
Lam. 4: 1
5: 4—AB
Eze. 7:19
19+A
16:13[g], 17
18: 8
22:18, 22
27:12
28: 4, 13
38:13
Dan. 11: 8
43 A[h]
Hos. 2: 8

Hos. 3: 2
8: 4
9: 6
13: 2
Joel 3: 5
Amos 2: 6
8: 6
Mic. 3:11
Nah. 2: 9
Hab. 2:19
Zeph. 1:11, 18
Hag. 2: 8
Zec. 6:11
9: 3
13: 9
14:14
Mal. 3: 3, 3

[a] B ἄργυρος. [b] A ἀργυροῦς.
[c] pro χρυσίον. [d] S[3] ἀργυροῦς.
[e] BS ἄργυρος. [f] C ἄργυρος.
[g] A ἄργυρος. [h] pro ἄργυρος.

ἀργυροκοπέω.

Jeremiah 6:29

ἀργυροκόπος.

Jud. 17: 4[a]
Jer. 6:29

[a] A χωνευτής.

ἄργυρος.

Exo. 27:11 B[a]
Pro. 10:20
17: 3
27:21 BS[a]
Ecc. 10:19 C[a]
Isa. 60: 9

Eze. 16:13 A[a]
22:20
Dan. 2:35
39+A
45
11:38, 43[b]

[a] pro ἀργύριον. [b] A ἀργύριον.

ἀργυρώνητος.

Gen. 17:12, 13
23, 27

Exo. 12:44

ἄρδην.

1 Ki. 7:31
Mal. 4: 5

ἀρεσκεία.

Proverbs 29:48

ἀρέσκω.

Gen. 19: 8
20:15
34:18
41:37
Lev. 10:20
Nu. 22:34 AB[a]
23:27
36: 6
Deu. 1:23
23:16
Jos. 9:31
17:16[b]
22:30, 33
24:15
Jud. 10:15 A[c]
14: 1+A
3 A[d]
7 A[e]
21:14
1 Sa. 18: 5 A
2 Sa. 3:19, 36

2 Sa. 19: 4
1 Ki. 3:10
9:12
12: p24/62
l67
20: 2
2 Ch. 30: 4
Est. 1:21
2: 4, 4, 9
5:13, 14
Job 31:10
Psa. 68:32
Pro. 12:21
24:18
Isa. 51:13 A[f]
59:15
Jer. 18: 4
Dan. 3:32
4:24
6: 1
Mal. 3: 4

[a] pro ἀρκέω. [b] A ἀρκέω.
[c] pro ἀγαθόω. [d] pro εὐθύς.
[e] pro εὐθύνω. [f] pro αἴρω.

ἀρεστός.

Gen. 3: 6
16: 6
Exo. 15:26
Lev. 10:19
Deu. 6:18
12: 8, 25

Deu. 12:28
13:18
21: 9
2 Ch. 12:10+A
Ezra 7:18
10:11

Neh. 9:24, 37
Pro. 21: 3
Isa. 38: 3
Jer. 9:14[a]
16:12[a]
18:12

[a] A ἐραστός.

ἀρετή.

Pro. 1: 7 A[a]
Isa. 42: 8, 12
43:21
63: 7
Isa. 63: 7+B[1]
Hab. 3: 3
Zec. 6:13

[a] pro ἀρχή.

ἀρετίζω.

1 Samuel 25:35

[ἀρήν] ἀρνός.

Gen. 30:32, 33
35
Exo. 12: 5[a]
23:19
34:26
Lev. 1:10
3: 7
Deu. 14:20
32:14
1 Sa. 7: 9
2 Sa. 6:13
1 Ki. 1: 9, 19
25
2 Ki. 3: 4—A
1 Ch. 29:21
Job 31:20 A[b]
Pro. 27:24
Isa. 1:11
5:17
11: 6
34: 6+AS
40:11
65:25
Jer. 28:40
Mic. 5: 7
6: 7 A[c]

[a] A ἀμνός. [b] pro ἀμνός.
[c] pro χίμαρος.

ἄρθρον.

Job 17:11

ἀριήλ.

1 Ch. 11:22
Isa. 29: 2
Eze. 43:15, 15
16

ἀριθμέω.

Gen. 13:16 A[a]
14:14
15: 5
16:10
32:12
41:49
Lev. 23:15, 16
Nu. 2: 4 A[b]
6 A[b]
11 A[b]
13 A[b]
15 A[b]
16 A[b]
24 A[b]
26 A[b]
31 A[b]
3:15 A[b]
16 A[b]
2 Sa. 24: 1, 10
1 Ki. 3: 8
2 Ki. 12:10
1 Ch. 21: 1, 2, 6
17
23: 3
27:24
2 Ch. 2:17
5: 6
25: 5
Ezra 1: 8
Job 3: 6
14:16
28:26
38:37
39: 2
Ps. 146: 4
Pro. 8:21
Ecc. 1:15
Isa. 33:18
Jer. 40:13

[a] pro ἐξαριθμέω.
[b] pro ἐπισκέπτομαι.

ἀριθμητός.

Job 14: 5
15:20
16:22
Job 21:33 A[a]
36:26 S[b]
27[c]

[a] pro ἀναρίθμητος.
[b] pro ἀριθμός. [c] S[1] ἀναρίθμητος.

ἀριθμός.

Gen. 34:30
41:49
Exo. 12: 4
16:16
23:26
Lev. 25:15
15—A
16
27:32
Nu. 1: 2, 18
20, 22
24, 26
28, 30
32, 34
Nu. 1:36, 38
40, 42
49
3:22
22 A[a]
28, 34
40, 43
9:20
14:34
15:12, 12
26:53
29:18, 21
24, 27
30, 33
Nu. 29:37
31:36
Deu. 4:27
25: 3
26: 5
28:62
32: 8
33: 6
Jos. 4: 5
Jud. 6: 5
7: 6, 12
11:33—A
21:23
1 Sa. 6: 4, 18
27: 7
2 Sa. 2:15
21:20
24: 2, 9
1 Ki. 7:40
18:31
1 Ch. 7: 2, 5, 7
9, 40
40—A
9:28
28—BS
11:11
16:19
21: 2, 5
22: 4, 16
23: 3, 24
27, 31
25: 1, 7
27: 1, 23
24
2 Ch. 2:17
12: 3
17:14
26:11, 11
12
29:32
2 Ch. 35: 7
Ezra 1: 9
2: 2
3: 4
6:17
8:34
Est. 9:11
Job 1: 5[b]
5: 9
9:10
21:21
34:24
36:26[c]
38:21
Psa. 38: 5
39: 6, 13
103:25
104:12, 34
146: 5
150: p 6
Ecc. 2: 3
5:17
7: 1—C
Cant. 6: 7
Isa. 2: 7, 7
10:19
34: 2, 16
40:26
Jer. 2:28, 28
32
11:13, 13
26:23
51:28
Eze. 4: 4, 5, 9
5: 3
12:16
20:37
Dan. 9: 2
Hos. 1:10

[a] pro ἐπίσκεψις.
[b] S[1] καθαρισμός. [c] S ἀριθμητός.

ἀριστάω.

Gen. 43:24
1 Sa. 14:24
1 Ki. 13: 7

ἀριστερός.

Gen. 13: 9, 9
14:15
24:49
48:13, 13
14
Lev. 14:15, 16
26, 27
Nu. 22:26
Deu. 2:27
5:32
17:11, 20
28:14
Jos. 1: 7
19:28+A
Jud. 3:21
5:26
7:20
16:29
1 Sa. 6:12
2 Sa. 2:19, 21
14:19
1 Ki. (3) 42
7:25, 35
2 Ki. 22: 2
23: 8
1 Ch. 6:44
12: 2
2 Ch. 3:17
4: 6, 7
18:18
23:10
34: 2
Neh. 8: 4[a]
Job 23: 9
Pro. 3:16
4:27, 27
Ecc. 10: 2
Isa. 9:20
30:21
54: 3
Eze. 1:10
4: 4
39: 3
Dan. 12: 7
Jon. 4:11

[a] A εὐώνυμος.

ἄριστον

2 Sa. 24:15
1 Ki. (3) p 46

ἀριώθ.

2 Kings 4:39

ἀρκεύθινος.

1 Ki. 6:29
2 Ch. 2: 8

ἄρκευθος.

1 Ki. 6:30+A
Hos. 14: 8

ἀρκέω.

Exo. 12: 4
Nu. 11:22, 22
Nu. 22:34[a]
Jos. 17:16 A[b]
1 Ki. 8:27
2 Ch. 6:18
Pro. 24:50, 51

[a] AB ἀρέσκω. [b] pro ἀρέσκω.

ἄρκος.

Jud. 1:35
1 Sa. 17:34, 36
37
2 Sa. 17: 8
2 Ki. 2:24
Isa. 11: 7
Isa. 59:11
Lam. 3:10
Dan. 7: 5
Hos. 13: 8
Amos 5:19—A[1]

ἀρκτοῦρος.

Job 9: 9

ἅρμα.

Gen. 41:43
46:29
50: 9
Exo. 14: 6, 7, 9
17, 18
23, 25
26, 28
15: 4, 19
Deu. 11: 4
Jos. 11: 4, 6, 9
24: 6
Jud. 4: 3, 7, 13
13, 15
15, 16
5:28, 28
1 Sa. 8:11, 11
12
13: 5
15:12
2 Sa. 1: 6
8: 4 *ter*
10:18
15: 1
1 Ki. 1: 5
(3) p 46
4:21
(26) A
7:19
10: p 22 *bis*
26+A
26, 26
29
12:18+A
p 24 l 10
l 74
18:44
21: 1, 21
25, 25
33
22:31, 32
33, 35
35, 35
38 A[a]
2 Ki. 2:11, 12
5: 9, 21
26
6:14, 15
17
7: 6
8:21, 21
9:21, 21
27
28—A
10: 2, 15
16
2 Ki. 13: 7, 14
18:24
19:23
23:11
1 Ch. 18: 4 *ter*
19: 6
7+BS
7, 18
28:18
2 Ch. 1:14 *ter*
17
8: 6, 9
9:25, 25
10:18
12: 3
14: 9
18:30, 31
32, 34
21: 9
35:24, 24
Psa. 19: 8
67:18
Cant. 1: 9
6:11
Isa. 2: 7
5:28
22: 7, 18
31: 1
37:24
43:17
66:15, 20
Jer. 4:13
6:23
17:25
22: 4
26: 9
27:36
28:22
29: 3
Eze. 23:24
26: 7, 10
27:20
43: 3
Dan. 11:40
Hos. 1: 7+A
10:13 A[b]
Joel 2: 5
Mic. 1:13
5:10
Nah. 2: 4, 5
3: 2
Hag. 2:22
Zec. 6: 1, 2, 2
3, 3
9:10[c]

[a] pro αἷμα. [b] pro ἁμάρτημα.
[c] S[1] τόξον.

ἁρμόζω.

2 Sa. 6: 5, 14
Ps. 150: p 6
Pro. 8:30
17: 7
Pro. 19:14
25:11+S[2]
Nah. 3: 8

ἁρμονία.

Eze. 23:42
Eze. 37: 7

ἀρνέομαι.

Genesis 18:15

ἀρνίον.

Ps. 113: 4
6—S[1]
Jer. 11:19
27:45

ἀρνός *vide* ἀρήν.

ἀροτήρ.

Isaiah 61: 5

ἀροτρίασις.

Genesis 45: 6

ἀροτριάω, —αζω.

Deu. 22:10
Jud. 14:18[a]
1 Ki. 19:19
Job 1:14
4: 8
Isa. 7:25, 25
28:24, 24
45: 9, 9
Jer. 33:18
Mic. 3:12

[a] A καταδαμάζω.

ἄροτρον.

1 Ch. 21:23
Isa. 2: 4
Joel 3:10
Mic. 4: 3

ἀροτρόπους.

Judges 3:31

ἄρουρα.

Gen. 21:33
1 Sa. 22: 6
1 Sa. 31:13

ἁρπαγή.

Lev. 6: 2
Ecc. 5: 7
Isa. 3:14
Isa. 10: 2ABS[a]
Nah. 2:12

[a] pro διαρπαγή.

ἅρπαγμα.

Lev. 6: 4
Job 29:17
Psa. 61:11
Isa. 42:22
61: 8
Eze. 18: 7, 12
Eze. 18:16, 18
19: 3, 6
22:25, 27
29
33:15
Mal. 1:13

ἁρπάζω.

Gen. 37:33
Lev. 6: 4
19:13
Deu. 28:31
Jud. 21:21, 23[a]
2 Sa. 23:21—A
Job 20:19
24: 2, 9, 19
Psa. 7: 3
9:30, 30
21:14
49:22
68: 5
Ps. 103:21
Isa. 10: 2
Eze. 18: 7, 12
16, 18
19: 3, 6
22:25, 27
Hos. 5:14
6: 1
Amos 1:11
3: 4
Mic. 3: 2
5: 8
Nah. 2:12

[a] A διαρπάζω.

ἅρπαξ.

Genesis 49:27

ἀρραβών.

Genesis 38:17, 18, 20

ἄρριζος.

Job 31: 8

ἀρρωστέω.

2 Sa. 12:15
13: 2, 6
1 Ki. 12: p 24 l 24
14: 1 A
17:17
2 Ki. 1: 2
2 Ki. 8: 7, 29
13:14
20: 1, 12
2 Ch. 22: 6
32:24

ἀρρωστία.

1 Ki. 12: p 24 l 24
l 27
17:17
2 Ki. 1: 2
8: 8, 9
13:14

Psa. 40: 4
Ecc. 5:12, 15
Ecc. 5:16
6: 2

ἄρρωστος.

1 Ki. 14: 5 A
Mal. 1: 8

ἄρσεν, -σην.

Gen. 1:27
5: 2
6:19, 20
7: 2, 2, 3
3,9,15
16
17:14, 23
34:24
Exo. 1:16, 17
18, 22
2: 2
12: 5
Lev. 1: 3, 10
3: 1, 6
4:23
6:29, 26
12: 2, 7
15:33
Lev. 18:22
20:13
22:19
27: 3, 5, 6
7
Nu. 1: 3
3:40
31:17, 18
Jos. 17: 2
Jud. 21:11[a], 11
12
Job 3: 3
Isa. 26:14
66: 7
Jer. 20:15
37: 6
Mal. 1.14
[a] A ἀρσενικός.

ἀρσενικός.

Gen. 17:10, 12
34:15, 22
25
Exo. 12:48
13:12, 12
15
23:17
34:19, 23
Lev. 6:18
Nu. 1:18, 20
22, 24
26, 28
30, 32
34, 36
38, 10
42
3:15, 22
Nu. 3:28, 34
39, 43
5: 3
18:10
26:62
31: 7, 17
Deu. 4:16
15:19
16:16
20:13
Jud. 21:11 A[a]
1 Ki. 11:15, 16
2 Ch. 31:16, 19
Ezra 8: 4
5—B
6 *to* 14
Eze. 16:17
[a] *pro* ἄρσεν.

ἄρσην *vide* ἄρσεν.

ἄρσις.

2 Sa. 11: 8
19:42
1 Ki. (3) *p* 1—A
p 46
5:15
1 Ki. 11:28
12:*p* 24/9
l 11
2 Ki. 8: 9
Psa. 80: 7

ἀρτάβη.

Isaiah 5:10

ἀρτήρ.

Nehemiah 4:17

ἄρτι.

2 Samuel 15:37—AB

ἀρτίως.

2 Samuel 15:34

ἀρτοκοπικός.

1 Chronicles 16: 3

ἀρτός (*ab* αἴρω).

Nu. 4:27 A[a]
Nu. 4:27
[a] *pro* ἔργον,

ἄρτος.

Gen. 3:19
14:18
18: 5
21:14
24:33
25:34
27:17
28:20
37 25
39 6
Gen. 41:54, 55
43:15, 30
31
45:23
47:15, 16
17, 17
19
49:20
Exo. 2:20
16: 3, 4, 8
Exo. 16:12, 15
29, 32
18:12
23:25
25:29
29: 2, 23
32, 34
34:28
39:18
40:21
Lev. 2: 4
7: 2, 3
8:26, 26
31, 32
22: 7, 11[a]
11, 13
23:14, 17
17, 18
19, 20
24: 5,5,6,7
26: 5, 26
26, 26
Nu. 4: 7
6:15, 19
13:19, 20
21 + A
21: 5, 5
Deu. 8: 3, 9
9: 9, 18
10:18
16: 3
23: 4
29: 6
Jos. 9:11, 18
Jud. 5: 8 + A
6:20 + A
7:13
8: 5,6,15
13:16
19: 5
8 + A
19
Ruth 1: 6
2:14
1 Sa. 1:24
2: 5
36 + A
36
9: 7
10: 3, 4
14:24, 24
28
16:20
17:17 A
20:34
21: 3, 4, 4
6 *qtr*
22:13
25:11, 18
28:20, 22
30:11, 12
2 Sa. 3:29, 35
35
6:19
9: 7, 10
10[b], 10
12: 3, 17
20, 20
21
16: 1, 2
1 Ki. 5: 9
7:34
11:18
12:*p* 24/30
ll 31,38
13: 8,9,15
16, 17
18, 19
22, 22
23
14: 3 A
17: 6
6 + A
11
18: 4, 13
20: 4, 5, 7
22:27
2 Ki. 4:8, 42 + A
42
6:22
18:32
25: 3, 29
1 Ch. 9:32
16: 3
23:29
2 Ch. 4:19
13:11
18:26
Ezra 10: 6
Neh. 5:15, 18
9:15
10:33
13: 2
Job 6: 6—S[1]
24: 5
28: 5
Psa. 13: 4
36:25
40:10
41: 4
77:20, 24
25
79: 6
101: 5, 10
103:14, 15
104:16[c], 40
126: 2
131:15
Pro. 6:26
9: 5, 17
12: 9, 11
20:13[c]
22: 9
28:19, 21
Ecc. 9: 7, 11
10:19
11: 1
Cant. 5: 1
Isa. 3: 1, 7
4: 1
21:14
28:28
30:20
23—S[1]
33:16
36:17
44:15, 16
19
55:10
58: 7, 10
65:25
Jer. 5:17—S[1d]
11:19
16: 7
44:12 + S[3]
21, 21
45: 9
48: 1
49:14—S[1]
51:17
52: 6, 33
Lam. 1:11—S
4: 4
5: 9
Eze. 4: 9, 15
16, 16
17
5:16
12:18, 19
13:19
14:13
16:19, 49
18: 7[e], 16
24:17, 22
44: 3, 7
48:18
Dan. 10: 3
Hos. 2: 5
9: 4, 4
Amos 4: 6
8:11
Hag. 2:12
Mal. 1: 7

[a] A ἔργον.
[b] A αὐτός.
[c] S[1] αὐτός
[d] S[2] ἀγρός.
[e] A ἀνήρ.

ἀρχαῖος.

Jud. 5:21[a]
1 Sa. 24:14
1 Ki. (3) 1
4:26
Job 21:28 A[b]
Psa. 43: 2
76: 6
78: 8
88:50
138: 5[c]
Ps. 142: 5
Isa. 22: 9, 11
23:16
25: 1
37:26
41: 4 S[d]
43:18
Lam. 1: 7
2:17
Eze. 21:21
[a] A καδησείμ.
[b] *pro* ἄρχων.
[c] S[1] δίκαιος.
[d] *pro* ἀρχή.

ἀρχή.

Gen. 1: 1, 16
16
2:10
10:10
13: 4[a]
40:13, 13
20, 20
21
41:13, 21
43:17, 19
49: 3
Exo. 6:25
12: 2
34:22
22 B[b]
36:24
Nu. 1: 2
4:22
24:20
26: 2
Deu. 11:12
17:18, 20
21:17
33:15, 27
Jos. 24: 2
Jud. 7:11[c], 16
17[d], 19[e]
19[e], 20
9:34, 37
43
44 A[f]
44
20:18—A
18—A
Ruth 1:22
1 Sa. 11:11
13:17, 17
18, 18
2 Sa. 7:10
14:26
17: 9
21: 9, 10
1 Ki. 7:21, 21
20: 9
12—B[g]
2 Ki. 17:25
1 Ch. 12:32 + A
16: 7
17: 9
26:10
29:12
2 Ch. 13:12
23: 8
Ezra 4: 6
8:18
9: 2—B
Neh. 9:17
12:46
Job 1:17 AS[2h]
37: 2—A
40:14
Psa. 73: 2
76:12
77: 2
101:26
109: 3
110:10
118:152
160
136: 6
138:17
Pro. 1: 7, 7[i]
Pro. 8:22
23—A
9:10
16: 1,5,12
17:14
Ecc. 3:11
5:10[k]
7: 9
10:13
Cant. 4: 8
Isa. 1:26
2: 6
9: 6,7,14
10:10[m]
19:11, 15
22:11
23: 7
40:21
41: 4[n], 26
27
42: 9, 10,
43: 9, 13
44: 8
45:21
48: 8, 16
51: 9
63:16, 19
Jer. 2: 3
13:21
22: 6
25:14
26: 1
28:58
30: 2
33: 1
37:20 + A
41: 1
Lam. 2:19, 19
4: 1
Eze. 10:11
16:25, 31
55
55 + A
55
21:20 + A
20, 20
21
29:14, 15
31: 3, 10
14
36:11
42:10, 12
43:14
48: 1,208[o]
Dan. 6:26
7:12, 14
26, 27
8: 1
9:21, 23
11:19 A[p]
41
Hos. 1: 2, 11
Amos 6: 1, 7
Obad. 20
Mic. 3: 1
4: 8
5: 2
Nah. 1: 6
3: 8, 10
Hab. 1:12
Zec. 12: 7
Mal. 3: 8 S[1o]

[a] A σκηνή.
[b] *pro* ἑορτή.
[c] A μέρος.
[d] A μέσος.
[e] A ἄρχω.
[f] *pro* ἀρχηγός.
[g] A κεφαλή.
[h] *pro* κεφαλή.
[i] A ἀρετή.
[k] S[2] ἀλλ' η.
[m] AS χώρα.
[n] S ἀρχαῖος.
[o] *pro* ἀπαρχή.
[p] *pro* ἰσχύς.

ἀρχηγός.

Exo. 6:14
Nu. 10: 4
13: 3, 4
14: 4
16: 2
24:17
25: 4
Deu. 33:21
Jud. 5: 2 + A
15—A
9:44[b]
11: 6[b], 11[b]
1 Ch. 5:24
1 Ch. 8:28 A[c]
12:20
26:26
2 Ch. 23:14
Neh. 2: 9
7:70, 71
11:16 A
17 + S[3]
Isa. 3: 6, 7, 7
30: 4
Jer. 3: 4
Lam. 2:10
Mic. 1:13
[a] A ἀρχή.
[b] A ἡγέομαι.
[c] *pro* ἄρχων.

ἀρχῆθεν.

2 Kings 19:25 + A

ἀρχιδεσμοφύλαξ.

Gen. 39:21, 22
23
Gen. 40: 3 + A
41:10 A[a]
[a] *pro* ἀρχιμάγειρος.

ἀρχιδεσμώτης.

Genesis 40: 4

ἀρχιερεύς.

Lev. 4: 3
Jos. 22:13
24:33[a]
1 Ki. 1:25 A[b]
1 Ch. 15:14 S[ab]
[a] A ἱερεύς.
[b] *pro* ἱερεύς.

ἀρχιεταῖρος.

2 Sa. 15:32
37 A[a]
2 Sa. 16:16
[a] *pro* ἑταῖρος.

ἀρχιευνοῦχος.

Dan. 1: 3, 7, 8
9, 10
Dan. 1:11, 18

ἀρχιμάγειρος.

Gen. 37:36
39: 1
41:10[a], 12
2 Ki. 25: 8
9—A
10 + A
11, 12
15, 18
2 Ki. 25:20
Jer. 47: 1, 2, 5
48:10
52:12, 14
16, 19
24, 26
Dan. 2:14
[a] A ἀρχιδεσμοφύλαξ.

ἀρχιοινοχοεία.

Genesis 40:13

ἀρχιοινοχόος.

Gen. 40: 1, 2, 5
9
20 A[a]
Gen. 40:21, 23
41: 9
[a] *pro* οἰνοχόος.

ἀρχιπατριώτης.

Joshua 21: 1

ἀρχισιτοποιός.

Gen. 40: 1, 2, 5
16
20 A[a]
Gen. 40:22
41:10
[a] *pro* σιτοποιός

ἀρχιστράτηγος.

Gen. 21:22, 32
26:26
Jos. 5:14, 15
1 Sa. 12: 9
1 Sa. 14:50
26: 5
2 Sa. 2: 8
1 Ki. 2:22, 32

1 Ki. 2:32—A
(3) p 46
1 Ch. 19:16, 18
1 Ch. 27:34
Dan. 8:11

ἀρχισωματοφύλαξ.

1 Sa. 28: 2
Est. 2:21

ἀρχιτεκτονέω.

Exo. 31: 4
35:32
Exo. 37:21

ἀρχιτεκτονία.

Exodus 35:32, 35

ἀρχιτέκτων.

Isaiah 3: 3

ἀρχίφυλος.

Deu. 29:10
Jos. 21: 1

ἄρχω.

Gen. 1:14+A
18, 26
28
2: 3
4: 7
6: 1
9:20
10: 8
11: 6
18:27
21: 2
41:54
44:12
45:26
Exo. 4:10
Nu. 10:46
Deu. 1: 5
2:31
3:24
15: 6, 6
16: 9, 9
28:12, 12
Jos. 3: 7
12: 5
17:12
Jud. 1:27, 35
5: 2+A
7:19 A[a]
8:22, 23
23, 23
9: 2 A[b]
9 A[c]
11 A[c]
13 A[c]
22
10:18
13: 5, 25
16:19, 22
17:11
19: 6 A[d]
20:31, 39
40+A
1 Sa. 3: 2, 12
9:17
10: 1
14:35
21:11 A[e]
22:14, 15
2 Sa. 7:29
2 Sa. 18:14
24:15
1 Ki. (3) p 46
2 Ki. 10:32
15:37
1 Ch. 1:10
17:27
27:24
29:12
2 Ch. 3: 1, 2, 3
20:22[f]
29:17, 27
27
31: 7, 10
21
34: 3, 3
36: 4—A
Ezra 3: 6, 8
5: 2
Neh. 4: 7
Est. 6:13
Job 6: 4, 9
20+S[2]
13:15
36:24
42: p 18
Psa. 76:11
Pro. 19:10
22: 7
29: 2
Isa. 11:10
14: 9
22:22—S[1]
32: 1, 5
40:23
63:19
Jer. 22:30
32:15
Eze. 9: 6, 6
13: 6
Dan. 5: 7, 16
11:10 A[g]
Hos. 5:11
7: 5
8: 4
Jon. 3: 4
Mic. 1:12
6:13

[a] pro ἀρχή. [b] pro κυριεύω.
[c] pro κινέω. [d] pro ἄγω.
[e] pro ἐξάρχω. [f] A ἐνάρχομαι.
[g] pro ἔρχομαι.

ἄρχων, ἄρχουσα.

Gen. 12:15
14: 7
25:16
27:29
31: 2
42: 6
45: 8
47: 5
49:10, 20
Exo. 2:14
Exo. 15:15
16:22
22:28
34:31
35:27
Lev. 4:22
18:21
20: 2, 3, 4
5
Nu. 1: 4, 16
Nu. 1:44
44 A[2][a]
2: 3, 5, 7
10, 12
14, 18
20, 22
25, 27
29
3:24, 30
32, 32
35
4:34, 46
7: 2 ter
3, 10
10, 11
11, 12
18, 24
30, 36
42, 48
54, 60
66, 72
78, 84
10: 4
16:13
17: 2, 6, 6
6
21:18
22: 8, 13
14, 15
18—A[1]
21[b], 35
40
23: 6, 17
21
25:14, 15
18
27: 2
30: 2
31:13, 26
32: 2[b], 28
34:18
22 to 28
36: 1, 1
Deu. 17:14, 15
15
20: 9
28:36
32:42
33: 5—A
5, 20
21
Jos. 9:20, 21
24, 24
25, 27
11:10
13:21
14: 1
17: 4
19:51
22:14 ter
30, 32
23: 2
24: 1+A
Jud. 4: 2, 7
5: 8—A
29
7:25
8: 3, 6, 14
15
15+A
16+A
9:30
10:18, 18[c]
11: 8[c], 9[c]
15:11 A[d]
16: 5[e], 8[e]
18[e], 18[f]
23[e], 27[e]
30[e]
1 Sa. 6: 4
9·16
10: 1, 2
13:14
17:55 A
18:30 A
2 Sa. 6: 2
10: 3, 16
18
18: 5—A
19: 6, 13
2 Sa. 23: 8, 18
19
24: 2, 4, 4
1 Ki. 1:19, 25
2: 5
(3) p 1
p 46 qnq
4: 2, 24
5:16
9:23 A
10: p 22
p 22—B
11: 1, 14
15, 21
12: p 24 l 9
l 71
15·20
16: 9
21:14, 15
17, 19
19+B
22:26 A[g]
31, 32
33
2 Ki. 4:13
5: 1
8:21
9: 5 ter
10: 1
23: 8
24:12, 14
25:19, 23
26
1 Ch. 2:10
4:38, 42
5: 6, 7, 15
24
7: 2, 3, 7
9, 11
40, 40
8: 6, 10
13, 28
28[h]
9: 9, 13
17, 33
34, 34
11: 6, 6, 10
15, 20
21, 42
12: 3, 9, 14
18, 18
23, 28
34
15: 5, 6, 7
8, 9, 10
12, 16
22, 22
27
19: 3
21: 2
22:17
23: 2, 8, 9
11, 16
17, 18
19, 20
24
24: 4, 4, 5
5, 6, 6
21, 31
25: 1
26:10, 12
21, 26
31, 32
27: 1, 3, 3
4, 5
28: 1 qtr
21
29: 6, 6, 12
24
2 Ch. 1: 2, 2
5: 2
8: 9, 9, 10
11:22
12: 5, 6, 10
16: 4
17:14
18:25, 25
30, 31
32
21: 4, 9, 9
2 Ch. 22: 8
23: 2, 13
13, 20
24: 6, 10
17, 23
28:12, 14
18—A
21
29:20, 30
30: 2, 6, 12
24
31: 8, 10
32: 6, 21
31
33:11, 14
34: 8, 9
35: 8, 8, 9
15, 25
25
Ezra 1: 5, 8
2:68
3:12
4: 2, 3
5:10
7:28, 28
8: 1, 17
20, 24
25, 29
29
9: 1, 2
10: 5, 8 S[1]
14, 16
Neh. 3: 7—ABS
9, 12
14
15—ABS
16, 17
18, 19
4:16, 19
5: 7, 14
7: 2, 5
8:13
9:32, 34
38
10:14
11: 1, 3, 13
12: 7, 12
22, 23
24
26+S[3]
31, 32
41
Est. 1: 3, 11
14, 16
16, 18
21
3:12, 12
8: 9
9: 3
Job 3:15
12:21, 24
21:28[i]
29:25
34:18
Psa. 2: 2
23: 7, 9
32:10—S[1]
44:17
46:10
67:26
28—S[1]
28, 28
75:13
81: 7
82:12, 12
86: 6
104:20, 21
22
106:40
112: 8, 8
117: 9
118:23, 161
145: 3
148:11
Ecc. 10: 7, 16
17
Isa. 1:10, 23
3: 4
14—S[1]
17
Isa. 8:21
9: 6+AS[2]
6
10: 8, 12
13: 2
14: 5
16: 4
19:11, 13
13
21: 5
22: 3, 18
23
23: 8
28:14
29:10
32: 1
33:22
34: 1, 12
12+AB*S
40:23
41: 1, 25
43: 4, 9, 27
28
47: 7
49: 7, 7, 23
55: 4
60:17
Jer. 1:18
2:26
4: 9
8: 1
17:25, 25
22: 4+A
24: 1
28:59
30: 3
31: 7
32: 4
33:10, 11
12, 16
21
37:21
39:32
41:19, 21
42: 4
43:12, 12
14
19+A
21
44:14, 15
45:22, 25
27
51: 9, 17
21—S[1]
52:10
Lam. 1: 1, 6
2: 2, 6, 9
5:12
Eze. 7:27
12:10, 12
17:12—A
19: 1
22:27
26:16
27: 8, 21
28: 2, 12
30:13
31:11
32:29, 30
34:24
37:22, 24
25
38: 2, 3
39: 1, 18
Dan. 2:10, 15
48
3: 2, 3
4: 6
5:11, 29
9: 6, 8
10:13 ter
20, 20
21
11: 5, 18
12: 1
Hos. 3: 4
5:10
6:10
7: 3, 5, 16
Hos. 8:10
9:15
10:14
12:11
13:10
Amos 1:15
Amos 2: 3+A
Mic. 5: 2
7: 3
Zeph. 1: 8
3: 3
Zec. 6:10

[a] pro ἀνήρ. [b] A ἀνήρ.
[c] A κεφαλή. [d] pro κυριεύω.
[e] A σατράπης. [f] A σατραπεία.
[g] pro βασιλεύς. [h] A ἀρχηγός.
[i] A ἀρχαῖος.

ἀρωδιός.

Lev. 11:19 AB[a] [a] pro ἐρωδιός.

ἄρωμα.

2 Ki. 20:13
1 Ch. 9:29:30
2 Ch. 9: 1, 9, 9
16:14
32:27
Est. 2:12
Cant. 1:3
4:10, 16
5: 1, 13
6: 1
8:14[a]

[a] AS[1] κοίλωμα.

ἀσάλευτος.

Exo. 13:16
Deu. 6: 8
Deu. 11:18

ἄσβεστος.

Job 20:26 AS*[a] [a] pro ἄκαυστος.

ἀσβόλη.

Lamentations 4: 8

ἀσέβεια.

Deu. 9: 4+A
5[a]
18:22
19:16
25: 2—B
1 Sa. 24:12
Job 35: 8
36:18
Psa. 5:11
31: 5
64: 4
72: 6
Pro. 1:19, 31
4:17
11: 5—S[1]
6 S[2][b]
28: 4, 13
29:25
Ecc. 8: 8
Isa. 59:20
Jer. 5: 6
6: 7
Lam. 1: 5
Eze. 12:19
14: 6
16:43, 58
Eze. 18:28, 30
31
21:24, 24
22:11
23:27, 29
35, 48
48, 49
33: 9
14 A[c]
Hos. 10:13
11:12
Amos 1: 3, 6, 9
11, 13
2: 1, 4, 6
3:14
5:12
Obad. 10
Mic. 1: 5, 5, 13
3: 8
6: 7, 12
7:18
Hab. 1: 3
2: 8, 17
17
Zeph. 1: 9[a]
Mal. 2:16

[a] A ἀνομία. [b] pro ἀπώλεια.
[c] pro ἁμαρτία.

ἀσεβέω.

Lev. 20:12
Deu. 17:13
18:20
25: 2
2 Sa. 22:22
Job 9:20, 21
10: 2, 3 A[a]
7, 15
34: 8, 10
Psa. 17:22
Pro. 8:36
Ecc. 7:18
Isa. 59:13
Jer. 2: 8
Jer. 2:29—A
3:13
22: 3
Lam. 3:41
Eze. 16:27[b]
28 A[c]
18:31[d]
Dan. 9: 5+A
Hos. 7:13
8: 1
Amos 4: 4[e], 4
Zeph. 3: 4—S[1]
11

[a] pro ἀδικέω. [b] A ἐκπορνεύω.
[c] pro ἐκπορνεύω. [d] A ποιέω.
[e] A ἀνομέω.

ἀσέβημα.

Lev. 18:17
Deu. 9:27
Lam. 1:14
4:22

ἀσεβής.

Gen. 18:23, 23, 25, 23
Exo. 9:27; 23: 7
Deu. 25: 1
Jud. 20:13 A[a]
Job 3:17; 8:13, 19, 20, 22; 9:24, 29; 10: 3; 11:20; 15, 20, 34; 16:11; 18: 5; 20: 5, 5 A[a], 29; 21: 7, 14+A, 16, 17, 28; 22:18; 24: 2, 6−S[1]; 27: 7, 8, 13; 32: 3[b]; 34: 8, 8, 18, 18, 26; 36: 6, 12, 18; 38:13, 15, 30; 40: 7
Psa. 1: 1, 4, 5, 6; 9: 6, 23, 34; 10: 5; 11: 9; 16: 9, 13; 25: 5, 9; 30:18; 36:28, 35, 38; 50:15; 57:11−S
Pro. 1: 7, 10, 22, 32; 2:22; 3:25, 33, 35; 4:14, 19; 9: 7; 10: 3, 6, 7, 11, 15, 16, 20, 24, 24+A, 25−S[1], 27, 28, 30, 32; 11: 4, 7, 8, 9[c], 10+AB[e]S[2], 11, 18, 19, 23, 31; 12: 5, 6, 7, 10, 12, 12 B[d], 21, 26+A, 26; 13: 5, 6 A, 9, 19, 22, 25; 14:11, 19, 32; 15: 6, 6−S[1], 8[e], 9, 14 S[1f], 18, 28, 29; 16: 2, 4; 17:23; 18: 3, 5, 22; 19:28; 20:26; 21: 4, 7, 10, 12, 12, 22, 26, 27, 29, 30; 24:15, 16, 20, 22, 30; 25: 5, 26; 28: 1, 2, 3, 12, 24, 28; 29: 2, 7, 16
Ecc. 3:16, 17; 7:16, 22-ACS[2], 26; 8:10, 13, 14, 14; 9: 2
Isa. 5:23; 11: 4; 13:11; 24:8+ABS; 25: 2, 5; 26: 7 S[1d], 10, 10, 19; 28:21; 29: 5; 33:14; 48:22; 55: 7; 57:21
Jer. 5:26; 12: 1; 23:19; 32:17; 37:23
Eze. 20:38; 33: 8, 9, 11[g], 11, 12[h], 14
Hos. 14: 9
Hab. 1: 4, 9, 13
Zeph. 1: 3[i]

[a] pro παράνομος. [b] A[1]S[4] εὐσεβής. [c] S[1] ἁμαρτάνω, S[2] ἁμαρτωλός. [d] pro εὐσεβής. [e] S ἁμαρτωλός. [f] pro ἀπαίδευτος. [g] A ἁμαρτωλός. [h] A ἄνομος. [i] S[1] βασιλεύς.

ἀσελεισήλ.

Jer. 45:14[a]

[a] A σαλαθιήλ.

ἄσημος.

Gen. 30:42 | Job 42:11

ἄσηπτος.

Exo. 25: 5, 9, 12, 27; 26:15, 26, 32; 27: 1, 6; 30: 1, 5; 35: 7, 24; 37: 4
Deu. 10: 3
Isa. 40:20

ἀσθένεια.

Job 37: 6
Psa. 15: 4
Ecc. 12: 4
Jer. 6:21; 18:23

ἀσθενέω.

Jud. 6:15[a]; 16: 7, 11, 17; 19: 9[b]
1 Sa. 2: 4, 4, 5 B[c], 5
2 Sa. 3: 1
2 Ki. 19:26
2 Ch. 28:15
Job 4: 4; 28: 4
Psa. 9: 4; 17:37; 25: 1 AS[d]; 26: 2; 30:11; 57: 8; 67:10; 87:10; 104:37; 106:12; 108:24
Pro. 24:16
Isa. 7: 4; 28:20; 29: 4; 32: 4; 44:12
Jer. 6:21; 18:15; 26: 6, 12, 16; 27:32
Lam. 1:14; 2: 8; 5:13
Eze. 17: 6[e]; 21:15; 34: 4
Dan. 11:14, 19, 33, 34, 35, 41
Hos. 4: 5, 5; 5: 5, 5; 11: 6; 14: 1, 9
Nah. 2: 6; 3: 3
Zeph. 1: 3
Zec. 12: 8
Mal. 2: 8; 3:11

[a] A ταπεινός. [b] A κλίνω. [c] pro πεινάω. [d] pro σαλεύω. [e] A εὐθηνέω.

ἀσθενής.

Gen. 29:17
Nu. 13:19
Jud. 16:13
1 Sa. 2:10
2 Sa. 13: 4
Job 4: 3; 36:15
Psa. 6: 3
Pro. 6: 8; 21:13; 22:22; 24:37 C[a], 73, 77
Eze. 17:14; 34:20

[a] pro ταπεινός.

ἀσίδα.

Job 39:13 | Jer. 8: 7

ἀσιτέω.

Esther 4:16

ἄσιτος.

Job 24: 6

ἀσκός.

Gen. 21:14, 15, 19
Jos. 9:10, 10
Jud. 4:19
1 Sa. 10: 3; 16:20
Job 13:28; 32:19
Psa. 32: 7; 77:13; 118:83
Jer. 13:12, 12

ᾆσμα.

Nu. 21:17
Psa. 32: 3; 39: 4; 95: 1; 97: 1; 149: 1
Ecc. 7: 6; 12: 4
Cant. 1: 1, 1
Isa. 5: 1; 23:15; 26: 1

ἀσμενίζω.

1 Samuel 6:19

ἄσοφος.

Proverbs 9: 8+AS[2]

ἀσπάζομαι.

Exo. 18: 7 | Jud. 18:15 A[a]

[a] pro ἐρωτάω.

ἀσπάλαξ.

Lev. 11:30[a]

[a] A[2] σπάλαξ.

ἀσπιδίσκη.

Exo. 28:13, 14, 25; 36:23, 26

ἀσπίς.

Deu. 32:33
1 Sa. 17: 6, 45
1 Ch. 5:18
2 Ch. 9:16, 16−B
Job 15:26; 20:14; 41: 6
Psa. 13: 3−A; 57: 5; 90:13; 139: 4
Isa. 11: 8, 8; 14:29; 30: 6, 6; 59: 5
Jer. 26: 3

ἄστεγος.

Pro. 10: 8; 26:28
Isa. 58: 7

ἀστεῖος.

Exo. 2: 2
Nu. 22:32
Jud. 3:17

ἀστήρ.

Gen. 1:16; 15: 5; 22:17; 26: 4; 37: 9
Deu. 4:19
Jud. 5:20
1 Ch. 27:23
Neh. 9:23
Psa. 8: 4; 135: 9[a]
Ecc. 12: 2
Isa. 13:10; 14:13; 47:13
Jer. 8: 2; 38:35[b]
Eze. 32: 7 A[c]
Dan. 12: 3
Joel 3:15
Obad. 4 S[1c]

[a] AS[1] ἄστρον. [b] A ἄστρον. [c] pro ἄστρον.

ἀστράγαλος.

Dan. 5: 5, 24 | Zec. 11:10

ἀστραπή.

Exo. 19:16
Deu. 32:41
2 Sa. 22:15
Psa. 17:15; 76:19; 96: 4; 134: 7; 143: 6
Jer. 10:13; 28:16
Eze. 1:13
Dan. 10: 6
Nah. 2: 5
Hab. 3:11
Zec. 9:14

ἀστράπτω.

2 Sa. 22:15−AB | Psa. 143: 6

ἀστρολόγος.

Isaiah 47:13

ἄστρον.

Exo. 32:13
Nu. 24:17
Deu. 1:10; 10:22; 28:62
Neh. 4:21
Job 3: 9; 9: 7; 15:15+A; 20:25[a]; 25: 5; 38: 7
Ps. 135: 9 AS[1b]; 146: 4; 148: 3
Isa. 34: 4; 45:12
Jer. 28: 9; 38:35 A[b]
Eze. 32: 7[c]
Dan. 8:10
Joel 2:10
Amos 5:26
Obad. 4[d]
Nah. 3:16−S[1]

[a] A ἀνήρ. [b] pro ἀστήρ. [c] A ἀστήρ. [d] S[1] ἀστήρ.

ἄσυλος.

Proverbs 22:23

ἀσύμφορος.

Proverbs 25:20

ἀσυνετέω.

Psa. 118:158[a]

[a] S[1] ἀσυνθετέω.

ἀσύνετος.

Deu. 32:21
Job 13: 2
Psa. 75: 6; 91: 7

ἀσυνθεσία.

Ezra 9: 2, 4; 10: 6
Jer. 3: 7[a]

[a] S ἀθεσία.

ἀσυνθετέω.

Ezra 10: 2, 10
Neh. 1: 8[a]; 13:27
Psa. 72:15; 77:57[b]; 118:158 S[1c]

[a] S[1] ἀθετέω. [b] S[2] ἀθετέω. [c] pro ἀσυνετέω.

ἀσύνθετος.

Jeremiah 3: 7, 8, 10, 11

ἀσφάλεια.

Lev. 26: 5
Deu. 12:10
Ps. 103: 5
Pro. 8:14; 11:15; 28:17
Isa. 8:15; 18: 4; 34:15

ἀσφαλής.

Pro. 3:18-BS[1]; 8:28; 15: 7

ἀσφαλίζω.

Neh. 3:15 ABS | Isa. 41:10

ἀσφαλτοπίσσα.

Exodus 2: 3

ἄσφαλτος.

Gen. 6:14; 11: 3; 14:10

ἀσφαλτόω.

Genesis 6:14

ἀσφαλῶς.

Genesis 34:25

ἀσχημονέω.

Deu. 25: 3
Eze. 16: 7, 22; 16:39; 23:29 A[a]

[a] pro αἰσχύνω.

ἀσχημοσύνη.

Exo. 20:26; 22:27; 28:38
Lev. 18: 6, 7, 7, 7, 8, 8, 9, 9, 10, 10, 10, 11, 11, 12, 13−A, 14, 15, 15, 16, 16[a], 17, 17, 18, 19; 20:11, 17, 17, 17, 18, 19, 20, 21
Deu. 23:13, 14
Ezra 4:14
Lam. 1: 8
Eze. 16: 8; 23:10 A[b], 18 A[b]
Hos. 2: 9
Nah. 3: 5 A[b]

[a] A γυνή. [b] pro αἰσχύνη.

ἀσχήμων.

Gen. 34: 7 | Deu. 24: 3

ἀσωτία.

Proverbs 28: 7

ἄσωτος.

Proverbs 7:11

ἀτάρ.

Job 6:21 | Job 7:11[a]

[a] A τοιγαροῦν pro ἀ. οὖν.

ἀτείχιστος.

Nu. 13:20 | Pro. 25:28

ἀτεκνία.

Psa. 34:12 | Isa. 47: 9

ἄτεκνος.

Gen. 15: 2; Lev. 20:20, 21 | Isa. 49:21; Jer. 18:21

ἀτεκνόω.

Gen. 27:15 A[a]; 31:38; 42:36; 43:13, 13; Deu. 32:25; 1 Sa. 15:33, 33; 2 Sa. 17: 8; 2 Ki. 2:19, 21 | Cant. 4: 2; 6: 5; Jer. 15: 7; Lam. 1:20; Eze. 36:12, 13; 14; Hos. 9:12, 14

[a] *pro* ἀποτεκνόομαι.

ἀτιμάζω.

Gen. 16: 4, 5; Deu. 27:16; 1 Sa. 2:30 A[a]; 10:27; 17:42 AB[b]; Est. 1:16 A[c]; 18; Pro. 14: 2, 21; 19:26; 22:10, 22; 24:52, 67; 27:22 | Pro. 28: 7; Isa. 5:15; 16:14; 23: 9; 53: 3; Eze. 16:59 A[a]; 61 A[d]; 17:18 A[a]; 28:24, 26; 36: 3, 5; Mic. 7: 6

[a] *pro* ἀτιμόω. [b] *pro* ἐξατιμάζω. [c] *pro* ἀδικέω. [d] *pro* ἐξατιμόω.

ἀτιμία.

Job 10:15[a]; 12:21; 40: 8; Psa. 82:17; Pro. 3:35; 6:33; 9: 7; 11: 2, 16; 12: 9, 11[b]; 16; 13:18; 14:35; 18: 3; Isa. 10:16; 22:18 | Jer. 3:25; 6:15; 13:26; 20:11; 23:40; 28:51; Eze. 16:52, 63; 36: 7, 15; 39:26; 44:12 + A; 13; Hos. 4: 7, 18; Nah. 3: 5; Hab. 2:16; 16 − S[1]

[a] A ἀνομία. [b] S[1] ἁμαρτία.

ἄτιμος.

Job 30: 4, 8; Isa. 3: 5 | Isa. 53: 3

ἀτιμόω.

1 Sa. 2:30[a]; 15: 9; 2 Sa. 10: 5; 1 Ch. 19: 5; Jer. 22:22, 28; 38:22 | Lam. 1:11; Eze. 16:54, 59[a]; 17:16, 18[a]; 19; Obad. 2

[a] A ἀτιμάζω.

ἀτιμώρητος.

Pro. 11:21; 19: 5, 9 | Pro. 28:20

ἀτμίς.

Gen. 19:28; Lev. 16:13; Eze. 8:11 | Hos. 13: 3; Joel 2:30

ἀτμός.

Ecclesiastes 9: 9 + B

ἄτοπος.

Job 4: 8; 11:11; 27: 6; 34:12 | Job 35:13; 36:21 − A[a]; Pro. 24:55

[a] BS[1] ἄδικος.

ἄτρακτος.

Proverbs 29:37

ἀτράπελος.

Job 39: 9 + A

ἀτραπός.

Jud. 5: 6[a]; Job 6:19; 19: 8 A[b] | Job 24:13; Pro. 7:25 + AS[2]

[a] A τρίβος. [b] *pro* πρόσωπον.

ἀτρύγητος.

Exo. 27:20 A[a]

[a] *pro* ἄτρυγος.

ἄτρυγος.

Exo. 27:20[a]

[a] A ἀτρύγητος.

ἀττάκης.

Leviticus 11:22

ἀττέλαβος, −λεβος.

Nahum 3:17

ἀτυχέω.

Proverbs 27:10

αὐγάζω.

Lev. 13:24, 25; 26, 28 | Lev. 13:38, 39; 14:56

αὔγασμα.

Leviticus 13:38, 39

αὐγέω.

Job 29: 3

αὐγή.

Isaiah 59:9

αὐθάδης.

Gen. 49: 3, 7 | Pro. 21:24

αὐθάδεια.

Isaiah 24: 8 + ABS

αὐθημερινός.

Job 7: 1

αὐθήμερος.

Deu. 24:17; Neh. 11:23 + S[3] | Pro. 12:16

αὐλαία.

Exo. 26: 1, 2, 2; 2, 3, 3; 4, 4, 5; 5, 6; 37: 1, 2, 2 | Exo. 37:10, 13; 14[a]; 40:17; Isa. 54: 2

[a] A πύλη.

αὖλαξ.

Nu. 22:24; Job 31:38 | Job 39:10; Psa. 64:11

αὐλάρχης.

2 Samuel 8:18

αὐλαρχία.

1 Ki. (3) *p* 46

αὐλή.

Exo. 27: 9, 9, 12; 13, 16; 17, 18; 19; 35:12; 37: 7, 7, 13; 14 A[a]; 15, 16 | Exo. 37:16, 18; 38:19, 20; 21; 39: 9[b], 9; 9, 20; 20; 40: 6 A[a]; 27 − A[g]

Lev. 6:16, 26; 8:31; Nu. 3:26, 26; 37; 4:26, 32; 32; 2 Sa. 17:18; 1 Ki. (3) *p* 1; 6:33; 33 − A; 7:45, 46; 49; 49 + A; 8:64; 2 Ki. 20: 4; 21: 5; 23:12; 1 Ch. 9:22, 25; 16:29; 23:28; 28: 6, 12; 2 Ch. 4: 9 *ter*; 6:13; 7: 7; 20: 5; 23: 5; 24:21; 29:16; 31: 2; 33: 5; Neh. 3:25; 8:16, 16; 13: 7; Est. 1: 5; 2:11, 19; 3: 2, 3; 4: 2A[c], 2[d]; 11; 5: 9, 13; 6: 4, 4, 5; 10 − A; 12; 7: 4; Psa. 28: 2; 64: 5; 83: 3, 11; 91:14; 95: 8, 9; 99: 4; 115:10; 121: 2 | Ps. 133: 1; 134: 2; Isa. 1:12; 30:32 AS[e]; 34:13; Jer. 19:14; 30: 6, 8; 8 + S[1]; 11; 33: 2; 39: 2 − S[1]; 8, 12; 40: 1; 42: 2, 4[f]; 43:10, 20; 44:21; 45: 6, 7 A[c]; 13, 28; 46:14[c], 15; Eze. 8: 7, 16; 10: 3, 4, 5; 40:16, 17; 17, 19; 20, 23; 23, 27; 27, 28; 31, 34; 37, 44; 44, 47; 41: 3; 42: 1, 3, 3; 7, 8, 9; 14; 43: 5; 44:17, 17; 19, 21; 27; 45:19; 46: 1, 20; 21[h], 21; 21, 21; 21 + A; 22; 22 − A; 22, 22; 47: 2; 16 − A; 17; 48: 1, 1; Dan. 2:49; Zec. 3: 7

[a] *pro* σκηνή. [b] B πύλη, A σκηνή. [c] *pro* πύλη. [d] S[3] πύλη. [e] *pro* τύμπανον. [f] S[3] ὁδός. [g] S[1] αὐτός. [h] B[1] αὐτός.

αὐλίζω.

Jud. 19: 2[a]; 19: 4[b], 6, 7; 9[c], 10; 11, 13; 15[d], 15[d]; 20[d]; 20: 4[d]; Ruth 1:16, 16; 3:13; 2 Sa. 12:16; 17:16; 19: 7; Neh. 4:22; 13:20, 21; Job 11:14; 15:28 | Job 19: 4; 29:19; 31:32; 38:19; 39:27; 41:13; Psa. 24:13; 29: 6; 54: 8; 90: 1; Pro. 19:23; Cant. 1:13 − B; 7:11; Jer. 38: 9; Dan. 4:20, 22

[a] A καταπαύω. [b] A ὑπνόω. [c] A μένω. [d] A καταλύω.

αὐλός.

1 Sa. 10: 5; 2 Sa. 6: 5; Isa. 5:12 | Isa. 30:29; Jer. 31:36, 36

αὐλών.

1 Sa. 17:3[a]; 1 Ch. 10: 7; 12:15 | 1 Ch. 27:29; 2 Ch. 20:26; Jer. 31: 8

[a] B κύκλῳ.

αὐξάνω.

Gen. 1:22, 28; 8:17; 9: 1, 7; 17: 6, 20; 21: 8, 20; 25:27; 26:22; 28: 3; 30:30; 35:11; 41:52[a]; 47:27; 48: 4; 49:22, 22; Exo. 1: 7; 23:30; Lev. 26: 9 | Nu. 24: 7; Jos. 4:14; Jud. 5:11[b]; 13:24 A[c]; 1 Ch. 14: 2; 17:10; 23:17; 2 Ch. 1: 1 B[d]; 11:23; Job 42:10; Ps. 101:24; Isa. 61:11; Jer. 3:16; 22:30; 23: 3; Dan. 3:30

[a] A ὑψόω. [b] A ἐνισχύω. [c] *pro* ἁδρύνω. [d] *pro* μεγαλύνω.

αὔρα.

1 Ki. 19:12; Job 4:16 | Ps. 106:29[a]; Eze. 8: 2 + A

[a] S[1] αὐτός.

αὔριον.

Gen. 30:33 A[a]; Exo. 8:10, 23; 29; 9: 5, 18; 10: 4; 16:23; 23 + B; 17: 9; 19:10; 32: 5, 30; Lev. 7: 6; 10: 6; Nu. 11:18; 14:25; 16: 7, 16; 41 B[a]; Deu. 6:20; Jos. 3: 5, 5; 4: 6; 7:13; 11: 6; 22:18, 24; 27, 28 | Jud. 19: 9; 20:28; 1 Sa. 9:16; 16 + A; 11: 9, 10; 11; 19: 2, 11; 20: 5, 18; 28:19; 2 Sa. 11:12; 1 Ki. 19: 2, 11; 21: 6; 2 Ki. 6:28; 7: 1, 18; 10: 6; 2 Ch. 20:16, 17; Est. 5: 8 − S[1]; 8, 12; 9:13; Pro. 3:28; 27: 1; Isa. 22:13

[a] *pro* ἐπαύριον.

αὐταρκέω.

Deuteronomy 32:10

αὐτάρχης.

Proverbs 24:31

αὐτόθι.

Joshua 5: 8

αὐτόματος.

Lev. 25: 5, 11; Jos. 6: 5 | 2 Ki. 19:29; Job 24:24

αὐτομολέω.

Jos. 10: 1, 4; 1 Sa. 20:30; 2 Sa. 3: 8 | 2 Sa. 10:19; Pro. 6:11 A[a]

[a] *pro* ἀπαυτομολέω.

αὐτοῦ, *adv.*

Gen. 22: 5; Nu. 22: 8; 32: 6 | Deu. 5:31; 2 Sa. 20: 4

αὐτόχθων.

Exo. 12:19, 48; Lev. 16:29; 17:15; 19:34; 20: 4; 23:42 | Lev. 24:16; Nu. 9:14; 15:13, 30; Jos. 9: 6; Jer. 14: 8; Eze. 47:22

αὐχήν.

Jos. 7: 8, 12
13:28—A
1 Ki. 7:19+A
2 Ch.29: 6
Ps. 128: 4
Jer. 19:15 S[a]

[a] pro τράχηλος.

αὐχμός.

Jeremiah 31:31

αὐχμώδης.

1 Sa. 23:14+AB
14
15, 19
1 Sa. 26: 1
Mic. 4: 8

ἀφαγνίζω.

Lev. 14:49, 52
Nu. 6: 2
8: 6, 21
Nu. 19:12, 13
19, 20
31:20

ἀφαίρεμα.

Exo. 29:27
28 A[a]
28, 28
35: 5
21—A
21, 22
21, 24
29
36: 3
39: 2,7,12
Lev. 7: 4, 22
24
8:27
Lev. 9:21
10:14, 15
14:21
Nu. 6:20
15:19, 20
20, 21
18:19, 24
26, 27
27, 28
28, 29
31:41, 52
Eze. 44:30
45:15

[a] pro ἀφόρισμα.

ἀφαίρεσις.

Nu. 36: 4 A[a]

[a] pro ἄφεσις.

ἀφαιρέω.

Gen. 21:25
30:23
31: 9, 16
31
40:19
48:17
Exo. 5: 8, 11
13:12[a]
29:27
33: 5, 23
34: 7, 9
35:24
Lev. 1:16
2: 9
4:10
6:10, 15
8:29
9:21
10:17
22:15[b]
Nu. 11:17
14:18
15:19, 20
18:19, 26
28, 29
30, 32
21: 7
31:28, 52
36: 3, 3, 4
Deu. 4: 2
12:32
Jos. 5: 9
Jud. 21: 6 A[c]
1 Sa. 5: 4
7:14
17:26 A, 36
39[d], 46
51
21: 6
24: 5,6,12
30:18
2 Sa. 4: 7[e]
16: 9
20:22, 22
1 Ki. 15:12
21:41
2 Ki. 6:32
1 Ch. 11:23
19: 4
Est. 4: 4
8: 2, 3
Job 1:21
9:21
19: 9
22: 6
24: 7, 10
36: 7
38:15
Psa. 75:13
Pro. 1:19
4:16
11:30
13:18
14:35
22: 9
24:30
26: 7
27:13
Ecc. 2:10[f]
3:14
Isa. 1:16, 25
3: 1, 18
4: 1
5: 5, 8
6: 7
7:17, 20
8: 8
9: 4, 14
10:13, 27
11:13
14:25, 25
16: 2
18: 5, 5
20: 2
22:17, 19
25
25: 8, 8
27: 9, 9
28:18
30:11, 11
38:14
40:27
Isa. 53:10
58: 9
Jer. 6: 2
11:15
33: 2
Eze. 21:26
23:25
26:16[g]
Eze. 36:26
45: 9
48:14
Dan. 5:20
Hos. 2: 9
Mic. 2: 8
Zech. 3: 4, 4
10:11

[a] A ἀφορίζω. [b] A προσφέρω.
[c] pro ἐκκόπτω. [d] A διαφέρω.
[e] B ἀναφαιρέω. [f] A ὑφαιρέω.
[g] A[1] καθαιρέω, A[2] αἱρέω.

ἀφάλλομαι.

Eze. 44:10
Nah. 3:17

ἀφανής.

Neh. 4: 8—ABS
Job 24:20

ἀφανίζω.

Exo. 8: 9
12:15
21:29, 36
Deu. 7: 2
13: 5
19: 1
Jud. 21:16
1 Sa. 24:22
2 Sa. 21: 5
22:38
2 Ki. 10:17, 28
21: 9
Ezra 6:12
Est. 3: 6, 13
9:24[a]
Job 2: 9
4: 9
22:20
39:24
Psa. 93:23
145: 9
Pro. 10:25—S[1]
12: 7
14:11
24:33
Cant. 2:15
Jer. 4:26
12: 4, 11
27:21, 45
28: 3
29: 4
Lam. 1: 4, 13
16
Lam. 3:11
4: 5
5:18
Eze. 4:17
6: 6
12:19
14: 9
19: 7
20:26
25: 3
30: 7 A[b], 9
11 A[c]
14 A[c]
34:25[d]
36: 4,5,34
34, 35
35, 36
Dan. 7:26
11:31, 44
Hos. 2:12
5:15
10: 2
14: 1
Joel 1:17, 18
2:20
Amos 7: 9
9:14
Mic. 5:14
6:13, 15
Hab. 1: 5
Zeph. 2: 9
3: 6
Zec. 7:14

[a] AS[3] ἀπόλλυμι. [b] pro ἐρημόω.
[c] pro ἀπολλυμι. [d] A ἀπόλλυμι.

ἀφανισμός.

Deu. 7: 2
1 Ki. 9: 7
13:34
2 Ki. 22:19
2 Ch. 29: 8—B
36:19
Ezra 4:22
Jer. 9:11
10:22
12:11, 11
18:16
19: 8
25: 9, 11
12
26:19
27: 3, 13
23
28:26, 29
37, 41
62
Eze. 4:16
6:14
Eze. 7:27
12:19, 20
14: 8, 15
15: 8
23:33
29:12+A
Dan. 9:18, 26
27+AB[2]
27+AB[2]
Hos. 5: 9
Joel 1: 7
2: 3
3:19, 19
Mic. 1: 7
6:16
7:13
Zeph. 1:13, 15
2: 4, 13
3: 1
Zec. 7:14
Mal. 1: 3

ἀφάπτω.

Deu. 6: 8
11:18
Jud. 20:34 A[a]
Pro. 3: 3
6:21

[a] pro φθάνω.

ἄφεδρος.

Lev. 12: 2, 5
15:19, 20
25 ter
26, 26
Lev. 15:33
Eze. 18: 6
36:17 A[a]

[a] pro ἀποκάθημαι.

ἀφειδῶς.

Proverbs 21:26

ἄφεσις.

Exo. 18: 2
23:11
Lev. 16:26
25:10, 10
11, 12
13, 28
28, 30
31, 33
40, 41
50, 52
54
27:17, 18
18, 21
23, 24
Nu. 36: 4[a]
Deu. 15: 1, 2, 2
3, 9
31:10
2 Sa. 7:14 A[b]
22:16
Est. 2:18
Isa. 58: 6
61: 1
Jer. 11: 8, 15
17, 17
Lam. 3:47
Eze. 46:17
47: 3
Joel 1:20
3:18

[a] A ἀφαίρεσις. [b] pro ἀφή.

ἁφή.

Lev. 13 passim
14: 3, 32
34, 35
36[a], 37
37—AB
39, 40
43, 44
48, 48
54
Deu. 17: 8, 8
21: 5
24:10
2 Sa. 7:14[b]
1 Ki. 8:38
2 Ch. 6:29
Pro. 24:46
Ecc. 6: 3 S[c]
Jer. 31: 9

[a] AB οἰκία. [b] A ἄφεσις.
[c] pro ταφή.

ἀφηγέομαι.

Exo. 11: 8
Jud. 1: 1
20:18+A
18
Ezra 6: 7—B
Eze. 11: 1
12:10
21:12, 25
22: 6, 25
Eze. 45: 8,9,16
17, 22
46: 2, 4, 8
10, 12
16, 17
18
48:21, 21
22, 22

ἄφθορος.

Esther 2: 2

ἀφίημι.

Gen. 4:13
18:26
20: 6
35:18
42:33
45: 2
50:17
Exo. 9:21
12:23
22: 5
32:32, 32
Lev. 4:20, 26
31, 35
5: 6, 10
13, 16
18
6: 7
16:10
19:22
Nu. 14:19
15:25, 26
28+A
22:13
Deu. 15: 2
26:10—B
Jos. 10:19
Jud. 1:34
2:21, 23
3: 1, 28
Jud. 9: 9 A[a]
11 A[a]
13 A[a]
15: 1 A[b]
16:26—A
Ruth 2:16 A[d]
1 Sa. 17:20 A
22 A
28 A
2 Sa. 15:16
16:10, 11
20: 3
1 Ki. 19: 3
2 Ki. 4:27
23:18
1 Ch. 16:21
2 Ch. 10: 4, 10
28:14
Ezra 6: 7
Neh. 9:17+S[3]
Job 39: 5, 14
42:10
Psa. 16:14
24:18
31: 1, 5
84: 3
104:14, 20
124: 3
Pro. 4:13
Ecc. 2:18
5:11
10: 4
11: 6
Cant. 3: 4
Isa. 22: 4, 14
Isa. 32:14
33:24
55: 7
Jer. 12: 7
Eze. 16:39

[a] pro ἀπολειπω. [b] pro δίδωμι.
[d] pro φαγω.

ἀφικνέομαι.

Gen. 28:12
38: 1
47: 9
Job 11: 7
Job 13:27
15: 8
16:20
Pro. 1:27

ἀφίστημι.

Gen. 12: 8
14: 4
19: 9
30:36
31:40, 49
Exo. 23: 7
Lev. 13:58
Nu. 8:25
12:10[a]
14: 9, 31
16:27
32: 9
Deu. 1:28
4: 9
7: 4
13:10, 13
32:15
Jos. 1: 8
3:16
8: 6 A[b]
16
22:18, 19
23
29 A[c]
29—A
Jud. 2:19+A
16:17, 19
20
1 Sa. 6: 3
14: 9
16:14, 23
18:12+A
13
19:10
28:15, 16
2 Sa. 2:22, 23
28
7:15 ter
12:10
22:23
23+B
1 Ki. 11:29
40+B
21:24
2 Ki. 1:18[d], 18
3: 3
10:29, 31
13: 2,6,11
14:24, 25
15: 9, 18
24, 28
17:18, 22
18: 6, 22
22: 2
23:19
19 A[e]
27, 27
24: 3
1 Ch. 17:13, 13
2 Ch. 13: 6[f]
14: 3, 5
15:17[g]
20:23 B[h]
2 Ch. 21: 8, 10
21:10
25:27
26:18
28:19, 22
24
29: 6
30: 7
35:19, 19
36: 5 ter
Neh. 9:26
Est. 6: 1
Job 7:16
14: 6
19:13
21:14
30:10
31:22
Psa. 6: 9
9:22
17:23
21:11
34:22
37:22
38:11
43:19
65:20
79:19
80: 7
118:29
Pro. 23:18
Ecc. 11:10
Isa. 33:14
40:27
52:11, 11
57: 8
59: 9, 11
13, 14
14
Jer. 2: 5
3:14
5:23[i]
6: 8
14: 3 S[1 k]
19
16: 5
17: 5, 13
39:40
40: 8
Lam. 3:11
4:15 ter
Eze. 6: 9+A
17:15
20: 8, 38
23:17, 18
18, 22
28
33: 8 A[m]
Dan. 2: 5, 8
6:18[n]
9: 5, 9
Hos. 5: 3[n]
Obad. 14 S[1 p]

[a] A ἀπέρχομαι. [b] pro ἀποσπάω.
[c] pro ἀποστρέφω.
[d] B ἀποστέλλω. [e] pro ποιέω.
[f] B ἀνίστημι. [g] A ἐξαίρω.
[h] pro ἀνίστημι. [i] A ἐξαφιστημι.
[k] pro ἀποστιλλω.
[m] pro φυλάσσω. [n] A γίνομαι.
[o] A ἄπειμι. [p] pro ἐφιστημι.

ἄφνω.

Jos. 10: 9
Pro. 1:27
Ecc. 9.12
10: 3 S[a]
Jer. 4:20
18:22
28: 8

[a] pro ἄφρων.

ἀφοβία.

Proverbs 15:16

ἄφοβος.

Pro. 3:24
Pro. 19:23

ἀφόβως.

Proverbs 1:33

ἀφοράω.

Jonah 4: 5

ἀφορία.

Hag. 2:17[a]

[a] S[1] ἀπορία.

ἀφορίζω.

Gen. 2:10
10: 5
Exo. 13:12 A[a]
19:12, 23
29:24, 26
27
Lev. 10:15
13: 4,5,11
21, 26
31, 33
50, 51
14:12, 38
46
20:25, 25
26
25:34
27:21
Nu. 8:11
12:14, 15
Nu. 15:20
18:24
Deu. 4:41
Jos. 14: 4
16: 9
21:13*to*18
21*to*32
16—A
22+A
2 Sa. 8: 1
Psa. 67·10
Pro. 8:27
Isa. 29:22
45:24 AS[2b]
52:11
56: 3
Eze. 45: 1,4,13
48: 9, 20
Mal. 2: 3

[a] *pro* ἀφαιρέω. [b] *pro* διορίζω.

ἀφόρισμα.

Exo. 29:24, 26
27, 28[a]
36:38
Lev. 10:14, 15
15
Lev. 14:12
Nu. 15:19
35: 3
Eze. 44:29

[a] A ἀφαίρεμα.

ἀφορισμός.

Eze. 20:31, 40
Eze. 48: 8

ἀφορμή.

Pro. 9: 9
Eze. 5: 7

ἀφρονεύομαι.

Jeremiah 10:21

ἀφρόνως.

Genesis 31:28

ἀφροσύνη.

Deu. 22:21
Jud. 19:23, 24
20: 6 A[a]
10 A[a]
1 Sa. 25:25+A
25
2 Sa. 13:12
Job 1:22
4: 6
21:23 ACS[b]
Psa. 37: 6
68: 6
Pro. 5: 5, 23
Pro. 9: 6
13: 2, 13
22
26: 4, 5
27:22
Ecc. 2:12, 13
4:17 S[2c]
7:26
9:17
10: 1, 3
13
Lam. 2:14

[a] *pro* ἀπόπτωμα.
[b] *pro* ἀπλοσύνη. [c] *pro* ἄφρων.

ἄφρων.

2 Sa. 13:13
Job 2:10
Job 5: 2, 3
30: 8
Job 34:36
Psa. 13: 1
38: 9
48:11
52: 2
73:18, 22
91: 7
93: 8
Pro. 1:22
6:12
7: 7
9: 4, 13
16
10: 1,5,18
21, 23
24+A
11:29, 30
12: 1, 15
16, 23
13:16, 20
14: 1, 3, 7
8, 9 A[a]
16, 18
24, 29
33
15: 2, 5, 7
20
16:22. 27
17: 2,7.10
12, 16
18, 21
24, 25
Pro. 18: 6,7,22
19:10, 13
25, 28
29
20: 1, 3
21:20
22: 3
23: 9
24: 9, 25
45, 57
26: 1
4*to*12
27: 3, 12
22
28:26
29:11, 20
Ecc. 2:14, 15
15, 16
16, 19
4: 5, 13
17[b]
5: 2, 3
6: 8
7: 5, 6, 7
10
10: 2,3[c],6
12, 14
15
Isa. 59: 7AS[1d]
Jer. 4:22
17:11

[a] *pro* παράνομος.
[b] S[2] ἀφροσύνη. [c] S ἄφνω.
[d] *pro* ἀπὸ φόνος.

ἀφυλάκτως.

Eze. 7:22
Eze. 23:39+A

ἀφυστερέω.

Nehemiah 9:20

ἀφφουσώθ.

2 Kings 15: 5

ἀφφώ

2 Ki. 2:14
2 Ki. 10:10

ἄφωνος.

Isaiah 53: 7

ἀχαβίν.

1 Ch. 21:20[a]

[a] A κρύπτω.

ἀχάτης.

Exo. 28:19
36:19
Eze. 28:13

ἄχει, ἄχι.

Gen. 41: 2
3+A
18
Gen. 41:19+A
Isa. 19: 7

ἀχρεῖος.

2 Samuel 6:22

ἀχρειόω.

2 Ki. 3:19
Psa. 13: 3
Psa. 52: 4
Jer. 11:16

ἄχρηστος.

Hosea 8: 8

ἄχρι.

Gen. 44:28[a]
Jud. 11:33—A
Job 32:11

[a] A ἔτι *pro* ἄ. νῦν

ἄχυρον.

Gen. 24:25, 32
Exo. 5: 7,7,10
11, 12
13, 16
18
Jud. 19:19
1 Ki. 4:21
Job 21:18
41:18
Isa. 11: 7
Isa. 17:13
30:24
65:25
Jer. 23:28
Nah. 3:14

ἀωρία.

Ps. 118:147
Isa. 59: 9
Zeph. 1:15[a]

[a] S[3] ταλαιπωρία

ἄωρος.

Job 22:16
Pro. 10: 6
11:30
Pro. 13: 2
Isa. 65:20

βαάλ.

1 Kings 6: 5

βάδ.

1 Sa. 2:18[a]

[a] AB βάρ.

βαδδίν.

Dan. 10: 5
Dan. 12: 6, 7

βαδίζω.

Gen. 42:19
44:25
Exo. 4:18, 19
6: 6
7:15
10:24
12:31
19:24
32: 7, 34
Deu. 5:30
10:11
13: 6[a]
Jud. 10:14 A[b]
2 Sa. 7: 3
14: 8
15: 9
18:21
24: 1
Est. 4:16, 17
Isa. 21: 6
26:20
40:31
Isa. 55: 1
Jer. 6:16, 25
11:10 AS[b]
12: 9
13: 1, 4, 6
17:19
19: 1
27: 4
30: 3
31· 2
35:13
38: 2
41: 2
42: 2[a]
43:19
51:35
Eze. 1: 9
3: 4, 11
Hos. 1: 2—A
Amos 7:12, 15
Jon. 1: 3
Mic. 7: 4

[a] A πορεύω. [b] *pro* πορεύω.

βαθμός.

1 Sa. 5: 5
2 Ki. 20: 9[a]
9—A
2 Ki. 20:10[a], 10[a]
11

[a] A ἀναβαθμός.

βάθος.

Jud. 5:30 A[a]
Job 28:11
Psa. 68: 3, 15
129: 1
Pro. 18: 3
Ecc. 7:25
Isa. 7:11
51:10
Eze. 26:20
Eze. 27:34
31:14, 18
32:18, 22
24
43:13, 14
Amos 9: 3
Jon. 2: 4
Mic. 7:19
Zec. 10:11

[a] *pro* βάμμα.

βάθρον.

Isa. 14:23 A[a]

[a] *pro* βάραθρον.

βαθύγλωσσος.

Eze. 3: 5[a]

[a] A βαρύγλωσσος.

βαθύνω.

Psa. 91: 6[a]
Jer. 29: 9
Jer. 30: SABS[b]

[a] BS[1] βαρύνω. [b] *pro* ἐμβαθύνω.

βαθύς.

Job 11: 8+A, 8
12:22
Psa. 63· 7
Pro. 18: 4
20: 5
22:14
Pro. 25: 3
Ecc. 7:25
Isa. 29:15
30:33
31: 6
Jer. 17: 9
Eze. 23:32
32:21
Dan. 2:22

βαθύφωνος.

Isaiah 33:19

βαθύχειλος.

Ezekiel 3: 5+A

βαίθ.

1 Kings 5:11

βαίνω.

Deuteronomy 28:56

βακτηρία.

Exo. 12:11
1 Sa. 17:40
2 Ki. 4:29, 29
31
Psa. 22: 4
Pro. 13:24
14: 3
Jer. 1:11
31:17

βακχούρια.

Nehemiah 13:31

βάλανος.

Gen. 35: 8, 8
Jud. 9: 6
Isa. 2:13
Isa. 6:13
Jer. 30: 9

βαλάντιον.

Job 14:17
Pro. 1:14

βάλλω.

Exo. 10:19[a]
Nu 22:38 B[b]
Jud. 6:19[c]
7:12[d]
8:25[e]
20:16+A
1 Sa. 14:42[f], 43
2 Sa. 20:22
1 Ki. 6: 3—A
2 Ki. 23: 4[g]
1 Ch. 25: 8
26:13, 14
2 Ch. 26:15
Neh. 10:34
11: 1[h]
Est. 3: 7
9:24+S[3]
Job 5:3 15:29
16:13
38: 6
Psa. 21:19
77: 9
125: 6[i]
147: 6
Pro. 1:14
Ecc. 3: 5
Isa. 19: 8, 8
29: 3
37:33
33 A[k]
Jer. 17: 8
47:10
Eze. 21:22
22, 22
23:24
47:22
48:29
Dan. 3:21[a]
22+A
24[a]
6:24 A[b]
Hos. 14: 5
Joel 3: 3
Obad. 11
Jon. 1: 7, 7
15 S[1m]
Mic. 2: 5
Nah. 3:10
Hab. 1:10
3:13

[a] A ἐμβάλλω. [b] *pro* ἐμβάλλω.
[c] A ἐγχέω. [d] A παρεμβάλλω.
[e] A ῥίπτω. [f] A λαμβάνω.
[g] B λαμβάνω. [h] BS[1] λαμβάνω.
[i] AS[1] αἴρω. [k] *pro* ἐπιβάλλω.
[m] *pro* ἐκβάλλω.

βάμμα.

Jud. 5:30, 30, 30[a]

[a] A βάθος.

βαπτίζω.

2 Ki. 5:14
Isa. 21: 4

βαπτός.

Eze. 23:15 A[a]

[a] *pro* παραβαπτός.

βάπτω.

Exo. 12:22
Lev. 4: 6, 17
9: 9
11:32
14: 6, 16
Lev. 14:51
Nu. 19·18
Deu. 33:24
Jos. 3:15
Ruth 2:14

1 Sa. 14:27
2 Ki. 8:15
Job 9:31
Psa. 67:24
Pro. 25:20 S[1a]
Dan. 4:30
5:21

[a] pro βλάπτω.

βάραθρον.

Isa. 14:23[a]

[a] A βάθρον.

βάρβαρος.

Psa. 113: 1 | Eze. 21:31

βαρέως.

Gen. 31:35 | Isa. 6:10

βάρις.

2 Ch. 36:19
Ezra 6: 2
Neh. 2: 8 + S[3]
Est. (9)14 + S[3]
Psa. 44: 9
Psa. 47: 4
14 − S[1]
Lam. 2: 5, 7
Dan. 8: 2

βαρκηνίμ.

Judges 8: 7, 16

βάρος.

Judges 18:21 − A

βαρύγλωσσος.

Ezekiel 3: 5 A[a]

[a] pro βαθύγλωσσος.

βαρυθυμέω.

Nu. 16:15 | 1 Ki. 11:22

βαρυκάρδιος.

Psalm 4: 3

βαρύνω.

Exo. 5: 9
7:14
8:15, 32
9: 7, 34
10: 1 A[a]
Jos. 19:48
Jud. 1:35
20:34 A[b]
1 Sa. 3: 2
5: 3, 6
6: 6, 6
31: 3
1 Ki. 12:4, 10, 14
p 24 l 55
l 55
1 Ch. 10: 3
2 Ch. 10:10, 14
Neh. 5:15
Job 35:16
Psa. 31: 4
37: 5
91: 6 B[1] S[1c]
Isa. 33:15
47: 6
59: 1
Lam. 3: 7
Eze. 27:25
Nah. 2: 9
3:15
Hab. 2: 6
Zec. 7:11
11: 8
Mal. 3:13

[a] pro σκληρύνω. [b] pro βαρύς.
[c] pro βαθύνω.

βαρυόπτομαι.

Genesis 48:10

βαρύς.

Gen. 48:17
Exo. 17:12
18:18 − A
Nu. 11:14
20:20
Jud. 20:34[a]
1 Sa. 4:18
5:11
1 Ki. 3: 9
10: 2
12: 4, 11
2 Ki. 6:14
18:17
2 Ch. 9: 1
10: 4, 11
25:19
Neh. 5:18
Job 6: 3
15:10[b]
23: 2
33: 7
Psa. 34:18
37: 5 − A
Pro. 27: 3, 3
Dan. 2:11
Nah. 3: 3

[a] A βαρύνω. [b] A[1] πρέσβυς.

βασανίζω.

1 Samuel 5: 3

βάσανος.

1 Sa. 6: 3, 4, 8
17
Eze. 3:20
7:19
Eze. 12:18
16:52, 54
32:24, 30

βασιλεία.

Gen. 10:10
14: 1
20: 9
Nu. 21:18, 18
24: 7, 7
32:33, 33
Deu. 3:10, 13
21
28:25
Jos. 11:10, 12
13:12, 21
27
30 − A
30, 31
1 Sa. 10:16, 18
11:14
13:13, 14
15:28
18: 8 + A
20:31
24:21
28:17
2 Sa. 3:10, 28
5:12
7:12, 16
12:26
16: 3, 8
19: 9
1 Ki. 1:46
2:12, 15
15, 22
35
(3)46 + A
(3) p 46
9: 5 − A
10:20
11:11, 13
14, 31
34, 35
12:21
p 24 l 12
26
16: p 28 − A
18:10, 10
20: 7 A[a]
2 Ki. 11: 1
14: 5
19:15, 19
24:12
25: 1, 27
1 Ch. 4:23
10:14
11:10
12:23
14: 2
16:20
17:11, 14
22:10
26:31
28: 5, 7
29:30, 30
2 Ch. 1: 1
2: 1, 12
3: 2
7:18
8: 6, 9
9:19
11: 1, 17
12: 1, 2, 8
13: 1, 8
15:10, 19
16: 1, 12
13
17: 5, 7, 10
20: 6, 29
30
21: 3, 4, 5
22: 9, 10
23:20
25: 3
26:21
2 Ch. 29: 3, 19
21
32:15
33:13 − A
34: 3, 3, 8
8 + A
35:19
36:20, 22
23
Ezra 1: 1, 2
4: 5, 6, 6
24 − B
6:15
7: 1, 13
23
8: 1
Neh. 9:22[b], 35
12:22
Est. 1: 4, 19
20, 22
2: 3, 16
18
3: 6, 7[c]
8, 13
4:11, 13
5: 3
6 + S[3]
11
6: 9 + S[3]
7: 2
8: 5, 12
13
9: 4, 16
20
10: 1, 2, 3
Psa. 21:29
44: 7
45: 7
67:33
78: 6
101:23 B S[1a]
102:19
104:13
30 B S[2a]
134:11
144:11, 12
13, 13
Ecc. 4:14
Isa. 1: 1
7: 8
9: 7
17: 3
23:17
37:16, 20
47: 5
62: 3
Jer. 1:2, 10, 15
15: 4
18: 7, 9
24: 9
28:59
32:12
34: 6
35: 8
41:17
52: 4
Eze. 17:13, 14
37:22
23 + A
Dan. 1: 1, 3, 20
2: 1, 37
39, 39
40, 41
42, 44
44, 44
3:30, 33
33
4:14, 15
22, 23
26, 27
28, 29
Dan. 4:31, 33
33
5: 7, 11
16, 18
20, 21
26, 28
29, 31
6: 1, 1, 3, 7
26, 26
28, 28
7:14, 14
17, 18
22, 23
23, 27
27, 27
Dan. 8: 1, 23
9: 1
2 + A
10:13, 13
11: 2, 4, 4
9, 17
20, 20
21, 21
Hos. 1: 4
Amos 6: 2
7:13
9: 8
Obad. 21
Mic. 4: 8
Nah. 3: 5

[a] pro βασιλεύς. [b] B βασιλεύς.
[c] A βασιλεύω.

βασίλειον.

2 Sa. 1:10
1 Ki. 4:(21) A
14: 8 A
2 Ki. 15:19 + A
2 Ch. 23:11
Est. 1: 9
2:13
Pro. 18:19
Nah. 2: 6

βασίλειος.

Exo. 19: 6
23:22
1 Ch. 28: 4

βασιλεύς.

Gen. 14: 1 qtr
2 qnq
5, 8, 8
8, 8, 8
9 qnq
10, 10
17 ter
18, 21
22
17: 6, 16
20: 2
23: 6
26: 1, 8
35:11
36:31, 31
39:20
40: 1, 1, 5
17 + A
41:46
45:21
47: 5
Exo. 1: 8, 15
17, 18
2:23
3:10, 11
18, 19
4:18
5: 4
6:11, 13
27, 29
14: 5[a], 8
Nu. 20:14
21: 1, 21
26, 26
29, 33
34
22: 4, 10
23: 7
31: 8, 8
32:33, 33
33:40
Deu. 1: 4, 4
2:24, 26
30, 31
32
3: 1, 2, 3
4, 6, 8
11, 21
4:46, 47
47
7: 8, 24
9:26
11: 3
29: 7, 7
31: 4
Jos. 2: 2, 3, 10
5: 1, 1
6: 2
Jos. 8: 1, 2, 14
23, 29
9: 1, 16
16, 16
10 passim
11: 1 qtr
2, 4, 5
10, 12
17, 18
12 passim
19 + A
13:10, 13
21, 27
30
16:10
23: 5
24: 9, 12[b]
33
Jud. 1: 7
3: 8, 10
12, 14
15, 17
19, 20
4: 2, 17
23, 24
24
5: 3, 6 A[c]
19, 19
8: 5, 12
18, 26
9: 6 + A
8
15 A[d]
25 − A
11:12, 13
14, 17
17, 17
19
19 − A
25, 28
17: 6
18: 1, 31
21:25
Ruth 4:22 + A
1 Sa. 2:10
8: 5, 6, 9
10, 11
18, 18
19, 20
22
10:18, 19
24, 25
11:15
12: 1, 2, 9
9, 12
12, 12
13, 13
14, 15
1 Sa. 12:17, 19
25
14:47
15: 1, 8, 11
17, 20
23, 26
32
16: 1[e]
17:25 A
55 A
56 A
18: 6 A
18 A
22, 22
23, 25
25 − A
26
27 + AB
27
19: 4
20: 5 + A
24
25 + A
29
21: 2, 8, 10
11, 12
22: 3, 4, 11
11, 14
14, 15
16, 17
17, 18
23:20, 20
24: 9, 15
25:36
26:14 + A
15, 15
16, 16
17, 19
20, 22
27: 2, 6
28:13
29: 3[f], 8
2 Sa. 2: 7
3: 3, 21
24, 31
32, 33
36, 37
38, 39
4: 8, 8
5: 2, 3, 3
3, 11
12, 17
6:12, 16
20
7: 1, 2, 3
18
8: 3, 5, 7
7, 8, 9
10, 11
12, 14
9: 2, 3, 3
4, 4, 5
6, 9, 11
11, 11
13
10: 1, 5, 6
19
11: 1, 2, 8
8, 9
18 + AB
18 − A
19, 20
22, 24
12: 7, 30
13: 4, 6, 6
13, 18
21, 23
24, 24
25, 26
27, 27
29, 30
31, 32
32, 33
33, 34
35, 35
36, 36
37
37 − A
39
14 passim
2 Sa. 14:27 + A
15: 2, 3
6, 9
10 − A
15 ter
16, 16
17, 18
19, 19
21, 21
21 + A
22
22 − AB
23
23 − A
25, 27
34, 34
35
16: 2, 2, 3
3, 4, 4
5, 6, 6
9, 9, 10
14, 16
17: 2, 16
17, 21
18: 4, 4, 5
5 − A
12, 12
13, 18
19, 20
21 − A
25, 25
26, 27
28 ter
29, 29
30, 31
31, 32
32, 33
19 passim
15 − A
19 + A
40[g]
20: 2, 3, 4
21, 22
21: 2, 5, 6
7, 8[h]
14
22:51
23:23
24: 2, 3, 3
3, 4, 4
9, 20
20, 21
22, 23
23, 24
1 Ki. 1 passim
9 + A
11 + A
17 + A
28 − B
45 + A
51 + A
53 − B
2:15, 17
18, 19
19, 19
20, 22
23, 25
26
29 − B
30, 30
31, 35
35
(3)36, 37
38, 38
39, 42
44, 45
46
p 46 + A
p 46 ter
3: 4 + A
13, 16
22, 23
24, 24
25, 26
27, 28
28
4: 1, 5, 7
18, 18
20, 20
21

1 Ki. 4:24+A
30
30−A
5: 1,1+A
13
6: 1,2,6
7: 1,2
26
31 ter
33+A
34
37+A
8: 1
1+A
2+A
5,14
14,62
63,63
64
66−B
9: 1,10
11,11
16 A
26,28
10: 3,6,9
10−A
12,12
13,13
15
16+A
17−B
18
21+A
22,22
p 22 bis
23,24
26,26
27,28
29,29
11: 1,5
14,18
20+A
27
27−AB
33,37
40
44−A
12: 1,2 A
3,6,12
12,13
15,16
16,18
18,23
p 24 t 1
t 5,14
t 20
t 78
27
27+A
28
13: 4,4,6
6,7,8
11
14: 14 A
19A,25
26,26
27,27
28,29
15: 7,9,16
17,17
18 ter
19,20
22,22
23,25
28,31
32 A,33
16: 5
6+AB
8+A
10+A
14
15+A
16,18
18+B
18,20
23,27
p 28−AB
p 28−A
p 28−A
p 28−A

1 Ki. 16 p 28−A
29,31
33
19: 15,16
20: 1,7[k]
10−B
13,18
21 passim
1+A
9+A
17−A
22 passim
4+A
26[m]
27+A
41−B
46−B
48 A
49 A
2 Ki. 1: 3,6
6−AB
9,11
11,13
15,18
18+A
18
3: 1−A
4,4,5
5,6,7
7,9,9
9,10
10,11
12 ter
13 ter
14,21
23,26
26
4:13
5: 5,5,6
7,8,8
6: 8,9,10
11,11
12,12
21,24
26,26
28,30
7: 2,6,6
6,9,11
12,14
14,15
17,17
18
8: 3,4,5
5,5,6
6,7,8
9,16
16,16
18,20
23,25
25+A
26,28
29,29
29+A
9: 3,6,12
14,15
15,16
16,16
18,19
21,21
27,29
34
10: 4,6,7
8,13
13
25 A[n]
34
11: 2,2,4
5,7,8
8,10
11,12
12,14
14,16
17,17
19 ter
20
12: 6,7,10
17
18 qtr
19
13: 1,3,4

2 Ki. 13: 7,8
10,12
12,13[o]
14,16
16,18
18
22+A
24
14: 1,1
5+A
8,9,9
11,11
13+A
13,14
15,15
16,17
17,18
22,23
23+A
28,29
15: 1,1
5,6
8,11
13,15
17,19
20,20
21,23
25,26
27,29
29−A
31,32
32,36
37
16: 1,3,5
5,6,7
7,7,8
8,9
9−A
9−AB
10 ter
11
11+A
12+A
12
12+A
15,15
16
17−A
18,18
19
17: 1,2,3
4 qtr
5,6,7
8,24
26,27
18 passim
17−A
28+A
19: 1,4,5
6,8,9
10+A
10,11
13,13
13−B
17,20
32,36
20: 6,12
14,18
20
21: 3,11
17,28
24,25
22: 3,3,9
9,10
10,11
12,12
16,18
23: 1,1,2
3,4,5
11,11
12,12
13,13
19
19+A
21,22
22,23
25,28
29,29
34
24: 1,5,7

2 Ki. 24: 7,7,10
11,12
12,12
13,13
15,15
16,17
20
25: 1,2,4
5,6,6
8,8,9
11,19
20,21
22,23
24,25
27 ter
28,30
1 Ch. 1:43
43+A
3: 2
4:23,31
41
5: 6,17
17,26
26
9: 1,18
11: 2,3,3
3,4
14: 1
2−ABS
8
15:29
16:21
17:10
18: 3,5,9
9,10
11−ABS
17
19: 1,5,7
9
20: 1,2
21: 2−A
3,4−B
6,20
23,24
24: 6,31
25: 1,2,5
6
26:26,30
32,32
27: 1[p],1
24,25
31,32
33,33
34
28: 1
1−AB
2+A
4,4
29: 1,6,9
10,11
20,22
24,25
25,29
2 Ch. 1:12,14
15,16
17,17
2: 8,11
11,12
4:11,16
17
5: 3,6
6: 3
7: 4
5−AB
5,6,11
8:10,11
15,18
9: 8,8,8
9,9,11
11,12
12,14
14,15
16,17
20,21
21,22
23,25
26,27
9:30+AB
10: 2,3+A
6,12

2 Ch. 10:13,13
15,16
16
18−B
18
12: 2,6,9
9
10−AB
10,11
13−AB
13: 5
16: 1,1,2
2,3,4
6,7,7
11
17:19,19
18: 3,3,4
5,5,7
7,8,9
9,11
12,14
14,15
17,19
25,25
26,28
28,29
29,30
30,31
32,33
34
19: 1,2,11
20:15,34
35−B
35
21: 2,6,8
12,13
17,20
22: 1,5−AB
5,6,6
11−B
11,11
11+B
23: 3 ter
5−A[1]
7,7,9
10,11
11,12
12,13
13,15
16,20
20,20
24: 6,8,11
11,12
14,16
17,17
21,23
25,27
25: 3,7,16
17−AB
17−B
18,18
21,21
23,23
24,25
25
26−B
26: 2,11
13,18
21
22+A[2]
23
27: 5,5,7
28: 2,5,5
6,7,7
16−AB
16
18−A
18−A
19,20
21,21
22,23
26,27
29:15,18
19,20
23,24
25
25−B
27,29
30
30: 2,4,6

2 Ch. 30:6,6,12
26
31: 3,13
32: 1,4,7
8,9,9
10,11
20,21
22,23
32
33:11,25
34:11,16
16,18
18,19
20,20
22,24
26,28
29,30
31
35: 3,3,4
4+AB
7,10
15,16
18,19
20 ter
21,23
23,27
36: 1,3,4
5,6,8
10,13
17,18
22,22
23
Ezra 1: 1,1,2
7,8
2: 1
3: 7,10
4: 2,3,5
5,7,8
11,12
13,13
14,14
15,16
17,19
20,22
23,24
5: 6,7,8
11,12
13,13
14
14−B
14−B
17 qtr
6: 1,3,3
4,8,10
12,13
14,15
22
7: 1,6
7,8
12,12
14,15
20,21
23,26
27,28
28
8: 1,22
22,25
36,36
9: 7,7,9
Neh. 1:11
2: 1,1,2
3,3,4
5,5
5+S[3]
6,6
7,7
8+S[3]
8,8,9
9,14
16 S[1n]
18,19
3:15
25
5: 4
14+S[3]
6: 6,7,7
7: 6
9:24 B[r]
22−S[1]
22,24

Neh. 9:32,32
34,37
11:23,24
13: 6 ter
26 ter
Est. 1: 2−S[1]
5,5,7
8,9,10
10,12
13+AS[3]
14,14
15,16
16,16
17
17−AS[1]
18,19
19+A
19,20
21,21
22+AS[3]
2 passim
3: 1,2,3
3,4,8
8,8,9
9,10
11,12
12,15
4: 2
5+A
7,8,8,9
11,11
11,16
5: 3,4
4+AS[3]
5,6,8
8+S[3]
8,9,11
12,14
14
6 passim
2−A
3−A
8−A
7: 1,2,3
4,5,6
7,8,8
9 ter
10
8: 1,1,2
3,4,4
7,8
9+S[3]
10
(9)14
9: 1,4,11
12,13
25
10: 1,2,3
Job 2:11,11
3:14
12:18
29:25
34:18
36: 7
39:22[s]
41:25
42 p 18 ter
Psa. 2: 2
6−B
10
5: 3
17:51
19:10
20: 1,8
23: 7
8−A[1]
9
10−A[1]
10
28:10
32:16
43: 5
44: 2,6,10
12,14
15,16
46: 3,7,8
47: 3,5
59: 9
60: 7
62:12

Psa. 67:13,15
25,30
71: 1,1,10
10,11
73:12
75:13
83: 4
88:19,28
94: 3
97: 6
98: 4−S[1]
100: 3 S[1t]
101:16,23[u]
104:14,20
30[v]
107: 9
109: 5
118:16
134:10,11
11
135:17,18
19,20
137: 4
143:10
144: 1
148:11
149: 2,8
Pro. 6: 8
8:15
13:17
14:28,35
16:10,12
13,14
15
19: 6,12
20: 2,8,26
28
21: 1
22:11,29
24:21,23
23,63
66,69
25: 1,2,3
5,6,15
28:16
29: 4,12
14
Ecc. 1: 1,12
2: 8
4:13
5: 8
8: 2,4
9:14
10:16,17
20
Cant. 1: 4,12
3: 9,11
7: 5
Isa. 6: 1,5
7: 1 ter
16−A
17,20
8: 4,6,7
13: 4,19
14: 4,9,16
18,28
32
19: 4,11
11,11
20: 1,4,6
23:11,15
24:21
32: 1
33:17,22
34:12
36: 1,2,2
4,4,6
8,13
13+B
13−S[1]
14,15
16,18
21
37: 1,4,5
6,8
8+AS
9,10
10,11
13,18
21,33

Isa. 37:37
38: 6, 9
39: 1, 3, 7
41: 2, 21
43:15
44: 6–S[1]
45: 1
13-AS[3]
49: 7, 23
51: 4
52:15
60: 3, 10
11–S[1]
12, 16
62: 2
Jer. 1: 2, 3, 3
18
2:26
3: 6–A
4: 9
8: 1, 19
13:13, 18
15: 4
17:19–S[1]
20, 25
19: 3, 4
13
20: 4, 5
21: 1, 2, 3
7, 10
11
22: 1, 2, 4
6
18–S
24
23: 5
24: 1, 1
1+A
8
25: 1–S[1]
3+A
3, 17
26: 1–A
2 ter
13, 17
27:17, 17
18, 18
41, 43
28:11, 20
27, 28
31, 33
34, 57
59
30: 6, 8
32: 4, 5, 6
8 ter
11-A[1]S[1]
11, 12
33: 1, 10
18, 21
22, 23
34: 2, 2, 2
2, 2, 2
5, 6, 7
9, 10
11, 17
35: 1, 2, 4
11, 14
36: 2, 3, 3
21, 22
37: 9
39: 1 ter
2–S[1]
2–S[1]
3–S[1]
3–S[1]
4+A
4–S[1]
28, 32
35, 36
40: 4
41: 1, 2, 2
4, 6, 7
8, 21
21
42: 1
43: 1, 2, 9
12, 16
20, 20
21 ter

Jer. 43:22, 24
25, 26
26, 27
28, 29
30
44: 1+A
3, 7, 17
17, 18
19, 20
21
45: 3–S
4, 5, 5
6, 7, 7
8, 10
11, 14
14, 15
16, 17
18+A
19, 22
22, 23
24, 25
25, 26
27
46: 1, 1, 3
3
47: 5, 7, 9
11, 14
48: 1, 2, 9
9, 10
18
49:11
50: 6, 10
51: 9, 17
21, 30
30, 30
31
52: 4, 5, 7
8, 9, 9
10, 11
12, 13
20, 25
26 ABS
26, 27
31 ter
32, 34
Lam. 2: 2, 6, 9
4:12
Eze. 1: 2
7:27+A
17:12, 12
16
19: 9
21:20, 21
24: 2
26: 7
7+A
7, 7
27:33, 35
28:17
29: 2
3+A
18, 19
30:10, 21
22, 24
25, 25
31: 2
32: 2, 10
11
29+A
31
Dan. 1: 1, 2
3, 4, 5
5, 5, 8
10, 10
13, 15
18, 19
19, 20
21
2 passim
15 A[w]
47+A
3: 1–A
2+A
3, 5, 7
9, 9, 10
12, 13
16, 17
18
19+A
22, 24

Dan. 3:24
25–B[1]
27
27+AB[2]
28–AB
28, 30
31
4:15
16+A
19, 20
21, 21
24, 25
27–A
28, 28
30+A
34
5: 1, 2, 3
5, 5, 6
7, 8, 8
9, 10
11
11+A
12, 13
13, 13
17
17+A
18
30–A
6: 2, 3, 6, 6
7, 8, 9
12 qtr
13, 14
15 ter
16, 16
17–A
18, 19
21, 21
22, 23
24, 25
7: 1, 24
24, 27
8: 1, 20
21, 21
22, 23
27

Dan. 9: 6, 8
10: 1
11: 2, 3, 5
6, 6, 7
8, 9, 11
11, 13
14, 15
15, 25
25, 27
36, 40
40
Hos. 1: 1, 1
3: 4, 5
5: 1, 13
7: 3, 5, 7
8:10
10: 3, 3, 6
7
11: 1, 5
13:10, 10
11
Amos 1: 1, 1, 15
2: 1
7: 1, 10
13
Jon. 3: 6, 7
Mic. 1: 1, 14
2:13
4: 9
6: 5
Nah. 3:18
Hab. 1:10
Zeph. 1: 1
3 S[1x]
5, 8
3: 8, 15[y]
Hag. 1: 1
2: 1, 22
22–S[1]
Zec. 7: 1, 2
9: 5, 9
11: 6
14: 5, 9, 10
16, 17
Mal. 1:14

[a] A Φαραώ. [b] A πόλις.
[c] pro ὁδός. [d] pro βασιλείω.
[e] AB βασιλεύω. [f] A φυλή.
[g] A λαος. [h] A Ἰωαθαν.
[i] B βασιλεύω. [k] A βασιλεία.
[m] A ἄρχων. [n] pro Βάαλ.
[o] B ἀδελφός. [p] AB λαός.
[q] pro στρατηγός.
[r] pro βασιλεία. [s] AS[1] βίλος.
[t] pro παράβασις.
[u] BS[1] βασιλεία. [v] BS[2] βασιλεία.
[w] pro Δανιήλ. [x] pro ἀσεβής.
[y] AS[2] βασιλεύω.

βασιλεύω.

Gen. 36:31, 31
32 to 39
37: 8, 8
Exo. 15:18
Jos. 13:10, 12
Jud. 4: 2
9: 6, 8, 10
12, 14
15[a], 16
18
1 Sa. 8: 7, 9, 11
22
11:12
12: 1, 12
14
14:47
15:11–A
35
16: 1
1 AB[b]
23:17
24:21, 21
27: 5
2 Sa. 2: 4, 9, 10
10, 11
3:17, 21
5: 4, 4, 5
5

2 Sa. 8:15
10: 1
15:10
16: 8
19:22
1 Ki. 1: 5, 11
13, 13
17, 18
24, 30
35, 43
2:11, 11
11+A
35–AB
(3) p 46
4: 1
6: 1
11:22
24 A
37, 42
44
12: 1, 17 A
20
p 24:12
ll 3, 4
14: 2 A
19 A
20 A
20 A

1 Ki. 14:21 ter
25, 31
15: 1, 1, 2
8, 9, 10
24, 25
25, 28
29, 33
16: 6, 8, 10
11–A
15, 16
21, 22
23, 23
28
p 28–A
p 28+B
p 28–A
p 28–A
28B[h], 29
29+A
22:40, 41
41, 42
42, 51
52, 52
2 Ki. 1:18
18+A
3: 1
1–A
27
8:13, 15
16, 17
17, 20
24, 25
26, 26
9:13, 29
10: 5, 35
36
11: 3, 12
21
12: 1, 1, 21
13: 1, 9, 10
24
14: 1, 2, 2
16, 21
23, 29
15: 1, 2, 2
5, 7, 8
10, 13
13
14+A
17, 22
23, 25
27, 30
32, 33
33, 38
16: 1, 2, 2
20
17: 1, 21
18: 1, 2, 2
19:37
20, 21
21: 1, 1, 18
19, 19
24, 26
22: 1, 1
23:30, 31
31, 33
34, 36
36
24: 6, 8, 8
17, 18
18
1 Ch. 1:43+A
43+A
44, 45
46, 47
48, 49
50
3: 4–B
4
11:10
12:31, 38
38–A
16:31

1 Ch. 18:14
19: 1
23: 1
29:22, 26
28
2 Ch. 1: 8, 9, 11
13
9:30, 31
10: 1, 17
11:22
12:13 ter
16
13: 1, 2
14: 1
17: 1
20:31 ter
21: 1, 5, 8
20
20–A
22: 1, 1, 2
2, 12
23: 3, 11
24: 1, 1, 27
25: 1+B
1, 1
26: 1
3–B
3, 23
27: 1, 1
8 A
8 A
9
28: 1, 1, 27
29: 1, 1
32:33
33: 1, 1, 20
21, 21
25
34: 1, 1
36: 2 ter
5, 5, 8
9, 9, 10
11, 11
Est. 1: 3, 11
2: 4
3: 7 A[d]
4:14
Job 34:30
42 p 18
Psa. 9:37
44: 5
46: 9
92: 1
95:10
96: 1
98: 1
145:10
Pro. 1: 1
8:15
9: 6–S[2]
24:57
Ecc. 4:14
Isa. 1: 1
7: 6
24:23
30:33
32: 1
36: 1
37:38
52: 7
Jer. 22:11, 15
23: 5
26: 1
35: 1+A
41: 5
44: 1 ter
52: 1, 1, 31
Eze. 17:16
20:33
Dan. 9: 1
Hos. 8: 4
Mic. 4: 7
Zeph. 3:15 AS[2b]

[a] A βασιλεύς. [b] pro βασιλεύς.
[c] B βασιλεύς. [d] pro βασιλεία.

βασιλικός.

Nu. 20:17
21:22
2 Sa. 14:26
Est. 1:19

Est. 2: 9, 23
(9)15
9: 3
Job 18:14
Dan. 6: 7

βασιλίσκος.

Psa. 90:13 | Isa. 59: 5

βασίλισσα.

1 Ki. 10: 1, 4, 10
13
2 Ch. 9: 1, 3, 9
12
Est. 1: 9, 11
12, 15
16, 17
19
2:22+A
4: 4
5: 3+S[3]
6, 12
7: 1, 2
3+S[3]
5+S[3]
Est. 7: 6, 7, 8
8: 7+A
9:12+S[3]
29–S[1]
30
Psa. 44:10
Cant. 6: 7, 8
Jer. 30, 6
36: 2
51:17, 18
19
25–S[1]
Dan. 5:10
10+A

βάσις.

Exo. 26:19, 19
19-AB[1]
21, 21
21–B
25 ter
32, 37
27:10
11–A[1]
11, 12
13, 14
15, 16
17, 18
29:12
30:18
28+A
31: 9
37: 4, 6, 8
9, 10
12, 13
15, 17
38:23, 26
39: 8, 9, 9
14–A
Exo. 39:29+A
Lev. 1:15
4: 7, 18
25, 30
34
5: 9
6:32
8:11, 15
9: 9
Nu. 3:36, 37
4:14, 31
31, 32
32
Deu. 12:27–B
2 Ki. 16:17
25:16+B[a]
2 Ch. 6:13
Cant. 5:15
Jer. 52:17–A
Eze. 16:31, 39
41:22
43:20

βασκαίνω.

Deuteronomy 28:54, 56

βάσκανος.

Pro. 23: 6 | Pro. 28:22

βάσταγμα.

2 Sa. 15:33
Neh. 13:15, 19
Jer. 17:21
Jer. 17:22–S[1]
24, 27

βαστάζω.

Jud. 16:30[a]
Ruth 2:16, 16
2 Ki. 18:14
Job 21: 3 A[b]

[a] A κλίνω. [b] pro αἴρω.

βάτος.

Exo. 3: 2 ter
3, 4
Deu. 33:16
Job 31:40

βάτος.

Ezra 7:22[ab] | Ezra 7:22–B[b]

[a] B ἀποθήκη. [b] (A βαδῶν.)

βάτραχος.

Exo. 8: 2, 3, 4
5, 6, 6
7, 8, 9
11, 12
Exo. 8:13
Psa. 77:45
104:30

βδέλλα.

Proverbs 24:50

βδέλυγμα.

Gen. 43:31 | Gen. 46:34

Exo. 8:26, 26
Lev. 5: 2
7:11
11:10, 11
12, 13
20, 23
41, 42
18:22, 26
27, 29
20:13
Deu. 7:25, 26
26
12:31
13:14
14: 3
17: 1, 4
18: 9, 12
12
20:18
22: 5
23:18
24: 6
25:16
27:15
29:17
32:16
1 Ki. 11: 6
5+A
33
14:24
20:26
2 Ki. 12: 8 B[a]
16: 3
17:32
21: 2, 11
23:13
2 Ch. 15: 8
28: 3
33: 2
34:33
36:14

Psa. 87: 9
Pro. 11: 1, 20
12:22
15: 8, 9, 26
16:12
20, 23
21:27
27:20
29:27, 27
Isa. 1:13
2: 8, 20
17: 8
41:24
44:19
66: 3, 17
Jer. 2: 7
4: 1
7:10—S[1]
30
11:15
13:27
16:18
39:35
51:22
Eze. 5: 9, 11
6: 9, 11
7: 8, 9, 3
4, 20
8:10
11:18, 21
16:22+A
20: 7, 8, 30
30:13+A
33:26 A, 29
36:31
Dan. 9:27
11:31
12, 11
Zec. 9: 7
Mal. 2:11

[a] pro βδέκ.

βδελυγμός.

1 Sa. 25:31
Nah. 3: 6

βδελυκτός.

Proverbs 17:15

βδελύσσω.

Gen. 26:29
Exo. 1:12
5:21
Lev. 11:11, 13
43
18:30
20:23, 25
21:14 A[a]
26:11
Deu. 7:26
23: 7, 7
1 Ki. 20:26
Job 9:31
15:16
19:19
30:10

Psa. 5: 7
13: 1
52: 2
55: 6
105:40
106:18
118:163
Pro. 8: 7
28: 9
Isa. 14:19
49: 7
66: 5
Hos. 9:10
Amos 5:10
6: 8
Mic. 3: 9

[a] pro ἐκβάλλω.

βεβαιόω.

Psa. 40:13
Psa. 118:28

βεβαίως.

Leviticus 25:30

βεβαίωσις.

Leviticus 25:23

βέβηλος.

Lev. 10:10
21: 9
1 Sa. 21: 4, 5
Eze. 4:14 A[2]B[*a]

Eze. 21:25
22:26
44:23

[a] pro ἕωλος.

βεβηλόω.

Exo. 31:13
Lev. 18:21
19: 8, 12

Lev. 19:29
20: 3
21: 6, 7, 9
Lev. 21:12, 14
15, 23
22: 2, 9, 15
32
Nu. 18:32
25: 1
30: 3
Neh. 13:17, 18
Psa. 9:26
54:21—S[1]
73: 7
88:32, 35
40
Isa. 48:11[a]
56: 2, 6
Jer. 16:18
41:16
Lam. 2: 2
Eze. 7:21, 22
13:19
20: 9, 13

Eze. 20:14, 16
21, 22
24, 39
44
22: 8, 26
26
23:38, 39
24:21
25: 3
28:18
36:20, 21
22, 23
23
39: 7
43: 7, 8
44: 7
Dan. 11:31
Amos 2: 7
Zeph. 3: 4
Mal. 1:12
2:10, 11

[a] S[1] βούλομαι.

βεβήλωσις.

Leviticus 21: 4

βεδέκ.

2 Ki. 12: 5, 5, 6
7, 8[a]

2 Ki. 12:12
22: 5, 6

[a] B βδέλυγμα.

βέλος.

Deu. 32:23, 42
2 Sa. 18:14
22:15
2 Ki. 9:24
13:15, 15
17, 17
19:32
2 Ch. 26:15
Job 6: 4
16: 9
20:25
30:14
34: 6
39:22 AS[*a]
Psa. 7:14
10: 2

Psa. 17:15
37: 3
44: 6
56: 5
63: 8
76:18
90: 5
119: 4
126: 4
143: 6
Isa. 5:28
7:24
37:33
49: 2
Lam. 3:12
Joel 2: 8

[a] pro βασιλεύς.

βελόστασις.

Jer. 28:27
Eze. 4: 2
17, 17

Eze. 21:22
26: 8 A[a]

[a] pro περίστασις.

βέλτιστος.

Gen. 47: 6, 11
Exo. 22: 5, 5

βελτίων, —τιον.

Gen. 29:19
Nu. 14: 3
Jud. 9: 2 A[a]
18:19 A[a]
Job 42:15
Pro. 8:19
24:40
Isa. 17: 3

Isa. 45: 9
Jer. 22:15
33:13, 14
42:15
45:20
47: 9
49: 6

[a] pro ἀγαθός.

βῆμα.

Deu. 2: 5
Neh. 8: 4

βηρύλλιον.

Exo. 28:20
36:20

Eze. 28:13

βία.

Exo. 1:13, 14
14:25
Neh. 5:14, 15
18
Isa. 17:13
28: 2—S[1]

Isa. 30:30
52: 4
63: 1
Eze. 44:18
Hab. 3: 6

βιάζω.

Gen. 33:11
Exo. 19:24
Deu. 22:25, 28
Jud. 13:15 A[a]
16 A[a]

Jud. 19: 7
2 Sa. 13:25, 27
2 Ki. 5:23+A
Est. 7: 8[b]
Jon. 1:13 B[1 c]

[a] pro κατέχω.
[b] A ἐκβιάζω.
[c] pro παραβιάζομαι.

βίαιος.

Exo. 14:21
Job 34: 6[a]
Psa. 47: 8
Isa. 11:15

Isa. 30:30 B[b]
58: 6
59:19

[a] S[1] βιβλίον.
[b] pro βιαίως.

βιαίως.

Isa. 30:30[a]
Jer. 18:14

[a] B βίαιος.

βιβάζω.

Lev. 18:23
Lev. 20:16

βιβλιαφόρος.

Esther 3:13

βίβλινος.

Isaiah 18: 2

βιβλιοθήκη.

Ezra 6: 1
Est. 2:23

βιβλίον.

Exo. 17:14
24: 7
Nu. 5:23
21:14[a]
Deu. 17:18
24: 3, 5
28:58, 61
29:20, 21
27
30:10
31: 9, 24
26
Jos. 18: 9
23: 6
24:26
1 Sa. 10:25
2 Sa. 1:18
11:14, 15
1 Ki. 5:(18) A
8:53[a]
11:41
14:19 A, 29
15: 7, 23
31
16: 5, 14
20, 27
p28—A
20: 8, 8, 9
11—B
22:39, 46
2 Ki. 1:18
5: 5, 6, 6
7
8:23
10: 1, 2, 6
7, 34
12:19
13: 8, 12
14: 6, 15
18, 28
15: 6, 11
15, 21
26, 31
36
16:19
19:14
20:12, 20
21:17, 25
22: 8
8—A
10, 11

2 Ki. 22:13, 13
16[a]
23: 2, 3, 21
24, 28
24: 5
1 Ch. 9: 1
27:24
2 Ch. 13:22
16:11
20:34
25:26[h]
27: 7
28:26
32:17, 32
34:14, 15
15, 16
18, 21
21, 24
30, 31
35:12 AB[c]
19, 27
36: 8
Ezra 4:15 AB[c]
6:18 AB[c]
7:11, 17
Neh. 7: 5
8: 1, 3, 5
8, 18
9: 3
10:34 B[d]
12 23
13: 1[e]
Est. 9:20
10: 2[e]
Job 19:23[f]
31: 6 S[1 g]
Psa. 39: 8
138:16
Ecc. 12:12
Isa. 29:11, 12
18
30: 8
34: 4
37:14
50: 1
Jer. 3: 8
25:13
28:60, 63
36:29
37: 2
39:10, 11
Jer. 39:12, 14
14, 16
25, 44
43: 2, 4, 8
10, 11
14A[h], 18
20 A[h]
25 A[h]

Jer. 43:29A[h], 32
51:31
Eze. 2: 9
27: 9
Dan. 12: 4
Nah. 1: 1
Mal. 3:16

[a] A βίβλος.
[b] B βυβλίον.
[c] pro βίβλος.
[d] pro νόμος.
[e] S[1] βίβλος.
[f] S βίβλος.
[g] pro βίαιος.
[h] pro χαρτίον.

βιβλιοφόρος.

Esther 8:10

βίβλος.

Gen. 2: 4
5: 1
Exo. 32:32, 33
Nu. 21:14 A[a]
Jos. 1: 8
1 Ki. 8:53 A[a]
2 Ki. 22:16 A[a]
2 Ch. 17: 9[b]
35:12[c]
Ezra 4:15[c]
6:18[c]

Neh. 13: 1 S[1 a]
Est. 10: 2 S[1 a]
Job 19:23 S[a]
37:19
42 p 18
Psa. 68:29
Jer. 36: 1
Dan. 7:10
9: 2
12: 1

[a] pro βιβλίον.
[b] B βύβλος.
[c] AB βιβλίον.

βιβρώσκω.

Exo. 12:46
13: 3
21:28
29:34
Lev. 6:16, 23
26, 30
7: 5, 6, 9
14[a]
11:13, 41
19: 6, 7, 23
22:30
Deu. 12:23
Jos. 5:12
9:11, 18

Jud. 14:14—A
1 Sa. 30:12
Job 5: 3
6: 6—S[1]
18:13
Isa. 9:18
28:28
51: 8, 8
Jer. 24: 2, 3, 8
37:16
Eze. 4:14
18:15[a]
Nah. 1:10

[a] A φάγω.

βίκος.

Jeremiah 19: 1, 10

βίος.

Ezra 7:26
Job 7: 1, 6, 16
8: 9
9:25
10: 5, 20
12:12
14: 5, 6, 14
15:20

Job 21:13
Pro. 3: 2, 16
4:10
5: 9
16:17
24:71
29:30, 32[a]
Cant. 8: 7

[a] AS[2] πλοῦτος.

βιότης.

Proverbs 5:23

βιόω.

Job 29:18
Pro. 7: 2

Pro. 9: 6+AS[?]

βιρά.

Nehemiah 7: 2

βλαβερός.

Proverbs 10:26

βλάπτω.

Pro. 25:20[a]

[a] S[1] βάπτω.

βλαστάνω.

Gen. 1:11
Nu. 17: 8, 8
Jud. 16:22[a]
2 Sa. 23: 5
Ecc. 2: 6

Isa. 27: 6
45: 8—S
55:10 A[b]
Joel 2:22

[a] A ἀνατέλλω.
[b] pro ἐκβλαστάνω.

βλαστός.

Gen. 40:10; 49:9
Exo. 38:15
Nu. 17:8
1 Ki. 7:11
2 Ch. 4:5
Job 15:30; 30:12
Eze. 17:8, 23; 19:10

βλασφημέω.

2 Ki. 19:4, 6, 22
Isa. 52:5

βλασφημία.

Eze. 35:12
Dan. 3:29

βλάσφημος.

Isaiah 60:3

βλέπω.

Gen. 45:12; 48:10
Exo. 4:11; 23:8
Nu. 21:20
Deu. 4:34; 28:32[a], 34; 29:4
Jos. 18:14
Jud. 9:36[b]; 13:19[c], 20[c]; 19:30[d]
1 Sa. 3:2; 4:15 AB[e]; 9:9, 9, 11; 18; 16:4; 25:35; 26:12
2 Sa. 14:24
1 Ki. 1:48; 17:23
2 Ki. 2:19; 9:17
1 Ch. 9:22; 21:3; 29:29, 29
2 Ch. 4:4; 4+A; 4+A; 4+A; 5:9, 9; 10:16
Neh. 2:17
Est. 2:15
Job 10:4
Psa. 9:32, 35; 39:13; 68:24
Pro. 4:25; 12:13; 16:25
Ecc. 8:16; 11:4, 7; 12:3
Cant. 1:6
Isa. 6:9, 9; 8:22; 21:3; 29:18 AS³ [f]; 38:14; 44:18
Jer. 5:21; 20:18; 49:2
Lam. 3:1
Eze. 8:3; 5+A; 14; 9:2; 11:1; 12:2[b], 2; 13:3, 6; 40:6, 19; 19, 20; 21, 22; 23, 23; 24, 32; 40, 44; 44, 45; 46; 42:7, 8, 15; 16; 43:1; 2+A; 4, 17; 44:1; 46:1; 9−A; 12, 19; 47:1[g], 2
Dan. 5:23
Amos 8:1[b]
Nah. 2:8 A[e]
Hag. 2:3
Zec. 4:2; 5:2

[a] A εἰμί. [b] A ὁράω. [c] A θεωρέω. [d] A ὄρος. [e] pro ἐπιβλέπω [f] pro ὁράω. [g] A ἐπιβλέπω.

βλέφαρον.

Job 16:16
Psa. 10:4; 131:4
Pro. 4:25; 6:4, 25; 24:36
Jer. 9:18

βοάω.

Gen. 4:10; 29:11; 39:14, 15; 18
Exo. 8:12; 14:15; 15:25; 17:4
Nu. 12:13
Deu. 15:9 A[a]; 22:24, 27
Jos. 6:10; 15:18
Jud. 4:10[b]; 6:7[c], 34[d]; 35+A; 7:23, 24; 9:54; 10:10, 12[e]; 14; 12:1[e], 2; 15:18 A[f]; 16:28 A[f]; 18:22, 23
1 Sa. 5:10; 7:8, 9; 8:18; 11:7; 12:8, 10; 14:26; 15:11; 20:38 A[g]; 24:9
2 Sa. 15:2; 18:26, 28; 20:4, 5, 10; 22:7, 42
1 Ki. 17:10, 11; 18:24; 21:39
2 Ki. 2:12; 4:1; 6:5, 26; 7:10, 11; 8:3, 5; 11:14; 18:18, 28; 20:11
1 Ch. 5:20; 16:32 A[h]; 21:26
2 Ch. 13:14, 15; 15; 14:11; 18:31; 20:9, 20; 23:13; 32:18, 20
Neh. 9:4; 28 S[g]
Est. 4:1
Job 2:12; 30:7; 35:9; 36:13; 37:3
Isa. 5:29, 30; 12:4; 14:7; 15:4, 5, 5; 22:2; 24:14 AS[i]; 27:5; 31:4; 33:7[k]; 34:14; 36:13 AS[g]; 40:3, 6, 6; 42:11−A; 13; 44:5[m]; 5-AS²; 23; 46:7; 54:1; 58:9
Jer. 12:6; 22:20; 31:31
Lam. 2:18; 3:8
Dan. 3:4; 5:7; 6:20
Hos. 7:14
Joel 1:19
Jon. 1:5 A[g]; 2:3−S¹
Hab. 1:2; 2:11

[a] pro καταβοάω. [b] A παραγγέλλω. [c] A κράζω. [d] B φοβέω. [e] A συνάγω. [f] pro κλαίω. [g] pro ἀναβοάω. [h] pro βομβέω. [i] pro φωνέω. [k] AS³ φοβέω. [m] A ἐρῶ.

βοή.

Exo. 2:23
1 Sa. 4:14, 14; 9:16
2 Ch. 33:13
Isa. 15:8; 24:11[a]
Eze. 21:22

[a] AS φωνή.

βοήθεια.

Jud. 5:23; 23−A
1 Sa. 18:3
1 Ch. 12:16
2 Ch. 28:21
Est. 4:14
Job 6:13; 31:21
Psa. 7:11; 19:3; 21:20; 34:2; 37:23; 48:15; 59:13; 61:8; 69:2; 70:12−B; 88:20, 44; 90:1; 107:13; 120:1, 2; 123:8
Pro. 21:31; 24:6[a]; 28:12
Isa. 8:20; 20:6; 30:5; 6+AS; 32; 31:1, 3; 47:15
Jer. 16:19; 29:4; 44:7
Lam. 3:56−A; 4:17
Dan. 11:34

[a] S¹ βοηθέω.

βοηθέω.

Gen. 49:25
Deu. 22:27; 28:29; 31−B; 32:38
Jos. 10:4, 6, 33
1 Sa. 7:12
2 Sa. 8:5; 18:3−A; 21:17
1 Ki. 1:7
2 Ki. 14:26
1 Ch. 12:1, 18; 19, 33; 36; 18:5; 19:19
2 Ch. 19:2; 26:13, 15; 28:16; 32:18
Ezra 5:2; 10:15
Est. 8:11; 9:16
Job 4:20; 20:14; 26:2; 29:12
Psa. 21:12; 27:7; 36:40−S¹; 39:14; 40:4; 43:27; 45:6; 53:6; 69:2+B*S; 6; 78:9; 85:17; 93:17, 18; 106:12, 41; 108:26; 118:86, 117; 175
Pro. 3:27[a]; 13:12; 18:19; 20:22; 24:6 S¹[b]; 28:18
Ecc. 7:20
Isa. 10:3; 30:2; 31:3; 41:6, 10; 14; 44:2; 49:8; 50:9; 66:15
Lam. 1:7
Eze. 30:8
Dan. 10:13; 11:34
Hos. 13:9

[a] A ποιέω. [b] pro βοήθεια.

βοηθός.

Gen. 2:18, 20
Exo. 15:2; 18:4
Deu. 33:7, 26; 29
Jud. 5:23+A
1 Sa. 7:12
2 Sa. 22:42
1 Ch. 12:18
Job 22:25; 29:12
Psa. 9:10, 35; 17:3; 18:15; 26:9; 27:7; 29:11; 32:20; 39:18; 45:2; 51:9; 58:18; 61:9; 62:8; 69:6; 70:7; 71:12; 77:35; 80:2; 93:22; 113:17, 18; 19; 117:6, 7; 118:114; 145:5
Isa. 8:13 S[a]; 17:10; 25:4; 50:7; 63:5
Eze. 12:14
Nah. 3:9

[a] pro φόβος.

βόθρος.

Jos. 8:29
1 Sa. 13:6
Psa. 7:16; 56:7; 93:13
Pro. 22:14; 26:27[a]
Ecc. 10:8
Eze. 26:20, 20; 31:14; 32:18, 21[b]; 22, 24; 29, 30
Amos 9:7
Zec. 3:9

[a] S βόθυνος. [b] B θόρυβος.

βόθυνος.

2 Sa. 18:17
2 Ki. 3:16, 16
Pro. 26:27 S[a]
Isa. 24:17, 18; 18; 47:11; 51:1
Jer. 31:28, 43; 44, 44

[a] pro βόθρος.

βοΐδιον.

Jeremiah 27:11

βόλβιτον.

Eze. 4:12, 15; 15
Zeph. 1:17

βολή.

Genesis 21:16

βολίς.

Exo. 19:13
Nu. 24:8; 33:55
Jos. 23:13
1 Sa. 14:14
Neh. 4:17
Psa. 54:22
Cant. 4:4
Jer. 9:8; 27:9
Eze. 5:16
Hab. 3:11
Zec. 9:14

βόλος.

Eze. 17:7[a], 10[a]

[a] A βῶλος.

βομβέω.

1 Ch. 16:32[a]
Jer. 31:36, 36; 38:35

[a] A βοάω.

βορά.

Job 4:11; 9:26; 38:39, 41

βόρβορος.

Jeremiah 45:6, 6

βορέας.

Job 26:7
Pro. 25:23; 27:16

βορρᾶς.

Gen. 13:14; 28:14
Exo. 26:18, 35; 27:11 A[a]; 37:9; 40:20
Lev. 1:11
Nu. 2:25; 3:35; 10:6; 34:3 A[b], 7; 9; 35:5
Deu. 2:3; 3:27
Jos. 15:5, 6, 8; 10, 11; 16:6; 17:9, 10, 10; 18:5, 12; 12, 16; 18, 19; 19; 19:14, 27; 24:31
Jud. 2:9; 7:1; 12:1[c]; 21:19
1 Sa. 14:5
1 Ki. 7:12
2 Ki. 16:14
1 Ch. 9:24; 26:14, 17; 18
2 Ch. 4:4; 14:10
Job 37:21
Psa. 47:3; 88:13; 106:3
Ecc. 1:6; 11:3
Cant. 4:16
Isa. 14:13, 31; 41:25; 43:6; 49:12
Jer. 1:13−S¹; 14, 15; 3:12, 18; 4:6; 6:1, 22; 10:22; 13:20; 16:15; 23:8; 25:9; 26:6, 10; 20, 24; 27:3, 9, 41; 29:2; 38:8
Eze. 1:4; 8:3, 5, 5; 5, 14; 9:2; 20:47; 21:4; 23:24; 26:7; 32:30; 38:6, 15; 39:2; 40:19, 20; 23, 35; 40, 44; 44, 46; 41:11; 42:1, 1, 2; 4, 7, 11; 13, 17; 17; 44:4; 46:9, 9, 19; 47:2, 15; 17; 17+A; 17+A; 48:1, 1, 10; 16, 17; 30, 31
Dan. 8:4; 11:6, 7, 8; 11, 13; 15, 40; 44
Joel 2:20
Amos 8:12
Zeph. 2:13
Zec. 2:6; 6:6, 8, 8; 14:4

[a] (A πορρᾶν) pro ἀπηλιωτής. [b] pro λίψ. [c] (A κεφεινα.)

βόσκημα.

2 Ch. 7:5−B
Isa. 7:25; 27:10; 32:14; 49:11
Jer. 32:22

βόσκω.

Gen. 29:6+A; 7, 9; 37:12, 16; 41:2
1 Ki. 12:16
Job 1:14
Isa. 5:17; 11:6, 7; 11:7 A[a]; 14:30; 30:23; 34:17; 49:9; 65:25
Jer. 38:10
Eze. 34:2, 2, 3

Eze. 34: 8,8,10
13,14
Eze. 34:14,15
16

[a] pro εἰμί.

βόστρυχος.

Jud. 16:14 A[a]
19 A[a]
Cant. 5: 2,11

[a] pro σειρά.

βοτάνη.

Gen. 1:11,12
Exo. 9:22,25
10:12,15
15
1 Ki. 18: 5
2 Ki. 19:26[a]
Job 8:12
Isa. 58:11+AS[2]
66:14
Jer. 14: 5
27:11
Zec. 10: 1

[a] vide χλωροβοτάνη.

βοτρύδιον.

Isaiah 18: 5

βότρυς.

Gen. 40:10
Nu. 13:24,24
25,25
32: 9
Deu. 1:24
Deu. 32:32
Cant. 1:14−B
7: 7,8
Isa. 65: 8
Mic. 7: 1

βούβαλος.

Deuteronomy 14: 5+A

βούκεντρον.

Ecclesiastes 12:11

βουκόλιον.

Exo. 13:12
Lev. 22:19,21
23:18
Deu. 7:13
28: 4,18
51
1 Sa. 8:16
14:32
15: 9,21
1 Sa. 27: 9
30:20
2 Sa. 12: 2,4
Ecc. 2: 7
Isa. 17: 2+AS[2]
65:10
Eze. 46: 6+A
Joel 1:18
Amos 6: 4

βουλευτής.

Job 3:14
Job 12:17

βουλευτικός.

Proverbs 24: 6

βουλεύω.

Gen. 50:20,20
2 Sa. 16:23
17: 7,21
1 Ki. 12: 6[a]
9 A[b]
28−A
2 Ki. 6: 8
1 Ch. 13: 1
2 Ch. 10: 6[c], 9[c]
20:21
25:17
30: 2,23
32: 3
Ezra 4: 5[d]
Neh. 5: 7
6: 7
Est. 3: 6
Job 26: 3 S[1 b]
Psa. 30:14
61: 5
70:10
82: 4,6
Pro. 15:22
Isa. 3: 9
7: 5
8:10
14:24,26
27
16: 3
19:12,17
23: 8,9
28:29
31: 6
32: 7,8
45:20
46:10,11
51:13
Jer. 18:23+A
27:45
29:21
30: 8
40:22 A[e]
Eze. 11: 2
Mic. 6: 5
Nah. 1:11[f]
Hab. 2:10

[a] A βούλομαι. [b] pro συμβουλεύω. [c] AB βούλομαι. [d] B βούλομαι. [e] pro βούλομαι. [f] A λογίζομαι.

βουλή.

Gen. 49: 6
Nu. 16: 2
Deu. 32:28
Jud. 19:30
Jud. 20: 7
2 Sa. 15:31,34
16:20,23
23
2 Sa. 17: 7,14
14,14
23
1 Ki. 12: 8,13
14
p 24 l 62
2 Ki. 18:20
1 Ch. 12:19
2 Ch. 10: 8,13
14
22: 5
Ezra 4: 5
10: 3 S[3 a]
8
Neh. 4:15
Est. 9:30
Job 5:12,13
10: 3
12:13
18: 7
22:18
29:21
38: 2
42: 3−S[1]
Psa. 1: 1,5
12: 3
13: 6
19: 5
20:12
32:10
10−S[1]
11
65: 5
72:24
88: 8
105:13,43
106:11
110: 1
Pro. 1:25,30
2:11,16
3:21
8:12,14
9:10[b]
11:13,14
15:22
19:21
Pro. 20: 5
21:30
22:20
24:72,72
25:28
Ecc. 2:12
Isa. 3: 9
4: 2
5:19
7: 5,7
8:10
9: 6
10:25
11: 2
14:26
19: 3,11
17
25: 1,7
28: 8
8−S[1]
29:15,15
30: 1
31: 6
32: 7,8
36: 5
41:21
44:25,26
46:10
47:13
55: 7,8,8
Jer. 18:18,23
19: 7,7
27:45
29: 8,21
30: 8
39:19
Eze. 7:26
11: 2
27: 9
Dan. 2:14
4:24
Hos. 10: 6
Mic. 4: 9,12
6:16 A[c]
Zec. 6:13
Jer. 45:21 A[a]
49:22[f]
Eze. 3: 7
18:23 A[a]
Eze. 33:11
Dan. 5:19 qtr
Jon. 1:14

[a] pro θέλω. [b] pro βουλεύω. [c] S[3] βουλή. [d] vide θεεβουλαθώθ [e] pro βεβηλόω. [f] A βουλεύω.

[a] pro βούλομαι. [b] S[1] βούλημα. [c] pro ὁδός.

βούλημα.

Pro. 9:10 S[1 a]

[a] pro βουλή.

βούλομαι.

Gen. 24: 5
Exo. 4:23
8: 2,21
9: 2
10: 3,7,27
16:28
22:17
36: 2
Lev. 26:21
Deu. 25: 7,8
Jud. 13:23 A[a]
Ruth 3:13
1 Sa. 2:25,25
8:19
15: 9
18:25
20: 3
22:17
24:11
28:23
31: 4
2 Sa. 2:23
6:10
20:11
24: 3
1 Ki. 12: 6 A[b]
13:33
16: p 28−A
20: 6
1 Ch. 10: 4
11:19
2 Ch. 10: 6 AB[b]
9 AB[b]
21: 7
25:16
Ezra 4: 5 B[b]
10: 3[c]
Est. 3:11
8:11
Job 9: 3
13: 3
21:14
30:14
34:14
35:13
36:12
37: 9
11 S[2 d]
39: 9
Psa. 35: 4
39: 9
69: 3
77:10 S[2 e]
113:11 S[1 e]
Pro. 1:10
12:20
18: 1
21: 7
Isa. 1:11,29
8: 6,6
30: 9,15
36:16
42:21,24
48:11 B[1 e]
53:10,10
65:12
66: 4
Jer. 6:10
13:10
32:14

βουνίζω.

Ruth 2:14,16

βουνός.

Gen. 31:46 ter
47,47
48 ter
51−A
52
Exo. 17: 9,10
Nu. 23: 9
Deu. 33:15
Jos. 5: 3
1 Sa. 7: 1
10: 5,10
13
13: 3
14: 2
22: 6
23:19,19
26: 1,1,3
2 Sa. 2:24,25
6: 3
3+A
17: 9
1 Ki. 14:23
15:22
2 Ki. 2:16−A
10: 8
16: 4
17:10
1 Ch. 11:31
Psa. 64:13
71: 3
77:58
113: 4
6−S[1]
148: 9
Pro. 8:25
Cant. 2: 8
4: 6
Isa. 2: 2,14
9:18
10:18,32
30:17,25
40: 4
41:15
42:15−AS
44:23
49:13+S[1]
54:10
55:12
65: 7
Jer. 2:20
3:23
4:24
13:27
16:16
27: 6
29:17
38:39
Eze. 6: 3,13
20:28
34: 6
35: 8
36: 4,6
Hos. 4:13
5: 8
9: 9
10: 8,9,9
Joel 3:18
Amos 9:13
Mic. 4: 1
6: 1,2 A[a]
Nah. 1: 5
Hab. 3: 6
Zeph. 1:10

[a] pro ὄρος.

βοῦς.

Gen. 13: 5
18: 7
26:14
30:43
32: 5,5 A[a]
7,15
33:13
34:28
41: 2,3,3
4,4,18
19,20
20,26
27
45:10
46:32
47: 1,17
50: 8
Exo. 9: 3
10: 9,24
12:32,38
20:10,17
23: 4,12
29: 1
34: 3
Lev. 1: 2,3
3: 1
4: 3,14
7:13
9: 2
16: 3
27:32
Nu. 7: 3,6,7
8,15
21,27
33,39
45,51
Nu. 7:57,63
69,75
81,87
88
8: 8,8
11:22
15: 3,8,24
28:11,19
27
29: 2,8,13
31:28,30
33,38
44
Deu. 5:14,21
7:13
8:13
12: 6,17
21
14: 4,22
25−B
15:19
16: 2
21: 3
25: 4
28: 4,18
51
32:14
Jud. 3:31
1 Sa. 6: 7,7,10
12,14
11: 7,7
14:32
15:14,15
16: 2
2 Sa. 17:29
24:22,22
2 Sa. 24:24
1 Ki. 1: 9 A[b]
(3): p 46
4:23
7:12,15
15,30
8: 5,63
18:23,23
19:19
19 A[c]
20,21
21
2 Ki. 5:26
16:17
1 Ch. 27:29,29
2 Ch. 13: 9
32:29
Ezra 6: 9
Neh. 10:36
Job 1: 3,14
6: 5
21:10
24: 3
40:10
Job 42:12
Psa. 8: 8
49:10
65:15
143:14
Pro. 7:22
14: 4,4
Isa. 1: 3
5:10
7:21,25
11: 7,7
30:24
32:20
65:25
Eze. 4:15
43:19,23
25
45:18
Dan. 4:22,29
30
5:21
Joel 1:18
Jon. 3: 7
Hab. 3:17

[a] pro παῖς. [b] pro μόσχος. [c] pro ζεῦγος.

βούτομον.

Job 8:11
Job 40:16

βούτυρον.

Gen. 18: 8
Deu. 32:14
Jud. 5.25
2 Sa. 17:20
Job 20:17
29: 6
Pro. 24:68
Isa. 7:15,22

βραγχιάω.

Psalm 68: 4

βραδύγλωσσος.

Exodus 4: 10

βραδύνω.

Gen. 43: 9
Deu. 7:10
Isa. 46:13

βραχίων.

Gen. 24:18,46
27:16
49:24
Exo. 6: 1,6
15:16
29:22,27
32:11
Lev. 7:22,23
24
8:25,26
9:21
10:14,15
Nu. 6:19,20
18:18
Deu. 3:24
4:34
5:15
6:21
7: 8+AB[a]
19
9:26,29
11: 2
18: 3
26: 8
29: 3+AB
33:20,27
Jud. 15:14,14 A[a]
16:12
2 Sa. 1:10
22:35
1 Ki. 8: 41+A
2 Ki. 9:24
17:36
2 Ch. 6:32
32: 8
Job 26: 2
31:22
35: 9
38:15
Job 40: 4
Psa. 9:36
17:35
36:17
43: 4,4
70:18
76:16
78:11
88:11,14
22
97: 1
135:12
Pro. 29:35
Cant. 8: 6
Isa. 9:20
15: 2
17: 5+AS[1]
26:11
30:30
40:10,11
44:12
51: 5,5,9
52:10
53: 1
59:16
62: 8
63: 5,12
Jer. 17: 5
21: 5
28:14
39:17,21
Eze. 4: 7
13:20
17: 9
20:33,34
30:21,22
24,25
25
Dan. 2:32

Dan. 10: 6 | Hos. 7:15
11: 6, 15 | 11: 3
22 | Zec. 11:17, 17
31+A |

[a] pro χείρ.

βραχύς.

Exo. 18:22 | Psa. 8: 6
Deu. 26: 5 | 93:17
28:62 | 104:12
1 Sa. 14:29, 43 | 118:87
2 Sa. 16: 1 | Isa. 57:17
19:36 |

βρέχω.

Gen. 2: 5 | Isa. 34: 3
19:24 | Eze. 22:24
Exo. 9:23 | 38:22
Psa. 6: 7 | Joel 2:23
77.24, 27 | Amos 4: 7 *qlr*
Isa. 5: 6 |

βρόμος.

Job 6: 7 | Joel 2:20
17:11[a] | [a] A δρόμος.

βροντάω.

1 Sa. 2:10 | Job 40: 4
7:10 | Psa. 17:14
2 Sa. 22:14 | 28: 3
Job 37: 3, 4 |

βροντή.

Job 26:14 | Ps. 103: 7
40: 4+A | Isa. 29: 6[a]
Psa. 76:19 | Amos 4:13

[a] A κραυγή.

βροτός.

Job 4:17 | Job 25: 4
9: 2 | 28: 4, 13
10: 4, 21 | 32: 9, 21
11:12 | 33:12
14: 1, 10 | 34:15
15:14 | 36:25, 28

βροῦχος.

Lev. 11:22 | Joel 2:25
1 Ki. 8:37 | Amos 7: 1
2 Ch. 6:28 | Nah. 3:15
Ps. 104:34 | 16—S[1]
Joel 1: 4, 4 |

βροχή.

Psa. 67:10 | Psa. 104:32

βρόχος.

Pro. 6: 5 | Pro. 22:25
7:21 |

βρυγμός.

Proverbs 19:12

βρύχω.

Job 16: 9 | Ps. 111:10
Psa. 34:16 | Lam. 2:16
36:12 |

βρῶμα.

Gen. 6:21 | 1 Ki. 10: 5
14:11 | 12*p*24*l*50
41:35, 35 | 1 Ch. 12:40
36, 48 | 2 Ch. 2:10
48, 48 | 9: 4
42: 2,7,10 | 11:11
43: 1,3,19 | Ezra 3: 7
21 | Job 6: 5
44: 1, 25 | 20:21
Lev. 11:34 | Psa. 68:22
25: 6, 37 | 73:14
Deu. 2: 6, 28 | 77:18
23:19 | 78: 2
2 Sa. 13: 5,7,10 | 106:18

Pro. 23: 6[a] | Joel 1:16
29:33 | 2:23
Isa. 3: 6 | Hab. 1:16
62: 8—S[1] | Hag. 2:12
Jer. 41:20 A[b] | Mal. 1: 7+AS[3]
Eze. 4:10 | 12

[a] C ἔδεσμα. [b] pro βρῶσις.

βρώσιμος.

Lev. 19:23 | Eze. 47:12
Neh. 9:25 |

βρῶσις.

Gen. 1:29, 30 | Psa. 43:12
2: 9, 16 | 52: 5
3: 6 | 77:30
9: 3 | 103:21
25:28 | Isa. 55:10
47:24 | Jer. 7:33[b]
Lev. 7:14 | 15: 3
19: 7 | 19: 7
25: 7 | 41:20[c]
Deu. 32:24 | Lam. 1: 6+S[1]
Jud. 14.14 A[a] | 11, 19
1 Sa. 2:28 | 4:10
2 Sa. 16: 2 | Eze. 29: 5 A[d]
19:42 | 47:12
1 Ki. 19: 8 | Dan. 1:10
Job 33:20 | Hab. 3:17, 17
34: 3 | Mal. 3.11
Psa. 13: 4 |

[a] pro βρωτός. [b] A κατάβρωμα. [c] A βρῶμα. [d] pro κατάβρωμα.

βρώσκω, vide βιβρώσκω.

βρωτός.

Jud. 14:14[a] | Job 33:20

[a] A βρῶσις.

βυβλίον.

2 Ch. 25:26 B[a] | [a] pro βιβλίον.

βύβλος.

2 Ch. 17: 9 B[a] | [a] pro βίβλος.

βυθός.

Exo. 15: 5 | Psa. 68: 3, 16
Neh. 9:11 | 106:24
Psa. 67:23 |

βύρσα.

Lev. 8:17 | Job 16:15
9:11 | 40:26

βύσσινος.

Gen. 41:42 | Est. 1: 6, 6
Exo. 28:35 | 6: 8
36:35 | (9)15
1 Ch. 15:27, 27 | Isa. 3:23
2 Ch. 5:12 | Eze. 16:13

βύσσος.

Exo. 25: 4 | Exo. 36:36, 36
26: 1, 31 | 37
36 | 37: 3, 5, 7
27: 9—8 | 14, 16
16, 18 | 21
28: 5, 6, 8 | 39:13+A
15, 29 | 2 Ch. 2:14
35 | 3:14
31: 4+A | Pro. 29:40
35: 6, 23 | Isa. 3:23
25, 35 | 19: 9
36: 9, 10 | Eze. 16:10
12, 15 | 27: 7
32, 36 |

βύω.

Psalm 57: 5

βῶλαξ.

Job 7: 5

βῶλος.

Job 38:28 | Eze. 17:10 A[a]
Eze. 17: 7 A[a] | [a] pro βόλος.

βωμός.

Exo. 34:13 | 2 Ch. 31: 1
Nu. 3:10 | Isa. 15: 2
23: 1, 2, 4 | 16:12
4, 14 | 17: 8
14, 29 | 27: 9
30 | Jer. 7:31, 32
Deu. 7: 5 | 11:13
12: 3 | 30: 2
Jos. 22:10, 10 | 31:35
11, 16 | 39:35
19, 23 | Hos. 10: 8
26, 34 | Amos 7: 9
Jud. 7: 1+A |

γαβής.

1 Chronicles 4: 9

γαβίν.

2 Kings 25:12

γαβίς.

Job 28:18

γάζα.

Ezra 5:17 | Est. 4: 7
6: 1 | Isa. 39: 2
7:20, 21 |

γαζαρηνοί.

Dan. 2:27 | Dan. 5: 7, 11
4: 4 | 15

γαζοφυλάκιον.

2 Ki. 23:11 | Neh. 12:44
Ezra 10: 6 | 13: 4, 5, 7
Neh. 3:30 | 8, 9
10:37—A | Est. 3: 9
38 | Eze. 40:17 A[a]

[a] pro παστοφόριον.

γαζοφύλαξ.

1 Chronicles 28: 1

γαί.

Numbers 33:44, 45

γαῖα.

2 Ki. 19:35 | Ezra 9: 1, 2
19:11[a] | 14—BS
1 Ch. 7:28 B[b] | Psa. 48:12
Ezra 3: 3—B | Eze. 36:24

[a] A γενεά. [b] pro Γάζης.

γαῖσος.

Joshua 8:18, 18

γάλα.

Gen. 18: 8 | Deu. 27: 3
49:12 | 31:20
Exo. 3: 8, 17 | 32:14
13: 5 | Jos. 5: 6
23:19 | Jud. 4:19
33: 3 | 5:25
34:26 | 1 Sa. 17:18 A
Lev. 20:24 | Job 10:10
Nu. 13:28 | 29: 6
14: 8 | Ps. 118:70
16:13, 14 | Pro. 24:68
Deu. 6: 3 | Cant. 4:11
11: 9 | 5: 1, 12
14:20 | Isa. 7:22
26: 9, 10 | 28: 9
15 | 60:16

Jer. 11: 5 | Eze. 20: 6, 15
39:22 | 34: 3
Lam. 4: 7 | Joel 3:18

γαλαθηνός.

1 Sa. 7: 9 | Amos 6: 4

γαλεάγρα.

Ezekiel 19: 9

γαλῆ.

Leviticus 11:29

γαμβρεύω.

Gen. 38: 8 A[a] | Ezra 9:14 B[a]
Deu. 7: 3

[a] pro ἐπιγαμβρεύω.

γαμβρός.

Gen. 19:12, 14 | Jud. 1:16[a]
14 | 4:11
Exo. 3: 1 | 15: 6 A[b]
4:18 | 19: 4,5 A[b]
18: 1, 2, 5 | 7, 9
6, 7, 8 | 1 Sa. 18:18 A
12, 12 | 22:14
15, 17 | 2 Ki. 8:27+A
24, 27 | Neh. 6:18
Nu. 10:29 |

[a] A πενθερός. [b] pro νυμφίος.

γάμος.

Gen. 29:22 | Est. 2:18
Est. 1: 5[a] | 9:22

[a] AS[3] πότος.

γαρέμ.

2 Ki. 9:13[a] | [a] A γὰρ ἕνα.

γαστήρ.

Gen. 16: 4,5,11 | Job 21:10
25:21, 23 | 31:15, 18
24 A[a] | 32:18, 19
30:41 | 38:29
31:10—A | 40:11
38:18, 21 | Psa. 16:14
25, 27[b] | 21:10
Exo. 2: 2, 22 | 11 S[2] [a]
21:22 | 30:10
Nu. 5:22 | 43:26
11:12 | 57: 4
Jud. 13: 3+A | 70: 6
5,5 A[a] | 109: 3
7, 7 | 126: 3
2 Sa. 11: 5, 5 | 138:13
2 Ki. 4:17 | Ecc. 5:14
8:12 | 11: 5
15:16 | Isa. 7:14
1 Ch. 7:23 | 8: 3
Job 3:10, 11 | 26:18
10:19 | 40:11
15: 2, 35 | Hos. 14: *a* 1
16:16 | Amos 1: 3, 13
20:14, 23 |

[a] pro κοιλία. [b] A κοιλία.

γαυρίαμα.

Job 4:10 | Isa. 62: 7[a]
13:12 | Jer. 31: 2[a]

[a] ABS ἀγαυρίαμα.

γαυριάω.

Job 3:14 | Job 39:21, 23

γαυρόομαι.

Numbers 23:24

γεδδούρ.

1 Samuel 30: 8

γείνω.

Gen. 6: 1 A[a]

[a] pro γίνομαι.

γεῖσος.

1 Ki. 7:46
Jer. 52:22 ter
Eze. 40:43
Eze. 41: 7[a]
43:13, 17

[a] A μέσος.

γείτων.

Exo. 3:22
12: 4
Ruth 4:17
2 Ki. 4: 3
Job 19:15
26: 5 S^1[a]
5
Psa. 30:12
Psa. 43:14
78: 4, 12
79: 7
88:12
Jer. 6:21
12:14
29:11

[a] pro γίγας.

γειώρας.

Exo. 12:19
Isa. 14: 1

γελάω.

Gen. 17:17
18:12, 13
15, 15
Job 19: 7[a]
22:19
Job 20:24
Psa. 51: 8
Ecc. 3: 4
Jer. 20: 8
Lam. 1: 7

[a] AS^2 λαλέω.

γελοιάζω.

Genesis 19:14

γελοιασμός.

Jeremiah 31:27

γελοιαστής.

Job 31: 5

γέλως.

Gen. 21: 6
Job 8:21
17: 6[a]
Pro. 10:23
Ecc. 2: 2
7: 3, 7
10:19
Jer. 20: 7
31:26
39
Lam. 3:14
Eze. 23:32 + A
Amos 7: 9
Mic. 1:10, 10

[a] S^* γλῶσσα.

γεμίζω.

Genesis 45:17

γέμω.

Gen. 37:25
2 Ch. 9:21
Job 32:19 A[a]
Psa. 9:28
13: 3 — A
Amos 2:13

[a] pro ζέω.

γενεά.

Gen. 6: 9
7: 1
9:12
15:16
17: 7, 9
10, 12
25:13
31: 3
43: 6
50:23
Exo. 1: 6
3:15 — A
15
12:14, 17
17 + A
42
13:18
16:32, 33
17:16, 16
20: 5
27:21
29:42
30: 8, 10
21, 31
31:13, 16
Exo. 34: 7
40:13
Lev. 3:17
6:18
7:26
10: 9
17: 7
20:18[a]
21:17
22: 3
23:14, 21
31, 41
43
24: 3
25:30, 41[b]
Nu. 9:10
10: 8, 30
13:23, 29
14:18 — B
15:14, 15
21, 23
38
18:23
32:13
35:29
Deu. 2:14
5: 9
7: 9
23: 3, 8
29:22
32: 5, 7, 7
32:20
Jos. 22:27[c], 28
Jud. 2:10, 10
3: 2
2 Ki. 19:11 A[d]
1 Ch. 16:15
Est. 9:27
27 — A
28
Job 8: 8
42:16
Psa. 9:27, 27
11: 8
13: 5
21:31
23: 6
32:11, 11
44:18, 18
47:14
48:12, 12
20
60: 7, 7
70:18
71: 5, 5
72:15
76: 9, 9
77: 4, 6, 8
8
78:13, 13
84: 6, 6
88: 2, 2, 5
5
89: 1, 1
Psa. 94:10
99: 5, 5
101:13, 13
19, 25
25
104: 8
105:31, 31
108:13
111: 2
118:90, 90
134:13, 13
144: 4, 4, 13
13
145:10, 10
Pro. 22: 4
27:23, 23
Ecc. 1: 4, 4
Isa. 13:20
24:22
34:10, 17
17
41: 4
51: 8, 8, 9
53: 8
58:11 + AS^3
11 + AS^3
12, 12
60:15, 15
61: 3, 4
Jer. 7:29
8: 3
10:25
Lam. 5:19, 19
Dan. 3:33, 33
4:31, 31
Joel 1: 3
2: 2, 2
3:20, 20
Zeph. 3: 9

[a] A γένος.
[b] A γῆ.
[c] A τέκνον.
[d] pro γαῖα.

γενεαλογέω.

1 Chronicles 5: 1

γένεσις.

Gen. 2: 4
5: 1
6: 9
10: 1, 32
11:10, 27
25:12, 19
31:13
32: 9
36: 1, 9
(37) 2
40:20
Exo. 6:24, 25
28:10
21 + A
Nu. 1:18
Nu. 3: 1
Ruth 2:11
4:18
1 Ch. 1:29
4: 2, 21
38
5: 7
7: 2, 4, 9
8:28
9: 9, 34
26:31
Ecc. 7: 2 ACS[a]
Eze. 4:14
16: 3, 4
Hos. 2: 3

[a] pro γέννησις.

γενετή.

Leviticus 25:47

γένημα vide γέννημα.

γεννάω.

Gen. 4:18[a], 18
18, 18
5 passim
6: 1, 1[a], 4
10
10: 1[a], 8
13, 15
21[a], 24
24, 24
25, 26
11 passim
28[a]
17:20
22:23
24: 4[h], 7[b]
25: 3, 19
26 A[c]
Gen. 46:20, 21
22 A[c]
48: 6
Exo. 6:20
Lev. 18: 9
Nu. 26:33, 58
60[d]
Deu. 4:25
23: 8
28:41
32:18
Jos. 5: 7
Jud. 11: 1[d]
Ruth 4:13 A[c]
18, 19
19, 20
20, 21
Ruth 4:21, 22
22
2 Sa. 5:14
2 Ki. 20:18
1 Ch. 1:10
11 A
1:13 A
18 ter A
19 A
20 A
34
2 passim
18 B[e]
41 — AB
46 + AB
3: 4
4: 2
2 — A[i]
8, 11
12, 14
14, 17
6: 4, 4, 5
5, 6, 6
7, 7, 8
8, 9, 9
10, 11
11, 12
12, 13
13, 14
14
7:15 — B
32
8: 1, 7, 8
9, 11
32, 33
33, 33
34, 36
36, 36
37
9:38, 39
39, 39
40, 42
1 Ch. 9:42, 42
43
2 Ch. 11:21
13:21
24: 3
Ezra 10:44
Neh. 12:10, 10
11, 11
Job 3: 3[a]
5: 7
12: 4[a]
15: 7[f]
38:21
42:13
p 18
Psa. 2: 7
44:17[b]
109: 3[g]
Pro. 8:25
11:19
17:17
23:22
Ecc. 3:15 A[h]
5:13
6: 3
Isa. 1: 2, 9 A[h]
9: 6[a]
39: 7
49:21
66: 9
Jer. 2:27
16: 2, 3, 3
Eze. 16:20 — A
18:10, 14
21:30
23:37
31: 6, 7 A[b]
36:12[i]
47:22
Hos. 5: 7
9:16
Zec. 13: 3, 3, 5

[a] A γίνομαι.
[b] AS γίνομαι.
[c] pro τίκτω.
[d] A τίκτω.
[e] pro λαμβάνω.
[f] BS γίνομαι.
[g] S^1 ἐκγεννάω.
[h] pro γίνομαι.
[i] A δίδωμι.

γέννημα, γένημα.

Gen. 40:17 A[a]
41:34
47:24
49:21
Exo. 22: 5
23:10
Lev. 19:25
23:39
25: 7, 12
15, 16
20, 21
22, 22
26: 4
Nu. 18:30, 30
Deu. 14:21, 21
27
16:15
22: 9, 9
26:10, 12
28: 4[b], 11
18, 42
51
30: 9
32:13, 22
33:14
Jud. 1:10
9:11
2 Ki. 8: 6
2 Ch. 31: 5
32:28
Job 39: 4
Psa. 64:11
106:37
Pro. 8:19
14: 4
15:29
Ecc. 5: 9
Cant. 6:10
Isa. 3:10
29: 1
30:23 — S^1
32:12
65:21
Jer. 2: 3
7:20
8:13
Lam. 4: 9
Eze. 36:30
48:18
Hos. 10:12
Amos 8: 6
Hab. 3:17
Zec. 8:12 — S^1

[a] pro γένος.
[b] A ἔκγονος.

γέννησις.

1 Ch. 4: 8
Ecc. 7: 2[a]
Isa. 45:10
Hos. 2: 3

[a] ACS γένεσις.

γεννητός.

Job 11: 3, 12
14: 1 — C
Job 15:14
25: 4

γένος.

Gen. 1:11, 11
12, 12
21, 21
24, 24
25 ter
6:20 ter
7:14 qtr
8:19
11: 6
17:14
19:38
25:17
26:10
34:16
35:20
40:17[a]
Exo. 1: 9[b]
5:14
Lev. 20:17
18 A[c]
21:13, 17
Jos. 4:14
Jos. 11:21[d]
2 Ch. 4: 3, 13
16:14
Est. 2:10
3: 7, 13
4: 4 S^1[e]
6:13
Job 8: 8
40:25 AC[f]
Pro. 19:20
Isa. 22: 4
42: 6
43:20
49: 6 — A
8 + S^1
Jer. 36:32
38: 1, 37
36
43:31
48: 1
Dan. 3: 5, 7, 10
15 — A

[a] A γέννημα.
[b] A ἔθνος.
[c] pro γενεά.
[d] A ὄρος.
[e] pro γίνομαι.
[f] pro ἔθνος.

γέρας.

Numbers 18: 8

γερουσία.

Exo. 3:16, 18
4:29
12:21
24: 9[a]
Lev. 9: 1, 3
Nu. 22: 4, 7, 7
Deu. 5:23
19:12
Deu. 21: 2, 3, 4
6, 19
22:15, 16
17, 18
25: 7, 8, 9
27: 1
29:10
Jos. 23: 2

[a] A πρεσβύτερος.

γέρων.

Job 32:10
Pro. 17: 6
Pro. 29:41 - AS^2

γεῦμα.

Exo. 16:31
Nu. 11: 8
Job 6: 6
Jer. 31:11

γεῦσις.

Daniel 5: 2

γεύω.

Gen. 25:30
1 Sa. 14:24, 29
43, 43
2 Sa. 3:35
19:35
Job 12:11
Job 20:18
34: 3
Psa. 33: 9
Pro. 29:36
Jon. 3: 7[a]

[a] A γίνομαι.

γέφυρα.

Isaiah 37:25

γεωμετρία.

Isaiah 34:11

γεωμετρικός.

Zechariah 2: 1

γεωργέω.

1 Chronicles 27:26

γεώργιον, -ος.

Gen. 26:14
Pro. 6: 7
9:12
16:32[a]
Pro. 24: 5, 45
29:34
Jer. 28:23

[a] $AC^2 S^2$ + γ.

γεωργός.

Gen. 9:20
49:15
2 Ch. 26:10[a]
Jer. 14: 4
28:23
38:24

Jer. 52:16
Joel 1:11
Amos 5:18

[a] A φιλογεωργός.

γῆ.

Gen. 1 *passim*
2: 1, 4, 4
5, 5
5+A
6, 6, 7
9, 11
12, 13
19
3: 1, 14
14, 17
19 *ter*
23
4: 2,3,10
11, 12
12, 14
14, 16
5:29
6: 1, 4, 5
6,7,11
11, 12
12, 13
13, 17
17, 20
7: 3, 4, 4
6,8,10
12, 14
17, 17
18, 19
21, 21
23, 23
24
8: 1, 3, 7
8,9,11
13, 13
14, 17
17, 19
21, 22
9: 1, 2, 2
7
7+A
10, 11
13, 14
16−A
16, 17
19, 20
10: 5, 8
10, 11
25, 32
11: 1, 2, 4
8, 9, 9
28, 31
32−A
12: 1, 1, 3
5
5+A
6−A
6,7,10
10
13: 6
6−A
7,9,10
12, 15
16, 16
17
14:19, 22
15: 7, 13
18
16: 3
17: 8, 8
18: 2, 18
25, 27
19: 1, 23
25
28+A
28, 31
31
20: 1, 15
21:21+A
23, 32
34
22: 2
18−A
23: 2,7,12
13

Gen. 23:15−A
19
24: 3,4,5,5
7 *ter*
8, 37
52, 62
25: 6
26: 1, 2, 3
3, 4, 4
12, 15
22
27:28, 39
46
28: 4, 12
13, 14[a]
14, 15
29: 1
30:25
31: 3, 13
13, 18
32: 3, 9
33: 3, 18
34: 2, 10
21, 21
30
35: 6, 12
12
16+A
21, 27
36: 5, 6, 6
7, 16
17, 20
21, 30
34, 43
(37) 1, 1
37:10
38: 9
40:15
41:19−A
29
30+A
30, 31
33, 34
34
36 *ter*
41, 43
44, 46
47, 48
52, 53
54, 54
55, 56
57
42: 5
6 *ter*
7, 12
13, 29
30, 30
32, 33
34
43: 1
2−A
10, 25
44: 8, 11
14
45: 6, 7, 8
9, 10
17, 18
19, 25
26
46: 6, 12
20, 27
28, 31
34
47 *passim*
27−A
48: 3, 4
5−B
7,7,12
16
21+A
21
49:15, 25
30
50: 5

Gen. 50: 7−A
8, 11
13, 24
24
Exo. 1: 7, 10
2:15, 15
22
3: 5,8,8,8
10, 11
17, 17
4: 3, 3
5: 5+A
12−A
6: 1, 4, 4
8, 11
13
26−A
27−A
28
7: 2,3,4,9
19, 21
8: 6,7,14
16, 16
17, 17
17+AB[a]
21, 22
22, 23
24, 24
25
9: 5, 9, 9
11, 14
15, 16
22, 22
23, 23
25, 26
29, 33
10: 5, 5
5−A
5, 6, 6
12 *ter*
13, 14
15 *qtr*
19, 21
22
11: 5, 6, 9
10, 10
12: 1, 12
12, 13
17, 19
25, 29
30, 33
40, 40
41, 42
48, 51
13: 3−A
5,5,11
14, 15
17
18−A
14: 3, 11
15:13
16: 1, 3, 6
14, 32
35+A
18: 3, 27
19: 1, 5
20: 2, 4, 4
11, 12
24
22:21
23: 9, 10
19, 20
22, 26
29, 29
30, 31
33
29:46
31:17
32: 1−B
4, 7, 9
11, 12
13
23+A
33: 1, 1, 3
16
34: 8, 10
12, 15
24, 26
Lev. 4:27
11: 2, 21

Lev. 11:29, 31
41, 42
43, 44
45, 16
14:34, 34
16:22
17:13
18: 3−AB
25, 25
27, 27
28
19: 9:23
29, 29
33, 34
36
20: 2,4,22
24, 24
25
22:24, 33
23:10, 22
39, 43
25: 2, 2, 4
5, 6, 7
9,9,10
18−A
19, 23
23, 24
24, 31
38, 38
41 A[b]
42, 45
55
26: 1, 4, 5
5, 6, 6
7+AB[a]
13, 19
20, 22
32, 33
34 *qtr*
36, 38
39, 41
42, 43
43, 44
45
27:21, 24
30, 30
Nu. 1: 1
3:13
5:17
8:17
9: 1, 14
14
15 A[c]
10: 9, 30
11:12, 31
12: 3
13: 3, 17
18, 19
20, 21
21, 22
26, 27
28, 28
29+A
30
33 *ter*
14: 2, 3, 6
7, 8, 8
9, 14
16, 21
23, 23
24, 30
31, 31
34, 36
36, 37
38
15: 2, 14
18, 19
41
16:13, 14
30, 31
32, 33
34
18:13, 20
20:12, 17
23, 24
21: 4, 22
24, 26
34, 35
22: 5, 5, 6
11, 11

Nu. 26:10, 15
53, 55
27:12
32: 4,4,5,7
8, 9, 9
11, 17
22, 22
29, 29
30, 30
32, 33
33
35+A
33: 1,4,37
38, 40
51, 52
53, 53
54, 55
55
34: 2,2,12
13, 17
18, 29
35:10, 14
28, 32
33 *ter*
34
36: 2
Deu. 1: 5, 7, 8
8, 21
22, 25
25, 27
30, 35
36
2: 5,9,12
19, 20
24, 27
29, 31
31
37 A[d]
3: 2,8,12
13+B
13, 18
20, 24
25, 28
4: 1,5,10
14, 17
18, 18
20−A
21, 22
22, 25
26, 26
32, 36
38, 39
40, 43
45, 46
46, 47
47
5: 6, 8, 8
14+B[e]
15, 16
31, 33
6: 1, 3, 4
10, 12
15, 18
21, 23
7: 1,6,13
13, 22
8: 1, 7, 8
8, 9, 9
10, 14
19
9: 4, 5, 6
12, 23
26, 28
28, 29
10: 7, 11
14, 19
11: 3, 6, 8
9,9,10
10, 11
11, 12
14, 17
17, 21
21, 25
29, 30
31
12: 1,1,10
16, 19
24, 29
29
13: 5, 7, 7

Deu. 13:10, 13[e]
15[e]
14: 2
15: 4,7,11
11, 15
23
16: 3,6+A
12, 20
17:14
18: 9
19: 1, 2, 3
8, 10
14
20: 1, 16
21: 1,8+A
23
22: 6
23: 7, 20
24: 6, 20
22, 24
25:15
17−A
19
26: 1, 2, 3
9+A
9,9,10
10
12+A
15, 15
27: 2, 3, 3
28: 1+A
1, 4, 8
10, 11
11, 12
18, 21
23, 24
25, 26
33, 42
49, 51
52, 56
63, 64
64
29: 1, 2, 2
8, 16
22, 22
23, 24
25, 27
28−A
28
30: 5,9,16
18, 19
20
31: 4,7,13
16, 20
20, 21
23, 28
32: 2
10−A
13, 22
24, 43
47, 49
49, 52
33:13, 16
17, 21
28
34: 1, 2, 2
2, 4
4+A[f]
5
6+A
11, 11
Jos. 1: 2,6,11
13, 14
15
2: 1, 2, 3
9
10−A
11, 24
24
3:11, 13
4: 7, 18[f]
24
5: 6 *ter*
11, 12
14
6:27
7: 2 A[g]
3+A
6, 9, 9
21+A

Jos. 7:22 A[e]
8: 1
9:12, 15
17, 30
10:40
41+A
42
11: 3−AB
16
16−B
16, 23
23
12: 1, 1
1−A
5−AB
13: 1, 2, 4
5, 7
21 A[h]
25
14: 1−A
4, 5, 7
9, 15
15: 8, 19
17: 5−B
6, 7 A[i]
12
18: 1, 3, 4
6, 8, 8
9
19:49, 51
21: 2
38+A
42, 43
22: 4, 9
9+A
9, 10
11, 13
15−AB
19, 19
32+A
32, 33
23: 5, 13
14, 15
24: 3, 7, 8
8, 13
15
17+A
18
Jud. 1: 2, 14
15, 26
27, 32
33
2: 1, 2, 6
12
21−A
3:11, 25
27−A
30
4:21
5: 4, 31
6: 4, 5
8−A
9, 10
11−AB
37, 39
40
7: 1 A[l]
8:28
9:37
10: 4−A
8
11: 3,5,12
13, 15
15, 17
18 *ter*
19, 21
21
26−A
29+A
12:12, 15
13:20
16:24
18: 2, 2, 7
9+A
9,9,10
10, 14
17
30−A
19:30−A
20: 1, 21

Jud. 20:25
21:12, 21
Ruth 1: 1, 7
2:10, 11
1 Sa. 1:21
2: 5,8,10
10
27−A
3:19, 21
4: 5, 12
5: 3+A
4+A
6: 1, 5, 5
7: 6
9: 2, 4, 4
4
5+A
16
13: 3, 7
17−B
19, 20
14:15, 24
29, 32
45
17:44, 46
46, 50
20:15, 31
41+A
21:11
22: 5
23:14, 23
27
24: 9
25:23, 41
26: 7,8,20
27: 1, 8
8−B
9
28: 3,9,13
14, 14
20, 23
29:11
30:16 *ter*
31: 9
2 Sa. 1: 2, 2
2:22
4:11
5: 6
25−A
7: 9, 23
8: 2
12+B
9:10
10: 2
12:16, 17
20
13:31
37−B
14: 4,7,11
14, 20
22, 33
15: 4, 23
32
17:12, 26
18: 8, 9
11, 28
19: 9
20:10
21:14, 14
22: 8, 43
23: 4
24: 6−B
8, 13
13, 20
25
1 Ki. 1:23, 31
40, 52
2: 2
(3) *p* 46
4:10, 18
18
(21) A
30
7:33
8: 9, 21
23, 27
34, 36
37+A
40, 41+A
43+A

1 Ki. 8:46, 47
47, 48
48, 51
53
53—A
60
9: 7, 8
11—A
26
10: 6, 7
12—A
13, 15
p 22 *bis*
23—B
24, 26
11:18+A
21, 22
22
22—AB
43—A
12 *p* 24 *l* 16
l 22
28, 32
13:34
14:17 A, 24
15:12, 20
16: 2
p 28—A
17: 7, 14
18: 1, 5^k
12, 42
19: 3—A
21: 7—B
27
22:36
47 A
2 Ki. 2:15, 19
3:20, 27
4:37, 38
5: 2,4,15
17+A
19
6:23
7:12 A^m
8: 1, 1, 2
3—A
6
10:10
33—B
11: 3, 14
18, 19
20
12: 1+B
13:18, 20
14:11+B
15: 5, 19
20, 29
16:15+A
17: 5,7,23
26, 26
27, 36
18:25, 32
32
32—B
32, 35
19: 7, 7
15, 15
17+A
19, 37
20:14
21: 8, 24
24
23:21, 30
33
33—B
35, 35
24: 2,7,14
15
25: 3, 12
19, 19
21, 21
22—A
24
1 Ch. 1:10,19 A
45
4:40
5: 9
11—B
23+A
25

1 Ch. 6:55—B
7:21
10: 9
11: 4—BS
13: 2
14:17
16:14, 18
23, 30
30, 31
33
17: 8, 21
19: 2, 3
21:12, 16
21
22: 2, 5, 8
18, 18
27:12
21—AB
26
28: 8
29:11, 15
30
2 Ch. 1: 9
2:12, 17
4:17
5:10
6: 5, 14
18, 25
27, 28
28+B
31, 32
33, 36
36, 37
38, 38
7: 3, 14
20, 21
22
8: 8
17—A
9: 5, 11
12, 14
23, 26
28
12: 8
13: 9
14: 1, 6, 6
7, 8, 8
15: 8
16: 9
17: 6, 10
19: 3
20: 7, 10
11+A
24, 29
22:12
23:13—AB
17, 20
21
26: 1, 21
28: 3 A^n
29: 9
30: 9, 25
31: 1+B
32:13, 17
19, 21
31
33: 6 A^n, 8
25, 25
34: 7, 8, 33
35:19
36: 1, 2, 3
4—A
4, 5, 14
21, 23
Ezra 1: 2—B
4: 4
5:11
6:21
9:11, 11
12
10: 2, 11
Neh. 4: 2-ABS
5
5:14
8: 6
9: 6—S^3
8
10—S^1
15, 22
22—B

Neh. 9:23, 24
24, 30
35, 36
10:28, 30
31, 35
37—A
38+S^1
11:35 S^3
Est. 10: 1
Job 1: 3
6+A
7,8,10
16+A
20+A
2: 2 A^o, 3
9, 12
3:14
5: 6, 10
22+A
7: 1,5,21
8: 9, 19
10: 9, 21
21
11: 8+A
9
12: 8, 15
17+A
17, 19
24—A
14: 5, 8
19
15:19, 20
16:13, 18
18: 4 A^p
10, 17
19:25
20: 4, 27
21:26
26+A
22: 8
24: 4, 13
18, 19
26: 7
27:16
28: 2,5,24
29:23
30: 8, 19
23
31: 8, 38
39
34:13, 15
35:11
37: 2,5,11
12, 16
38: 4, 13
14, 14
16 AO^t
19, 26
37, 38
39:14, 24
40: 8
41:16, 24
42: 6
p 18
Psa. 1: 4
2: 2,8,10
7: 6
8: 2, 10
9:37, 39
11: 7
15: 3
16:11, 14
17: 8
18: 5
20:11
21:28, 30
30
23: 1
24:13
26:13
32: 5,8,14
33:17
36: 3,9,11
22, 29
34
38:13—AS
40: 3
41: 7
43: 4, 26
44:13—AS

Psa. 44:17
45: 3, 7, 9
10, 11
46: 3,8,10
47: 3, 11
49: 1, 4
51: 7
54:10 S^{1m}
56: 6, 12
57: 3, 12
58:14
59: 4
60: 3
62: 2, 10
64: 6
9 S^{1q}
10
65: 1, 4
66: 3, 5, 7
8
67: 9, 33
68:35
35+S^1
70:20
21—BS
71: 6
11+S
16, 16
17, 19
72: 9, 25
73: 7,8,12
17, 20
74: 4, 9
75: 9
108*S^{2r}
13
76:19
77:12
40—S^1
51—B
69
78: 2
79:10
80: 6, 11
81: 5, 8
82:11, 19
84: 2, 10
12, 13
87:13
88:12, 28
40, 45
89: 2
93: 2
94: 3+AS^2
4
95: 1,9,11
13
96: 1, 4, 5
9
97: 3, 4, 9
98: 1
99: 1
100: 6, 8
101:16+AS
20, 26
102:11
103: 5,9,13
14, 24
30, 32
35
104: 7, 11
16, 23
27, 30
32, 35
35, 36
105:17, 22
24, 38
106:34
35—S^1
107: 6
108:15
109: 6
111: 2
112: 6, 7
113: 7, 23
24
118:19, 64
87, 90
119
120: 2

Ps. 123: 8
133: 3
134: 6,7,12
135: 6, 21
136: 4
137: 4
138:15
139:11—A
12
140: 7, 7
141: 6
142: 3, 6
10+A
145: 4, 6
146: 6, 8
147: 4
148: 7, 11
11, 13
Pro. 1:11, 12
2:21
21+AS
22
3:19
8:16, 23
25+S
29
9:12
10:30
12:11
15: 6
17:24
24:27, 37
51, 56
59
25: 3, 25
28:19
29:41
Ecc. 1: 4
3:21
5: 1, 8
7:21
8:14, 16
10: 7—S^1
17
11: 2, 3
12: 6 S^1, 7
Cant. 2:12, 12
Isa. 1: 2,7,19
2: 7,8,10
10, 19
19, 21
3:26
4: 2
5: 8, 26
30
6: 3, 11
12
7:16, 22
24
8: 9, 19
22
9: 1, 19
11: 4,4,12
16
12: 3
13: 5, 18
14: 1, 2, 7
9, 12
15, 16
20, 21
21, 25
16: 1, 4
18: 1, 2, 6
6
19: 3, 24
25+B^1
21: 1, 9
23: 1, 8, 9
10, 13
17—AS
24: 3, 3, 4
4
5+ABS
6, 6
10+S
11—B
11-ABS
13, 14
16, 17
18, 19

Isa. 24:19, 20
21
25: 8
26: 1, 9, 9
10, 15
18, 18
19, 19
21, 21
21+A
28: 2, 22
24
29: 4 *ter*
30:23
23—S^1
24
32: 2, 13
33: 9, 17
34: 1,5 S^{1s}
7, 9, 9
15
35: 6, 7
36:10—A
17 *ter*
20
37: 7, 11
16, 20
38:11
11—AS
39: 3
40:12, 21
22, 23
24, 28
41: 2, 5, 9
18—S
19, 24
42: 4,5 A^{tt}
5, 10
43: 6+AS
6
20+S
44:23, 24
45: 8, 9
12, 18
19, 22
46:11
47: 1,1-AS
48:13
16+AS^1
19
20+S^1
20
49: 6,8,12
13, 23
51: 6, 6
6+A
13, 16
23
52:10
53: 2, 8
54: 5, 9
55: 9, 10
57:13
58:14
60: 2, 18
21
61: 7, 11
62: 4, 4
4—AS
7, 11
63: 3, 3, 6
11 AB*S^u
65:16, 16
17, 25
66: 1, 8^v
16, 22
Jer. 1: 1, 14
15, 18
2: 6 *qtr*
7, 15
18 A^w
18 A^w, 31
3: 2, 16
18, 18
19—S^1
4: 5, 7
7+S^1
16, 20
23—S^1
27, 28
5:19

Jer. 5:19—A
30
6: 8, 12
19, 20
22, 29 A^x
7: 7, 20
22, 25
33, 34
8: 2, 16
16, 19
9: 3, 12
19, 21
22, 24
10:11, 11
12, 13
18, 22
11: 4,5,19
12: 4,5,11
12, 12
14
15—S^1
13:13
14: 2, 4, 8
13, 15
18^y
15: 3,4,10
14
16: 3, 4, 4
13—A^1
13, 14
15, 15
18, 19
17: 6, 13
26
26—AS
18:16
19: 7
12+S^1
22:10, 12
26, 27
28, 29
29
23: 3,5,10
15, 24
7, 8, 8
24: 5,6,8^z
9, 10
25: 5,9,11
13
26: 8, 10
12, 13
27: 3, 8, 9
13+A
16^z, 18
19+A
21, 22
23, 25
28, 34
38
41+A
41, 46
28: 2, 4, 5
7,9,15
16, 25
27, 28
28+A
29, 29
36 AS^1
41, 43
49—S
50
50+S^1
52, 54
29: 2,2,22
31:21
32:12, 15
16, 17
18, 19
19—S^1
19, 24
33: 6, 17
20
34: 4, 5, 8
9
35: 8, 16
36: 7
37: 3
38: 8, 12
16, 23
24^{aa}

Jer 38:32, 37
39: 8, 15
17, 26
21, 22
22
29 A^y
37, 41
43, 44
40: 2,9,11
13
41: 1, 13
17, 20
22
42: 7, 11
15, 19
43:29
31—S
44: 2
7—S^1
8 A^m
12, 19
46:16 A^m
47: 3, 5, 6
7, 9
11+AS
11, 12
48: 2, 18
49:10, 12
13, 14
16, 17
50: 4,5,11
12
51: 1—S
1—A
8,8,9^a
13—A
14, 14
15—A
21, 22
26, 26
27, 28
28
52: 6, 25
25, 27
Lam. 2: 1, 2
2+A
9, 10
10, 11
15
3:33
4:12, 21
Eze. 1: 2, 15
19, 21
6:14
7: 2, 2, 7
21, 23
27
8: 3, 12
17
9: 9, 9
10:16, 19
11:15, 16
17, 24
12: 6, 12
13, 19
19, 19
20, 22
13: 9, 14
14:13, 15
16, 17
17, 19
15: 8
16: 3, 29
17: 4,5,13
18: 2+A
19: 4,7,12
13
20: 5, 6, 6
6, 6
8+AB
9
10+A
15 *ter*
28, 32
30, 38
42, 42
21: 2, 30
32
22:24, 29
30 *b*^{bb}

Eze. 23:15, 16
27, 48
24: 7, 7
25: 3, 6, 9
26: 11, 16
20, 20
27: 29, 30
33
28: 17, 18
26
29: 5[ee], 9
10, 12
12—A
14, 14
19, 20
30: 4—A
11—A
11
12+A
12, 13
13+A
14, 25
31: 12, 14
16, 18
32: 4, 4
5+A
6, 8, 9
15
18 A[dd]
18, 23
24
24—AB
26—AB
32—AB
33: 2, 2, 3
24 *ter*
25 A
26 A
28, 29
34: 6, 13
13, 25
27, 27
28, 29
35: 14
36: 5, 6
17
18+A
20, 24
28, 34
35
37: 12, 14
21, 22
25
38: 2, 8, 8
9, 11
11[e], 12
16, 16
18, 19
20 *ter*
39: 13, 13
14, 14
15, 16
18, 26
40: 2
42: 6
43: 2
45: 1, 1, 4
7, 8
9+A
22
46: 3
9—A
47: 13, 14
15, 18
21
48: 12[ee]
14, 29
Dan. 1: 2
12+A
2: 35, 39
3: 31
4: 7, 8, 12
12, 17
19, 20
32, 32
6: 25, 27
7: 4, 17
23, 23
8: 5, 5, 7
10, 18

Dan. 9: 6, 7, 15
10: 9, 15
11: 9, 16
19, 28
28, 39
40, 41
42, 42
12: 1, 2
Hos. 1: 2, 11
2: 3, 12
15, 18
18, 21
22, 23
4: 1, 1, 2
3, 3
6: 3
7: 16
8: 1
9: 3
10: 1
11: 11
12: 9
13—A
13: 4, 4, 5
15
Joel 1: 2, 6, 10
14
2: 1, 3
10, 18
20—S[1]
21, 30
3: 2, 16
19
Amos 1: 11
2: 7, 10
10
3: 1, 2, 5
5, 11
14
4: 13
5: 2, 7, 8
7: 2, 10
11, 12
17 *ter*
8: 4, 8, 9
11
9: 5, 6, 6
7, 8, 9
15, 15
Obad. 3, 20
Jon. 1: 13
2: 7
4: 2
Mic. 1: 2, 3
10—A
4: 3+A
13
5: 4, 5, 6
6, 11
6: 2, 4
7: 2, 13
17
Nah. 1: 5
2: 13
3: 13
Hab. 1: 6
2: 8, 14
17, 20
3: 3, 6, 7
9, 12
Zeph. 1: 2, 3, 18
18
2: 3, 5, 11
14
3: 8, 10
20
Hag. 1: 10, 11
11
2: 4, 6, 21
Zec. 1: 10, 11
11, 21
2: 6
12+A
3: 9
4: 10, 14
5: 3, 6, 9
11
6: 5, 6, 6
7+S[3]
7—S[1]

Zec. 6: 7, 7, 8
8
7: 5, 14
14
8: 7, 7
12—S[1]
9: 1, 10
16
10: 10
11: 6, 6

Zec. 11: 7+S[1]
16
12: 1, 3, 12
13: 2, 2
5—A
8—AS[3]
14: 9, 10
17
Mal. 3: 11, 12
4: 5

[a] A θάλασσα. [b] *pro* γενεά.
[c] *pro* σκηνή. [d] *pro* ἐγγύς.
[e] A πόλις. [f] A ξηρός.
[g] *pro* Γαι. [h] *pro* Σιών.
[i] *pro* πηγή. [k] A πεδίον.
[m] *pro* πόλις. [n] *pro* γε.
[o] *pro* σύμπας. [p] *pro* ὄρος.
[q] *pro* πέρας. [r] *pro* καρδία.
[s] *pro* ἀπώλεια. [t] *pro* πηγνύμι.
[u] *pro* θάλασσα. [v] S[2] γυνή.
[w] *pro* ὁδός. [x] *pro* πῦρ.
[y] A ὁδός. [z] A οἶκος.
[aa] AS πόλις. [bb] *pro* ὀργή.
[cc] A ἀγρός. [dd] *pro* ἰσχύς.
[ee] A ἅγιος.

γηγενής.

Psa. 48: 3
Pro. 2:18
Pro. 9:18
Jer. 39:20

γῆρας, γῆρος.

Gen. 15:15
21: 2, 7
25: 8
37: 3
43:38
44:20, 29
31
48:10
2 Sa. 19:33[a]
1 Ki. 11: 3
14: 4 A
15:23
1 Ch. 29:28
Psa. 70: 9, 18
91:11, 15
Pro. 16:31
24:52
Isa. 46: 4

[a] A οἶκος.

γηράσκω.

Gen. 18:13
24:36
27: 1, 2
Jos. 23: 2
Ruth 1:12
1 Sa. 8: 1, 5
1 Sa. 12: 2
2 Ch. 24:15
Job 14: 8
29:18
Psa. 36:25
Pro. 23:22

γίγαρτον.

Numbers 6: 4

γίγας.

Gen. 6: 4, 4
10: 8, 9, 9
14: 5
Nu. 13:34
Deu. 1:28
Jos. 12: 4
13:12
2 Sa. 21:11, 22
1 Ch. 1:10
11:15
14: 9, 13
20: 4, 6, 8
Job 26: 5[a]
Psa. 18: 6
32:16
Pro. 21:16
Isa. 3: 2
13: 3
14: 9
40:24, 25
Eze. 32:12, 21
27
27 A[b]
39:18, 20

[a] S[1] γείτων. [b] *pro* πᾶς.

γίνομαι.

Var. Lec. tantum.

Gen. 4:18 A[a]
6: 1[b]
1 A[a]
7: 6[c]
10: 1 A[a]
21 A[a]
11:28 A[a]
17:17 A[d]
24: 4 AS[a]
7 AS[a]
25: 3+A
Exo. 20:12—A
22:14—A[1]
33: 7—A
Lev. 13:52 A[g]
Lev. 20: 2[e]
Nu. 4:40—A
14:24+AB
Deu. 4:36[f]
16:12[c]
17:12 A[g]
22: 7[c]
27:16+A
23—A
Jos. 6:10—AB
9:33—A
13:28—A
31+A[2]
Jud. 6: 8+A
9:35+A
Jud. 10: 4 A[g]
11: 5+A
35+A
12: 5+A
9 A[g]
14 A[g]
13: 2 A[g]
14:20[h]
16:14—A
25+A
30 A[g]
17: 8 A[i]
12[c]
18, 19[c]
20 A[d]
19: 2 A[g]
30+A
Ruth 1:19—AB
4:13—B
1 Sa. 1: 1 A[g]
5:10—A
18: 1 A
6 A
10 A
17 A
19 A
29+A
30 A
23:26 A[g]
27: 6—A
2 Sa. 18:25 A[k]
24:13—A
1 Ki. 6(11) A
8: 1—A
8+A
9: 9+A
11(25) A
14: 8 A
9 A
16:11—A
18:17—A
36+A
46+A
20: 1+A
4—A
22:13[m]
2 Ki. 11: 8 AB[g]
1 Ch. 16:19[n]
40 S[1] [o]
17:22 ABS
2 Ch. 6: 6—B
20:26—A
Ezra 4:15—B
5:17 B[p]
10: 3[q]
Neh. 4: 2—ABS
6: 6 AS[g]
Est. 4: 4[r]
9:14—A
Job 1:13 A[g]
3: 3 A[a]
12: 4 A[a]
14: 5+A
15: 7 BS[s]
19:15+A
34:26+A
40:27—BS[1]
Psa. 44:17 AS[a]
86: 4—S[1]
89: 2[s]
103:48—S
Pro. 1:23—S[1]
19:25[c]
Ecc. 3:13[t]
Isa. 1: 9[t]
9: 6 A[a]
26:16+S[1]
48:20+S[1]
Jer. 1:13—S[1]
5: 7[u]
12:11 A[p]
15: 9 S[1] [v]
18:21[w]
20:14 A[d]
31:39—S[1]
38: 9 S[g]
43:27—S[1]
49: 7—S[1]
Eze. 11:11 A
22:24—A
24:20—A
26:17+A
28:14—A
31: 7[t]
8+A
32:23+A
36: 3 A[x]
Dan. 6:18 A[y]
8:11+A
9:12[z]
Hos. 7: 6 A[aa]
Amos 7:10 A[bb]
Jon. 3: 7 A[cc]

[a] *pro* γεννάω. [b] A γείνω.
[c] A εἰμί. [d] *pro* τίκτω.
[e] A προσγεννάω. [f] A ποιέω.
[g] *pro* εἰμί. [h] A συνοικέω.
[i] *pro* ἔρχομαι. [k] *pro* πορεύω.
[m] A καινός. [n] A λέγω.
[o] *pro* ἐντέλλω. [p] *pro* τίθημι.
[q] S[3] ποιέω. [r] S[1] γένος.
[s] S[1] ἑδράζω. [t] A γεννάω.
[u] S εἰμί. [v] *pro* κενόω.
[w] A ἵστημι. [x] *pro* ἀναβαίνω.
[y] *pro* ἀφίστημι. [z] A γράφω.
[aa] *pro* ἐγγίνομαι.
[bb] *pro* δύναμαι. [cc] *pro* γεύω.

γινώσκω.

Gen. 2:17
3: 5, 7, 22
4: 1, 9, 17
25
8:11
9:24
12:11
15: 8, 13
13
18:21
19: 8
20: 6, 7
21:26
22:12
24:14, 16
21, 44
27: 2
29: 5, 5
30:26, 29
33:13
38: 9, 16
Gen. 38:26
39: 8, 23
42, 33, 34
41:27
Exo. 2:25
6: 7
7: 5, 17
9:29
10: 2
14: 4[a], 18
16: 6, 12
18:11
22:10
25:21
29:42, 46
30: 6, 36
31:13
33:13
Lev. 4:14, 23
28
5: 3, 4, 17
Nu. 11:23
12: 6
14:34
16: 5, 28
30
17: 4
22:19
31:17
18 A[b]
35
32:23
Deu. 4:39
7: 9, 15
8: 5
9: 3, 6, 24
11: 2
18, 21
19:17 B[c]
20: 6
33: 9 A[2d]
34:10
Jos. 3: 7, 10
4:24
22:22, 31
23:13, 14
Jud. 2: 7, 10
3: 1, 2, 4
4: 9
6:29[e], 37
11:39
13:16, 21
14: 4, 18[f]
16: 9
14+A
20
17:13
18: 5, 14
14[g]
19:22, 25
20:34
21:11 A[b]
12
Ruth 3: 4, 14
4: 4
1 Sa. 1:19
2:10
3: 7, 20
4: 6
6: 9
10:24
12:17
14:29, 38
17:18 A, 46
47
18:28+A
20: 3, 3, 7
9, 9
33—A
39—A
21: 2
22: 3, 6, 17
23: 9, 22
23
24:12, 21
25:17
26: 4, 12
28: 1, 1, 2
14, 14
2 Sa. 3:25, 25
36, 37
5:12
14: 1, 20
22
15:11
17:19
18:29
19: 6, 20
35
22:44
24: 2, 13
1 Ki. 1: 4, 11
18
2: 5, 9, 32
(3) *p* 1
37, 37
42, 42
44 A[b]
44 AB[b]
8:38, 39
43, 43
1 Ki. 8:60
14: 2 A
17:24
18:36, 37
21: 7, 13
22, 28
41 A[d]
2 Ki. 2: 3, 3, 5
5
4: 1, 9, 39
5: 7, 8, 15
7:12
17:26
19:19, 27
1 Ch. 12:32, 32
14: 2
21: 2
28: 9, 9
29:17
2 Ch. 6:29, 30
30, 33
33
12: 8
13: 5
25:16
32:13
33:13
Ezra 4:15
5:17, 17
Neh. 2:16
4:11
15A[h], 15
6:16
9:10
13:10
Est. 4:11
Job 5:24, 25
27
6:17 A[d]
9:11
11: 6
12: 9, 20
19: 3, 6, 13
29
20: 4
21:19
22:13
23: 3, 5
24:14
27:22 C[i]
28: 7
34: 4, 33
35:15
36: 5, 26
37: 6
38:31+A
39: 1
Psa. 1: 6
4: 4
9:11, 17
21
13: 3—A
4
17:44
19: 7
34: 8, 11
15
35:11
36:18
38: 5, 7
39:10
40:12
43:22
45:11
47: 4
49:11
50: 5
52: 5
55:10
58:14
66: 3
68: 6, 20
70:15
72:11, 16
22
73: 5, 9
76:20
77: 3, 6
78: 6 S[2d]
10

Psa. 80: 6
81: 5
82:19
86: 4
87:13
88:16
89:11
90:14
91: 6
93:11
94:10
99: 3
100: 4
102:14
103:19
108:27
118:75, 79
125
152–S[1]
134: 5
137: 6
138: 1, 2, 4
14, 23
23
139:13
141: 4
143: 3[k]
Pro. 1: 2
4: 1
9:10
10: 9
13:15, 20
15:14
22:17
24:12, 12
22, 26
27+AC
27: 1
29:20
Ecc. 1:16[m], 17
2:14
3:12, 14
4:13
6: 5, 10
7:26, 26
8: 5, 5, 7
12, 16
17
9: 5, 5, 11
12
10:14, 15
11: 2, 5, 5
6, 9
Cant. 1: 8
6:11
Isa. 1: 3, 3
5:19
7:15, 16
8: 4, 9
9: 9
11: 9
15: 4
19:21
26:11
29:15, 24
30:15
33:13
37:20
40:13, 21
21, 28
41:20, 22
23, 26
42:16, 25
43:10, 19
44:18, 19
20
45: 3, 4, 6
20, 21
47: 8, 10
11, 11
48: 4, 6
7, 8, 8
49:23
50: 4, 7
51:12
52: 6
56:10
58: 2, 3[n]
59: 8A[b], 12
60:16

Isa. 61: 9
63:16
66:14
Jer. 2:16
19–S[1]
23
3:13
4:22 A[d]
5: 1, 4
6:15[n], 27
8: 7, 7
9: 3, 16
24
11:18, 19
12: 3
13:12, 12
14:20
15:12, 15
16:21
17: 9
18:23
22:16, 16
27:24[o]
24+S[3]
31:30
33:15, 15
35: 9
37:24[m]
38:19, 34
39: 8
40: 3
43:19
45:24
47:14, 15
48: 4
49:10, 19
51: 3, 15
28
Eze. 2: 5
6:13
7: 4 A[d]
27
10:20
12:15, 16
13: 9, 23[a]
17:24
20: 5, 9, 12
20
26+A
22:16
23:49
26: 6
28:22, 23
24, 26
29: 6, 9, 16
21
30: 8, 19
25, 26[a]
32: 9, 15
33:29, 33
34:15[p], 27
30
35: 4, 9
11, 12
15
36:11, 23
36, 38
37: 6, 13
14, 28
38:16, 23
23
39: 6, 7, 7
8, 22
23, 28
Dan. 1: 4
2: 3, 9, 22
30
4: 6, 14
22, 23
29
5:21, 22
23
6:10, 15
9:25
11:32, 38
12: 7
Hos. 2: 8
5: 3
6: 3, 3
7: 9[a], 9

Hos. 8: 2
9: 2
11: 3, 12
13: 4
Joel 3:17 S[3d]
Amos 3: 2, 10
5:12
Jon. 1:10, 12
4: 2, 11
Mic. 3: 1
4: 9, 12
6: 5

Nah. 1: 7
3:17
Hab. 2:14
3: 2
Zeph. 3: 5–A
Zec. 2: 9
4: 5
6:15[a]
7:14
11:11
Mal. 2: 4 S[d]

[a] A ἐπιγινώσκω. [b] pro εἰδέω. [c] pro προΐστημι. [d] pro ἐπιγινώσκω. [e] A εἶπον. [f] A εὑρίσκω. [g] A εἰδέω. [h] pro ἀκούω. [i] pro φείδομαι. [k] S γνωρίζω. [m] S ἐπιγινώσκω. [n] A προσέχω. [o] S φεύγω. [p] A[2] ἐπιγινώσκω.

γλαύξ.

Lev. 11:15
19+AB
Deu. 14:14

γλεῦκος.

Job 32:19

γλυκάζω.

Ezekiel 3: 3

γλυκαίνομαι.

Exo. 15:25
Job 20:12
21:33
Psa. 54:15
Pro. 24:13

γλύκασμα.

Neh. 8:10
Pro. 16:24

γλυκασμός.

Cant. 5:16
Joel 3:18
Amos 9:13

γλυκερός.

Proverbs 9:17

γλυκύς.

Jud. 14:14, 18
Psa. 18:11
118:103
Pro. 16:21
27: 7
Ecc. 5:11
11: 7
Cant. 2: 3
Isa. 5:20, 20

γλυκύτης.

Judges 9:11

γλύμμα.

Exo. 28:11
35:10 A[a]
Isa. 45:20
60:18

[a] pro κατακάλυμμα.

γλυπτός.

Exo. 34:13
Lev. 26: 1
Deu. 4:16, 23
25
5: 8+A
7: 5, 25
12: 3
27:15
Jud. 2: 2
3:19, 26
17: 3, 4
18:14
17+A
18, 20
24, 30
31
2 Ki. 17:41
21: 7[a]
2 Ch. 28: 2
33: 7, 15
19
2 Ch. 34: 4
Psa. 77:58
96: 7
105:19, 26
38
Isa. 10, 10
42: 8, 17
44:17
46: 1
48: 5
Jer. 8:19
10:14
27:38
28:17, 52
Eze. 21:21
Hos. 11: 2
Mic. 1: 7
5:13
Nah. 1:14
Hab. 2:18

[a] A κρυπτός.

γλυφή.

Exo. 25: 6
28:21
35: 8
1 Ki. 7:27
2 Ch. 2: 7, 14
Eze. 41:25, 25

γλύφω.

Exo. 28: 9
36:13
2 Ch. 2: 7, 14
3: 5, 7
Isa. 44: 9, 10
Eze. 41:18
Hab. 2:18

γλῶσσα.

Gen. 10: 5, 20
31
11: 7
Exo. 11: 7
Jos. 7:21
10:21
Jud. 7: 5
6 A[a]
2 Sa. 23: 2
Neh. 13:24+S[3]
Job 5:21
6:30
17: 6 S[*b]
20:12, 16
29:10
33: 2
Psa. 5:10
9:28
11: 4, 5
13: 3–A
14: 3
15: 9
21:16
30:21
33:14
34:28
36:30
38: 2, 4
44: 2
49:19
50:16
51: 4, 6
54:10
56: 5
63: 4, 9
65:17
67:24
70:24
72: 9
77:36
20
80: 6
108: 2
118:172
119: 2, 3
125: 2
136: 6
138: 4
Ps. 139: 4
Pro. 3:16
6:17, 24
10:20, 31
12:18, 19
15: 2, 4
17: 4, 20
18:21
21: 6, 23
24:23 ter
25, 15, 23
26:28
27:20
29:43
Cant. 4:11
Isa. 3: 8
19:18
28:11
29:24
32: 4
35: 6
41:17
45:23
50: 4
57: 4
59: 3
66:18
Jer. 5:15–A
9: 3, 5, 8[c]
18:18
23:31–B
Lam. 4: 4
Eze. 3: 6, 26
36: 3
Dan. 1: 4
3: 4
7–A
29, 31
5:19
6:25
7:14
Hos. 7:16
Mic. 6:12
Zeph. 3: 9, 13
Zec. 8:23
14:12

[a] pro χείρ. [b] pro γέλως. [c] A καρδία.

γλωσσόκομον.

2 Sa. 6:11 A[a]
2 Ch. 24: 8, 10
2 Ch. 24:11, 11

[a] pro κιβωτός.

γλωσσότμητος.

Leviticus 22:22

γλωσσοχαριτέω.

Proverbs 28:23

γλωσσώδης.

Psa. 139:12
Pro. 21:19

γνάθος.

Jud. 4:21 A[a]
22 A[a]
Jud. 5:26 A[a]

[a] pro κρόταφος.

γναφεύς.

2 Ki. 18:17
Isa. 7: 3 ABS[a]
Isa. 36: 2 ABS[a]

[a] pro κναφεύς.

γνοφερός.

Job 10:21

γνόφος.

Exo. 10:22
14:20
20:21
Deu. 4:11
5:22
Jos. 24: 7
2 Sa. 22:10
1 Ki. 8:12 A, 53
2 Ch. 6: 1
Job 3: 5
9:17
17:13
22:13
Job 23:17
27:20[a]
Psa. 17:10
96: 2
Pro. 7: 9 A[b]
Isa. 44:22
60: 2
Jer. 23:12
Eze. 34:12, 12
Joel 2: 2
Amos 5:20
Zeph. 1:15

[a] S λαίλαψ. [b] pro γνοφώδης.

γνοφόω.

Lamentations 2: 1

γνοφώδης.

Exo. 19:16
Pro. 7: 9[a]

[a] A γνόφος.

γνώμη.

Ezra 4:19, 21
22
5: 3, 5, 9
13, 17
6: 1, 3, 8
11, 12
14, 14
Ezra 7:13, 21
23
Psa. 82: 4
Pro. 2:16
12:26+A
Dan. 2:14, 15

γνωρίζω.

Exo. 21:36
Ruth 3: 3
1 Sa. 6: 2
10: 8
14:12
16: 3
28:15
2 Sa. 7:21
1 Ki. 1:27
8:53
1 Ch. 16: 8
Ezra 4:14, 16
5:10
7:24, 25
Neh. 8:12
9:14
Job 34:25
Psa. 15:11
24: 4
31: 5
38: 5
76:15
77: 5
89:12
97: 2
102: 7
Ps. 105: 8
142: 8
143: 3 S[a]
144:12
Pro. 3: 6
9: 9
15:10
22:19
Jer. 11:18
16:21
Eze. 20: 5, 11
43:11
44:23
Dan. 2: 5, 6, 10
15, 17
23, 23
28, 29
30, 45
4: 3, 4
5: 7, 8, 15
16, 17
7:16
8:19
Hos. 8: 4
Amos 3: 3

[a] pro γινώσκω.

γνώριμος.

Ruth 2: 1
3: 2
2 Sa. 3: 8
Pro. 7: 4

γνωριστής.

2 Kings 23:24

γνῶσις.

Jos. 23:13+A
1 Sa. 2: 3
1 Ki. 7: 2 B[a]
1 Ch. 4:10
Psa. 18: 3
72:11
93:10
118:66
138: 6
Pro. 2: 6
8: 9, 10
Pro. 8:12
9: 6
13:16, 19
16: 5
19:23
21:11
22:20, 21
24:26
27:21
29: 7
Ecc. 1:16, 17

Ecc. 1:18, 18; 2:21, 26; 7:13; 8: 6; 9:10; 12: 9
Isa. 11: 2
Jer. 10:14
Jer. 28:17; 47:14
Dan. 1: 4; 12: 4
Hos. 4: 6; 10:12
Mal. 2: 7

[a] pro ἐπίγνωσις.

γνώστης.

1 Sa. 28: 3, 9
2 Ki. 21: 6
2 Ch. 35:19

γνωστός.

Gen. 2: 9
Exo. 33:16
2 Ki. 10·11
Ezra 4:12, 13; 5: 8
Neh. 5:10
Psa. 30:12
Psa. 54:14; 75: 2; 87: 9, 19
Isa. 19:21
Eze. 36:32
Dan. 3:18
Zec. 14: 7

γνωστῶς.

Exo. 33:13
Pro. 27:23

γογγύζω.

Exo. 16: 7 A[a]; 17: 3 AB[a]
Nu. 11: 1; 14:27, 27; 29; 16:41; 17: 5
Jud. 1:14
Psa. 58:16; 105 25
Isa. 29:24; 30:12
Lam. 3:38

[a] pro διαγογγύζω.

γόγγυσις.

Numbers 14:27

γογγυσμός.

Exo. 16: 7, 8, 8; 9, 12
Nu. 17: 5, 10
Isa. 58: 9

γομόρ, γόμορ.

Exo. 16:16, 18; 22, 32; 33, 36
1 Sa. 16:20; 25:18
2 Ki. 5:17 AB[a]
Eze. 45:11; 11—A; 11, 13; 13+A; 14
Hos. 3: 2

[a] pro γόμος.

γόμος.

Exo. 23: 5
2 Ki. 5:17[a]

[a] AB γομόρ.

γομφιάζω.

Ezekiel 18: 2

γομφιασμός.

Amos 4: 6

γονεύς.

Est. 2: 7
Pro. 29:15

γονορρυέω.

Le . 22: 4[a]

[a] AB γονορρυής.

γονορρυής.

Lev. 15: 4, 4, 6; 7, 8, 9; 11, 12; 13, 32
Lev. 15:33; 22: 4 AB[a]
Nu. 5: 2
2 Sa. 3:29

[a] pro γονορρυέω.

γόνος.

Leviticus 15: 3

γόνυ.

Gen. 30: 3; 48:12
Deu. 28:35
Jud. 4:21+A; 7: 5, 6; 16:19
1 Ki. 8:54; 18:42; 19:18; 18—A
2 Ki. 1:13; 4:20; 9:24
1 Ch. 29:20
2 Ch. 6:13
Ezra 9: 5
Job 3:12; 4: 4; 16:10
Ps. 108:24
Isa. 35: 3; 45:23; 66:12
Dan. 5: 6; 6:10; 10.10
Nah. 2:10

γράμμα.

Exo. 36:39
Lev. 19:28
Jos. 15:15, 16; 49; 21:29
Jud. 1:11, 12
Est. 4: 3—S[3]
Est. 4: 8+S[3]; 6: 1, 2; 8: 5, 10; 9: 1
Isa. 29:11, 12; 12
Dan. 1: 4

γραμματεία.

Psalm 70:15 B[?]S[a]

[a] pro πραγματεία.

γραμματεύς.

Exo. 5: 6, 10; 14, 15; 19
Nu. 11:16
Deu. 20: 5, 8, 9
Jos. 1:10; 3: 2; 9: 6; 23: 2; 24: 1
Jud. 5:14—A
2 Sa. 8:17; 20:25
1 Ki. (3) p 46; 4: 3
2 Ki. 12:10; 18:18, 37; 19: 2; 22: 3, 8, 10; 12; 25:19
1 Ch. 2:55; 5:12; 18:16; 23: 4; 24: 6; 27: 1; 32+A
2 Ch. 19:11
2 Ch. 24:11; 26:11; 34:13, 15[a]; 18, 20
Ezra 4: 8, 9, 17; 23; 7: 6, 11; 12, 21; 25
Neh. 8: 1, 4[b]; 9, 13; 12:26, 36; 13:13
Est. 3:12; 8: 9; 9: 3
Job 37:19
Psa. 44: 2
Isa. 22:15 A[c]; 36: 3; 11+AS; 22; 37: 2
Jer. 8: 8; 43:10, 12; 12, 23; 44:15, 20; 52:25

[a] (A γραμματαίαν.) [b] S[1] ἱερεύς.
[c] pro ταμίας.

γραμματεύω.

1 Ch. 26:29
Jer. 52·25

γραμματική.

Daniel 1:17

γραμματικός.

Isaiah 33:18

γραμματοεισαγωγεύς.

Exo. 18:21+A; 25+A
Deu. 1:15
Deu. 16:18; 29:10; 31:28

γραπτός.

2 Ch. 36:22
Ezra 1: 1

γραφεῖον.

Job 19:24

γραφή.

Exo. 32:16, 16
Deu. 10: 4
1 Ch. 15:15; 28:19
2 Ch. 2:11; 21:12; 24:27; 30: 5, 18; 35: 4
Ezra 2:62; 4: 7
Ezra 6:18; 7:22
Neh. 7:64
Psa. 86: 6
Eze. 13: 9
Dan. 5: 7, 8, 15; 16, 17; 24, 25; 6: 8; 10:21

γραφίς.

Exo. 32: 4
1 Ki. 6:27
Isa. 8: 1
Eze. 23:14

γράφω.

Exo. 24: 4, 12; 31:18; 32:15 A[a]; 15, 32; 34: 1, 27; 28; 36.39
Nu. 5:23; 33: 2
Deu. 4:13; 5 22; 6: 9; 9:10, 10; 10: 2, 4; 11:20; 17:18; 24: 3, 5; 27: 3, 8; 28:58, 61; 61; 29:20, 21; 27; 30:10; 31: 9, 19; 22, 24; 32:44
Jos. 1: 8; 9: 4, 5; 5+A; 7; 18: 9; 23: 6; 24:26
Jud. 8:14[b]
1 Sa. 10:25
2 Sa. 1:18; 11:14, 15
1 Ki. 2: 3; 6:27; 8:53; 11:41; 14:19 A, 29; 15: 7, 23; 31; 16: 5, 14; 20, 27; p 28—A; 20: 8, 9; 11—B; 22:39, 46[c]
2 Ki. 1:18; 8:23; 10: 1, 6, 34; 12:19; 13: 8, 12; 14: 6, 15; 18, 28; 15: 6, 11; 15, 21; 26, 31; 36; 16:19; 17:37; 20:20; 21:17, 25; 22:13; 23: 3, 21; 24, 28; 24: 5
1 Ch. 4:41; 16.40; 24: 6; 29:29
2 Ch. 9:29; 12:15; 13:22; 16:11; 20:34; 23:18; 24:27; 25: 4, 26; 26:22; 27: 7; 28:26; 30: 1; 31: 3; 32:17, 32; 33:19; 34:21, 24; 31[d]; 35:12, 19; 25, 26; 27; 36: 8
Ezra 3: 2, 4; 4: 6, 7, 7; 8; 5: 7, 10; 6: 2; 8:34
Neh. 6: 6; 7: 5; 8:14, 15; 9:38; 10:34, 36; 12:22, 23; 13: 1
Est. 1:19; 3:10, 12; 6: 2—S[1]; 8: 5, 8, 8; 9, 10; 9: 1, 20; 22 AS[e]; 23, 29; 31; 10: 1, 2
Job 19:23; 42:18
Psa. 39: 8; 68:29; 101:19; 138:16
Pro. 3: 3+A; 8:15
Ecc. 12:10
Isa. 4: 3; 8: 1; 10: 1 ter; 19; 22:16; 30: 8; 65: 6
Jer. 17:13[f]; 22:30; 25:13; 28:60, 60; 37: 2
Jer. 38:33[g]; 39:10, 12; 25, 44; 43: 2, 4, 17; 18, 27; 28, 29; 32; 51:31
Eze. 2:10, 10; 13: 9; 24: 2
Eze. 37:16, 16; 20
Dan. 5: 5, 5; 6: 9, 25; 7: 1; 9:11; 12 A[h]; 13; 12: 1
Hab. 2: 2
Mal. 3:16

[a] pro καταγράφω.
[b] A ἀπογράφω. [c] B ἐγγράφω.
[d] A ἐγγραφω. [e] pro στρέφω.
[f] S[3] ἐγγραφω. [g] A ἐπιγράφω.
[h] pro γίνομαι.

γρηγορέω.

Neh. 7: 3
Jer. 1:12—S[1]; 5: 6; 38:28, 28
Jer. 51:27
Lam. 1:14
Dan. 9:14

γρηγόρησις.

Daniel 5:11, 14

γρύζω.

Exo. 11: 7
Jos. 10:21

γρύψ.

Lev. 11:13
Deu. 14:12

γυμνός.

Gen. 3: 1, 7, 10; 11; 27:16
1 Sa. 19:24
2 Ch. 28:15
Job 1:21, 21; 22: 6; 24: 7, 10; 26: 6; 31:19
Pro. 23:31
Ecc. 5:14
Isa. 20: 2, 3, 4; 32:11; 58: 7
Eze. 16: 7, 22; 39; 18: 7, 16; 23:29
Hos. 2: 3
Amos 2:16; 4: 3
Mic. 1: 8

γυμνότης.

Deuteronomy 28:48—B

γυμνόω.

Genesis 9:21

γύμνωσις.

Genesis 9:22, 23, 23

γυναικεῖα.

Genesis 18:11

γυναικεῖος.

Gen. 31:35 A[a]
Lev. 18:22[b]
Deu. 22: 5
Est. 2:11, 17

[a] pro γύνη. [b] AB γύνη.

γυναικών.

Esther 2: 3, 9, 13, 14

γύναιον.

Job 24:21[a]

[a] ABS[1] ἀγύναιος.

γυνή.

Gen. 2:22, 23; 24; 3: 1, 1, 2; 4, 6, 8; 12, 13; 13, 15; 16, 17; 20, 21; 4: 1, 17; 19, 23
Gen. 4:23, 25; 6: 2, 18; 18; 7: 7, 7, 13; 13; 8:16, 16; 18, 18; 11:29 ter; 31; 12: 5, 11

Gen. 12:11, 12
14, 17
18, 19
19, 20
13: 1
14:16
16: 1, 3, 3
17:15, 19
18: 9, 10
19:15, 16
26
20: 2, 2, 3
7, 11
12, 14
17, 18
21:21
23:19
24: 3, 4, 5
7, 8, 15
36, 37
38, 39
40, 44
51, 67
25: 1, 10
20, 21
21
26: 7, 7, 8
9, 10
11, 34
27:46
28: 1, 2, 6
6, 9, 9
29:21, 28
30: 4, 9, 13
26
31:17, 32
35ᵃ, 50
32:22
33: 5
34: 4, 8, 12
16, 21
29
36: 2, 6, 10
10, 12
13, 14
17, 18
18—A
39
37: 1
38: 6, 8, 9
12, 14
20
39: 7, 8, 9
19
41:45
44:27
45:19
46: 5, 19
26
49:31, 31
Exo. 1:19
2, 7, 9
21, 22
3:22
4:20
6:20, 23
25
11: 2+A
15:20
18: 2, 5, 6
19:15
20:17
21: 3, 3, 4
4, 5, 22
22, 28
29
22:16, 17
24
32: 2
3+A
35:22, 25
26, 29
36: 6
Lev. 12: 2
13:29, 38
15:18, 19
25
18: 8, 11
14, 15
16

Lev. 18:16 Aᵇ
17, 18
19, 20
22 ABᶜ
23
19:20
20:10, 10
11, 13
14, 16
16, 18
21, 27
21: 7, 7
13—ABᵉ
14
24:10, 11
26:26
Nu. 5: 6, 12
14, 14
15, 18
18, 19
21, 21
22, 24
25, 26
27, 28
29, 30
30, 31
6: 2
12: 1, 1
14: 3
16:27
21:30
25: 8, 15
26:59
30: 4, 17
31: 9, 17
18, 35
32:26, 30
36: 3, 3, 4
6, 6, 8
12
Deu. 2:34
3: 6, 19
5:21
13: 6
17: 2, 5, 17
20: 7, 14
21:11, 11
13, 15
22: 5, 13
14, 16
19, 22
22, 22
24, 29
30
24: 3, 5, 6
7, 7
25: 5, 5, 7
7, 9, 11
27:20
23—A
28:30, 54
29:11, 18
31:12
Jos. 1:14
2: 1, 4
6:21, 22
23
8:25
9: 8
15:16, 17
Jud. 1:12, 13
3: 6
4: 4, 4, 9
17, 21
5:24 *ter*
8:30
9:49, 51
53, 54
11: 1, 2, 2
2
12: 9 Aᵈ
13: 2, 3, 6
9, 10
11, 11
13, 19
20, 21
22, 23
24
14: 1, 2, 2
3, 3, 7

Jud. 14:10, 15
16, 20
15: 1, 1, 6
16: 1, 4
27, 27
19: 1, 26
27
20: 4, 4 Aᵉ
21: 1, 7, 7
10+A
11, 14
14+A
16, 16
18, 18
21, 22
23
Ruth 1: 1
2—B
4, 5
3: 8, 11
14
4: 5, 10
10, 11
13—B
14
1 Sa. 1: 2, 4, 15
18, 19
23, 26
2:20, 20
22+A
4:19, 20
14:50
15: 3, 33
33
18: 7
17 A
19 A
27
19:11
21: 4, 5
22:19
25: 3, 3, 14
37, 39
40, 42
43, 44
27: 3, 3, 9
11
28: 7, 7, 8
9, 11
12, 12
13—AB
21, 23
24
30: 2, 2, 3
5, 5, 18
22
2 Sa. 1:26
2: 2, 2
3: 5, 8, 14
5:13
6:19
11: 2, 2, 3
3, 5, 11
21, 22
26, 27
12: 8, 9, 9
10, 10
11, 11
15, 24
14: 2, 2, 4
5
8—AB
9
12—B
13, 17
18, 18
19, 27
27
15:16
17:19, 20
20
19: 5
20: 3, 16
17, 21
22
1 Ki. 2:17, 21
3:16, 17
17, 18
19—A
22, 24

1 Ki. 4:11
15—B
30—A
30—A
7: 2
9:16 A
10: 8
11: 1—B
1
3+A
4, 7, 19
19, 26
12 *p* 24
18—B
ll 19, 19
ll 25, 29
ll 31, 36
l 40
14: 2 A
2 A
4 A
5 A
6 A
17 A
16:31
17: 9, 10
12, 15
17, 19
24
19: 1
20: 5, 7, 25
21: 3, 5, 7
2 Ki. 4: 1, 8, 9
17, 37
5: 2
6:26, 28
30
8: 1, 2, 3
5, 5, 6
18
14: 9
22:14 Aᶠ
23: 7
24:15
1 Ch. 1:50+A
2:18, 24
26, 29
35
3: 3
4: 5, 18
19
7: 4, 15
16, 23
8: 8, 9, 29
9:35
14: 3
16: 3
2 Ch. 8:11
11:18, 21
21, 23
13:21
15:13
20:13
21: 6, 14
22:11
24: 3
25:18
28: 8
29: 9
34:22
Ezra 2:61
10: 1, 2, 3
10, 11
14, 17
18—S¹
19—S¹
44
Neh. 4:14
5: 1
6:18
7:63
8: 2, 3
10:28
12:43
13:23, 26
27
Est. 1: 9, 10
20
2: 3, 4, 7
8

Est. 2:12—S¹
14, 15
4:11
5:10, 14
6:13, 13
7: 8
8:11+S³
Job 2: 9, 10
11: 3, 12
14: 1
15:14
19:17
25: 4
31: 9, 10
11
38:30
42 *p* 18
Ps. 108: 9
127: 3
Pro. 5: 3, 3, 18
6:24, 26
29
7: 5, 10
9:13
11:16, 16
22
12: 4, 4
14: 1
18:22, 22
19:14
21:19
24:51, 55
58, 71
25:24
27:15
29:28
48—C
48
Ecc. 7:27, 29
9: 9
Cant. 1: 8
5: 9, 18
Isa. 4: 1
13: 8, 16
19:16
27:11
32: 9
49:15ᵍ, 15
54: 6, 6
66: 8 S²ʰ
Jer. 3: 1, 1, 20
5: 8
6:11, 12

Jer. 7:18
8:10
9:20, 20
13:21
14:16
16: 1
18:21
27:37
28:22, 30
29:23
36: 6
6—S¹
23
42: 8—A
45:22, 23
47: 7
48:16
50: 6
51: 7, 9, 15
15, 20
24, 25
Lam. 2:20
4:10
5:11
Eze. 8:14
9: 6
16:30, 32
34, 41
18: 6, 6
11, 15
22:11
23: 2, 10
43+A
44, 48
24:18+A
30:17ⁱ
44:22
Dan. 6:24
11:17, 37
Hos. 1: 2
2: 2
3: 1
12:12, 12
Amos 7:17
Nah. 3:13
Zec. 5: 7, 9
12:12+A
12, 12
13, 13
14
14: 2
Mal. 2:14, 14
15

ᵃ A γυναικεῖος. ᵇ *pro* ἀσχημοσύνη. ᶜ *pro* γυναικεῖος. ᵈ *pro* θυγάτηρ. ᵉ *pro* παλλακή. ᶠ *pro* μήτηρ. ᵍ A μήτηρ. ʰ *pro* γῆ. ⁱ A πόλις.

Jer. 28:26
38:38, 40
Eze. 41:15
43:20
Eze. 45:19
Zeph. 1:16
3: 6
Zec. 14:10

γωνιαῖος.

Job 38: 6

δαβείρ, δαβίρ.

1 Ki. 6: 9, 16
18
19+A
19, 21
20+A
29
1 Ki. 7:35
8: 6, 8
2 Ch. 3:16
4:20
5: 7, 9

δαιμόνιον.

Deu. 32:17
Psa. 90: 6
95: 5
105:37
Isa. 13:21
34:14
65: 3, 11

δάκνω.

Gen. 49:17
Nu. 21: 6, 8, 8
9
Deu. 8:15
Ecc. 10: 8, 11
Jer. 8:17
Amos 5:19
9: 3
Mic. 3: 5
Hab. 2: 7

δάκρυ, δάκρυον.

2 Ki. 20: 5
Psa. 6: 7
38:13
41: 4
55: 9
14+
8ᵃ S²
79: 6, 6
114: 8
125: 5
Ecc. 4: 1
Isa. 25: 8
38: 5
Jer. 9: 1, 18
13:17
14:17
38:16
Lam. 1: 2
2:11, 18
Hos. 13: 3ᵃ
Mic. 2: 6
Mal. 2:13

ᵃ A καπνοδόχη.

δακρύω.

Job 3:24
Lam. 1: 2 Aᵃ
Eze. 27:35
Mic. 2: 6

ᵃ *pro* κλαίω.

δακτύλιος.

Gen. 38:18, 25
41:42
Exo. 25:11 *ter*
13, 14
25
25—A
26
26:29
27: 4, 7
30: 4
35:22
36:23, 24
25, 27
Exo. 36:28, 29
29
38: 3, 10
10+A
10+A
18, 24
Nu. 31:50
Est. 3:10
8: 2, 8, 8
10
Isa. 3:20—S¹
Dan. 6:17, 17

δάκτυλος.

Exo. 8:19
29:12
31:18
Lev. 4: 6, 17
25, 30
34
8:15
9: 9
14:16, 16
27
16:14, 14
19
Deu. 9:10
2 Sa. 21:20, 20
1 Ki. 7: 3
1 Ch. 20: 6
2 Ch. 10:10
Job 29: 9
Psa. 8: 4
143: 1
150 *p* 6
Pro. 6:13
7: 3
Cant. 5: 5
Isa. 2: 8
17: 8
31: 7 S¹ᵃ
59: 3
Jer. 52:21
Dan. 2:41, 42
5: 5

ᵃ *pro* χείρ.

δαλός.

Isa. 7: 4
Eze. 24: 9ᵃ
Amos 4:11
Zec. 3: 2
12: 6

ᵃ B λαός.

γῦρος.

Job 22:14
Isa. 40:22

γυρόω.

Job 26:10

γύψ.

Lev. 11:14
Deu. 14:13
Job 5: 7
Job 15:23
28: 7
39:27

γωλάθ.

2 Chronicles 4:12, 13

γωληλά.

Nehemiah 2:13

γωνία.

Exo. 26:23, 24
27: 2
1 Sa. 14:38
1 Ki. 7:20
2 Ki. 14:13
2 Ch. 4:10
25:23
26: 9, 9
9+Bᵃ
2 Ch. 26:15
28:24
Neh. 3:19, 20
24, 25
Job 1:19
Ps. 117:22
Pro. 7: 8, 12
21: 9
25:24

δαμάζω.

Daniel 2:40, 40

δάμαλις.

Gen. 15: 9
Nu. 7:17, 23
20, 35
41, 47
53, 59
65, 71
77, 83
88
19: 2, 6, 9
10
Deu. 21: 3, 4, 4
6
Jud. 14:18
1 Sa. 16: 2
1 Sa. 28:24
1 Ki. 12:28, 32
2 Ki. 10:29
17:16
Psa. 67:31
Isa. 5:18
7:21
15: 5
Jer. 26:20
Hos. 4:16
10:11
Joel 1:17
Amos 4: 1

δανείζω, –νίζω.

Deu. 15: 6, 6, 8
10
28:12[a], 12
44, 44
Neh. 5: 4
Psa. 36:21, 26
Pro. 19:17
20: 4
22: 7
Isa. 24: 2, 2

[a] A ἐκδανείζω.

δάνειον.

Deu. 15: 8, 10
Deu. 24:13

δανειστής.

2 Ki. 4: 1
Ps. 108:11
Pro. 29:13

δαπάνη.

Ezra 6: 4, 8

δαρόμ.

Eze. 20:46[a]

[a] AB δαγών.

δάσος.

2 Sa. 18: 9[a]
Ps. 131: 6AS[1 b]
Isa. 9:18

[a] A δράσος. [b] pro πεδίον.

δασύπους.

Lev. 11: 5
Deu. 14: 7

δασύς.

Gen. 25:25
27:11, 23
Lev. 23:40
Deu. 12: 2
2 Ki. 1: 8
Neh. 8:15
Isa. 57: 5
Eze. 6:13+A
Hab. 3: 3

δαψιλεύομαι.

1 Samuel 10: 2

δεβραθά.

2 Kings 5:19

δέησις.

Jos. 18: 4
1 Ki. 8:28
30[a], 38
45
49+A
52, 52
54
9: 3
2 Ch. 6:19; 19
21, 29
35, 39
40
Job 8: 6
16:20
27: 9
36:19
40:22
Psa. 5: 3
6:10
9:13[b]
16: 1
20: 3[c]
21:25
27: 2, 6
30:23
33:16
38:13
39: 2
54: 2
60: 2
65:19 S[2 d]
85: 6
87: 3
101: 1, 18
Ps. 105:44
114: 1
118:169
129: 2
139: 7
140: 1
141: 3, 7
142: 1
Ps. 144:19
Isa. 1:15
Jer. 3:21
11:14
14:12
Lam. 3:55–A
Dan. 9: 3, 17
23

[a] A φωνή. [b] A φωνή, S κραυγή. [c] S[2] θέλησις. [d] pro προσευχή.

δεῖ.

Lev. 4: 2
Ruth 4: 5
2 Sa. 4:10
2 Ki. 4:13, 14
Ezra 9: 3+A
Est. 1:15
4:16–BS
Job 15: 3–A
19: 4
Pro. 22:14
23: 2
Isa. 30:29
50: 4
Eze. 13:19, 19
Dan. 2:28, 29
29, 46
6:15

δείδω.

Job 3:19, 25
7: 2
26:13
29:14AS[1 a]
Job 31:35
38:40
41: 1
Isa. 60:14

[a] pro ἐνδύω.

δείκνυμι, –νύω.

Gen. 12: 1
41:25, 28
39
48:11
Exo. 13:21
15:25
25: 8, 40
26:30
33: 5
18+A
Lev. 13:49
Nu. 8: 4
13:27
16:30
22:41
23: 3
24:17
Deu. 1:33
3:24
4: 5, 36
5:24
32:20
34: 1, 4
Jos. 7:14, 14[a]
14[a]
Jud. 1:24, 25
4:22
13:23[b]
1 Sa. 12:23
2 Sa. 15:25
1 Ki. 13:12
2 Ki. 6: 6
8:10, 13
11: 4
16:14
20:13, 13
15
2 Ch. 23: 3
Est. 1: 4, 11
4: 8
Job 28:11
33:23
34:32[c]
Psa. 4: 7
49:23
58:11
59: 5
70:20
77:11
84: 8
90:16
Ecc. 2:24
3:18
Cant. 2:14
Isa. 11:11
30:30
39: 2, 2
40:14, 14
48: 9, 17
53:11
Jer. 18:17
24: 1
45:21
Eze. 11:25
40: 4 ter
43:10
Hos. 5: 9
Amos 7: 1, 4, 7
17
Mic. 4: 2
Nah. 3: 5
Hab. 1: 3
Zec. 1: 9, 20
3: 1
8:12

[a] A ἐνδείκνυμι. [b] A φωτίζω. [c] A διδάσκω.

δείλαιος.

Hos. 7:13
Nah. 3: 7

δείλη.

Gen. 24:63
Exo. 18:13[a], 14
1 Sa. 20: 5
30:17
2 Sa. 1:12
1 Ki. 17: 6
2 Ch. 2: 4
13:11, 11
Est. 2:14
Jer. 31:33
Zeph. 2: 7

[a] A ἑσπέρα.

δειλία.

Lev. 26:36 A[a]
Job 13:11 A[b]
Psa. 54: 5
88:41
Pro. 19:15

[a] pro δουλεία. [b] pro δίνα.

δειλιαίνω.

Deuteronomy 20: 8

δειλιάω.

Deu. 1:21
31: 6, 8
Jos. 1: 9
8: 1
10:25
Psa. 13: 5
Psa. 26: 1
77:53
103: 7
118:161
Isa. 13: 7
Jer. 15: 5

δειλινός.

Gen. 3: 8
Exo. 29:39, 41
Lev. 6:20
1 Ki. 18:29
2 Ch. 31: 3–A

δειλός.

Deu. 20: 8
Jud. 7: 3
Jud. 9: 4[a]
2 Ch. 13: 7

[a] A θαμβέω.

δεινός.

2 Sa. 1: 9
Job 2:13
Job 33:15

δεινῶς.

Job 10:16
Job 19:11

δειπνέω.

Proverbs 23: 1

δεῖπνον.

Dan. 1:16
Dan. 5: 1

δέκα.

Jos. 15:44[a]
Jud. 6:27[b]
2 Sa. 15:16–A[e]
1 Ki. 7:40+A
12 p 24/52[c]
2 Ki. 16:17+A
20: 9–A
25:25–B
2 Ch. 4: 1–A
2 Ch. 27: 8 A
36: 9+A
Ezra 1:10–A[d]
8:24[c]
Est. 9:12+S[3]
13–A
18+S[3]
Jer. 48: 1[e], 2[e]
Dan. 7: 7+A

[a] A ἐννέα. [b] A τρισκαίδεκα. [c] B δώδεκα. [d] B ἕξ pro 410. [e] S δώδεκα.

δεκάδαρχος.

Exo. 18:21, 25
Deu. 1:15 AB[a]

[a] pro δέκαρχος.

δεκαδύο.

2 Ki. 1:18[a]
Est. 8:12+S[*]

[a] A δύο.

δεκαεννέα.

Joshua 19:38+A

δεκάπηχυς.

1 Kings 7:47

δεκαπλασίων.

Daniel 1:20

δέκαρχος.

Deuteronomy 1:15[a]

[a] AB δεκάδαρχος.

δεκάς.

Neh. 10:38[a]

[a] AS[1] δεκατή.

δεκάτη.

Gen. 14:20
28:22
Lev. 27:30, 31
32
Nu. 29: 7
Deu. 14:21
1 Sa. 1:21
Neh. 10:37–A
38, 38
38 AS[1 a]
12:44
13: 5, 12

[a] pro δεκάς.

δέκατος.

Gen. 8: 5[a]
Lev. 16:29 AB[1]
19: 5 AB[b]
25: 9–A[1]
2 Ki. 25: 1[c]
Ezra 10:16[d]
Jer. 39: 1[e]
Jer. 46: 1+A
52:12[f]
Eze. 29: 1[g]
32: 1[g], 1[h]
33:21[i]
45:11–A

[a] A ἑνδέκατος. [b] pro δεκτός. [c] A δεύτερος. [d] S[3] δωδικατος. [e] B[?] δωδέκατος. [f] S[1] δέκα. [g] A ἑνδέκατος, B δωδέκατος. [h] A[1] ἑνδ– aut δωδ– [i] AB δωδέκατος.

δεκατόω.

Nehemiah 10:37

δεκάχορδος.

Psa. 32: 2
91: 4
Psa. 143: 9

δεκτός.

Exo. 28:34
Lev. 1: 3, 4
17: 4
19: 5[a]
22:19, 20
23:11
Deu. 33:16, 23
24
Job 33:26–S[1]
Pro. 10:24
11: 1
12:22
Pro. 14: 9, 35
15: 8, 28
16: 5, 13
22:11
Isa. 49: 8
56: 7
58: 5
60: 7
61: 2
Jer. 6:20
Mal. 2:13

[a] AB δέκατος.

δένδρον.

Gen. 18: 4, 8
23:17
Nu. 13:21
Deu. 12: 2
20:19
22: 6
Job 14: 7
19:10
40:16, 17
Pro. 11:30
13:12
15: 4
Isa. 2:13
16: 9
17: 8[a]
27: 9
57: 5
Eze. 6:13
47: 7
Dan. 4: 7, 8
11, 17
20, 23
Hos. 4:13

[a] A ἄλσος.

δεξαμενή.

Exodus 2:16

δεξιός, δεξιά.

Gen. 13: 9, 9
24:49
48:13, 13
14, 17
18
Exo. 14:22, 29
15: 6, 6, 12
29:20 sex
22
Lev. 7:22, 23
8:23 ter
24 ter
25, 26
9:21
14:14 ter
16
17 ter
25 ter
27
28 ter
Nu. 18:18
20:17
22:26
Deu. 2:27
5:32
17:11, 20
28:14
32:40
33: 2
Jos. 1: 7
23: 6
Jud. 3:16, 21
5:26
7:20
16:29
1 Sa. 6:12
11: 2
23:19, 24
2 Sa. 2:19, 21
14:19

2 Sa. 16: 6
20: 9
24: 5
1 Ki. 2:19
(3)42
6:12
7:25—B
25, 33
22:19
2 Ki. 11:11—A
22: 2
23:13
1 Ch. 6:39
12: 2
2 Ch. 3:17, 17
4: 6, 7, 8
10
18:18
23:10
34: 2
Neh. 8: 4
12:31—ABS[1]
Job 23: 9
30:12
40: 9
Psa. 15: 8, 11
16: 7
17:36
19: 7
20: 9
25:10
43: 4
44: 5, 10
47:11
59: 7
62: 9
72:23
73:11—S[1]
76:11
77:54
79:16, 18
88:11, 26
43
89:12
90: 7

Psa. 97: 1
107: 7
108: 6, 31
109: 1, 5
117:15, 16
16—S[1]
120: 5
136: 5
137: 7
138:10
141: 5
143: 8, 8, 11
11
Pro. 3:16
4:27, 27
Ecc. 10: 2
Cant. 2: 6
8: 3
Isa. 9:20
30:21
41:10, 13
44:20
45: 1
48:13
51:16+A
54: 3
63:12
Jer. 22:24
Lam. 2: 3—S[1]
4
Eze. 1:10
4: 6
10: 3
16:46
21:16, 21
39: 3
47: 1, 2
Dan. 12: 7
Jon. 4:11
Hab. 2:16
Zec. 3: 1
4: 3, 11
6:13
11:17, 17
12: 6

δέον, τα δέοντα.

Exo. 16:22
21:10
1 Ki. 4:22

Pro. 21:31
Dan. 11:26

δέρμα.

Gen. 27:16
Exo. 25: 5, 5
26:14, 14
29:14
35: 7, 7
23, 23
23+A
39:21
21+AB
Lev. 4:11
6:38
11:32[a]
13: 2, 2, 3
3, 4, 4
5, 6, 7
8, 10
11, 12
12, 13
18, 20
21, 22
24, 24
25, 26
27, 28
30, 31
32, 33

Lev. 13:34, 34
35, 36
38, 39
39, 41
48, 48
49, 49
51, 51
56
15:17
16:27
Nu. 4: 6
11 A[b]
12 A[b]
19: 5
Job 2: 4, 4
10:11
19:20, 26[c]
30:30
Jer. 13:23
Lam. 3: 4
4: 8
5:10
Eze. 37: 6, 8
Mic. 3: 2, 3

[a] A δερμάτινος.
[b] pro δερμάτινος. [c] AS[2] σῶμα.

δερμάτινος.

Gen. 3:21
Lev. 11:32 A[a]
13:52, 53
57, 58
59

Nu. 4: 8, 10
11[b], 12[b]
14, 14
31:20
2 Ki. 1: 8

[a] pro δέρμα. [b] A δέρμα.

δέρρις.

Exo. 26: 7, 7, 8
8, 8, 9
9—A[1]
9, 10
10, 11
12
12—AB
12—B
13, 13

Nu. 4:25
Jud. 4:18+A
21+A
1 Ch. 17: 1
Ps. 103: 2
Cant. 1: 5
Jer. 4:20
10:20, 20
Zec. 13: 4

δέρω.

Lev. 1: 6AB[2a]
2 Ch. 29:34 A[a]
2 Ch. 35:11 B[a]

[a] pro ἐκδέρω.

δεσμεύω.

Gen. 37: 7
49:11
Jud. 16:11[a]
1 Sa. 24:12

Job 26: 8
Ps. 146: 3
Amos 2: 8

[a] A δεσμός.

δέσμη.

Exodus 12:22

δέσμιος.

Ecc. 4:14[a]
Lam. 3:33

Zec. 9:11, 12

[a] AS δεσμός.

δεσμός.

Gen. 42:27, 35
35
Lev. 26:13
Nu. 19:15
30:14
Jud. 15:13, 14
16:11 A[a]
1 Sa. 25:29
2 Ch. 33:11
Ezra 7:26 A[b]
Job 38:31
39: 5
Psa. 2: 3
106:14
115: 7
Pro. 7:22
Ecc. 4:14 AS[c]

Ecc. 7:27
Isa. 28:22
42: 7
49: 9
52: 2
Jer. 2:20
5: 5
34: 1
37: 8
Eze. 3:25
4: 8
Dan. 4:12, 20
Hos. 11: 4
Nah. 1:13
Hab. 3:13
Hag. 1: 6
Mal. 4: 2

[a] pro δεσμεύω. [b] pro παράδοσις. [c] pro δέσμιος.

δεσμωτήριον.

Gen. 39:22, 22
23—A
40: 3, 5

Jud. 16:21[a]
25[a]
Isa. 24:22

[a] A φυλακή.

δεσμώτης.

Gen. 39:20
Jer. 24: 1—S[1]

Jer. 36: 2

δεσπόζω.

1 Ch. 29:11
Psa. 21:29
58:14

Psa. 65: 7
88:10
102:19

δεσποτεία, -τία.

Ps. 102:22 AS[2a]
Psa. 144:13

[a] pro δυναστεία.

δεσπότης.

Gen. 15: 2, 8
Jos. 5:14
Job 5: 8[a]
Pro. 6: 7
17: 2
22: 7
24:33
29:25[b]

Isa. 1:24
3: 1
10:33
Jer. 1: 6
4:10
14:13+A
15:11
Jon. 4: 3

[a] A παντοκράτωρ. [b] S σωτήρ.

δεῦρο.

Gen. 12: 1—A
19:32
24:31
31:44
37:13
Exo. 3:10
Nu. 10:29
22: 6, 11
17
23: 7, 7
13, 27
24:14
Jud. 4:22
9:10, 12
14
11: 6
18:19[a]
19:11, 13
1 Sa. 9: 5, 9[b]
10
14: 1, 6
16: 1
17:44
20:21
23:27
2 Sa. 13:11

2 Sa. 15:22
18:22
1 Ki. 1:12, 13
53
13:15
15:19
18: 5
2 Ki. 1: 3[c]
3:13
4: 3, 7
25, 29
5: 5, 19
6: 3+A[a]
3
7: 9
8: 1, 8, 10
9: 1
10:16
2 Ch. 16: 3
25:17
Neh. 6: 2, 7
Pro. 7:18
Ecc. 2: 1
9: 7
Cant. 4: 8, 8
Dan. 12: 9, 13

[a] A ἔρχομαι. [b] A δεῦτε.
[c] A πορεύω.

δεῦτε.

Gen. 11: 3, 4, 7
37:20, 27
Exo. 1:10
Jos. 10: 4
Jud. 9:15
1 Sa. 9: 9 A[a]
2 Ki. 1: 2, 6
6: 2, 13
19
7: 4, 14
14: 8
22:13
Neh. 2:17
Job 17:10
Psa. 33:12

Psa. 45: 9
65: 5, 16
82: 5
94: 1, 6
Isa. 1:18
2: 3, 5
9:10
27:11
56: 9
Jer. 11:19
18:18 18
28:10
Dan. 3:26
Jon. 1: 7
Mic. 4: 2

[a] pro δεῦρο.

δευτερεύω.

1 Ch. 16: 5[a]
Est. 4: 8

[a] AS δεύτερος.

δευτερονόμιον.

Deu. 17:18
Jos. 9: 5

δεύτερος.

Exo. 4: 8[a]
Jos. 5: 2—B
Jud. 6:28[b]
1 Sa. 14:49—A
17:13 A
1 Ki. 6:25—B
7: 4—B
(9)+A
16:29—A
2 Ki. 1:18+A

1 Ch. 16: 5 AS[c]
26: 2—B
4—B
11—B
16—A
20:22—B
Neh. 11:17+S[3]
Est. 8: 9+S[1]
Psa. 47: 1—A
Eze. 10:14 A

[a] AB ἔσχατος. [b] A σιτευτός.
[c] pro δευτερεύω.

δευτερόω.

Gen. 41:32
1 Sa. 26: 8
2 Sa. 20:10
1 Ki. 18:34, 34

1 Ki. 21:20—A
Neh. 13:21
Jer. 2:36

δευτέρωσις.

2 Ki. 23: 4
2 Ki. 25:18

δέχομαι.

Gen. 4:11
33:10
50:17
Exo. 29:25 A[a]
32: 4

Lev. 7: 8
19: 7
22:23[b], 25
27
Deu. 30: 1
Deu. 32:11
33: 3, 11
Jud. 13:23 A[a]
2 Ch. 7: 7
29:16, 22
30:16
Ezra 8:30
Job 2:10
4:12
8:20
36:18
40:19
Psa. 49: 9
Pro. 1: 3, 9[c]
2: 1
4:10
9: 9
10: 8

Pro. 16:17
21:11
24:23, 23
24
Isa. 22: 3 A[d]
40: 2
Jer. 2:30
5: 3
7:28
9:20
17:23—A
32:14
Hos. 4:11
10: 6
Amos 5:11
Zeph. 3: 2, 7
Zec. 1: 6

[a] pro λαμβάνω.
[b] A[2]B[1] προσδέχομαι.
[c] A ἔλω. [d] pro δέω B.

δέω (A).

Gen. 19:18
25:21
43:19
44:18
Exo. 4:10, 13
5:22—A
32:11, 31
Nu. 12:11, 13
Deu. 3:23
9:18, 25
25
15:11 A[a]
Jos. 7: 7
Jud. 13: 8 A[b]
1 Sa. 13:12
1 Ki. 8:33, 47
59
9: 3
13: 6, 6
2 Ki. 1:13
13: 4
2 Ch. 6:24, 37
Est. 8: 3+S[3]

Job 5: 8
8: 5
9:15
11:19
17: 1
19:16
30:24
34:19
36:13 S[1c]
Psa. 27: 2[d]
29: 9
63: 1
118:58
141: 2[e]
Pro. 26:25
Isa. 37: 4—AS[3]
Jer. 33:19
Dan. 6:11
9:13
Hos. 12: 4
Zec. 8:21
Mal. 1: 9

[a] pro ἐπιδέω A.
[b] pro προσεύχομαι. [c] pro δέω B.
[d] A κράζω. [e] A προσεχω.

δέω (B).

Gen. 38:28
42:24
Jud. 15: 4[a], 10
12, 13
13
16: 5, 6, 7
8, 10
11, 12
13
21 A[b]
2 Sa. 3:34
2 Ki. 5:23+A
7:10
10+A
12:20
17: 4
25: 7
2 Ch. 33:11
36: 2, 6
Job 32:19
19+A

Job 36:13[c]
39:10
40:21[d], 24
Ps. 149: 8
Pro. 15: 7
25:12
Cant. 7: 5
Isa. 3:10
22: 3[e]
42: 7
43:14
45:14
Jer. 40: 1
52:11
Eze. 3:25
16: 4
27:24
37:17
Hos. 10: 6
Nah. 3:10

[a] A μέσος. [b] pro ἐπιδέω B.
[c] S[1] δέω A. [d] A εἰλέω.
[e] A δέχομαι.

δῆγμα.

Micah 5: 5

δηλαϊστός.

Eze. 5:15[a]

[a] A δήλαιος.

δῆλος.

Nu. 27:21
Deu. 33: 8
1 Sa. 14:41

1 Sa. 28: 6
Hos. 3: 4

δηλόω.

Exo. 6: 3
33:12
Deu. 33:10
Jos. 4: 7
1 Sa. 3:21
1 Ki. 8:36
2 Ch. 6:27
Est. 2:22
Psa. 24:14
41: 9ᵃ
50: 8
147: 9
Isa. 42: 9
Jer. 16:21
Dan. 4:15
ᵃ AS² ᾠδή.

δήλωσις.

Exo. 28:26
Lev. 8: 8
Psa. 118:130

δημηγορέω.

Proverbs 24:66

δῆμος.

Nu. 1:20, 22
24, 26
28, 30
32, 34
36, 38
40, 42
2:34
3:15, 18
19, 20
20, 21
21, 21
24
27 *quq*
29, 30
33 *ter*
35, 39
4: 2
4+A
18
22—A
24, 29
33, 34
36, 37
38, 40
41, 42
42, 44
45, 46
11:10
13: 3
18: 2
23:10
26 *passim*
24—A
26—A
Nu. 26:44—AB
44—B
27: 1, 4
36: 6, 8
12, 12
Jos. 7:14, 14
17, 17
17+A
13:15, 23
24, 28
28—AB
28—A
29, 31
15: 1, 12
16: 5, 8
17: 2, 2
18:11, 20
21, 28
19: 8ᵃ, 10
16, 23
24—B
31, 47
21: 4,7,10
20, 26
33, 34
40
Jud. 13: 2—A
17: 7
9+A
18: 2ᵇ
11ᵇ
19ᵇ
Neh. 4:13
ᵃ A κλῆρος. ᵇ A συγγένεια.

διαβάθρα.

2 Samuel 23:21—A

διαβαίνω.

Gen. 31:21, 52
52
32:10, 22
23
Exo. 21:21 Aᵃ
Nu. 32: 7ᵇ
29, 30
32
33: 8, 51
35:10
Deu. 3:21, 25
27, 28
4:21, 22
22, 26
9: 1
11: 8, 29
31
12:10
27: 2, 3, 4
12
28: 1+A
30:18
31: 2, 13
32:47
Jos. 1: 2, 11
14
Jos. 2:23
3: 1, 11
14, 17
17
4: 1,7,10
11, 11
12, 13
22, 23
5: 1
22:19
24:11
Jud. 3:28
6:33+A
8: 4
10: 9
11:29 Aᶜ
29 Aᶜ
32 Aᶜ
12: 3 Aᶜ, 5
19:18 Aᵈ
1 Sa. 13: 7, 7
14: 1, 4, 6
8
20:29ᵉ
26:13
27: 2+A
2 Sa. 2:29
10:17
15:22
23ᶠ
33
16: 9
17:16, 21
22, 24ᵍ
19:18, 18
31, 33
36, 37
38, 39
39, 40
40, 40
24: 5
1 Ki. (3)37
2 Ki. 2: 8,9,14
2 Ki. 4: 8
1 Ch. 12:15
19:17
Job 19: 8
Psa. 67: 8
118:136 Aʰ
Pro. 9:18
24:64
Isa. 16: 8
43: 2
45:14
14—AS
47: 2
Jer. 6: 5 Aⁱ
Eze. 47: 5
Amos 5: 5ᵇ
6: 2
ᵃ pro διαβιόω. ᵇ A ἀναβαίνω.
ᶜ pro παρέρχομαι.
ᵈ pro παραπορεύομαι.
ᵉ AB διασώζω. ᶠ A παρέρχομαι.
ᵍ A διέρχομαι. ʰ pro καταβαίνω.
ⁱ pro ἀναβαίνω.

διαβάλλω.

Nu. 22:22ᵃ
Dan. 3: 8
Dan. 6:24
ᵃ AB ἐνδιαβάλλω.

διάβασις.

Gen. 32:22
Jos. 2: 7
4: 8
Jud. 3:28
12: 5, 6
1 Sa. 14: 4
2 Sa. 19:18, 18
Isa. 51:10
Jer. 28:32

διάβημα.

2 Sa. 22:37
Job 31: 4
Psa. 16: 5, 5
17:37
21:15 S¹ ᵃ
36:23, 31
39: 3
72: 2
Psa. 84:14
118:133
139: 5
Pro. 4:12
16: 1
20:24
Cant. 7: 1
ᵃ pro ὀστέον.

διαβιάζομαι.

Numbers 14:44

διαβιβάζω.

Gen. 32:23
Nu. 32: 5, 30
Jos. 7: 7
2 Sa. 19:15, 41

διαβιόω.

Exo. 21:21ᵃ
ᵃ A διαβαίνω.

διαβοάω.

Gen. 45:16
Lev. 25:10

διαβολή.

Nu. 22:33
Pro. 6:24

διάβολος.

1 Ch. 21: 1
Est. 7: 4
8: 1—S¹
Job 1: 6,7,7,9
12, 12
Job 2:1,2,2,3ᵃ
4, 6, 7
Ps. 108: 6
Zec. 3: 1, 2, 2
ᵃ A Σατανᾶς.

διαβουλεύομαι.

Genesis 49:23

διαβουλία.

Psa. 5:11
Hos. 11: 6

διαβούλιον.

Psa. 9:23
Eze. 11: 5
Hos. 4: 9
Hos. 5: 4
7: 2

διαγγέλλω.

Exo. 9:16
Jos. 6:10
Psa. 2: 7
Lev. 25:9, 9
Psa. 58:13

διάγγελμα.

1 Kings 4:20

διαγινώσκω.

Nu. 33:56
Deu. 2: 7
Deu. 8: 2
Pro. 14:33

διαγλύφω.

Exo. 28:11
11+A
2 Ch. 4: 5
Eze. 41:19, 20

διαγογγύζω.

Exo. 15:24
16: 2,7ᵃ,8
17: 3ᵇ
Nu. 14: 2, 36
Nu. 16:11
Deu. 1:27
Jos. 9:24
ᵃ A γογγύζω. ᵇ AB γογγύζω.

διαγραφή.

Ezekiel 43:12

διαγράφω.

Jos. 18: 4
Est. 3: 9—S²
Cant. 8: 9
Eze. 4: 1
Eze. 8:10
42: 3
43:11, 11

διάγω.

2 Sa. 12:31ᵃ
2 Ki. 16: 3
17:17
21: 6
23:10
2 Ch. 28: 3
33: 6
Job 12:17
Psa. 77:13
135:14, 16
Eze. 16:25ᵇ
20:37
23:37
Zec. 13: 9
ᵃ A ἀπάγω. ᵇ A ἄγω.

διαδέχομαι.

1 Ch. 26:18 *ter*
2 Ch. 31:12
Est. 10: 3

διάδηλος.

Genesis 41:21

διάδημα.

Est. 1:11
2:17
6: 9+S³
Est. (9)15
Isa. 62: 3

διαδίδωμι.

Gen. 49:20 Aᵃ
27 Aᵃ
Jos. 13: 6
ᵃ pro δίδωμι.

διάδοχος.

1 Ch. 18, 17
2 Ch. 26:11
2 Ch. 28: 7

διαδύω.

2 Samuel 17:49

διάζομαι.

Jud. 16:14 Aᵃ
Isa. 19:10 S³ ᵇ
ᵃ pro λαμβάνω.
ᵇ pro ἐργάζομαι.

διαζωννύω.

Eze. 23:15 Aᵃ
ᵃ pro ζωννύω.

διαθερμαίνω.

Exo. 16:21
1 Sa. 11: 9, 11
2 Ki. 4:34

διάθεσις.

Job 37:15 Sᵃ
Psa. 72: 7
ᵃ pro διάκρισις.

διαθήκη.

Gen. 6:18
9: 9, 11
12, 13
15, 16
17
15:18
17: 2, 4, 7
7,9,10
11, 13
13, 14
19, 19
21
21:27, 32
26:28
31:14
Exo. 2:24
6: 4, 5
19: 5
23:22, 32
24: 7, 8
25:14+A
27:21
31: 7, 16
34:10, 12
15, 27
28
39:15
Lev. 2:13
24: 8
26: 9
11 ABᵃ
15, 25
42 *ter*
44, 45
Nu. 10:33
14:44
18:19
25:12+A
12, 13
Deu. 4:13, 23
31
5: 2, 3
7: 2,9,12
8:18
9: 5,9,11
10: 8
17: 2
29: 1, 1, 9
12, 14
20, 21
25
27+A
31: 9, 16
20, 25
26
33: 9
Jos. 3: 3, 6, 6
8, 11
13, 14
15
15—A
17
4: 7,9,10
11, 16
18
6: 8,9,11
12—A
13
7:11, 15
9: 6, 12
13, 17
21, 22
23:16
24:25
33+A
Jud. 2: 1,2,20
8:33
9: 4+A
46+A
20:27
1 Sa. 4: 3+A
4+A
4+A
5+A
5: 4
6: 3, 18
7: 1, 1
11: 1, 2
1 Sa. 20: 8
22: 8
23:18
2 Sa. 3:12, 13
21
5: 3
6:10
10:19+Bᵃ
15:24
23: 5
1 Ki. 2:26
3:15
5:12
6:18
8: 1,6+A
9, 21
23
15:19, 19
19:14—A
21:34ᵇ, 34
2 Ki. 11: 4
4+A
17
13:23
17:35, 38
18:12
23: 2, 3, 3
3, 21
1 Ch. 11: 3
15:25, 26
27, 28
29
16: 4,6,15
17, 37
17: 1
22 19
28: 2, 18
2 Ch. 5: 2, 7
6:11, 14
13: 5
15:12
16: 3
21: 7
23: 3, 16
25: 4
29:10—A²
10
34:30, 31
31, 32
Ezra 10: 3
Neh. 1: 5
9: 8, 32
13:29
Job 5:23+A
31: 1
40:23
Psa. 24:10, 14
43:18
49: 5, 16
54:21—S¹
73:20
77:10, 37
82: 6
88: 4, 29
35, 40
102:18
104: 8, 10
105:45
110: 5, 9
131:12
Pro. 2:17
Isa. 24: 5
28:15, 18
33: 8
42: 6
49: 6—A
8
54:10
55: 3
56: 4, 6
59:21
61: 8
Jer. 3:16
11: 2, 3, 6
10
14:21
22: 9
27: 5

Jer. 38:31, 32
32, 33
39:40
41: 8, 10
13, 15
16 A[c]
18
18–AS[1]
Eze. 16: 8, 29
59, 60
60, 61
62
17:13, 14
15, 16
18, 19
30: 5
34:25
37:26, 26
44: 7
Dan. 9: 4, 27
27 + AB[2]
11:22, 28
30, 30
32
Hos. 2:18
6: 7
8: 1
10: 4
12: 1
Amos 1: 9
Obad. 7
Zec. 9:11
11:10
14 A[d]
Mal. 2: 4, 5, 8
10, 14
3: 1

[a] pro σκηνή. [b] A Δαμασκός. [c] pro ὄνομα. [d] pro κατασχεσις.

διαθρύπτω.

Lev. 2: 6
Isa. 58: 7
Nah. 1: 6

διαίρεσις.

Jos. 19:51
Jud. 5:15 A[a]
16[b]
1 Ch. 24: 1–A[1]
26: 1, 10
12, 19
27: 1, 1, 2
2, 4, 4
1 Ch. 27: 4–AB
5, 6
7 to 15
2 Ch. 8:14, 14
35: 5, 10
12
Ezra 6:18
Ps. 135:13

[a] pro μερίς. [b] A διέρχομαι.

διαιρέω.

Gen. 4: 7
15:10, 10
32: 7
33: 1[a]
Exo. 21:35, 35
Lev. 1:12, 17
5: 8
Nu. 31:27, 42
Jos. 18: 4[b], 5
22: 8
Jud. 7:16
9:43
1 Sa. 15:29
2 Sa. 19:29
1 Ki. 3:25, 26
2 Ki. 2: 8
1 Ch. 4:38 B[c]
23: 6
24: 3, 4, 5
Job 21:21
Psa. 67:13
Pro. 16:19
17: 2
Isa. 9: 3
30:28
Eze. 37:22
Dan. 2:41
5:28
11: 4, 39
Amos 5: 9

[a] A ἐπιδιαιρέω. [b] AB διέρχομαι. [c] pro διέρχομαι.

διαίρω.

Neh. 4:17 S[a]   [a] pro αἴρω.

δίαιτα.

Job 5: 3, 24
8: 6, 22
11:14
18: 6, 14
Job 20:19, 25
22:23, 28
39: 6

διαιτάω.

Job 30: 7

διακαθιζάνω.

Deuteronomy 23:13

διακαθίζω.

2 Sa. 11: 1[a]   [a] A καθίζω.

διακάμπτω.

2 Kings 4:34

διάκενος.

Numbers 21: 5

διακλάω.

Lam. 4: 4[a]   [a] A κλάω.

διακλέπτω.

2 Samuel 19: 3, 3

διακομίζω.

Joshua 4: 3, 8

διακονία.

Esther 6: 3 A[a], 5 A[a]

[a] pro διάκονος.

διάκονος.

Est. 1:10
2: 2
6: 1[a]
Est. 6: 3[b], 5[b]
Pro. 10: 5

[a] ABS διδάσκαλος. [b] A διακονία.

διακοπή.

Jud. 5:17 A[a]
21:15
2 Sa. 5:20, 20
6: 8, 8
1 Ch. 13:11, 11
1 Ch. 14:11, 11
Job 28: 4
Pro. 6:15
Mic. 2:13

[a] pro διέξοδος.

διακόπτω.

Gen. 38:29
2 Sa. 5:20
20 A[a]
20
6: 8
1 Ki. (3) p 1
2 Ki. 3:26
14:13 A[b]
1 Ch. 13:11
1 Ch. 14:11
15:13
Psa. 28: 7
73: 5 S[1c]
Jer. 52: 7
Amos 9: 1
Mic. 2:13
Hab. 3:14

[a] pro κόπτω. [b] pro καθαιρέω. [c] pro ἐκκόπτω.

διακόσιοι.

Gen. 11:17[a]
Exo. 30:23–A[1]
Nu. 1:33[b]
2:21 [a c]
1 Sa. 30:12 + A
21–A
1 Ki. 21:15[a]
Neh. 7:12[d]
Neh. 7:24–AB
69 + AS
71–A
Cant. 8:12[e]
Eze. 48:17–A
17–A
17–A
17–A

[a] A τριακόσιοι. [b] B τριακόσιοι. [c] B τετρακόσιοι. [d] S ὀκτακόσιοι. [e] S[1] δισχίλιοι.

διακούω.

Deu. 1:16
Job 9:33[a]

[a] A διακρίνω.

διακρίβεια.

1 Kings 11:33 + A

διακρίνω.

Exo. 18:16
Lev. 24:12
Deu. 33: 7
1 Ki. 3: 9
1 Ch. 26:29
Job 9:14
33 A[a]
12:11
15: 5
21:22
23:10
Psa. 49: 4
Psa. 81: 1
Pro. 24:77 S[b]
77
Ecc. 3:18
Jer. 15:10
Eze. 17:20 + A
20:35, 36
34:17, 20
44:24
Joel 3: 2, 12
Zec. 3: 7

[a] pro διακούω. [b] pro κρίνω.

διάκρισις.

Job 37:15[a]   [a] S διαθεσις.

διακρύπτω.

1 Sa. 3:17 A[a]   [a] pro κρύπτω.

διακύπτω.

Jud. 5:28 A[a]
2 Sa. 6:16
2 Sa. 24:20
2 Ki. 9:30
Psa. 13: 2
52: 3
Psa. 84:12
91: 8
Lam. 3:49
Eze. 41:16, 16

[a] pro παρακύπτω.

διαλανθάνω.

2 Samuel 4: 6

διαλέγω.

Exo. 6:27
Jud. 8: 1[a]
Isa. 63: 1

[a] A κρίνω.

διαλείπω.

1 Sa. 10: 8
13: 8
1 Ki. 15.21–A
2 Ch. 29:11
Isa. 5:14
Jer. 8: 6
Jer. 9: 5
14:17
17: 8
38:16
51:18

διάλεκτος.

Esther 9:26

διάλευκος.

Gen. 30:32[a], 33
35, 35
Gen. 30:39, 40
31:10, 12

[a] A διαραντός.

διαλλάσσω.

Jud. 19: 3 A[a]
1 Sa. 29: 4
Job 5:12
Job 12:20, 24
36:28
37: 4 + C

[a] pro ἐπιστρέφω.

διάλλομαι.

Canticles 2: 8

διαλογή.

Psalm 103:34

διαλογίζομαι.

2 Sa. 14:14 A[a]
19:19 AB[a]
Psa. 9:23
20:12
34:20
35: 5 AS[a]
76: 6
Ps. 118:59
139: 9
Pro. 16:30[b]
17:12
Isa. 19:10 A[c]
Jer. 27:45 A[a]

[a] pro λογίζομαι. [b] ACS λογίζομαι. [c] pro ἐργάζομαι.

διαλογισμός.

Psa. 39: 6
55: 6
91: 6
93:11
138: 2, 20
145: 4
Isa. 59: 7, 7
Jer. 4:14[a]
Jer. 27:45 A[b]
Lam. 3:59, 60
Dan. 2:29, 30
4:16
5: 6, 10
7:28
11:24 A[b]

[a] B[2]S λογισμός. [b] pro λογισμός.

διάλογος.

Job 7:13 A[a]   [a] pro λόγος.

διάλυσις.

Nehemiah 1: 7

διάλυτος.

Exo. 36:31 A[a]   [a] pro ἀδιάλυτος.

διαλύω.

1 Ki. 19:11
Neh. 1: 7
Job 30:17
Pro. 6:35[a]
Isa. 58: 6
Dan. 5: 6
Jon. 1: 4 AS[2b]

[a] A διά. [b] pro συντρίβω.

διαμαρτάνω.

Nu. 15:22[a]
Jud. 20:16 A[b]

[a] A διαμαρτυρέω. [b] pro ἐξαμαρτανω.

διαμαρτυρέω, –ρομαι.

Gen. 43: 2 A[a]
Exo. 18:20
19:10, 21
23
21:29, 36
Nu. 15:22 A[b]
Deu. 4:26
8:19
30:19
31:28
32:46
1 Sa. 8: 9, 9
21: 2
2 Ki. 17:13, 15
2 Ch. 24:19
Neh. 9:26, 34
13:21 AS[c]
Psa. 49: 7
80: 9
Jer. 6:10
39:10, 44
Eze. 16: 2
20: 4
Zec. 3: 6
Mal. 2:14

[a] pro μαρτυρέω. [b] pro διαμαρτάνω. [c] pro ἐπιμαρτύρομαι.

διαμαρτυρία.

Genesis 43: 2

διαμένω.

Exo. 36:10
Neh. 11:23 + S[3]
Psa. 5: 6
18:10
60: 8
71:17
Ps. 101:27
118:89, 90
91
Jer. 3: 5
39:14

διαμερίζω.

Gen. 10:25
49: 7
Deu. 32: 8
Jos. 21:42
Jud. 5:30
2 Sa. 6:19
1 Ch. 1:19 A
16: 3
Neh. 9:22 A[a]
Job 31: 2 S[1a]
Psa. 16:14
21:19
54:22
59: 8
107: 8
Isa. 34:17
Eze. 47:21[b]
Mic. 2: 4[b]
Zec. 14: 1

[a] pro μερίζω. [b] A διαμετρέω.

διαμερισμός.

Eze. 48:29
Mic. 7:12, 12

διαμετρέω.

2 Sa. 8: 2
Psa. 59: 8
107: 8[a]
Eze. 40: 5, 6
9 + A
11, 13
19, 20
23, 24
27, 28
32, 35
47, 48
41: 1, 2, 3
Eze. 41: 4, 5, 13
15, 26
42:15, 16
17, 18
19
45: 3
47: 3, 4, 4
5
21 A[b]
Mic. 2: 4 A[b]
Zec. 2: 2

[a] S ἐκμετρέω. [b] pro διαμερίζω.

διαμέτρησις.

2 Ch. 3: 3–A[2]
4: 2
Jer. 38:39
Eze. 42:15
45: 3

διαναπαύω.

Genesis 5:29

διαναφέρω.

Lev. 4:10 AB[a]   [a] pro ἀναφέρω.

διανέμω.

Deuteronomy 29:26

διανεύω.
Psalm 34:19

διανήθω.
Exo. 28: 8, 29
35: 6—A[1]
Exo. 36:10, 12
15

διανθίζω.
Esther 1: 6

διανίστημι.
Deu. 6: 7[a]
Deu. 11:19
[a] A ἀνίστημι.

διανοέομαι.
Gen. 6: 5, 6
8:21
Exo. 31: 4
2 Sa. 21:16
2 Ch. 2:14
11:22
Psa. 72: 8
Jer. 7:31
19: 5
Dan. 1: 4
Zec. 8:14, 15

διανόημα.
Pro. 14:14
15:24
Isa. 55: 9
Eze. 14: 3, 4

διανόησις.
2 Chronicles 2:14

διάνοια.
Gen. 8:21
17:17
24:15, 45
27:41
34: 3
45:26
Exo. 9:21
28: 3
35: 9 A[a]
22, 25
26, 29
• 34, 35
36: 1
8+A
Lev. 19:17
Nu. 15:39
22:18
32: 7[b]
Deu. 4:39
6: 5[b]
7:17
28:28, 47[b]
Deu. 29:18
Jos. 5: 1
14: 8 A[a]
22: 5[b]
1 Ch. 29:18
Job 1: 5[b], 8
9: 4
36:28
37: 4+C
Pro. 2:10
4: 4 S[a]
9:10
13:15
27:19[c]
Isa. 14:13[d]
35: 4
55: 9
57:11
59:15
Jer. 38:33[e]
Eze. 14: 4
[a] pro καρδία. [b] A καρδία.
[c] ACS[2] καρδία. [d] S καρδία.
[e] S[1] καρδία.

διανοίγω.
Gen. 3: 5, 7
Exo. 13: 2, 12
12, 13
15
34:19
Nu. 3:12
8:16
18:15
2 Ki. 6:17, 17
20
Job 11: 5 C[a]
27:19
29:19
31:32 C[a]
38:32
Pro. 20:13
29:38, 43
Isa. 5:14
Lam. 2:16
3:45
Eze. 3:10
20:26
21:22
24:27
Hos. 2:15
Nah. 2: 6
Hab. 3:14
Zec. 11: 1
12: 4
13: 1
[a] pro ἀνοίγω.

διανυκτερεύω.
Job 2: 9

διαπαντός.
Psa. 39:17+B
Ps. 118:119+S[1]

διαπαρατηρέομαι.
2 Samuel 3:30

διαπαρθενεύω.
Ezekiel 23: 3, 8

διαπαύω.
Lev. 2:13
Hos. 5:13

διαπειλέω.
Ezekiel 3:17

διαπέμπω.
Proverbs 16:28

διαπεράω.
Deu. 30:13
Isa. 23: 2

διαπετάννυμι.
2 Sa. 17:19
1 Ki. 6:25, 32
(32) A
8: 7, 22
38, 54
1 Ch. 28:18
2 Ch. 3:13
5: 8
6:12, 13
2 Ch. 6:29
Psa. 43:21
87:10
104:39
142: 6
Lam. 1:13, 17
2: 6
Eze. 16: 8

διάπηγα.
1 Ki. 7:17+A, 18+A

διαπίπτω.
Nu. 5:21, 22
27
Deu. 2:14, 15
16 B[a]
Jos. 21:45
Neh. 8:10
Job 14:18[b]
Jer. 18: 4 S[a]
19:12, 13
Nah. 2: 6
[a] pro πίπτω. [b] A πίπτω.

διαπλατύνω.
Ezekiel 41: 7

διαπληκτίζομαι.
Exodus 2:13

διαπνέω.
Cant. 2:17
Cant. 4: 6, 16

διαπονέω.
Ecclesiastes 10: 9

διαπορεύω.
Gen. 24:62[a]
Nu. 11: 8
31:23
Jos. 15: 3
Jud. 9:25 A[b]
1 Sa. 12: 2
20: 3
2 Sa. 5:10[a]
1 Ki. 9: 8
18:35
2 Ki. 4: 9
6:26, 30
2 Ch. 7:21
30:10
Job 2: 2
22:14
Psa. 8: 9
38: 7
57: 8
Psa. 67:22
76:18
81: 5
90: 6
100: 2
103:26
Pro. 5:16
9:12
Isa. 11:15
30:25
34:10+S[2]
Jer. 18:16[c]
Eze. 20:26
21:16
33:15, 28
39:15
Zeph. (2) 15[c]
Zec. 9: 8
[a] A πορεύω. [b] pro παραπορεύομαι. [c] A παραπορεύομαι.

διάπρασις.
Leviticus 25:33

διαπρίω.
1 Chronicles 20: 3

διάπτωσις.
Jeremiah 19: 6, 14

διαραντός.
Gen. 30:32 A[a] [a] pro διάλευκος.

διαρπαγή.
Nu. 14: 3, 31
Deu. 1:38+A
2 Ki. 21:14
Ezra 9: 7
Est. 7: 4—A
Isa. 5: 5
5 A[a]
10: 2[b]
Isa. 42:24
Eze. 23:46
25: 7
Dan. 3:29[c]
11:33
Hab. 2: 7
Zeph. 1:13
Mal. 3:10
[a] pro καταπάτημα.
[b] ABS ἁρπαγή. [c] A διαρπάζω.

διαρπάζω.
Gen. 34:27, 29
Deu. 28:29
Jud. 9:25[a]
21:23 A[b]
1 Sa. 14:36
23: 1
2 Ki. 7:16
17:20
Est. 3:13
9:10, 15
16
Psa. 34:10
43:11
88:42
108:11
Isa. 5:17
42:22
Jer. 21:12
22: 3
27:11
Eze. 7:21[c]
22:29
Dan. 2: 5
3:29 A[d]
Amos 3:11
Mic. 2: 2, 2
Nah. 2: 9, 9
Zeph. 2: 4, 9
Zec. 14: 2
[a] A ἀναρπάζω. [b] pro ἁρπάζω.
[c] A διαφθείρω. [d] pro διαρπαγή.

διαρραίνω.
Proverbs 7:17

διαρρήγνυμι.
Gen. 37:29, 34
44:13
Lev. 10: 6
21:10
Nu. 14: 6
Jos. 7: 6
Jud. 11:35
16: 9 A[a]
1 Sa. 4:12
15:27, 28
28:17
2 Sa. 1: 2, 11
11—A
3:31
13:19, 31
31
14:30
15:32
23:16
1 Ki. 11:11, 11
30
20:16
27
2 Ki. 2:12, 14
5: 7, 8, 8
6:30
11:14
18:37
19: 1
22:11[b], 19
1 Ch. 11:18
2 Ch. 23:13
25:12
34:19, 27
Ezra 9: 3, 5
Neh. 9:21
Est. 4: 1
Job 1:20 ABS[c]
28:10[d]
Psa. 2:3
29:12
73:15
77:13, 15
104:41
106:14
115: 7
140: 7[e]
Pro. 23:21
Isa. 33:20
45: 1
Jer. 5: 5
37: 8
43:24
48: 5
Eze. 13:20, 21
Hos. 13: 8
14: 1
Joel 2:13
Nah. 1:13
[a] pro διασπάω. [b] A ῥήγνυμι.
[c] pro ῥήγνυμι. [d] ABCS ῥήγνυμι.
[e] S[2] ῥήγνυμι.

διαρρίπτω, —τέω.
Job 41:10
Isa. 62:10

διαρτάω.
Numbers 23:19

διαρτίζω.
Job 33: 6, 6

διασαλεύω.
Hab. 2:16 S[3 a] [a] pro σαλεύω.

διασαφέω.
Deuteronomy 1: 5

διασάφησις.
Gen. 40: 8
Ezra 5: 6
Ezra 7:11

διασείω.
Job 4:14[a]
[a] A[1] συμπίπτω, A[2]S συσσείω.

διασκεδάννυμι.
Gen. 17:14
Exo. 32:25, 25
Lev. 26:15, 44
Nu. 15:31
Deu. 31:16, 20
Jud. 2: 1
2 Sa. 15:31, 34
17:14
1 Ki. 12 p 24 l 61
15:19
2 Ch. 16: 3
Ezra 4: 5
9:14
Neh. 4:15
Job 16:12
24:17+A
38:24
Psa. 32:10
88:34
118:126
Ecc. 12: 5
Isa. 8:10
9: 4, 11
14:27
19: 3
24: 5+S
32: 7
44:25
Jer. 11:10
14:21
Hab. 1: 4
Zec. 11:10, 11
14
Mal. 2: 2

διασκευάζω.
Joshua 4:12

διασκευή.
Exodus 31: 7

διασκορπίζω.
Gen. 49: 7 A[a]
Nu. 10:35
Deu. 30: 1, 3
Neh. 1: 8
Job 37:10—C
Psa. 21:15
52: 6
58:12, 16
67: 2, 31
88:11
91:10
105:27
140: 7
Jer. 9:16
10:21
13:14
23: 1, 2
27:37
28:20, 20
21, 22
Jer. 28:22, 22
23 ter
Eze. 5: 2, 10
6: 5
10: 2
11:16
12:15
20:23
23 A[a]
34, 41
22:15
28:25
29:13
46:18
Dan. 4:11
11:24
Zec. 1:19, 21
21
11:16 A[b]
13: 7 AS[2 c]
[a] pro διασπείρω.
[b] pro σκορπίζω. [c] pro ἐκσπάω.

διασκορπισμός.
Jer. 24: 9
Eze. 6: 8
Eze. 13:20
Dan. 12: 7

δίασμα.
Judges 16:13, 14

διασπασμός.
Jeremiah 15:3

διασπάω.
Jud. 14: 6 A[a]
6 A[a]
16: 9[b]
9 A[c]
12[d]
Job 19:10
Isa. 58: 6
Jer. 2:20
4:20
10:20

Hos. 13: 8
Zeph. 3:10 S[1e]

[a] pro συντρίβω.
[b] A διαρρήγνυμι. [c] pro ἀποσπάω
[d] A σπάω. [e] pro διασπείρω.

διασπείρω.

Gen. 9:19
10:18, 32
11: 4, 8, 9
49: 7[a]
Exo. 5:12
Lev. 26:33
Deu. 4:27
28:64
32: 8, 26
1 Sa. 11:11
13: 8, 11
14:23, 34
2 Sa. 18: 8
20:22
1 Ki. 12p 24 l 72
22:17
2 Ki. 25: 5
2 Ch. 18:16
Est. 3: 8
9:19
Psa. 43:12
Isa. 11:12
24: 1
32: 6[b]
33: 3
35: 8
Isa. 41:16
56: 8
Jer. 13:24[b]
15: 7 S[1b]
18:17
23: 3+S
25:15
30: 5
39:37
47:15
52: 8
Eze. 5:12 A[c]
11:17
12:14, 15
17:21
20:23[a]
22:15
29:12
30:23, 26
32:15
34: 5, 6, 6
12
36:19
Dan. 9: 7
Joel 3: 2
Zeph. 3:10—A[d]

[a] A διασκορπίζω. [b] A διαφθείρω.
[c] pro σκορπίζω. [d] S[1] διασπάω.

διασπορά.

Deu. 28:25
30: 4
Neh. 1: 9
Ps. 138: 1+A[2]
146: 2
Isa. 49: 6
Jer. 13:14 S[1a]
15: 7[b]
41:17

[a] pro διαφθορά. [b] A διαφθορά.

διαστέλλω.

Gen. 25:23
30:28, 35
40
Lev. 5: 4, 4
10:10
11:47
16:26
22:21
Nu. 8:14
16: 9
35:11
Deu. 10: 8
19: 2, 7
29:21
Jos. 20: 7
Jud. 1:19
Ruth 1:17
1 Sa. 3: 1
1 Ki. 8:53
2 Ki. 2:11
6:10+A
1 Ch. 23:13
2 Ch. 10:10
23:18
Ezra 8:24
10: 8, 11
16
Neh. 8: 8
Psa. 65:14
67:15
105:33
Jer. 22:14
Eze. 3:18, 18
19, 20
21, 21
22:26, 26
24:14
39:14
42.20
Hos. 13:15
Mic. 6: 8
Nah. 1:12
Mal. 3:11

διάστημα.

Gen. 32:16
1 Ki. 6:10
7:46
Eze. 41: 6, 8, 8
Eze. 42: 5, 5
12, 13
45: 2
48:15, 17

διαστολή.

Exo. 8:23
Nu. 19: 2
Nu. 30: 7

διαστρέφω.

Exo. 5: 4
23: 6
Nu. 15:39
32: 7
Deu. 32: 5
Jud. 5: 6
2 Sa. 22:27 A[a]
1 Ki. 18:17, 18
Job 37:11
Psa. 17:27
Pro. 4:27
6:14
Pro. 8:13
10: 9
11:20
16:30
Ecc. 1:15
7:14
12: 3
Isa. 59: 8
Eze. 13:18, 19
22, 22
14: 5 A[b]
16:34[c], 34[c]
Mic. 3: 9
Hab. 1: 4

[a] pro στρεβλόω. [b] pro πλαγιάζω. [c] A ἐκστρέφω.

διαστροφή.

Proverbs 2:14

διαστρώννυμι.

1 Samuel 9:25

διασφαγή.

Nehemiah 4: 7

διασφραγίζω.

Jer. 39:10 AS[a] [a] pro σφραγίζω.

διασχίζω.

Exo. 14:21 A[a]
1 Ch. 20: 3—AB
Psa. 34:15
[a] pro σχίζω.

διασώζω.

Gen. 19:19, 20[a]
35: 3
Nu. 10: 9
21:29
Deu. 20: 4
Jos. 6:26
9:21
10:20, 20
28, 30
37, 39
40 A[b]
11: 8
Jud. 3:26, 26
29
12: 4, 5
21:17
1 Sa. 19:10[c]
17, 18[a]
20:29 AB[d]
22: 1, 20
23:13
2 Sa. 1: 3
2 Ki. 10:24
19:30
37 A[b]
Ezra 9:14
15—A
Job 21:10, 20
22:30
29:12
36:12
Pro. 10: 5
Ecc. 8: 8
9:15
Isa. 37:38
Jer. 8:20
Eze. 17:15, 15[a]
Dan. 11:41
Hos. 13:10
Amos 2:15
9: 1
Jon. 1: 6
Mic. 6:14, 14
Zec. 8:13

[a] A σώζω. [b] pro σώζω.
[c] A ἐκσπάω. [d] pro διαβαίνω.

διαταγή.

Ezra 4:11

διάταγμα.

Ezra 7:11

διάταξις.

1 Ki. 6: 5
13+A
2 Ch. 31:16, 17
Ps. 118:91
Eze. 42:20
43:10

διατάσσω.

Jud. 3:23—A
5: 9
1 Sa. 13:11
1 Ki. 11:18
1 Ch. 9:33
2 Ch. 5:11
Pro. 9:12
Eze. 21:19, 20
42:15, 20
44: 8
Dan. 1: 5

διατείνω.

Psa. 84: 6
139: 6
Isa. 21:15
40:22

διατελέω.

Deu. 9: 7
Jer. 20: 7, 18

διατήκω.

Hab. 3: 6[a] [a] S[1] τήκω.

διατηρέω.

Gen. 17: 9, 10
37:11
Exo. 2: 9
9:16
12: 6
34: 7
Nu. 18: 7
28: 2
Deu. 7: 8
33: 9
Job 2: 6 A[a]
Psa. 11: 8
Pro. 21:23
22:12
Isa. 56: 2
Dan. 7:28[b]

[a] pro διαφυλάσσω.
[b] A συντηρέω.

διατήρησις.

Exo. 16:33, 34
Nu. 17:10
Nu. 18: 8
19: 9

διατίθημι.

Gen. 9:17
15:18
21:27, 32
26:28
31:44
Exo. 24: 8
34:12 A[a]
15 A[a]
Deu. 4:23
5: 2, 3
7: 2
9: 9
29: 1, 12
14, 25
31:16
20+A
Jos. 7:11
9:12, 13
17, 21
22
24:25
Jud. 2: 2
1 Sa. 11: 1, 2
18: 3 A
22: 8
23:18
2 Sa. 3:12, 13
21
5: 3
1 Ki. 5:12
8: 9, 21
15:19
21:34
2 Ki. 11: 4, 17
17:35, 38
2 Ki. 23: 3
1 Ch. 11: 3
16:16
19:19
2 Ch. 5:10
6:11
7:18
16: 3
21: 7
23: 3, 16
29:10
34:31
Ezra 10: 3
Neh. 9: 8, 38
Psa. 49: 5
82: 6
83: 6
88: 4
104: 9
Isa. 55: 3
61: 8
Jer. 11:10
38:31, 32
33
39:40
41:13[b]
Eze. 16:30
17:13
34:25
37:26
Hos. 2:18
10: 4
11: 8, 8
12: 1
Zec. 11:10

[a] pro τίθημι. [b] BS τίθημι.

διατίλλω.

Job 16:12

διατόνιον.

Exodus 35:10

διατόρευμα.

1 Kings 7:17+A

διατρέπω.

Jud. 18: 7—A
Est. 7: 8
Job 31:34

διατρέφω.

Gen. 7: 3
50:20 A[a]
21
Jos. 14:10
Ruth 4:15
2 Sa. 19:32, 33
20: 3
1 Ki. 17: 4, 9
18: 4
Neh. 9:21
Psa. 30: 4
32:19
54:23
Pro. 22: 9

[a] pro τρέφω.

διατρέχω.

Exo. 9:23
1 Sa. 17:17 A
1 Ki. 18:26
Nah. 2: 5

διατριβή.

Lev. 13:46
Pro. 12:11
14:24
Pro. 20:45
Jer. 30:11

διατρίβω.

Lev. 14: 8
Jer. 42: 7
Hab. 3: 6

διαφανής.

Exo. 30:34
Est. 1: 6[a]
Isa. 3:22
[a] AS ἐπιφανής.

διαφαύσκω, —φώσκω.

Gen. 44: 3
Jud. 16: 2—A
19:26
1 Sa. 14:36
2 Sa. 2:32

διαφέρω.

1 Sa. 17:39 A[a]
Pro. 20: 2
Pro. 27:14
Dan. 7: 3, 19[b]

[a] pro ἀφαιρέω. [b] A διάφορος.

διαφεύγω.

Deu. 2:36
Jos. 8:22
10:28, 30
33
2 Ki. 9:15
Pro. 19: 5
Isa. 10:14
Jer. 11:15
Amos 9: 1

διαφθείρω.

Jud. 2:19
6: 4[a], 5
16: 7[b], 8[b]
20:21, 25
35, 42
Ruth 4: 6
1 Sa. 2:25
6: 5
13:17
14:15
23:10
26: 9 A[c]
15
2 Sa. 1:14
11: 1
14:11
20:20 A[d]
24:16, 16
2 Ki. 8:19
13:23
18:25, 25
19:12
Psa. 13: 1
52: 2
56: 1
57: 1
58: 1
74: 1
77:38, 45
Ecc. 5: 5
Isa. 32: 6 A[e]
36:10—A[f]
Isa. 49:19 AS[3g]
Jer. 5:26
6: 5, 28
12:10
13: 7
24 A[e]
15: 6
7 A[e]
27:45
28: 1, 25
25
Lam. 2: 5, 6, 8
Eze. 7:21 A[h]
16:52 A[d]
20:44
23:11
28:17
Dan. 2: 9, 44
4:20
6:23
7:14
8:24, 24
25
9:26
11:17
Mic. 2:10
Nah. 2: 3
Zeph. 3: 7 AS[2d]
Mal. 1:14
2: 8
3:11

[a] B καταφθείρω. [b] A ἐρημόω.
[c] pro ταπεινόω. [d] pro φθείρω.
[e] pro διασπείρω. [f] S[1] καταφθείρω. [g] pro καταφθείρω.
[h] pro διαρπάζω.

διαφθορά.

Job 33:28
31+A
Psa. 9:16
15:10
29:10
34: 7
54:24
106:20
139:12 AS[a]
Pro. 28:10
Jer. 13:14[b]
Jer. 15: 3, 7 A[c]
28: 8
Lam. 4:20
Eze. 19: 4, 8
21:31
Dan. 3:25
6:23
10: 8
Hos. 11:
13:
Zeph. 3: 6[d]

[a] pro καταφθορά. [b] S[1] διασπορά.
[c] pro διασπορά. [d] S[1] καταφθορά.

διαφλέγω.

Psalm 82:15

διαφορέω.

Jer. 37:16[a] — [a] S[1] βιαφοβέω.

διαφόρημα.

Jer. 37:16[a] — [a] S[1] βιαφόρημα.

διάφορος.

Lev. 19:19
Deu. 22: 9[a]
Ezra 8:27
Dan. 7:7,19 A[b]

[a] B δίφορος. [b] *pro* διαφέρω.

διαφυλάσσω.

Gen. 28:15, 20
Lev. 19:20
Deu. 7:12
32:10
Jos. 24:17
Job 2: 6[a]
Psa. 30: 7[b]
Psa. 40: 3 AS[c]
90:11
Pro. 2: 8
6:24[d]
Jer. 3: 5 AS[c]
Hos. 12:13
Zec. 3: 7[e]

[a] A διατηρέω. [b] BS φυλάσσω. [c] *pro* φυλάσσω. [d] S[1] φυλάσσω. [e] A φυλάσσω.

διαφωνέω.

Exo. 24:11
Nu. 31:49
Jos. 23:14
1 Sa. 30:19
1 Ki. 8:56
Eze. 37:11

διαφωτίζω.

Neh. 8: 3[a] — [a] S[1] φωτίζω.

διαχέω.

Lev. 13:22, 23
27, 28
32, 34
35, 36
51, 53
55
14:39, 44
48
1 Sa. 30:16
Job 21:24
Pro. 23:32
Jer. 2:20
3:13
Eze. 30:16
Zec. 1:17

διαχρίω.

Lev. 2: 4
Lev. 7: 2

διάχρυσος.

Psalm 44:10

διάχυσις.

Lev. 13:22—AB
27, 35
Lev. 14:48

διαχωρέω.

Pro. 16:28 C[a] — [a] *pro* διαχωρίζω.

διαχωρίζω.

Gen. 1: 4, 6, 7
14, 18
13: 9, 11
14
30:32, 40
Nu. 32:12
Jud. 13:19[a]
2 Sa. 1:23, 23
1 Ch. 12: 8 A[b]
2 Ch. 25:10
Pro. 16:28[c]
Eze. 34:12

[a] A θαυμαστός. [b] *pro* χωρίζω. [c] C διαχωρέω.

διάψαλμα.

Psa. 2:2+ABS
3: 3, 5
4: 3, 5
7: 6
9:17, 21
19: 4
20: 3
23: 6—A
31: 4—A
5
Psa. 31: 7—A
33:11—A[1]
38: 6
8—ABS
12—A
43: 9—A
45: 4
8—A[1]
46: 5—A
47: 5—A
Psa. 48:14
16—A
49: 6—A[1]
15—A[1]
51: 5, 7
53: 5
54: 8, 20
56: 3—S
4+S
7
58: 6, 14
59: 6
60: 5
61: 5, 9
65: 4, 7, 15
66: 2, 5
67: 4+B
8
14+BS
20, 33
74: 4
75: 4, 10
Psa. 76: 4, 10
16
79: 8—S
80: 8—A
81: 2
82: 9—A
83: 5—A
9—A
84: 3—A[1]
86: 3—A[1]
6—A
87: 8—A[1]
88: 5—A
38—A[1]
46, 49
93:15—A[1]
139: 4
6—A
9—A
142: 6—A
Hab. 3: 3, 9, 13

διαψεύδω.

2 Kings 4:16

δίγλωσσος.

Proverbs 11:13

διγομία.

Jud. 5:16[a] — [a] A μοσφαιθάμ.

διδακτός.

Isaiah 54:13

διδασκαλία.

Pro. 2:17
Isa. 29:13

διδάσκαλος.

Est. 6: 1 ABS[a] — [a] *pro* διάκονος.

διδάσκω.

Deu. 4: 1, 10
14
5:31
6: 1
11:19
20:18
31:19, 22
32:44
Jud. 3: 2
2 Sa. 1:18
22:35
1 Ch. 5:18
25: 7
2 Ch. 17: 7, 9, 9
Ezra 7:10
Neh. 8: 8
Job 6:24
8:10
10 A[a]
10: 2
13:23
21:22
22: 2
32: 9
33: 4, 33
34:32 A[b]
36: 2
37:19
42: 4
Psa. 17:35
36—S[1]
24: 4, 5, 9
33:12
50:15
Psa. 70:17
93:10, 12
118:12, 26
64, 66
68, 99
108
124
135
171
131:12
142:10
143: 1
Pro. 1:23
4: 4, 11
5:13
6:13
22:21
24:26
Ecc. 12: 9
Cant. 3: 8
Isa. 9:15
29:13
55:12
Jer. 9:14, 20
12:16
13.21
38:18, 34
39:33
33+BS
Eze. 44:23
Dan. 1: 4
12: 4
Hos. 10:11

[a] *pro* ἐξάγω. [b] *pro* δείκνυμι.

διδαχή.

Psalm 59: 1

δίδραχμος, -ον.

Gen. 20:14, 16
Gen. 23:15, 16
Exo. 21:32
30:13 *qtr*
15
Lev. 27: 3, 4, 5
5, 6, 6
7, 7
Lev. 27:16, 25
Nu. 3:47
Deu. 22:29
Jos. 7:21, 21
Neh. 5:15
10:32

διδυμεύω.

Cant. 4: 2
Cant. 6: 5

δίδυμος.

Gen. 25:24
38:27
Deu. 25:11
Jos. 8:29
Cant. 4: 5
7: 3

δίδωμι.

Gen. 1:29
3: 6, 12
12
4:12
9: 2, 3, 12
12: 7
13:15, 17
14:20, 21
15: 2, 3, 7
18
16: 3, 5
17: 8, 16
20
18: 7
20:14, 16
21:14, 27
23: 4, 9, 9
11, 11
24: 7, 32
35, 36
41, 53
53
25: 5, 6, 34
26: 3, 4
27:17, 28
28: 4, 4, 13
20, 22
29:19, 19
21[a], 24
26, 27
28, 29
32—A
30: 1, 4, 6
9, 14
18, 18
28, 31
31, 35
31: 7, 9
32:16
34: 8, 9, 11
12, 12
14, 16
21
35: 4, 12
12, 12
38: 9, 14
16, 17
18, 18
26
39: 4, 8
21, 22
40:11, 13
21
41:45
42:25, 27
37
43:13, 22
23[a]
45:18, 21
21, 22
22
46:18, 25
47:11, 15
16, 17
19, 22
22, 24
48: 4, 9, 22
49:20[b]
27[b]
Exo. 2: 9
3:21
4:11, 15
Exo. 4:21
5: 7, 10
13, 16
18, 21
6: 4, 8, 8
7: 1, 9
8:23
9: 5, 23
10:25
11: 3
12:25, 36
13: 5, 11
16: 8, 15
29, 29
17: 2, 14
20:12
21: 4, 13
22, 23
30, 32
34
22: 7, 10
17, 29
30 A[c]
23:27
24:12
25:15, 20
30:12, 13
14, 15
16, 33
31: 6, 6, 18
32:13, 24
29
33: 1
34:16, 20
35:34
36: 1, 2
Lev. 5:16
6:17
7:22, 24
26
10:14, 17
14:34, 34
15:14
17:11
18:20, 21
23
19:20, 23
20: 2, 3, 4
15, 24
22:14, 22
23:10, 38
24:19, 20
20
25:2, 2, 19
24, 37
37, 38
26: 4, 4, 6
20, 20
46
27: 9
Nu. 3: 9, 9, 48
51
5:10, 18
20, 21
21
6:26
7: 5, 6, 7
8, 9
8:19
10:29
11:13, 13
18, 21
Nu. 11:29, 29
13: 3
14: 1 A[d], 4
8, 23
15: 2, 21
16:14
17: 3, 6
18: 6, 8, 8
11, 12
12, 19
21, 24
26, 28
19: 3
20: 8, 12
19, 21
24
21:16, 23
22:18
24:13
25:12
26:54, 62
27: 4, 7, 9
10, 11
12, 20
31:29, 30
41, 47
32: 5, 7, 9
29, 32
33, 40
33:53
34:13
35: 2, 2, 4
6, 6, 7
8, 8, 13
14, 14
36: 2
Deu. 1: 8, 13
20, 25
36, 39
2: 5, 5
5+B
9, 9, 12
19, 19
25, 29
3:12, 13
15, 16
18, 19
20, 20
4: 1, 8, 21
38, 40
5:16, 22
29, 31
6: 3, 10
18+A
22, 23
23
7: 3, 13
16
8:10, 18
9: 6, 10
11, 23
10: 4, 11
18
11: 9, 14
15, 17
17, 21
26, 29
31, 32
12: 1, 9, 15
21
13: 1, 12
17
14:20, 25
15: 4, 7, 9
10 *ter*
14
16: 5, 10
17, 18
20
17: 2, 14
18: 3, 4, 9
14, 18
19: 1, 2, 8, 8
10, 14
21+AB[e]
21+AB[e]
20:14, 16
21: 1, 17
23
22:16, 19
Deu. 22:29
24: 3—A[2]
5, 6
25:15, 19
26: 1, 2, 3
9, 10
11, 12
13, 14
15, 15
27: 2, 3
28: 1+A
1, 8, 11
12, 21
25, 31
32, 52
53, 55
65
29: 4, 8
30: 1, 7, 15
18+A
19, 20
31: 7, 9
20—A
32: 3, 49
33: 8
34: 4
Jos. 1: 2, 3, 6
11, 13
14, 15
15
2: 9
5: 6
6:24
7:19, 19
8: 1
9:30
11:20, 23
12: 6, 7
13: 7, 8, 8
14, 15
24, 29
31+A
14: 3, 4, 13
15:13, 13
16, 17
19 *qtr*
16:10
17: 4, 4
18: 3, 4, 7
19:49, 50
20: 2, 4 A
8
21: 2, 3, 8
9, 11
12
13—A
21, 42
42, 42
43, 43
22: 4, 7, 7
23:13, 15
24: 3, 4, 7
13, 25
32, 33
Jud. 1: 2, 4 A[e]
12, 13
15 *ter*
20
2: 1+A
3: 6
5:11, 25
6: 1[f], 9
13[f]
7: 7[f], 16
8: 5, 6, 7
15, 24
25, 25
9: 4, 29
11:30[f], 30[f]
12: 3[f]
14: 9, 12
13, 19
15: 1[f], 2
6, 12[f]
18 A[h]
16: 5, 23[f]
17: 4, 10
18:10[f]
20: 7, 13
28[f], 36

Jud. 21: 1, 7
14, 18
18, 22
Ruth 1: 6, 9
2:18
3:17
4: 3, 7, 8
11, 12
13
1 Sa. 1: 4, 5, 6
6, 11
11, 16
17, 27
2: 9, 10
15, 16
28
6: 5
8: 6, 14
15
9: 8, 23
23
10: 4
12:13, 17
18
14:41
41 − A
41
15:28
17:10,17 A
25 A
44 [f], 46
18: 2 A, 4 A
8, 8
17 A
19 A
19 A
21, 27
20: 10 − A
21: 3, 6, 9
10
22: 7, 10
10, 13
15
24: 8
25: 8, 11
27, 41
27: 5, 6
28:17, 19
30:11, 12
22
2 Sa. 4: 8, 10
9: 9
10:10
12: 8
8 + A
8, 11
14: 7
16: 8
18:11, 33
19:42
20: 3, 21
21: 6, 6, 9
10
22:14, 36
41, 48
24: 9, 15
23
1 Ki. 1:48
2: 5 − B
17, 21
35 *ter*
3: 6, 7, 9
12, 13
25, 26
27, 27
4:25
30 − A
5: 3,5,6 [i]
7,9,10
11, 11
12
6: 9, 10
18
7: 4
34 A [k]
47
8:32, 32
34, 36
36, 39
40, 48

1 Ki. 8:50, 56
9: 6, 7
11 [m], 12
13
16 A
10: 9, 10
10, 13
13, 17
p 22, 24
27, 27
11:11, 13
18
18 + A
19, 31
35, 36
38 + A
12: 4, 9
p 21 *t* 8
ll 17,18
l 51
20
13: 3, 5, 7
8
26 + A
14: 7 A
8 A
15 A
15: 4, 18
16: 2, 3
17:14, 19
23
18: 1,9,23
23 + A
26 + A
19:21
20: 2 *ter*
3
4 + A
6 *ter*
7, 15
22
21: 5, 13
28
22: 6,6,12
15 + A
23
2 Ki. 3:10
13 A [a]
4:42, 43
43
44 + A
5: 1 [n], 17
22, 23
6:28, 29
8: 6, 19
9: 9 [o]
10:15, 15
11:10, 12
12: 7, 9, 9
11, 14
15, 15
13: 3, 5
14: 9
15:19, 20
16:17
17:20
18:15, 16
23, 23
19: 7, 18
21: 8
22: 5, 5, 7
8,9,10
23: 5, 11
33
35 *qtr*
25:28, 30
1 Ch. 2:35
5: 1, 20
6:48, 55
56, 57
64, 65
67
9: 2
14:10, 10
17
16:18, 28
28
29 − BS
17:22
19:11

1 Ch. 21: 5, 14
22, 22
23, 23
25
22: 9, 12
18, 19
25: 5
28: 5, 11
15, 16
19
29: 3, 7, 8
14, 19
25
2 Ch. 1: 7, 10
12, 12
2:10, 11
12, 14
3:16 [o]
5: 1
6:25, 27
27, 30
31, 38
7:19, 20
20
8: 2, 9
9: 8, 8, 9
9, 12
16, 23
27
10: 4, 9
11:11, 16
23
12: 7
13: 5
16: 1
17: 2,5,19
18: 5, 11
14, 22
20: 3,7,10
11, 22
21: 3, 3, 7
22:11
23: 9, 11
15
24:10, 12
25: 9,9,16
18
26: 8
27: 5
28:15
18 A,21
29: 6, 8
30: 8, 12
31: 4, 14
15, 19
32:24, 25
29, 33
33: 8
34: 9, 10
10, 11
15, 16
17, 18
35: 8,8,25
36: 4
4 − A
4, 23
Ezra 1: 2, 7
2:69
3: 7
4:13, 20
5:12, 14
16
6: 4, 5 − B
6, 8, 9
7: 6,6,10
11, 19
20, 20
27
8:20, 36
9: 8, 8, 9
9, 11
12, 13
10:11, 19
Neh. 1:11
2: 1, 6, 7
8, 8, 9
12, 17
4: 5
5: 7
7: 5, 70

Neh. 7:70 + AS [3]
71 [p]
71 − AB
9:8,8 + S [3]
10, 13
15, 15
17, 20
20, 22
24, 27
27, 29
30, 35
35, 36
37
10:29, 30
32
12:47
13: 5, 10
25, 26
Est. 1:19
2: 3, 9
3:10
4: 8
5: 6 + S [3]
8 + S [3]
6: 9
9 + S [3]
7: 2 + S [3]
3
8: 2, 7-A
9:13
Job 1:12, 21
22
2: 4 A [q]
3:20
5:10
6: 8, 8
7: 3
13:22
15: 2, 10
20
19:23
22:27
28:15
31:31, 35
32: 4
33: 5
34:19 A [r]
36
35: 4, 7
36: 6, 31
37: 9
38:36
39:34
42:10 [s], 11
15
Psa. 1: 3
2: 8
4: 8
13: 7
14: 5
15:10
17:14, 36
41, 48
19: 5
20: 3, 5, 7
27: 4, 4
28:11
36: 4, 21
38: 9
43:12
45: 7
48: 8
50:18
52: 7
54: 7, 23
56: 4
59: 6, 13
60: 6
65: 2, 9
66: 7
67:12, 34
35, 36
68:22
71: 1, 15
73:14
76:18
77:20, 24
29 S [1 t]
46, 66
80: 3

Psa. 83: 7, 12
84: 8, 13
13
85:16
98: 7
103:12, 27
28
104:11, 44
105:15, 46
107:13
110: 5, 6
111: 9
113: 9, 24
119: 3
120: 3
123: 6
126: 2
131: 4
134:12
135:21, 25
143:10
144:15
145: 7
146: 9
147: 5
Pro. 1: 4
2: 3, 6
3:28, 34
4: 9
6: 4, 31
9: 9
12:14
13:15
17:14
22: 9, 9
16, 26
23:12, 26
31
24:31, 71
74
26: 8, 23
28:17, 27
29:13, 17
23, 33
40
Ecc. 1:13, 13
16
2:21, 26
26, 26
3:10, 11
4:17 S [2 u]
5: 5, 17
18
6: 2
7: 3
22 S [v]
8: 9, 15
16, 17
9: 9
10: 6
11: 2
12: 7, 11
Cant. 1:12
2:13
6:10
7:12, 13
8: 1,7,11
Isa. 7:14
8:18, 20
20
9: 6
13:10, 10
22:21, 21
22
22 −
BS [1]
25:10
26:12
29:11, 12
30:20
32: 3
33:16
35: 2
36: 8, 8
40:23, 29
41: 2, 2
27
42: 1, 5, 6
8, 12
24

Isa. 43: 4, 16
20, 28
44: 3
45: 3
46:13
47: 6, 6
48:11
49: 4, 6 [w]
8
50: 4, 6
51:23 [x]
53: 9, 10
55: 4, 10
56: 5, 5
57:15, 15
18
58:10
59:21
60:17
61: 3, 8
62: 8
66: 3, 9
Jer. 1: 9
2:15
3: 8, 15
19
4:16
5:14, 24
6:21 : 27
7: 7, 14 [y]
8:10
9: 1, 2
11, 13
11: 5
12: 7,8,10
13:16, 20
14:13, 22
15: 9, 13
20
16:13, 15
17:10
18:21
19: 7, 12
20: 4, 4, 5
21: 7, 8
22:29
23:39, 40
24: 7,9,10
25: 5, 9
27: 5
28:25, 30
55
29:16
31: 9, 34
32:16, 17
33: 4, 6, 6
15
34: 4, 5
36: 6, 11
21, 26
26
37: 3, 16
21
38:21, 33
33 − A
35
39: 3 − S [1]
12, 16
19 [z], 22
24, 25
28, 30
40
41: 3 − A
17, 18
20, 21
22
42: 5 [aa]
15
43:20
44: 4, 18
21
45: 7, 16 [f]
18 [f], 19
46:14, 17 [f]
47: 5, 11
49:12, 15
50: 3
51:10, 30
30, 35
52:11, 32

Jer. 52:34
Lam. 1:11, 13
14
2: 7, 18
3:29
5: 6
Eze. 2: 8
3: 3, 8
9 + A
17, 20
25
4: 2, 2, 5
8, 15
6: 5 + A
13
7: 8, 9
3,4,20
8:16 + A
9: 4, 10
10: 7
11:15, 17
19 *ter*
21
12: 6
13:11
15: 4, 6, 6
7 [bb], 8
16: 7, 12
17, 19
21
33 − A
34 B [1 cc]
34, 36
38 + A
41, 43
47 + B [1]
61
17: 5, 15
18, 19
22 + A
18: 7, 8
13, 16
19: 8
20:11, 12
15, 25
28, 42
21, 11, 11
22: 4, 31
23: 7, 25
25, 31
42, 46
49
24: 8
25: 4, 5, 7
10, 14
17
26: 4, 8, 8
14, 17
19, 21
27:10, 12
13, 14
16, 17
18
19 + A
22
28: 2,6,17
18, 26
29: 4,5,10
12, 19
20, 21
30: 8, 12
13 + A
14, 16
21 *ter*
24 [n], 25
31:10
14, 14
32: 5,7 A [dd]
8, 15
22
23 + A
23
24, 26
26

Eze. 32:29 − A
29, 32
33: 2,7,24
27, 28
34:29 [ee]
26 [ff]
27 [f], 27
35: 3,7,12
36: 5
12 A [gg]
26 *ter*
27, 28
30
37: 6,6,14
19, 22
25
39: 4,4,11
21
43: 8, 19
44:28, 30
45: 6, 16
19
46:16, 17
47:11, 14
23
48:12
Dan. 1: 2,9,12
16, 17
2:16, 21
23, 37
38, 48
4:13, 14
22, 29
5:17, 18
19, 21
21, 28
7: 4,6,11
12, 14
22, 25
27
8:12, 13
9: 3, 10
27
10: 1, 12
15
11: 4 + A
17, 21
31
12:11
Hos. 2: 5, 8
12, 15
5: 4
9:14, 14
14 + A
13:10, 11
Joel 2:11, 17
19, 22
23, 30
3: 3
16 − S [1]
Amos 1: 2
3: 4
4: 6
9:15
Obad. 2
Jon. 1: 3 − S [1]
14 − S [1]
Mic. 1:14
3: 5
5: 3
6: 7
7:20
Hab. 3:10
Zeph. 3: 5, 20
Hag. 2: 9
Zec. 3: 7, 9
7:11
8:12
12 − S [1]
12
10: 1
11:12
12: 7 A [hh]
Mal. 2: 2, 5, 9

[a] A φέρω. [b] A διαδίδωμι.
[c] *pro* ἀποδίδωμι. [d] *pro* ἐνδίδωμι.
[e] *pro* παραδίδωμι.
[f] A παραδίδωμι. [g] A ἀφίημι.
[h] *pro* εὐδοκέω. [i] A δουλεύω.
[k] *pro* λαμβάνω. [m] A οἰκοδομέω.

[n] A τίθημι. [o] A ἐπιδίδωμι.
[p] BS[1] τίθημι. [q] pro ἐκτίω.
[r] pro εἰδέω. [s] A προστίθημι.
[t] pro φέρω. [u] pro δόμα.
[v] pro τίθημι. [w] AS τίθημι.
[x] A ἐμβάλλω. [y] A λαλέω.
[z] A ἀποδίδωμι. [aa] A ἵστημι.
[bb] A στηρίζω. [cc] pro προσδίδωμι.
[dd] pro φαίνω. [ee] A εἰμί.
[ff] A ἀποστέλλω. [gg] pro γεννάω.
[hh] pro σώζω.

διεγγυάω.

Nehemiah 5: 3

διεκβάλλω.

Jos. 15: 4,7,8[a] | Jos. 15:11, 11
9,9,11 | 16: 7

[a] B ἐκβάλλω.

διεκβολή.

Jer. 12:12 | Obad. 14
Eze. 47: 8[a], 11 | Zec. 9:10
48:30 | [a] A ἐκβολή.

διελαύνω.

Jud. 4:21 A[a] | Jud. 5:26 A[b]

[a] pro διεξέρχομαι.
[b] pro διηλόω.

διελέγχω.

Job 9:33 A[a] | Mic. 6: 2
Isa. 1:18 | [a] pro ἐλέγχω.

διεμβάλλω.

Exo. 40:16 | Nu. 4:11, 14[a]
Nu. 4: 6, 8 | [a] A ἐμβάλλω.

διεξάγω.

Habakkuk 1:4

διεξέρχομαι.

Jud. 4:21[a] | Job 20:25
2 Sa. 2:23[b] | Eze. 12: 5

[a] A διελαύνω. [b] A ἐξέρχομαι.

διέξοδος.

Nu. 34: 4, 5, 8
9, 12
Jos. 15: 4,7,11
16: 3, 8
17: 9
18:12, 14
19
19:14, 22
20, 33
Jud. 5:17[a]
2 Ki. 2:21
Psa. 1: 3
67:21
106:33[b]
35—S[1]
118:136
143:14

[a] A διακοπή. [b] S[1] ἔξοδος.

διέρχομαι.

Gen. 4: 8
15:17
22: 5
41:46
Exo. 12:12[a]
14:20
32:27
Lev. 26: 5
7+AB[a]
Nu. 20:17, 18
20
31:23, 23
Deu. 2: 7
Jos. 3: 2
16: 3
6 A[b]
7 A[b]
18: 4
4 AB[c]
4[d], 13
14
14 A[e]
Jos. 18:15, 17
18
19:12, 13
27, 34
Jud. 5:16 A[f]
11:18 A[g]
20 A[e]
15:14 A[h]
21:20 A[g]
1 Sa. 2:30, 35
6:20
9: 4 qlr
27
27+A
12: 2
14:23
26:22
30:31
2 Sa. 7: 7
11:27[d]
15:34, 34[i]
17:22, 24
2 Sa. 17:24 A[i]
20:14
24: 2
1 Ki. 3: 6
18: 5, 6
2 Ki. 4:31, 42
14: 9
1 Ch. 4:38[k]
17: 6
21: 4—8
2 Ch. 15:12
17: 9
20:10
23:15
30: 5
Ezra 8:35 B[b]
Neh. 12:31—ABS[l]
Est. 6:11
Job 41: 7
Psa. 17:13
41: 5, 8
47: 5 A[a]S[b]
65: 6, 12
72: 7, 9
87:17
89: 4
102:16
103:10, 20
104:13, 18
123: 4, 5
Pro. 28:10
Cant. 4: 8
Isa. 13:20[m]
21: 1
41: 3
43: 2
52: 1
59:14
Jer. 2:10 S[b]
8:20
13: 1
22: 8[n]
31:32
44: 4
Lam. 4:21
5:18
Eze. 5:17
9: 4
14:17
16: 6, 8
29:11
11—A
44: 2
47: 3, 4, 4
5
Joel 3:17
Amos 6: 2
8: 5
Jon. 2: 4
Mic. 2:13
5: 8
Nah. 1:14
Hab. 1:11
Zec. 10:11

[a] B ἔρχομαι. [b] pro ἔρχομαι.
[c] pro διαιρέω. [d] A ἔρχομαι.
[e] pro παρέρχομαι.
[f] pro διαίρεσις. [g] pro πορεύω.
[h] pro τήκω. [i] pro διαβαίνω.
[k] B διαιρέω. [m] S εἰσέρχομαι.
[n] S ἔρχομαι.

διετηρίς.

2 Samuel 13:23

διευλαβέομαι.

Deu. 28:60 | Job 6:16[a]

[a] A εὐλαβέομαι.

διηγέομαι.

Gen. 24:66
29:13
37: 9
40: 8, 9
41: 8, 12
Exo. 10: 2
18: 8
24: 3
Nu. 13:28
Jos. 2:23
Jud. 5:11[a]
6:13
1 Sa. 11: 5
1 Ki. 13:11
2 Ki. 8: 4, 6
1 Ch. 16: 9
Est. 1:17[b]
6:13
10: 3[c]
Psa. 9: 2—S[1]
18: 2
21:23
Psa. 25: 7
47.13, 14
49:16[d]
54:18
63: 6
65:16
72:15
74: 2
77: 3
86: 6
87:12
104: 2
117:17[e]
118:85
144: 5
6—S[1]
Isa. 43:21
53: 8
Jer. 23:27, 28
28, 32
Eze. 17: 2
Joel 1: 3

[a] A φθέγγομαι. [b] S[3] ἐπιδιηγέομαι.
[c] AS ἡγέομαι. [d] AS[2] ἐκδιηγέομαι.
[e] AS[1] ἐκδιηγέομαι.

διήγημα.

Deu. 28:37 | Eze. 17: 2
2 Ch. 7:20

διήγησις.

Jud. 5:14—A | Hab. 2: 6
7:15 A[a] | [a] pro ἐξήγησις.

διηθέω.

Job 28: 1

διηλόω.

Judges 5:26[a], 26[b]

[a] A ἀποτρίβω. [b] A διελαύνω.

δίθυμος

Pro. 26:20[a] [a] AS[2] ὀξύθυμος.

διΐημι.

Deuteronomy 32:11

διϊκνέομαι.

Exodus 26:28

διΐστημι.

Exo. 15: 8 | Isa. 59: 2
Pro. 17: 9 | Eze. 5: 1

δικάζω.

Jud. 6:31, 31[a]
31[b]
32[c]
1 Sa. 7: 6, 15
16, 17
8: 5,6,20
12: 7[d]
24:13, 16
Psa. 34: 1
42: 1
73:22
Jer. 15:10
Lam. 3:37
Hos. 4: 4
Mic. 7: 2

[a] A ἀντιδικέω. [b] A ἐκδικέω.
[c] A δικαστήριον. [d] A δικαιόω.

δίκαιος.

Gen. 6: 9
7: 1
18:23, 23
24, 24
25, 25
26, 28
20: 4
Exo. 9:27
18:21
23: 7, 8
Lev. 19:36 ter
Nu. 23:10
Deu. 4: 8
16:18, 19
20
25: 1, 15
15
32: 4
1 Sa. 2: 2, 9
24:18
2 Sa. 4:11
1 Ki. 2:32
8:32
2 Ki. 10: 9
2 Ch. 6:23
12: 6
Ezra 9:15—A
Neh. 9: 8, 33
Job 1: 1
8+AS[2]
2: 3 A[a]
5: 5
6:29
8: 3
9: 2, 15
20, 23
10:15
11: 2
12: 4
13:18
15:14
17: 8
22:15, 19
24: 4, 11
25: 4
27: 5, 17
28: 4[b]
31: 6
32: 1, 2
33:12
34: 5, 10
12 A[c]
17
35: 2, 7
Job 36: 3,7,10
17
37:22
40: 3
Psa. 1: 5, 6
2:12
5:13
7:10, 11
12
10: 3, 5, 7
13: 5
30:19
31:11
32: 1
33:16, 18
20, 22
36:12, 16
17, 21
25
26+A
29, 30
32, 39
51: 8
54:23
57:11, 12
63:11
67: 4
68:29
74:10
91:13
93:21
96:11, 12
111: 4, 6
114: 5
117:15, 20
118:137
124: 3, 3
128: 4
138: 5 S[1d]
139:14
140: 5
141: 8
144:17
145: 8
Pro. 1:11
2:16
3: 9, 32
33
4:18, 25
6:17
9: 9
10: 3, 6, 7
11, 16
17—AS[2]
Pro. 10:18, 20
21, 22
24, 25
28, 30
31, 32
11: 1, 4, 7
8, 9, 10
11+B[e]
15, 16
18, 19
23, 28
31
12: 3, 5, 7
10, 13
17, 21
25, 26
13: 5, 9, 9
11, 21
22, 23
25
14: 9, 19
32
15: 6—S[1]
28, 28
29
16: 1, 5, 11
13
33 S[1e]
33
17: 4
7—S
15
15 S[e]
15, 26
26
18: 5, 10
17
19:22
20: 8
21: 2, 3, 7
12, 15
18, 26
23:24, 31
24:15, 16
35, 39
25:26
28: 1, 12
18 S[1f]
21, 28
28
29: 2, 4, 6
7, 16
26, 27
Ecc. 3:16, 17
Ecc. 7:16, 16
17, 21
8:14, 14
9: 1, 2
Isa. 3:10
5:23, 23
26:21
32: 1
41:10
45:21
22+A[g]
47: 3
51: 1
53:11
54:17[g]
57: 1 ter
58: 2
59: 4
60:21
61: 8
64: 5
Jer. 11:20
12: 1
20:12
23: 5
37:16 S[h]
38:23
40: 5
Lam. 1:18
4:13
Eze. 3:20, 21
21
13:22
18: 5, 8, 9
11, 20
24, 26
23:45
33:12, 12
13, 18
45:10 ter
Dan. 9:14
12: 3
Hos. 14: 9
Joel 3:19
Amos 2: 6
5:12
Jon. 1:14—S[1]
Hab. 1: 4, 13
2: 4
Zeph. 3: 5
Zec. 7: 9
8:16 A[i]
9: 9
Mal. 3:18

[a] pro ἄκακος. [b] A δικαιοσύνη.
[c] pro κρίσις. [d] pro ἀρχαῖος.
[e] pro ἄδικος. [f] pro δικαίως.
[g] S[1] ἅγιος. [h] pro ἀδικία.
[i] pro εἰρηνικός.

δικαιοσύνη.

Gen. 15: 6
18:19
19:19
20: 5, 13
21:23
24:27, 49
30:33
32:10
Exo. 15:13
34: 7
Lev. 19:15
Deu. 9: 4, 5, 6
33:19, 21
Jos. 24:14
Jud. 5:11, 11
1 Sa. 2:10
12: 7
26:23
2 Sa. 8:15
22:21, 25
1 Ki. 3: 6, 9
8:32
10: 9
1 Ch. 18:14
29:17
2 Ch. 6:23
9: 8
Neh. 2:20
Job 8:6 22:28
24:13
27: 6
28: 4 A[a]
29:14
33:13 ACS[2b]
26
35: 8
Psa. 4: 2, 6
5: 9
7: 9, 18
9: 5, 9
10: 7
14: 2
16: 1, 15
17:21, 25
21:32
22: 3
30: 2
34:24[c], 27
28
35: 7, 11
36: 6
37:21[d]
39:10, 11
44: 5, 8
47.11
49: 6

Psa. 50:16, 21
51: 5
57: 2
64: 6
66: 5+S^1
68:28
70: 2, 15
16, 19
21[e], 24
71: 1, 2, 4
7
84:11, 12
14
87:13
88:15, 17
93:15
95:13
96: 2, 6
97: 2, 9
98: 4
102:17
105: 3, 31
110: 3
111: 3, 9
117:19
118: 7, 10
62, 75
106, 121
123, 138
142, 142
144, 160
164, 172
131: 9
142: 1, 11
144: 7
Pro. 1: 3, 22
2: 9, 20
3: 9, 16
8: 8, 15
18, 20
20 AS^2 [f]
10: 2
11: 4+A
5
6−S^1
21, 30
12:27
13: 2, 6 A
14:34
15: 6, 9
29
16: 5, 4
11, 12
17, 31
17:14, 23
20: 7, 28
21:16, 21
25: 5
Ecc. 5: 7
Isa. 1:21, 26
5: 7, 16
9: 7
10:22
11: 5
16: 5
26: 2, 9

Isa. 26:10
32:16, 17
17
33: 5, 6
15
38:19
39: 8
41: 2
42: 6
6+S^1
45: 8, 8
13
19, 23
24
46:12, 13
48: 1, 18
49:13+S^1
51: 5, 6, 8
54:14
56: 1
57:12
58: 2, 8
59: 9−S^3
14, 17
60:17
61: 3
3+S^1
8, 11
62: 1, 2
63: 1, 7
64: 6
Jer. 4: 2
9:24
22: 3, 13
15
23: 5
27: 7
Eze. 3:20, 20
14:14, 20
18: 5, 17
19, 20
21[g]
22, 24
24, 26
27
33:12, 13
13, 14
16, 18
19
45: 9
Dan. 8:12
9: 7, 8
18, 24
Hos. 2:19
10:12, 12
Joel 2:23
Amos 5: 7, 24
6:12
Mic. 6: 5
7: 9
Zeph. 2: 3
Zec. 8: 8
Mal. 2:17
3: 3
4: 2

[a] pro δίκαιος. [b] pro δίκη.
[c] S^1 ἐλεημοσύνη. [d] S^2 ἀγαθωσύνη.
[e] S^2 μεγαλωσύνη.
[f] pro δικαίωμα. [g] A δικαίωμα.

δικαιόω.

Gen. 38:26
44:16
Exo. 23: 7
Deu. 25: 1
1 Sa. 12: 7 A[a]
2 Sa. 15: 4
1 Ki. 8:32
2 Ch. 6:23
Job 33:32
Psa. 18:10
50: 6
72:13
81: 3
142: 2

Isa. 1:17
5:23
42:21
43: 9, 26
45:25
50: 8
53:11
Jer. 3:11
Eze. 16:51, 52
52
21:13
44:24
Mic. 6:11
7: 9

[a] pro δικάζω.

δικαίωμα.

Gen. 26: 5
Exo. 15:25, 26
21: 1, 9, 31
24: 3
Lev. 25:18
Nu. 15:16
27:11
30:17
31:21
35:29
36:12
Deu. 4: 1, 5, 6
8, 14
40, 45
5: 1, 31
6: 1, 2, 4
17, 20
24[a]
7:11, 12
8:11
10:13
11: 1
17:19
26:16, 17
27:10
28:45
30:10, 16
33:10
Ruth 4: 7
1 Sa. 2:12
8: 3, 9, 11
10:25
27:11
30:25
2 Sa. 19:28
22:23
1 Ki. 2: 3
3:28
8:45, 59
59−B
2 Ki. 17: 8, 13
19, 34
37
23: 3
2 Ch. 6:35
19:10

2 Ch. 33: 8+A
Job 34:27
Psa. 17:23
18: 9
49:16
88:32
104:45
118: 5, 8
12, 16
20 S^1 [b]
23, 24
26, 27
33, 48
54, 56
64, 68
71, 80
83, 93
94, 112
117, 118
124, 135
141, 145
155, 171
147: 8
Pro. 2: 8
8:20[c]
19:28
Jer. 11:20
18:19
Eze. 5: 6, 6, 7
7
11:20
18: 9
21 A[d]
20:11
13+A
13, 16
18, 19
21, 24
25
36:27
43:11
44:24
Hos. 13: 1
Mic. 6:16
Mal. 4: 6

[a] A κρίμα. [b] pro κρίμα.
[c] AS^2 δικαιοσύνη.
[d] pro δικαιοσύνη.

δικαίως.

Gen. 27:36
Deu. 1:16
16:20

Pro. 24:77
28:18[a]

[a] S^1 δίκαιος.

δικαίωσις.

Leviticus 24:22

δικαστήριον.

Jud. 6:32 A[a] [a] pro δικάζω.

δικαστής.

Exo. 2:14
Jos. 9: 6
23: 2
24: 1

1 Sa. 8: 1, 2
24:16
Isa. 3: 2

δίκη.

Exo. 21:20
Lev. 26:25
Deu. 32:41, 43
Job 20:16
33:13[a]
Psa. 9: 5
34:23
42: 1
73:22

Ps. 139:13
Pro. 22:23 A[b]
Lam. 3:57[c]
Eze. 25:12
Hos. 13:14
Joel 3:14 14
Amos 7: 4
Mic. 7: 9

[a] ACS^2 δικαιοσύνη. [b] pro κρίσις.
[c] A ἀδικία.

δίκτυον.

1 Ki. 7: 5, 5
5−A
27, 28

1 Ki. 7:28
2 Ch. 4:12, 13
13

Job 18: 8
Pro. 1:17
29: 5
Cant. 2: 9
Jer. 52:22, 23
Lam. 1:13

Eze. 12:13
17:20
19: 8
32: 3
Hos. 5: 1
7:12

δικτυόομαι.

1 Kings 7: 6

δικτυωτός.

Exo. 27: 4
38:24
Jud. 5:28 A[a]

2 Ki. 1: 2
Eze. 41:16

[a] pro τοξικός.

δίμετρος.

2 Kings 7: 1, 16, 18

δίνη, −να.

Job 13:11[a]

Job 28:10[b]

[a] A δειλία. [b] C θίς.

διοδεύω.

Gen. 12: 6
13:17
Psa. 88:42[a]
Isa. 59: 8
Jer. 2: 6
9:12

Jer. 27:13
Eze. 5:14
14:15
36:34 A[b]
Zeph. 3: 6
Zec. 7:14

[a] A παραπορεύομαι.
[b] pro παροδεύω.

δίοδος.

Deu. 13:16
Pro. 7: 8
Isa. 11:16[a]

Jer. 2:28
7:34
14:16 A[b]

[a] A ὁδός. [b] pro ὁδός.

διοικέω.

1 Kings 21:27+A

διοικητής.

Ezra 8:36

διοικοδομέω.

Nehemiah 2:17

διόλου.

1 Kings 10: 8

διορύω.

Job 6:19

διορθόω.

Pro. 16: 1
Isa. 16: 5

Isa. 62: 7
Jer. 7: 3, 5, 5

διορθρίζω.

1 Sa. 29:10 A[a] [a] pro ὀρθρίζω.

διορίζω.

Exo. 26:33
Lev. 20:24
Jos. 5: 6
15:47
2 Ch. 32: 4
Job 35:11

Isa. 45:18, 24[a]
Eze. 41:12[b], 12
13, 15
42: 1, 10
47:18
20 A[c]

[a] AS^2 ἀφορίζω. [b] B αἰθρίζω.
[c] pro ὁρίζω.

διόρυγμα.

Exo. 22: 2
Jer. 2:34

Zeph. 2:14

διορύσσω.

Job 24:16
Eze. 12: 5, 7

Eze. 12:12[a]
[a] A ὀρύσσω.

δίπηχυς.

Numbers 11:31

διπλασιάζω.

Eze. 21:14

Eze. 43: 2

διπλασιασμός.

Job 42:10

διπλοΐς.

1 Sa. 2:19
15:27
24: 5, 6, 12

1 Sa. 28:14
Job 29:14
Ps. 108:29

διπλόος, −οῦς.

Gen. 23: 9, 17
19
25: 9
43:14
49:30
50:13
Exo. 16: 5, 22
22: 4, 7, 9
25: 4
28:16

Exo. 35: 6
36:16, 16
Deu. 21:17
2 Ki. 2: 9
Ezra 1:10−AB
Job 11: 6
42:10
Isa. 40: 2
Jer. 16:18[a]
Zec. 9:12

[a] B διὰ πάσας.

δισσός.

Gen. 43:11
45:22
Pro. 20:10, 23

Pro. 29:40
Jer. 17:18

δίστομος.

Jud. 3:16
Ps. 149: 6

Pro. 5: 4

δισχίλιοι.

Exo. 39: 7 A[a]
1 Ki. 7:12+A
1 Ch. 26:32[b]

Neh. 7:69[c]
71−AB[d]

[a] A 2400 pro 1500 [b] A χίλιοι.
[c] AS ἑξακισχίλιοι. [d] S^1 χιλιάς.

διτάλαντος.

2 Kings 5:23, 23 A[a]
[a] pro δύο τάλαντα.

διυλίζω.

Amos 6: 6

διυφαίνω.

Exodus 36:31

διφθέρα.

Exodus 39:21

δίφορος.

Deuteronomy 22: 9 B[a]
[a] pro διάφορος.

δίφρος.

Deu. 17:18+A
Jud. 3:24+A
1 Sa. 1: 9
4:13, 18

1 Sa. 28:23
2 Ki. 4:10
Job 29: 7
Pro. 9:14

διχηλέω.

Lev. 11: 3, 4, 4
5, 6, 7
26

Deu. 14: 6, 7, 7
8

διχοτομέω.

Exodus 29:17

διχοτόμημα.

Gen. 15:11, 17
Exo. 29:17

Lev. 1: 8
Eze. 24: 4, 4

δίψα.

Deu. 8:15
2 Ch. 32:11[a]
Neh. 9:15
Psa. 68:22
103:11
Ps. 106:33
Isa. 5:13 AS[b]
41:17
Amos 8:11

[a] A θλίψις. [b] pro δίψος.

διψάω.

Exo. 17: 3
Jud. 4:19
15:18
Ruth 2: 9
2 Sa. 17:29
Job 18: 9
22: 7
29:23
Psa. 41: 3
62: 2
106: 5
Pro. 25:21, 25[a]
28:15
Isa. 21:14
Isa. 25: 4, 5
29: 8, 8
32: 2, 6[b]
35: 1, 6, 7
40:28+S
41:18
43:20+S
48:21
49:10
53: 2
55: 1
65:13
Jer. 38:25

[a] S[1] ζάω. [b] S[1] πεινάω.

δίψος.

Exo. 17: 3
Deu. 28:48—B
32:10
Jud. 15:18
Neh. 9:20
Psa. 61: 5
Isa. 5:13[a]
Isa. 44: 3
50: 2
Jer. 2:25
Lam. 4: 4
Hos. 2: 3
Amos 8:13

[a] AS δίψα.

διψώδης.

Proverbs 9:12

διωγμός.

Pro. 11:19
Lam. 3:19

διωθέω.

Ezekiel 34:21

διώκω.

Gen. 31:23
Exo. 15: 9
Lev. 26: 7, 8, 8
17
17—A
36, 36
Deu. 16:20[a]
19: 6
30: 7
32:30
Jos. 2: 8[b]
20: 5 A
23:10
Jud. 4:16, 22
7:23[b]
8: 4—A
5, 12
9:40[b]
20:43[c]
1 Sa. 30:10 B[d]
2 Sa. 18:16
20: 7, 10
13
21: 5
22:38
24:13
2 Ki. 5:21
9:27
25: 5
1 Ch. 12:15 S[e]
Ezra 9: 4
Est. 8:14+S[3]
Job 19:22
Psa. 7: 2
33:15
68: 5 S[e]
Ps. 108:31 S[1 d]
Pro. 9:12—S
12:11
15: 9
21: 6
28: 1, 19
Ecc. 3:15
Isa. 1:23
5:11
13:14
16: 4
17: 2, 13
30:16, 28
31: 8 A[f]
41: 3
51: 1
Jer. 17:18
20:11
29:31 ter
Lam. 1: 3 S[d]
6+S[1]
6
4:19
5: 5
Eze. 25:13
35: 6
Hos. 6: 3
12: 1
Amos 1:11
2:16
6:12
Mic. 2:11
Nah. 1: 8
3: 2
Hab. 2: 2
Hag. 1: 9

[a] A φυλάσσω. [b] A καταδιώκω. [c] A καταπαύω. [d] pro καταδιώκω. [e] pro ἐκδιώκω. [f] pro μάχαιρα.

διώροφος.

Genesis 6:16

διώρυξ.

Exo. 7:19
8: 5
Isa. 19: 6
Isa. 27:12
33:21
Jer. 38: 9

διωστήρ.

Exo. 38: 4, 10
11
Exo. 39:15
40:18

δόγμα.

Est. 4: 8+S[3]
9: 1+S[3]
Eze. 20:26[a]
Dan. 2:13
3:10, 12
Dan. 3:29
4: 3
6: 8, 9, 10
12, 13
15, 26

[a] AB δόμα.

δογματίζω.

Esther 3: 9

δοκέω.

Gen. 19:14
38:15
Exo. 25: 2
35:21, 22
26
Jos. 9:31
Est. 1:19
3: 9
5: 4
8: 5, 8
Job 1:21
15:21
Job 20: 7, 22
Pro. 2:10
14:12
16:25
17:28
26:12[a]
27:14
29:24
Jer. 34: 4
Dan. 4:14, 22
20
5:21

[a] A[1] δοξάζω.

δοκιμάζω, —μόω.

Jud. 7: 4 A[a]
Job 34: 3
Psa. 16: 3
25: 2—S[1]
65:10
67:31
80: 8
94: 9
138: 1, 23
Pro. 8:10
Pro. 17: 3
27:21
Jer. 6:27, 27
9: 7
11 20
12: 3
17:10
20:12
Zec. 11:13
13: 9, 9

[a] pro ἐκκαθαίρω.

δοκιμαστής.

Jeremiah 6:27

δοκίμιον.

Psa. 11: 7
Pro. 27:21

δόκιμος.

Gen. 23:16
1 Ki. 10:18
1 Ch. 28:18
1 Ch. 29: 4
2 Ch. 9:17
Zec. 11:13

δοκός.

Gen. 19: 8
1 Ki. 6:15, 16
2 Ki. 6: 2, 5
2 Ch. 34:11
Cant. 1:17

δόκωσις.

Ecclesiastes 10:18

δόλιος.

Psa. 5: 7
11: 3, 4
16: 1
30:19
42: 1
51: 6
108: 2, 2
119: 2, 3
Pro. 11: 1
Pro. 12: 6, 17
24, 27
13: 9, 13
14:25
20:23
26:23 S[a]
Jer. 9: 8
Zeph. 3:13

[a] pro λεῖος.

δολιότης.

Nu. 25:18
Psa. 37:13
49:19
Psa. 54:24
72:18

δολιόω.

Nu. 25:18
Psa. 5:10
Psa. 13: 3—A
104:25

δολίως.

Jeremiah 9: 4

δόλος.

Gen. 27:35
34:13
Exo. 21:14
Lev. 19:16
Deu. 27:24
2 Sa. 14:20 B[a]
2 Ki. 9:23[b]
Job 13: 7, 16
15:35[c]
31: 5
23+S[1]
Psa. 9:28
23: 4
31: 2
33:14
34:20
35: 4
Psa. 51: 4
54:12
138: 4+S[2]
Pro. 10:10
12: 5[d], 20
16:28[e]
26:23, 24[f]
26
Isa. 9: 5
53: 9
Jer. 5:27
9: 6, 6
Eze. 35: 5
Dan. 8:25, 25
11:23
Mic. 6:11
Zeph. 1: 9

[a] pro λόγος. [b] A δοῦλος. [c] A πόνος. [d] S[1] λόγος. [e] S χολος. [f] B[1] λόγος.

δολόω.

Psa. 14: 3
Psa. 35: 3

δόμα.

Gen. 25: 6
47:22
Exo. 28:34
Lev. 7:20
23:38
Nu. 3: 9
18: 6, 7
11, 29
27: 7
28: 2
Deu. 12:11+A
23:23
1 Sa. 18:25
2 Sa. 19:42
1 Ki. 13: 7
2 Ch. 2:10
17:11
21: 3
2 Ch. 31:14
32:23
Psa. 67:19
Pro. 18:16
19:17
Ecc. 3:13
4:17[a]
5:18
Eze. 20:26 AB[b]
31
46: 5, 16
17
Dan. 2: 6, 48
5:17
Hos. 9: 1
10: 6
Mal. 1: 3 ABS[c]

[a] S[2] δίδωμι. [b] pro δόγμα. [c] pro δῶμα.

δόμος.

Ezra 6: 4, 4

δόξα.

Gen. 31: 1, 16
45:13
Exo. 15: 7, 11
16: 7, 10
24:16, 17
28: 2, 36
29:43
33: 5
18+A
19, 22
40:28, 29
Lev. 9: 6, 23
Nu. 12: 8
14:10, 21
22
16:19, 42
20: 6
23:22
24: 8, 11
27:20
Deu. 5:24
Jos. 7:19
1 Sa. 2: 8
4:22
22+A
6: 5
1 Ki. 3:13
8:11
1 Ch. 16:24-ABS
27, 28
29—BS
22: 5
29:12, 25
28
2 Ch. 1:11, 12
2: 6
3: 6
5:13, 14
7: 1, 2, 3
17: 5
2 Ch. 18: 1
26:18
30: 8
32:27, 33
Neh. 9: 5
Est. 1: 4
5: 1, 11
6: 3
10: 2
Job 19: 9
29:20
37:21
39:20
40: 5
Psa. 3: 4
7: 6
8: 6
16:15
18: 2
20: 6, 6
23: 7
8—A[1]
9
10—A[1]
10
25: 8
28: 1, 2, 3
9
29:13
44:14
48:15, 17
18
56: 6
8+S
9, 12
61: 8
62: 3
65: 2
67:35
70: 8—S[1]
71:19
19—S[1]
72:24
78: 9
83:12
84:10
95: 3—A[1]
7, 8
96: 6
101:16, 17
103:31
105:20
107: 2
2+S[2]
6
111: 3, 9
112: 4
113: 9
137: 5
144: 5, 11
12
149: 5, 9
Pro. 3:16, 35
8:18
11:16
14:28
16: 1
1+AS[a]
18:11, 12
20: 3, 29
21:21
22: 4
25: 2, 2
26: 8, 11
28:12
29:23
Ecc. 6: 2
10: 1
Isa. 2:10, 19
21
3: 8, 18
20
Isa. 4: 2, 5
6: 1, 3
8: 7[c]
10: 3, 12
16
11: 3
12: 2
14:11
16:14
17: 3, 4, 4
20: 5
21:16
22:22—S[1]
23, 25
24:14, 15
26:10
28: 1, 4[b]
5
30:18+AS
27, 30
33:17
35: 2, 2
40: 5, 6, 26
42: 8, 12
43: 7
45:24[e]
46:13 S[1]
48:11
52: 1, 14
53: 2
58: 8
60: 1, 2, 13
19, 21
61: 3 ter
62: 2, 8[e]
8, 8[f]
63:12, 14
15
64:11
66:11, 12
18, 19
19
Jer. 2:11
13:11, 16
18, 20
14:21
17:12
23: 9
31:11
18—S[1]
Lam. 2:11
15+
AB[d]S
Eze. 2: 1
3:12, 23
23
8: 4
9: 3
10: 4, 4, 18
19, 22
11:22, 23
27: 7, 10
39:21
43: 2, 2, 4, 5
44: 4
Dan. 4:27
5:18
10: 8[g]
11:20, 21
39
Hos. 4: 7
9:11
10: 5
Mic. 1:15
5: 4
Hab. 2:14, 16
16—S[1]
Hag. 2: 3, 7, 9
Zec. 2: 5, 8
10: 8 S[1 h]
Mal. 1: 6
2: 2

[a] S δύναμις. [b] B ζωή. [c] S[1] εἰρήνη. [d] pro δόξασμα. [e] B* δεξιά. [f] pro ἰσχύς. [g] A ἔχω. [h] pro εἰσδέχομαι.

δοξάζω.

Exo. 15: 1, 2, 6
Exo. 15:11, 21

Exo. 34:29, 30
35
Lev. 10: 3
Deu. 33:16
Jud. 9: 9
13:17
1 Sa. 2:29, 30
30
15:30
2 Sa. 6:20, 22
10: 3
2 Ki. 12:11 A[a]
1 Ch. 17:18
19: 3
Ezra 7:27
8:36
Est. 3: 1
6: 6, 6, 7
9, 11
10: 3
Psa. 14: 4
21:24
36:20
49:15, 23
85: 9, 12
86: 3
Psa. 90:15
Pro. 13:18
26:12 A[1 b]
Isa. 4: 2
5:16
10:15
24:23
25: 1
33:10
42:10—S[1]
43: 4, 23
44:23
49: 3 AS[c]
5
52.13
55: 5
60: 7, 13
66: 5
Lam. 1: 8
5:12
Eze. 39:13
Dan. 4:31, 34
5:23
11:38, 38
Mal. 1: 6, 11

[a] pro ἐκδίδωμι. [b] pro δοκέω.
[c] pro ἐνδοξάζω.

δόξασμα.

Isa. 46:13[a]
Lam. 2: 1

[a] S[1] δόξα.

δοξαστός.

Deuteronomy 26:19

δορά.

Gen. 25:25
Mic. 2: 8

δορατοφόρος.

1 Chronicles 12:24—A

δορκάδιον.

Isaiah 13:14

δορκάς.

Deu. 12:15, 22
14: 5
15:22
2 Sa. 2:18
1 Ki. (3) p 46
4:23
1 Ch. 12: 8
Pro. 6: 5
Cant. 2: 9
4: 5
7: 3
8:14

δόρκων.

Canticles 2:17

δόρυ.

1 Sa. 13:19, 22
17: 7, 45
47
18:10 A
11 A
19: 9, 10
10
20:33
21: 8
22: 6
26: 7, 8
11, 12
16, 22
2 Sa. 1: 6
2:23, 23
21:16, 19
2 Sa. 23: 7, 18
21—A
21 B[a]
21, 21
1 Ki. 10:16, 16
14:26
1 Ch. 11:23 ter
12: 8, 34
20: 5
2 Ch. 11:12
14: 8
25: 5
26:14
Job 41:17
Jer. 26: 4
Mic. 4: 3[b]

[a] pro ῥάβδος. [b] A ζιβύνη.

δόσις.

Gen. 47:22, 22
Pro. 21:14
Pro. 25:14

δότης.

Proverbs 22: 8

δοτός.

1 Samuel 1:11

δουλεία.

Gen. 30:26
Exo. 6: 6
13: 3, 14
20: 2
Lev. 25:39
26:30[a], 45
Deu. 5: 6
6:12
7: 8
8:14
13: 5, 10
Jud. 6: 8—A
1 Sa. 14:40, 40
1 Ki. 5: 6
9: 9
21 A
12: 4
1 Ch. 25: 6—AB
2 Ch. 10: 4
2 Ch. 12: 8, 8
Ezra 6:18
8:20
9: 8, 9
Neh. 3: 5
5:18
9:17
10:32, 37
Est. 7: 4
Ps. 103:14
146: 8—A
Pro. 26: 9
Isa. 14: 3
Jer. 41:13
Lam. 1: 3
Eze. 29:18, 18
20 A[b]
Mic. 6: 4

[a] A δειλία. [b] pro λειτουργία.

δουλεύω.

Gen. 14: 4
15:14
25:23
27:29, 40
29:15, 18
20, 25
30
30:26, 26
29
31: 6, 41
Exo. 14: 5, 12
12
21: 2, 6
23:33
Lev. 25:39
Deu. 13: 4+A
15:12, 18
28.64
Jud. 2: 7
3: 8, 14
9:28, 28
38
10: 6[a], 6
10[a], 13[a]
16[a]
1 Sa. 2:24
4: 9—B
9—B
7: 3, 4
8: 8
11: 1
12:10, 10
14, 20
23, 24
17: 9
26:19
2 Sa. 10:19
16:19, 19
22:44
1 Ki. (3) p 46
4(21) A
5: 6 A[b]
9: 6
9—A
12: 4, 7
p 244 56
16:31
22:54
2 Ki. 10:18, 18
17:41
18: 7
21: 3
25:24
1 Ch. 19:19
28: 9
2 Ch. 7:22
10: 4
24:18
30: 8
33: 3, 16
22
34:33
35: 5
Neh. 9:35
Job 21:15
36:11
39: 9
Psa. 2:11
17:44
21:31
71:11
80: 7
99: 2
101:23
105:36
Pro. 10:24+A
11:29
12: 9
Isa. 14: 3
19:23
43:23 AS[2 c]
53:11
56: 6
60:12
65: 8, 13
13, 13
14, 15
Jer. 2:20
31 A[d]
5:19
19—A
8: 2
11:10
13:10
16:11, 13
22: 9
25: 6, 11
34: 5—S
6+A
41: 9
42:13
Eze. 20:40
29:18[c], 20
Dan. 7:14, 27
Hos. 12:12
Zeph. 3: 9
Zec. 2: 9
Mal. 3:14, 17
18, 18

[a] A λατρεύω. [b] pro δίδωμι.
[c] pro δουλόω. [d] pro κυριεύω.
[e] A δουλόω.

δούλη.

Exo. 21: 7
Lev. 25:44
Jud. 19:19 A[a]
Ruth 2:13
3: 9, 9
1 Sa. 1:11
11+A
11, 16
18
8:16
25:24, 24
25, 27
28, 31
41
28:21, 22
2 Sa. 14: 6, 7, 12
15[b], 15
16, 19
20:17
1 Ki. 1:13, 17
3:20+A
2 Ki. 4: 2, 16
2 Ch. 28:10
Neh. 5: 5 B[c]
Isa. 14: 2
56: 6
Joel 2:29
Nah. 2: 7

[a] pro παιδίσκη. [b] AB λαός.
[c] pro δοῦλος.

δοῦλος.

Lev. 25.44
26:13
Deu. 32:36
Jos. 9:29
14: 7 A[a]
24:30
Jud. 2: 8
6:27
9:28
15:18
19:19 A[a]
1 Sa. 2:27
3: 9, 10
8:14:15
16, 17
12·19
13: 3
14:21, 41
16:16
17: 9, 9, 32
34, 36
58 A
18: 5A, 30A
19: 4
20: 7, 8, 8, 8
22: 8, 14
15, 15
23:10, 11
11
25:10, 39
26:17, 18
19
27: 5, 5, 12
28: 2
29: 3, 8
30:13
2 Sa. 3:18
6:20
7: 5, 8, 19
20, 21[b]
21, 25
25+A
27, 27
28, 29
29
8: 2, 6
14
9: 2, 6, 8
10, 10
11, 11
12
10: 2, 19
11: 9, 11
13, 17
21, 24
12:18
13:24, 24
35
14:19, 20
22, 22
30, 30
15: 2, 8, 21
34
18:29, 29
19: 5, 7, 14
17—A
20, 26
26, 27
28, 35
35, 36
37, 37
21:22
24:10, 21
1 Ki. 1:19, 26
26, 27
33, 47
51
(3)38, 39
39, 40
40, 41
3: 6, 7, 8
9, 9 A[c]
5: 6, 6, 9
8:23, 24
25
26+A
28+A
28, 29
30
34 B[c]
36[d]
36 B[c]
52, 53
56, 59
66
11:11, 13
26, 32
34, 36
38
12: 7, 7
p 244 7
14: 8 A
18 A
15:29—A
16: 2 A[c]
18: 9, 12
36
20:28
21: 9, 32
39, 40
22:50 A
50 A
2 Ki. 1:13
14+A
4: 1 ter
5: 6, 15
17, 17
18, 18
25
6: 3
8:13, 19
9: 7, 7
23 A[e]
10:10, 19
19
21—A
21, 22
23—A
23, 23
12:20, 21
14: 5, 25
16: 7
17: 3, 13
23
18:12, 24
19:34
20: 6
21: 8, 10
22: 9, 12
24: 1, 2
1 Ch. 17: 4[f], 7
18, 26
2 Ch. 2: 8
6:23, 42
28:10
36:20
Ezra 2:55—8
65
4:15
5:11
9: 9, 11
Neh. 1: 6, 6, 11
2:10, 19
20
5: 5[g]
7:57
60—S
67
9:14, 36
36—ABS
10:29
11: 3
Job 40:23
Psa. 18:12, 14
26: 9
30:17
33:23
34:27
35: 1—A
68:37
77:70, 71
78: 2, 10
79: 5
85: 2, 4
88: 4, 21
40, 51
89:13, 16
101:15, 29
104: 6, 17
25, 26
42
108:28
115: 7
7—A[1]
118:17, 23
38, 49
65, 76
84, 91
122
124
125
135
140
176
Ps. 122: 2
131:10
133: 1
134: 1, 9
12 AS[c]
14
135:22[h]
142: 2, 12
143:10
Pro. 9: 3
Ecc. 2: 7
5:11
7:22
10: 7, 7
Isa. 14: 2
42:19
45:14
48:20[d]
49: 3, 5, 7
56: 6
63:17
65: 9
Jer. 2:14
3:22
7:25
25: 4
26:27
42:15 A[a]
51: 4 A[a]
Lam. 5: 8
Eze. 28:26
34:23
37:24, 25
25
38:17
Dan. 3:26
6:20
9: 6, 10
11, 17
Joel 2:29
Amos 3: 7
Jon. 1: 9
Hag. 2:23
Zec. 1: 6
3: 8
Mal. 1: 6
4: 6

[a] pro παῖς. [b] A λόγος.
[c] pro λαός. [d] A λαός.
[e] pro δόλος. [f] AS παῖς.
[g] B δούλη. [h] S[2] λαός.

δουλόω.

Gen. 15:13
Pro. 27: 8[a]
Isa. 43:23—BS[1 b]
Eze. 29:18 A[c]

[a] C καταδουλόω. [b] AS[2] δουλευω.
[c] pro δουλεύω.

δοχή.

Gen. 21: 8
26:30
Est. 1: 3
Est. 5: 4, 5
8—S[1]
12, 14

δράγμα.

Gen. 37: 7[a], 7
7[b], 7[b]
41:47
Lev. 23:10, 11
12, 15
Deu. 24:21
Jud. 15: 5 A[c]
Ruth 2: 7, 15
Neh. 13:15
Ps. 125: 6
128: 7
Hos. 8: 7
Mic. 4:12

[a] A δράχμα. [b] A δράγχμα.
[c] pro στάχυς.

δράκων.

Exo. 7: 9, 10
12
Deu. 32:33
Job 4:10
7:12
20:16
26:13
38:39
40:20
Psa. 73:13, 14
90:13
Ps. 103:26
148: 7
Isa. 27: 1 ter
Jer. 9:11
27: 8
28:34
Lam. 4: 3
Eze. 29: 3
32: 2
Amos 9: 3
Mic. 1: 8

δράξ.

Lev. 2: 2
5:12
6:15
1 Ki. 17:12
Ecc. 4: 6, 6
Isa. 40:12
Eze. 10: 2[a]
13:19

[a] A χείρ.

δράσσομαι.

Lev. 2: 2
5:12
Nu. 5:26
Psa. 2:12

δραχμή.

Gen. 24:22
Exo. 39: 2
Ezra 2:69 A[a]
8:27+A

[a] pro μνᾶ.

δράω.

2 Chronicles 35:19—AB

δρέπανον.

Deu. 16: 9
24: 1
1 Sa. 13:20, 21
Isa. 2: 4
18: 5
Jer. 27:16
Joel 3:10, 13
Mic. 4: 3
Zec. 5: 1, 2

δρομεύς.

Job 7: 6 AS[2a]
9:25
Pro. 6:11, 11[b]
Pro. 24:49
Amos 2:14

[a] pro λαλιά. [b] A ἀνήρ.

δρόμος.

2 Sa. 18:27, 27
Job 17:11 A[a]
38:34 A[b]
Ecc. 9:11
Jer. 8: 6
23:10[c]

[a] pro βρόμος. [b] pro τρόμος.
[c] B δρυμός.

δρόσος.

Gen. 27:28, 39
Exo. 16:13
Nu. 11: 9
Deu. 32: 2
33:13, 28
Jud. 5: 4—A
6:37, 38
39, 40
2 Sa. 1:21
17:12
1 Ki. 17: 1
Job 24:20
29:19
38:28
Ps. 132: 3
Pro. 3:20
19:12
26: 1
Cant. 5: 2
Isa. 18: 4
26:19
Dan. 4:12, 20
22, 30
5:21
Hos. 6: 4
13: 3
14: 5
Mic. 5: 7
Hag. 1:10
Zec. 8:12

δρυμός.

Deu. 19: 5
20:10 A[a]
Jos. 17:15, 18
18
Jud. 4:16 A[b]
1 Sa. 14:25
2 Sa. 18: 6, 6
8, 17
1 Ki. 7:39
10:17, 21
2 Ki. 2:24
19:23
1 Ch. 16:33
2 Ch. 9:16, 20
27: 4
Psa. 28: 9
49:10[c]
73: 5
79:14
82:15
95:12
103:20
131: 6
Ecc. 2: 6
Cant. 2: 3
Isa. 7: 2
9:18
10:18
14: 8 S[1 d]
21:13
27: 9
29:17
32:15, 19
37:24
44:14
56: 9
65:10
Jer. 5: 6
10: 3
12: 8
21:14
23:10 B[e]
26:23
27:32
33:18
Eze. 15: 2, 6
20:46, 47
34:25
Eze. 39:10
Hos. 13: 8
Amos 3: 4
Mic. 3:12
Mic. 5: 8
7:14
Zec. 11: 2

[a] pro ἀγρός. [b] pro Ἀρισώθ.
[c] AS[2] ἀγρός. [d] pro Λιβανος.
[e] pro δρόμος.

δρῦς.

Gen. 12: 6
13:18
14:13
18: 1
Deu. 11:30
Jud. 4:11
6:11 A[a]
19 A[a]
9:37+A
1 Sa. 10: 3
1 Sa. 17:19 A
2 Sa. 18: 9, 9
10, 14
1 Ki. 13:14
1 Ch. 10:12
Jer. 2:34
Eze. 6:13+A
Hos. 4:13
Amos 2: 9
Zec. 11: 2

[a] pro τερέμινθος.

δύναμαι.

Gen. 13: 6 A[a]
16
15: 5
19:19, 22
24:50
29: 8
30: 8
31:35
32:25
34:14
36: 7
37: 4
41:49
43:31
44: 1, 22
26, 26
45: 1, 3
48:10
Exo. 2: 3
4:13
7:18, 21
24
8:18
9:11
10: 5
12:39
15:23
18:18—A
23
19:23
33:20
40:29
Lev. 26:37
Nu. 9: 6
11:14
13:31, 32
14:16
22: 6, 11
18, 37
24:13
Deu. 1: 9, 12
7:17, 22
9:28
12:17
14:23
16: 5
17:15
21:16
22: 3, 19
29
24: 6
28:27, 35
31: 2
Jos. 7:12, 13
9:25
15:63
17:12
24:19
Jud. 1:19, 32
2:14
8: 3
11:35
14:13, 14
16: 5
18: 7+A
21:18
Ruth 4: 6, 6
1 Sa. 3: 2
6:20
10:26 A[b]
17: 9, 9, 33
39
26:25, 25
2 Sa. 3:11
12:23
17:17[c]
1 Ki. 3: 9
5: 3
8:11, 64
10:p 22
13: 4, 16
21: 9
22:22
2 Ki. 3:26
4:40
16: 5
18:23, 29
1 Ch. 21:30
2 Ch. 5:14
7: 2
18:21
20:37
29:34
30: 3, 17
32:13, 13
14, 14
15
Ezra 2:59
Neh. 4: 2—ABS
10
6: 3
7:61
Est. 6:13
8: 6, 6
Job 4:20
6: 7
7:20
10:13, 15
16:14[d]
20:14
30:24
32: 3
33: 5, 20
35: 6, 14
40: 9
42: 2
Psa. 17:39
20:12
35:13
39:13
77:19, 20
128: 2
138: 6
Pro. 17:16
24:56
73
26:15
Ecc. 1: 8, 15
15
6:10
7:14
8:17, 17
Cant. 7: 6 S[e]
8: 7
Isa. 7: 1
8: 8
11: 9
16:12
20: 6
24:20
28:20
29:11
36: 8, 9
14, 19
44:20
46: 2
47:11, 12
56:10
57:20
59:14
60:20 S[1 f]
Jer. 1:19
2:13
3: 5
5: 4, 22
6:10
11:11
13:23
14: 9
15:20
18: 6
19:11
20: 7, 9
10, 11
Jer. 29:11
30:12
43: 5
45: 5, 22
51:22
Lam. 1:14
4:14
Eze. 7:19+A
33:12
47: 5
Dan. 2:10, 26
47
3:29
4:15, 15
34
5: 8, 15
16, 16
6:20
10:17
Hos. 5:13
8: 5
9: 4 A[e]
11: 4
12: 4
Amos 7:10[g]
Obad. 7
Jon. 1:13
Hab. 1:13 AS[3 h]
Zeph. 1:18

[a] pro χωρέω. [b] pro δύναμις.
[c] A ἐνδύω. [d] A δυνατός.
[e] pro ἡδύνω. [f] pro δύνω.
[g] A γίνομαι. [h] οὐ δ. pro ὀδύνῃ

δύναμις.

Gen. 21:22, 32
26:26
Exo. 6:26
7: 4
9:16 A[a]
12:17, 41
51
14:28
15: 4
Nu. 1: 3, 3, 20
22, 24
26, 28
30, 32
34, 36
38, 40
42, 45
52
2: 3, 4, 6
8, 9, 10
11, 13
15, 16
18, 19
21, 23
24, 25
26, 28
30
31+A
32
6:21
10:14, 14
15, 16
18:18
19, 20
22, 22
23, 24
25, 25
26, 27
28
31: 6, 9, 14
21, 48
33: 1
Deu. 3:24
6: 5
8:17, 18
11: 4, 4—A
16:17
Jos. 4:24
5:14
6:17 A[b]
Jud. 3:29
4: 2, 7
5:31[c]
6:12[d]
Jud. 8: 6[e], 21
9:29
11: 1[d]
18: 2
20:44[f], 46[f]
21:10
Ru. 3:11 | 4:11
1 Sa. 2: 4, 10
4: 4+A
10:26[g]
14:48, 52
17:20 A
55 A
18:17 A
31:12
2 Sa. 6: 2, 18
19
8: 9
10: 7, 16
18
11:16
13:28
17:10, 10
25
19:13
20:23
22:33, 40
23:36 A[h]
24: 4, 9
1 Ki. 1:19, 25
42, 52
2: 5
4: 4[c]
10: 2
11:15 A[i]
28
15:20
17: 1
18:15
21: 1, 15
19, 25
25, 28
2 Ki. 2:16
3:14
4:13
5: 1
6:14, 15
7: 6
9: 5, 16
11:15
17:16
18:17, 20
19:20, 31
2 Ki. 21: 3, 5
23: 4, 5
24:16
25: 1, 5, 5
10—B[k]
19, 23
26
1 Ch. 5:18, 24
7: 2, 5, 7
9, 11
11, 40
8:40 9:13
11:26
12:18
21—A
22, 22
13: 8
18: 9
19:16, 18
20: 1
21: 2
25: 1
26:26
27: 3, 4
29: 2, 11
2 Ch. 9: 1
13: 3 ter
14: 8, 8, 9
13
16: 4, 7, 8
17: 2, 14
16, 17
18:18
20:21—A
22: 9
23:14
24:23, 24
24
25: 7, 9
10, 13
26:11, 13
13, 14
28: 9
33:11[c], 14
34: 8 A[m]
36: 4
Ezra 2:69
4:23
8:22
10:13
Neh. 1:10
2: 9
4: 2
5: 5
11: 6
Est. 2:18
8:11+S[3]
Job 11: 6
20+A
12:13
26: 3
28:11
37:13
39:19
40: 5, 11
41: 3, 13
Psa. 17:33, 40
20: 2, 14
23:10
29: 8
32: 6, 16
17
43:10
45: 2, 8, 12
47: 9, 14
48: 7
53: 3
58: 6, 12
17
59:12, 14
62: 3
65: 3
67:12, 13
20, 34
35, 36
68: 7
73:13[n]
76:15
79: 5, 8
Psa. 79:15, 20
83: 2, 4, 9
8, 9, 13
88: 9, 11
18
92: 1
102:21
107:12, 14
109: 2, 3
117:15
16—S[1]
121: 7
135:15
137: 3
139: 8
144: 4, 6
12 A[o]
148: 2
150: 1
Pro. 29:47[p]
Ecc. 9:10, 16
10:10, 17
12: 3
Cant. 2: 7
3: 5
5: 8
8: 4+ABS
Isa. 8: 4, 7 S[q]
34: 4—AS
36: 2
3+S[3]
22
42:13
60:11
Jer. 3:23
6: 6
16:21
26: 2
28: 3
39: 2—S[1]
40:12—A[l]
41: 7, 21
42:11
11—AS[l]
44: 5, 7, 10
11, 11
45: 3
46: 1
47: 7
7+A
13
48:11, 13
16
49: 1, 8
50: 4, 5
52: 4, 8
14, 25
Eze. 17:17
26:12
27:10, 11
18, 27
28: 4, 5, 5
29:18, 18
19
32:23
31+A
38: 4, 15
Dan. 2:23
4:32
8: 9, 10
10, 13
10: 1
11: 7, 10 A[r]
13, 25
25, 26
31 A[o]
Hos. 10:13
Joel 2:11, 25
Amos 6:14—A
Obad. 11, 13
Hab. 3:19
Zeph. 1:13
2: 9
Hag. 2:22—S[1]
22+A
Zec. 1: 3[s], 3[t]
4: 6
7: 4
9: 4

[a] pro ἰσχύς. [b] pro Σαβαώθ.

[c] A δυναστεία. [d] A ἰσχύς.
[e] A στρατεία. [f] A δυνατός.
[g] A δύναμαι.
[h] πολλὺς δ. pro πολυδυνάμεως.
[i] pro στρατιά. [k] A εὐπορία.
[m] pro πόλις. [n] S[1] δυναστεία.
[o] pro δυναστεία.
[p] AB[1]S[1] δυνατός. [q] pro δόξα.
[r] pro ἀνὰ μέσος. [s] S[1] παντοκράτωρ. [t] A παντοκράτωρ.

δυναμόω.

Psa. 51:9 B[1]S[1] [a]
67:29
Ecc. 10:10
Dan. 9:27
27+AB[2]

[a] pro ἐνδυναμόω.

δυναστεία.

Exo. 6: 6
Jud. 5:31 A[a]
1 Ki. 15:23
16: 5, 27
p 28—A
22:46
2 Ki. 10:34
13: 8, 12
14:15, 28
20:20
1 Ch. 29:12, 30
2 Ch. 20: 6
33:11 A[a]
Job 37: 5
Psa. 19: 7
20:14
64: 7
65: 7
70:16, 18
73:13 S[1] [a]
Psa. 77: 4, 26
79: 3
88:14
89:10
102:22[b]
105: 2, 8
144: 6+ ABS[1]
11, 12[c]
146:10
150: 2
Pro. 18:18[d]
Jer. 25:14
28:30
Eze. 22:25
Dan. 11:31[e]
Amos 2:16
Mic. 3: 8
Nah. 2: 4

[a] pro δύναμις. [b] AS[2] δεσποτία.
[c] A δύναμις. [d] AC δυνάστης.

δυναστεύμα.

1 Kings (3) p 46

δυναστεύω.

2 Ki. 10:13
1 Ch. 16:21
Pro. 19:10
Jer. 13:18
Eze. 22:25+A

δυνάστης.

Gen. 49:24
50: 4
Lev. 19:15
Jud. 5: 9 A[a]
1 Sa. 2: 8
1 Ch. 28: 1
29:24
2 Ch. 23:20
Job 5:15
6:23
9:22
12:19
13:15
15: 5, 20
27:13
29:12
36:22
Psa. 71:12
Pro. 1:21
8: 3, 15
14:28
17:26
18:16
18 AC[b]
23: 1
24:72
25: 6, 7
Isa. 5:22
Jer. 41:19
Dan. 3:27
Amos 6: 7
Nah. 3:18
Hab. 3:14

[a] pro ἑκουσιάζομαι.
[b] pro δυναστεία.

δυνατέω.

2 Ch. 14:11 A[a] [a] pro ἀδυνατέω.

δυνατός.

Gen. 26:16
32:28
47: 5
Exo. 8:26
17: 9—A
18:21, 25
Nu. 13:31
22:38
Deu. 1:28
2:21
3:18
Jos. 6: 2
8: 3
10: 7
Jud. 5: 3+A
7[a]
14+A
21
22 A[b]
23
6:12 A[b]
11: 1 A[c]
Jud. 18:26[d]
20:44 A[e]
46 A[e]
Ruth 2: 1
1 Sa. 2: 4, 9, 10
9: 1
14:52
17: 4, 51
2 Sa. 1:19, 21
22, 25
27
2: 7
10: 7
16: 6
17: 8, 10
20: 7
23: 8, 9
16, 17
22, 23
1 Ki. 1: 8, 10
2 Ki. 5: 1
9:16
15:20
24:14, 16
1 Ch. 5: 2
9:26
10:12
11:10, 11
12, 19
22, 24
26
12: 1, 4, 8
21, 24
25, 28
30
19: 8
24: 4
26: 6, 7, 9
12, 30
31, 32
27: 6
2 Ch. 8: 9
13: 3, 3, 17
17: 7, 13
2 Ch. 17:14, 16
17, 18
25: 5, 6
26:12, 17
28: 6, 7
32: 3, 21
35: 3
Neh. 11:14
Est. 9:16+S[1]
Job 16:14 A[f]
20:19[g]
36: 5
Psa. 17:18
21+ABS
23: 8, 8
44: 4, 6
51: 3
77:65
88: 9, 20
102:20
111: 2
119: 4
126: 4
Pro. 3:28
29:47 AB[1]S[1] [e]
Ecc. 9:11
Cant. 3: 7, 7
4: 4
Isa. 8: 8
Jer. 30:19
48:16
50: 6
51:20
Eze. 3: 8
20: 6 B[a] [h]
Dan. 3:17
11: 3
Joel 3:10 S[1] [i]
Mic. 4: 7[d]
Nah. 2: 4
Zeph. 1:15
3:17
Mal. 1:14

[a] A φράζω. [b] pro ἰσχυρός.
[c] pro ἐπαίρω. [d] A ἰσχυρός.
[e] pro δύναμις. [f] pro δύναμαι.
[g] AOS[2] ἀδυνατός. [h] pro κηρίον.
[i] pro ἀδυνατός.

δυνατῶς.

1 Chronicles 26: 8

δύνω, δύω.

Gen. 28:11
Exo. 15:10
Lev. 22: 7
Deu. 23:11
Jud. 14:18 A[a]
19:14
2 Sa. 2:24
3:35
1 Ki. 22:36
2 Ch. 18:34
Job 2: 9
Pro. 11: 8 A[b]
Ecc. 1: 5
Isa. 29: 4
60:20[c]
Joel 2:10
3:15
Amos 8: 9
Jon. 2: 6
Mic. 3: 6

[a] pro ἀνατέλλω. [b] pro ἐκδύνω.
[c] B[1]S[1] δύναμαι.

δύο.

Gen. 31:41—A[1]
Exo. 26:19-AB[1]
21—B
27: 7+A
28:12—B
34:28+A
29—A
36:25+A
38: 1+A
Lev. 10: 1—A
12: 6+A
Deu. 9:15—A
17—A
10: 3+A
25:11+A
Jos. 2: 4—A
9:16+A
13: 8—B
Jos. 19:30+A
Jud. 7:25+A
11: 2+A
16:25+A
19: 6—A
9—A
Ruth 1: 1—B
8—B
2 Sa. 8: 2—A
5—A
23:20—A
1 Ki. 6(32) A
20:11—B
21:15+A
2 Ki. 5:23—AB
9:32[a]
15:23[b]
21: 5[c], 19[d]
1 Ch. 26:17+A
Neh. 7:34-BS[e]
71-AB[f]
Job 9:33+A
42: 7—B
Eze. 4: 5+AB
Eze. 40: 9[b]
30+A
39+A
42: 6—A
Zec. 1: 8+A

[a] A τρεῖς. [b] A δέκα.
[c] A πᾶς. [d] A[2] δωδέκα.
[e] A τέσσαρες. [f] S[1] ἑβδομήκοντα.

δυσβάστακτος.

Proverbs 27: 3

δύσις.

Psalm 103:19

δυσκολία.

Job 34:30

δύσκολος.

Jeremiah 29: 9

δύσκωφος.

Exodus 4:11

δυσμή.

Gen. 15:12, 17
Exo. 17:12
22:26
Nu. 22: 1
33:48, 49
50
35: 1
36:12
Deu. 1: 1
11:24, 30
30
16: 6
24:15
Jos. 1: 4
5:10
10:13, 27
11:16
13: 7
15: 3
23: 4
Jud. 20:33+A
2 Sa. 2:20
2 Sa. 4: 7
1 Ch. 6:78
7:28
12:15
26:16, 18
18, 30
2 Ch. 4: 4
Psa. 49: 1
67: 5
74: 7
102:12
106: 3
112: 3
Isa. 9:12
43: 5
45: 6
51: 3-AS[3]
59:19
Eze. 27: 9, 9
Amos 6:14
Zec. 8: 7
Mal. 1:11

δυστοκέω.

Genesis 35:16

δύσχρηστος.

Isaiah 3:10

δύω vide δύνω.

δώδεκα.

Nu. 7:84—A
86+A
Jos. 4: 2+A
Jos. 4: 5—A
1 Ki. 2:12+A
10:20—A

δωδεκάμηνος.

Daniel 4:26

δωδέκατος.

2 Ch. 34: 3[a]
Est. 2:16[b]
Est. 8:12—AS
Eze. 29: 1[a]

[a] A δέκατος. [b] S[3] δέκατος.

δῶμα.

Deu. 22: 8
Jos. 2: 6, 6, 8
Jud. 9:51
16:27
1 Sa. 9:25, 26
2 Sa. 11: 2, 2
16:22
18:24
2 Ki. 19:26
23:12
2 Ch. 28: 4
Neh. 8:16
Ps. 101: 8
128: 6
Pro. 25:24
Isa. 15: 3
Isa. 22: 1
37:27
Jer. 19:13
31:38
Jer. 39:29
Zeph. 1: 5[a]
Mal. 1: 3[b]

[a] S εἴδωλον. [b] ABS δόμα.

δωρεά.

Dan. 2: 6
Dan. 5:17

δωρεάν.

Gen. 29:15
Exo. 21: 2, 11
Nu. 11: 5
1 Sa. 19: 5
25:31
2 Sa. 24:24
1 Ki. 2:31
1 Ch. 21:24
Job 1: 9
Psa. 34: 7, 19
Psa. 68: 5
108: 3
118:161
119: 7
Isa. 52: 3, 5
Jer. 22:13
Lam. 3:51
Eze. 6:10+A
Mal. 1:10

δωρέω.

Gen. 30:20
Lev. 7: 5
Est. 8: 1
Pro. 4: 2

δωροδέκτης.

Job 15:34

δωρολήπτης.

Proverbs 15:27

δῶρον.

Gen. 4: 4
24:53
30:20
32:13, 18
20, 21
33:10
43:10, 14
24, 25
Exo. 23: 7, 8, 8
Lev. 1: 2, 2, 3
10, 14
14
2: 1, 1, 4, 4
5, 7, 12
13, 13
3: 1, 2, 6
7, 8, 12
4:23, 32
5:11
6:20
7: 3, 4, 6
19, 28
9: 7, 15
17: 4
21: 6, 8, 17
21, 22
22:18, 25
27
23:14
27: 9, 11
Nu. 5:15
6:14, 21
7: 3, 10
11, 12
13, 17
19, 23
25, 29
31, 35
37, 41
43, 47
49, 53
55, 59
61, 65
67, 71
73, 77
79, 83
9: 7, 13
15: 4, 25
18: 9
28: 2, 24
31:50
Deu. 10:17
12:11
Deu. 16:19, 19
27:25
Jud. 3:15, 17
18, 18
5:19[a]
9:31 A[b]
1 Sa. 8: 3
10:27
1 Ki. (3) p 46
4(21) A
8:64+A
64+A
10:25
15:19
2 Ki. 8: 9+B
16: 8
1 Ch. 16:29
18: 2, 6
2 Ch. 9:24
17: 5, 11
19: 7
26: 8
32:23
Neh. 13:31
Job 8:20
20: 6
31: 7
36:18
Psa. 14: 5
25:10
44:13
67:30
71:10, 10
75:12
Pro. 4: 2
6:35
15:27
17:23
21:14
22: 9
Isa. 1:23
5:23
8:20
18: 7
33:15
39: 1
45:13
60: 7+S[1]
66:20
Jer. 28:59
40:11
47: 5
Eze. 20:39

Eze. 22:12
23+A
Dan. 11:39
Hos. 8: 9
Amos 5:11
Mic. 3:11
[a] A πλεονεξία. [b] pro κρυφῆ.

ἔα.

Job 25: 6

ἔαρ.

Gen. 8:22
Nu. 13:21
Psa. 73:17
Zec. 14: 8

ἐάω.

Gen. 38:16
Exo. 32:10
Deu. 9:14
Jos. 19:47
Jud. 11:37
2 Sa. 15:34
1 Ki. 12:30—AB
Est. 3: 8
Job 7:19
9:18, 28
10:14 A[a]
20
31:34
Dan. 4:12, 20
23
[a] pro ποιέω.

ἑβδομάς.

Exo. 34:22
Lev. 23:15, 16[a]
25: 8
Nu. 28:26
Deu. 16: 9, 9
10, 16
2 Ch. 8:13
Dan. 9:24, 25
25, 26
27, 27
27+AB[2]
27+AB[2]
10: 2, 3
[a] AB[2] ἕβδομος.

ἑβδομήκοντα.

1 Ch. 21: 5—B[a] Ezra 8:14[b]
[a] A ὀγδοήκοντα. [b] B ὀγδοήκ-.

ἑβδομηκοστός.

1 Kings 8: 2+A

ἕβδομος.

Exo. 31:15[a]
1 Ki. 8: 2+A
16:10+A
15+A
1 Ch. 26: 5—B
Neh. 8: 1+S[1]
Jer. 52:31[b]
[a] A σάββατον. [b] S ἑπτά.

Ἑβραῖος.

Gen. 39:14, 17
40:15
41:12
43:31
Exo. 1:15, 16
19
2: 6, 7
11, 13
3:18
5: 3
Exo. 7:16
9: 1, 13
10: 3
21: 2
Deu. 15:12, 12
1 Sa. 4: 6, 9
13:19
14:11
17: 8
Jer. 41: 9, 9, 14

ἐγγαστρίμυθος.

Lev. 19:31
20: 6, 27
Deu. 18:11
1 Sa. 28: 3, 7, 7
8, 9
1 Ch. 10:13
2 Ch. 33: 6
35:19
Isa. 8:19
19: 3
44:25

ἐγγελάω.

Psa. 2: 4 A[a] [a] pro ἐκγελάω.

ἐγγίζω.

Gen. 12:11
18:23
19: 9
27:21, 22
26, 27
41
33: 3
35:16
37:18
44:18
45: 4—A
Gen. 45: 4—A
47:29
48: 7, 10
13
Exo. 3: 5
19:21, 22
24: 2, 2
32:19
34:30
Lev. 10: 3
21: 3, 3 A[a]
Lev. 21:21[b], 23
25:25
Nu. 24:17
Deu. 4: 7
13: 7
15: 9
20: 2
21: 3, 6
22: 2, 2 B[c]
25: 5
31:14
Jud. 9:52
19:13[d]
20:23[e]
Ruth 2:20
1 Sa. 17:41 A
48+A
2 Sa. 11:20[f]
15: 5
18:25
19:42
20:16
17 A[g]
1 Ki. 2: 1, 7
8: 59
20: 2
2 Ki. 2: 5
4: 6, 27
5:13
2 Ch. 18:23[h]
Ezra 4: 2
9: 1
Job 19:21+A
33:22
Psa. 26: 2
31: 6, 9
37:12
54:19, 22
68: 4 B[i]
87: 4
90: 7, 10
106:18
118:169 AS[k]
148:14
Pro. 3:15
5: 8
Pro. 10:14
19: 7
Ecc. 4:17 S[2 m]
Isa. 5: 8, 19
8:15
26:17
29:13
30:20
33:13
38:12
41: 1, 5, 21
21, 22
45:21
46:13
50: 8, 8
51: 5
54:14
55: 6
56: 1
58: 2
65: 5
Jer. 23:23
28: 9
Lam. 3:56—A
4:19
Eze. 7: 7
9: 1, 6
12:23
22: 4, 5
23: 5
40:46
42:13
43:19
44:13
45: 4
Dan. 6:20
Hos. 12: 6
Amos 6: 3
9:10
Jon. 3: 6
Mic. 2: 9
4:10—A
Hab. 3: 2
Zeph. 3: 2
Hag. 2:14
[a] pro ἐκδίδωμι. [b] AB προσεγγίζω. [c] pro ἐπίσταμαι. [d] A ἔρχομαι. [e] A προσεγγίζω. [f] A ἐργάζομαι. [g] pro προσεγγίζω. [h] A ποιέω. [i] pro ἐλπίζω. [k] pro (ἐγγυσάτω). [m] pro ἐγγύς.

ἐγγίνομαι.

Hos. 7: 6[a] [a] A γίνομαι.

ἐγγίων

Ruth 3:12
Neh. 13: 4—S[1]

ἐγγλύφω.

Exo. 36:21[a] Job 19:24
[a] B ἐγγράφω.

ἔγγονος.

Deu. 7:13[a]
2 Sa. 21:18[a]
Pro. 23:18 A[b]
Isa. 14:29 A[b]
30: 6 S[b]
Isa. 48:19 S[b]
49:15 S[b]
61: 9 S[b]
65:23 S[b]
[a] AB ἔκγονος. [b] pro ἔκγονος.

ἔγγραπτος.

Psalm 149: 9

ἐγγράφω.

Exo. 36:21 B[a]
1 Ki. 22:46 B[b]
2 Ch. 34:31 A[b]
Jer. 17:13 S[3 b]
[a] pro ἐγγλύφω. [b] pro γράφω.

ἐγγυάω.

Pro. 6: 1
17:18, 18
Pro. 19:28
28:17

ἐγγύη.

Proverbs 22:26

ἐγγύθεν.

Jos. 6:13—A
9:22
Eze. 7: 8

ἐγγύς, -ύτατος, ἔγγιστα.

Gen. 19:20
45:10
Exo. 13:17
32:27
Lev. 21: 2
25:25+AB
Nu. 27:11
Deu. 2:19, 37[a]
4:46
30:14
32:35
34: 6
Jud. 3:20
1 Ki. 8:46
20: 2 AB[b]
2 Ch. 6:36
Est. 1:14
9:20
Job 6:15
13:18
17:12
19:14
Psa. 14: 3
21:11
Psa. 33:10
37:12
84:10
118:151
141:18
Pro. 27:10
Ecc. 4:17[c]
Isa. 13: 6
57:19
Jer. 12: 2
31:16, 24
32:12
42: 4
Eze. 6:12
23:12
30: 3
Dan. 9: 7
Joel 1:15
2: 1
3:14
Obad. 15
Zeph. 1: 7, 14
14
[a] A εἰς γῆ. [b] pro ἐγγίζω. [c] S[2] ἐγγίζω.

ἐγείρω.

Gen. 41: 4, 7
49: 9
Exo. 5: 8[a]
23: 5 A[b]
Jud. 2:16, 18
3: 9, 15
7:19[c], 19
16:14 A[d]
1 Sa. 2: 8
5: 3
2 Sa. 12:17
18:31 A[e]
1 Ki. 11:14
23 A
2 Ki. 4:31
1 Ch. 10:12
22:19
2 Ch. 21: 9
22:10
Ps. 107: 3 S[1 f]
112: 7
126: 2
Pro. 6: 9, 22
10:12
11:16
15: 1, 18
Pro. 17:11
21:14
28: 2
29:22[g]
23 S[2 h]
Ecc. 4:10, 10
Cant. 2: 7
3: 5
8: 4
Isa. 5:11
10:26[i]
14: 9
26:19
41:25
45:13
Jer. 6:22 B[f]
27: 9
28:11, 12
Eze. 21:28
38:14[k]
Dan. 4:10+A
10:10
12: 2 A[f]
Joel 3:12 A[f]
Mic. 3: 5
[a] A πορεύω. [b] pro συναίρω. [c] A ἔγερσις. [d] pro ἐξυπνίζω. [e] pro ἐπεγείρω. [f] pro ἐξεγείρω. [g] AS ὀρύσσω. [h] pro ἐρείδω. [i] AS ἐπεγείρω. [k] A ἐξεγείρω.

ἔγερσις.

Jud. 7:19 A[a] Psa. 138: 2
[a] pro ἐγείρω.

ἐγκάθετος.

Job 19:12
Job 31: 9

ἐγκάθημαι.

Gen. 49:17
Exo. 23:31, 33
34:12, 15
Lev. 18:25[a]
Nu. 13:19, 20
14:45
Nu. 22: 5, 11
Deu. 1:46, 46
2:10, 12
3:29
Jud. 2: 2
1 Ki. 11:16[b]
Psa. 9:29
Isa. 8:14
Isa. 9: 9 AS[2 c]
Eze. 29: 3
[a] A ἐγκαταλείπω. [b] A κάθημαι. [c] pro κάθημαι.

ἐγκαθίζω.

Jos. 8: 9
1 Ki. 20:10[a]
Eze. 35: 5
[a] A καθίζω.

ἐγκαίνια.

Ezra 6:16, 17
Neh. 12:27, 27
Dan. 3: 2[a]
[a] A ἐγκαινισμός.

ἐγκαινίζω.

Deu. 20: 5, 5
1 Sa. 11:14
1 Ki. 8:63
2 Ch. 7: 5
15: 8[a]
Psa. 50:12
Isa. 16:11[b]
41: 1
45:16
[a] B ἀνακαινίζω. [b] AS ἐγκεν-

ἐγκαίνισις.

Nu. 7:88 A[a] [a] pro ἐγκαίνωσις.

ἐγκαινισμός.

Nu. 7:10, 11
84
2 Ch. 7: 9
Psa. 29: 1
Dan. 3: 2 A[a], 3
[a] pro ἐγκαίνια.

ἐγκαλέω.

Exo. 22: 9
Pro. 19: 5
Zec. 1: 4

ἐγκαλύπτω.

Pro. 26:26 B[a] [a] pro ἐκκαλύπτω.

ἔγκαρπος.

Jeremiah 38:12

ἔγκατα, -τον.

Gen. 43:29[a]
1 Ki. 17:22+A
Job 21:24
Psa. 50:12
108:18
[a] A ἔντερον.

ἐγκατακρύπτω.

Amos 9: 3[a] [a] A ἐγκρύπτω.

ἐγκατάλειμμα.

Deu. 28: 5, 17
Ezra 9:14
Psa. 36:37, 38
Psa. 75:11
Jer. 11:23

ἐγκαταλείπω.

Gen. 24:27
28:15
Lev. 18:25 A[a]
26:43
Nu. 10:31
Deu. 4:31
12:19
28:20
31: 6, 8
16 A[b]
32:15, 18
Jos. 1: 5
22: 3
24:20
Jud. 2:12, 13
20
10: 6, 10
13
Ruth 2:20
1 Sa. 8: 8
12:10
1 Ki. 6(13) A
8:57
9: 9
11:33[c]
12: 8, 13
14:10 A
1 Ki. 19:10, 14
20:21
2 Ki. 2: 2[a], 4, 6
4:30
7: 7
8: 6 A[b]
9: 8
14:26
17:16
21:22
22:17
1 Ch. 14:12
28:20
2 Ch. 7:19, 22
10:13
11:14
12: 1, 5, 5
13:10, 11
15: 2[d], 2
21:10
24:18, 20
20, 24
25
29: 6
32:31
34:25
Ezra 8:22

Ezra 9: 9, 10
15 S[3b]
Neh. 5:10
9:17, 19
28, 31
10:39
13:11
Job 20:13
Psa. 9:11, 35
15:10
21: 2
26: 9[c]
9 S[2f]
10
36: 8, 25
28, 33
37:11, 22
39:13
70: 9, 11
18
88:31
93:14
118: 8, 87
139: 9
Pro. 2:13
4: 2, 6
24:14
27:10
28: 4
Isa. 1: 4, 8, 9
28
6:12[g]
16: 8
17: 9
9 AS[b]
10 A[b]
24:12
Isa. 32:14
41: 9, 17
42:16
49:14
54: 7 B[b]
58: 2
60:15
62:12[h]
65:11
Jer. 1:16
2:13
4:29
5: 7
9:13, 19
12: 7
14: 5
16:11, 11
17:11, 13
19: 4
22: 9
28: 9
30:14
32:24[i]
Eze. 8:12
9: 9
20: 8
23: 8
24:21
36: 4[i]
Hos. 4 10
5: 7
11: 9
Jon. 2: 9
Mal. 2:10, 11
14, 15
16

[a] pro ἐγκάθημαι. [b] pro καταλείπω. [c] AB καταλείπω. [d] B καταλείπω. [e] B[2]S[2] ἀποσκορακίζω. [f] pro ὑπερεῖδον. [g] ABS καταλείπω. [h] S καταλείπω. [i] A καταλείπω.

ἐγκαταλιμπάνω.
Psalm 118:53

ἐγκαταλοχίζω.
2 Ch. 31:18[a]
[a] A καταλοχία.

ἐγκαταπαίζω.
Job 40:14 | Job 41:24

ἐγκαυχάομαι.
Psa. 51: 3
73: 4
Psa. 96: 7
105:47

ἔγκειμαι.
Gen. 8:21
34:19
Est. 9: 3

ἐγκισσάω.
Gen. 30:38
39 – A
Gen. 30:41, 41
31:10

ἐγκλείω.
Ezekiel 3:24

ἔγκληρος.
Deuteronomy 4:20

ἐγκλοιόω.
Proverbs 6:21

ἐγκοίλια.
Leviticus 1: 9, 13

ἔγκοιλος.
Leviticus 13:30, 31

ἐγκόλαμμα.
Exodus 36:13

ἐγκολαπτός.
1 Ki. 6:27[a] | 1 Ki. 6(32) A
[a] B ἐκκολαπτός.

ἐγκολάπτω.
1 Ki. 6(32) A | 1 Ki. 6:32[a]
[a] A εἰσκολ- B ἐκκολ-

ἐγκολλάω.
Zechariah 14:5

ἔγκοπος.
Job 19: 2
Ecc. 1: 8
Isa. 43:23

ἐγκοτέω.
Gen. 27:41 | Psa. 54: 4

ἐγκότημα.
Jeremiah 31:39

ἐγκρατεύομαι.
Gen. 43:30
1 Sa. 13:12
Est. 5:10 + S[3]

ἐγκρατέω.
Exodus 9: 2

ἐγκρίς.
Exo. 16:31 | Nu. 11: 8

ἐγκρούω.
Judges 16:13

ἐγκρύπτω.
Jos. 7:21, 22 B[a]
Pro. 19:24[b]
Eze. 4:12[c]
Hos. 13:12
Amos 9: 3 A[d]

[a] pro κρύπτω. [b] O ἐκκρύπτω. [c] A κατακρύπτω. [d] pro ἐγκατακρύπτω.

ἐγκρυφίας.
Gen. 18: 6
Exo. 12:39
Nu. 11: 8
1 Ki. 17:12, 13
1 Ki. 19: 6
Eze. 4:12
Hos. 7: 8

ἐγκτάομαι.
Genesis 34:10

ἔγκτημα.
Nu. 31: 9 A[a]
[a] pro ἔγκτητος.

ἔγκτησις.
Lev. 25:13[a]
16, 16[a]
2 Ki. 4:13 B[b]

[a] AB* κτῆσις. [b] pro ἔκστασις.

ἔγκτητος.
Lev. 14:34
22:11
Nu. 31: 9[a]
[a] A ἔγκτημα.

ἐγκυλίω.
Proverbs 7:18

ἐγκύπτω.
1 Ki. 6:27 + A | Cant. 6: 9 A[a]*
[a] pro ἐκκύπτω.

ἐγκωμιάζω.
Pro. 12: 8
27: 2, 21
Pro. 28: 4
29: 2

ἐγκώμιον.
Est. 2:23 | Pro. 10: 7

ἐγρήγορος.
Lamentations 4:14

ἐγχειρέω.
Jer. 28:12 ABS[a] | Jer. 29:17
[a] pro ἐγχειρίζω.

ἐγχείρημα.
Jer. 23:20 | Jer. 37:24

ἐγχειρίδιος.
Exo. 20:25
Jer. 27:42
Eze. 21: 3, 4, 5

ἐγχειρίζω.
2 Ch. 23:18
Jer. 18:22
Jer. 28:12[a]
[a] ABS ἐγχειρέω.

ἐγχέω.
Exo. 24: 6
Jud. 6:19 A[a]
2 Ki. 4:40, 41
Jer. 31:11
Eze. 24: 3[b]

[a] pro βάλλω. [b] A ἐκχέω.

ἐγχρίω.
Jeremiah 4:30

ἐγχρονίζω.
Pro. 9:18 A[a]
10:28
Pro. 23:30
[a] pro χρονίζω.

ἐγχώριος.
Gen. 34: 1
Exo. 12:49
Lev. 18:26
Lev. 24:22
Nu. 15:29
Jos. 9:28

ἐδαφίζω.
Ps. 136: 9
Isa. 3:26
Eze. 31:12
Hos. 10:14
14: a1
Nah. 3:10

ἔδαφος.
Nu. 5:17
1 Ki. 6:15, 16
28
7:44 + A
44 + A
Job 9: 8
Ps. 118:25
Isa. 25:12
26: 5
29: 4
Jer. 38:37
Eze. 41:16, 16
20
Dan. 6:24

ἔδεσμα.
Gen. 27: 4, 7, 9
14, 17
31
1 Sa. 15: 9
Psa. 54:15
Pro. 23: 3, 6 C[a]
Dan. 6:18
[a] pro βρῶμα.

ἔδομαι vide ἐσθίω.

ἕδρα.
Deu. 28:27
1 Sa. 5: 3, 6 A[a]
9, 9, 12
6: 4
1 Sa. 6: 5 + A
11 + A
17 – A
[a] pro ναῦς.

ἑδράζω.
1 Ki. (3) p 16 + A
Psa. 89: 2 S[1a]
Pro. 8:25
[a] pro γίνομαι.

ἕδρασμα.
1 Kings 8:13 A

ἔδω vide ἐσθίω.

ἐθέλω vide θέλω.

ἐθισμός.
Gen. 31:35 | 1 Ki. 18:28 – B[a]
[a] A κρῖμα.

ἔθνος.
Gen. 10: 5, 5, 20
31, 32
32
12: 2
14: 1, 5, 9
15:14
17: 4, 5, 6
16, 16
20, 20
27
18:18, 18
20: 4
21:13, 18
22:18
25:16, 23
26: 4
27:29
28: 3
35:11, 11
36:40
46: 3
48: 4, 19
49:10
Exo. 1: 9
9 A[a]
9:24
15:14
19: 5, 6
21: 8
23:11, 18
22, 22
27
32:10
33:13, 16
34:10, 24
Lev. 18:24, 28
19:16
20: 2, 23
24, 26
21: 1
25:44
26:33, 38
45
Nu. 13:29, 32
14:12, 15
21:18
23: 9
24: 7, 8, 20
25:15
Deu. 1:28
2:10, 21
25
4: 6, 6, 7
8, 19
27, 27
33, 34
34, 38
6:14
7: 1, 1, 6
7, 7, 14
16, 17
19, 22
8:20
9: 1, 4
4 + A
5, 14
10:15
11:23, 23
12: 2 A[b]
29, 30
13: 7
14: 2
15: 6, 6
17:14
Deu. 18: 9, 14
19: 1
20:15
26: 5, 19
28: 1, 10
12, 12
32, 33
36, 37
49, 49
50, 64
65
29:16, 18
24
30: 1, 3
31: 3
32: 8, 8, 21
21, 28
42 A[c]
43
33:17, 19
Jos. 4:24
23: 3, 4, 4
7, 9, 12
13
24: 4, 17
18, 33
Jud. 2:12[d], 20
21, 23
3: 1
4: 2, 13
16
1 Sa. 8: 5, 20
2 Sa. 7:23, 23
22:44, 50
1 Ki. 4:27 + A
11: 2
14:24
18:10
2 Ki. 6:18
16: 3
17: 8, 11
15, 26
29, 29
29
29 – AB
32, 32
33, 41
18:33
19:12, 17
21: 2, 9
1 Ch. 14:17
16:20, 20
24 - ABS
26, 28
31, 35
17:21, 21
18:11
29:11
2 Ch. 7:20
15: 6, 6
20: 6
28: 3
32: 7, 13
14, 15
17, 23
33: 2, 9
36:14
Ezra 4:10
6:21
9: 7, 11
Neh. 5: 8
9 - ABS[1]
17
6: 9, 16

Neh. 9:30 S[3][e]
13:26
Est. 1: 3,5,11
3: 8 *ter*
11, 12
14
4: 1, 11
8:17
10: 3
Job 12:23, 23
17: 6
34:29
40:25, 25[f]
Psa. 2: 1, 8
9: 6, 12
16, 18
20, 21
37
17:44, 50
21, 28, 29
32:10, 12
42: 1
43: 3, 12
15–S[1]
45: 7, 11
46: 2, 4, 9
48: 2
56:10
58: 6, 9
64: 8
65: 7, 8
66: 3[g],5,5
67:31
71:11, 17
77:55
78: 1, 6
10, 10
79: 9
81: 8
82: 5
85: 9
88:51
93:10
95: 3–A[i]
5,7,10
97: 2
101:16–S[1]
104: 1, 13
13, 44
105: 5, 27
34, 35
44 S[c]
47
107: 4
109: 6
110: 6
112: 4
113:10, 12
116: 1
117:10
125: 2
134:10, 15
147: 9
149: 7
Pro. 11:26
14:28, 34
24:39, 61
66
28:15, 17
29: 9, 18
Isa. 1: 4
2: 2, 3, 4
4, 4
5:26
8: 9, 10
9: 1
10: 6,7,13
11:10, 10
12
12: 4
13: 4
4–S[1]
4, 4
14: 2,6,6,9
12, 18
26, 32
16: 8
17:12, 12
13
18: 2, 2, 7

Isa. 23: 3
24:13
25: 6, 7, 7
29: 7–S[1]
8
30: 6, 28
33: 3,8,12
34: 1, 2
36:18, 20
37:12, 26
40:15, 17
41: 2,5,28
42: 1, 4, 6
43: 9
45: 1, 20
49: 1, 6, 7
8, 22
51: 4, 5
52: 5, 10
10+S[1]
15
54: 3
55: 4, 4, 5
56: 7
60: 2, 3, 5
11, 12
12, 16
22
61: 6,9,11
62: 2, 10
63: 3
64: 2
65: 1
66: 8, 12
18, 19
19, 20
Jer. 1: 5, 10
2:11
3:17
19 S[h]
19
4: 2,7,16
5: 9, 15
15, 29
6:18, 22
7:28
9:16, 26
10: 2,3,25
12:17
14:22
16:19
18: 7, 8, 9
13
22: 8
25: 9, 11
12, 13
15
26:12
28–ABS
28–S[1]
27: 2, 3, 9
12, 23
41, 46
28: 7, 20
27–S[1]
27, 28
41, 44
49 S[1][i]
58
29:15, 16
30: 9
31: 2
32: 1+A
1,3,17
18, 18
33: 6
34: 6, 9
35:11, 14
38: 7, 10
36
43: 2
51: 8
Lam. 1: 1,3,10
2: 9
4:15, 18
20
Eze. 4:13
5: 5, 6, 7
7,8,15
6: 8, 9

Eze. 7:24+A
11:16, 17
12:15, 16
16:14
19: 4, 8
20: 9, 14
22, 23
32
22:4,15,16
23:30
25: 7, 8
10+A
26: 2, 3, 5
7, 16
27:33, 36
28: 7, 19
25[k], 25
29:12, 13
15, 15
30: 3, 11
23, 26
31: 6, 11
12, 12
16
32: 2,9,10
12, 16
18
34:13, 28
29
35:10
36: 3+A
3,3,4,5
6,7,13
14, 15
15 A[m]
19, 20
21, 22
23, 23
24, 30
36
37:21, 22
22
28–A
38: 6, 8, 8
9, 12
12, 15
16, 22
38:23

Eze. 30: 4,7,21
23, 27
27, 27
28
Dan. 3: 4+A
8:22
11:23
12: 1
Hos. 8: 8, 10
9:17
Joel 1: 6
2:17, 17
19
3: 2, 2, 8
9, 11
12, 12
Amos 6: 1, 14
9: 9, 12
Obad. 1,2,15
16–BS[1]
Mic. 4: 2, 3, 3
3,7,11
5: 7,8,15
7:16
Nah. 3: 3, 4, 5
Hab. 1: 6, 17
2: 5,8,13
3: 6, 12
Zeph. 2: 1,9,11
11
3: 8
Hag. 2: 7,7,14
22
Zec. 1:15
21–A[l]
2: 8, 11
7:14
8:13, 22
23
9:10
12: 3, 3, 9
14: 2,3,16
18, 19
Mal. 1:11, 11
14
2: 9
3: 9 S[1][e]
12

[a] *pro* γένος.
[b] *pro* τόπος.
[c] *pro* ἐχθρός.
[d] A αὐτός.
[e] *pro* ἔτος.
[f] AC γένος.
[g] S[1] λαός.
[h] *pro* τέκνον.
[i] *pro* γῆ.
[k] A χώρα.
[m] *pro* λαός.

ἔθω.

Numbers 24: 1

εἰδέω, εἴδω, εἶδον, οἶδα.

Gen. 1: 4, 8
10, 13
18, 21
25, 31
2: 9, 19
3: 5, 6, 6
6: 2,5,12
7: 1
8: 6+A
8, 13
9:22, 23
11: 5
12:12, 14
15
13:14
16: 4, 5
13, 14
18: 2,2,19
19: 1, 28
33, 35
21:9,16,19
22: 4, 13
14
24:30, 63
64
25:27
26: 8, 28
27: 6

Gen. 28: 6,8,16
29:10, 31
32
30: 1, 9
31: 2,6,10
12, 32
42, 44
32: 1, 2
25, 30
33: 1, 5
10, 10
34: 2
37: 4, 9
14, 25
38:2,14,15
39: 3, 6
13, 14
40: 5, 6, 8
16, 16
41: 1, 11
11, 19
22
42: 1, 7, 9
12, 23
27, 35
43: 6, 15
17, 21
28

Gen. 44:15, 23
26, 28
31, 34
45:13, 27
48: 8, 17
19, 19
49:15
50:11, 15
23
Exo. 1: 8
2: 2, 5
3: 4,4,7,7
7, 19
4:14, 31
5: 2, 21
8:10, 15
22
9: 7, 14
34
10: 7, 10
23, 26
28
11: 7
13:17
14:10+A
13, 30
31
16:13, 15
29, 32
18:14
23: 5, 9
24:10
32: 1, 1, 5
22, 23
25
33:12, 13
17, 20
20
34:29, 30
35
39:23
Lev. 5:18
9:24
13: 7, 21
26, 31
53, 56
14:36, 48
20.17, 17
23:43
Nu. 4:20
11:15, 16
12: 8
14:23
17: 9
20:29
21: 8
22: 2, 6
23, 25
27, 33
23:13
24: 1, 4
16, 20
21, 23
25: 7
27:12
31:18[a]
32: 1
35:23
Deu. 1: 8, 19
21, 31
39
3:19, 27
4: 5, 12
15, 19
35, 42
5:24
7:19
8: 3
16–A
16
9: 2, 16
10:21
11: 2,2,28
12:13
13: 2, 3, 6
13
15:15[b]
19: 4[c]
20: 1
21: 1, 11

Deu. 22: 1
26: 7
28:68
29: 3 A[d]
4, 16
17
31:13, 21
29
32:17, 17
19, 36
39, 39
40
33:21
34: 6
Jos. 1: 8[e]
2: 1
3: 3
5: 6, 13
7:21
8:14, 14
15
21–A
10: 2
18: 9
20: 5 A
22:10, 22
28
23: 4
24: 7, 29
Jud. 1:24
3:24
4: 8
6:22, 22
28–A
9:36, 43
48, 55
11:35
12: 3
13:22[f]
14: 1, 8
11–A
15:11
16: 1, 5
18, 24
18: 7
9+A
9[g]
14 A[h]
26
19: 3, 17
24
20:36
39–A
41
21:11[a]
Ruth 1:18
2:11, 18
3:11
1 Sa. 2:12
5: 3, 7
6:13, 19
9:17
10:11, 11
14
12:12, 16
17, 24
13: 6, 11
14: 3, 16
17, 29
29, 38
52
15:35
16: 6, 16
17, 18
18 A[i]
17:24 A
28 A
28 A
42, 51
55 A
55 A
18:15, 28
19: 5
15+A
20
20: 3, 12
30
21: 8, 14
22:15, 22
23:15, 17

1 Sa. 23:22+A
23
24:12, 16
25:11, 17
23, 25
26: 3, 16
28: 5, 9
12, 21
29: 9
31: 5, 7
2 Sa. 1: 5,7,10
2:26
3:13, 25
26, 38
6:16
7:20
10: 6,9,14
15, 19
11: 2, 16
20, 22
12:22
13: 5, 5, 6
28, 34
14:24, 28
30, 32
15:27, 28
16:12
17: 8, 10
18, 23
18:10, 21
24, 26
29
19:22
20:12, 12
24:13, 17
20
1 Ki. 2:15
(3) 44[a]
44[k]
3: 7, 28
5: 3, 6
6[m]
8:30
9:12, 27
10: 4
11:28
12:16
p 24 *l* 33
13:25
14: 4 A
16:18
18:12
17–A
30+A
21: 7, 22
31
22: 3, 19
32, 33
2 Ki. 2:10, 12
15, 24
3:14
15 A[n]
22, 26
4:25
5: 7, 21
6:13, 17
17, 20
20, 21
30, 32
32
7:14
8:12, 29
9:11, 16
17, 22
26, 27
32–A
10:10, 16
23
11: 1, 14
12:10
13: 4, 21
14:26
16:10, 12
17:26
19:16
20: 5, 15
15
23:16, 29
1 Ch. 10: 5, 7
12:17

1 Ch. 15:29
17:18
19: 6, 10
15, 16
19
21:12, 15
16, 20
23, 28
28:10
20 A[o]
29:17
2 Ch. 2: 7, 8, 8
13, 14
8:18
9: 3, 6
12: 7
15: 9
18:16, 18
31, 32
19: 6
20:12, 17
24
22:10
23:13
24:11, 22
31: 8
32: 2, 31
Ezra 3:12
4:14
7:25, 25
Neh. 4:14
9: 9
10:28
13:15, 23
Est. 4:14
5: 9, 13
8: 6[p]
(9)15
Job 2:12
3: 9, 16
4: 8, 16
6:19, 21
7: 7
8: 9
9: 2, 5
11
21, 25
28
10: 7, 13
18
11: 8, 11
11
12:24
13: 2, 18
14:21
15: 9,9,23
18:21
19:14, 19
25
20: 7
7+C
17
21:14, 20
27
22:19
23: 2,4 S[1][q]
8, 10
17
24:11, 13
26:14
27:12[r]
28:10, 13
23, 24
26
29: 8, 11
16
30:23, 25
31: 6
32: 5,8,10
11
34:16[r],17[s]
19[t]
35: 5
5+A
13
36:12, 25
28
37: 4
4+C
14

Job 38: 5, 12[p]
17, 21
42: 2,3,11
16
Psa. 9:14
10: 7
13: 2
15:10
16: 2−S[1]
24:18, 19
26:13
32:13
33: 9, 13
34:21, 22
36:25, 35
37
40: 7
44:11
45: 9
47: 6 9
48:11 52: 3
54:10
57: 9, 11
58: 5
63: 3
65: 5
68:33
73: 9
76:17, 17
78: 6 S[1u]
79:15
83:10
85:17
89:15, 16
94: 9
96: 4, 6
97: 8
105: 5, 44
106:24
108:25
113: 3
118:37, 96
153,158
159
127: 5, 6
138:16, 24
24+A[s]
Pro. 3:13, 28
4:17, 19
27
6: 6
7: 7, 23
9:18
19: 7
22: 8
23: 2, 33
35
24:12, 12
25: 7
26:12
28:22
29:20
Ecc. 1:10, 14
17
2: 1, 3
12, 13
19, 24
3:10, 13
16, 21
22, 22
4: 1, 3, 4
7, 15
17
5: 7, 12
17, 17
6: 1, 5, 6
8
7: 1, 14
15
15−S[2]
16, 28
30
8: 1, 1, 9
10, 16
17, 17
9: 1, 9
11, 13
10: 5, 7
Cant. 3: 3, 11
6: 8, 10

Cant. 6:10
7:12
Isa. 1: 1, 1
5:13, 19
6: 1, 5, 9
10
9: 2
10:24
13: 1
14:10
21: 6, 7
22: 9, 11
26:10, 11
13, 14
28: 4
29:23
30:19
33:15, 19
34:15
37:17
38: 5, 11
11−AS
11
39: 4 *ter*
40:26
41: 5, 20
42:16, 18
20, 22
44:16, 20
45: 5, 15
46: 5
49:18
51: 7
53: 2, 3
55: 5
56:10, 11
11
57: 1, 11
58: 3, 7
59: 8[a], 8
15, 16
60: 4, 8
63:15
64: 4
Jer. 2:10, 10
19, 23
3: 2, 6, 7
8
4:22, 24
26
5: 1
6:16, 16
7: 9, 12
9: 6
10:23, 25
11:18, 20
13:20
14:18
15:14
16:13
19: 4
20:12
22:10 S[d]
28
23:11, 13
18
24: 7
32:16
36:32
37: 6
38:26, 34
40:11 B[v]
48:13
49:14, 18
51:17
Lam. 1: 7, 8, 9
10, 11
12, 18
20
2: 9, 14
14, 16
20
3:49, 58
59
5: 1
Eze. 1: 1, 4
15, 18
27, 27
2: 1, 9
3:13, 23

Eze. 8: 2, 4
7+A
9, 10
10+A
10: 1, 8[w]
9, 15
20, 22
11: 1, 24
12: 3, 6
13:23
16: 6, 8
50−A
18:14
28+A
19: 5, 11
20:28
23:11, 13
14
31:10
33: 3, 6
37: 8
39:15
40: 4
43: 3 *qtr*
44: 4, 5
Dan. 1:10, 13
2: 8, 8, 9
21
26−A
41, 41
43, 45
4: 2

Dan. 4: 6−A
15, 17
20
7: 1
8: 2+A
3,4,6,7
15, 20
9:18, 21
10: 5, 7, 7
8, 20
12: 5
Hos. 5:13
6:10
9:10
13−B
Joel 2:14
Amos 1: 1
3: 9
5:16
6: 2
9: 1
Jon. 3: 9, 10
Mic. 1: 1
Hab. 1: 1, 5
2: 1
3: 7
Hag. 2: 3
Zec. 1:18
2: 1, 2
4:13
5: 1, 5, 9
6: 1

[a] A γινώσκω. [b] AB εἰμί.
[c] A ἀκουσίως. [d] *pro* ὁράω.
[e] A συνίημι. [f] A ὁράω.
[g] A εὑρίσκω. [h] *pro* γινώσκω.
[i] *pro* εἶδος. [k] AB γινώσκω.
[m] B ἰδίως. [n] *pro* λαμβάνω.
[o] *pro* ἰδού. [p] A ἐπείδω.
[q] *pro* εἶπον. [r] ABCS εἰ δέ.
[s] AB εἰ δέ. [t] A δίδωμι.
[u] *pro* ἐπιγίνωσκω. [v] *pro* εἰσφέρω. [w] A ἰδού. [x] B[2] S[1] *pro* ὁδός.

εἶδος.

Gen. 29:17
32:30, 31
39: 6
41: 2, 3, 4
18, 19
Exo. 24:10, 17
26:30
28:29
Lev. 13:43
Nu. 8: 4
9:15, 16
11: 7, 7
12: 8
Deu. 21:11
Jud. 8:18+A
13: 6[a], 6[a]
1 Sa. 16:18[b]

1 Sa. 25: 3
2 Sa. 11: 2
13: 1
Est. 2: 2, 3, 7
Job 33:16
41: 9
Pro. 7:10
Cant. 5:15
Isa. 52:14
53: 2, 2, 3
Jer. 11:16
15: 3
Lam. 4: 8
Eze. 1:14+A
16, 16
26
8: 2+A

[a] A ὅρασις. [b] A εἰδέω.

εἴδω *vide* εἰδέω.

εἴδωλον.

Gen. 31:19, 34
35
Exo. 20: 4
Lev. 19: 4
26:30
Nu. 25: 2, 2
33:52
Deu. 5: 8−A
29:17
32:21
1 Sa. 17:43 A[a]
31: 9
1 Ki. 11: 2, 5, 5
(5)+A
7, 33
2 Ki. 17:12
21:11, 21
23:24
1 Ch. 10: 9
16:26

2 Ch. 11:15
14: 5
15:16
17: 3
23:17
24:18
28: 3
33:22
34: 7
35:19
Psa. 96: 7
113:12
134:15
150 *p* 6
Isa. 1:29
10:11
27: 9
30:22
37:19
41:28

Isa. 48: 5
57: 5
Jer. 9:14
14:22
16:19
Eze. 6: 4
5+A
6, 13
13
8:10
16:16
18:12
23:30
33:25+A

Eze. 30:17
18+A
25
37:23
44:12
Hos. 4:17
8: 4
13: 2
14: 8
Mic. 1: 7
Hab. 2:18
Zeph. 1: 5 S[b]
Zec. 13: 2

[a] *pro* θεός. [b] *pro* δῶμα.

εἴθε.

Job 9:33

εἰκάζω.

Jeremiah 26:23

εἰκάς.

Zechariah 7: 1+A

εἰκῆ.

Proverbs 28:25

εἰκοσαετής.

Exo. 30:14
39: 3
Lev. 27: 3
Nu. 1: 3, 18
20, 22
24, 26
28, 30
32, 34
36, 38
40, 42
45
4:23, 30

Nu. 4:35, 39
43, 47
8:24
14:29
26: 2, 4
32:11
1 Ch. 23:24, 27
27:23
2 Ch. 25: 5
31:17
Ezra 3: 8

εἴκοσι.

Exo. 27:11−A
39: 1[a]
Lev. 27: 5[b]
Jos. 19:30+A
2 Sa. 19:17−A
1 Ki. 8: 1−A
1 Ch. 15: 5[c]
6[d]

2 Ch. 3: 4−A[1]
4: 1−A
7: 5−B
27: 8 A
Ezra 2:41[e]
Neh. 7:30[f]
69+AS[3]
Eze. 40:30+A

[a] A τριάκοντα. [b] A εἰκοστός.
[c] BS δέκα. [d] ABS πεντήκοντα.
[e] B τεσσεράκοντα.
[f] ABS[1] εἰκοσιεῖς.

εἰκοσιδύο.

Neh. 7:17[a] | Neh. 11:12-BS[1]

[a] B εἰκοσιοκτώ.

εἰκοσιοκτώ.

Ezra 8:11[a] | Neh. 7:27−B

[a] B ἑβδομήκοντα ὀκτώ.

εἰκοσιπέντε.

Gen. 11:25[a]
1 Ki. 16 *p* 28−A

Eze. 40:27+A
[a] A εἰκοσιεννέα.

εἰκοσιτρεῖς.

Nehemiah 7:24−AB, 26−B

εἰκοστός.

1 Ki. 15: 8−A
16: 6+AB
10+A

1 Ki. 16:15+A
2 Ch. 7:10[a]
Neh. 9: 1[b]

[a] A εἰκάς. [b] S εἰκάς.

εἴκω.

1 Ki. 12: 7+A
Est. 4:15 S[1a]

Job 6: 3, 25
[a] *pro* ἥκω.

εἰκών.

Gen. 1:26, 27
5: 1, 3
9: 6
Deu. 4:16
1 Sa. 6:11+A
2 Ki. 11:18
2 Ch. 33: 7
Psa. 38: 7
72:20
Isa. 40:19, 20
Eze. 7:20
8: 5+A

Eze. 16:17
23:14
Dan. 2:31, 31
32, 34
35
3: 1, 2, 3
3, 5, 7
11, 12
14, 15
18
Hos. 13: 2

εἰλέω, εἱλέω.

2 Ki. 2: 8
Job 40:21 A[a]

Isa. 11: 5
[a] *pro* δέω (B).

εἶμι.

Exo. 32:26 | Pro. 6: 6

εἴν, ἴν.

Exo. 29:40, 40
30:24
Lev. 23:13
Nu. 15: 4, 5, 6
7, 9, 10
28: 5, 7

Nu. 28:14 *ter*
Eze. 4:11
45:24
46: 5, 7
11, 14

εἶπον.

Var. lec. tantum.

Gen. 22: 7+A
7[a]
11−A
27:18+A
29:26 A[b]
31:51−A
43:15[c]
45: 4−A
50:16[d]
Exo. 4:26−B
32:14+A
27 A[e]
33:15 A[e]
34:10[f]
Nu. 15: 1[f]
16:34+A
22:18−A[1]
28[e]
32[a]
Deu. 12:20 A[g]
Jos. 5:15 A[e]
23: 4 B[h]
Jud. 2: 3+A
5: 1 A[e]
6:29 A[i]
7: 3+A
9:27 B[k]
54−A
11:15−A
13:13 A[g]
15:13[m]
16:24+A
17: 2 A[n]
18: 8[a]
Ruth 4: 1 AB[o]
1 Sa. 2:30 AB[e]
3: 5−A
4:21+A
10:16+A
16:18−A
17:37+A
43−A
18:22+A
20:26 A[g]
32+A
22: 7+AB
23: 7−A
29: 9+A
2 Sa. 13:32−A
14: 4−A
19:21[a]
1 Ki. 2:14+A
(3)42+A
13: 2−B

1 Ki. 16 *p* 28−A
18: 8 A[e]
20: 4+A
21:11−A
29−A
28−A
37−A
22:16+B
28+A
2 Ki. 2:24+A
3:21[p]
4:15+A
5:11−A
15−A
22+A
6: 5+A
7 A[g]
9:12−A
10:23−A
13:17−B
20:19+A
2 Ch. 18:19+A
27−AB
20:20−B
23:13+A
31:10−A
Neh. 6: 6+S[3]
13:19−B
Est. 4:15+A
5:12−A
6:10+A
Job 1: 9−A
17[a]
23: 4[q]
29: 1[a]
32: 6[a]
39:33 A[e]
Ps. 117: 4−S
Pro. 7:13 S[1r]
Ecc. 3:18[s]
Isa. 21: 9+S[1]
22:14+S[2]
30:16+AS
36:10−A
13−S
47: 4+AS[2]
48: 5−A[1]
49:15−S[1]
66:22 S[1e]
Jer. 1:12−S[1]
13−S[1]
19[a]
3:19[a]
14:10 S[e]

Jer. 19:12 S[e]
22:21 −A
23:17 −AS
28:61 −S[1]
29:13[a]
37:12[a]
39: 3 −S[1]
42: 6 A[e]
17 −A
44:17 −AS
47:15 −S[1]
50: 2 A[e]
51:26[a]
26 −A[1]
Lam. 3:24 −AB
Lam. 3:56 −A
Eze. 9:10 +A
12:10 +A
17:22 +A
Dan. 2: 4 A[o]
5 +A
27[d]
3: 9 +A
25 −B[1]
4:16 +A
5:17[u]
Jon. 2: 3 −S[1]
Zec. 6: 7 −S[1]
Mal. 3: 8 AS[3g]

[a] A λέγω. [b] pro ἀποκρίνω. [c] A ἐντέλλω. [d] B λέγω. [e] pro λέγω. [f] A λαλέω. [g] pro ἐρῶ. [h] vide ἐπιρρίπτω. [i] pro γινώσκω. [k] pro πίνω. [m] A ὄμνυμι. [n] pro προσεῖπον. [o] pro λάλεω. [p] A ἐπάγω. [q] S[1] εἰδέω. [r] pro προσεῖπον. [s] S[1] ἐπάγω. [t] A εἰ. [u] A ἀποκρίνω.

εἴρ.

Daniel 4:10, 14, 20

εἰρέω, *vide* ἐρῶ.

εἰρηνεύω.

1 Ki. 22:45
2 Ch. 14: 5, 6
20:30
Job 3:26
5:23
Job 5:23 +A
24
15:21
16:12
20:22 C[a]

[a] pro πληρόω.

εἰρήνη.

Gen. 15:15
26:29
Exo. 18:23
Lev. 26: 6
Nu. 6:26
25:12
Deu. 20:10
Jos. 9:21
Jud. 4:17
6:23, 24
8: 9
11:13, 31
18: 6
15 −A
19:20
21:13
1 Sa. 1:17
7:14
10: 4
16: 4, 5
17:18 A
22 A
20: 7, 13
21, 42
25: 5, 35
29: 7
30:21
2 Sa. 3:21, 22
23, 24
8:10
11: 7 *ter*
15: 9, 27
17: 3
18:28, 29
32
19:24, 30
1 Ki. 2: 5 −B
6, 13
13, 33
(3) *p* 46
4:24
5:12
21:18
22:17, 27
28
2 Ki. 4:23
26 *qtr*
2 Ki. 5:19, 21
22 +A
9:11, 17
18, 18
19, 19
22, 22
31
10:13
20:19 −B
22:20 −A
1 Ch. 4:40
12:17, 18
18, 18
18:10
22: 9
2 Ch. 15: 5
18:16, 26
27
19: 1 +A
34:28
Ezra 4: 7, 16
17
5: 7
9:12
Job 5:24 +A
11:18
Psa. 4: 9
13: 3 −A
27: 3
28:11
33:15
34:27
36:11
37: 4
40:10
54:19
71: 3, 7
72: 3
73: 3
84: 9, 11
118:165
119: 6
121: 6, 7, 8
124: 5
127: 6
147: 3
Pro. 3: 2, 17
Pro. 3:23
4:27
12:20
16: 5
17: 1
Ecc. 3: 8
Cant. 8:10[a]
Isa. 9: 6
6 +AS[2]
6 +AS[3]
7
14:30
26: 3, 12
27: 5
5 −B
29:24
32: 4, 17
18
33: 7 +AS[2]
7
38:16 +S[2]
39: 8
41: 3
45: 7
24 S[1 b]
48:18
52: 7
53: 5
54:10, 13
57: 2, 19
19
59: 8, 8
60:17
66:12
Jer. 4:10
6:14 *ter*
8:15
12: 5, 12
14:13, 19
Jer. 15: 5
16: 5
23:17
32:23
35: 9
36: 7, 7
7 −S[1]
11
37: 5
40: 6
6 +S
9
41: 5
45: 4
50:12
Lam. 3:17
Eze. 7:25
13:10
10 +A
10, 16
16
34:25, 27
29
37:26
38: 8, 11
14
39: 6, 26
Dan. 3:31
6:25
10:19
Mic. 2: 8
3: 5
5: 5
Nah. 1:14
Hag. 2: 9, 9
Zec. 8:10, 12
19
9:10
Mal. 2: 5, 6

[a] S χάρις. [b] pro δόξα.

εἰρηνικός.

Gen. 34:21
37: 4
42:11, 19
31, 33
34
Nu. 21:21
Deu. 2:26
20:11
23: 6
1 Sa. 10: 8
11:15
13: 9
2 Sa. 6:17, 18
20:19
24:25
1 Ki. (3) *p* 1
1 Ki. 3:15
8:63, 64
64
9:25 A
2 Ki. 16:13
1 Ch. 12:38
Psa. 34:20
36:37
119: 7
Pro. 7:14
Jer. 9: 8
45:22
Obad. 7
Mic. 7: 3
Zec. 6:13
8:16[a]

[a] A δίκαιος.

εἰρηνοποιέω.

Proverbs 10:10

εἴρω *vide* ἐρῶ.

εἷς.

Exo. 26:19 −AB[1]
21 −B
27 −A
Jos. 10:30 +A
Jud. 15: 7 +A
1 Sa. 2:36 +A
6: 7 +A
1 Ki. 4: 8 −A
9 −A
11 −A
13 −A
15 −A
16 −A
18 −A
6:22 −B
23 +B
24 −B
7: 5 −A
18: 6 −A
22: 8[a]
2 Ki. 2:16 −A
24:18 −A
1 Ch. 1:19 A
17: 6 +A
2 Ch. 3:12 A
9:15 +AB
16:13 +A
Ezra 10:16 −B
17 −S[1]
Psa. 23: 1 −S
Isa. 27:12 +AS
30: 9 +AS[3]
Jer. 28:60 +AS
52: 1[b]
Eze. 8: 7 +A
8 +A
10: 9 +A
14 A
25:15[c]
34:23[d]
Eze. 40:12 +A
12 +A
Dan. 9: 2 +A
27 +AB[2]

[a] A ἔτι. [b] A δεύτερος. [c] A αἰών. [d] A ἕτερος.

εἰσάγω.

Gen. 6:19
7: 2
8: 9
12:15
29:13, 23
39:14, 17
43:15, 16
17[a], 17
47: 7
Exo. 2:10
3: 8 −A
6: 8[b]
13: 5, 11
15:17
18: 7
23:10 A[1 c]
20, 23
25:13
26:29
27: 7
33: 3
Lev. 10:18
18: 3
20:22
Nu. 14: 3, 8, 16
24, 31
15:18
16:14
20:12
27:17
Deu. 4:27, 38
6:10
23 +A
7: 1
8: 7
9: 4, 28
11:29
21:12
26: 9
30: 5
31:20, 21
23
Jos. 2: 3 A[d]
Jud. 2: 1
12: 9 A[e]
19: 4 A[f]
21 A[e]
1 Sa. 7: 1
9:22
16:12, 17
17:57 A
19: 7
20: 8, 8
21:14, 15
27:11
2 Sa. 5: 2
11:15
1 Ki. (3) 1
46 +A
4:30 −A
7: 2 A[c]
12:20 A[g]
p 24 *l* 58
1 Ki. 12 *p* 24 *l* 63
21:39[b]
2 Ki. 9: 2
20:20[h]
1 Ch. 11: 2
2 Ch. 25:23
28:13
29: 4
36: 4
10 A[e]
Neh. 1: 9
9:23
Est. 1:11
3: 9 +S[3]
Psa. 65:11
77:54
Pro. 23: 7
25:17
Ecc. 8:10[i]
Cant. 2: 4
3: 4
8: 2 −S[1]
Isa. 14: 2
56: 7
58: 7
60:11
Jer. 2: 7 S[k]
3:14
22: 7 A[m]
33:23
34: 9, 10
42: 2 A[e], 4
44:14
Lam. 3:13
Eze. 8: 7, 14
16
17:13
19: 9
20:15, 28
37, 42
27:15
34:13
36:24
37:12, 21
40: 3, 17
19 A[k]
24 A[k]
28, 32
35, 41
48
41: 1
42: 1, 1
43: 5
44: 4, 7
46:19
47: 1
Dan. 1: 3, 18
18
2:24, 25
4: 3
5: 7, 13
Zec. 8: 8
10:10

[a] A εἰσφέρω. [b] B ἐξάγω. [c] pro συνάγω. [d] pro ἐξάγω. [e] pro εἰσφέρω. [f] pro κατέχω. [g] pro καλίω. [h] AB εἰσφέρω. [i] C ἄγω. [k] pro ἄγω. [m] pro ἐπάγω.

εἰσακούω.

Gen. 21:17
34:17, 24
42:21, 22
Exo. 2:24
3:18
4: 1, 8, 9
5: 2
6: 5, 9, 12
12, 30
7: 4, 13
Exo. 7:10, 22
8:15, 19
9:12
11: 9, 10[a]
16: 7, 8, 9
12, 20
28
22:23, 27
23:21
Nu. 14:22
Nu. 16: 8
20:16
21: 3
27:20
Deu. 1:43, 45
3:26
4:30
9:19, 23
10:10[b]
11:13 B[c]
28 A[c]
13: 8
18 A[c]
15: 5
19: 9 A[c]
21:18
23: 5
26: 7
27:10
28: 1 A[c]
2 A[c]
9 A[c]
15
45[d]
58, 62
30: 2[e], 8
10, 16
17, 20
33: 7
34: 9
Jos. 22: 2 A[f]
Jud. 2: 2, 17
20[e]
3: 9 +A
5:16 A[c]
6:10
11:28 A[c]
28 +A
13: 9[g]
19:25[d]
20:13 A[c]
1 Sa. 12:15 A[e]
2 Sa. 12:18
1 Ki. 3:11
8:29, 30
30, 32
34, 36
39, 43
45, 49
52
2 Ki. 10: 6
19: 4
1 Ch. 21:28 A[h]
2 Ch. 6:21, 23
25, 27
30, 33
7:14
34:21[h]
Neh. 9:17, 28
Est. 1:12
Job 5: 1 A[f]
9:14 A[f]
15
16 A[f]
16
22:27
27: 9[i], 10
30:20 AS[c]
33:26 +S[1]
34:28
35:12
36:10
37:22 AC[h]
Psa. 3: 5 A[h]
4: 2, 2, 4
5: 4
6: 9
10 −S[1 i]
9:38
12: 4
16: 1
6 AS[1 h]
6
17:42
21: 3, 25[g]
26: 7, 7
27: 2, 6
30:23
33: 7, 18
37:16
Psa. 38:13
39: 2
53: 4
54: 3, 17
18, 20
57: 6
60: 2, 6
63: 2
64: 3
65:18, 19
68:17, 34
83: 9
85: 1[k]
7[m]
90:15[m]
91:12 BS[1 c]
98: 6[n]
101: 2, 3[o]
105:25, 44
114: 1
119: 1
129: 2
140: 1
142: 1
1 A[h], 7
144:19 S[2 h]
150 *p* 6
Pro. 1:28
8: 6, 34
12:15
21:13[o]
28: 9
Ecc. 9:16[p]
Isa. 1:15, 19
20
19:22[s]
32: 9[d]
37: 4, 17
42:23
46: 7[q]
55: 3[r]
58: 9
59: 1
Jer. 6:10[e]
7:13 S[c]
16
24 A[c]
26[t]
11:10[u], 11
14
13:11[u]
14:12
17:23 A[c]
24[i]
27 ABS[a]
18:19, 19[g]
19:15
23:22 S[c]
25: 4
7 AS[c]
33: 5
5 AS[c]
36:12
40: 6 +AS
42: 8 A[c]
14 A[c]
15[v]
44:14[w]
47: 3 A[c]
49:21 A[c].
Eze. 3: 6, 7, 7
8:18 +A
13:19
20: 8, 30
Dan. 1:14
9: 6, 10
11 A[c]
14, 17
19[d]
Hos. 9, 17
Jon. 2: 3
Mic. 3: 4
7 B[h]
5:15
7: 7
Hab. 1: 2
3: 1
Zeph. 3: 2
Zec. 1: 4 −A
4

Zec. 6:15, 15
7:11, 12
Zec. 7:13, 13
Mal. 3:16

[a] A θέλω. [b] B ἀκούω.
[c] pro ἀκούω. [d] A ἀκούω.
[e] A ὑπακούω. [f] pro ὑπακούω.
[g] A ἐπακούω. [h] pro ἐπακούω.
[i] AS² ἀκούω. [k] AS ἐπακούω.
[l] AS² ἐπακούω. [n] B ἐπακούω.
[m] S ἐπακούω. [p] ACS ἀκούω.
[r] AS¹ ἀκούω. [s] AS³ ἐπακούω.
[q] ABS ἀκούω. [t] BS ἀκούω.
[u] A ἀκούω. S ὑπακούω.
[o] AB ἀκούω. [w] AS ἀκούω.

εἰσάπαξ.

2 Sa. 23: 8
Dan. 2:35

εἰσβλέπω.

Job 6:28[a]
21: 5[a]
Isa. 37:17

[a] A ἐμβλέπω.

εἴσδεκτος.

Leviticus 22:21, 29

εἰσδέχομαι.

Jer. 23: 3
Eze. 11:17
20:34, 41
22:19, 20
20
Hos. 8:10
Mic. 4: 6
Hab. 2: 5
Zeph. 3: 8, 19
20
Zec. 10: 8[a], 10

[a] S¹ εἰς δόξαν.

εἰσδύω.

Jeremiah 4:29

εἰσείδω.

Exo. 2:25 A[a] [a] pro ἐπείδω.

εἴσειμι.

Exo. 28:23, 31
1 Sa. 16: 6

εἰσέρχομαι.

Gen. 6:18, 20
7: 1, 7, 9
13, 15
16
12:11, 14
16: 2, 4
19: 3, 5, 8
9, 23
31, 33
34, 35
20: 3, 13
24:31, 32
67
27:33 A[a]
29:21, 23
30
30: 3, 4, 10
16, 16
31:33, 33
34:25, 27
38: 2, 8, 9
16, 16
18
39:11, 14
17
40: 6
41:21, 21
43:25, 29
44:14
46: 6, 8
26, 27
Exo. 1: 1, 19
3:18
5: 1, 15
6:11
7:10, 23
8: 1, 3
9: 1, 19
10: 1, 3
12:23, 25
14:16, 17
Exo. 14:20, 22
23
23+A
15:19
16:22
20:21
21: 3
24: 3, 18
29:30
33: 8[b], 9
34:35
35:29
40:29
Lev. 9:23
12: 4
14: 8, 34
36, 36
44, 48
16: 3, 23
26, 28
18:14, 19[c]
19:23
21:11
23:10
25: 2
Nu. 4: 5, 15
20
5:22, 24
27
6: 6
8:15, 22
24
12:14
14:24, 30
15: 2
16:43
17: 8
19: 7
20:24
25: 8
27:17, 21
Nu. 31:24
32: 9
Deu. 1: 8 A[d]
37, 38
39
4: 1, 21
34
6:18
8: 1
9: 1
11: 5 A[a]
8, 31
12: 5 A[a]
16:20
17:14
18: 9
19: 5
20:19
21:13
23: 1
2-AB[i]
3, 3, 8
10-B
11
24: 1, 2, 12
25: 5
26: 1, 3
27: 3
31: 7
32:44[e], 52
33: 7 A[a]
34: 4
Jos. 1:11, 11
2: 1[b], 1, 4
3: 8
6: 5, 6
22, 23
8:19[f]
10, 19
14:11
19:27
23: 7
24: 6
Jud. 3:20
24 A[g]
4:21, 22
6:19
7:13 A[a]
19
8:15+A
9: 5
27 A[b]
41[i]
46 A[a]
11:18
34 A[a]
13: 6[h]
15: 1, 1
16: 1
18: 9+A
9[b]
10 A[a]
10[k]
15, 18
20 A[a]
19:15, 15
16 A[a]
22[b], 23
20: 8 A[m]
Ruth 2:18
3:15, 16
17
4:13-B
1 Sa. 1:18, 19
24
4:13, 14
5: 3
10-A
11
6:14
9:13, 13[b]
10: 5, 5, 14
22 A[a]
12: 8
14:11, 26
16:21
20:10, 41
43
21:15
23: 7
1 Sa. 24: 4
26:6, 6[n], 15
28:21
30: 1
2 Sa. 1: 2
2:24
3: 7, 24[o]
4: 5, 7
5: 6, 6, 8
6: 9
7:18
10:14
11: 4
7-A
11
12: 1, 16
20, 20
24
13: 5, 6
14: 4, 33
33
15:32 A[a]
37
16:15
16 A[a]
21, 22
17: 6, 17
18, 25
18: 9
19: 3, 5, 8
25
20: 3, 3, 8[f]
22
24:13
13 A[a]
1 Ki. 1:13, 14
15, 23
28, 32
35+A
42[h], 42
47, 53
2:13, 19
10: 2
11: 2, 2
17, 18
12:21
p24 l36
l37, 40
l46, 51
l74
13: 7, 8
22, 25
14: 4 A
5 A
5 A
6 A
6 A
12 A
13 A
17 A
16:10
17:12, 13
18
18:12
19: 9
20: 5
5+A
13-8[b]
21:30, 33
22:25, 30
30
2 Ki. 3:24, 24
4: 4, 11
32, 33
36, 37
5: 4, 5, 25
6:20
7: 4, 5, 8
8, 8, 9
10, 10
12
8:14
9: 2, 2, 5
6, 11
34
10:17, 21
23, 24
25
11: 5, 9[p]
13, 16
2 Ki. 11:18, 19
18:21, 37
19: 1
23 A[a]
32, 33
20: 1, 14
22: 9
24:11
25:26
1 Ch. 2:21
7:23
11: 5
14:15[q]
19:15 A[a]
2 Ch. 1:10
7: 2
8:11
12:11
18:24, 29
29
20:28
23: 6, 6, 12
14[r], 17
19, 20
24:17
26:16, 17
27: 2
29:16, 17
18
30: 8
25 B[a]
32:21 A[a]
Ezra 2:68[s]
9:13 S³[a]
Neh. 2: 8
6:10, 11
11+S³
9:15
10:29
13: 1
Est. 1:12 S¹[a]
19
2:12, 15
16
4: 2, 4, 8
9, 11
11[t], 16
5:10, 14
6: 4+S³
4
5+S³
7: 1
9:25
Job 13:16
14: 3
15:28
33:26
37: 7
41: 4
Psa. 5: 8
17: 7
23: 7, 9
25: 4
36:15
42: 4
48:20
50: 2
62:10
65:13
68: 2, 28
70:16
72:17
78:11
87: 3
94:11
99: 2, 4
104:23
108:18
117:19, 20
118:170
131: 3, 7
142: 2
Pro. 5:10 A[a]
6:29
11: 2
23:10
27:10
28:10
Cant. 5: 1
Isa. 2:10, 21
Isa. 7:24
13:20
20 S[u]
16:12
19:23
20: 1
24:10
26: 2, 20
30:29
36: 6, 22
37:24, 33
34-AS
47: 1+AS
5
Jer. 2: 7
4: 5
8:14
9:21[b]
14:18
16: 5, 8
17:25
21:13
22: 4
28:51
30: 4
33:21
34:18
37:20
39: 5, 23
41: 3, 10[b]
42:11[v], 11
43: 5, 20
45:11
46: 3
48: 6, 7
17+A
49:14, 15
18, 19
22
50: 2, 7, 7
11
51: 8 AS[a]
Lam. 1:10, 10
22
4:12
Eze. 3: 4, 11
15, 24
4:14
7:22
8: 9, 10
9: 2
10: 2, 2, 6
11:16, 18
12:16
13: 9
16: 7, 8, 10
17: 3
20:38
21:20, 20
22: 3 B[l][a]
36:20, 20
21, 22
37:10, 21
40: 4, 6
41: 3
42:14
43: 4
44: 2, 3, 9
16, 25
46: 2, 8, 9
10
Dan. 2:16+A
17
5:10, 15
6:10
10: 3
11: 6, 7, 9
10 A[n]
15, 17
30, 40
41
Hos. 7: 1
9: 4, 10
11: 9
Joel 1:13
2: 9
Amos 4: 4
6: 1
14-A
Obad. 5, 5, 11
Obad. 13
Jon. 3: 4[w]
Mic. 4: 8
Nah. 2:11
Hab. 3:16
Hag. 1:14
Zec. 1:21 A[x]
5: 4
6:10
7: 3

[a] pro ἔρχομαι. [b] A ἔρχομαι.
[c] AB προσέρχομαι.
[d] pro εἰσπορεύω.
[e] A προσέρχομαι. [f] B ἔρχομαι.
[g] pro ἐπέρχομαι. [h] pro εἰσφέρω.
[i] A καθίζω. [k] A ἥκω.
[m] pro ἀπέρχομαι. [n] A εἰσπορεύω.
[o] A ἀπέρχομαι. [p] A ἐπέρχομαι.
[q] ABS ἐξέρχομαι. [r] A [illegible]ρχομαι.
[s] AB ἔρχομαι. [t] S ἔρχομαι.
[u] pro διέρχομαι. [v] A ἀναβαίνω.
[w] AS² εἰσπορεύω.
[x] pro ἐξέρχομαι.

εἰσκολάπτω.

1 Ki. 6:32 A[a] [a] pro ἐγκολάπτω.

εἰσκύπτω.

1 Samuel 13:18

εἰσοδιάζομαι.

2 Ki. 12: 4
2 Ch. 34:14

εἰσόδιος.

Daniel 11:13

εἴσοδος.

Gen. 30:27
Jos. 13: 5
Jud. 1:14[a], 24
25
1 Sa. 16: 4
17:52
29: 6
2 Sa. 3:25
1 Ki. 2:13
3: 7
8:65
2 Ki. 11:16
14:25
16:18
19:27+A
23:11
1 Ch. 9:19
13: 5-A
2 Ch. 7: 8
2 Ch. 16: 1
23: 4, 13
26: 8
33:14
Psa. 73: 5[b]
120: 8
Pro. 8: 3, 34
Isa. 37:28
66:11
Jer. 8: 7
Eze. 27: 3[c]
42: 9
43:11+A
44: 5
46:19
47:15, 20
20
48: 1
Mal. 3: 2

[a] A εἰσπορεύω.
[b] S¹ ὁδός, S² ἔξοδος. [c] A ὁδός.

εἰσπηδάω.

Amos 5:19-A[l]

εἰσπορεύω.

Gen. 6: 4
7:16
23:10, 18
44:30
Exo. 1: 1
11: 4
14:28
23:27
28:29, 30
30:20, 21
33: 8
34:12, 34
38:27
Lev. 10: 9
14:46
16: 2, 17
23
Nu. 4: 3
19 A[a]
23, 30
35, 39
43, 47
7:89
13:22
15:18
19:14
Nu. 33:40
34: 2, 8
Deu. 1: 7, 8[b]
22
4: 5, 14
6: 1
7: 1
9: 5
10:11
11:10, 11
12:29
23:20
28: 6, 19
21, 63
30:16
31: 2, 16
Jos. 2: 2, 3, 18
3:15
6: 1, 13
10: 19[c]
15:18 A[d]
Jud. 1:14 A[e]
7:17
20:10+A
Ruth 4:11
1 Sa. 5: 5

1 Sa. 9:14
11:11
18: 6 A
13, 16
23: 3[c]
26: 5[c]
6 A[f], 7
2 Sa. 15:37[e]
1 Ki. 14:28
15:17
16:18 A[g]
2 Ki. 3:24
4: 8, 10
5:18
9:31
11: 8, 8, 9
15
1 Ch. 9:25
24:19
27: 1
2 Ch. 12:11
15: 5
18:14 A[g]
23: 4, 7, 7
26:11—AB
31:16
Ezra 9:11
Est. 2:13, 14
14
Psa. 40: 7
95: 8

Isa. 30:29
Jer. 17:19, 20
27
19: 3—S
22: 2
23:19 S[1] [d]
43:29, 29
Eze. 8: 5+A
10: 3
20:29
23:39, 44
44, 44
26:10, 10
42: 9, 12
43: 3
44:17, 21
27
46: 8, 9, 9
9, 10
Dan. 4: 4
5: 8
10:20[b]
11:16
Hos. 4:15
Joel 3:11, 13
Amos 2: 7
5: 5
Jon. 3: 4 AS[3] [f]
Hag. 2:16
Zec. 8:10
Mal. 3: 2

[a] *pro* προσπορεύω. [b] A εἰσέρχομαι. [c] A πορεύω. [d] *pro* ἐκπορεύω. [e] *pro* εἴσοδος. [f] *pro* εἰσέρχομαι. [g] *pro* πορεύω. [h] A ἐκπορεύω.

εἰσσπάω.

Genesis 19:10

εἰσφέρω.

Gen. 27:10, 18
25, 33
37:32
43:17 A[a]
47:14
Exo. 4: 6, 6, 7
7
16: 5, 5 A[b]
23:19
26:33
34:26 A[c]
40: 4, 4, 19
Lev. 4: 5[d], 16
6:30
16:12, 15[d]
27
Nu. 31:54
Deu. 7:26
11:14
28:38
Jos. 6:19, 24
Jud. 9:27[e]
12: 9[f]
19: 3[g], 21[f]
1 Sa. 5: 1, 2
9: 7 A[h], 7
17:18 A
2 Sa. 9:10
13:10, 10
1 Ki. 7: 2[f], 37
8: 6
14:26
15:15, 15
2 Ki. 12:13, 16

2 Ki. 20:20 AB[a]
22: 4
23:34
1 Ch. 9:28
13: 5, 12
16: 1
22:19
2 Ch. 5: 1, 7
15:18
24: 6, 9, 10
11[d]
28:27
30:15
31: 6
12 A[h]
34: 9, 16
36:10[f], 18
Neh. 3: 5
10:39[i]
Est. 6: 1
Job 39:12
Cant. 1: 4
Isa. 2:19
23: 3
Jer. 17:24
40:11[k]
48: 5
Lam. 5: 9
Dan. 1: 2
6:18
Joel 3: 5
Hag. 1: 6, 9
Mal. 1:13
3:10

[a] *pro* εἰσάγω. [b] *pro* συνάγω. [c] *pro* τίθημι. [d] A φέρω. [e] A εἰσέρχομαι. [f] A εἰσάγω. [g] A πορεύω. [h] *pro* φέρω. [i] B φέρω. [k] B εἰδέω.

εἰσφορά.

Exodus 30:13, 14, 15, 16

ἕκαστος.

Gen. 10: 5
11: 7

Gen. 13:11
26:31[a]

Gen. 37:19
41:11—A[1]
42:21, 25
35
43:20, 32
44: 1, 11
11, 13
49:28
Exo. 1: 1
5: 4, 8
7:12
11: 2
12: 3, 3, 4
22
16:16, 16
18
21—S
29
29+A
18:16
26: 5
28:21
30:12
32:27 *ter*
27—B
29
33: 8, 10
35:21
36: 4, 21
Lev. 6:40
10: 1
19: 3, 11
25:10, 10
13+AB[2]
46
Nu. 1: 4+A
4, 4
2:17, 34
4:19
5:10
7: 3, 5
11:10
16:17 *ter*
18
17: 2, 9
25: 5
26:54
31:53
32:18
35: 8
36: 7, 8, 9
Deu. 1:41
3:20
12: 8
16:17
24:18
Jos. 1:15
3:12
4: 2, 4, 5
6: 5
24:28, 33
Jud. 2: 6+A
7:21 A[b]
9:49+A
15: 7 A[c]
21:25+A
Ruth 1: 8, 9
1 Sa. 4:10
5: 4
8:22
9: 9
10:11, 25
13: 2, 20
20
14:34 *ter*
20:15, 41
41
25:10, 13
26:23
27: 3
30: 6, 22
2 Sa. 2: 3, 16
27
6:19—A
19
13:29 A[b]
1 Ki. (3) *p* 46
4:20, 21
(25) A
7:22

1 Ki. 8:31, 38
66
10:25—A
12:24
p 24 *l* 69
l 70—B
ll 72, 81
14: 8 A
21:20
20—A
24
22:17, 36
2 Ki. 9:13
14: 6—B
18:33
1 Ch. 16:43
28:16, 17
2 Ch. 6:23 A[d]
9:16—B
24
11: 4
18: 9, 16
23: 8, 10
25: 4, 22
31: 1, 2
16 B[e]
36: 4
Neh. 4:22-ABS
11:20 S[3]
23+S[3]
Est. 2:11
3: 4
9:19—A
Job 1: 4
2:11, 12
42:11
Psa. 6: 7
7:12
11: 3
41: 4, 11
61:13
144: 2
Pro. 5:22
24:12
Isa. 14:18 A[f]
36:16, 18
41: 6
42:25
56:11
Jer. 1:15
5: 8
6: 3
9: 4, 5
12:15
15—S[1]
16:12
17:10
18:11, 12
19: 9
22: 8
23:14, 27
30—B
35, 35
25: 5
26:16
27:16, 16
28: 6, 9
30: 5
32:12
33: 3
38:30, 34
34
39:19
41: 9
9—S[1]
10
10—AB
15, 16
16, 17
17+AS[3]
42:15
43:16
44:10
Eze. 1: 9, 23
7:16
8:11, 12
9: 1[g], 2
10:22
18:30
20: 7, 39

Eze. 22: 6, 11
11, 11
24:23
33:20
45:20
46:18
47:14
Joel 2: 7, 8
Amos 1:11+A
Jon. 1: 5, 7
3: 8
Mic. 4: 4, 4, 5
7: 2

Zeph. 2:11
Hag. 1: 9
2:22
Zec. 3:10
7: 9, 10
8: 4, 10
16, 17
10: 1
11: 6, 9
13: 4
14:13
Mal. 2:10
3:16

[a] A ἄνθρωπος. [b] *pro* ἀνήρ. [c] *pro* ἔσχατος. [d] *pro* αὐτός. [e] *pro* ἐκτός. [f] *pro* ἄνθρωπος. [g] A αὐτός.

ἑκάτερος.

Gen. 40: 5+A
Eze. 1:11, 12
23 B[a]

Eze. 1:23 B[a]
37: 7

[a] *pro* ἕτερος.

ἑκατόν.

Gen. 11:24—A
Exo. 37: 9—A[2]
9—A[2]
39: 4—A
1 Sa. 18:27—A
1 Ki. 8:63—B
9:28[a]
2 Ki. 3: 4—A

2 Ch. 3: 4—A[2]
7: 5—B
17:18—A
Ezra 7:22—B
Neh. 7:26—B
27—B
33+AS

[a] A τετρακόσιοι.

ἑκατονταετής.

Genesis 17:17

ἑκατονταπλάσιος.

2 Samuel 24: 3

ἑκατονταπλασίως.

1 Chronicles 21: 3

ἑκατόνταρχος.

Exo. 18:21, 25
Nu. 31:14, 48
52, 54
Deu. 1:15
1 Sa. 8:12
22: 7
2 Sa. 18: 1
2 Ki. 11: 4, 9, 10

2 Ki. 11:15, 19
1 Ch. 13: 1
26:26
27: 1
29: 6
2 Ch. 1: 2—A[1]
23: 1, 14
25: 5

ἑκατοντάς.

1 Sa. 20: 2
2 Sa. 18: 4

1 Ch. 28: 1

ἑκατοστεύω.

Genesis 26:12

ἐκβαίνω.

Jos. 4:16, 17
18

Isa. 24:18

ἐκβάλλω.

Gen. 3:24
4:14
21:10
Exo. 2:17
6: 1
10:11
11: 1
12:33, 39
23:18, 28
29, 30
31
33: 2
34:11, 24
Lev. 1:16
14:40
21: 7, 14[a]
22:13

Nu. 21:32
22: 6:11
30:10
Deu. 11:23
24: 2 A[2] [b]
29:28
33:27
Jos. 15: 8 B[c]
24:12 A[d]
18
Jud. 5:21 A[e]
6: 9
9:41
11: 2, 7
1 Sa. 26:19
2 Sa. 7:23
1 Ki. 2:27

2 Ki. 16: 6
1 Ch. 17:21
2 Ch. 11:14, 16
13: 9
15: 8
20:11
23:14
29: 5, 16
16
Ezra 10: 3
Job 22:22 B[f]
24:12
31:39 A[f]
Psa. 16:11
43: 3
49:17
77:55
79: 9

Ps. 108:10
Pro. 18:22, 22
22:10
24:58
27:15
Ecc. 3: 6
Isa. 2:20
5:29
22:17
Jer. 12:14, 15
22:28
23:31—B
Lam. 3:16
Eze. 44:22
Hos. 9:15
Jon. 1:15[g]
2:11
Zec. 7:14

[a] A βδελύσσω. [b] *pro* ἐμβάλλω. [c] *pro* διεκβάλλω. [d] *pro* ἐξαποστέλλω. [e] *pro* ἐκσύρω. [f] *pro* ἐκλαμβάνω. [g] AS[2] ἐμβάλλω, S[1] βάλλω.

ἐκβιάζω.

Jud. 14:15[a]
Est. 7: 8 A[b]

Psa. 37:13
Pro. 16:26

[a] A πτωχεύω. [b] *pro* βιάζω.

ἐκβλαστάνω.

Nu. 17: 5
Job 38:27

Isa. 55:10[a]

[a] A βλαστάνω.

ἐκβλύζω.

Proverbs 3:10

ἐκβοάω.

2 Kings 4:36

ἐκβολή.

Exo. 11: 1
Eze. 47: 8 A[a]

Jon. 1: 5

[a] *pro* διεκβολή.

ἐκβράζω.

Nehemiah 13:28

ἐκβρασμός.

Nahum 2:10

ἐκγελάω.

Neh. 2:19
4: 1
Psa. 2: 4[a]

Psa. 36:13
58: 9

[a] A ἐγγελάω.

ἐκγεννάω.

Ps. 109: 3 S[1] [a]

[a] *pro* γεννάω.

ἔκγονος.

Gen. 48: 6
Deu. 7:13 AB[a]
28: 4, 4 A[b]
11, 11
18, 51
53
29:11[c]
30: 9, 9
31:12
2 Sa. 21:16
18 AB[a]

Pro. 23:18[d]
24:20, 34
35, 36
37
Isa. 11: 8
14:29[d], 29
30: 6[e]
48:19[e]
49:15[e]
61: 9[e]
65:23[e]

[a] *pro* ἔγγονος. [b] *pro* γέννημα. [c] A τέκνον. [d] A ἔγγονος. [e] S ἔγγονος.

ἐκγράφω.

Proverbs 25: 1

ἐκδανείζω, -νίζω.

Exo. 22:25
Deu. 23:19

Deu. 28:12 A[a]

[a] *pro* δανείζω.

ἐκδέρω.

Lev. 1: 6[a]
2 Ch. 29:34[b]
35:11[c]
Mic. 2: 8
3: 8

[a] AB² δέρω. [b] A δέρω.
[c] B δέρω.

ἐκδέχομαι.

Gen. 43: 8
44:32
2 Sa. 19:38 A[a]
Job 34:33 S[a]
Ps. 118:122 AS[b]
Isa. 57: 1
Isa. 66: 4 B[a]
Hos. 8: 7
9: 6
Mic. 2:12, 12
Nah. 3:18

[a] pro ἐκλέγω. [b] pro ἐνδέχομαι.

ἐκδέω.

Joshua 2:18

ἐκδιδύσκω.

1 Sa. 31: 8
2 Sa. 23:10
Neh. 4:23
Hos. 7: 1

ἐκδίδωμι.

Exo. 2:21
Lev. 21: 3[a]
Jud. 1:14, 15
2 Ki. 12:11[b]
Jer. 31:17

[a] A ἐγγίζω. [b] A δοξάζω.

ἐκδιηγέομαι.

Job 12: 8
Psa. 49:16 AS²[a]
117:17 AS¹[a]
Eze. 12:16
Hab. 1: 5

[a] pro διηγέομαι

ἐκδικάζω.

Lev. 19:18
Deu. 32:43[a]

[a] A ἐκδικέω.

ἐκδικέω.

Gen. 4:15, 24
Exo. 21:20, 21
Lev. 26:25
Nu. 31: 2
Deu. 18:19
32:41 + A²
43A[a], 43
Jud. 6:31 A[b]
15: 7 — A
16:28 A[c]
1 Sa. 3:13
14:24
15: 2
18:25 — A
24:13
2 Ki. 9: 7
2 Ch. 22: 8
Psa. 36:28[d]
98: 8
Isa. 57:16
Jer. 5: 9, 29
9: 9
15: 3
23: 2, 34
25:12
26:10, 25
27:15, 18
Jer. 27:18, 21
28:36 — A
44, 52
Eze. 7: 3, 27
16:38
19:12
20: 4
23:25, 45
24: 8
25:12, 12
Hos. 1: 4
2:13
4: 9
8:13
9: 9
12: 2
Joel 3:21 A[e]
Amos 3: 2, 14
14
Obad. 21
Nah. 1: 2
2 - ABS
2
9 — S¹
Zeph. 1: 8, 9, 12
3: 7
Zec. 5: 3, 3
Ps. 140: 7
Isa. 59:17
66:15
Jer. 11:20
20:10, 12
26:10, 21
27:15, 27
28, 31
28: 6, 11
11
36 — A
Lam. 3:59
Eze. 5:15
9: 1
Eze. 14:21
16:38, 41
20: 4
23:10, 45
45
24: 8
25:11, 12
14, 14
15, 15
17, 17
30:14
Hos. 9: 7
Mic. 5:15
7: 4

[a] pro ἐκδικάζω. [b] pro δικάζω.
[c] pro ἀνταποδίδωμι.
[d] AS² ἐκδιώκω. [e] pro ἐκζητέω.
[a] A ἀνταπόδομα.

ἐκδικησία.

Judges 16:28 A[a]

[a] pro ἀνταπόδοσις.

ἐκδίκησις.

Exo. 7: 4
12:12
Nu. 31: 2, 3
33: 4
Deu. 32:35
Jud. 11:36
14: 4[a]
Jud. 15: 7 + A
2 Sa. 4: 8
22:48
Psa. 17:48
57:11
78:10
93: 1, 1

ἐκδικητής.

Psalm 8: 3

ἐκδιώκω.

Deu. 6:19
1 Sa. 30:10 A[a]
1 Ch. 8:13
12:15[b]
Psa. 36:28 AS²[c]
43:17
68: 5[b]
100: 5
Ps. 118:157
Jer. 27:44
29:20
Dan. 4:22, 29
30
5:21
Joel 2:20

[a] pro καταδιώκω. [b] S διώκω.
[c] pro ἐκδικέω.

ἐκδοξάζω.

Haggai 1: 8

ἐκδύνω, —δύω.

Gen. 37:23
Lev. 6:11
16:23
24 A[a]
Nu. 20:26, 28
1 Sa. 18: 4 A
19:24
31: 9
1 Ch. 10: 9
Est. 5: 1
Job 11:15
19: 9
Job 30:13
Pro. 11: 8[b]
Cant. 5: 3
Isa. 32:11
52: 2[c]
Lam. 4: 3
Eze. 16:39
23:26
26:16
44:19
Hos. 2: 3

[a] pro ἐνδύω. [b] A δύνω.
[c] B ἐκλύω.

ἐκεῖσε.

Job 39:29

ἐκζέω.

Gen. 49: 4
Exo. 16:20[a]
1 Sa. 5: 6
6: 1
Job 30:27
Eze. 24: 5 + A
47: 9

[a] A² ζέω.

ἐκζητέω.

Gen. 9: 5 + A¹
5, 5
42:22
Exo. 10:11[a]
18:15
Lev. 10:16
Deu. 4:29 A[b]
29
12: 5, 30
30 + A
17: 4, 9
23:21, 21
Jos. 2:22
22:23
Jud. 6:29 A[c]
14: 4 A[b]
1 Sa. 20:15
2 Sa. 4:11
1 Ki. (3)40
14: 5 A
2 Ki. 1:16[d]
16 + A
22:13
1 Ch. 10:14 A[b]
1 Ch. 13: 3 A²[b]
15:13[e]
2 Ch. 1: 5
12:14
14: 4, 7[f], 7
15: 2, 13
16:12 A[h]
17: 3, 4
19: 3
20: 3, 4
22: 9 A[b]
25:20
26: 5
28:23
30:19
31:21
Ezra 4: 2
6:21
9:12
10:16
Psa. 9:11, 13
25
34 AS[b]
13: 2
Psa. 21:27
24:10
26: 4, 8[g]
30:24
33: 5, 11
43:22
52: 3
60: 8
68: 7 S[b]
33
76: 3
77: 7
34 S[b]
104:45
110: 2
118: 2, 10
15 S¹[b]
22, 33
34 S¹[i]
45, 56
94
100[k]
145, 155
121: 9
141: 5
Pro. 11:27
27:21
21 ACS[b]
29:10
Ecc. 1:13
Isa. 1:12, 17
8:19 — AS
19
9:13 AS³[h]
16: 5
31: 1 AS[b]
34:16 A[b]
Jer. 10:21 AS[b]
36:13[k]
43:24 A[b]
44: 7
Eze. 3:18, 20
33: 6, 8
34: 6[a], 8
10, 11
12
16 A[b]
39:14
Dan. 9: 3
Hos. 5: 6
7:10
10:12
Joel 3:21[m]
Amos 5: 4, 5, 6
14
9:12
Mic. 6: 8
Zec. 8:21, 22
Mal. 2: 7

[a] A ζητέω. [b] pro ζητέω.
[c] pro ἐρευνάω.
[d] A ἐπερωτάω, B ζητέω.
[e] ABS ζητέω. [f] B ζητέω.
[g] S¹ ζητέω. [h] pro κατανοέω.
[i] pro ἐξερευνάω. [k] S ζητέω.
[m] A ἐκδικέω.

ἔκθαμβος.

Daniel 7: 7

ἔκθεμα.

Est. (9)14 A[a]
17 — S¹
Eze. 16:23

[a] pro πρόσταγμα.

ἐκθερίζω.

Lev. 19: 9, 9
Lev. 23: 5

ἐκθηλάζω.

Isaiah 66:11

ἐκθλιβή.

Micah 7: 2

ἐκθλίβω.

Gen. 40:11
Lev. 22:24
Jos. 19:47
Jud. 1:34
2:15
18 — A
10:12 A[a]
16:16[b]
1 Sa. 10:18 A[a]
1 Ki. 8:37 A[a]
2 Ki. 13:22
Psa. 17:39
Psa. 34: 5
41:10
42: 2
118:157 AS¹[c]
Pro. 12:13
Isa. 29: 2[c]
Lam. 4:12
Eze. 34:21
Amos 6:14
Mic. 7: 2
Zeph. 1:17

[a] pro θλίβω. [b] A κατεργάζομαι.
[c] S¹ ἐκλείπω.

ἔκθλιψις.

Eze. 12:18 A[a] [a] pro θλίψις.

ἐκκαθαίρω.

Deu. 26:13
Jos. 17:15[a]
Jud. 7: 4[b]

[a] A ἐκκαθαρίζω. [b] A δοκιμάζω.

ἐκκαθαρίζω.

Deu. 32:43
Jos. 17:15 A[a]
Jos. 17:18
Jud. 20:13[b]
Isa. 4: 4

[a] pro ἐκκαθαίρω. [b] A ἐξαίρω.

ἐκκαίω.

Exo. 22: 6
Nu. 11: 1, 3
Deu. 29:20
32:22
Jud. 15: 5[a], 14[b]
2 Sa. 22: 9, 13
24: 1
1 Ki. 20:21
2 Ki. 22:13[c], 17
2 Ch. 34:21, 25
Neh. 10:34
Est. 1:12 + S³
Job 3:17[d]
Psa. 2:13
38: 4
72:21 S²[e]
77:38
78: 5
88:47
105:18
Ps. 117:12
120: 6 S¹[f]
Pro. 6:19
14: 5, 25
19: 9
24:23 S[f]
29: 8
Isa. 50:11
Jer. 1:14
4: 4
7:20 S[g]
15:14
51: 6
Eze. 20:48
24:10 A[h]
11 A[i]
Dan. 3:19, 19
22
Obad. 18
Nah. 2:13

[a] A ἐξάπτω. [b] A ὀσφραίνομαι.
[c] B ἐκχέω. [d] A πάνω.
[e] pro εὐφραίνω. [f] pro συγκαίω.
[g] pro καίω. [h] pro ἀνακαίω.
[i] pro προσκαίω.

ἐκκαλέω.

Gen. 19: 5
Deu. 20:10

ἐκκαλύπτω.

Proverbs 26:26[a]

[a] B ἐγκαλύπτω, S¹ συγκαλύπτω.

ἐκκενόω.

Gen. 24:20
Jud. 20:31[a], 32[b]
2 Ch. 24:11
Psa. 74: 9
136: 7, 7
Cant. 1: 3
Isa. 51:17
Eze. 5: 2, 12
12:14[c]
28: 7
30:11
Dan. 9:25

[a] A ἐξέλκω. [b] A ἐκσπάω.
[c] A ἐκχέω.

ἐκκεντέω.

Nu. 22:29
Jos. 16:10
Jud. 9:54
1 Ch. 10: 4
Isa. 14:19
Jer. 44:10
Lam. 4: 9

ἐκκήρυκτος.

Jeremiah 22:30

ἐκκινέω.

2 Ki. 6:11
Pro. 16:17 S[a]

[a] pro ἐκκλίνω.

ἐκκλάω.

Leviticus 1:17

ἐκκλείω.

Exo. 23: 2[a]
Job 34:20
Psa. 67:31 S¹[b]

[a] A ἐκκλίνω. [b] pro ἀποκλείω.

ἐκκλησία.

Deu. 4:10
9:10
18:16
23: 1[a]
2 - AB¹
3, 3, 8
32: 1
Jos. 9: 8
Jud. 20: 2
21: 5, 8
1 Sa. 17:47
1 Sa. 19:20
1 Ki. 8:14, 22
55, 65
12: 3 + A
1 Ch. 13: 2, 4
28: 2, 8
29: 1, 10
20, 20
2 Ch. 1: 3, 5
6: 3, 3
12, 13

2 Ch. 7: 8
10: 3
20: 5, 14
23: 3
28:14
29:23, 28
31—A
32
30: 2,4,13
17, 23
24, 25
25
Ezra 2:64
10: 1,8,12
14+AS
Neh. 5: 7, 13
7:66
Neh. 8: 2, 17
13: 1
Job 30:28
Psa. 21:23, 26
25: 5, 12
34:18
39:10
67:27
88: 6
106:32
149: 1
Pro. 5:14
Lam. 1:10
Eze. 32: 3+A
23+A
Joel 2:16
Mic. 2: 5

[a] A² οἶκος.

ἐκκλησιάζω.

Lev. 8: 3
Nu. 20: 8
Deu. 4:10
Deu. 31:12, 28
1 Ch. 13: 5 BS[a]
Est. 4:16

[a] pro ἐξεκκλησιάζω.

ἐκκλησιαστής.

Ecc. 1: 1,2,12
7:28
Ecc. 12: 8, 9
10

ἐκκλίνω.

Gen. 18: 5
19: 2, 3
38:16
Exo. 10: 6
23: 2, 2 A[a]
Nu. 20:17, 21
21:22
22:23, 26
33, 33
Deu. 2:27
5:32
16:19—AB
17:11
20: 3
24:19
27:19
29:18
31:29
Jos. 1: 7
23: 6
Jud. 2:17
4:18[b], 18[b]
18[b]
10:16[c]
14: 5 A[d], 8
18: 3, 15
19:11, 12
15
20: 8 A[e]
45 A[f]
47 A[f]
Ruth 4: 1, 1
1 Sa. 8: 3, 3
12:20
14: 7
15: 6, 6
17:53
18:11 A
25:14
2 Sa. 2:19, 21
21
3:27
6:10
1 Ki. 11: 2
3+A
4, 9
15: 5
16 p 28—A
22:43
2 Ki. 4: 8, 10
11
5:12
1 Ch. 13: 9, 13
2 Ch. 20:10, 32
34: 2, 33
Neh. 9:19
Neh. 13:26
Job 23:11
24: 4
29:11
31: 7
34:27
36:19
39:32
Psa. 13: 3
16:11
26: 9
33:15
36:27
43:19
52: 4
54: 4
100: 4
108:23
118:21
50 S¹ [g]
51, 102
115, 157
124: 5
138:19
140: 4
Pro. 1:15
3: 7
4: 5 A
15, 27
5:12
7:25
9: 4, 16
10:25
14:16, 27
15:24, 27
16:17[a]
17:23
18: 5
24: 7
28: 9
Isa. 9:20
10: 2
66:12
Jer. 5:23, 25
14: 8
18:14
Lam. 3:34
Eze. 16:27
Dan. 9: 5, 11
Hos. 5: 6
Joel 2: 7
Amos 2: 7
5:12
Zeph. 1: 6
Mal. 2: 8
3: 5, 7

[a] pro ἐκκλείω. [b] A ἐκνεύω. [c] A μεθίστημι. [d] pro ἔρχομαι. [e] pro ἐπιστρέφω. [f] pro ἐπιβλέπω. [g] pro ζάω. [h] S ἐκκινέω.

ἐκκλύζω.

Leviticus 6:28

ἐκκολαπτός.

1 Ki. 6:27 B[a] [a] pro ἐγκ-

ἐκκολάπτω.

Exo. 36:13—A¹
1 Ki. 6:32 B[a]
Pro. 24:52 A[b]

[a] pro ἐγκ- [b] pro ἐκκόπτω.

ἐκκόπτω.

Gen. 32: 8 A[a]
36:35
Exo. 21:27
34:13—A
Nu. 16:14
Deu. 7: 5
12: 3
20:19, 20
Jos. 15:16—A
Jud. 6:25 A[b]
26 A[c]
28 A[b]
16:21[d]
21: 6[e]
1 Ki. 15:13
2 Ch. 14: 3, 14
15
31: 1 A[a]
Job 14: 7
Job 19:10
42 p 18
Psa. 73: 5[f]
Pro. 24:52[g]
Isa. 9:10 AS[a]
27: 9
Jer. 6: 6
10: 3
22: 7
26:13 A[a]
23
31: 2
51: 7
8 ABS[a]
Dan. 4:11
9:26
Mic. 5:14
Zec. 12:11

[a] pro κόπτω. [b] pro ὀλοθρεύω. [c] pro ἐξολοθρεύω [d] A ἐξορύσσω. [e] A ἀφαιρέω. [f] S¹ διακόπτω. [g] A ἐκκολάπτω.

ἐκκρέμαμαι.

Genesis 44:30

ἐκκρούω.

Deuteronomy 19: 5

ἐκκρύπτω.

Pro. 19:24 C[a] [a] pro ἐγκρύπτω.

ἐκκύπτω.

Ps. 101:20
Cant. 2: 9
Cant. 6: 9[a]
Jer. 6: 1

[a] A¹ ἀναβαίνω, A² ἐγκύπτω.

ἐκλαμβάνω.

Job 3: 5
22:22[a]
Job 31:39[b]

[a] B ἐκβάλλω. [b] A ἐκβάλλω.

ἐκλάμπω.

2 Sa. 22:29
Eze. 43: 2
Dan. 12: 3 A[a]

[a] pro λάμπω.

ἐκλατομέω.

Nu. 21:18
Deu. 6:11

ἐκλέγω.

Gen. 6: 2
13:11
Nu. 16: 5, 7
17: 5
Deu. 1:33
4:37
7: 7
10:15
12: 5, 11
14, 18
21, 26
14: 2, 22
Deu. 14:23, 24
15:20
16: 2, 6, 7
11, 15
16
17: 8, 10
15
18: 5, 6
21: 5 A[a]
26: 2
30:19
31:11
Jos. 9:33
24:15[b], 22
Jud. 5: 8[c]
10:14
1 Sa. 2:28[d]
8:18, 18
10:24
12:13
13: 2
16: 8, 9, 10
17: 8, 40
2 Sa. 6:21
16:18
19:38[e]
24:12
13—A
15
1 Ki. 3: 8
8:16
16—A
16, 44
48
11:13, 32
34, 36
14:21
18:23, 25
2 Ki. 21: 7
23:27
1 Ch. 15: 2
16:41
19:10
21:10, 11
28: 4, 5
2 Ch. 6: 5, 5
6—8
6, 34
38
2 Ch. 7:12, 16
12:13
33: 7
35:19
Neh. 1: 9
9: 7
Job 29:25
34:33[f]
Psa. 32:12
46: 5
64: 5
77:67, 68
70
83:11
104:26
131:13
134: 4
Pro. 17: 3 S¹ [g]
21:47
Isa. 7:15
16—S¹
14: 1
40:20
41: 8, 9, 24
43:10
44: 1, 2, 13
49: 7
56: 4
58: 5, 6
65:12
66: 3, 4[h], 4
Eze. 20:38[i]
Dan. 11:35
12:10
Joel 2:16
Zec. 3: 2

[a] pro ἐπιλέγω. [b] A αἱρέω. [c] A αἱρετίζω. [d] A ἐπιλέγω. [e] A ἐκδέχομαι. [f] S ἐκδέχομαι. [g] pro ἐκλεκτός. [h] B ἐκδέχομαι. [i] B ἐλέγχω.

ἐκλείπω.

Gen. 8:13, 13
11: 6
18:11
21:15
25: 8, 17
29, 30
35:29
47:13, 15
15, 16
18
49:10, 33
Exo. 13:22
Nu. 11:33
Deu. 15:11
28:65
32:36
Jos. 3:13, 16
4: 7
5:12
9:29
Jud. 5: 6, 7, 7
8: 5[a], 15[b]
1 Sa. 2:33
9: 7
16:11
2 Sa. 3:29
20:18, 18
1 Ki. 17:14, 16
2 Ki. 7:13
2 Ch. 4:18
6:16
Est. 9:28
Job 6:15
13:19
14: 7
21:19
31:26
Psa. 9: 7
11: 2
17:38
30:11
36:20, 20
38:11
54:12
63: 7
Psa. 67: 3, 3
68: 4
70: 9, 13
71:19
72:19, 26
77:33
83: 3
89: 7, 9, 9
101: 4, 28
103:29, 35
106: 5
118:81, 82
123
141: 4
142: 7
Pro. 3: 3
4:21[c]
10:20
24+A
24:10, 46
Isa. 7: 8
15: 6
19: 5, 6, 13
21:16
29: 2 S¹[d]
20
38:12—AS
14
51: 6
53: 3
54:10
55:13
56: 5
58:11
59:21
66:20
Jer. 4:31
6: 4, 15
29, 29
7:28
9:10
14: 4, 6
15:10
18:14
24:10
Jer. 26:28
28:30, 58
31:11
34: 6
38:40
42:19
43:23, 29[e]
44:21
49:17, 22
51:12, 18
27, 27
Lam. 1:19
2:11, 11
3:22—AB
4:17, 22
Eze. 15: 4
22:15
Eze. 24:11
34:16, 21
47:12
Hos. 4: 3
13: 2
Amos 8:13
Jon. 2: 8
Nah. 1: 4
Hab. 2:13
3:17
Zeph. 1: 2, 2, 3
3
2: 9
3: 6
Zec. 11: 9, 9
16 S² [f]
13: 8

[a] A πειράω. [b] A ἐκλύω. [c] S¹ λείπω. [d] pro ἐκθλίβω. [e] A ἐκτρίβω. [f] pro ἐκλιμπάνω.

ἐκλείχω.

Nu. 22: 4, 4
1 Ki. 18:38
1 Ki. 22:38

ἔκλειψις.

Deu. 28:48
Neh. 3:21
Pro. 14:28
Isa. 17: 4
Eze. 5:16

ἐκλεκτός.

Gen. 23: 6
41: 2, 4, 5
7, 18
20
Exo. 14: 7
30:23
Nu. 11:28
Deu. 12:11
Jud. 20:15, 34
1 Sa. 24: 3
26: 2
2 Sa. 8: 8
21: 6
22:27, 27
1 Ki. (3) p 46 bis
4:23
23+A
23
2 Ki. 3:19+A
8:12
19:23
1 Ch. 7:40
9:22
16:13
18: 8
Ezra 5: 8
Neh. 5:18
Job 37:10
Psa. 17:27, 27
77:31
88: 4
4+S¹
20
104: 6, 43
105: 5, 23
140: 4
Pro. 8:19
12:24
Pro. 17: 3[a]
Cant. 5:15
6: 8, 9
Isa. 22: 7, 8
28:16
40:30
42: 1
43:20
45: 4
49: 2
54:12
65: 9, 15
23
Jer. 3:19
10:17
22: 7
26:15
31:15
32:20
38:39
Lam. 1:15
5:13, 14
Eze. 7:20
17: 3 A[b]
22[c]
19:12, 14
25: 9
27:20
22 A[d]
24
31:16
Dan. 11:15
Amos 5:11
Hab. 1:16
Hag. 2: 7
22+A
Zec. 7:14
11:16

[a] S¹ ἐκλέγω. [b] pro ἐπίλεκτος. [c] A ἐπίλεκτος. [d] pro χρηστός.

ἐκλευκαίνομαι.

Daniel 12:10—A

ἔκλευκος.

Leviticus 13:24

ἐκλιμία.

Deuteronomy 28:20

ἐκλιμπάνω.

Zec. 11:16[a] [a] S² ἐκλείπω.

ἐκλογίζομαι.
2 Ki.12:15 | 2 Ki.22: 7

ἐκλοχίζω.
Canticles 5:10

ἔκλυσις.
Isa. 21: 3
Jer. 20: 3
Eze. 23:33[a]
[a] A ἐκχέω.

ἐκλύτρωσις.
Numbers 3:49

ἐκλύω.
Gen. 27:40
49:24
Deu. 20: 3
Jos. 10: 6
18: 3
Jud. 8:15 A[a]
1 Sa. 14:28
30:21 AB[b]
2 Sa. 4: 1
16: 2[c], 14
17: 2, 29
21:11
15 A[d]
1 Ki. 20: 4+A
21:43
2 Ch. 15: 7
Ezra 4: 4
Neh. 6: 9
Job 19:25
20 28 S[e]
30:16 S[2f]
Pro. 3:11
6: 3
23:20 C[g]
Isa. 13: 7
29: 9
46: 2
51:20
52: 2 B[h]
Jer. 4:31
12: 5
30:13
45: 4
Lam. 2:12, 19
Eze. 7:17
31:15
[a] pro ἐκλείπω. [b] pro ὑπολείπω.
[c] B λύω. [d] pro πορεύω.
[e] pro ἑλκύω. [f] pro ἐκχέω.
[g] pro ἐκτείνω. [h] pro ἐκδύω.

ἐκμιαίνω.
Jer. 32: 2[a] [a] ABS μαίνομαι.

ἐκμετρέω.
Deu. 21: 2
Ps. 107: 8 S[a]
Hos. 1:10
[a] pro διαμετρέω.

ἐκμιαίνω.
Lev. 18:20, 23
25[a]
Lev. 19:31
[a] AB μιαίνω.

ἐκμυελίζω.
Numbers 24: 8

ἐκμυκτηρίζω.
Psa. 2: 4
21: 8
Psa. 34:16

ἐκνεύω.
Jud. 4:18 A[a]
18 A[a]
18 A[a]
18:26+A
2 Ki. 2:24
23:16
Mic. 6:14
[a] pro ἐκκλίνω.

ἐκνήφω.
Gen. 9:24
1 Sa. 25:37
Joel 1: 5
Hab. 2: 7, 19

ἔκνηψις.
Lam. 2:18 | Lam. 3:48

ἑκουσιάζομαι.
Jud. 5: 2[a], 9[b]
Ezra 2:68
3: 5
Ezra 7:13, 15
16[c]
Neh. 11: 2
[a] A προαίρεσις, B ἀκουσιάζομαι.
[b] A δυνάστης. [c] B ἀκουσιάζομαι.

ἑκουσιασμός.
Ezra 7:16

ἑκούσιος.
Lev. 7: 6
23:38
Nu. 15: 3
29:39
Deu. 12: 6–8
Ezra 1: 4, 6
Ezra 3: 5
8:28
Neh. 5: 8
Psa. 67:10
118:108
Pro. 27: 6

ἑκουσίως.
Exo. 36: 2 | Psa. 53: 8

ἐκπειράζω.
Deu. 6:16, 16
8: 2 B[a]
Deu. 8:16
Psa. 77:18
[a] pro πειράζω.

ἐκπέμπω.
Gen. 24:54, 56
59
1 Sa. 20:20
1 Sa. 24:20
2 Sa. 19:31
Pro. 17:11

ἐκπεράω.
Numbers 11:31

ἐκπεριπορεύομαι.
Joshua 15: 3

ἐκπετάζω, –τάννυμι.
Exo. 9:29
33 A[a]
Ezra 9: 5
Job 26: 9[b]
Pro. 13:16
Isa. 54: 3
Isa. 65: 2
Lam. 1:10
Eze. 12:13
17:20
19: 8
[a] pro ἐκτείνω. [b] A σκέπω.

ἐκπέτομαι.
Job 20: 8
Pro. 7:10
Lam. 4:19[a]
Hos. 9:11
11:11 A[b]
Nah. 3:16
[a] A ἐξάπτω. [b] pro ἐξίστημι.

ἐκπηδάω.
Deu. 33:22
1 Ki. 21:39, 39
Est. 4: 1

ἐκπιέζω, –άζω.
Jud. 6:38[a]
18: 7–A
1 Sa. 12: 3
Pro. 24:68
Eze. 22:29
Zeph. 3:19
[a] A ἀποπιάζω.

ἐκπικραίνω.
Deuteronomy 32:16 A[a]
[a] pro παραπικραίνω.

ἐκπίνω.
Job 6: 4
Isa. 51:17[a]
Zec. 9:15
[a] A πίνω.

ἐκπίπτω.
Deu. 19: 5
2 Ki. 6: 5
Job 14: 2
15:30, 33
24: 9
Ecc. 10:10
Isa. 6:13[a]
14:12
28: 1, 4
40: 7
[a] A ἐκσπάω.

ἐκπλήσσω
Ecclesiastes 7:17

ἐκπλύνω.
Isaiah 4: 4

ἐκποιέω.
1 Ki. 21:10
2 Ch. 7: 7[a]
Eze. 46: 7[b], 11
[a] A ποιέω. [b] A εὐποιέω.

ἐκπολεμέω.
Exo. 1:10
Deu. 20:10, 19
Jos. 9: 2
10: 4
Jos. 22:12
23: 3, 10
Jud. 9:52 A[a]
10: 9 A[a]
[a] pro παρατάσσω.

ἐκπολιορκέω.
Jos. 7: 3[a] | Jos. 10: 5, 34[b]
[a] A ἐμπολιορκέω.
[b] AB πολιορκέω.

ἐκπορεύω.
Gen. 2:10
24:11, 13
15, 43[a]
45
34:24 A[b]
Exo. 5:20
7:15
8:20 A[c]
13: 4, 8
14: 8
16:29
25:31, 32
34
35+A
33: 7, 11
34:34
40:15
Nu. 1: 3, 20
22, 24
26, 28
30, 32
34, 36
38, 40
42, 45
12:12
26: 2
31:27, 28
36
32:24
Deu. 8: 3, 7
11:10
23: 4, 23
24:11
25:17
28: 6, 19
31: 2
Jos. 2:10
6: 1
15: 3, 3[d]
4[e], 18[f]
Jud. 1:24
2:15 B[g]
8: 1 A[g]
30
9:33
11:31, 34
13:14
1 Sa. 11: 7
14:11
17: 8, 20 A
35, 55 A
18: 5 A, 13
16
20:11
24:15
2 Sa. 16: 5, 5
18: 4
19: 7, 19
1 Ki. 2:30
4:29
8: 9
1 Ki. 10:29
15:17
21:18
22:35
2 Ki. 11: 7, 8
9–B
1 Ch. 5:18
7:11
12:33, 36
27: 1
2 Ch. 15: 5–A
23: 7
26:11
33:14[e]
Job 3:16
29: 7
38: 8, 24
29
39:21
25+A
41:10, 11
12
Psa. 18: 6
40: 7
67: 8
87: 9
88:35
Pro. 3:16
Isa. 36:16
Jer. 5: 6
6:25
17:16
19–S[1]
21–S[1]
19:10
21: 9
22:10
23:19[b]
32:18
45: 2
Eze. 1:13
9: 7
12: 4
14:22
33:30
44:19
46:10
47: 1, 8, 12
Dan. 7:10+A
10:20 A[i]
11:30
Amos 5: 3[c], 3[c]
Mic. 1: 3
Zec. 2: 3
5: 3, 5, 6
9
6: 1, 5, 6
6, 6, 7
8
8:10
[a] A ἐξέρχομαι. [b] pro ἐμπορεύομαι. [c] pro ἐξέρχομαι.
[d] A περιπορεύω. [e] A πορεύω.
[f] A εἰσπορεύω. [g] pro πορεύω.
[h] S[1] εἰσπορεύω. [i] pro εἰσπο-

ἐκπορθέω.
Job 12: 6

ἐκπορνεύω.
Gen. 38:24
Exo. 34:15, 16
Exo. 31:16–A
Lev. 17: 7
19:29, 29
20: 5, 6
21: 9
Nu. 15:39
25: 1
Deu. 22:21
31:16
Jud. 2:17
8:27, 33
2 Ch. 21:11, 13
13
Jer. 3: 1
Eze. 6: 9, 9[a]
Eze. 16:16, 17
20, 26
26
27 A[b]
28[c], 28
30, 33
20:30
23: 3, 5, 30
43–A
Hos. 1: 2, 2
2: 5
4:12, 13
18
5: 3
[a] B πορνεύω. [b] pro ἀσεβέω.
[c] A ἀσεβέω.

ἐκπρεπής.
1 Ki. 8:53 AB[a] [a] pro εὐπρεπής.

ἐκπριόω.
Proverbs 24:11

ἔκρηγμα.
Ezekiel 30:16

ἐκρήγνυμι.
Job 18:14

ἐκριζόω.
Jud. 5:14[a]
Jer. 1:10
Dan. 7: 8
Zeph. 2: 4
[a] τιμωρέω.

ἐκρίπτω.
Jud. 6:13[a]
9:17[b]
15: 9, 15[b]
Psa. 1: 4
Pro. 5:23
Jer. 22:28
Zeph. 2: 4
[a] A ἀπωθέω. [b] A ῥίπτω.

ἐκρυέω.
Deu. 28:40 | Isa. 64: 6

ἔκρυσις.
Ezekiel 40:38

ἐκσαρκίζω.
Ezekiel 24: 4

ἐκσιφωνίζω.
Job 5: 5

ἐκσπάω.
Jud. 3:22
16:14 A[a]
20:32 A[b]
1 Sa. 17:35
51+A
19:10 A[c]
Job 29:17 AOS[*d]
Psa. 21:10
24:15
128: 6
Isa. 6:13 A[e]
Jer. 22:24
Eze. 11:19
17: 9
21: 3, 5
Amos 3:12, 12
4:11
9:15
Hab. 2: 9
Zec. 3: 2
13: 7[f]
[a] pro ἐξαίρω. [b] pro ἐκκενόω.
[c] pro διασώζω. [d] pro ἐξαρπάζω.
[e] pro ἐκπίπτω.
[f] AS[2] διασκορπίζω.

ἐκσπερματίζω.
Numbers 5:28

ἔκστασις.
Gen. 2:21
15:12
27:33
Nu. 13:33
Deu. 28:28
Jud. 16:14+A
1 Sa. 11: 7
14:15, 15
2 Ki. 4:13[a]
2 Ch. 14:14

2 Ch. 15: 5
17:10
20:29
29: 8
Psa. 30: 1—S
23
67:28
115: 2
Pro. 26:10
Jer. 5:30
Eze. 17: 3 A[b]
26:16
27:35
32:10
Dan. 10: 7
Hab. 3:14
Zec. 12: 4
14:13

[a] B ἔγκτησις. [b] pro ἔκτασις.

ἐκστραγγίζω.

Ezekiel 23:34 +A

ἐκστρατεύω.

Pro. 24:62 AS[a] [a] pro στρατεύω.

ἐκστρέφω.

Deu. 32:20
Eze. 13:20
16:34 A[a]
Eze. 16:34 A[a]
Amos 6:12
Zec. 11:16[b]

[a] pro διαστρέφω. [b] A ἐκτρίβω.

ἐκσύρω.

Jud. 5:21[a] [a] A ἐκβάλλω.

ἐκταράσσω.

Psa. 17: 5
Psa. 87:17[a]

[a] B ταράσσω.

ἔκτασις.

Eze. 17: 3[a] [a] A ἔκστασις.

ἐκτάσσω.

Nu. 32:27
2 Ki. 25:19
Neh. 4:16 AS[a]
Neh. 5:15 S[1 a]
Dan. 1:10

[a] pro ἐκτινάσσω.

ἐκτείνω.

Gen. 3:22
8: 9
14:22
19:10
22:10
48:14
Exo. 3:20
4: 4, 4
6: 8
7: 5, 19
8: 5, 6
16, 17
9:22, 23
33[a]
10:12, 21
22
14.16, 21
26, 27
15:12
25:19
38:19
40:17
Nu. 14:30
Deu. 25:11
Jos. 8:18, 18
19
Jud. 3:21
5:15+A
26
6:21
9:33, 44
44[b]
15:15
20:37—A
1 Sa. 1:16
14:27
17:49
2 Sa. 6: 6
15: 5
22:33 A[c]
24:16
1 Ki. 8:41+A
1 Ki. 13: 4, 4
2 Ki. 6: 7
21:13
1 Ch. 13: 9, 10
21:16
Ezra 6:12
Neh. 5:13 S[1 c]
9:15
13:21
Est. 4:11
8: 4
Job 26: 7
28: 9
30:12
36:30
Psa. 54:21—S[1]
59:10
79:12
103: 2
107:10 S[1 d]
124: 3
137: 7
Pro. 1:17, 24
23:20[e], 32
24:67
29:37[f], 38
Isa. 1:15
44:24
Jer. 1: 9
6:12
10:12
15: 6
21: 5[g]
28:15, 25
29:23
Lam. 2: 8
Eze. 1:11, 22
23
2: 9
6:14
8: 3
17+A
Eze. 10: 7
13: 9
14: 9, 13
16:27
17: 6
25:7, 13, 16
30:25
32: 4
35: 3
Eze. 37: 6
Dan. 11:42
Hos. 5: 1
7: 5
11: 4
Zeph. 1: 4
2:13
Zec. 1:16[h]
12: 1

[a] A ἐκπετάννυμι. [b] A ἐκχέω.
[c] pro ἐκτινάσσω.
[d] pro ἐπιβάλλω. [e] C ἐκλύω.
[f] S[1] ἐκτενής. [g] A ἐντείνω.
[h] A ἐκτίθημι.

ἐκτελέω.

Deu. 32:45[a]
2 Ch. 4: 5

[a] A συντελέω.

ἐκτέμνω.

Isaiah 38:12

ἐκτενής.

Pro. 29:37 S[1 a] [a] pro ἐκτείνω.

ἐκτενῶς.

Joel 1:14
Jon. 3: 8

ἐκτήκω.

Lev. 26:16
Job 31:16[a]
Psa. 38:12
118:139
Ps. 118:158
138:21
Eze. 24:10 A[b]

[a] A τήκω. [b] pro τήκω.

ἐκτίθημι.

Est. 3:14
4: 3, 8
8:13
(9)14, 17
17-AS[1]
Est. 9:14[a]
Job 36:15
Dan. 3:20
6: 8[b]
Zec. 1:16 A[c]

[a] S[1] ἐπιτίθημι. [b] AB[1] ἐχθές.
[c] pro ἐκτείνω.

ἐκτίκτω.

Isaiah 55:10

ἐκτίλλω.

1 Ki. 14:15 A ?
Psa. 51: 7
Ecc. 3: 2
Jer. 24: 6
40:10
Jer. 51:34
Dan. 4:11, 20
7: 4
11: 4

ἐκτιναγμός.

Nahum 2:10

ἐκτινάσσω.

Exo. 14:27
Jud. 7:19
16:20[a]
2 Sa. 22:33[b]
1 Ki. 5: 9
Neh. 4:16[c]
5:13[d], 13
13, 15[e]
Job 38:13
Ps. 108:23
126: 4
135:15
Isa. 28:27 AS[f]
52: 2
Dan. 4:11
7:20
Nah. 2: 3, 3

[a] A ἀποτινάσσω. [b] A ἐκτείνω.
[c] AS ἐκτάσσω. [d] S[1] ἐκτείνω.
[e] S[1] ἐκτάσσω. [f] pro τινάσσω.

ἐκτίω, —τίνω.

Job 2: 4[a] [a] A δίδωμι.

ἐκτοκίζω.

Deuteronomy 23:19, 20, 20

ἐκτομίας.

Lev. 22:24[a] [a] A ἐκτομίς.

ἐκτομίς.

Lev. 22:24 A[a] [a] pro ἐκτομίας.

ἐκτός.

Jud. 3:31+A
5:28—A
8:26[a]
20:15[b]
17[b]
1 Ki. (3) p 46
4:23
10:13
15: 5+A
2 Ch. 9:12
17:19
23:14
31:16[c]
Pro. 24:23
Cant. 4: 1, 3
Isa. 26:13
Dan. 11: 4

[a] A πλήν. [b] A χωρίς.
[c] B ἕκαστος.

ἕκτος.

1 Ch. 26: 3—B
5—B
Eze. 45:13[a]

[a] A ἑκατόν.

ἐκτρέπω.

Amos 5: 8

ἐκτρέφω.

Gen. 45: 7, 11
47:17
2 Sa. 12: 3
1 Ki. 11:20
12: 8, 10
2 Ki. 10: 6
2 Ch. 10:10
Job 31:18
39: 3
Psa. 22: 2
Pro. 23:24
Isa. 23: 4
49:21
Eze. 31: 4
Hos. 9:12
Jon. 4:10
Zec. 10: 9

ἐκτρέχω.

Jud. 13:10 A[a]
1 Ki. 18:16

[a] pro τρέχω.

ἐκτρίβω.

Gen. 19:13, 14
29
34:30
41:36
45:11
47:18
Exo. 9:15
12:13
23:23
32:10
Lev. 6.28
Nu. 14:15
15:31
19:13
32:21
Deu. 2:12, 22
23
4: 3, 26
26, 31
Deu. 7:20
28:24, 52
Jos. 6:18
7: 9
Jud. 8:12 A[a]
1 Ki. 16:12+A
2 Ch. 20:23
32:21
Neh. 9:24
Job 9:17
30:13, 23
Isa. 22:17
Jer. 9:21
11:19
31:18
43:29 A[b]
Eze. 43: 8
Amos 8: 4
Zec. 11:16 A[c]

[a] pro ἐξίστημι. [b] pro ἐκλείπω.
[c] pro ἐκστρέφω.

ἔκτριψις.

Numbers 15:31

ἐκτρυγάω.

Leviticus 25: 5

ἐκτρώγω.

Micah 7: 4

ἔκτρωμα.

Nu. 12:12
Job 3:16
Ecc. 6: 3

ἐκτυπόω.

Exo. 25:32, 33
35
Exo. 28:32
36:39[a]

[a] A ἐντυπόω.

ἐκτύπωμα.

Exodus 28:32

ἐκτύπωσις.

1 Kings 6:32

ἐκτυφλόω.

Exo. 21:26
23: 8
Deu. 16:19 A[a]
2 Ki. 25: 7
Isa. 56:10
Jer. 52:11
Zec. 11:17, 17

[a] pro ἀποτυφλόω.

ἐκφέρω.

Gen. 1:12
14:18
24:53
Exo. 4: 6, 7
12:39, 46
Lev. 4:12, 21
6:11
14:45
16:27
26:10
Nu. 13:33
14:36
17: 8[a], 9
20: 8
Deu. 14:27
22:15, 19
24:13
28:38
Jos. 7:23
10:22 A[b]
18: 6, 8
Jud. 6:18[c], 19
30[d]
19:22[d]
Ruth 2:18
2 Sa. 12:30
1 Ki. 17:13
21:42[d]
2 Ki. 10:22, 26
15:20
23: 6
24:13
1 Ch. 9:28—BS
20: 2, 3 A[b]
2 Ch. 34:14
Ezra 1: 7, 8
5:14
14—B
6: 5
8:17
10:19—S[1]
Neh. 5:11
6:19
9:15
Psa. 36: 6
68:32—S[1]
Pro. 10:18
29:11
Ecc. 5: 1
Cant. 2:13
Isa. 40:26
42: 1, 3
54:16
Jer. 8: 1
17:22—S[1]
27:25
28:10, 44
Eze. 12: 4, 7
17:23
24: 6
46:20
Dan. 5: 2, 3
Amos 4: 3
6:10
Hag. 1:11
Zec. 4: 7
5: 4

[a] A ἐξανθέω. [b] pro ἐξάγω.
[c] A φέρω. [d] A ἐξάγω.

ἐκφεύγω.

Jud. 6:11
2 Sa. 17: 2 A[a]
Job 15:30
Pro. 10:19
Pro. 12:13
Isa. 66: 7
Amos 5:19 A[a]

[a] pro φεύγω.

ἐκφοβέω.

Lev. 26: 6
Deu. 28:26[a]
Job 7:14
33:16
Eze. 32:27
Eze. 34:28
39:26
Mic. 4: 4
Nah. 2:11[b]
Zeph. 3:13

[a] A ἀποσοβέω. [b] S[1] ἐκφορέω.

ἔκφοβος.

Deuteronomy 9:19

ἐκφορά.

2 Ch. 16:14
2 Ch. 21:19, 19

ἐκφορέω.

Nah. 2:11 S[1 a] [a] pro ἐκφοβέω.

ἐκφόριον.

Lev. 25:19
Deu. 28:33
Jud. 6: 4 A[a]
Hag. 1:10
Mal. 3:10

[a] pro καρπός.

ἐκφύρω.

Jeremiah 3: 2

ἐκφυσάω.

Eze. 22:20[a], 21
Hag. 1: 9
Mal. 1:13

[a] A ἐμφυσάω.

ἐκφύσημα.

Ezekiel 22:21+A

ἐκχέω, ἐκχύω.

Gen. 9: 6, 6
37:22
38: 9
Exo. 4: 9
29:12
30:18
Lev. 4: 7, 12
18, 25
30, 34
8:15
9: 9
14:41
17: 4, 13
Nu. 19:17
35:33, 33
Deu. 12:16, 24
15:23
19:10
21: 7
Jud. 6:20
9:44 A[a]
20:37
1 Sa. 1:15
7: 6
25:31
2 Sa. 20:10, 15
1 Ki. 2:31
13: 3, 5
2 Ki. 16:13[b]
19:32
21:16
22:13 B[c]
24: 4
1 Ch. 22: 8, 8
28: 3
2 Ch. 36: 5
Job 12:21
16:13
30:16[d]
Psa. 13: 3—A
21:15
34: 3
41: 5
44: 3
61: 9
68:25
72: 2
78: 3, 6, 10
101: 1
105:38
106:40

Ps. 141: 3
Pro. 1:16 AS[2]
6:17
Ecc. 11: 3
Isa. 57: 6
59: 7
Jer. 6: 6, 11
7: 6
20 A[c]
10:25
14:16
22: 3, 17
Lam. 2: 4, 11
12, 19
4: 1, 11
13
Eze. 7: 8
9: 8
12:14 A[f]
14:19
16:15, 36
38+A
18:10
20: 8, 13
21
21:31
22: 3, 4, 6
9, 12
22, 27
31
23: 8
33 A[g]
24: 3 A[h], 7
30:15
33:25 A
36:18
18+A
39:29
Dan. 11:15
Hos. 5:10
12:14
Joel 2:28, 29
3:19
Amos 5: 8
9: 6
Zeph. 1:17
3: 8
Zec. 12:10
Mal. 3: 3 S[2] [e]
10

[a] pro ἐκτείνω. [b] AB προσχέω. [c] pro ἐκκαίω. [d] S[2] ἐκλύω. [e] pro χέω. [f] pro ἐκ[illegible]ω. [g] pro ἔκλυσις. [h] pro ἐγχέω.

ἔκχυσις.

Lev. 4:12
1 Ki. 18:28

ἐκχύω vide ἐκχέω.

ἐκχωρέω.

Nu. 16:45
Jud. 7: 3[a]

Amos 7:12

[a] A ἐξορμάω.

ἐκψύχω.

Jud. 4:21+A
Eze. 21: 7

ἑκών.

Exo. 21:13
Job 36:19

ἐλαία.

Gen. 8:11
Exo. 27:20
30:24
Deu. 8: 8
28:40, 40
Jud. 9: 8, 9
15: 5

2 Sa. 15:18—A
30
2 Ki. 18:32
Neh. 5:11 BS[1] [a]
8:15
Job 15:33
Psa. 51:10
Ps. 127: 3
Isa. 17: 6
24:13
Jer. 11:16
Hos. 14: 6
Mic. 6:15

Hab. 3:17
Hag. 2:19
Zec. 4: 3, 11
12
14: 4—A
4

[a] pro ἐλαιών.

ἐλάϊνος.

Leviticus 24: 2

ἐλαιολογέω.

Deuteronomy 24:22

ἔλαιον.

Gen. 28:18
35:14
Exo. 27:20
29: 2
2—A
7, 21
23, 40
30:24
25—A[1]
25, 31
31:11
35:14, 19
28
38:25
39:16, 17
40: 7
Lev. 2: 1, 2, 4
4, 5, 6
7, 15
16
5:11[a]
6:15, 21
40
7: 2 ter
8: 2, 10
12, 26
30
9: 4
10: 7
14:10, 10
12, 15
16, 17
18, 21
21, 24
26, 27
28, 29
21:10, 12
23:13
24: 2
Nu. 4: 9, 16
16
5:15
6:15, 15
7:13, 19
25, 31
37, 43
49, 55
61, 67
73, 79
8: 8
11: 8
15: 4, 6, 9
18:12
28: 5, 9, 12
12, 13
20, 28
29: 3, 9, 14
35:25
Deu. 7:13
8: 8
11:14
12:17
14:22
18: 4
28:40, 51
32:13
33:24

Ruth 3:10 A[b]
1 Sa. 10: 1
16: 1, 13
2 Sa. 1:21
14: 2
1 Ki. 1:39
5:11
17:12, 14
16
2 Ki. 4: 2, 6, 7
7
9: 1, 3, 6
18:32
20:13
1 Ch. 9:29
12:40
27:28
2 Ch. 2:10, 15
11:11
31: 5
32:28
Ezra 3: 7
6: 9—A
7:22—B
Neh. 5:11—BS[1]
10:37, 39
13: 5, 12
Est. 2:12
Psa. 4: 8
5: 8 AS[b]
22: 5
44: 8
54:22
88:21 AB[2]S[b]
91:11 AB[2]S[b]
101: 1 A[b]
103:15
108:18, 24
118:64 A[b]
129: 7 A[b]
140: 5
150 p 6
Pro. 21:17
Ecc. 7: 1
9: 8
10: 1
19—AC
Isa. 1: 6
Jer. 47:10, 12
48: 8
Eze. 16: 9, 13
18, 19
23:41
27:17
32:14
45:14, 14
24, 25
46: 5, 7, 11
14, 15
Hos. 2: 5, 8, 22
12: 1
Joel 1:10
2:19, 24
Mic. 6:15
Hag. 1:11
2:12

[a] B λίβανος. [b] pro ἔλεος.

ἐλαιών.

Exo. 23:11
Deu. 6:11
Jos. 24:13
1 Sa. 8:14
2 Ki. 5:26
1 Ch. 27:28

Neh. 5:11[a]
9:25—S[1]
Jer. 5:17—S[1]
Amos 4: 9

[a] BS[1] ἐλαία.

ἔλασμα.

Habakkuk 2:19

ἐλασσόω.

Nu. 26:54
33:54
1 Sa. 2: 5
21:15
2 Sa. 3:29

Psa. 8: 6
33:11
Jer. 37:19
51:18[a]
Eze. 24:10

[a] A ἐλαττονέω.

ἐλάσσων.

Gen. 1:16
25:23
27: 6
Exo. 16:17, 18[a]
Lev. 25:16—A
Nu. 26:54

Nu. 33:54
35: 8, 8
Job 16: 6
Pro. 13:11
22:16

[a] A[2] ὀλίγος.

ἐλάτη.

Gen. 21:15
Cant. 5:11

Eze. 31: 8

ἐλάτινος.

Ezekiel 27: 5

ἐλατός.

Nu. 10: 2
16:38
1 Ki. 10:16, 17

2 Ch. 9:15, 16
Psa. 97: 6

ἐλαττονέω.

Gen. 8: 3, 5
18:28
Exo. 16:17+A
18
30:15
Lev. 25:16

1 Ki. 11:22
17:14, 16
Pro. 11:24
14:34
Jer. 51:18 A[a]

[a] pro ἐλασσόω.

ἐλαύνω.

Exo. 25:11
1 Ki. 9:27
Isa. 33:21

Isa. 41: 7
Zec. 10: 4 A[a]

[a] pro ἐξελαύνω.

ἔλαφος.

Deu. 12:15, 22
14: 5
15:22
2 Sa. 22:34
1 Ki. (3) p 46
4:23
Job 39: 1
Psa. 17:34
28: 9

Psa. 41: 2
103:18
Pro. 5:19
7:23
Cant. 2: 9, 17
8:14
Isa. 34:15
35: 6
Jer. 14: 5

ἐλαφρός.

Exo. 18:26
Job 7: 6
9:25

Job 24:18
Eze. 1: 7

ἐλάχιστος.

Jos. 6:26, 26
1 Sa. 9:21
2 Ki. 18:24
Job 18: 7

Job 30: 1
Pro. 24:59
Isa. 60:22
Jer. 29:21

ἐλεγμός.

Lev. 19:17
Nu. 5:18, 19
23, 24
24, 27
2 Ki. 19: 3
Psa. 37:15

Psa. 38:12
149: 7
Isa. 37: 3
50: 2[a]
Hab. 2: 1 S[1] [b]

[a] AS[3] ἀπειλή. [b] pro ἔλεγχος.

ἔλεγξις.

Job 21: 4
Job 23: 2

ἔλεγχος.

Job 6:26
13: 6
16:21
23: 4, 7
Psa. 72:14
Pro. 1:23, 25
30
5:12
6:23
12: 1

Pro. 13:18
15:10
16: 1, 17
27: 5
28:13
29:15
Eze. 13:14
Hos. 5: 9
Hab. 2: 1[a]

[a] S[1] ἐλεγμός.

ἐλέγχω.

Gen. 21:25
31:37, 42
Lev. 6: 5[a]
19:17
2 Sa. 7:14
1 Ch. 12:17
16:21
2 Ch. 26:20
Job 5:17
9:33[b]
13: 3, 10
15
15: 3, 6
22: 4
32:12
33:19
39:32, 34
Psa. 6: 2
37: 2
49: 8, 21
93:10
104:14

Ps. 140: 5
Pro. 3:11, 12[c]
9: 7, 8, 8
10:10
15:12
18:17
19:25
24:29[d], 40
28:23
29: 1
Isa. 2: 4 AS[3] [e]
11: 3, 4
29:21
Jer. 2:19
Eze. 3:26
20:38 B[f]
Hos. 4: 4
Amos 5:10
Mic. 4: 3 A[e]
Hab. 1:12
Hag. 2:14

[a] B λέγω. [b] A διελέγχω. [c] AS παιδεύω. [d] S ἐξελέγχω. [e] pro ἐξελέγχω. [f] pro ἐκλέγω.

ἐλεέω, ἐλεάω.

Gen. 33: 5, 11
43:29
Exo. 23: 3
33:19, 19
Nu. 6:25
Deu. 7: 2
13:17
28:50
30: 3
Jud. 21:22+A
2 Sa. 12:22
2 Ki. 13:23
2 Ch. 36:17
Job 19:21, 21
24:21
27:15
41: 3
Psa. 6: 3
9:14
24:16
25:11
26: 7
29:11
30:10
36:26
40: 5, 11
50: 3
55: 2
56: 2, 2
66: 2+S[2]
85: 3, 16
114: 5
118:29, 58
132
122: 3, 3
Pro. 12:13
13: 9
14:21, 31
17: 5
19:17
21:10, 26
22: 9

Pro. 28: 8
Isa. 9:17, 19
12: 1
13:18
14: 1
27:11
30:18
19, 19
33: 2
44:23
23 A[a]
49:10, 13
15
52: 8, 9
54: 7, 8
55: 7
59: 2
Jer. 3:12 A[b]
6:23
7:16
12:15
27:42
37:18
38:20, 20
49:12
Lam. 3:22—AB
4:16
Eze. 5:11
7: 9, 4
8:18
9: 5, 10
24:14
39:25
Hos. 1: 6, 6, 7
8
2: 1, 4
23 A[c]
23 A[c]
14: 3
Amos 5:15
Zec. 1:12, 17
Mal. 1: 9+S[2]

[a] pro λυτρόω. [b] pro ἐλεήμων. [c] pro ἀγαπάω.

ἐλεημοσύνη.

Gen. 47:29
Deu. 6:25
24:15
Psa. 23: 5
32: 5
34:24 S[1 a]
102: 6
Pro. 3: 3
14:22
15:27
Pro. 19:22
20:28
21:21
29:45
Isa. 1:27
28:17
38:18
59:16
Dan. 4:24
9:16

[a] pro δικαιοσύνη.

ἐλεήμων.

Exo. 22:27
34: 6
2 Ch. 30: 9
Neh. 9:17, 31
Psa. 85:15
102: 8
110: 4
111: 4
114: 5
Ps. 144: 8
Pro. 11:17
19:11
20: 6
28:22
Jer. 3:12[a]
Joel 2:13
Jon. 4: 2

[a] A ἐλεέω.

ἔλεος.

Gen. 19:19
24:12, 14
44, 49
39:21
40:14
Exo. 20: 6
34: 7
Nu. 11:15
14:19
Deu. 5:10
7: 9, 12
13:17
Jos. 2:12, 12
14
11:20
Jud. 1:24
6:17[a]
8:35
21:22 – A
Ruth 1: 8
2:20
3:10[b]
1 Sa. 15: 6
20: 8, 14
15
2 Sa. 2: 5, 6
3: 8
7:15
9: 1, 3, 7
10: 2, 2
15:20
16:17
22:51
1 Ki. 2: 7
3: 6, 6
8:23
21:31
1 Ch. 16:34, 41
17:13
19: 2, 2
29:12 + A
2 Ch. 1: 8
5:13
6:14, 42
7: 3, 6
20:21
24:22
32:32
Ezra 3:11
7:28
9: 9
Neh. 1: 5
9:32
13:14, 22
Job 6:14
10:12
37:12
Psa. 5: 8[c]
6: 5
12: 6
16: 7
17:51
Psa. 20: 8
22: 6
24: 6, 7, 10
25: 3
30: 8, 17
22
31:10
32: 5, 18
22
35: 6, 8, 11
39:11, 12
41: 9
47:10
50: 3
51:10
56: 4, 11
58:11, 17
18
60: 8
61:13
62: 4
65:20
68:14, 17
76: 9
83:12
84: 8, 11
85:13
87:12
88: 1, 3, 15
21[d], 25
29, 34
50
89:14
91: 3, 11[d]
93:18 – A[1]
97: 3
99: 5
100: 1[b]
102: 4, 11
17
105: 1, 7, 45
106: 1, 8, 15
21, 31
43
107: 5
108:16
21 + AS[1]
21, 26
113: 9
116: 2
117: 1, 2, 3
4 – S
29
118:41
41 S[1 e]
64[b], 76
88, 124[f]
149[g]
159
120: 7[b]
135: 1 to 26
23 – S[1]
Ps. 137: 2, 8
140: 5
142: 8, 12
143: 2
146:11
Pro. 3:16
14:22, 22
Isa. 16: 5
45: 8
47: 6
54: 7, 8, 10
56: 1
60:10
63: 7, 7, 15
64: 4
Jer. 2: 2
9:24
16:13
39:18
40:11
Jer. 43: 7
44:20
45:26
49: 2, 12
Lam. 3:22 – AB
31
Eze. 18:19
21 – A
Dan. 1: 9
9: 4, 20
Hos. 2:19
4: 1
6: 4, 6
12: 6
Jon. 2: 9
Mic. 6: 8
7:18, 20
Hab. 3: 2
Zec. 7: 9

[a] A χάρις. [b] A ἔλαιον. [c] AS ἔλαιον. [d] AB?S ἔλαιον. [e] pro λόγος. [f] AS[1] λόγιον. [g] S λόγιον.

ἐλευθερία.

Leviticus 19, 20

ἐλεύθερος.

Exo. 21: 2, 5, 26
27
Deu. 15:12, 13
18
21:14
1 Sa. 17:25 A
1 Ki. 20: 8
11 – B
Neh. 13:17
Job 39: 5
Psa. 87: 6
Pro. 25:10
Ecc. 10:17
Jer. 36: 2
41: 9, 14
16

ἐλεφάντινος.

1 Ki. 10:18
22 + A
22:39
2 Ch. 9:17, 21
Psa. 44: 9
Cant. 5:14
7: 4
Eze. 27:15
Amos 3:15
6: 4

ἐλέφας.

Ezekiel 27: 6

ἑλικτός.

Lev. 6:21
1 Ki. 6:12

ἕλιξ.

Genesis 49:11

ἑλίσσω.

Job 18: 8
Ps. 101:27[a]
Isa. 34: 4

[a] S[1] ἀλλάσσω.

ἕλκος.

Exo. 9: 9, 10
11, 11
Lev. 13:18, 19
20, 22
23, 27
Deu. 28:27, 35
2 Ki. 20: 7
Job 2: 7
Pro. 25:20

ἑλκύω.

Deu. 21: 3
2 Sa. 22:17
Neh. 9:30
Job 20:28[a]
28:18
39:10
Psa. 9:30
Ps. 118:131
Ecc. 2: 3
Cant. 1: 4
Jer. 14: 6
38: 3
45:13
Hab. 1:15

[a] S ἐκλύω.

ἕλκω.

Jud. 5:14 – A
20: 2[a], 15[a]
17[a], 25[a]
35[a], 46[a]
Ecc. 1: 5
Isa. 10:15
Dan. 7:10

[a] A σπάω.

ἔλλειμμα.

2 Sa. 21: 2[a]

[a] AB αἷμα.

Ἕλλην.

Isa. 9:12
Zec. 9:13

ἑλληνικός.

Jer. 26:16
Jer. 27:16

ἐλλογέω.

Isa. 65:16 S[1 a]

[a] pro εὐλογέω.

ἐλλουλίμ.

Jud. 9:27[a]

[a] A χορός.

ἐλμωνί.

2 Kings 6: 8

ἕλος.

Exo. 2: 3, 5
7:19
8: 5
Isa. 19: 6
Isa. 33: 9
35: 7, 7
41:18
42:15

ἐλούλ.

Nehemiah 6:15

ἐλπίζω.

Gen. 4:26
Jud. 9:26[a]
20:36
2 Ki. 18: 5, 24
1 Ch. 5:20
2 Ch. 13:18
Job 24:23
Psa. 4: 6
5:12
7: 2
9:11
12: 6
15: 1
16: 7
17: 3, 31
20: 8
21: 5, 5, 6
9
24:20
25: 1
26: 3
27: 7
30: 2, 7, 15
20, 25
31:10
32:18, 21
22
33: 9, 23
35: 8
36: 3, 5, 40
37:16
39: 4
40:10
41: 6, 12
42: 5
43: 7
51:10
54:24
55: 4, 5, 12
Psa. 56: 2
61: 9 – S[1]
11
63:11
68: 4[b]
70: 1, 14
77:22
83:13
85: 2
90: 2, 4, 14
111: 7
113:17, 18
19
117: 9, 9
118:42
114 S[1 c]
129: 6
6 – S[1]
130: 3
140: 8
142: 8
143: 2
144:15
146:11
Isa. 11:10
18: 7[d]
25: 9
26: 4, 8
29: 8
30:12
38:18
42: 4
51: 5, 5
Jer. 13:25
51:14
Eze. 36: 8
Hos. 10:13
Mic. 7: 5

[a] A πείθω. [b] B ἐγγίζω. [c] pro ἐπελπίζω. [d] S ἀνέλπιστος.

ἐλπίς.

Deu. 24:17
Jud. 18: 7
7 + A
9 + A
10[a]
27 – A
2 Ch. 35:26
Job 2: 9
4: 6
5:16
6: 8
7: 6
8:13
11:18, 20
14: 7
Job 17:15
19:10
27: 8
30:15
Psa. 4: 9
13: 6
15: 9
21:10
39: 5
59:10
60: 4
61: 8
64: 6
70: 5
72:28
Psa. 77: 7, 53
90: 9
93:22
107:10
141: 6
145: 5
Pro. 1:33
10:28
11: 7, 23
13:12
14:26
22:19
23:18
24:14
26:12
29:20
Ecc. 9: 4
Isa. 24:16
26: 3 – AS
28: 4, 5, 10
Isa. 28:10, 13
13, 15
17, 18
19
30:32
31: 2
32: 9, 10
47:10
Jer. 2:36
17: 5, 7
31:13
Lam. 3:18
Eze. 28:26, 26
29:16
34:27, 28
37:11
Hos. 2:18
Mic. 2: 8
Zeph. (2)15
Zec. 9: 5 A[b]

[a] A πείθω. [b] pro παράπτωμα.

ἐμβαθύνω.

Jer. 30: 8[a]

[a] ABS βαθύνω.

ἐμβαίνω.

Jud. 15: 6 A[a]
2 Ch. 1:17[b]
Jon. 1: 3 ABS[2 a]
Nah. 3:14

[a] pro ἀναβαίνω. [b] A ἀναβαίνω.

ἐμβάλλω.

Gen. 31:34
37:22
39:20
40:15
43:21
44: 1, 2
Exo. 2: 3
10:19 A[a]
15:25
16:33
23:15, 20
40:18
Nu. 4:10, 12
14 A[b]
14
5:17
19: 6
22:38[c]
23: 5, 12
16
Deu. 10: 2, 5
11:18
24: 2[d]
26: 2
31:19
Jos. 7:11
18:10
1 Sa. 18:25 – A
2 Ki. 4:39, 41
2 Ch. 24:10
Job 18: 8
Psa. 39: 4
Pro. 7: 5
11:21
16: 5
22:18
Isa. 28:16
37: 7
19 ABS[e]
29
51:23 A[f]
Jer. 11:19
20: 2
22: 7
34: 6
44:21
Eze. 4: 9
24: 4
26:12
Dan. 3: 6, 11
15, 20
21 A[g]
24 A[g]
6: 7, 12
16, 24[g]
Amos 4: 2 – A
Jon. 1:12
15 AS[2 h]
Hag. 2:16
Zec. 11:13

[a] pro βάλλω. [b] pro διεμβάλλω. [c] B βάλλω. [d] A[2] ἐκβάλλω. [e] pro ἀναβάλλω. [f] pro δίδωμι. [g] A βάλλω. [h] pro ἐκβάλλω.

ἐμβατεύω.

Joshua 19:49, 51

ἐμβιβάζω.

2 Ki. 9:28 A[a]
Pro. 4:11

[a] pro ἐπιβιβάζω.

ἐμβλέπω.

Jud. 16:27 A[a]
1 Sa. 16: 7
1 Ki. 8: 8
Job 2:10
6:28 A[b]
21: 5 A[b]
Psa. 39: 5 AB[c]
Isa. 5:12, 30
30 + S[2]
8:22
17: 7
22: 8, 11
51: 1, 2, 6

[a] pro θεωρέω. [b] pro εἰσβλέπω. [c] pro ἐπιβλέπω.

ἐμβρίμημα.
Lamentations 2: 6

ἐμεκαχώρ.
Joshua 7:24, 26

ἔμετος.
Proverbs 26:11

ἐμέω.
Isa. 19:14 | Amos 5:19 A[1 a]

[a] pro ἐμπίπτω.

Ἐμμανουήλ.
Isaiah 7:14

ἐμμένω.
Nu. 23:19
Deu. 19:15
27:26
Isa. 7: 7 AS[a]
8:10
Isa. 28:18
30:18
Jer. 38:32
51:25, 25, 29

[a] pro μένω.

ἐμμολύνω.
Proverbs 24: 9

ἔμμονος.
Lev. 13:51, 52–AB[1] | Lev. 14:44

ἔμπαιγμα.
Psa. 37: 8 A[a] | Isa. 66: 4

[a] pro ἐμπαιγμός.

ἐμπαιγμός.
Psa. 37: 8[a] | Eze. 22: 4

[a] A ἔμπαιγμα.

ἐμπαίζω.
Gen. 39:14, 17
Exo. 10: 2
Nu. 22:29
Jud. 16:25 A[a]
27 A[b]
19:25
20: 5+A
1 Sa. 6: 6
31: 4
1 Ch. 10: 4
2 Ch. 36:16
Job 40:24 A[a]
Ps. 103:26
Pro. 23:35
27: 7
Isa. 33: 4
Jer. 10:15
Eze. 22: 5
Nah. 2: 4
Hab. 1:10
Zec. 12: 3, 3

[a] pro παίζω. [b] pro ἐν παιγνίᾳ.

ἐμπαίκτης.
Isaiah 3: 4

ἐμπαραγίνομαι.
Proverbs 6:11

ἐμπαρρησιάζομαι.
Job 22:26 A[a] [a] pro παρρ-

ἐμπεριπατέω.
Lev. 26:12
Deu. 23:14
Jud. 18: 9+A
2 Sa. 7: 6
Job 1: 6+A
7
2: 2
Pro. 24:66

ἐμπήγνυμι.
Jud. 3:21
1 Sa. 26: 7
2 Sa. 18:14
Psa. 9:16
Psa. 31: 4[a]
37: 3
68: 3, 15
Lam. 2: 9

[a] A πηγνύω.

ἐμπίπλημι, ἐμπλήθω.
Gen. 42:25
Exo. 15: 9
28: 3, 37
31: 3
Exo. 35:31, 35
40:29[a]
Lev. 19:29 A[b]
26:26
Nu. 14:21
Deu. 6:11, 11
8:10, 12
11:16
14:28
24: 2
26:12 A[c]
27: 7
31:20
32:15
33:23
34: 9
Jud. 17: 5 A[d]
12 A[d]
Ruth 2:14, 18
1 Sa. 20: 3[e]
2 Ki. 3:25
2 Ch. 5:13, 14
30: 5 B[b]
Neh. 9:25
Job 8:21
9:18
15: 2
19:22
20:11
22:18
23: 4
31:31 A[b]
33:24
38:39
40: 8
Psa. 21:27
62: 6
77:29
80:14
90:16
102: 5
103:28 B[b]
104:40
106: 9
144:16
147: 3
Pro. 6:30
8:21
12:11
13:25
18:20[f]
20:13
24: 4, 50
51
25:16 S[b]
27:20
Ecc. 1: 7
Ecc. 1: 8 ACS[b]
8 S[d]
4: 8
5:11
6: 3 ACS[b]
Isa. 2: 6, 7, 7
8
6: 4[f g]
9:20
11: 3, 9
13:21[g]
14:21
21: 3
22: 2
7 S[2 b]
23:18
27: 6[b]
29:19
31: 4
33: 5
34: 6, 7
44:16
58:10, 11
65:20
66:11
Jer. 15:17
26:10[i]
27:10
19 A[b]
38:14, 25
48: 9
Eze. 7:19
11: 6
16:28, 28
29
24:13
27:25, 33
28:13
32: 4, 5, 6
35: 8
39:20
Hos. 4:10
7: 6
13: 6
Joel 2:19
24 A[b]
26
Amos 4: 8
Mic. 3: 8
6:12 A[b]
14
Hab. 2: 5, 14[k]

[a] AB πίμπλημι. [b] pro πίμπλημι. [c] pro εὐφραίνω. [d] pro πληρόω. [e] A πληρόω. [f] S πίμπλημι. [g] A πίμπλημι. [h] B πίμπλημι. [i] BS πίμπλημι. [k] S[2] πίμπλημι.

ἐμπίπρημι, ἐμπρήθω.
Nu. 31:10
Deu. 13:16
Jos. 6:24
8:19
11: 9, 11
13, 13
16:10
Jud. 1: 8
9:49 A[a]
52
12: 1
15: 6[b]
18:27
20:48[c]
1 Sa. 30: 1 A[a]
2 Sa. 14:30, 30
1 Ki. 9:16 A
15:13
18:10
2 Ki. 10:26
25: 9, 9
2 Ch. 36:19, 19
Neh. 1: 3
Jer. 28:32
52:13, 13
Eze. 16:41
23:25 A[d]
47[b]
Mic. 1: 7

[a] pro ἐμπυρίζω. [b] A ἐμπυρίζω. [c] A ἐξαποστέλλω. [d] pro καταφάγω.

ἐμπίπτω.
Gen. 14:10
Exo. 21:33
Jud. 15:18
18: 1
1 Sa. 29: 3
2 Sa. 24:14, 14
2 Ki. 7: 4
2 Ki. 25:11, 11
1 Ch. 21:13, 13
Psa. 7:16
56: 7
Pro. 12:13
13:17
17:12, 16
Pro. 17:20
22:14
26:27
28:10, 14
Ecc. 10: 8
Isa. 10: 4
Isa. 24:18
47:11
Jer. 31:32 S[a]
44
Amos 5:19[b]

[a] pro ἐπιπίπτω. [b] A[1] ἐμέω.

ἐμπιστεύω.
Deu. 1:32
Jud. 11:20[a]
2 Ch. 20:20 *ter*
Jon. 3: 5 BS[1 b]

[a] A θέλω. [a] pro πιστεύω.

ἐμπλατύνω.
Exo. 23:18
34:24 A[a]
Deu. 12:20
19: 8
Deu. 33:20
Pro. 18:16
Amos 1:13
Mic. 1:16

[a] pro πλατύνω.

ἐμπλέκω.
Proverbs 28:18

ἐμπλήθω *vide* ἐμπίπλημι.

ἐμπλόκιον.
Exo. 35:22
36:22, 25
25
Nu. 31:50
Isa. 3:18
20–S[1]

ἔμπνευσις.
Psalm 17:16

ἐμπνέω.
Deu. 20:16
Jos. 10:28, 30
35, 37
Jos. 10:39, 40
11:11, 11
14

ἐμποδίζω.
Jud. 5:22[a] | Ezra 4: 4

[a] A ἀποκόπτω.

ἐμποδοστατέω.
Judges 11:35+A

ἐμποδοστάτης.
1 Chronicles 2: 7

ἐμποιέω.
Exodus 9:17

ἐμπολάω.
Amos 8: 5

ἐμπολιορκέω.
Jos. 7: 3 A[a] [a] pro ἐκπολ-

ἐμπορεύομαι.
Gen. 34:10, 21
21[a]
42:34
2 Ch. 9:14
Pro. 3:14
Pro. 29:32
Eze. 27:13, 21
Hos 12: 1
Amos 8: 6

[a] A ἐκπορεύω.

ἐμπορία.
Deu. 33:19
Isa. 23:18, 18
45:14
Eze. 27:13, 15
Eze. 27:16, 24
28: 5, 16
18
Nah. 3:16–S[1]

ἐμπόριον.
Isa. 23:17 | Eze. 27: 3

ἔμπορος.
Gen. 23:16
37.28
1 Ki. 10:15, 28[a]
2 Ch. 1:16
Isa. 23: 8
Eze. 27:12, 15
17, 18
20, 21
22, 22
Eze. 27:23, 23
25
25+A
36
38:13

[a] A πόρος.

ἐμπρήθω *vide* ἐμπίπρημι.

ἔμπροσθεν.
Gen. 24: 7
32: 3–A
16
33: 3, 14
41:43
45: 5, 7
46:28
48:20
Nu. 14:43
Jos. 3: 6
4: 5, 11
12, 23
23
5: 1
6: 9
8: 6
Jud. 1:10 A[a]
11, 23
3: 2, 27
4:14, 23[b]
18:21
20:32 A[c]
39 A[c]
Ruth 4: 7
1 Sa. 2:29
8:20
9: 9, 9, 15
19, 27
10: 5, 8
17:41 A
18:13
23:24
25:19
30:20
2 Sa. 3:31 A[d]
5:24
6: 4–A
10:15, 16
19
15: 1
19:17
20: 8
24:13
1 Ki. 1: 5
3:12
8: 5
16:25, 30
33
18:46
22:54
2 Ki. 4:31
5:23
9:17
10:29 B[e]
17: 2
18: 5
2 Ki. 21:11
23:25
1 Ch. 4:40
9:20
14:15
15:24
17:13
19:16
21:30
22: 5
29:25
2 Ch. 1:12
3:15
5: 6
9:11
13:13
14–A
15: 8
20:21–A
35:19
Ezra 4:18
Neh. 8: 1
12:36
Job 21:33
29: 2
41:13
42:10, 12
Psa. 79:10
104:17
Ecc. 1:10, 16
2: 7, 9
4:16
Isa. 41:26
43:10
45: 1, 1,
58: 8
Jer. 7:12, 24
Lam. 5:21
Eze. 2:10
36:11
38:17
Dan. 6:10
7: 7
7+A
8, 10
24
Joel 2: 3, 23
Jon. 3: 2
Mic. 2: 8
7:20
Hag. 2: 3
Zec. 1: 4
7: 7, 12
8:11
Mal. 3: 4

[a] pro πρότερον. [b] A ἐνώπιον. [c] pro πρῶτος. [d] pro ἐνώπιον. [e] pro ἀπὸ ὄπισθεν.

ἐμπρόσθιος.
Exo. 28:14 | 1 Sa. 5: 4

ἔμπτυσμα.
Isaiah 50: 6

ἐμπτύω.
Nu. 12:14 | Deu. 25: 9

ἐμπυρίζω.
Lev. 10: 6, 16
Jos. 8:28
Jud. 9:49[a]
Jud. 14:15 A[b]
15: 5 A[c]
6 A[d]

1 Sa. 30:1[a],3,14
2 Sa. 14:30, 31
1 Ki. 4:30—A
16:18+B
18
2 Ch. 35:19
Psa. 9:23
59: 2
Psa. 73: 7
79:17
Isa. 3:14
Jer. 4:26
28:25, 30
58
50:12
Eze. 23 47 A[d]

[a] A ἐμπιπρήμι. [b] pro κατακαίω. [c] pro καίω. [d] pro ἐμπίπρημι.

ἐμπυρισμός.

Lev. 10: 6
Nu. 11: 3
Deu. 9:22
1 Ki. 8:37

ἔμπυρος.

Eze. 23:37
Amos 4: 2

ἐμφαίνω.

Psalm 79: 2

ἐμφανής.

Exo. 2:14
Isa. 2: 2
Isa. 65: 1
Mic. 4: 1

ἐμφανίζω.

Exo. 33:13
18—A
Est. 2:22
Isa. 3: 9

ἐμφανῶς.

Psa. 49: 3
Pro. 9:14
Zeph. 1: 9

ἐμφραγμός.

Micah 5: 1

ἐμφράσσω.

Gen. 26:15, 18
2 Ki. 3:19, 25
2 Ch. 32: 3,4,30
Job 5:16
Psa. 62:12
106:42
Isa. 22: 7
Lam. 3: 9
Dan. 6:22
12: 4, 9
Mic. 5: 1
Zec. 14: 5 A[a]
5—A, 5

[a] pro φράσσω.

ἐμφύρω.

Eze. 22: 6 B*[a] [a] pro συμφύρω.

ἐμφυσάω.

Gen. 2: 7
1 Ki. 17:21
Job 4:21
Eze. 21:31
Eze. 22:20 A[a]
37: 9
Nah. 2: 1

[a] pro ἐκφυσάω.

ἐναγκαλίζομαι.

Pro. 6:10
Pro. 24:48

ἐνακούω.

Nahum 1:12

ἐναλλάξ.

Genesis 48:14

ἐνάλλομαι.

Job 6:27
16: 4, 10
Job 19: 5

ἔναντι.

(*Often interchanged with* ἐναντίον.)

Gen. 12:19
19:13
38: 7
Exo. 6:12
28:12
12+A
Exo. 28:26, 26
31, 34
29:10
11—A
23, 24
25, 26
Exo. 29:42
30: 8, 16
32:11[a]
34:34
39:12
40:21, 23
Lev. 1: 5, 11
3: 1,7,12
13
4: 2, 4, 4
6, 15
15, 17
5:19
6: 7, 14
25, 32
7:20, 28
8:26, 27
29
9: 2, 4, 5
21
10: 1,2,15
17, 19
12: 7
14:11, 12
16, 18
20, 23
24, 27
29, 31
15:14, 15
30
16: 1,7,10
13, 15
30
19:22
23:11, 28
40
24: 6, 8
26:45
27:11
Nu. 3: 4, 4, 7
5:16, 18
25, 30
6:16, 20
7: 3
8: 9, 10
11, 13
13, 13
13—A
15, 21
22, 22
10: 9, 10
11: 1, 10
18
14:37
15:15, 25
28
16: 2, 7, 9
16, 17
38, 40
17: 7
18:19
20: 3, 13
25
26:61
27: 2 *qtr*
3,5,14
19, 19
21, 21
Nu. 31: 3, 50
54
32:13, 20
21, 22
22, 22
23, 27
29, 30
32
35:12
36: 1 *ter*
Deu. 1:41
6:18
9:25
10: 8
15:20
16:14+A
18: 5
19:17 *ter*
21: 9
25: 2—B
9
26: 5
10 A[b]
10, 13
27: 7
29:15+A[2]
31: 7
34:12
Jos. 7:12[c], 23
18: 6,8,10
19:51
20: 9
22:22
Jud. 3:12
12 A[d]
4: 1 A[d]
6: 1 A[d]
10: 6 A[d]
20:26 A[d]
26 A[d]
2 Sa. 21: 9
1 Ch. 11: 3
16:37
2 Ch. 1: 5
6:12, 13
7: 4, 6
20:13, 18
30: 9[e]
Job 2: 1[f]
2 A[d]
13: 7, 7
15: 4, 13
25
16:20, 21
19:28
22:23
25: 4
27:10
34:10, 10
35: 2
Ps. 108:14
Pro. 3:32
14:19
Isa. 8: 4
23:18, 18
Jer. 3:25
12:13
16:10

[a] A κατέναντι. [b] pro ἀπέναντι. [c] A[2] πρόσωπον. [d] pro ἐνώπιον. [e] B ἀντί. [f] A ἐνώπιον.

ἐναντιόομαι.

Proverbs 20: 8

ἐναντίος, ἐναντίον.

Gen. 6: 8, 11
13
7: 1
10: 9, 9
13: 9, 13
16: 4, 5
6 A[a]
17:18
18: 3, 22
19:14, 19
27
20:15
Gen. 21:11, 12
23:11, 12
13, 18
24:12, 40[b]
27: 7, 12
20
28: 8
29:20—A
30:27, 30
40, 41
31:32
32: 5
Gen. 33: 8[c], 10
14, 15
34:10, 11
18, 18
21
35:21
38:10
39: 4,9,21
40: 9
41:37, 37
46
42:24
43: 8, 13
14, 32
44:14, 18
47: 2, 6, 7
15, 18
19, 25
29
50: 4
Exo. 3:21
4:21, 30
5:21, 21
6:30
7: 9,9,10
10, 10
20, 20
8:26, 26
9: 8,8,10
11, 13
10: 3, 16
11: 3 *qtr*
10
12:36
13:22
15:26
16: 9, 33
34
17: 6
18:12
19:11
24:17
25:29
27:21
28:23
33:13, 13[d]
19
34:21, 28
40: 5[d], 32
Lev. 1: 3
3: 2—A
4: 7
13: 5
23:20
24: 4
25:23
26: 7,8,17
40
27: 8
Nu. 1:53
2: 2
3: 6
7: 3
9: 6
11:11, 20
14: 5, 27
19: 5
20:8,12,27
22:32
24: 1
25: 6, 6
27:19, 22
22
33:3 36:6
Deu. 1:23[d], 45
4: 6
6:25
9:16, 17
18, 18
10:11
12: 7, 12
18, 18
25, 28
13:16, 18
14:25
15:18
16:11, 16
17: 2
18: 7, 13
20:18
Deu. 22:17
24: 3,6,15
25: 2, 3
28:25, 31
29:10, 15
31:11, 29
Jos. 4:13, 14
5:13
6: 7,8,13
26—A
7: 6, 20
11: 6
13: 4
28—A
17: 4 *ter*
18: 4
19:12, 13
20: 3
22:16, 27
29[e], 31
24: 1 A[f]
Jud. 1:10
3: 7
8:11+A
Ruth 4: 4, 4
1 Sa. 13: 5
17:30 A
2 Sa. 12:11, 12
18: 6 A[g]
22:13
1 Ki. 11:19
22:53[i]
2 Ki. 15:25
19:14
1 Ch. 2: 3
4:40
6:32
13: 8
16: 1,6,37
39
17: 24, 27
19: 3—S
10
21: 7, 23
22: 8, 18
18
23:13
24: 2, 31
29:15, 22
25+AB
2 Ch. 1: 2
6:14, 16
19, 24
7: 6, 17
19
10: 6, 8
12: 2
13:15
14:12, 13[d]
18: 9
20: 9, 9
21: 6
22: 4
23:17
25: 8, 14
26:19
27: 6
28:14
29: 6, 11
19, 23
30: 4, 4
31:20
33: 2[d], 6
23
34: 2, 18
24, 27
31
36: 5
Ezra 9:15
Job 1: 9, 22
2: 1—S[i]
10
4:17
8: 4
9: 4
11: 4
13: 3, 15
16
15:15, 25
26
Job 18: 3
19:15
22:26
25: 5
31:28
32: 1, 2
34:26, 37
35:14
Psa. 17: 9 B[h]
30:20
33: 1
37:10, 12
38: 2
49: 3
51:11
68:20
72:16[i]
76: 3
77:12
79: 3
84:14[k]
87: 2
88:37
94: 6[m]
96: 3
97: 2
100: 7[n]
101: 1[o]
105:46
108:15
115: 5—AS
6, 9
118:46, 168
137: 1
141: 3[h]
Pro. 8: 7
Pro. 14: 7
Isa. 37:14
40:10
41: 2
43: 4
49: 4, 5
53: 2, 7
59:12
61:11
65: 3, 12
66: 4
Jer. 1:17
2:22
7:30[d]
8:14
12: 3
14: 7, 20
15: 9
18:10, 23
19:7;25:16
47: 4, 10
Eze. 17:15
18:18
28:17, 18
33:31
38:23
43:11, 24
44: 3, 11
46: 3, 9
Dan. 1:18
3:32
6:10
9:20
10:12, 16
Amos 3:10—A
Nah. 1:11

vide ἔναντι *et* ἐνώπιον.

[a] pro ἐν τ. χερσί [b] S ἐνώπιον. [c] A ἐν. [d] A ἐνώπιον. [e] A ἀπεναντίον. [f] pro ἀπέναντι. [g] pro ἐξεναντίας. [h] pro πρόσωπον. [i] S[2] ἐνώπιον. [k] AS[2] ἐνώπιον. [m] S[1] ἐνώπιον. [n] AS ἐνώπιον. [o] S ἐνώπιον.

ἐναποθνήσκω.

1 Samuel 25:37

ἔναρα.

Joshua 13:21—A

ἐνάρχομαι.

Exo. 12:18
Nu. 9: 5
16:47
Deu. 2:24, 25
Deu. 2:31
Jos. 10:24
2 Ch. 20:22 A[a]
Pro. 13:12

[a] pro ἄρχω.

ἔνατος.

Jer. 52: 4[2][a] [a] A ἕβδομος.

ἐναφίημι.

Ezekiel 21:17

ἐνδεής.

Deu. 15: 4,7,11
24:16
Job 30: 4
Pro. 3:27
7: 7
9: 4, 13
16
11:12, 16
12:11
Pro. 13:25
15:21
18: 2
21:17
24:45
28:16
Isa. 41:17
Eze. 4:17

ἔνδεια.

Deu. 28:20, 57
Job 30: 3
Pro. 6:11, 11
32
10:21
14:23
17:14
Pro. 24:49
27: 7
Isa. 25: 4
Eze. 4:16
12:19
Amos 4: 6

ἐνδείκνυμι.

Gen. 50:15, 17
Exo. 9:16
Jos. 7:14 A[a]
Jos. 7:14 A[a]
15, 16
17, 18

[a] pro δείκνυμι.

ἕνδεκα.

Jos. 15:51[a]

[a] A δέκα.

ἐνδέκατος.

1 Ki. 16 p28 − A
Eze. 26: 1[a]

[a] A δωδέκατος.

ἐνδελεχισμός.

Exo. 29:38, 42
30: 8
Nu. 28: 6, 23
Ezra 3: 5
Neh. 10:33, 33
Dan. 11:31[a]
12. 11

[a] A (−λεχιστόν.)

ἐνδελεχῶς.

Exo. 29:38
Lev. 24: 3
Nu. 28: 3
Dan. 6:16, 20

ἔνδεσμος.

1 Ki. 6:14
14 A[a]
Pro. 7:20
Eze. 13:11

[a] pro σύνδεσμος.

ἐνδέχομαι.

Psa. 118:122[a]

[a] AS ἐκδέχομαι.

ἐνδέω.

Deu. 8: 9
15: 8[a]
Deu. 15:10 − A
Pro. 28:27

[a] A ὑστερέω.

ἐνδέω.

Exo. 12:34
1 Sa. 25:29
Eze. 28:13

ἐνδιαβάλλω.

Nu. 22:22 AB[a]
Psa. 37:21
70:13
Ps. 108: 4, 20
29

[a] pro διαβάλλω.

ἐνδιαλλάσσω.

1 Kings 22:47 A

ἐνδιατρίβω.

Proverbs 23:16

ἐνδιδύσκω.

2 Sa. 1:24
13:18
Pro. 29:39 ABS[a]

[a] pro ἐνδύω.

ἐνδίδωμι.

Gen. 8: 3
3 + A
Nu. 14: 1[a]
Pro. 10:30
Eze. 8:11

[a] A δίδωμι.

ἐνδογενής.

Leviticus 18: 9

ἔνδοθεν.

Nu. 18: 7
1 Ki. 6:19 + A

ἔνδον.

Lev. 11:33, 33
Deu. 21:12
Deu. 22: 2

ἐνδοξάζω.

Exo. 14: 4, 17
18
Exo. 33:16
2 Ki. 14:10
Psa. 88: 8
Isa. 45:25
49: 3[a]
Eze. 28:22
38:23

[a] AS δοξάζω.

ἔνδοξος.

Gen. 34:19
Exo. 34:10
Nu. 23:21
Deu. 10:21
Jos. 4: 4
Jud. 18:21 + A
1 Sa. 9: 6
18:23
22:14
2 Sa. 23:19, 23
1 Ch. 4: 9
11:21, 25
2 Ch. 2: 9
36:14
Neh. 4:19 + S[1]
Est. 1: 3
6: 9
Job 5: 9
9:10
Job 34:24
Ps. 149: 8
Pro. 25:27
Isa. 5:14
10:33
11: 4 S[a]
12: 4
13:19
22:17, 24
23: 8, 9, 9
24:15
26:15
32: 2
48: 9
59:19
60: 9
64: 3, 11
Nah. 3:10

[a] pro ταπεινός.

ἐνδόξως.

Exodus 15: 1, 21

ἐνδόσθια.

Exo. 12: 9
29:17
Lev. 4: 8, 8
Lev. 6:33, 33
8:16

ἐνδυάζω.

Psalm 140: 4 S[1][a]

[a] pro συνδοιάζω.

ἔνδυμα.

2 Sa. 1:24
20: 8
2 Ki. 10:22
Est. 6: 9 + S[3]
10 + S[3]
Psa. 68:12
132: 2
Pro. 29:40
Isa. 63: 2
Lam. 4:14
Dan. 3:21 + A
7: 9
Zeph. 1: 8

ἐνδυναμόω.

Jud. 6:34 AB[a]
1 Ch. 12:18 A[a]
Psa. 51: 9[b]

[a] pro ἐνδύω. [b] B[1]S[1] δυναμόω.

ἔνδυσις.

Job 41: 4

ἐνδύω.

Gen. 3:21
27:15
38:19
41:42
Exo. 28:37
29: 5, 8, 30
40:11, 12
Lev. 6:10, 10
11
8: 7, 7, 13
16: 4, 4, 24
24[a], 32
21:10
Nu. 20:26, 28
Deu. 22: 5, 11
Jud. 6:34[b]
1 Sa. 17: 5, 38
2 Sa. 6:14
14: 2
17:17 A[c]
1 Ki. 22:30
1 Ch. 12:18[d]
2 Ch. 5:12
6:41
9:18
18: 9, 29
24:20
2 Ch. 28:15
Est. 4: 1
Job 8:22
10:11
29:14[e]
39:19
Psa. 34:13, 26
64:14
92: 1, 1
103: 1
108:18, 29
131: 9, 16, 18
Pro. 23:21
29:39[f], 44
Cant. 5: 3
Isa. 22:21
49:18
50: 3
51: 9
52: 1, 1
59:17
61:10
Jer. 10: 9
26: 4
Eze. 7:27
9: 2, 3, 11
10: 2, 6, 7
Eze. 16:10
23: 6, 12
38: 4
42. 14
44:17, 17
19
Dan. 5: 7, 16
Dan. 5:29
10: 5
12: 6, 7
Jon. 3: 5
Zeph. 1: 8
Zec. 3: 3, 4
13: 4

[a] A ἐκδύω. [b] AB ἐνδυναμόω. [c] pro δύναμαι. [d] A ἐνδυναμόω. [e] AS[1] δείδω. [f] ABS ἐνδιδύσκω.

ἐνεγγυάομαι.

Proverbs 6: 3

ἐνέδρα.

Jos. 8: 7, 9, 14
Job 25: 3
Psa. 9:29

ἐνεδρεύω.

Deu. 19:11
Jos. 8: 4
Jud. 9:25[a]
32, 34
43
16: 2
21:20
1 Sa. 15: 5
2 Sa. 3:27
Job 24:11
38:40
Psa. 9:30
30 − A
Pro. 7:12
26:19
Lam. 3:10
4:19

[a] A ἔνεδρον.

ἔνεδρον.

Nu. 35:20, 22
Jos. 8: 2, 12
18, 19
21 − A
Jud. 9:25 A[a]
35
16: 9, 12
Jud. 20:29, 33
36, 37
37, 38
39 − A
1 Ki. 21:40
2 Ch. 13:13, 13
Obad. 7

[a] pro ἐνεδρεύω.

ἐνείδω.

Genesis 20:10

ἐνειλέω.

1 Sa. 21: 9[a]

[a] A λαμβάνω.

ἔνειμι.

1 Ki. 10:17
2 Ch. 24:15 A[a]
Job 27: 3
28:14[b]
Job 28:14[b]
34:13[c]
36: 2 A[a]
Pro. 14:23

[a] pro εἰμί. [b] ACS εἰμί. [c] O ἐν αὐτῇ, S εἰμί.

ἐνείρω.

Job 10:11

ἕνεκα, −κεν.

Gen. 18:30 − A
31 + A
1 Ki. 8:41 + A
Isa. 43:25 − AS
Eze. 13:19 − A
Jon. 1: 8 + A
14 − S[1]

ἐνενήκοντα.

Ezra 2:58[a]
Dan. 12:11[b]

[a] B 70. [b] B* τεσσεράκοντα.

ἐνενηκονταοκτώ.

Ezra 2:16[a]

[a] B ἐνενηκονταδύο.

ἐνεός.

Pro. 17:28
Isa. 56:10

ἐνεργέω.

Nu. 8:24[a]
Pro. 21: 6
Pro. 29:30
Isa. 41: 4

[a] A ἔργον.

ἐνεργός.

Ezekiel 46: 1

ἐνευλογέω.

Gen. 12: 3[a]
18:18
22:18
26: 4 A[b]
Gen. 28:14
1 Sa. 2:29
Psa. 9:24
71:17 S[2][b]

[a] A εὐλογέω. [b] pro εὐλογέω.

ἐνευφραίνομαι.

Proverbs 8:31[a], 31[b]

[a] A εὐφραίνω. [b] BS εὐφραίνω.

ἐνεχυράζω.

Exo. 22:26
Deu. 24: 8, 8, 12
19
Job 22: 6
Job 24: 3
34:31
Eze. 18:16

ἐνεχύρασμα.

Exo. 22:26
Eze. 33:15[a]

[a] A ἐνέχυρον.

ἐνεχυρασμός.

Ezekiel 18: 7, 12, 16

ἐνέχυρον.

Deu. 24:12, 13
14, 15[a]
Eze. 33:15 A[b]

[a] A ἱμάτιον. [b] pro ἐνεχύρασμα.

ἐνέχω.

Gen. 49:23
Eze. 14: 4, 7

ἔνθα καὶ ἔνθα.

2 Ki. 2: 8, 14[a]
2 Ki. 5:25

[a] A ἔνθεν καὶ ἔνθεν.

ἔνθεμα.

Canticles 4: 9

ἐνθέμιον.

Exodus 38:16, 16

ἔνθεν καὶ ἔνθεν.

Exo. 26:13
32:15
37:13
Jos. 9: 6
1 Sa. 14: 4 + 8
16
1 Ki. 10:19, 20
2 Ki. 2:14 A[a]
4:35
2 Ch. 9:18, 19
Eze. 40: 6 + A
10, 10
Eze. 40:12, 12
16, 21
26, 34
37
39 + A
41, 48
48, 49[b]
41: 1, 2, 3
15, 19
19, 26
47: 7, 12

[a] pro ἔνθα καὶ ἔνθα. [b] B ἔνθεν...ἐντεῦθεν.

ἐνθρονίζω.

Est. 1: 2 S[3][a]

[a] pro θρονίζω.

ἐνθυμέομαι.

Gen. 6: 6, 7[a]
Deu. 21:11
Jos. 6:18
7:21
Isa. 10: 7
37:29 S[b]
Lam. 2:17
17 A[c]

[a] A θυμόω. [b] pro θυμόω. [c] pro ἐντέλλω.

ἐνθύμημα.

1 Ch. 28: 9
Ps. 118:118
Jer. 3:17[a]
7:24[a]
Eze. 14: 5, 7, 22
23
16:36
18: 6, 15
Eze. 20:16, 24
31
22: 3, 4
23: 7, 30[a]
37, 49
24:14, 14
44:10
Mal. 2:16

[a] A ἐπιθύμημα.

ἐνθύμιος.

Psalm 75:11, 11

ἐνιαύσιος.

Exo. 12: 5
29:38
Lev. 9: 3
12: 6
14:10, 10
23:12, 18
19
Nu. 6:12, 14
14
7:15, 17
21, 23
27, 29
33, 35
39, 41
45, 47
51, 53
57, 59
63, 65

Nu. 7:69, 71
75, 77
81, 83
87
88—AB
88
8: 8
15:27
28: 3,9,11
19, 27
29: 2,8,13
17, 20
23, 26
29, 32
36
Eze. 46:13
Mic. 6: 6

ἐνιαυτός.

Gen. 1:14
17:21
26:12
47:17, 28
Exo. 12: 2
23:14, 16
17, 29
30:10
10+A
34:22, 23
24
Lev. 16:34
23:40
25: 5, 10
10, 11
15, 29
30, 50
52, 53
53
54 A[a]
27:17, 18
23, 24
Nu. 10:11
14:34
28:14
Deu. 11:12, 12
14:21, 21
27
15:20, 20
16:16
24: 7
31:10
Jos. 5:12
Jud. 10: 8 A[b]
11:40
1 Sa. 1: 7, 7
7:16, 16
2 Sa. 11: 1
21: 1, 1
1 Ki. (3) p 1
4: 7
5:11
6: 5
8:59[c]
9:25 A
10:14, 25
25
12 p 24/76
14:21, 25

1 Ki. 15: 9[d]
16 p 28—A
18: 1
21:22, 26
22: 2
2 Ki. 8:26
13:20
17: 4
18: 9, 10
24:18[d]
25: 8—A
27
1 Ch. 27: 1
2 Ch. 8:13
9:13, 24
24—A
22: 2
24: 5,5,23
27: 5, 5
36:10
Neh. 10:32, 34
34, 35
35
Job 3: 6
Psa. 64:12
89:10 B[e]
Pro. 2:19
Isa. 6: 1
21:16, 16
29: 1, 1
32:10
34: 8
37:30, 30
61: 2
63: 4
Jer. 11:23
17: 8
23:12
31:44
35:16
39: 1, 1
43: 1
51:31
52:31
Eze. 4: 6
15: 4
Dan. 11:13
Zec. 14:16

[a] pro ἔτος. [b] pro καιρός. [c] A αὐτός. [d] A ἔτος. [e] pro αὐτός.

ἐνιουδαΐζω.

Est. (9)17 S[1a] [a] pro Ἰουδαΐζω.

ἐνίστημι.

1 Kings 12 p 24/75

ἐνισχύω.

Gen. 12:10
Gen. 33:14
43: 1
47: 4, 13
48: 2
Deu. 3:28 A[a]
32:13
Jud. 1:28
3:12
5:11 A[b]
12+A
12+A
11+A
9:24[c]
16:28
20:22
2 Sa. 10:21
22:40
2 Ki. 12: 8
15:19+A
25: 3
1 Ch. 4:23
15:21[d]
19:13—BS

Gen. 32:28
2 Ch. 1: 1[e]
24:13
Ezra 1: 6[f]
9:12
Neh. 10:29
Ps. 147: 2
Isa. 33:23
41:10
42: 6
45: 5—AS
57:10
Jer. 6: 1
9: 3
Eze. 27: 9
30:25
34: 4, 16
Dan. 6: 7
10:18, 19
11: 5, 5
Hos. 10:11
12: 3, 4
Joel 3:16
Hag. 2:22+A

[a] pro κατισχύω. [b] pro αὐξάνω. [c] A κατισχύω. [d] BS ἰσχύω. [e] B κατενισχύω. [f] A ἰσχύω.

ἐννακόσιοι.

Neh. 7:39[a]
Neh. 11: 8[b]

[a] S[1] ἑκατόν. [b] S[1] πεντακόσιοι.

ἔννευμα.

Proverbs 6:13

ἐννεύω.

Pro. 6:13
Pro. 10:10

ἐννοέω.

Job 1: 5
Isa. 41:20
Dan. 9:23

ἔννοια.

Pro. 1: 4
2:11
3:21
4: 1
5: 2
8:12

Pro. 16:22
18:15
19: 7
23: 4, 19
24: 7

ἐννόμως.

Proverbs 29:43

ἐννοσσεύω.

Psa. 103:17
Jer. 22:23

ἐνοέω.

2 Samuel 20:15

ἐνοικείοω.

Esther 8: 1

ἐνοικέω.

Lev. 26:32
Jud. 6:10 A[a]
2 Ki. 19:26
22:16, 19
Isa. 5: 3, 9
21:14
22:21
21—A[g]
23: 2
6 AS[b]
24: 1, 6
17[c]
26: 5,9,18
21[c]
27: 5
32:18, 19
33:24

Isa. 34: 1+A
37:26 AS[d]
40:22
49:19 A[b]
65:21, 22
66:10 A[e]
Jer. 29: 2 A[b]
19 BS[b]
30: 1
31: 9 A[f]
33: 9 A[b]
34: 9
38:24
49:17
51: 2 A[f]
8 AS[b]
Dan. 9: 7[g]

[a] pro κάθημαι. [b] pro κατοικέω. [c] S κατοικέω. [d] pro οἰκέω. [e] pro ἀγαπάω. [f] pro ἔνοικος. [g] A κατοικεω.

ἔνοικος.

Jud. 5:23 A[a]
Jer. 31: 9[b]
Jer. 51: 2[b]

[a] pro κατοικέω. [b] A ἐνοικέω.

ἐνοπλίζω.

Nu. 31: 5
32:17, 27
29, 30

Nu. 32:32
Deu. 3:18
Jos. 6: 7

ἔνοπλος.

1 Kings 22:10

ἐνορκίζω.

Neh. 13:25 A[a] [a] pro ὁρκίζω.

ἐνόρκιος.

Numbers 5:21

ἔνορκος.

Nehemiah 6:18

ἐνοχλέω.

Gen. 48: 1
Deu. 29:18 AB[a] [a]
1 Sa. 19:14

1 Sa. 30:13
Dan. 6: 2
Mal. 1:13

[a] pro ἐν χολῇ.

ἔνοχος.

Gen. 26:11
Exo. 22: 3
34: 7
Lev. 20: 9, 11
12, 13
16, 27

Nu. 14:18
35:27, 31
Deu. 19:10
Jos. 2:19, 19
Job 15: 5
Isa. 54:17

ἐνσείω.

2 Kings 8:12

ἐνσιτέω.

Job 40:25

ἐνσκολιεύομαι.

Job 40:19

ἔνταλμα.

Job 23:11, 12[a]
Isa. 29:13
Isa. 55:11

[a] A ἐντολή.

ἐντάσσω.

Ezra 7:17
Job 15:22 A[a]
Dan. 5:24, 25

Dan. 6:10
10:21
Amos 7: 8

[a] pro ἐντέλλω.

ἐνταῦθα.

Gen. 38:21
22 A[a]
48: 9
Nu. 23: 1, 1
Jud. 4:20 A[a]
16: 2 A[a]
18: 3 A[b]
1 Sa. 7:12
9:11
10:22

1 Sa. 14:33, 34
36, 38
16:11+A
17: 3, 3
21: 8, 9
23: 3
2 Sa. 11:12
1 Ki. 19: 9, 13
2 Ki. 2: 2, 4
Psa. 72:10

[a] pro ὧδε. [b] pro τόπος.

ἐνταφιάζω.

Genesis 50: 2, 2

ἐνταφιαστής.

Genesis 50: 2, 2

ἐντείνω.

1 Ki. 22:34 A[a]
1 Ch. 5:18 A[b]
2 Ch. 18:33 A[b]
Psa. 7:13
10: 2
36:14
44: 5
57: 8
63: 4
77: 9
Isa. 5:28
Jer. 4:29

Jer. 9: 3
21: 5 A[c]
26: 9
27:29
Lam. 2: 4[d]
3:12
Hos. 7:16
Hab. 3: 9, 9
Zec. 9:13

[a] pro ἐπιτείνω. [b] pro τείνω. [c] pro ἐκτείνω. [d] A ἐντέλλω.

ἐντέλλω.

Gen. 2:16
3:11, 17
6:22
7: 5,9,16
12:20
21: 4
27: 8
28: 1, 6
32: 4, 17
19
42:25
43:15 A[a]
44: 1
45:19
50:12+A
Exo. 4:28
7: 2, 6
10, 13[b]
20
12:28, 50
23:15, 22
25:21
29:35
31:11
32: 8
34:11, 18
32, 32[b]
34
40:14[c]
Lev. 6: 9
7:26, 28
28
8: 5, 21
29, 34
35
9: 5,7,10
10:13
17: 2
24: 2
27:34
Nu. 1:54
2:33
34 A[d]
3:42
8:20
9: 8
27:19, 19
22
28: 2
30: 1, 17
31: 7
32:25
34: 2, 13
29
36: 2,5,12
Deu. 1: 3, 16
18, 19
41
2: 4, 37
3:18, 21
28
4: 2, 2, 5
13, 14
40
5:12, 16
32, 33
6: 1, 2, 4
6, 17
20, 24
25
7:11
8: 1, 11
9:12, 16
10: 5, 13
11: 8, 13

Deu. 11:22, 27
[illegible]
12:11, 14
21, 28
32
13: 5, 18
15: 5, 11
15
18:18
19: 7, 9
20:17
24:10, 20
22, 24
26:13, 14
16
27: 1,4,10
11
28: 1, 13
14, 15
45
29: 1
30: 2,8,11
16
31: 5, 10
14, 23
25, 29
32:46
33: 4
34: 9
Jos. 1: 7,9,10
11, 13
16, 18
3: 3, 8
4: 8, 10
12, 16
17
6:10
8: 4, 8
9: 4, 6, 8
10:27, 40
11: 9, 15
23
13: 6
14: 2, 5
17: 4
18: 8
21: 2, 8
22: 2, 2, 5
23:16
Jud. 2:20
3: 4
4: 6
13:14
19:30+A
21:10, 20
Ruth 2: 9, 15
3: 6
1 Sa. 13:13, 14
14
17:20 A
18:22
20:29
21: 2, 2
25: 7, 15
21, 30
2 Sa. 4:12
5:25
7: 7
9:11
11:19
13:28, 28
29
14: 8, 19
17:14, 23
18: 5

2 Sa. 18: 5—A
12
21:14
24:19
1 Ki. 1:35
2: 3
(3) p1
43, 46
5: 6
6: 2
8:58
9: 4
11:10, 10
11, 38
13: 9, 17
21
15: 5
17: 4, 9
22:31
2 Ki. 11: 5,9,15
14: 6
16:13, 16
17:13, 15
27, 34
35
18: 6, 12
20: 1
21: 8, 8
22:12
23: 4, 21
1 Ch. 6:49
14:16
15:15
16:15, 40[e]
17: 6—BS
22: 6, 13
17
24:19
2 Ch. 7:13, 17
18:30
19: 9
23: 8, 14
25: 4
33: 8
34:20
36:23
Ezra 4: 3
Neh. 1: 7, 8
5:14
7: 2
8: 1, 14
9:14
13:13+S[3]
Est. 2:10, 15[f]
20
4: 8, 17

Est. 8: 9
Job 15:22[c]
36:32
37:11
Psa. 7: 7
32: 9
41: 9
43: 5
67:29
77: 5[h], 23
90:11
104: 8
110: 9
118: 4, 138
132: 3
148: 5
Pro. 3: 2
6: 3
Isa. 5: 6
13: 4, 11
23:11
34:16
45:11, 12
48: 5
Jer. 1: 7, 17
7:22. 23
23, 31
11: 4, 4
13: 5, 6[i]
14:14
17:22
19: 5
23:32
27:21
28:59
29: 7
39:23
42: 6, 10
14, 18
43: 5,8,26
45:10, 27
Lam. 1:10, 17
2: 4 A[k]
17[m]
3:36
Eze. 9:11
10: 6
12: 7
24:18
37: 7, 10
Amos 2:12
6:11
9: 3, 4, 9
Nah. 1:14
Zec. 1: 6
Mal. 4: 6

[a] pro εἶπον. [b] A λαλέω. [c] A συντάσσω. [d] pro συντάσσω. [e] S[1] γίνομαι. [f] AS[3] λέγω. [g] A ἐντάσσω. [h] S[1] τίθημι. [i] B ἀνατέλλω. [k] pro ἐντείνω. [m] A ἐνθυμέομαι.

ἔντερον.

Gen. 43:29 A[a]   [a] pro ἔγκατα.

ἐντεῦθεν.

Gen. 37:17
42:15
50:25
Exo. 11: 1
13: 3, 19
17.12, 12
32: 7
33: 1, 15
Nu. 11:31, 31
22:24, 24
Deu. 9:12

Jos. 4: 3+A
8:22, 22
Jud. 7: 9+A
18
Ruth 2: 8
2 Sa. 2:13, 13
1 Ki. 17: 3
Jer. 2:36
45:10
Eze. 40:49 B[a]
Dan. 12: 5, 5

[a] pro ἔνθεν.

ἐντήκω.

Eze. 4:17[a]   Eze. 24:23

[a] AB[1] τήκω.

ἐντίθημι.

Ezra 5: 8   Pro. 8: 5

ἐντιμιόω.

2 Kings 1:13, 14

ἔντιμος.

Nu. 22:15
Deu. 28:58
1 Sa. 26:21
Neh. 2:16
4:14, 19
5: 5, 7
6:17
7: 5
Job 28:10[a]

Job 34:19
Psa. 71:14
Isa. 3: 5
13:12, 12
16:14
28:16
43: 4
Dan. 2:37

[a] AC τίμιος.

ἐντίμως.

Numbers 22:17

ἐντολή.

Gen. 26: 5
Exo. 12:17
15:26
16:28
24:12
Lev. 4:13, 22
27
5:17
6: 2
22:31
26: 3, 15
27:34
Nu. 15:22, 31
39, 40
36:12
Deu. 4: 2, 40
5:29, 31
6: 1, 2
17
24+A
25
7: 9, 11
8: 1, 2, 6
11
10:13
11: 1—8
8, 13
22, 27
28
13: 4+A
18
15: 5
16:12
17:19, 20
19: 9
26:13, 13
18
27: 1, 10
28: 1
13 A[a]
14[b], 15
45
30: 8, 10
11, 16
16+A
Jos. 5: 6
22: 3, 5, 5
Jud. 2:17 A[c]
3: 4
1 Sa. 13:13
1 Ki. 2: 3
(3) 43
3:14
6(12) A
8.58, 61
9: 4, 6
11:11
34+A
38
13:21
14: 8 A
2 Ki. 17:13, 16
19, 34
37
18: 6, 36
21: 8
23: 3

1 Ch. 28: 7, 8
29:19
2 Ch. 7:19
8:13, 14
15
12: 1
14: 4
17: 4
19:10
24:20, 21
29:15, 25
25
30:16
34:22, 31
35:10, 15
16
Ezra 7:11
9:10, 14
10: 3
Neh. 1: 5, 7, 9
9:13, 14
16, 29
34
10:29, 32
11:23
12:24, 45
13: 5
Job 23:12 A[d]
Psa. 18: 9
77: 7
88:32
102:18
110: 7
111: 1
118: 4,6,10
15, 19
21, 32
35, 40
45, 47
48
57 S[1e]
60, 63
66, 69
73, 78
86, 87
96, 98
100, 104
110, 115
127, 128
131, 134
139 AS[1 e]
143
151 A[f]
159, 166
168, 172
173, 176
Pro. 2: 1
4: 4
6:23
7: 1, 2
10: 8
13:13
15: 5
19:16
Ecc. 8: 5
12:13
Isa. 48:18

Jer. 19:15[b]
42:16
18—S
Eze. 18:21

Eze. 18:31+A
Dan. 9: 4, 5
Mal. 2: 1, 4

[a] pro φωνή. [b] A λόγος. [c] pro λόγος. [d] pro ἔνταλμα. [e] pro νόμος. [f] pro ὁδός.

ἐντομίς.

Lev. 19:28
21: 5

Jer. 16: 6

ἐντός.

Est. 4:11 A[a]
Job 18:19 A[b]
Psa. 38: 4
102: 1

Ps. 108:22
Cant. 3.10
Isa. 16:11
Dan. 10:16

[a] pro ἐσώτερος. [b] pro ἐν τοῖς.

ἐντρέπω.

Exo. 10: 3
Lev. 26:41
Nu. 12:14
Jud. 3:30
8:28 A[a]
11:33 A[a]
2 Ki. 22:19
2 Ch. 7:14
12: 7,7,12
30:11[b], 15
34:27
36:12
Ezra 9: 6
Job 32:21
Psa. 34: 4, 26

Psa. 39:15, 15[c]
68: 7
69: 3
70:24
82:18
Isa. 16: 7, 12
24:23+S[1]
41:11
44:11—S[3]
45:16, 17
50: 7
54: 4
Jer. 27:12—BS
Eze. 36:32

[a] pro συστέλλω. [b] B τρέπω. [c] AS[2] καταισχύνω.

ἔντριτος.

Ecclesiastes 4:12

ἔντρομος.

Psa. 17: 8
76:19

Dan. 10:11

ἐντροπή.

Job 20: 3
Psa. 34:26
43:16

Psa. 68: 8, 20
70:13
108:29

ἐντρυφάω.

Neh. 9:25 A[a]
Isa. 55: 2
57: 4

Jer. 38:20
Hab. 1:10

[a] pro τρυφάω.

ἐντρύφημα.

Ecclesiastes 2: 8

ἐντυπόω.

Exo. 36:39 A[a]   [a] pro ἐκτυπόω.

ἐνυπνιάζω.

Gen. 28:12
37: 5, 6, 9
10
41: 5
Deu. 13: 1, 3, 5
Jud. 7:13
Isa. 29: 7, 8

Isa. 56:10
Jer. 23·25
34: 7
36: 8
Dan. 2: 1, 3
Joel 2:28

ἐνυπνιαστής.

Genesis 37:19

ἐνύπνιον.

Gen. 37: 5, 6, 8
9,9,10
20

Gen. 40: 5
5+A
5, 8, 9
Gen. 40:16
41: 1, 7, 8
11, 11
15, 15
25, 26
32
42: 9
Deu. 13: 1, 3, 5
Jud. 7:13, 13
15
1 Sa. 28: 6, 15
1 Ki. 3:15
Job 7:14
20: 8
33:15
Psa. 72:20
Ecc. 5: 2—S[1]
6
Isa. 29: 7 A[a]
8
65: 4

Jer. 23:25, 27
28, 28
32
36: 8
Dan. 1:17
2: 1, 2, 3
4, 5, 6
6, 7, 9
9, 26
28, 36
45
4: 2, 3, 4
5+A
6, 15
16
5:12
7: 1, 1
Joel 2:28
Mic. 3: 7
Zec. 10: 2

[a] pro καθ᾽ ὕπνους.

ἔνυστρον.

Deu. 18: 3   Mal. 2: 3,3-S[1]

ἐνφώθ.

Judges 8:26+A

ἐνώπιος, —ον.

Gen. 11:28
16:13, 14
17: 1[a]
24:51
30:33, 38
31:35, 37[a]
44:32[a]
48:15[b]
Exo. 3: 6
14: 2
21: 1
22: 8, 9
23:15, 17
25:29
32:33
33:11, 11
17
34: 9, 10
20, 23
Lev. 4: 4,17A[c]
18, 24
13:37
29:17
24: 3, 8
25:53
Nu. 13:34, 34
17:10
19: 3
32: 4, 5[a]
Deu. 1: 8, 42
4: 8, 10
25[d], 34
44
5: 5 A[e]
6.22
11:26[a], 32
12. 8[a]
16:16
29: 2
31: 5+A
11
Jos. 9: 5
10: 8
24:25
Jud. 2:11[a]
3:12[f]
4: 1[f], 15
23 A[g]
6: 1[f], 18
8:28[h]
9:39[h]
10: 6[f]
15 A[i]
11: 9, 11
12: 3 A[k]
13: 1[a], 15[a]

Jud. 14: 1+A
7 A[i]
16:25
25—A
18: 6
20:23, 26[f]
26[f], 28
32, 35[h]
39[a], 42
21: 2, 25[m]
1 Sa. 1: 9, 11
12, 15
24, 26
2:11, 11
17, 18
21
28+A
30, 35
3:1,18,21
4: 2, 3
5: 3, 4
6:20
7: 6, 6
10—A
8: 6 A[i]
9:24, 24
10:19, 25
11:10, 15
15
12: 2, 2, 3
3,7,17
14:18, 36
40
15:17, 19
21, 30
30, 33
16: 6, 10
16, 21
22
17:57 A
19: 7, 24
20: 1, 1
3 A[i]
25+A
21: 7, 13
23:18
25:23
26:19, 24
28:22, 25
25
29: 8, 10
2 Sa. 2:14, 17
3:31[n], 34
36, 36
4:10
5: 3, 20

2 Sa. 6: 5,7,14
16, 17
21
21—A
7:16, 18
19
25+A
29
10: 3
11:13
13: 9
16:19 *ter*
18: 7,9,14
24
19:13
18—A
27+AB
22:25[a]
24: 4
1 Ki. 1: 2+A
25, 28
28, 32
2: 4, 26
(3) *p* 1, 45
3: 6, 10
16, 22
24
8:22, 23
25, 25
28, 33
46, 50
59, 62
64, 65
65
9: 3, 4, 6
10: 8
11: 8
33+A
33, 36
38
12: 6
p 24 *l* 6
ll 62,67
14:22
15: 3,5,11
26, 34
16: 7, 19
25
p 28—A
30
32 A[o]
17: 1
18:15
19:11, 11
19
20: 2, 20
25
22:10, 21
43 A[t]
2 Ki. 1:18
3:14
4:12, 38
43
5: 1, 2, 3
15—B[b]
16
6: 1, 22
8: 9, 18
27
12: 2
14:24
18:22
20: 3, 3 A[i]
22:10, 19
23: 2 B[p],3
37 A[t]
24:19[m]
25: 8, 29
1 Ch. 17:17
29:10
2 Ch. 1: 6, 10
14: 2, 7[q]
13
18:20
20:32
24: 2
25: 2
26: 4
27: 2
28: 1

2 Ch. 29: 2
33:22
34:31
36: 2,9,12
Ezra 4:23
7:19
8:21, 29
9: 9, 15
10: 1, 11
Neh. 1: 4,6,11
2: 1, 1, 5
6
4: 2
8: 2, 5
9: 8, 11
24, 24
28, 32
35
Est. 2: 9,15 A[r]
5: 7
6: 1+S^{3}
13
7: 3
8: 5+AS^{3}
5+S^{3}
Job 1:6
2: 1 A[s]
2[f]
14: 3—A
26: 6
31:3[p]
42: 7
Psa. 5: 9
9:20, 25
14: 4
15: 8
17: 7, 13
23, 25
18:15
21:26, 28
30
22: 5
35: 3
37:18
38: 6
40:13
49: 8
50: 5, 6
53: 5
55: 9, 14
60: 8
61: 9
65:11 BS^{1}[t]
67: 4,5—S^{1}
8
68:23
71: 9, 14
78:10, 11
85: 9, 14
87: 3
89: 8[u]
95: 6
97: 6
99: 2
105:23
114: 9[v]
118:169[a]
170
140: 2
141: 3
142: 2
Pro. 3: 4
5:21
8: 9
11: 1
12:15
20:10, 23
22:14
25: 6, 26
Ecc. 3:11 S^{1}[w]
Cant. 8:12
Isa. 1: 7
5:21
9: 3
13:16
24:23
38: 3, 3
48:19[x]
49:16
52:10

Isa. 65: 6[v]
66:22, 23
Jer. 7:10, 11
10: 9
18: 4
Lam. 1: 5 S[a]
6 A[a]
Eze. 2:10
5: 8, 14
6: 4
8: 1
10: 2, 10
12: 3, 3, 5
6, 7
16:41, 50
20: 9,9,14
22
21:23
22:16 A[i]
28: 9, 25
37:20
38:16
39:27
Dan. 1: 4—B^{1}
5,9,13
19
2: 2,9,10

Dan. 2:11, 24
25, 27
36
3: 3, 13
27+AB^{2}
4: 3, 4
5+A
16+A
5:13, 15
17
22 A[c]
23
6: 1, 13
22
7:13+A
8: 4, 6[y]
7, 15
9:18
Hos. 2:10[a]
6: 2
Zeph. 3:20
Hag. 2: 3, 14
Zec. 8: 6, 6
11:12
12: 8
Mal. 2:17
3:16

vide ἐναντίον.

[a] A ἐναντίον. [b] B ἐναντίον. [c] *pro* κατενώπιον. [d] A ἔναντι, B ἐναντίον. [e] *pro* ῥῆμα. [f] A ἔναντι. [g] *pro* ἔμπροσθεν. [h] A πρόσωπον. [i] *pro* ὀφθαλμός. [k] *pro* χείρ. [m] A ὀφθαλμός. [n] A ἔμπροσθεν. [o] *pro* ἐν οἴκῳ. [p] *pro* ἐν ὠσίν. [q] A ἐν ᾧ. [r] *pro* παρὰ πάντων. [s] *pro* ἔναντι, [t] *pro* ἐπὶ τ. νῶτον. [u] S^{2} ἐναντίον. [v] S^{1} ἐναντίον. [w] *pro* ἐν καιρῷ [x] *pro* πρόσωπον. [y] A ἀνὰ μέσον.

ἐνωτίζομαι.

Gen. 4:23
Exo. 15:26
Nu. 23:18
Jud. 5: 3
Neh. 9:30
Job 32:11
11+A
33: 1
31+A
31[a]
34: 2, 16
37:13
Psa. 5: 2
16: 1
38:13
48: 2
53: 4

Psa. 54: 2
83: 9
85: 6
134:17[b]
139: 7
142: 1
Isa. 1: 2
28:23
42:23
44: 8
51: 4
Jer. 8: 6
13:15
23:18
Hos. 5: 1
Joel 1: 2

[a] A προσέχω. [b] A ἀκούω.

ἐνώτιον.

Gen. 24:22, 30
47
35: 4
Exo. 32: 2, 3
35:22
Jud. 8:24, 24

Jud. 8:25, 26
Pro. 11:22
25:12
Isa. 3:20
Eze. 16:12
Hos. 2:13

ἕξ.

Lev. 12: 5[a]
Jud. 12: 7[b]
2 Sa. 21:20—A
1 Ch. 4:27[c]

2 Ch. 13: 9 A[d]
27: 8 A
Eze. 41: 8—A

[a] A εἷς. [b] B ἑξήκοντα. [c] AB τρεῖς. [d] *pro* ἐν.

ἐξαγγέλλω.

Psa. 9:15
55: 9
70:15[a]
72:28

Psa. 78:13
106:22
118:13, 26
Pro. 12:16

[a] S ἀναγγέλλω.

ἐξαγοράζω.

Daniel 2: 8

ἐξαγορεύω.

Lev. 5: 5
16:21
26:40
Nu. 5: 7
1 Ki. 8:31
Ezra 10: 1[a]

Neh. 1: 6
9: 2, 3
Job 31:34
Psa. 31: 5
Dan. 9:20

[a] B^{1} προσαγο-

ἐξαγριαίνω.

Dan. 8: 7[a]

[a] A ἐξαγριόω.

ἐξαγριόω.

Dan. 8:7 A[a]

[a] *pro* ἐξαγριαίνω.

ἐξάγω.

Gen. 1:20, 21
24
8:17
11:31
15: 5, 7
19: 5,8,12
17
20:13
38:24
40:14
41:14
43:22
48:12
Exo. 3: 8, 10
11, 12
6: 6, 7
8 B[a][a]
13 A[b]
26, 27
7: 4, 5
8:18
12:17, 42
51
13: 3,9,14
16
14:11, 11
16: 3,6,32
18: 1
19:17
20: 2
29:46
32: 1,7,11
12, 23
33: 1
Lev. 19:36
22:33
23:43
24:14, 23
25:38, 42
55
26:13, 45
Nu. 15:36, 41
19: 3
20:10, 16
21: 5
23:22
27:17
Deu. 1:27
4:20, 37
5: 6, 15
6:12, 21
23
7: 8, 19
8:14, 15
9:12, 26
28, 28
29
13: 5, 10
17: 5
21:19
22:21, 24
26: 8
29:25
Jos. 2: 3[c]
6:22, 23
10:22[i]
23, 24
15: 9 A[e]

Jos. 24: 5, 31
Jud. 2:12
6: 8—A
13 A[f]
30 A[g]
19:22 A[g]
24, 25
1 Sa. 12: 8
2 Sa. 5: 2
12:31
13: 9,9,18
22:20
49—A
1 Ki. 8:16, 21
51, 53
9: 9
20:10—B
13
21:39 B[a]
42 A[g]
22:34
2 Ki. 10:22
11:15
21:15—A
23: 4
25:27
1 Ch. 11: 2
19:16
20: 3[d]
2 Ch. 1:17
7:22
18:33
23:11
35:23, 24
Neh. 9: 7, 18
Job 8:10[h]
10:18
12:22
15:13
23: 7
Psa. 17:20
24:17
30: 5
65:12
67: 7
77:16
103:14
104:37, 43
106:14, 28
134: 7
135:11
141: 8
142:11
Isa. 42: 7
43: 8, 17
48:21
65: 9
Jer. 16:13
15:19
20: 3
28:16
33:23
38:32
39:21
42: 3[i]
45:22, 23
46:14
52:31

Eze. 11: 7, 9
14:22
20: 6, 9
10+A
14, 22
34
20:36+A
38[k], 41
28:18
34:13

Eze. 37: 1
42:15
43: 1
46:21
47: 2
Dan. 9:15
11:32 A[m]
Hos. 9:13
Joel 1: 5 S^{1}[n]
Mic. 7: 9

[a] *pro* εἰσάγω. [b] *pro* ἐξαποστέλλω. [c] A εἰσάγω. [d] A ἐκφέρω. [e] *pro* ἄγω. [f] *pro* ἀνάγω. [g] *pro* ἐκφέρω. [h] A διδάσκω. [i] A ἄγω. [k] A ἐξαίρω. [m] *pro* ἐπάγω. [n] *pro* ἐξαίρω.

ἐξαίρεσις.

Genesis 49: 5

ἐξαίρετος.

Gen. 48:22
Job 5: 5[a]

[a] A ἐξαιρέω.

ἐξαιρέω.

Gen. 32:11
37:21, 22
Exo. 3: 8
18: 4, 8, 9
10
Lev. 14:40, 43
Nu. 35:25
Deu. 23:14
25:11
32:39
Jos. 2:13
9:32
10: 6
24:10
Jud. 9:17 A[a]
10:15
14: 9, 9
18:28 A[a]
1 Sa. 4: 7, 8
7: 3
10:18
12:10, 11
21
14:48
17:37, 37
26:24
30: 8,8,18
22
2 Sa. 14: 6
19: 5, 9[b]
22: 1,2,20
23:12
1 Ki. 1:12
2 Ki. 17:39
18:29, 30
30, 34
35, 35
19:12—AB
12
1 Ch. 16:35
2 Ch. 25:15
32:17, 17
Job 5: 4, 5 A[c]
19
10: 7
36:21
Psa. 30: 2—S
3
36:40
49:15

Psa. 58: 2
63: 2
70: 2—S^{1}
81: 4
90:15
114: 8
118:153
139: 2, 5[b]
142: 9
143: 7
11—S^{1}
Isa. 10:12
31: 5
38:14
42:22
43:13
44:17, 20
47:14
48:10
50: 2—S^{3}
57:13
60:16
61: 4 S[d]
Jer. 1: 8
17[e], 19[f]
15:21
20:13
21:12
22: 3
38:11
41:13
49:11
Eze. 7:19+A
33:5,9[b],12
34:10, 27
Dan. 3:15, 17
28
6:14, 14
16, 20
27
8: 4, 7
Hos. 2:10
5:14
Mic. 5: 8
7: 3
Nah. 2: 2
Zeph. 1:18
Zec. 5: 7
11: 6

[a] *pro* ῥύομαι. [b] A ῥύομαι. [c] *pro* ἐξαίρετος. [d] *pro* ἐξερημόω. [e] A^{1} ἐξαίρω. [f] S ἐξαίρω.

ἐξαίρω.

Gen. 20: 1
35: 5
41:44
49:33
Exo. 13:20

Exo. 14:19, 19
15:22
19: 2 A[a]
28:34
Lev. 9:22

Nu. 1:51
2: 9[b]
16[b], 17[b]
24[b], 31[b]
34
4: 5, 15
9:19
20 A[a]
10: 2, 5, 6
6, 6, 12
13, 14
17, 18
21, 22
25, 28
29, 33
35, 34
11:35
12:15
13: 1
21:11
24: 2
33:52, 52
Deu. 7: 1
16:19
17: 7, 12
19:19
21: 9, 21
22:21, 22
24
24: 9
28:63
29:28
Jos. 7:12, 13
Jud. 1:20+A
21 A[c]
27[d], 28
28, 29
30, 31
32, 33
2: 3[e], 21
23
11:23, 24[f]
16:11[g]
20:13 A[h]
1 Sa. 20:15, 15
15 A[i]
2 Sa. 14: 7, 11
16
1 Ki. 2:31
8:25
9: 5, 7
14:24
15:14
16 p 28—A
p 28—A
22:44
2 Ki. 14: 4
15: 4, 35
16: 3
17: 8
18: 4
21: 2
23:24
1 Ch. 5:25
2 Ch. 7:18, 20

2 Ch. 15:17 A[k]
17: 6
19: 3
33: 9
Ezra 8:31
Psa. 39:15
Pro. 12: 3
20:13
Ecc. 7:27
10: 9
Isa. 16: 6
30:22 AS[3m]
62:10
Jer. 1:17 A[1n]
19 S[o]
4: 7
12:17
18: 7
27:34
28: 9, 20
26 S[p]
31:10
Lam. 1: 6[p], 15
Eze. 1: 4, 19
19, 20
21, 21
2: 2[q]
3:14
6: 6
10:16
19 A[r]
11:18, 22
13:11, 13
14: 8, 13
17
16:27, 42
50
17:17
20:15, 23
38 A[s]
39
45: 9
Dan. 2:35
7: 19
Hos. 2: 2, 17
10: 8
Joel 1: 5[t], 9[u]
Amos 1: 8
2: 9[v]
6: 7, 8
9: 8, 8
Obad. 9, 10
Mic. 5:11
12 A[v]
7:18
Nah. 1: 2
2: 1[w]
Zeph. 1: 3, 4
Zec. 4: 1 B[x]
9: 7
10: 2 S[3o]
11: 8
12: 9
13: 2

[a] pro ἀπαίρω. [b] A ἀναζεύγνυμι. [c] pro κληρονομέω. [d] A κληρονομέω. [e] A προστίθημι. [f] A κατακληρονομέω. [g] A ἐκσπάω. [h] pro ἐκκαθαρίζω. [i] pro εὑρίσκω. [k] pro ἀφίστημι. [m] pro μιαίνω. [n] pro ἐξαιρέω. [o] pro ξηραίνω. [p] AS[1] ἐξέρχομαι. [q] A ἐξεγείρω. [r] pro ἐξέρχομαι. [s] pro ἐξάγω. [t] S[1] ἐξάγω. [u] S[1] ἐξέρχομαι. [v] pro ἐξολοθρεύω. [w] S[3] ἀναλίσκω. [x] pro ἐξεγείρω.

ἐξαίσιος.

Job 4:12
12+A
5: 9
9:10, 24
18:12
Job 20: 5
22:10
34:24
37:15

ἐξαίφνης.

Job 1:19
Pro. 21:22

Isa. 47: 9, 9
Jer. 6:26
15: 8
Mic. 2: 3
Hab. 2: 7
Mal. 3: 1

ἑξάκις.

Jos. 6:13—AB
15 B[a]
2 Ki. 13:19
Job 5:19

[a] pro ἑπτάκις.

ἐξακολουθέω.

Job 31: 9
Isa. 56:11
Jer. 2: 2
Amos 2: 4

ἐξακονάω.

Psa. 51: 4 BS[1a]
Eze. 21:11

[a] pro ἀκονάω.

ἑξακόσιοι.

Jud. 18:17+A
1 Sa. 27: 2[a]
30: 9[a]
2 Sa. 15:18—A
1 Ki. 5:16[b]
2 Ch. 9:15+AB
Neh. 7:10[c]
11—A[d]

[a] B τετρακόσιοι. [b] A πεντακόσιοι. [c] S ἑπτακόσιοι. [d] BS ὀκτακόσιοι.

ἐξακριβάζω, —βόω.

Nu. 23:10
Job 28: 3

ἐξάλειπτρον.

Job 41:22

ἐξαλείφω.

Gen. 7: 4, 23
23
9:15
Exo. 17:14
32:32, 33
Lev. 14:42, 43
48
Nu. 5:23
27: 4
Deu. 9:14
25: 6, 19
29:20
Jud. 15:16, 16
21:17
2 Ki. 14:27
1 Ch. 29: 4
Neh. 13:14
Psa. 9: 6
50: 3, 11
68:29
108:13, 14
Pro. 6:33
Isa. 43:25
Jer. 18:23
Eze. 6: 6+A
9: 8
20:17
22:30
25:15
Hos. 11: 9

ἐξάλειψις.

Job 15:23+A
Eze. 9: 6
Mic. 7:11

ἐξαλλάσσω.

Gen. 45:22[a]

[a] A ἀλλάσσω.

ἐξάλλομαι.

Isa. 55:12
Joel 2: 5
Mic. 2:12
Nah. 3:17
Hab. 1: 8

ἔξαλλος.

2 Sa. 6:14
Est. 3: 8

ἐξαμαρτάνω.

Jud. 20:16[a]
1 Ki. 14:16 A
15:26, 30
34
16: 2, 13
19, 26
20:22
22:53
2 Ki. 1:18
3: 3
10:29, 31
2 Ki. 13: 2, 6, 11
14:24
15: 9, 18
24, 28
17:21
21:11, 16
23:15
Neh. 9:33
Ecc. 5: 5
Hab. 2:10
Zeph. 1:17

[a] A διαμαρτάνω.

ἐξαμαρτωλός.

Psalm 138:19 S[1a]

[a] pro ἁμαρτωλός.

ἑξάμηνος.

2 Ki. 15: 8
1 Ch. 3: 4—B

ἐξαναλίσκω.

Exo. 32:12
33: 3, 5
Lev. 26:22, 33
44
Nu. 14:35
16:21, 45
17:12
25:11
32:13
Deu. 2:15
5:25
Deu. 7:22
9: 4
28:21, 42
Jos. 24:20
Jer. 9:16
10:25
25:16
Lam. 3:65
Eze. 20:13
35:15[a]

[a] A ἐξολοθρεύω.

ἐξανατέλλω.

Gen. 2: 9
Ps. 103:14
111: 4
Ps. 131:17
146: 8

ἐξανθέω.

Exo. 28:29
36:32
Lev. 13:12 AB[a]
12, 20
22, 25
27, 39
57
Nu. 17: 8 A[b], 8
Psa. 71:16
91:14
Ps. 102:15
131:18
Cant. 6:10[c]
Isa. 18: 5[d]
27: 6
35: 2
Hos. 7: 9
14: 8
Nah. 1: 4

[a] pro ἀνθέω. [b] pro ἐκφέρω. [c] A ἀνθέω. [d] ABS ἀνθέω.

ἐξανίστημι.

Gen. 4:25
18:16
19: 1[a], 32
34
Exo. 10:23[a]
21:19
Lev. 19:32
Nu. 25: 7
Jos. 8: 7, 18
19
Jud. 3:20
5: 7 A[b]
12 A[b]
Ruth 3: 8 A[c]
1 Ki. 1:49 A, B[c]
2:19
1 Ki. 18:27
Est. 7: 7
7+S[3]
Job 4: 4
Isa. 29: 8, 8
37:36 AS[b]
61: 4
Jer. 28:29[d]
Eze. 7:10
25:15
Dan. 3:24
Hos. 6: 2[e]
10:14
Obad. 1
Jon. 3: 6

[a] A ἀνίστημι. [b] pro ἀνίστημι. [c] pro ἐξίστημι. [d] S[1] ἀνίστημι. [e] AB ἀνίστημι.

ἐξαντλέω.

Pro. 20: 5
Hag. 2:16

ἐξαπατάω.

Exo. 8:29[a]

[a] A ἀπατάω.

ἐξάπινα.

Lev. 21: 4
Nu. 4:20
6: 9
Jos. 11: 7
2 Ch. 29:36
Psa. 63: 5
72:19
Isa. 48: 3

ἐξαπίνης.

Nu. 35:22
Pro. 6:15
Pro. 29: 1
Isa. 47:11

ἐξαπορέω.

Psalm 87:16—A[1]

ἐξαποστέλλω.

Gen. 3:23
8:10, 12
19:29
Gen. 24:40[a]
25: 6
26:27[b], 29

Gen. 26:31
31:27, 42
32:13
45: 1, 24
Exo. 3:12[b], 20
4:21, 23
23
5: 1, 2, 2
6: 1, 11
13[c]
7: 2, 14
16
8: 1, 2, 8
20, 21
21[d]
28 A[e]
29, 32
9: 1, 2, 7
13, 14
17, 28
35
10: 3, 4, 7
20, 27
11: 1, 1[b]
10
13:15, 17
14: 5
18:27
21:2 A[f], 26
27
24: 5
Lev. 14: 7, 53
16:21, 22
26
18:24
20:23
26:25
Nu. 5: 2, 3, 4
13: 4[b]
Deu. 9:23[h]
15:12, 13
13, 18
21:14
22:19, 29
24: 3, 5, 6
28:20 A[e]
Jos. 2:21
22: 6, 7
24:12, 12[g]
28 A[e]
Jud. 1:25
2: 6
3:15[b], 18
19—A
5:15 A[e]
6: 8, 14
35[n]
35+A
7: 8
24 A[e]
9:23
11: 7
17 A[e]
38 A[e]
12: 9
15: 5
18: 2 A[e]
19:25, 29 A[e]
30+A
20: 6[b]
12 A[e]
48 A[i]
1 Sa. 5:10, 11[b]
11
6: 3, 3[b]
6, 8
9:19, 26
10:25
13: 2
16:20
19:17, 17
20: 5, 13
22, 29
2 Sa. 3:14[b], 24
10: 4
11:12
13:16, 17
1 Ki. 2:25
8:66
11:21, 22

1 Ki. 11:22
12 p 24 l 16
l 21
15:12
18—A
19
16 p 28—A
21:31, 34
2 Ki. 1:16 A[e]
3: 7
5: 5, 24
8:12
11:12
15:37
22: 3 A[e]
24: 2
2 Ch. 36:15
Est. 4:15
8: 5 AS[3e]
10
9:19+ABS
20[b], 22
Job 12:19
14:20
22: 9
30:11
39: 3
Psa. 17:15, 17
19: 3
42: 3
56: 4, 4
77:45, 49
80:13
103:10[h], 30
104:17 A[2e]
20 BS[1e]
26, 28
105:15
109: 2
134: 9
143: 6, 7
150 p 6
Isa. 27: 8
50: 1, 1
66:19
Jer. 1: 7
3: 1, 8
7:25
8:17
15: 1
24: 5
25:16 A[k]
17
27:33
28: 2
33:22
35:16
41: 9
10 S[e]
14[h], 16
Eze. 2: 3
3: 5, 6
5:16 AB[e]
17
13:20
14:13, 21[m]
17: 7, 15
23:16, 40
28:23+A
31: 4
Hos. 8:14
Joel 2:19, 25
3:13
Amos 1: 4 AB[e]
7, 10
12
2: 2, 5
4:10
7:10
8:11
Obad. 1, 7
Mic. 1:14
6: 4
Hag. 1:12
Zec. 1:10
2:11[b]
4: 9
7: 2, 12
8:10
9:11

Mal. 2: 2, 4
16
Mal. 3: 1

[a] S ἀποστέλλω. [b] A ἀποστέλλω. [c] A ἐξάγω. [d] B ἐπαποστέλλω. [e] pro ἀποστέλλω. [f] pro ἀπέρχομαι. [g] A ἐκβάλλω. [h] B ἀποστέλλω. [i] pro ἐμπίπρημι. [k] pro ἐπαποστέλλω. [m] A ἐπαποστέλλω.

ἐξάπτω.

Exo. 30: 8[a]
Nu. 8: 3
Jud. 15: 5 A[b]
Pro. 22:15
Lam. 4:19 A[c]
Eze. 20:47
24:11+A

[a] A[1] ἅπτω. [b] pro ἐκκαίω. [c] pro ἐκπέτομαι.

ἐξαριθμέω.

Gen. 13:16, 16[a]
15: 5
Lev. 15:13, 28
25: 8
Nu. 23:10
31: 5
Deu. 16: 9, 9
Job 31: 4
Psa. 21:18
89:11
138:18
Eze. 44:26
Hos. 1:10

[a] A ἀριθμέω.

ἐξαρκέω.

Numbers 11:23

ἐξαρπάζω.

Job 29:17[a]

[a] ACS[1] ἐκσπάω.

ἔξαρσις.

Nu. 10: 6
Jer. 12:17

ἐξαρτάω.

Exo. 28: 7[a]

[a] AB ἐξαρτίζω.

ἐξαρτίζω.

Exo. 28: 7 AB[a]

[a] pro ἐξαρτάω.

ἐξάρχω.

Exo. 15:21
32:18 ter
Nu. 21:17
1 Sa. 18: 7
1 Sa. 21:11[a]
29: 5
Ps. 146: 7
Isa. 27: 2

[a] A ἄρχω.

ἐξασθενέω.

Psa. 63: 9 B[2]S[a]

[a] pro ἐξουθενόω.

ἐξαστράπτω.

Eze. 1: 4, 7
Nah. 3: 3

ἐξατιμάζω.

1 Sa. 17:42[a]

[a] AB ἀτιμάζω.

ἐξατιμόω.

Eze. 16:61[a]

[a] A ἀτιμάζω.

ἐξαφίστημι.

Jer. 5:25 A[a]

[a] pro ἀφίστημι.

ἐξεγείρω.

Gen. 28:16
41:21
Nu. 10:35
24:19
Jud. 5:12, 12
12+A
12, 12
16 A[a]
16:20 A[b]
1 Sa. 26:12
2 Sa. 12:11
19:18
23:18
1 Ki. 16: 3
2 Ch. 36:22
Ezra 1: 1, 5
Est. 8: 4
Job 5:11
14:12+A
Psa. 3: 6
7: 7
31:23
43:24
56: 9 ter
58: 5
72:20
Psa. 77:65
79: 3
107: 2+S[2]
3[c], 3
118:62
138:18
Pro. 25:23
Cant. 2: 7
3: 5
4:16
8: 4, 5
Isa. 38:16
41: 2
51: 9 ter
17, 17
52: 1, 1
Jer. 6:22[i]
27:41
28: 1, 38
39—S[1]
38:26
Eze. 2: 2 A[e]
21:16
23:22
38:14 A[f]
Dan. 7: 4 A[e]
11:25
12: 2[g]
Joel 3: 7, 9
12[g]
Amos 2: 9 A[e]
Jon. 1: 4, 11
13
Hab. 1: 6
2:19
3:13
Hag. 1:14
Zec. 2:13
4: 1[h], 1
9:13[i]
11:16
13: 7

[a] pro ἄγγελος. [b] pro ἐξυπνίζω. [c] S[1] ἐγείρω. [d] B ἐγείρω. [e] pro ἐξαίρω. [f] pro ἐγείρω. [g] A ἐγείρω. [h] B ἐξαίρω. [i] A ἐπεγείρω.

ἐξέδρα.

Eze. 40:44, 45
46
41:10, 11
42: 1, 4
6 A[a], 7
7, 8, 9
Eze. 42:10, 11
12, 13
13, 13
44:19
46:19, 23
23

[a] pro ἐξώτερος.

ἐξεικονίζω.

Exodus 21:22, 23

ἔξειμι.

Exodus 28:31

ἐξεκκλησιάζω.

Lev. 8: 4
Nu. 1:18 A[a]
20:10
Jos. 18: 1
Jud. 20: 1
2 Sa. 20:14
1 Ki. 8: 1
2+A
12:21
1 Ch. 13: 5[b]
15: 3[c]
28: 1
2 Ch. 5: 2, 3
11: 1
15: 9
24: 6
Jer. 33: 9
43: 9

[a] pro συνάγω. [b] BS ἐκκλησιάζω. [c] A συνάγω.

ἐξελαύνω.

Zec. 9: 8
Zec. 10: 4[a]

[a] A ἐλαύνω.

ἐξελέγχω.

Pro. 24:29 S[a]
Isa. 2: 4[b]
Mic. 4: 3[c]

[a] pro ἐλέγχω. [b] AS[3] ἐλέγχω. [c] A ἐλέγχω.

ἐξέλευσις.

2 Samuel 15:20—A

ἐξελίσσω.

1 Kings 7:45

ἐξέλκω.

Gen. 37:28
Jud. 20:31 A[a]
Job 20:15
Job 36:20
Pro. 24:68

[a] pro ἐκκενόω.

ἐξεμέω.

Job 20:15
Pro. 23: 8
Pro. 25:16
Jer. 32: 2, 13

ἐξεναντίας.

Exo. 14: 2, 9
36:26
Jos. 8:11
Jud. 9:17
20:34
43 A[a]
1 Sa. 10:10
17: 2, 8
21 A
26:20
2 Sa. 10: 9—A
9, 10
11:15
18: 6[b], 13
1 Ki. 20:10—B
13
1 Ki. 21:27
22:35
2 Ki. 2: 7, 15
3:22
1 Ch. 19:11, 17
2 Ch. 18:34
Neh. 3:25, 27
28, 29
30
Psa. 22: 5
34: 3
Eze. 47: 3
Dan. 10:13
Obad. 11
Hab. 1: 3, 9

[a] pro ἀπέναντι. [b] A ἐναντίον.

ἐξεργάζομαι.

Psa. 7:14
Psa. 30:20

ἐξερεύγομαι.

Exo. 8: 3
Psa. 44: 2
118:171
Ps. 143:13
144: 7[a]

[a] A ἐρεύγομαι.

ἐξερευνάω.

Deu. 13:14 A[a]
Jud. 5:14
18: 2 A[b]
1 Sa. 23:23
1 Ch. 19: 3
Psa. 63: 7, 7
108:11
118: 2, 34[c]
Ps. 118:69, 115
129
Pro. 2: 4
Lam. 3:39
Joel 1: 7
Amos 9: 3
Obad. 6
Zeph. 1:12

[a] pro ἐρευνάω. [b] pro ἐξιχνιάζω. [c] S[1] ἐκζητέω.

ἐξερεύνησις.

Psalm 63: 7

ἐξερημόω.

Lev. 26:31, 32
Jud. 16:24 A[a]
2 Ki. 19:24
Isa. 37:26
50: 2
61: 4, 4[b]
Jer. 25: 9
Eze. 6: 6
Eze. 12:20
19: 7
36: 4[c]
Hos. 13:15
Amos 7: 9 A[a]
Nah. 1: 4
Zeph. 3: 6
Hag. 1: 4

[a] pro ἐρημόω. [b] S ἐξαιρέω. [c] A ἐρημόω.

ἐξέρπω.

Psalm 104:30

ἐξέρχομαι.

Gen. 4:16
8: 7, 16
18, 19
9:10, 18
22
10:11, 14
12: 1, 4, 5
14: 8, 17
15: 4, 14
17: 6
19: 6, 14
14, 15
23
30 A[a]
24: 5
43 A[b]
50, 63
25:25, 26
27: 3, 30
28:10
30:16
31:13[c], 33
34: 1, 6, 26
35:11
Gen. 38:28, 29
30
39:12, 13
15, 18
41:46
42:15
43:30
44: 4, 28
46:26
47:10, 18
Exo. 1:10
2:11, 13
3:13[d]
4:14
8:12, 20[e]
29, 30
9:29, 33
10: 6, 18
11: 8 ter
12:22, 31
41
13: 3
15:20
16: 1, 4, 27
Exo. 17: 6, 9
10—A
18: 5[f], 7
21: 3, 3, 4
11, 22
22: 6
23:15
32:24
34:18, 34
35:20
Lev. 8:33
9:23, 24
10: 2, 7
14: 3, 38
15, 16, 32
16:17, 18
24
21:12
22: 4
24:10
25:28, 30
31, 33
41, 54
27:21
Nu. 1: 1
9: 1
10: 9
11:20, 20
24, 31
12: 4, 4, 5
16:27, 35
46
20:11, 18
20
21:23, 28
33
22: 5, 11
32, 36
24: 7, 24
26: 4
27:17, 21
30: 3, 13
31:13
33: 1, 3, 54
34: 4, 9
35:26
Deu. 1:44
2:23, 32
3: 1
4:15, 46
6: 4
9: 7
13:13
15:16
16: 1, 3, 6
20: 1
21: 2, 10
23: 9, 10
12—B[1]
24: 7
28: 7, 25
57
29: 7
Jos. 2: 5, 8, 19
5: 4, 6
8: 5, 6, 14
19, 22
9:18
23 A[f]
11: 4
14:11
16: 2
18:11, 11
19: 1, 10
17, 24
32, 40
21: 4
Jud. 1:10—A
3:10
19+A
23
23—A
24
4:14[d], 18
22
9:15, 20
20, 27[d]
29, 35
38, 39
42, 43
Jud. 10:17 [e]
11: 3[h], 31
36
14:14
14+A
15:19
16:12[i], 20
19:23, 27
20: 1, 14
20, 21
25, 28
31
21:21, 21
24[e]
Ruth 1: 7, 13
2:22[k]
1 Sa. 1:23
2: 3
4: 1, 3
7:11—A
8:20
9:11, 14
26
11: 3, 10
13:10, 17
23
14:11
17: 4
18: 6, 30 A
19: 3
20:35
21: 5
23:13
13 AB[f]
15[i]
24: 9+A
14
26:20
28: 1-A, 1
30:21
2 Sa. 2:12, 13
23 A[m]
5:24
6:20
10: 8
11: 8, 8, 13
17, 23
13:39
15:16, 17
16: 5, 7
7—A
11
18: 2, 2, 3
6, 24
19: 7
20: 7, 7
8
8—A
21:17
24: 4, 20
1 Ki. 2:30
(3)36, 42
46
8:10, 19
44
9:12
11:29
12 ρ 24 l 21
ll 35, 41
l 47
12:25
13:12 A[f]
19:11, 13
21:16, 17
17
18+A
19, 21
31, 33
39
22:21, 22
22
2 Ki. 2:21, 23
24
3: 6
4:18, 21
37, 39
5:2, 11, 27
6:15
7:12, 12
12+A

2 Ki. 7:16
9:11, 15
21, 21
24
10: 9, 25
13: 5
18:31
19: 9, 31
35
20:18
23:17
24: 7, 12
25: 4
1 Ch. 1:12 A
2:53
12:17
14: 8
15ABS[n]
15
19: 9
21: 4–8
21
24: 7
25: 9
26:14
2 Ch. 1:10
5:10, 11
6: 9, 34
14: 9, 10
15: 2
18:20, 21
21
19: 2, 4
20:10, 11
17, 20
20
21–A
22, 23[o]
21:15, 19
22: 7 AB[f]
7
23:14
14 A[n]
24: 5
25: 5
26: 6, 18
20
28: 9
31: 1
32:21
Neh. 2:13
8:15, 16
Est. 5: 9
7: 8+S[n]
(9)14, 15
Job 1:12, 21
2: 7
3:11
5: 6, 15
8:16
23:11
24: 5
26: 4
27:13 A[f]
28: 5
31:34, 40
33:28 A[f]
37: 1, 8 A[p]
20+A
39: 4
Psa. 16: 2
18: 5
43:10
59:12
72: 7
80: 6
103:23
107:12
108: 7
145: 4
150 p6
Pro. 7:15
24:23, 68
68
Ecc. 4:14
5:14
7:19
10: 5
Cant. 1: 8
3:11

Cant. 5: 6[q]
7:11
Isa. 2: 3
7: 3
19 S[1 f]
11: 1, 16
14:29, 29
28:29
36: 3
37: 9
32 A[r]
36
38:12
42:13
45:23
48: 1, 3, 20
49: 9, 17
51: 4, 5
52:11, 11
12
55:11, 12
57:16
62: 1
66:24
Jer. 1: 5
2:36
4: 4, 7
7:25
9: 3
4+A
11:11
14:18
15: 1, 2
19: 2
20:18
22:11, 22
23:15
26: 9
27: 8
28:32
31: 7
36: 2
37:19, 21
23, 23[s]
38: 4, 9, 39
44: 5, 7, 12
45: 8, 17
17, 18[t]
21
48: 6
50:12
51:17
52: 7
Lam. 1: 6 AS[1 u]
3: 7, 37
Eze. 3:22, 23
23
5: 4
7:10+A
10: 7, 18
19[v]
12: 4, 6, 7
12, 12
15: 7
16:14
19:14
21: 4, 20
24: 6, 12
30: 9
36:20
38: 8
39: 9
42:14
44: 3
46: 3, 8, 9
9, 9, 10
12, 12
Dan. 2:13, 14
15
3:26, 26
5: 5
8: 9
9:22, 23
11:11
Hos. 6: 5
Joel 1: 9 S[1 u]
2:16
3:18
Jon. 4: 5
Mic. 1:11

Mic. 2:13, 13 | Zec. 1:21[w]
4: 2, 10 | 5: 5
5: 2 | 9:14
Nah. 1:11 | 10: 4
Hab. 1: 4, 7 | 14: 2, 3, 8
3: 5, 13 | Mal. 4: 2

[a] *pro* ἀναβαίνω.
[b] *pro* ἐκπορεύω. [c] A ἀπέρχομαι.
[d] A ἔρχομαι. [e] A ἐκπορεύω.
[f] *pro* ἔρχομαι. [g] *pro* συνάγω.
[h] A συνεκπορεύω. [i] A κάθημαι.
[k] AB πορεύω. [m] *pro* διεξέρχομαι. [n] *pro* εἰσέρχομαι.
[o] AB ἔρχομαι. [p] *pro* ἐπέρχομαι.
[q] S ἀπέρχομαι. [r] *pro* εἰμί.
[s] S ἐπέρχομαι. [t] S[1] ἔρχομαι.
[u] *pro* ἐξαίρω. [v] A ἐξαίρω.
[w] A εἰσέρχομαι.

ἔξεστι.

Ezra 4:14 | Est. 4: 2

ἐξετάζω.

Deu. 13:14 A[a] | 1 Ch. 28: 9 A[a]
19:18 | Psa. 10: 4, 5

[a] *pro* ἐτάζω.

ἐξετασμός.

Jud. 5:16[a] | Pro. 1:32

[a] A ἐξιχνιασμός.

ἐξεύρεσις.

Isaiah 40:28

ἐξευφραίνω.

Eze. 23:41 A[a] [a] *pro* εὐφραίνω.

ἐξέχω.

Exo. 38:15 | Neh. 3:25, 26
Nu. 21:13 | 27
1 Ki. 7:14, 15 | Eze. 42: 5, 6
15

ἐξηγέομαι.

Lev. 14:57 | Job 12: 8
Jud. 7:13 | 28:27
2 Ki. 8: 5 | Pro. 28:13
1 Ch. 16:24-ABS

ἐξήγησις.

Jud. 7:15[a] [a] A διήγησις.

ἐξηγητής.

Gen. 41: 8, 24 | Pro. 29:18

ἐξηγορία.

Job 22:22 | Job 33:26

ἑξήκοντα.

Gen. 5:25[a] | 2 Ch. 11:21[d]
2 Ki. 25:19[b] | Ezra 6: 3–B
1 Ch. 9:13[c] | Neh. 7:66[e]

[a] A[2] ὀγδοήκοντα. [b] A ἑπτά.
[c] A ἐνενήκοντα. [d] B τριακοντα.
[e] B[1] ὀκτώ.

ἑξηκονταετής.

Leviticus 27: 3[a], 7

[a] A ἑξηκοστοῦ ἔτους.

ἐξηλιάζω.

2 Samuel 21: 6, 9, 13

ἑξῆς.

Exo. 10: 1 | Deu. 3: 6
Deu. 2:34 | Jud. 20:48+A

ἐξηχέω.

Joel 3:14

ἐξικνέομαι.

Jud. 5:15[a] [a] A ἀκριβασμός.

ἐξιλάομαι, ἐξιλάσκομαι.

Gen. 32:20 | Nu. 5: 8
Exo. 30:10, 15 | 6:11
16 | 8:12, 19
32:30 | 21
Lev. 1: 4 | 15:25, 28
4:20, 26 | 28
31, 35 | 16:46, 47
5: 6, 10 | 25:13
13, 16 | 28:22, 30
18 | 29: 5, 11
6: 7, 30 | 31:50
37 | 35:33
8:15, 34 | Deu. 21: 8
9: 7, 7 | 1 Sa. 3:14
10:17 | 6: 3
12: 7, 8 | 2 Sa. 21: 3
14:18, 19 | 1 Ch. 6:49
20, 21 | 2 Ch. 29:24, 24
29, 31 | 30:18
53 | Neh. 10:33
15:15, 30 | Ps. 105:30
16: 6, 10 | Pro. 16:14
11, 16 | Eze. 16:63
17, 17 | 43:20, 22
18, 20 | 22, 26
24, 27 | 45:15, 17
30, 32 | 18, 20
33 *ter* | Dan. 9:24
34 | Hab. 1:11
17:11, 11 | Zec. 7: 2
19:22 | 8:22
23:28 | Mal. 1: 9

ἐξίλασις.

Nu. 29:11 | Hab. 3:17+A

ἐξίλασμα.

1 Sa. 12: 3 | Psa. 48: 8

ἐξιλασμός.

Exo. 30:10+A | Eze. 7:25
Lev. 23:27, 28 | 43:23
Nu. 5: 8 A[a] | 45:19
1 Ch. 28:11 | [a] *pro* ἱλασμός.

ἐξιππάζομαι.

Habakkuk 1:8

ἐξίπταμαι *vide* ἐκπέτομαι.

ἕξις.

Jud. 14: 9 A[a] | Dan. 7:15
1 Sa. 16: 7 | Hab. 3:16[b]

[a] *pro* στόμα. [b] S[3] ἰσχύς.

ἐξισόω.

Exo. 37:16 | Exo. 38:15

ἐξίστημι.

Gen. 27:33 | Jud. 4:21–A
42:28 | 5: 4 A[a]
43:32 | 8:12[b]
45:26 | 9:44 A[c]
Exo. 18: 9 | Ruth 3: 8[d]
19:18 | 1 Sa. 4:13
23:27 | 13: 7
Lev. 9:24 | 14:15
Jos. 2:11 | 16: 4
10:10 | 17:11
Jud. 4:15 | 21: 1
1 Sa. 28: 5 | Isa. 42:14
2 Sa. 17: 2 | 52:14
22:15 | 60: 5
1 Ki. 1:49[e] | Jer. 2:12
9: 8 | 4: 9
2 Ki. 4:13 | 9:10
2 Ch. 7:21 | 18:16
15: 6 | 30:12
Job 5:13 | Eze. 2: 6, 6
12:17 | 21:14
26:11 | 26:16
36:28 | 27:31 A
37: 4+C | 35
Isa. 7: 2 | 31:15+A
10:31 | 32:10
13: 8 | Dan. 2: 1, 3
16: 3 | Hos. 3: 5
28: 7 | 5: 8
29: 9[f] | 11:10, 11[h]
32:11 | Mic. 7:17
33: 3 | Hab. 3: 2
41: 2

[a] *pro* στάζω. [b] A ἐκτρίβω.
[c] *pro* ἵστημι. [d] A ἐξανίστημι.
[e] B ἐξανίστημι. [f] S[1] ἵστημι.
[h] A ἐκπέτομαι.

ἐξιχνιάζω.

Jud. 18: 2, 2[a] | Job 28:27
Job 5:27 | 29:16
8: 8 | Ps. 138: 3
10: 6 | Ecc. 12: 9
13: 9 | [a] A ἐξερευνάω.

ἐξιχνιασμός.

Jud. 5:16 A[a] [a] *pro* ἐξετασμός.

ἐξοδεύω.

Jud. 5:27[a] [a] A ταλαίπωρος.

ἐξοδία.

Deu. 16: 3 | 2 Sa. 11: 1
33:18 | Eze. 26:18+A
1 Sa. 18:30 A | Mic. 7:15
2 Sa. 3:22

ἐξοδιάζω.

2 Kings 12:12

ἐξόδιος.

Lev. 23:36 | 2 Ch. 7: 9
Nu. 29:35 | Neh. 8:18
Deu. 16: 8 | Psa. 28: 1

ἔξοδος.

Exo. 19: 1 | Psa. 73: 5 S[2 b]
23:16 | 74: 7
Nu. 33:38 | 104:38
35:26 | 106:33 S[1 c]
Jud. 5: 4, 31[a] | 113: 1
1 Sa. 29: 6 | 120: 8
2 Sa. 1:20 | 143:13
3:25 | Pro. 1:20
22:43 | 4:23
1 Ki. (3):37 | 8:35, 35
3: 7 | 24:35, 42
6: 1 | 25:13, 26
10:28, 29 | Isa. 37:28
21:34 | 51:20
2 Ki. 19:27 | Jer. 11:13
1 Ch. 5:16 | Lam. 2:19, 21
20: 1 | 4: 1, 5, 8
2 Ch. 1:16 | 14
9:28 | Eze. 16:25 A[d]
16: 1 | 42:11
23: 8 | 43:11
32:30 | 44: 5
Neh. 4:21 | 47: 3
Job 38:27 | Dan. 9:25
Psa. 18: 7 | Mic. 5: 2
64: 9

[a] A ἀνατολή. [b] *pro* εἴσοδος.
[c] *pro* διέξοδος. [d] *pro* ὁδός.

ἐξοικοδομέω.
Nehemiah 3:15—ABS

ἔξοικος.
Job 6:18

ἐξοκέλλω.
Proverbs 7:21

ἐξολεθρεύω vide ἐξολοθ—

ἐξόλλυμι.
Pro. 10:31
11:17
Pro. 15:27

ἐξολόθρευμα.
1 Samuel 15:21

ἐξολόθρευσις.
Jud. 1:17 A[a]
Ps. 108:13
Eze. 9:1

[a] pro ἀνάθεμα.

ἐξολοθρεύω, ἐξολεθ—
Gen. 17:14
Exo. 8:24
12:15, 19
22:20[a]
30:33
31:14
Lev. 17: 4,9,14
18:29
19: 8
20:17, 18
22: 3
23:29
26:30
Nu. 4:18 A[b]
9,13
15:30
19:20
Deu. 1:27
2:34
3: 6,6
4:38
6:15
7: 4,10
17,23
24
9: 3
3+A
4+A
5,8,14
19,20
25,26
10:10
12:29,30
18:12
20:19
20 A[b]
28:20,45
48,61
63
31: 3,4
33:19
Jos. 2:10
7:25
9:30
10: 1,28
32,37
39,40
11:11,12
14,20
20,21
21
13: 6,12
13
14:12
15:14
17:12,13[c]
13,18
Jos. 22:33
23: 4,5,5
9,13
15
24: 8
Jud. 1:17,19[d]
2: 3+A
4:24
6:26[e]
Ruth 4:10
1 Sa. 2:31,33
15: 3
8+A
9,9
15,18
20
24:22
28: 9
2 Sa. 4:11
7: 9
21: 5
1 Ki. 2: 4
10 p 22
11:15,16
12 p 24 l 42
14:10 A
15:29
16:33—A
18: 5
20:21,26
2 Ki. 9: 7,8
18: 4
23:14
1 Ch. 17: 8
21:12,12
15 ter
2 Ch. 8: 8
20: 7,10
23,23
21: 7
22: 4
28: 3
32:14
33: 2
34:11
36: 5
Psa. 11: 4
17:41
33:17
36: 9,22
28,34
38,38
43: 3
53: 7
72:27
81: 8 S[1 f]
82: 4,11
Psa. 91: 8
100: 8
105:23,23
34
108:15
142:12
144:20
Isa. 10: 7
22:25—AS
29:20
48: 9,19
Jer. 4: 7
27:16
26—S
28:11,53
55,62
29: 4
31: 8
43:29
Eze. 6: 3,6
14:19,21
21: 3
4—A
25: 7,13
Eze. 25:16
31:12
35:15 A[g]
Dan. 9:26
Hos. 8: 4
Joel 1:16
Amos 1: 5,8
2: 3
Obad. 14
Mic. 5: 9,10
11,12[b]
13
Nah. 1:14
2:13
3:15
Zeph. 1:11
2:11
3: 7
Hag. 2:22 AS[2 h]
Zec. 9:10,10
13: 2,8
14: 2
Mal. 2:12

[a] B ὀλεθρεύω. [b] pro ὀλοθρεύω. [c] A ὀλέθρευσις. [d] A κληρονομέω. [e] A ἐκκόπτω. [f] pro κατακληρονομέω. [g] pro ἐξαναλίσκω. [h] A ἐξαίρω.

ἐξομολογέομαι.
Gen. 29:35
2 Sa. 22:50
1 Ki. 8:33,35
1 Ch. 16: 4,8,34
23:30
29:13
2 Ch. 5:13,13
6:24
7: 6
20:21
21—A
23:12
30:22
31: 2
Psa. 6: 6
7:18
9: 2
17:50
21:26+S[2]
27: 7
29: 5,10
13
32: 2
34:18
41: 6,12
42: 4,5
43: 9
44:18
48:19
51:11
53: 8
56:10
66: 4,4,6
6
70:22
Psa. 73:19
74: 2,2
75:11
85:12
87:11
88: 6
91: 2
96:12
98: 3
99: 4
104: 1
105: 1,47
106: 1,8,15
21,31
107: 4
108:30
110: 1
117: 1,19
21,28
28,29
118: 7,62
121: 4
135: 1,2,3
26
137: 1,2,4
138:14
139:14
141: 8
144:10
Isa. 45:23 AS[3 a]
Jer. 40:11
Dan. 2:23
6:10
9: 4

[a] pro ὄμνυμι.

ἐξομολόγησις.
Jos. 7:19
1 Ch. 25: 3
2 Ch. 20:22
Neh. 12:27+S
Job 8:21[a]
Psa. 41: 5
94: 2
95: 6
Psa. 99: 1,4
103: 1
110: 3
146: 7
148:13
Isa. 51: 3
Jon. 2:10

[a] A ἀγαλλίασις.

ἐξόπισθεν.
2 Ki. 17:21
1 Ch. 17: 7
1 Ch. 19:10
Psa. 77:71

ἐξοπλίζω.
Nu. 31: 3
Nu. 32:20

ἐξορκίζω.
Gen. 24: 3
Jud. 17: 2 A[a]
1 Ki. 22:16 B[b]

[a] pro ἀράομαι. [b] pro ὁρκίζω.

ἐξορμάω.
Jud. 7: 3 A[a]

[a] pro ἐκχωρέω.

ἐξορύσσω.
Jud. 16:21 A[a]
1 Sa. 11: 2
Pro. 29:22

[a] pro ἐκκόπτω.

ἐξουδενόω, —νέω.
Jud. 9:38
1 Sa. 8: 7 B[a]
10:19[b]
15: 9,23
23,26
26
16: 1,7
2 Sa. 6:16
12:10
2 Ki. 19:21
1 Ch. 15:29
2 Ch. 36:16 B[a]
Job 30: 1
Psa. 14: 4
21:25
43: 6
50:19
52: 6
57: 8
58: 9
Psa. 59:14
68:34
72:20,22
77:59
88:39
101:18
105:24
107:14
118:118
141
Pro. 1: 7 C[a]
Ecc. 9:16
Cant. 8: 1,7,7
Eze. 21:10
Dan. 11:21
Zec. 4:10
Mal. 1: 7 S[2 c]
7[d], 12
2: 9

[a] pro ἐξουθενόω. [b] B ἐξουθενέω. [c] pro ἀλισγέω. [d] S[3] ἐξουθενόω.

ἐξουδένωμα.
Psa. 89: 5
Dan. 4:14

ἐξουδένωσις.
Psa. 30:19
106:40
Ps. 118:22
122: 3,4

ἐξουθενέω, —νόω.
1 Sa. 2:30
8: 7,7[a]
10:19 B[b]
2 Ch. 36:16[a]
Psa. 63: 9[c]
Pro. 1: 7[d]
Jer. 6:14
Eze. 22: 8
Amos 6: 1
Mal. 1: 7 S[3 b]

[a] B ἐξουδενόω. [b] pro ἐξουδενέω. [c] B[2]S ἐξασθενέω. [d] C ἐξουδενέω.

ἐξουθένημα.
Psalm 21: 7

ἐξουσία.
2 Ki. 20:13
Ps. 113: 2
135: 8,9
Pro. 17:14
Ecc. 8: 8[a]
Isa. 39: 2—ABS
Jer. 28:28+A
Dan. 3: 2,3,33
4:23,31
31
5: 4+AB[2]
7: 6,14
14,27
11: 5+A

[a] ACS ἐξουσιάζω.

ἐξουσιάζω.
1 Ki. 4(21) A
Ezra 7:24
Neh. 5:15
9:37—S[1]
Ecc. 2:19
5:18
6: 2
Ecc. 7:20
8: 4,8
8 ACS[a]
9
9:17
10: 4,5

[a] pro ἐξουσία.

ἐξουσιαστής.
Isaiah 9: 6+AS[2]

ἐξοχή.
Job 39:28

ἐξυβρίζω.
Gen. 49: 4
Eze. 47: 5

ἐξυπνίζω.
Jud. 16:14[a]
20[b]
1 Ki. 3:15
Job 14:12

[a] A ἐγείρω. [b] A ἐξεγείρω.

ἐξυπνόω.
Psa. 120: 4 S[a]

[a] pro ὑπνόω.

ἔξω.
Gen. 9:22
15: 5
19:17
24:11,29
31
39:12,13
15,18
Exo. 12:46
21:19
29:14
33: 7,7
8—A
Lev. 4:12,21
6:11
8:17[a]
9:11
10: 4,5
13:46
14: 3,8,40
41,45
53
16:27
17: 3,4
18: 9
24:14,23
Nu. 5: 3,4
12:14,15
15:35,36
19: 3,9
31:13,19
35: 4,5,27
Deu. 23:10—B
12—B[1]
12—B[1]
13
24:13,13
25: 5
Jos. 2:19
6:23
22:19
Jud. 12: 9
19:25
1 Sa. 9:26
2 Sa. 13:17,18
1 Ki. 8: 8
20:13
2 Ki. 10:24
16:18
23: 4
1 Ch. 26:29
2 Ch. 5: 9
24: 8
29:16
32: 3,5
33:14
15 A[b]
Ezra 10:13
Neh. 13: 8,20
Est. 9:19—S[1]
Job 1:10,10[c]
2: 8
31:32
39: 3[d]
40: 8+AS
Psa. 30:12
40: 7
Pro. 7:12
Cant. 8: 1
Isa. 42: 2
51:23
Dan. 3:26+A
4:20
Amos 4: 5

[a] A παρέξω. [b] pro ἔξωθεν. [c] A ἔξωθεν. [d] A ἄνευ.

ἔξωθεν.
Gen. 6:14
7:16
20:18
Exo. 25:10
26:35
27:21
38: 2
40:20
Lev. 24: 3
Deu. 32:25
Jud. 9:51
12: 9
1 Ki. 6:10
7:46+A
46
2 Ki. 4: 3
23: 6
2 Ch. 33:15[a]
Job 1:10 A[b]
Ps. 150 p 6
Jer. 6:11
Jer. 9:21
10:17
11: 6
21: 4
28: 4
40:10
44:21
51: 6,9,17
21
Lam. 1:20
Eze. 7:15
40: 5,14
15
43 A[c]
41: 9,17
25
42: 7
43:21
46: 2 A[c]
47: 2

[a] A ἔξω. [b] pro ἔξω. [c] pro ἔσωθεν.

ἐξωθέω.
Deu. 13: 5
2 Sa. 14:13,14
14
15:14
23: 6
2 Ki. 17:21
Psa. 5:11
35:13
48:15+AS[2]
Pro. 2:22

Isa. 41: 2
Jer. 8: 3
16:15
23: 2[a],3,8
24: 9
25:15
26:28
Jer. 27: 6,17
28:35
Joel 2:20
3: 6
Mic. 2: 9
4: 6[a]

[a] A ἀπωθέω.

ἔξωσμα.

Lamentations 2:14

ἐξώτατος.

1 Ki. 6:28
Neh. 11:16 A

ἐξώτερος.

Exo. 26: 4
1 Ki. 6:27
Est. 6: 4+S[3]
Job 18:17
Eze. 10: 5
40:19, 20
31, 37
Eze. 41:15, 17
42: 1 A[a],3
6[b],7,8
9, 14
44: 1, 19
46:20, 21

[a] pro ἐσώτερος. [b] A ἐξέδρα.

ἑορτάζω.

Exo. 5: 1
12:14, 14
23:14
Lev. 23:39, 41
Nu. 29:12
Deu. 16:15
1 Sa. 30:16
1 Ki. (3) p 46
Psa. 41: 5
75:11
Isa. 30:29
Nah. 1:14
Zec. 14:16, 18
19

ἑορτή.

Exo. 10: 9
12:14
13: 6
23:15, 16
16, 18
32: 5
34:18, 22
22[c], 25
Lev. 22:21
23: 2, 2, 4
6, 34
37, 44
Nu. 10:10
15: 3
28: 2, 17
29:12, 39
Deu. 16: 8, 10
13
14—A
16 ter
31:10
33:10 A[2 b]
Jud. 21:19
1 Ki. 8: 2+A
65
12:32, 32
33, 33
2 Ki. 23:16
1 Ch. 23:31
2 Ch. 2: 4
5: 3
7: 8, 9
8:13 qtr
30:13, 21
2 Ch. 30:22, 26
31: 3
35:17
Ezra 3: 4, 5
6:22
Neh. 8:14, 18
10:33
Psa. 73: 4[c], 8
80: 4
117:27
Isa. 1:14
Jer. 38: 8
Lam. 1: 4
2: 6, 6, 7
22
Eze. 23:34
36:38
44:24
45:17, 17
21, 23
25
46: 9, 11
Dan. 8:19 A[1 b]
Hos. 2:11
9: 5
12: 9
Amos 5:21
8:10
Nah. 1:14
Zeph. 3:17
Zec. 8:19
14:16, 18
19
Mal. 2: 3

[a] B ἀρνή. [b] pro ὀργή.
[c] S[1] ὀργή.

ἐπαγγελία.

Est. 4: 7
Psa. 55: 9
Amos 9: 6

ἐπαγγέλλω.

Est. 4: 7
Pro. 13:12

ἐπάγω.

Gen. 6:17
7: 4
8: 1
Gen. 18:19
20: 9
26:10
Gen. 27:12
Exo. 10: 4, 13
11: 1
15:19, 26
26
28:39
32:21, 34
33: 5
34: 7
Lev. 22:16
26:25, 36
Deu. 23:13
28:49, 61
29:27
Jos. 23:15
24: 7
Jud. 4: 7[a]
9:24
1 Sa. 5: 6
15:23
30:22 A[b]
2 Sa. 17:14
1 Ki. 8:46[c]
9: 9
20·21
29, 29
2 Ki. 22:16, 20
1 Ch. 4:10
2 Ch. 7:22
34:24, 28
Est. 9:25
Job 10:17[d]
15: 7
22:17
34:28
38: 5
42:11
Psa. 7:12
77:26
87: 8
Pro. 6:22
26:11
Ecc. 3:18 S[1 e]
Isa. 1:25
7:17
10:12 ABS[f]
24
15: 7, 9
24:21
26:14, 21
Isa. 27: 1
31: 3
42:25
48: 9
63: 7
Jer. 4: 6
5:15
6:19
11:11, 23
15: 8
17:18
18:22
19: 3, 15
22: 7[g]
23:12
25:13[h], 15
16
28:64
31:44
39:42, 42
40: 6 A[i]
43:31
49:17
51: 2[k], 35
Lam. 1:21
Eze. 5: 1, 17
6: 3
11: 8
13:13
14:15, 17
19 A[m]
22, 22
22:13 B[n]
23:22
26: 7
28: 7
29: 8
30:24
33: 2
39:21
Dan. 9:12, 14
11:32[o]
Hos. 13:15
Amos 1: 8
5: 9
Zeph. 3:17
Hag. 1:11
Zec. 3: 8 S[3 p]
13: 7[q]

[a] A ἀπάγω. [b] pro ἀπάγω.
[c] A ἐπαίρω. [d] A ἐπεγείρω.
[e] pro εἶπον. [f] pro ἐπισκέπτομαι.
[g] A εἰσάγω. [h] A πατάσσω.
[i] pro ἀνάγω. [k] S ἄγω.
[m] pro ἐπαποστέλλω.
[n] pro πατάσσω. [o] A ἐξάγω.
[p] pro ἄγω. [q] S[3] ἐπιστρέφω.

ἐπαγωγή.

Deu. 32:36
Isa. 10: 4 AS[a]
Isa. 14:17

[a] pro ἀπαγωγή.

ἐπᾴδω.

Deu. 18:11
Psa. 57: 6
Ecc. 10:11
Jer. 8:17[a]

[a] A[1] ἐπιλανθάνω, A[2] ἐπιλαλέω.

ἐπαινετός.

Ezekiel 26:17

ἐπαινέω.

Gen. 12:15
Psa. 9:24
33: 3
43: 9
55: 5
62: 4, 12
63:11
101: 9
Ps. 104: 3
105: 5
116: 1[a]
144: 4[b]
147: 1
Ecc. 4: 2
8:10, 15

[a] S[1] αἰνέω. [b] A[1] αἰνέω.

ἔπαινος.

1 Ch. 16:27
2 Ch. 21:20
Psa. 21: 4, 26
31:28

ἐπαίρω.

Gen. 7:17
13:10
Exo. 7:20
10:13
14:16
17:11
Nu. 6:26
20:11
Jud. 2: 4
9: 7
11: 1[a]
21: 2 A[b]
Ruth 1: 9, 14
1 Sa. 20:33
2 Sa. 5:12
13:36
18:24, 28[c]
20:21
1 Ki. 1: 5
8: 1+A
46 A[d]
11:27
12 p 24 l 12
2 Ki. 9:32
14:10
18:29
19:10[e]
1 Ch. 21:16
2 Ch. 25:19
35: 3 A[b]
Ezra 4:19
7:28
Neh. 8: 6-BS[1]
Job 31:21
41:17+CS[2]
Psa. 8: 2
23: 7, 9
27: 9
36:35
46:10
72:18
73: 3
74: 6
77:26 B[1 f]
92: 3, 3
101:11
105:26
133: 2
Pro. 3: 5
19:18
24:17, 36
Isa. 6: 1, 4
Jer. 13:15
29: 6
Lam. 4: 2
Eze. 10:15+A
17:14
18: 6
Dan. 11:14
Obad. 3
Hab. 3:10
Zeph. 1:11
Zec. 1:21

[a] A δυνατός. [b] pro αἴρω.
[c] A ἀνταίρω, B μισέω.
[d] pro ἐπάγω. [e] A ἐπερωτάω.
[f] pro ἀπαίρω.

ἐπαισχύνομαι.

Job 34:19[a]
Ps. 118: 6 AS[1 b]
Isa. 1:20 AS[1 b]

[a] A αἰσχύνω. [b] pro αἰσχύνω.

ἐπαιτέω.

Psalm 108:10

ἐπακολουθέω.

Lev. 19: 4, 31
20: 6
Nu. 14:24
Deu. 12:30
Jos. 6: 8
Jos. 14: 8, 9, 14
Job 26: 3
31: 7
Pro. 7:22
Isa. 55: 3

ἐπακούω.

Gen. 16:11
17:20
21:17
25:21
27:13[a]
30: 6, 17
22, 33
35: 3
Deu. 26:14 B[b]
14 B[c]
Jos. 10:14
22: 2 B[b]
Jud. 2:17 A[b]
13: 9 A[d]
1 Sa. 7: 9
8:18
28:15
30:24[e]
2 Sa. 21:14
22: 7, 42[f]
24:25
1 Ki. 18:21, 26
26
36—A
36—A
37, 37
2 Ki. 13: 4
1 Ch. 5:20
21:26, 28[g]
29:23 B[n]
2 Ch. 6:19
2 Ch. 11: 4[a]
24:17
25:16
30:20, 27
32:24
33:10[h], 13
13, 19
Ezra 8:23
Job 8: 6
33:12, 13
37:22[i]
38:34 S[b]
Psa. 3: 54
16: 6[k]
17:45 A[b]
19: 2, 7, 10
21:25 A[d]
33: 5
51:11 S[1 e]
59: 7
64: 6
68:14, 18
80: 8
85: 1 AS[d]
7 AS[2 d]
90:15 AS[2 d]
98: 6 B[1],8
101: 3 S[3]
107: 7
117: 5, 21
28
Ps. 118:26, 145
137: 3
142: 1[g]
144:19[m]
Pro. 15:29[n]
21:13[a]
13 S[d]
29:12 BS[b]
Ecc. 10:19
Cant. 5: 6 A[b]
Isa. 8: 9
10:30
30—S
19:22 A[d]
Isa. 30:19
41:17
45: 1
49: 8
50: 2 S[1 b]
10 S[b]
55: 3 AS[3 d]
65:21 AS[b]
Jer. 18:19 A[d]
Hos. 2:21, 21
22, 22
Mic. 3: 7[o]
Zec. 10: 6
13: 9

[a] A ὑπακούω. [b] pro ὑπακούω.
[c] pro ποιέω. [d] pro εἰσακούω.
[e] B ὑπακούω. [f] AB ὑπακούω.
[g] A εἰσακούω. [h] A ἀκούω.
[i] AC εἰσακούω. [k] AS[1] εἰσακούω.
[m] S[2] εἰσακούω [n] S ὑπακούω.
[o] B εἰσακούω.

ἐπακρόασις.

1 Samuel 15:22

ἔπαλξις.

1 Ki. (3) p 1
Cant. 8: 9
Isa. 21:11
Isa. 54:12
Jer. 27:15

ἐπανάγω.

Zechariah 4:12

ἐπαναγωγή.

Ezekiel 25: 9 B[a]

[a] pro ἐπάνω πηγῆς.

ἐπανακαινίζω.

Job 10:17

ἐπαναπαύω.

Nu. 11:25, 26
Jud. 16:26+A
2 Ki. 2:15
5:18
2 Ki. 7: 2, 17
Isa. 11: 2 S[a]
Eze. 29: 7
Mic. 3:11

[a] pro ἀναπαύω.

ἐπανάστασις.

2 Kings 3: 4

ἐπαναστρέφω.

Gen. 18:10
Exo. 14:28
Lev. 22:13
Nu. 35:28
Deu. 3:20
Deu. 24: 6
21 A[a]
22
Job 16:22

[a] pro ἀναστρέφω.

ἐπανατρυγάω.

Lev. 19:10
Deu. 24.23

ἐπανέρχομαι.

Gen. 33:18[a]
50: 5[b]
Lev. 25:13
Job 7: 7
Pro. 3:28

[a] A ἔρχομαι.
[b] A ἐπέρχομαι, B ἀπέρχομαι.

ἐπανήκω.

Lev. 14:39
Pro. 3:28
Pro. 7:20

ἐπανθέω.

Job 14: 7[a]

[a] A ἀνθέω.

ἐπανίστημι.

Deu. 19:11
22:26
Deu. 33:11
Jud. 6:31[a]

Jud. 9:18
43 A[b]
1 Sa. 4:15
17:35
2 Sa. 14: 7
18:32
22:40 AB[c]
49 A[d]
1 Ki. 6(18) A
2 Ki. 16: 7
Job 17: 8
19:19
20:27
22:15 A[1e]
27: 7
29: 8 A[f]
30: 5, 12
Psa. 3: 2
17:40, 49
26: 3, 12
43: 6
53: 5
58: 2
85:14
91:12
108:28
123: 2
Isa. 9:11
14:22
31: 2
Lam. 3:61
Dan. 11: 2, 14
Mic. 7: 6

[a] A ἵστημι. [b] pro ἀνίστημι. [c] pro ἐφίστημι. [d] pro ἐπεγείρω. [e] pro πατέω. [f] pro ἵστημι.

ἐπάνω.

Gen. 1: 2, 2, 7
29
7:18
20 A[a]
18: 2
22: 9
40:17, 17
42:27
Exo. 30:14
39: 3
Lev. 27: 7
Nu. 1: 3, 18
20, 22
24, 26
28, 30
32, 34
36, 38
40, 42
45
3:15, 22
28, 34
39, 40
43
4: 3, 23
30, 35
39, 43
47
8:24
14:29
26: 2, 4, 62
32:11
Deu. 28:13
Jos. 9:11[b]
Jud. 1:14+A
36 A[c]
36
13:20
Ruth 3:15
1 Sa. 9: 2
10:23
16:13
17: 6 AB[d]
39
1 Sa. 18: 4 A
30:25
2 Sa. 1: 9
5:20, 20
24:20, 21
1 Ki. (3) p 1
2 Ki. 3:21 A[e]
15:35
1 Ch. 23: 3, 24
27
2 Ch. 4:12 A[d]
13
24:20
25: 5
26:19
31:16, 17
Ezra 3: 8
Neh. 8: 5
12:31
31 ABS[1]
(38) S[3]
Job 33:12
Ps. 107: 5
Ecc. 5: 7
Isa. 10: 9
14:13, 14
18: 2
Jer. 16:16, 16
42: 4
43:10
50:10
52:32
Eze. 1:11, 27
10: 1
25: 9[f]
37: 8
47:16
Dan. 6: 2
12: 6, 7
Hag. 2:15 A[a]
19+A
Zec. 4: 2 ter
3

[a] pro ὑπεράνω. [b] A ἐπί. [c] pro ἀνάβασις. [d] pro ἐπί. [e] pro εἶπον. [f] B ἐπαναγωγή.

ἐπάνωθεν.

Exo. 25:19
26:14
38: 5[a]
Jud. 3:21−A
4:15−A
8:13−A
2 Sa. 11:21 B[b]
13: 9, 9
24:25
1 Ki. 2: 4
7: 9, 12
15, 48
8: 7
2 Ki. 2: 3, 5[c]
13, 14
10:31 AB[d]
17:21, 23
25: 5, 21
28
1 Ch. 29:25
2 Ch. 5: 8
Neh. 12:37
Job 18:16
Eze. 1:22
40:43
Amos 2: 9[c]

[a] A ἄνωθεν. [b] pro ἀπὸ ἄνωθεν. [c] A ἀπάνωθεν. [d] pro ἀπανωθεν.

ἐπαξονέω.

Nu. 1:14[a] [a] A ἐπισκέπτομαι.

ἐπαοιδή.

Exo. 8: 7 A[a]
Deu. 18:11
Isa. 47:12

[a] pro φαρμακία

ἐπαοιδός.

Exo. 7:11, 22
8: 7, 18
19
Lev. 19:31
20: 6, 27
1 Sa. 6: 2
2 Ch. 33: 6
Isa. 47: 9
Dan. 1:20
2: 2, 10
27
4: 4, 6
5:11

ἐπαποστέλλω.

Exo. 8:21 B[a]
Deu. 28:48
32:24[b]
1 Ki. 12 p 24 l 37
Job 20:23
Jer. 9:16[c]
25:16[d]
Eze. 14:19[e]
21 A[a]

[a] pro ἐξαποστέλλω. [b] B ἀποστέλλω. [c] S[1] ἀποστέλλω. [d] A ἐξαποστελλω. [e] A ἐπάγω.

ἔπαρμα.

Ezra 6: 3

ἔπαρσις.

Nu. 33: 2 A
2 Ki. 19:25
Ps. 140: 2
Lam. 3:46
Eze. 24:25, 25
Zec. 12: 7

[a] pro ἄπαρσις.

ἐπαρυστήρ.

Exodus 25:38

ἐπαρυστρίς.

Exo. 38:17
Nu. 4: 9
1 Ki. 7:35
Zec. 4: 2, 12

ἐπαρχία.

Esther 4:11+S[3]

ἔπαρχος.

Ezra 5: 3, 6
6: 6, 13
Ezra 8:36
Neh. 2: 7, 9

ἔπαυλις.

Gen. 25:16
Exo. 8:11, 13
14: 2, 9
Lev. 25:31
Nu. 22:39
31:10
32:16, 24
36[a], 41
41
34: 4
Jos. 13:23, 28
15:28, 36
45, 47
47, 54[b]
Jos. 15:60
19:23 A[c]
Jud. 10: 4
1 Ch. 4:32, 33
Neh. 11:25, 27
12:28, 29
Psa. 68:26
143:14[d]
Pro. 3:33
Isa. 34:13
35: 7
42:11
62: 9
65:10

[a] A πόλις. [b] A κώμη. [c] pro κώμη. [d] S[2] πλατεῖα.

ἐπαύριον.

Gen. 19:34
30:33[a]
Exo. 9: 6
18:13
32: 6
Lev. 23:11, 15
16
Nu. 11:32
16:41[b]
17: 8
33: 3
Jud. 6:38
Jud. 9:42
21: 4
1 Sa. 5: 3+A
4+A
18:10 A
20:27
30:17
31: 8
2 Sa. 11:12
2 Ki. 8:15
1 Ch. 29:21
Jon. 4: 7

[a] A αὔριον. [b] B αὔριον.

ἐπαφίημι.

Job 10: 1
13:15
39:11
Eze. 16:42
22:20 A[a]

[a] pro χωνεύω.

ἐπεγείρω.

1 Sa. 3:12
22: 8
2 Sa. 18:31
22:49[a]
1 Ch. 5:26
2 Ch. 21:16
Job 10:17 A[b]
Isa. 10:26 AS[c]
13:17
19: 2
Isa. 19: 2+
AB[a]S[2]
42:13
43:11
Jer. 29: 7
Amos 6:14
Mic. 5: 5
Nah. 1: 8
Zec. 9:13 A[d]

[a] A ἐπανίστημι. [b] pro ἐπάγω. [c] pro ἐγείρω. [d] pro ἐξεγείρω.

ἐπεί.

Gen. 50: 4[a]
Exo. 1:21[a]
2: 3[b]
Jud. 6: 8+A
Job 35: 7−A

[a] AB ἐπειδή. [b] A ἐπειδή.

ἐπειδή.

Gen. 15: 3
18:31
19:19
23:13
41:39
Exo. 34:33
Deu. 2:16
Job 9:29
Pro. 1:24
Jer. 25: 8
31: 7
36:31
Eze. 28: 6

ἐπείδω.

Gen. 4: 4
13:10
16:13
31:49
Exo. 2:25[a]
1 Ch. 17:17
Est. 8: 6 A[b]
Job 38:12 A[b]
Psa. 21:18
30: 8
53: 9
91:12
111: 8
Jer. 31:19
42:18
Obad. 12, 13

[a] A εἰσείδω. [b] pro εἰδέω.

ἔπειμι.

Exo. 8:22
9: 3[a]
Deu. 32:29
1 Ki. 10:16
1 Ch. 20: 1
2 Ch. 9:15
Pro. 3:28
27: 1

[a] A εἰμί.

ἐπεισφέρω.

Judges 3:22

ἔπειτα.

Nu. 19:19+A
Isa. 16: 2

ἐπέκεινα.

Gen. 35:16
Lev. 22:27
Nu. 15:23
32:19
1 Sa. 10: 3
18: 9 AB
20:22, 38
Isa. 18: 1, 2
Jer. 22:19
Eze. 39:22
43:27
Amos 5:27
Mic. 4: 5
Hag. 2:18

ἐπέκτασις.

Job 36:29 AS[2a] [a] pro ἀπέκτασις.

ἐπελπίζω.

2 Ki. 18:30
Psa. 51: 9
118:43, 49
Ps. 118:74, 81
114[a]
147

[a] S[1] ἐλπίζω.

ἐπεναντίος.

Job 33:10 C[a] [a] pro ὑπεναντίος.

ἐπενδύτης.

Lev. 8: 7 A[a]
1 Sa. 18: 4 A
2 Sa. 13:18

[a] pro ὑποδύτης.

ἐπερείδω.

Proverbs 3:18

ἐπέρχομαι.

Gen. 42:21
50: 5 A[a]
Exo. 10: 1
Lev. 11:34[b]
14:43
16: 9, 10
Nu. 5:14, 14
30
6: 5
8: 7
Jos. 24:20
Jud. 3:24[c]
9:57
18:17+A
20:33[d]
1 Sa. 7:13 A[e]
11: 7
30:23
2 Sa. 15: 4 A[f]
17: 2
19: 7
1 Ki. 19:19 B[g]
2 Ki. 11: 9 A[h]
2 Ch. 20: 9
22: 1
32:26
Neh. 5: 9 S[g]
Job 1:19−S[1i]
2:11
3: 5
4:15
5:21 S[f]
15:19
19:29
20:22, 28
21:17
23: 6, 17
25: 3
27: 9
13 O[f]
31:12
37: 8[k]
Job 39:15 S[1m]
40:15
Psa. 89:19
Pro. 3:25, 25
4:14, 15
5: 6
16:33
18: 3
19:11
26: 2, 11
27:12, 12[n]
Ecc. 2:12[o]
16 AS[2f]
Isa. 7:25
13:13
28:18
32:15 AS[f]
41: 4, 22
23
42:23
44: 7
45:11
48: 3
63: 4[p]
65:17
Jer. 29: 49
37:23 S[r]
Eze. 33: 4[q]
39:11
47: 9, 9 A[f]
Dan. 9:11
11:13
Hos. 10:11
Amos 5:17 A[f]
Mic. 3:11
5: 5, 6
Nah. 3:19
Zeph. 2: 2−S[3]
2
Zec. 9: 8
12: 9 A[f]

[a] pro ἐπανέρχομαι. [b] A ἀπέρχομαι. [c] A εἰσέρχομαι. [d] A παλαιω. [e] pro προσέρχομαι. [f] pro ἔρχομαι. [g] pro ἀπέρχομαι. [h] pro εἰσέρχομαι. [i] A ἔρχομαι. [k] A ἐξέρχομαι. [m] pro ἐπιλανθάνω. [n] A ἔρχομαι, C παρέρχομαι. [o] S[2] ἀπέρχομαι. [p] B ἔρχομαι. [q] AS ἔρχομαι. [r] pro ἐξέρχομαι.

ἐπερωτάω.

Gen. 24:23
57 A[a]
26: 7
38:21
43: 6
Nu. 23: 3, 15
27:21
Deu. 4:32
18:11
32: 7
Jos. 9:20
Jud. 1: 1
8:14
18: 5[b]
20:18 A[a]
23 A[a]
23+A
28−A
1 Sa. 9: 9
10:22
14:37
17:56 A
1 Sa. 22:13 A[a]
23: 2, 4[c]
28: 6, 16
30: 8
2 Sa. 2: 1
5:23
11: 7
14:18
16:23
20:18
1 Ki. 12 p 24
l 25 B[a]
l 26
22: 5, 7, 8
2 Ki. 1: 2 A[d], 2
16 A[c]
8: 6
9−A
19:10 A[f]
1 Ch. 10:13
14:19[g]
Job 8: 8

Job 12: 7 A[a]
Psa. 34:11[b]
136: 3[i]
Pro. 17:28
Ecc. 7:11
Isa. 10: 3
30: 2
65: 1
Jer. 21: 2
23:33 S[a]
Jer. 37:14
41:17 A[a]
Eze. 14: 7, 10
20: 1, 3
21:21
Dan. 2:10, 11
27[b]
Hos. 4:12
Hag. 2:11
Zec. 4: 4, 12

[a] pro ἐρωτάω. [b] B ἐρωτάω. [c] AB ἐρωτάω. [d] pro ἐπιζητέω. [e] pro ἐκζητέω. [f] pro ἐπαίρω. [g] BS ἐρωτάω. [h] AS ἐρωτάω. [i] S[1] ἐρωτάω.

ἐπερώτημα.

Daniel 4:14

ἐπερώτησις.

Genesis 43: 6

ἐπέτειος.

Deuteronomy 15:18

ἐπευκτός.

Jeremiah 20:14

ἐπεύχομαι.

Deu. 10: 8 | 1 Ch. 23:13

ἐπέχω.

Gen. 8:10, 12
1 Ki. 22: 6, 15
2 Ki. 4:24
2 Ch. 18: 5, 14
Job 18: 2
Job 27: 8
28:28 C[a]
30:26
Jer. 6:11
Joel 1:13 S[1 a]

[a] pro ἀπέχω.

ἐπήκοος.

2 Ch. 6:40 | 2 Ch. 7:15

ἐπήλυτος.

Job 20:26

ἐπιβαίνω.

Gen. 24:61
Lev. 15: 9[a]
Nu. 22:22—A
30
Deu. 1:36
11:25
33:26, 29
Jos. 1: 3
14: 9
15: 6
Jud. 5:10
10: 4
12:14
1 Sa. 5: 5
25:20, 42
30:17
2 Sa. 18: 9
19:26
1 Ki. 12:33 A[b]
13:13
2 Ki. 4:24
9:25
Neh. 2:12
Est. 6: 8
Job 6:21
17: 6 B[c]
30:21[d]
Psa. 17:11
67: 5, 34
75: 7
90:13
Pro. 21:22
Jer. 10: 5
17:25
18:15
22: 4
26: 4, 9
27:21
24[e]
Eze. 10:18
Amos 4:13
Mic. 1: 3
5: 5, 6
Nah. 3:17
Hab. 2: 1
3: 8
Zec. 1: 8
9: 9

[a] A καθίζω. [b] pro ἀναβαίνω. [c] pro ἀποβαίνω. [d] A ἀποβαίνω. [e] B[2]S ἐπιτίθημι.

ἐπιβάλλω.

Gen. 2:21
22:12
39: 7
46: 4
48:14, 17
Exo. 5: 8
7: 4
20:25
21:22, 30
30
Lev. 10: 1
19:19
Nu. 4: 6, 7, 8
14
11:31
16:18, 46
47
19: 2
Deu. 12: 7, 18
15:10
20:19
24: 1, 7
27: 5
28: 8, 20
Jos. 7: 6
9: 4
2 Sa. 18:12
1 Ki. 21: 6
2 Ch. 30: 3
Est. 6: 2
Job 27.12
Psa. 80:15
107:10[a]
Pro. 18:17
20:26
23: 2
Isa. 5:25
11: 8, 14
15
19:16
25:11
34:11, 17
37:33[b]
Hos. 7:12
Zec. 8:23 S[c]
23 S[c]

[a] S[1] ἐκτείνω [b] A βάλλω. [c] pro ἐπιλαμβάνω.

ἐπίβασις.

Psa. 103: 3 | Cant. 3:10

ἐπιβάτης.

2 Ki. 7:14
9:17, 18
19
18:23
Est. (9)14+S[3]
Job 39:18
Jer. 28:21[a]
Eze. 27:29

[a] A ἀναβάτης.

ἐπιβατός.

Nehemiah 4:13+S[1]

ἐπιβιβάζω.

2 Sa. 6: 3
1 Ki. 1:33
2 Ki. 9:28[a]
13:16, 16
23:30
2 Ch. 23:20[b]
Psa. 65:12
Hos. 10:11
Hab. 3:15, 19

[a] A ἐμβιβάζω. [b] A ἀναβιβάζω.

ἐπιβλέπω.

Gen. 19:26, 28
Exo. 14:24
Lev. 26: 9
Nu. 12:10
21: 9
Deu. 9:27
Jud. 5:28+A
6:14 A[a]
20:40, 42[b]
45[c], 47[c]
1 Sa. 1:11, 11
2:29
32+A
4:15[d]
7: 2
9:16
13:17, 18
18
14:13
16: 7[e]
17:41 A
24: 9
2 Sa. 1: 7
2:20
9: 8
1 Ki. 7:12 qtr
8:28
18:43, 43
19: 6
2 Ki. 3:14
13:23
2 Ch. 6:19
16: 9
20:24
Psa. 12: 4
24:16
32:13, 14
39: 5[f]
65: 7
68:17
73:20
79:15
Psa. 83:10
85:16
101:18, 20
103:32
118: 6, 132
141: 5
Pro. 24:47[g]
Ecc. 2:11, 12
Isa. 63: 5
64: 9
66: 2
Jer. 4:23, 25
Lam. 1:11
2:20
3:62
4:16
5: 1
Eze. 10:11
17: 5
20:46
21: 2
36: 9
47: 1 A[h]
Hos. 3: 1[i]
11: 4
Amos 5:22
Jon. 2: 5
Mic. 7: 7
Nah. 2: 8[k]
Hab. 1: 3, 5, 13
13
2:15
3: 6
Hag. 1: 9
Zec. 1:16 B[a]
4:10
6: 7
10: 4
12:10
Mal. 2:13
3: 1

[a] pro ἐπιστρέφω. [b] A κλείω. [c] A ἐκκλίνω. [d] AB βλέπω. [e] A ἐπιστρέφω. [f] AB[1] ἐμβλέπω. [g] BS[1] ἀποβλέπω. [h] pro βλέπω. [i] A ἀποβλέπω. [k] A βλέπω.

ἐπίβλημα.

Isaiah 3:22

ἐπιβόλαιον.

Jud. 4:18—A | Eze. 13:18, 21[a]

[a] A περιβόλαιον.

ἐπιβουλεύω.

Proverbs 17:26

ἐπιβουλή.

Esther 2:22

ἐπίβουλος.

1 Sa. 29: 4
2 Sa. 2:16
19:22
1 Ki. 5: 4
Est. 7: 6+S[3]
Hab. 2: 7

ἐπιβρέχω.

Psalm 10: 6

ἐπιβρίθω.

Job 29: 4[a]

[a] S[1] ἐπιτρίβω.

ἐπιγαμβρεύω.

Gen. 34: 9
38: 8[a]
1 Sa. 18:22+A
22, 23
1 Sa. 18:26, 27
2 Ch. 18: 1
Ezra 9:14[b]

[a] A γαμβρεύω. [b] B γαμβρεύω.

ἐπιγαμία.

Jos. 23:12 | 1 Ki. (3) p 46+A

ἐπιγελάω.

Proverbs 1:26

ἐπιγεμίζω.

Nehemiah 13:15

ἐπιγινώσκω.

Gen. 27:23
31:32, 32
37:32, 33
38:15, 25
26
41:31
42: 7, 8, 8
Exo. 14: 4 A[a]
Deu. 1:17
16:19
21:17
33: 9[b]
Jud. 18: 3
Ruth 2:10, 19
3:14, 18
1 Sa. 26:17
2 Sa. 19: 7
1 Ki. 21:41[c]
Ezra 3:13
Neh. 6:12
13:24
Est. 3: 5
4: 1
Job 2:12
4:16
6:17[c d]
7:10
24:13, 16
17
34:27
Psa. 78: 6[e]
102:16
141: 5
Pro. 14: 8
Pro. 24:38, 53
27:23
Ecc. 1:16 S[a]
Isa. 61: 9
63:16
Jer. 4:22[c]
5: 5
6:15 S[a]
24: 5
37:24 S[a]
Lam. 4: 8
Eze. 5:13
6: 7, 10
14
7: 9, 4[c]
11:10, 12A
12:20
13:14, 21
23 A[a]
14: 8, 23
15: 7
16:62
17:21
20:38, 42
44, 48
21: 5
22:22
24:24, 27
25: 5, 7
11, 14
17
30:26 A[a]
34:15 A[2 a]
Hos. 2:20
Hos. 5: 4
7: 9 A[a]
14: 9
Joel 2:27
3:17[f]
Jon. 1: 7
Hab. 3: 2
Hag. 2:19
Zec. 2:11
4: 9
6:10, 14
15 A[a]
Mal. 2: 4[g]

[a] pro γινώσκω. [b] A[2] γινώσκω. [c] A γινώσκω. [d] C ἀναγινώσκω. [e] S[1] εἰδέω, S[2] γινώσκω. [f] S[3] γινώσκω. [g] S γινώσκω.

ἐπιγνωμοσύνη.

Proverbs 16:23

ἐπιγνώμων.

Pro. 12:26
13:10
Pro. 17:27
29: 7

ἐπίγνωσις.

1 Ki. 7: 2[a]
Pro. 2: 5
Hos. 4: 1, 6
6: 6

[a] B γνῶσις.

ἐπίγνωστος.

Job 18:19

ἐπιγονή.

2 Ch. 31:16, 18 | Amos 7: 1

ἐπιγράφω.

Nu. 17: 2, 3
Pro. 7: 3
Isa. 44: 5
Jer. 38:33 A[a]

[a] pro γράφω.

ἐπιδείκνυμι.

Est. 2: 3 A[a]
Pro. 12:17
Isa. 37:26

[a] pro ἐπιλέγω.

ἐπιδέκατος.

Nu. 18:21, 24
26 ter
28
Deu. 12:11, 17
14:22, 27
26:12, 12
2 Ch. 31: 5, 6, 6
12
Isa. 6:13
Amos 4: 4
Mal. 3: 8

ἐπιδέξιος.

Ezra 5: 8 | Pro. 27:16

ἐπιδέω (A).

Deu. 2: 7
15: 7, 8, 9
Deu. 15:10, 11[a]
Job 6:22

[a] δέω (A).

ἐπιδέω (B).

Jud. 16:21[a]
Jer. 28:63
Dan. 3:21

[a] A δέω (B).

ἐπιδιαιρέω.

Gen. 33: 1 A[a]

[a] pro διαιρέω.

ἐπιδίδωμι.

Gen. 49:21
1 Sa. 14:13
2 Ki. 9: 9 A[a]
Est. 9:11
Amos 4: 1

[a] pro δίδωμι.

ἐπιδιηγέομαι.

Esther 1:17 S[3 a]

[a] pro διηγέομαι

ἐπιδιπλόω.

Exodus 26: 9

ἐπιδιώκω.

Genesis 44: 4

ἐπίδοξος.

Proverbs 6: 8

ἐπιδύω, -δύνω.

Deu. 24:17
Jos. 8:29
Jer. 15: 9

ἐπιεικεύομαι.

Ezra 9: 8[a]

[a] B ἐπισκευάζω.

ἐπιεικής.

Psalm 85: 5

ἐπιεικῶς.

1 Sa. 12:22
2 Ki. 6: 3

ἐπιζάω.

Genesis 47:28

ἐπιζήμιος.

Exodus 21:22

ἐπιζητέω.

Jud. 6:29[a]
1 Sa. 20: 1
2 Sa. 3: 8
2 Ki. 1: 2[b], 3
6[c]
3:11
8: 8
2 Ki. 22:18
2 Ch. 18: 6
Est. 8: 7
Ecc. 7:29[d]
Isa. 62:12
Hos. 3: 5
5:15 A[e]

[a] A ἀνετάζω. [b] A ἐπερωτάω. [c] AB ζητέω. [d] A ζητέω. [e] pro ζητέω.

ἐπίθεμα.

Exo. 25:16
Lev. 7:24
8:29
14:24
23:15, 17
20
Nu. 6:20, 20
18:11, 18
1 Ki. 7: 4, 4
4—B
5, 5
5—A
6
8+A
9

ἐπίθεσις.

2 Ch. 25:27
Eze. 23:11

ἐπιθυμέω.

Gen. 31:30
49:14
Exo. 20:17, 17
34:24
Nu. 11: 4
Deu. 5:21, 21
7:25
12:20
14:25
25—B
18: 6
1 Sa. 2:16
20: 4
2 Sa. 3:21
23:15
1 Ki. 11:37
1 Ch. 11:17
2 Ch. 8: 6
Job 33:20
Psa. 44:12
105:14
118:20, 40
Pro. 21:26
23: 3, 6
24: 1
Ecc. 6: 2
Cant. 2: 3
Isa. 1:29
26: 9
43:24
58: 2,2,11
Jer. 17:16
Amos 5:18
Mic. 2: 2

ἐπιθύμημα.

Nu. 16:15
1 Ki. 21: 6
Isa. 27: 2
32:12
Jer. 3:17 A[a]
7:24 A[a]
Lam. 1: 6+S[1]
7, 10
Lam. 1:11
2: 4
Eze. 23:30 A[a]
24:16, 21
25
Dan. 11:38
Hos. 9:16

[a] pro ἐνθύμημα.

ἐπιθυμητής.

Numbers 11:34

ἐπιθυμητός.

2 Ch. 20:25
32:27
36:10
Ezra 8:27
Psa. 18:11
105:24
Pro. 1:22
21:20
Isa. 32:14
Jer. 12:10
Eze. 26:12
Dan. 11: 8, 43
Hos. 13:15
Amos 5:11
Nah. 2: 9

ἐπιθυμία.

Gen. 31:30
49: 6
Nu. 11: 4, 34
35
33:16, 17
Deu. 9:22
12:15, 20
21
2 Ch. 8: 6
Job 20:20
Psa. 9:24, 38
20: 3
37:10
77:29, 30
102: 5
105:14
Ps. 111:10
126: 5
139: 9
Pro. 6:25
10:24
11:23
12:12
13: 4, 12
19
21:25, 26
Cant. 5:16
Jer. 2:24
Dan. 9:23
10: 3, 11
19
11:37

ἐπιθύω.

1 Ki. 12:33
13: 1, 2A[a]
1 Ki. 13: 2
Hos. 2:13

[a] pro θύω.

ἐπικάθημαι.

2 Samuel 16: 2

ἐπικαθίζω.

Gen. 31:34
Lev. 15:20
2 Sa. 13:29
22:11[a]
1 Ki. 1:38, 44
2 Ki. 10:16
Eze. 32: 4

[a] A καθίζω.

ἐπικαλέω.

Gen. 4:26
12: 8
13: 4
21:33
26:25
33:20
48:16
Exo. 29:45, 46
Nu. 21: 3
Deu. 4: 7
12: 5, 11
21, 26
14:22, 23
15: 2
16: 2,6,11
15+A[1]
17: 8+A
10+A
26: 2
28:10
33:19
Jos. 21: 9
Jud. 6:24[a]
15:19[b]
1 Sa. 12:17, 18
23:28
2 Sa. 6: 2
20: 1
22: 4, 7
1 Ki. 7: 7, 7
8:43, 43
52
13: 2, 4
16:24
17:21
18:24, 25
26, 27
28
2 Ki. 5:11
23:17, 17
1 Ch. 4:10
13: 6
16: 8
2 Ch. 6:20, 33
33
7:14
28:15
Est. 4: 8
9:26
Job 5: 1, 8
17:14[c]
27:10
Psa. 4: 2
13: 4
17: 4, 7
19: 8 S[2d]
10
24:14+A
30:18
41: 8
48:12
49:15
52: 5
55:10
74: 2
78: 6
79:19
80: 8
85: 5
88:27
90:15[e]
98: 6, 6
101: 3
104: 1
114: 2, 4
115: 4,8-S[1]
117: 5
137: 3
144:18
18—S[1]
146: 9
Pro. 1:28
2: 3
8:12
18: 6
21:13
Isa. 18: 7+S
43: 7
55: 5, 6
63:19 A[f]
64: 7
Jer. 4:20
7:10, 11
14, 30
10:25
11:14
14: 9
15:16
20: 8
39:34
41:15
Lam. 3:54—A
56—A
Eze. 10:13
20:29
Dan. 9:18, 19
10: 1
Hos. 7: 7, 11
Joel 2:32
Amos 4: 5, 12
9:12
Jon. 1: 6
Mic. 6: 9
Zeph. 3: 9
Zec. 13: 9
Mal. 1: 4

[a] A καλέω. [b] A ἐπίκλητος. [c] ACS προσκαλέω. [d] pro μεγαλύνω. [e] AS[2] κράζω. [f] pro καλέω.

ἐπικάλυμμα.

Exo. 26:14
39:21
2 Sa. 17:19
Job 19:29—A

ἐπικαλύπτω.

Gen. 7:19 A[a]
20
8: 2[b]
Exo. 14:26
26:12 A[c]
Nu. 4:11
11A[a], 13
2 Sa. 15:30, 30
1 Ki. 19:13
Job 16:18
Psa. 31: 1
43:20
Pro. 28:13
Jer. 3:25
14: 4
Eze. 1:11, 23

[a] pro καλύπτω. [b] A ἀποκαλύπτω. [c] pro ὑποκαλύπτω.

ἐπικαταλαμβάνω.

Numbers 11:23

ἐπικαταράομαι.

Nu. 5:18, 19
22, 23
24, 24
27
Nu. 22:17
23: 7
Ps. 150 p6
Mal. 2: 2

ἐπικατάρατος.

Gen. 3:14, 17
4:11
9:25
27:29
49: 7
Deu. 27:15 to 22
23
23—A
24, 25
26
28:16, 16
17, 18
19, 19
Jos. 6:26
Jos. 9:29
Jud. 5:23[a]
21:18
1 Sa. 14:24, 28
26:19
Ps. 118:21
Pro. 24:39
Isa. 65:20
Jer. 11: 3
17: 5
20:14, 15
31:10
Mal. 1:14

[a] A καταράσις.

ἐπίκειμαι.

Exo. 36:40
Job 19: 3
Job 21:27

ἐπίκλητος.

Nu. 1:16
26: 9
28:18, 26
29: 1,7,12
Jos. 20: 9
Jud. 15:19 A[a]
Amos 1: 5

[a] pro ἐπικαλέω

ἐπικλίνω.

Gen. 24:14
1 Ki. 8:58

ἐπικλύζω.

Deu. 11: 4
Isa. 66:12

ἐπικοιμάομαι.

Deu. 21:23 A[a]
1 Ki. 3:19[b]

[a] pro κοιμάω. [b] A κοιμαω.

ἐπικοσμέω.

Ecc. 1:15[a]

[a] A κοσμέω.

ἐπικραταιόω.

Ecclesiastes 4:12

ἐπικρατέω.

Gen. 7:18, 19
41:57
47:20
1 Ki. 9:23 A
Ezra 4:20
Lam. 2:22
Eze. 29: 7 A[a]
Amos 6: 5[b]

[a] pro ἐπικροτέω. [b] AB ἐπικροτέω.

ἐπικρέμαμαι.

Isa. 22:24
Hos. 11: 7

ἐπικροτέω.

Pro. 17:18
Isa. 55:12
Jer. 5:31
Eze. 29: 7[a]
Amos 6: 5 AB[b]

[a] A ἐπικρατέω. [b] pro ἐπικρατέω.

ἐπικρούω.

Jeremiah 31:26

ἐπικρύπτω.

2 Sa. 19: 4 A[a]

[a] pro κρύπτω.

ἐπικυλίω.

Joshua 10:27

ἐπιλαλέω.

Jer. 8:17 A[2a]

[a] pro ἐπᾴδω.

ἐπιλαμβάνω.

Gen. 25:26
Exo. 4: 4, 4
Deu. 9:17
25:11
Jud. 12: 6
16: 3
21 A[a]
19:25
29 A[a]
20: 6 A[a]
2 Sa. 13:11
15: 5[b]
1 Ki. 1:50
6:10
11:30
2 Ki. 2:12
4:27
Job 8:15
16: 7
30:18
Job 38:13
Psa. 34: 2
47: 7[c]
Pro. 4:13
7:13
Isa. 3: 6
4: 1
5:29
27: 4
Jer. 30:14
38: 4 BS[d]
32
51:23
Eze. 29: 7
30:21
41: 6
Joel 2: 9
Zec. 8:23[e], 23[e]
14:13

[a] pro κρατέω. [b] A καταλαμβάνω. [c] A ὑπολαμβάνω. [d] pro ἔτι λαμβάνω. [e] S ἐπιβάλλω

ἐπιλάμπω.

Isa. 4: 2[a]

[a] A λάμπω.

ἐπιλανθάνω.

Gen. 27:45
40:23
41:30, 51
Deu. 4: 9, 23
31
6:12
8:11, 14
19
9: 7
24:21
25:19
26:13
31:21
32:18
Jud. 3: 7
1 Sa. 1:11+A
12: 9
2 Ki. 17:38
Job 8:13
9:27
11:16
19:14
28: 4
39:15[a]
Psa. 9:13, 18
19, 32
33
12: 2
30:13
41:10
43:18, 21
25
44:11
49:22

Psa. 58:12
73:10, 23
76:10
77: 7, 11
87:13
101: 5
102: 2
105:13, 21
118:16, 30
61, 83
93, 109
139, 141
153, 176
136: 5, 5
Pro. 2:17
3: 1
4: 4
5+A
24:73, 75
Ecc. 2:16
9: 5[b]
Isa. 23:16
41:21
49:14, 15
15, 15
Isa. 51:13[c]
54: 4
65:11, 16
Jer. 2:32, 32
3:21
8.17 A[1 d]
13:25
14: 9
18:15
20:11
23:27, 27
40
27: 5, 6
37:14
51: 9
Lam. 2: 6
3:17
5:20
Eze. 22:12[c]
23:35
Hos. 2:13
4: 6, 6
8:14
13: 6
Amos 8: 7

[a] S[1] ἐπιργομαι. [b] AS πλήθω.
[c] B ἀπολαυσάτω. [d] pro ἐπᾴδω.

ἐπιλέγω.

Exo. 17: 9
18:25
Deu. 21: 5[a]
Jos. 8: 3
1 Sa. 2:28 A[b]
2 Sa. 10: 9
2 Sa. 17: 1
1 Ki. 14:10 A
10 A
22:47 A
Est. 2: 3[c]

[a] A ἐκλέγω. [b] pro ἐκλέγω.
[c] A ἐπιδείκνυμι.

ἐπιλείπω.

Obad. 5[a]
Zeph. 3: 3 S[1 b]

[a] ABS ὑπολείπω. [b] pro ὑπολείπω

ἐπίλεκτος.

Exo. 15: 4
24:11
Jos. 17:16, 18
Eze. 17: 3[a]
22 A[b]
Eze. 23: 6, 7, 12
23
24: 5
Joel 3: 5

[a] A ἐκλεκτός. [b] pro ἐκλεκτός.

ἐπιληπτεύομαι.

1 Sa. 21:15
Jer. 30: 3+AS

ἐπίληπτος.

1 Sa. 21:14, 15
2 Ki. 9:11

ἐπίλοιπος.

Lev. 27:18
Deu. 19:20
21:21
Jud. 7: 6 A[a]
21.16 A[b]
2 Ki. 4: 7[c]
Isa. 38:10, 12[d]
Jer. 32: 6
34:10[e]
51:14
Dan. 2:18
7: 7, 19
Mic. 5: 3

[a] pro κατάλοιπος.
[b] pro περισσός. [c] A ὑπόλοιπος.
[d] A λοιπος. [e] S ὑπόλοιπος.

ἐπιμαρτύρομαι.

1 Ki. (3)42
Neh. 9:29, 30
13:15, 21[a]
Jer. 39:25
Amos 3:13

[a] AS διαμαρτύρομαι.

ἐπιμέλεια.

Est. 2: 3
Ps. 106:30 S[1 a]
Pro. 3: 8, 22
Pro. 13: 4
28:25

[a] pro ἐπὶ λιμένα.

ἐπιμελέομαι.

Gen. 44:21
Pro. 27:21

ἐπιμελῶς.

Gen. 6: 5
8:21
Ezra 6: 8, 12
Ezra 6:13
Pro. 13:24

ἐπιμένω.

Exo. 12:39[a]
[a] A ὑπομένω.

ἐπιμερίζω.

Job 31: 2 A[a]
Job 39:17[b]

[a] pro μερίζω. [b] ABS μερίζω.

ἐπιμίγνυμι.

Pro. 14:10
Eze. 16:37

ἐπίμικτος.

Exo. 12:38
Nu. 11: 4
Neh. 13: 3
Eze. 30: 5

ἐπιμύλιος.

Deu. 24: 8
Jud. 9:53[a]

[a] A μύλος.

ἐπινεύω.

Proverbs 26:24

ἐπινοέω.

Job 4:18
Job 9: 7+BS

ἐπίνοια.

Jeremiah 20:10

ἐπινυστάζω.

Proverbs 6: 4

ἐπιξενόομαι.

Proverbs 21: 7

ἐπίορκος.

Zechariah 5: 3

ἐπιπαραγίνομαι.

Joshua 10: 9 A[a]
[a] pro παραγίνομαι.

ἐπιπείθομαι.

Deu. 32:37
Job 31:24
Isa. 30:32
vide πείθω.

ἐπίπεμπτος.

Lev. 5:16
6: 5[a]
22:14
27:13, 15
Lev. 27:19, 27
31
Nu. 5: 7

[a] A[1]B πεμπτός.

ἐπιπέμπω.

Proverbs 6:19

ἐπιπίπτω.

Gen. 14:15
15:12, 12
45:14
14 A[a]
46:29
50: 1
Exo. 15:16
Lev. 11:32, 35[b]
37, 38
Nu. 35:23
Jos. 2: 9
11: 7[c]
1 Sa. 26:12[b]
31: 4
2 Sa. 17: 9
2 Ki. 4:37 A[d]
1 Ch. 10: 4[e]
Neh. 6:16[c]
Est. 7:8 9:4 S[3f]
Job 4:13
6:16, 27
13:11
18:16
33:15
Psa. 15: 6[g]
54: 5
57: 9 BS[1 d]
68:10
77:28[g]
104:38
Ecc. 9:12
Jer. 31:32[e h]
Eze. 24: 6 B[d]
Dan. 10: 7

[a] pro κλαίω. [b] AB[1] πίπτω.
[c] A πίπτω. [d] pro πίπτω.
[e] AS πίπτω. [f] pro προσπίπτω.
[g] S πίπτω. [h] S ἐμπίπτω.

ἐπιπληθύνω.

Gen. 7:17[a]
[a] A πληθύνω.

ἐπιποθέω.

Deu. 13: 8
32:11
Psa. 41: 2, 2
61:11
83: 3
Ps. 118:20, 131
174
Jer. 13:14
Zeph. 3: 2 S[1 a]

[a] pro πείθω.

ἐπιπολάζω.

2 Kings 6: 6

ἐπίπονος.

Jeremiah 51:33

ἐπιπορεύομαι.

Lev. 26:33
Eze. 39:14

ἐπιρραντίζω.

Leviticus 6:27

ἐπιρρέω.

Job 22:16

ἐπιρρίπτω.

Nu. 35:20, 22
Jos. 10:11
23: 4[a]
2 Sa. 20:12
1 Ki. 19:19
Job 27:22[b]
Psa. 21:11
Psa. 54:23
Jer. 15: 8
28:63 S[c]
Eze. 43:24
Amos 8: 3
Nah. 3: 6

[a] B ὅπερ εἶπα. [b] A ἀπορρίπτω.
[c] pro ῥίπτω.

ἐπίσαγμα.

Leviticus 15: 9

ἐπισάττω.

Gen. 22: 3
24:32 A[a]
Nu. 22:21
Jud. 19:10
2 Sa. 16: 1
17:23
19:26
1 Ki. (3)40
12:11
13:13, 13
23, 27 A
27 A
2 Ki. 4:24
Jer. 26: 4

[a] pro ἀποσάττω.

ἐπισείω.

Jud. 1:14
1 Sa. 26:19
2 Sa. 24: 1
1 Ch. 21: 1

ἐπισημαίνω.

Job 14:17

ἐπίσημος.

Gen. 30:42
Est. 5: 4

ἐπισιτίζω.

Joshua 9:10

ἐπισιτισμός.

Gen. 42:25
45:21
Exo. 12:39
Jos. 1:11
9:11, 17
Jos. 9:20
Jud. 7: 8
20:10
1 Sa. 22:10
Psa. 77:25

ἐπισκιάζω.

Genesis 32:31

ἐπισκεπάζω.

Lamentations 3:42, 43

ἐπισκέπτομαι.

Gen. 21: 1
50:24, 25
Exo. 3:16
4:31
13:19
32:34
39: 2
Lev. 13:36
Nu. 1: 3, 3
18 A[a]
19, 44
47[b]
2: 4[c], 6[c]
8, 9
11[c], 13[c]
15[c], 16[c]
19, 21
23, 24[c]
26[c], 28
30, 31[c]
3:15, 15[c]
16[c], 39
40, 42
4:23, 27
29, 30
32, 34
37, 38
41, 42
45, 46
46, 48
49, 49
16: 5
26:54, 63
64, 64
27:16
Jos. 8:10
Jud. 15: 1
20:15, 15
17
21: 3, 9[d]
Ruth 1: 6
1 Sa. 2:21
11: 8
13:15
14:17, 17
15: 4
17:18 A
20: 6, 6, 18
18, 19
25, 27
2 Sa. 2:30
18: 1
24: 2, 4
1 Ki. 21:15, 15
26, 27
2 Ki. 3: 6
9:34
10:19, 19
1 Ch. 26:31
2 Ch. 24: 6
Ezra 1: 2
4:15, 19
5:17
6: 1
7:14
Neh. 7: 1
12.12
Job 2:11+A
11
35:15
Psa. 8: 5
16: 3
26: 4
58: 6
64:10
79:15
88:33
105: 4
Isa. 10:12[e]
Jer. 3:16
5: 9, 29
9: 9, 25
11:22
13:21
15:15
23: 2
29: 9
34: 6
36:10, 32
37:20
39:41
43:31
51:13, 13
29
Lam. 4:22
Eze. 20:40
23:21
34:11
12 A[f]
Hos. 4.14
Zeph. 2: 7
Zec. 10: 3, 3
11:16
16 S[1 f]
Mal. 3:10 BS[1 g]

[a] pro ἐπαξονέω. [b] A συνεπισκέπτομαι. [c] A ἀριθμέω.
[d] A ἀποσκοπέω. [e] ABS ἐπάγω.
[f] pro ζητέω. [g] pro ἐπιστρέφω.

ἐπισκευάζω.

Exo. 30: 7
1 Sa. 3: 3
2 Ch. 24: 4, 12
12—A
2 Ch. 29: 3
34:10
Ezra 9: 8 B[a]

[a] pro ἐπιεικεύομαι.

ἐπισκευή.

2 Ki. 12:11 A[a] [a] pro ἐπίσκοπος.

ἐπίσκεψις.

Exo. 30:13, 14
39: 3
Nu. 1:21[a], 23
25, 27
29, 31
33, 35
37, 39
41, 43
44, 45
2:32, 32
3:22, 22[b]
34, 36
Nu. 3:39, 43
4:36. 37
40—A
41, 44
45
16:29
26: 7, 14
18[a], 21
23, 27
31, 38
41, 45
50, 51

Nu. 26:62, 63
2 Sa. 24: 9
1 Ch. 21: 5
23:11, 24
24: 3, 19
1 Ch. 26:30
Jer. 11:23[c]
23:12
28:18
31:44

[a] B ἐπισκοπή. [b] A ἀριθμός. [c] B* ἐπισκοπή.

ἐπισκιάζω.

Exo. 40:29
Psa. 90: 4
Ps. 139: 8
Pro. 18:11

ἐπισκοπέω.

Deu. 11:12
2 Ch. 34:12
Est. 2:11
Pro. 19:23

ἐπισκοπή.

Gen. 50:24, 25
Exo. 3:16
13:19
30:12, 12
Lev. 19:20
Nu. 1:21 B[a]
4:16
7: 2
14:29
16:29
26:18 B[a]
47
Deu. 28:25 AB[b]
Job 5:24+A
6:14
7:18
Job 10:12
24:13
29: 4
31:14
34: 9, 9
Ps. 108: 8
Pro. 29:13
Isa. 10: 3
23:17
24:22
29: 6
Jer. 6:15
10:15
11:23 B[a]
Eze. 7:22

[a] pro ἐπίσκεψις. [b] pro ἐπὶ κοπήν.

ἐπίσκοπος.

Nu. 4:16
31:14
Jud. 9:28
2 Ki. 11:15, 18
12:11[a]
2 Ch. 34:12, 17
Neh. 11: 9, 14
22
Job 20:29
Isa. 60:17

[a] A ἐπισκευή.

ἐπίσπαστρον.

Exodus 26:36

ἐπισπάω.

Gen. 39:12
Isa. 5:18
Nah. 3:14—S[1]

ἐπισπεύδω.

Est. 6:14
Pro. 6:18

ἐπισπλαγχνίζομαι.

Pro. 17: 5[a] [a] A σπλαγχνίζω.

ἐπισπουδάζω.

Gen. 19:15 A[a]
Pro. 13:11
Pro. 20:21

[a] pro σπουδάζω.

ἐπισπουδαστής.

Isaiah 14: 4

ἐπίσταμαι.

Gen. 47: 5
Exo. 4:14
9:30
Nu. 20:14
22:34
24:16
32:11
Deu. 20:20
22: 2[a]
28:33, 36
64
29:26
31:27
Jos. 2: 5, 9
3: 4
Jos. 14: 6
2 Ch. 2: 7, 12
Neh. 2: 5+S[3]
Job 7:20
13: 2
14:21
32:21
33:31+A
34: 2
37:15
38: 4, 20
33
42: 3
Pro. 9:13
10:21
Pro. 14:22
15: 2
29: 7
Isa. 29:11, 12
12
37:28
41:20
48: 8
55: 5
Isa. 66:18+S
Jer. 1: 5, 6
2: 8
17:16
Eze. 11: 5
17:12
28:19
37: 3

[a] B ἐγγίζω.

ἐπιστάτης.

Exo. 1:11
5:14
1 Ki. (3) p1
5:16
2 Ki. 25:19
2 Ch. 2: 2
31:12
Jer. 36:26
52:25

ἐπιστέλλω.

1 Ki. 5: 8 A[a]
Neh. 6:19 B[a]

[a] pro ἀποστέλλω.

ἐπιστέφω.

Jer. 2:24 S[1 a] [a] pro ἐπιστρέφω.

ἐπιστήμη.

Exo. 31: 3
35:31
36: 1, 2
Nu. 24:16
Deu. 32:28
2 Ch. 2:12
Neh. 8: 8
Job 12:12, 16
21:22
22: 2
26:12
28:12, 28
Job 32: 7
34:35
36: 3
38:36
39:26
Ecc. 1:17
Isa. 33: 6
Jer. 3:15
Eze. 28: 3, 4, 5
7, 17
Dan. 1:20

ἐπιστήμων.

Deu. 1:13, 15
4: 6
Isa. 5:21

ἐπιστήριγμα.

2 Samuel 22:19

ἐπιστηρίζω.

Gen. 28:13
Jud. 16:26+A
26
29 A[a]
29
2 Sa. 1: 6
Psa. 31: 8
37: 3
70: 6
87: 8
Cant. 8: 5
Isa. 36: 6

[a] pro ἵστημι.

ἐπιστοιβάζω.

Leviticus 1: 7[a], 8, 12

[a] AB[2] στοιβάζω.

ἐπιστολή.

2 Ch. 30: 1, 6
Ezra 4: 6—B
8, 11
5: 6
Neh. 2: 7, 8, 9
6: 5, 17
19
Est. 3:14
Est. 8:13
13+S[3]
9:26, 29
30+S[1]
Isa. 18: 2
39: 1
Jer. 36: 1

ἐπιστρατεύω.

Isa. 29: 7, 8
31: 4
Zec. 14:12—S[1]

ἐπιστρέφω.

Gen. 8:12
21:32
24:49
37:30[a]
44:13
50:14 A[b]
Exo. 4:18 A[c]
20
Exo. 5:22
7:23
10: 8 A[c]
16:10
32:31 A[b]
34:31
Nu. 10:36
13:26 A[c]
Nu. 14:25
16:50
21:33
23: 5
Deu. 1: 7, 24
40
2: 1, 3, 8
3: 1
4:30, 39
9:15
10: 5
20: 5 A[c]
6 A[c]
7 A[c]
28:60
30: 2, 8, 9
10
31:18 A[c]
20
Jos. 7:12 A[b]
8:24[d]
10:21 A[c]
11:10[f]
13:28—A
19:27, 34
20: 4 A, 6 A
Jud. 6:14[e], 18
7: 3[f], 3[f]
15 A[b]
8: 9 A[g]
13[a], 33[f]
9:56[f], 57[f]
11: 8[h], 9
13, 31
35 B[c]
39[i]
14: 8 A[b]
15: 4[k], 19
17: 3+A
18:21, 23
26[a]
19: 3[m]
20: 8[n]
41[f], 48[o]
21:14[f]
Ruth 1: 6 A[c], 7
10, 11
12, 14
15, 22
22
4: 3, 15
1 Sa. 4:19
7: 3
10: 9
14:21[p], 26
27
15:12, 27[f]
16: 7 A[q]
17:30 A
57 A
18: 2 A
6+A
22:18, 18[f]
23:23+A
26:21, 23
27: 9 A[r]
30:19
22 A[c]
2 Sa. 2:23[f]
26 A[c]
3:12, 26
27
6:20
10: 5
11: 1
12:23, 31
14:13, 21
24 A[c]
15: 8, 8, 19
20, 20
25, 27
34
16: 3, 8, 12
17: 3, 3
18:30, 30
19:10, 11
12, 14
15, 39
43
1 Ki. 2:30[s], 32[c]
1 Ki. 2:33[f]
(3) 41 A[r]
8:33, 34[s]
35 A[c]
44, 47
47, 48
12: 2 A, 21
26, 27
27+A
13: 4, 6, 6
9, 11[f]
16, 17
18, 19
20, 22
23, 26
29, 33
33
17:21
18:43, 44[t]
19: 6, 7
21: 9[a], 22
26
22:27, 28
28, 34
2 Ki. 1: 5, 5, 6
6—AB
2:13, 18 A[r]
25[t]
3: 4, 27[t]
4:22, 31
35, 38
5:10, 14
15, 21
26
7: 8, 15
8: 3, 6, 29
9:18
19—A
23, 36
13:25[f], 25
14:22[f], 28
16: 6[f], 18
17: 3
19: 8[f], 9[f]
20: 2 AB[c]
5
9—A
10, 11
21: 3[f]
22: 9 A[c]
23: 1, 16
20, 25
34
24: 1
1 Ch. 10:14[u]
12:19
23 A[c]
16:43
21:20
2 Ch. 6: 3, 24
26, 37
37, 38
10:12
11: 1
12:11
14:15
15: 4
18:26, 27
27, 33
19: 1[d], 4
20:27
22: 6
24:19
25:10[t], 24
26: 2, 20
28:15[t]
30: 6, 6, 9
9 A[c], 9
31: 1
33: 3
13—A
19
35:19
36:10, 13
Ezra 2: 1
6:22
9:14[f]
10:16
Neh. 1: 9
2: 6, 15
Neh. 2:20
4: 5
12+S[3]
15
5:11
7: 6
8:17
9:17, 26
28, 29
35 A[c]
13: 2[v]
9
Est. 6:12
7: 8
Job 7:10
22:23
30:15
33:23
31+A
36:10
Psa. 6: 5, 11[u]
7: 8, 13
17
13: 7
18: 8
21:28
22: 3
50:15
52: 7 B[2]S[c]
55:10
58: 7, 15
59: 2
67:23, 23
70:20, 21
72:10
77:34, 39
41
57 B[1]S[c]
79: 4, 8, 15
20
84: 2 A[c], 5
7, 9
89: 3, 13
93:15
103: 9[d], 29
114: 7
118:59[a], 79
125: 1, 4
145: 4
Pro. 17: 8
Ecc. 1: 6, 7
2:20
3:20
4: 1, 7
5:14
9:11[x]
12: 2, 7, 7
Cant. 6:12 qtr
Isa. 6:10
9:13[w]
19:22
31: 6
44:22
45:13, 22
46: 8
49: 6
55: 7
63:15, 17
Jer. 2:21[y]
27 S[z]
3:10[f], 12
14, 22
22
4: 1, 1
5: 3
6: 9
8: 4 AS[r], 5
9: 5
11:10
12:15, 17
15:19
18: 8
22:10[a]
27 A[c]
24: 7
26:21[e u]
Jer. 27: 9
29: 3[aa]
34:13
35: 6
37:21 A[c]
38:13 S[1 c]
16, 18
18
39:33 S[c]
37
40: 7 BS[3 c]
11 S[c]
41:10
15[bb]
16, 16
22
45:26 AS[c]
49:12
51:14 ter
28
Lam. 1:11, 12
16, 19
2: 8[w]
8 BS[c]
14
3: 3, 39
5:21, 21
Eze. 1: 9, 12
17
7:13
8:17+A
10:11, 11
16
14: 6, 6
18:30
32+A
26: 2
34: 4 A[c]
16 AB[1 c]
35: 2
38:12
42:17, 18
19
44: 1
47: 6—B
Dan. 4:31, 33
33
9:25
10:20
11:13, 18
18, 19
28, 29
29, 30
30
Hos. 2: 7, 9
3: 5
5: 4, 15
6: 1, 10
7:10
11: 5
12: 6
14: 1, 2, 7
Joel 2:12, 13
14
3: 1
Amos 4: 6, 8, 9
10, 11
9:14
Jon. 1:13
Mic. 5: 3
7:19
Zeph. 2: 7 S[1 c]
3:20
Hag. 2:17
Zec. 1: 3, 3
16[cc]
4: 1
5: 1
6: 1
8: 3
10: 9, 10
13: 7 S[3 dd]
Mal. 1: 4
2: 6
3: 7 ter
10[ee], 18

[a] A ἀναστρέφω. [b] pro ὑποστρέφω. [c] pro ἀποστρέφω. [d] B ἀποστρέφω. [e] A ἐπιβλέπω. [f] A ἀποστρέφω. [g] pro ἐπι-

στροφή. [h] A ἔρχομαι. [i] A ἀνακάμπτω. [k] A συνδέω. [m] A διαλλάσσω. [n] A ἐκκλινω. [o] A ἀποκλείω. [p] B ἀναστρέφω. [q] pro ἐπιβλέπω. [r] pro ἀναστρέφω. [s] AB ἀποστρέφω. [t] A ὑποστρέφω. [u] S ἀποστρέφω. [v] BS στρέφω. [w] AS ἀποστρέφω. [x] S ὑποστρέφω. [y] S[1] ἐπιστρέφω. [z] pro στρέφω. [aa] S[1] στρέφω. [bb] A στρέφω. [cc] B ἐπιβλέπω. [dd] pro ἐπάγω. [ee] BS[1] ἐπισκέπτομαι.

ἐπιστροφή.

Jud. 8: 9[a]
Cant. 7:10
Eze. 42:11
47: 7, 11

[a] A ἐπιστρέφω.

ἐπισυνάγω.

Gen. 6:16
38:29
1 Ki. 18:20[a]
2 Ch. 5: 6
20:26
Psa. 30:14 AS[b]
101:23 AS[2b]
105:47
146: 2
Isa. 9: 5
52:12[c]
Jer. 12: 6
Eze. 16:37
40:12
Mic. 4:11
Hab. 2: 5
Zec. 12: 3
14: 2

[a] A συνάγω. [b] pro συνάγω. [c] S[1] συνάγω.

ἐπισυνίστημι.

Lev. 26:16 AB[a]
Nu. 14:35
16:19
26: 9[b]
Nu. 27: 3
Jer. 20:10[c], 10
Eze. 2: 6

[a] pro ἐφίστημι. [b] A ἐφίστημι. [c] S[1] ἐφίστημι.

ἐπισύστασις.

Nu. 16:40
Nu. 26: 9

ἐπισυστρέφω.

Numbers 16:42

ἐπισφραγίζω.

Nehemiah 9:38

ἐπίσχω.

Judges 20:28+B

ἐπιτάσσω.

Gen. 49:33
Est. 1: 8
3: 2 A[a]
12[b]
Est. 8: 8, 11
Ps. 106:29–S[1c]
Eze. 24:18
Dan. 6: 9

[a] pro προστάσσω. [b] A προστάσσω. [c] S[2] ἐπιτιμάω.

ἐπιτείνω.

1 Ki. 22:34[a] [a] A ἐντείνω.

ἐπιτελέω.

Lev. 6:22
Nu. 23:23
Jud. 11:39 A[a]
20:10+A
1 Sa. 3:12
Est. (9)14
9:27–S[1]
Zec. 4: 9

[a] pro ποιέω.

ἐπιτήδειος.

1 Chronicles 28: 2

ἐπιτήδευμα.

Lev. 18: 3, 3
Deu. 28:20
Jud. 2:19
1 Sa. 2: 3
25: 3
1 Ki. 15:12
1 Ch. 16: 8
Neh. 9:35
Job 14:16
Psa. 9:12

Psa. 13: 1
27: 4
76:13
80:13, 13
98: 9
105:29
39–A
Pro. 20:11
Jer. 4: 4, 18
7: 3
5–A
11:18
17:10
18:11
23: 2, 22
25: 5
33: 3
Jer. 42:15
Eze. 6: 9
9+A
8:15
14: 6
20: 7, 8, 18
39, 39
43, 44
21:24
36:31
Hos. 9:15
12: 2
Mic. 2: 7, 9
3: 4
7:13
Zeph. 3:11
Zec. 1: 4, 6

ἐπιτηδεύω.

Jer. 2:33
Mal. 2:11

ἐπιτίθημι.

Gen. 9:23
11: 6
21:14
22: 6, 9, 9
28:11 A[a]
37:34
42:26
43:17
44:13
48:18
Exo. 3:22
18:11
21:14
22:25
25:11, 17
20
25–A
29, 37
26:32, 35[b]
28:14, 24
25, 26
33
29: 3–A
6, 6, 10
12 A[a]
13, 15
17, 19
20, 24
30:10+A[2]
34:33
36:14, 24
25, 26
26, 27
28, 33
40
37: 4
38:24
40: 4, 5[c]
16, 17
18 A[d]
19[e], 20[f]
23
Lev. 1: 4, 7, 9
10, 13
15, 17
2: 1, 2, 9
15
3: 2, 8, 13
4: 4, 7, 15
18, 24
25, 29
30, 34
34, 35
5:11, 12
6:12
7:20
8: 7, 8, 8
9, 9, 14
15, 18
22, 23
24, 26
27
9: 9, 13
14, 17
20
10: 1[c]
Lev. 14:14, 17
18, 24
25, 28
29
16: 8, 13
18, 21[e]
21
23:20
24: 6, 7, 14
Nu. 4: 6, 10
12, 13
14, 14
5:15, 25
6:18, 19
27
8: 2, 10
12
11:11, 17
25
15:38
16: 7, 7, 17
18–A[2]
40, 46
27:18, 23
Deu. 7:15, 15
11:25
14: 1
22:14, 17
26: 6
28:48
33:10
34: 9
Jos. 10:24, 24
Jud. 6:19 A[a]
8:31 A[a]
9:24 A[a]
48 A[a]
49
16: 3 A[a]
18:19
Ruth 3:15
1 Sa. 6:18
23:27
27: 8, 10
30: 1, 14
2 Sa. 13:19, 19
1 Ki. 13:29
14:27
16(?)28–A
18:23–A
23, 23
25, 33
21:31
2 Ki. 4:29, 31
5:11
11:16
13:16
18:14, 14
20: 7
24:17[c]
1 Ch. 13: 7
2 Ch. 3:16 B[a]
4: 6 A[a]
23:13, 13
24:21, 25
26
2 Ch. 25:13, 27
28:17, 18
29:23
33:24, 25
Neh. 9: 7
Est. 2:17
9:14 S[1h]
Job 29: 9
31:27
40:27
Psa. 3: 7[i]
20: 6
58: 4
61: 4
Isa. 1: 6
44: 3
Jer. 27:24 B[2]S[k]
Jer. 29:10
Lam. 3:52
Eze. 21:26
23: 5[m], 7
9, 12
16, 20
27:30
40:42
43:20
Dan. 1: 7
5:12
6:17
Mic. 7:16
Zec. 3: 5
5–S[1]
6:11
Mal. 1: 7, 12

[a] pro τίθημι. [b] AB τίθημι. [c] A τίθημι. [d] pro ὑποτίθημι. [e] A[1] τίθημι. [f] AB[2] τίθημι. [g] A προσάγω. [h] pro ἐκτίθημι. [i] AS συνεπιτίθημι. [k] pro ἐπιβαίνω. [m] A προστίθημι.

ἐπιτιμάω.

Gen. 37:10
Ruth 2:16
Psa. 9: 6
67:31
Ps. 105: 9
106:29 S[2a]
118:21
Zec. 3: 2, 2

[a] pro ἐπιτάσσω.

ἐπιτίμησις.

2 Sa. 22:16
Job 26:11
Psa. 17:16
75: 7
Psa. 79:17
103: 7
Ecc. 7: 6

ἐπιτρέπω.

Gen. 39: 6
Est. 9:14–A
Job 32:14

ἐπιτρέχω.

Gen. 24:17
1 Ki. 10:20 A[a]

[a] pro κατατρέχω.

ἐπιτρίβω.

Job 29: 4 S[1a] [a] pro ἐπιβρίθω.

ἐπίτριψις.

Psalm 92: 3+AS[2]

ἐπιτυγχάνω.

Gen. 39: 2
Pro. 12:27

ἐπιφαίνω.

Gen. 35: 7 A[a]
Nu. 6:25
Deu. 33: 2
Psa. 30:17
66: 2
79: 4, 8, 20
117:27
Ps. 118:135
Jer. 36:14
Eze. 17: 6
39:28
Dan. 9:17
Zeph. 2:11[b]

[a] pro φαίνω. [b] AS[1] ἐπιφανής.

ἐπιφάνεια.

2 Sa. 7:23
Amos 5:22

ἐπιφανής.

Jud. 13: 6 A[a]
1 Ch. 17:21
Est. 1: 6 AS[b]
Pro. 25:14
Joel 2:11, 31
Hab. 1: 7
Zeph. 2:11 AS[1c]
3: 1
Mal. 1:14
4: 4

[a] pro φοβερός. [b] pro διαφανής. [c] pro ἐπιφαίνω.

ἐπιφαύσκω.

Job 25: 5
31:26
Job 41: 9

ἐπιφέρω.

Gen. 1: 2
7:18
37:22
1 Sa. 22:17
24: 7, 11
26: 9, 11
1 Sa. 26:23
2 Sa. 1:14
Est. 8: 7
Job 15:12
Pro. 26:15
Zec. 2: 9

ἐπιφημίζω.

Deuteronomy 29:19

ἐπιφυλλίζω.

Lam. 1:22
2:20
Lam. 3:50

ἐπιφυλλίς.

Jud. 8: 2
Lam. 1:22
2:20
Obad. 5[a]
Mic. 7: 1
Zeph. 3: 7

[a] S[1] ὑποφυλλίς.

ἐπιχαίρω.

Psa. 34:19, 24
26
37:17
40:12
Pro. 17: 5, 18
24:17
Eze. 25: 3, 6, 15
Hos. 10: 5
Obad. 12
Mic. 4:11
7: 8

ἐπιχαρής.

Job 31:20

ἐπίχαρις.

Nahum 3: 4

ἐπίχαρμα.

Exodus 32:25

ἐπίχαρτος.

Proverbs 11: 4

ἐπιχειρέω.

2 Ch. 20:11
Ezra 7:23
Est. 9:25

ἐπίχειρον.

Jer. 31:25
Jer. 34: 4

ἐπιχέω, –χύω.

Gen. 28:18
35:14
Exo. 29: 7
Lev. 2: 1, 6, 15
5:11
8:12
11:38
14:15, 26
21:10
Nu. 5:15
1 Sa. 10: 1
1 Ki. 18:34
2 Ki. 3:11
4: 5
9: 3, 6
Job 36:27
Zec. 4:12

ἐπίχυσις.

Job 37:17

ἐπιχύω vide ἐπιχέω.

ἐπιχώρησις.

Ezra 3: 7

ἐπιψοφέω.

Eze. 25: 6 AB[a] [a] pro ψοφέω.

ἐπόζω.

Exo. 7:18, 21
Exo. 16:20, 24

ἐποίκιον.

1 Chronicles 27:25

ἐποικτείρω.
Job 24:21+A

ἐπονείδιστος.
Pro. 18: 1
19:26
Pro. 25:10
27:11

ἐπονομάζω.
Gen. 4:17, 25
26
5: 2,3,29
19:22 A[a]
21:31
25:25
26:18, 21
22
30:11
Exo. 2:10, 22
15:23
16:31
17: 7, 15
Exo. 20:24
Lev. 24:11
Nu. 13:17, 25
32:38, 41
42
Deu. 2:11, 20
3: 9,9,14
12: 5
Jos. 7:26
22:34
Jud. 2: 5[b]
1 Ch. 28: 3
2 Ch. 12:13

[a] pro καλέω. [b] A καλέω.

ἐπόπτομαι.
Psa. 5: 4
34:17
117: 7
Mic. 4:11
7:10

ἐπουράνιος.
Psa. 67:15
Dan. 4:23 A[a]

[a] pro οὐράνιος.

ἔποψ.
Lev. 11:19
Deu. 14:16[a]
Zec. 5: 9

[a] A ὕποψ.

ἑπτά.
Gen. 41:27[4]−A
Exo. 29:38+A[2]
Nu. 12:14[2]−A
28:17−A
24[a]
Jud. 16:11+A
1 Ki. 6: 5+A
8:65+A
21:15[b]
1 Ch. 3: 4−B
Ezra 2:39−B

[a] A[2] δύο. [b] B 60 pro 7000.

ἑπταετής.
Judges 6:25

ἑπτάκις.
Gen. 4:24
33: 3
Lev. 4: 6, 17
8:11
14: 7, 16
27, 51
16:14, 19
25: 8
26:18, 24
28
Nu. 19: 4
Jos. 6:15[a]
1 Ki. 18:43
43+B
44
2 Ki. 4:35
5:10, 14
Ps. 118:164
Pro. 24:16

[a] B ἑξάκις.

ἑπτακισχίλιοι.
Nu. 31:36[a]
2 Ch. 17:11+A

[a] B πεντακισχίλιοι.

ἑπτακόσιοι.
Gen. 5:26[a]
Nu. 2:26[b]
4:36[c]
26:38[d]
Jud. 8:26[e]
2 Ch. 15:11[c]
17:11+A
Ezra 2:33[f]
Neh. 7:11[g]
69+AS[3]

[a] A[2] 782 pro 802. [b] B πεντακόσιοι. [c] A τριακόσιοι, B διακόσιοι. [d] A πεντακόσιοι. [e] A ἑπτά. [f] B ἑξακόσιοι. [g] BS ὀκτακόσιοι.

ἑπτάμηνος.
Ezekiel 39:13, 14

ἑπταπλάσιος.
Psa. 78:12[a]
Pro. 6:31
Isa. 30:26

[a] S ἑπταπλασίων.

ἑπταπλασίων.
2 Sa. 12: 6
Psa. 78:12 S[a]

[a] pro ἑπταπλάσιος.

ἑπταπλασίως.
Psa. 11: 7
Dan. 3:19

ἐπωμίς.
Exo. 25: 6
28: 4, 6, 7
8, 12
15, 25
29: 5, 5
35: 8, 27
36: 9, 11
14, 15
26, 27
Exo. 36:28
28−B
29 ter
30
Lev. 8: 7, 7
1 Sa. 21: 9+A
Eze. 40:48
41: 2, 3

ἐπωρύω.
Jon. 1:11 A[a]
13 A[a]
Zec. 11: 8

[a] pro πορεύω.

ἐραστής.
Jer. 4:30
22:20
22−A
Lam. 1:19
Eze. 16:33, 36
Eze. 16:37
23: 5,9,22
Hos. 2: 5,7,10
12, 13

ἐραστός.
Jer. 9:14 A[a]
Jer. 16:12 A[a]

[a] pro ἀρεστός.

ἐράω.
1 Sa. 19: 2
2 Sa. 20:18 B[a]
Est. 2:17
Pro. 4: 6

[a] pro ἐρωτάω.

ἐργάβ.
1 Sa. 6:11, 15
1 Sa. 20:19[a]

[a] A ἔργον.

ἐργάζομαι.
Gen. 2: 5, 15
3:23
4: 2, 12
29:27
Exo. 5:18
20: 9
31: 4, 5
34:21
35: 9
36: 4, 6, 8
Lev. 25:40
Nu. 3: 7
8:11, 15
19, 25
26
31:51
Deu. 5:13
15:19
21: 3, 4
2 Sa. 9:10
11:20 A[a]
1 Ch. 25: 1
27:26
2 Ch. 2:10
Job 24: 6
33:29
31+A
34:32
Psa. 5: 6
6: 9
7:16
13: 4
14: 2
Psa. 27: 3
35:13
43: 2
52: 5
57: 3
58: 3, 6
63: 3
73:12
91: 8, 10
93: 4, 16
100: 8
118: 3
124: 5
140: 4, 9
Pro. 3:30
10:29
12:11
28:19
29:36
Ecc. 5: 8
Isa. 5:10
19: 9, 9
10[b]
23:10
28:24
30:24
44:12, 12
15
45: 9
Jer. 22:13
34: 5, 7, 9
9, 10
35:14
Jer. 37: 8, 9
41:14, 18
47: 9
Eze. 27:19
36:34
48:18, 19
19
Hos. 6: 8
7: 1
Mic. 2: 1
Hab. 1: 5
Zeph. 2: 3
Zec. 13: 5−A

[a] pro ἐγγίζω.
[b] A διαλογίζομαι, S[3] διάζομαι.

ἐργαλεῖον, –λίον.
Exo. 27:19
39:10, 21
Exo. 39:21

ἐργασία.
Gen. 29:27
Exo. 26: 1
39: 1
Lev. 13:51
Nu. 31:20
Ruth 2:12
1 Ch. 6:48, 49
9:13
26: 8, 29
30
28:13, 20
2 Ch. 4:11, 22
8:16
15: 7
2 Ch. 24:12
31:21
34:13, 13
17
Ps. 103:23
106:23
Pro. 6: 8
Ecc. 9: 1
Isa. 1:31
41:24
Eze. 15: 3, 4, 5
5
Jon. 1: 8

ἐργάσιμος.
Lev. 13:48, 49
1 Sa. 20:19

ἐργάτις.
Proverbs 6: 8

ἐργοδιωκτέω.
2 Chronicles 8:10

ἐργοδιώκτης.
Exo. 3: 7
5: 6, 10
13
1 Ch. 23: 4
2 Ch. 2:18

ἔργον.
Gen. 2: 2, 2, 3
3:17
5:29
8:21
20: 9
39:11
40:17
46:33
47: 3
Exo. 1:11, 11
14 ter
2:23, 23
5: 4, 4, 5
9, 13
6: 9
12:16
18:20
20: 9, 10
23:12, 16
16, 24
24:10
26:31, 36
27: 4
28: 6, 11
14, 15
22, 28
35
30:35, 35
31: 3, 5, 5
14, 15
15
32:16
34:10
35: 2,2,21
24, 29
32, 33
35, 35
36: 1, 2, 3
4, 4, 5
Exo. 36: 7, 10
11, 15
15, 22
30, 35
37
37: 3,5,16
38:24, 25
39: 1, 21
23
40:27
Lev. 7:14
11:32
16:29
22:11 A[a]
23: 3, 3, 7
8, 21
25, 28
30, 31
35, 36
Nu. 3: 7,8,26
31, 36
4: 3,4,16
23, 27[b]
30, 31
33
35+A
39, 43
47 ter
49
7: 5
8:11, 15
19
24 A[c]
26
16:28
28:18, 25
26
29: 1,7,12
35
Deu. 2: 7
4:28
5:13, 14
11: 7
14:28
15:10
16: 8, 15
23:20
24:21
26: 6
27:15
28:12
30: 9
31:29
32: 4
33:11
Jos. 4:24[d]
24:29
Jud. 2: 7, 10
13:12 A[e]
16:11
19:16
1 Sa. 8:16
14:47−A
15: 9
20:19 A[f]
2 Sa. 23:20
1 Ki. (3) p 1 bis
5:16, 16
7: 2,2,6,6
7+A
7+A
8, 11
12+A
14, 15
19, 19
26, 31
32, 37
45
9:23 A
23 A
11:28
13:11
16: 7
18:36
2 Ki. 12:11, 14
15
19:18
22: 5, 5, 9
17
23:19
1 Ch. 9:19, 31
33
11:22
22:15, 15
23: 4, 24
28
25: 1, 1
29: 1
5−AB
6, 7
2 Ch. 3:10
4: 6
16: 5
17: 4, 13
20:37
23:18
24:12, 13
13
29:34, 35
31:21
32:19, 30
34:10, 10
12, 13
16+A
25
35: 2
Ezra 2:69
3: 8, 9
4:24
5: 8
6: 7, 22
10:13
Neh. 2:16
4:11, 15
16, 17
19, 21
22
5:16, 16
6: 3, 3, 9
Neh. 6:16
7:70, 71[g]
10:33
11:12
16 A
22
13:10, 30
Est. 3: 9+S[3]
Job 1: 3, 10
4:17
10: 3
11: 4, 11
13:27
14:15
21:16
22: 3
24:14
33: 9+A
34:21, 25
36: 3,9,23
24
37:11, 14
39:11
Psa. 8: 4, 7
9:17
16: 4
27: 4, 4, 5
5
32: 4, 15
43: 2
44: 2
45: 9
61:13
63:10
65: 3, 5
76:12, 13
77: 7
85: 8
89:16, 17
17+AS
91: 5, 6
94: 9
101:26
102:22
103:13, 23
24, 31
104: 1[h]
105:13, 35
39−A
106:22, 24
108:20
110: 2, 3, 6
7
113:12
117:17
134:15
137: 8
138:14
142: 5
144: 4,9,10
14, 17
Pro. 8:22
10:16
11:18
13:19
16: 2,4,11
18: 9
20: 6, 12
21: 8
22: 8,8,29
24:12, 12
29:33, 35
Cant. 7: 1
Isa. 2: 8
3:10, 11
24
5:12, 12
17: 8
19:14, 15
28:21, 21
29:15, 23
32:17
37:19
40:10
45:11
54:16
58:13
59: 6 ter
60:21
62:11

Isa. 64: 4, 8
65: 7, 22
66:18
19+S[1]
Jer. 1:16
7:13
10: 3,9,15
11: 4
17:22, 24
18: 3
25: 6
27:25, 29
28:10, 18
31:10, 30
33:13−S[1]
38:16
39:19
51: 8, 9 A[i]
Lam. 3:63
4: 2
Eze. 1:16
Eze. 6: 6+A
16:30
23:43
44:14
Dan. 2:49
3:12
30+A
4:34
8:27
Hos. 13: 2
14: 3
Joel 2:11, 20
Amos 8: 7
Jon. 3:10
Mic. 5:13
6:16
Nah. 2:13
Hab. 1: 5
3: 2, 17
Hag. 1:14
2:14, 17

[a] *pro* ἀρτός. [b] A ἄρτος.
[c] *pro* ἐνεργέω. [d] A χρόνος.
[e] *pro* ποίημα [f] *pro* ἐργάβ.
[g] B ἔτος. [h] S[1] μεγαλεῖος.
[i] *pro* κακός.

ἐρεθίζω.

Nu. 14: 8 B[a]
Deu. 21:20
Pro. 19: 7
25:23

[a] *pro* αἱρετίζω.

ἐρεθισμός.

Deu. 28:22
Deu. 31:27

ἐρεθιστής.

Deuteronomy 21:18

ἐρείδω.

Gen. 49: 6
Job 17:10[a]
Pro. 3:26
4: 4
5: 5
Pro. 9:12
11:16
24:63
29:23[b], 35
37[c]

[a] S[2] κρίνω. [b] B ἐρίζω, S[2] ἐγείρω.
[c] S ἐρίζω.

ἔρεισμα.

Proverbs 11:26

ἔρεος.

Lev. 13:47, 48, 52, 59−A

ἐρεύγομαι.

Lev. 11:10
Psa. 18: 3
144: 7 A[a]
Eze. 22:25 A[b]
Hos. 11:10
Amos 3: 4, 8

[a] *pro* ἐξερεύγομαι.
[b] *pro* ὠρύομαι.

ἐρευνάω.

Gen. 31:33, 33
35, 37
44:12[a]
Deu. 13:14[b]
Jud. 6:29[c]
2 Sa. 10: 3
1 Ki. 21: 6
2 Ki. 10:23
Pro. 20:27
Jer. 27:26
Joel 1: 7

[a] (A ἤραυνα.) [b] A ἐξερευνάω.
[c] A ἐκζητέω.

ἐρέω vide ἐρῶ.

ἐρημία.

Isa. 60:12
Eze. 35: 4, 9

ἐρημικός.

Psa. 101: 7
Psa. 119: 4

ἐρημίτης.

Job 11:12

ἔρημος.

Gen. 12: 9
13: 1, 3
14: 6
16: 7
21:14, 20
21
24:62
36:24
37:22
Exo. 3: 1, 18
4:27
5: 1, 3
7:16
8:20, 27
28
13:18, 20
14: 3, 11
12
15:22, 22
16: 1,3,10
14, 32
17: 1
18: 5
19: 1, 2
23:29, 31
Lev. 7:28
16:10, 21
22
26:31, 33
33
Nu. 1: 1, 19
3: 4, 14
9: 1, 5
10:12, 12
31
13: 1,4,18
22, 23
27
14: 2, 16
22, 25
29, 32
33, 33
35
15:32
16:13
20: 1, 4
21: 1,5,11
13, 20
23
23:28
24: 1
26:61, 64
65
27: 3, 14
14
32:13, 15
33: 6, 8, 8
11, 12
15, 16
36 *ter*
34: 3
Deu. 1: 1, 19
31, 40
2: 1, 7, 8
26
4:43
45+A
6: 4
7:22
8: 2, 15
16
9: 7, 28
11: 5, 24
29: 5
32:10, 51
34: 3
Jos. 1: 4
5: 5
12: 8
14:10
15: 1[a], 21
16: 1+A
1
20: 8
21:36, 42
24: 7
Jud. 1:16
8: 7, 16
Jud. 11:16, 18
22
20:42, 45
47
1 Sa. 4: 8
17:28 A
23:14, 14
24, 25
25
24: 2
25: 1, 4, 7
14, 21
26: 2, 2, 3
3
2 Sa. 2:24
15:18−A
23, 28
16: 2
17:16, 29
1 Ki. 2:34
(3) *p* 46
9:18 A
19: 4, 15
2 Ki. 2: 8
3: 8
1 Ch. 5: 9
6:78
12: 8
21:29
2 Ch. 1: 3
8: 4
20:16, 20
24
24: 9
26:10
Ezra 9: 9
Neh. 2:17
9:19, 21
Job 1:19
15:28
38:26
39: 6
Psa. 28: 8, 8
54: 8
62: 1, 2
64:13
67: 8
74: 7
77:15, 19
40
40 S[1 b]
52
94: 8
105: 9, 14
26
106: 4, 33
35
135:16
Pro. 9:12
21:19
Cant. 3: 6
Isa. 1: 7
5: 9, 17
6:11
13: 9
14:17, 23
15: 6−S[1]
16: 1, 8
8 AS[1 c]
17: 9
21: 1, 1
24:12
30: 6
32:15, 16
34:11
35: 1, 1, 2
6
40: 3
41:18
42:11
43:19, 20
44:26
48:21
49: 8, 19
50: 2
51: 3, 3−A
52: 9
54: 1
Isa. 58:12
61: 4, 4[d]
62: 4
63:13
64:10, 10
Jer. 2: 6, 15
24, 31
4:11, 26
27
7:34 S[e]
9: 2, 10
12, 26
12:10, 12
13:24
17: 6, 6
22: 6
23:10
27:12
29:14
31: 6
32:10
38: 2
40:10, 12[f]
41:22[g]
51: 2
Lam. 4: 3, 19[h]
5: 9
Eze. 5:14
6:14
13: 4
14: 8
19:13
20:10, 13
Eze. 20:13+A
13, 15
17, 18
21−A
23, 35
36
23:42
25:13
26:20
29: 9, 10
12 A[i]
30:12
33:28, 29
34:25
35: 3, 4, 7
12
14−A
15
36: 2, 33
35, 38
38: 8
Dan. 9:17
Hos. 2: 3, 14
9:10
13: 5, 15
Joel 1:19, 20
2:22
Amos 2:10
5:25
Zeph. 2:13
Hag. 1: 9
Zec. 14:10
Mal. 1: 3, 4[k]

[a] A ὅριον. [b] *pro* ἄνυδρος
[c] *pro* θάλασσα. [d] S[1] αἰώνιος.
[e] *pro* ἐρήμωσις. [f] A ἐρημόω.
[g] A ἄβατος. [h] A ὄρος.
[i] *pro* ἐρημόω. [k] AS[2] ἐρημόω.

ἐρημόω.

Gen. 47:19, 19
Lev. 26:22, 30
43
Jud. 16: 7 A[a]
8 A[a]
24[b]
2 Ki. 19:17
Ezra 4:15
Neh. 2: 3−S[1]
Job 14:11
Psa. 68:26
78: 7
Isa. 1: 7
6:11
11:15
23:13
24: 1, 10
33: 8
34:10
10+S[1]
37:18, 25
42:15−AS
44:27
49:17
Isa. 51:10
54: 3
60:12
Jer. 3: 2
10:25
28:36
33: 9
40:10
12 A[c]
Lam. 1:*a* 1
Eze. 26: 2, 19
29:12[d], 12
30: 7, 7[e], 7
32:15
33:24, 27
28, 29
35: 3, 7
36: 4 A[f]
10
38:12
Dan. 8:11
Amos 3:11
7: 9[b]
Mal. 1: 4 AS[2 e]

[a] *pro* διαφθείρω. [b] A ἐξερημόω.
[c] *pro* ἔρημος. [d] A ἔρημος.
[e] A ἀφανίζω. [f] *pro* ἐξερημόω.

ἐρήμωσις.

Lev. 26:34, 35
2 Ch. 30: 7
36:21−B
Psa. 72:19
Jer. 4: 7
7+S[1]
7:34[a]
Jer. 22: 5
32: 4
51: 6, 22
Dan. 8:13
9: 2, 27
27
12:11

[a] S ἔρημος.

ἐρίζω.

Gen. 26:35
1 Sa. 12:14, 15
2 Ki. 14:10
Pro. 29:23 B[a]
24 S[1 b]
37 S[a]

[a] *pro* ἐρείδω. [b] *pro* μερίζω.

ἔριθος.

Isaiah 38:12

ἐρικτός.

Leviticus 2:14

ἔριον.

Deu. 22:11
Jud. 6:37
Ps. 147: 5
Pro. 29:31
Isa. 1:18
Isa. 51: 8
Eze. 27:18
34: 3
44:17
Dan. 7: 9

ἐριστός.

(Exo. 39:21 B *pro* εἰς τά.)

ἔριφος.

Gen. 27: 9, 16
37:31
38:17, 20
23
Exo. 12: 5
Lev. 1:10
Jud. 6:19
13:15, 19
14: 6
Jud. 15: 1
1 Sa. 16:20
2 Ch. 35: 7, 8
Cant. 1: 8
Isa. 11: 6
Jer. 28:40
Eze. 43:22, 25
45:23
Amos 6: 4

ἑρμηνευτής.

Genesis 42:23

ἑρμηνεύω.

Ezra 4: 7
Job 42 *p* 18

ἑρπετόν.

Gen. 1:20, 21
24, 25
26, 28
30
6: 7, 19
20
7:14, 21
23
8: 1, 17
19
9: 3
Lev. 11:20, 21
23, 29
31, 41
42, 43
Lev. 11:44
20:25
22: 5
Deu. 4:18
14:18
1 Ki. 4:29
Ps. 103:25
148:10[a]
Isa. 16: 1
Eze. 8:10+A
38:20
Hos. 2:12, 18
4: 3
Hab. 1:14

[a] (S[1] ἑρπετινα.)

ἕρπω.

Gen. 1:26, 28
30
6:20
7: 8
8: 1−A
Lev. 11:41, 42
43, 46
Deu. 4:18
Psa. 68:35[a]
Eze. 38:20

[a] S[1] πέρας.

ἐρύθημα.

Isaiah 63: 1

ἐρυθροδανόω.

Exo. 25: 5
26:14
Exo. 35: 7, 23
39:21

ἐρυθρός.

Exo. 10:19
13:18
15: 4, 22
23:31
Nu. 14:25
21: 4
33:10, 11
Deu. 1: 1, 40
2: 1
11: 4
Jos. 2:10
4:23
24: 6−A
6
Jud. 11:16 A[a]
Neh. 9: 9
Ps. 105: 7,9,22
135:13, 15
Isa. 63: 2

[a] *pro* Σίφ.

ἐρυσίβη.

Deu. 28:42
1 Ki. 8:37
Psa. 77:46
Hos. 5: 7
Joel 1: 4
2:25

ἔρχομαι.

Gen. 10:19, 19
30
11:31
12: 5+A
13: 3, 10
18
14: 5, 7
16: 8
18:21, 22
19: 1, 22
22: 3, 9
23: 2
24:30, 41
42, 63
25:18, 29
26:27
27:30, 33[a]
35
29: 6, 9
30:38, 38
31:24
32: 6, 6, 8
11
33: 1, 14
18
18 A[b]
34: 5,7,20
35: 6:16
27
37:10, 10
14, 19
23, 25
35
39:16
41:14, 29
35, 50
54, 57
42: 5, 5, 6
10, 12
15, 29
43:20, 21
44:12
45:25
46: 1
47: 1, 1, 5
15, 18
48: 1, 2, 5
7, 7
49: 6, 10
50:18
Exo. 2: 8, 15
3: 1
13 A[c]
16
5:20
8:25
10:26
12:12 B[d]
15:23, 27
16: 1, 35
17: 6+A
8
18: 5 A[c]
16
19: 1, 2, 7
22: 9
33: 8 A[e]
35: 9
Lev. 13:16
25:22, 25
27:32
Nu. 11:26
13:23 AB[f]
24, 27
28
20: 1, 6
21: 1, 23
27
22: 7,9,14
16, 16
20, 37
39
25: 6
31:14, 21
33: 9
Deu. 1:19, 20
24, 31
9: 7

Deu. 11: 5[a]
12: 5[a]
13: 2
14:28
16: 7[g]
17: 3[a], 9
26: 3
28:15, 45
29: 7, 22
30: 1
33: 7[a], 16
Jos. 2: 1 A[e]
22
3: 1
8:11
19 B[e]
9:10, 12
23[h]
11: 7, 21
16: 6[i], 7[i]
18: 4 A[d]
20: 6 A
22:10
Jud. 2: 6[g]
3:27
4:14 A[c]
20
5:18, 23
6: 4, 5[k]
11, 18
7:13[a], 13
8: 4
9:26
27 A[c]
31[k]
37[k]
46[a], 52
11: 7
8 A[m]
12[n], 16
18[k], 33
34[a]
12: 1 A[o]
13: 6 A[e], 6
8, 9[k]
10
11−A
12, 17
14: 5[p]
15:14
17: 8[a], 9
18: 2[k], 7[k]
8[k]
9 A[e]
10[a]
13+A
13
19 A[r]
20[a], 27
19:10[k]
11[e]
13 A[t]
16[a]
17
22 A[e]
26
29+A
20: 3−A
4
10−A
11+A
26, 34[k]
21: 2[k], 8
22
Ruth 1: 2
19−AB
2: 3−B
4,7,12
3: 4, 7, 7
14
1 Sa. 1:19+A
2:13, 14
15, 27
31
3:10
4: 3,5,12
13
7: 1

1 Sa. 9: 5
13 A[e]
15, 16
10: 8,9,10
13, 22[a]
11: 4, 5, 9
9
12:12
14: 5,5,20
15: 5
16: 4, 11
17:12 A
20 A
22 A
34, 43
45
19:16, 22
23
20: 1,9,24
37
21: 1, 10
22: 1, 5
23:10, 13[u]
15 A[c]
27
24: 4
25: 9, 12
26, 33
40
26: 1, 10
27: 1 A[v], 9
28: 4, 8
29: 4, 8
30: 3,9,17
26
31: 4, 7, 8
2 Sa. 1: 2−A
2, 4, 23
29
3:20, 23[w]
24, 35
4: 4
5: 3, 13
20
7:14
11:10
27 A[d]
12: +ter
13: 5,6,24
30, 36
14: 3, 15
29, 31
32
15: 2, 4[x]
18, 28
32[a]
34 A[d]
16: 5, 14
16[a]
17:20, 27
18:27
19:10, 11
15, 15
20
20: 8 B[e]
12, 14
23:19, 23
24: 6, 7, 7
13[a], 18
21
1 Ki. 1:22
23+B
42 A[e]
49[g]
2:28, 30
8: 3+A
18, 31
41+A
9:28
10: 1,2,10
12, 13
14, 22
11:18, 18
43−A
12:1, 3+A
p 24 l 22
l 34
13:10, 11
12[h], 14
29+A

1 Ki. 14: 3 A
17:10−AB
18: 7[g]
46+A
19: 3, 4
20: 4+A
13 A[e]
21:43
22:15, 37
2 Ki. 1: 9+A
13
2: 2, 3, 4
15
3:20
4: 1, 7[y]
25
25−AB
25, 27
39+A
5: 6, 8, 9
15, 22
24
6: 4, 14
23, 32
32
7: 5, 6
8: 1,3,7,9
9:18, 19
20, 30
10: 2, 7, 8
12+A
21
13:20, 20
14:13
15:14
29−A
16: 6
11+A
12+A
18:17, 18
32
19: 3, 5
23[a], 28
33
20:17
24:10
25: 1, 2, 8
23, 25
1 Ch. 2:24, 55
4:39, 41
5: 9
7:22
10: 4, 7, 8
11: 1,3,18
21, 25
12: 1, 16
19, 22
23, 38
13: 9
14: 9
15:29
16:33
17:16
18: 5
19: 2, 3, 5
7, 7, 9
15[a], 15
17
20: 1
21:4,11,21
2 Ch. 1:13
5: 4
6:22, 32
32
8: 3, 18
9: 1, 1, 6
21
10: 1, 1, 3
3+B
5, 12
11: 1, 16
12: 3, 4, 5
13:13
14: 9, 11
16: 7
18:14
19:10
20: 1, 2, 4
12, 24
25 AB[c]

2 Ch. 21:12, 19
22: 7, 7[u]
23: 2
24:11, 23
25: 7, 10
14,18,18
28: 9, 12
20
30: 1,5,11
12, 25[z]
27
31: 8
32: 1, 1, 4
21[a]
34: 9
35:22
36: 5
Ezra 2: 2
68 AB[e]
3: 8, 8
4:12
5: 3, 16
7: 8, 9
8:15, 18
18, 31
32, 35[aa]
9:13[bb]
10: 8, 14
Neh. 1: 2
2: 7,9,11
19
4: 3,8,11
12
5:17[cc]
6:10
10+S[3]
17
7: 7+S[3]
9:33[rc]
13: 6,7,21
22
Est. 1:12[dd]
4: 2
11 S[e]
5: 4, 8
Job 1: 6,6,14
15, 15
16, 16
17, 17
18
19 A[ee]
19
2: 1, 1, 2
3: 4, 7, 9
25, 26
5:21[ff]
21+A
26[g]
6: 8
9:32
18: 9, 11
19:12
23: 3
27:13[gg]
28: 8 A[o]
29:13
31:32
33:28[h]
38:11, 16
22
42:11
p 18
Psa. 21:31
34: 8
35:12
43:18
47: 5[hh]
50: 2
51: 2, 2
53: 2
54: 6, 16
68: 3
70:18
78: 1
79: 3
95:13, 13
97: 8+AS[2]
101: 2
104:19, 31
34, 40

Ps. 117:26
118:41, 77
125: 6
Pro. 1:11, 26
27
27−C
2:10
5:10[a]
6:15
7:18
9: 5
14:12, 13
15
18: 3
21: 6+AS[2]
23:35
27:12 A[ee]
Ecc. 1: 4
2:16[ii]
6: 4
9:14
11: 8
12: 1
Cant. 2:10, 13
13
4: 8, 16
7: 1, 11
Isa. 1:12
5:19, 26
7:19[ks]
9: 8
13: 3, 5, 9
14: a1, 31
21: 1, 2, 9
23: 1, 10
27: 6, 11
28:15
30:27
32:10
15[mm]
36: 7 S[1 nn]
17
37: 5, 29
34
38: 1
39: 3, 6
40:10
41: 5, 25
44: 7
47:13
48: 5
49:12 AS[oo]
18
50: 2
63: 4 B[ee]
66: 7, 18
Jer. 2:10[pp]
4:16
6:22
7:10, 32
9:17
21 A[e]
25−S[1]
10:22
12: 9, 12
13:20
14: 3
16:14
17: 6,8,15
19: 6, 14
22: 8 S[1 d]
23
23: 5, 7
26:13, 20
21
27:26, 41
28:52, 56
61−S[1]
29: 4 AS[ee]
10
30: 2
31:12, 16
21
32:18
33: 2
34: 2
35: 9
37: 3
38:27, 31
38

Jer. 30: 7, 8
41:10 A[e]
43: 6
44: 4, 16
19
45:18 S[1 c]
25, 27
47: 4, 6, 8
10, 12
13
48: 1, 5
51: 8[qq]
52: 4,5,12
Lam. 1: 4
5: 4
Eze. 1: 4
2: 2
3:24
9: 2
14: 1, 4, 7
16:33
17:12
19: 9−A
20: 1, 3
21: 7,7,27
22: 3[rr]
23:17, 40
40
24:24
33: 4 A[ee]
3, 6, 6
21, 22
22, 31
33
36: 8
37: 9+A, 9
38: 8, 13
18
39:17

Eze. 43: 2
47: 8, 9[x]
Dan. 1: 1
2: 2, 24
3: 2
4: 5, 33
6:19
7:13, 22
8:5,6,17
17
9:13, 23
26
10.12, 13
14, 20
20
11:10[x]
10[ss]
Hos. 10: 9+A
12
Joel 2:31
Amos 4:2
5:17[x]
6: 3[tt]
7: 1
8:11
9:13
Jon. 1: 8
2: 8
Mic. 1: 9
Hab. 2: 3
Zec. 1:21
2:10
9: 9
12: 9[x]
14: 1, 16
18
Mal. 3: 1
4: 1, 1
4, 5

[a] A εἰσέρχομαι. [b] pro ἐπανέρχομαι. [c] pro ἐξέρχομαι. [d] pro διέρχομαι. [e] pro εἰσέρχομαι. [f] pro ἀπέρχομαι. [g] A ἀπέρχομαι. [h] A ἐξέρχομαι. [i] A διέρχομαι. [k] A παραγίνομαι. [m] pro ἐπιστρέφω. [n] A ἥκω. [o] pro παρέρχομαι. [p] A ἐκκλίνω. [q] A γίνομαι. [r] pro δεῦρο. [s] A εἰμί. [t] pro ἐγγίζω. [u] AB ἐξέρχομαι. [v] pro ἀνίημι. [w] AB ἄγω. [x] A ἐπέρχομαι. [y] A ἀνίστημι. [z] B εἰσέρχομαι. [aa] B διέρχομαι. [bb] S[3] εἰσέρχομαι. [cc] S[1] ἔχω. [dd] S[1] εἰσέρχομαι. [ee] pro ἐπέρχομαι. [ff] S ἐπέρχομαι. [gg] A ἐξέρχομαι, C ἐπέρχομαι. [hh] A[2]S διέρχομαι. [ii] AS[2] ἐπέρχομαι. [kk] S[1] ἐξέρχομαι. [mm] AS ἐπέρχομαι. [nn] pro λέγω. [oo] pro ἥκω. [pp] S διέρχομαι. [qq] AS εἰσέρχομαι. [rr] B[1] εἰσέρ. [ss] A ἄρχω. [tt] A εὔχομαι.

ἐρῶ, εἴρω, ἐρέω, ῥέω.

Gen. 10: 9
12:12
15:13
18: 5
31:16
32: 4, 18
20
37:20
41:28
42:14
43: 6
44: 4
45:21, 27
46:31, 34
Exo. 3:13, 13
14, 15
16, 18
4: 1,1,15
22
7: 9, 16
8: 1, 10
20
9: 1, 13
10:29

Exo. 12:27
13:14
14: 3
19: 3, 6
20.22
22:28
23:13[a]
22
33:17
Lev. 1: 2
12: 2
15: 2
17: 2,8,12
18: 2
19: 2, 14
21: 1
22:18
23: 2, 10
24:15
25: 2
27: 2
Nu. 5:12, 19
21, 22
6: 2

Nu. 8: 2
11:18
14:15
15: 2, 18
38
18:24, 26
30
21:27
23:23
24:13
28: 2, 3
33:51
34: 2
35:10
Deu. 4: 6
6:21
12:20[b]
20: 3, 8
21: 7, 20
22:16
25: 7, 8, 9
26: 3, 5
13
27:14*to*22
23
23 − A
24, 25
26
28:67, 67
29:22, 24
25
31:17
32: 7, 40
Jos. 1: 3
7: 8
8: 6
9:17
22:27, 28
Jud. 4:20
7:18
9:29
13:13[b]
16:15 A[c]
19:30 + A
21:22
1 Sa. 3:9 10:2
11: 9
16: 2
18:25
20: 6, 26[b]
25: 6
2 Sa. 5: 6, 8
7: 8
11:21, 25
13: 5
14:15
15:10
15 A[d]
34
16:10
19:13
1 Ki. 1:13, 34
2:31
9: 8, 9
12*p*24*l*36
*l*41, 52
2 Ki. 4:26
6: 7[b]
19: 6
10 + A
20: 5
22:18
1 Ch. 16:36
17: 7
21:10 A[d]
2 Ch. 7:21, 22
10:10
18:26
34:26
Est. 1: 1 S[1e]
Job 9:12
10: 2
11:10
15:18[f]
19:28, 29
20: 7
21:28
22:29
23: 5
32:11-BS[1]
Job 33:31 + A
34: 5, 34
35: 3 ACS[2]
36: 3
37:18
38:35
39:25 A[g]
Psa. 10: 1
34:10
41:10
51: 8
57:12
86: 5
90: 2
105:48
121: 1
125: 2
138:20
144: 6, 11
Pro. 5:12
8: 6
23:35
24:69
25: 7
Ecc. 1:10
7:27-AC[h]
8: 4
12: 1
Isa. 2: 3
3: 7
7: 4
8:17, 21
10: 9
12: 1, 4
14:4 + ABS
10, 16
24
19:11
20: 6
23:12
24:16
25: 9
29:11, 12
12, 15
16
37: 6, 10
41: 6, 7
26
43: 6
44: 5, 5 A[i]
20
45: 9
14 + A
49:20, 21
51:16
57:14
58: 9
65: 8, 24
Jer. 2:23, 27
3:12, 16
4:11
5:19
7:28, 32
8: 8
10:11
11: 3
13:12, 13
21
14:17
15: 2
16:11, 14
19
17:20
19: 3, 11
21: 3, 8
22: 2, 8, 9
23:33, 35
38, 7
28:35, 35[k]
62, 64
31:14
32:13, 14
16
33: 4
34: 3
36:24
38:23
41: 2
43:29
44: 7
Jer. 45:26
50:10
Lam. 2:15
Eze. 2: 4
3:11, 27
4:13
5: 4, 6
6: 3
12:19
13: 2 + A
2, 7, 12
18
14: 4
16: 3
17: 3
18:19
19: 2
20: 3, 5, 27
47
21: 3, 7, 9
28, 28
22: 3
24: 3
27 A[m]
25: 3
26:17
27: 3
28: 9
32: 2, 21
33: 2, 17
33
Eze. 30:35
37: 4, 19
21
38:11, 13
44: 6
Dan. 2:36
4:32
8:26
12: 6
Hos. 1:10
2: 7, 23
23
10: 3, 8
Joel 2:17
Amos 5:16
6:10 *ter*
Jon. 3: 7
Mic. 3: 1
4: 2
Nah. 3: 7
Hab. 2: 6
Zeph. 3:16
Zec. 1: 3
6:12
11:12
12: 5
13: 3, 5, 6
6, 9, 9
Mal. 1: 4, 5
3: 8[n]

[a] A λαλέω. [b] A εἶπον.
[c] *pro* λέγω. [d] *pro* αἱρέω.
[e] *pro* αἴρω. [f] A ἀναγγέλλω.
[g] *pro* λέγω. [h] S[2] εἶπον.
[i] *pro* βοάω. [k] A[2] ἐπί.
[m] *pro* λαλέω. [n] AS[3] εἶπον.

ἐρωδιός.

Lev. 11:19[a]
Deu. 14:15
Psa. 103:17

[a] AB[1] ἀρωδιός.

ἔρως.

Pro. 7:18
Pro. 24:51

ἐρωτάω.

Gen. 24:47, 57[a]
32:17, 29
29
37:15
40: 7
43: 6, 26
44:19
Exo. 3:13
13:14
Deu. 6:20
13:14
Jos. 4: 6, 21
Jud. 4:20
13: 6, 18
18: 5 B[b]
15[c]
20:18[a]
23[a]
1 Sa. 10: 4
17:22 A
19:22
22:10, 13[a]
15
23: 4 AB[b]
25: 5, 8
30:21
2 Sa. 5:19
8:10
20:18, 18
2 Sa. 20:18[d]
1 Ki. 12*p*24
*l*25[e]
1 Ch. 10:14 + A
14:10 BS[b]
14
18:10
Ezra 5: 9, 10
Neh. 1: 2
Job 12: 7[a]
21:29
38: 3
40: 2
42: 4
Psa. 34:11 AS[b]
121: 6
136: 3 S[1b]
Isa. 41:28
45:11
Jer. 6:16
18:13
23:33[f]
27: 5
31:19
37: 6
43:17
44:17[a]
45:14, 27
Dan. 2:27 B[b]

[a] A ἐπερωτάω. [b] *pro* ἐπερωτάω.
[c] A ἀσπάζομαι. [d] B ἐράω.
[e] B ἐπερωτάω. [f] S ἐπερωτάω.

ἐσβειέ, –βί.

Jeremiah 26:17

ἔσθησις.

Proverbs 8:10 + A

ἐσθίω, ἔσθω, ἔδω.

Gen. 6:21
39: 6
40:17
47:22
49:27
Exo. 12: 8, 9
11, 15
18, 20
20, 43
45, 48
13: 6, 7
16: 3, 12
22:31
23:11, 11
15
29:32, 33
33
Lev. 3:17
6:16, 16
18, 26
30, 30
7:13, 15
16
11:11, 34
40, 47
47
14:47
17:10, 13
14
19: 8, 8, 26
22: 4, 6
8 A[a]
16
23: 6
26:16
Nu. 11: 5
15:19
18:11, 13
31
24: 8
28:17 − A
Deu. 12:22, 22
15:22[b]
32:38
Jos. 24:13
Jud. 14: 9
14 + A
1 Sa. 1: 7, 8
9:13
14:30, 32
34
30:16
2 Sa. 9:10, 11
13
12: 3
19:28
1 Ki. 1:25
2: 7
1 Ki. (3)*p*46*bis*
4(20) A
(25) A
8:65
17:15
18:19
20: 5
22:27
2 Ki. 4:40, 41
42, 43
25:29
1 Ch. 12:39
2 Ch. 18:26
Job 1: 4
13 + AS[2]
18
5: 5
32:22
40:10
Psa. 13: 4 S[c]
40:10
52: 5 BS[1c]
105:20
126: 2
Pro. 1:31
13:25
18:21
23: 7
25:27
Ecc. 5:10
10:16
Isa. 9:20
24: 6
26:11
28: 8
29: 8
30:27
46: 1 A[d]
65: 4
66:17
Jer. 2: 3
19: 9, 9
21:14[e]
37:16[f], 16
52:33
Lam. 4: 5
Eze. 22: 9
45:21
Dan. 1:13, 15
4:30
7: 7, 19
Hos. 9: 4
Joel 2:26
Amos 6: 4
Nah. 3:12
Hab. 3:14
Zec. 7: 6
Jos. 7: 6
8:29
10:26
Jud. 19: 9, 16
20:23, 26
21: 2
Ruth 2: 7, 17
1 Sa. 14:24
23:24
2 Sa. 11: 2, 13
1 Ki. 22:35, 35
1 Ch. 16:40
23:30
2 Ch. 18:34
Ezra 3: 3
4:20 AB[b]
Job 4:20
7: 4, 4
Psa. 29: 6
54:18
58: 7, 15
64: 9
89: 6
103:23
Ecc. 11: 6
Isa. 17:14
21:13
Jer. 6: 4 A[c]
Eze. 12: 4, 7
24:18
33:22
46: 3
Dan. 6:14
8:14, 26
Zec. 14: 7

vide φάγω.

[a] *pro* φάγω. [b] A φάγω.
[c] *pro* κατεσθίω. [d] *pro* αἴρω.
[e] A κατέδω. [f] S ἐχθρός.

ἑσπέρα.

Gen. 1: 5, 8, 13
19, 23
31
8:11
19: 1
29:23
30:16
49:27
Exo. 12: 6, 18
18
16: 6, 8, 12
13
18:13 A[a]
27:21
Lev. 11:24, 25
26, 27
28, 31
32, 39
40, 40
14:46, 47
47
15: 5, 6, 7
Lev. 15: 8, 9, 10
10, 11
16, 17
18, 19
21, 22
23, 27
17:15
22: 6
23:32, 32
24: 3
Nu. 9: 3, 11
15, 21
19: 7, 8
10
11 + A[2]
19, 21
22
28: 4, 8
Deu. 16: 4, 6
23:11
28:67, 67
Jos. 5:10

[a] *pro* δείλη. [b] *pro* πέραν.
[c] *pro* ἡμέρα.

ἑσπερινός.

Lev. 23: 5
2 Ki. 16:15
Ezra 9: 4, 5
Ps. 140: 2
Pro. 7: 9
Dan. 9:21

ἕσπερος.

Job 9: 9
Job 38:32

ἑστιατορία.

2 Kings 25:30, 30

ἐσχάρα.

Exo. 27: 4, 4, 5
5
30: 3[a]
Lev. 2: 7
6:39
2 Ch. 4:11
Job 41:10
Pro. 26:21
Jer. 43:22, 23
23

[a] A ἐσχαρίς.

ἐσχαρίς.

Exo. 30: 3 A[a] [a] *pro* ἐσχάρα.

ἐσχαρίτης.

2 Samuel 6:19

ἐσχατίζω.

Jud. 5:28 A[a] [a] *pro* αἰσχύνω.

ἔσχατος.

Gen. 33: 2
49: 1
Exo. 4: 8 AB[a]
Lev. 23:16
27:18
Nu. 2:31
10:25
24:14
31: 2
Deu. 4:30
8:16
13: 9
17: 7
24: 5, 5
28:49
31:27, 29
29
32:20
34: 2
Jos. 1: 4
10:14
24:27
Jud. 15: 7[b]
Ruth 3:10
1 Sa. 29: 2
2 Sa. 2:26
13:15 − A
19:11, 12
23: 1
24:25
1 Ki. 9:26
17:13
1 Ch. 23:27
2 Ch. 9:29
12:15
16:11
20:34
25:26
26:22
28:26
35:27
Ezra 8:13
Neh. 5:15
8:18
Job 8: 7, 13
11: 7
18:20
23: 8
42:12
Psa. 72:17
134: 7
138: 5, 9
Pro. 5:11
19:20
23:32
25: 8
29:21, 44
Ecc. 1:11, 11
4:16
7: 8
10:13
Isa. 2: 2
8: 9
37:24

Isa. 41:22, 23
45:22
46:10
47: 7
48:20
49: 6
62:11
Jer. 6:22
9: 2
10:13
16:19
17:11
23:20
25:18
27:12, 41
28:16, 32
32:18
38: 8

Jer. 37:24
Lam. 1: 9
Eze. 35: 5
38: 6,8,15
16
39: 2
Dan. 2:28
8: 3, 19
23
10:14
11: 4, 29
12: 8
Hos. 3: 5
Joel 2:20
Jon. 2: 6
Mic. 4: 1
Hag. 2: 9
Zec. 14: 8

[a] *pro* δεύτερος. [b] A ἕκαστος.

ἔσω.

Gen. 39:11
Lev. 10:18[a]
Nu. 3:10
1 Ki. 6:15
(18) A
(22) A
7:22

2 Ki. 7:11
2 Ch. 4: 4
29:16, 18
Job 1:10
Eze. 9: 6
44:17+A

[a] A ἕως.

ἔσωθεν.

Gen. 6:14
Exo. 25:10
36:27
38: 2
Lev. 14:41
1 Ki. 6:15−B
15
16+A
18
7:17+A
46
2 Ki. 6:30
11:15

2 Ch. 3: 4
Psa. 44:14 AB[2] S[2 a]
Eze. 1:27+A
7:15
40: 9+A
9, 15
16, 16
19, 22
26, 43[b]
41:17
42:15
46: 2[b]

[a] *pro* Ἐσεβών. [b] A ἔξωθεν.

ἐσώτατος.

1 Ki. 6:17+A
25, 28
33

1 Ki. 7:36
49+A
Job 28:18

ἐσώτερος.

Exo. 26:33
Lev. 16: 2, 12
15
1 Sa. 24: 4
1 Ki. 6:27
1 Ch. 28:11, 20
2 Ch. 4:22
23:20
Est. 4:11[a]
Isa. 22:11
Eze. 8: 3+A
16

Eze. 10: 3
40:17, 23
27, 28
34, 44
44
41: 3, 17
42: 1[b], 3
43: 5
44:17, 17
21, 27
45:19
46: 1

[a] A ἐντός. [b] A ἐξώτερος.

ἐτάζω.

Gen. 12:17
Deu. 13:14−S[a]
1 Ch. 28: 9[a]
29:17
Est. 2:23[b]
Job 32:11

Job 33:27[c]
36:23
Psa. 7:10
138:23
Jer. 17:10
Lam. 3:39

[a] A ἐξετάζω. [b] S[3] ἀνετάζω.
[c] S[1] ἑτοιμάζω.

ἑταίρα.

Jud. 11: 2[a]
2 Sa. 13:16 B[b]

Pro. 19:13

[a] A ἕτερος. [b] *pro* ἕτερος.

ἑταῖρος.

Jud. 4:17−A

Jud. 14:11 A[a]
Jud. 14:20 A[b]
2 Sa. 13: 3
15:37[c]
16:17, 17
1 Ki. 2:22
4: 5
16:11+A
Job 30:29

Job 31:10 S[d]
Pro. 22:24
27:17[e]
Ecc. 4: 4[f]
Cant. 1: 7[g]
8:13[h]
Jer. 6:12 A[d]
8:10 A[d]

[a] *pro* κλητός. [b] *pro* φιλιάζω.
[c] A ἀρχιεταῖρος. [d] *pro* ἕτερος.
[e] AC ἕτερος. [f] AS ἕτερος.
[g] CS ἕτερος. [h] S ἕτερος.

ἔτασις.

Job 10:17
12: 6

Job 31:14

ἐτασμός.

Genesis 12:17

ἑτερόζυγος.

Leviticus 19:19

ἕτερος.

Gen. 4:25
8:10, 12
17:21
26:21, 22
29:19, 27
30
30:24
31:49, 49
37: 9, 9
41:19
42:13
43:21
Exo. 1: 8
16:15, 15
20: 3
22: 5
20 A[a]
23:13
26: 3 *qtr*
6,6,17
17
28: 7, 7
30: 9
34:14
Lev. 14:42[b], 42
27:20
Nu. 14: 4,4,24
36: 9
Deu. 4:28
5: 7
6:14
7: 4
8:19
11:16, 28
13: 2,6,13
17: 3
18:20
20: 5, 6, 7
24: 4
28:14, 30
32, 36
64
65−A
29:22, 26
28
30:17
Jos. 23:16
24: 2, 16
20[c]
Jud. 2:10, 12
17, 19
9:37[d]
10:13
11: 2 A[q]
34−A
Ruth 2: 8, 22
1 Sa. 8: 8
17:30 A
19:21
21: 9
26:19
28: 8

2 Sa. 13:16[e]
18:26, 26
1 Ki. 3:22
9: 6, 9 A[f]
11: 4 A[g]
10
14: 9 A
2 Ki. 5:17
17: 7, 35
37, 38
22:17
1 Ch. 2:26
16:20
23:17
2 Ch. 3:11, 11
12 A
12 A
7:19, 22
34:25 A[f]
Ezra 1:10
Neh. 2: 1
Job 1:16, 17
18 S[h]
18:19
30:24
31: 9, 10[i]
Psa. 47:14
77: 4, 6
101:19
104:13
108: 8
Pro. 27:17 AC[k]
Ecc. 4: 4 AS[k]
7:23
Cant. 1: 7 CS[k]
8:13 S[k]
Isa. 6: 3, 3
13: 8, 8
28:11
30:10
34:14, 14
16, 16
42: 8
44: 5, 25
47: 8, 10
10
48:11
Jer. 3: 1
5:19 A[f]
6:12[m]
8:10[m]
16:13
18: 4
24: 2
39:20, 39
39
42:15[n]
43:28, 32
51: 3, 5, 8
15+A
Eze. 1: 8+A
8+A

Eze. 1:23[o], 23[o]
3:13, 13
11:19
12: 3
17: 7
34:23 A[p]
42:14
44:19
Dan. 2:11, 39
44
3:29

Dan. 5:17
7: 6,8,20
24−B[1]
8: 3, 8−B
9: 2
11: 4
12: 5
Hos. 3: 3−B
Joel 1: 3
Amos 3:15
Zec. 2:3 11:7

[a] *pro* θάνατος. [b] AB στερεός.
[c] A ἀλλότριος. [d] A εἷς.
[e] B ἑταίρα. [f] *pro* ἀλλότριος.
[g] *pro* αὐτός. [h] *pro* ἄλλος.
[i] A ἄλλος, S ἑταῖρος.
[k] *pro* ἑταῖρος. [m] A ἑταῖρος.
[n] AS ἀλλότριος. [o] B ἑκάτερος.
[p] *pro* εἷς. [q] *pro* ἑταίρα.

ἔτι.

Gen. 44:28 A[a]
2 Sa. 18:18−A
1 Ki. (3) *p* 1[b]
22: 8 A[c]

Eze. 37:22[d]
Hos. 2:16[d]
Joel 2:27[d]

[a] *pro* ἄχρι νῦν. [b] (B ἔτει).
[c] *pro* εἷς. [d] A οὐκέτι.

ἑτοιμάζω.

Gen. 24:14, 31
44
43:15, 24
Exo. 15:17
16: 5
23:20
Nu. 23: 1,4,29
Jos. 1:11
9:10
1 Sa. 2: 3
7: 3
13:13
20:31
23:22
2 Sa. 5:12
7:12, 24
1 Ki. 2:12, 24
5:17
6:18+A
2 Ki. 12:11
1 Ch. 9:32
12:39
14: 2
15: 1,3,12
17:11
22: 3, 5, 5
14, 14
28: 2
29: 2,3,16
2 Ch. 1: 4
2: 7, 9
3: 1
8:16
12: 1
26:14
27: 6
29:19, 36
31:11, 11
35: 4,6,12
14, 14
15, 16
Ezra 3: 3
Est. 5:14
6: 4, 14
7: 9, 10
Job 12: 5
15:28
18:12
27:16
28:27
33:27 S[1 a]
38:25, 41

Job 41: 1
Psa. 7:13, 14
9: 8
10: 2
20:13
22: 5
23: 2
56: 7
64: 7, 10
67:11
77:19, 20
88: 3, 5
98: 4
102:19
118:60
73+S[1]
131:17
146: 8
Pro. 3:19
6: 8
8:27, 35
9: 2
16:13
19:29
21:31
23:12
24:42, 60
Isa. 14:21
21: 5, 5
28:24 S[1 b]
30:33
40: 3
44: 7
54:11
65:11
Jer. 26:14
28:12, 15
Eze. 4: 3, 7
20: 6[c]
21:20+A
28+A
38: 7, 7, 8
Dan. 12:11+A
Amos 4:12
Mic. 7: 3
Nah. 2: 6
3: 8−S[3]
8−S[3]
Hab. 2:12
Zeph. 1: 7
3: 7
Zec. 5:11

[a] *pro* ἐτάζω. [b] *pro* προετοιμάζω
[c] A ὄμνυμι.

ἑτοιμασία.

Ezra 2:68
3: 3

Psa. 9:38
64:10

Psa. 88:15
Eze. 43:11+A
Dan. 11: 7, 20

Dan. 11:21
Nah. 2: 4
Zec. 5:11

ἕτοιμος.

Exo. 15:17
19:11, 15
34: 2
Lev. 16:21−B[1]
Nu. 16:16
Deu. 32:35
Jos. 4: 3
8: 4
1 Sa. 13:21
23:23+A
26: 4
2 Sa. 23: 5
1 Ki. (3) 45
8:39, 43
49
2 Ch. 6: 2, 30

2 Ch. 6:33, 39
Est. 3:14
8:13
Psa. 16:12
32:14
37:18
56: 8, 8
92: 2
107: 2, 2
111: 7
Eze. 21:10, 11
11
Hos. 6: 3
Mic. 4: 1
6: 8

ἑτοίμως.

Ezra 7:17, 21
26

Dan. 3:15

ἔτος.

Gen. 5: 3, 4
5 *to* 23
25 *to* 28
30, 31
6: 1, 3
7: 6, 11
8:13
9:28, 29
11:10 *to* 26
32
12: 4
14: 4, 4, 5
15:13
16: 3, 16
17: 1, 17
24, 25
21: 5
23: 1
25: 7,7,17
17, 20
26
26:34
29:18, 20
27, 30
31:38
41 *ter*
35:28
37: 1
41: 1, 26
26, 27
27, 27
29, 30
34, 35
36, 46
47, 48
50, 53
54
45: 6,6,11
47: 8
9 *qtr*
18, 18
28, 28
50:22, 26
Exo. 6:16, 18
18, 20
20
7: 7, 7
12:40, 41
16:35
21: 2, 2
23:10
11+A
40:15
Lev. 19:23, 24
25
25: 3, 3, 4
8 *qtr*
10, 11
13−A
15−A
16

Lev. 25:16−A
20, 21
21, 22
22, 27
28, 40
50 *ter*
51, 52
52, 54[a]
27: 5, 18
Nu. 1: 1, 18
4: 3, 3
9: 1
13:23
14:33, 34
32:13
33:38, 39
Deu. 1: 3
2: 7, 14
8: 4
14:27
15: 1,9,12
18
26:12
29: 5
31: 2, 10
32: 7
34: 7
Jos. 5: 5
14: 7, 10
10
24:30, 33
Jud. 2: 8
3: 8, 11
14, 30
4: 3
5:31
6: 1
8:28
9:22
10: 2, 3, 8
11:26
12: 7,9,11
14
13: 1
15:20
16:31
Ruth 1: 4
1 Sa. 2: 9
4:15; 18
7: 2
29: 3
2 Sa. 2:10, 10
11
4: 4
5: 4, 4, 5
5
13:38
14:28
15: 7
19:32, 34[b]
35

2 Sa. 21: 1
24:13
1 Ki. 2:11 *ter*
12+A
(3)1,38,39
5:17
6: 1, 1, 4
5+A
7:39
8: 1−A
9:10
10:22
11:42
12 *p*24 *l*3
ll 4, 28
14:20 A, 21
15: 1, 2
8−A
9 A[c]
10, 25
25, 28
33, 33
16: 6+AB
8+A
8
10+A
15+A
15 B[d]
23 *ter*
p 28−A
p 28−A
p 28−A
29, 29
17: 1
22: 1, 41
42, 42
52, 52
2 Ki. 1:18, 18
18+A
3: 1−A
1
8: 1, 2, 3
16, 17
17, 25
26
9:29
10:36
11: 3, 4, 21
12: 1, 1, 6
13: 1, 1-A
1, 10
10−A
10
14: 1, 2, 2
17, 21
23, 23
15: 1
1+A
2, 2, 8
8+A
13, 17
17, 23
23, 27
27, 30
32, 33
33
16: 1, 2, 2
17: 1, 1, 5
6
18: 1, 2, 2
9, 10
10, 13
19:29, 29
20: 6
21: 1, 1, 19
19
22: 1, 1, 3
23:23, 31
36, 36
24: 1, 8, 12
18 A[c]
18
25: 1, 2, 27
1 Ch. 2:21
8: 4−6
4
20: 1
21:12
26:31
29:27 *ter*

2 Ch. 3: 2
8: 1
9:21, 30
11:17, 17
12: 2, 13
13
13: 1, 2
14: 1, 6
15:10, 19
16: 1, 12
13
17: 7−AB
7
18: 2
20:31, 31
21: 5, 5, 20
20−A
22: 2, 12
23: 1
24: 1, 1, 15
25: 1, 1, 25
26: 1, 3, 3
27: 1, 1, 5
8 A
8 A
28: 1, 1-A
29: 1, 1
33: 1, 1, 21
21
34: 1, 1, 3
3, 8
35:19
36: 2, 5, 5
5, 9
11
11−AB
11
21, 22
Ezra 1: 1
3: 8
4:24
5:11, 13
6: 3, 15
7: 7, 8
Neh. 1: 1
2: 1
5:14 *ter*
7:71 B[e]
9:21, 30[f]
10:31
13: 6
Est. 1: 3
2:16
3: 7
8: 9[g]
Job 10: 5
15:20
16:22
32: 8
36:11, 26
38:21
42:16, 16
Psa. 30:11
60: 7
76: 6
77:33
89: 4, 5, 9
10 *ter*
15
94:10
101:23, 28
Pro. 3: 2, 16
4:10
9:11, 18
10:27
13:23
Ecc. 6: 3, 3, 6
11: 8
12: 1−S[1]
Isa. 5: 6+S[1]
7: 8
14:28
16:14, 14
20: 1
3−AS
3
23:15, 15
16
36: 1
38: 5, 10

Isa. 65:20, 20
Jer. 1: 2, 3
25: 1−S[1]
3, 3, 11
12
26: 2
28:59
35: 1, 3
36:10
41:14, 14
43: 9
46: 1 A[h], 2
52: 1, 1, 4
5, 31
Eze. 1: 1, 2
8: 1
20: 1
22: 4
24: 1
26: 1
29: 1, 11
12−A
13, 17
30:20
31: 1
32: 1, 17
33:21

Eze. 38: 8+A
8, 17
39: 9
40: 1, 1
46:17
Dan. 1: 1, 5
21
2: 1
3: 1
5:31
7: 1
8: 1
9: 1
2+A
2[i], 2
10: 1
11: 1, 6
Joel 2: 2, 25
Amos 1: 1
2:10
5:25
Hab. 3: 2
Hag. 1: 1
2: 1, 10
Zec. 1: 1, 7, 12
7: 1, 3, 5
Mal. 3: 4, 9[k]

[a] A ἐνιαυτός. [b] B ἡμέρα. [c] *pro* ἐνιαυτός. [d] *pro* ἡμέρα. [e] *pro* ἔργον. [f] S[1] ἔθνος. [g] A μήν. [h] *pro* μήν. [i] A ἡμέρα. [k] S[1] ἔθνος.

εὖ.

Gen. 12:13, 16
32: 9, 12
40:14
Exo. 1:20
20:12−A
Nu. 10:29, 32
Deu. 4:40
5:16, 29, 33
6:3, 18, 24[a]
8:16
10:13
12:25, 28
15:16
19:13

Deu. 22: 7
28:63
30: 5
Jos. 24:20
Ruth 3: 1
Job 24:21−A
Pro. 3:27
27+A
Isa. 41:23
53:11
Jer. 7:23−S[1]
13:23
Eze. 21:15, 15
36:11

[a] A πολυήμερος.

εὐαγγελία.

2 Sa. 18:20, 27 | 2 Ki. 7: 9

εὐαγγελίζομαι.

1 Sa. 31: 9
2 Sa. 1:20
4:10
18:19, 20
20, 26
31
1 Ki. 1:42
1 Ch. 10: 9
Psa. 39:10

Psa. 67:12
95: 2
Isa. 40: 9, 9
52: 7, 7
60: 6
61: 1
Jer. 20:15
Joel 2:32
Nah. 1:14

εὐαγγέλιον.

2 Sa. 4:10 | 2 Sa. 18:22, 25

εὐάλωτος.

Proverbs 24:63

εὐαρεστέω.

Gen. 5:22, 24
6: 9
17: 1
24:40
39: 4
48:15

Exo. 21: 8
Jud. 10:16+A
Psa. 25: 3
34:14
55:14
114: 9

ἐυάρμοστος.

Ezekiel 33:32

εὖγε.

Job 31:29
29+AC
39:25

Psa. 34:21, 21
25, 25
39:16, 16

Psa. 69: 4, 4
Eze. 6:11, 11
26: 2

Eze. 36: 2
2+A

εὐγένεια.

Ecc. 7: 8[a]

[a] AS εὐτονία.

εὐγενής.

Job 1: 3

εὔγνωστος.

Pro. 3:15
5: 6

Pro. 26:26

εὐδοκέω.

Gen. 24:26, 48
33:10
Lev. 26:34, 34
41
Jud. 11:17[a]
15: 7+A
18[b]
19:10[a]
25[a]
20:13[c]
2 Sa. 22:20
1 Ch. 29: 3, 23
2 Ch. 10: 7
Job 14: 6
Psa. 39:14
43: 4
48:14AS[2 d]
50:18, 21

Psa. 67:17
76: 8
84: 2
101:15
118:108[e]
118:10, 11
119: 4
150 *p* 6
Ecc. 9: 7
Isa. 54:17 A[f]
62: 4−AS
Jer. 2:19
36 S[1 f]
14:10 AS[f]
12
Hab. 2: 4
Hag. 1: 8
Mal. 2:17

[a] A θέλω. [b] A δίδωμι. [c] A ἀκούω. [d] *pro* εὐλογέω. [e] S[1] εὐλογέω. [f] *pro* εὐοδόω.

εὐδοκία.

1 Ch. 16:10
Psa. 5:13
18:15
50:20
68:14

Psa. 88:18
105: 4
140: 5
141:16
Cant. 6: 3

εὐδοκιμέω.

Genesis 43:22

εὐεκτέω.

Proverbs 17:22

εὔελπις.

Proverbs 19:18

εὐεργεσία.

Psalm 77:11

εὐεργετέω.

Psa. 12: 6
56: 3

Psa. 114: 7

εὔζωνος.

Jos. 1:14 | Jos. 4:13

εὐήκοος.

Proverbs 25:12

εὔηχος.

Job 30: 7 | Psa. 150: 5

εὐθαλέω.

Daniel 4: 1

εὐθαλής.

Daniel 4:18

εὔθετος.

Psalm 31: 6

εὐθέως.

Jos. 6:11 | Job 5: 3

εὐθηνέω.

Job 21: 9, 23
Psa. 67:18
72:12
122: 4
127: 3
Jer. 12: 1

Jer. 17: 8
Lam. 1: 5
Eze. 17: 6 A[a]
Dan. 4: 1
Hos. 10: 1
Zec. 7: 7

[a] *pro* ἀσθενέω.

εὐθηνία.

Gen. 41:29, 31
34, 47
48, 53
Psa. 29: 7

Ps. 121: 6, 7
Eze. 16:49
Dan. 11:21, 24

εὐθής *vide* εὐθύς.

εὐθύνω.

Nu. 22:23
Jos. 24:23
Jud. 14: 7[a]

1 Sa. 18:20, 26
Pro. 20:24

[a] A ἀρέσκω.

εὐθύς, εὐθής.

Gen. 15: 4
24:45
33:12
38:29
Nu. 23: 3
Jos. 8:14
Jud. 14: 3[a]
17: 6[b]
21:25
1 Sa. 12:23
29: 6
2 Sa. 1:18
17: 4
19: 6, 18
1 Ki. 11:33, 38
14: 8 A
15: 5, 11
16 *p* 28−A
20:23, 25
22:43
2 Ki. 10: 3, 15
30
12: 2
14: 3
15: 3[b], 34
16: 2
18: 3
22: 2
1 Ch. 13: 4
2 Ch. 14: 2
20:32
24: 2
25: 2
26: 4
27: 2
28: 1
29: 2
31:20
34: 2
Ezra 8:21
Neh. 9:13
Est. 8: 5+S[3]
Job 3:11
Psa. 7:11
10: 2
18: 9
24: 8, 21

Psa. 26:11
31:11
32: 1, 4
35:11
36:14
48:15
50:12
57: 2
63:11
72: 1
77:37
91:16
93:15
96:11
106: 7, 42
110: 1
111: 2, 4
118:137
124: 4+S[1]
4
139:14
142:10
Pro. 2:13, 16
19, 21
11: 3 A
11+AS[2]
20:11
21:29
27:21
28:10
29:10
Ecc. 7:30
Isa. 26: 7
33:15
40: 3, 4
42:16
45:13
59:14
Jer. 3: 2
41:15
Eze. 23:40
33:17, 17
20
46: 9
Dan. 11:17
Hos. 14: 9

[a] A ἀρέσκω. [b] A ἀγαθός.

εὐθύτης.

Jos. 24:14
1 Ki. 3: 6
9: 4
Psa. 9: 9
10: 7
16: 2−S[1]

Psa. 25:12
36:37
44: 7
66: 5
74: 3
95:10

Psa. 97: 9
98: 4
110: 8
118: 7
Ecc. 12:10
Cant. 1: 4
7: 9
Dan. 6:22

εὐιλατεύω.

Deu. 29:20 | Psa. 102: 3

εὐίλατος.

Psalm 98: 8

εὐκαιρία.

Psa. 9:10, 22 | Psa. 144:15

εὔκαιρος.

Psa. 103:27[a]

[a] A καιρός.

εὐκαταφρόνητος.

Jeremiah 20:16

εὐκλεής.

Jeremiah 31:17

εὐκληματέω.

Hosea 10: 1

εὔκολος.

2 Samuel 15: 3

εὐλάβεια.

Jos. 22:24 | Pro. 28:14

εὐλαβέομαι.

Exo. 3: 6
Deu. 2: 4
1 S. 18:15, 29
Job 3:25 A[a]
6:16 A[b]
13:25
19:29
Pro. 2: 8
24:28
Isa. 51:12+AS
57:11
Jer. 4: 1
5:22
15:17
22:25
Nah. 1: 7
Hab. 2:20
Zeph. 1: 7
3:12
Zec. 2:13
Mal. 3:16

[a] pro φροντίζω.
[b] pro διευλαβέομαι.

εὐλαβής.

Lev. 15:31 | Mic. 7: 2 AE[?a]

[a] pro εὐσεβής.

εὔλαλος.

Job 11: 2

εὐλογέω.

Gen. 1:22, 28
2: 3
5: 2
9: 1
12: 2, 2[a]
3, 3
3 A[b]
14:19, 19
17:16, 16
20
22:17, 17
24: 1, 35
48, 60
25:11
26: 3, 4[c]
12, 24
29[a]
27: 4, 7, 10
19, 23
25, 27
27, 29
29, 30
31, 33
33, 34
Gen. 27:38, 41
28: 1, 3, 6
6
30:27, 30
31:55
32:26, 29
35: 9
39: 5
43:27[a]
47: 7, 10
48: 3, 9, 15
16, 20
20
49:25, 28
28
Exo. 12:32
20:11, 24
23:25
39:23
Lev. 9:22, 23
Nu. 6:23, 24
27
22: 6, 6, 12
23:11, 20
Nu. 23:20, 25
25
24: 1, 9, 9
10, 10
Deu. 1:11
2: 7
7:13, 13
8:10
12: 7
14:23, 28
15: 4, 4, 6
10, 14
18
16:10+A
15
18: 5
21: 5
23:20
24:15, 21
26:15
27:12
28: 3, 3, 4
5, 6[a]
6[b], 12
30: 9[d], 16
33: 1, 11
20, 24[e]
Jos. 9: 6
14:13
17:14
22: 6, 7, 33
24:10
Jud. 5: 2, 9, 24
24
9:19+A
13:24
17: 2 A[f]
Ruth 2: 4, 19
3:10
1 Sa. 2: 9, 20
9:13
13:10
23:21
25:14, 33
26:25
2 Sa. 2: 5
6:11, 12
18, 20
20
7:29, 29
8:10
13:25
14:22
19:39
21: 3
24:23
1 Ki. 1:47
(3)45
8:14, 55
66
10: 9
20:10−B
13
2 Ki. 4:29, 29
10:15
1 Ch. 4:10, 10
13:14
16: 2, 36
43
17:27 ter
18:10
26: 5
29:10, 20
20
2 Ch. 6: 3
9: 8
20:26
30:27
31: 8, 10
Neh. 8: 6
9: 5, 5
Neh. 11: 2
Job 1:10, 11
21
2: 5
11: 3
29:13
31:20
42:12
Psa. 5:13
15: 7
25:12
27: 9
28:11
33: 2
36:22
44: 3
48:14[g], 19
61: 5
62: 5
64:12
65: 8
66: 2, 7, 8
67:27
71:15, 17
17[h]
19 S[2][f]
95: 2
102: 1, 2, 20
21, 22
22
103: 1, 35
106:38
108:28
111: 2
112: 2
113:20 ter
21, 23
26
117:26, 26
118:108 S[1][i]
127: 4, 5
128: 8
131:15, 15
133: 1, 2, 3
134:19, 19
20, 20
144: 1, 2, 10
21
147: 2
Pro. 3:33
11:25
20:21
22: 8
24:34
27:14
28:20
29:48
Isa. 12: 1
19:24, 25
25
25: 3, 3
4+AS
36:16
38:18, 19
20
43:20
51: 2
61: 9
64:11
65:16, 16[k]
23
Jer. 4: 2
17: 7
38:23
Eze. 3:12
Dan. 2:19, 20
3:23
4:31
5: 4+AB[2]
Hag. 2:19

[a] A εὐλογητός.
[b] pro ἐνευλογέω.
[c] A ἐνευλογέω.
[d] A πολυωρέω.
[e] B εὐλογητός.
[f] pro εὐλογητός.
[g] AS[2] εὐδοκέω.
[h] S[2] ἐνευλογέω.
[i] pro εὐδοκέω.
[k] S[1] ἐλλογέω.

εὐλογητός.

Gen. 9:26
Gen. 12: 2 A[a]
Gen. 14:20
24:27, 31
26:29 A[a]
43:27 A[a]
Exo. 18:10
Deu. 7:14
28: 6 A[a]
6 A[a]
33:24 B[a]
Jud. 17: 2[b]
Ruth 2:20
4:14
1 Sa. 15:13
25:32, 33
39
2 Sa. 6:21−A
18:28
22:47
1 Ki. 1:48
5: 7
8:15, 56
1 Ch. 29:10
2 Ch. 2:12
6: 4
Ezra 7:27
Psa. 17:47
27: 6
30:22
40:14
65:20
67:20, 20
36
71:18, 19[c]
88:53
105:48
118:12
123: 6
134:21
143: 1
Dan. 3:28
Zec. 11: 5

[a] pro εὐλογέω.
[b] A εὐλογέω.
[c] S[2] εὐλογέω.

εὐλογία.

Gen. 27:12, 35
36, 36
38, 41
28: 4
33:11
39: 5
49:25 ter
26 ter
28
Exo. 32:29
Lev. 25:21
Nu. 23:11
Deu. 11:26, 27
29
12:15
16:17
23: 5
28: 2, 8
30: 1, 19
19 A[a]
33: 1, 13
23
Jos. 9: 7
15:19
24:10
Jud. 1:15
1 Sa. 25:27
30:26+A
2 Sa. 7:29
2 Ki. 5:15
18:31
1 Ch. 5: 1, 2
2 Ch. 20:26, 26
Neh. 9: 5
13: 2
Job 29:13
Psa. 3: 9
20: 4, 7
23: 5
36:26
83: 7
108:17
128: 8
132: 3
Pro. 10: 6, 22
11:11+AB[a]S[2]
26
24:10
Isa. 27: 9
44: 3
65: 8
Eze. 34:26
44:30
Joel 2:14
Zec. 8:13
Mal. 2: 2, 2
3:10

[a] pro ζωή.

εὐμεγέθης.

1 Samuel 9: 2

εὐμετάβολος.

Proverbs 17:20

εὐμήκης.

Deuteronomy 9: 2

εὔνοια.

Est. 2:23 | Est. 6: 4

εὐνοῦχος.

Gen. 39: 1
40: 2, 7
1 Sa. 8:15
1 Ki. 22: 9
2 Ki. 8: 6
9:32
20:18
23:11
24:12, 15
25:19
1 Ch. 28: 1−AB
2 Ch. 18: 8
Neh. 1:11 BS[1][b]
Est. 1:10, 12
15
21 S[1][a]
2: 3, 14
15, 21
23
4: 4, 5
6: 2, 14
7: 9
Isa. 56: 3, 4
Jer. 36: 2
48:16
52:25

[a] pro Μουχαῖος.
[b] pro οἰνοχόος.

εὐοδία.

Proverbs 25:15

εὐοδιάζω.

Zechariah 9:17

εὔοδος.

Nu. 14:41
Pro. 11: 9
Pro. 13:13

εὐοδόω.

Gen. 24:12, 21
27, 40
42, 48
56
39: 3, 23
Deu. 28:29
Jos. 1: 8, 8
Jud. 4: 8
18: 5[a]
1 Ki. 22:12, 15
1 Ch. 13: 2
22:11, 13
2 Ch. 7:11
13:12
14: 7
18:11, 14
20:20
24:20
2 Ch. 26: 5
31:21
32:30
35:13
Ezra 5: 8
Neh. 1:11
2:20
Ps. 117:25
Pro. 17: 8[b]
28:13
Isa. 46:11
48:15
54:17[c]
55:11
Jer. 2:36[d]
12: 1
14:10[e]
Dan. 8:12[a]

[a] A κατευοδόω.
[b] S ἀδικέω.
[c] A εὐδοκέω.
[d] S[1] εὐδοκέω.
[e] AS εὐδοκεω.

εὐόδως.

Proverbs 24:64

εὐπαθέω.

Job 21:23 | Psa. 91:16

εὐπάρυφος.

Eze. 23:12[a]

[a] A εὐπάρφυρος.

εὐποιέω vide εὖ et ποιέω.

εὐπορέω.

Lev. 25:26[a] | Lev. 25:28[b], 49

[a] A εὑρίσκω.
[b] AB εὑρίσκω.

εὐπορία.

2 Ki. 25:10 A[a]

[a] pro δύναμις.

εὐπόρφυρος.

Eze. 23:12 A[a]

[a] pro εὐπάρυφος.

εὐπρέπεια.

2 Sa. 15:25
Job 5:24+A
36:11
Psa. 25: 8
49: 2
92: 1
Ps. 103: 1[a]
Pro. 29:44
Jer. 23: 9
Lam. 1: 6
Eze. 16:14

[a] AS[2] μεγαλοπρέπεια.

εὐπρεπής.

2 Sa. 1:23
23: 1
1 Ki. 8:53[a]
Job 18:15
Eze. 32:19+A
Zec. 10: 3

[a] AB ἐκπρεπής.

εὐπρόσωπος.

Genesis 12:11

εὑρετής.

Proverbs 10:20

εὑρετός.

Judges 9: 6—A

εὕρημα.

Jer. 45: 2
46:18
Jer. 51:35

εὔριζος.

Psalm 47: 3

εὑρίσκω.

Gen. 2:20
4:14, 15
5:24
6: 8
8: 9
11: 2
16: 7
18: 3,26A[a]
28, 29
30
30+A
31
31—A
32
19:19
26:12, 19
32
27:20
30:14, 27
31:32, 33
33, 35
37
32: 5, 19
33: 8, 10
15
34:11
36:24
37:15, 17
32
38:20, 22
23
39: 4
41:38
44: 6, 8, 9
10, 12
16, 16
17, 34
47:14, 25
29
50: 4
Exo. 5:11
9:19—AB
12:19
14: 9
15:22
16:25, 27
21:17
22: 2, 4, 6
7, 8
33:13, 13
16, 17
34: 9
35:23, 24
Lev. 5:11
6: 3, 4
12: 8
14:21, 22
30, 32
25:26 A[b]
26
28 AB[b]
47
Nu. 6:21
11:11, 15
15:32, 33
20:14
31:50
32: 5
35:27
Deu. 4:29, 30
17: 2
18:10
20:11
21: 1, 17
22: 3, 14
Deu. 22:17, 20
22, 23
25, 27
28, 28
24: 3, 3
28: 2
31:17, 17
21+A
Jos. 2:22
10:17
Jud. 1: 5A[c]
5:30
6:12 A[d]
13, 17
9:33
14:12
18 A[e]
15:15
17: 8, 9
18: 9 A[f]
20:48, 48
21:12
Ruth 1: 9
2: 2, 10
13
3: 1 A[g]
1 Sa. 1:18
9: 4, 4, 8
11, 13
13, 20
10: 2, 2, 3
7, 16
21
12: 5
13:15, 16
19, 22
22
14:17, 30
16:22
20: 3, 15[h]
21, 29
36
21: 3
23:17
24:20
25: 8,8,28
26:18
27: 5
29: 3, 6, 8
30:11
31: 3
8—A
2 Sa. 7:27
14:22
15:25
16: 4
17:12, 20
20: 6
1 Ki. 1: 3, 52
11:19, 29
12p24l45
13:14, 24
28
14:13 A
15:18
18: 5, 10
12—B
19:19
20:20, 20
21:36
37—A
2 Ki. 2:16 D[i]
17
4:29, 39
7: 9
2 Ki. 9:21, 35
10:13, 15[k]
12: 5,9,10
18
14:14
16: 8
17: 4
18:15
19: 4, 8
20:13
22: 8,9,13
23:2,18A[m]
24
25:19, 19
1 Ch. 4:40, 41
10: 3, 8
17:25
20: 2
24: 4
26:31
28: 9
29: 8, 17
2 Ch. 2:17
5:11
15: 2,4,15
19: 3
20:16, 25
21:17
22: 8
25: 5
13 B[n]
24
29:16, 29
30:21, 25
31: 1
32: 4
34:14, 15
17, 21
30, 32
33
35: 7, 17
18, 19
Ezra 2:62
4:15, 19
6: 2
7:16
8:15, 25
10:18—S[1]
Neh. 5: 8
7: 5, 5
64
8:14
9: 8, 32
13: 1
Est. 1: 5
2: 9, 15
17
5: 8
6: 2
7: 3
8: 5
Job 11: 7
12:12+A
17:10—S[2]
19:28
20: 8
23: 3
28:12, 13
20
32:13
33:10
34:11
37:12—A
22
39:30
42:15
Psa. 9:36
16: 3
20: 9, 9
35: 3
36:10, 36
45: 2
68:21
72:10
75: 6
83: 4
88:21
106: 4
114: 3, 3
Ps. 118:143
162
131: 5, 6
Pro. 1:28
2: 5, 20
3: 3, 13
4:22
5: 4
7:15
8: 9, 17
12: 2
14: 6
16: 5,5,31
18:22, 22
19: 7, 8
20: 6
21:21
24:14
25:16
29:28
Ecc. 3:11
7:15, 25
27, 28
28, 29
29, 29
30
8:17 ter
9:10, 15
11: 1
12:10
Cant. 3: 1, 2, 3
4
4+S
5: 6, 7, 8
8: 1, 10
Isa. 30:14
34:14
35: 9
37:36
41:12
48:17
51: 3
55: 6
58: 3
59: 5
65: 1,8,18
Jer. 2: 5, 24
34, 34
5: 1, 26
6:16
10:18
11: 9
14: 3
27: 7, 20
24
31:27
36:13—S
38: 2
48: 3,8,12
49:16
51:33
52:25, 25
Lam. 1: 3,6,19
2:16
Eze. 22:30
27:33
28:15
Dan. 1:19, 20
2:25, 35
5:11, 14
27
6: 4, 4, 5
11, 22
23
11:19
12: 1+A
Hos. 2: 6, 7
5: 6
6: 3
9:10
12: 4, 8, 8
14: 8
Amos 2:16
8:12
Jon. 1: 3
Mic. 1:13
Zeph. 3:13
Zec. 12: 5
Mal. 2: 6

[a] pro εἰμί. [b] pro εὐπορέω. [c] pro καταλαμβάνω. [d] pro ὁράω. [e] pro γινώσκω. [f] pro εἰδέω. [g] pro ζητέω. [h] A ἐξαίρω. [i] pro αἴρω. [k] B λαμβάνω. [m] pro ῥύομαι. [n] pro πορεύω.

εὖρος.

Exo. 25:22
26: 2—A[a]
8
27: 1, 12
13, 18
28:16
30: 2
36:16
37: 2, 16
38: 4 A[a]
Deu. 3:11
2 Ch. 3: 3
8 A[b]
4: 1
6:13
Job 11: 9
38:18
Eze. 40:11, 21
25, 27
Eze. 40:29, 33
36, 47
48, 49
41: 2 ter
4 A[b]
4, 5, 7
9, 10
11, 12
14, 22
42:11, 20
43:13, 14
14, 17
45: 1, 3, 5
6
46:22
48: 8,9,13
13
Dan. 3: 1

[a] pro εὐρύς. [b] pro μῆκος.

εὐρύς.

Exodus 38: 4[a], 10, 24

[a] A εὖρος.

εὐρυχωρία.

Genesis 26:22

εὐρύχωρος.

Jud. 18:10 A[a]
2 Ch. 18: 9
Psa. 30: 9
103:25
Isa. 30:23
33:21
Hos. 4:16

[a] pro πλατύς.

εὐρωτιάω.

Joshua 9:11—A

εὐσέβεια.

Pro. 1: 7
13:11
Isa. 11: 2
33: 6

εὐσεβής.

Job 32: 3A[1]S[1a]
Pro. 12:12[b]
13:19
Ecc. 3:16
Isa. 24:16
26: 7, 7[c]
32: 8
Mic. 7: 2[d]

[a] pro ἀσεβής. [b] B ἀσεβής. [c] S[1] ἀσεβής. [d] AB[2] εὐλαβής.

εὔσημος.

Psalm 80: 4

εὔσκιος.

Jeremiah 11:16

εὐσταθέω.

Jeremiah 30: 9

εὐστόχως.

1 Ki. 22:34
2 Ch. 18:33

εὐστροφία.

Proverbs 14:35

εὐσυναλλάκτως.

Proverbs 25:10

εὐσχήμων.

Proverbs 11:25

εὐτάκτως.

Proverbs 24:62

εὐτονία.

Ecc. 7: 8 AS[a]

[a] pro εὐγένεια

εὐτόνως.

Joshua 6: 8

εὐφραίνω.

Lev. 23:40
Deu. 12: 7, 12
18
14:20+A[2]
25—A
16:11, 14
15
20: 6, 6
24: 7
26:11, 12[a]
27: 7
28:30, 63
63
30: 9, 9
32:43, 43
33:18
Jud. 5:11 A[b]
9:13[c], 19
19
16:23
19: 3[d]
1 Sa. 2: 1
6:13
11: 9, 15
16: 5
2 Sa. 1:20
1 Ki. 1:40, 45
4(20)A
8:65
1 Ch. 16:10, 31
33
29: 9, 9
2 Ch. 6:41
7:10
15:14
20:27
23:13, 21
29:36
30:25
Ezra 6:22
Neh. 12:43 ter
Est. 5: 9, 14
(9)15+S[3]
Job 21:12
31:25
Psa. 5:12
9: 3
13: 7
15: 9
18: 9
20: 2, 7
29: 2
30: 8
31:11
32:21
33: 3
34:15, 27
39:17
42: 4
44: 9
45: 5
47:12
52: 7
57:11
62:12
63:11
64:11
65: 6
66: 5
67: 4
68:33
69: 5
72:21[e]
76: 4
84: 7
85: 4, 11
86: 7
Psa. 88:43
89:14
14—BS[1]
91: 5
93:19 AS[2 f]
95:11
96: 1,8,12
103:15, 31
34
104: 3, 38
105: 5
106:30, 42
108:28
112: 9
117:24
118:74
121: 1
125: 3
149: 2
Pro. 2:14
8:30
31 A[g]
31 BS[g]
10: 1
12:20, 25
14:10
15:13, 20
16: 1
17:21, 21
22
22:18
23:15, 24
25
27:11
29: 2,3,25
44
Ecc. 2:10
3:12, 22
4:16
5:18
8:15
10:19
11: 8, 9
Cant. 1: 4
Isa. 9: 3, 3
3+AS
17
12: 6
14: 8, 29
16:10
24: 7, 14
25: 9
26:19
28:22
26—S[1]
30:29, 29
35: 1
41:16
42:11, 11
44:23
45: 8
49:13
52: 8
54: 1
56: 7
61:10
62: 5, 5
65:13, 19
66:10
Jer. 7:34
20:15
27:11
38: 7, 12
13
Lam. 2:17
4:21
Eze. 23:41[h]

Hos. 7: 3
9: 1
Joel 2:21, 23
Amos 6:13
Hab. 1:16
Zeph. 3:14, 17
Zec. 2:10
8:19[i]
10: 7

[a] A ἐμπίπλημι. [b] pro ὑδρεύω.
[c] A εὐφροσύνη. [d] A πάρειμι.
[e] S[2] ἐκκαίω. [f] pro ἀγαπάω.
[g] pro ἐνευφραίνομαι.
[h] A ἐξευφραίνω. [i] S[1] εἰμί.

εὐφροσύνη.

Gen. 31:27
Nu. 10:10
Deu. 28:47
Jud. 9:13 A[a]
2 Sa. 6:12
1 Ki. 1:40
1 Ch. 12:40
15:16, 25
29:17
2 Ch. 20:27
23:18
29:30
30:21, 23
26
Ezra 3:12, 13
13 A[b]
6:16, 22
Neh. 8:12, 17
12:27
43 + S[3]
43, 44
Est. 1: 4
(9)16
17 − S[1]
17 − S[1]
9:17, 18
19
19 + ABS
22
Job 3: 7
20: 5
Psa. 4: 8
15:11
29:12
44:16
50:10
67: 4
96:11
99: 2
104:43
105: 5
136: 6
Pro. 10:28
14:13
21:15, 17
24:67
29: 6
Ecc. 2: 1, 2, 3
10, 26
5:19
7: 5
8:15
9: 7
Cant. 3:11
Isa. 9: 3
12: 3
14: 7, 11
16:10
22:13
24: 8
11
11 − ABS
25: 6
29:19, 19
32:13, 14
35: 7, 10
10, 10
44:23
48:20
49:13
51: 3, 11
11
52: 9
55:12
60:15
61: 3, 7, 10
10
65:14, 18
18
66: 5
Jer. 15:16
16: 9
25:10
31:33
38:13 A[c]
40: 9, 11
Lam. 2:15
Eze. 35:14
36: 5
Hos. 2:11
Joel 1: 5, 16
Zeph. 3:17
17 S[1 d]
Zec. 8:19

[a] pro εὐφραίνω. [b] pro φωνή.
[c] pro χαρμονή. [d] pro ἀγάπησις.

εὐχάριστος.

Proverbs 11:16

εὐχερής.

Proverbs 14: 6

εὐχερῶς.

Pro. 12:24[a] [a] A ἐχθρός.

εὐχή.

Gen. 28:20
31:13
Lev. 7: 6
22:21, 23
29
23:38
27: 2
Nu. 6: 2, 4
5 + A
6, 7, 8
9, 12
12, 13
Nu. 6:18, 19[a]
21, 21
15: 3, 8
21: 2
29:39
30: 3, 4, 5
5, 6, 7
8, 9, 10
11, 12
13, 14
15
Deu. 12: 6 − AB
Deu. 12:17, 26
23:17 + A
18, 21
Jud. 11:30, 39
1 Sa. 1:11, 21
2: 9
2 Sa. 15: 7, 8
1 Ki. 2:23 A[b]
Job 6: 70[c]
11:17
16:17
22:27
Psa. 21:26
40:14
55:13
60: 6 S[2 d]
Psa. 60: 9
64: 2
65:13
115: 5 − AS
9
Pro. 7:14
15: 8, 29
19:13
24:70
Ecc. 5: 3
Isa. 19:21
Jer. 11:15
Jon. 1:16
2: 8 BS[1 d]
Nah. 1:15
Mal. 1:14

[a] A κεφαλή. [b] pro ψυχή.
[c] pro ὀργή. [d] pro προσευχή.

εὔχομαι.

Gen. 28:20
31:13
Exo. 8: 8, 9, 28
29, 30
9:28
10:18
Lev. 27: 2, 8
Nu. 6: 2, 5, 13
18, 19
20, 21
21, 21
11: 2
21: 2, 7, 7
30: 3, 4, 10
Deu. 9:20, 26
12:11, 17
23:21, 22
23
Jud. 11:30, 39
1 Sa. 1:11
2: 9
2 Sa. 15: 7, 8
2 Ki. 20: 2
Job 22:27
33:26
42: 8, 10
Psa. 73:12
131: 2
Pro. 20:25
Ecc. 5: 3, 3, 4
4
Isa. 19:21
Jer. 7:16 − A
22:27
Amos 6: 3 A[a]
Jon. 1:16
2:10

[a] pro ἔρχομαι.

εὔχρηστος.

Proverbs 29:31

εὔψυχος.

Proverbs 24:66

εὐώδης.

Exodus 30:23, 23 − A[1]

εὐωδία.

Gen. 8:21
Exo. 29:18, 25
41
Lev. 1: 9, 13
17
2: 2, 9, 12
3: 5, 11
16
4:31
6:15, 21
8:21, 28
17: 4, 6
23:13, 18
Nu. 15: 3, 5, 7,
Nu. 15:10, 13
14, 24
18:17
28: 2, 6, 8
13, 24
27
29: 2, 6, 8
11, 13
36
Ezra 6:10
Eze. 6:13
16:19
20:28, 41
Dan. 2:46

εὐώνυμος.

Exo. 14:22, 29
Nu. 20:17
Jos. 13: 3
23: 6
2 Sa. 16: 6
1 Ki. 22:19
2 Ki. 11:11
2 Ch. 3:17
4: 8
Neh. 8: 4 A[a]
Cant. 2: 6
8: 3
Eze. 16:46
21:16
Zec. 4: 3
11 − S[1]
12: 6

[a] pro ἀριστερός.

ἐφαδανῶ

Dan. 11:45[a] [a] A ἐνφανδ-

ἐφάλλομαι.

1 Sa. 10: 6
11: 6 − A
1 Sa. 16:13

ἐφαμαρτάνω.

Jeremiah 39:35

ἐφάπτω.

Amos 6: 3
Amos 9: 5

ἐφέλκω.

Nu. 9:19
Jos. 24:29

ἔφηλος.

Leviticus 21:20

ἐφημερία.

1 Ch. 9:33
23: 6
25: 8
26:12
28: 1, 13
21
2 Ch. 5:11
13:10
2 Ch. 23: 8, 18
31: 2, 2, 15
16, 17
35: 4
Neh. 12: 8, 24
24
13:30

ἐφθός.

Nu. 6:19
1 Sa. 2:15

ἐφίστημι.

Gen. 24:43[a]
Exo. 1:11
7:23
Lev. 17:10
19:16
20: 3, 5, 6
26:16[b], 17
Nu. 1:50
14:14
23: 6, 17
26: 9 A[c]
Jos. 6:26, 26
7:26
8:29
Jud. 3:19[i]
Ruth 2: 5, 6
1 Sa. 17:51
22:17
2 Sa. 1:10
8: 3
22:40[e]
1 Ki. (3) p 46
16:34
2 Ki. 4:38
1 Ch. 18: 3
Neh. 6: 1
8:13
Job 11: 9 + A
Job 14:20
26:11 A[f]
Pro. 9:18
22:17
23: 5
27:23
Isa. 1:26
3: 4
21: 4
41:22
63: 5[g]
Jer. 5:27[h]
20:10 S[1 c]
21: 2
26:14
27:44
28:12, 27
29:20
36:10
51:11
Eze. 24: 3
31:15
44:24
Amos 9: 1
Obad. 14[i]
Hag. 2: 5
Zec. 1:10, 11

[a] A?S ἵστημι. [b] AB ἐπισυνίστημι.
[c] pro ἐπισυνίστημι.
[d] A παραστήκω. [e] AB ἐπανίστημι.
[f] pro πετάννυμι. [g] S ἵστημι.
[h] S συνίστημι.
[i] A ἵστημι, S[1] ἀφίστημι.

ἐφοδεύω.

Deuteronomy 1:22

ἐφοδιάζω.

Deu. 15:14
Jos. 9:18

ἐφόδιος.

Deuteronomy 15:14

ἐφοράω.

Job 21:16[a]
22:12
28:24
31:23
Ps. 112: 6
Ps. 137: 6
Eze. 8:12 A[b]
9: 9 − A
Zec. 9: 1

[a] A καθαρός. [b] pro ὁράω.

ἐφούδ, ἐφώδ.

Jud. 8:27
Jud. 17: 5

Jud. 18:14
17 + A
18, 20
1 Sa. 2:18, 28
14: 3
18
1 Sa. 14:18 − A
22:18
23: 6, 9
30: 7
8 + A

ἐχθές.

Gen. 31: 5
Jos. 3: 4
20: 5 A
Ruth 2:11
1 Sa. 4: 7
10:11
14:21
19: 7
20:27
1 Sa. 21: 5
2 Sa. 5: 2
15:20
2 Ki. 9:26
13: 5
1 Ch. 11: 2
Job 30: 3
Psa. 89: 4
Dan. 6: 8 AB[1 a]

vide χθές.
[a] pro ἐκτίθημι.

ἔχθρα.

Gen. 3:15
Nu. 35:20, 22
Pro. 6:35
10:18
15:17
25:10
Pro. 26:26
Isa. 63:10
Jer. 9: 8
Eze. 35: 5, 11
Mic. 2: 8

ἐχθραίνω.

Nu. 25:17, 18
Deu. 2: 9, 19
Psa. 3: 8
34:19

ἐχθρεύω.

Exo. 23:22
Nu. 33:55
1 Sa. 18:29 + A

ἐχθρία.

Genesis 26:21

ἐχθρός.

Gen. 14:20
49: 8
Exo. 15: 6, 9
23: 4, 5, 22
Lev. 26: 7, 8, 17
25, 32
34, 36
37, 38
39, 41
44
Nu. 10: 9, 35
14:42
23:11
24: 8, 8, 10
18
32:21
35:23
Deu. 1:42
6:19
12:10
20: 1, 3, 4
14
21:10
23: 9, 14
25:19
28: 7, 25
31, 48
53, 55
57, 68
30: 7
32:27, 31
41, 42[a]
43
33: 7, 11
27, 29
Jos. 7: 8, 12
12, 13
10:13, 19
25
13:28 − A
21:44, 44
22: 8
23: 1
Jud. 2:14[b], 14
18[c]
Jud. 3:28
5:31
8:34 A[d]
11:36
16:23, 24
1 Sa. 2: 1
4: 3
10: 1
12:10, 11
14:24, 30
47
18:25 − A
19:17
20:15, 15
22: 8, 13
24: 5, 20
25:26, 29
26: 8
29: 8
30:26
2 Sa. 3:18
4: 8 *ter*
5:20
7: 1, 9, 11
12:14
18:19, 32
19: 9
22: 1, 4, 18
38, 41
49 − A
24:13
1 Ki. 3:11
8:33, 37
44, 46
46 + A
48
20:20
2 Ki. 17:39
21:14, 14
1 Ch. 12:17
14:11
17: 8, 10
21:12, 12
22: 9
2 Ch. 6:24, 28

2 Ch. 6:34, 36
36
20:27
25: 8
Ezra 8:22, 31
Neh. 4:10, 15
5: 9
6: 1, 16
9:28
Est. 7: 6
9:10, 22
Job 6:23−A
8:22
19:11−S[1]
22:25
27: 7
31:29
34:26+A
36:16
38:23
Psa. 5: 9
6: 8, 11
7: 5, 6, 7
8: 3, 3
9: 4, 7, 14
26
12: 3, 5
16: 9, 14
17: 1, 4, 18
21+ABS
38, 41
40
20: 9
24: 2, 10
26: 2, 6
11
29: 2
30: 9, 12
16
34:24+S[1]
36:20
37:17−S[1]
20
40: 3, 6, 8
12
41:10
11 AS[2][d]
42: 2
43: 6, 11
14+A
17
44: 6
53: 7, 9
54: 4, 13
55: 8, 10
58: 2, 11
60: 4
63: 2
65: 3
67: 2, 22
24
68: 5, 10
70:10
71: 9
73: 3, 10
18
76: 5−S[2]
77:53, 61
66
79: 7
80:15, 16
82: 3
88:11, 23

Psa. 88:24, 43[e]
43, 52
91:10+A[2]S
10, 12
96: 3
101: 9
104:24
105:10, 41[f]
42
106: 2
107:14[g]
109: 1, 2
111: 8
117: 7
118:98, 139
126: 5
131:18
135:24
137: 7
138:21, 22
142: 3, 9
12
Pro. 6: 1
12:24 A[h]
15:28
20:22
24:17
25:21
26:24, 25
27: 6
Isa. 1:24
9:11
11:13
42:13
62: 8
Jer. 6:25
12: 7
15: 9, 11
14
18:17
19: 7, 9
20: 4, 5
21: 7
23:16
26:10
27: 7
28:35 S[1]
37:14
16 S[k]
16
38:16
41:20, 21
51:30, 30
Lam. 1: 2, 5, 7
9, 16
21
2: 3, 4, 5
7[m], 16
17, 22
3:45, 51
4:12
Eze. 35: 5
36: 2
39:23
Dan. 4:16
Hos. 8: 3
Amos 9: 4
Mic. 4:10
5: 9
7: 6, 8, 10
Nah. 1: 2, 8
3:11, 13
Zeph. 3:15

a A ἔθνος. b A προνομεύω.
c A κριτής. d pro θλίβω.
e AS[V] θλίβω. f S ἔθνος.
g A θλίβω. h pro [illegible].
i pro μόχθος. k pro ἔσθω.
m B αὐτοῦ.

ἐχῖνος.

Isa. 13:22
14:23
Isa. 34:11, 15
Zeph. 2:14

ἔχω.

Gen. 1:29, 30
Gen. 7:23
Gen. 8:11
16: 4, 5, 11
18:10, 31
19:15
23: 8
24:15, 45
34:14
37:24
38:23, 24
25
41:23, 38
43:25, 26
44:19
49:23
Exo. 2: 2+A
21:22
26: 3[a]
28:28, 30
33:12
36: 2, 31
Lev. 6:10
11:21
21:23
22:20, 22
25:27 AB[e][b]
30
Nu. 2: 2, 5, 7
12, 14
17, 20
22, 27
29, 34
7: 9
16: 3
19: 2
15+AB[f]
22: 5, 11
29
27:18
34: 3
Deu. 2:25
4:38
11:30
24:17
28:30
30:20
Jos. 5: 8
6: 8
8:20−A
17:17
Jud. 4:11
6:20−A
9:37
13: 3+A
5, 7
18: 7−A
19:14
1 Sa. 4:18
19: 3
23: 6
2 Sa. 11: 5
13:23
14:30
15:18−A
16:13
21: 1
1 Ki. 1: 9
7:22
9:26
13:23
14:10 A
2 Ki. 8:12
15:16
1 Ch. 2:32
10: 8
23: 2, 6
27:34
28:12
2 Ch. 11:21
13:20
18:16
Neh. 2: 6
3:23
4: 3, 12
18
5:17 S[1][c]
8: 4, 10
9:33 S[1][c]
Est. 3:11
4: 2
(9)15
Job 1:11, 14
2: 3
4:11, 21
6: 5
10:13
17: 8, 9
18:14, 20
19:20
20:18+A
21: 6, 10
17
24: 8
27:10
30: 9, 16
31:16, 35
42:10+A
Psa. 16: 2−B
37:15
67:26
93:15
113:13, 13
14, 14
15, 15
134:16, 16
17
17+A
17+A
17+A
139: 6
140: 6
Pro. 1: 9 A[d], 22
3:27
6: 7
7:10
12:10
13: 5, 7
16:32+AC[2]S[2]
18: 2
20: 9
22:27
23: 3
24:5, 36, 37
26:12
27:24, 25
28:23
29:20
Ecc. 7:13+S[a]
10:20−B
Cant. 2:14
8: 8
Isa. 1:30
3: 6, 24
6: 5, 5, 6
7:14 AS[c]
8: 6
13: 8, 16
17
27:11
28: 2−S[1]
31: 9
37: 3
40:11
43: 8
45: 9
47:14
53: 2
54: 1
55: 1
57: 8
62:11
Jer. 3: 3−S
9: 8
15:18
17: 5
18:15
27:42
45:19
49:16
Eze. 1: 8+A
15, 19
3:13 8:11
9: 1, 2, 3
10: 6, 9, 9
9+A
16
16+A
19
11:22
12: 2, 2
Eze. 17: 3
34: 4
40:43
41:22
42: 1, 1, 6
43: 6, 8
44:18, 18
48:13, 18
21
Dan. 3:15, 16
4: 5
6+A
5: 4+AB[2]
7: 4+AB[2]
8: 6, 17[f]
20
10: 4
8 A[g]
Dan. 10:16
11:13 A[h]
Hos. 4: 6
7:11
8: 7
13:11
14: 1
Amos 1: 3, 13
2: 8
3: 4
5:20
6:13
Mic. 1:11
Nah. 3:12
Hab. 1:14
Zec. 5: 9
8: 4
9:11

a A συνέχω. b vide ὑπερέχω.
c pro ἔρχομαι. d pro δέχομαι.
e pro λαμβάνω. f A ἀνὰ μέσον.
g pro δόξα. h pro ἄγω.

ἕψημα, ἕψεμα.

Gen. 25:29, 30
34
2 Ki. 4:38, 39
2 Ki. 4:40
Hag. 2:12

ἕψω.

Gen. 25:29
Exo. 12: 9
16:23, 23
23:19
29:31
34:26[a]
Lev. 6:28, 28
8:31
Nu. 11: 8
Deu. 14:20
16: 7
1 Sa. 2:13
1 Sa. 9:24
2 Sa. 13: 8
1 Ki. 19:21
2 Ki. 4:38
6:29
1 Ch. 2:30
2 Ch. 35:13
Lam. 4:10
Eze. 24: 5
46:20, 24
Zec. 14:21

a B προσφέρω.

ἐωθινός.

Exo. 14:24
1 Sa. 11:11[a]
Psa. 21: 1
Amos 7: 1
Jon. 4: 7

a A πρωϊνός.

ἕωλος.

Eze. 4:14[a]

a A[2]B* βέβηλος.

ἕως.

Lev. 10:18 A[a]
1 Ch. 5:10 AB[b]
1 Ch. 17:24−ABS

a pro ἔσω. b pro αὐτῶν.

ἑωσφόρος.

1 Sa. 30:17
Job 3: 9
11:17
38:12
Job 41: 9
Ps. 108: 9
109: 3
Isa. 14:12

ζάκχος.

1 Chronicles 28:11, 20

ζάω.

Gen. 1:20, 24
2: 7, 19
3:20, 22
5: 3
4−A[2]
5, 6, 7
9, 10
12, 13
15, 16
18, 19
21, 25
26, 27
28, 30
8:21
9: 3, 10
Gen. 9:12, 15
16, 28
11:11 to 26
12:13
17:18
19:19, 20
20: 7
21:19
25: 6, 7
26:19
27:40, 46
31:32
35:28
42: 2, 18
43: 6, 7, 26
Gen. 43:27
45: 3, 26
28
46:30
47:19
50:22
Exo. 4:18
19:13
21:35
22: 4
33:20
Lev. 11:10
13:10, 14
14: 4, 5, 6
6, 6, 7
49, 50
51, 51
52, 52
53
16:10, 20
21, 21
18: 5, 18
25:35, 36
Nu. 4:19
5:17
14:21, 21
28, 38
16:30, 33
48
19:17
21: 8, 9
24:23
Deu. 4: 1, 4, 10
33, 33
42
5: 3, 24
26, 26
6:24
8: 1, 3, 3
11: 8
12: 1, 19
16:20
19: 4, 5
30: 6, 16
19
31:13, 27
32:39, 40
33: 6
Jos. 3:10
4:14
8:23
9:27
Jud. 8:19
15:19[a]
17:10 A[b]
Ruth 2:20
3:13
1 Sa. 1:26, 28
5:12
10:24
14:39, 45
15: 8, 9
17:26 A
36
55 A
19: 6
20: 3, 3
14, 21
31
25:26, 26
34
26:10, 16
28:10
29: 6
2 Sa. 1:10
2:27
4: 9
11:11
12: 5, 18
21, 22
22
14:11, 19
15:21, 21
34
16:16
18:14
18−A
19: 6
20: 3
22:47
1 Ki. 1:25, 29
31, 34
39
2:24
(3) p 1
3:22+A
22, 23
23, 25
26
26+A
8:40
12: 6
p 24 l 26
17: 1, 12
22+A
23
18:10, 15
20:15
21:18, 18
32, 32
22:14
2 Ki. 1: 2
2: 2, 2, 4
4, 6, 6
3:14
4:7, 16, 17
30, 30
5:16, 20
7: 4, 12
8: 8, 9
10 A[b]
10, 14
10:14
14+A
19
21−A
11:12
13:21
14:17
18:32
19: 4, 16
20: 1
2 Ch. 6:31
10: 6
18:13
23:11
25:25
Neh. 2: 3
5: 2
6:11
9:29
Est. 6:13
Job 7:16
8:17
12:10
14:14
18:19
21: 7
27: 2
33:31+A
39:29 S[1][c]
42:16, 16
Psa. 17:47
21:27, 30
26:13
37:20
38: 6
40: 3−B
41: 3
48:10
51: 7
54:16
55:14
57:10
68:29, 33
71:15
83: 3
88:49
113:26
114: 9
117:17
118:17, 25
37, 40
50[f], 77
88, 93
107, 116
144, 149
154, 156
159
170 A[e]

Ps. 118:175
170 S[c]
123: 3
137: 7
141: 6
142: 2, 11
Pro. 1:12
3:22
9: 6 + S^2
11, 18
25:25 S^1[f]
28:16
Ecc. 4: 2,2,15
6: 3, 6
7: 3, 15
9: 4, 4, 5
10:19
11: 8
Cant. 4:15
Isa. 8:19
37: 4, 17
38: 1
11 – AS
16, 19
49:18
55: 3
Jer. 2:13 AS^2[b]
4: 2
5: 2
11:19
12:16
16:14, 15
21: 9, 9
22:24
23: 7, 8
26:18
29, 12, 12
42: 7
45: 2
2 – A
16, 17
17, 20
51:26
52:33
Lam. 3:38
4:20
Eze. 3:18[g], 21

Eze. 5:11
7:13 + A
13:19, 22[e]
14:16, 18
20
16:22, 48
17:10, 19
18: 3, 9, 13
17, 19
21, 22
23, 28
32 + A
20: 3, 11
13 + A
13, 21
25, 31
33
33:10, 11
11
13 + A
15, 16
19, 27
34: 8
35: 6, 11
37: 3, 6, 9
10, 14
47: 9 *ter*
Dan. 2: 4, 30
3: 9
4:14, 31
5:10
6: 6, 20
21, 26
12: 7
Hos. 1:10
4:15
6: 2
14: 7
Amos 5: 4, 6, 14
8:14, 14
Jon. 4: 3, 8
Hab. 2: 4
Zeph. 2: 9
Zec. 1: 5
13: 3
14: 8

[a] A ἀναψύχω. [b] *pro* ζωή. [c] *pro* ζητέω. [d] S^1 ἐκκλίνω. [e] *pro* ῥύομαι. [f] *pro* διψάω. [g] A ζητέω.

Eze. 5:13
8: 5 + A
16:38, 42
23:25
35:11 + A
36: 6

Eze. 38:19
Zeph. 1:18
3: 8
Zec. 1:14
8: 2

[a] A ζυγός.

ζέα.

Isaiah 28:25

ζέμα, ζέμμα.

Jud. 20: 6 – A
Eze. 24:13 + A

ζεύγνυμι.

Gen. 46:29
Exo. 14: 6
1 Sa. 6: 7, 10
2 Sa. 20: 8
1 Ki. 18:44
2 Ki. 9:21, 21

ζεῦγος.

Lev. 5:11
Jud. 17:10 A[a]
19: 3, 10
2 Sa. 10: 1
1 Ki. 19:19[b], 21
2 Ki. 5:17
9:25
Job 1: 3, 14
42:12
Isa. 5:10

[a] *pro* στολή. [b] A βοῦς.

ζέω.

Exo. 16:20 A^2[a]
Job 32:19[b]
Eze. 24: 5
5 + B

[a] *pro* ἐκζέω. [b] A γέμω.

ζῆλος.

Nu. 25:11, 11
Deu. 29:20
2 Ki. 19:31
Job 5: 2
Psa. 68:10
78: 5
118:139
Pro. 6:34 – S^1
27: 4

Ecc. 4: 4
9: 6
Cant. 8: 6
Isa. 9: 7
11:13[a]
26:11
37:32
42:13
63 15

ζηλοτυπία.

Numbers 5:15, 18, 25, 29

ζηλόω.

Gen. 26:14
30: 1
37:11
Nu. 5:14, 14
30
11:29
25:11, 13
Deu. 32:19
Jos. 24:19
2 Sa. 21: 2
1 Ki. 19:10, 10
14, 14
2 Ki. 10:16
18 A[a]

Psa. 36: 1
72: 3
Pro. 3:31
4:14
6: 6
23:17
24: 1, 19
Isa. 11:11, 13
Eze. 31: 9
39:25
Joel 2:18
Zec. 1:14
8: 2, 2

[a] *pro* συναθροίζω.

ζήλωσις.

Numbers 5:14, 14, 30

ζηλωτής.

Exo. 20: 5
34:14
Deu. 4:24
Deu. 5: 9
6:15
Nah. 1: 2

ζηλωτός.

Gen. 49:22
Exo. 34:14

ζημία.

2 Ki. 23:33 – B
Ezra 7:26
Pro. 27:12

ζημιόω.

Exo. 21:22
Deu. 22:19
Pro. 17:26
Pro. 19:19
21:11
22: 3

ζητέω.

Gen. 19:11
37:15, 16
43: 8, 20
Exo. 2:15
4:19, 24
10:11 A[a]
33: 7
Lev. 10:16
Nu. 16:10
35:23
Deu. 4:29[b]
13:10
22: 2
Jud. 4:22
14: 4[b]
18: 1
Ruth 3: 1[c]
1 Sa. 9: 3
10: 2, 14
21
13:14
14: 4
16:16
19: 2, 10
22:23, 23
23:10, 14
15, 25
24: 3, 10
25:26, 29
26: 2, 20
27: 1, 4
28: 7, 7
2 Sa. 3:17
4: 8
5:17
11: 3

2 Sa. 12:16
14:16
16:11
17: 3, 20
20:19
21: 1, 2
1 Ki. 1: 2, 3
10:24
11:22, 40
12 *p*24 *l* 12
18:10
19:10, 14
21: 7
2 Ki. 1: 6 AB[d]
16 B[a]
2:16, 17
6:19
1 Ch. 4:39
10:13, 14[h]
13: 3[e]
14: 8
15:13 ABS[a]
16:10, 11
11
21: 3, 30
22:19
28: 8, 9
2 Ch. 7:14
9:23
11:16
14: 7 B[a]
15:12, 15
16:12[b]
18: 4, 7
20: 4
22: 9, 9[b]

2 Ch. 25:15
26: 5
33:12
34:3, 21, 26
Ezra 2:62
7: 6, 10
8:21, 22
23
Neh. 2: 4[f], 10
5:12, 18
7:64
12:27
Est. 2: 2, 21
6: 2 – A
Job 6: 5
9:26
38:41
39: 8, 29[g]
Psa. 4: 3
9:31[h], 36
23: 6, 6
26: 8 + S^2
8 S^1[a]
8
33:15
34: 4
36:10, 25
32, 36
37:13, 13
39: 7 AS[i]
15, 17
53: 5
62:10
68: 7[k]
69: 3, 5
70:13, 24
77:34[k]
82:17
85:14
103:21
104: 3, 4, 4
118:100 S[a]
176[m]
Pro. 1:28
2: 3 + AB^2C^2
4
8:17 S[n]
17
9: 6
11:27
14: 6
15:14
16: 5, 5
17: 9, 16
18: 1, 15
23:35
27:21[o]
28: 5
29:10 A[p]
Ecc. 3: 6, 15
7:26
29 A[d]
30
8:17

Ecc. 12:10
Cant. 3: 1, 1, 2
2
5: 6, 17
Isa. 8:19
9:13[a]
21:12, 12
31: 1[a]
34:16[b]
40:20
41:12, 17
45:19
51: 1
55: 6
58: 2
65: 1, 10
Jer. 2:24, 33
4:30
5: 1, 1
10:21[h]
11:21
19: 7
21: 7
22:25
25:16
27: 4, 6, 20
33:21
36: 7
13 S[a]
13 – AS
37:17
43:24[b]
51:30, 30
35
35 – A
Lam. 1:11, 19
3:26
Eze. 3:18 A[r]
7:25, 26
13:22 A[r]
22:30
26:21 + A
34: 4, 6 A[a]
12[s]
16[b]
36:37[t]
Dan. 1:20
2:13, 18
4:33
6: 4
7:16, 19
8:15
Hos. 2: 7
5:15[u]
Amos 8:12
Mic. 3: 2
Nah. 3: 7, 11
Zeph. 1: 6
2: 3, 3
Zec. 6: 7 + S^2
11:16[v]
12: 9
Mal. 2:15
3: 1

[a] *pro* ἐκζητέω. [b] A ἐκζητέω. [c] A εὑρίσκω. [d] *pro* ἐπιζητέω. [e] A^2 ἐκζητέω. [f] AB συζητέω. [g] S^1 ζάω. [h] AS ἐκζητέω. [i] *pro* αἰτέω. [k] S ἐκζητέω. [m] S ζάω. [n] *pro* φιλέω. [o] ACS ἐκζητέω. [p] *pro* μισέω. [q] AS^3 ἐκζητέω. [r] *pro* ζάω. [s] A ἐπισκέπτομαι. [t] A ζήτημα θήσομαι. [u] A ἐπιζητέω. [v] S^1 ἐπισκέπτομαι.

ζήτημα.

Eze. 36:37 A[a]

[a] *vide* ζητέω.

ζιβύνη.

Isa. 2: 4
Jer. 6:23
Mic. 4: 3 A[a]

[a] *pro* δόρυ.

ζιοῦ.

1 Kings 6: 4

ζυγός.

Gen. 27:40
Lev. 19:35, 36
26:13
Nu. 19: 2
Deu. 21: 3
2 Ch. 10: 4, 4, 9
10, 11
11, 14
Job 6: 2
31: 6
39:10
Psa. 2: 3
61:10
Pro. 11: 1
16:11
20:23
Isa. 5:18
9: 4
10:27, 27
11:13 A[a]
14: 5, 5, 25

Isa. 14:29
40:12, 15
46: 6
47: 6
Jer. 2:20
5: 5
34: 6, 9
35: 2, 4, 11
14
37: 8
39:10
Lam. 3:27
Eze. 5: 1
34:27
45:10
Dan. 5:27
8:25
Hos. 12: 7
Amos 8: 5
Mic. 6:11
Zeph. 3: 9

[a] *pro* ζῆλος.

ζυγόω.

1 Ki. 7:43
Eze. 41:26[a]

[a] A ξυλόω.

ζῦθος.

Isaiah 19:10

ζύμη.

Exo. 12:15, 15
19
13: 3, 7
23:18
Exo. 34:25
Lev. 2:11
Deu. 16: 3, 4

ζυμίτης.

Leviticus 7: 3

ζυμόω.

Exo. 12:34, 39
Lev. 6:17
Lev. 23:17
Hos. 7: 4

ζυμωτός.

Exo. 12:19, 20
13: 7
Lev. 2:11

ζωγραφέω.

Isa. 49:16
Eze. 23:14, 14

ζωγρεία, –ρία.

Nu. 21:35
Deu. 2:34

ζωγρέω.

Nu. 31:15, 18
Deu. 20:16
Jos. 2:13
6:25
Jos. 9:26
2 Sa. 8: 2
2 Ch. 25:12

ζωή.

Gen. 1:30
2: 7, 9
3:14, 17
20, 22
24
6:17
7:11, 15
22
8:13
23: 1
25: 7, 17
27:16
45: 5
47: 8, 9, 9
9, 28
Exo. 1:14
6:16, 18
20
Deu. 4: 9
6: 2
16: 3

Deu. 17:19
28:66, 66
30:15, 19
19[a], 20
32:47
Jos. 1: 5
10:10 – A
Jud. 6: 4
16:30
17:10[b]
1 Sa. 7:15
18:18 A
25:29
2 Sa. 1:23
15:21
19:34
1 Ki. (3) *p* 46
4 (21) + A
11:34
15: 5, 6 A
2 Ki. 8:10[a], 14

2 Ki. 25:29, 30
Ezra 6:10
Job 3:20
7: 1, 7
15+A
9:21
10:12, 21
11:17
12:18 A[a]
16:13 AS[2d]
21:22
33:22, 28
30[e]
36:14
Psa. 7: 6
15:11
16:14
20: 5
22: 6
25: 9
26: 1, 4
29: 6
30:11
33:13
35:10
36: 7 BS[1 f]
41: 9
48:19
55: 8
62: 4, 5
65: 9
87: 4
102: 4
103:33
127: 5
132: 3
142: 3
145: 2
Pro. 2:19
3: 2, 16
18
4:10, 13
22, 23
5: 6, 9
6:23
8:35
9:11, 18
10: 3, 11
16, 17
11:19, 30
12:27
13:12, 14
14:27
15: 4, 24

Pro. 16:15, 17
17, 22
18: 4, 21
19:23
21:21
22: 4
23: 3
27:25, 25
Ecc. 2: 3, 17
3:12
5:17, 19
6: 8
7: 1—C
1—C
8:15
9: 3, 9, 9
9
Isa. 4: 3
26:14
28: 4 B[g]
38:12, 20
53: 8
57:15
65:22
Jer. 2:13[h]
8: 3
17:13
21: 8
42: 7+A
8+A
Lam. 3:52, 57
Eze. 1:20, 21
3:21
7:13+A
13
10:17
16: 6
18: 9, 13
17, 19
21, 28
26:20
31:17
32:23, 24
26, 27
32
33:13+A
15, 15
37: 5
10+A
Dan. 7:12
12: 2
Hos. 10:12
Jon. 2: 7
Mal. 2: 5

[a] A εὐλογία. [b] A ζάω. [c] pro ζώνη. [d] pro χολή. [e] AS[2] ψυχή. [f] pro ὁδός. [g] pro δόξα. [h] AS[2] ζάω.

ζωμός.

Jud. 6:19, 20
Isa. 65: 4

Eze. 24:10

ζώνη.

Exo. 28: 4, 35
36
29: 9
36:37
Lev. 8: 7, 13
16: 4
Deu. 23:13
1 Sa. 18: 4 A

1 Ki. 2: 5
2 Ki. 1: 8
3:21
Job 12:18[a]
Ps. 108:19
Isa. 3:24
5:27
Eze. 9: 2,3,11

[a] A ζωή.

ζωννύω, —νυμι.

Exo. 29: 9
Lev. 8: 7, 13
16: 4
Jud. 18:11[a]
1 Sa. 17:39
25:13
2 Sa. 20: 8[b]
1 Ki. 20:27
2 Ki. 4:29
9: 1

Neh. 4:18
Job 38: 3
40: 2
Ps. 108:19 S[1 c]
Isa. 3:24
11: 5
Eze. 9:11[a]
16:10
23:15[d]

[a] A περιζώννυμι. [b] AB περιζώννυμι. [c] pro περιζώννυμι. [d] A διαζωννύω.

ζωογονέω.

Exo. 1:17, 18
22
Lev. 11:47, 47
Jud. 8:19

1 Sa. 2: 6
27: 9, 11
1 Ki. 21:31
2 Ki. 7: 4

ζῶον.

Gen. 1:21
Job 38:14
Psa. 67:11
103:25
144:16
Eze. 1: 5, 13
13
14+A

Eze. 1:15, 19
19
20+A
22
3:13
10:15, 20
47: 9
Hab. 3: 2

ζωοποιέω.

Jud. 21:14—A
2 Ki. 5: 7
Neh. 9: 6

Job 36: 6
Psa. 70:20
Ecc. 7:13

ζωοποίησις.

Ezra 9: 8, 9

ζωπυρέω.

2 Kings 8: 1, 5, 5, 5

ζῶσις.

Isaiah 22:12

ζώω.

Psa. 79:19
Psa. 84: 7

ἡγεμονία.

Gen. 36:30
Nu. 1:52

Nu. 2:17[a]

[a] A τάγμα.

ἡγεμονικός.

Psalm 50:14

ἡγεμών.

Gen. 36:15 to 18
19
19+A
21, 29
29 qtr
30 qtr
40 qtr
41 ter
42 ter
43 ter
Exo. 15:15
1 Ch. 1:51 mult
Job 42: p 18
Psa. 54:14

Psa. 67:28—S[1]
Jer. 28:23
28 A[a]
57
45:17
46: 3 AS[a]
3
47: 7, 13
48:11, 13
16
49: 1, 8
50: 4, 5
Eze. 17:13[b]
23:23

[a] pro ἡγέομαι. [b] A ἡγέομαι.

ἡγέομαι.

Gen. 49:10, 26
Exo. 13:21
23:23, 27
Deu. 1:13, 15
5:23
Jos. 13:21
Jud. 9:51+A
11: 6 A[a]
11 A[a]
1 Sa. 15:17
22: 2
25:30
2 Sa. 2: 5
3:38
4: 2
5: 2
6:21
7: 8
1 Ki. 1:35
9: 5
10:26
12 p 24 l 71

1 Ki. 14: 7 A, 27
15:13
16: 2, 16
2 Ki. 1: 9+A
13
20: 5
1 Ch. 5: 2
7:10
9:11, 20
11: 2
12:21, 27
13: 1
16: 5
17: 7
26:24+A
27: 4—AB
8, 16
2 Ch. 5: 2
6: 5
7:18
9:26
11:11, 22

2 Ch. 17: 2,7,15
18:16
19:11, 11
20:27
28: 7
31:13
Est. 1:16
5:11
10: 3 AS[b]
Job 18:24
19:11—S[1]
30: 1, 19
33:10
35: 2
41:18, 19
22
42: 6
Ps. 103:17
Pro. 5:10
16:18
24:66
29:26

Jer. 4:23
20: 1
28:28[c]
46: 3[d]
Eze. 17:13 A[e]
19:11
20:46
23: 6, 12
43: 7, 7, 9
44: 3
45: 7
Dan. 3: 2,3,30
9:25, 26
11:22
Mic. 2: 9, 13
3: 9, 11
5: 2+A
7: 5
Nah. 3: 4
Hab. 1:14
Mal. 1: 8

[a] pro ἀρχηγός. [b] pro διηγέομαι. [c] A ἡγεμών. [d] AS ἡγεμών. [e] pro ἡγεμών.

ἥγημα.

Ezekiel 17: 3

ἥγησις.

Judges 5:14+A

ἡγητέον.

Proverbs 26:23

ἡδέως.

Est. 1:10
Pro. 3:24

Pro. 9:17

ἤδη.

Gen. 27:36 A[a]
2 Sa. 14:17[b]

Ecc. 9: 7—AC

[a] pro ἰδού. [b] A εἴη δή.

ἡδονή.

Nu. 11: 8

Pro. 17: 1

ἡδύνω.

Job 24: 5
Ps. 103:34
140: 6
146: 1

Pro. 13:19
Cant. 7: 6[a]
Jer. 6:20
Hos. 9: 4[b]

[a] S δύναμαι. [b] A δύναμαι.

ἡδύς.

Est. 1: 7
Ps. 134: 3 A[a]
Pro. 12:11
14:23

Cant. 2:14
Isa. 3:24
44:16
Jer. 38:26

[a] pro καλός.

ἥδυσμα.

Exo. 30:23, 34
1 Ki. 10: 2, 10
10, 25

2 Ch. 9:24
Ecc. 10: 1
Eze. 27:22

ἡδυσμός.

Exodus 30:34

ἡδύφωνος.

Ezekiel 33:32

ἡδώ.

Job 36:30[a]

[a] A τόξον, BS[1] ᾠδή.

ἡθάμ.

Psalm 73:15—8

ἥκω.

Gen. 6:13
18:10
41:30
42: 7, 9
45:16, 18
46:31
47: 4, 5
Exo. 3: 9
18:23
20:24
Lev. 13: 9
14:35
Nu. 22:36, 38
Deu. 12: 9, 26
28: 2
32:17
33: 2
Jos. 2: 3
9:12, 15
23:14 A[a]
15
Jud. 11:12 A[b]
16: 2
18:10 A[c]
1 Sa. 2:34, 36
4: 6,7,16
9:12
10: 3, 7
15:12
16: 2, 5
20:19
22: 5
23: 7—A
25: 8
26: 3, 4
29: 6,9,10
2 Sa. 3:23
14:32
17:12
1 Ki. 8:42
13:21
19:15, 15
2 Ki. 8: 7
20:14, 14
23:18
1 Ch. 12:17
2 Ch. 20: 2
32: 2
35:21
Neh. 2:10
Est. 4:13[d]
Job 3:24
4: 5
15:21
16:22
36:18 A[e]
Psa. 36:13
39: 8
41: 3
49: 3
64: 3
67:32
85: 9
100: 2
101:14
108:17
120: 1
125: 6
Pro. 6: 3, 11
24:40, 49
Ecc. 5:14
Cant. 2: 8
Isa. 2: 2
3:14
4: 5
7:17
8:21
10: 3, 28
29
13: 6

Isa. 18: 6
19: 1
27:13
30:28
32:19
35: 4, 10
37: 3
39: 3, 3, 6
42: 9
45:20, 24
47: 9,9,11
11, 11
49:12[f]
51:11
59:19, 19
20
60: 1, 4, 5
6,7,13
61: 5
66:15, 18
23
Jer. 1:15
2: 3, 31
3:18
4:12, 15
16
5:12
6: 3, 26
8:16
10: 9
16:19
17:26
23:17, 19
25:15
26:18, 22
27: 4,5,27
31
28:13, 33
53, 60
29: 5
31: 8
32:16[g]
37:23
38:12, 12
39:24, 29
43:14
47: 4+AS
Eze. 7: 2, 2, 6
7, 10
12, 25
21:25, 29
23:24, 42
24:14, 26
30: 4, 9
32:11
33:33
38: 8,9,11
15
39: 8
47: 9
Dan. 11: 7, 21
24, 29
44, 45
Hos. 6: 3
9: 7, 7
13:13
Joel 1:15
Amos 8: 2
Mic. 1:15
4: 8, 10
7: 4, 12
Hab. 1: 9
2: 3
3: 3
Hag. 1: 2
2: 7
Zec. 6:10, 15
8:20, 22
14: 5, 21
Mal. 3: 1

[a] pro ἀνήκω. [b] pro ἔρχομαι. [c] pro εἰσέρχομαι. [d] S[1] εἴκω. [e] pro εἰμί. [f] AS ἔρχομαι. [g] A ἐκεῖ.

ἤλεκτρον.

Eze. 1: 4, 27

Eze. 8: 2

ἡλιάζομαι.

2 Samuel 21:14

ἡλικία.

Job 20:18
Eze. 13:18

ἥλιος.

Gen. 15:12, 17
19:23
28:11
32:31
37: 9
Exo. 16:21
17:12
22: 3, 26
Lev. 22: 7
Nu. 21:11
25: 4[a]
Deu. 4:19, 41
47, 49
11:30
16: 6
17: 3
23:11
24:15, 17
33:14
Jos. 1: 4, 15
4:19
8:29
10:12, 13
13, 27
12: 1
13: 5, 7, 8
15: 7, 10
19:27, 34
23: 4
Jud. 5:31
9:33
11:18
14:18
19:14
20:43
21:19
1 Sa. 11: 9
2 Sa. 2:24
3:35
12·11, 12
23: 4
1 Ki. 8:53
22:36
2 Ki. 3:22
10:33
23: 5, 11
11
2 Ch. 18:34
Neh. 7: 3
8: 3
Job 1: 3
2: 9
8:16
9: 7
25: 5+A
31:26
Psa. 18: 6
49: 1
57: 9
Psa. 71: 5, 17
73:16
88:37
103:19, 22
112: 3
120: 6
135: 8
148: 3
Ecc. 1: 3, 5, 5
9
13 S[2 b]
14
2: 3, 11
17, 18
19, 20
22
3: 1 S[2 b]
16
4: 1, 3, 7
15
5:12, 17
6: 1, 5
7: 1—C
12
8: 9, 15
15, 17
9: 3, 6, 9
9, 11
13
10: 5
11: 7
12: 2
Cant. 1: 6
6: 9
Isa. 9:12, 12
11:11, 14
13:10
24:23+S[1]
30:26, 26
38: 8 *ter*
41:25
45: 6
49:10
59:19
60:19, 20
Jer. 8: 2
15: 9
38:35
Eze. 8:16
32: 7
Joel 2:10, 31
3:15
Amos 8: 9
Jon. 4: 8, 8
Mic. 3: 6
Nah. 3:17
Hab. 3:11
Mal. 1:11
4: 2

[a] A λαός. [b] *pro* οὐρανός.

ἡλιούπολις.

Gen. 41:45
Jer. 50:13

ἧλος.

Jos. 23:13
1 Ki. 7:36
2 Ki. 12:13
1 Ch. 22: 3
2 Ch. 3: 9
Ecc. 12:11
Isa. 41: 7
Jer. 10: 4

ἡμέρα.

Gen. 1: 5, 5, 8
13
14+A
14, 14
16, 18
19, 23
31
Gen. 2: 2, 2, 3
4, 17
3: 5, 14
17
4: 3
5: 1, 2, 4
5, 8, 11
Gen. 5:14, 17
20, 23
27, 31
6: 3, 4, 5
7: 4, 4, 10
11, 12
13, 17
24
8: 3, 6, 10
12, 22
22
9:29
10:25
11:32
15:18
17:12, 14
23, 26
18:11
19:37, 38
21: 4, 8, 34
22: 3
24: 1, 55
25: 7, 8
24
26:32, 33
27: 2, 41
44, 45
29: 7, 14
20—A
21
30:14, 33
35, 36
31: 2, 5, 22
23, 39
40
32:32
33:13, 16
34:25
35: 3, 4, 20
28, 29
37:34
38:12
39:10, 10
11
40: 4, 12
13, 18
19, 20
20
41: 1
42:17, 18
43: 8
44:32
47: 8, 9, 9
9, 9, 26
28, 29
48:15, 20
49: 1
50: 3 *ter*
4, 10
Exo. 2:11, 13
23
3:18
4:10, 18
5: 3, 7, 8
13, 14
19
6:28
7:25
8:22, 27
9:18, 18
24—A
10: 6, 6
13, 22
23—A
23, 28
12:14
15 *qtr*
16, 16
17, 17
18, 18
19, 51
13: 3, 6, 6
7, 8, 10
10, 21
22
14:27, 30
15:22
16: 1, 4, 4
5 *ter*
22, 26
Exo. 16:26, 27
29 *qtr*
30
19: 1, 11
11, 15
16
20: 8, 9, 10
11 *ter*
21:21
36—A
22:30, 30
23:12, 12
15, 26
24:16, 16
18
29:30, 35
36, 37
38
38+A[2]
31:15 *ter*
17, 17
32:28, 34
34:18, 21
21+A
28
35: 2, 2, 3
38:26
40: 2, 31
32
Lev. 6: 5, 20
7: 5, 6, 7
8, 25
26, 28
8:33, 33
33 AB[1]
33, 34
35, 35
9: 1
12: 2, 2, 3
4, 4, 5
5, 6
13: 4, 5, 5
6, 14
21, 26
27, 31
32, 33
34, 46
50, 51
54
14: 2, 8, 9
10, 23
38, 39
46, 57
57
15: 3, 13
14, 19
24, 25
25, 25
26, 28
29
16:30
19: 6, 6, 7
22:27, 27
28, 30
23 *passim*
40-AB[1]
24: 8
25: 9, 29
26:34, 35
27:23
Nu. 3: 1, 13
4:16
6: 4, 5, 5
6, 8, 9
9, 10
11, 12
12, 13
13
7: 1, 10
11, 11,
12, 18
24, 30
36, 42
48, 54
60, 66
72, 78
84
8:17
9: 3, 5, 6
6, 11
Nu. 9:15, 16
18, 19
20, 21
21+A
22
10:10, 33
33, 34
11:19 *qtr*
20, 21
31, 31
32, 32
12:14
14—A
15
13:21, 21
26
14:14, 34
34, 34
15:23, 32
33—A
19:11
12 *qtr*
14, 16
19 *ter*
20:15, 29
22:30
24:14
25:18
28: 3, 9, 16
17—A
17—A
18, 24
24, 25
26
29: 1, 12
12, 17
20, 23
26, 29
32, 35
30: 6, 8, 9
13, 15
15, 15
16
31:19 *ter*
24
32:10
33: 3, 8
Deu. 1: 2, 33
46, 46
2: 1, 14
21, 22
25, 30
3:14
4: 9, 10
10, 10
15, 20
26, 30
32, 32
40
5: 1, 12
13, 14
14+B[*]
15, 24
29
6: 2, 24
8:16—A
9: 7, 9, 10
11, 18
24, 25
10: 8, 10
15
11: 1, 4, 21
21, 31
12: 1
14:22
16: 3 *ter*
4, 4, 8
8, 13
15
17: 9, 12
19
18: 5+A
16
19: 9, 17
20:19
21:13, 16
23
23: 6
26: 3, 16
27: 2, 9, 11
Deu. 28:29, 33
66
29: 4
30.20
31:10, 13
14, 17
17, 18
22, 29
32: 7
20—A
35, 35
44, 48
33:12, 25
34: 6, 8, 8
Jos. 1: 5, 8, 11
2:16, 22
3: 2, 4, 7
15
4: 9, 14
18
5: 9, 10
12
6:10, 12
14, 15
15—AB
25, 26
7:26
8:25
28, 29
9:18, 22
32, 33
33
10:12, 13
14, 27
28, 32
35
11:18
13: 1, 1, 13
14: 9, 12
12, 14
15:63
16:10
20: 6 A
22: 3, 3, 17
22—B
29
23: 1, 1, 2
8, 9
24: 7, 25
27, 29
29, 31
31
Jud. 1:21, 26
2: 7, 7, 18
3:20[a], 30
4: 8, 14
23
5: 1, 6, 6
6:24, 27
32
8:28
9:19, 45
10: 4, 15
11: 4+A
40 *ter*
12: 3
13: 7, 10
14: 8, 10
12, 14
15, 17
17, 18
15: 1, 1, 19
20
16:16[b]
17: 6, 10
18: 1 *ter*
12
30—A
31, 31
19: 2, 4, 5
8, 8, 9
11, 30
30
30+A
30+A
20:15, 21
22, 24
25, 26
27—B
28, 30
Jud. 20:35, 46
21:19, 19
25
Ruth 1: 1+A
4: 5
1 Sa. 1: 3, 3, 4
11, 15
20, 21
24, 24
28
2:19 *ter*
31, 32
34, 35
3: 1, 2
12
4: 1, 12
5: 5
6:15, 16
18+A
7: 2, 2, 6
10, 13
15
8: 8, 8, 18
18
9:12, 13
15, 24
10: 8, 9
11: 3, 11
13
12: 2, 5, 18
13: 8, 11
22
14: 1, 18
21, 23
24, 31
36, 37
45, 45
52
15:35
16:13
17:10
12 A
16 A
46
18. 2 A
9 AB
10 A
27+A
29+A
19: 7, 24
20: 6, 19
26
27—A
31
34+A
21: 5, 6, 7
10, 13
22: 4, 8, 13
18, 22
23:14
24: 5, 11
25: 7, 8, 15
16, 16
38
26:10
27: 1, 6, 6
7
7+A
11
28: 1, 2, 18
20
29: 3 *ter*
6, 6, 8
8
30: 1, 12
25
31: 6, 13
2 Sa. 1: 1, 2
2:11, 17
3: 9—A
35, 37
38
4: 3, 5, 8
5: 8
6: 8, 9, 23
7: 6, 6, 11
12
8: 7
11:12
12:18
2 Sa. 13:23, 32
37
14: 2, 26
26, 28
16:12, 23
18: 7, 8, 18
20 *ter*
19: 2, 2, 3
13, 19
24, 24
34
34 B[c]
20: 3, 4
21: 1, 9, 10
12
22: 1, 19
23:10, 20
24: 8, 13
15, 18
1 Ki. 1: 1, 30
2: 1, 8, 11
25, 26
(3) *p* 1
37, 37
42
p 16 *bis*
3: 2+A
6, 11
13+A
14, 18
4(21)+A
22
(25)+A
5: 1
8: 8+A
16, 24
29, 29
40, 59
59, 59
61, 64
65, 65
65+A
65+A
66
9: 3, 9, 13
10:12, 21
p 22
11:12
14—A
(25) A
34, 36
39A, 42
12: 5, 7, 7
12, 12
19
p 24 *l* 57
l 59
32, 33
13: 3, 11
14:14 A
19 A
20 A
29, 30
15: 5, 6 A
7, 14
16, 23
31
32 A
16: 5, 14
15[a]
16+A
16, 20
27
p 28—A
p 28—A
34—B
17: 7, 14
15+A
18: 1
19: 4, 8
20:27, 29
29
21:29 *ter*
22:25, 35
39
46—B
47 A
2 Ki. 1:18
2:17, 22
3: 6, 9

2Ki. 4: 8, 11
6:29
7: 9, 9
18 A[c]
8: 6, 19
20, 22
23
10:27, 32
34, 36
12: 2, 19
13: 3,8,12
22
14: 7, 15
18, 28
15: 5,6,11
14, 15
19, 21
26, 29
31, 36
37
16: 6, 19
17:23, 34
37, 41
18: 4
19: 3, 3
25+A
20: 1, 5, 6
8, 17
17
19−B
20
21:15−A
15, 17
25
23:22, 22
28, 29
24: 1, 5
25:29, 30
30, 30
1 Ch. 1:19 A
4:41, 41
43
5:10, 17
17, 26
7: 2, 22
9:25, 33
10: 6, 12
11:22
12:22, 22
39
13: 3, 11
12
14 A[f]
16: 7, 23
24, 37
37
17: 5,5,10
11
21:12
22: 9
23: 1
26:17, 17
17−A
18
27:24
28: 7
29:15, 21
22, 28
2 Ch. 1:11
5: 9
6: 5, 15
20, 31
7: 8, 9, 9
16
8: 8, 13
13, 14
14, 16
9:29
10: 5,7,12
12, 19
12:15
13:18, 20
14: 1
15: 3, 11
17
18: 7, 24
34
20:25, 26
26
21: 7,8,10,

2 Ch. 21:15, 15
19 *qtr*
24: 2, 11
11, 14
15, 18
26: 5,5,21
28: 6
29:17 *qtr*
30:21 *ter*
22, 23
23, 26
31:16, 16
32:24, 26
34:33
35: 1−AB
16, 17
18
36: 5, 8, 9
21−B
Ezra 3: 4 *qtr*
6
4: 2, 5, 7
15[g], 19
6: 9,9,15
22
8:15, 32
33
9: 7 *ter*
15
15+S[1]
10: 8,9,13
16
17−S[1]
Neh. 1: 4, 6
2:11
4: 9, 16
22
5:14, 18
18
6:15, 17
8: 2, 3, 9
10, 11
13, 17
17
18 *scr*
9: 1, 10
12, 19
32, 32
10:31, 31
11:23+S[3]
12: 7, 12
22, 23
23, 26
26, 43
44, 46
47
47−S[1]
47, 47
13: 1,6,15
15, 15
17, 19
22, 23
Est. 1: 1, 2, 4
5,5,10
2:11, 12
14, 18
3: 4, 7−A
7, 7
12+S[3]
13, 14
4: 8, 11
16, 16
5: 1, 4
9+S[3]
6: 1
7: 2
8: 1, 12
13
9: 2[h], 11
17, 19
19+AS
21
21+S[3]
22
22−S
22
26−A
27, 28
Job 1: 4, 5, 5
6, 13

Job 2: 1, 13
3: 1, 3
4 ACS[3]
5−S[1]
6, 6, 8
6:14
7: 4
14: 5, 14
15:10, 24
17:11, 12
20:28
21:30, 30
24:16
29: 2+A
2
30:16, 26
27
32: 4
36:11
38:23
42:17
Psa. 1: 2
7:12
12: 3
17: 1, 19
18: 3, 3
19: 1, 10
20: 5
21: 3
22: 6, 6
24: 5
26: 4, 5
31: 3, 4
33:13
34:28
36:13, 19
26
37: 7, 13
38: 5, 6
40: 2
41: 4, 4, 9
11
43: 2, 2, 9
16, 23
48: 6
49:15
51: 3
54:11, 24
55: 2, 3, 3
5−S
6, 10
58:17
60: 7 *ter*
9, 9
67:20, 20
70: 8, 15
24
71: 7, 15
72:10, 14
73:16, 22
76: 3, 6
77: 9, 14
33, 42
80: 4
83:11
85: 3, 7
87: 2, 10
18
88:17, 30
46
89: 4,9,10
14, 15
90: 5, 16
91: 1
92: 1, 5
93:13
94: 8
95: 2, 2
101: 3, 3, 4
9, 12
24, 25
102:15
108: 8
109: 3, 5
114: 2
117:24
118:84, 91
97, 104
120: 6
127: 5

Ps. 135: 8
136: 7
137: 3
138:12−A
16
139: 3, 8
142: 5
143: 4
144: 2
145: 4
Pro. 4:18
6:34
7:20
8:21
30
34−S[1]
10:27
11: 4+A
16: 2, 4
21:26, 31
23:17
24:10, 10
25.19
27:15
29:44
Ecc. 2: 3, 16
23
5:16, 17
19
6: 3
7: 1−C
2,2,11
15, 15
16
8: 8,8,13
15, 16
9: 9
9+BCS
9+B
11: 1, 8, 9
12: 1, 1, 3
Cant. 2:17
3:11, 11
4: 6
8: 8
Isa. 1:13
2: 2, 11
12, 17
20
3: 7, 18
4: 2, 5
5:30
7: 1, 17
17, 18
20, 21
23
9: 4, 14
10: 3, 18
20, 27
11:10, 11
16
12: 1, 4
13: 6,9,13
14: 3
4+AS
17: 4, 7, 9
11, 11
18: 4
19:16, 18
19, 21
23, 24
20: 6−A
21: 8
22: 5,8,12
20, 25
23:15
25: 9
26: 1
27: 1, 2, 3
12, 13
28: 5, 19
24
29:18
30: 8, 23
25, 26
33
31: 7
32:10
34: 8, 10
37: 3,3,26

Isa. 38:10, 13
13, 20
39: 6, 6, 8
45: 9−AS[2]
47: 9
48: 7
49: 8
51: 9, 13
52: 6
58: 2, 2, 3
5, 13
60:11, 19
20
61: 2
62: 6
63: 4,9,11
65: 2,5,22
22
66: 8
Jer. 1: 2,3,18
2:32
3: 6, 16
17, 18
25
4: 9
5:18
6: 4, 4[b]
11
7:22, 25
25, 25
32
9: 1
25−S[1]
11: 4, 5
12: 3
13: 6
14:17
15: 9
16: 9, 14
19
17:11, 16
17−S[1]
18[m], 21
22−S[1]
22, 24
24−S[1]
27, 27
18:17
19: 6
20: 7, 8
14, 14
18
23: 5,6,20
7
25: 3, 18
26:10, 10
21
27: 4, 20
27, 31
28: 2, 52
29: 4, 23
30: 2
31:12, 16
32:19, 20
33:18
35: 3
37: 3, 7, 8
24
38: 6, 19
27, 29
31, 32
33, 35
36, 38
39:14, 20
20, 31
31, 39
41:13
42: 1, 7, 7
8, 19
43: 2 *ter*
6, 30
44:16, 21
46:17
48: 4
49: 7
51: 6, 10
22
52:11−A
33, 34
34, 34

Lam. 1: 7,7,12
13, 21
2: 2,7,16
17, 18
21, 22
22
3: 3, 14
56−A
61
4:19
5: 4 AB[n]
20, 21
Eze. 1:28
2: 3
3:15, 16
4: 4
4+A
5, 5, 6
6, 8, 9
9, 10
5: 2
7: 7, 10
12
19+A
12: 3, 4, 7
22, 23
25, 27
13: 5
16: 4, 5
22+AB
43+A
56, 60
20: 5,6,29
31
21:25, 29
22: 4, 14
24−A
23:19
39+A
24: 2 *ter*
25
26
27
26:18
27:27
28:14, 15
15
15+A
29:21
30: 2, 3, 3
9,9,18
31:15
32:10
33:12, 12
12+A
34:12, 12
36:33
38: 8, 10
14, 16
17, 17
18, 18
19
39: 8, 11
13, 22
40: 1
43:18, 22
25, 25
26, 27
44:26, 27
45:21, 22
23 *qtr*
25+A
25
46: 1, 1, 2
4,6,12
13
48, 35
Dan. 1: 5,5,12
14, 15
18
2:28, 44
4:31
5:11
6: 7, 10
12, 13
7: 9, 13
22
8:14, 26
9: 3 A[c], 7
15

Dan. 10: 2, 2, 3
4
12−A
13, 14
14
11:20, 33
12:11, 12
13, 13
Hos. 1: 1, 1, 5
11
2: 3, 13
15, 15
16, 18
21
3: 3, 4, 5
4: 5
5: 9
6: 2, 2
7: 5
9: 5, 5, 7
7, 9
10:14
12: 1, 9
Joel 1: 2,2,15
15
2: 1
1+A
2,2,11
29, 31
3: 1, 14
18
Amos 1: 1,1,14
14
2:16
3:14
4: 2
5: 8, 18
18, 20
6: 3
8: 3, 9, 9
10, 11
13
9:11, 11
13
Obad. 8, 11
11
12 *qtr*
13 *ter*
14, 15
Jon. 2: 1
3: 3, 4, 4
Mic. 1: 1

Mic. 2: 1, 4
3: 6
4: 1, 6
5: 2, 10
7: 4, 11
11, 11
12+A
14, 15
20
Nah. 1: 7
2: 4, 6
3:17
Hab. 1: 5
3:16
Zeph. 1: 1, 7, 8
9, 10
12, 14
14, 15
15
15−A
15 *ter*
16, 18
2: 2, 3
3: 8, 11
17
Hag. 2:15, 18
18, 19
23
Zec. 2:11
3: 9, 10
4:10
6:10
8: 4, 6, 9
9, 10
11, 15
23
9:12, 16
11, 11
12: 3, 4, 6
8, 8, 9
11
13: 1, 2, 4
8+AS[3]
14: 1, 3, 3
4, 5[o]
5, 6, 7
7, 7, 8
9, 13
20, 21
Mal. 3: 2,4,17
4: 1, 1, 3
4

[a] A καιρός. [b] A νύξ.
[c] *pro* ἔτος. [d] B ἔτος.
[e] *pro* ὥρα. [f] *pro* μήν.
[g] A χρόνος. [h] S[1] ὥρα.
[i] *pro* νύξ. [k] A ἑσπέρα.
[m] A λιμός. [n] *pro* ὕδωρ.
[o] S[3] πρόσωπον.

ἡμίεφθος.

Isaiah 51:20

ἡμίονος.

Gen. 12:16
45:23
1 Sa. 21: 7
23: 9
2 Sa. 13:29
18: 9 *ter*
1 Ki. 1:33, 38
44
10:25
18: 5

2 Ki. 5:17
1 Ch. 12:40−A[1]
2 Ch. 9:24
Ezra 2:66
Neh. 2: 8+S[3]
7:69+AS
Psa. 31: 9
Isa. 66:20
Eze. 27:14+A
Zec. 14:15

ἡμίσευμα.

Numbers 31:36, 42, 43, 47

ἡμισεύω.

Psalm 54:24

ἥμισυς.

Exo. 24: 6, 6
25: 9 *ter*
10, 16
22

Exo. 26:12−AB
16
27: 5
30:13, 13

Exo. 30:15, 23
38: 1+A
1+A
1+A
24
39: 2
Lev. 6:20, 20
Nu. 12:12
15: 9, 10
28:14
31:29, 30
32:33
34:13, 14
15
Deu. 3:12, 13
29: 8
Jos. 1:12
4:12
9: 6, 6
12: 2, 5, 6
13: 7, 8, 25
29, 31
31
14: 2
18: 7
21: 5, 6, 25
27
22: 1, 7, 7
9, 10
11, 13
15, 21
30, 31
32, 33
34
Jud. 16: 3−A
2 Sa. 10: 4
18: 3
19:40
1 Ki. 3:25, 25
7:17+A
18, 21
10: 7
13: 8
1 Ki. 16: 9, 21
21
1 Ch. 2:54
5:18, 23
26
6:61, 70
71
12:31, 37
19: 4
26:32
27:20, 21
2 Ch. 9: 6
Neh. 3: 9, 12
16-BS[1]
17, 18
4:16, 16
21 A[a]
21
8: 3[b]
12:32
38 S[3]
40 S[3]
13:24
Est. 5: 3
6+S[3]
7: 2
Ps. 101:25
Isa. 44:16
16-AS[1]
19
Jer. 17:11
Eze. 16:51
40:12, 42
43:17
Dan. 7:25
9:27
27+AB[?]
12: 7
Zec. 14: 2, 4
4+A
4, 4, 8
8

[a] pro ἡμεῖς.
[b] A μέσος, B*S[3] μεσόω.

ἡνία.

Nahum 2: 4

ἡνίκα.

Jud. 3:18[a]
11:35 A[b]
15:14+A
17 A[b]
Jud. 16:22+A
1 Sa. 1:24+A
Pro. 8:28 AS[b]

[a] A ὡς. [b] pro ὡς.

ἡνίοχος.

1 Ki. 22:34
2 Ch. 18:33

ἧπαρ.

Gen. 49: 6
Exo. 29:13, 22
Lev. 3: 4, 10
15
4: 9
6:34
Lev. 7:20
8:16, 25
9:10, 19
1 Sa. 19:13, 16
Pro. 7:23

ἡπατοσκοπέω.

Ezekiel 21:21

ἠρεμάζω.

Ezra 9: 3, 4

ἥρως.

Genesis 46:28, 29

ἥσσων, ἧττον.

1 Sa. 30:24
Job 5: 4
13:10
Job 20:10
Isa. 23: 8
Dan. 2:39

ἡτυχάζω.

Gen. 4: 7
Exo. 24:14

Jud. 3:11, 30
5:31
8:28
18: 7, 9[a]
27
Ruth 3:18
2 Ki. 11:20
2 Ch. 14: 1
23:21
Neh. 5: 8
Job 3:13, 26
11:19
14: 6
32: 1, 7
Job 37: 7, 16
Psa. 75: 9
106:30
Pro. 1:33
7:11
15:15
26:20
Isa. 7: 4
Jer. 26:27
29: 6, 7
Lam. 3:26
Eze. 32:14
38:11
Zec. 1:11

[a] A σιωπάω.

ἡσυχῇ.

Jud. 4:21 A[a]
Isa. 8: 6

[a] pro κρυφῇ.

ἡσυχία.

Jos. 5: 8
1 Ch. 4:40
22: 9
Job 34:29
Pro. 7: 9
11:12
Eze. 38:11

ἡσύχιος.

Isaiah 66: 2

ἡττάω.

1 Ki. 16:22+A
Isa. 8: 9 ter
13:15
19: 1
20: 5
30:31
Isa. 31: 4, 9
33: 1
51: 7
54:17
Jer. 31: 1+AS

ἥττημα.

Isaiah 31: 8

ἧττον vide ἥσσων.

ἠχέω.

Exo. 19:16
Ruth 1:19
1 Sa. 3:11
4: 5
1 Ki. 1:41, 45
2 Ki. 21:12
Job 30: 4
Psa. 45: 4
82: 2
Isa. 16:11
17:12
51:15
Jer. 5:22[a]
10: 3
27:42
28:55
Hos. 5: 8

[a] S ἰσχύω.

ἦχος.

1 Sa. 4:15
14:19
Psa. 9: 7
41: 5
64: 8
76:18
150: 3
Pro. 11:15
Isa. 13:21
Jer. 28:16, 42
29: 3
Joel 3:14
Amos 5:23

ἠχώ.

Job 4:13

θάλασσα.

Gen. 1:10, 22
26, 28
9: 2
12: 8
13:14
14: 3
22:17
28:14 A[a]
14
32:12
41:49
Exo. 10:19, 19
13:18
14: 2, 2, 9
16, 16
Exo. 14:21 ter
22, 23
26, 27
27, 28
29, 30
15: 1, 4, 4
8, 10
19 ter
21, 22
20:11
23: 31, 31
26:22, 27
27:12
37:10
Lev. 11: 9, 10
Nu. 2:18
3:23
10: 6
11:22, 31
13:30
14:25
21: 4
33: 8, 10
11
34: 3, 5, 6
6, 7, 11
12
35: 5
Deu. 1: 1−AB
40
2: 1
3:17, 17
27
5:14+B[a]
11: 4, 24
30:13, 13
33:19, 23
34: 2
Jos. 1: 4
2:10
3:16−A
16
4:23
5: 1
8: 9, 12
9: 1
11: 4
12: 3 ter
7
13: 7, 7, 27
15: 2, 4, 5
5, 8, 10
11, 12
12, 47
16: 3, 3, 6
8, 8
17: 9−A
10
18:12, 14
14, 19[b]
19
19:11, 22
26, 29
34, 34
46
22: 7
23: 4
24: 6, 6, 7
Jud. 5:17
7:12
9:37
11:16
1 Sa. 13: 5
2 Sa. 8: 8
17:11
22:16
1 Ki. 2:35
(3) p 1 bis
p 46
4(20)+A
25
5: 9
9+A
7:10, 12
12, 12
25, 30
30
9:26, 27
10:22, 29
18:32, 35
38, 43
2 Ki. 14:25
16:17
25:13, 16
1 Ch. 9:24
16:32
18: 8
2 Ch. 2:16
4: 2, 4, 6
10, 15
8:18
20: 2
Ezra 3: 7
Neh. 9: 6, 9, 11
11
Est. 10: 1
Job 7:12
9: 8
11: 9
12: 8
14:11
26:12
28:14
36:30
38: 8, 16
22 S[1 c]
41:21, 22
Psa. 8: 9, 9
23: 2
32: 7
45: 3
64: 6, 8
65: 6
67:23
68: 3, 35
71: 8, 8
73:13
76:20
77:13, 27
53
79:12
88:10, 13
26
92: 4
94: 5
95:11
97: 7
103:25
105: 7, 9, 22
106: 3, 23
113: 3, 5
134: 6
135:13, 15
138: 9
145: 6
Pro. 8:29+AS[2]
23:34
Ecc. 1: 7, 7
Isa. 2:16
5:30
9: 1+AS[2]
10:22, 26
11: 9, 14
15
16: 8[d]
17:12
18: 2
19: 5
23: 2, 4, 4
11
24:14, 15
27: 1+S
42:10
43:16
48:18
19+S
49:12
50: 2
51:10, 10
15
60: 5
63:11[e]
Jer. 5:22
6:23
15: 8
22:20
26:18
27:42
28:36, 42
29:22
31:32
32: 8
38:35
52:17−A
20, 20
Eze. 26: 3, 5, 12
16, 17
17+A
18+A
27: 3, 4, 9
25, 26
27, 29
32+A
33, 34
28: 2, 8
Eze. 32: 2
38:20
39:11
41:12
42:18, 18
45: 7 ter
47: 8, 10
15, 17
18, 19
20, 20
48: 1, 2, 3
4, 5, 6
7
8+A
8, 10
16
17−A
18, 21
21[f], 23
24, 25
26, 27
28, 31
Dan. 2:38−B
7: 2, 3
8: 4
11:45
Hos. 1:10
Hos. 4: 3
Joel 2:20, 20
Amos 5: 8
8:12−[f]
12
9: 3, 6
Jon. 1: 4, 4
9, 11
11, 12
12, 13
15, 15
2: 4
Mic. 7:12, 12
19
Nah. 1: 4
3: 8
Hab. 1:14
3: 8−S[1]
15
Zeph. 1: 3
2: 5, 7
Hag. 2: 6, 21
Zec. 9: 4
10+S[?]
10
10:11, 11
14: 4, 8, 8

[a] pro γῆ.
[b] A Βαιθαλαγα.
[c] pro χάλαζα.
[d] AS[1] ἔρημος.
[e] AB*S γῆ.
[f] A ἀνατολή.

θάλλω.

Gen. 40:10
Job 8:11
Pro. 15:13
26:20

θαλπιώθ.

Canticles 4: 4

θάλπω.

Deu. 22: 6
1 Ki. 1: 2, 4
Job 39:14

θαμβέω.

Jud. 9: 4 A[a]
1 Sa. 14:15
2 Sa. 22: 5
2 Ki. 7:15
Dan. 8:17
18+A

[a] pro δειλός.

θάμβος.

1 Sa. 26:12
Ecc. 12: 5
Cant. 3: 8
Cant. 6: 3, 9
Eze. 7:18

θαμμούζ.

Ezekiel 8:14

θανατηφόρος.

Nu. 18:22
Job 33:23

θάνατος.

Gen. 2:17
3: 4
21:16
25:11
Exo. 5: 3
9: 3, 15
10:17
19:12
21:12, 15
16, 17
22:19, 20[a]
31:14
15+A
Lev. 20: 2, 9
10
11−B[1]
12
13 AB[1]
15, 16
27
24:16, 17
21
26:25
Lev. 27:29
Nu. 6: 9+A
12:12
14:12
15:35
16:29
26:10, 65
35:16, 17
18, 21
21, 31
Deu. 19: 6
21:22
22:26
28:21
30:15, 19
31:14, 27
Jos. 2:13, 14
Jud. 5:18
13: 7, 22
15:13
16:16 A[b]
30
21: 5

Ruth 1:17
1 Sa. 1:11
5: 6
11+A
14:39, 44
15:32, 35
20: 3, 14
31
22:16
2 Sa. 1:23
3:33
12: 5, 14
14:14
15:21
18:33
19:28
20: 3
21: 1
22: 5, 6, 6
24:13, 15
15
1 Ki. 2:26
(3)37, 42
3:26, 27
8:37
2 Ki. 1: 4,6,16
2:21
4:40
8:10
11:15−A
15: 5
20: 1
1 Ch. 21:12, 14
2 Ch. 6:28
7:13
20: 9
32:11, 24
33
Ezra 7:26
Est. 4: 8, 8
Job 3: 5, 21
22+A
23
5:20
7:15−A
9:23
12:22
15:34
16:16+AS^2
17:14
18:13
20:15+A
24:17−A
17
27:15
28: 3, 22
30:23
33:18, 22
24, 30
38:17
Psa. 6: 6
7:14
9:14
12: 4
17: 5, 6
21:16
22: 4
32:19
33:22
43:20
48:15
54: 5, 16
55:14
67:21

Psa. 72: 4
77:50, 50
87: 7
88:49
106:10, 14
18
114: 3, 8
115: 6
117:18
Pro. 2:18
5: 5
7:27
8:36
10: 2
11: 4+A
19
12:27
14:27
16:14
18: 6, 21
21: 6
23:14
24: 8, 11
25:10
Ecc. 3:19, 19
7: 2, 27
8: 8
Cant. 8: 6
Isa. 9: 2, 8[c]
27: 8
28:15, 18
38: 1
39: 1
53: 8,9,12
Jer. 8: 3
9:21
13:16
14:12, 15
15: 2, 2
16: 4
18:21, 23
21: 6, 7, 8
24:10
33: 8, 11
16
41:17
45:15−A
50:11
11−S^1
51:43+A
Lam. 1:20
Eze. 3:18
5:12, 17
6:11, 12
7:15, 15
12:16
14:19, 21
18:13, 23
32
28: 8
10+A
23+A
23
31:14
33: 8, 11
14, 27
38:22
Hos. 13:14, 14
Amos 4:10
Jon. 4: 9
Hab. 2: 5
3:13
Zec. 5: 3
3+AS

[a] A ἕτερος. [b] pro ἀποθνήσκω.
[c] S^1 λόγος.

Jud. 9:54
13:23
15:13
16:30, 30
20:13
21: 5[b]
1 Sa. 2: 6
5:10, 11
11:12
14:45
17:35
50A, 51
19: 1, 2, 5
11, 11
15, 17
20: 8
33−A
33
22:17, 18
18+A
21
24: 8 A[c]
28: 9
30: 2, 15
2 Sa. 1: 9, 10
16
3:30, 37
4: 7
8: 2−A
13:28, 32
14: 6,7,32
18:15
19:21, 22
20:19
21: 1, 4, 9
17
22:11
1 Ki. 1:51, 52
2: 8, 24
26, 34
(3) p 1
3:26, 27

1 Ki. 11:40
12p24l13
13:24
26+A
15:28
16:10
17:18, 20
18: 9
19:17, 17
2 Ki. 5: 7
7: 4
11: 2,2,15
20
14: 6, 19
15:10, 14
25, 30
16: 9
17:26
21:23
23:29
25:21
2 Ch. 22:11
23:15, 17
21
24:22, 25
25: 3, 27
Job 5: 2
26:13
Psa. 36:32
43:23
68: 1
78:11
101:21
108:16
Ecc. 10: 1
Jer. 8:17
45:15
50: 3
Lam. 3:52
Eze. 3:18
18:13[b]
33: 8, 14

[a] pro τελευτάω. [b] A ἀποθνήσκω.
[c] pro θύω.

θανάτωσις.

1 Samuel 26:16

θανουρίμ.

Nehemiah 3:11

θάπτω.

Gen. 23: 4, 6, 6
8, 11
13, 15
19
25: 9, 10
35: 8−A
19, 29
47:29, 30
49:29, 31
31, 31
50: 5, 5, 6
7, 13
14, 26
Nu. 11:34
20: 1
33: 4
Deu. 10: 6
21:23
34: 6
Jos. 24:31, 31
33
Jud. 2: 9
8:32
10: 2, 5
12: 7, 10
12, 15
16:31
Ruth 1:17
1 Sa. 25: 1
28: 3
31:13
2 Sa. 2: 4,5,32
3:32
4:12
17:23

2 Sa. 21:12 A[a]
14
1 Ki. 2:10, 29
31, 34
11:15, 43
12p24l1
13:29+A
30
31, 31
14:13 A
18 A, 31
15: 8, 24
16: 6, 28
p28−AB
22:37, 51
2 Ki. 8:24−A
9:10, 28
34, 35
10:35
12:21
13: 9
13−B
20, 21
14:16, 20
15: 7−A
38−A
16:20
21:18, 26
23:30
1 Ch. 10:12
2 Ch. 9:31
12:16+B
16
14: 1
16:14

2 Ch. 21: 1, 20
22: 9
24:16, 25
25
25:28
26:23
27: 9
28:20 B^{1b}
27
32:33
33:20
35:24

2 Ch. 36: 8
Psa. 78: 3
Jer. 7:32
8: 2
14:16
16: 4
20: 6
22:19
Eze. 39:14, 15
15
Hos. 9: 6

[a] pro κλέπτω. [b] pro θλίβω.

θαρσείς, θαρσίς.

Eze. 1:16
Dan. 10: 6

θαρσέω, θαρρέω.

Gen. 35:17
Exo. 14:13
20:20
1 Ki. 17:13
Pro. 1:21

Pro. 20:29
Joel 2:21, 22
Zeph. 3:16
Hag. 2: 5
Zec. 8:13, 15

θάρσος.

2 Ch. 16: 8
Job 4: 4

Job 17: 9

θαῦμα.

Job 17: 8
18:20

Job 20: 8 S^{1a}
[a] pro φάσμα.

θαυμάζω.

Gen. 19:21
Lev. 19:15
26:32
Deu. 10:17
28:50
2 Ki. 5: 1
2 Ch. 19: 7
Job 13:10
21: 5
22: 8
32:21
34:19
41: 1

Job 42:11
Psa. 47: 6
Pro. 18: 5
Ecc. 5: 7
Isa. 9:14
14:16
41:23
52: 5, 15
61: 6
Jer. 4: 9−AS^1
Dan. 3:24
8:27
Hab. 1: 5

θαυμάσιος.

Exo. 3:20
Nu. 14:11 A[a]
Deu. 34:12
Jos. 3: 5 A[b]
Jud. 6:13
1 Ch. 16: 9, 12
24−ABS
Neh. 9:17
Job 37: 4
Psa. 9: 2−S^1
25: 7
39: 6
70:17
71:18
74: 2
76:12, 15
77: 4, 11
12, 32
85:10

Psa. 87:11, 13
88: 6
95: 3
104: 2, 5
105: 7
22 AS^{2b}
106: 8, 15
21, 24
31
110: 4
118:18, 27
130: 1
135: 4
138:14
144: 5
Jer. 21: 2
Dan. 12: 6
Joel 2:26
Hab. 1: 5

[a] pro σημεῖον.
[b] pro θαυμαστός.

θαυμαστός.

Exo. 15:11
34:10
Deu. 28:58, 59
Jos. 3: 5[a]
Jud. 13:18
19 A[b]
Job 42: 3
Psa. 8: 2, 10
41: 5
64: 6
67:36
92: 4, 4

Psa. 97: 1
105:22[c]
117:23
118:129
Pro. 6:30
Isa. 3: 3
9: 6+AS^2
25: 1
Dan. 8:24
9: 4
Amos 3: 9
Mic. 7:15

[a] A θαυμάσιος. [b] pro διαχωρίζω.
[c] AS^2 θαυμάσιος.

θαυμαστόω.

2 Sa. 1:26
2 Ch. 26:15
Psa. 4: 4
15: 3

Psa. 16: 7
30:22
138: 6, 14

θαυμαστῶς.

Psa. 44: 5
Psa. 75: 5

θέα.

Isa. 2:16
Isa. 27:11

θεάομαι.

2 Chronicles 22: 6

θεέ, θεείμ.

1 Ki. 14:28
Eze. 40: 6+A
7, 7, 8
10, 12
12, 13

Eze. 40:13, 14
16, 21
24, 29
33, 36

θεεβουλαθώθ.

Job 37:11[a]

[a] (pro θ. εἰς) A κατωτάτω θεἰς, S^1 ἔθετο βουλαθ εἰς, S^2 ἔνθα ἐβούλετο θεἰς.

θεηλάθ.

Ezekiel 40: 7

θεῖον.

Gen. 19:24
Deu. 29:23
Job 18:15
Psa. 10: 6

Isa. 30:33
34: 9
Eze. 38:22

θεῖος.

Exo. 31: 3
35:31
Job 27: 3

Job 33: 4
Pro. 2:17

θεκέλ.

Daniel 5:25, 27

θέλημα.

2 Sa. 23: 5
1 Ki. 5: 8,9,10
9:11
2 Ch. 9:12
Est. 1: 8
Job 21:21
Psa. 1: 2
15: 3
27: 7
29: 6, 8
39: 9
102: 7, 21
106:30
110: 2
142:10

Ps. 144:19
Ecc. 5: 3
12: 1, 10
Isa. 44:28
48:14
58: 3, 13
62: 4
Jer. 9:24
23:17, 26
Dan. 4:32
8: 4
11: 3, 16
36
Mal. 1:10

θέλησις.

2 Ch. 15:15
Psa. 20: 3 S^{2a}

Pro. 8:35
Eze. 18:23−A

[a] pro δέησις.

θελητής.

2 Ki. 21: 6 A[a]
23:24

Mic. 7:18

[a] pro τέμενος.

θελητός.

1 Sa. 15:22
Mal. 3:12

θέλω, ἐθέλω.

Gen. 24: 8
37:35
39: 8

Gen. 48:19
Exo. 2: 7, 14
8:32

Exo. 10: 4
11:10 A[a]
Nu. 20:21
22:14
Deu. 1:26
2:30
10:10
21:14
23: 5, 22
25: 7, 7
29:20
Jos. 24:10
Jud. 11:17 A[b]
20 A[c]
13:23[d]
19:10 A[b]
25 A[b]
20: 5
1 Sa. 14:15
18:22
26:23
2 Sa. 2:21
12:17
13: 9, 14
16, 25
14:29, 29
15:26
23:16, 17
1 Ki. 9: 1
10: 9, 13
21: 8, 35
22:50 A
2 Ki. 8:19
13:23
24: 4
1 Ch. 11:18
19:19
28: 4, 9
2 Ch. 7:11[e]
9: 8
36: 5
Neh. 1:11
Est. 1: 8
5: 3
6: 6, 6, 7
11
Job 23:13

Job 33:32
Psa. 5: 5
17:20
21: 9
33:13
34:27, 27
36:23
39: 7, 15
40:12
50:18
67:31
69: 2+S^1
72:25
77:10[f]
108:17
111: 1
113:11[g]
118:35
134: 6
146:10
Pro. 1:30
21: 1
Ecc. 8: 3
Cant. 2: 7
3: 5
8: 4
Isa. 1:19, 20
5:24
9: 5
28: 4, 12
55:11
56: 4
66: 3
Jer. 5: 3, 3
8: 5
9: 6
11:10
27:33
38:15
39:33 A[h]
45:21[d]
Eze. 3: 7
18:23[d], 32
20: 8
Hos. 6: 6
11: 5
Mal. 3: 1

[a] *pro* εἰσακούω. [b] *pro* εὐδοκέω
[c] *pro* ἐμπιστεύω. [d] A βούλομαι.
[e] $B^?$ ποιέω. [f] S^2 βούλομαι.
[g] S^1 βούλομαι. [h] *pro* ἀκούω.

θέμα.

Lev. 24: 6, 6
7

1 Sa. 6: 8, 11
15

θεμέλιος.

Deu. 32:22
2 Sa. 22: 8, 16
1 Ki. 6: 2
7:46
2 Ki. 16:18
2 Ch. 31: 7+B
Ezra 4:12
5:16
Job 9: 6
18: 4
22:16
Psa. 17: 8, 16
81: 5
86: 1
136: 7
Pro. 8:29
Isa. 13: 5—A^1
13
14:15

Isa. 24:18
25: 2
28:16, 16
40:21
44:23
54:11
58:12
Jer. 6: 5
28:26
Lam. 4:11
Eze. 13:14
30: 4
Hos. 8:14
Amos 1: 4,7,10
12, 14
2: 2, 5
Mic. 1: 6
6: 2
Nah. 1:10—S^1

θεμελιόω.

Jos. 6:26, 26
1 Ki. 6: 4
7:47
16:34
2 Ch. 8:16[a]
31: 7
Ezra 3: 6, 10
7: 9—AB
Job 38: 4

Psa. 8: 4
23: 2
47: 9
77:69
86: 5
88:12
101:26
103: 5, 8
118:90, 152

Pro. 3:19
8:23
18:19
Cant. 5:15
Isa. 14:32
44:28
48:13

Isa. 51:13, 16
Amos 9: 6
Hag. 2:18
Zec. 4: 9
8: 9
12: 1

[a] A τελειόω.

θεμελίωσις.

Ezra 3:11, 12

θεός.

(*vide etiam* κύριος).

Adonai.

Neh. 4:14
Psa. 76: 3

Isa. 3:17
Hab. 3:19

El.

Gen. 14:18, 19
20, 22
16:13
17: 1
21:33
31:13
35: 1, 3
11
49:25
Exo. 15: 2, 11
20: 5
34:14, 14
Nu. 12:13
16:22
23:19, 22
23
24: 4+AB
8, 16
23
Deu. 3:24
4:24, 31
5: 9
6:15
7: 9, 21
10:17
32: 4, 12
18, 21
33:26
Jos. 3:10[a]
1 Sa. 2: 3
Job 27: 2[b]
9[c]
Psa. 5: 5
9:32
16: 6
17: 3, 31
33, 48
18: 2
21: 2, 2, 11
28: 1, 3
35: 7
41: 9, 10
42: 4
43:21
51: 7
54:20
56: 3
62: 2
67:20, 21
21, 25
36

Psa. 72:11, 17
76:10
14—S^1
15
77: 7, 8, 18
19, 34
35—S^1
41
79:11
80:10, 10
81: 1
82: 2
83: 3
88: 7, 8, 27
93: 1, 1
94: 3—AS^2
98: 8
103:21
105:14, 21[d]
106:11
117:27, 28
135:26[e]
138:17, 23[a]
139: 7
145: 5
149: 6
150: 1
Isa. 5:16
8:10[f]
9: 6+S^2
10:21
12: 2
31: 3
43:10, 12
44:10, 15
17, 17
45:14, 15
20, 22
46: 9
Jer. 39:18
Eze. 28: 2, 2, 9
Dan. 11:36
36+A
36+A
Hos. 1:10
11: 9, 12
Mic. 2: 1
7:18
Nah. 1: 2
Mal. 1: 9
2:10, 11

[a] A κύριος. [b] ACS^4 κύριος.
[c] AC κύριος. [d] S^1 κύριος.
[e] AS^1 κύριος. [f] A κύριος ὁ θ.

El Elohim.

Gen. 33:20

Gen. 46: 3

El Jehovah.

Jeremiah 28:56

El Shaddai.

Gen. 28: 3
43:13

Gen. 48: 3
Exo. 6: 3

Elah.

Ezra 4:24
5: 1[a], 2
2, 5, 8

Ezra 5:11, 12
13, 14
16, 17

Ezra 6: 3, 5, 5
7, 7, 8
9, 10
12, 12
14, 16
17, 18
7:14, 15[b]
16, 17
18, 19
19, 20
21, 23
23, 24
25, 25
26
Jer. 10:11
Dan. 2:11, 18
19, 20
23, 28
37, 44
45, 47
47, 47

Dan. 3:12, 14
15, 17
18, 25
26, 28
28, 28
29, 29
32
4: 5, 5, 6
15
5: 3—A
4, 11
14, 18
21—A
23, 23
26
6: 5, 7, 10
11, 12
16, 20
20, 22
23, 26
26

[a] A κύριος ὁ θ. [b] B κύριος.

Eloah.

Deu. 32:15, 17
2 Ch. 32:15
Neh. 9:17
Job 3:23[a]
29: 2, 4[b]
31: 2
35:10
37:14[c]
39:17, 32
Psa. 17:32

Psa. 49:22
113: 7
138:19
Pro. 24:28
Isa. 44: 8
Dan. 11:37, 38
38, 39
Hab. 1:11
3: 3

[a] A κύριος. [b] ACS^2 κύριος.
[c] C κύριος.

Elohim.

Var. Lec. tantum.

Gen. 19:29[1][a]
24: 3[2]—A
31:50—A
48:15[2][b]
Exo. 18:19[1]—A
34:16[2]—A
Deu. 6:14[2]—B
12:30+A
25:18[a]
Jos. 2:11[2][c]
22:16[d]
34[e]
Jud. 4:23[d]
6:20[a]
7:14[a]
9:57[a]
10:10[d]
16:28—A
1 Sa. 5:10[2]—A
14:18+A
17:26 A
43[f]
18:10 A
20: 9+A
2 Sa. 7:25+A
15:29—B
23: 1[d]
1 Ki. 13:14[2]—A
29—A
14: 9 A
18:39[1]—A
19: 8+A
20:10—B
2 Ki. 1:16+A
4:16+A
25[2]—AB
5: 8+A
17:27—B
31—B
1 Ch. 14:11—BS
16: 1[2][a]
17:20—ABS
19:13—BS
25: 6[2]—AB
28: 8[1]—B
2 Ch. 15:18[g]
33: 7[1][a]
34: 9[a]
Ezra 1: 3[3]—B

Ezra 9: 6—B
Neh. 10:37—A
39[d]
11:16 A
12:40 S^3
13: 1[h]
Job 28:23[i]
Psa. 13: 5[k]
19: 6[m]
42: 4[3]—ABS^1
49:23—S^2
52: 5[n]
55: 2[b], 5[2][n]
12[o]
62:12[n]
65:16[o]
67: 9[2]—S^1
17—S^1
32[n]
34—S
68:30+S
70:12[2]—B
72:28[b]
77:59[n]
103:33—A^1
114: 5[p]
142:10—A
Ecc. 3:13[q]
7:30[a]
8: 2—AS
Isa. 25: 9[m]
28:26—S^1
40: 1[a]
52:12[r]
57:21[r]
59: 2—A
64: 4—A^1
Jer. 28: 5[d]
51:15+A
Eze. 10:19[d]
Dan. 9:19[d]
20+A
Hos. 9: 8[2][a]
Joel 2:17[d]
Amos 8:14[1][d]
Jon. 4: 7[d], 8[d]
9[d]

[a] A κύριος. [b] B κύριος.

[c] B ὅς. [d] A κύριος ὁ θ.
[e] A θεὸς θεός. [f] A εἴδωλον.
[g] AB κύριος ὁ θ. [h] S^1 κύριος.
[i] ACS^2 κύριος. [k] S^2 κύριος ὁ θ.
[m] S κύριος ὁ θ. [n] S^1 κύριος.
[o] BS^1 κύριος. [p] S^1 κύριος ὁ θ.
[q] C κύριος. [r] AS κύριος ὁ θ.

Jah Jah.

Isaiah 38:11

Jah Jehovah.

Isaiah 26: 4

Jehovah.

Gen. 4: 1, 4, 16
6: 6, 7
12:17
13:10, 10
13, 14
15: 6, 7
16: 5
18: 1, 14
25:21
30:24, 27
31:49
38: 7, 10
Exo. 4: 1[a]
11[a], 30
31
5: 2+A
17, 21
6:26
8:29, 30
9: 5
10:11[b]
18[b]
13:21
14:31
15: 1[b]
16: 7, 8, 9
33
19: 3, 7, 8
8, 18
21, 21
23, 24
22:11
24: 2, 3, 5
16
28:23
32:30
35:30
36: 2
Lev. 21:21
22:18
Nu. 9:19
15:30
16: 5, 11
22:13, 22
23, 24
25, 26
27, 28
31, 32
35
23: 3, 5, 8
12, 16
26
24:13
Deu. 2:15[b]
4:20[a]
8: 3
9:26
12:21
26:17
29:20
31:27
Jos. 5: 6
6:11
9:33
10:12[a], 14
14: 7[b]
15:13
17: 4, 14
19:50[b]
22:19[b]
1 Sa. 2: 1, 24
3: 7
4: 3
5: 3
14: 3

1 Sa. 16: 7, 8[b]
19: 9[b]
20:13[h]
22:10
26:19
2 Sa. 12:20
1 Ki. 5: 7
20: 3
22:19[a]
2 Ki. 2: 2[b]
1 Ch. 10:13[b]
13:14
15:15
16:26
25: 6[b]
26:27
29:21
2 Ch. 24: 6
Psa. 29: 9
68:32
83:12
97: 4[c]
Pro. 3: 5, 7, 19
33
5:21
6:16[d]
15:29
16: 1, 5
20[e]
17:15
18:22[f], 22
19:17
21: 1, 3
24:21
Isa. 4: 2
6:12
7:17
8:17, 18
9:11
10:20, 26
11: 2, 3
14: 2+AS
27
23:16
24:21
25:10
27: 1[g]
12[i]
28:13[h]
30: 9, 18
33: 5
36:15, 18
20
37:20, 22
38: 7, 20[d]
20, 22[i]
39: 6[g]
40:27, 28
31
41: 4, 14
42:12, 19
24
43:11
44: 5, 5
6—B^1
6, 23
23
45:21
49:13
51:13
54:13
58: 8, 9, 11
13
61: 9
65:23

Jer. 1: 2
4: 4
9:20[h]
11:10

Jer. 27:15
Hos. 3: 1
Mal. 2:17

[a] A κύριος ὁ θ. [b] A κύριος.
[c] AB[2]S κύριος. [d] AS κύριος.
[e] AC κύριος. [f] AS[2] κύμιος.
[g] S[1] κυριος. [h] B κύριος, AS κ. ὁ θ.
[i] AS[3] κύριος ὁ θ.

Jehovah Elohim.

Gen. 2: 5, 7
8[a], 9
19, 21
22[a]
3:22[a]
28:13
Exo. 3:18, 18
4: 5[a]
8:27[a]
28[a]
10: 7[a]
29:46
Deu. 12:31[a]
13: 3[a]
16:21[a]
19: 1
30: 5[a]

2 Ki. 2:14[a]
5:11[b]
1 Ch. 15:12, 13
14[a]
22:19[a]
2 Ch. 33:18[a]
36:23
Ezra 1: 3–8
7:28[b]
8:28
9: 8[a]
Isa. 41:13
48:17–A[1]
51:15
Jer. 3:21, 25
8:14
Joel 1:14[c]

[a] A κύριος ὁ θ. [b] A κύριος.
[c] AS[3] κύριος ὁ θ.

Shaddai, Tzoor, etc.

Gen. 28:19
31:13–A
Exo. 16:34 B[a]
Nu. 24: 4, 16
Deu. 32: 4, 8, 15
18, 30
31, 31
2 Sa. 5:21
Neh. 10:38[b]
11: 2 S[1] [c]
Job 6:10
Psa. 17:32, 47
27: 1
30: 3
61: 3, 7, 8
70: 3
72:26

Psa. 90: 1
94: 1
131: 2, 5
143: 1
Ecc. 5: 5
Isa. 8: 8
13: 6
19: 3
30:29
49: 7
60:16
Jer. 3:19
Eze. 20:28
Hos. 11: 7
Amos 2: 7
8:14

[a] pro μαρτύριον. [b] S[3] θησαυρός.
[c] pro λαός.

Nihil in Hebrew.

Gen. 3:11–A
17:19–A
24: 7
35: 9
14–A
43:27
49:24
50:24
Exo. 3:12–A
16, 16
18:20
34:13
Lev. 21:23
Nu. 23: 3, 6, 15
31:41
Deu. 7: 5
9:26
32:18, 43
33:12
Jos. 9:33–A
10:13
24:17–A
25, 33
33
1 Sa. 2: 3
4: 4+A
22+A
9: 7
16: 7
2 Sa. 2: 5+A
6: 7
23: 4
24:16–A
1 Ki. 14: 3 A
17: 1

1 Ki. 21:23
22:17–A
2 Ki. 5: 3
19:20
23:16
1 Ch. 16:40
26:28–A
28: 6
Ezra 3: 8+A
Neh. 10:38
Job 2:10
15: 8–ABCS
34:27
39:17+A
Psa. 13: 3–A
17: 8
23: 6
43:10+AS[2]
49: 3
54: 9+S[2]
67:33
74: 6
78:13+S[2]
83: 8
84: 7
85: 4+S[1]
133: 1
Pro. 1: 7
4:27
16: 2, 5
21: 8
22: 8
24:24, 26

Pro. 21:69, 70
76
Ecc. 2:26+C
5: 5
7:14
Isa. 2: 2
5:19+S[a]
26: 9
33:22
40: 5
45: 6–ABS
23[a]
25–S[1]
58: 2+A
59: 8+S[1]

Jer. 1: 1
4: 2
12: 4
27:29
39:19–S
Eze. 10:22
28:26
Dan. 3:23
4:15+B
24
5: 4+AB[2]
22, 23
6:13
Hos. 11:12
Mal. 2:16+A

[a] S[1] κύριος.

θεὸς θεός.

El Elohim Jehovah.

Joshua 22:22

θεὸς θεὸς κύριος.

El Elohim Jehovah.

Joshua 22:22

Elohim Jehovah.

Psalm 49: 1

θεὸς ὁ κύριος.

Jehovah Elohim.

2 Ch. 33:12[a] [a] A κύριος ὁ θ.

θεὸς σαδδαΐ.

El Shaddai.

Ezekiel 10: 5

θεοσέβεια.

Gen. 20:11
Job 28:28

θεοσεβής.

Exo. 18:21
Job 1: 1, 8
Job 2: 3

θεράπαινα.

Exo. 11: 5
21:26, 27
Job 19:15

Job 31:13, 31
Pro. 29:33
Isa. 24: 2

θεραπεία.

Gen. 45:16
1 Sa. 15:23 B[a]
Est. 2:12

Est. 5: 1
Joel 1:14
2:15

[a] pro θεραφῖν.

θεραπεύω.

2 Sa. 19:24
2 Ki. 9:16
Est. 2:19
6:10

Pro. 14:19
19: 6
29:26
Isa. 54:17

θεράπων.

Gen. 24:44
50:17
Exo. 4:10
5:21
7: 9, 10
10, 20
8: 3, 4, 9
11, 21
24, 29
31
9: 8, 14
20, 30
34
10: 1, 6, 7
11: 3
12:30
14: 5, 8, 31
33:11
Nu. 11:11
12: 7, 8

Nu. 32:31
Deu. 3:24
9:27
29: 2
34:11
Jos. 1: 2
9: 4, 6
2 Ki. 25:30 A[a]
1 Ch. 16:40
Job 1: 8 A[b]
2: 3
3:19
7: 2
19:15+A
16
31:13
42: 7, 8[c]
8, 8
Pro. 18:14
27:25

[a] pro διὰ παντός. [b] pro παῖς.
[c] A παῖς.

θεραφεῖν, –φίν.

Jud. 17: 5
18:14
17+A
18, 20

1 Sa. 15:23[a]
2 Ki. 23:24
2 Ch. 35:19
[a] B θεραπεία.

θερίζω.

Lev. 23:10, 22
22
Ruth 2: 3, 4, 5
6, 7, 9
14
1 Sa. 6:13
8:12
13:21
2 Ki. 4:18
Job 4: 8
5: 5 A[a]

Job 5:26
8:12–S[1]
24: 5+A
6–A
Ps. 125: 5
128: 7
Pro. 22: 8
Ecc. 11: 4
Jer. 9:22
12:13

[a] pro συνάγω.

θερινός.

Jud. 3:20
24–A

Dan. 2:35
Amos 3:15

θερισμός.

Gen. 8:22
30:14
Exo. 23:16
34:22
Lev. 19: 9
9–AB[1]
9
23:10, 10
22 ter
Jos. 3:15
Jud. 15: 1
Ruth 1:22
2:23
23+A

1 Sa. 6:13
8:12
12:17
2 Sa. 21: 9, 9, 10
24:15
Job 14: 9
18:16
29:19
Isa. 16: 9
18: 5
Jer. 5:16–S[1]
24
27:16

θέριστρον.

Gen. 24:65
38:14, 19
1 Sa. 13:20

Cant. 5: 7
Isa. 3:23

θερμαίνω.

1 Ki. 1: 1, 2
Job 31:20
Psa. 38: 4
Ecc. 4:11 C[a]
11

Isa. 44:15, 16
16
Eze. 24:11[b]
Hos. 7: 7
Hag. 1: 6

[a] pro θέρμη. [b] A συμφρύγω.

θερμασία.

Jeremiah 28:39

θερμαστρεύς.

1 Kings 7:26, 31

θέρμη.

Job 6:17
Psa. 18: 7

Ecc. 4:11[a]
[a] C θερμαίνω.

θερμός.

Jos. 9:18
1 Sa. 21: 6

Job 37:16
Jer. 38: 2

θέρος.

Gen. 8:22
Psa. 73:17
Pro. 6: 8

Pro. 24:60 26:1
Jer. 8:20
Zec. 14: 8

θεσβίτης.

1 Ki. 20:17
2 Ki. 1: 3, 8

2 Ki. 9:36
Mal. 4: 4

θέσις.

1 Kings 11:36

θεσμός.

Pro. 1: 8
Pro. 6:20

θετός.

Nehemiah 3:15+S[1]

θεωρέω.

Jos. 8:20[a]
Jud. 13:19 A[b]
20 A[b]
16:27[c]
Psa. 21: 8
26: 4
30:12
49:18
63: 9
65:18
67:25
72: 3

Pro. 16: 1
29:34
Ecc. 7:12
Dan. 2:29+A
31, 34
3:27
4: 7, 10
5: 5
7: 2, 4, 6
7, 9, 11
13, 21

[a] A ὁράω. [b] pro βλέπω.
[c] A ἐμβλέπω.

θεωρητός.

Daniel 8: 5+A

θήκη.

Exo. 25:26
Isa. 3:26
Isa. 6:13

θηλάζω.

Gen. 21: 7
32:15
Exo. 2: 7, 9, 9
Nu. 11:12
Deu. 32:13, 25
33:19
1 Sa. 1:23
15: 3
22:19
1 Ki. 3:21, 25

Job 3:12
20:16
Psa. 8: 3
Cant. 8: 1
Isa. 60:16
66:11
Jer. 51: 7
Lam. 2:11, 20
4: 3, 4
Joel 2:16

θηλυκός.

Nu. 5: 3
Deu. 4:16

θηλυμανής.

Jeremiah 5: 8

θῆλυς.

Gen. 1:27
5: 2
6:19, 20
7: 2, 2, 3
3, 9, 15
16
Exo. 1:16, 22
Lev. 3: 1, 6
4:28, 32
5: 6
12: 5, 7

Lev. 15:33
27: 4, 5, 6
7
Nu. 31:15
Jud. 5:10–A
1 Ki. 10:26
2 Ch. 9:25
Job 1: 3, 14
42:12
Pro. 24:66
Amos 6:12

θημωνιά, θιμωνιά.

Exo. 8:14, 14
Job 5:26

Cant. 7: 2
Zeph. 2: 9

θήρ.

1 Sa. 20:20+A
Job 5:23

θήρα.

Gen. 25:28
27: 3, 5, 7
19, 25
30, 31
33
Exo. 22:13
Nu. 23:24
Psa. 10:12
34: 8
123: 6

Ps. 131:15[a]
Pro. 11: 8
12:27
Isa. 31: 4
Hos. 5: 2
9:13
Amos 3: 4
Nah. 2:12, 13
3: 1

[a] AS[1] χήρα.

θήρευμα.

Lev. 17:13
Ecc. 7:27
Jer. 37:17

θηρευτής.

Psa. 90: 3
Jer. 16:16

θηρεύω.

Gen. 27: 3,5,33
Lev. 17:13
Job 18: 7
38:30
Psa. 58: 4
93:21
123: 7
Ps. 139:12
Ecc. 9:12, 12
Jer. 5: 6
16:16
28:41
Lam. 3:51, 51
4:18

θηριάλωτος.

Gen. 31:39
Exo. 22:13, 31
Lev. 5: 2
7:14
Lev. 17:15
22: 8
Eze. 4:14
44:31

θηριόβρωτος.

Genesis 44:28

θηρίον.

Gen. 1:24, 25
30
2:19, 20
3: 1, 14
6:19
7:14, 21
8: 1, 17
19
9: 2,5,10
37:20, 33
33
Exo. 23:11, 29
Lev. 11:27
17:13
25: 7
26: 6, 22
Deu. 7:22
28:26
32:24
Jos. 23: 5
1 Sa. 17:44 A[a]
46
2 Sa. 21:10
23:11
2 Ki. 14: 9
2 Ch. 25:18, 18
Job 5:22
23+A
37: 7
39:15
40:10
41:16
Psa. 49:10
67:31
73:19
78: 2
103:11, 20
148:10
Isa. 5:29
13:21
18: 6, 6
35: 9
43:20
Isa. 46: 1
56: 9, 9
Jer. 7:33
10: 2 S[1 b]
12: 9
15: 3
16: 4
19: 7
34: 5
41:20
Eze. 5:17
14:15, 15
21
17:23 A[c]
29: 5
31: 6, 13
32: 4
33:27
34: 5,8,25
28
38:20
39: 4, 17
Dan. 2:38
4: 9, 11
12, 13
18, 20
22, 29
5:21
7: 3, 5, 6
6, 7
7+A
7, 11
12, 17
19, 19
23
8: 4
Hos. 2:12, 18
4: 3
13: 8
Hab. 2:17
Zeph. 2:14, 14
(2)15

[a] *pro* κτῆνος. [b] *pro* σημεῖον.
[c] *pro* ὄρνεον.

θησαυρίζω.

2 Ki. 20:17
Psa. 38: 7
Pro. 1:18
2: 7
13:22
Pro. 10:27[a]
Amos 3:10
Mic. 6:10
Zec. 9: 3

[a] A ὀρύσσω.

θησαύρισμα.

Proverbs 21: 6

θησαυρός.

Gen. 43:22
Deu. 28:12
32:34
Jos. 6:19, 24
Jud. 18: 7—A
1 Ki. 7:37
14:26, 26
15:18
18—B
2 Ki. 12:18
14:14
16: 8
18:15
20:13, 15
24:13, 13
1 Ch. 9:26
26:20, 20
22, 24
26
27:25, 25
27, 28
2 Ch. 5: 1
8:15
12: 9, 9
16: 2
25:24
32:27
36:18, 18
Ezra 2:69
5:14
Neh. 7:70, 71
10:38 S[3 a]
39
Neh. 12:44
13:12
Job 3:21
38:22, 22
Psa. 32: 7
134: 7
Pro. 2: 4
3:14
8:21
10: 2
15:16
21:20
Isa. 2: 7
33: 6, 6
39: 2+S[1]
2, 4
45: 3
Jer. 10:13
15:13
20: 5
27:25, 37
28:13, 16
30: 4
48: 8
Eze. 27:24
28: 4, 13
Dan. 1: 2—A
Joel 1:17
3: 5 A[b]
Amos 8: 5
Mic. 6:10
Mal. 3:10

[a] *pro* θεός. [b] *pro* ναός.

θησαυροφύλαξ.

Ezra 5:14

θίασος.

Jeremiah 16: 5

θίβις.

Exodus 2: 3, 5, 6

θίγω.

Exodus 19:12

θίς.

Gen. 48:26
Deu. 12: 2
Job 15: 7
28:10 C[a]

[a] *pro* δίνη.

θλαδίας.

Lev. 22:24
Deu. 23: 1

θλάσμα.

Amos 6:11

θλάω.

Jud. 10: 8
1 Sa. 12: 4—A
2 Sa. 22:39
2 Ki. 18:21
Job 20:10 A[a]
Job 20:19[b]
Isa. 36: 6
42: 3[c]
Eze. 29: 7

[a] *pro* ὄλλυμι. [b] A θραύω.
[c] A συνθλάω.

θλίβω.

Exo. 3: 9
22:21
23: 9
Lev. 19:33
25:14, 17
26:26
Deu. 23:16
28:52, 53
55, 57
Jos. 19:47, 47
Jud. 4: 3
6: 9
Jud. 8:34[a]
10: 8[b], 9
12[c]
11: 7 A[d]
1 Sa. 10:18[c]
28:15
30: 6
2 Sa. 13: 2
22: 7
1 Ki. 8:37[c]
2 Ki. 13: 4
2 Ch. 6:28
2 Ch. 28:20[e], 22
33:12
Ezra 4: 1
Neh. 4:11
9:27 *ter*
Est. 8:11+S[3]
Job 20:22
36:15
Psa. 3: 2
12: 5
17: 7
22: 5
26: 2, 12
30:10
41:11[f]
43: 8
55: 2
59:14
68:18, 20
77:42
80:15
88:43 AS[2 g]
Ps. 101: 3
105:11, 42
44
106: 6, 13
19, 28
118:157[b]
119: 1
142:12
Isa. 11:13
18: 7
19:20
28:14
29: 7
49:26
51:13, 13
Jer. 37:20
Lam. 1: 3, 5, 5
7, 10
17, 20
2:17
Eze. 18:18
Mic. 5: 9

[a] A ἐχθρός. [b] A σαθρόω.
[c] A ἐκθλίβω. [d] *pro* χρήζω.
[e] A πατάσσω, B* θάπτω.
[f] AS[2] ἐχθρός. [g] *pro* ἐχθρός.
[h] AS[1] ἐκθλίβω.

θλιμμός.

Exo. 3: 9
Deu. 26: 7

θλῖψις.

Gen. 35: 3
42:21, 21
Exo. 4:31
Deu. 4:29
28:53, 55
57
31:17
21+A
Jud. 10:14
1 Sa. 1: 6, 6
10:19
24:20
26:24
2 Sa. 4: 9
22:19
1 Ki. 1:29
22:27, 27
2 Ki. 13: 4
19: 3
2 Ch. 15: 6
18:26, 26
20: 9
32:11 A[a]
Neh. 9:27, 37
Job 15:24
Psa. 4: 2
9:10, 22
19: 2
21:11
24:17, 22
31: 7
33: 5 AS[2 b]
7, 18
20
36:39
43:25
45: 2
49:15
53: 9
54: 4
58:17
59:13
65:11, 14
70:20
76: 3
Psa. 77:49
80: 8
85: 7
90:15
106:39
107:13
114: 3
117: 5
118:143
137: 7
141: 3
142:11
Pro. 1:27
21:23
24:10
Isa. 8:22
10: 3, 26
26:16, 16
28:10, 10
13, 13
30: 6, 20
33: 2
37: 3
57:13
63: 9
65:16
Jer. 6:24
10:18
11:16
15:11
27:43
Eze. 12:18[c]
18:18
Dan. 12: 1, 1
Hos. 6: 1
7:12
Obad. 12, 14
Jon. 2: 3—S[1]
Mic. 2:12
Nah. 1: 7
9—S[1]
2: 2
Hab. 3:16
Zeph. 1:15—A
Zec. 8:10

[a] *pro* δίψα. [b] *pro* παροικία.
[c] A ἔκθλιψις.

θνησιμαῖος.

Lev. 5: 2 *ter*
7:14
11: 8, 11
24, 25
26, 27
28, 35
Lev. 11:36, 37
38, 39
40, 40
17:15
22: 8
Deu. 14: 8, 20
1 Ki. 13:25, 25
2 Ki. 9:37
Psa. 78: 2
Isa. 5:25
Jer. 16:18
Jer. 41:20
43:30
Eze. 4:14
44:31

θνήσκω.

Gen. 50:15
Exo. 4:19
12:30
14:30
21:34 A[a]
35
Lev. 11:31, 32
Nu. 16:48, 49
49
19:11, 13
18
25: 9
33: 4
Deu. 25: 5[b]
26:14
Jud. 3:25
16:30
19:28 A[c]
Ruth 1: 8
2:20
4: 5,5,10
10
1 Sa. 4:17, 19
22+A
17:51
24:15
31: 5, 7
2 Sa. 1: 5, 19
2: 7
4: 1, 10
2 Sa. 9: 8
12:18, 18
19 *ter*
23
14: 2
16: 9
1 Ki. 3:20, 21
22, 23
23
11:21
12 *p* 24 *l* 15
ll 41, 43
l 44
14:11 A
11 A
16: 4, 4
20:14, 15
16, 24
24
22:37
2 Ki. 4:32
8: 5
13—A
2 Ch. 22:10
Job 39:30
Pro. 13:14
Ecc. 4: 2
Isa. 14:19
Jer. 16: 7
22:10

[a] *pro* τελευτάω. [b] A τελευτάω.
[c] *pro* νεκρός.

θνητός.

Job 30:23
Pro. 3:13
Pro. 20:24
Isa. 51:12

θολερός.

Habakkuk 2:15

θορυβέω.

Jud. 3:26
Nah. 2: 4

θόρυβος.

Ezra 10: 9
Pro. 1:27
23:29
Jer. 30: 2
Eze. 7: 7, 11
32:21 B[a]
Mic. 7:12+A

[a] *pro* βόθρος.

θραέλ.

Ezekiel 41: 8

θράσος.

Ezekiel 19: 7

θρασυκάρδιος.

Pro. 14:14
Pro. 21: 4

θρασύς.

Nu. 13:29
Pro. 9:13
13:17
Pro. 18: 6
21:24
28:26

θραῦσις.

Nu. 16:47, 48
49, 50
2 Sa. 17: 9
18: 7
2 Sa. 24:15, 21
25
Ps. 105:23, 30

θραῦσμα.

Lev. 13:30, 31[a]
31[b], 32
32, 33
33, 34
Lev. 13:34, 34
35, 36
37, 37
14:54

[a] AB τραῦμα. [b] A τραῦμα.

θραυσμός.

Nahum 2:10

θραύω.

Exo. 15: 6
Nu. 16:40
24:17
Deu. 20: 3
28:33
1 Sa. 20:34—B
2 Sa. 12:15
2 Ch. 6:24
2 Ch. 20:37
Job 20:19 A[a]
Isa. 2:10, 19
21
42: 4[b]
58: 6[c]
Jer. 28:30
Eze. 21: 7, 15

[a] *pro* θλάω. [b] S[1] σβέννυμι. [c] S τρέφω.

θρεπτός.

Esther 2: 7

θρηνέω.

Jud. 11:40
2 Sa. 1:17
3:33
2 Ch. 35:25
Jer. 9:17
22:10
28: 8—S[1]
Lam. 1:*a*1
Eze. 7:12
Eze. 8:14
32:16 *ter*
18
Joel 1: 5,8,11
13
Mic. 1: 8
2: 4
Zeph. 1:11
Zec. 11: 3

θρήνημα.

Ezekiel 27:32

θρῆνος.

2 Sa. 1:17
2 Ch. 35:25, 25
Isa. 14: 4
Jer. 7:29
9:10, 18
20
38:15
Lam. 1:*a*1
Eze. 2:10
19: 1
Eze. 19:14 AB[a]
14
26:17
27: 2, 32
28:12
32: 2, 16
Amos 5: 1, 16
8:10
Mic. 2: 4

[a] *pro* θρόνος.

θρίξ.

Exo. 25: 4
35: 6, 26
36:10
Lev. 13: 3, 4, 4
10, 20
21, 25
26, 30
31, 32
36, 37
14: 8, 9, 9
Nu. 6: 5, 18
Jud. 16:22
20:16
1 Sa. 14:45
2 Sa. 14:11, 26
1 Ki. 1:52
Ezra 9: 3
Job 4:15
Psa. 39:13
67:22
68: 5
Pro. 23: 7
Isa. 7:20
Eze. 16: 7
Dan. 3:27
4:30
7: 9

θροέω.

Canticles 5: 4

θρονίζω.

Est. 1: 2[a]

[a] S[3] ἐνθρονίζω.

θρόνος.

Gen. 41:40
Exo. 11: 5
12:29
Jud. 3:20
1 Sa. 2: 8
2 Sa. 3:10
7:13, 16
14: 9
1 Ki. 1:13, 17
20, 24
27, 30
35, 37
37, 46
1 Ki. 1:47, 47
48
2: 4, 12
19, 19
24, 33
(3)45
3: 6
5: 5
7:44
8:20, 25
9: 5
10: 9, 18
19, 19
1 Ki. 10:19+A
19 A[a]
16:11
22:10, 19
2 Ki. 10: 3, 30
11:19
13:13[b]
15:12
21: 4 A[c]
25:28, 28
1 Ch. 17:12, 14
22:10
28: 5
29:23
2 Ch. 6:10, 16
7:18
9: 8, 17
18, 18
18: 9, 18
23:20
Neh. 3: 7-ABS
Job 12:18
26: 9—S[1]
36: 7
Psa. 9: 5, 8
10: 4
44: 7
46: 9
88: 5, 15
30, 37
45, 46[d]
92: 2
93:20
96: 2
102:19
121: 5, 5
131:11, 12
Pro. 8:27
11:16
12:23
16:12
20: 8, 28
25: 5
29:14
Isa. 6: 1
9: 7
14: 9, 13
16: 5
22:23
66: 1
Jer. 1:15
3:17
13:13
14:21
17:12, 25
22: 2, 4
30
25:17
43:30
50:10
52:32
32+A
Lam. 5:19
Eze. 1:26, 26
10: 1
19:11[e]
26:16
43: 7
Dan. 4: 1+A
5:20
7: 9, 9
Jon. 3: 6
Hag. 2:22
Zec. 6:13

[a] *pro* τόπος. [b] B πατήρ. [c] *pro* ὄνομα. [d] AS χρόνος. [e] AB θρῆνος.

θρυλλέω.

Job 31:30

θρύλλημα.

Job 17: 6
Job 30: 9

θυγάτηρ.

Gen. 5: 4,7,10
13, 16
19, 22
26, 30
6: 1, 2, 4
11:11, 13
13, 15
17, 19
21, 23
25, 29
19: 8, 12
14, 15
16, 30
30, 36
24: 3, 13
23, 24
37, 43
47, 47
48
25:20
26:34, 34
27:46, 46
28: 1, 2, 6
8, 9
29: 6,9,10
16, 18
23, 24
28, 29
30:21
31:26, 28
31, 41
43 *ter*
50, 50
55
34: 1, 1, 3
5, 7, 8
9,9,16
16, 17
19, 21
Gen. 34:21
36: 2 *ter*
3,6,14
18—A
25, 39
37:35
38: 2
41:45, 50
46: 7, 7
7[a], 15
15, 18
20, 25
Exo. 2: 1, 5, 6
7, 8, 9
10, 16
20, 21
3:22
6:20, 23
25
10: 9
20:10
21: 4, 7, 9
31
32: 2
34:16 *ter*
Lev. 10:15
12: 6
18:10, 10
10—A
11
17 *qtr*
19:29
21: 2, 9
22:12, 13
24:11
26:29
Nu. 18:11, 19
21:29
25: 1, 15
Nu. 25:18
26:30, 37
37, 59
27: 1, 7, 8
9
30:17
36: 2, 6, 8
10, 11
Deu. 5:14
7: 3, 3
12:12, 18
31
13: 6
16:11, 14
18:10
22:16, 17
17
23:17, 17
28:32, 41
53, 56
32:19
Jos. 7:24
15:16, 17
16:10
17: 3, 3, 6
Jud. 1:12, 13
27 *sex*
3: 6, 6
11:26 A[b]
26 A[b]
34, 34
35, 40
40
12: 9, 9[c]
14: 1, 2, 3
19:24
21: 1, 7
14—A
18, 21
21
Ruth 1:11, 12
13
2: 2,8,22
3: 1, 10
11, 16
18
1 Sa. 1: 4+A
16
2:21
8:13
14:49, 50
17:25 A
18:17 A
19 A
20, 27
25:44
30: 3,6,19
2 Sa. 1:20, 20
24
3: 3,7,13
5:13
6:16, 20
23
11: 3
12: 3
13:18
14:27
17:25
19: 5
21: 8,8,10
11
1 Ki. (3)1, *p*1
p 46+A
4:11, 15
30—A
30—A
7:45
9: 9,16 A
24 A
11: 1
12 *p*24*l*5
*l*19
15: 2, 10
16 *p*28—A
31
21: 7
22:42
2 Ki. 8:18, 26
9:34
11: 2
2 Ki. 14: 9
15:33
17:17
18: 2
19:21, 21
21:19
22: 1
23:10, 31
36
24: 8, 18
1 Ch. 1:41+A
50+A
2: 3, 21
34, 35
49
3: 2, 5
4:18, 27
7:15—B
24—B
14: 3
15:29
23:22
25: 5
2 Ch. 2:14
8:11
11:18, 18
20, 21
21
13: 2
19 A[d]
21
20:31
21: 6, 17
22: 2
11—B
11
24: 3
25:18
27: 1
28: 8
29: 1, 9
31:18
36: 2, 5
Ezra 2:61
9: 2, 12
12
Neh. 3:12
4:14
5: 2
5—S[1]
5
6:18
7:63
10:28, 30
30
11:25+S[3]
25+S[3]
27+S[3]
28+S[3]
30+S[3]
31+S[3]
13:25, 25
Est. 2: 7
15—S[1]
9:29
Job 1: 2, 13
18
2: 9
42:13, 15
15+A
Psa. 9:15
44:10, 11
13, 14
47:12
72:28
96: 8
105:37, 38
136: 8
143:12
Pro. 24:50
29:47
Ecc. 12: 4
Cant. 1: 5
2: 2, 7
3: 5, 10
11-8S[1]
5: 8, 16
6: 8
7: 1, 4
8: 4
Isa. 1: 8
3:16, 17
4: 4
10:30, 32
16: 1—A
2
22: 4
23:12
32: 9
37:22, 22
43: 6, 20
45:11+AS
47: 1, 1, 5
49:22
52: 2
56: 5
60: 4
62:11
Jer. 3:24
4:11, 31
5:17
6: 2, 23
26
7:31
8:19, 21
22
9: 1,7,20
11:22
14:16—S
17
16: 2, 3
19: 9
26:11, 19
24
27:39, 42
30: 3, 4
31:18+A
36: 6
6—S[1]
38:21+A
22
39:35
42: 8
48:10
50: 6
52: 1
Lam. 1: 6, 15
2: 1, 2, 4
5,8,10
Lam. 2:11, 13
13, 15
18+S[1]
18
3:47, 50
4: 3,6,10
21, 22
22
Eze. 5:14
13:17
14:16, 18
20, 22
16:20, 27
28, 30
30, 45
45+B
46, 46
48, 48
49, 49
53, 53
55
55+A
55, 57
57
22:11
23: 2,4,10
10, 26
47
24:21, 25
26: 6, 8
30:18
32:16, 18
44:25
Dan. 11: 6, 17
Hos. 1: 3, 6
4:13, 14
Joel 2:28
3: 8
Amos 7:17
Mic. 1: 8, 13
15
4: 8,8,10
13
5: 1
7: 6
Zeph. 3:14 *ter*
Zec. 2: 7, 10
9: 9, 9

[a] A υἱός. [b] *pro* ὅριον. [c] A γυνή. [d] *pro* κώμη.

θύελλα.

Exo. 10:22
Deu. 4:11
Deu. 5:22

θυΐα.

Numbers 11: 8

θυΐσκη.

Exo. 25:28
38:12
Nu. 4: 7
7:14, 20
26, 32
38, 44
50, 56
62, 68
74, 80
Nu. 7:84, 86
86+A
86
1 Ki. 7:36
2 Ki. 25:14
1 Ch. 28:17—AB
2 Ch. 4:21
24:14
Jer. 52:19

θύλακος.

2 Kings 5:23

θῦμα.

Gen. 43:15
Exo. 29:28
34:15+B
25[a]
Deu. 18: 3[b]
1 Sa. 25:11
2 Sa. 6:13
2 Ki. 10:24[a]
2 Ch. 7: 4
Pro. 9: 2
17: 1
Eze. 40:41, 41[a]
42
46:24

[a] A θυμίαμα. [b] A θυσία.

θυμιάζω *vide* θυμιάω.

θυμίαμα.

Gen. 37:25
43:10
Exo. 23:18[a]
29:18[b]
30: 1, 7, 8
9, 27
35, 37
31:11
34:25[a]
25A[c]
35:14, 19
28
38:25
39:16
40:25
Lev. 4: 7, 18
10: 1
16:12, 13
13
Nu. 4:16
7:14, 20
26, 32
38, 44
50, 56
62, 68
74, 80
86
Nu. 16: 7, 17
18, 35
40, 46
47
Deu. 33:10
1 Sa. 2:28, 29
3:14
2 Ki. 10:24 A[e]
1 Ch. 6:49
28:18
2 Ch. 2: 4
13:11
26:16, 19
29: 7
Psa. 65:15
140: 2
Pro. 27: 9[d]
Isa. 1:13
39: 2
43:24 AS[e]
Jer. 17:26
51:21
Eze. 8:11
16:18
23:41
40:41 A[c]
Mal. 1:11

[a] A[1] θυσίασμα. [b] AB[2] θυσίασμα.
[c] pro θῦμα. [d] (S θυμίασιν.)
[e] pro θυσίασμα.

θυμιατήριον.

2 Ch. 26:19
Eze. 8:11

θυμιάω, –άζω.

Exo. 23:18 A[1 a]
30: 7[b], 7, 8
40: 5, 25
1 Sa. 2:15, 16
28
1 Ki. 1:23 A[c]
(3) p 1
3: 2, 3
9:25 A
11: 7
16 p 28 – A
22:44
2 Ki. 12: 3
14: 4
15: 4, 35
16: 4, 13
17:11
35 A[c]
36 A[a]
18: 4
22:17
23: 5, 5, 8
1 Ch. 6:49
23:13
2 Ch. 2: 4, 6
13:11
2 Ch. 26:16, 18[b]
18 A[a]
19
28: 4, 25
29: 7, 11
30:14
32:12
34:25[c]
Cant. 3: 6
Isa. 65: 3 A[d], 3
7
Jer. 7: 9
11:12, 13
17
18:15
19: 4, 13
31:35
39:29
51: 3, 5, 8
15, 17
18, 19
21, 23
25
Hos. 11: 2
Hab. 1:16

[a] pro θύω. [b] B[1] θύω.
[c] A θύω. [d] pro θυσιάζω.

θυμός.

Gen. 27:45
49: 6, 7
Exo. 11: 8
15: 8
22:24
32:12, 19
Lev. 10: 6
26:24, 28
41
Nu. 12: 9
14:34
18: 5
22:22
25: 3, 4, 11
32:10, 13
14
Deu. 6:15[a]
7: 4
9:19
13:17
Deu. 29:23, 24
27, 28
31:17
32:22, 24
33, 33
Jos. 7:26
Jud. 2:14, 20
3: 8
6:39
9:30[b]
10: 7 – A
14:19[b]
1 Sa. 17:28 A
20:34
28:18
2 Sa. 11:20
22:16
2 Ki. 5:12
13: 3
19:27
2 Ki. 22:17
23:26
24: 3, 20
2 Ch. 12: 7
25:10
28:11 – B
13 – B
29: 8 A[c]
10
30: 8
34:21, 25
35:19, 19
36: 5, 16
Ezra 8:22
10:14 – A
Est. 2: 1
7:10
Job 3:17
6: 4
10: 1 + A
13:13
15:13
19:29
20:16, 23
24:22
31:11
36:13, 18
37: 1
Psa. 2: 5, 13
6: 2, 8
9:35
29: 6
30:10
36: 8
37: 2
57: 5
68:25
73: 1
77:38, 49
49
84: 4, 5
87: 8
89: 7, 11
101:11
105:23 – S[1]
40
123: 3
Pro. 6:34 – S[1]
11: 4 + A
15: 1
16:14
18:14
20: 2
21:14
24:18, 23
27: 4
29:11
Ecc. 2:23
5:16
7: 4, 10
11:10
Isa. 1:24
5:25 S[c]
25
7: 4
9:12, 17
19, 21
10: 4 AS[c]
5, 25
26
12: 1
13: 3, 9, 13
13
14: 3, 6, 6
27: 8
28: 2, 21
21
30:27, 27
30, 30
33
31: 4
Isa. 34: 2
37:29
42:25
48: 9
51:13, 13
17, 17
20, 22
54: 8
59:19
63: 3, 5
65: 5
66:15
Jer. 2:35
4: 4, 8, 26
6:11
7:20
10:24, 25[b]
15:14
18:20[d], 23
20:16
21: 5
23:20
25:16
32:23
37:24 – S[1]
39:31, 37
40: 5
43: 7
49:18, 18
51: 6
6 + S
Lam. 1:12
2: 2 + A
2, 3, 4
3: 1, 42
46
4:11, 11
Eze. 5:13
15 + A
15
16 A[e]
7: 8
8:18
9: 8
13:13, 13
15
14:19
16:38, 42
19:12
20: 8, 13
21, 33
34
21:17
22:20 + A
22, 31
23:25
24: 8, 13
25:14
30:15
36: 5, 6, 18
38:18
39:29
43: 8
Dan. 2:12
3:13, 19
9:16
11:44
Hos. 8: 5
11: 9
13:11
Amos 6:12
Jon. 3: 9
Mic. 5:15
Nah. 1: 2, 6, 6
Hab. 3: 8, 12
Zeph. 2: 2
3: 8
Zec. 6: 8
8: 2
10: 3, 4

[a] AB[1] θυμόω. [b] A ὀργή.
[c] pro ὀργή. [d] S[1] θύρα.
[e] pro λιμός.

θυμόω.

Gen. 6: 7 A[a]
30: 2
39:19
Gen. 44:18
Exo. 4:14
32:10, 11
Lev. 10:16
Nu. 11: 1, 10
33
22:27
24:10
Deu. 1:37
4:21
6:15 AB[1 b]
9: 8, 20
11:17
Jos. 7: 1
Jud. 9:30 A[c]
10: 7 A[c]
14:19 A[c]
1 Sa. 11: 6
19:22
20:30
2 Sa. 3: 8
6: 7
11:22
12: 5
13:21
19:42
22: 8
2 Ki. 1:18
5:11
17:18
20 – AB
23:26
1 Ch. 13:10
2 Ch. 16:10
25:10
26:19, 19
Est. 3: 5
5: 9
Job 21: 4
32: 5
Ecc. 7:10
Isa. 5:25[d]
13:13
37:29[e]
54: 9
Jer. 30:12[f]
Eze. 21: 9
Dan. 11:30
Hos. 7: 5
11: 7
12:14

[a] pro ἐνθυμέομαι. [b] pro θυμός.
[c] pro ὀργίζω. [d] S ὀργίζω.
[e] S ἐνθυμέομαι.
[f] A κοιμάω, S[1] ἀθυμέω.

θυμώδης.

Pro. 11:25
15:18
22:24
Pro. 24:72
29:22
Jer. 37:23

θύρα.

Gen. 6:16
18: 1, 2, 10
19: 6, 9, 10
11, 11
Exo. 12:22 *ter*
23
21: 6
26:36 – AB[1]
29: 4, 10
10
11 – A
32, 42
33: 8, 9, 10
10
37: 5 – A[1]
38:20, 26
39: 8, 20
40: 5, 6, 10
26
Lev. 1: 3, 5
3: 2, 8
9 B[a]
13
4: 4, 7, 14
18
8: 3, 4, 33
35
10: 7
12: 6
14:11, 23
38
15:14, 29
16: 7
17: 4, 4, 5
6, 7 A[a]
9
19:21
Nu. 3:25 – A[1]
4:25, 31
6:10, 13
18
10: 3
11:10
12: 5
16:18, 19
27, 50
20: 6
25: 6
27: 2
Deu. 15:17
22:21
31:14, 14
Deu. 31:15, 15
Jos. 2:19 – A
19:51
20: 4 A
Jud. 3:23, 24
25
4:20
9:35, 40
44 – A
52
11:31
16: 3
18:16
17 + A
19:22, 26
27, 27
1 Sa. 2:22 + A
3:15
21:13, 13
23: 7
2 Sa. 10: 8
11: 9, 23
13:17, 18
1 Ki. 6:29, 31
31, 31
(32) A
7:36, 36
42
16:34
2 Ki. 4: 4, 5, 15
33
5: 9
6:32, 32
7: 3
9: 3, 10
10: 8
12:13
18:16
23: 8
1 Ch. 9:21, 27
2 Ch. 4: 9, 22
22
18: 9
28:24
29: 3, 7
Neh. 3: 1, 3
4 S[1 b]
6, 13
14
15 – ABS
20, 21
6: 1, 10
Neh. 7: 1, 3
Job 5: 4
31: 9, 32
34
Psa. 73: 6
77:23
140: 3
Pro. 5: 8
8:34
9:14
14:19
26:14
Ecc. 12: 4
Cant. 5: 2
7:13
8: 9
Isa. 26:20
Isa. 45: 1, 2
57: 8
Jer. 18:20 S[1 e]
30: 9
Eze. 8: 8
38:11
40:11
48
41: 4[c], 11[e]
11, 11
24
42: 9
46:12
Dan. 3:26
Zec. 11: 1
Mal. 1:10

[a] pro θυσία. [b] pro χείρ.
[c] pro θυμός. [d] A θύρωμα.
[e] A θυρίς.

θυρεός.

Jud. 5: 8 – A
1 Sa. 17:41 A[a]
2 Sa. 1:21, 21
2 Ki. 19:32
1 Ch. 12: 8, 34
2 Ch. 9:15
15 + AB
15
11:12
12: 9, 10
14: 8
2 Ch. 23: 9
25: 5
26:14
Neh. 4:16
Psa. 34: 2
45:10
Cant. 4: 4
Isa. 21: 5
37:33
Eze. 23:24

[a] A θυραιόν.

θυρεοφόρος.

1 Chronicles 12:24

θυρίς.

Gen. 8: 6
26: 8
Jos. 2:15, 18
Jud. 5:28
1 Sa. 19:12
2 Sa. 6:16
1 Ki. 6: 8
2 Ki. 9:30, 32
13:17
1 Ch. 15:29
Pro. 7: 6
Cant. 2: 9
Isa. 24:18
Jer. 9:21
22:14
Eze. 40:16, 16
22, 25
25, 29
33, 36
41:11 A[a]
16 *ter*
26
Dan. 6:10
Joel 2: 9

[a] pro θύρα.

θύρωμα.

1 Ki. 6:29
7:36, 42
42
1 Ch. 22: 3
2 Ch. 3: 7
4: 9
Eze. 40:38, 48
Eze. 41: 3 *ter*
4 A[a]
22, 23
24 *ter*
25
42: 4, 11
12

[a] pro θύρα.

θυρωρός.

2 Sa. 4: 6
2 Ki. 7:11
Eze. 44:11

θυσία.

Gen. 4: 3, 5
31:54
46: 1
Exo. 10:25
12:27
18:12
24: 5
29:34, 41
42
30: 9
32: 6
34:15 + A
Lev. 1: 9, 13
17
2: 1, 1, 2
3, 3, 4
5, 6, 7
8, 9, 10
Lev. 2:11, 13
14, 14
15
3: 1, 3, 6
9[a]
4:10, 26
31, 35
5:13
6:14, 15
15, 20
21, 21
23, 39
40
7: 1, 2, 3
5, 6, 7
10, 11
19, 19
22, 24

Lev. 7:27, 27
9: 4, 17
18
10:12, 14
14:10, 20
21, 31
17: 5, 5
7[b], 8
19: 5
21: 6, 21
22:21, 29
23:13, 13
16, 18
18, 19
37
26:31
Nu. 4:16
5:15, 15
18, 18
25, 25
26
6:15, 17
17, 18
7:13, 17
19, 23
25, 29
31, 35
37, 41
43, 47
49, 53
55, 59
61, 65
67, 71
73, 77
79, 83
87, 88
8: 8
10:10
15: 3, 4, 5
6
6−A
8, 9
24
16:15
23: 3, 3
15
25: 2, 2
28: 5, 8, 9
13, 20
26, 28
31+A
31
29: 3, 6, 6
9, 11
14, 16
18, 19
21, 22
24, 25
27, 28
30, 31
33, 34
37, 38
39
Deu. 12:27−B
18: 3 A[c]
27: 7[d]
32:38
33:19
Jos. 9: 4
22:23, 23
26
27−A
27, 28
29, 29
Jud. 6:18
13:19, 23
16:23 A[e]
1 Sa. 1:21, 24
2:17, 19
29, 29
3:14
6:15
9:12, 13
10: 8
11:15
15:22, 22
16: 3, 5
20: 6, 29
26:19
2 Sa. 14:17

2 Sa. 15:12+A
1 Ki. 8:62, 63
64, 64
12:27
18:29
2 Ki. 3:20
5:17 A[e]
10:19
21−A
16:13
15 qtr
1 Ch. 9:31
21:23
23:29
29:21, 21
2 Ch. 7: 1, 5
12[f]
29:31
31−A
30:22
31: 2
33:16
Ezra 7:17
9: 4, 5
Neh. 10:33
Job 1: 5
20: 6
Psa. 4: 6
19: 4
26: 6
39: 7
40: 5,8,14
23
50:18, 19
21
95: 8
105:28
106:22
115: 8
140: 2
Pro. 7:14
15: 8
16: 5
21: 3, 27
Ecc. 4:17
Isa. 1:11
19:21
34: 6
43:23
23-BS[1]
24
56: 7
57: 6, 7
65: 4
66:20
Jer. 6:20
7:21, 22
14:12
17:26
26:10
Eze. 39:17, 17
19
42:13
44:11, 15
29
45:15, 17
17, 23
46: 5
Dan. 8:11, 12
13
9:21
27+AB[2]
27
12:11+A
Hos. 3: 4
6: 6
8:13
9: 4
Joel 1: 9, 13
2:14
Amos 4: 4
5:21, 22
25
Jon. 1:16
Zeph. 1: 7, 8
3:10
Zec. 9: 1
Mal. 1: 8, 10
11, 13

Mal. 2:12, 13
Mal. 3: 3, 4

[a] B θύρα. [b] A θύρα.
[c] pro θῦμα. [d] A θυσιαστήριον.
[e] pro θυσίασμα. [f] A θυσιάζω.

θυσιάζω.

Exo. 22:20
Lev. 7: 6
24: 9
Jud. 2: 5[a]
16:23[b]
2 Sa. 15:12
1 Ki. 1: 9, 19
25[b]
22:44
2 Ki. 12: 3
14: 4
15: 4, 35
16: 4
17:35[c]
23:20

1 Ch. 21:28
2 Ch. 7: 5
12 A[d]
33:17−AB
34: 4
Ezra 4: 2
6: 3
Neh. 4: 2-ABS
3
Ecc. 9: 2, 2
Isa. 65: 3[b]
Hos. 4:13
12:11
Zec. 14:21

[a] A θύω. [b] A θυμιάζω.
[c] A θυμιάω. [d] pro θυσία.

θυσίασμα.

Exo. 23:18 A[1 a]
29:18 AB[2 a]
34:25 A[a]
Lev. 2:13
Nu. 18: 9
Deu. 12: 6−B

Deu. 12:11
Jud. 16:23[b]
2 Ki. 5:17[b]
Ezra 6: 3
Neh. 12:42
Isa. 43:24[c]

[a] pro θυμίαμα. [b] A θυσία.
[c] AS θυμιαμα.

θυσιαστήριον.

Gen. 8:20, 20
12: 7, 8
13: 4, 18
22: 9, 9
26:25
33:20
35: 1, 3, 7
Exo. 17:15
20:24, 25
26
21:14
24: 4, 6
27: 1, 1, 3
5, 5, 6
7
28:39
29:12+A
12, 12
13, 16
18, 21
21, 25
36, 37
37, 37
38, 38
44
30: 1, 18
20, 27
28
31: 8
32: 5
35:17
38:22, 23
24 ter
27
39:10, 10
15
40: 5, 6, 8
9, 9, 24
26, 27
Lev. 1: 5, 7, 8
9, 11
11, 12
13, 15
15, 15
16, 17
2: 2, 8, 9
12
3: 2, 5, 5
8, 11
13, 16
4: 7, 7, 10
18, 18

Lev. 4:19, 25
25, 26
30, 30
31, 34
34, 35
5: 9, 9, 12
6: 9, 9, 10
10, 12
13, 14
15, 32
35
7:21
8:11, 11
15 ter
16, 19
21, 24
28, 30
9: 7, 8, 9
9, 10
12, 13
14, 17
18, 20
24
10: 9, 12
14:20
16:12, 18
18, 20
25, 33
17: 6, 11
21:23
22:22
Nu. 3:31
4:11, 13
14
5:25, 26
7: 1, 10
10, 11
84, 88
10:38, 39
46
18: 3, 5, 7
17
Deu. 12:27−B
27−B
16:21
26: 4
27: 5, 5, 6
7 A[a]
33:10
Jos. 9: 3, 4
33
33−A

Jos. 22:19, 28
29, 29
Jud. 2: 2
6:24, 25
26, 28
28, 30
31, 32
13:20
20+AB
21: 4
1 Sa. 2:28, 33
7:17
14:35, 35
2 Sa. 24:18, 21
25, 25
1 Ki. 1:50, 51
53
2:28, 29
29
(3) p1
3: 4, 15
6:19
7:34
8:22, 31
54, 64
:25 A
12:32, 33
33
13: 1, 2, 2
2, 3, 4
4, 5, 5
32
16:32
18:26
31+A
32−A
32, 33
33, 35
19:10, 14
2 Ki. 11:11, 18
18
16:10, 10
11, 12
12+A
13, 14
14, 15
15
18:22, 22
21: 3, 4, 5
23: 9, 12
12, 15
15, 16
16, 17
20
1 Ch. 6:49, 49
16:40
21:18, 22
26, 26
29
22: 1
28:18
2 Ch. 1: 5, 6
4: 1, 11
19

2 Ch. 5:12
6:12, 22
7: 7, 9
8:12
14: 3, 5
15: 8
23:10, 17
17
26:16, 19
28:24
29:18, 19
21, 22
22
22−B
24, 27
30:14
32:12, 12
33: 4, 5, 15
16
34: 4, 5, 7
35:16
Ezra 3: 2, 3
7:17
Neh. 10:34
Psa. 25: 6
42: 4
50:21
82:13[b]
83: 4
117:27
Isa. 6: 6
19:19
56: 7
60: 7
Lam. 2: 7
Eze. 6: 4, 5, 6
13
8: 5+A
16
9: 2
40:46, 47
41:22
43:13, 13
18, 20
22, 26
27
45:19
47: 1
Dan. 9:27+AB[2]
Hos. 3: 4
4:18
8:11, 11
12
10: 1, 2, 8
12:11
Joel 1: 9, 13
2:17
Amos 2: 8
3:14, 14
9: 1, 1 A[c]
Zec. 9:15
14:20
Mal. 1: 7, 10
2:13

[a] pro θυσίαν σωτηρίου.
[b] AS ἁγιαστήριον.
[c] pro ἱλαστήριον.

θύω.

Gen. 31:54
46: 1
Exo. 3:18
5: 3, 8, 17
8: 8, 25
26, 26
27, 28
29
12:21
13:15
20:24
23:18[a]
24: 5
30: 7 B[1 b]
32: 8−B
34:15
Lev. 17: 5, 7
19: 5, 5, 6
22:29, 29
Nu. 22:40

Deu. 12:15, 21
15:21
16: 2, 4, 5
6
17: 1[c]
18: 3
27: 7
32:17
33:19
Jud. 2: 5 A[d]
6:18[e]
12: 6[f]
16:23 A[d]
1 Sa. 1: 3−A
4, 21
2:12, 14
15, 16
19
6:15+A
10: 8+A

1 Sa. 11:15
15:15
21−B
16: 2, 5
24: 8[g]
25:11
28:24
1 Ki. 3: 3, 4
8: 5, 62
63, 63
11: 7
12:32
13: 2[h]
16 p 28−A
19:21
2 Ki. 17:36[i]
1 Ch. 15:26
29:21
2 Ch. 5: 6
7: 4
11:16
15:11
18: 2
25:14
26:18 B[b]
18[i]
28: 3+AB
23
29:22, 22
22−B
24

2 Ch. 30:15, 17
22
33:16, 22
34:25 A[b]
35: 1, 6, 11
Neh. 12:43
Psa. 4: 6
26: 6
49:14
53: 8
105:37, 38
106:22
115: 8
Pro. 16: 5
Isa. 22:13
66: 3
Jer. 1:16
2:28
11:19
Eze. 16:20
20:28
39:17, 19
Hos. 4:13, 14
8:13
11: 2
13: 2
Jon. 1:16
2:10
Hab. 1:16
Mal. 1:14

[a] A[1] θυμιάω. [b] pro θυμιάζω.
[c] A προσφέρω. [d] pro θυσιάζω.
[e] AB τιθημι. [f] A σφάζω.
[g] A θανατόω. [h] A ἐπιθύω.
[i] A θυμιάζω.

θωδαθά.

Neh. 12:27[a] [a] ABS θωλαθά.

θώραξ.

1 Sa. 17: 5, 5
39+A
1 Ki. 22:34
2 Ch. 18:33
26:14

Neh. 4:16
Job 41: 4, 17
Isa. 59:17
Jer. 26: 4
Eze. 38: 4

ἴαμα.

2 Ch. 36:16
Job 23: 5[a]
Ecc. 10: 4
Isa. 26:19

Isa. 58: 8[b]
Jer. 26:11
37:17[c]
40: 6

[a] AS[2] ῥῆμα. [b] S[2] ἱμάτιον.
[c] A ἱμάτιον.

ἰαμίν.

2 Ki. 25:14[a] [a] A ἱμάτιον.

ἰάομαι.

Gen. 20:17
Exo. 15:26
Lev. 14: 3, 48
Nu. 12:13
Deu. 28:27, 35
30: 3
32:39
1 Sa. 6: 3
1 Ki. 18:31+A
32−A
2 Ki. 2:21, 22
20: 5, 8
2 Ch. 6:30 AB[a]
7:14
30:20
Neh. 4: 2-ABS
Job 5:18
12:21
13: 4
Psa. 6: 3
29: 3
40: 5
59: 4
102: 3
106:20

Ps. 146: 3
Pro. 12:18
18: 9
26:18[b]
Ecc. 3: 3
Isa. 6:10
7: 4
19:22, 22
30:26, 26
53: 5
57:18, 19
61: 1
Jer. 3:22
6:14
15:18
17:14, 14
19:11
28: 8, 9
Lam. 2:13
Hos. 5:13
6: 1
7: 1
11: 3
14: 4
Zec. 11:16

[a] pro ἱλάσκομαι. [b] S[2] πειράω.

ἴασις.

Job 18:14
Psa. 37: 4, 8
Pro. 3: 8, 22
4:22
15: 4
16:24
29: 1
Isa. 19:22
Isa. 19:22-ABS
Jer. 8:15, 22
14:19, 19
Eze. 30:21
Nah. 3:19
Zec. 10: 2
Mal. 4: 2

ἴασπις.

Exo. 28:18
36:18
Isa. 54:12
Eze. 28:13

ἰατρεία.

2 Ch. 21:18
Jer. 31: 2

ἰατρεῖον.

Exodus 21:19

ἰατρεύω.

2 Ki. 8:29
9:15
2 Ch. 22: 6, 9
Jer. 28: 9
37:13, 17
40: 6+AS
6

ἰατρός.

2 Ch. 16:12
Job 13: 4
Psa. 87:11
Pro. 14:30
Isa. 26:14
Jer. 8:22

ἶβις.

Lev. 11:17
Deu. 14:15
Isa. 34:11

ἰγνύα.

1 Kings 18:21

ἰδέα.

Gen. 5: 3
Dan. 1:13, 13
Dan. 1:15

ἰδεόγραφος.

Psalm 150:p6

ἰδιοποιέομαι.

2 Samuel 15: 6

ἴδιος.

Gen. 14:14
15:13
47:18
Deu. 15: 2
Est. 5:10
6:12
Job 2:11
7:10, 13
24:12
Pro. 5:18, 19
Pro. 5:20
6: 2, 2
9:12
11:24
13: 8
16:23
20:25
22: 7
27: 8, 8, 15
Eze. 21:30

ἰδίως.

1 Ki. 5: 6 B[a]

[a] *pro* εἰδέω.

ἰδιώτης.

Proverbs 6: 8

ἰδού.

Gen. 27:36[a]
29: 9−A
31:51−A
32: 6−A
41: 6−A
Exo. 34:29+A
Lev. 14:37−AB
Nu. 22:11+B
Deu. 20:16+A
Jos. 2: 2+A
Jud. 1:24−A
4:14+A
Jud. 9:38+A
15: 2+A
21: 9+A
19−A
1 Sa. 14:26−A
15:12+A
19: 9+A
2 Sa. 9: 6−A
1 Ki. 8:53−A
16:20−A
27−A
18:11−B
1 Ki. 19:11−AB
21:31+A
22:46−A
2 Ki. 2: 2+B
5:11−A
22−A
7: 3+A
10:34+A
14:15+A
15: 6+B
21−A
22:20−A
1 Ch. 28:20−B[b]
2 Ch. 8: 9+A
20:17+B
24:27−A
26:22+A[2]
Ezra 9:15-BS[1]
Neh. 9:36-ABS
Est. 10: 2−S[1]
Job 32:11+A
33:31+A
Psa. 67:34−S[1]
91:10+A[2]S
Cant. 2:11−S[1]
Isa. 40:10−S[1]
Jer. 4:10-AS[1]
6:19[c]
9:25−S[1]
23:29−AS
30−B
31−B
26:27-AS[1]
29:16+A
39: 3−S[1]
42:17−A
51: 2−S
27+A
34−S
Eze. 4: 8−B[2]
8: 7+A
16+A
10: 8 A[d]
25: 7+A
36: 7+A
37: 2+A
25+A
Dan. 3:25 A[e]
Amos 9: 9+A

[a] A ἤδη. [b] A εἰδέω. [c] AS Ἰούδα. [d] *pro* εἰδέω. [e] *pro* ὧδε.

ἱδρύω.

Psa. 143:12[a]

[a] ABS[1] ἁδρύνω.

ἱδρώς.

Genesis 3:19

ἱέραξ.

Lev. 11:16−A
Deu. 14:14+A
Deu. 14:16−A
Job 39:26

ἱερατεία.

Exo. 29: 9
35:19
39:19
40:13
Nu. 3:10
18: 1, 7, 7
25:13
Jos. 18: 7
1 Sa. 2:36
Ezra 2:62
Neh. 7:64
13:29, 29
Hos. 3: 4

ἱεράτευμα.

Exo. 19: 6
Exo. 23:22

ἱερατεύω.

Exo. 28: 1, 3, 4
37
29: 1, 44
30:30
31:10
40:11, 13
Lev. 7:25
16:32
Nu. 3: 3, 4
Nu. 16:10
Deu. 10: 6
Jos. 24:33
1 Sa. 2:28
1 Ch. 6:10
24: 2
2 Ch. 31:19
Eze. 44:13
Hos. 4: 6

ἱερεία.

2 Kings 10:20

ἱερεύς.

Gen. 14:18
41:45, 50
46:20
47:22, 22
26
Exo. 2:16
3: 1
18: 1
19:22, 24
29:30
35:18
36: 8
37:19
Lev. 1: 5, 7
8−A[1]
9, 11
12, 13
15, 15
Lev. 1:17
2: 2, 2, 8
9, 9, 16
3: 2, 5, 8
11, 13
16
4: 5, 6, 7
10, 16
17, 18
20, 25
26, 30
31, 31
34, 35
35
5: 6
8 *ter*
10, 12
12, 13
Lev. 5:13, 16
16, 18
18
6: 7, 10
12, 18
22, 23
26, 29
35, 36
37, 38
39
7: 4, 21
22, 24
10:16+A
12: 6, 7, 8
13 *passim*
14 *passim*
16+A
15:14, 15
15, 29
30, 30
16:20, 24
32, 33
17: 5, 6
19:22
21: 1, 9, 10
21
22: 4, 10
11, 12
13, 14
23:10, 11
20, 20
27: 8 *ter*
11, 12
12, 14
14, 18
21, 23
Nu. 3: 3, 6, 9
32
4:16, 28
33
5: 8, 9, 10
15, 16
17, 17
18, 18
19, 21
21, 23
25, 26
30
6:10, 11
11, 16
17, 19
20, 20
7: 8
10: 8
15:25, 28
16:37, 39
18:28
19: 3, 6, 7
7
25: 7, 11
26: 1
3−A
63
27: 2, 19
21, 22
31: 6, 12
13, 21
26, 29
31, 41
51, 54
32: 2, 28
33:38
34:17
35:25, 28
28, 32
36: 1
Deu. 17: 9−B
12, 18
18: 1, 3, 3
19:17
20: 2
21: 5
24:10
26: 3, 4
27: 9
31: 9
Jos. 3: 3, 6, 6
8, 13
14, 15
15, 17
Jos. 4: 9, 10
16, 17
18
6: 6, 8, 9
12, 13
13, 16
20
9: 6
14: 1
17: 4
19:51
20: 6 A
21: 1, 4
13+A
19, 20[a]
22:30, 31
32
24:33 A[b]
Jud. 17: 5, 10
12, 13
18: 4, 6
17+A
18−A
18, 19
19, 19
20, 24
27, 30
1 Sa. 1: 3, 9, 12
2:11, 12
12, 13
14, 15
15, 35
3: 1
5: 5
6: 2
14: 3, 19
19, 36
21: 1, 2, 4
5, 6, 9
22: 9
11+A
11, 17
17, 18
18, 19
21
23: 9
30: 7
2 Sa. 8:17
15:27, 35
35
17:15
19:11
20:25, 26
1 Ki. 1: 7, 8, 19
25[c], 26
32, 34
38, 39
42, 44
45
2:22, 26
27, 35
35
(3) p 46
4: 2+A
4
5+A
8: 3
4+A
6, 10
11
12:31, 32
13: 2, 33
33
2 Ki. 10:11, 19
21−A
21−A
11: 9, 10
15, 15
18, 18
12: 2, 4, 5
6, 7, 7
8, 9, 9
10, 16
16:10, 11
11+A
15, 16
17:28, 32
19: 2
22: 4, 8
10
2 Ki. 22:12, 14
23: 2, 4, 4
8, 8, 9
20, 24
25:18
1 Ch. 9: 2, 10
30, 31
13: 2
15:11, 14[d]
24
16: 6, 39
39
18:16
17 BS[e]
23: 2
24: 6, 6, 31
27: 5
28:13, 21
2 Ch. 4: 6, 9
5: 5, 7, 11
11, 12
14
6:41
7: 2, 6, 6
8:14, 14
15
11:13, 15
13: 9 *ter*
10, 12
14
15: 3−B
17: 8
19: 8, 11
22:11
23: 4, 6, 8
8−AB
11−AB
14 *ter*
17
18 *ter*
24: 2, 5, 11
12, 20
25
26:17, 17
18, 19
19, 20
20
29: 4, 16
21, 22
24, 26
34 *ter*
30: 3, 15
16, 21
24, 25
27
31: 2, 2, 4
9, 10
15, 17
19
34: 5, 9, 14
18, 30
35: 2, 8, 8
10, 11
14, 14
18, 19
36:14
Ezra 1: 5−A
2:36, 61
63, 69
70
3: 2−B
8, 10
12
6: 9, 16
18, 20
20
7: 5, 7, 11
13, 16
21, 24
8:15, 24
29, 30
33
9: 1
10: 5-BS[1]
10, 16
18−S[1]
Neh. 2:16
3: 1, 1, 20
22, 28
5:12
Neh. 6:14 BS[1f]
7:39, 63
65, 70
71[g], 72
8: 2
4 S[1h]
9, 13
9:32, 34
38
10: 8, 28
34, 36
37, 38
39
11: 3, 10
20 S[3]
12: 1, 7, 12
22, 26
30, 35
41 S[3]
44, 44
13: 4, 5, 13
28, 30
Job 12:19
Psa. 77:64
98: 6
109: 4
131: 9, 16
Isa. 24: 2
28: 7
37: 2
40: 2
61: 6
66:21
Jer. 1: 1
2: 8, 26
4: 9
5:31
6:13
8: 1
13:13
14:18
18:18
19: 1
20: 1
21: 1
23:11, 33
34
30: 3
31: 7
33: 7, 8, 11
16
34:13
35: 1, 5
36: 1, 25
26, 26
38:14
39:32
41:19
44: 3
52:24, 24
Lam. 1: 4, 19
2: 6, 20
4:13, 16
Eze. 1: 2
7:26
22:26
40:45, 46
42:13, 14
43:19, 24
27
44:15, 21
22, 30
30, 31
45: 4, 19
46: 2, 19
20
48:10, 11
13
Hos. 4: 4, 9
5: 1
6: 9
Joel 1: 9, 13
2:17
Amos 1:15
3:12
7:10
Mic. 3:11
Zeph. 1: 4
3: 4
Hag. 1: 1, 12

Hag. 1:14
2: 2, 4, 11
12, 13
Zec. 3: 1, 8
Zec. 6:11, 13
7: 3, 5
Mal. 1: 6
2: 1, 7

[a] A ὕριον. [b] *pro* ἀρχιερεύς.
[c] A ἀρχιερεύς. [d] S* ἀρχιερεύς.
[e] *pro* Χερεθί. [f] *pro* προφήτης.
[g] S ἱερός. [h] *pro* γραμματεύς.

ἱερόν.

1 Ch. 9:27
29: 4
2 Ch. 6:13
Eze. 27: 6
Eze. 28:18
45:19
Dan. 9:27

ἱερός.

Jos. 6: 8
Ezra 6: 3—A
Neh. 7:71 S[a]
[a] *pro* ἱερεύς.

ἱερωσύνη.

1 Chronicles 29:22

ἱκανός.

Gen. 30:15
33:15
Exo. 4:10
12: 4
36: 7
Lev. 5: 7
12: 8
25:26, 28
Ruth 1:20
21—A
1 Sa. 18:30 A
1 Ki. 16:31
2 Ki. 4: 8
2 Ch. 30: 3
Job 21:15
31: 2
39:32
Pro. 24:50
25:16
Isa. 40:16, 16
Jer. 31:30
Eze. 1:24+A
34:18
Joel 2:11
Obad. 5
Nah. 2:12
Hab. 2:13
Zec. 7: 3

ἱκανόω.

Gen. 32:10
Nu. 16: 7
Deu. 1: 6
2: 3
3:26
1 Ki. 12:28
19: 4
1 Ki. 21:11
1 Ch. 21:15
Cant. 7: 9
Eze. 44: 6
45: 9
Mal. 3:10

ἱκανῶς.

Job 9:31

ἱκετεύω.

Job 19:17
Psa. 36: 7
Zeph. 3:10+S[2]

ἱκετηρία.

Job 40:22

ἱκέτης.

Psa. 73:23
Mal. 3:14

ἰκμάς.

Job 26:14
Jer. 17: 8

ἴκτερος.

Lev. 26:16
1 Ki. 8:37+A
2 Ch. 6:28
Jer. 37: 6
Amos 4: 9

ἰκτῖνος.

Lev. 11:14
Deu. 14:13

ἱλαρός.

Job 33:26[a]
Pro. 19:12
Pro. 22: 8
[a] ACS[2] καθαρός.

ἱλαρότης.

Proverbs 18:22

ἱλαρύνω.

Psalm 103:15

ἱλαρῶς.

Job 22:26

ἱλάσκομαι.

Exo. 32:14
2 Ki. 5:18, 18
24: 4
2 Ch. 6:30[a]
Psa. 24:11
Psa. 64: 4
77:38
78: 9
Lam. 3:41
Dan. 9:19
[a] AB ἰάομαι.

ἱλασμός.

Lev. 25: 9
Nu. 5: 8[a]
1 Ch. 28:20
Ps. 129: 4
Eze. 44:27
Dan. 9: 9
Amos 8:14
[a] A ἐξιλασμός.

ἱλαστήριος.

Exo. 25:16, 17
18, 19
19, 20
21
31: 7
35:11
38: 5, 7, 7
8
Lev. 16: 2, 2, 13
14, 14
15, 15
Nu. 7:89
Eze. 43:14 *ter*
17, 20
Amos 9: 1[a]
[a] A θυσιαστήριον.

ἵλεως.

Gen. 43:22
Exo. 32:12
Nu. 14:19, 20
Deu. 21: 8
1 Sa. 14:45+A
2 Sa. 20:20, 20
23:17
1 Ki. 8:30, 34
36, 39
50
1 Ch. 11:19
2 Ch. 6:21, 25
27, 39
7:14
Isa. 54:10
Jer. 5: 1, 7
27:20
38:34
43: 3
Amos 7: 2

ἰλύς.

Psa. 39: 3[a]
Psa. 68: 3[b]
[a] ABS ὕλις. [b] B[1]S ὕλη.

ἱμάς.

Job 39:10
Isa. 5:18, 27

ἱμάτιον.

Gen. 9:23
27:27
28:20
37:29, 34
38:14, 19
39:12, 12
13, 15
16, 18
41:13
Exo. 12:34
19:10, 14
22: 9, 26
27
Lev. 6:27
10: 6
11:25, 28
32, 40
40
12: 4 A[a]
13: 6, 34
45, 47
47, 47
49, 51
52, 53
55, 56
57, 58
59
14: 8, 9, 47
47, 55
15: 5, 6, 7
Lev. 15: 8, 10
11, 13
17, 21
22, 27
16: 4—A
26, 28
17:15, 16
19:19
21:10, 10
Nu. 4: 6, 7, 8
9, 11
12, 13
14
8: 7, 21
14: 6
15:38
19: 7, 8, 10
19, 21
20:28
31:24
Deu. 8: 4
10:18
21:13
22: 3—8
17
24:15 A[b]
15, 19
29: 5
Jos. 7: 6
9:11, 19
Jud. 8:25, 26[c]
11:35
14:12, 13
19—A
17:10
1 Sa. 4:12
19, 13, 24
21: 9
24:12+A
28: 8
2 Sa. 1: 2, 11
11—A
3:31
12:20
13:31, 31
14: 2, 30
15:32 A[d]
19:24
20:12
1 Ki. 1: 1
11:29, 30
12 *p* 24 *l* 50
20:16
2 Ki. 2:12
4:39
5: 7, 8, 8
26
6:30
7:15
9:13
11:14
18:37
19: 1
22:11, 19
25:14 A[e]
29
2 Ch. 34:19:27
Ezra 9: 3, 5
Neh. 4:23
9:21
Est. 4: 1
Est. 5: 1
Job 1:20
13:28
24: 7
Psa. 21:19
44: 9
101:27
103: 2, 6
108:18, 19
Pro. 6:27
24:27
25:20
27:13
Ecc. 9: 8
Cant. 4:10[f], 11
Isa. 3: 6, 7
4: 1
9: 5
14:19
33: 1
37: 1
50: 9
51: 6, 8
58: 8 S[2g]
59: 6, 17
61:10
63: 1, 2
3 S[1a]
Jer. 30: 7
37:17 A[g]
43:24
48: 5—S[1]
50:12
Eze. 16:16, 39[h]
18: 7+A
42:14
Hos. 2: 5, 9
Joel 2:13
Amos 2: 8
Hag. 2:12, 12
Zec. 3: 3, 4, 5

[a] *pro* αἷμα. [b] *pro* ἐνέχυρον.
[c] A περιβόλαιον. [d] *pro* χιτών.
[e] *pro* ἱαμίν. [f] S μύρον.
[g] *pro* ἴαμα. [h] A ἱματισμός.

ἱματιοφύλαξ.

2 Kings 22:14

ἱματισμός.

Gen. 24:53
Exo. 3:22
11: 2
12:35
21:10
Jos. 22: 8
Ruth 3: 3
1 Sa. 27: 9
1 Ki. 10: 5, 25
22:30
2 Ki. 7: 8
2 Ch. 9: 4, 24
18:29
Psa. 21:19
44:10
Pro. 27:24
Isa. 3:18
Eze. 16:18
39 A[a]
23:26
26:16
Zec. 14:14
[a] *pro* ἱμάτιον.

ἱμείρω.

Job 3:21[a]
[a] ABCS ὁμείρω.

ἴν *vide* εἴν.

ἴνδαλμα.

Jeremiah 27:30

ἰξευτής.

Amos 3: 5
Amos 8: 1, 1

ἰός.

Psa. 13: 3—A
139: 4
Pro. 23:32
Lam. 3:13
Eze. 24: 6, 6, 11
12, 12

ἰουδαΐζω.

Est. (9)17[a]
[a] S[1] ἐνιουδαΐζω.

ἰουδαϊστί.

2 Ki. 18:26, 28
2 Ch. 32:18
Neh. 13:24
Isa. 36:11, 13

ἱππάζομαι.

Jer. 27:42
Eze. 23: 6, 12

ἱππάρχης.

2 Samuel 1: 6

ἱππασία.

Jer. 8:16
Hab. 3: 8

ἱππεύς.

Gen. 49:17
50: 9
Exo. 14: 9
1 Sa. 8:11
13: 5
2 Sa. 8: 4
10:18
1 Ki. 1: 5
4(26) A
10 *p* 22 *bis*
26, 28[a]
21:20
2 Ki. 2:12
13: 7, 14
18:24
1 Ch. 19: 6
7+BS
2 Ch. 1:14, 14[b]
16 B[b]
8: 6, 9
9:25
16: 8
2 Ch. 23:15
Ezra 8:22
Neh. 2: 9
Est. (9)14
Job 1:17
Isa. 21: 7
22: 7
Jer. 4:29
26: 4
Eze. 23: 6, 12
26: 7—A
10
27:14
38: 4
Dan. 11:40
Hos. 1: 7
Joel 2: 4
Amos 2:15
Nah. 2: 4
3: 3
Hab. 1: 8
[a] A ἵππος. [b] *pro* ἵππος.

ἱππεύω.

2 Ki. 9:16[a]
Eze. 23:23
Mic. 1:13
[a] A σπεύδω.

ἱππόδρομος.

Gen. 35:19—A
Gen. 48: 7, 7

ἵππος.

Gen. 14:11, 16
21
47:17
49:17
Exo. 9: 3—A[1]
14: 7, 9, 17
18, 23
15: 1, 19, 21
Deu. 11: 4
17:16, 16
20: 1
Jos. 11: 4, 6, 9
17:16, 18
24: 6
Jud. 5:22
2 Sa. 15: 1
1 Ki. (3) *p* 46 *bis*
4:21
(26) A
10:25
26+A
26
28 A[a]
29—A
12 *p* 24 *l* 11
16: 9
18: 5
21: 1, 20
21, 25
25
22: 4, 4
2 Ki. 2:11
3: 7, 7
5: 9
6:14, 15
17
2 Ki. 7: 6—A
7, 10
13, 14
9:18, 19
33
10: 2
11:16
14:20
18:23
23:11
1 Ch. 18: 4
2 Ch. 1:14 A[a]
16[b], 17
9:21, 23
28
12: 3
21: 9
25:28
Ezra 2:66
4:23
Neh. 3:28
7:68+AS
Est. 6: 8, 9
9+S[3]
10+S[3]
11
11—A
Job 30:18—S[1]
19
Psa. 19: 8
31: 9
32:17
75: 7
146:10
Pro. 21:31
26: 3

Ecc. 10: 7
Cant. 1: 9
Isa. 2: 7
5:28
22: 6
30:16
31: 1, 1, 3
36: 8, 9
43:17
63:13
66:20
Jer. 4:13
5: 8
6:23
8: 6, 16
16
12: 5
17:25
22: 4
26: 4, 9
27:36, 42
28:21
27−S[1]
38:40
Eze. 17:15

Eze. 23: 6, 12
20, 23
24+A
26: 7, 10
11
27:14
38: 4, 15
39:20
Hos. 1: 7
14: 3
Joel 2: 4
Amos 4:10
6: 7, 12
Mic. 5:10
Nah. 3: 2
Hab. 1: 8
3: 8, 15
Hag. 2:22
Zec. 1: 8, 8
6: 2, 2, 3
3, 6
9:10
10: 3, 5
12: 4, 4
14:15, 20

[a] pro ἱππεύς. [b] B ἱππεύς.

ἵπταμαι.

Job 20: 8

ἶρις.

Exodus 30:24

ἴσος.

Exo. 26:24
24
24−B
30:34, 34
Lev. 6:40
Nu. 12:12
Deu. 13: 6
1 Ki. 7:19+A
Job 5:14
11:12
13:12
24:20
27:16

Job 28: 2
30:19
40: 4+A
10
41: 3
Pro. 25:10
Isa. 61:23
Eze. 40:5, 5, 6
7 ter
7−A, 8
8, 9+A
41: 8
45:11

ἰσότης.

Job 36:29 | Zec. 4: 7

ἰσόψυχος.

Psalm 54:14

ἰσόω.

Job 28:17, 19 | Psa. 88: 7

ἵστημι.

Gen. 6:18
9:11
12: 8
17: 7, 19
21
18: 2, 22
19:17, 27
21:28, 29
23:17
24:13, 30
31
43A[2]S[a]
26: 3
28:18, 22
29:35
30: 9
21+A
40
31:25, 45
48
33:19, 20
35:14, 20
41: 1, 17
46
43: 8, 14
44:32

Gen. 47: 2, 7
Exo. 3: 5
4:25
26−B
6: 4
7:15 A[b]
8:20
9:11, 13
14:13[c], 19
20
17: 6, 9
20:18, 21
24:10
32:26
33: 8, 9
10, 10
21
34: 2
40: 2, 15
16, 16
27
Lev. 9: 5
14:11
16: 7, 10
18:23
26: 9

Lev. 27: 8, 11
12, 14
17
Nu. 3: 6
5:16, 18
30
8:13
9: 8, 15
17
10:12, 21
11:16, 24
12: 5
16:18, 27
48
21: 9
22:24
27: 2, 19
21, 22
30: 5, 6, 8
8, 12
12, 14
15, 15
35:12
Deu. 4:10, 11
5: 5, 31
8:18
9: 5
10:10
16:22
19:14, 15
17[d]
24:13
25: 8
27: 2, 4, 12
13
29: 1, 10
13
31:14, 14
15, 15
32: 8
Jos. 2:11
3: 4, 8
13
16 ter
17
4: 9, 10
20
5:13, 15
6:26+A
10:12, 13
13, 19
17: 4
18: 5, 5
20: 4 A
6 A?
24: 1, 26
Jud. 4:20
6:31 A[e]
7: 5, 21
8:27
9: 7, 35
44[f]
15: 5+A
16:25, 29[g]
18:16[h]
18−A
30[i]
20: 2
39−A
Ruth 2: 7
4: 7
1 Sa. 1:23
6:14
7:12
9:27
10:19 AB[1 j]
13:14
14: 9
15:13
17: 3, 3
8[k]
19: 3, 20
20:38
24:21
26:13
28:20
30: 9
2 Sa. 1: 9
2:25
14:26

2 Sa. 15: 2, 17
18−A
24
17:17
18: 4, 12
18
18−A
30
20: 4, 11
12, 12
15
21: 5, 12
22:34
24:18
1 Ki. 1:28
2: 4
3:15, 16
6(12) A
7: 7 ter
11+A
22
8:11 A[m]
14
22 A[n]
55
10: 9
19−A
20
12:15
p 24 l 36
13: 1, 24
24−A
25, 28
15: 4, 4
16:32
19:11, 13
21:38, 39
22:19, 21
35, 36
2 Ki. 2: 7, 7, 13
3:21
4: 6, 12
15
5: 9
11−B
15
6:31
7:12 B[n]
8: 9
10: 4, 4, 9
11:11[i], 14
13: 6, 18
15:20
18:17, 28
19:26
23: 3, 3, 10
24
25: 8
1 Ch. 6:32, 33
39
9:22
11:14
15:16, 17
16:17
21: 1, 15
16, 18
23:28, 30
25: 1
28: 2
2 Ch. 3:13, 17
5:12, 14
6:12, 13
7: 6, 6
8:14
9: 8, 18
19
10: 6, 8
18:18 B[o]
20, 34
20: 9, 13
20, 21
23:10, 19
25:14
14+B
26:18
29: 3, 11
25, 26
30: 5, 16
33: 3, 19
34:31[i], 32

2 Ch. 35: 2, 5, 10
19
Ezra 2:68
3: 8, 9, 10
6:18
8:25, 26
29, 33
9:15
10:13, 14
Neh. 3: 1
3 A[p]
6, 13
14
15-ABS
4: 9, 13
13
5:13
6: 7
7: 1, 3
8: 4, 4, 5
9: 2−S[1]
3, 4, 8
10:32[q]
12:31−ABS[1]
40 S[3]
40 S[3]
44
13:11, 19
30
Est. 4: 2
6: 5
9:21, 27
30, 30
31
Job 6: 2, 2
8:15
14: 2
20:19
28:15
29: 8[r]
30:20, 28
31: 6
32:16
33: 5
37:13, 19
39:26
40:12
41:15
Psa. 1: 1
17:34, 39
20:12
23: 3
25:12
30: 9
35:13
37:12, 12
39: 3
77:13[s]
81: 2
103: 6
104:10
105:23, 30
106:25, 29
108: 6
118:38, 106
121: 2
131: 7
133: 1
134: 2
118: 6
Pro. 8: 2
14:11
15:25 S[1 t]
Ecc. 1: 4
2: 9
4:12, 15[u]
8: 3
Cant. 2: 9+ACS[2]
Isa. 3:13
6: 2
17: 5
21: 6, 8, 8
22:22 S[2 v]
23
29: 9 S[1 w]
36: 2, 13
40:12, 20
22

Isa. 44: 7, 11
12[x], 13
13, 26
46: 6, 10
47:12, 13
48:13
49: 1, 6
51:14, 16
63: 5 S[a]
66:22
Jer. 4: 6
5:26
6:16
7:10
11: 5
14: 6
15: 1, 19
17:19
18:20
21 A[y]
19:14
23:18
20-S[1 z]
22
26:21
27:44
28:50
29:20
31:11, 19
33: 2
35: 5, 6
38:21
39: 9, 10
12 AS[o]
41:18 AS[1]
42: 5 A[v]
14, 16
43:21
47:10
52:12
Lam. 1:14
Eze. 1:21, 21
24
25+A
2: 1, 2
3:23, 24
8:11
9: 2
10: 3, 6, 9
17, 17
19
11:23
13: 5
17:14
21:21
22:30
24:11
27:29
31:14
33:26 A
37:10
40: 3
42:16
43: 6, 6
44:11, 15
46: 2
47:10
Dan. 1: 4, 5, 19
2: 2, 31
3: 1
2+AB
3, 3
3+A
5, 7, 12
14, 18
5:27
6: 7, 8, 15
7: 4, 5, 16
8: 3, 4, 6
7, 13
15, 17
18, 22
25
9:12
10:11, 13
16, 17
11: 1, 4, 6
7 B[1 n]
8, 11
14, 15

Dan. 11:15, 16
16, 21
25
12: 1, 5
Hos. 10: 9
Amos 6: 5
7: 7
Obad. 14 A[s]
Jon. 1:15
Mic. 2:11
5: 4

Nah. 2: 8
3: 9[aa]
Hab. 2: 1
3: 6, 11
Zec. 1: 8
2: 3
3: 1, 1, 3
4, 5, 7
11:12+A
12
14: 4, 12

[a] pro ἐφίστημι. [b] pro εἰμί.
[c] A στήκω. [d] B γινώσκω.
[e] pro ἐπανίστημι. [f] A ἐξίστημι.
[g] A ἐπιστηρίζω. [h] A στηλόω.
[i] A ἀνίστημι. [j] pro καθίστημι.
[k] B ἀνίστημι. [m] pro στήκω.
[n] pro ἀνίστημι.
[o] pro παρίστημι. [p] pro στεγάζω.
[q] B ποιέω. [r] A ἐπανίστημι
[s] S[2] παρίστημι. [t] pro στηρίζω.
[u] ACS ἀνίστημι. [v] pro δίδωμι.
[w] pro ἐξίστημι. [x] AS[3] τετραίνω.
[y] pro γίνομαι, [z] S[3] ἀνίστημι.
[aa] ABS εἰμί.

ἱστίον.

Exo. 27: 9, 11
12, 13
14, 15
35:12
37: 7
11−B

Exo. 37:16
39:20
Nu. 3:26
4:26
Isa. 33:23

ἱστός.

Isa. 30:17
33:23
38:12

Isa. 59: 5, 6
Eze. 27: 5

ἰσχίον.

2 Samuel 10: 4

ἰσχνόφωνος.

Exo. 4:10 | Exo. 6:30

ἰσχυρός.

Gen. 14: 5
41:31
50:10
Exo. 19:19
Nu. 13:19, 32
20:20
22: 6 A[a]
24: 4−B
21
Deu. 2:10 A[b]
4:38
7: 1
9: 1, 14
10:17
11:23
Jos. 4:24
6:20
10: 2
23: 9
Jud. 5:13, 22[c]
23 A[d]
6:12[e]
9:51[e]
14:14, 18
18:26 A[f]
2 Sa. 15:12
22:18 A[a]
31, 32
33, 48[e]
23: 5
1 Ki. 11:28
2 Ki. 24:15
1 Ch. 5:24
7: 2, 4, 5
7, 9, 11
40
8:40
9:13
12: 8
Ezra 4:20

Neh. 1: 5
9:31, 32
Job 22:13
33:29
31+A
34:31
36:22, 26
37: 4, 9
17
Psa. 7:12
41: 3+AS[2]
Pro. 6: 2
8:28, 29
14:29 B[1]S[1 g]
16:32
21:14
24: 5, 61
65
27:25
Ecc. 6:10
Isa. 8: 7, 11
9: 6+AS[2]
21:17
26: 1[h]
27: 1
3 AS[i]
28: 2
33:16[k]
43:16, 17
53:12
Jer. 1:18 S[i]
5:16
9:23
26: 5, 6
27:34
29:23
31:11
37:21
39:18
40: 3

Lam. 1:15
Eze. 26:17 + A
30:22
34: 4, 16
20
Dan. 1:15
2:37, 40
42
3:20, 33
6:20[m]
Dan. 7: 7
8: 9, 24
11:23
Joel 1: 6
2: 2,5,11
Amos 2: 9
5:12
Mic. 4: 3, 7 A[f]
Zeph. 1:16 A[i]

[a] *pro* ἰσχύς. [b] *pro* ἰσχύω.
[c] A δυνατός. [d] *pro* ὑπερέχω.
[e] A ὑψηλός. [f] *pro* δυνατός.
[g] *pro* ἰσχυρῶς. [h] S ὀχυρός.
[i] *pro* ὀχυρός. [k] A ὀχυρός.
[m] A μέγας.

ἰσχυρόω.

Isaiah 41: 7

ἰσχυρῶς.

Deu. 12:23
Jud. 8: 1[a]
Pro. 14:29[b]
29:35

[a] A κραταιῶς. [b] B[1] S[1] ἰσχυρός.

ἰσχύς.

Gen. 4:12
31: 6
49: 3
Exo. 9:16[a]
15: 6, 13
32:11, 18
Lev. 5: 7 A[b]
26:20
Nu. 14:13, 17[c]
22: 6[d]
24:18
Deu. 3:24, 24
4:37
8:17, 18
9:26 + A
26, 29
26: 8
32:13
33:11, 25
27
Jos. 6: 2
8: 3
10: 7
17:17
Jud. 5:13 + A
6:12 A[e]
14
11: 1 A[e]
16: 5, 6, 9
14 + A
15, 17
19, 30
Ruth 2: 1
1 Sa. 2: 9, 10
28:20, 22
30: 4
2 Sa. 6: 5
22:18[d]
24: 2, 4
1 Ki. 19: 8
2 Ki. 5: 1
15:20
17:36
19: 3
23:25
24:14
1 Ch. 5: 2
12:21, 25
28, 30
16:27, 28
26: 7 + A
29:11, 12
2 Ch. 3:17
6:41
13:20
20: 6, 12
25: 6
26:13
28: 6
35:19
Neh. 4:10
8:10
Est. 10: 2
Job 4: 2
5: 5
6:11, 12
12, 22
25
9:19
12:16
16: 5
19:20 A[n]
23: 6
26: 2, 12
30: 2, 18
31:39
36:5,20,22
37:22
39:11, 21
40:11
Psa. 17: 2
21:16
28: 4, 11
30:11
32:16
37:11
38:11
60: 4
64: 7
70: 9[f]
77:61
101:24
102:20
110: 6
117:14
146: 5
Pro. 5:10
8:14
14: 4, 26
15: 6
6 − S[1]
18:10
21:60
27:23
29:44
Ecc. 4: 1 − C
Cant. 2: 7
3: 5
5: 8
8: 4
Isa. 1:31
2:10, 19
21
3: 1, 1
10:13, 13
33
11: 2
23: 4, 11
28: 6
29: 2
Isa. 30:15
33:11, 13
37: 3
40: 9, 10
26, 29
31
41: 1
42:13
44:12
45: 1
47: 5, 9
49: 4, 5
26
51: 9
52: 1
58: 1
61: 6
62: 8[g]
63: 1, 15
Jer. 9:23
10:12
15:10, 12
16:19
20: 5
23:10
28:15, 53
29:17
34: 4
39:17
Lam. 1: 6, 14
Eze. 7:24
19:11 + A
12, 14
24:21, 25
26:11
27:12
30: 6, 15
18, 21
31:18
32:12, 12
Eze. 32:16, 18[h]
20, 26
29, 30
31
33:28
34:27[i]
Dan. 1: 4
2:20 + A
3: 4, 20
4:11, 27
5: 7
8: 6,7,22
24
24 + A
10: 8,8,16
17
11: 1,6,10
15, 17
19[k], 25
Hos. 6: 9
7: 9
8: 7
Joel 2:22
Amos 2:14
3:11
5: 9
6:13
Mic. 3: 8
4:13
5: 4
7:16
Nah. 1: 3
2: 2
3: 9
Hab. 1:11
3: 4
16 S[3 m]
Zec. 4: 6
14:14

[a] A δύναμις. [b] *pro* ἰσχύω.
[c] A χείρ. [d] A ἰσχυρός.
[e] *pro* δύναμις. [f] S ψυχή.
[g] S δόξα. [h] A γῆ.
[i] A καρπός. [k] A ἀρχή.
[m] *pro* ἕξις. [n] *pro* ὕλη.

ἰσχύω.

Gen. 31:29
Exo. 1: 9, 12
20
Lev. 5: 7[a]
27: 8
Deu. 2:10[b]
16:10
28:32
31: 6,7,23
Jos. 1: 6, 7, 9
14, 18
10:25
14:11, 11
Jud. 6: 2[c]
7:11
1 Ki. 2: 2
8:41 + A
1 Ch. 15:21 BS[d]
16:11
21: 4 − B[e]
22:13
28: 7, 10
20
29:14
2 Ch. 2: 6
15: 7
17:13
19:11
25: 8[e]
32: 7
Ezra 1: 6 A[d]
Job 26: 9, 31[f]
Psa. 12: 5
Pro. 7: 1
18:19
Isa. 1:24
3: 1, 1
2 − S[1]
25
5:22
8: 9
9 − S[1]
10:21
22: 3
23: 8, 11
25: 8
28:22
35: 3, 4
41: 7
46: 2
49:25
50: 2
2 − S[3]
59: 1
Jer. 5: 6
22 S[g]
20:11
31:14
Dan. 4: 8, 17
19
7:21
8: 8
10:19, 19
Joel 3:10

[a] A ἰσχύς. [b] A ἰσχυρός.
[c] A κατισχύω. [d] *pro* ἐνισχύω.
[e] A κραταιόω. [f] B ἀκούω.
[g] *pro* ἠχέω.

ἴσως.

Gen. 32:20
1 Sa. 25:21

Jer. 5: 4
33: 3
Jer. 43: 3, 7
Dan. 4:24

ἰταμία.

Jer. 29:17
Jer. 30: 4

ἰταμός.

Jer. 6:23
Jer. 27:42

ἰτέα.

Lev. 23:40
Ps. 136: 2
Isa. 44: 4

ἰχθυηρός.

Nehemiah 3: 3

ἰχθυϊκός.

2 Chronicles 33:14

ἰχθυρός.

Nehemiah 12:39

ἰχθύς.

Gen. 1:26, 28
9: 2
Exo. 7:18, 21
Nu. 11: 5
Deu. 4:18
1 Ki. 4:29
Neh. 13:16
Job 12: 8
Psa. 8: 9
104:29
Ecc. 9:12
Isa. 50: 2
Eze. 29: 4
4 + A
5
38:20
47: 9, 10
10
Dan. 2:38 − B
Hos. 4: 3
Hab. 1:14
Zeph. 1: 3

ἰχνεύω.

Proverbs 23:30

ἴχνος.

Gen. 42: 9, 12
Deu. 11:24
28:35, 65
Jos. 1: 3
Jud. 5:28 A[a]
1 Sa. 5: 4
2 Sa. 14:25
1 Ki. 5: 3
18:44
2 Ki. 9:35
2 Ki. 19:24
Job 9:26
11: 7
38:16
Psa. 17:37
76:20
Pro. 5: 5
24:54
Eze. 32:13
43: 7

[a] *pro* πούς.

ἰχώρ.

Job 2: 8
Job 7: 5

κάβος.

2 Kings 6:25

κάδιον.

1 Samuel 17:40, 40

κάδος.

2 Ch. 2:10 A[a]
Isa. 40:15

[a] *pro* μέτρον.

καθαγιάζω.

Lev. 8: 9
27:26
1 Ch. 26:20

καθαιρέω.

Gen. 24:18, 46
27:40
44:11
Exo. 24:24, 24
34:13
Lev. 11:35
14:45
Nu. 1:51
4: 5
10:17
Deu. 7: 5
28:52
Jos. 8:29
10:27

Jud. 2: 2[a]
6:25, 28[b]
30[b]
31[b]
32[b]
9:45
1 Ki. 19:14
2 Ki. 3:25, 25[c]
10:27 + A
14:13[d]
16:17
23: 7,8,12
2 Ch. 30:14
Ezra 6:11
Neh. 1: 3
2:13
4: 3
Job 19: 2
Psa. 9: 7
10: 3
27: 5
51: 7
59: 3
79:13
88:41
Pro. 21:22
Ecc. 3: 3
10: 8
Isa. 5: 5
14:17 − A
22:10
28:27
49:17
Jer. 4: 7
7 + S[1]
13:18
24: 6
29:17
38:40
40: 4[e]
49:10
51:34
52:14
Lam. 2: 2, 17
Eze. 16:39
26: 4 A[e]
12
16 A[1 f]
16 A[1 g]
36:36
Zec. 9: 6

[a] A κατακαίω. [b] A κατασκάπτω.
[c] A κάθημαι. [d] A διακόπτω.
[e] *pro* καταβάλλω.
[f] *pro* ἀφαιρέω. [g] *pro* καθέζομαι.

καθαίρω.

2 Sa. 4: 6
Jer. 28:39 S[a]
Jer. 38:28

[b] *pro* καρόω.

καθαρίζω.

Gen. 35: 2
Exo. 20: 7
29:36, 37
30:10
34: 7
Lev. 8:15
9:15 − A[1]B
12: 7, 8
13: 6,7,13
17, 23
28, 34
35, 37
59
14: 2, 4, 7
8, 11
11, 14
17, 18
19, 20
23, 25
28, 29
31, 48
57
15:13, 28
28
16:19, 20
30, 30
22: 4
Nu. 6: 9
9 A[1]P[a]
8:15
12:15
14:18
30: 6,9,13
31:23, 24
Deu. 5:11
19:13
Jos. 22:17
1 Sa. 20:26
2 Ki. 5:10, 12
13, 14
2 Ch. 29:15 − B
34:3, 5, 8
Ezra 6:20
Neh. 12:30, 30
13: 9, 22
30
Job 1: 5
Psa. 11: 7
18:13, 14
38: 9 S[1 b]
50: 4, 9
Pro. 25: 4
Isa. 53:10
57:14
66:17
Jer. 13:27
32:15
40: 8
Lam. 4: 7
Eze. 24:13 + A
13
36:25, 25
33
37:23
39:13, 14
16
43:26
44:26
Dan. 8:14
Hos. 8: 5
Mal. 3: 3, 3

[a] *pro* ξυράω. [b] *pro* ῥύομαι.

καθαριότης.

Exo. 24:10
2 Sa. 22:21, 25
Psa. 17:21, 25

καθαρισμός.

Exo. 29:36
30:10
Lev. 14:32
15:13
Nu. 14:18
1 Ch. 23:28
Neh. 12:45
Job 1: 5 S[1 a]
7:21
Psa. 88:45
Pro. 14: 9

[a] *pro* ἀριθμός.

καθαρός.

Gen. 7: 2,2,3,3
8—A
8, 8
8—A
8:20, 20
20: 5, 6
24: 8
44:10
Exo. 25:10, 16
22, 27
28, 30
36, 38
39
27:20
28: 8—AB
13, 14
22, 32
30: 3,4,35
31: 8
36:22, 38
38: 2
5—B
9
11+A
25
39:16
Lev. 4:12
6:11
7: 9
10:10
11:32, 36
37, 47
13: 6, 13
17, 34
37, 39
40, 41
58
14: 4, 7, 8
9, 49
53
15: 8, 12
13
17:15
20:25, 25
22: 7
24: 2, 4, 6
7
Nu. 5:17, 28
8: 7
9:13
18:11, 13
19: 3, 9, 9
12, 12
Nu. 19:18, 19
Deu. 12:15, 22
14:11, 19
15:22
23:10
1 Sa. 20:26
2 Ch. 3: 4, 5, 8
4:16, 20
21
9:15+B
15
13:11
Ezra 2:69—A
6:20
Neh. 2:20
Job 4: 7, 17
8: 6
9:30
11: 4, 13
15
14: 4
15:15
16:17
17: 9
21:16 A[a]
22:25, 30
25: 4+A
5[b]
28:19
33: 3, 3, 9
26 ACS[2] [c]
Psa. 23: 4
50:12
Pro. 8:10+B[*]
12:27
14: 4
20: 9
25: 4
Ecc. 9: 2
Isa. 1:16, 25
14:19, 20
35: 8
47:11
65: 5
Jer. 4:11
Eze. 22:26
36:25
44:23
Dan. 2:32 AB[2] [d]
7: 9
Hab. 1·13
Zec. 3: 5,5–S[1]
Mal. 1:11

[a] pro ἐφοράω. [b] A ἄμεμπτος.
[c] pro ἱλαρός. [d] pro χρηστός.

κάθαρσις.

Lev. 12: 4, 6
Jer. 32:15
Eze. 15: 4

καθέδρα.

1 Sa. 20:18, 25
25
1 Ki. 8:13 A
10: 5, 19
2 Ki. 16:18
17:25
2 Ki. 19:27
2 Ch. 9: 4, 18
Psa. 1: 1
106:32
138: 2
Lam. 3:62

καθέζομαι.

Lev. 12: 5
Job 39:27
Jer. 37:18
Eze. 26:16[a]

[a] A[1] καθαιρέω.

κάθεμα.

Isa. 3:19
Eze. 16:11

καθεύδω.

Gen. 28:13
39:10
Deu. 11:19[a]
Ruth 3: 7+A
1 Sa. 3: 2[b],3,5
5, 6, 9
1 Sa. 19: 9
26: 5, 5, 7
7
2 Sa. 4: 5, 6, 7
12: 3
1 Ki. 18:27
Psa. 87: 6
Pro. 3:24
6:22
Cant. 5: 2
Isa. 51:20
Eze. 4: 9
Dan. 12: 2
Amos 6: 4
Jon. 1: 5

[a] A κοιτάζω. [b] B[1] κάθημαι.

καθήκω.

Gen. 19:31
Exo. 5:13, 19
16:16, 18
21—B
36: 1
Lev. 5:10
Lev. 9:16
Deu. 21:17
1 Sa. 2:16
Eze. 21:27
Hos. 2: 5

καθηλόω.

Psalm 118:120

καθήλωμα.

1 Kings 6:19+A

κάθημαι.

Gen. 18: 1
19: 1, 30
21:16
16 A[a]
23:10
38:11, 11
Exo. 11: 5
12:29
16:29 AB[a]
17:12
18:14
24:18 A[b]
Lev. 8:35
12: 4
13:46
15: 6
23 A[a]
Nu. 32: 6
Deu. 6: 7
11:19
Jos. 5: 8
Jud. 3:20
24+A
4: 5
5:10
16 A[a]
6:10[c]
18 A[a]
13: 9
16: 9
12 A[d]
17:10
18: 7, 8
Ruth 3:18 4:4
1 Sa. 1: 9+A
22, 23
3: 2 B[1] [e]
4: 4
13+A
5: 7
12: 2
14: 2
20: 5, 19[f]
22: 5,6,23
23:14, 18
24: 4
27: 5[f], 5
11
30:24
2 Sa. 6: 2
7: 2
16: 3, 18
18:24
19: 8
23:10
1 Ki. 1:17, 20
24, 27
30, 35
48
(3)36
3: 6+A
7:45
8:25
9:16 A
11:16 A[g]
1 Ki. 11:43—A
12:17 A
13:14, 20
17: 9+A
19
20:11 A[b]
22:10, 19
2 Ki. 1: 9
2: 2, 4, 6
18
3:25 A[i]
4:38
6:32, 32
7: 3
9: 5
13+A
10:30
14:10
15:12
18:27
19:15
1 Ch. 13: 6
2 Ch. 6:16
18: 9,9,18
25:19 AB[a]
26:21
32:10
Ezra 9: 3, 4
Neh. 2: 6
6+S[3]
11: 6
Est. 5:13+S[3]
Job 2: 8
9–S[1] [f]
38:40
Psa. 46: 9
49:20
68:13
79: 2
98: 1
106:10
109: 1
126: 2
Pro. 3:24
6:10
Ecc. 10: 6
Cant. 5:12
8:13
Isa. 6: 1
9: 2 A[k]
9[m]
19: 1
36:11+A
12
37:16
42: 7
47: 8
Jer. 8:14
13:13
13 A[h]
15:17
17:25
21: 9
22: 2,4,30
28:30
Jer. 30: 8, 9
31:18, 19
43
32:15, 16
39:12+A
40: 4 A[i]
43:12, 22
30
47:10
51: 1[n], 13
15, 26
Lam. 3:28
Eze. 8: 1,1,14
23:41
33:31
44: 3
Dan. 7: 9
Hos. 3: 3, 4
Jon. 4: 5
Zec. 3: 8
5: 7
8: 4
9:12[o]

[a] pro καθίζω. [b] pro εἰμί.
[c] A ἐνοικέω. [d] pro ἐξέρχομαι.
[e] pro καθεύδω. [f] A καθίζω.
[g] pro ἐγκάθημαι.
[h] pro κατοικέω. [i] pro καθαιρέω.
[k] pro πορεύω. [m] AS[2] ἐγκάθημαι.
[n] S κατοικέω. [o] A καὶ τίθημι.

κάθιδρος.

Jeremiah 8: 6

καθιζάνω.

Job 12:18[a]
Pro. 18:16

[a] A καθίζω.

καθίζω.

Gen. 8: 4
21:16[a]
22: 5
27:19
37:25
38:14
43:32
48: 2
Exo. 2:15
12:22
16: 3, 29[b]
32: 6
Lev. 15: 4, 6
9 A[c]
22, 23[a]
26
Nu. 11: 4
Deu. 1:45
17:18
21:13
25: 2
Jos. 5: 2
Jud. 5:16[a],17[d]
6:11, 18[a]
8:29[e]
9:41 A[f]
11:17
15: 8—A
19: 4, 6
7—A
15
20:26, 47
21: 2, 23[c]
Ruth 2:14
3: 1
4: 1 *ter*
2, 2
1 Sa. 1:23
2: 8
5:11
13:16
19: 2, 18
20: 5,19A[g]
25, 25
22: 5
23:14
24: 1—A
25:13
26: 3
27: 3
5 A[g],7
28:23
30:10, 21
2 Sa. 1: 1
2:13
5: 9
6:11
7: 1, 18
10: 5
2 Sa. 11: 1 A[b],1
12, 12
13:20
14:28
15:25+A
29
19: 8, 37
22:11 A[i]
1 Ki. 1:13, 46
2:12, 19
19
(3)38
8:20
11(24)A
16:11
17: 5
19: 4
20: 9
10 A[k]
12—B
13
22: 1
2 Ki. 7: 4
11:19
13: 5, 13
17:28
25:24
1 Ch. 11: 7
13:14
17:16
19: 5
20: 1
28: 5
29:23
2 Ch. 6:10
23:20
25:19[b]
Ezra 2:70
8:32
10: 2[m], 9
10[m]
14[m],17
18–S[1] [m]
Neh. 1: 4
6: 7
7:72
8:17
11: 1, 1, 2
3, 3, 4
25
13:16, 23
27
Job 2: 9 A[g]
6:29
12:18 A[n]
29:25
36: 7
Psa. 1: 1
9: 5
Psa. 25: 4, 5
28:10
112: 8
118:23
121: 5
131:13
136: 1
142: 3
Pro. 9:14
20: 8
22:10
23: 1
29:41
Cant. 2: 3
Isa. 14:13
16: 5
30: 8
47: 1
1—AS
5,8,14
52: 2
Jer. 3: 2
13:18—A
15:17
16: 8 A[o]
29:19
30:11
Jer. 31:18
33:10
39: 5 S[p]
37[q]
44:16, 21
45:13, 28
46: 3, 14
47: 6
48:17
49:10, 10
13
Lam. 1:*a*1,1, 3
2:10
3: 6
Eze. 3:15
14: 1
20: 1
36:35
Dan. 7:10, 26
11:10
Hos. 14: 7
Joel 3:12
Jon. 3: 6
4: 5
Mic. 7: 8
Zec. 6:13[r]
Mal. 3: 3

[a] A κάθημαι. [b] AB κάθημαι.
[c] pro ἐπιβαίνω. [d] A παροικέω.
[e] A κατοικέω. [f] pro εἰσέρχομαι.
[g] pro κάθημαι. [h] pro διακαθίζω. [i] pro ἐπικαθίζω.
[k] pro ἐγκαθίζω. [m] S[3] λαμβάνω.
[n] pro καθιζάνω.
[o] pro συγκαθίζω. [p] pro καθίημι.
[q] A κατοικίζω. [r] B[1]S[1] καθίημι.

καθίημι.

Exo. 17:11
1 Ch. 21:27 A[a]
Jer. 39: 5[b]
Zec. 6:13 B[1]S[1] [c]
11:13

[a] pro κατατίθημι.
[b] A ἀποθνήσκω, S καθίζω.
[c] pro καθίζω.

κάθισις, A κάθησις.

Jer. 20: 9
Jer. 30: 8

καθίστημι.

Gen. 39: 4, 5
41:33, 34
41, 43
47: 5
Exo. 2:14
5:14
18:21
Nu. 3:10, 32
4:19
21:15
31:48
Deu. 1:13, 15
16:18 A[a]
17:14
15 *qter*
19:16
20: 9
25: 6
28:13, 36
32:25
Jos. 6:23
8: 2
9:33
10:18
20: 3, 9
Jud. 11:11 A[b]
1 Sa. 1: 9, 26
3:10
5: 3
8: 1, 5
10:19[c], 19
23
12: 7, 16
18: 5 A,13
19:20
22: 9
29: 4, 10
30:12
2 Sa. 3:39
6:21
15: 4
17:25
18: 1
1 Ki. 3 *p*1
4: 5, 7
20
5:16
11:28
2 Ki. 7:17
10: 3
22: 5, 9
25:22, 23
1 Ch. 6:31
9:29
11:25
12:18
22: 2
26:32
2 Ch. 11:15, 22
12:10
17: 2
19: 5, 8
21: 5
24:11
25: 3
23 A[d]
28:15
29: 4
31:13
33:14
34:10
36: 1—A
4
Ezra 7:25
Neh. 12:14
13:19

Est. 2: 3
8: 2
Job 16:12
Psa. 2: 6
8: 7
9:21
17:44
44:17
96: 1
104:21
108: 6
Pro. 29:14
Isa. 3:13
40: 8
62: 6
Jer. 1:10
6:17
Jer. 20: 1
23: 3
26: 4
36:15
37:24−S[1]
47: 5,7,11
48: 2,18
51:28[e]
Eze. 34:18
Dan. 1:11
2:21,24
38,48
40
3:12
5:11
6: 1,3

[a] pro ποιέω. [b] pro τίθημι.
[c] AB[1] ἵστημι. [d] pro κατασπάω.
[e] A καταβαίνω, S παροικέω.

καθοδηγέω.

Job 12:23
Jer. 2: 6
Eze. 39: 2

κάθοδος.

1 Ki. 9:25 A
Ecc. 6: 6
Ecc. 7:23

καθόλου.

Exo. 22:11[a]
Eze. 13: 3, 22
Eze. 17:14
Amos 3: 3, 4
[a] A ὅλος.

καθομολογέω.

Exodus 21: 8, 9

καθοπλίζω.

Jeremiah 26:9

καθοράω.

Nu. 24: 2
Job 10: 4
Job 39:26

καθόρμιον.

Hosea 2:13

καθυβρίζω.

Pro. 19:28
Jer. 28: 2

καθυμνέω.

2 Chronicles 30:21

καθυπνόω.

Proverbs 24:18

καθυστερέω.

Exo. 22:29
1 Ch. 26:27

καθυφαίνω.

Exodus 28:17

καινίζω.

Isa. 61: 4
Zeph. 3:17

καινός.

Deu. 20: 5
22: 8
32:17
Jos. 9:19
Jud. 5: 8[a]
15:13
16:11−A
12
1 Sa. 6: 7
23:15, 16
18, 19
2 Sa. 6: 3
3+A
1 Ki. 11:29, 30
12 *p* 24 *l* 50
22:13 A[b]
2 Ki. 2:20
1 Ch. 13: 7
2 Ch. 20: 5
Job 6: 6 AS[c]
7: 3 S[c]
6 S[c]
16 AS[c]
29:20 C[c]
Psa. 32: 3
39: 4
Psa. 95: 1
97: 1
106: 9 S[c]
143: 9
149: 1
Ecc. 1:10
Isa. 8: 1
41:15
42: 9[a], 10
43:19
48: 6
62: 2
Isa. 65:15[d]
17[e], 17
66:22, 22
Jer. 33:10
38:22
31−S[1]
43:10
Lam. 3:23−AB
Eze. 11:19
18:31, 31
36:26, 26

[a] A κενός. [b] pro γίνομαι.
[c] pro κενός. [d] S[1] αἰώνιος.
[e] S[1] καπνός.

καινότης.

1 Ki. 8:53
Eze. 47:12

καίπερ.

Pro. 6: 8
Jon. 1:13+B[1]

καίριος.

Proverbs 15:23

καιρός.

Gen. 1:14
6:13
17:21, 23
26
18:10, 14
21: 2, 22
26: 1[a]
29:34
30:20, 41
38: 1
Exo. 8:32
9: 4−A[1]
14
13:10−B
23:14, 15
17
34:18, 23
24
Lev. 15:25
23: 4
26: 4
Nu. 9: 3,7,13
14: 9
16:14 B[b]
22: 4
23:23
Deu. 1: 9, 16
18
2:34
3: 4,8,12
18, 21
23
4:14
5: 5
9:19, 20
10: 1,8,10
16: 6, 16
28:12
31:10
32:35+A
Jos. 5: 2
11:10, 21
Jud. 3:29 A[c]
4: 4
10: 8[d], 14
11:26
12: 6
13:23
14: 4
21:14
22 A[b]
24
1 Sa. 1:20
4:20
9:16
18:19 A
20:12
2 Sa. 11: 1
20: 5
23: 5
1 Ki. 11: 3, 29
14: 1 A
15:23
16:22
18:29
2 Ki. 4:16, 17
8:22
16: 6
18:16
20:12
24:10
1 Ch. 9:25, 25
11:11, 20
12:32
21:28, 29
29:30−B
2 Ch. 7: 2, 8
8:13
15: 3
16: 7, 10
21:10, 19
25:27
28:16
30: 3
35:17
Ezra 5: 3
8:34
10:13[e], 14
Neh. 4:22
6: 1[f]
9:27
10:34
12:17+S[3]
13:21, 31
Est. 2:12
12+A
4:14, 14
8: 9+S[3]
Job 5:26
10: 4
28: 3+A
38:32
39: 1, 18
Psa. 1: 3
9:26
20:10
31: 6
33: 2
36:19, 39
68:14
70: 9
71: 3
80:16
101:14, 14
103:19
27 A[g]
105: 3
118:20, 126
Pro. 5: 3, 19
6:14
Pro. 8:30
17:17
18: 1
Ecc. 3: 1 *to* 8
11[b], 17
7:18
8: 5, 6
9: 8, 11
12, 12
10:17
Cant. 2:12
Isa. 8:22
18: 7
30: 8
33: 2
38: 1
39: 1
49: 8
50: 4+A
54: 9 S[2 i]
60:22
64: 9
Jer. 2:27, 28
3:17
4:11
5:24
6:15
19 S[k]
8: 1, 7, 7
15
10:15
11:12, 14
14
14: 8, 19
15:11, 11
16:21
18:23
26:21
27: 4, 16
20, 26
27, 31
28: 6, 18
Lam. 1:15, 21
Lam. 4:19, 19
Eze. 4:10, 10
11, 11
7: 7, 12
12:27
16: 8, 8
21:25, 29
22: 3,4,30
30: 3+A
35: 5+A
5
Dan. 2: 8,9,21
4:13, 20
22, 29
33
6:10, 13
7:12, 12
22, 25
25
25+A
25, 25
8:17, 19
9:25, 27
11: 6, 13
14, 24
27, 29
35, 35
40
12: 1 *qtr*
4, 7, 7
7,9,11
Hos. 2: 9
Joel 3: 1
Amos 5:13, 13
Mic. 2: 3
3: 4
5: 3
Hab. 2: 3
3: 2
Zeph. 3:16, 19
20, 20
Hag. 1: 2, 4

[a] A χρόνος. [b] pro κλῆρος.
[c] pro ἡμέρα. [d] A ἐνιαυτός.
[e] B τόπος. [f] S[1] λαός.
[g] pro εὔκαιρος. [h] S[1] ἐνώπιον.
[i] pro χρόνος. [k] pro καρπός.

καίω.

Exo. 3: 2
27:20−A
20, 21
35: 3
Lev. 4:12
6: 9, 12
12, 13
13:56 A[a]
24: 2, 3, 4
Deu. 4:11
5:23
7:25[b]
9:15
32:22
Jud. 15: 5[c]
2 Sa. 23: 7[d]
1 Ki. 13: 2−A
Neh. 4: 2−ABS
Job 15:34[b]
31:12
41:10, 11
Psa. 7:14
49: 3
Isa. 4: 5
5:24
9:18, 18
10:16, 16
17, 18
30:27, 33
Isa. 33:14
34: 9
44:15
16+AS[1]
50:11
62: 1
65: 5
Jer. 7:18, 20[e]
15:14
20: 9
21:12
30:16
39:29
29 A[f]
41: 2
43:27 AS[1 f]
44: 8, 10
45:18
50:12
Eze. 1:13
39: 9, 9
Dan. 3: 6, 11
15, 17
20, 21
23, 26
Hos. 7: 4
7+A
Mal. 4: 1

[a] pro πλύνω. [b] A κατακαίω.
[c] A ἐμπυρίζω. [d] B τίθημι.
[e] S ἐκκαίω. [f] pro κατακαίω.

κακία.

Gen. 6: 5
31:52
Exo. 22:23
Exo. 23: 2
32:12
14+A
Deu. 31:18
Jud. 9:56 A[a]
57 A[a]
16:18 A[b]
20: 3 A[a]
12 A[a]
13 A[a]
34
41 A[a]
1 Sa. 6: 9
12:17, 19
20, 25
17:28 A
20: 7,9,33
23: 9
24:12
25:17, 28
39
29: 6, 7
2 Sa. 3:25, 39
13:15−A
16
15:14
16: 8
24:16
1 Ki. 1:52
(3)44, 44
9: 9
11:22
13:33
14:10 A
16: 7
20:29, 29
21: 7
2 Ki. 6:33
14:10
1 Ch. 21: 8, 15
2 Ch. 7:22
25:19
Neh. 9: 9 S[3 c]
Est. 8: 3
Job 4: 6
17: 5
20:12
22: 5
27: 5 S[d]
Psa. 35: 5
Psa. 49:19
51: 3, 5
106:34
Pro. 1:16 AS[3]
13:16
14:18, 32
16:30[e]
19: 7, 9
26:11
Ecc. 5:12
7: 4, 15
16
12: 1
Isa. 29:20
Jer. 1:16
2:19
3: 2−A
4:14, 18
6: 7
7:12
8: 6
11:15, 17
12: 4
13:22 A[f]
15: 7
13 A[g]
16:18[h]
28:24[i]
Lam. 1:22
Eze. 6: 9+A
16:23, 37
57
20:43
22:12
Dan. 9:14+A
Hos. 7: 1, 2, 3
9:15, 15
10:15
Joel 2:13
Amos 3: 6
Jon. 1: 2, 7
8+A
3:10[e]
4: 2
Nah. 3:19
Zec. 7:10
8:17

[a] pro πονηρία. [b] pro καρδία.
[c] pro ταπείνωσις. [d] pro ἀκακία.
[e] A κακός. [f] pro ἀδικία.
[g] pro ἁμαρτία. [h] AS ἀδικία.
[i] A ἀδικία.

κακολογέω.

Exo. 21:16
22:28
1 Sa. 3:13
Pro. 20:20
Eze. 22: 7

κακοπάθεια.

Malachi 1:13

κακοπαθέω.

Jonah 4:10

κακοποιέω.

Gen. 31: 7, 29
43: 5
Lev. 5: 4
Nu. 35:23
Jud. 19:23[a]
1 Sa. 12:25
25:34
26:21
2 Sa. 20: 6
24:17+A
1 Ki. 16:33−A
1 Ch. 21:17, 17
Ezra 4:13, 15
Pro. 4:16
6:18
11:15
19: 7
Isa. 11: 9
Jer. 4:22
10: 5
[a] A πονηρεύομαι.

κακοποίησις.

Ezra 4:23

κακοποιός.

Pro. 12: 4
Pro. 24:19[a]
[a] S[1] κακότης.

κακός, κακόν.

Gen. 19:19
24:50
26:29
44:34
48:16
50:15
Exo. 5:19
Lev. 25:36 A[a]
Nu. 11:23
32:11, 23
Deu. 1:39
29:21
30:15
31:17, 17
21+A
29
32:23
Jud. 2:15
6:13
15: 3 A[b]
1 Sa. 10:19
20:13
24:18
25:26, 39
2 Sa. 12:11, 18
17:14
18:32
19: 7,7,35
1 Ki. 3: 9
20:21
22:8,18,23
2 Ki. 8:12−A
21:12
22:16, 20
1 Ch. 7:23
2 Ch. 18:7,17,22
20: 9
34:24, 28
Neh. 13:18
Est. 7: 7
9:25
Job 1: 5
2:3,10,11
4:12
5:5,19,21
6:23+A
13: 4, 26
16: 2
22:23 S[1c]
27:15+A
28:28
30:26
Psa. 7: 5
9:27
11: 3+AS[2]
14: 3
20:12
22: 4
26: 5
27: 3
33:14, 15
17
34: 4, 26
36:27
37:13, 21
39:13, 15
40: 6, 8
53: 7
55: 6
69: 3
70:13, 20
24
72:18+S[2]
87: 4
89:15
90:10
106:26, 39
108: 5
120: 7
139:12
Pro. 1:18, 18
28, 33
2:12, 14
14, 16
3: 7, 29
30, 31
4:27
5:14

Pro. 6:3,11,11
14, 18
8:13
9: 7,8,12
12
10:23, 29
11:27
12:12, 20
21, 26
13:10, 10
12 A[d]
17, 21
14: 6, 16
19, 22
22, 24
25
15: 2,3,14
15, 15
23[e], 27
28
16: 2,4,12
17, 22
27, 28
28, 30
30 A[f]
17:4,11,12
13, 13
16, 20
18: 3, 6
19: 6, 27
20:30
21:12, 26
22: 8
14 *bis*
16+AS[2]
24: 1, 10
16, 34
35, 36
37
25:19, 19
27:12, 21
28: 5, 10
14, 20
29:30+A
Ecc. 4:17[g]
9: 2, 12[h]
Isa. 7:16
13:11
26:15, 15
28: 9
31: 2
45: 7
46: 7
57:12
Jer. 1:14
2: 3, 27
4: 6
5:12
6: 1, 19[i]
7: 6, 24
9: 3,3,14
11:11, 12
17, 23
13:23
14: 8, 16
15:11
16:10, 19
18: 8,8,11
20
19: 3
15+A
15
21:10
23:12, 17
25:16+S
28:60, 61[k]
31: 2
32:18
33: 3, 13
19, 19
36:11
39:23, 42
42:17−A
43: 3, 31
46:16
47: 2
48:11
49: 6, 10

Jer. 49:17
51: 2, 5, 7
9[m], 9
9,9,17
23, 35
Lam. 1:21
3:37
Eze. 6:10+A
14:22, 22
20:44
Dan. 7:24
9:12, 13
Joel 3:13

Amos 6: 3
9: 4, 10
Jon. 3:10 A[f]
4: 6
Mic. 1:12
2: 1, 3
3:11
4: 9
7: 3
Hab. 2: 9, 9
Zeph. 3:15
Zec. 1:15
Mal. 1: 8, 8

[a] *pro* τόκος. [b] *pro* πονηρία. [c] *pro* ἄδικος. [d] *pro* ἀγαθός. [e] S² ἄκακος. [f] *pro* κακία. [g] S καλός. [h] B καλός. [i] S κατά. [k] B Χαλδαῖος. [m] A ἔργον.

κακότης.

Pro. 24:19 S[1a] [a] *pro* κακοποιός.

κακουργία.

Psalm 34:17

κακοῦργος.

Proverbs 21:15

κακουχέω.

1 Ki. 2:26, 26
1 Ki. 11:39 A

κακοφροσύνη.

Proverbs 16:18

κακόφρων.

Pro. 11:22
Pro. 19:19

κακόω.

Gen. 15:13
16: 6
19: 9
Exo. 1:11
5:22, 23
22:21, 22
23
23: 9+A
Nu. 11:11
16:15
20:15
24:24, 24
29: 7
30:14
Deu. 8: 2,3,16
26: 6
Jos. 24: 4, 20
Ruth 1:21−A
1 Ki. 17:20
Job 20:26
22: 9
24:24
30:11
31:30

Psa. 26: 2
37: 9
43: 3
88:23
93: 5
105:32
106:39
Ecc. 7:23
8: 9
10:15[a]
Isa. 41:23
50: 9
53: 7
Jer. 25: 6
32:15
38:28
51:27
Eze. 33:12
Dan. 10:12
Hos. 9: 7
Zeph. 1:12
Zec. 8:14
10: 2

[a] A σκοτόω, CS κοπόω.

κακῶς.

Exo. 22:28
Lev. 19:14
20: 9, 9

Isa. 8:21
Jer. 7:10
Eze. 34: 4

κάκωσις.

Exo. 3: 7, 17
Nu. 11:15
Deu. 10: 3
Est. 8: 6
Psa. 17:19

Psa. 43:20
Isa. 53: 4
Jer. 2:28
11:14
28: 2

καλαβώτης.

Lev. 11:30 AB[a]
Pro. 24:63

[a] *pro* χαλαβώτης.

κάλαθος.

Jeremiah 24: 1, 2, 2

καλαμάομαι.

Deu. 24:22
Jud. 20:45
Isa. 3:12

Isa. 24:13, 13
Jer. 6: 9, 9

καλάμη.

Exo. 5:12
15: 7
Job 24:24
41:20
Psa. 82:14
Isa. 1:31
5:24
17: 6

Isa. 27: 4
Joel 2: 5
Amos 2:13
Obad. 18
Mic. 7: 1
Nah. 1:10
Zec. 12: 6
Mal. 4: 1

καλάμινος.

2 Ki. 18:21
Isa. 36: 6

Eze. 29: 6

καλαμίσκος.

Exo. 25:30, 31
31, 31
32, 32
33, 34

Exo. 25:34, 34
36
38:14, 15

κάλαμος.

Exo. 30:23−A[1]
1 Ki. 14:15 A?
Job 40:16
Psa. 44: 2
67:31
Cant. 4:14
Isa. 19: 6
35: 7[a]
42: 3
Eze. 40: 3, 5, 5

Eze. 40: 5, 6, 7
7, 7
7−A
8, 8
9+A
41: 8
42:12, 16
17, 18
19, 20[b]

[a] S ποίμνιον. [b] A μέτρον.

καλέω.

Gen. 1: 5, 5, 8
10, 10
2:19, 19
20, 23
3: 9, 20
11: 9
12:18
16:11, 13
14, 15
17: 5, 15
19
19:22[a], 37
38
20: 8, 9
21: 3, 12
17
22:11, 14
15
24:57, 58
25:26, 30
26: 9, 20
33, 33
27: 1, 36
42
28:19
29:32, 33
34, 35
30: 6,8,13
18, 20
21, 24
31: 4, 47
47, 48
54
32: 2, 28
30
33:17
35: 7,8,10
10−A
15, 18
18
38: 3, 4, 5
29, 30
39:14
41: 8, 14
45, 51
52

Gen. 46:33
47:29
48: 6
49: 1
50:11
Exo. 1:18
2: 7,8,20
3: 4
8: 8, 25
9:27
10:16, 24
12:16, 21
31
19: 3, 7[b]
20
24:16
33: 7, 19[b]
34: 5,6,15
31
36: 2
Lev. 9: 1
10: 4
13:45
23: 2,4,21
37
Nu. 11: 3, 34
12: 5
16:12
22: 5, 20
37
23:11
24:10
25: 2
Deu. 5: 1
25: 8, 10
29: 2
31: 7, 14
32: 3
Jos. 5: 3, 9
19:48
24: 9
Jud. 1:17, 26
2: 5 A[c]
4: 6, 13
6:24 A[d]
32

Jud. 8: 1
10: 4
12: 1
13:24
14:15
15:17, 19
16:18−A
19, 25
25
18:12, 29
21:13
Ruth 1:20, 20
21
4:14, 17
17
1 Sa. 1:20
3: 4, 5, 5
6 *ter*
8 *ter*
9, 10
4:21
6: 2
7:12
9: 9, 22
26
16: 3, 5, 8
19: 7
22:11
26:14
28:15
29: 6
2 Sa. 1: 7, 15
2:16, 26
5: 9, 20
6: 8
9: 2, 9
11:13
12:24, 25
28
13:17, 23
14:33
17: 5
18:18
18+A
21: 2
1 Ki. 1: 9, 10
19, 19
25, 26
28, 32
2:28[e]
(3)36, 42
9:13
12: 3+A
20[f]
18: 3
20:12−B
21: 7
22: 9, 13
2 Ki. 1: 3, 9
3:10, 13
4:12, 12
15+A
15, 22
36, 36
6:11
8: 1[g]
9: 1
10:19
12: 7
14: 7
18: 4
1 Ch. 4: 9
6:63
7:16, 23
11: 7
13:11
14:11
15:11
22: 6
23:14
2 Ch. 3:17
10: 3
18: 8, 12
20:26
24: 6
Ezra 2:61
4:18
8:21
Neh. 5:12
7:63

Est. 2:14
3:12
4:11[h]
5:10
12−A
12
6: 5
8: 9
9:26
Job 9:16
13:22
14:15
19:16
38:34
42:14
p 18
Psa. 49: 1
104:16
146: 4
Pro. 1:24
16:21
21:24
27:16
Ecc. 6:10
Cant. 3: 1
2+AC
5: 6
Isa. 1:26
4: 1, 3
7:14
8: 3, 4
9: 6
13:19
19:18
21: 8, 11
22:12, 20
35: 8
40:26
41: 2, 4, 4
9, 25
42: 6
43: 1, 22
44: 7[i]
45: 3, 4
46:11
47: 1, 5
48: 1,8,12
13, 15
49: 1, 6
50: 2
51: 2
54: 5, 6
56: 7
58: 5, 12
13
60:14, 18
61: 2, 3, 6
62: 2, 4, 4
4, 12
12[k]
63:19[m]
65: 1, 12
15
66: 4
Jer. 3: 4, 17
19[n]
6:30
7:13
9:17
11:16
19: 6
20: 3
23: 6
26:17, 19
30: 7
32:15
37:17
41: 8, 15
17, 17
42: 2+A
43: 4
44:17
45:14
49: 8
Lam. 1:15, 19
21
2:22
4:15
Eze. 8:18+A
9: 3

Eze. 36:29
38:21
39:12
Dan. 2: 2
5:12
6:16
Hos. 1: 4, 6, 9
Hos. 1:10
2:16, 16
11:12
Amos 5:16
7: 4
Zec. 8: 3
11: 7, 7

a A ἐπονομάζω. b B λαλέω.
c pro ἐπονομάζω.
d pro ἐπικαλέω. e AB κλίνω.
f A εἰσάγω. g A κλίνω.
h A κληρόω. i S[1] λαλέω.
k S[1] συγκαλέω. m A ἐπικαλέω.
n S[1] παρακαλέω.

καλλιόω.

Canticles 4:10, 10

καλλονή.

Psa. 46: 5
Psa. 77:61

κάλλος.

Gen. 49:21
Deu. 33:17
1 Sa. 16:12
17:42
Est. 1:11
Psa. 29: 8
44: 3, 4, 12
Pro. 6:25
11:22
29:48
Isa. 2:16
Isa. 37:24
53: 2
62: 3
Eze. 16:14, 15
25
27: 3, 4, 11
28: 7, 7, 12
17, 17
31: 8
Zec. 11: 7

κάλλυντρον.

Leviticus 23:40

καλλωπίζω.

Gen. 38:14
Ps. 143:12
Jer. 10: 4[a]
26:20

a S[1] κολάπτω.

καλός.

Gen. 1: 4, 8, 10
13, 18
21, 25
31
2: 9, 9, 12
17:18
3: 5, 6, 22
6: 2
12:14
15:15
18: 7
24:16, 50
25: 8
27: 9, 15
29:17
30:20
39: 6
41: 2, 4, 5
18, 20
22, 24
26, 26
35
44: 4
49:14, 15
Lev. 27:10, 10
12, 14
33
33 −AB
Nu. 10:29
11:18
13:20
24: 1, 5, 13
Deu. 1:14
6:10, 18
8:12
12:25, 28
13:18
21: 9, 11
Jos. 7:21 +A
21:45
23:15
1 Sa. 25: 3 A[e]
2 Sa. 11: 2
13: 1
14:25 +A
27
19:27 +AB
1 Ki. 1: 3, 4
12 p24 l45
14:13 A
18:24
21: 3 +A
22: 8, 13
15, 18
1 Ch. 29:28
2 Ch. 14: 2
31:20
Est. 1:11
2: 2, 3, 7
Job 10: 3
13: 9 −A
33:31 +A
34: 2 + ACS[3]
4
Psa. 34:12[b]
132: 1
134: 3[c]
150 p6
Pro. 2:10, 11
3: 4, 17
15: 2, 23
16: 1, 24
17:26
18: 5
20:23
22: 1, 17
23: 8
24: 4, 14
38 −S
25:27
29:29, 36
Ecc. 3, 11
4:17 S[d]
Ecc. 5:17
9:12 B[d]
Cant. 1: 5, 8, 15
15, 16
2:10, 13
4: 1, 1, 7
5: 9, 17
6: 3, 9
Isa. 1:17
3:25
5: 9, 20
20
22:18
27: 2
41: 7
65: 2[e]
Jer. 2:33
4:22 AS[f]
12: 6
18:11
22:15 +A
17
47: 4
Lam. 4: 9
Eze. 16:13
17: 8
20:25
24: 4
31: 3, 7
34:18
Dan. 1: 4
Hos. 4:13
10:11
Joel 3: 5
Amos 5:14, 15
8:13
Jon. 4: 3, 8
Mic. 2: 7
3: 2
6: 8
Nah. 3: 4
Zec. 1:13
9:17
11:10, 12
Mal. 2:13[g], 17

a pro ἀγαθός. b A ἀγαθός.
c A ἡδύς. d pro κακός.
e AS[3] ἀληθινός, S[1] ἀληθής.
f pro καλῶς. g A ἄλλος.

κάλος.

Nu. 3:37[a]
Nu. 4:32[a]

a A κλάδος.

κάλυμμα.

Exo. 27:16
34:33, 34
35
39:21[a]
40: 5
Nu. 3:25
4: 8, 10
Nu. 4:11, 12
14, 14
25[b]
25 B[c]
25[a]
31 AB[2] c
1 Ch. 17: 5[d]

a A κατακάλυμμα. b AB[2] κατακάλ-
c pro κατακάλυμμα.
d AS κατάλυμα.

καλυπτήρ.

Exo. 27: 3
Nu. 4:13, 14

καλύπτω.

Gen. 7:19[a]
Exo. 8: 6
10: 5, 15
14:28
15: 5, 10
16:13
21:33
24:15, 16
26:13
27: 2
28:38
40:28
Lev. 3·14 A[b]
13:12, 13
16:13
17:13
Nu. 4: 8, 9
11[a], 12
15
9:15, 16
16:33, 42
22:11
Deu. 23:13
Jos. 24: 7
1 Sa. 19:13
1 Ki. 7:27
Neh. 4: 6
Job 15:27
21:26
22:11
23:17
36:30, 32
Psa. 31: 5
43:16
54: 6
68: 8
77:53
79:11
84: 3
103: 9
105:11, 17
139:10
Pro. 10: 6, 11
12, 18
26:23
Ecc. 6: 4
Isa. 29: 4 B[c]
60: 2, 6
Eze. 7:18
16: 8
24: 7, 8
26:10 A[b]
30:18
32: 7
38:16
40:43
41:20, 20
Hos. 2: 9
10: 8
Obad. 10
Hab. 2:17
3: 3
Mal. 2:13, 16

a A ἐπικαλύπτω.
b pro κατακαλύπτω.
c pro ἀνακαλύπτω.

καλώδιον.

Jud. 15:13, 14
Jud. 16:11, 12 −A

καλῶς.

Gen. 26:29
32:12 +A
Lev. 5: 4
2 Sa. 3:13
1 Ki. 2:18
8:18
2 Ki. 25:24
2 Ch. 6: 8
Est. 2: 9
6:10 −S[3]
Job 13: 8 +A
Psa. 32: 3
127: 2
Pro. 23:24
24:64
Isa. 23:16
Jer. 1:12 −S[1]
4:22[a]
Hos. 2: 7
Mic. 1:11
Zeph. 3:20
Zec. 8:15

a AS καλός.

καμάρα.

Isaiah 40:22

καμηλοπάρδαλις.

Deuteronomy 14: 5

κάμηλος.

Gen. 12:16
24:10, 10
11, 14
19, 20
22, 30
31, 32
32, 35
44, 46
46, 61
63, 64
30:43
31:17, 34
32: 7 −A
15
37:25
Exo. 9: 3
Lev. 11: 4
Deu. 14: 7
Jud. 6: 5
7:12
8:21, 26
1 Sa. 15: 3
27: 9
30:17
1 Ki. 10: 2
2 Ki. 8: 9
1 Ch. 5:21
12:40
27:30
2 Ch. 9: 1
14:15
Ezra 2:67
Neh. 7:69 +AS
Job 1: 3, 17
42:12
Isa. 21: 7
30: 6
60: 6, 6
Jer. 30: 7, 10
Eze. 25: 5
27:21
Zec. 14:15

καμιναῖος.

Exodus 9: 8, 10

κάμινος.

Gen. 19:28
Exo. 19:18
Nu. 25: 8
Deu. 4:20
Job 41:11
Pro. 16:30
17: 3
Isa. 48:10
Jer. 11: 4
Eze. 22:20, 22
Dan. 3: 6, 11
15, 17
19, 20
21, 22
23, 26

καμμύω.

Isa. 6:10
29:10
Isa. 33:15
Lam. 3:43

κάμνω.

Job 10: 1 −S[1]
Job 17: 2

κάμπη.

Joel 1: 4
2:25
Amos 4: 9

καμπή.

Nehemiah 3:24, 31

κάμπτω.

Jud. 5:27 A[a]
7: 5 A[b]
6 A[b]
2 Sa. 22:40
2 Ki. 1:13
9:24
1 Ch. 29:20
2 Ch. 29, 29
Job 9:13
Isa. 45:23
58: 5
Dan. 6:10

a pro κατακλίνω. b pro κλίνω.

καμπύλος.

Proverbs 2:15

καμψάκης, καψ—

1 Ki. 17:12, 14
16
1 Ki. 19: 6

κάνθαρος.

Habakkuk 2:11

κανοῦν.

Gen. 40:16, 17
17, 18
Exo. 29: 3, 3, 23
32
Lev. 8: 2, 26
Lev. 8:31
Nu. 6:15, 17
19
Jud. 6:19 A[a]

a pro κόφινος.

κανών.

Micah 7: 4

κάπηλος.

Isaiah 1:22

καπνίζω.

Gen. 15:17
Exo. 19:18
20:18
Ps. 103:32
Ps. 143: 5
Isa. 7: 4
42: 3

καπνοδόχη.

Hos. 13: 3 A[a] a pro δάκρυον.

καπνός.

Exo. 19:18, 18
Jos. 8:20
21 −A
Jud. 20:38, 40
2 Sa. 22: 9
Job 41:11
Psa. 17: 9
36:20
67: 3
101: 4
Pro. 10:26
Cant. 3: 6
Isa. 4: 5
6: 4
14:31
34:10
51: 6
65: 5
17 S[1] a
Joel 2:30
Nah. 2:13

a pro καινός.

κάππαρις.

Ecclesiastes 12: 5

κάρα.

Jer. 4: 9 S[1] a a pro καρδία.

καρδία.

Gen. 6: 5
20: 5, 6
42:28
50:21
Exo. 4:21
7: 3, 13
14, 22
8:15, 19
32
9: 7, 12
14, 34
35
10: 1, 20
27
11:10
14: 4, 5
5 +B
8
8 +A
17
25: 2
31: 6
35: 5, 9[a]
21
36: 2
Lev. 26:36, 41
Nu. 22:38 A[b]
32: 7 A[c], 9
Deu. 1:28
2:30
Deu. 4: 9, 29
5:29
6: 5 A[c], 6
12 +A
8: 2, 5
14, 17
9: 4, 5
10:12
11:13, 16
18
12:20 A[d]
13: 3
15: 7, 9, 10
17:17, 20
18 21
19: 6
20: 3, 8, 8
26:16
28:47 A[e]
65, 67
29: 4, 19
19
30: 1, 2, 6
6, 6, 10
14, 17
32:46
Jos. 2:11
7: 5
11:20
14: 8[a]

Jos. 22: 5 A[e]
23:14
24:23
Jud. 1:15
5: 9, 15
16
9: 3
16:15, 17
18, 18[e]
25
18:20
19: 3, 5, 6
8,9,22
Ruth 2:13
3: 7
1 Sa. 1: 8, 13
2: 1, 35
4:13, 20
6: 6, 6
7: 3, 3
9:19, 20
10: 9, 26
12:20, 24
13:14
14: 7 *ter*
16: 7
17:28A, 32
21:12
24: 6
25:25
31 + A
36, 37
27: 1
28: 5
29:10 − A
Sa. 6:16
7: 3, 21
27
13:20, 28
33
14: 1
15: 6, 13
17:10, 10
18: 3, 3
14, 14
19: 7, 14
19
24:10
1 Ki. 2: 4, 35
(3) 44
3: 6,9,12
4:25
8:17, 18
18, 23
38, 39
39, 47
48, 58
61, 66
9: 3, 4
10: 2, 24
11: 2
3,3,4,9
10 − A
10 − A
12:26, 27
33
14: 8 A
15: 3,3,14
18:37
2 Ki. 5:26
9:24
10:15
15 − A
15, 15
30, 31
12: 4
14:10
20: 3
22:19
23: 3, 25
1 Ch. 12:17
16:10
17:19
22:19
28: 2, 9, 9
29: 9, 17
17, 18
18, 19
2 Ch. 1:11
6: 7, 8, 8

2 Ch. 6:14, 30
30, 37
38
7:10, 16
9:23
11:16
12:14
13: 7
15:12, 17
16: 9
17: 6
19: 3, 9
20:33
22: 9
24: 4
25: 2, 19
26:16
29:10, 31
30: 8[f], 12
19, 22
32: 6, 25
26, 31
34:27, 31
35:19
36:13
Ezra 6:22
7:10, 27
Neh. 2: 2, 12
5: 7
6: 8
7: 5
9: 8
Est. 5: 9 + S[3]
Job 1: 5 A[e]
8:10
11:13
12: 3, 24
15:12
17: 4, 11
22:22
23:16
31: 7,9,27
29
33: 3, 23
34:10
34 − C
36: 5, 13
28, 34
37: 4 + C
23
38: 2
41:15
Psa. 4: 5, 8
5:10
7:10, 11
9: 2, 27
32, 34
38
10: 2
11: 3, 3
12: 3, 6
13: 1
14: 2
15: 9
16: 3
18: 9, 15
19: 5
20: 3 S[2 d]
21:15, 27
23: 4
24:17
25: 2
26: 3,8,14
27: 3, 7
30:13, 25
31: 5, 11
32:11, 15
21
33:10
34:25
35:11
36: 4, 11
15[e], 31
37: 9, 11
38: 4
39: 9[h], 11
13
40: 7
43:19, 22
44: 2, 6

Psa. 45: 3
47:14
48: 4
50:12, 19
52: 2
54: 5, 22
56: 8, 8
57: 3
60: 3
61: 5,9,11
63: 7, 11
65:18
68:21 S[1 d]
72: 1,7,13
21, 26
26
73: 8
75: 6, 10[i]
76: 7
77: 8, 18
37, 72
80:13
83: 3, 6
84: 9
85:11, 12
89:12
93:15, 19
19 S[1 d]
94: 8, 10
96:11
100: 2, 3, 5
101: 5
103:15, 15
104: 3, 25
106:12
107: 2, 2
108:16, 22
110: 1
111: 7, 8
118: 2,7,10
11, 32
34, 36
58, 69
70, 80
111, 112
145, 161
124: 4
130: 1, 2A[d]
137: 1
138:23
139: 3
140: 4
142: 4
146: 3
Pro. 2: 2
3: 1,3 + A
5
4: 4[k], 21
23
5:12
6:14, 18
7: 3, 10
25
8: 5
10: 8, 20
22
24 + A
12:20, 23
25
13:12
14:10, 30
30, 33
33
15: 7, 11
13, 14
22, 28
16: 1,1,23
17: 3, 10
21, 22
18: 4, 12
15, 22
19:21
20: 5, 9
21: 1,2,12
22:11, 15
17, 18
20[m]
23:12, 15
15, 17
19, 26

Pro. 23:34
24: 2,6,12
25: 3, 20
20
26:23, 24
25 AC[d]
27: 9, 11
19 ACS[2e]
21, 21
23
28:14, 26
29:20
Ecc. 1:13, 16
16, 17
2: 1, 3, 3
10, 10
15, 15
20, 22
23
3:11, 17
18
5: 1, 19
7: 3
4 − B
5, 5, 8
22, 23
26, 27
8: 5,9,11
16, 17
17
9: 3, 3, 7
10: 2, 2, 3
11: 9
9 − B
10
Cant. 3:11
5: 2
8: 6
Isa. 1: 5
6:10, 10
9: 9
14:13 S[e]
15: 5
19: 1
21: 4
29:13
32: 4, 6
38: 3
40: 2
44:18
19 + AS
20, 25
46: 8, 12
47: 7,8,10
49:21
51: 7
57: 1, 11
15
17 S[2 n]
59:13
21 S[1 o]
60: 5
61: 1
63:17
65:14, 16
17
66:14
Jer. 3:10, 15
16, 17
4: 9[p], 9
14, 18
19
19 − S[1]
5:23, 24
7:24, 31
8:18
9: 8 A[q]
14, 26
11:20
12: 3, 11
13:22
14:14
15:16
16:12
17: 5,9,10
18:12
19: 5
20:12
22:17
23: 9, 16

Jer. 23:17, 20
26, 26
24: 7, 7
28:50
29:17, 23
23
31:29, 36
36
36:13
37:21, 24
38:21
33 S[1 e]
33
39:35, 39
40, 41
51:21
Lam. 1:20, 22
2:11, 18
19
3:21, 32
40, 64
5:15, 17
Eze. 3:10
6: 9
11:19 *ter*
21, 21
13: 2 + A
3, 17
22
14: 3, 4, 5
7
17:22
22 + A
18:31
20:16
21: 7, 15
22:14
27: 4, 25
26[r], 27
28: 2 *qtr*
5, 6, 6
8, 17
29:16 + A
32: 9
33:31

Eze. 36:26 *ter*
38:10
40: 4
44: 5, 5, 7
9
Dan. 1: 8
2:30
4:13, 13
5:20, 21
22
7: 4, 28
8:25
10:12
11:12, 25
27, 28
Hos. 2:14
4:11
7: 2, 6
7 + A
11, 14
10: 2
11: 8
13: 6, 8
Joel 2:12, 13
Amos 2:16
Obad. 3, 3
Joh. 2: 4
Nah. 2: 7, 10
Hab. 1:16 − S[2]
2:16 − S[3]
3:16 S[2 s]
Zeph. 1:12 − A
(2)15
3:14
Hag. 1: 5, 7
2:15, 18
18
Zec. 7:10, 12
8:17
10: 7, 7
12: 5
Mal. 1: 1
2: 2, 2
4: 5, 5

[a] A διάνοια. [b] *pro* στόμα.
[c] *pro* διάνοια. [d] *pro* ψυχή.
[e] A κακία. [f] A τράχηλος.
[g] S[1] ψυχή. [h] AS κοιλια.
[i] B*S[2] γῆ. [k] S διάνοια.
[m] BS ψυχή. [n] *pro* ὁδός.
[o] *pro* στόμα. [p] S[1] κάρα.
[q] *pro* γλῶσσα. [r] A μέσος.
[s] *pro* κοιλία.

καρδιόω.

Canticles 4: 9, 9

καρησίμ.

2 Chronicles 35:19

καρόω.

Jer. 28:39[a]
[a] S καθαίρω.

καρπάσινος.

Esther 1: 6

καρπίζω.

Jos. 5:12 | Pro. 8:19

κάρπιμος.

Genesis 1:11, 12

καρπόβρωτος.

Deuteronomy 20:20

καρπός.

Gen. 1:11, 12
29
3: 2[a],3,6
4: 3
30: 2
43:10

Exo. 10:12, 15
Lev. 19:23 − A
24, 25
23:40
25: 3
26: 4, 20

Lev. 27:30
Nu. 13:21, 27
28
Deu. 1:25
7:13
11:17
26: 2
Jud. 6: 4[b]
1 Sa. 5: 4
2 Ki. 19:29, 30
Neh. 9:36
37 − ABS
10:35, 37
Job 22:21
Psa. 1: 3
4: 8
20:11
57:12
66: 7
71:16
77:46
84:13
103:13
104:35[c]
106:37
120: 3
127: 2
131:11
Pro. 1:31
3: 9
10:16
11:30
12:14
13: 2
15: 4 S[2 d]
6 − S[1]
18:20, 20
21
19:22
27:18
29:34, 38

Pro. 29:49
Ecc. 2: 5
Cant. 2: 3
4:13
5: 1
8:11 − A
12
Isa. 27: 6
37:30
Jer. 2: 7
6:19[e]
12: 2
17: 8, 10
27:27
36: 5, 28
38:12
Lam. 2:20
Eze. 17: 8,9,23
19:10
25: 4
34:27
27 A[f]
36: 8, 30
47:12, 12
Dan. 4: 9
11 A[g]
11, 18
Hos. 9:16
10: 1,1,12
13
14: 2, 8
Joel 2:22
Amos 2: 9
6:12
9:14
Mic. 6: 7
7:13
Nah. 3:12 S[2 h]
Hag. 2:19
Zec. 8:12
Mal. 3:11

[a] A[2] πᾶς. [b] A ἐκφόριον.
[c] S[1] χόρτος. [d] *pro* πνεῦμα.
[e] S καιρός. [f] *pro* ἰσχύς.
[g] *pro* κλάδος. [h] *pro* σκοπός.

καρποφορέω.

Habakkuk 3:17

καρποφόρος.

Psa. 106:34
148: 9
Jer. 2:21

καρπόω.

Lev. 2:11 Deu. 26:14

κάρπωμα.

Exo. 29:25, 38
41
30: 9
40: 6,8,26
Lev. 1: 4,9,13
14, 17
2: 9, 10
16
3: 3, 5, 9
11, 14
16
6:15, 17
18, 35
7:15, 20
25
8:21, 28
10:12, 13

Lev. 10:15
22:27
23:37
Nu. 15: 3 A[a]
5, 10
13, 14
25
18: 9, 17
28: 2,3,13
19, 24
29: 8, 11
13, 36
Deu. 18: 1
Jos. 22:26, 27
28, 29
Job 42: 8 A[b]

[a] *pro* ὁλοκαύτωμα.
[b] *pro* κάρπωσις.

κάρπωσις.

Lev. 4:10, 18
22:22
Job 42: 8[a]
[a] A κάρπωμα.

καρπωτός.

2 Samuel 13:18, 19

κάρταλλος.

Deu. 26: 2, 4
2 Ki. 10: 7
Jer. 6: 9

καρτερέω.

Job 2: 9
Isa. 42:14

καρύα.

Canticles 6:10

καρύϊνος.

Gen. 30:37
Jer. 1:11

καρυΐσκος.

Exodus 25:32, 33, 35

κάρυον.

Gen. 43:10
Nu. 17: 8[a]

[a] (B καροία.)

καρυωτά.

Exodus 38:16

κάρφος.

Genesis 8:11

Καρχηδόνιος.

Eze. 27:12
25+A
Eze. 38:13[a]

[a] A Χαλκηδόνος.

κασία.

Psa. 44: 9
Eze. 27:17

κασσιτέρινος.

Zechariah 4:10

κασσίτερος.

Nu. 31:22
Eze. 22:18, 20
Eze. 27:12

καταβαίνω.

Gen. 11: 5, 7
12:10
15:11
18:21
24:16, 45
26: 2
28:12
37:35
38: 1
42: 2, 3, 38
43: 2+A
3, 12
14, 19
44:23, 26
26, 26
45: 9
46: 3, 4
Exo. 2: 5
3: 8
11: 8
19:10, 11
14, 18
20, 21
24, 25
24:16
32: 1, 7, 15
34−A
33: 9
34: 5, 29, 29
Lev. 9:22
Nu. 11: 9, 9, 17
25
12: 5
14:45
16:30, 33
20:15, 28
31:11, 11
12
Deu. 9:12, 15
Deu. 9:21
10: 5, 22
26: 5
28:24, 43
31:15
32: 2
Jos. 2:23
3:13, 16
16, 16
15: 7, 10
17: 9−A
18:13, 16
16, 16
17, 18
19:47
24: 4
Jud. 1: 9, 34
3:27, 28
28
4:14, 15
5:11
13−A
13−A
14
7: 9, 10
10, 11
11, 24[a]
9:36, 37
11:37
14: 1, 5, 7
10, 19
15: 8, 8+A
11, 12
16:31
20:45[b]
Ruth 3: 6
1 Sa. 6:21
9:25, 27
10: 5, 8, 8
1 Sa. 13:12, 20
14:36, 37
15:12
17: 8
28A, 28A
22: 1
23: 4, 6, 8
11, 20
25
24: 8
25: 1, 20
20
26: 2, 10
30:24
2 Sa. 1:21
5:17, 24
11: 8, 9, 10
10, 13
17:18
19:16, 20
24, 31
21:15
22:10
23:13, 13
20−A
21−A
1 Ki. 1:25, 38
2: 8
(3) p 1
6(32) A
18:44
20:16, 18
18
22: 2
2 Ki. 1: 4, 6, 9
10, 10
11, 12
12, 14
15, 15
16
3:12
5:14
6:18, 33
7:17
8:29
9:16, 16
32
10:13
13:14
20:11+A
1 Ch. 7:21
11:15, 22
23
2 Ch. 7: 1, 3
18: 2
20:16
22: 6
Neh. 3:15
6: 3, 3
9:13
Job 7: 9
17:16, 16
36:16
38:30
Psa. 7:17
17:10
Psa. 21:30
27: 1
29: 4, 10
54:16
71: 6
87: 5
103: 8
106:23, 26
113:25
118:136[e]
132: 2, 2, 3
138: 8
142: 7
143: 5
Pro. 24:27
Ecc. 3:21
Cant. 5: 1
6: 1, 10
Isa. 5:14
14:11, 15
19
25:12
30: 2
31: 1, 4
32:19
34: 5
38: 8, 8
42:10
47: 1
52: 4
55:10
63:14
Jer. 18: 2, 3
22: 1
27:27
28:14
31:15
18−S[1]
43:12, 14
51:28 A[d]
Eze. 22:24+A
24: 8 A[1][e]
26:16, 20
20
27:29
30: 6
31:12, 15
16, 17
18
32:18
19+A
21, 24
24, 27
29, 30
30
47: 1, 8, 15
Dan. 4:10, 20
Amos 6: 2
8: 8, 9: 5
Obad. 16
Jon. 1: 3, 5
2: 7
Mic. 1: 3−A
12
Nah. 3: 7
Hag. 2:22[f]

[a] A ἀνίστημι. [b] A προσκολλάω. [c] A διαβαίνω. [d] pro καθίστημι [e] pro ἀναβαίνω. [f] A ἀναβαίνω.

καταβάλλω.

2 Sa. 20:15
2 Ki. 3:19, 25
6: 5
19: 7
2 Ch. 32:21
Job 12:14[a]
16: 9, 14
Psa. 36:14
72:18
105:26, 27
139:11
Pro. 7:26
18: 8
25:28
Isa. 16: 9[b]
Isa. 26: 5
Jer. 19: 7
Eze. 6: 4
23:25
26: 4, 4[c]
9, 12
29: 5
30:22
31:12
32:12
33: 4 A[d]
39: 3
Dan. 11:12
Hag. 2:22+A

[a] A καταστρέφω. [b] S καταλαμβάνω. [c] A καθαιρέω. [d] pro καταλαμβάνω.

καταβαρύνω.

2 Sa. 13:25
14:26
Joel 2: 8

κατάβασις.

Jos. 8:24
10:11
Jud. 1:16
1 Sa. 23:20
2 Sa. 13:34
1 Ki. 7:15
Eze. 48: 1
Mic. 1: 4

καταβιάζω.

Gen. 19: 3[a]
Exo. 12:33

[a] A παραβιάζομαι.

καταβιβάζω.

Deu. 21: 4
Jos. 2:18
Jud. 7: 5 A[a]
Jer. 28:40
Lam. 1: 9
Eze. 26:20
28: 8
31:16, 18
32:18

[a] pro καταφέρω.

καταβιόω.

Amos 7:12

καταβλέπω.

Genesis 18:16

καταβοάω.

Exo. 5:15
22:23, 27
Deu. 15: 9[a]
24:17

[a] A βοάω.

καταβόσκω.

Exodus 22: 5 *ter*

κατάβρωμα.

Nu. 14: 9
Deu. 28:26
31:17
Jer. 7:33 A[a]
Eze. 21:32
Eze. 29: 5[b]
33:27
34: 5, 8, 10
35:12[c]

[a] pro βρῶσις. [b] A βρῶσις. [c] A κατάσχεσις.

κατάβρωσις.

Genesis 31:15

καταβρώσκω.

Neh. 2: 3, 13
Eze. 39: 4

κατάγαιος.

Genesis 6:16

καταγγέλλω.

Pro. 17: 5 A[a] [a] pro καταγελάω.

καταγελάω.

Gen. 38:23
2 Ch. 30:10
Job 5:22
9:23
21: 3
30: 1
39: 7, 18
Job 39:22
41:20
Psa. 24: 2
Pro. 17: 5[a]
24:52
29: 9
Mic. 3: 7

[a] A καταγγέλλω.

κατάγελως.

Psa. 43:14−S[1], AS[2] χλευασμός.

καταγηράσκω.

Isaiah 46: 4

καταγίνομαι.

Exo. 10:23
Nu. 5: 3
Deu. 9: 9

καταγινώσκω.

Deu. 25: 1
Pro. 28:11

κατάγνυμι.

Deu. 33:11
2 Sa. 22:35
Jer. 31:25
Lam. 3:65 A[a]
Zec. 1:21
9: 4 AS[1][b]
12: 4 S[1][b]

[a] pro καταδιώκω.
[b] pro πατάσσω.

καταγράφω.

Exo. 17:14
32:15[a]
Nu. 11:26
1 Ch. 9: 1
2 Ch. 20:34
Job 13:26
Hos. 8:12

[a] A γράφω.

κατάγω.

Gen. 37:25, 28
39: 1, 1
42:20 A[a]
38
43:10
44:21, 29
31
45:13
Jud. 7: 4 A[b]
16:21 A[b]
1 Sa. 2: 6
19:12
30:15, 15
16
1 Ki. 1:33
2: 6, 9
(3) p 1
5: 9
6:32
17:23
18:40
2 Ki. 11:19
Psa. 21:16
30:18
54:24
55: 8
Psa. 58:12
77:16
Pro. 5: 5
7:27
Isa. 9: 3
26: 5, 5
63: 3, 6
Jer. 9:18
13:17
14:17
19: 8[c]
37: 6 S[1][d]
Lam. 1:13, 16
2:10, 18
3:47
Eze. 26:11
44:14[c]
Hos. 7:12
Joel 3: 2
Amos 3:11
9: 2
Obad. 3, 4
Hab. 3:12
Zec. 6:13 S[1][e]
9:10 S[1][e]

[a] pro ἄγω. [b] pro καταφέρω. [c] A τάσσω. [d] pro κατέχω. [e] pro κατάρχω.

καταδαμάζω.

Jud. 14:18 A[a] [a] pro ἀροτριάω.

καταδείκνυμι.

Gen. 4:21
Isa. 40:26
41:20
Isa. 43:15
45:18

καταδέομαι.

Gen. 42:21
Isa. 57:10

κατάδεσμος.

Isaiah 1: 6

καταδέχομαι.

Exo. 35: 5
Deu. 32:29

καταδέω.

Nu. 19:15
1 Ki. 21:38
Isa. 46: 1
Eze. 30:21
34: 4, 16

καταδιαιρέω.

Psa. 47:14−S[1]
54:10
Ps. 135:13
Joel 3: 2

καταδικάζω.

Job 34:29
Psa. 36:33
93:21
Ps. 108: 7
Lam. 3:35
Dan. 1:10

καταδιώκω.

Gen. 14:14, 15
31:36
33:13
35: 5
Exo. 14: 4, 8, 9
23
Deu. 1:44
11: 4
28:22, 45
Jos. 2: 5, 7
8 A[a]
16, 16
22
7: 5
8:16, 17
17—A
24
10:10, 19
11: 8
24: 6
Jud. 7:23 A[a]
25
9:10 A[a]
1 Sa. 7:11—A
17:52
23:25, 28
24:15
25:29
26:18, 20
30: 8, 8
10[b], 22
2 Sa. 2:19, 24
28
2 Sa. 17: 1
20: 6
1 Ki. 21:20
1 Ch. 10: 2
2 Ch. 13:19
14:13
Neh. 9:11
Psa. 7: 6
17:38
22: 6
30:16
34: 3, 6
37:21
68:27
70:11
82:16
108:16, 31[c]
118:84, 86
150
161
141: 7
142: 1, 3
Pro. 12:26
13:21
Jer. 15:15
52: 8
Lam. 1: 3[c]
3:11, 65[d]
Hos. 2: 7
8: 3
Joel 2: 4
Mic. 2:11

[a] pro διώκω.
[b] A ἐκδιώκω, B διώκω.
[c] S διωκω. [d] A κατάγνυμι.

καταδολεσχέω.

Lamentations 3:20

καταδουλόω.

Gen. 47:21
Exo. 1:14
6: 5
Ezra 7:24
Pro. 27: 8 C[a]
Jer. 15:14
Eze. 29:18
34:27

[a] pro δουλόω.

καταδυναστεία.

Exo. 6: 7
Jer. 6: 6
Eze. 22:12
Eze. 45: 9
Amos 3: 9

καταδυναστεύω.

Exo. 1:13
21:17
Deu. 24: 9
1 Sa. 12: 3, 4
2 Sa. 8:11
2 Ch. 21:17
Neh. 5: 5, 5
Isa. 29: 5—AS
Jer. 7: 6
22: 3
27:33, 33
Eze. 18: 7, 12
Eze. 18:16
22: 7, 29
45: 8
46:18
Hos. 5:11
12: 7
Amos 4: 1
8: 4
Mic. 2: 2
Hab. 1: 4
Zec. 7:10
Mal. 3: 5

κατάδυσις.

1 Kings 15:13

καταδύω, —δύνω.

Exo. 15: 5
Jer. 28:64
Amos 9: 3
Mic. 7:19

καταθαρσέω.

2 Chronicles 32: 8

καταθλάω.

Psa. 41:11
Isa. 63: 3

καταθύμιος.

Isa. 44: 9
Mic. 7: 3

καταιγίς.

Psa. 10: 6
49: 3
54: 9
68: 3, 16
80: 8
82:16
106:25, 29
118: 8
Pro. 1:27
10:25—S[1]
Isa. 5:28
Isa. 17:13
21: 1
28:15, 17
18
29: 6
40:24
41:16
57:13
66:15
Jer. 4:13
Lam. 5:10

καταισχύνω.

Jud. 18: 7—A
Ruth 2:15
2 Sa. 10: 6
16:21[a]
19: 5
2 Ki. 19:26
Psa. 6:11 AS[2 b]
13: 6
21: 6
24: 2, 3, 20
30: 2, 18
33: 6
34: 4
36:19
39:15
15 AS[2 c]
43: 8, 10
52: 6
69: 3
70: 1
73:21
118:31, 116
126: 6
Pro. 19:26
20: 4 S[b]
Isa. 1:29 A[b]
3:15
28:16
Isa. 50: 7 S[1 b]
54: 4
Jer. 2:36, 36
6:15, 15
15[d]
7:19
9:19
10:14
15: 9
17:13[e], 18
18[f]
26:24
27: 2, 38
28:17
30:12
31:13, 13
21
Eze. 24:12
Hos. 2: 5
4:19
Joel 1:11 S[2 g]
2:26, 27
Mic. 3: 7
7:16
Zeph. 3:11, 20
Zec. 10: 5
13: 4

[a] A αἰσχύνω. [b] pro αἰσχύνω.
[c] pro ἐντρέπω. [d] AS αἰσχύνω.
[e] S[1] αἰσχύνω. [f] A πτοέω.
[g] pro ξηραινω.

κατακαίω.

Gen. 38:24
Exo. 3: 2, 3
12:10
29:14, 34
32:20
34:13
Lev. 4:12, 21
21
6:30
7: 7, 9
8:17, 32
9:11
13:52, 52
55, 57
16:27, 28
19: 6
20:14
21: 9
Nu. 16:37, 39
39
19: 5, 5, 8
17
Deu. 7: 5
25 A[a]
9:21
12: 3, 31
29:23
Jos. 7:15
11: 6
Jud. 2: 2 A[b]
14:15[c]
1 Sa. 31:12
2 Ki. 17:31
23: 4, 5
6—A
11, 11
2 Ki. 23:15, 16
20
1 Ch. 14:12
2 Ch. 15:16
34: 5
Job 1:16
15:34 A[a]
Psa. 45:10
82:15
Pro. 6:27, 28
Isa. 1:31
9:19
27: 4
33:12, 12
43: 2, 2
44:16, 19
47:14
64: 2
Jer. 7:31
19: 5
21:10
30: 2
39:29[d]
41:22
43:25, 27[e]
28, 29
32
45:17, 23
50:13
Eze. 5: 2, 4
20:47
39:10
43:21
Dan. 11:18 AB[f]
Amos 2: 1

[a] pro καίω. [b] pro καθαιρέω.
[c] A ἐμπυρίζω. [d] A καίω.
[e] AS[1] καιω. [f] pro καταπαύω.

κατακάλυμμα.

Exo. 26:14
35:10[a]
37:16 A[b]
38:19
39:21 A[c]
40:17, 19
Nu. 3:25, 31
Nu. 4: 6
25 AB[2 c]
25[d]
25 A[c]
31, 31[e]
Isa. 14:11
47: 2

[a] A γλύμμα. [b] pro καταπέτασμα
[c] pro κάλυμμα. [d] B κάλυμμα.
[e] AB[2] κάλυμμα.

κατακαλύπτω.

Gen. 38:15
Exo. 26:34
29:22
Lev. 3: 3
9—AB
14[a]
4: 8
6:33
9:19
Nu. 4: 5
22: 5
2 Ch. 18:29
Est. 6:12+S[3]
Isa. 6: 2, 2
11: 9
26:21
Jer. 26: 8
28:42, 51
Eze. 26:10[a], 19
32: 7
38: 9
Hab. 2:14

[a] A καλύπτω.

κατακάμπτω.

Psa. 37: 7
Psa. 56: 7

κατάκαρπος.

Psa. 51:10
Hos. 14: 6
Zec. 2: 4

κατακάρπωσις.

Leviticus 6:10, 11

κατάκαυμα.

Exo. 21:25, 25
Lev. 13:24, 24
25, 28
28
Nu. 19: 6
Jer. 31:34
Hos. 7: 4

κατακαυχάομαι.

Jer. 27:10, 38
Zec. 10:12

κατάκειμαι.

Pro. 6: 9
Pro. 23:34

κατακενόω.

Gen. 42:35
2 Sa. 13: 9

κατακεντέω.

Jer. 28: 4
Eze. 23:47

κατακλάω.

Ezekiel 19:12

κατακλείω.

Jeremiah 39: 3—S[1]

κατακληροδοτέω.

Deu. 1:38 A[a]
Deu. 21:16 A[a]

[a] pro κατακληρονομέω.

κατακληρονομέω.

Nu. 13:31
33:54
34:13, 18
35: 8[a]
Deu. 1:38[b]
2:21
22—B[1]
3:20, 28
12: 2 A[c]
10, 29
15: 4
18:14
19: 1, 14
21:16[b]
Deu. 25:19 A[c]
29: 1
31: 3, 7
Jos. 12: 1
13:32
14: 1, 1
18: 2 A[c]
19:51
21: 3, 43
22:19
23: 5
24: 8
Jud. 2: 6
11:24 A[c]
Jud. 11:24 A[d]
18: 9 A[c]
1 Sa. 2: 8
2 Sa. 7: 1
1 Ch. 28: 8—B
Psa. 36:34
81: 8[f]
104:44 AS[2 c]
Isa. 14: 2
Jer. 3:18
Eze. 22:16
Eze. 45: 8
9+A
46:18
47:13, 14
Amos 2:10
Obad. 17, 17
19, 19
Hab. 1: 6
Zec. 2:12
8:12

[a] B κληρονομέω. [b] A κατακληροδοτέω. [c] pro κληρονομεω.
[d] pro ἐξαίρω.
[f] S[1] ἐξολοθρεύω.

κατακληροῦμαι.

1 Sa. 10:20, 21
21
1 Sa. 14:42, 42
47—A

κατακλίνω.

Exo. 21:18
Nu. 24: 9
Jud. 5:27—A
Jud. 5:27[a]
1 Sa. 16:11

[a] A κάμπτω.

κατάκλιτον.

Isaiah 3:23

κατακλύζω.

Job 11:19
Psa. 77:20
Jer. 29: 2, 2
Eze. 13:11, 13
Eze. 38:22
Dan. 11:10, 22
22, 26

κατακλυσμός.

Gen. 6:17
7: 6, 7
10, 17
9:11, 11
15, 28
10: 1, 32
Gen. 11:10
Psa. 28:10
31: 6
Dan. 9:26
Nah. 1: 8

κατακολουθέω.

Jeremiah 17:16

κατακονδυλίζω.

Amos 5:11

κατακοντίζω.

Job 30:14

κατάκοπος.

Jud. 5:26 A[a]
Job 3:17
Job 16: 7[b]

[a] pro κοπιάω. [b] C κατὰ τόπον

κατακόπτω.

Gen. 14: 5, 7
Nu. 14:45
Jos. 10:10
11: 8
Jud. 20:43[a]
2 Ch. 15:16
28:24
34: 7
7 A[b]
Isa. 18: 5 AS[c]
Isa. 27: 9
Jer. 20: 4
21: 7
Eze. 5: 2
Dan. 7:23
Amos 1: 5
Mic. 1: 7
4: 3
Zeph. 1:11
Zec. 11: 6

[a] A κόπτω. [b] pro κόπτω.
[c] pro ἀποκόπτω.

κατακοσμέω.

Exo. 39: 6
Isa. 61:10

κατακράζω.

2 Ki. 2:23 B[*a] [a] pro καταπαίζω.

κατακρατέω.

1 Sa. 14:42
1 Ki. 12 p24 l73
2 Ch. 12: 1, 4
Jer. 8: 5
27:15, 43
Jer. 47:10
Mic. 1: 9
4: 9
Nah. 3:14, 14

κατακρημνίζω.

2 Chronicles 25:12

κατακρίνω.

Esther 2: 1

κατακρούω.

Jud. 16:14 A[a] [a] pro πηγνύμι.

κατακρύπτω.

Gen. 35: 4
Jos. 10:16
1 Ki. 18: 4[a]
2 Ki. 7: 8
2 Ch. 18:24
22:12
Psa. 50:21
55: 7

Isa. 2:18
Jer. 13: 4, 6
43:19[b]
26—S[1]
50: 9, 10
Eze. 4:12 A[c]
Amos 9: 2[d]

[a] AB κρύπτω. [b] A κρύπτω.
[c] pro ἐγκρύπτω. [d] A κατορύσσω.

κατακτάομαι.

2 Chronicles 28:10

κατακυλίνδω, —λίω.

Jud. 5:27[a]
1 Sa. 14: 9

Jer. 28:25
[a] A συγκάμπτω.

κατακύπτω.

2 Kings 9:32

κατακυριεύω.

Gen. 1:28
9: 1, 7[a]
Nu. 21:24
32:22, 29
Jos. 24:33 A[b]
Psa. 9:26, 31

Psa. 18:14
48:15
71: 8
100: 2
118:133
Jer. 3:14

[a] A πληθύνω. [b] pro κυριεύω.

καταλαλέω.

Nu. 12: 8
21: 5, 7
Job 19: 3
Psa. 44:17 AS[3] [a]
49:20
77:19

Ps. 100: 5
118:23
Pro. 20:13
Hos. 7:13
Mic. 3: 7
Mal. 3:13, 16[b]

[a] pro παραλαλέω. [b] A λαλέω.

καταλαμβάνω.

Gen. 19:19
31:23, 25
44: 4
Exo. 15: 9
22: 4 AB[a]
Lev. 26: 5, 5
Nu. 21:32
32:23
Deu. 19: 6
28:15, 45
Jos. 2: 5
8:19
10:19
11:10
19:18
Jud. 1: 5[b]
6B[1c], 8
7:24
9:45, 50[d]
18:22—A
1 Sa. 30: 8 *ter*
2 Sa. 5: 7 AS[e]
12:26, 27
29
15: 5 A[f]
14
21:11
1 Ki. 9:16 A
18:44
2 Ki. 18:10

2 Ki. 25: 5
2 Ch. 9:20†
22: 9
25:23—A
33:11
Neh. 9:25
Job 5:13
34:24
Psa. 7: 6
17:38
39:13
68:25[g]
70:11
Pro. 1:13
2:16, 19
19
11:27
13:21
16:32
Isa. 10:14
16: 9 S[h]
20: 1 AS[e]
35:10
37: 8
51:11
59: 9—S[3]
Jer. 3: 8
10:19
28:24
40:16[i]

Jer. 52: 8
Lam. 1: 3
Eze. 33: 4[k]
Hos. 2: 7
10: 9

Amos 9:13
Obad. 6[i]
Mic. 6: 6, 6
Zec. 1: 6
14:16 A[a]

[a] pro καταλείπω. [b] A εὑρίσκω.
[c] pro λαμβανω.
[d] A προκαταλαμβάνω.
[e] pro προκαταλαμβάνω.
[f] pro ἐπιλαμ- † A κατειλέω.
[g] S[1] λαμβάνω. [h] pro καταβάλλω
[i] S καταλείπω. [k] A καταβάλλω.

καταλέγω.

Deuteronomy 19:16

κατάλειμμα.

Gen. 45: 7
Jud. 5:13—A
1 Sa. 13:15
2 Sa. 14: 7[a]
1 Ki. 12:24 *l* 79
15: 4
2 Ki. 10:11
19:31

Job 22:20
Isa. 10:22
14:22, 30
37:30
Jer. 27:26
29:10
32:24[b]
47:11

[a] A λῆμμα. [b] ABS κατάλυμα.

καταλείπω.

Gen. 2:24
7:23
14:10
33:15
39:12, 13
15, 18
42:38
44:22, 22
Exo. 2:20 8:31
10: 5, 5
15 A[a]
12:10
46+A
14:28
16:19, 20
23, 24
22: 4[b]
29:34
39:13
Lev. 2:10
5:13
6:16
7: 5, 7
8:32
10: 6, 12
12, 16
14:17, 18
29
19: 6, 10
25:52
26:36, 39
Nu. 9:12
11:26
21:35
26:65
32:15
33:55
Deu. 2:34
3: 3, 11
4:27
7:20
28:51, 54
54, 55
62
29:25
31:16[c], 17
Jos. 8:17
17—A
22
10:28, 30
33, 39
40
11: 8, 11
14, 22
22
13: 2, 12
17: 6
18: 2
21: 5, 20

Jos. 21:40
23: 4, 7
24:16
Jud. 2:21
4:16
6: 4[d]
8:10
9: 5[e]
Ruth 1: 3, 5, 16
2:11, 14
18
1 Sa. 2:11
30:13
31: 7
2 Sa. 13:30
14: 7
17:13
1 Ki. 11:33 AB[f]
19:18, 20
2 Ki. 2:2 AB[f]
3:25
4:43, 44
7:13
8: 6[e]
10:11, 11
14, 17
21
25:11, 22
22
1 Ch. 4:43
10: 7
16:37
28: 9, 9
2 Ch. 1:14
8: 7, 8
10: 8
15: 2 B[f]
21:17
28: 6
30: 6
31:10, 10
34:21[g]
Ezra 1: 4
9: 8
15—A[h]
Neh. 1: 2, 3
3—A
3: 8
6: 1
Job 6:18
Psa. 48:11
Pro. 12:11
14:26
20: 7
Isa. 3:20
4: 2, 3
6:11
12 ABS[f]
7: 3, 16, 22

Isa. 10: 3, 14
19, 20
21
11:11, 11
16
13:12, 14
16:14
17: 2, 6, 6
9[i]
10[e]
18: 6
21:10
23:15
24: 6, 12
14
27:10
28: 5, 6
30:17
18+AS
37: 4, 31
32
38:10, 12
39: 6
40:21
54: 6, 7[k]
62: 4
12 S[f]
65:15
66:19

Jer. 2:17, 19
8: 3
9: 2
17:13
21: 7
29:10
31:28
32:24 A[f]
34: 9
41: 7+A
7
44:10
45: 4, 22
47: 6
48:10
49:2, 16 S[1m]
50: 6
51: 7
52:16
Lam. 2:22
5:20
Eze. 36: 4 A[f], 4
36
39:14
Dan. 10:13
11:30
Obad. 6 S[m]
Zec. 11:17
14:16[b]

[a] pro ὑπολείπω. [b] AB καταλαμβάνω. [c] A ἐγκαταλείπω.
[d] A ὑπολείπω. [e] A ἀπολείπω.
[f] pro ἐγκαταλείπω. [g] A περιλείπω. [h] S[3] ἐγκαταλείπω.
[i] AS ἐγκαταλείπω. [k] B ἐγκαταλείπω. [m] pro καταλαμβάνω.

κατάλειψις.

Genesis 45: 7

καταλέω.

Exo. 32:20 | Deu. 9:21

κατάληψις.

Deuteronomy 20:19

καταλιθοβολέω.

Exo. 17: 4 | Nu. 14:10

κατάλιθος.

Exo. 28:17 | Exo. 36:17

καταλιμπάνω.

Gen. 39:16
2 Sa. 5:21

1 Ki. 18:18

καταλλαγή.

Isaiah 9: 5

καταλλάσσω.

Jeremiah 31:39

καταλογίζομαι.

Isaiah 11:10

κατάλοιπος.

Lev. 5: 9
Nu. 3:26
Deu. 3:13
Jud. 7: 6[a]
1 Sa. 13: 2
2 Sa. 10:10
12:28
1 Ki. 12:23
21:30, 30
1 Ch. 4:43
6:61, 70
77
7:24
12:38
19:11
24:20

2 Ch. 9:29
21:14
32:32 B[b]
34: 9
36:20
Ezra 3: 8
4: 3, 9
10, 10
17, 17
6:16
7:18, 20
Neh. 2:16—S[1]
4:14, 19
6: 1, 14
7:71—AB
10:28

Neh. 11: 1
Psa. 16:14
Isa. 9: 1 S[2] [b]
15: 9
21:17[c]
46: 3
Jer. 6: 9
8: 3
15: 9
23: 3
24: 8
29: 4, 4, 5
7
32:23
38: 7
46: 3
47:15
48:16
49: 2, 10
50: 5[d]
51:12, 28
52:16[c]
Eze. 5:10

Eze. 9: 8
11:13
17:21
23:25, 25
25:16
34:18
36: 3
Joel 1: 4 *ter*
Amos 1: 8
6: 9
9: 1, 12
Mic. 2:12
3: 1, 9
7:18
Zeph. 2: 7, 9, 9
3:13
Hag. 1:12, 14
2: 2
Zec. 8: 6, 11
12
11: 9[e]
14: 2

[a] A ἐπίλοιπος. [b] pro λοίπος.
[c] S λοιπός. [d] AS λοιπός.
[e] BS λοιπός.

καταλοχία.

2 Chronicles 31:18 A[a]
[a] A ἐν κ. pro ἐγκαταλοχίζω.

καταλοχισμός.

1 Ch. 4:33
5: 7, 17

1 Ch. 9:22
2 Ch. 31:17

κατάλυμα.

Exo. 4:24
15:18
1 Sa. 1:18
9:22
2 Sa. 7: 6
1 Ch. 17: 5 AS[a]

1 Ch. 28:13
Jer. 14: 8
32:24 AB S
40:12
Eze. 23:21

[a] pro κάλυμμα
[b] pro κατάλειμμα.

κατάλυσις.

Jeremiah 29:21

καταλύω.

Gen. 19: 2, 2
24:23, 25
26:17
42:27
43:20
Nu. 22: 8
25: 1
Jos. 2: 1
3: 1
Jud. 19: 9+A
15 A[a]
15 A[a]
20 A[a]
20: 4 A[a]
Ruth 4:14
2 Sa. 17: 8
1 Ki. 19: 9
2 Ki. 25:10 A[b]
2 Ch. 23: 8
Ezra 5:12[c]

Psa. 8: 3
88:45
Isa. 38:12
Jer. 5: 7
7:34
16: 9
28:43
29:17
30: 9
32:10
44:13
45:22
Lam. 5:15
Eze. 16: 8
21:30
23:17
26:13, 17
Zeph. 2: 7
Zec. 5: 4

[a] pro αὐλίζω.
[b] pro κατασπάω. [c] B λύω.

καταμανθάνω.

Gen. 24:21
34: 1
Lev. 14:36

Jud. 5:28+A
Job 35: 5

καταμαρτυρέω.

1 Ki. 20:10—B
13

Job 15: 6
Pro. 25:18

καταμένω.

Gen. 6: 3 | Nu. 20: 1

Nu. 22: 8
Jos. 2:22
Jos. 7: 7
2 Ki. 12:20+A

καταμερίζω.

Lev. 25:46
Nu. 32:18
34:29[a]
Deu. 19: 3
Jos. 13:14

[a] A καταμετρέω.

καταμερισμός.

Joshua 13:14

καταμετρέω.

Nu. 34: 7,8,10
29 A[a]
Eze. 45: 1
Eze. 48:14
Amos 7:17
Mic. 2: 4

[a] pro καταμερίζω.

καταμίγνυμι.

Exodus 28:14

καταμόνας, κατὰ μόνας.

Gen. 32:16
Jud. 7: 5
17: 3 A[a]
Psa. 4: 9
Psa. 32:15
140:10
Jer. 15:17
Lam. 3:28

[a] pro υἱός.

καταμωκάομαι.

2 Ch. 30:10
Jer. 45:19

καταναλίσκω.

Lev. 6:10
Deu. 4:24
7:22
9: 3
1 Ch. 21:26
Isa. 30:14
66:16 A[a]
Isa. 66:17 A[b]
Jer. 3:24
27: 7ABS[3b]
Zeph. 1:18
3: 8
Zec. 9: 4,15

[a] pro κρίνω. [b] pro ἀναλίσκω.

κατανέμομαι.

Psalm 79:14

κατανίστημι.

Numbers 16: 3

κατανοέω.

Gen. 3: 6
42: 9
Exo. 2:11
19:21
33: 8
10+A
Nu. 32: 8,9
1 Ki. 3:21
Job 23:15
30:20
Psa. 9:35
Psa. 21:18
36:32
90: 8
93: 9
118:15[a], 18
141: 5
Isa. 5:12
57: 1
59:16
Hab. 3: 2

[a] S[1] ἐκζητέω.

καταντάω.

2 Samuel 3:29

κατάντημα.

Psalm 18: 7

κατάνυξις.

Psa. 59: 5
Isa. 29:10

κατανύσσω.

Gen. 27:38−A
34: 7
Lev. 10: 3
1 Ki. 20:27, 29
Psa. 4: 5
29:13
Psa. 34:15
108:16
Isa. 6: 5
47: 5
Dan. 10: 9
15−B

καταξαίνω.

Jud. 8: 7 A[a]
16+A
Jud. 8:16 A[a]

[a] pro ἀλοάω.

καταξηραίνω.

Jos. 2:10
Hos. 13:15

κατάξηρος.

Numbers 11: 6

καταπαίζω.

2 Ki. 2:23[a]
Jer. 2:16
Jer. 9: 5

[a] B[a] κατακράζω.

καταπανουργεύομαι.

Psalm 82: 4

καταπάσσω.

Est. 4: 1
Job 1:20+A
Job 2:12
Jer. 6:26

καταπατέω.

Jos. 19:48 A[a]
Jud. 5:21
9:27 A[b]
1 Sa. 14:48
17:53
23: 1−A
2 Ch. 25:18
Job 28: 8 S[b]
39:15
Psa. 7: 6
55: 2,3
56: 4
90:13
138:11
Isa. 10: 6
Isa. 16: 4, 8, 9
18: 2,7
25:10
28: 3, 28
41:25, 25
63: 3, 3, 6
18+A
Eze. 26:11
32: 2, 13
34:18
Hos. 5:11
Amos 4: 1
5:12
Zec. 12: 3,3
Mal. 4: 3

[a] pro κατοικέω. [b] pro πατέω.

καταπάτημα.

Isa. 5: 5[a]
7:25
14:25
22: 5
18−B
Isa. 28:18
Lam. 2: 8
Eze. 26: 4
Mic. 7:10

[a] A διαρπαγή.

καταπάτησις.

2 Kings 13: 7

κατάπαυσις.

Exo. 34:21[a]
35: 2[a]
Lev. 25:28 AB[b]
Nu. 10:36
Deu. 12: 9
Jud. 20:43+A
1 Ki. 8:56
1 Ch. 6:31
2 Ch. 6:41
Psa. 94:11
131:14
Isa. 66: 1

[a] A καταπαύω.
[b] pro κατάσχεσις.

καταπαύω.

Gen. 2: 2,3
8:22
49:33
Exo. 5: 5
10:14
16:13
20:11
31:17, 18
33:14
34:21
21 A[a]
33
35: 2 A[a]
Nu. 25:11
Deu. 3:20
5:33
12:10
25:19
32:26 A[b]
33:12
Jos. 1:13, 15
Jos. 3:13
10:20
11:23
21:44
22: 4
23: 1
Jud. 8: 3+A
18: 2A[c]
20:43+A
43 A[d]
Ruth 2: 7
2 Sa. 21:10
1 Ki. 12:24
1 Ch. 23:25
2 Ch. 14: 6, 7
15:15
16: 5
20:30
32:22
Ezra 9:13+S[3]
Neh. 4:11
Neh. 6: 3
Job 21:34
26:12
Psa. 54: 7
73: 8
84: 4
Ecc. 10: 4
Lam. 3:11
Lam. 5:14, 14
Eze. 1:24
30:13+A
Dan. 9:27+AB[2]
11:18[e]
Hos. 1: 4
11: 6

[a] pro κατάπαυσις. [b] pro παύω
[c] pro αὐλίζω. [d] pro διώκω.
[e] AB κατακαίω.

καταπείθω.

2 Sa. 17:16[a]
Eze. 16:15

[a] A καταπίνω.

καταπελματόω.

Joshua 9:11

καταπενθέω.

Exodus 33: 4

καταπέτασμα.

Exo. 26:31, 33
33, 33
34, 35
37
27:21
30: 6
35:11
37: 3, 5
16[a]
38:18
39: 4, 20
40: 3,5,19
Exo. 40:20, 24
Lev. 4: 6, 17
16: 2, 12
15
21:23
24: 3
Nu. 3:10. 26
4: 5, 32
18: 7
1 Ki. 6:33−A
2 Ch. 3:14

[a] A κατακάλυμμα.

καταπέτομαι.

Proverbs 27: 8

καταπήγνυμι.

1 Sa. 31:10
Job 39:17 S[1 a]
Hos. 5: 2
9: 8

[a] pro κατασιωπάω.

καταπηδάω.

Gen. 24:64
1 Sa. 25:23

κατάπικρος.

2 Samuel 17: 8

καταπίνω.

Gen. 41: 7, 24
Exo. 7:12
15: 4[a], 12
Nu. 16:30, 32
34
21:28
26:10
Deu. 11: 6
2 Sa. 17:16 A[b]
Job 7:19
8:18
Psa. 34:25
57:10
68:16
105:17
106:27
123: 3
Ps. 140: 6
Pro. 1:12
19:28
21:20
23: 7
Isa. 9:16
16: 8
25: 8
28: 4
7−AS
49:19
Jer. 28:34, 44
Lam. 2:16
3:48
Hos. 8: 8
Jon. 2: 1
Hab. 1:13

[a] A καταποντίζω.
[b] pro καταπείθω.

καταπίπτω.

Neh. 8:11
Job 15:23+A
Ps. 144:14
Isa. 49:19 S[1 a]

[a] pro πίπτω.

καταπιστεύω.

Micah 7: 5

καταπλάσσω.

Job 37:10[a]
Isa. 38:21

[a] AS[2] καταπλήσσω.

κατάπληξις.

Ezra 3: 3−B

καταπλήσσω.

Jos. 5: 1
Job 7:14
Job 13:21
37:10AS[2 a]

[a] pro καταπλάσσω.

καταπολεμέω.

Joshua 10:25

καταποντίζω.

Exo. 15: 4 A[a]
2 Sa. 20:19, 20
Psa. 54:10
68: 3, 16
Ps. 123: 4
Ecc. 10:12
Lam. 2: 2, 5, 5

[a] pro καταπίνω.

καταποντισμός.

Psalm 51: 6

καταπραΰνω.

Psa. 82: 2
88:10
Pro. 15:18

καταπρονομεύω.

Nu. 21: 1
Jud. 2:14[a]

[a] A προνομεύω.

καταπτήσσω.

Jos. 2:24
Pro. 24:65
Pro. 28:14
29: 9

κατάπτωμα.

Psalm 143:14

κατάρα.

Gen. 27:12, 13
Nu. 23:25
Deu. 11:26, 28
29
23: 5
27:13
28:15, 45
29:27[a]
30: 1, 19
Jos. 9: 7
Jud. 9:57
2 Sa. 16:12
1 Ki. 2: 8
3 p 1
2 Ki. 22:19
Neh. 13: 2
Job 31:30
Ps. 108:17, 18
Pro. 3:33
Isa. 64:10
65:23
Jer. 24: 9
29:14 AS[b]
33: 6
36:22
51: 8, 12
Dan. 9:11
Zec. 8:13
Mal. 2: 2

[a] A ἀρά. [b] pro κατάρασις.

καταράομαι.

Gen. 5:29
8:21
12: 3, 3
27:29
Lev. 24:11, 14
15, 23
Nu. 22: 6 A[a]
6,6,12
23: 8 B[a]
8,8,13,
25, 27
24: 9,9,10
Deu. 21:23
23: 4
Jud. 5:23, 23
9:27
1 Sa. 17:43
2 Sa. 16: 5, 7, 9
10, 10
11, 13
2 Sa. 19:21
1 Ki. 2: 8
3 p 1
2 Ki. 2:24
9:34
Neh. 10:29
13: 2, 25
Job 3: 1,5−S[1]
8, 8
24:18
Psa. 36:22
61: 5
108:28
Pro. 24:33, 34
27:14
Ecc. 7:22, 23
10:20, 20
Jer. 15:10
Mal. 2: 2

[a] pro ἀράομαι.

κατάρασις.

Nu. 23:11 | Jer. 20:14[a]
Jud. 5:23+A |

[a] AS κατάρα.

καταργέω.

Ezra 4:21, 23 | Ezra 6: 8
5: 5 |

καταργυρόω.

Exodus 27:17

καταριθμέω.

Gen. 50: 3 | 2 Ch. 31:19
Nu. 14:29 |

καταρράκτης,
καταράκτης.

Gen. 7:11 | Psa. 41: 8
8: 2 | Jer. 20: 2, 3
Lev. 11:17 | 36:26
Deu. 14:16 | Mal. 3:10
2 Ki. 7: 2, 19 |

καταρράσσω,
καταράσσω.

Psa. 36:24 | Hos. 7: 6
73: 6 |

καταρρεμβεύω,
–ρομβεύω.

Numbers 32:13

καταρρέω.

1 Sa. 2:33 | 1 Sa. 21:13

καταρρήγνυμι.

Jos. 9:10 | Ps. 144:14
Job 32:19 A[a] | 145: 8
Psa. 88:45 | Pro. 27: 9
101:11 |

[a] pro ῥήγνυμι.

καταρρίπτω.

Lamentations 2: 1

καταρρυέω.

Jeremiah 8:13

καταρτίζω.

Exo. 15:17[a] | Psa. 17:34
Ezra 4:12, 13 | 28: 9
16 | 39: 7
5: 3, 9, 11 | 67:10, 29[b]
6:14 | 73:16
Psa. 8: 3 | 79:16
10: 3 | 88:38
16: 5 |

[a] A κατεργάζομαι.
[b] S[2] κατεργάζομαι.

κατάρχω.

Nu. 16:13 | Joel 2:17
1 Ki. 10 p 22 | Nah. 1:12
12 p 24 l 66 | Zec. 6:13[a]
Neh. 9:28 | 9:10[a]

[a] S[1] κατάγω.

κατασβεννύω.

Pro. 15:18 | Pro. 28: 2

κατασιγάω.

Ezekiel 27:32+A

κατασιωπάω.

Nu. 13:31 | Job 37:19
Neh. 8:11 | 39:17[a]

[a] S[1] καταπήγνυμι.

κατασκάπτω.

Deu. 12: 3 | Pro. 14: 1[a]
Jud. 6:28 A[a] | 24:46
30 A[a] | 29: 4
31 A[a] | Jer. 1:10
32 A[a] | 2:15
8: 9 | 5:10
17 A[b] | 27:15
1 Ki. 18:31+A | 28:58, 58
32–A | Eze. 13:14
19:10 | 16:39
2 Ki. 21: 3 A[c] | 36:35
1 Ch. 20: 1 | Hos. 10: 2
2 Ch. 32: 5[d] | Joel 1:17
36:19 | Amos 3:14
Pro. 11:11 | 9:11[e]

[a] pro καθαιρέω. [b] pro καταστρέφω. [c] pro κατασπάω. [d] A κατασπάω. [e] A καταστρέφω.

κατασκεδάζω.

Exodus 24: 8

κατασκέπτομαι.

Nu. 10:34 | Jos. 7: 2, 3
13: 3, 17 | Jud. 1:23[a]
18, 22 | 18:2, 14, 17
24, 26 | 2 Sa. 10: 3
33, 33 | Job 39: 8
14: 6, 7, 34 | Ecc. 1:13
36, 38 | 2: 3
21:32 | 7:26

[a] A κατά.

κατασκευάζω.

Nu. 21:27 | Isa. 43: 7
2 Ch. 32: 5 | 45: 7, 9
Pro. 23: 5 | Jer. 26: 9 A[a]
Isa. 40:19, 28 |

[a] pro παρασκευάζω.

κατασκευή.

Exo. 27:19[a] | Nu. 32:16 A[c]
35:24 AB[b] | 1 Ch. 29:19
36: 7 | 2 Ch. 26:15
Nu. 8: 4 |

[a] A ἀποσκευή. [b] pro παρασκευή. [c] pro ἀποσκευή.

κατασκηνόω.

Nu. 14:30 | Psa. 67:17, 19
35:34, 34 | 68:37
Deu. 33:12, 28 | 73: 2
Jos. 22:19 | 77:55, 60
Jud. 5:17 A[a] | 84:10
17 A[a] | 101:29
18:28[b] | 103:12
2 Sa. 7:10 | 119: 5
1 Ki. 6(13) A | 138: 9
1 Ch. 17: 9 | Pro. 1:33
23:25 | 2:21
2 Ch. 6: 1[c], 2[b] | 8:12
Ezra 6:12 | Jer. 7:12
7:15 | 17: 6
Neh. 1: 9 | 23: 6
Job 18:15 | 28:13
29:25 | Eze. 25: 4
Psa. 5:12 | 43: 7, 9
7: 6 | Dan. 4: 9, 18[b]
14: 1 | Joel 3:17, 21
15: 9 | Obad. 3
22: 2 | Mic. 4:10
36: 3, 27 | 7:14
29 | Zec. 2:10, 11
64: 5[d] | 8: 3, 8

[a] pro σκηνόω. [b] A κατοικέω. [c] A[2] κατοικέω. [d] S[1] κατοικέω.

κατασκήνωσις.

1 Ch. 28: 2 | Eze. 37:27

κατάσκιος.

Jer. 2:20 | Hab. 3: 3
Eze. 20:28 | Zec. 1: 8

κατασκοπεύω.

Gen. 42:30 | Jos. 6:22, 23
Exo. 2: 4 | 25, 25
Deu. 1:24 | 14: 7
Jos. 2: 1, 2, 3 |

κατασκοπέω.

2 Sa. 10: 3 | 1 Ch. 19: 3

κατάσκοπος

Gen. 42: 9, 11 | 1 Sa. 26: 4
14, 16 | 2 Sa. 15:10
31, 34 |

κατασμικρύνω.

2 Samuel 7:19

κατασοφίζομαι.

Exodus 1:10

κατασπαταλάω.

Pro. 29:21 | Amos 6: 4

κατασπάω.

2 Sa. 11:25 | 2 Ch. 30:14
2 Ki. 10:27 | 31: 1
11:18 | 32: 5 A[d]
21: 3[a] | 18
23:12, 15 | 33: 3
25:10–B[b] | 34: 4[e], 7
2 Ch. 23:17 | Pro. 15:25
24: 7 | Mic. 1: 6, 10
25:23[c] | Zeph. 3: 6
26: 6 | Zec. 11: 2

[a] A κατασκάπτω.
[b] A καταλύω. [c] A καθίστημι.
[d] pro κατασκάπτω.
[e] A καταστρέφω.

κατασπείρω.

Lev. 19:19 | Job 18:15
Deu. 22: 9 |

κατασπεύδω.

Exo. 5:10, 13 | 1 Ch. 21:30
9:19 | 2 Ch. 26:20
10:16 | 35:21
Deu. 33: 2 | Est. 5: 5
1 Sa. 21: 8 A[a] | Dan. 4:16+A

[a] pro κατὰ σπουδήν.

κατασπουδάζομαι.

Job 23:15

καταστασιάζω.

Exodus 38:22

καταστενάζω.

Exo. 2:23 | Eze. 9: 4
Jer. 22:23 | 21: 6
Lam. 1:11 |

καταστηρίζω.

Job 20: 7[a]

[a] AC στηρίζω.

καταστολή.

Isaiah 61: 3

καταστραγγίζω.

Leviticus 5: 9

καταστρατοπεδεύω.

Joshua 4:19

καταστρέφω.

Gen. 13:10 | Deu. 29:23, 23
19:21, 25 | Jud. 7:13 A[a]
29 | 8:17[b]
2 Ki. 21:13 | Isa. 1: 7
2 Ch. 34: 4 A[c] | 13:19
Ezra 6:12 | Jer. 20:16
Job 9: 5 | 27:40
11:10 | 29:19
12:14 A[d] | Lam. 4: 6
15, 19 | Dan. 11: 8+AB[2]
18: 4 | Amos 4:11, 11
24:22 | 9:11 A[f]
28: 9 | Jon. 3: 4
Psa. 88:40 | Hag. 2:22, 22
Pro. 10:32 S[2] [e] | 22+A
14: 1 A[f] | Mal. 1: 4, 4

[a] pro ἀναστρέφω. [b] A κατασκάπτω. [c] pro κατασπάω. [d] pro καταβάλλω. [e] pro ἀποστρέφω. [f] pro κατασκάπτω.

καταστροφή

Gen. 19:29 | Job 21:17
2 Ch. 22: 7 | 27: 7
Job 8:19 | Pro. 1:18, 27
15:21 | Hos. 8: 7

καταστρώννυμι, –ύω.

Nu. 14:16 | Job 12:23

κατασύρω.

Jer. 29:11[a]

[a] A κατερευνάω.

κατασφάζω.

Eze. 16:40 | Zec. 11: 5

κατασφραγίζω.

Job 9: 7 | Job 37: 6

κατάσχεσις.

Gen. 17: 8 | Jos. 22: 4, 9
47:11 | 19, 19
48: 4 | 1 Ch. 4:33
Lev. 25:24, 25 | 7:28
27, 28[a] | 9: 2
32, 33 | 13: 2
33, 34 | 2 Ch. 11:14
41, 45 | Neh. 11: 3
27:16, 21 | Psa. 2: 8
22, 24 | Eze. 33:24
28 | 35:12 A[c]
Nu. 13: 3 | 36: 2, 3, 5
15: 2 A[b] | 12
20:24+A | 44:28, 28
27: 4, 7, 12 | 45: 5, 6, 7
32: 5, 22 | 7, 8
29, 32 | 46:16, 18
33:54, 54 | 18
35: 2, 8, 28 | 48:20, 21
36: 3 | 22+A
Deu. 32:49+A | 22
Jos. 21:12, 41 | Zec. 11:14[d]

[a] AB κατάπαυσις. [b] pro κατοίκησις. [c] pro κατάβρωμα. [d] A διαθήκη.

κατατάσσω.

Job 7:12 | Job 35:10
15:23 |

κατατείνω.

Leviticus 25:43, 46, 53

κατατέμνω.

Lev. 21: 5 | Isa. 15: 2
1 Ki. 18:28 | Hos. 7:14

κατατέρπω.

Zeph. 3:14[a]

[a] S[1] τέρπω.

κατατήκω.

Jos. 5: 1 A[a] | Mic. 4:13[b]

[a] pro τήκω. [b] A λεπτύνω.

κατατίθημι.

1 Ch.21:27[a]
Psa. 40: 9
Jer. 39:14 S[b]

[a] A καθίημι. [b] pro τίθημι.

κατατοξεύω.

Exo. 19:13
Nu. 24: 8
2 Ki. 9:16
Psa. 10: 2
63: 5, 5

κατατρέχω.

Lev. 26:37
Jud. 1: 6
1 Ki. 19:20[a]
Job 16:10

[a] A ἐπιτρέχω.

κατατρίβω.

Deu. 8: 4
29: 5
Pro. 5:11

κατατρυφαω.

Psalm 36: 4, 11

κατατρώγω.

Proverbs 24:23

κατατυγχάνω.

Job 3:22

καταφάγω.

Gen. 31:15, 38
37:20, 33
41: 4, 20
43: 1
Exo. 10:15
15: 7
Lev. 9:24
10: 2
Nu. 11: 1
16:35
21:28
26.10
Deu. 28:39, 57
32:22
42 A[e]
Jud. 6:21
9:15, 20[b]
20
2 Sa. 2:26
11:25 A[a]
18: 8, 8
1 Ki. 12 p 24
ll 13, 41
14:11 A
11 A
16: 4, 4
18:38
20:23
24 A[a]
24 A[a]
2 Ki. 1:10, 10
12, 12
14
9:10, 36
2 Ch. 7: 1, 13
Job 1:16[c]
22:20
Psa. 20:10
68:10
77:45, 63
78: 7
104:35, 35
Pro. 24:52
Ecc. 6: 2 S[1 a]
Isa. 10:18
Isa. 31: 8
50: 9
Jer. 2:30
5:14
8:16
10:25
12: 9 A[a]
12
17:27
26:10, 14
27:32
28:34
30:16
Lam. 2: 3
4:11
Eze. 2:10
15: 7
19:14
20:47
23:25[d]
28:18
36: 8[e]
Dan. 7:23
Hos. 2:12
5: 7
7: 7, 9
8: 7, 14
13: 8[c]
Joel 1: 4 *ter*
20
2:25
Amos 1: 4, 7, 10
12, 14
2: 2, 5
4: 9
5: 6
7: 2, 4, 4
Obad. 18
Mic. 3: 3
Nah. 2:13
3:13, 15
15
Zec. 11: 1, 16
12: 6

vide κατεσθίω.

[a] *pro* φάγω. [b] B φάγω. [c] S[1] καταφλέγω. [d] A ἐμπίπρημι. [e] A φάγω.

καταφαίνω.

Genesis 48:17

καταφερής.

Joshua 7: 5

καταφέρω.

Gen. 37: 1
Deu. 1:25
22:14
Jud. 7: 4[a], 5[b]
16:21[a]
2 Sa. 14:14[d]
1 Ki. 1:53
Isa. 17:13 A[c]
28: 2
2 — S[1]
Eze. 47: 2
Dan. 5:20
Mic. 1: 4

[a] A κατάγω. [b] A καταβιβάζω. [c] *pro* φέρω. [d] B καταφθείρω.

καταφεύγω.

Gen. 19:20
Lev. 26 25
Nu. 35:25, 26
Deu. 4:42
19: 5
Jos. 10:27
20: 9
Ps. 142: 9
Isa. 10: 3
17: 3
54:15
55: 5
Jer. 27: 5
Zec. 2:11

καταφθάνω.

Jud. 20:42 A[a] [a] *pro* φθάνω.

καταφθείρω.

Gen. 6:12, 12
13, 17
9:11
Exo. 18:18
Lev. 26:39
Jud. 6: 4 B[a]
2 Sa. 14:14 B[b]
2 Ch. 12: 7
24:23
25:16
2 Ch. 26:16
27: 2
35:21
Isa. 10:27
13: 5
24: 1
32: 7
36:10 S[1 a]
49:19[c]

[a] *pro* διαφθείρω. [b] *pro* καταφέρω. [c] AS[3] διαφθείρω.

καταφθορά.

2 Ch. 12:12
Psa. 48:10
Ps. 139:12[a]
Zeph. 3: 6 S[1 b]

[a] AS διαφθορά. [b] *pro* διαφθορά.

καταφιλέω.

Gen. 31:28, 55
33: 4 — A
45:15
Exo. 4:27
Ruth 1: 9, 14
1 Sa. 20:41
2 Sa. 14:33
2 Sa. 15: 5
19:39
20: 9
1 Ki. 2:19
19:20
Psa. 84:11

καταφλέγω.

Job 1:16 S[1 a]
Ps. 104:32
Ps. 105:18

[a] *pro* καταφάγω.

καταφλογίζω.

Psalm 17: 9

κατάφοβος.

Proverbs 29:16

καταφρονέω.

Gen. 27:12
Pro. 13:13, 13
15
18: 3
19:16
23:22
Pro. 25: 9
Jer. 2:36
Hos. 6: 7
Hab. 1:13
Zeph. 1:12

καταφρονητής.

Hab. 1: 5
2: 5
Zeph. 3: 4

καταφυγή.

Exo. 17:15
Exo. 21:14
Nu. 35:27, 28
Deu. 19: 3
2 Sa. 22: 3
Psa. 9:10
17: 3
30: 3, 4
31: 7
45: 2
58:17
Psa. 70: 3
89: 1
90: 2, 9
93:22
103:18
143: 2
Isa. 25:12
Jer. 16:19
Dan. 11:39

καταφύτευσις.

Jeremiah 38:22

καταφυτεύω.

Exo. 15:17
Lev. 19:23
Deu. 6:11
Jos. 21:13 A[a]
2 Sa. 7:10
1 Ch. 17: 9
Psa. 43: 3
79: 9, 10
Pro. 29:34
Isa. 65:21
Jer. 1:10 — A
Jer. 11:17
18: 9
24: 6
36: 5 S[a]
38:28
Eze. 17:22, 23
36:36
Amos 9:14 AB[a]
14 A[b]
15
Zeph. 1:13

[a] *pro* φυτεύω. [b] *pro* ποιέω.

καταχαίρω.

Proverbs 1:26

καταχαλάω.

Joshua 2:15

καταχαλκόω.

2 Chronicles 4: 9

καταχέω.

Gen. 39:21
Job 41:14
Psa. 88:46

καταχρίω.

Exodus 2: 3

καταχρύσεος.

Deuteronomy 1: 1

καταχρυσόω.

Exo. 25:10, 12
27
26:29, 29
30: 3, 5
37: 4, 6
38: 2, 11
Exo. 38:18
39: 6
2 Ch. 3: 4, 5
8 A[a]
9:17

[a] *pro* χρυσόω.

κατάχυσις.

Job 30:16

καταχώννυμι.

Zechariah 9:15 — S[2]

καταχωρίζω.

1 Ch. 27:24
Est. 2:23

καταψύχω.

Genesis 18: 4

κατέδω.

Exo. 10: 5, 5, 12
Lev. 26:29, 38
Deu. 28:38, 51
2 Sa. 22: 9
Job 18:13
20:26
Isa. 1:20
33:11
61: 6
Jer. 5:16 — S[1]
17 *ter*
21:14 A[a]

[a] *pro* ἔδω.

κατείδω.

Exo. 10: 5
Deu. 26:15

κατειλέω.

2 Ch. 9:20 A *pro* καταλαμβάνω.

κατεμβλέπω.

Exodus 3: 6

κατέναντι.

Gen. 2:14
4:16
50:13
Exo. 19: 2
32: 5
11 A[a]
Nu. 17: 4
25: 4[b]
Jud. 19:10 A[c]
2 Sa. 10:17 A[c]
1 Ki. 20:13 + A
2 Ki. 1:13
15.10 + A
1 Ch. 5:11
8:32
19: 7, 14
24: 6
26:15
16-A, 18
2 Ch. 2: 6
4:10
5:12[f]
6:12, 22
24, 28
8:14
2 Ch. 32:12
Neh. 3:10, 23
12 37
Psa. 5: 6
25: 3
Ecc. 4:12
6: 8
Isa. 38:20
Lam. 3:34
Eze. 1: 9 A[c]
3: 8, 8
11: 1
40:10, 27
41
41:13, 14
42: 1, 4, 19[e]
44: 4
47:20
Dan. 5: 1, 5
6:10, 22
Joel 1:16
Amos 3:12
4: 3
Mic. 2: 8
Zec. 14: 4 — A

[a] *pro* ἔναντι. [b] B ἀπέναντι. [c] *pro* ἀπέναντι. [d] A κατὰ ἀνατολή. [e] A κατὰ πρόσωπον. [f] A κατεναντίον.

κατεναντίον.

2 Sa. 22:23
2 Ch. 34:27
Neh. 12:24
Psa. 43:16[a]

[a] A κατενώπιον.

κατενισχύω.

2 Ch. 1: 1 B[a] [a] *pro* ἐνισχύω.

κατεντευκτής.

Job 7:20

κατενώπιον.

Lev. 4:17[a]
Jos. 1: 5
3: 7
21:44
Jos. 23: 9
Psa. 43:16 A[b]
Dan. 5:22[a]

[a] A ἐνώπιον. [b] *pro* κατεναντίον.

κατεπείγω.

Exodus 22:25

κατέπω.

Numbers 14:37

κατεργάζομαι.

Exo. 15:17 A[a]
35:33
39: 1
Nu. 6: 3
Deu. 28:39
Jud. 16:16 A[b]
1 Ki. 6:33
Psa. 67:29 S[2 a]
Eze. 34: 4
36: 9

[a] *pro* καταρτίζω.
[b] *pro* ἐκθλίβω.

κατεργασία.

1 Chronicles 28:19

κάτεργος.

Exo. 30:16
Exo. 35:21

κατερευνάω.

Jer. 20:11 A[a] [a] *pro* κατασύρω.

κατέρχομαι.

2 Samuel 16:21

κατεσθίω, —θω.

Gen. 40:17
Nu. 12:12
Nu. 13:33
Deu. 28:55

Psa. 13: 4[a]
52: 5[b]
Pro. 21:37—A
Isa. 1: 7
9:12
29: 6
Isa. 30:30
Eze. 22:25
34: 3
36:13
Joel 2: 5
Zec. 11: 9

vide κατοφάγω.

[a] S ἐσθίω. [b] BS[1] ἔσθω.

κατευθύνω.

Jud. 12: 6
14: 6 A[a]
19 A[a]
15:14 A[a]
1 Sa. 6:12
2 Sa. 19:17
1 Ki. 11:43—A
1 Ch. 29:18
2 Ch. 12:14
17: 5
19: 3
20:33
30:19
32:30
Psa. 5: 9
7:10
36:23
39: 3
68: 5
77: 8
89:17
17+AS
100: 7
101:20
Ps. 118: 5, 133
139:12
140: 2
Pro. 1: 3
4:26
9:15
13:13
15: 8, 21
21: 2
23:19
29:27
Jer. 15:11
21:12
Eze. 17: 9, 10
15
18:25[b], 25
25
Dan. 3:30
6:28
8:24, 25
11:27, 36
Hos. 4:10
Zec. 11:16
Mal. 2: 6

[a] *pro* ἅλλομαι. [b] A κατορθόω.

κατευοδόω.

Jud. 18: 5 A[a]
Psa. 1: 3
36: 7
44: 5
Psa. 67:20
Pro. 17:23
Dan. 8:11
12 A[a]

[a] *pro* εὐοδόω.

κατέχω.

Gen. 22:13
24:56
39:20
42:19
Exo. 32:13
Jos. 1:11
Jud. 13:15[a]
16[a]
19: 4[b]
Ruth 1:13
2 Sa. 1: 9
2:21
4:10
6: 6
6+AB
1 Ki. 1:51
2:28, 29
2 Ki. 3:10 A[c]
12:12
1 Ch. 13: 9
2 Ch. 15: 8
Neh. 3: 4
Neh. 3: 4—B
4—A
5
Job 15:24
23: 9
27:17
34:14
Psa. 68:37
72:12
118:53
138:10
Pro. 18:22
19:15
Cant. 3: 8
Isa. 40:22
Jer. 6:24
13:21
27:16
37: 6[d]
Eze. 33:24
Dan. 7:18, 22

[a] A βιάζω. [b] A εἰσάγω.
[c] *pro* παρέρχομαι. [d] S[1] κατάγω.

κατήγορος.

Proverbs 18:17

κατισχύω.

Gen. 49:24
Exo. 1: 7
7:13
17:11, 11
18:23
Deu. 1:38
2:30
3:28[a]
Jos. 11:20
17:13
23: 6
Jud. 6: 2 A[b]
7: 8[c]
9:24 A[d]
1 Sa. 19: 8
2 Ki. 14: 5
22: 5
24: 2
1 Ch. 5:20
11:10
15:26
21: 6[e]
1 Ch. 22:12
29:12
2 Ch. 8: 3
11:12, 17
17
12:13
13:18, 21
14:11, 11
15: 8
16: 9
17: 1
22: 9
24: 5
25: 8
8 A[b]
11
26: 7, 8, 9
15, 16
27: 5, 6
28:23
31: 4
32: 4, 5, 5
34:10
2 Ch. 35: 2
36:13
Job 18: 9
Psa. 88:22
Isa. 22: 4
24:20
42:25
50:11
54: 2
63:12
Jer. 8:21
15:18
Eze. 3: 8
13:22
30:24
Dan. 11: 6, 7, 12
21, 32
Hos. 7:15
14: 8
Hag. 2: 4 *ter*
Zec. 8: 9, 13
10: 6, 12

[a] A ἐνισχύω. [b] *pro* ἰσχύω.
[c] A κρατέω. [d] *pro* ἐνισχύω.
[e] A προσοχθίζω.

κατοδυνάω *vide* κατωδυνάω.

κατοικεσία.

Ps. 106:36
Lam. 1: 7[a]
Eze. 6:14[b]

[a] A μετοικεσία. [b] A κατοικία.

κατοικέω.

Gen. 9:27
11: 2, 31
12: 6
13: 6, 6, 7
12, 12
18
14: 7, 12
13
16:12
19:25+A
25, 29
30, 30[a]
20:15
21:20, 21
22:19
24:62
25:11, 18
18
26: 2, 6, 17
34:10, 10
15, 22
30
35:21
36: 8[a], 20
(37) 1
45:10
46:34
47: 4, 5
6 A[b]
11 A[b]
27
49:13
50:22
Exo. 2:15 A[c]
12:13 A[d]
40[e]
15:14, 15
Lev. 18: 3
20:22
23:42, 42
25:10, 18
19
26: 5, 35
Nu. 13:20, 29
30 *ter*
33
14:14, 25
21: 1, 25
31
32—A
Nu. 21:34
23: 9
32:17, 17
39, 40
33:40, 52
53, 53
55, 55
35: 2, 3, 25
28, 32
33, 34
Deu. 1: 4, 4, 6
44
2: 4, 8, 20
22, 23
29, 29
3: 2, 19
4:46
8:12
9:28
11:30, 31
12:10, 10
29
13:12, 13
15
17:14
19: 1
23:16, 16
25: 5
26: 1
29:16
30:20
33:19
Jos. 1:14
2:24
6:25 AB[b]
7: 9
8: 5
20 A[f]
25
9: 9, 13
16, 17
22, 28
30
33—A
10: 1, 6, 6
12: 2, 4
13: 6, 13
21
14: 4
15:15, 63
Jos. 15:63
16:10 *ter*
17:11, 11
11+A
12, 16
19:48[g]
48, 50
20: 4 A
6 A
21: 2, 43
22:33
24: 2 B[h], 8
11, 15
18, 32
Jud. 1: 9, 10
11, 16
17, 19
21, 21
27 *qnq*
29, 29
30 *ter*
31 *qtr*
32, 32
33 *qnq*
35
3: 3, 5
4: 2
5:15+A
23[i]
8:11 A[k]
29 A[m]
9:21 A[c]
10: 1 A[c]
18
11: 3 A[c]
8[t], 21
18: 1
7+A
9+A
28 A[n]
20:15 A[c]
21:10 A[c]
12 A[c]
21 A[c]
23 A[m]
Ruth 1: 4
1 Sa. 6:21
12: 8 A[b]
11
22: 4
23: 5
27: 8
31: 7, 11
2 Sa. 2: 3
5: 6
7: 2, 5, 6
9:13
11:11
1 Ki. (3) *p* 46
4(25) A
30—A
8:27, 53
53
12:25
13:11, 25
15:18
17:20
20: 8
11—B[o]
2 Ki. 16: 6
17: 6, 27
29, 32
22:14
23: 2
1 Ch. 2:55
4:22, 23
23, 28
40
43+A
5: 8, 9
10, 11
16, 22
23
7:29
8: 6, 13
13, 28
29, 32
9: 2, 3
16, 34
9:35, 38
1 Ch. 10: 7[p], 11
11: 4
5+A
12:15
30 S[q]
17: 1, 1, 4
5
22:18
29:15 B[h]
2 Ch. 2: 3
6: 1 A[2 n]
2[n], 18
8:11
10: 2, 17
11: 5
15: 5
16: 2
19: 4, 8
10
20: 7, 8, 15
18, 20
23, 23
21:11, 13
22: 1
26: 7
28:18
30:25
31: 4, 6
32:12, 22
26, 33
33: 9
34:22, 27
28, 30
32
35:18
Neh. 3:13
8:14
9:24
11:21 S[3]
Est. 9:19+ABS
Job 4:19
42 *p* 18
Psa. 2: 4
9:12
21: 4
22: 6
23: 1
26: 4
32: 8, 14
48: 2
64: 5 S[1 a]
9
67: 7, 11
17
68:26, 36
74: 4
82: 8
83: 5
90: 1
97: 7
100: 7
106:34
36 A[1 b]
112: 5
122: 1
124: 1
131:14
132: 1
134:21
139:14
Pro. 21:63
Isa. 6:11
8:18
9: 1+AS[2]
2
10:14, 24
31
12: 6
13:20, 22
14:23
16: 7
18: 3, 3
20: 6
23: 6[r], 18
24: 5, 6
17 S[1 s]
26:21 S[a]
27:10
32:16, 18[t]
33: 5
Isa. 34:11
40:22
42:10, 11
11
44:26
45:18
49:19[u], 20
51: 6
54: 3 A[b]
57:15
62: 5
65: 9
66:10 S[2 v]
Jer. 1: 1, 14
2: 6, 15
4: 3—A
4, 7, 29
6: 8 AS[b]
12—S[1]
8: 1, 16
9:11, 26
10:17, 18
11: 2, 9, 12
23
12: 4
13:13, 13[a]
17: 6, 25
25 A[b]
18:11
19: 3, 12
20: 6
21: 6, 13
22: 6, 23
23:14
24: 8
25: 2, 5, 9
26: 8, 19, 19
27: 3, 13
21—S[1]
34[w], 35
39 *ter*
40
40 A[h]
45
28: 1, 12
24, 29
35, 35
37, 43
62
29: 2[a], 2, 9
19[x], 21
30:11
31:28[a]
33: 9[a], 15
36: 5, 28
39:32
41:22
42: 7 A[c]
9, 13
17—A
43:31
45: 2
47: 9
49:15, 18
22
50: 2 A[c], 4
5[y]
51: 1, 1 S[z]
8[r], 27
28[aa]
Lam. 4:12, 21
5:19
Eze. 2: 6
Eze. 3:15
7: 7
11:15
12: 2, 19
19, 20
15: 6
16:46, 46
25:16
26:17+A
17
19 AB[b]
20
27: 3, 8, 35
28: 2, 26
26, 26
29: 6, 11
31: 6, 17
32:15
33:24
34:25, 27
28
35: 9
36:10, 17
28
37:25 *ter*
38: 8
11 A[c]
11, 12
39: 6, 9
45: 5
Dan. 2:38
4: 9, 18
18 A[a]
32
9: 7 A[a]
Hos. 4: 1, 3
9: 3, 3
10: 5
11: 5
Joel 1: 2, 14
2: 1
3:20
Amos 1: 5, 8
3:12
5:11
6: 8
8: 8
9: 5, 14
Jon. 4:11
Mic. 1:11, 11
12, 13
15
6:12, 16
7:13
Nah. 1: 5
3: 8
Hab. 2: 8, 17
Zeph. 1: 4, 11
13, 18
2: 5
3: 1, 6
Zec. 1:11
2: 4, 7
7: 7, 7
8:20
21+S[1]
21
9: 5, 6
11: 6
12: 5, 6, 7
8, 10
13: 1
14:11, 11

[a] A οἰκέω. [b] *pro* κατοικίζω.
[c] *pro* οἰκέω. [d] *pro* εἰμί.
[e] A παροικέω. [f] *pro* κάτοικος.
[g] A καταπατέω. [h] *pro* παροικέω.
[i] A ἔνοικος. [k] *pro* σκηνόω.
[m] *pro* καθίζω. [n] *pro* κατασκηνόω. [o] A κάθημαι.
[p] S κατοικίζω. [q] *pro* κατ' οἶκος.
[r] AS ἐνοικέω. [s] *pro* ἐνοικέω.
[t] B οἰκέω. [u] A ἐνοικέω.
[v] *pro* ἀγαπάω. [w] S παροικέω.
[x] BS ἐνοικέω. [y] S μετοικεσία.
[z] *pro* κάθημαι. [aa] AS παροικέω.

κατοίκησις.

Gen. 10:30
Gen. 27:39

Exo. 12:40[a]
Nu. 15: 2[b]
2 Sa. 9:12
1 Ki. 8:30
2 Ki. 2:19
2 Ch. 6:21

[a] A παροίκησις. [b] A κατάσχεσις.

κατοικητήριος.

Exo. 12:20
15:17
1 Ki. 8:13 A
39, 43
49
2 Ch. 6:30, 33
39
2 Ch. 30:27
Psa. 32:14
75: 3
106: 4, 7
Jer. 9:11
21:13
Nah. 2:11, 12

κατοικία.

Exo. 35: 3
Lev. 3:17
7:16
23: 3, 14
17, 21
31
Nu. 24:21
31:10[a]
35:29
1 Ch. 6:54
7:28
Psa. 86: 7
131:13
Jer. 3: 6, 8, 12
Eze. 6: 6
14 A[b]
28: 2
34:13
48:15
Dan. 2:11
4:22, 20
32
5:21
Hos. 11: 7
14: 4
Obad. 3
Zeph. 2: 5

[a] B οἰκία. [b] pro κατοικεσία.

κατοικίζω.

Gen. 3:24
47: 6[a]
11[a]
Exo. 2:21
Lev. 23:43
Nu. 21:15
Deu. 2:12, 21
22, 23
Jos. 6:25[b]
7: 7
24:13
1 Sa. 12: 8[a]
2 Ki. 17:24, 24
32
1 Ch. 9: 18[c]
10: 7 S[d]
2 Ch. 8: 2
Ezra 4:10
Psa. 4: 9
28:10
Psa. 67: 7
92: 1
106:36[a]
112: 9
Isa. 54: 3[a]
Jer. 6: 8[e]
7: 3, 7
12:15
17:25[a]
39:37 A[f]
47: 7[g]
Eze. 26:19[b], 20
29:14
36:11, 33
38:12, 14
39:26
Hos. 2:18
12: 9
Zec. 10: 6

[a] A κατοικέω. [b] AB κατοικέω. [c] pro ἀποικίζω. [d] pro κατοικέω. [e] AS κατοικέω. [f] pro καθίζω. [g] B ἀποικίζω.

κατοικοδομέω.

Genesis 36:43

κάτοικος.

Gen. 50:11
Jos. 8:20[a]
Pro. 29:41–AS[2]

[a] A κατοικέω.

κατοίομαι.

Habakkuk 2: 5

κατόπισθε.

Gen. 37:17
Jud. 18:12 A[a]
19: 3 A[a]
Ruth 2: 2, 3[b], 9
2 Sa. 2:10, 27
15:34
16:18
20:14
1 Ki. 13:14
2 Ki. 6:32
2 Ch. 25:27
Neh. 4:13
Pro. 24:42
Eze. 3:12
41:15
44:10
Zec. 6: 6
7:14

[a] pro ὀπίσω. [b] A ὄπισθεν.

κατοπίσω.

Judges 18:22+A

κάτοπτρον.

Exodus 38:26

κατορθόω.

1 Ki. 2:35
1 Ch. 16:30
28: 7
2 Ch. 29:35
33:16
35:10, 16
Psa. 95:10
118: 9, 128
Pro. 2: 7, 9
4:18
9: 6
Pro. 11:10
12: 3, 19
14:11
25: 5
Isa. 9: 7
Jer. 10:23
Eze. 18:25 A[a]
29 ter
Mic. 7: 2
Zec. 4: 7

[a] pro κατευθύνω.

κατόρθωσις

2 Ch. 3:17
Psa. 96: 2

κατορύσσω.

Gen. 48: 7
Jos. 21:32, 33
Jer. 13: 7
32:19
Eze. 39:12, 13
13
Amos 9: 2 A[a]

[a] pro κατακρύπτω.

κατορχέομαι.

Zechariah 12:10

κατοχεύω.

Leviticus 19:19

κατόχιμος.

Leviticus 25:46

κάτοχος.

Jonah 2: 7

κάτω.

Gen. 35: 8
Exo. 20: 4
Deu. 28:43, 43
32:22
Jos. 2:11
15:19
16: 3
18:13
1 Ki. 8:23
9:17 A
2 Ki. 19:30
1 Ch. 7:24
27:23
2 Ch. 8: 5
32:30
Neh. 4:13
Job 37:11 A[a]
Psa. 62:10
85:13
87: 7
138:15
Ecc. 3:21
5: 1+S[1]
Isa. 5:30+S[2]
8:22
37:31
51: 6
Jer. 38:37
Lam. 3:54–A
Eze. 1:27
8: 2
31:16+A

[a] vide θεεβουλαθώθ.

κατωδυνάω.

Exo. 1:14
Eze. 9: 4

κατώδυνος.

1 Sa. 1:10
22: 2
1 Sa. 30: 6
2 Ki. 4:27

κάτωθεν.

Exo. 26:24
27: 5
28:29[a]
36:28–B
32
Exo. 38:24
Deu. 33:13
Isa. 14: 9
Eze. 41: 7

[a] A κυκλόθεν.

καυθμός.

Isa. 15: 3 S[1a] [a] pro κλαυθμός.

καυλός.

Exo. 25:30
38:14
Nu. 8: 4

καῦμα.

Gen. 8:22
31:40[a]
Deu. 32:10
2 Sa. 4: 5
Job 24:24
30:30
Pro. 10: 5
25:13
Isa. 4: 6
18: 4
Jer. 17: 8
43:30

[a] A καύσων.

καῦσις.

Exo. 39:17
Lev. 6: 9
2 Sa. 23: 7
2 Ch. 13:11
Isa. 4: 4–A
40:16
44:13
Dan. 7:11

καύσων.

Gen. 31:40 A[a]
Job 27:21
Isa. 49:10
Jer. 18:17
28: 1
Eze. 17:10
19:12
Hos. 12: 1
13:15
Jon. 4: 8

[a] pro καῦμα.

καυχάομαι.

Jud. 7: 2
1 Sa. 2: 3
10 quater
1 Ki. 21:11
1 Ch. 16:35
Psa. 5:12
31:11
48: 7
Psa. 93: 3
149: 5
Pro. 20: 9
25:14
27: 1
Jer. 9:23 ter
24, 24

καύχημα.

Deu. 10:21
26:19
33:29
1 Ch. 16:27
29:11
Psa. 88:18
Pro. 11: 7
Pro. 17: 6
19:11
Jer. 13:11
17:14
28:11
Zeph. 3:19, 20
Zec. 12: 7

καύχησις.

1 Ch. 29:13
Pro. 16:31
Jer. 12:13
Eze. 16:12, 17
Eze. 16:39
23:26, 42
24:25

καψάκης vide καμψάκης.

κέγχρος.

Isa. 28:25–AS, Eze. 4: 9

κέδρινος.

Lev. 14: 4, 6, 49
51, 52
Nu. 19: 6
2 Sa. 5:11
7: 2, 7
1 Ki. 5: 8
6:14, 15
(18) A
7:39, 39
1 Ki. 9:11
1 Ch. 14: 1
17: 1, 6
22: 4, 4
2 Ch. 2: 8
3: 5
Ezra 3: 7
Cant. 8: 9

κέδρος.

Nu. 24: 6
Jud. 9:15
1 Ki. 4:29
5:10
6:13
(18) A
19+A
33
7:44+A
48, 49
10:27
2 Ki. 14: 9
19:23
2 Ch. 1:15
2: 3
2 Ch. 9:27
25:18
Psa. 28: 5, 5
36:35
79:11
91:13
103:16
148: 9
Cant. 1:17
5:15
Isa. 2:13
9:10–S[1]
14: 8
37:24
41:19

Isa. 60:13
Jer. 22: 7, 14
23
Eze. 17: 3, 22
23
Eze. 27: 5
Amos 2: 9
Zeph. 2:14
Zec. 11: 1, 2

κεῖμαι.

Jos. 4: 6
2 Sa. 8:10 B[a]
13:32
Ezra 6: 1
Isa. 9: 4
30:33
Jer. 24: 1

[a] pro ἀντίκειμαι.

κειράδες.

Jer. 31:31[a], 36[a] [a] A κίδαρις.

κειρία.

Proverbs 7:16

κείρω.

Gen. 31:19
38:12, 13
Deu. 15:19
1 Sa. 25: 2, 4, 7
11
2 Sa. 13:23, 24
14:26 ter
Job 1:20
Pro. 17:19 A[a]
Pro. 27:24
Cant. 4: 2
6: 5
Isa. 53: 7
Jer. 7:29
30:1[b]
52:31–AS
Mic. 1:16

[a] pro χαίρω. [b] AB[1] κεράννυμι.

κεκρυμμένως.

Jeremiah 13:17

κέλευσμα.

Proverbs 24:62

κενολογέω.

Isaiah 8:19

κενός.

Gen. 31:42
37:24[a]
Exo. 3:21
5: 9
23:15
34:20
Lev. 26:16, 20
Deu. 15:13
16:16
32:47
Jud. 5: 8 A[b]
7:16
9: 4
11: 3[c]
Ruth 1:21
3:17
1 Sa. 6: 3
2 Sa. 1:22, 22
2 Ki. 4: 3
Neh. 5:13
Job 2: 3, 9
6: 5, 6[d]
7: 3[e], 6[e]
16[d]
9:17
15: 3+A
31, 35
20:18
21:34
Job 22: 6, 9
27:12, 12
29:20[f]
31:34–C
33:21
34:19
39:16
Psa. 2: 1
7: 5
24: 3
30: 7
106: 9[e]
Pro. 23:29
Isa. 29: 8
30: 7
32: 6
42. 9 A[b]
45:18
59: 4
65:23
Jer. 6:29
14: 3
18:15
26:11
27: 9
28:58
Hos. 12: 1
Mic. 1:14
Hab. 2: 3

[a] A ἐκεῖνος. [b] pro καινός. [c] A λιτός. [d] AS καινός. [e] S καινός. [f] C καινός.

κενοτάφιον.

1 Samuel 19:13, 16

κενόω.

Jer. 14: 2
Jer. 15: 9[a]

[a] S[1] γίνομαι.

κεντέω.

Job 6: 4

κέντρον.

Pro. 26: 3
Hos. 5:13
Hos. 13:14

κενῶς.

Isaiah 49: 4

κεπφωθείς, A **κεφφω-**

Proverbs 7:22

κεραμεοῦς.

Daniel 2:41+A²

κεραμεύς.

1 Ch. 4:23
Psa. 2: 9
Isa. 29:16
41:25, 25
Isa. 45: 9, 9
Jer. 18: 2, 3, 6
6
Lam. 4: 2

κεράμιον.

Isa. 5:10
30:14
Jer. 42: 5

κέραμος.

2 Samuel 17:28–A

κεράννυμι.

Deu. 28:66 Aᵃ
Pro. 9: 2, 5
Isa. 5:22
Isa. 19:14
Jer. 30:10AB¹ᵇ

ᵃ pro κρεμάννυμι. ᵇ pro κείρω.

κέρας.

Gen. 22:13
Exo. 27: 2, 2
29:12
30: 2,3,10
Lev. 4: 7, 18
25, 30
34
8:15
9: 9
16:18
Deu. 33:17, 17
1 Sa. 2: 1, 10
16: 1, 13
2 Sa. 22: 3
1 Ki. 1:39, 50
51
2:28, 29
22:11
1 Ch. 25: 5
2 Ch. 18:10
Job 42:14
Psa. 17: 3
21:22
68:32
74: 5,6,10
10
88:18, 25
91:11
111: 9
Ps. 117:27
131:17
148:14
Isa. 5: 1
Jer. 31:12, 25
Lam. 2: 3, 17ᵃ
Eze. 29:21
34:21
41:22
43:15, 20
Dan. 7: 7+A
7
8 *ter*
11, 20
20+A
21, 24
8: 3
3+A
5, 6, 7
8, 8, 9
20, 21
22
Amos 3:14
6:13
Mic. 4:13
Hab. 3: 4
Zec. 1:18, 19
21 *ter*

ᵃ A κεφαλή.

κέρασμα.

Psa. 74: 9
Isa. 65:11

κεράστης.

Proverbs 23:32

κερατίζω.

Exo. 21:28, 31
32, 35
Deu. 33:17
1 Ki. 22:11
2 Ch. 18:10
Psa. 43: 6
Jer. 27:11
Eze. 32: 2
34:21
Dan. 8: 4

κερατίνη.

Jud. 3:27
6:34
7: 8, 16
18, 18
19, 20
20, 22
2 Sa. 15:10
18:16
2 Sa. 20: 1, 22
1 Ki. 1:34, 39
41
2 Ki. 9:13
2 Ch. 15:14–B
Neh. 4:18, 20
Psa. 97: 6

κεραστής.

Exodus 21:29, 36

κεραυνός.

Job 38:35

κεραυνόω.

Isaiah 30:30

κέρκος.

Exo. 4: 4, 4
Jud. 15: 4, 4, 4
Pro. 26:17

κέρκωψ.

Proverbs 26:22

κεφάζ, AB **καιφάζ.**

Canticles 5:11

κεφάλαιος.

Lev. 6: 5
Nu. 4: 2
Nu. 5: 7
31:26, 49

κεφαλή.

Gen. 3:15
8: 5
11: 4
28:11, 12
18
40:16, 17
19
48:14, 14
17 *ter*
18
49:26
Exo. 12: 9
16:16
26:24ᵃ
29: 6,7,10
15, 17
19
30: 2
Lev. 1: 4,8,10
12, 15
3: 2,8,13
4: 4, 11
15, 24
29, 33
5: 8
8: 9, 12
14, 18
20, 22
9:13
10: 6
13:12, 29
30, 40
41, 44
45
14: 9, 18
29
16:21, 21
19:27
21: 5, 10
10
24:14
Nu. 1: 2, 18
20, 22
24, 26
28, 30
32, 34
36, 38
40, 42
3:47
Nu. 5:18
6: 5, 5, 7
9, 9, 11
12, 18
19 Aᵇ
8:12
Deu. 21: 6, 12
28:13, 23
44
32:42
33:16
Jos. 7: 6
Jud. 5:26, 30
7:25
8:28
9:25, 30ᶜ
53, 57
10:18 Aᵈ
11: 8 Aᵈ
9 Aᵈ
11
13: 5
16:13, 14
17, 19
22
1 Sa. 1:11
4:12
5: 4
10: 1
14:45
17: 5, 38
46, 51
54,57 A
19:13, 16
25:39
26: 7, 16
29: 4
2 Sa. 1: 2, 10
16
2:16, 25
3: 8, 29
4: 7, 7, 8
8, 12
12:30, 30
13:19, 19
14:26, 26
15:30, 30
32
16: 9
2 Sa. 18: 9
20:21, 22
22:44
1 Ki. 2:32, 33
33
(3)37, 44
7: 4,7+A
8, 21
21, 27
8: 1+A
8, 32
19: 6
20:12 Aᵉ
21:31, 32
2 Ki. 2: 3, 5
4:19, 19
6:25, 31
32
9: 3,6,30
10: 6, 7, 8
19:21
25:27
1 Ch. 10: 9, 10
12:19
20: 2, 2
23: 3, 24
25: 1
2 Ch. 3:15, 16
4:12 *ter*
5: 9
6:23
Ezra 9: 3, 6
Neh. 4: 5
9: 1–ABS
Est. 6: 9+S³
12
Job 1:17ᶠ, 20
20+A
2: 7
12+A
16: 4
19: 9
20: 3
40:26
Psa. 3: 4
7:17
17:44
20: 4
21: 8
22: 5
26: 6
37: 5
39:13
43:15
59: 9
65:12
67:22
68: 5
73:13, 14
82: 3
107: 9
108:25
109: 6, 7
117:22
132: 2
139: 8, 10
140: 5
Pro. 4: 9
10: 6, 22
11:26
23:23
Ecc. 2:14
9: 8
Cant. 2: 6
4: 8
Cant. 5: 2, 11
7: 5, 5
8: 3
Isa. 1: 5, 6
3:24
7: 8
8–S¹
9,9,20
8: 8
9:14
15: 2
19:15
35:10
10
37:22
43: 4
51:11
59:17
61: 7
Jer. 2:36
7:29
9: 1
13:18
14: 4
18:16
31:37
38: 7
52:31
Lam. 1: 5
2:10, 15
17 Aᵍ
3: 5, 53
5:16
Eze. 1:22, 25
26+A
5: 1
7:18
9:10
10: 1
11:21
13:18
16:12, 43
17:19
22+A
22:31
23:15, 42
24:23
26:16
27:30
29:18
32:27
33: 4
44:18, 20
20
Dan. 1:10
2:28, 32
38
3:27
4: 2
7: 1, 6, 9
15, 20
Joel 3: 4, 7
Amos 2: 7
5:11+A
8:10
9: 1
Obad. 15
Jon. 2: 6
4: 6, 6, 8
Hab. 3:13, 14
Zec. 1:21
3: 5
5–S¹
6:11

ᵃ A κεφαλίς. ᵇ pro εὐχή. ᶜ A κορυφή. ᵈ pro ἄρχων. ᵉ pro ἀρχή. ᶠ AS² ἀρχή. ᵍ pro κέρας.

κεφαλίς.

Exo. 26:24 Aᵃ
32, 37
27:17
37: 4,6,15
17
38:20, 20
39: 4, 4, 5
5, 6
Exo. 40:16
Nu. 3:36
4:31
1 Ki. 7: 9+A
17+A
Ezra 6: 2
Psa. 39: 8
Eze. 2: 9, 10
Eze. 2:10
Eze. 3: 3

ᵃ pro κεφαλή.

κεφουρέ.

1 Ch. 28:17–B
Ezra 1:10

κηλιδόω.

Jeremiah 2:22

κημός.

Psa. 31: 9
Eze. 19: 4, 9

κῆπος.

Deu. 11:10
1 Ki. 20: 2, 2
2 Ki. 21:18, 18
26
25: 4
Neh. 3:16, 26
Est. 7: 7, 8
Ecc. 2: 5
Cant. 4:12, 12
15, 16
5: 1, 1
6: 1,1,10
Cant. 8:13
Isa. 1:29
58:11
61:11
65: 3
66:17
Jer. 36:28
52: 7
Eze. 36:35
Amos 4: 9
9:14

κηρίον.

1 Sa. 14:27ᵃ
Psa. 18:11
117:12
118:103+S¹
Pro. 16:24
Pro. 24:13
27: 7
Cant. 4:11
Eze. 20: 6ᵇ, 15

ᵃ B σκῆπτρον. ᵇ B* δυνατός.

κηρός.

Psa. 21:15
57: 9
67: 3
Psa. 96: 5
Isa. 64: 2
Mic. 1: 4

κήρυγμα.

2 Ch. 30: 5
Pro. 9: 3
Jon. 3: 2

κήρυξ.

Gen. 41:43
Dan. 3:

κηρύσσω.

Gen. 41:43
Exo. 32: 5
36: 6
2 Ki. 10:20
2 Ch. 20: 3
24: 9
36:22
Est. 6: 9, 11
Pro. 1:21
8: 1
Isa. 61: 1
Dan. 5:29
Hos. 5: 8
Joel 1:14
2: 1, 15
3: 9
Jon. 1: 2
3: 2, 4, 5
7
Mic. 3: 5
Zeph. 3:14
Zec. 9: 9

κῆτος.

Gen. 1:21
Job 3: 8
9:13
26:12
Jon. 2: 1, 1
2–S¹
11

κίβδηλος.

Lev. 19:19
Deu. 22:11

κιβωτός.

Gen. 6:14, 14
15, 15
16, 16
18, 19
7: 1, 7, 9
13, 15
16, 17
18, 23
8: 1, 4, 6
9, 9, 10
13, 16
19
Gen. 9:10, 18
Exo. 25: 9, 13
13
14–A
15, 20
20, 21
26:33, 34
30: 6, 26
31: 7
35:11
38: 1,5,11
39:15

Exo. 40: 3—B
3, 5
18—A
18, 19
19
Lev. 16: 2
Nu. 3:31
4: 5[a]
7:89
10:33, 35
14:44
Deu. 10: 1, 2, 3
5, 8
31: 9, 25
26
Jos. 3: 3, 6, 6
8, 11
13, 14
15, 15
17
4: 7, 9, 10
11, 16
18
6: 8, 9, 11
12, 13
9: 6, 6
22:19 A[b]
24:33
Jud. 20:27
1 Sa. 3: 3
4: 3, 4, 4
5, 6, 11
13, 17
18, 19
21, 22
22 + A
5: 1, 2, 3
4, 7, 8
8, 8, 10
10—A
10, 11
11
6: 1, 2, 3
8, 11
13, 15
18, 19
20, 21
7: 1, 1, 2
14:18 + A
2 Sa. 6: 2, 3, 4
4—A
6, 7, 9
10
11[c]
12, 12
13, 15
16, 17
7: 2
11:11
15:24, 24
25, 29
1 Ki. 2:26
3:15
6:18
8: 1, 3
4 + A
5, 6, 7
7, 9, 21
2 Ki. 12: 9, 10
1 Ch. 6:31
13: 3, 5, 6
7, 9
10, 12
13—S
14
15: 1, 2
2—BS
3, 12
14, 15
23, 24
24, 25
26, 27
28, 29
16: 1, 4, 6
37, 37
17: 1
22:19
28: 2, 18
2 Ch. 1: 4
5: 2, 4
5 + A
6, 7, 8
8, 10
6:11, 41
8:11
35: 3
Ps. 131: 8
Jer. 3:16

[a] A σκηνή. [b] pro σκηνή. [c] A γλωσσόκομον.

κίδαρις.

Exo. 28: 4, 35
36
29: 9
36:36
Lev. 8:13
16: 4
Jer. 31:31 A[a]
36 A[a]
Eze. 21:26
44:18
Zec. 3: 5
5—S[1]

[a] pro κειράδες.

κιθάρα.

Gen. 4:21
31:27
2 Ch. 9:11
Job 21:12
30: 9, 31
Psa. 32: 2
42: 4
56: 9
70:22
80: 3
91: 4
Psa. 97: 5, 5
107: 3
146: 7
150: 3
Isa. 5:12
16:11
23:16
24: 8
30:32
Dan. 3: 5, 7
10, 15

κιθαρίζω.

Isaiah 23:16

κινδυνεύω.

Ecc. 10: 9
Isa. 28:13
Jon. 1: 4

κίνδυνος.

Psalm 114: 3

κινέω.

Gen. 7:14, 21
Gen. 8:17, 19
9: 2
11: 2
20: 1
Lev. 11:44, 46
Nu. 14:44
Jud. 6:18 A[a]
9: 9[b]
11[b]
13[b]
20:37[c]
1 Sa. 1:13
2 Sa. 15:20
1 Ki. 14:15 A
2 Ki. 19:21
23:18
2 Ch. 35:15
Job 13:25
Job 16: 4
Psa. 21: 8
103: 5 A[d]
Pro. 17:13
Cant. 2:17
4: 6
Isa. 22:25
33:20
37:22
41: 7
46: 7
Jer. 10: 5
14:10
18:16
31:17
Lam. 2:15
Zeph. 3: 1

[a] pro χωρίζω. [b] A ἄρχω. [c] A ὁρμάω. [d] pro κλίνω.

Gen. 7:21

κίνησις.

Job 16: 5
Psa. 43:15

κιννάμωμον, κινα—

Exo. 30:23
Pro. 7:17
Cant. 4:14
Jer. 6:20

κινύρα.

1 Sa. 10: 5
16:16, 16
23
2 Sa. 6: 5
1 Ki. 10:12
1 Ch. 13: 8
15:16, 21
28
1 Ch. 16: 5
25: 1, 3, 6
2 Ch. 5:12
20:28
29:25
Neh. 12:27—ABS[1]

κιρνάω.

Psalm 101:10

κισσάω.

Psalm 50: 7

κιχράω.

1 Sa. 1:28
Ps. 111: 5
Pro. 13:11

κίων.

Jud. 16:25[a]
26[a]
Jud. 16:29[a]
1 Ki. 15:15, 15

[a] A στύλος.

κλάδος.

Lev. 23:40, 40
Nu. 3:37 A[a]
4:32 A[a]
Jud. 9:48[b]
49[b]
Isa. 17: 6
55:12
Jer. 11:16
Eze. 31: 5, 6, 7
8, 9, 12
Dan. 4: 9, 11[c]
11, 18
Hos. 14: 6
Zec. 4:12

[a] pro κάλος. [b] A φορτίον. [c] A καρπός.

κλαίω.

Gen. 21:16
27:38—A
29:11
33: 4
37:35
42:24
43:29, 29
45:14[a], 14
15
46:29
50: 1, 17
Exo. 2: 6
Lev. 10: 6
Nu. 11: 4, 10
13, 18
20
14: 1
Nu. 20:29
25: 6
Deu. 1:45
21:13
34: 8
Jud. 2: 4
9: 7
11:37, 38
14:16, 17
15:18[b]
16:28[b]
20:23, 26
21: 2
Ruth 1: 9, 14
1 Sa. 1: 7, 8
10[c], 10
4:19
1 Sa. 11: 4, 5
13:16
20:41
24:17
30: 4, 4
2 Sa. 1:12, 24
24 + B
3:16, 32
32, 34
12:21:22
13:36, 36
15:23
30—B
30
18:33
19: 1
1 Ki. 18:45
20:27
2 Ki. 8:11, 12
13:14
20: 3
22:19
2 Ch. 34:27
Ezra 3:12
10: 1 ter
Neh. 1: 4
8: 9, 9
Job 2:12
30:25
Job 31:38
Psa. 77:64
94: 6
125: 6
136: 1
Ecc. 3: 4
Isa. 15: 2, 5
16: 9
22: 4
30:19
33: 7
38: 3
Jer. 9: 1
13:17
22:10, 10
18—A
27: 4
31: 5
41: 5, 5
5 A[d]
48: 6
Lam. 1:a1, 2
2[e], 15
Eze. 24:16, 23
27:31 A
Hos. 12: 4
Joel 1: 5, 18
2:17
Mic. 2: 6

[a] A ἐπιπίπτω. [b] A βοάω. [c] B λέγω. [d] pro κόπτω. [e] A δακρύω.

κλάσμα.

Lev. 2: 6
6:21
Jud. 9:53
19: 5 A[a]
1 Sa. 30:12
2 Sa. 11:21, 22
Eze. 13:19

[a] pro ψωμός.

κλαυθμός.

Gen. 45: 2
46:29
Deu. 34: 8
Jud. 21: 2
2 Sa. 13:36
2 Ki. 20: 3
Ezra 3:13
Job 16:16
30:31
Psa. 6: 9—S[1]
29: 6
101:10
Isa. 15: 3[a]
16: 9
Isa. 22:12
30:19
38: 3
65:19
Jer. 3:21
22:10
31: 5, 32
38: 9, 15
16
Lam. 5:13
Joel 2:12
Mic. 7: 4
Mal. 2:13

[a] S[1] καυθμός.

κλαυθμών.

Jud. 2: 1, 5
2 Sa. 5:23, 24
Psa. 83: 7

κλάω.

Jud. 9:53[a]
Jer. 16: 7
Jer. 27:23[b]
Lam. 4: 4 A[c]

[a] A συνθλάω. [b] AS συγκλάω. [c] pro διακλάω.

κλεῖθρον.

Neh. 3: 3
6—A
13, 14
Job 26:13
38:10
Cant. 5: 5

κλείς.

Jud. 3:25
1 Ch. 9:27
Job 31:22
Isa. 22:22—B

κλείω.

Gen. 7:16
Jos. 2: 5, 7
Jud. 9:51[a]
20:42 A[b]
1 Sa. 23:20
2 Ch. 28:24
Neh. 6:10
7: 3
Neh. 13:19
Job 12:14[c]
Ecc. 12: 4
Cant. 4:12, 12
Isa. 22:22
24:10
60:11
Eze. 44: 1, 2, 2
Eze. 46: 1, 3, 12
Dan. 6:18

[a] A ἀποκλείω. [b] pro ἐπιβλέπω. [c] A ἀποκλίνω.

κλέμμα.

Gen. 31:39, 39
Exo. 22: 3, 4

κλέος.

Job 28:22
Job 30: 8

κλέπτης.

Exo. 22: 2
Deu. 24: 9
Job 24:14
30: 5
Psa. 49:18
Pro. 29:24
Isa. 1:23
Jer. 2:26
29:10
Hos. 7: 1
Joel 2: 9
Obad. 5
Zec. 5: 3, 4

κλέπτω.

Gen. 30:33
31:19, 30
32
40:15
44: 4, 8
Exo. 20:14
21:17
22: 1, 7, 7
8, 12
Lev. 19:11
Deu. 5:19
24: 9
Jos. 7:11
2 Sa. 19:41
21:12[a]
2 Ki. 11: 2
2 Ch. 22:11
Job 17: 3
Pro. 6:30, 30
24:32
Jer. 7: 9—S[1]
23:30—B
Obad. 5

[a] A θάπτω.

κληδονίζω.

Deu. 18:10
2 Ki. 21: 6
2 Ch. 33: 6

κληδονισμός.

Deu. 18:14 A[a]
Isa. 2: 6

[a] pro κληδών.

κληδών.

Deu. 18:14[a]

[a] A κληδονισμός.

κλῆμα.

Nu. 13:24
Psa. 79:12
Jer. 31:32
Eze. 8:17 + A
15: 2
Eze. 17: 6, 7, 23
19:11
Joel 1: 7
Nah. 2: 3
Mal. 4: 1

κληματίς.

Deu. 32:32
Isa. 18: 5

κληροδοσία.

Psa. 77:55
Ecc. 7:12 ACS[a]

[a] pro κληρονομία.

κληροδοτέω.

Ezra 9:12[a]
Psa. 77:55

[a] A κληρονομέω.

κληρονομέω.

Gen. 15: 3, 4, 4
7, 8
21:10
22:17
24:60
28: 4
47:27
Exo. 23:30
Lev. 20:24
Nu. 14:24, 31
18:20, 23
24
21:35
26:53, 55
Nu. 27:11
32:19
33:54
34:17
35: 8 B[a]
Deu. 1: 8, 21
39
2: 9, 24
31
3:12[b]
4: 1, 5, 14
22, 26
38, 47
5:33

Deu. 6: 1, 18
7: 1
8: 1
9: 1, 4, 5
6, 23
10:11
11: 8, 8, 10
11, 23
29, 31
31+A
12: 2[c], 29
16:20
17:14
19:14+A[2]
20:16
21: 1
23:20
25:19[c]
26: 1[l]
28:21, 63
30: 5, 5, 16
18
31:13
32:47
33:23
Jos. 1:15
12: 7[c]
14: 2
16: 4
17: 6, 14
18: 2[c], 3
19: 9
22: 9
24: 4[e]
Jud. 1:18, 19
19 A[f]
20, 21[g]
27 A[h]
3:13
11: 2, 21
22+A
23, 24[e]
24, 24

Jud. 18: 9[c]
1 Ki. 20:15, 16
18, 19
2 Ki. 17:24
1 Ch. 28: 8 B[i], 8
Ezra 9:11
12 A[k]
Neh. 9:15, 22
23, 25
Psa. 5: 1
24:13
36: 9, 11
22, 29
43: 4
68:36
82:13
104:44[m]
118:111
Pro. 3:35
11:29
13:22
Isa. 14:21
17:14
34:17
49: 8
53:12
54: 3
57:13
58:11+AS[3]
60:21
61: 7
63:18
65: 9, 9
Eze. 7:24+A
33:25 A
26 A
35:10
36:12
Hos. 9: 6
Obad. 20
Zeph. 2: 9
Zec. 9: 4

[a] *pro* κατακληρονομέω.
[b] B προνομεύω. [c] A κατακληρονομέω. [d] A κλῆρος.
[e] A κληρονομία. [f] *pro* ἐξολοθρεύω. [g] A ἐξαίρω.
[h] *pro* ἐξαίρω. [i] *pro* οἰκοδομέω.
[k] *pro* κληροδοτέω.
[m] AS[2] κατακληρονομέω.

κληρονομία.

Gen. 31:14
Exo. 15:17
Nu. 18:20−A
23
24:18, 18
26:54 *ter*
56
27: 7, 8, 9
10, 11
32:18
34: 2
35: 8
36: 2, 2, 3
3, 4, 4
4, 4, 7
7, 8, 8
9, 12
Deu. 2:12
3:20
9:26 A[a]
12: 9
19:14
32: 9
33: 4
Jos. 1:15
11:23
12: 6[b]
7 A[c]
13: 1, 7, 14
14, 23
28
15:20
16: 5, 8, 9
17: 4
18: 7, 20

Jos. 18:28
19: 1, 8, 9
10, 16
23, 31
39, 47
24: 4 A[c]
Jud. 2: 6, 9
18: 1, 1
20: 6
21:17, 23
24
Ruth 4: 5, 6, 10
1 Sa. 10: 2
26:19
2 Sa. 14:16
20: 1, 19
21: 3
1 Ki. 8:36, 51
53
12:16
*p*24 *l*70
20: 3
4+A
6
2 Ki. 21:14
1 Ch. 16:18
21:12
2 Ch. 6:27
10:16
20:11
31: 1
Job 31: 2
42:15
Psa. 2: 8
15: 5, 5, 6

Psa. 27: 9
32:12
36:18
46: 5
60: 6
67:10
73: 2
77:62, 71
78: 1
93: 5, 14
104:11
105: 5, 40
110: 6
126: 3
134: 12, 12
135:21, 22
Ecc. 7:12[d]
Isa. 17:14
19:25
47: 6
49: 8
54:17
58:14
63:17
Jer. 2: 7
3:19

Jer. 10:16
12: 7, 8, 9
14, 15
16:18
27:11
28:19
Lam. 5: 2
Eze. 11:15
25: 4, 10
44:28, 28
45: 1
46:16, 16
17+A
17, 18
18+A
47:14, 22
23
48:28
Joel 2:17
3: 2
6+S[3]
Mic. 1:14, 15
2: 2
7:14, 18
Zec. 4: 7
Mal. 1: 3

[a] *pro* μερίς. [b] A κλῆρος.
[c] *pro* κληρονομέω.
[d] ACS κληροδοσία.

κληρονόμος.

Jud. 18: 7−A
2 Sa. 14: 7
Jer. 8:10

Jer. 13:25 S[a]
Mic. 1:15

[a] *pro* κλῆρος.

κλῆρος.

Gen. 48: 6
49:14
Exo. 6: 8
Lev. 16: 8−AB
8, 8, 9
10
Nu. 16:14[a]
18:21, 24
24, 26
26:55, 56
62
27: 7
32:19
33:53, 54[b]
34:13, 14
15
35: 2
36: 2, 3, 3
9
Deu. 2: 5, 9, 19
19
3:18
4:21
5:31
9:29
10: 9, 9
11:31
12: 1, 12
14:26, 28
15: 4
7+A
17:14+A
18: 1, 1, 2
2
19:10, 14
21:23
24: 6
25:15
19+A
26: 1 A[c]
2+A
29: 8
Jos. 12: 6 A[d], 7
13: 6
14: 2, 3, 9
13, 14
17: 4, 6, 14

Jos. 17:17
18: 6, 8, 10
11, 11
19: 1, 1, 2
8 A[e]
9[f], 9
10, 17
24, 32
40, 40
51
21: 4, 10
23: 4
24:31
Jud. 1: 3, 3
20: 9
21:22[g]
1 Ch. 6:54, 61
63, 65
24: 5, 7[b]
31
25: 8, 9[h]
26:13, 14
14, 14
Neh. 10:34, 34
11: 1
Est. 3: 7, 7
9:24, 26
Psa. 21:19
30:16
67:14
124: 3
Pro. 1:14
18:18 S[2][i]
Isa. 34:17
57: 6
Jer. 12:13
13:25[k]
Eze. 24: 6
47:22
48:29
Dan. 12:13
Hos. 5: 7
Joel 3: 3
Obad. 11
Jon. 1: 7 *ter*
Mic. 2: 5
Nah. 3:10

[a] B καιρός. [b] A κληρωτί.
[c] *pro* κληρονομέω.
[d] *pro* κληρονομία. [e] *pro* δῆμος.
[f] A υἱός. [g] A καιρός.
[h] A ὁλόκληρος. [i] *pro* σιγηρός.
[k] S κληρονόμος.

κληρουχία.

Nehemiah 11(20) S[3]

κληρόω.

1 Sa. 14:41
Est. 4:11 A[a]

Job 20:23 C[b]
Isa. 17:11, 11

[a] *pro* καλέω. [b] *pro* πληρόω.

κληρωτί.

Nu. 33:54 A[a]
Jos. 21: 4, 5

Jos. 21: 6+A
7, 8

[a] *pro* κλῆρος.

κλῆσις.

Jeremiah 38: 6

κλητός.

Exo. 12:16
Lev. 23: 2, 3
4[a], 7
8, 21
24, 27
35, 36

Lev. 23:37
Nu. 28:25
Jud. 14:11[b]
2 Sa. 15:11
1 Ki. 1:41, 49
Zeph. 1: 7

[a] AB καὶ αὗται. [b] A ἑταῖρος.

κλίβανος.

Gen. 15:17
Exo. 8: 3
Lev. 2: 4[a]
6:39
11:35

Lev. 26:26
Psa. 20:10
Lam. 5:10
Hos. 7: 4, 6, 7
Mal. 4: 1

[a] AB λίβανος.

κλίμα.

Jud. 20: 2+A

Ps. 118:102 S[1][a]

[a] *pro* κρῖμα.

κλιμακτήρ.

Eze. 40:22, 26
31, 34

Eze. 40:37
43:17

κλῖμαξ.

Gen. 28:12
Neh. 3:15

Neh. 12:37

κλίνη.

Gen. 48: 2
49:33
Exo. 8: 3
Deu. 3:11, 11
1 Sa. 19:13, 15
16
2 Sa. 3:31
4: 7
1 Ki. 17:19
20: 4
2 Ki. 1: 4
6−A
16
4:10, 21
32
11: 2

2 Ch. 16:14
22:11
24:25
Est. 1: 6
7: 8
Job 7:13
Psa. 6: 7
40: 4
131: 3
Pro. 7:16
26:14
Cant. 1:16
3: 7
Eze. 23:41
Amos 6: 4

κλίνω.

Jud. 7: 5[a]
6[a]
9: 3
16:30 A[b]
19: 8
9 A[c]
11 A[d]
1 Sa. 4: 2
14:32
2 Sa. 19:14
22:10
1 Ki. 2:28 AB[e]
28
20:27+A
2 Ki. 8: 1 A[e]
19:16

2 Ki. 20:10
Ezra 7:28
9: 5, 9
Job 38:37
Psa. 16: 6
17:10
20:12
30: 3
44:11
45: 7
48: 5
61: 4
70: 2
74: 8
77: 1
85: 1

Psa. 87: 3
101: 3, 12
103: 5[f]
114: 2
118:36
112
143: 5
Pro. 21: 1
Isa. 24:20
33:23

Isa. 37:17−AS
Jer. 6: 4
17:22
31:12, 12
41:14
42:15
51: 5
Dan. 9:18
Zec. 14: 4

[a] A κάμπτω. [b] *pro* βαστάζω.
[c] *pro* ἀσθενέω. [d] *pro* προβαίνω.
[e] *pro* κωλύω. [f] A κινέω.

κλίτος, κλιτύς.

Exo. 25:11 *ter*
13, 17
18 *ter*
31, 31
26:18, 20
27, 27
28, 28
27: 4, 9, 9
11−B
14, 15
28:24
30: 4
37: 9
9−A[2]

Exo. 37:10, 11
38: 3, 3, 10
10
40:20+AB
22
Nu. 34: 3
35: 5 *qtr*
1 Ki. 7:25
2 Ch. 20: 4
Psa. 90: 7
127: 3
Eze. 46:21, 22
22+A
47: 1, 2

κλοιός.

Gen. 41:42
Deu. 28:48
Jud. 8:26+A
1 Ki. 12: 4, 4, 9
10, 11
11, 14
14
*p*24 *l*55
1 Ch. 18: 7

Job 40:21 A[a]
Pro. 1: 9
Isa. 43:14 AS[2][b]
Jer. 34: 1
35:10, 12
13, 13
Eze. 34:27+A
Dan. 8:25
Hab. 2: 6

[a] *pro* κρίκος. [b] *pro* πλοῖον.

κλοπή.

Gen. 40:15
Pro. 9:17

Jer. 31:27
Hos. 4: 2

κλοποφορέω.

Genesis 31:26

κλύδων.

Pro. 23:34
Jon. 1: 4, 11

Jon. 1:12

κλυδωνίζομαι.

Isaiah 57:20

κλώθω.

Exo. 25: 4
26: 1, 1, 31
36, 36
27: 9−B
16, 16
18
28: 6, 8, 15
15, 20
33
31: 4+A

Exo. 35: 6
36: 9, 10
12, 15
32, 36
37: 3, 5, 7
14, 16
Lev. 14: 4
6 A[a]
49, 51
52

[a] *pro* κλωστός.

κλών.

Job 18:13

Job 40:17

κλῶσμα.

Nu. 15:38

Jud. 16: 9 A[a]

[a] *pro* στρέμμα.

κλωστός.

Lev. 14: 6[a]

[a] A κλώθω.

κναφεύς.

Isa. 7: 3[a]

Isa. 36: 2[a]

[a] ABS γναφεύς.

κνήμη.

Deu. 28:35
Jud. 15: 8
Ps. 146:10
Cant. 5:15
Isa. 47: 2
Dan. 2:33

κνημίς.

1 Samuel 17: 6

κνήφη.

Deuteronomy 28:27

κνίδη.

Job 31:40

κνίζω.

Amos 7:14

κόθωνος.

Ezra 2:69[a]   [a] A χιτών.

κοιλάς.

Gen. 14: 8, 10
17
37:14
Lev. 14:37
Nu. 14:25
Jos. 17:16
19:47
Jud. 1:19, 34
5:14 + A
15
6:33
7: 1, 8, 12
18:28
1 Sa. 6:13
17: 2, 19A
21: 9
31: 7 − A
2 Sa. 5:18, 22
18:18
2 Sa. 23:13
1 Ki. 21:23, 28
1 Ch. 11:15
14: 9, 13
18:12, 13
2 Ch. 20:26
25:11
Psa. 59: 8
64:14
83: 7
107: 8
Cant. 2: 1
Jer. 21:13
Hos. 1: 5
2:15
Joel 3: 2, 12
14[a], 14
Mic. 1: 4
[a] S^1 κοῖλος.

κοίλασμα.

Isaiah 8:14

κοίλη.

Jonah 1: 5

κοιλία.

Gen. 3:14
25:23, 24[a]
30: 2
38:27 A[b]
41:21, 21
Exo. 20:13, 22
Lev. 3: 3, 3
9 − AB
9, 14
14 − A^1
4:11
8:21, 25
9:14, 19
11:42
Nu. 5:21, 22
27
Deu. 7:13
28: 4, 11
18, 53
30: 9
Jud. 3:21, 22
13: 5[a]
16:17
Ruth 1:11
2 Sa. 7:12
16:11
20:10
1 Ch. 17:11
2 Ch. 21:15, 15
18, 19
32:21
Job 1:21
2: 9
3:11
10:18
15:35
Job 20:15 + A
30:27
31:15
38: 8
Psa. 21:11[c], 15
39: 9 AS[d]
70: 6
131:11
Pro. 18:20
20:27, 30
24:15, 70
26:22 S^2[e]
Cant. 5: 4, 14
7: 2
Isa. 8:19
16:11
44: 2, 24
46: 3
48: 8, 19
49: 1, 5, 15
Jer. 1: 5
4:19
19 − BS^1
28:34
Lam. 1:20
2:20
Eze. 3: 3
7:19
Dan. 2:32
Hos. 9:16
12: 3
Jon. 2: 1
2 − S^1
3
Mic. 6: 7
Hab. 3:16[f]

[a] A γαστήρ. [b] pro γαστήρ. [c] S^2 γαστήρ. [d] pro καρδία. [e] pro σπλάγχνον. [f] S^2 καρδία.

κοῖλος.

Exo. 27: 8
Lev. 13:32, 34
Jos. 9:11
Joel 3:14 S^1[a]
[a] pro κοιλάς.

κοιλοσταθμέω.

1 Kings 6:13, 15

κοιλόσταθμος.

Haggai 1: 4

κοίλωμα.

Gen. 23: 2
1 Ki. 7: 3
Cant. 2:17
Cant. 8:14 AS^1[a]
Eze. 43:14
[a] pro ἄρωμα.

κοιμάω.

Gen. 19: 4, 32
33, 33
34, 34
35, 35
24:11 A[a]
54
26:10
28:11, 11
30:15, 16
31:54
32:13, 21
34: 2, 7
35:21
39: 7, 12
14, 17
41:21
47:30
49: 9
Exo. 22:16, 19
27
23:18
34:25
Lev. 14:47
15: 4, 18
24, 24
26, 33
18:22
19:13, 20
20:11, 12
13, 18
20
26: 6
Nu. 5:13, 19
23:24
Deu. 16: 4
21:23[b]
22:22, 22
23, 25
25, 28
29
24:14, 15
27:20, 21
22, 23
23 − A
31:16
Jos. 2: 8
6:11
Jud. 5:27
16: 3, 14
Ruth 3: 4 ter
7, 8, 13
14
1 Sa. 3: 9, 15
9:25
2 Sa. 7:12
11: 4, 9, 11
13
12:11
16 + A
24
13: 5, 6, 8
11, 14
31
1 Ki. 1: 2, 21
2:10
3:19 A[c]
1 Ki. 11:21, 43
44 − A
12 p 24 l 1
14:20 A, 31
15: 8, 24
16: 6, 28
p 28 − A
17:19 A[a]
19: 5, 6
20: 4
22:40, 51
2 Ki. 4:11, 20
32 A[a]
34
8:24
9:16 + A
10:35
13: 9, 13
14:16, 22
29
15: 7, 22
38
16:20
20:21
21:18
24: 6
1 Ch. 17:11
2 Ch. 9:31
16:13
21: 1
26: 2, 23
27: 9
28:27
32:33
33:20
36: 8
Job 3:13
7: 4
8:17
14:12
20:11
21:13, 26
22:11
27:19
20 + A
39: 9
40:16
Psa. 3: 6
4: 9
40: 9
56: 5
67:14
Pro. 4:16
Ecc. 2:23
4:11
Isa. 1:21
5:27
14: 8, 18
21:13
43:17
50:11
57: 8
65: 4
Jer. 3:25
30:12[1]
51:33
Lam. 2:21
Eze. 4: 4, 4, 6
23: 8
31:18
32:19 + A
20, 21
27, 28
Eze. 32:29 + A
29, 30
32
34:14
Dan. 6:18
8:27

[a] pro κοιμίζω. [b] A ἐπικοιμάομαι. [c] pro ἐπικοιμάομαι. [d] pro θυμόω.

κοιμίζω.

Gen. 24:11[a]
Jud. 16:19
2 Sa. 8: 2
1 Ki. 3:20, 20
17:19[a]
2 Ki. 4:21, 32[a]
2 Ch. 16:14
Job 24: 7, 10
Nah. 3:18
[a] A κοιμάω.

κοινός.

Job 30: 1 A[a]
Pro. 1:14
15:23
Pro. 21: 9 S^1[b]
9
25:24
[a] pro κύων. [b] pro οἶκος.

κοινωνέω.

2 Ch. 20:35
Job 34: 8
Pro. 1:11
Ecc. 9: 4

κοινωνία.

Leviticus 6: 2

κοινωνός.

2 Ki. 17:11
Pro. 28:24
Isa. 1:23
Mal. 2:14

κοιτάζω.

Lev. 15:20
Deu. 6: 7
11:19 A[a]
Ps. 103:22
Cant. 1: 7
Jer. 40:12
Dan. 4:12
Zeph. 2:14
3:13
[a] pro καθεύδω.

κοιτασία.

Leviticus 20:15

κοίτη.

Gen. 40: 4
Exo. 10:23
21:18
Lev. 15: 4, 5, 10
17, 18
21, 23
24, 24
26, 26
32
18:20, 22
23
19:20
20:13
22: 4
Nu. 5:13, 20
31:17, 18
35
Jud. 21:11, 12
2 Sa. 4: 5, 11
11: 2, 13
13: 5
17:28
1 Ki. 1:47
1 Ch. 5: 1
Job 7:13
33:15, 19
36:28
37: 4 + C
7
38:40
Psa. 4: 5
35: 5
40: 4
149: 5
Pro. 7:17
Cant. 3: 1
Isa. 11: 8
17: 2
56:10
57: 7
Jer. 10:22
27: 6
Eze. 23:17
Dan. 2:28, 29
4: 2, 7, 10
7: 1
Hos. 7:14
Mic. 2: 1, 12

κοιτών.

Exo. 8: 3
Jud. 3:24 + A
15: 1 A[a]
2 Sa. 4: 7
13:10
1 Ki. 21:30
2 Ki. 6:12
Ecc. 10:20
Eze. 8:12
Joel 2:16
[a] pro ταμεῖον.

κόκκινος.

Gen. 38:28, 30
Exo. 25: 4
Exo. 26: 1, 31
36
27:16
28: 5, 8, 15
29
31: 4
35: 6
23 + A
25, 35
36: 9, 10
12, 16
32, 37
37: 3, 5, 16
21
39:13
Lev. 14: 4, 6
49, 51
52
Nu. 4: 8
19: 6
Jos. 2:18
2 Sa. 1:24
2 Ch. 2: 7, 14
3:14
Cant. 4: 3
6: 5
Isa. 1:18
3:23
Jer. 4:30

κόκκος.

Lam. 4: 5[a]   [a] A κόλπος.

κολαβρίζω.

Job 5: 4

κολακεύω.

Job 19:17

κολάπτω.

Exo. 32:16
1 Ki. 7:46, 49[a]
Jer. 10: 4 S^1[b]
[a] B κολλάω. [b] pro καλλωπίζω.

κόλασις.

Jer. 18:20
Eze. 14: 3, 4, 7
18:30
Eze. 43:11
44:12

κολεός.

1 Sa. 17:51 + A
2 Sa. 20: 8
1 Ch. 21:27
Jer. 29: 6
Eze. 21: 3, 4, 5

κολλάω.

Deu. 6:13
10:20
28:60
29:20
Ruth 2: 8
21 B[a]
2 Sa. 20: 2
1 Ki. 7:49 B[b]
11: 2
2 Ki. 1:18
3: 3
5:27
18: 6
Job 29:10
Job 38:38
41: 7, 14
Psa. 21:16
24:21
43:26
62: 9
100: 3
101: 6
118:25, 31
136: 6
Jer. 13:11, 11
Lam. 2: 2
4: 4
[a] pro προσκολλάω.
[b] pro κολάπτω.

κόλλη.

Isaiah 44:13

κολλύρα.

2 Samuel 13: 6 B[a]
[a] pro κολλυρίς.

κολλυρίζω.

2 Samuel 13: 6, 8

κολλύριον.

1 Kings 12 p 24 l l 30, 32, 39

κολλυρίς.

2 Sa. 6:19
13: 6[a]
8
2 Sa. 13:10
1 Ki. 14: 3 A
[a] B κολλύρα.

κολοβόκερκος.

Leviticus 22:23

κολοβόρριν.

Leviticus 21:18

κολοβόω.

2 Samuel 4:12

κολοκύνθη.

Jonah 4: 6, 6, 7, 9, 10

κόλπος.

Gen. 16: 5
Exo. 4: 6 *ter*
7 *ter*
Nu. 11:12
Deu. 13: 6
28:54, 56
Ruth 4:16
2 Sa. 12: 3, 8
1 Ki. 3:20, 20
17:19
22:35, 35
Job 19:27[a]
23:12
31:34-C
Psa. 34:13
73:11
Psa. 78:12
88:51
128: 7
Pro. 6:27
16:33
17:23
19:24
24:27
26:15
Ecc. 7:10
Isa. 49:22
65: 6, 7
Jer. 39:18
Lam. 2:12
4: 5 A[b]
Hos. 8: 1

[a] S[1] κόπος. [b] *pro* κόκκος.

κόλπωμα.

Ezekiel 43:13

κολυμβήθρα.

2 Ki. 18:17
Neh. 2:14
3:15, 16
Ecc. 2: 6
Isa. 7: 3
22: 9, 11
36: 2
Nah. 2: 8

κόμη.

Lev. 19:27
Nu. 6: 5
Job 1:20
16:12
Job 38:32
Eze. 24:23
44:20

κομίζω.

Gen. 38:20
Lev. 20:17
1 Sa. 2:22+A
Ezra 6: 5-B
Job 22: 8 A[a]
Psa. 39:16
Eze. 16:52, 54
58[b]
Hos. 2: 9

[a] *pro* οἰκίζω. [b] A κοσμέω.

κόνδυ.

Gen. 44: 2, 4, 9
10, 12
Gen. 44:16, 17
Isa. 51:17, 22

κονδυλίζω.

Amos 2: 7
Mal. 3: 5

κονδυλισμός.

Zephaniah 2: 8

κονία.

Deu. 27: 2, 4
Job 28: 4
38:38
Isa. 27: 9
Amos 2: 1

κονίαμα.

Daniel 5: 5

κονιάω.

Deu. 27: 2, 4
Pro. 21: 9

κονιορτός.

Exo. 9: 9
Deu. 9:21, 21
28:24
2 Ki. 9:17, 17
Job 21:18
Cant. 3: 6
Isa. 3:24
5:24
10: 6
17:13
Isa. 29: 5
Eze. 26:10
Dan. 2:35
Nah. 1: 3

κοντός.

1 Sa. 17: 7
Eze. 39: 9

κόνυζα.

Isaiah 55:13

κοπάζω.

Gen. 8: 1
6+A
8, 11
Nu. 11: 2
16:48, 50
Jos. 14:15
Jud. 15: 7[a]
20:28+A
Ruth 1:18
2 Sa. 13:39
2 Sa. 23:10 A[b]
Est. 2: 1
7:10
Ps. 105:30
Jer. 14:21
Eze. 43:10
Hos. 8:10[c]
Amos 7: 5
Jon. 1:11, 12

[a] A ποιέω. [b] *pro* κοπιάω.
[c] A[1] κοπιάω.

κοπανίζω.

1 Ki. (3) *p* 46
1 Ki. 4:22

κοπετός.

Gen. 50:10
Est. 4: 3
Psa. 29:12
Isa. 22:12
Jer. 6:26
9:10
Eze. 27:31 A
Joel 2:12
Amos 5:16, 16
17
Mic. 1: 8
Zec. 12:10, 11
11

κοπή.

Gen. 14:17
Deu. 28:25[a]
Jos. 10:20
[a] AB ἐπισκοπή.

κοπιάω.

Deu. 25:18, 18
Jos. 24:13
Jud. 5:26[a]
1 Sa. 6:12
14:31
17:39
2 Sa. 17: 2
23: 7, 10[b]
Job 2: 9
20:18
39:16
Psa. 6: 7
48: 9
68: 4
126: 1
Pro. 4:12
Ecc. 2:18[c]
Isa. 5:27
16:12
Isa. 30: 5
31: 3
33:24
40:28, 30
31
43:22
45:14
46: 1
47:13, 15
49: 4
57:10
63:13
65:23
Jer. 2:24
17:16
28:58
Lam. 5: 5
Hos. 8:10 A[1d]

[a] A κατάκοπος. [b] A κοπάζω.
[c] AS μοχθέω. [d] *pro* κοπάζω.

κόπος.

Gen. 31:42
Deu. 1:12
Jud. 10:16
Neh. 5:13
Job 3:10 A[a]
4: 2
5: 6, 7
11:16
19:27 S[1 b]
Psa. 9:28
35 A[a]
24:18
54:11 S[a]
128 S[1 c]
Psa. 72: 5, 16
87:16
89:10
93:20
106:12
139:10-A[1]
Jer. 20:18
51:33
Hos. 12: 3
Mic. 2: 1
Hab. 1: 3
3: 7
Zec. 10: 2
Mal. 2:13

[a] *pro* πόνος. [b] *pro* κόλπος.
[c] *pro* τόκος.

κοπόω.

Ecc. 10:15 CS[a] [a] *pro* κακόω.

κοπρία.

1 Sa. 2: 8
2 Ki. 9:37
Neh. 2:13
3:13, 14
12:31-ABS[1]
Job 2: 8
Ps. 112: 7
Isa. 5:25
Jer. 32:19
Lam. 4: 5

κόπρος.

Exo. 29:14
Lev. 4:11
8:17
16:27
Nu. 19: 5
1 Ki. 14:10 A
2 Ki. 6:25
18:27
Psa. 82:11
Isa. 30:22
36:12
Eze. 4:12

κόπτω.

Gen. 23: 2
32: 8[a]
50:10
Exo. 27:20
29:40
Lev. 21: 2
Nu. 13:24, 25
Deu. 19: 5
25:18
Jos. 10:20
11: 8
Jud. 1: 4[b], 5[c]
17[e]
6:30 A[d]
9:48, 49
20:13 A[e]
1 Sa. 25: 1
28: 3
2 Sa. 1:12
3:31
5:20[f], 24
11:26
1 Ki. 5: 6, 6, 11
11:15
12 *p* 24/45
13:29+A
30, 31
14:13 A
18 A
2 Ki. 17:15+A
19:23
2 Ch. 2: 8, 10
16
31: 1[a]
34: 4, 7[g]
Est. 5:14
Ecc. 3: 4
12: 5
Isa. 9:10[h]
10:15
14: 8
15: 3
32:12
37:24
44:14
Jer. 4: 8
8: 2
16: 4, 5, 6
22:18
23:29
26: 5, 13[a]
23
29: 6
30: 3
31:37
32:20
41: 5[i]
48: 5-S[1]
51: 8[k]
Eze. 6: 9
9: 5, 7, 8
20: 43[m]
24:16, 23
39:10
Joel 1:13
Mic. 1: 8, 11
Hag. 1: 8
Zec. 7: 5
12:10[n], 12
14:12-S[1]

[a] A ἐκκόπτω. [b] AB[a] πατάσσω.
[c] A πατάσσω. [d] *pro* ὀλοθρεύω.
[e] *pro* κατακόπτω. [f] A διακόπτω.
[g] A κατακόπτω. [h] AS ἐκκόπτω.
[i] A κλαιω. [k] ABS ἐκκόπτω.
[m] A[2] ὁράω. [n] S[1] ὁράω.

κόπωσις.

Ecclesiastes 12:12

κόραξ.

Gen. 8: 6
Lev. 11:16-AB
Deu. 14:14+A[2]
1 Ki. 17: 4, 6
Job 38:41
Ps. 146: 9
Pro. 24:52
Cant. 5:11
Isa. 34:11
Zeph. 2:14-S[1]

κοράσιον.

Ruth 2: 8, 21[a]
22, 23
3: 2
1 Sa. 9:11, 12
20:30
25:42
1 Ki. 12 *p* 24/40
Est. 2: 2, 3, 7
8-S[1]
9, 9, 12
12+A
Joel 3: 3
Zec. 8: 5

[a] AB παιδάριον.

κορέννυμι.

Deuteronomy 31:20

κόρη.

Deu. 32:10
Psa. 16: 8
Pro. 7: 2
20:20
Zec. 2: 8

κόριον.

Exo. 16:14, 31
Nu. 11: 7

κόριον.

Deu. 28:57[a] [a] AB χόριον.

κόρος.

Lev. 27:16
Nu. 11:32
1 Ki. 3 *p* 46 *bis*
4:22, 22
5:11
2 Ch. 2:10, 10
27: 5
Ezra 7:22
Eze. 45:13

κορύνη.

2 Samuel 21:16

κορυφή.

Gen. 49:26
Exo. 17: 9, 10
19:20, 20
24:17
38:16
Nu. 14:40, 44
20:28
21:20
23: 9, 14
28
Deu. 3:27
28:35
33:15, 15
16
34: 1
Jos. 15: 8, 9
Jud. 6:26
9: 7
36 A[a]
Jud. 16: 3
1 Sa. 26:13
2 Sa. 14:25
1 Ki. 18:42+A
2 Ki. 1: 9
Psa. 7:17
67:22
Pro. 1: 9
Isa. 28: 1
Eze. 6:13+A
8: 3
17:22
43:12
Hos. 4:13
Joel 2: 5
Amos 1: 2
9: 3
Mic. 4: 1

[a] *pro* κεφαλή.

κορώνη.

Jeremiah 3: 2

κοσμέω.

2 Ch. 3: 6
Est. 1: 6
Ecc. 1:15 A[a]
7:14
Jer. 4:30
Eze. 16:11, 13
58 A[b]
23:40, 41
Mic. 6: 9

[a] *pro* ἐπικοσμέω. [b] *pro* κομίζω.

κόσμιος.

Ecc. 12: 9[a] [a] C κόσμος.

κόσμος.

Gen. 2: 1
Exo. 33: 5, 6
Deu. 4:19
17: 3
2 Sa. 1:24, 24
Pro. 17: 6
20:29
28:17
29:17
Ecc. 12: 9 C[a]
Isa. 3:18+AS
19, 20
24, 26
Isa. 13:10[b]
24:21
40:26
49:18-AS
18
61:10
Jer. 2:32
4:30
Eze. 7:20
16:11
13+A
23:40
Nah. 2: 9

[a] *pro* κόσμιος. [b] S[1] οἶκος.

κόσυμβος.

Exo. 28:35 A[a]
Isa. 3:18
[a] *pro* κυσυμβωτός.

κοσυμβωτός.

Exo. 28: 4, 35[a] [a] A κόσυμβος.

κότος.

Joel 2:31 S[a] [a] *pro* σκότος.

κοτύλη.

Lev. 14:10, 12
15, 21
Lev. 14:24
Eze. 45:14 *ter*

κουρά.

Deu. 18: 4
Jos. 5:12 B[a]
Neh. 3:15
Job 31:20

[a] *pro* χώρα.

κουρεύς.

Jud. 16:19 A[a]
Eze. 5: 1

[a] *pro* ἀνήρ.

κουφίζω.

Exo. 18:22
1 Sa. 6: 5
1 Ki. 12: 4, 9, 10
p 24 *l* 56
Ezra 9:13
Job 21:30
Jon. 1: 5

κοῦφος.

1 Sa. 18:23
2 Sa. 1:23
2:18
2 Ki. 3:18
20:10
1 Ch. 12: 8
Ecc. 9:11
Isa. 18: 2
19: 1
30:16, 16
Jer. 4:13
26: 6
Lam. 4:19

κούφως.

Isaiah 5:26

κόφινος.

Jud. 6:19[a]
Psa. 80: 7

[a] A κανοῦν.

κόχλαξ.

1 Samuel 14:14

κράζω.

Gen. 41:55
Exo. 5: 8
22:23
32:17
Nu. 11: 2
Jos. 6:16
Jud. 1:14
3: 9, 15
4: 3
6: 7 A[a]
8 + A
10:12 A[a]
18:22 + A
24
2 Sa. 13:19
19: 4, 28
Job 6: 5
19: 7
30:20, 28
34:19
35: 9, 12
38:41
Psa. 3: 5 4: 4
16: 6
17: 7, 42
21: 3, 6, 25
26: 7
27: 1, 2 A[b]
29: 3, 9
30:23
31: 3
33: 7, 18
54:17
56: 3
60: 3
64:14
65:17
Psa. 68: 4
76: 2
85: 3, 7
87: 2, 10
14
90:15 AS[2c]
106: 6, 13
19, 28
118:145
146, 147
119: 1
129: 1
140: 1, 1
141: 2, 6
Isa. 6: 3, 4
14:31
15: 4
19:20
26:17
31: 4
42: 2
65:14, 24
Jer. 4: 5
11:11, 12
22:20
29: 2
30: 3
31: 3, 20
32:20
40: 3
Lam. 3: 8
Eze. 27:30
Hos. 8: 2
Joel 1:14
Mic. 3: 4
Hab. 1: 2
Zec. 7:13

[a] *pro* βοάω. [b] *pro* δέω (A).
[c] *pro* ἐπικαλέω.

κραιπαλάω.

Psa. 77:65
Isa. 24:20
Isa. 29: 9

κρᾶμα.

Canticles 7: 2

κρανίον.

Jud. 9:53
2 Ki. 9:35

κράσπεδον.

Nu. 15:38, 38
39
Deu. 22:12
Zec. 8:23

κραταιός.

Exo. 3:19
6: 1
13: 3, 9, 14
16
Deu. 3:24
4:34
5:15
6:21
7: 8, 19
21
9:26
29 − A
11: 2
26: 8
29: 3 + AB
34:12
Jos. 24: 4
Jud. 5:13 − A
1 Sa. 14:52
2 Sa. 11:16
22:31 − A
1 Ki. 12 *p* 24 *l* 24
17:17
18: 2
19:11
2 Ch. 6:32
Ezra 6: 4 − B
Neh. 1:10
9:32
Job 9: 4
26: 2
30:21
Psa. 23: 8
46:10
53: 5
58: 4
70: 7
85:14
134:10
135:12, 18
140: 6[a]
Pro. 23:11
Cant. 8: 6
Jer. 21: 5
30:21
Eze. 3: 9, 14
20:33, 34
Dan. 2:37
8:24
9:15
Amos 2:14
16 − A
Hab. 3: 4

[a] S[2] κριτής.

κραταιότης.

Psalm 45: 4

κραταιόω.

Jos. 18: 1 A[a]
Jud. 3:10 − A
Ruth 1:18
1 Sa. 4: 9
17:50 A
23:16
30: 6
2 Sa. 1:23
2: 7
3: 1
10:11, 11
12
11:23, 25
25
22:18, 33
23: 3
1 Ki. 21:22, 23[b]
23, 25
2 Ki. 3:26
12: 6, 7, 12
14
22: 6
1 Ch. 21: 4 A[c]
2 Ch. 21: 4
23: 1
31: 8
2 Ch. 35:22
Ezra 6:22
7:28
10: 4
Neh. 2:18
6: 9
Job 36:20[d]
22[e]
Psa. 9:20
26:14
30:25
37:20
63: 6
68: 5
73:13
79:16, 18
88:14
102:11
104: 4, 24
116: 2
138: 6, 17
141: 7
Lam. 1:16
Dan. 4:33
5:20

[a] *pro* κρατέω. [b] B[2] κρατέω.
[c] *pro* ἰσχύω. [d] S[1] κρατέω.
[e] S κραταιῶς.

κραταίωμα.

1 Sa. 2:32 + A
Psa. 24:14
27: 8
Psa. 30: 4[a]
42: 2
Jer. 31: 1 + AS

[a] AS κραταίωσις.

κραταιῶς.

Jud. 8: 1 A[a]
1 Sa. 2:16
Job 36:22 S[b]
Pro. 22: 3

[a] *pro* ἰσχυρῶς. [b] *pro* κραταιόω.

κραταίωσις.

Psa. 30: 4 AS[a]
59: 9
Psa. 67:36

[a] *pro* κραταίωμα.

κρατέω.

Gen. 19:16
21:18
Deu. 2:34
3: 4
Jos. 18: 1[a]
Jud. 7: 8 A[b]
20[c]
8:12
16:21[d]
26[e]
29 − A
19:29[d]
20: 6[d]
Ruth 3:15
1 Sa. 15:27
17:35
2 Sa. 1:11
2:16
3: 6, 29
6: 6
13:14
20: 9
1 Ki. 21:23 B[af]
2 Ki. 4: 8
11:12 AB[g]
12: 5
1 Ch. 19:12, 12
2 Ch. 25: 5
Neh. 3: 6
7 − ABS
8 *to* 14
16 *to* 24
27 *to* 32
4:17, 21
5:16
Est. 1: 1
Job 9:19
26: 9 − S[1]
36:20 S[1f]
Psa. 55: 1
72: 6, 23
136: 9
Pro. 8:16
12:24
14:18
16:32
17: 2
18:21
24:27
26:17
28:22
Ecc. 2: 3
9:12 + S[2]
Cant. 3: 4
7: 8
Isa. 32:17
41:13
42: 6
45: 1
Jer. 6:23
20: 7
Eze. 7:13
21:11
22:14
Dan. 5:12
10: 8
11: 2, 6
Amos 2:14
Nah. 2: 1
Hab. 1:10

[a] A κραταιόω. [b] *pro* κατισχύω.
[c] A λαμβάνω. [d] A ἐπιλαμβάνω.
[e] *vide* χειραγωγέω.
[f] *pro* κραταιόω. [g] *pro* κροτέω.

κρατήρ.

Exo. 24: 6
25:30, 32
33, 35
Pro. 9: 2, 3
Cant. 7: 2

κράτιστος.

1 Sa. 15:15
Psa. 15: 6, 6
Psa. 22: 5
Amos 6: 2

κράτος.

Gen. 49:24
Deu. 8:17
Jud. 4: 3
Ezra 8:22
Job 12:16
21:23
Psa. 58:10
61:12
75: 4
Psa. 85:16
88:10
89:11
Pro. 27:23
Isa. 22:21
40:26
Dan. 4:27
11: 1

κραυγάζω.

Ezra 3:13

κραυγή.

Gen. 18:20, 21
19:13
Exo. 3: 7, 9
11: 6
12:30
1 Sa. 4: 6, 6
5:12
2 Sa. 6:15
22: 7
1 Ki. 12 *p* 24 *l* 47
Neh. 5: 1, 6
9: 9
Est. 4: 3
Job 16:18
31:28, 28
39:25
Psa. 5: 2
9:13 S[a]
17: 7
101: 2
143:14
Ecc. 9:17
Isa. 5: 7
29: 6 A[b]
30:19
58: 4
Isa. 65:19
66: 6 − S[1]
Jer. 4:19
8:19
14: 2
18:22
20:16
26:12
27:46
28:54
29:22
Jer. 31: 5, 34
32:22
38:35
Eze. 21:22
27:28
30 A[c]
Amos 1:14
2: 2
Jon. 1: 2
2: 3
Zeph. 1:10, 16

[a] *pro* δέησις. [b] *pro* βροντή.
[c] *pro* φωνή.

κρεάγρα.

Exo. 27: 3
38:23
Nu. 4:14
1 Sa. 2:13, 14
1 Ch. 28:17
2 Ch. 4:11, 16
Jer. 52:18

κρεανομέω.

Leviticus 8:20

κρέας.

Gen. 9: 4
Exo. 12: 8
46 + A
46
16: 3, 8, 12
21:28
22:31
29:14, 31
32, 34
Lev. 6:27
7: 5, 7, 8
9, 9, 10
11
8:17, 31
32
9:11
11: 8, 11
16:27
22:30
Nu. 11: 4, 13
13
18 *qtr*
21, 33
18:18
19: 5
Deu. 12:15, 20
20, 20
23
27 − B
27
Deu. 14: 8
16: 4
28:53
32:42 − B
Jud. 6:19, 20
21, 21
1 Sa. 2:13, 15
15 − B
1 Ki. 17: 6 + A
6
Job 10:11
Psa. 49:13
Pro. 23:20
Isa. 22:13
44:16, 19
65: 4
66:17
Jer. 7:21
11:15
37:16
Eze. 4:14
11: 3, 7
11 A
24:10
39:17, 18
Dan. 10: 3
Hos. 8:13
Mic. 3: 3
Hag. 2:12
Zec. 11:16

κρείσσων.

Exo. 14:12
Jud. 8: 2
11:25 + A
15: 2 A[a]
1 Ki. 10: 4
Est. 1:19
Psa. 36:16
62: 4
83:11
Pro. 3:14
8:11, 19
12: 2, 9
13:12
15:16, 17
Pro. 15:29
16:19, 32
32
17: 1
19:22
21: 9, 19
24: 5
25: 7, 24
27: 5, 10
28: 6
29: 1
Isa. 56: 5
Eze. 32:21

[a] *pro* ἀγαθός.

κρεμαστός.

Jud. 6: 2[a]
1 Ki. 7: 6, 6

[a] A ὀχύρωμα.

κρεμάω, −μάννυμι.

Gen. 40:19, 22
41:13
Deu. 21:22, 23
28:66[a]
Jos. 8:29
10:26, 26
2 Sa. 4:12
18: 9 AB[b]
9, 10
Est. 2:23
5:14
6: 4

Est. 7:10
8: 7
9:13, 14
23, 25
Job 26: 7[b]
Ps. 136: 2
Cant. 4: 4
Lam. 5:12
Eze. 15: 3
17:23
27:10, 11

[a] A κεράννυμι. [b] pro περιπλέκω [c] A κρεμνάω.

κρεμνάω.

Job 26: 7 A[a] [a] pro κρεμάω.

κρημνός.

2 Chronicles 25:12, 12

κρήνη.

2 Sa. 2:13 ter
4:12
1 Ki.(3) p 1
1 Ki. 22:38
2 Ki. 20:20

κρηπίς.

Jos. 3:15
4:18
1 Ch. 12:15
Joel 2:17

κριθή.

Gen. 26:12
Exo. 9:31, 31
Lev. 27:16
Deu. 8: 8
Ruth 1:22
2:17, 23
3: 2, 15
17
2 Sa. 14:30
17:28
21: 9, 10
1 Ki. 4:21
2 Ki. 7: 1, 16
18
1 Ch. 11:13
2 Ch. 2:10, 15
27: 5
Job 31:40
Isa. 28:25
30:24
Jer. 48: 8
Eze. 4: 9
13:19
45:13
Hos. 3: 2
Joel 1:11
Hag. 2:16, 16

κρίθινος.

Nu. 5:15
Jud. 5: 8 + A
7:13
2 Ki. 4:42
Eze. 4:12

κρίκος.

Exo. 26: 6,6,11
11
27:10, 11
37: 6
38:10[a], 19
Exo. 38:10
Job 38: 6[a]
40:21[b]
Isa. 58: 5

[a] A στύλος. [b] A κλοίος.

κρῖμα.

Exo. 18:22
23: 6
Lev. 18: 4, 5
20:22
26:15, 43
46
Nu. 35:24, 29
36:12
Deu. 4: 1[a], 8
45
5: 1, 31
6: 1, 4, 20
24 A[b]
7:11
8:11
12: 1 A[c]
21:22
26:16, 17
32:41
Jud. 13:12 A[c]
1 Sa. 2:10
2 Sa. 8:15
22:23
1 Ki. 2: 3
3:11, 28
6(12) A
10: 9, 9
18:28 A[d]
2 Ki. 11:14
2 Ki. 17:26, 26
27, 33
34, 37
40
1 Ch. 15:13
16:12, 14
18:14
22:13
28: 7
2 Ch. 4: 7, 20
6:39
7:17
9: 8[e]
19:10
24:24
30:16
33: 8
Ezra 7:10, 26
Neh. 1: 7
8:18 − BS[1]
9:13, 29
10:29
Job 9:15, 19
13:18
14: 3
19: 7
20 + AS[2]
23: 4, 7
29:14
Job 31:13
32:10
34: 5, 6
36: 6, 15
17
40: 3
Psa. 9:17, 26
10: 2
17:23
18:10
35: 7
36: 6
47:12
71: 1
80: 5
88:15, 31
96: 2, 8
102: 6
104: 5, 7
118: 7, 13
20[f], 30
39, 43
52, 62
75
102[g]
106, 108
120, 121
132, 149
156, 160
164
170 A[h]
175
145: 7
147: 8, 9
149: 9
Pro. 1: 3
2: 9
8: 8 A[i]
12: 5
21:15
28: 5
Ecc. 5: 7
Isa. 1:27
5:16
9: 7
10: 2
16: 5
28:26 − S[1]
32:16
Jer. 4:12
5: 1
Jer. 7: 5 A[c]
8: 7
9:24
12: 1
21:12
22:13, 15
23: 5
26:28[e]
28: 9, 10
37:18
39: 7 AS[c]
8
Eze. 5: 8, 10
15
7:27
11: 9
18: 5 − 8
8, 27
22:29
23:25, 25
28:22, 26
30:19
33: 2 + A
14, 16
19
34:16
36:27
37:24
44:24
45: 9
Dan. 5:16
7:22
9: 5, 20
Hos. 2:19
5: 1, 11
6: 5
10: 4
12: 6
Amos 5: 7, 15
24
6:12
Mic. 3: 1, 8, 9
6: 8
7: 9
Hab. 1: 4, 4, 7
12
Zeph. 2: 3
3: 5, 8
Zec. 7: 9
8:16

[a] A ῥῆμα. [b] pro δικαίωμα. [c] pro κρίσις. [d] pro ἰθισμός. [e] A κρίσις. [f] S[1] δικαίωμα. [g] S[1] κλίμα. [h] pro λόγιον. [i] pro ῥῆμα.

κρίνον.

Exo. 25:30, 33
33
35 + A
Nu. 8: 4
1 Ki. 7: 7 + A
8, 11
2 Ch. 4: 5
Cant. 2: 1, 2, 16
4: 5
5:13
6: 1, 2
7: 2
Isa. 35: 1
Hos. 14: 5

κρίνω.

Gen. 15:14
16: 5
18:25
19: 9
26:21
30: 6
31:53
49:16
Exo. 5:21
18:13, 22
22, 26
26
Lev. 19:15
Nu. 35:24
Deu. 1:16, 17
16:18
25: 1 − B
32:36
Jud. 3:10, 30
4: 4, 5 A[a]
8: 1 A[b]
Jud. 10: 2, 3
11:27, 27
12: 7, 8, 9
11
11 + A
13, 14
15:20
16:31
21:22
Ruth 1: 1
1 Sa. 2:10
4:18
24:16
25:39
2 Sa. 18:19, 31
19: 9
1 Ki. 3: 9, 28
7:41
8:32
2 Ki. 15: 5
23:22
1 Ch. 16:33
2 Ch. 1:10, 11
6:23
19: 6, 8
20:12
24: 6, 22
26:21
Ezra 4: 9
7:25
Job 7:18
8: 3
9: 3
10: 2
13:19
17:10 S[2] [c]
22:13
23:13
27: 2
31:13
35:14
36:31
37:22
39:34
Psa. 2:10
5:11
7: 9, 9
9: 5, 9, 9
20, 39
25: 1
34:24
36:33
42: 1
50: 6
53: 3
57: 2, 12
66: 5 + S[1]
5
71: 2, 4
74: 3
81: 2, 3, 8
93: 2
95:10, 13
13
97: 9, 9
108: 7
109: 6
118:154
134:14[d]
Pro. 17:15
22:23
23:11
24:35, 73
Pro. 24:76, 77[e]
28:25
29: 7, 9, 14
Ecc. 3:17
6:10
Isa. 1:17, 23
2: 4
5: 3
11: 3, 4
16: 5
19:20
41: 6
43:26
49:25
50: 8, 8
51:22
66:16[f]
Jer. 2: 9
9 − S[1]
35
5:28, 28
11:20
21:12
22:16
27:34
28:36
32:17
37:13
Lam. 3:35, 58
Eze. 7: 8, 14
11:10
11 A
18:30
20:36
21:30
22: 2
23:36
24:14 ter
33:20
34:22
35:11
36:19
38:22
44:24
Dan. 9:12
Hos. 2: 2, 2
13:10
Mic. 3:11
4: 3
6: 1
Zec. 7: 9
8:16

[a] pro κρίσις. [b] pro διαλέγω. [c] pro ἐριδω. [d] S[1] οἰκτείρω. [e] S διακρίνω. [f] A καταναλίσκω.

κριός.

Gen. 15: 9
22:13, 13
30:40
31:10, 12
38
32:14
Exo. 25: 5
26:14
29: 1, 3, 15
15
16 + A
17, 18
19, 19
21, 22
26, 27
31, 32
35: 7, 23
39:21
Lev. 5:15, 16
18
6: 6, 31
32
8: 2, 18
18, 19
20, 21
22 ter
29
9: 2, 4, 18
19
16: 3, 5
Lev. 19:21, 22
23:18
Nu. 5: 8
6:14, 17
19
7:15, 17
21, 23
27, 29
33
35 − A
39, 41
45, 47
51, 53
57, 59
63, 65
69, 71
75, 77
81, 83
87, 88
15: 6, 11
23: 1, 2, 4
14, 29
30
28:11, 12
14, 19
20, 27
28
29: 2, 3, 8
9, 13
14, 14
Nu. 29:17, 18
20, 21
23, 24
26, 27
29, 30
32, 33
36, 37
Deu. 32:14
1 Sa. 15, 22
2 Ki. 3: 4
1 Ch. 15:26
29:21
2 Ch. 13: 9
15:11 + A
17:11
29:21, 22
32
Ezra 6: 9, 17
7:17
8:35
10:19 − S[1]
Job 42: 8
Psa. 28: 1
Psa. 64:14
65:15
113: 4, 6
Isa. 1:11
34: 6, 7
60: 7
Jer. 28:40
32:20, 20
21, 22
Lam. 1: 6
Eze. 27:21
34:17, 22
22
39:18
43:23, 25
45:23, 24
46: 4, 5, 6
7, 11
Dan. 8: 3, 4, 6
7 qtr
20
Mic. 6: 7

κρίσις.

Gen. 14: 7
18:19, 25
19: 9
Exo. 6: 6
15:25
18.15
22: 9
23: 2, 3, 6
24:14
28:15, 23
24, 26
26
Lev. 19:15, 35
25:18
Nu. 27: 5, 11
21
35:12
Deu. 1:17, 17
4: 5, 14
10:18
11: 1, 32
12: 1[a]
16:18
19 − AB
17: 8 qtr
9, 11
18: 3
19: 6
24:19
25: 1
27:19
30:10, 16
32: 4
33:21
Jos. 20: 3, 6 A
9
24:25
Jud. 4: 5[b]
13:12[a]
18: 7[c]
1 Sa. 24:16
25:39
2 Sa. 15: 2, 2, 4
6
1 Ki. 8:49 + A
11:33 + A
2 Ki. 1: 7
17:34
25: 6
1 Ch. 6:32
23:31
24:19
2 Ch. 8:14
9: 8 A[d]
19: 6, 8, 10
20: 9
35:13
Ezra 3: 4
Est. 1:13
Job 6:29 + AS[2]
9:32
13: 6
22: 4
Job 34: 4, 12[e]
35: 2
39:32
Psa. 1: 5
9: 5, 8
24: 9
32: 5
34:23
36:28, 30
71: 2
75: 9, 10
93:15
98: 4 − S[1]
4
100: 1
105: 3
110: 7
111: 5
118:84, 137
154
121: 5
139:13
142: 2
Pro. 6:19, 34
15:18
16:10
18: 5
19:28
22:23[f]
23:11, 29
24:38 − S
68
26:17
28: 2
Ecc. 3:16
8: 5, 6
11: 9
12:14
Isa. 1:17, 21
23, 24
3:13, 13
14
4: 4
5: 7
10: 2
11: 4
26: 8
28: 6, 6, 17
32: 1, 7
33: 5, 15
34: 5, 8, 8
35: 4
40:14, 27
41: 1, 21
42: 1, 3, 4
49: 4, 25
51: 4, 7
53: 8
54:17
56: 1
58: 2, 2, 4
59: 4, 8, 9
11, 14

Isa. 59:15
63: 1
Jer. 1:16
4: 2
5: 4,5,28
28, 28
7: 5[a]
10:24
17:11
22: 3, 16
16
26:28 A[d]
27:34
31:21
Jer. 32:17
33:11, 16
37:13
39: 7[g]
52: 9
Lam. 3:34, 58
Eze. 39:21
41:24
Dan. 4:34
Hos. 4: 1
12: 2
Mic. 6: 2, 2
Hab. 1: 3
Mal. 3: 5, 5

[a] A κρῖμα. [b] A κρίνω. [c] A σύγκρισις. [d] *pro* κρῖμα. [e] A δίκαιος. [f] A δίκη, S[1] ψυχή. [g] AS κρῖμα.

κριτήριον.

Exo. 21: 6
Jud. 5:10[a]
1 Ki. 7:44
Dan. 7:10, 26

[a] A λαμπήνη.

κριτής.

Deu. 1:15, 16
16:18
17: 9, 12
19:17, 18
21: 2
25: 2—B
29:10
31:28
Jud. 2:16, 17[a]
18, 18
18 A[b]
18, 19
Ruth 1: 1
1 Sa. 24:16
2 Sa. 7:11
15: 4
2 Ki. 23:22
1 Ch. 17: 6+A
10
23: 4
28: 1
2 Ch. 1: 2
19: 5, 6
26:11
2 Ch. 34:13
Ezra 7:25
10:14
Job 9:24
12:17
13: 8
Psa. 7:12
49: 6
67: 6
74: 8
140: 6 S[2 c]
148:11
Isa. 1:26
30:18
33:22
63: 7
Eze. 25:16+A
Dan. 9:12
Hos. 7: 7
Amos 2: 3
Mic. 7: 3
Hab. 1: 3
Zeph. 3: 3

[a] A αὐτός. [b] *pro* ἐχθρός. [c] *pro* κραταιός.

κρόκη.

Lev. 13:48, 49
51, 52
53, 55
Lev. 13:56, 57
58, 59

κρόκινος.

Pro. 7:17[a]
[a] AS[2] κρόκος.

κροκόδειλος.

Leviticus 11:29

κρόκος.

Pro. 7:17 AS[2 a]
Cant. 4:14

[a] *pro* κρόκινος.

κρόμμυον.

Numbers 11: 5

κροσσός, κρωσσός.

Exo. 28:22, 24
Exo. 36:22

κροσσωτός.

Exo. 28:14, 14
Psa. 44:14

κρόταφος.

Jud. 4:21[a]
22[a]
Jud. 5:26[a]
Ps. 131: 4

[a] A γνάθος.

κροτέω.

2 Ki. 11:12[a]
Job 27:23
Psa. 46: 2
97: 8
Lam. 2:15
Eze. 6:11
21:12, 14
17
25: 6
Nah. 3:19

[a] AB κρατέω.

κρούω.

Jud. 19:22
Cant. 5: 2

κρύβδην.

2 Sa. 12:12 A[a]
[a] *pro* κρυβῆ.

κρυβῆ.

Gen. 31:26 A[a]
Ruth 3: 7 A[a]
1 Sa. 19: 2 B[a]
2 Sa. 12:12[b]

[a] *pro* κρυφῆ. [b] A κρύβδην.

κρύβω *vide* κρύπτω.

κρυπτός.

Deu. 15: 9
29:29
1 Ki. 6: 8
2 Ki. 21: 7 A[a]
Isa. 22: 9
Isa. 29:10
Jer. 29:11
Eze. 8:12
40:16
41:26

[a] *pro* γλυπτός.

κρύπτω, κρύβω.

Gen. 3: 8, 10
4:14
18:17
31:20
37:26
Exo. 2: 3, 12
Nu. 5:13
Deu. 7:20
Jos. 2: 4,6,16
6:25
7:19, 21
22[a]
10:17
Jud. 9: 5
1 Sa. 3:17[b], 17
18
10:22
13: 6
14:11, 22
19: 2
20: 2, 5[c]
19, 24
23:19
23+A
2 Sa. 14:18
17: 9
19: 4[d]
1 Ki. 17: 3
18: 4 AB[e], 13
22:25[f]
2 Ki. 6: 5,9,29
7: 8+A
12
11: 2, 3
1 Ch. 21:20 A[g]
2 Ch. 22:11, 11
Job 5:21
13:20, 24[h]
14:13
15:18
17: 4
18:10
20:12
23:12
24: 4
28:21
29: 8
31:33
34:22, 29
38: 2, 2
40: 8
Job 42: 3—S[1]
3
Psa. 9:16
16:14
26: 5
30: 5, 20
34: 7, 8
37:10 ABS
39:11, 11
53: 2
54:13
63: 6
68: 6[k]
77: 4
118:11
138:15
139: 6
141: 4
Pro. 1:11
2: 1
7: 1
10:14
11:13
12:16
17: 9, 9
25: 2
4 A[m]
26:15, 26
27: 5
Isa. 2:10
29:14
32: 2, 2
42:22
49: 2[n], 2[o]
Jer. 4:29
13: 5
16:17+S[1]
17
18:20, 22
23:24
27: 2
29:11
39:27
43:19 A[e]
45:14, 25
49: 4
Lam. 3:55—A
Eze. 12: 6,7,12
Hos. 6: 9
13:14
Obad. 6

[a] B ἐγκρύπτω. [b] A διακρύπτω. [c] A πορεύω. [d] A ἐπικρύπτω. [e] *pro* κατακρύπτω. [f] B[1] κρύφιος. [g] *pro* μεθ' ἀχαβίν. [h] A ἀποκρύπτω. [i] *pro* ἀποκρύπτω. [k] S[2] ἀποκρύπτω. [m] *pro* τύπτω. [n] S[1] σκεπάζω. [o] AS[3] σκεπάζω.

κρύσταλλος.

Nu. 11: 7
Job 6:16
38:29
Ps. 147: 6
Ps. 118: 8
Isa. 54:12
Eze. 1:22

κρυφαῖος.

Exo. 17:16
Jer. 23:24
Lam. 3:10

κρυφαίως.

Jer. 44:17
Jer. 47:15

κρυφῆ.

Gen. 31:26[a]
Exo. 11: 2
Deu. 28:57
Jud. 4:21[b]
9:31[c]
Ruth 3: 7[a]
1 Sa. 19: 2[d]
Job 13:10
Ps. 138:15
Isa. 29:15
45:19
48:16

[a] A κρυβῆ. [b] A ἠτυχῆ. [c] A δῶρον. [d] B κρυβῆ.

κρύφιος.

Jud. 3:19
Ruth 4: 1
1 Ki. 22:25 B[1 a]
Psa. 9: 1
18:13
Psa. 43:22
45: 1—A
50: 8
Pro. 9:17

[a] *pro* κρύπτω.

κρωσσός *vide* κροσσός

κτάομαι.

Gen. 4: 1
12: 5, 5
25:10
33:19
36: 6
39: 1
46: 6
47:19, 20
22, 23
49:30
50:13
Exo. 15:16[a]
21: 2
Lev. 22:11
25:14
15—A
28, 30
44, 45
50
27:22, 24
Deu. 28:68
32: 6
Jos. 24:32
Ruth 4: 4, 5, 5
8, 9, 10
2 Sa. 12: 3
24:21, 24
21, 24
1 Ki. 16:24
2 Ki. 12:12
22: 6
Neh. 5: 8, 16
Psa. 73: 2
77:54
138:13
Pro. 1: 5, 14
3:31
4: 4+S[2]
5 A
5 A
16:22
17:16, 21
18:15
19: 8
22: 9
29:47
Ecc. 2: 7
Isa. 1: 3
26:13
43:24
57:13
Jer. 13: 1, 2
16:19
19: 1
39: 7,8,8[b]
9
15 AS[3 c]
25, 43
44
Eze. 5: 1
7:12, 13
8: 3
Amos 8: 6
Zec. 11: 5

[a] A λυτρόω. [b] A κτῆσις. [c] *pro* κτίζω.

κτείνω.

Pro. 24:11
Pro. 25: 5

κτῆμα.

Job 20:29
27:13[a]
Pro. 12:27
23:10
Pro. 29:34
Hos. 2:15
Joel 1:11

[a] AS[2] ὀργή.

κτῆνος.

Gen. 1:25, 26
28
2:20
3:14
6: 7, 19
20
7: 2, 2, 8
8, 14
21, 23
8: 1, 17
19, 20
9:10
13: 2
5 A[a]
7, 7
26:14, 14
29: 7
30:29, 43
31: 9, 43
43
33:13, 17
34: 5, 23
36: 6
46:32
47: 1, 4, 5
16, 16
17, 17
18
Exo. 9: 3, 4, 4
4+A
6, 6, 7
19, 19
20, 21
22, 25
10:26
11: 5, 7
12:12, 29
38
13: 2, 12
15
17: 3
19:13
20:10, 17
22: 5, 10
19
Lev. 1: 2
5: 2
7:15, 16
11: 2, 2, 3
3, 26
39, 46
19:19
20:16, 16
25 *ter*
21:18
25: 7
26:22
27: 9, 10
10, 11
11, 26
28
Nu. 3:13, 41
41, 45
45
8:17
16:32
18:15, 15
20: 4,8,11
19
31: 9, 11
26, 28
30, 47
32: 1, 1, 4
16, 24
26, 30
35: 3
Deu. 2:35
3: 7, 19
19
4:17
5:14, 21
7:14
11:15
Deu. 14: 4, 6, 6
20:14—B
27:21
28:11, 51
30: 9
Jos. 1:14
8: 2
27+A
14: 4, 4—A
21: 2
22: 8
Jud. 6: 5 A[b]
20:48
1 Sa. 17:44[c]
23: 5
1 Ki. 4:29
18: 5 A[a]
2 Ki. 3: 9, 17
1 Ch. 4:39, 41
5: 9
7:21
2 Ch. 20:25
26:10
32:28
Ezra 1: 4, 6
Neh. 2:12, 12
14
9:37—S[1]
10:36
Job 1: 3, 10
36:28
37: 4+C
42:12
Psa. 8: 8
35: 7
48:13, 21
49:10
77:48, 50
103:14
106:38
134: 8
146: 9
148:10
Pro. 12:10
24:65, 65
Ecc. 3:18, 19
19, 21
Isa. 30:23
46: 1
63:14
Jer. 7:20
9:10
12: 4
21: 6
27: 3
28:62
30:10
38:12, 27
39:43
40:10, 10
12
43:29
Eze. 8:10+A
14:13, 17
19, 21
24: 5
25:13
27:20
29: 8, 11
32:13, 13
35: 7
36:11
41:31
Joel 1:20
2:22
Jon. 3: 7, 8
4:11
Mic. 5: 8
Zeph. 1: 3
Hag. 1:11
Zec. 2: 4
8:10
14:15

[a] *pro* σκηνή. [b] *pro* κτήσις. [c] A θηρίον.

κτηνοτρόφος.

Gen. 4:20
46:32, 34
Nu. 32: 4

κτηνώδης.

Psalm 72:22

κτῆσις.

Gen. 23: 4, 9, 18
20
36: 43
46: 6
49:30, 32
50:13
Lev. 14:34
20:24
25:10
13AB[1 a]
16AB[1 a]
Jud. 6: 5[b]
18:21
2 Ki. 3:17
1 Ch. 28: 1—AB
2 Ch. 14:15[b]
Ezra 8:21
Job 36:33
Ps. 104:24 B[c]
Pro. 1:13[d]
8:18
10:15[e]
Ecc. 2: 7
Jer. 39: 7
8 A[f]
11, 12
14, 16
Eze. 38:12, 13

[a] pro ἔγκτησις. [b] A κτῆνος.
[c] pro κτίσις. [d] A κτίσις.
[e] S[1] κτίσις. [f] pro κτάομαι.

κτίζω.

Gen. 14:19, 22
Exo. 9:18
Lev. 16:16
Deu. 4:32
32: 6 A[a]
Psa. 32: 9
50:12
88:13, 48
101:19
103:30
148: 5
Pro. 8:22
Ecc. 12: 1
Isa. 22:11
45: 7, 8
46:11
54:16, 16
Jer. 38:22
39:15[b]
Eze. 28:14, 15
Hos. 13: 4, 4
Amos 4:13
Hag. 2: 9
Mal. 2:10

[a] pro πλάσσω. [b] AS[3] κτάομαι.

κτίσις.

Psa. 73:18—S
103:24
104:21[a]
Pro. 1:13 A[b]
10:15 S[1 b]

[a] S κτῆσις. [b] pro κτῆσις.

κτίστης.

2 Samuel 22:32

κύαθος.

Exo. 25:28
38:12
Nu. 4: 7
Jer. 52:19

κύαμος.

2 Sa. 17:28
Eze. 4: 9

κυβερνάω.

Proverbs 12: 5

κυβέρνησις.

Pro. 1: 5
11:14
Pro. 24: 6

κυβερνήτης.

Pro. 23:34
Eze. 27: 8, 27
Eze. 27:28

κύβος.

Est. 1: 6
Job 38:38

κυδοιμός.

Job 39:25

κῦδος.

Isaiah 14:25

κύησις.

Ruth 4:13

κυκλόθεν.

Exo. 28:20 A[a]
Jos. 21:44
23: 1
Jud. 2:14
8:34
1 Sa. 10: 1+AB
12:11
1 Ki. (3) 1
p 46
4:24
5: 4
6:9, 9+A
10+A
10
33—A
7:11, 11
22
18:32
2 Ki. 25.10—B[b]
1 Ch. 22: 9, 18
2 Ch. 4: 2, 3
14: 7
15:15
20:30
32:22
33:14
Ezra 1: 6
Neh. 12·28
Job 1:10 A[c]
18: 9+A
10+A
Psa. 30:14
Isa. 30:32
Jer. 6:25
Jer. 17:26
20:10
10+B[1]
26: 5
27:29
28: 2
30: 7
31:17
39:14 A[c]
Lam. 2:22
Eze. 1:18, 28
5:17
10:12—A
16:33, 37
19: 8
23:22
37: 2
40:16, 25
41: 5, 11
12
17 A[c]
19
42:15
43: 2, 12
13, 17
17
45: 1, 2, 2
Joel 3:11, 12
Amos 3:11
Zec. 2: 5
7: 7
12: 6
14:14

[a] pro κάτωθεν. [b] A κύκλῳ.
[c] pro κύκλῳ.

κύκλος, κύκλῳ.

Gen. 23:17
35: 5
41:48
Exo. 7:24
16:13
19:12
25:10, 23
23, 24
27:17
28:28, 29
30
29:16, 21
30: 3, 3
36:31, 33
34
37:18
38: 3+A
39: 9, 9
10+A
40: 6
27—A[g]
Lev. 1: 5, 11
3: 2, 8, 13
6:32
8:15, 19
24
9:12, 18
14:41
16:18
17: 6
25:31, 44
Nu. 1:50, 53
2: 2
3:37
4:32
11:24, 31
32
16:24, 27
34
22: 4
32:33
34:12
35: 2, 4
Deu. 12:10
13: 7
17:14
21: 2
25:19—A[1]
Jos. 6: 3, 20
Jos. 15·12
18:20
19: 8[a]
21:11, 41
42
24:33
Jud. 7·18, 21
20:29
1 Sa. 14:17
17: 3 B[b]
26: 5, 7
31: 9
2 Sa. 5: 9
7: 1, 1—A
22:12
1 Ki. (3) p 1
p 46+A
4:27+A
6:27
7: 9+A
10
10+A
21, 40
18:35
2 Ki. 11: 8, 11
25: 1, 4
10 A[c]
17
1 Ch. 4:33
6:55
10: 9
11: 8
28:12
2 Ch. 4: 3
14:14
17:10
23: 7, 10
34: 6
Neh. 5:17
6:16
Est. 1: 6
Job 1:10[d]
18:11—A
19: 8, 10
29: 5
41: 5
Psa. 3: 7
11: 9
17:12
Psa. 33: 8
43:14—S[1]
49: 3
75:12
77:28
78: 3, 4
88: 9
96: 2, 3
124: 2, 2
127: 3
Ecc. 1: 6
Cant. 3: 7
Isa. 6: 2
9:18
19: 7
42:25
49:18
60: 4
Jer. 1:15
4:17
6: 3
12: 9—A
15:14
21:14
25: 9
27:14, 32
31:39
38:39
39 A[e]
39:44[d]
40:13
52: 4, 7[f]
14, 21
22, 23
Lam. 1:17
2: 3
Eze. 1: 4
27+A
Eze. 1:27
2: 6
4: 2
5: 2, 5, 6
7, 7, 12
14, 15
6: 5, 13
8:10
12:14
16:57, 57
23:24
26: 8
27:11+A
11
28:24 A[g]
26
31: 4
4+A
32:24+A
34:26 A[g]
36: 3, 36
37: 2
40: 5, 14
16, 17
29
30 A
33, 36
36+A
43
41: 6, 7, 8
10, 16
16, 17[d]
42:20
43:20
46:23 ter
Nah. 3: 8
Zec. 12: 2

[a] A περικύκλος. [b] pro αὐλῶν.
[c] pro κυκλόθεν. [d] A κυκλόθεν.
[e] pro λίθος. [f] A κυκλόω.
[g] pro περικύκλος.

κυκλόω.

Gen. 2:11, 13
Exo. 13:18
Nu. 34: 4, 5
Deu. 2: 1, 3
32:10
Jos. 6: 7
Jud. 11:18
16: 2
19:22[a]
20: 5[a]
1 Sa. 7:16
2 Sa. 18:15
22: 6
24: 6
1 Ki. 5: 3
7: 3
10+A
11
22:32
2 Ki. 3: 9, 25
6:15
8:21
11: 8
2 Ch. 4: 3
18:31
21: 9
23: 2, 7
Job 1:17
16:13
19:12
22:10
Psa. 7: 8
21:17
25: 6
26: 6
31: 7, 10
47:13
48: 6
54:11
58: 7, 15
87:18
90: 4
108: 3
117:10, 11
11, 12
Ecc. 1: 6 ter
7:26
9:14
12: 5
Cant. 3: 2, 3
5: 7
Isa. 29: 3
37:33
Jer. 52: 7 A[b]
Lam. 3: 5
Eze. 31:15 B[a c]
43:17
Hos. 7: 2
11:12
Jon. 2: 4, 6
Hab. 2:16
Zec. 14:10

[a] A περικυκλόω. [b] pro κύκλῳ.
[c] pro κωλύω.

κύκλῳ vide κύκλος.

κύκλωμα.

2 Ch. 4: 2
Job 13:27 A[a]
33:11 A[b]
37:11
Ps. 139:10
Eze. 43:17
48:35

[a] pro κώλυμα. [b] pro ξύλον.

κύκνος.

Lev. 11:18
Deu. 14:15

κυλίκιον.

Est. 1: 7[a]

[a] S[1] κυκλίκινον.

κυλίω.

Jos. 10:18
Jud. 7:13 A[a]
1 Sa. 14:33
2 Ki. 9:33
33—A
Pro. 26:27, 27
Ecc. 10: 8+A
8+A
Amos 2:13[b], 13
5:24
Zec. 9:16

[a] pro στρέφω. [b] A κωλύω.

κῦμα.

Exo. 15: 8
Job 6:15
11:16
38:11
Psa. 41: 8
45: 4 S[1 a]
64: 8
88:10
106:25, 29
Isa. 48:18
51:15
Jer. 5:22
28:42
38:35
Eze. 26: 3
Jon. 2: 4
Zec. 10:11

[a] pro ὕδωρ.

κυμαίνω.

Isa. 5:30
17:12
Jer. 6:23
26: 7

κυμάτιον.

Exo. 25:10, 23
24
Exo. 38: 3+A

κυμβαλίζω.

Nehemiah 12:27

κύμβαλον.

1 Sa. 18: 6
2 Sa. 6: 5
1 Ch. 13: 8
15:16, 19
28
16: 5, 42
1 Ch. 25: 1, 6
2 Ch. 5:12, 13
29:25
Ezra 3:10
Ps. 150: 5, 5

κύμινον.

Isaiah 28:25, 27, 27

κυνηγέω.

Genesis 25:27

κυνηγός.

Gen. 10: 9, 9
1 Ch. 1:10

κυνικός.

1 Samuel 25: 3

κυνόμυια.

Exo. 8:21, 21
22, 24
24, 29
Exo. 8:31
Psa. 77:45
104:31

κυοφορέω.

Ecclesiastes 11: 5

κυπαρίσσινος.

1 Ki. 6:21+A
Neh. 8:15
Eze. 27:24

κυπάρισσος.

2 Ki. 19:23
Job 40:12
Cant. 1:17
Isa. 37:24
41:19
Isa 55:13
60:13
Eze. 27: 5
31: 3, 8

κυπρίζω.

Canticles 2:13, 15

κυπρισμος.

Canticles 7:12

κύπρος.

Cant. 1:14−B
Cant. 4:13

κύπτω.

Gen. 43:27
Exo. 4:31
12:27
34: 8
Nu. 22:31
1 Sa. 24: 9
28:14
2 Sa. 17:19 A[a]
1 Ki. 1:16, 31
1 Ki. 18:42
2 Ch. 20:18
Neh. 8: 6
Job 22:29
Psa. 9:31
Isa. 2: 9
46: 6
51:23

[a] pro ψύχω.

κυρεία, −ρία.

Isa. 40:10
Dan. 4:19
Dan. 6:26
11: 3, 4, 5

κυρία.

Gen. 16: 4, 8, 9
1 Ki. 17:17
2 Ki. 5: 3
Ps. 122: 2
Pro. 24:58
Isa. 24: 2

κυριεύω.

Gen. 3:16
37: 8, 8
Exo. 15: 9
Nu. 21:18
24: 7
Jos. 12: 2
15:16
24:33[a]
Jud. 9: 2[b], 2
14: 4
15:11[c]
2 Ch. 14: 7
20: 6
Ps. 105:11
Isa. 3: 4, 12
Isa. 7:18
14: 2, 2
19: 4
42:19
Jer. 2:31[d]
37: 3
Lam. 5: 8
Dan. 2:39
3:27
4:22, 29
5:21
6:24
11: 3, 4, 5
43

[a] A κατακυριεύω. [b] A ἄρχω.
[c] A ἄρχων. [d] A δουλεύω.

κύριος.

(*vide etiam* θεός.)

Adon.

Gen. 18:12
19: 2, 18
23: 6, 11
15
24: 9, 10
10, 12
12, 14
18, 27
27, 27
35, 36
36, 37
39, 42
44, 48
48, 49
51, 54
56, 65
31:35
32: 4,5,18
33: 6, 13
14, 14
15
30: 2, 3, 7
8,8,16
19, 20
40: 1, 7
42:10, 30
33
43:19
44: 5, 7, 8
9, 16
16, 18
19, 21
22, 24
Gen. 44:33
45: 8, 9
47:18 *ter*
25
Exo. 21: 4, 4, 5
6, 6, 8
32
32:22
Nu. 11:28
12:11
32:25, 27
36: 2, 2
Deu. 10:17, 17
23:15, 15
Jos. 3:11, 13
Jud. 3:25
4:18
6:13[a]
19:11, 12
Ruth 2:13
1 Sa. 1:15, 26
16:16
20 38
22:12
24: 7−B
9, 11
25:10, 14
17, 24
25
25−AB
26, 26
27, 27
28, 28
1 Sa. 25:29, 30
31 *ter*
41+A
26:15, 15
16, 17
18, 19
29: 4, 8
10
30:13, 15
2 Sa. 1:10
2: 5, 7
3:21
4: 8
9: 9, 10
10, 11
10: 3
11: 9, 11
11, 13
12: 8, 8
13:32, 33
14: 9, 12
15, 17
17, 18
19, 19
20, 22
15:15, 21
21
16: 3, 4, 9
18:28, 31
32
19:19, 19
20, 26
27, 27
28, 30
35, 37
20: 6
24: 3,3,21
22
1 Ki. 1: 2+A
2, 11
13, 17
18, 20
20, 21
24, 27
27, 31
33, 36
37, 37
43, 47
(3)38
3:17, 26
11:23 A
12:27
16:24
18: 7,8,10
11, 13
14
21: 4, 9
22:17
2 Ki. 2: 3,5,16
19
2 Ki. 4:16, 28
5: 1, 3, 4
18, 20
22, 25
6: 5, 12
15, 22
23, 26
32
8: 5, 12
14
9: 7, 11
31
10: 2, 3, 3
6, 9
18:23, 24
27, 27
19: 4, 6
1 Ch. 12:19
21: 3 *ter*
23
2 Ch. 2:14, 15
13: 6
Neh. 8:10
Job 3:19
Ps. 11: 5
44:12
96: 5−S
104:21
109: 1
113: 7
122: 2
134: 5
135: 3, 3
146: 5
Pro. 27.18
Isa. 1:24
19: 4
24: 2
26:13
36: 8, 12
12
37: 6
Jer. 22:18−A
34: 3, 3
41: 5−S
44:20
Dan. 1:10
10:16, 17
17, 19
12: 8
Hos. 12:14
Amos 4: 1
Mic. 4:13
Zec. 1: 9
4: 4,5,13
14
6: 4, 5
Mal. 1: 6, 6
3: 1

[a] A κύριος κ.

Adon Jehovah.

Isaiah 19: 4

Adonai.

Gen. 18: 3, 27
30, 31
32
20: 4
Exo. 4:10, 13
5:22
15:17
34: 9
Nu. 14:17
Jud. 6:15
1 Ki. 3:10
22: 6
2 Ki. 7: 6
19:23
Ezra 10: 3+S³
Neh. 1:11−ABS¹
Psa. 2: 4
15: 2[a]
34:17, 22
23
36:13
37:10+AS
23
38: 8
Psa. 39:18
43:24
50:17
53: 6
54:10
56:10
58:12
61:13
65:18
67:12, 18
23, 27
33
70:16
72:20
76: 8
77:65
78:12
85: 3
4−S¹
5, 8, 9
88:50, 51
89: 1
109: 3
120: 2, 8
6−S¹
Isa. 3:18
4: 4
6: 1, 8
11
7:14, 20
8: 7
9: 8, 17[b]
10:12
11:11
21: 6,8,16
28: 2
29:13
30:20
37:24
38:16
49:14[c]
Lam. 1:14, 15
15
Lam. 2: 1−A
2, 5, 7
18, 19
20
3:30, 35
36, 57
Eze. 18:25, 29
33:17, 20
Dan. 1: 2
9: 7, 8
16, 17
19 *ter*
Amos 7: 7, 8
9: 1
Mic. 1: 2
Zec. 9: 4
Mal. 1:14

[a] S¹ θεός. [b] AS θεός.
[c] A θεός.

Adonai Jehovah.

Deu. 9:26[a]
Jos. 7: 7[a]
1 Ki. 2:26
Psa. 68: 7[b]
72:28
Isa. 10:23[c],24[d]
22: 5, 15
28:22
52: 4[e]
56: 8
61: 1
65:13, 15
Jer. 2:22[f]
7:20
14:13
26:10
27:31
30: 5
39:17[a]
51:26[g]
Eze. 2: 4[a]
3:11[a],27[a]
5: 5[h], 7[h]
8[h],11[h]
6: 3[h], 3[h]
11[b]
7: 2[h], 5
8: 1[b]
9: 8[h]
11: 7[b], 8[h]
13[h],16[h]
17[b],21[h]
12:19[h],23[h]
25[h],28[b]
28[h]
13: 3[h], 8[h]
8[b], 9[b]
13[h]
16[h],18[h]
14: 4[b],11[b]
14[h], 16
18, 20
21[h], 23
15: 6[h], 8
16: 3, 8[b]
14[h], 19
23, 30
36[h], 43
48, 59[b]
63
17: 3,9,16
Eze. 17:10, 22
18: 3[h], 9[h]
23[a],30[h]
32[h]
20: 3,3[h],5[f]
27[h],30[i]
31, 33[h]
36[f],44[h]
21: 7[ef]
24[i],26[i]
28[f]
22:12[a], 28
23:22[i],32[k]
34[i],35[h]
49
24: 3[h], 6[h]
9[h],14[b]
21[i],24
25: 3, 3[h]
6[f], 8[h]
12[h],13[h]
14, 15[h]
16[h]
26: 3[h], 5[a]
7[h], 14
27: 3[m]
28: 2[f], 6[i]
10−A²
22, 24[f]
29: 3[f], 8[f]
13[n],16[f]
30: 2, 6
31:10[n]
32: 3[h],14[h]
33:11[h]
35:11[a], 14
36: 4,4,6[h]
22[h]
32[ef]
37: 5[a], 9[a]
12[h],19[h]
38:14[i],21[a]
39: 1[a], 5[a]
10, 13
17, 20[a]
43:27
Amos 1: 8
4: 2, 5[a]
6: 8
7: 4[f], 4
5[a], 6

[a] A κύριος κ. [b] S κύριος κ.
[c] AS θεός. [d] S¹ κ. ὁ θεός.
[e] B κύριος κ. [f] A κ. ὁ θεός.
[g] AS κύριος κ. [h] A Ἀδωναὶ κ.
[i] A κ. κ. ὁ θεός.
[k] A Ἀδωναὶ κ. κ. ὁ θ.
[m] A Ἀδωναὶ κ. κ. [n] AB κ. ὁ θεός.

El.

Nu. 23: 8
2 Sa. 22:48
Job 5: 8
8: 3, 5
13[a], 20
9: 2
12: 6
Job 13: 7
15: 4, 13
25−C
16:11
18:21
19:22
21:14, 22
Job 22: 2, 17
23:16
25: 4
27:11, 13
31:14
23−B
28
32:13
33:14
34: 5, 10
Job 34:12, 23
37
35: 2, 13
36: 5
37:13
38:41
40: 4, 14
Psa. 15: 1[b]
73: 8[c]
Isa. 40:18

[a] A θεός. [b] S¹ θεός.
[c] S θεός.

Eloah.

Job 3: 4
4: 9, 17
5:17
6: 8[a]
9
10: 2
11: 5, 6, 7
15: 8
Job 16:20, 21
19: 6, 21
26
21: 9
27: 8
31: 6
33:26

[a] A θεός.

Elohim.

Gen. 21: 2, 6
Exo. 3: 4
13:19
18: 1
20: 1
Lev. 2:13
Jud. 8: 3
1 Sa. 2:25
4:22
5: 2
6: 5
10:26
11: 6−A
14:15
16:15
23:14, 16
26: 8
2 Sa. 2:27
6: 3, 7
12
15:24
23: 3 A[a]
1 Ki. 3: 5, 11
4:25
10:24
11:23 A
12:22
1 Ch. 15: 2−BS
17: 3
24: 5
26:20, 32[b]
28: 2, 12
21[b]
29: 1,7,13
17
2 Ch. 4:19
5: 1
8:10
13:12, 15
16
15: 1
19: 3
20: 7[b], 20
24: 5, 13
20
25: 8,8,20
24
26: 5 *ter*
7
28:24
30:12
31:13, 21
32:29, 31
34:32
36:19
Ezra 9: 6−B
Job 1: 9[b]
2: 9, 10
5: 8
20:29
32: 2
34: 9
Psa. 52: 7[c]
76: 2
Pro. 3: 4
Isa. 7:13
61:10
62: 5
Mal. 2:17

[a] pro χριστός. [b] A θεός.
[c] S² θεός.

Jah.

Psa. 67: 5
76:12
88: 9
93: 7, 12
101:19
113:25, 26
117: 5, 14
Ps. 117:17, 18
19
121: 4
129: 3
134: 3, 4
146: 1
150: 6

Jah Jehovah.

Isaiah 12: 2

Jehovah.

Var. Lec. tantum.

Gen. 8:20[a]
14:22−A
Exo. 4:10[1a]
9:29[1]−B[a]
10: 9[b]
13−B
13:15[a]
14:13[c]
16: 7[a]
19:22[2d]
29:11−A
Lev. 3: 9[c]
7:19+AB
Lev. 20: 8[c]
Nu. 12: 8−A
18:28[2]−B
22:31[a]
26:65−A
28:16−A
29: 8[1]−AB
Deu. 5: 3−A
6:19−A
9: 4+A
5[2]−B
8[2]−B
20+A

Deu. 9:22[e]
11: 4[a]
17[2a]
18: 6+A
23: 2-AB[1]
26:10[1]-A
28: 9[1e]
Jos. 5: 6+A
6:26-A
11:15+A
22:22+A
29[2]-A
23: 1[c]
24:19[e]
Jud. 1:22[f]
2:13+A
3: 1[g]
15+A
5:23[1]-A
23+A
6:13[b]
34[a]
13: 1[2]-A
20:26+A
1 Sa. 3: 3+A
9+A
6: 1+A
8+A
11-B
12:11+A
18:12+A
20:14+A
28:10+A
2 Sa. 6:16+A
21[3]-A
7:25+A
16:12+A
24:12-A
1 Ki. 5: 3[2]-B
7:34-B
49+A
8: 4+A
6+A
10+A
11+A
12 A
9: 9[2]-B
25 A
25 A
12:15+A
13:26+A
26+A
14:5 A, 11 A
14 A
15 A
15 A
18 A
15:18-B
29-A
17: 5-A
22+A
2 Ki. 3:12-B
6:20[2]-B
33[2]-A
11: 3-B
12: 9[2h]
17:15-B
18:16+A
19:15+A
22: 3-A
19+AB
24: 2[1]-B
1 Ch. 6:32-B
9:19-B
20-B
14:10-A[2]
15: 3[i]
25+A
16: 8-BS
11-S
29[1]-BS
17:27-BS
21:28-B
23: 4-AB
28:13[2]-B
2 Ch. 7:12[c]
8:12[2]-AB
19:10[a]
24:12[3]-A
29:11-B

2 Ch. 29:15[2]-B
32:26[k]
33: 9-A
16[1]-B
36:18-AB
Ezra 1: 1[2]-B
5-B
7-B
3: 5[1]-B
6:22-B
7:27[2]-B
8:28[1e]
35-B
Neh. 8: 1-BS[1]
10[2]-ABS
10:35-B
Job 1: 6[m], 8[a]
2: 1[2]-S[1]
42:10[1n]
11[m]
Psa. 3: 4-A
6: 3[2]-B
10[1]-S[1]
24: 6-B
25: 2-S[1]
6-B
34:10[h]
27[o]
35: 1-A
36:10-S[1]
38:13-B
45: 9[p]
12 A[1q]
53: 8-B
55:11[k]
69: 2+S
70: 1[k]
83: 3[m]
13[r]
88: 7[2m]
90: 2[s]
91:10+A[2]S
97: 8+AS[2]
112: 1[2]-S[1]
113:19[2]-S
114: 1[m]
115: 5-AS
8-S[1]
117: 4-S
16[2]-S[1]
118:16[t]
134: 6-S[2]
13+AS[1]
139: 5-S
141: 2[2a]
Pro. 1: 7[u]
16: 1[u]
11[v]
17: 3[a]
19:14[u]
22:23-S[1]
Isa. 5:12[m]
8:11[e]
14: 3[p], 5[w]
19:20[2]-S[1]
25: 9-AS
28:21-A
30:30[w]
31: 1[w]
33: 6[m]
36:10[2]-A
37:14[1]-AS[3]
17[1]-AS
17[3] AS
18 ABS
42:10[m]
45: 8[x]
18[2]-ABS
19-A
49:26-A
52: 9-S[1]
55: 6[y]
60:14+ABS
20[z]
62: 4-AS

Isa. 62: 9-S[1]
63: 7+A
66:23-A[1x]
Jer. 1:12-S[1]
13-S[1]
2: 9+AB[a]S[a]
4: 3-A
5: 3-A
11-AS
9: 3-ABS
6-ABS
25-S[1]
11:21[1e]
15: 2[c]
16:10[1]-S[1]
18:23[h]
20:3+ABS
25:12+A
16[1]-S
29[2]-B
35[2]-A
25:12+A
26:23[eo]
27:20+A
28: 7[o]
12-S[1]
57-S[1]
33:10+A
19[2]-A
34:18[q]
35: 6+A
38:38[2z]
39: 3-S[1]
41:12-S[1]
43:27-S[1]
49:15[2]-S[1]
19-S[1]
51:34-S
52:17[2]-A
Lam. 1:11-A
2: 7-BS
8+A

Lam. 3:22-AB
24-AB
39-A
54-A
Eze. 7:19+A
9: 4+A
9[2]-A
11: 5[1]-B
12 A
13: 7+A
20:26+A
21: 3[c]
9[aa]
24:20[bb]
26:14[1]-A
34: 9+A
36:36[2h]
37:14[2h]
39: 7[h]
41:22-B[1]
48:35+A
Dan. 9:14[1e]
Joel 1: 9[2]-ABS
3:16[1]-S[1]
Amos 3:15-B
4: 3[e]
5: 8[e]
9: 6[e], 12[e]
Jon. 1:14[3]-S[1]
2:11-ABS[1]
Nah. 1: 2[2]-ABS
Hab. 3: 2+S
Zeph. 1: 5-A
2: 2[1]-S[3]
Hag. 1:13[1]-S[1]
13[2]-AS[2]
Zec. 4:10+AS
14:12-S[1]

[a] A θεός. [b] AB[a] κ. ὁ θεός. [c] AB θεός. [d] A πλῆθος. [e] A κ. ὁ θεός. [f] A Ἰούδας. [g] A Ἰησοῦς. [h] A κύριος κ. [i] A[2] θεός. [k] B θεός. [m] S[1] θεός. [n] C[1] θεός. [o] S θεός. [p] AS[2] θεός. [q] S κ. ὁ θεός. [r] S[2] κ. ὁ θεός. [s] B[1]S[1] θεός. [t] S[1] κύριος κ. [u] BS θεός. [v] C θεός. [w] AS θεός. [x] S[1] κ. ὁ θεός. [y] AS[3] θεός. [z] S[1] λαός. [aa] A[2] Ἀδωναὶ κ. [bb] A Ἀδωναὶ κ.

Jehovah Adon.

Nehemiah 10:29[a]

[a] S[3] θεός.

Jehovah Adonai.

Psa. 67:21[a]

[a] S[2] κύριος κ.

Jehovah Elohim.

Exo. 8:10
9:30[a]
Nu. 10: 9
Deu. 4: 5[b]
9: 5
15:20[b]
18: 5[b], 12[b]
30: 1[b], 3
3[b], 6
Jos. 4: 5
22:29[b]
23:13, 15
15[b]
24:24
1 Sa. 12:14
13:13
2 Sa. 5:10[b]
7:22[c], 25
1 Ki. 15: 4[b]
17:14[b], 20
1 Ch. 11: 2[b]

1 Ch. 22:18
2 Ch. 36: 5
Psa. 83:12
Isa. 60: 9
Jer. 5:14
7:28
14:22-AS
21: 4
23: 2
33:13
40: 4[d]
41: 2, 13[b]
42:17-A
44: 3, 7
45:17
49: 5, 9, 13
20, 20
50: 1[b], 1[b]
2
51:32
Amos 6:14-A

[a] B θεός. [b] A κ. ὁ θεός. [c] AB κυριος κ. [d] AS κ. ὁ θεός.

Jehovah Sabaoth Elohim.

Jer. 28:33
35: 2, 14
36: 8
38:23
39:15

Jer. 42:13, 18
49:15, 18
50:10
51:11

Artz, Baal, Shaddai, etc.

Gen. 27:29, 37
49:23
Exo. 21: 8, 28
20, 29
34, 34
36
22: 8, 11
12[a], 14
15
Nu. 22:13
Jos. 9: 9[b]
Jud. 19:22, 23
27 A[c]
1 Sa. 17:32
2 Ki. 4: 7 A[d]
2 Ch. 15: 5
Job 6: 4, 14

Job 13: 3
15:25
21:20
22: 3, 23
26
24: 1
31:35, 39
Ps. 103:16 S[1e]
Isa. 1: 3
17:10
54: 5
Jer. 43:13[f]
Lam. 3:38 A[g]
Dan. 2:38, 47
4:14, 16
21
5:23†

[a] A πλησίος. [b] A Ἰησοῦς. [c] pro ἀνήρ. [d] pro ἄνθρωπος. [e] pro πεδιον. [f] S[1] κ. ὁ θεός pro λαός. [g] pro τίς. † κ. ὁ θεός.

Nihil in Hebrew.

Gen. 4:10
16: 8
39: 4
43: 2-A
Exo. 8:27-A
10: 7+A
23 B[b]
32
17:15-A
18: 9+A
19:24
24: 1, 16
28:12+A
29:10
31:14-A
34:10, 34
35: 3
39:12
Lev. 1:10
2: 4, 12
14
3: 1
2-A
13, 16
4: 2
6:29, 32
10: 1, 18
11:45
14:20
16:15
21:24+A
23: 3, 13
24:16
25:36
Nu. 1:53+B
2: 2+A
5: 9
11:25+A
15: 5
16:22
20:16
29: 8-A
11
31: 3
Deu. 4:31-AB[1]
5:14+B[1]
6: 4
10+B
25+B
7: 7-AB
8-A
13
8:18-A
9:28+A
11:25+A
13:17+A
14:16

Deu. 19: 8
30: 8+B
31:11[c], 23
32: 4, 37
43
Jos. 1:13+A
3: 6, 6
14-B
15-A
4: 8, 9
16
6: 9
9:33
10:10, 35
13:14
22:19-A
24: 5+A
7, 8
11-A
31, 33
Jud. 2: 1[d]
16-A
17+A
4: 8
24+A
5:14+A
6: 8+A
16
7: 3+A
15
8:22-A[2]
10:15+A
13:19+A
19:26+A
20: 2-A
3+A
28-A
Ruth 3:13+B
1 Sa. 1: 6
8-A
9, 11
14, 24
24
2:10, 10
11, 14
23
4: 7
5: 3
6:13, 20
7:13
10: 1, 2
12:23
14:26
15:13, 23
16:12
17:47
20:21+B
22:11+A

1 Sa. 22:18
23: 9
24:16
25:30+A
30:23
2 Sa. 2: 5-A
5: 8, 23
6:21-A
14:15-AB
22
15:20
22: 8
23: 1
4-A
24:22
1 Ki. 2:29, 35
(3)46+A
6: 6+A
(11)A
7:31
8: 1-A
21, 53
11:10-A
33+A
12:30-AB
14:16 A
16:24
p 28-A
18:31+A
36-A
19: 4+A
12+A
20:27, 28
22: 7
2 Ki. 1:18, 18
8:13+A
11: 4+A
13:23
16:18, 18
17:12
20-A
23
26+A
32
21: 9
22: 9, 9
1 Ch. 10:14+A
15:27
16: 9
21:17
18+A[2]
24
23: 5
28:20
29:12
2 Ch. 3: 1
5:14+A[2]
23: 1-B
25: 4
26:18
28:13[e]
18-A
29:31-A
35:18
19 qnq
36: 2, 5, 5
5, 5
Ezra 1: 9+B
6:22+A
7:15
Neh. 8: 8
8+S
9: 3
Job 1:20+AS[2]
21, 22
7: 2
13:11+A
32: 9+C
33:23
36:12, 33
37: 1
39:34
42: 4
9+S[2]
Psa. 2: 7, 12
5: 6-S
11
12: 6
16: 8+S[2]
19: 5+AS[2]

Psa. 21:32
24:14+AB
21-S
25:11+AS[2]
26: 6+A
28: 1
30: 5-BS[1]
20-S
23-AS
32: 5+AS[2]
33:21+AS[2]
34:18+B
23
24-S
39:17
41: 7+AS[1]
42: 4+B
43:27
47:12-S[1]
50:20-S[1]
54:24
58: 2+S[1]
67:20
69: 5+S[2]
71:17+S[2]
74:10+S[1]
78: 8+S
9
82: 4+A
83: 6-S[2]
12
84: 8+AB
87: 3-S
89: 4+AS[2]
93:19-AS[2]
23+AS[2]
94: 4-AS
96:10
97: 1
101:26-S[1]
102:11
105:44-S
110: 9+S[2]
118: 7+AS[1]
64+S[1]
68, 85
93+S
94+S[1]
97
124+A
168-S[1]
170-S[1]
120: 7-S[1]
124: 3-AS[1]
135:23-S[1]
137: 1
8+BS[1]
138:13
141: 8-S[2]
142: 8
8+S[2]
144:14
Pro. 3:18, 34
7: 1
8:26
10: 6
17:11
21:27
22:11
23:11
24: 7, 12
29:23
Isa. 2: 1+AS
11
4: 5+A
5:13
8:10
9: 4+AS
10:12+S
12: 2+S
14:26
19:17+A
20+AS
23:18
24: 5+A
25: 1+AS
26:20
27: 4[f]

Isa. 27: 4+S[1]
28: 2+S[1]
29:24+S
30:12+AS
33:18+A
22+A[2]
22
37:4-AS[3g]
17, 17
30+S[1]
39: 6+A
44:14
49:15−S[1]
53: 1
57: 6+S
15+AS[3]
15+AS[1]
58: 6
63: 7
9+AS[1]
64: 2+AS[3]
65: 8+AS[2]
Jer. 1:17
2:31
3: 2+A
19
5: 1, 13
6:16
7:23+S
10:12
14: 8
16:21+S
20: 9
23:36+AS[3]
26:10
27:21
28:15-ABS
27+S[1]
57, 59
32:19
35: 7
38:36+A
39: 1+A
19, 19
43: 7+A
45:27
Lam. 1:13+A
Lam. 2: 8+A
3:22−AB
4:21
Eze. 3:14+A
23−AB
4:15+A
16+A
7:10
11: 2
20+A
25+A
18:31+A
33:20+A
34:15
35:13+A
36:32+A
37: 7+A
23
28+A
38:20
43: 2+A
44:11+A
Dan. 2:47+A
3:23
27+AB[2]
9: 7+A
9+A
18
19+A
Hos. 6: 9+A
Joel 2: 1+A
Amos 5: 1
25+A
7: 4−A
9:12+A
Jon. 1: 9
Hab. 3: 9
Zeph. 1: 6
Hag. 1: 6+A
Zec. 1:17+A
19, 21
3: 1
5: 2+S
14:18+A
Mal. 1: 2+S
2: 4+A
4: 1+A

[a] A θεός. [b] pro Μωυσῆς.
[c] A κ. ὁ θεός. [d] A κύριος κ.
[e] B κ. ὁ θεός. [f] AS[3] κ. ὁ θεός.
[g] S[1] κ. ὁ θεός.

κύριος Ἀδωναΐ.

Adonai.

Jud. 13: 8[a] [a] A κύριος.

Ἀδωναΐ κύριος.

Adonai Jehovah.

Jud. 16:28[a]
Eze. 33:25+A
Eze. 36:23+A
33[b], 37[c]

[a] A κύριος κ. [b] A κ. ὁ θεός.
[c] A κ. κ. ὁ θεός.

Ἀδωναΐ κύριος Ἐλωί.

Jehovah 1 Sa. 1:11

κύριος ὁ θεός.

Adon.

Zeph. 1: 9[a] [a] S[3] κύριος.

Adon Jehovah.

Exodus 23:17

Adon Jehovah Elohim.

Exo. 34:23 | Isa. 51:22

Adonai.

Psalm 67:20

Adonai El.

Psa. 85:15 | Dan. 9: 4

Adonai Elohim.

Psa. 37:16
85:12
Dan. 9: 3, 9, 15

Adonai Jehovah.

Deu. 3:24[a]
Isa. 25: 8[b]
Jer. 26:10
27:25[c]
Eze. 4:14[d]
43:18, 19
44: 6, 9, 12
15, 27
45: 9, 9, 15
18
Eze. 46: 1, 16[e]
47:13, 23
48:29
Amos 3: 7, 8
11
7: 1[c]
9: 8
Obad. 1
Zeph. 1: 7

[a] A κύριος κ. [b] A θεός.
[c] A κύριος. [d] A κ. κ. θεός.
[e] A Ἀδωναΐ κ.

Adonai Jehovah Sabaoth.

Jeremiah 2:19

El.

Isaiah 43:12

El Jehovah.

Psa. 84: 9 | Isa. 42: 5

Elah, Elohim.

Gen. 6:12, 13[a]
22
8:15
9:12
Exo. 8:25[b]
Lev. 19:14[1]
21: 7, 8
25:17, 43
Deu. 31:17
Jos. 24:27
Jud. 20:27[c]
1 Sa. 6: 3
1 Ki. 8:26
18:36
21:23 A[d]
1 Ch. 17:25-BS[c]
2 Ch. 2: 5[e]
9: 8
17: 4
20:12, 33
34: 3
Ezra 7:12[b]
9: 9
Neh. 13:14
Psa. 79: 8
Isa. 51:20
Eze. 8: 4
34:31
Dan. 9:17
10:12[b]
Hos. 2:23
Mic. 6: 8

[a] A θεός. [b] B θεός. [c] A κύριος.
[d] pro θεός. [e] AB θεός.

Jehovah.

Gen. 4: 6, 9[a]
13[b], 15
15, 26
5:29
6: 3, 5
8
7: 1, 16
8:21, 21
10: 9
24:40
29:31
30:30[b]
Exo. 8:22[c]
10:24, 26
12:31
13: 5, 8, 9[b]
11
15:26[b]
19:22[d]
20: 7[b]
34:14
Lev. 18: 5
19:12, 14
16, 28
32, 37
20:26
22: 3, 9
Deu. 1:41, 45[b]
2:14[b]
3:20, 21
4: 3, 21[e]
35, 39
5:11[b]
6:12, 18
7:15
8: 1[b]
20[b]
9:18
10:13
12:11[f], 14
25, 26
14: 2
15: 2, 4, 20
Deu. 16: 2, 15
16
17:10
18: 5, 7[b]
12
21: 9[a]
24: 6
28: 7, 11
13, 24[b]
64
29: 4
30: 8, 9
31: 4[b]
Jos. 1:15
2:10, 12
5: 1
22:23
23:15[b]
Jud. 3:28
Ruth 3:10[b]
1 Sa. 1: 3, 20
15:25
2 Sa. 15:31
1 Ki. 5: 5
8:59, 60[b]
11:10
18:18, 24
21:28
2 Ch. 30: 8
35: 1
Job 39:31
Psa. 91:16
Isa. 26:12
41:17, 21
42: 6, 8, 13
21
43: 1, 10
43:14, 15
44: 2
45: 1, 3, 5
6, 7, 11
Jer. 5:18
16: 1
Jer. 23:30−B
37, 38
27: 5
39:28[g]
40: 4[h]
Eze. 4:13
35:15
Hos. 6: 1
Hos. 14: 2
Joel 2:12
Jon. 2: 3−S[1]
Mic. 4:10
Nah. 3: 5
Zec. 10: 3, 12
Mal. 3: 6

[a] A θεός. [b] A κύριος.
[c] B κ. ὁ κύριος. [d] A θεός.
[e] AB* κύριος. [f] AB θεός.
[g] S κύριος. [h] ABS κύριος.

Jehovah El.

Psa. 9:33 | Psa. 30: 6

Jehovah Elohim.

Var. Lec. tantum.

Exo. 5: 3[a]
10: 8[b]
20:10[c]
Deu. 12:27−B
27−B
16:11[1b]
23:23[b]
26:10[1]−B
28:52+A
53+A
30: 7[d]
Jos. 10:42[d]
21:17[c]
Jud. 5: 3[c]
1 Sa. 6:20−B
1 Ki. 1:17[b], 36[b]
2: 3[b]
8:28[c]
13: 6[b]
14: 7 A
13 A
16:26−B
1 Ki. 16:33−B
2 Ki. 17:14+A
1 Ch. 22: 1[c]
2 Ch. 9: 8[2e]
29: 6[f]
30: 6[a]
Ezra 1: 2[b]
7: 6[2b]
9: 5[b]
15−A
10:11[g]
Neh. 9: 3[h], 3[i]
7−S[1b]
10:34[b]
Psa. 19: 8[c]
103: 1[k]
Isa. 55: 5[m]
Dan. 9: 4[1], 14[c]
20[c]
Mic. 4: 5[c]
Zec. 9:16[d]

[a] AB θεός. [b] B θεός.
[c] A θεός. [d] A κύριος.
[e] A λαός. [f] AB κύριος.
[g] BS θεός. [h] ABS θεός.
[i] BS[1] θεός. [k] B κ. κύριος.
[m] AS[3] θεός.

Jehovah Jehovah El.

Exo. 34: 6[a] [a] A κύριος κ. ὁ θεός.

Jehovah Sabaoth.

Jeremiah 26:18

Jehovah Sabaoth Elohim.

Jer. 34: 3
36: 4
Jer. 46:16
51: 2, 25

Nihil in Hebrew.

Lev. 2:13
8:35
10:23
Deu. 6:23+A
23+A
14:22+A
16:14+A
27: 7+A
28: 1+A
29:15+A[2]
30: 4−A
Deu. 30:16
18+A
Jos. 4:23
24:10[a]
1 Sa. 14:41
1 Ki. 8:65
Psa. 7: 7[b]
111: 4+A
Eze. 27:36+A
Amos 5: 7+A

[a] A κύριος. [b] S θεός.

κύριος κύριος.

Adonai Jehovah.

Jud. 6:22
2 Sa. 7:18, 19[a]
19[b], 20[a]
28, 29
1 Ki. 8:53−A
Psa. 70: 5
Isa. 22:12[c]
28:16[c]
30:15[c]
40:10[c]
48:16[c]
49:22[d]
50: 4[c], 5[c]
Isa. 50: 7[e], 9[d]
61:11
Eze. 12:10
13:20
14: 6[f]
20:39, 40
47[k], 49
21:13
22: 3[f]
19[fh]
31
23:28[f], 46[i]
26:15[k], 19
Eze. 26:21[f]
28:12[b], 25[f]
29:19[i], 20[i]
30:10[i], 13[i]
22
31:15[i], 18
32: 8[f], 11[i]
16, 31[g]
32[f]
33:27
34: 2, 8
10[i], 11[f]
15, 17
20[f], 30
31
Eze. 35: 3[b], 6
36: 2, 3[fi]
5[b], 13[i]
14[i], 15[g]
37: 3[b]
21[n]
38: 3[i], 10[f]
17[n], 18[f]
39: 8[f], 25[f]
29
Amos 5: 3
7: 2, 17[b]
8: 3[b], 9[g]
Mic. 1: 2[b]

[a] AB κύριος. [b] A κύριος.
[c] AS κύριος. [d] AB[1]S κύριος.
[e] AS[3] κύριος. [f] A κ. κ. ὁ θεός.
[g] A κ. ὁ θεός. [h] B κύριος.
[i] A Ἀδωναΐ κ. [k] A Ἀδωναΐ κ. κ.
[n] A Ἀδωναΐ κ. ὁ θ.

Jehovah.

1 Ch. 17:24
Jer. 28:62[a]
Eze. 20:38[b]

[a] S κύριος. [b] A κ. ὁ θεός.

Jehovah Adon.

Psalm 8: 2, 10

Jehovah Adonai.

Psa. 108:21
139: 8
Psa. 140: 8[a]
[a] A[1]S[1] κύριος.

κυρίος Ἐλωί.

Jehovah Jud. 5: 5

κύριος κύριος ὁ θεός.

Adonai Jehovah.

Amos 9: 5

κύριος θεὸς σαβαώθ.

Jehovah 1 Sa. 1:20

κύριος σαβαώθ.

Adonai Jehovah.

Isaiah 7: 7

κυρόω.

Gen. 23:20 | Lev. 25:30

κυρτός.

Lev. 21:20 | 1 Ki. 21:11

κύτος.

Psa. 64: 8[a] | Dan. 4: 8, 17
[a] B ὕδωρ.

κυψέλη.

Haggai 2: 16

κύω.

Isaiah 59: 4, 13

κύων.

Exo. 11: 7
22:31
Deu. 23:18
Jud. 7: 5
1 Sa. 17:43
43−A
24:15
2 Sa. 3: 8
9: 8
16: 9
1 Ki. 12p24l44
14:11 A
16: 4
20:19
19−A
1 Ki. 20:23, 24
22:38
2 Ki. 8:13−A
9:10, 36
Job 30: 1[a]
Psa. 21:17, 21
58: 7, 15
67:24
Pro. 7:22
26:11, 17
Ecc. 9: 4
Isa. 56:10, 11
66: 3
Jer. 15: 3

[a] A κοινός.

κώδιον.

Neh. 3:15−S[1], (S[3] κωλίων.)

κώδων.

Exo. 28:29, 30
36:33, 33
Exo. 36:34
2 Ch. 4:13

κώθων.

Esther (9)17–S¹

κωθωνίζω.

Esther 3:15

κωλεά.

1 Samuel 9:24

κῶλον.

Lev. 26:30, 30
Nu. 14:29, 32
33
1 Sa. 17:46, 46
Isa. 66:24

κώλυμα.

Job 13:27ᵃ

ᵃ A κύκλωμα.

κωλύω.

Gen. 23: 6
Exo. 36: 6
Nu. 11:28
1 Sa. 25:26
2 Sa. 13:13
Job 12:15
Psa. 39:10
118:101
Ecc. 8: 8
Isa. 28: 6
43: 6
Eze. 31:15+A
15ᵃ
Amos 2:13 Aᵇ
Mic. 2: 4

ᵃ B κυκλόω. ᵇ pro κυλίω.

κωμάρχης.

Esther 2: 3

κώμη.

Nu. 21:32
32:42
Jos. 10:39
13:30
15:24, 28
32, 36
41, 44
45
46–A
47, 47
51
54 Aᵃ
57, 59
59
60+A
62
16: 7, 9
17:11 *ter*
11+A
11, 16
18:24, 28
19: 6, 7, 16
23ᵇ, 31
47
21:12
1 Sa. 6:18
1 Ch. 2:23, 23
5:16
6:54, 56
7:28 *qtr*
29, 29
29+A
29, 29
8:12
9:16 18:1
27:25
2 Ch. 13:19, 19
19ᶜ
14:14
28:18
18–B
18
32:28
Neh. 6: 2
11:25+S³
Job 38:32
Cant. 7:11
Isa. 32:14
42:11
Jer. 19:15
30:14
Eze. 38:13ᵈ

ᵃ pro ἔπαυλις. ᵇ A ἔπαυλις. ᶜ A θυγατηρ. ᵈ A χώρα.

κώπη.

Ezekiel 27: 6

κωπηλάτης.

Eze. 27: 8, 9
26, 27
Eze. 27:29, 35

κωφεύω.

Jud. 16: 2
18:19
2 Sa. 13:20
2 Sa. 19:10
2 Ki. 18:36
Job 6:24
Job 13: 5, 13
19
Job 33:31, 33

κωφός.

Exo. 4:11
Lev. 19:14
Psa. 37:14
57: 5
Isa. 29:18
Isa. 35: 5
42:18, 19
43: 8
44:11
Hab. 2:18

κωφόω.

Psalm 38: 3, 10

λαβή.

Judges 3:22

λαβίς.

Exo. 38:17
Nu. 4: 9
2 Ch. 4:21
Isa. 6: 6

λάβρος.

Job 38:25, 34
Pro. 28: 3

λάγανον.

Exo. 29: 2–A
23
Lev. 2: 4
7: 2
Lev. 8:26
Nu. 6:15, 19
2 Sa. 6:19
1 Ch. 23:29

λαγχάνω.

1 Samuel 14:47

λαγωός.

Psalm 103:18 AS²ᵃ

ᵃ pro χοιρογρύλλιος.

λάθρα.

Deu. 13: 6
1 Sa. 18:22
26: 5
Job 31:27
Ps. 100: 5
Hab. 3:14

λαθραίως.

1 Samuel 24: 5

λάθριος.

Proverbs 21:14

λαῖλαψ.

Job 21:18
27:20 Sᵃ
Job 38: 1
Jer. 32:18

ᵃ pro γνόφος.

λάκκος.

Gen. 37:20, 22
24, 24
28, 29
29
40:15
Exo. 12:29
21:33
33–A
34
Lev. 11:36
Nu. 20:17
Deu. 6:11
Jud. 15:19ᵃ
1 Sa. 13: 6
2 Sa. 17:18, 19
21
23:15, 16
20
2 Ki. 18:31
1 Ch. 11:17, 18
22
2 Ch. 26:10
Neh. 9:25
Psa. 7:16
Psa. 27: 1
29: 4
39: 3
87: 5, 7
142: 7
Ecc. 12: 6
Isa. 36:16ᵇ
51: 1
Jer. 2:13
6: 7
41:16
45: 6 *ter*
7, 10
11, 13
Lam. 3:53
54–A
Eze. 31:16
32:23+A
Dan. 6: 7, 12
16, 17
19, 20
23, 23
24, 24
Zec. 9:11

ᵃ A τραῦμα. ᵇ B χαλκός.

λαλέω.

Var. Lec. tantum.

Gen. 29: 6+A
Exo. 4:16ᵃ
7:13 Aᵇ
19: 7 Bᶜ
23:13 Aᵈ
33:19 Bᵉ
34:10 Aᵉ
32 Aᵇ
Nu. 15: 1 Aᵉ
36 Aᶠ
Deu. 13:17+A
Jos. 20: 4 A
Jud. 9:38ᵍ
18: 7+A
Ruth 4: 1ʰ
1 Sa. 17:23 A
23 A
28 A
31 A
18: 1 A
2 Sa. 7:25²+A
11:18–A
1 Ki. 6(12)A
8:24²+A
26+A
12: 9 Aᵍ
13:26+A
27 A
14: 2 A, 5 A
11 A
18 A
15:29–A
20: 4+A
2 Ki. 1: 6–AB
18:26³–A
1 Ch. 17:23²–ABS
2 Ch. 6:15¹–A
Est. 2: 1–A
3: 4ⁱ
Job 2:13–S
13: 8+A
19: 7 AS²ᵏ
39:13+A
Psa. 36:30ᵐ
80: 9–AS²
144: 6+ABS¹
Ecc. 8: 4+ACS²
Isa. 15: 4 ASⁿ
16: 9 ASⁿ
44: 7 S¹ᵒ
Jer. 7:14 Aᵒ
18: 8 Aᵖ
19: 5+A
23:25–S
35–A
25: 2–S¹
28:12–S¹
41 S¹ᑫ
41: 3+A
42:14+BS
17–A
43: 2ʳ
3+A
4ʳ
Eze. 3:18+AB
13: 7+A
24:27ˢ
29: 3+A
Dan. 2: 4ᵗ
7:11+A
Jon. 4: 2+A
Hag. 2: 1ᵘ
Mal. 3:16 Aᵛ

ᵃ AB² προσλαλέω. ᵇ pro ἐντέλλω. ᶜ pro καλέω. ᵈ pro ἐρῶ. ᵉ pro εἶπον. ᶠ pro συντάσσω. ᵍ pro λέγω. ʰ AB εἶπον. ⁱ AS³ λέγω. ᵏ pro γελάω. ᵐ S¹ μελετάω. ⁿ pro Ἐλεαλή. ᵒ pro δίδωμι. ᵖ pro λογίζομαι. ᑫ pro ἁλίσκομαι. ʳ A χρηματίζω. ˢ A ἐρῶ. ᵗ A εἶπον. ᵘ S¹ λαμβάνω. ᵛ pro καταλαλέω.

λάλημα.

1 Ki. 9: 7
Eze. 23:10
Eze. 36: 3

λαλητός.

Job 38:14

λαλιά.

Job 7: 6ᵃ
29:23
33: 1
Psa. 18: 3
Ecc. 3:18
Ecc. 7:15
Cant. 4: 3
6: 5
Isa. 11: 3

ᵃ AS² δρομεύς.

λαμβάνω.

Gen. 2:15, 21
22, 23
3: 6, 19
22, 23
4:19
6: 2, 21
8: 9, 20
9:23
11:29, 31
12: 5, 19
19
14:11, 12
21, 23
24
15: 9, 10
16: 3
Gen. 17:23
18: 4, 5, 7
8
19:14, 15
20: 2, 3, 14
21:14, 18
24, 27
30
22: 2, 6, 6
10, 13
23:13
24: 3, 4, 7
7, 10
22, 37
38, 40
48, 51
Gen. 24:65, 67
25: 1, 20
21 Aᵃ
26:34
27: 3, 9, 14
15, 35
36, 36
46
28: 1, 2, 6
6, 9, 11
18
29:23
30: 9, 15
15, 37
41
31: 1
10–A
17, 32
34, 45
50
32:13, 22
23
33:11, 11
34: 2, 4, 9
16, 17
21, 25
26, 28
36: 2, 6
37:24, 31
38: 2, 6, 18
28
39:20
40:11
42:16, 24
33, 36
43:10, 11
12, 14
14, 17
44:29
45:19
47:23
48:13, 22
Exo. 2: 1, 2, 3
9, 22
4: 9, 9, 17
20, 25
6: 7, 20
23, 25
7: 9, 15
19
9: 8, 10
10:26
12: 3, 5, 7
21, 22
13:19
14: 7
15:14, 15
20
16:33
17: 5, 5, 12
18: 2, 12
20: 7, 7
21:10, 14
23: 8
24: 6, 7, 8
25: 2, 2, 3
27:20
28: 5, 9, 23
29: 1, 5, 7
12, 13
15, 16
19–A
20, 21
22, 25ᵇ
26, 31
30:12, 16
23, 34
32:20
33: 7
34: 4, 16
35: 5
36: 3
40: 7, 18
Lev. 4: 5, 30
34
5: 1, 17
7: 8, 24
8: 2, 10
15, 16
23, 25
Lev. 8:26, 28
29, 30
9: 2, 3, 5
15
10: 1, 12
12: 8
14: 4, 6, 10
12, 14
15, 21
24, 25
42, 42
49, 51
15:14, 29
16: 5, 7, 12
14, 18
22
17:16
18:17, 18
19: 8, 15
17
20:14, 17
21
21: 7, 13
14, 14
22: 9
23:40
24: 2, 5, 15
25:36
Nu. 1: 2, 17
49
3: 6, 12ᶜ
40, 41
45, 47
47, 49
50
4: 2, 9, 12
14, 22
5:17, 17
25, 31
6:19
7: 5, 6
8: 6, 8, 8
16, 18
9:13
11:12, 12
12: 1, 1
13:21
14:34
16: 6, 15
17, 18
39, 46
47
47+A
17: 2, 9
18: 1, 1, 6
22, 23
26, 28
32
19: 2, 4, 6
17, 18
20: 8, 9, 25
21:25, 26
25: 4, 7
26: 2
27:18, 22
30:16
31:11, 26
29, 30
47, 49
51, 54
32:39, 41
42
34:14, 15
18
35:31, 32
Deu. 1:15, 23
25
2: 6, 35
3: 4, 8, 14
4:20, 34
5:11, 11
7: 3, 25
9: 9, 21
10:17
12:26
14:24
15:17
16:19
19:12
20: 7, 7

Deu. 21: 3, 11
22: 6,7,13
14, 15
18, 30
24: 3, 5, 6
7,7,21
25: 5, 7, 8
26: 2, 4
27:25
28:30, 56
29: 8
30: 4, 12
13
31:26
Jos. 2: 4
4: 8 AB[d]
20
6:18
7: 1, 21
24
8: 1
21—A
9:10, 17
20
10: 1, 28
30, 32
35, 39
42 A[e]
11:12, 16
17
19[f]
19, 23
15:10, 17
16:10
18: 7
21:42
24: 3, 26
33
Jud. 1: 6[g], 24
3: 6, 21
25
4: 6, 21
5:19
6:20, 25
26, 27
7: 5 A[h]
5 A[h]
8
20 A[i]
8:16, 21
9:43[j], 48
48 A[k]
11: 5[j], 13
15
13:19, 23[b]
14: 2, 3, 3
8
11—A
19
15: 4,6,15
16:12, 14[m]
31
17: 2, 2, 4
18:17+A
18, 20
24, 27
19: 1, 28[n]
29
20:10, 10
21:22, 23
Ruth 1: 4
4: 2, 13
16
1 Sa. 2:14, 15
16, 16
4: 3, 11
17, 19
22
22+A
5: 1, 2
6: 7,8,10
7: 9, 12
14
8: 3, 11
13, 14
16
9: 3, 22
10: 1,4,23
11: 7
12: 3 *ter*

1 Sa. 12: 4
14:32
42 A[o]
15:21
16: 2, 11
13, 20
23
17:17 A
20 A
34, 40
49, 51
54
18: 2 A
19:13, 14
20
20:21, 31
21: 6, 8
9 A[p]
9, 9
24: 3, 12
25:11, 18
21, 27
27+A
35, 39
40, 43
26:11, 12
22
27: 9
28:24
30:11, 16
18, 19
20
31: 4, 12
13
2 Sa. 1:10
2: 8, 21
3:14, 15
4: 7
5:13, 21
7: 8
8: 1, 7, 7
8
9: 5
10: 4
11: 4, 5
12: 4, 4, 9
10, 11
30
13: 8,9,10
19
14: 2, 14
17:13, 19
18:14, 17
18—AB
18, 18
19:30
20: 3, 6
21: 8, 10
12
22:17[a]
23: 6, 16
24:22
1 Ki. 1:33, 39
(3) 1
p 46+A
3:20, 24
4:15
30—A
7: 1, 3[q]
45
8:31
9:28
10:28
11: 1, 12
13, 18
31, 34
35, 37
12 *p* 24 *l* 29
l 31, 50,
l 52, 53
14: 3 A
26 *ter*
26+A
15:18
16:31
17:10, 11
11, 19
23+A
18: 4, 26
31, 34

1 Ki. 19: 4, 10
14, 21
21: 6, 21
33, 34
22: 3, 26
2 Ki. 2: 3, 5, 8
14, 20
20
3:14, 15[r]
26, 27
4: 1, 17
29, 36
37, 41
5: 5, 15
16, 16
20, 20
23
23—A
24, 26
26
6: 2,7,13
7: 8, 13
14
8: 8,9,15
9: 1,3,13
17, 25
10: 6, 7
15 B[s]
11: 2, 4, 9
19
12: 4—A
4 B[t], 5
7, 8, 9
18
13:15, 15
18, 18
25, 25
14:13 A[u]
14, 21
15:29
16: 8
18:32
19: 4, 14
20: 7
7+A
17, 18
23: 4 B[o]
16, 30
34
24: 7, 12
25:14, 15
18, 19
20
1 Ch. 2:18[a], 19
21, 23
4:18
7:15, 21
23
10: 4,9,12
11:8+ABS
18
14: 3
15:15
16:29
17: 7
18: 1, 7, 8
11
19: 4
20: 2
21:18 A[z]
23, 24
23:22
24:31
26:27
27:23
2 Ch. 5: 4
6:22
8:18
11:18, 20
12: 9 *ter*
13:21
14:15
16: 2, 6[v], 6
18:25
19: 7
22:11
23: 1, 8, 20
24: 3
26: 1
28:18, 21

2 Ch. 36: 1, 4
Ezra 1: 4, 7
2:61
5:15
9: 2, 12
10: 2 S3[w]
10 S3[w]
14 S3[w]
18 S3[w]
44
Neh. 2: 1
5: 2,3,15
6:18
7:63
10:30
11: 1 BS1[o]
13:25
Est. 6:10+S3
11
8: 2
Job 2: 8
15:35
16:12
31:37
34:31
35: 7
38:14
40:23
42: 8, 8
p 18
Psa. 14: 3, 5
17:17
23: 4, 5
30:14
48:16, 18
67:19
68:25 S1[x]
74: 3
77:71
80: 3
81: 2
108: 8
115: 4
138: 9 S1[d]
20
Pro. 7:20
8:10
9: 7
11:21
17:23
18:22
22:25, 27
Ecc. 5:14, 18
Isa. 2: 4
6: 6
7:14[y]
8: 1, 3, 4
10: 9,9,10
10, 29
14: 2, 4
15: 7
19: 9
20: 1[s]
21: 3
22: 6
23: 5, 16
26:11, 18
28: 4, 19
30:28
31: 4
33:14
36: 1[aa]
17
37:14
38:21
39: 6, 7
40:24[bb]
41:16
44:15
47: 2, 3
49:24, 25
25
51:22
52: 5
57:11, 13
64: 1, 3
66:21
Jer. 3:14
9:10, 18
13: 4, 6, 7,

Jer. 15:15
16: 1
20:10
23:39
25: 9
26:11
27:24
28: 8, 26
32
30: 7, 7
31: 1, 41
32: 1, 3
34:17
35:10
36: 6
6—S1
22
38: 4[cc]
19
39: 3—S1
11, 14
23, 28
33
41:22
42:13
43: 2, 14
14, 21
21, 28
32
45:10, 11
11
46:14
47: 1, 2
49:16
50: 5, 9
52:17, 19
24
25+A
26, 31
Lam. 4:16
Eze. 3:10
4: 1, 3, 4
5, 6, 9
5: 1, 1, 2
3, 4
10: 6, 7, 7
14:10
15: 3, 3
16:16, 17
18, 20
32, 39
52
17: 3,5,12
13, 13
22
18: 8, 13
17, 19
20, 20
19: 1, 5
22:12, 12
25

Eze. 23:10, 25
26, 29
35, 49
24: 5, 16
25
26:17
27: 2,5,32
28:12
29:14
19+A
30: 4+A
32: 2, 24
30 A[dd]
33: 2, 6, 6
25 A
36: 7, 24
30
37:16, 16
19, 21
38:13
39:10, 26
43:11, 20
21, 22
44:10
12+A
13, 22
22
45:11, 18
19
20—B
46:18
Dan. 2: 6
11:12
Hos. 1: 2, 3
4: 8
5:14
13: 1
14: 2 *ter*
Joel 3: 5
Amos 2:11
4: 2
5: 1, 12
6:10
9: 3
Jon. 1:15
4: 3
Mic. 1:11
2: 4
6:16
Hab. 1: 3
2: 6
Zeph. 3:18
Hag. 2: 1 S1[ee]
12, 23
Zec. 6:10, 11
13
11: 7, 10
13, 15
14:21
Mal. 1: 8, 9
2: 3,9,13

Isa. 62: 1
Eze. 1:13
Dan. 5: 5
Dan. 10: 6
Nah. 2: 5
Zec. 12: 6—S1

[a] *pro* συλλαμβάνω.
[b] A δέχομαι. [c] A ἀλείφω.
[d] *pro* ἀναλαμβάνω.
[e] *pro* πατάσσω. [f] A παραδίδωμι.
[g] B1 καταλαμβάνω.
[h] *pro* λάπτω. [i] *pro* κρατέω.
[j] A παραλαμβάνω. [k] *pro* αἴρω.
[m] A διάζομαι. [n] A ἀναλαμβάνω.
[o] *pro* βάλλω. [p] *pro* ἐνειλέω.
[q] A δίδωμι. [r] A εἰδέω.
[s] *pro* εὑρίσκω. [t] *pro* ἀναβαίνω. [u] B γεννάω.
[v] A ἄγω. [w] *pro* καθίζω.
[x] *pro* καταλαμβάνω. [y] AS ἔχω.
[z] AS καταλαμβάνω. [aa] A συλλαμβάνω. [bb] AS3 ἀναλαμβάνω.
[cc] BS ἐπιλαμβάνω. [dd] *pro* ἀποφέρω. [ee] *pro* λαλέω.

λαμπάδιον.

Exo. 38:16, 16
1 Ki. 7:35
Zec. 4: 2, 3

λαμπάς.

Gen. 15:17
Exo. 20:18
Jud. 7:16
Jud. 7:20—A
15: 4, 4, 5
Job 41:10

λαμπήνη.

Jud. 5:10 A[a]
1 Sa. 26: 5, 7
Isa. 66:20

[a] *pro* κριτήριον.

λαμπηνικός.

Numbers 7: 3

λαμπρότης.

Psa. 89:17
109: 3
Isa. 60: 3
Dan. 12: 3

λαμπτήρ.

Pro. 16:28
20:20
Pro. 21: 4
24:20

λάμπω.

Pro. 4:18
Isa. 4: 2 A[a]
9: 2
Lam. 4: 7
Dan. 12: 3[b]

[a] *pro* ἐπιλάμπω. [b] A ἐκλάμπω.

λανθάνω.

Lev. 4:13
5: 3,4,15
Nu. 5:13, 27
2 Sa. 17:22
18:13
Job 24: 1
28:21
34:21
Isa. 40:26

λαξευτήριον.

Psalm 73: 6

λαξευτός.

Deuteronomy 4:49

λαξεύω.

Exo. 34: 1, 4
Nu. 21:20
23:14
Deu. 3:27
Deu. 10: 1, 3
Isa. 9:10
Eze. 40:42, 43

λαός.

Gen. 14:16
19: 4
28: 7, 12
13
25: 8, 23
23, 23
26:11
32: 7
33:15
34:22
35: 6
41:40, 55
42: 6
47:21
48:19
49:16, 29
33
50:20
Exo. 1:20, 22
3: 7, 10
12, 21
4:16, 21
23, 30
31, 31
5: 1, 4, 5
6,7,10
12, 16
22, 23
23
6: 7
7: 4,14,16
8: 1,3,4,8
8+A
9,9,11
20, 21
21, 22
Exo. 8:23, 23
29, 29
31, 32
9: 1, 2, 7
13, 14
15, 17
27
10: 3, 4
11: 2, 3, 8
12:27, 31
33, 34
36
13: 3, 17
17, 18
22
14: 3, 5, 5
6, 13
31
15:13, 16
16, 24
16: 4, 27
30
17: 1, 2, 3
3, 4, 5
5, 6, 13
18: 1
1+A
13, 13
14 *ter*
15, 18
19, 21
22, 23
26
19: 5, 7, 8
8, 8
9, 9, 10

Exo. 19:11, 12
14, 15
16, 17
18, 21
23, 24
25
20:18, 18
21
22:25 A[1b]
28
23:22
24: 2, 3, 3
7, 8
30:33, 38
31:14
32: 1, 1, 3
6,7,11
12, 14
17, 21
22, 25
28, 30
31, 34
35
33: 1, 3, 4
5,8,10
10, 12
13, 16
16
34: 9, 10
10
36: 5, 6
Lev. 4: 3, 27
7:10, 11
15, 17
9: 7, 15
15, 18
22, 23
23, 24
16:15, 24
24 – A
17: 4,9,10
18:29
19: 8, 18
20: 3, 5, 6
21: 4
14 – A
15
23:29, 30
26:12
Nu. 5:21, 27
9:13
11: 1, 2, 8
11, 12
13, 14
16, 17
18, 21
24, 24
29, 32
33, 33
34, 35
35
12:15
13: 1, 19
31, 33
14: 1,9,11
13, 14
15
16 – A
19, 39
15:26, 30
16:41, 46
47, 47
20: 1,3,24
21: 2, 4, 5
6 *ter*
7, 7
16 – A
23, 29
33, 34
35
22: 3, 5, 5
6, 11
12, 17
41
23: 9, 24
24:14, 14
25: 1, 2, 4
4 A[c]
27:13
31: 2, 3

Nu. 33:14
Deu. 2: 4, 16
32, 33
3: 1, 2, 3
28
4: 6, 10
20
5:28
7: 6, 6
9: 2,6,12
13, 13
26, 27
29
10:11
13: 9
14: 2,2,20
16:18
17: 7, 13
16
18: 3
20: 1, 2, 5
8, 9, 9
11
21: 8, 8
26:15, 18
19
27: 9, 11
12, 15
16, 17
18, 19
20, 21
22, 23
23 – A
24, 25
26
28: 9
29:13
31: 7, 12
16
32: 6,9,36
43, 43
44 + A
44, 50
50
33: 3, 5, 7
21[a], 29
Jos. 1: 2,6,10
11, 11
3: 3, 5, 6
6, 14
14, 16
17
4: 1,2,10
10, 11
19
6: 4, 5, 7
10, 20
20, 20
7: 3, 3, 5
7, 11
13, 16
24[b]
8: 3
5 + A
10, 10
11, 14
9: 6
10: 5,7,21
29 A[d]
33
11: 7
14: 8
17:14, 15
17
24: 2, 16
19, 21
22, 24
25, 27
28
Jud. 1:16
2: 3 + A
4, 6, 7
4:13
5: 2,9,11
12 + A
13 – A
14 + A
18
7: 1, 2, 3
3, 4, 5

Jud. 7: 6, 7, 8
8: 5
9:29, 32
33, 34
35, 36
36, 37
38, 42
43, 43
45, 48
48
10:16 + A
18
11:11, 20
21, 23
12: 2
14: 3, 16
17
16:24, 30
18: 7
9 + A
10, 20
22 + A
27
20: 2 + A
2, 8
10 + A
16 – A
25 + A
26, 31
31
21: 2, 4, 9
10 + A
15
Ruth 1: 6, 10
14, 15
16, 16
2:11
3:11
4: 4,9,10
11
1 Sa. 2: 8, 12
23, 24
4: 3,4,17
5:10, 11
6: 4, 19
19
7: 9
8: 7, 10
19, 21
9: 9, 12
13, 16
16, 16
17
10: 1,1,11
17, 23
23, 24
24, 25
25
11: 4, 4, 5
7, 11
12, 14
15
12: 5,6,18
19, 20
22, 22
13: 2, 5, 6
7, 8
11, 14
15 *ter*
16, 22
14: 3, 15
17, 20
23, 24
24, 26
26, 27
28 *ter*
30 *to* 34
39, 40
41, 41
42, 42
45 *ter*
15: 1 + A
4, 8, 9
15, 20
21, 24
30
17:27 A
30 A
18: 5 A
13, 16

1 Sa. 23: 8
24:10
26: 5, 7, 7
14, 15
27:12
30: 6,6,21
21
31: 9
2 Sa. 1: 2
4 – A
4, 12
2:26, 27
28, 30
3:31, 32
34, 35
36, 36
37
5: 2
2 – AB
12
6: 2, 18
19, 19
21
7: 7
8 – A
10, 11
23 *ter*
24, 24
8:15
10: 6, 10
12, 13
11: 7, 17
12:28, 29
31, 31
13:34
14:13, 15
15 AB[f]
15:12
18 – A
23, 23
24, 30
16: 6
14 – A
15 A[g]
18
17: 2, 3, 3
8, 9
16, 22
29, 29
18: 1, 2, 2
4
5 – A
6, 7, 8
8 – A
16, 16
19: 2, 2, 3
3, 8, 8
9, 39
40 A[h]
40, 40
20:12, 15
22
22:28, 44
44, 48
23:10, 11
24: 2, 2, 3
4, 9
10, 15
15, 16
17, 21
1 Ki. 1:39, 40
(3) *p* 1
3: 2 – B
8, 8, 9[i]
9
4:30
5: 7
16 + A
6(13) A
8:16, 16
30 – A
32, 33
34[k]
36 A[m]
36, 36[k]
38 + A
41, 43
43, 44
51, 52
53, 56

1 Ki. 8:59 – B
60, 66
66
9: 7, 23 A
10 *p* 22
12: 3, 6, 7
9, 10
13, 15
16, 23
p 24 *t* 54
t 57, 59
t 60, 61
t 61, 64
t 65, 67
t 69, 72
t 79
27, 27
28, 30
31
13:33
14: 2 A, 7 A
7 A
15:22 + A
16: 2[i], 2
16, 21
21, 21
22
22 – B
18:21 + A
21, 22
24, 30
30
36 – A
37, 37
39, 40
19:21
20: 9
12 – B
13 + A
21: 8, 10
15, 42
42
22: 4, 4
28 + A
44
2 Ki. 3: 7, 7
4:13, 41
42, 43
6:30
7:16, 17
20
8:21
9: 6
10: 9, 18
11:13, 13
14, 17
17, 17
18, 19
20
12: 3, 8
13: 7
14: 4, 21
15: 4, 5
10 + A
35
16:15
18:26
20: 5
21:24, 24
22: 4, 13
23: 2, 3, 6
21, 30
35
25: 3, 11
18, 19
22, 26
1 Ch. 5:25
10: 9
11: 2, 13
12:18
13: 4
14: 2
16: 2, 8
20
24 ABS
36, 43
17: 6, 7, 9
10
13 S[1n]
21 *ter*

1 Ch. 17:22, 22
18:14
19: 6,7,11
13 – BS
14
20: 3, 3
21: 3
3 + A
5, 17
17, 22
22:18
23:25
24: 1 AB[h]
24
28: 2, 21
29: 9, 14
17, 18
2 Ch. 1: 9, 10
10, 11
14
2:11, 18
6: 5, 5, 6
21, 24
25, 27
27, 29
32, 33
33, 34
39
7: 4,5,10
10, 13
14
8: 7, 10
9: 8 A[o]
10: 5, 6, 7
9, 10
12, 15
16
13: 9, 17
14:13
16:10
17: 9
18: 2, 3, 3
27
19: 4
20: 7 – B
21, 25
33
21: 9, 14
19
23: 5,6,10
12, 13
16, 16
17, 20
20, 21
24:10, 20
23, 23
25:11, 15
15
26: 1, 21
27: 2
29:36, 36
30: 3, 13
18, 20
24, 27
31: 4,8,10
32: 4, 6, 8
13, 13
14, 15
17, 17
18
19 – B
33:10, 17
25, 25
34:30
35: 3, 5, 7
8, 12
13
36: 1,4,14
15, 16
23
Ezra 1: 3
2: 2 – B
70
3: 1
3 – B
11, 13
13 – B
13
4: 4, 4
5:12

Ezra 6:12
7:13, 16
25
8:15, 36
9: 1, 1, 2
11, 14
10: 1, 2, 9
11, 13
Neh. 1: 8, 10
4:13, 14
19, 22
5: 1, 13
15, 18
19
6: 1 S[1p]
7: 4, 5
7[q]
71 – AB
72
8: 1,3,5,5
5, 6, 7
7, 8, 9
9,9,11
12, 13
16
9:10 – S[1]
22, 24
30, 32
10:14, 28
28, 30
31, 34
11: 1,1,2[r]
24
12:30
38 S[3]
13: 1
24 + S[3]
24 + S[3]
Est. 4: 8
11 + S[3]
7: 3[s], 4
8: 6
11 + S[3]
Job 18:19
31:30
34 A[t]
34:30
36:20, 31
Psa. 2: 1
3: 7, 9
7: 8, 9
9: 9
13: 4, 7
17:28, 44
44, 48
21: 7, 32
26: 4 S[1u]
27: 8, 9
28:11, 11
32:10, 12
34:18
43: 3, 13
15
44: 6, 11
13
18 – A[1]
46: 4, 10
47:10
49: 4, 7
52: 5, 7
55: 1, 8
56:10
59: 5
61: 9 – S[1]
66: 3 S[1v]
4, 4, 5
6, 6
67: 8, 31
36
71: 2, 3, 4
72:10
73:14, 18
76:15, 16
21
77: 1, 20
52, 62
78:13
80: 9, 12
14
82: 4

Psa. 84: 3, 7, 9
86: 6
88: 4 + S[1]
16, 20
93: 5,8,14
94: 4 – AS
7
95: 3, 10
13
96: 6
97: 9
98: 1, 2
99: 3
101:19, 23
104:13, 20
24, 25
43, 44
105: 4, 40
48
106:32
107: 4
110: 6, 9
112: 8
113: 1
115: 5 – AS
9
116: 1
118:11 + S[1w]
124: 2
134:12[x], 14
135:16
22 S[2m]
143: 2, 15
15
148:11, 14
14
149: 4, 7
Pro. 14:28
24:39
29: 2
Ecc. 4:16
Isa. 1: 3, 4, 7
10
2: 4, 6
3: 5,7,12
12, 13
14, 15
5:13, 25
6: 5, 8, 9
10
7: 2,8,17
8: 6, 11
12
9: 2, 3, 9
13, 16
19
10: 2, 6
22, 24
11:11, 16
13:14
14:20, 32
18: 2, 7, 7
19:25
24: 2
25: 3, 8
26: 2, 11
20
27:11
28: 5, 11
14
29:13, 14
30: 5,9,19
26
32:13, 18
33: 3, 19
19, 24
34: 1, 5
35: 2
40: 1
42: 5, 22
43: 8, 21
45:13
47: 6
48:20 A[m]
21
49:13, 13
51: 4,7,16
22
52: 4, 5, 6
53: 8

Isa. 55: 5
56: 3
57:14
58: 1,2
60: 5,21
61: 9–AS[3]
62:10,12
63: 8,14
64: 9
65: 2,3,10
18,19
22
Jer. 1:18
2:11,13
31,32
4:10,11
11,22
5:14,21
23,26
31
6:14,19
21,22
26,27
7:12,16
23,33
8: 5,7,19
21,22
9: 1,1,2
7,9
11: 4,11
14
12:14
16–A
16,16
13:11,12
14: 6+A
10,11
16,17
15: 1,7
7–S
20
16: 5,10
17:19
18:15
19: 1,11
14
21: 7,8
22: 2,4
23: 2,8
13
14+S
22,32
32,33
34
7 S[y]
24: 7
25: 1
2–S[1]
26:16,24
27: 6,16[z]
41
28:11,58
30: 1
32: 6
33: 7,8,8
9,11
12,16
17,18
23,24
34:13
35: 1,5,7
10,11
15
36: 1,10
37: 3,18
38: 1,7,14
33
38 S[1 aa]
39:21,38
42
40: 9
41: 8,10
19
42:16
43: 6
6 A[bb]
7[z],9
10
13[cc],14
44: 2,12

Jer. 44:18
45: 1[dd],4
4
46:14
47: 5,6
48:10,13
16
49: 1,8
50: 1,4
51:15,20
20,21
24
52: 6,16
25,25
Lam. 1: 1,7,11
18
2:11
3:14,44
47
4: 3,6
10
Eze. 3: 5,6,11
7:23,27
9: 9
11: 1,20
12:19
13: 9,10
17,18
19,19
21,23
14: 1–AB
8,9,11
17: 9,15
18:18
20:34,35
41,41
21:12,12
22:29
23:24
24: 9 B[ee]
18,19
25: 7,14
26:11,20
27: 3
28:25
30:11
31:12
32: 3,9
33: 2,2,3
6+A
6,12
17,30
31
31+A
34:30
36: 8,12
15[ff]
20,28
30 A[gg]
37:13,18
23,27
38:14,16
39: 7,13
42:14
44:11,11
19,19
23
45: 8
9+A
9,16,22
46: 3,9,18
18,20
24
Dan. 2:44
3: 4,7,7
29,31
5:19
6:25
7:14
8:24
9: 6,15
16,19
20,24
10:14
11:14
32+A
32,33
12: 1,1
7+A
Hos. 1: 9,9,10

Hos. 2: 1,23
23
4: 4,6,8
9,11
14
6:10
7: 8
9: 1
10: 5,10
14
11: 7,12
Joel 2: 2,5,6
16,17
18,19
26,27
3: 2,3,16
Amos 1: 5
3: 6
7: 8,15
8: 2
9:10,14
Obad. 13
Jon. 1: 8
2: 5 B[1 u]
3: 6 S[3 w]
Mic. 1: 2,9
2: 4,8,9
11
12 A[x]
3: 3,5
4: 1,3,5
13
5: 7,8

Mic. 6: 2 B[hh]
2,3,5
15,16
7:14
Nah. 3: 4[ii]
13,18
Hab. 2: 5,8,10
13
3:10,13
16
Zeph. 1:11
2: 8,9
3: 9,12
20
Hag. 1: 2,12
12,13
14
2: 2,4,14
Zec. 2:11
7: 5
8: 6,7,8
11,12
20,22
9:16
10: 9[kk]
11:10
12: 2,4,6
13: 9
14: 2
12–S[1]
14
Mal. 1: 4

[a] A Ἰσραήλ. [b] pro ἀδελφός. [c] pro ἥλιος. [d] A αὐτός. [e] pro Ἰσραήλ. [f] pro δούλη. [g] pro ἀνήρ. [h] pro βασιλεύς. [i] A δοῦλος. [k] B δοῦλος. [m] pro δοῦλος. [n] pro υἱός. [o] pro κυρίῳ θεῷ. [p] pro καιρός. [q] B υἱός. [r] S[1] θεός. [s] ABS[1] λόγος. [t] pro πλῆθος. [u] pro ναός. [v] pro ἔθνος. [w] pro λόγος. [x] AS δοῦλος. [y] pro οἶκος. [z] A τόπος. [aa] pro κύριος. [bb] pro Ἰούδα. [cc] S[1] κύριος ὁ θεός. [dd] S[1] ὄχλος. [ee] pro δαλός. [ff] A ἔθνος. [gg] pro λιμός. [hh] pro ὄρος. [ii] AS[2] φυλή. [kk] A ἀλλήλων.

λάπτω.

Judges 7: 5[a], 5[a], 6, 7

[a] A λαμβάνω.

λάρος.

Lev. 11:15
Deu. 14:14

λάρυγξ.

Job 6:30
12:11
20:13
29:10
34: 3
Psa. 5:10
13: 3–A
21:16

Psa. 68: 4
113:15
118:103
134:17+A
136: 6
140: 6
Cant. 2: 3
7: 9

λατομέω.

Exo. 21:33–A
Deu. 6:11
1 Ch. 22: 2
2 Ch. 26:10

Neh. 9:25
Job 28: 2
Isa. 22:16
51: 1

λατόμητος.

2 Ki. 12:12
2 Ki. 22: 6

λατόμος.

1 Ki. (3) p1
5:15
2 Ki. 12:12
1 Ch. 22: 2

2 Ch. 2: 2,18
24:12
Ezra 3: 7

λατρεία.

Exo. 12:25,26
13: 5

Jos. 22:27
1 Ch. 28:13–B

λατρευτός.

Exo. 12:16
Lev. 23: 7,8,21
25,35
36
Nu. 28:18,25

Nu. 28:26
29: 1
7+A
12,35

λατρεύω.

Exo. 3:12
4:23
7:16
8: 1,20
9: 1,13
10: 3,7,8
11,24
26,26
12:31
20: 5
23:24,25
Lev. 18:21
Nu. 16: 9
Deu. 4:19,28
5: 9
6:13
7: 4,16
8:19
10:12,20
11:13,16
28
12: 2
13: 2,6,13
17: 3
28:14,36
47,48
29:18,26
30:17

Deu. 31:20–B
Jos. 22: 5,27
23: 7,16
24: 2,14
14,14
15,15
15,16
18,19
20,21
22,24
29
Jud. 2:11,13
19
3: 6,7
10: 6 A[a]
10 A[a]
13 A[a]
16 A[a]
2 Sa. 15: 8
2 Ki. 17:12,16
33,35
21:21,21
2 Ch. 7:19
Eze. 20:32
Dan. 3:12,14
17,18
28
6.16,20

[a] pro δουλεύω.

λάτρις.

Job 2: 9

λάφυρα.

1 Chronicles 26:27

λαχανεία.

Deuteronomy 11:10

λάχανον.

Gen. 9: 3
1 Ki. 20: 2,2

Psa. 36: 2
Pro. 15:17

λέαινα.

Job 4:10
Dan. 7: 4

λεαίνω.

2 Sa. 22:43
Job 14:19

Psa. 17:43

λέβης.

Exo. 16: 3
1 Sa. 2:14,15
2 Sa. 17:28
1 Ki. 7:26,31
2 Ki. 4:38,39
40,41
41
25:14
2 Ch. 4:16
35:13

Psa. 59:10
107:10
Ecc. 7: 7
Jer. 1:13–S[1]
Eze. 11: 3,7
11 A
24: 3,6
Amos 4: 2
Mic. 3: 3
Zec. 14:20,21

λέγω.

Var. Lec. tantum

Gen. 19:38–A
22: 7 A[a]
41:51+A
44: 4+A
50:16 B[a]
24–A
Exo. 3:12–A
14–A
12:13+B

Exo. 14: 5+A
18: 4–A
32:22+A
27[b]
33:15[b]
36: 5+A
Lev. 6: 58[c]
16: 2+A
Nu. 22:25[b]

Nu. 22:32 A[a]
26: 1+A
Deu. 9:13–A
27: 1–B
Jos. 2: 2–A
4: 3+A
5:15[b]
17:17+A
22: 8+A
24+A
24: 2+A
2+A
Jud. 2: 1–A
5: 1[b]
6:32–A
8: 9+A
9:38 A[d]
11:15+A
15: 2–A
16:15[e]
18: 8 A[a]
19:30+A
1 Sa. 1:10 B[f]
2:16–A
30[g]
17:26 A
27 A
2 Sa. 7:27+A
19:21 A[h]
24:12–A
1 Ki. 1:23+A
3:22+A
6(11) A
12: 9[h]
13:27 A
14: 7 A
17: 8+A
18: 8[b]
20:10–B
21: 5–A
33+A
22:27+A
2 Ki. 10:21–A
17:13[i]
19:10+A
1 Ch. 16:19 A[k]
17: 3+A
21: 9–B
2 Ch. 2:11–AB
6:15–A
10:10–AB
20:21–A
25:17–B
Ezra 9:11–B
Neh. 1: 8–S[1]
Est. 1:18[m]
2:15+S[3 n]
3: 4 AS[3 d]
Job 1:17 A[a]
25: 5+A
29: 1 A[a]
32: 6[a]

Job 33:31+A
34:31–S[1]
39:25[c]
33[b]
Ps. 118:82–A
Isa. 7: 5+AS
22:13–B
26: 1+AS[3]
36: 7[o]
39: 6+A
43:12+A
57: 6+S
66:22[p]
Jer. 1: 4+A
13–S[1]
19 A[a]
2: 9+
AB[r]S[a]
3: 2+A
4: 3–A
5:11–AS
9:25–S[1]
14:10[p]
19:12[p]
23:16–S
29–B
30–B
33+S[3]
28:27+S[1]
29:13 A[a]
33:18+A
37:12 A[a]
38:31 AS[q]
39: 3–S[1]
3–S[1]
42: 6[b]
43:14–S[1]
50: 2[b]
51:26 A[a]
Eze. 3:12+AB
11:20+A
13: 7+A
18:31+A
27:36+A
33:20+A
36:23+A
32+A
37:18+A
28+A
Dan. 2:15+A
27 B[a]
Amos 5:25+A
6:14–A
Hag. 1: 2–S[2]
6+A
Zec. 2: 4–S[1]
5[r]
4: 4–A
5–A
13+S[3]
8:18–BS[1]
Mal. 1: 2+S

[a] pro εἶπον. [b] A εἶπον. [c] pro ἐλέγχω. [d] pro λαλέω. [e] A εἴρω. [f] pro κλαίω. [g] AB εἶπον. [h] A λαλέω. [i] B λόγος. [k] pro γίνομαι. [m] A ἄγω. [n] pro ἐντέλλω. [o] S[1] ἔρχομαι. [p] S εἶπον. [q] pro φημί. [r] A φημί.

λεῖμμα.

2 Kings 19: 4[a]

[a] B λῆμμα.

λεῖος.

Gen. 27:11
1 Sa. 17:40–A[a]
Pro. 2:20

Pro. 12:13
26:23[b]
Isa. 40: 4+A

[a] B τέλειος. [b] S δόλιος.

λείπω.

Job 4:11
Pro. 4:21 S[1]

Pro. 11: 4
19: 4

[a] pro ἐκλείπω.

λειτουργέω.

Exo. 28:31, 39
29:30
30:20
35:18
36:34
38:27
39:12, 13
Nu. 1:50
3: 6, 31
4: 3, 9
12, 14
23, 24
26, 30
35, 37
39, 41
43
8:22
24+A
26
16: 9
18: 2, 6, 7
21, 23
Deu. 10: 8
17:12
18: 5, 7
1 Sa. 2:11, 18
3: 1
2 Sa. 19:18
1 Ki. 1: 4, 15
8:11
19:21
2 Ki. 6:15 A[a]
23:14
1 Ch. 6:32

1 Ch. 15: 2
16: 4, 37
23:13, 28
32
26:12
27: 1
2 Ch. 5:14
8:14
11:14
13:10
15:16
17:19
22: 8—A
23: 6
29:11, 11
31: 2
35: 3
Neh. 10:36
Ps. 100: 6
Jer. 52:18
Eze. 40:46
42:14
43:19
44:11 *ter*
12, 15
16, 17
19, 27
45: 4, 4, 5
46:24
Dan. 7:10
Joel 1: 9, 13
13
2:17

[a] *pro* λειτουργός.

λειτούργημα.

Nu. 4:32 | Nu. 7: 9

λειτουργησίμος.

1 Chronicles 28:13

λειτουργία.

Exo. 37:19
Nu. 4:24, 27
27, 28
33
7: 5, 7, 8
8:22
24+A
25
16: 9
18: 4, 6, 7
21, 21
23, 31
2 Sa. 19:18
1 Ch. 6:32, 48

1 Ch. 9:13, 19
28
23:24, 26
28
24: 3, 19
26:30
28:13, 20
21
2 Ch. 8:14
31: 2, 4, 16
35:10, 15
16
Ezra 7:19
Eze. 29:20[a]

[a] A δουλεία.

λειτουργικός.

Exo. 31:10
39:13
Nu. 4:12, 26

Nu. 7: 5
2 Ch. 24:14

λειτουργός.

Jos. 1: 1 A[a]
2 Sa. 13:18
1 Ki. 10: 5
2 Ki. 4:43
6:15[b]
2 Ch. 9: 4

Ezra 7:24
Neh. 10:39
Ps. 102:21
103: 4
Isa. 61: 6

[a] *pro* ὑπουργός. [b] A λειτουργέω

λειχήν.

Lev. 21:20 | Lev. 22:22

λείχω.

1 Ki. 20:19, 19
Psa. 71: 9

Isa. 49:23
Mic. 7:17

λεκάνη.

Jud. 5:25 | Jud. 6:38

λέξις.

Est. 1:22
3:12
8: 9

Job 36: 2
38: 1

λεπίζω.

Genesis 30:37, 37, 38

λεπίς.

Lev. 11: 9—A
10, 12

Nu. 16:38
Deu. 14: 9, 10

λέπισμα.

Genesis 30:37

λέπρα.

Lev. 13: 2, 3, 8
9, 11
12, 12
13, 15
20, 22
25, 25
27, 29
30, 30
42, 43
47, 49

Lev. 13:51, 52
57, 59
14: 3, 7, 32
34, 44
54, 55
57
Deu. 24:10
2 Ki. 5: 3, 6, 7
27
2 Ch. 26:19

λεπράω.

Lev. 22: 4[a] | Nu. 12:10, 10

[a] A λεπρός.

λεπρός.

Lev. 13:44, 45
14: 2, 3
22: 4 A[a]
Nu. 5: 2
2 Sa. 3:29

2 Ki. 5:11
7: 3, 8
2 Ch. 26:20, 21
21, 23

[a] *pro* λεπράω.

λεπρόω.

2 Ki. 5: 1, 27 | 2 Ki. 15: 5

λεπτός.

Gen. 41: 3, 4, 6
7, 19
20, 23
24, 27
27
Exo. 16:14
30: 7, 36
32:20

Lev. 13:30
16:12
Deu. 9:21
1 Ki. 19:12
2 Ch. 34: 7
Isa. 27: 9
30:14, 22
Jer. 28:34

λεπτύνω.

2 Sa. 22:43
2 Ki. 23: 6, 15
2 Ch. 23:17
34: 4
Psa. 17:43
28: 6
Isa. 41:15

Jer. 31:12
Dan. 2:34, 35
40, 40
44, 45
6:24
7: 7, 19
Mic. 4:13 A[a]

[a] *pro* κατατήκω.

λέπυρον.

Cant. 4: 3 | Cant. 6: 6

λέσχη.

Proverbs 23:29

λευκαίνω.

Lev. 13:19
Psa. 50: 9

Isa. 1:18, 18
Joel 1: 7

λευκανθίζω.

Lev. 13:38[a], 39[a] Cant. 8: 5

[a] AB λευκαθίζω.

λεύκη.

Hosea 4:13

λευκός.

Gen. 30:32 A[a]
35, 37
37
31: 8, 8
49:12
Exo. 16:14, 31
Lev. 13: 3, 4, 4
10, 10
13, 16
17, 19

Lev. 13:20, 21
24, 25
26, 42
43
Ecc. 9: 8
Cant. 5:10
Isa. 41:19
Dan. 7: 9
Zec. 1: 8
6: 3, 6

[a] *pro* ῥαντός.

λέων.

Gen. 49: 9, 9
Nu. 23:24
24: 9
Deu. 33:20, 22
Jud. 14: 5, 8, 8
9, 18
1 Sa. 17:34, 36
37
2 Sa. 1:23
17:10
23:20
1 Ki. 7:15, 15
22
10:19
20—A
13:24
24—A
25
26+A
28, 28
21:36, 36
2 Ki. 17:25, 26
1 Ch. 11:22
12: 8
2 Ch. 9:18, 19
Job 4:10, 11
6: 7
10:16
28: 8
38:39
Psa. 7: 3
9:30—A
16:12
21:14, 22
34:17
57: 7
90:13
Pro. 19:12
20: 2
22:13
24:65
26:13
28: 1, 15

Ecc. 9: 4
Cant. 4: 8
Isa. 5:29, 29
11: 6, 7
30: 6, 6
31: 4
35: 9
38:13
65:25
Jer. 2:15, 30
4: 7
5: 6
12: 8
27:17, 44
28:38, 38
29:20
32:24
Lam. 3:10
Eze. 1:10
10:14 A
19: 2, 2, 3
5, 6, 6
22:25
32: 2
41:19
Dan. 4:30
6: 7, 12
16, 18
19, 20
22, 24
24, 27
Hos. 5:14
11:10
Joel 1: 6
Amos 3: 4, 8, 12
5:19
Mic. 5: 8
Nah. 2:11 *ter*
12, 12
13
Zeph. 3: 3
Zec. 11: 3

λεωπετρία.

Eze. 24: 7, 8 | Eze. 26: 4, 14

λήθη.

Lev. 5:15
Nu. 5:27

Deu. 8:19
Job 7:21

λῆμμα.

2 Sa. 14: 7 A[a]
2 Ki. 9:25[b]
19: 4 B[c]
Job 31:23
Jer. 23:33, 33[d]
34, 36
36, 38
38

Lam. 2:14
Nah. 1: 1
Hab. 1: 1, 7
Hag. 2:14
Zec. 9: 1
12: 1
Mal. 1: 1

[a] *pro* κατάλειμμα. [b] A ῥῆμα. [c] *pro* λεῖμμα. [d] S[1] ῥῆμα.

ληνός.

Gen. 30:38, 41
Exo. 22:29
Nu. 18:27, 30
Deu. 15:14 A[a]
16:13
Jud. 6:11
2 Ki. 6:27
Neh. 13:15

Psa. 8: 1
80: 1[b]
83: 1
Pro. 3:10
Isa. 63: 2
Jer. 31:33
Lam. 1:15
Hos. 9: 2

Joel 1:17
2:24

Joel 3:13

[a] *pro* οἶνος. [b] A ἀλλοιόω.

ληστήριον.

2 Ch. 22: 1 | 2 Ch. 36: 5-A, 5

ληστής.

Jer. 7:11
12: 9 A[a]
18:22

Eze. 22: 9+AB
Hos. 7: 1
Obad. 5

[a] *pro* ὕαινα.

λῆψις.

Proverbs 15:27, 29

λίαν.

Gen. 1:31
4: 5
1 Sa. 11:15
2 Sa. 2:17
1 Ki. 3: 4+A

Job 31:31
Ps. 138:17
Jer. 24: 3, 3
30: 8
31:29[a]

[a] A σφόδρα.

λίβανος.

Exo. 30:34
Lev. 2: 1, 2
4 AB[a]
15, 16
5:11 B[b]
11
6:15
24: 7
Nu. 5:15

Neh. 13: 5, 9
Cant. 3: 6
4: 6
Isa. 43:23
60: 6
66: 3
Jer. 6:20
17:26
48: 5

[a] *pro* κλίβανος. [b] *pro* ἔλαιον.

λιβανωτός.

1 Chronicles 9:29

λιγύριον.

Exo. 28:19
36:19

Eze. 28:13

λιθάζω.

2 Samuel 16: 6, 13

λίθινος.

Gen. 35:14
Exo. 24:12
31:18
32:15
34: 1, 4, 4
Deu. 4:13
5:22
9: 9, 10
11
10: 1, 1A[a],

Deu. 10: 3
1 Ki. 8: 9
2 Ki. 16:17
Ezra 6: 4
Est. 1: 6
Eze. 11:19
36:26
40:42
Dan. 5: 4, 23

[a] *pro* ξύλινος.

λιθοβολέω.

Exo. 8:26
19:13
21:28, 29
32
Lev. 20: 2, 27
24:14, 16
23
Nu. 15:35, 36
Deu. 13:10
17: 5
21:21

Deu. 22:21, 24
Jos. 7:25
1 Sa. 30: 6
1 Ki. 12:18
20:10—B
13, 14
15+A
2 Ch. 10:18
24:21
Eze. 16:40
23:47

λίθος.

Gen. 2:12
11: 3
28:11, 18
22
29: 2, 3, 3
8, 10
31:15, 16
46

Exo. 7:19
15: 5
17:12
19:13
20:25
21:18, 28
24: 4
25: 6, 6

Exo. 28: 9,9,10
10, 11
12—B
12, 17
21
35: 8,8,13
27, 27
33
36:13, 14
17, 21
Lev. 14:40, 42
42, 43
45
20: 2, 27
24:16, 23
26: 1
Nu. 14:10
15:35, 36
35:17, 23
Deu. 4:28
8: 9
13:10
17: 5
21:21
22:21, 24
27: 2, 3, 4
5, 6, 8
28:36, 64
29:17
Jos. 4: 3, 5, 6
7, 8, 9
11, 20
21
7:25, 26
8:29
9: 4, 5
10:11, 11
18, 27
15: 6
18:17
24:26, 27
Jud. 9: 5, 18
20:16
1 Sa. 6:14, 15
18
7:12, 12
14:33
17:40, 43
49, 49
50 A
25:37
2 Sa. 5:11
12:30
16: 6, 13
17:13
18:17
20: 8
1 Ki. 1: 9 A[a]
5:17
6: 2
2+A
2, 11
7:46, 47
47
48+A
10: 2, 10
11
22—A
27
12:18
15:22
18:31, 32
38
20:13
2 Ki. 3:19, 25
25
12:12, 12
19:18
22: 6
23:15
1 Ch. 12: 2
20: 2
22: 2, 14
15
1 Ch. 29: 2 ter
8
2 Ch. 1:15
2:14
3: 6
9: 1, 9, 10
27
10:18
16: 6
26:14, 15
32:27
34:11
Ezra 5: 8
Neh. 4: 2—ABS
3
9:11
Est. 1: 6, 6
Job 5:23+A
6:12
8:17
14:19
28: 3, 3, 6
31:24
38: 6, 38
41: 6, 15
Psa. 18:11
20: 4
90:12
101:15
117:22
Pro. 3:15
8:11, 19
24:46
26: 8, 27
27: 3
29:28
Ecc. 3: 5, 5
10:8+A, 9
Cant. 5:14
Isa. 8:14
9:10
13:12
27: 9
28:16
37:19
54:11, 12
12
60: 6+AS[1]
17
62:10
Jer. 2:27
3: 9
18: 3
28:26, 26
63
38:39[b]
50: 9, 10
52: 4—ABS
Lam. 3:52
4: 1, 7
Eze. 1:26
10: 1, 9
13:11, 13
16:40
20:32
23:47
26:12
27:22
28:13, 14
16
38:22
Dan. 2:34, 35
45
6:17
11:38
Mic. 1: 6
Hab. 2:11, 19
Hag. 2:15, 15
Zec. 3: 9, 9
4: 7, 10
5: 4, 8
9:15, 16
12: 3

[a] *pro* αἰθῆ. [b] A κύκλος.

λιθόστρωτος.

2 Ch. 7: 3
Est. 1: 6
Cant. 3:10

λιθουργέω.

Exodus 35:33

λιθουργικός.

Exo. 28:11
Exo. 31: 5

λικμάω.

Ruth 3: 2
1 Ki. 14:15 A
Job 27:21
Isa. 17:13
30:22, 24
41:16
Jer. 30:10
Jer. 38:10
Eze. 26: 4
29:12
30:23, 26
36:19
Dan. 2:44
Amos 9: 9, 9

λικμήτωρ.

Proverbs 20:26

λικμός.

Amos 9: 9

λιμαγχονέω.

Deuteronomy 8: 3

λιμήν.

Psalm 106:30[a], 35 S[b]

[a] S[1] ἐπιμέλεια. [b] *pro* λίμνη.

λίμνη.

Psa. 106:35[a]
113: 8
Cant. 7: 4

[a] S λιμήν.

λιμοκτονέω.

Proverbs 10: 3

λιμός.

Gen. 12:10, 10
26: 1, 1
41:27, 30
30, 31
36, 36
50, 54
54, 56
57
42: 5
43: 1
45: 6, 11
47: 4, 13
13, 20
Exo. 16: 3
Deu. 28:48
32:24
Ruth 1: 1
2 Sa. 21: 1
24:13
1 Ki. 8:37
18: 2
2 Ki. 4:38
6:25
7: 4
8: 1
25: 3
1 Ch. 21:12
2 Ch. 6:28
20: 9
32:11
Job 5:20
18:11
30: 3, 4
Psa. 32:19
36:19
104:16
Isa. 5:13
8:21
14:30
51:19
Jer. 5:12
11:22
14:12, 13
15, 15
16, 18
15: 2, 2
16: 4
17:18 A[a]
18:21
21: 7, 9
24:10
31: 6
39:24, 36
41:17
45: 2, 9
49:16, 17
22
51:12, 13
18, 27
52: 6
Lam. 2:19, 21
4: 9
5:10
Eze. 5:12, 16[b]
17
6:11, 12
7:15, 15
12:16
14:13, 21
34:29
36:30, 30[c]
Amos 8:11 ter

[a] *pro* ἡμέρα. [b] A θυμός. [c] A λαός.

λιμώσσω.

Psalm 58: 7, 15

λίνεος.

Exo. 28:38
Lev. 6:10, 10
13:48, 52
16: 4 ter
4—A
23, 32
Deu. 22:11
Jer. 13: 1
Eze. 44:17, 18
18

λινοκαλάμη.

Joshua 2: 6

λίνον.

Exo. 9:31, 31
1 Sa. 23:18+A
Pro. 29:31
Isa. 19: 9
42: 3
43:17

λιπαίνω.

Deu. 32:15
Neh. 9:25
Psa. 22: 5
Ps. 140: 5
Pro. 5: 3
Hab. 1:16

λιπαρός.

Jud. 3:29[a]
Neh. 9:35
Isa. 30:23

[a] A μαχητής.

λίπασμα.

Nehemiah 8:10

λίσσομαι.

Job 17: 2

λιτανεύω.

Psalm 44:13

λιτός.

Jud. 11: 3 A[a] [a] *pro* κενός.

λίψ.

Gen. 13:14
20: 1
24:62
28:14
Exo. 27: 9
37: 7
Nu. 2:10
3:29
10: 6[a]
34: 3[b], 3
4, 4
35: 5
Deu. 1: 7
3:27[a]
33:23
Jos. 15: 1[a], 2[a]
2[a], 3[a]
4[a], 7[a]
8—A
Jos. 15:10[a]
11[c]
17: 9, 10
18: 5, 13
13, 14
14, 15
16, 19
19
19: 8
2 Ch. 28:18
32:30
33:14
Psa. 77:26
Isa. 43: 6
Eze. 47:19, 20
48:28
Dan. 8: 4+A
5

[a] A νότος. [b] A βορρᾶς. [c] A[1] Βαλά.

λοβός.

Exo. 29:13, 20
20, 22
Lev. 3: 4, 10
15
4: 9
6:34
7:20
Lev. 8:16, 23
24, 25
9:10, 19
14:14, 17
25, 28
Amos 3:12

λογεῖον *vide* λόγιον.

λογίζομαι.

Gen. 15: 6
31:15
Lev. 7: 8
17: 4
25:31
27:23
Nu. 18:27, 30
Deu. 2:11, 20
3:13
1 Sa. 1:13
18:25—A
2 Sa. 4: 2—A
14:13
14[a]
19:19[b]
43
1 Ki. 10:21
2 Ch. 5: 6
9:20
Neh. 6: 2, 6
13:13
Job 31:28
34:37[c]
41:20, 23
Psa. 31: 2
34: 4
35: 5[d]
40: 8
43:23
51: 4
105:31
118:119
139: 3, 5
143: 3
Pro. 16: 1
30AOS[e]
17:28
24: 8
Ecc. 10: 3
Isa. 5:28
10: 7
13:17
29:16, 17
32:15
33: 8
40:15, 15
17
41:19
Isa. 44:19+AS
53: 3, 4, 12
Jer. 11:19
18: 8[f], 11
18
23:27
27:45[g]
29:21
30: 8
31: 2—S[1]
33: 3
36:11
43: 3—A
Lam. 4: 2
Eze. 11: 2
38:10
Dan. 4:32
11:24, 25
Hos. 7:15
8:12
Amos 6: 5
Mic. 2: 1, 3
Nah. 1: 9
11 AB
Zec. 8:17

[a] A διαλογίζομαι. [b] AB διαλογίζομαι. [c] A εἰμί. [d] AS διαλογίζομαι. [e] *pro* διαλογίζομαι. [f] A λαλέω. [g] *pro* βουλεύω.

λόγιον, λογεῖον.

Exo. 28:15, 22
23, 24
24, 26
29: 5
5—B
35:27
36:15, 16
22, 24
25, 27
29, 29
Lev. 8: 8, 8
Nu. 24: 4, 16
Deu. 33: 9
Psa. 11: 7, 7
17:31
18:15
104:19
106:11
118:11
25 A[2]S[a]
38
Ps. 118:41 A[a]
50, 58
65AS[1a]
67, 76
82, 103
107S[1a]
115, 123
124AS[1b]
133, 140
148
149 S[b]
158, 162
169
170[c]
172
147: 4
Isa. 5:24
28:13
30:11, 27
27

[a] *pro* λόγος. [b] *pro* ἔλεος. [c] A κρίμα.

λογισμός.

2 Sa. 14:14+A
Psa. 32:10, 11
Pro. 6:18
12: 5
15:22, 26
19:21
Ecc. 7:28, 30
9:10
Isa. 32: 7 A[a]
66:18
Jer. 4:14B[2]S[b]
Jer. 11:19
18:11, 18
27:45[c]
28:29
29:21
30: 8
36:11
Eze. 38:10
Dan. 11:24[c], 25
Mic. 4:12
Nah. 1:11

[a] *pro* λόγος. [b] *pro* διαλογισμός. [c] A διαλογισμός.

λογιστής.

2 Chronicles 26:15

λόγος.

Gen. 4:23
29:13
34:18
Exo. 4:28
5: 9
18:19
19: 7, 8
20: 1
24: 3, 8
33:17
34:27, 28
Exo. 35: 1
Lev. 8:36
Nu. 5:21 B[a]
11:23
12: 6
16:31
21:21
Deu. 1: 1, 18
32, 34
2:26
3:26

Deu. 4: 9, 30
5:28, 28
9:10
10: 4
12:28
13: 3, 14
16:19
18:19+A
22:14, 17
20
27: 3, 26
28:14 A[h]
29: 1, 9
31: 1, 12
24, 28
32:44
45+A
46, 46
47, 47
33: 3
Jos. 2:20
14: 7
20: 4 A
22:30, 32
23:14, 14
Jud. 2: 4, 17[c]
3:19, 20
5:29[i]
8: 3
9: 3, 30
11:11, 28
37[d]
13:12[d]
16:16
18: 7[d], 7
9+A
28
20: 7
21:11+A
Ruth 4: 7
1 Sa. 3:17, 18
19
8:21
11: 4
15: 1+A
11, 24
16:18
17:31 A
18: 8, 26
20:21
22:15
24: 8, 10
25: 9−A
24
28:10, 20
21
29:10
30:24
2 Sa. 1: 4
3: 8, 13
7:17
21 A[e]
28
11:18, 19
12: 9
13:21, 22
35
14: 3, 13
17, 19
20[f], 21
22
15: 3
16:23
17: 4, 6
18:13
19:11, 20
42, 43
43, 43
20:17, 18
21
22: 1
23: 1, 2
24: 3, 4, 11
19
1 Ki. 1: 7, 14
2: 4, 14
23
3:10+A
4:20
5: 7

1 Ki. 6: 5
(11)A
(12)A
8:56, 56
59
10: 3, 3, 6
7
11:10, 41[g]
12: 6, 7
16+A
22, 24
p 24 l 49
l 82
30
13: 1, 2, 4
5, 9, 11
17, 20
32
14:29, 29
15: 7, 7
23, 23
31, 31
16: 1, 5, 5
14, 14
20, 20
27, 27
p 28−A
17: 1
2 A[h]
18:21
20: 4+A
27
21: 9, 12
33, 35
22:13, 13
39, 39
46, 46
2 Ki. 1: 7, 18
18
4:13
5:13, 18
6:11, 12
30
7: 1
8:23, 23
9: 5, 36
10:34, 34
11: 5
12:19, 19
13: 8, 8
12, 12
14:15, 15
18, 18
28, 28
15: 6, 6, 11
11, 12
15, 15
21, 21
26, 26
31, 31
36, 36
16:19, 19
17: 9
13 B[i]
18:20, 27
28
29−A
36, 37
19: 4, 4, 6
16, 21
20: 9, 19[k]
16, 19
20
20−A
21:17, 17
25, 25
22:11, 13
13, 16
18
23: 2, 3, 16
17, 24
28, 28
24: 2, 5, 5
25:30
1 Ch. 10:13
11: 3, 10
12:23
13: 4
15:15
16:15

1 Ch. 17: 3, 15
23
21: 6, 12
19
22: 8
23:27
25: 5
26:32 A[m]
32
27: 1, 1, 24
28:21
29:29 qtr
2 Ch. 6:10
8:13, 14
15
9: 2, 2
2+B
5, 5, 6
29 ter
10: 6, 7, 9
15
11: 2, 4
12: 7, 12
15, 15
13:22, 22
15: 8
16:11
18:12, 18
19: 3, 6
11, 11
20:34, 34
23: 4
25:26
26:22
27: 7
28:26
29:30, 36
30: 4, 5, 12
31: 5, 16
32: 1, 8, 32
33:18, 18
19, 19
34:16
18−AB
19−B
21, 21
24, 26
27, 28
30, 31
35: 6, 19
22, 26
27
36: 5, 5, 8
8, 16
21
Ezra 1: 1
3: 4
7:11, 12
8:17
9: 3, 4
Neh. 1: 1, 4, 8
2:18, 20
5: 6, 8, 9
13
13+S[3]
13 S[3 h]
6: 5+S[3]
7, 8, 12
19, 19
8: 9, 12
13
9: 8
12:23, 47
13:17
Est. 1: 1
20 AS[3 n]
21
2: 1, 22
3: 4
4: 9, 12
5: 5
6: 1+S[3]
10
7: 3 ABS[1 o]
8+S[3]
8: 5+S[3]
17+S[3]
9:20, 26
31
Job 2:13+AC

Job 4:12
7:13[p]
9: 3
11:12[q]
14: 3
15: 3
16: 4 A[h]
19: 2, 28
21: 2
22: 4
26:14 S[1 r]
14
32:11+A
11, 15
33:32
34: 3
41: 3
Psa. 7: 1
16: 4
17: 1
18: 4
21: 2
32: 4, 6
40: 9
44: 2
49:17
50: 6
54:22
55: 5, 6, 11
58:13
63: 6
64: 4
90: 3
102:20, 20
104: 8, 19
27, 28
42
105:12, 24
106:20
108: 3
111: 5
118: 9, 16
17, 25[s]
28, 41[t]
42, 42
43, 49
65[u], 74
81, 89
101
107[v]
114[w]
130
130[x]
142 S[1 u]
147, 154
160, 161
120: 5[y]
130: 3
138: 4−S[3]
140: 4
144:14
147: 4, 7, 8
148: 8
Pro. 1: 2, 3, 6
23, 24
29[z]
4: 4, 10
20
5: 1, 7
7: 1, 2, 5
12: 5 S[1 aa]
6, 25
13: 5
14:15
15: 1
16:13, 21
24
17:14
18: 4, 13
19: 7
22:12, 17
17, 21
21
23: 8, 9, 12
16
24:23, 24
28, 29
31, 41
68, 69
70

Pro. 25: 2, 11
12, 27
26: 6, 18
18, 22
24 B[1 aa]
27:11
29:12, 19
20
Ecc. 1: 8
5: 1, 1, 2
6
6:11[bb]
7: 9, 22
8: 2, 3
9:16, 17
10: 1 B[cc]
12, 13
14, 20
12:10, 10
11, 13
Cant. 5: 6
Isa. 1:10
10 S[1 n]
2: 1, 3
8:10
9: 8 S[1 dd]
10:22, 23
11: 4
28:14, 23
29: 4, 4, 11
18, 21
30:12, 12
21
31: 2
32: 2, 7
7[ee], 9
36: 5, 12
13, 14
21, 22
37: 4, 4, 6
17, 22
38: 4
39: 5, 8
41:26
45:23
50: 4
51:16
58:13
59:13
66: 2, 5
Jer. 1: 2, 4, 9
11
12−S[1]
13−S[1]
2: 4, 31
3:12
5:13, 14
6:19
7: 2, 4, 8
28
8: 9 AS[n]
9:12, 20
20
10: 1
11: 1, 2
3[ff], 6
6, 10
13: 2, 3, 8
10
14: 1, 17
15:16, 10
17:15, 20
18: 1, 2, 5
18, 18
22
19: 2, 3
15 A[b]
20: 1, 8, 8
21: 1, 11
22: 1, 2, 4
5, 29
23:16, 17
18, 22
28, 28
29, 29
30−B
36, 38
24: 4
25: 1, 8, 13
26: 1

Jer. 27: 1
28:59, 60
61
32:16, 16
33: 1, 2, 5
7, 10
12, 15
20, 21
34:10, 13
15[v]
35: 6, 7, 9
12
36: 1, 10
23, 30
37: 1, 2, 4
38:10, 20
23
39: 1, 6, 8
20
40: 1
41: 1, 4, 5
6, 8, 12
42: 1, 12
13
43: 1, 2, 4
8, 10
11, 13
16, 16
17, 18
20, 24
27−S[1]
27, 28
32, 32
44: 2, 6
17
45: 1, 4
14, 19
20, 21
24, 27
27
46:15, 16
47: 1
49: 3
4−A[1]
4, 5, 7
15, 16
50: 1, 1, 8
51: 1, 16
17, 20
24, 26
28, 31
31
Eze. 1: 2
24+A
2: 6, 7
3: 4, 6, 10
16, 17
6: 1, 3
7: 1
9:11+A
11:14, 25
12: 1, 8, 17
21, 23
25, 25
26, 28
28+A
13: 1, 2, 6
8
14: 2, 12
15: 1
16: 1, 35
17: 1, 11
18: 1
20: 2, 45
47
21: 1, 8, 18
22: 1, 17
23
23: 1
24: 1, 15
20−A
25: 1, 3
26: 1
27: 1
28: 1, 11
20
29: 1, 17
30: 1, 20
31: 1
32: 1, 17

Eze. 33: 1, 7
8+A
23
34: 1, 7
9+A
35: 1
36: 1, 4, 16
37: 4, 15
38: 1
Dan. 2: 5, 11
4:14
14 A[h]
28, 30
6: 2, 12
7:11, 16
25, 28
9: 2, 12
23, 25
10: 1, 1, 6
9, 11
11, 12
12, 15
12: 4[gg], 9
Hos. 1: 1, 2
4: 1
13: 1
14: 2
Joel 1: 1
2:11
Amos 1: 1
3: 1
4: 1

Amos 5: 1, 10
6:13
7:10, 16
8:11, 12
Jon. 1: 1
3: 1, 6[hh]
4: 2
Mic. 1: 1, 2
2: 7
4: 2
6: 1
7: 3
Hab. 3: 5
Zeph. 1: 1
2: 5
Hag. 1: 1, 3, 12
2:10, 20
Zec. 1: 1, 6, 7
13
4: 6, 8
6: 9
7: 1, 4, 7
8, 12
8: 1, 9
16, 18
9: 1
11:11
12: 1
Mal. 1: 1
2:17
3:13

[a] *pro* ὅρκος. [b] *pro* ἐντολή.
[c] A ἐντολή. [d] A ῥῆμα.
[e] *pro* δοῦλος. [f] B δόλος.
[g] B ῥῆμα. [h] *pro* ῥῆμα.
[i] *pro* λέγω. [k] A τόπος.
[m] *pro* πρόσταγμα.
[n] *pro* νόμος. [o] *pro* λαός.
[p] A διάλονος. [q] A[1] ἄλογος.
[r] *pro* ὁδός. [s] A[2]S λόγιον.
[t] A λόγιον, S[1] ἔλεος.
[u] AS[1] λ γιον. [v] S[1] λόγιον.
[w] S[1] λαός. [x] AS[1] ἐντολή.
[y] S[1] νόμος. [z] CS[2] φόβος.
[aa] *pro* δόλος. [bb] S ὀλίγος.
[cc] *pro* ὀλίγος. [dd] *pro* θάνατος.
[ee] A λογισμός. [ff] S φωνή.
[gg] B λοιπός. [hh] S[3] λαός.

λόγχη.

Jud. 5: 8[a]
1 Sa. 17: 7
Neh. 4:13, 16
21
Job 16:13
41:17
Eze. 26: 8
39: 9

[a] A σειρομάστης.

λοιδορέω.

Gen. 49:23
Exo. 17: 2, 2
21:18
Nu. 20: 3, 13
Deu. 33: 8
Jer. 36:27 S[a]

[a] *pro* συλλοιδορέω.

λοιδόρησις.

Exodus 17: 7

λοιδορία.

Exo. 17: 7
Nu. 20:24
Pro. 10:18
20: 3

λοίδορος.

Pro. 25:24
26:21
Pro. 27:15

λοιμεύομαι.

Proverbs 19:19

λοιμός.

1 Sa. 1:16
2:12
10:27
25:17, 25
29:10
30:22
2 Ch. 13: 7
Psa. 1: 1
Pro. 19:25
21:24
22:10
24: 9

Pro. 29: 8 A[a]	Eze. 30:11
Isa. 5:14	31:12
Jer. 15:21	32:12
Eze. 7:21	Dan. 11:14[b]
18:10	Hos. 7: 5
28: 7	

[a] pro ἄνομος. [b] B λοιπός.

λοιπός.

Gen. 45: 6	2 Ki. 24: 5
Exo. 28:10	25:11
29:12, 34	1 Ch. 16:41
30:12, 21	29:29
Lev. 2: 3	2 Ch. 13:22
23:22	20:34
Deu. 8:20	24:27
17:14	25:26
Jos. 6:13, 13	26:22
13:27	27: 7
17: 2	28:26
21:34	32:32[a]
Jud. 20:45—A	33:18
47—A	35:26—AB
1 Sa. 8: 5	27+A
15:15	36: 8
1 Ki. 11:41	Ezra 4: 7
14:29	Neh. 11:20 S³
15: 7, 23	Est. 1: 3, 18
31	2: 3
16: 5, 14	9:16
20, 27	Isa. 9: 1[b]
16 p 28—A	17: 3
22:39, 46	21:17 S[c]
2 Ki. 1:18	38:12 A[d]
8:23	44:15, 17
10:34	19
12:19	Jer. 48:16
13: 8, 12	50: 5 AS[c]
14:15, 18	6
28	52:16 S[c]
15: 6, 11	Eze. 34:18
15, 21	36: 5
26, 31	Dan. 7:12, 20
36	11:14 B[e]
16:19	12: 4 B[f]
20:20	Amos 4: 2
21:17, 25	Zec. 11: 9 BS[c]
23:28	

[a] B κατάλοιπος. [b] S² κατάλοιπος. [c] pro κατάλοιπος. [d] pro ἐπίλοιπος. [e] pro λοιμός. [f] pro λόγος.

λουτήρ.

Exo. 30:18, 28	2 Sa. 8: 8
31: 9	1 Ki. 3 p 1
38:26, 27	7:16
Lev. 8:11	10:21
Nu. 4:14	2 Ki. 16:17
1 Sa. 2:14+A	2 Ch. 4: 3, 6, 14

λουτρόν.

Cant. 4: 2 | Cant. 6: 5

λουτρών, λυτ—

2 Kings 10:27

λούω.

Exo. 2: 5	Lev. 22: 6
29: 4	Nu. 19: 7, 8, 19
40:10	Deu. 23:11
Lev. 8: 6	Ruth 3: 3
11:40+A	2 Sa. 11: 2
40	12:20
14: 8, 9	1 Ki. 20:19
15: 5, 6, 7	22:38
8, 10	2 Ki. 5:10, 12[a]
11, 13	13
16, 18	Psa. 6: 7
21, 22	Cant. 5:12
27	Isa. 1:16
16: 4, 24	Eze. 16: 4, 9
26, 28	23:40
17:15, 16	

[a] A πορεύω

λοφιά.

Jos. 15: 2, 5 | Jos. 18:19

λοχεύω.

Gen. 33:13 | Psa. 77:71

λύκος.

Gen. 49:27	Jer. 5: 6
Pro. 28:15	Eze. 22:27
Isa. 11: 6	Hab. 1: 8
65:25	Zeph. 3: 3

λυμαίνομαι.

Exo. 23: 8	Isa. 65: 8, 25
2 Ch. 16:10	Jer. 28: 2
Psa. 79:14	31:18
Pro. 18: 9, 22	Eze. 16:25
23: 8	Dan. 6:22
25:26	Amos 1:11
27:13	

λυπέω.

Gen. 4: 5	Isa. 8:21
45: 5	19:10
Deu. 15:10	15: 2
1 Sa. 29: 4	32:11
2 Sa. 13:21	57:17
19: 2	17
2 Ki. 13:19	Jer. 15:18
Neh. 5: 6	Lam. 1:22
Est. 1:12	Eze. 16:43
2:21	Dan. 6:14
6:12	Jon. 4: 1, 4, 9
Job 31:39	9
Psa. 54: 3	Mic. 6: 3
Pro. 25:20	

λύπη.

Gen. 3:16, 16	Pro. 24:74
17	25:20
5:29	Isa. 1: 5
42:38	35:10
44:29, 31[a]	40:29
Pro. 10: 1, 10	50:11
22	51:11
14:13	Jon. 4: 1
15:13	

[a] A ὀδύνη.

λυπηρός.

Gen. 34: 7	Pro. 17:22
Pro. 14:10	26:23
15: 1	

λύσις.

Ecclesiastes 8: 1

λύτρον.

Exo. 21:30, 30	Nu. 3:51
30:12	18:15
Lev. 19:20	35:31, 32
25:24, 26	Pro. 6:35
51, 52	13: 8
Nu. 3:12, 46	Isa. 45:13
48, 49	

λυτρόω.

Exo. 6: 6	Lev. 27:31, 33
13:13, 13	Nu. 18:15, 15
15	17
15:13	Deu. 7: 8
16 A[a]	9:26
34:20 ter	13: 5
Lev. 19:20	15:15
25:25, 30	21: 8
33, 48	24:20
49 ter	2 Sa. 4: 9
54	7:23, 23
27:13, 13	1 Ki. 1:29
15, 19	1 Ch. 17:21, 21
20, 20	Neh. 1:10
27, 28	Psa. 7: 3
29, 31	24:22

Psa. 25:11	Pro. 23:11
30: 6	Isa. 35: 9
31: 7	41:14
33:23	43: 1, 14
43:27	44:22, 23[b]
48: 8, 8, 16	24
54:19	51:11
58: 2	52: 3
68:19	62:12
70:23	63: 9
71:14	Jer. 15:21—S
73: 2	27:34
76:16	38:11
77:42	Lam. 3:57
102: 4	5: 8
105:10	Dan. 4:24
106: 2, 2	Hos. 7:13
118:134	13:14
154	Mic. 4:10
129: 8	6: 4
135:24	Zeph. 3:15
143:10	Zec. 10: 8

[a] pro κτάομαι. [b] A ἐλεέω.

λύτρωσις.

Lev. 25:29, 29	Psa. 48: 9
48	110: 9
Nu. 18:16	129: 7
Jud. 1:15 ter	Isa. 63: 4

λυτρωτής.

Lev. 25:31, 32	Psa. 77:35
Psa. 18:15	

λυχνία.

Exo. 25:30, 30	Lev. 24: 4
31	Nu. 3:31
31—A	4: 9
32, 33	8: 2, 3, 4
34, 35	4
35+A	1 Ki. 7:35
26:35	2 Ki. 4:10
30:27	1 Ch. 28:15
31: 8	2 Ch. 4: 7, 20
35:16	13:11
38:13	Jer. 52:19—S
39:16	Zec. 4: 2
40: 4, 22	11—S¹

λύχνος.

Exo. 25:37, 37	2 Ch. 13:11
27:20	21: 7
30: 7, 8	29: 7
38:16, 17	Job 18: 6
39:17, 17	21:17
40: 4, 23	29: 3
Lev. 24: 2, 4	Psa. 17:29
Nu. 4: 9	118:105
8: 2, 2, 3	131:17
1 Sa. 3: 3	Pro. 6:23
2 Sa. 21:17	20 27+A
22:29	29:36
1 Ki. 7:35	Jer. 25:10
2 Ki. 8:19	Zeph. 1:12
1 Ch. 28:15	Zec. 4: 2, 2
2 Ch. 4:20, 21	

λύω.

Gen. 12:27	Ps. 104:20
Exo. 3: 5	145: 7
Jos. 5:15	Isa. 5:27
2 Sa. 16: 2 B[a]	14:17
Ezra 5:12 B[b]	40: 2
Job 5:20[c]	58: 6
39: 2, 5	Jer. 47: 4
42: 9	Dan. 3:25
Ps. 101:21	5:12

[a] pro ἐκλύω. [b] pro καταλύω. [c] A ῥύομαι.

λῶμα.

Exo. 28:29, 20	Exo. 36:32, 33
30	34, 40

μαγειρεῖον.

Ezekiel 46:23

μαγειρεύω.

Lamentations 2:21

μαγείρισσα.

1 Samuel 8:13

μάγειρος.

1 Sa. 9:23, 24	Eze. 46:24
Lam. 2:20	

μαγίς.

Judges 7:13

μάγος.

Dan. 1:20	Dan. 4: 4
2: 2, 10	5: 7, 11
27	15

μαδαρόω.

Nehemiah 13:25—ABS

μαδάω.

Lev. 13:40, 41 | Eze. 29:18

μαελέθ.

Psa. 52: 1 | Psa. 87: 1

μαζουρώθ.

2 Ki. 23: 5 | Job 38:32

μάθημα.

Jer. 13:21[a]

[a] A μαθητής.

μαθητής.

Jer. 13:21 A[a]

[a] pro μάθημα.

μαῖα.

Gen. 35:17	Exo. 1:18, 19
38:28	19, 20
Exo. 1:15, 17	21

μαιμάσσω, —μάω.

Job 38: 8[a] | Jer. 4:19—S¹

[a] A μαιόομαι.

μαίνομαι.

Jer. 32: 2 ABS[a] | Jer. 36:26

[a] pro ἐκμαίνω.

μαιόομαι.

Exo. 1:16	Job 38: 8 A[b]
Job 26: 5[a]	

[a] S¹ ματαιόω. [b] pro μαιμάω.

μακαρίζω.

Gen. 30:13	Ps. 143:15
Nu. 24:17	Cant. 6: 8
Job 29:10, 11	Isa. 3:12
Psa. 40: 3	9:16
71:18	Mal. 3:12, 15

μακάριος.

Gen. 30:13	Psa. 39: 5
Deu. 33:29	40: 2
1 Ki. 10: 8, 8	64: 5
2 Ch. 9: 7, 7	83: 5, 6, 13
Job 5:17	88:16
Psa. 1: 1	93:12
2:13	105: 3
31: 1, 2	111: 1
32:12	118: 1, 2
33: 9	126: 5

Ps. 127: 1, 2
136: 8, 9
143:15
145: 5
Pro. 3:13
8:32+AS²
34
Pro. 20: 7
28:14
Ecc. 10:17
Isa. 30:18
31: 9
32:20
56: 2
Dan. 12:12

μακαριστός.

Pro. 14:21
16:20
Pro. 29:18

μακράν vide μακρός.

μακρόβιος.

Isaiah 53:10

μακροημερεύω.

Deu. 5:33
6: 2
11: 9, 21[a]
Deu. 32:47
Jud. 2: 7

[a] A πολυημερεύω.

μακροήμερος.

Deu. 4:40[a] [a] A μακροχρόνιος.

μακρόθεν.

Gen. 21:16[a]
16+A
22: 4
37:18
Exo. 2: 4
20:18, 21
24: 1
Deu. 28:49
29:22
Jos. 9:12, 15
1 Sa. 26:13
1 Ki. 8:41+A
2 Ki. 2: 7
19:25+A
2 Ch. 6:32
Ezra 3:13
Neh. 12:43
Psa. 9:22
37:12
137: 6
138: 2
Pro. 25:25
29:32
Isa. 60: 4, 9
Jer. 4:16
6:20
8:19
26:27
28:50
38:10[b]
Eze. 23:40
Hab. 1: 8

[a] A μακρός. [b] ADS μακρός.

μακροθυμέω.

Job 7:16
Pro. 19:11
Ecc. 8:12+S²

μακροθυμία.

Pro. 25:15
Isa. 57:15
Jer. 15:15

μακρόθυμος.

Exo. 34: 6
Nu. 14:18
Neh. 9:17
Psa. 7:12
85:15
102: 8
144: 8
Pro. 14:29
Pro. 15:18, 18
16:32
17:27
Ecc. 7: 9
Dan. 4:24
Joel 2:13
Jon. 4: 2
Nah. 1: 3

μακρός, μακράν.

Gen. 21:16 A[a]
44: 4
Exo. 8:28
33: 7
Nu. 9:10, 13
Deu. 12:21
13: 7
14:23, 23
19: 6
20:15
30:11
Jos. 3: 4, 16
8: 4
9:28
Jud. 18: 7
9+A
Jud. 18:28
2 Sa. 7:19
15:17
1 Ki. 8:46
1 Ch. 17:17
2 Ch. 6:36
Ezra 6: 6
Neh. 4:19
Est. 9:20
Job 11: 9
12:12 A[b]
30:10
36: 3
Psa. 21: 2
64: 6
118:155
Pro. 2:16
4:24
5: 8
7:19
13:19
15:29
19: 7
22:15
24:31
27:10
28:16
Ecc. 7:25
Isa. 5:18, 26
27: 9
46:12
Isa. 57: 9, 19
59:11, 14
Jer. 2: 5
30:28
38:10 AS[a]
Eze. 6:12
11:15
12:22, 27
17: 3
22: 5
Dan. 9: 7
Joel 3: 8
Mic. 4: 3
Zec. 6:15
10: 9

[a] pro μακρόθεν. [b] pro πολύς.

μακρότης.

Deu. 30:20
Psa. 20: 5
22: 6
90:16
Psa. 92: 5
Ecc. 8:12
Lam. 5:20
Dan. 7:12

μακροχρονέω, –νίζω.

Deu. 17:20[a]
Deu. 32:27

[a] A μακροχρόνιος.

μακροχρόνιος.

Exo. 20:12
Deu. 4:40 A[a]
Deu. 5:16
17:20 A[b]

[a] pro μακροήμερος.
[b] pro μακροχρονίζω.

μάκρυμμα.

Ezra 9: 1, 11[a]

[a] (S¹ μακρυνσει.)

μακρύνω.

Jud. 18:22
Psa. 21:20
39:12
54: 8
55: 1
70:12
72:27
87: 9, 19
102:12
108:17
118:150
Ps. 119: 5
128: 3
Pro. 5: 7 S¹[a]
Ecc. 3: 5
7:25
8:13
Isa. 6:12
49:19
54: 2
Jer. 34: 8
Lam. 1:16

[a] pro ἄκυρος.

μάλα.

2 Sa. 14: 5
1 Ki. 1:43
2 Ki. 4:14

μάλαγμα.

Isa. 1: 6
Eze. 30:21

μαλακία.

Gen. 42: 4
44:29
Exo. 23:25
Deu. 7:15
28:61
2 Ch. 6:29
16:12
2 Ch. 21:15, 15
18, 19
24:25
Job 33:19
Isa. 38: 9
53: 3

μαλακίζω.

Gen. 42:38
2 Sa. 13: 5
2 Ch. 16:12, 12
Job 24:23
Isa. 38: 1, 9
39: 1
53: 5
Dan. 8:27

μαλακός.

Pro. 25:15
Pro. 26:22

μαλακύνω.

Job 23:16

μαλακῶς.

Job 40:22

μᾶλλον.

Gen. 19: 9
29:30
Nu. 13:32
14:12
Deu. 9: 1, 14
11:23
Job 20: 2
30:26
42:12+A
Psa. 63:11
Pro. 5: 4
Pro. 15:18
16: 5
18: 2
21: 3
26:12
28:23
29:20
Isa. 13:12, 12
54: 1
Jer. 8: 3+A
Jon. 1:11, 13

μάν.

Exo. 16:31, 32
33
Exo. 16:35[a], 35

[a] A μάννα.

μαναά.

2 Ki. 8: 8, 9
17: 3, 4
20:12
2 Ch. 7: 7
Neh. 13: 5, 9A[a]
Eze. 45:25
46: 5, 7, 11
14, 14
15, 20
Dan. 2:46

[a] pro μάννα.

μάνδρα.

Jud. 6: 2 A[a]
1 Sa. 13: 6
2 Sa. 7: 8
1 Ch. 17: 7
2 Ch. 32:28
Psa. 9:30–A
Ps. 103:22
Cant. 4: 8
Jer. 4: 7
Eze. 31:14
Amos 3: 4
Zeph. 2: 6

[a] pro τρυμαλιά.

μανδραγόρας.

Gen. 30:14, 14
15, 15
Gen. 30:16
Cant. 7:13

μανδύας.

Jud. 3:16
1 Sa. 17:38, 39
18: 4 A
2 Sa. 10: 4
20: 8
1 Ch. 19: 4

μανή.

Daniel 5:25, 26

μανθάνω.

Exo. 2: 4
Deu. 4:10
5: 1
14:22
17:19
18: 9
31:12, 13
1 Ch. 25: 8
Est. 4: 5
Job 34:36
Ps. 105:35
118: 7, 71
73
Pro. 6: 8
17:16
22:25
Isa. 1:17
2: 4
8:16
26: 9, 10
28:19
29:24, 24
32: 4
47:12
Jer. 9: 5
10: 2[a]
12:16, 16
13:23
Eze. 19: 3, 6
Dan. 7:16–θ¹
Mic. 4: 3

[a] A πορεύω.

μανία.

Psa. 39: 5
Hos. 9: 7[a], 8

[a] A μνεία.

μανιάκης.

Daniel 5: 7, 16, 29

μάννα.

Exo. 16:35 A[a]
Nu. 11: 6, 7, 9
Deu. 8: 3, 16
Jos. 5:12, 12
Neh. 9:20
Neh. 13: 9[b]
Psa. 77:24
Jer. 17:26
48: 5

[a] pro μάν. [b] AS² μαναά.

μαντεία.

Nu. 23:23
Deu. 18:10, 14
2 Ki. 17:17–A
Isa. 16: 6
41:25
Jer. 14:14
Eze. 13: 7, 8, 23
21:21, 23
Mic. 3: 6

μαντεῖον.

Nu. 22: 7
Pro. 16:10
Eze. 21:22

μαντεύομαι.

Deu. 18:10
1 Sa. 28: 8
2 Ki. 17:17
Jer. 34: 7
Eze. 12:24
Eze. 13: 6, 23
21:21, 23
29
22:28
Mic. 3:11

μάντις.

Jos. 13:22
1 Sa. 6: 2
Jer. 36: 8
Mic. 3: 7
Zec. 10: 2

μαραίνω.

Job 15:30
Job 24:24

μαρμάρινος.

Canticles 5:15

μαρσίππιον, μαρσύππιον.

Pro. 1:14
Isa. 46: 6

μάρσιππος.

Gen. 42:27, 27
28
43:11, 17
20, 20
20 A[a]
21, 22
Gen. 44: 1, 1, 2, 8
11, 11
12, 13
Deu. 25:13
Mic. 6:11

[a] pro χείρ.

μαρτυρέω, –τύρομαι.

Gen. 31:46
47 A[a]
48 ter
43: 2[b]
Nu. 35:30
Deu. 19:15, 18
31:19[c], 21
2 Ch. 28:10
Lam. 2:13

[a] pro μάρτυς. [b] A διαμαρτυρέω.
[c] A μαρτύριον.

μαρτυρία.

Gen. 31:47[a]
Exo. 20:16
Deu. 5:20
Psa. 18: 8
Pro. 12:19
25:18

[a] A μάρτυς.

μαρτύριον.

Gen. 21:30
31:44
Exo. 16:34[a]
25: 9, 15
20, 21
26:33, 34
27:21
28:39
29: 4, 10
10
11–A
30, 32
42, 44
30: 6, 16
18, 20
21, 26
26
27+θ
36, 36
31: 7, 18
32:15
33: 7
35:11, 21
37: 5, 19
38:26, 27
39: 8, 10
Exo. 39:21
40: 2, 3
5+A
5, 6, 10
18, 19
20
20+AB
22, 24
26+A²
28, 29
Lev. 1: 1, 3, 5
3: 2, 8, 13
4: 4, 5, 7
7, 14
16, 18
18
6:16, 26
30
8: 3, 4, 31
33, 35
9: 5, 23
10: 7, 9
12: 6
14:11, 23
15:14, 29
16: 2, 7, 13

Lev. 16:16, 17
20, 23
33
17: 4, 4, 5
6, 9
19:21
24: 3
Nu. 1: 1, 50
53, 53
2: 2, 17
3: 7, 8, 10
25, 25
38
4: 3, 4, 5
15, 23
25, 25
26, 28
30, 31
33, 35
37, 39
41, 43
47
5:17
6:10, 13
18
7: 5, 89
89
8: 9, 15
19, 22
24, 26
9:15
10: 3, 11
11:16
12: 4, 4, 5
14:10
16:18, 19
42, 43
50
17: 4, 4, 7
8, 10
18: 2, 4, 6
21, 22
23, 31
19: 4
20: 6
25: 6
27: 2
31:54
Deu. 4:45
6:17, 20
9:15−8
31:14 *ter*
15
15−A[1]B[1]
19 A[b]
26
Jos. 4:16
Jos. 18: 1
19:51
22:27, 28
34
24:27, 27
Ruth 4: 7
1 Sa. 2:22+A
9:24
13: 8, 11
20:35
1 Ki. 2: 3+A
8: 4, 4
2 Ki. 11:12
17:15
23: 3
1 Ch. 6:32
9:21
23:32
29:19
2 Ch. 1: 3, 13
5: 3
23:11
24: 6
34:31
Neh. 9:34
Job 15:34
16: 8
Psa. 24:10
77: 5, 56
79: 1
80: 6
92: 5
98: 7
118: 2, 14
22, 24
31, 36
46, 59
79, 88
95, 99
111, 119
125, 129
138, 144
146, 152
157, 167
168
121: 4
131:12
Pro. 29:14
Isa. 55: 4
Jer. 37:20
51:23
Hos. 2:12
Amos 1:11
Mic. 1: 2
7:18
Zeph. 3: 8

[a] S θεός. [b] *pro* μαρτυρέω.

μάρτυς.

Gen. 31:44
47 A[a]
47[b]
50−A
51−A
Exo. 23: 1
Lev. 5: 1
Nu. 5:13
23:18
35:30, 30
Deu. 17: 6 *ter*
7
19:15 *ter*
16, 18
Jos. 24:22
Ruth 4: 9, 10
11
1 Sa. 12: 5 *ter*
6
20:23, 42
1 Ki. 17:20
Job 16:19
Psa. 26:12
34:11
88:38
Pro. 6:19
12:17, 19
14: 5, 5, 25
19: 5, 9
21:28
24:43
Isa. 8: 2
43: 9, 10
10, 12
12+A
44: 8
Jer. 36:23
39:10, 25
44
49: 5
Mal. 3: 5

[a] *pro* μαρτυρία. [b] A μαρτυρέω.

μασαναί, μεσ−

2 Ki. 22:14
2 Ch. 34:22

μασμαρώθ.

Jeremiah 52:19

μασσάομαι.

Job 30: 5

μαστιγόω.

Exo. 5:14, 16
Deu. 25: 2−8
3, 3
1 Ki. 12*p*24*l*66
2 Ch. 25:16
Job 15:11
30:21
Psa. 72: 5, 14
Pro. 3:12
17:10
19:25
27:22
Jer. 5: 3

μαστίζω.

Numbers 22:25

μάστιξ.

1 Ki. 12:11, 14
*p*24*l*66
2 Ch. 10:11, 14
Job 5:21
21: 9
Psa. 31:10
34:15
37:18
38:11
Psa. 72: 4
88:33
90:10
Pro. 19:29
26: 3
Isa. 50: 6
Jer. 6: 7
Nah. 3: 2

μαστός.

Gen. 49:25
Job 3:12
24: 9
Psa. 21:10
Cant. 1: 2, 4
13−9
4: 5, 10
10
6:10
7: 3, 7, 8
12
8: 1, 8, 10
Isa. 28: 9
32:12
66:11
Jer. 18:14
Lam. 2:20
4: 3
Eze. 16: 4, 7
23: 3, 21
Hos. 2: 2
9:14
Joel 2:16

μάταιος.

Exo. 20: 7, 7
23: 1
Lev. 17: 7
Deu. 5:11, 11
1 Ki. 16: 2, 13
26
2 Ki. 17:15−A
2 Ch. 11:15
Job 20:18
Psa. 5:10
11: 3
23: 4
59:13
61:10
93:11
107:13
Pro. 12:11
21: 6
24:31
26: 2
29:18
Isa. 1:13
2:20
22: 1
28:29
29: 8
30: 7, 7, 15
15, 28
29+AS[2]
Isa. 31: 2
32: 6
33:11
44: 9
45:19
49: 4
59: 4
Jer. 2: 5
4:30[a]
8:19
10: 3, 15
28:18
Lam. 2:14, 14
4:17
Eze. 8:10
11: 2
13: 6, 7, 8
9, 19
21:29
22:28
Hos. 5:11 6:8
12: 1
Amos 2: 4[b]
Jon. 2: 9
Mic. 1:14
Zeph. 3:13
Zec. 10: 2
11:17
Mal. 3:14

[a] A μάτην. [b] A αἷμα.

ματαιότης.

Psa. 4: 3
25: 4
30: 7
37:13
38: 6
39: 5
51: 9
61:10
77:33
118:37
138:20
143: 4, 8, 11
Pro. 22: 8
Ecc. 1: 2*quater*
14
2: 1, 11
15[a], 17
19, 21
23, 26
3:19
4: 4, 7, 8
16
5: 6, 9
6: 2, 4, 9
Ecc. 6:11
7: 1−6
7, 16
8:10, 14
14
Ecc. 9: 1, 9
9+CS
11: 8, 10
12: 8 *ter*

[a] S[1] μάτη.

ματαιόω.

1 Sa. 13:13
26:21
2 Ki. 17:15−A
1 Ch. 21: 8
Job 26: 5 S[1a]
Jer. 2: 5
23:16
28:17[b]

[a] *pro* ματόομαι. [b] A μωραίνω.

ματαίως.

1 Ki. 20:25
Job 35:16
Psa. 3: 8
Psa. 34:19[a]
72:13
88:48

[a] A ἀδίκως.

μάτη.

Ecc. 2:15 S[1a] [a] *pro* ματαιότης.

μάτην.

1 Ki. 20:20
Psa. 34: 7
38: 7, 12
40: 7
62:10
126: 1, 1, 2
Pro. 3:30
Isa. 27: 3
Isa. 28:17
29:13
30: 5
41:29
Jer. 2:30
4:30 A[a]
8: 8
Eze. 14:23

[a] *pro* μάταιος.

μάχαιρα.

Gen. 22: 6, 10
27:40
31:26
34:25, 26
48:22
Exo. 15: 9
17:13
22:24
Lev. 26: 8, 25
33
Nu. 14:43
21:24
22:29, 31
Deu. 13:15
20:13
32:25, 41
42−8
33:29
Jos. 5: 2, 3
8:24 B*[a]
10:11
28 B[1b]
30 B*[b]
19:48
21:42
24:31
Jud. 1: 8 A[a]
3:16, 21
22
7:22 A[a]
8:20 A[a]
9:54[a]
19:29 A[a]
20:38 A[c]
1 Sa. 25:13+A
13+A
2 Sa. 2:16
11:25
15:14
18: 8
20: 8, 8, 10
23:10
1 Ki. 3:24, 24
18:28
2 Ki. 10:37
1 Ch. 5:18
21: 5, 5−8
12
2 Ch. 23: 9, 14
21+A
29: 9
Job 1:15, 17
Job 39:23
Psa. 56: 5
150*p*6
Pro. 5: 4
12:18
21:23, 37
25:18
Isa. 1:20
2: 4, 4
3:25, 25
10:34
13:15
14:19
21:15
22: 2
27: 1
31: 8, 8, 8[d]
34: 5, 6
37: 7, 38
41: 2
49: 2
51:19
65:12
Jer. 2:30
4:10
5:12
9:16
11:22
12:12
14:12, 13
15, 16
18[e]
15: 2[f], 2[f]
3, 9
16: 4
18:21−S[1]
21
19: 7
20: 4, 4
21: 7, 7, 9
24:10
25:16
26:10, 14
16
27:16, 21
35, 36
36, 37
37
29: 6
31: 2, 10
32: 2, 13
15, 17
Jer. 32:24
33:23
34: 6
38: 2
39:24, 36
41:17
Lam. 1:20
Eze. 5: 2, 12
26: 6, 8, 9
11, 15
28: 7, 23
30: 4, 5, 6
11, 17
21, 22
31:17, 18
32:12, 19
Eze. 32:21, 22
23+A
24, 26
27, 28
29
29+A
30
31+A
32
33:27
35: 5, 8
38: 4, 8
21+A
21
39:23
Zec. 11:17

[a] *pro* ῥομφαία. [b] *pro* ξίφος. [c] *pro* μάχη. [d] A διώκω. [e] A ῥομφαία. [f] S[1] χαρά.

μαχβάρ.

2 Kings 8:15[a]
[a] A ναβρά, B χαββά.

μαχείρ.

1 Ki. 5:11[a] [a] A μαχάλ.

μάχη.

Gen. 13: 7, 8
Jos. 4:13
Jud. 11:25 A[a]
20:38[b]
2 Sa. 22:44
Job 38:23
Pro. 15:18
Pro. 17: 1, 14
19
24:67, 68
25: 8, 10
26:20, 21
Isa. 58: 4

[a] *pro* μάχομαι. [b] A μάχαιρα.

μαχητής.

Jos. 6: 3 A[a]
Jud. 3:29 A[b]
5:23+A
12: 2[c]
2 Sa. 15:18−A
24: 9
1 Ch. 28: 1
Jer. 20:11
26: 9, 12
12
Jer. 27: 9, 36
37
28:30, 56
Joel 2: 7
3: 9, 11
Amos 2:14
Obad. 9
Hab. 1: 6+A
Zec. 9:13
10: 5, 7

[a] *pro* μάχιμος. [b] *pro* λιπαρός. [c] A ἀντιδικέω.

μάχιμος.

Jos. 5: 6
6: 3[a], 7
9, 13
2 Ki. 19:25
Pro. 21:19

[a] A μαχητής.

μάχομαι.

Gen. 26:20, 22
31:36
Exo. 21:22
Lev. 24:10
Deu. 25:11
Jos. 9:24
Jud. 11:25[a], 25
2 Sa. 14: 6
2 Ki. 3:23
2 Ch. 27: 5
Neh. 5: 7
13:11, 17
25
Cant. 1: 6
Isa. 27: 8
28:20
Jer. 40: 5

[a] A μάχη.

μαωζείμ.

Daniel 11:38

μεγαλαυχέω.

Psa. 9:39
Eze. 16:50
Zeph. 3:11

μεγαλεῖος.

Deu. 11: 2
Psa. 70:19
Psa. 104:1 S[1a]
105:21 A[2b]

[a] *pro* ἔργον. [b] *pro* μέγας.

μεγαλειότης.

Jer. 40: 9[a] [a] S μεγαλωσύνη.

μεγαλοπρέπεια.

Psa. 6: 2
20: 6
28: 4
67:35
70: 8
Psa. 95: 6
103: 1AS[2][a]
110: 3
144: 5, 12

[a] pro εὐπρέπεια.

μεγαλοπρεπής.

Deuteronomy 33:26

μεγαλοπτέρυγος.

Ezekiel 17: 3, 7

μεγαλορρημονέω.

Psa. 34:26
37:17
54:13
Eze. 35:13
Obad. 12

μεγαλορρημοσύνη.

1 Samuel 2: 3

μεγαλορρήμων.

Psalm 11: 4

μεγαλόσαρκος.

Ezekiel 16:26

μεγαλόφρων.

Proverbs 21: 4

μεγαλύνω.

Gen. 12: 2
19:19
43:33
Nu. 15: 3, 8
Jud. 5:13+A
1 Sa. 2:21
26+A
3:19
12:24
26:24, 24
2 Sa. 5:10
7:22
25+A
26
22:51
1 Ki. 1:37, 47
10:23
1 Ch. 11: 9−BS
17:24-ABS
29:12, 25
2 Ch. 1: 1[a]
9:22
Ezra 9: 6
Est. 9: 3+S[3]
Job 7:17
19: 5
Psa. 11: 5
17:51
19: 6, 8[b]
33: 4
34:27
39:17
40:10
56:11
Psa. 68:31
69: 5
91: 6
103: 1, 24
125: 2, 3
137: 2
Pro. 8:16
Ecc. 1:16
2: 4, 9
Isa. 42:21
Jer. 5:27
31:26, 42
38:14
Lam. 1: 9
2:13
4: 6
Eze. 9: 9
16: 7
24: 9
38:23
Dan. 2:48
4: 8, 17
19, 19
30
8: 4, 8, 9
10, 25
11:36, 37
Joel 2:20, 21
Amos 8: 5
Mic. 1:10
5: 4
Zeph. 2: 8, 10
Zec. 12: 7, 11
Mal. 1: 5

[a] B αὐξάνω.
[b] S[1] ἀγαλλιάω, S[2] ἐπικαλέω.

μεγάλωμα.

Jeremiah 31:17

μεγαλώνυμος.

Jeremiah 39:19

μεγάλως.

Nu. 6: 2
1 Ch. 29: 9
Neh. 12:43
Job 4:14
15:11
17: 7

Job 24:12 A[a]
30:30
Zec. 11: 2

[a] pro μέγας.

μεγαλωσύνη.

Deu. 32: 3
2 Sa. 7:21, 23
1 Ch. 17:19
22: 5
29:11
Psa. 70:21 S[2][a]
78:11
144: 3
Ps. 144: 6−S[1]
150: 2
Pro. 18:10
Jer. 40: 9 S[b]
Dan. 4:19, 33
5:18, 19
7:27
Zec. 11: 3

[a] pro δικαιοσύνη.
[b] pro μεγαλειότης.

μέγας.

Gen. 1:16, 16
21
10:12
12: 2, 17
15:12, 18
17:20
18:18, 20
19:11
20: 9
21: 8, 13
18
26:13
27:33, 34
29: 2
38:11, 14
39:14
45: 7, 28
46: 3
50: 9, 10
11
Exo. 1: 9
2:11
3: 3
6: 6
7: 4
9: 3
11: 3, 6
12:30
14:31
18:11
19:16
23:31
32:10, 11
21, 30
31
33:13−A[1]
Lev. 21:10
Nu. 11:33
13:29
14:12, 19
22:18
34: 6, 7
35:25, 28
28, 32
Deu. 1: 7, 17
19, 28
28
2: 7, 10
21
4: 6, 7, 8
11+B
32
34−B[1]
36, 37
38
5:22, 25
6:10, 22
7: 1
1+A
19, 19
21, 23
8:15, 17
9: 1, 1, 2
14
26+A
26
26 A[a]
29
10:17, 21
11: 7−B
23, 24
Deu. 15: 9
18:16
25:13, 14
26: 5
5+A
8, 8
27: 2, 14
28:59
29: 3, 3
24, 28
34:12
Jos. 1: 4
6:20
7: 1−A
9, 26
9: 1
10: 2, 10
20
11: 2, 8
13: 7, 7
14:12
15:12, 47
17:17
19:28
20: 6 A
22:10
23: 4, 9
24: 4, 26
Jud. 2: 7
5:15, 16
11:33
15: 8, 18
16: 5, 6
15, 23
21: 2, 5
1 Sa. 2:14, 17
4: 5, 6
10, 17
5: 6, 9, 9
6: 9, 14
15, 18
19
7:10
10: 2
12:16, 17
22
14:20, 24
33, 45
17:25 A
19: 5, 8
22 A[b]
20: 2−B
41
22:15
23: 5
25: 2, 36
28:12
30: 2, 16
19
2 Sa. 3:38
7: 9
13:15, 15
16, 36
15:23
18: 7, 9, 17
17, 17
29
19: 4, 32
20: 8
23:10, 12
2 Sa. 24: 6+A
1 Ki. 1:40
2:22
(3)p1
3: 4, 6, 6
15
4:13
6: 2
7:46, 47
49
8:41+A
55, 65
10:18
12p24l19
18:27, 28
45
19:11
21:13, 21
28
22:31
2 Ki. 3:27
4: 8
38−B
5: 1, 13
6:23, 25
7: 6
8: 4
10:19
21−A
12:10
16:15
17:21, 36
18:19, 28
28
20: 3
22: 4, 8, 13
23: 2, 4, 26
25:26
1 Ch. 9:31
11:14
12:14, 22
16:25
17: 8
22: 8
25: 8
26:13
29: 1
2 Ch. 1: 8, 10
2: 5, 5, 9
3: 5
4: 9
6:32
7: 8
9:17
13:17
15:14
16:14
18:30
20:19, 27
21:14
24:11, 25
26:15
28: 5
30:21, 26
31:15
32:18
34: 9, 21
30
35:19
36:18
Ezra 3:11, 12
13
4:10
5: 8, 11
9: 7, 13
10:12
Neh. 1: 3, 5
10−S[1]
3: 1, 20
27
4:14
5: 1, 7
6: 3
16+S
7: 4
8: 6, 12
17
9: 4−AB
18
19 A[c]
25, 26
Neh. 9:27, 32
37
11:14-ABS[1]
12:31-ABS[1]
43
13: 5
27+S[3]
28
Est. 1: 5+S[3]
4: 1, 3
10: 3
Job 1: 3, 19
2:12, 13
3: 8, 19
5: 9
9: 4, 10
22
10:17
21:12[d]
30: 4
36:24
37: 4, 21
38: 7
40:17
42: 3
Psa. 18:14
20: 6
21:26
39:10
46: 3
47: 2, 3
50: 3
75: 2
76:14
85:10
10−AS
13
88: 8
94: 3, 3
95: 4
98: 2, 3
103:25, 25
105:21[e]
107: 5
108:26+S[1]
110: 2
113:21
130: 1
134: 5
135: 4, 7
17
137: 5
144: 3
146: 5, 5
150p6
Pro. 2: 3+AB[g]C[2]
15:16
16:32+AC[g]S[2]
18:11
20: 6, 10
24: 5
26:25
27:14
28:16
29: 6
Ecc. 2:21
9:13, 14
14
10: 1, 4, 6
6+S
Isa. 1:13
5: 9, 14
7:20+AS
8: 1
9: 2, 6, 7
14
10:12
18: 7
19:22+AS
22: 5, 18
24
26: 4
27: 1, 13
29: 6
33: 4, 19
21, 22
34: 6
36: 4, 13
Isa. 36:13
38: 3
39: 2+AS
49: 6
54: 7
60:22
Jer. 4: 5, 6
6: 1, 13
22+AS[2]
10:22
11:16
21: 5, 6
22: 8
27:22, 41
28:54, 55
31: 3
32:18, 24
33:19
34: 4
35: 8
37: 7
38:34
39:17, 18
19
19−S
21, 37
42
40: 3
43: 7
48: 9
49: 1, 8
50: 9
51: 7, 12
15, 26
35
52:13
Eze. 1: 4
3:12
8: 6
9: 1
11:13
17: 3
6+A
7, 8, 9
17, 23
21:14
25:17
29: 3, 18
31:10
36:23[f]
37.10 A[c]
Eze. 38:15, 19
39:17
43:14, 14
47:10, 15
19, 20
48:28
Dan. 2:10, 31
35, 45
48
3: 3, 33
4:27
5: 1−A
6:20 A[g]
7: 2, 3
7+A
8
11−A
17+A
20
8: 8, 21
9: 4, 12
10: 1, 4, 7, 8
11: 2, 13
25, 25
12: 1
Hos. 1:11
Joel 2:11
11+ABS
25, 31
Amos 6:11
Jon. 1: 2, 4, 10
12, 16
2: 1
3: 2, 3, 5
4: 1, 6
11−A
Nah. 1: 3
Zeph. 1:10, 14
Hag. 1: 1, 12
14
2: 2, 4, 9
Zec. 1: 2, 14
15
3: 1, 8
4: 6, 7
6:11
7:12
8: 2, 2
14: 4, 13
Mal. 1:11, 14
4: 4

[a] pro ὑψηλός.
[b] pro ἅλως.
[c] pro πολύς.
[d] A μεγάλως.
[e] A[2] μεγαλεῖος.
[f] A ἅγιος.
[g] pro ἰσχυρός.

μέγεθος.

Exo. 15:16
1 Sa. 16: 7
1 Ki. 6:21
7:21
2 Ki. 19:23
Cant. 7: 7
Eze. 17: 6+A
19:11, 11
31: 3, 5, 10
14

μεγιστᾶνες.

2 Ch. 36:18
Est. (9)14+S[3]
Pro. 8:16
Isa. 34:12−B[g]S[1]
Jer. 14: 3
24: 8
25:17
27:35
32: 5
41:10
Eze. 30:13
Dan. 3:24
4:33
5: 1, 2, 3
9, 23
6:17
Jon. 3: 7
Nah. 2: 6
3:10
Zec. 11: 2

μέγιστος.

Job 26: 3
Job 31:28

μέθη.

Pro. 20: 1
24:74
Isa. 28: 7
Jer. 28:57
Eze. 23:32
39:19
Joel 1: 5
Hag. 1: 6

μεθίστημι.

Deu. 17:17
Deu. 30:17

Jos. 14: 8
Jud. 7: 5+A
9:29
10:16 A[a]
1 Sa. 6:12
1 Ki. 15:13
18:29, 29
2 Ki. 3: 2−A
12: 3
2 Ki. 17:23
23:33
2 Ch. 15:16
Isa. 54:10, 10
59:15
Dan. 2:21
7:12, 26
11:31
Amos 5:23
[a] *pro* ἐκκλίνω.

μεθοδεύω.
2 Samuel 19:27

μεθόριος.
Joshua 19:27+A

μεθύσκω.
Psa. 22: 5
Pro. 4:17
23:31
Jer. 28: 7
Hab. 2:15

μέθυσμα.
Jud. 13: 4[a], 7[a]
14[a]
1 Sa. 1:11, 15
Jer. 13:13
Hos. 4:11
Mic. 2:11
[a] A σίκερα.

μέθυσος.
Pro. 23:21
Pro. 26: 9

μεθύω.
Gen. 9:21
43:33
Deu. 32:42
1 Sa. 1:13, 14
25:36
2 Sa. 11:13
1 Ki. 16: 9
21:16
Job 12:25
Psa. 35: 9
64:10, 11
106:27
Cant. 5: 1
Isa. 7:20 AS^{a}
19:14
24:20
28: 1
Isa. 34: 5, 7
36:12 S^{1b}
49:26
51:21
55:10
58:11
Jer. 26:10
28:39, 57
31:26
32:13
38:14, 25
Lam. 3:15
4:21
Hos. 14: 7
Joel 1: 5
Nah. 3:11
[a] *pro* μισθόω. [b] *pro* μεθ' ὑμῶν.

μεθωεσίμ.
Ezra 2:62

μείζων.
Gen. 4:13
10:21
25:23
26:13
29:16
48:19
Jos. 19: 9
1 Sa. 14:30
17:13 A
1 Sa. 17:14 A
28 A
18:17 A
2 Sa. 13:15−A
1 Ki. 11:19
2 Ch. 17:12
Eze. 8: 6, 13
15
Dan. 7:20

μέλαθρον.
1 Ki. 6: 9
7: 9, 9
1 Ki. 7:41

μελαθρόω.
1 Kings 7:42

μελάνθιον.
Isaiah 28:25, 27, 27

μελανόω.
Job 30:30 A[a]
Cant. 1: 6
[a] *pro* σκοτόω.

μέλας.
Lev. 13:37
Cant. 1: 5
Cant. 5:11
Zec. 6: 2, 6

μέλει.
Job 22: 3

μελετάω.
Jos. 1: 8
Job 6:30
27: 4
Psa. 1: 2
2: 1
34:28
36:30
30 S^{1a}
37:13
62: 7
70:24
76: 7, 13
89: 9
118:16, 47
Ps. 118:70, 117
148
142: 5, 5
Pro. 8: 7
11: 2
15:28
19:27
24: 2
Isa. 16: 7
27: 8
33:18
38:14
59: 3, 13
[a] *pro* λαλέω.

μελέτη.
Job 33:15
37: 1
Psa. 18:15
38: 4
48: 4
118:24, 77
Ps. 118:92, 97
99, 143
174
Ecc. 12:12
Lam. 3:61

μέλι.
Gen. 43:10
Exo. 3: 8, 17
13: 5
16:31
33: 3
Lev. 2:11
20:24
Nu. 13:28
14: 8
16:13, 14
Deu. 6: 3
8: 8
11: 9
26: 9, 10
15
27: 3
31:20
32:13
Jos. 5: 6
Jud. 14: 8, 9, 18
1 Sa. 14:27, 29
43
2 Sa. 17:29
1 Ki. 12 *p* 24 *l* 31
ll 32, 39
14: 3 A
2 Ki. 18:32
2 Ch. 31: 5
Job 20:17
Psa. 18:11
80:17
118:103
Pro. 5: 3
16:24
24:13
25:16, 27
Cant. 4:11
5: 1
Isa. 7:15, 22
Jer. 11: 5
39:22
48: 8
Eze. 3: 3
16:13, 19
20: 6, 15
27:17

μελίζω.
Lev. 1: 6
Jud. 19:29
20: 6
1 Sa. 11: 7
1 Ki. 18:23, 33
Mic. 3: 3

μέλισσα.
Deu. 1:44
Ps. 117:12
Pro. 6: 8
Isa. 7:18

μελισσών.
Jud. 14: 8
1 Sa. 14:25, 26

μέλλω.
Gen. 25:22
43:24
Exo. 4:12
Job 3: 8
19:25
26: 2
Pro. 15:18
Isa. 9: 6+AS^{2}
15: 7
28:24+AS
47:13
48: 6
59: 5
Jer. 38:10

μέλος.
Exo. 29:17
Lev. 1: 6, 12
Lev. 8:20, 20
9:13
Jud. 19:29[a]
Job 9:28
Eze. 2:10
Eze. 24: 6
Mic. 2: 4
[a] A μερίς.

μέμψις.
Job 15:15+A
33:10, 23
Job 39: 7

μένω.
Gen. 24:55
45: 9
Exo. 9:28
Lev. 13: 5, 23
28, 37
Nu. 30: 5, 9, 10
13
Jud. 16: 2+A
19: 9 A[a]
1 Sa. 20:11
2 Sa. 18 14−A
1 Ki. 8:16+B
2 Ki. 7: 9
9: 3
Job 15:23, 29
21:11
36: 2
Psa. 9: 8
32:11
88:37
101:13
110: 3, 10
111: 3, 9
Ps. 116: 2
Pro. 15:22
19:21
Ecc. 7:16
Isa. 5: 2, 4, 7
11
7: 7[b]
8:17
10:32
14:20, 24
27: 9
30:18
32: 8
40: 8
46: 7
59: 9
66:22
Jer. 26:15
Eze. 48: 8+B
Dan. 4:23
6:26
Zec. 14:10
[a] *pro* αὐλίζω. [b] AS ἐμμένω.

μερίζω.
Exo. 15: 9
Nu. 26:53, 55
56
Deu. 18: 8
33:21
Jos. 13: 7
14: 5
18: 6
1 Sa. 23:28
30:24
1 Ki. 16:21
18: 6
Neh. 9:22[a]
Neh. 13:13
Job 31: 2[b]
39:17 ABS^{c}
40:25 S^{2d}
Pro. 8:21
14:18
19:14
29:24[e]
Isa. 53:12
Jer. 12:14
28:34
Hos. 10: 2
[a] A διαμερίζω. [b] A ἐπιμερίζω, S^{1} διαμερίζω. [c] *pro* ἐπιμερίζω. [d] *pro* μεριτεύομαι. [e] S^{1} ἐρίζω, S^{2} συμμερίζω.

μέριμνα.
Job 11:18
Psa. 54:23
Pro. 17:12

μεριμνάω.
Exo. 5: 9, 9
2 Sa. 7:10
1 Ch. 17: 9
Psa. 37:19
Pro. 14:23
Eze. 16:42

μερίς.
Gen. 14:24, 24
23: 9 A[a]
31:14
33:19
43:33 *ter*
Exo. 29:26
Lev. 6:17
7:23
8:29
Nu. 18:20, 20
31:36
Deu. 9:26[b]
10: 9
12:12
14:26, 28
18: 1, 8
32: 9
Jos. 14: 4
15:13
18: 5, 6, 7
7, 9
19: 9, 47
21:42
Jos. 22:25, 27
24:32, 32
Jud. 5:15[c]
19:29 A[d]
Ruth 2: 3
3: 7
4: 3
1 Sa. 1: 4, 5
9:23
30:24, 24
2 Sa. 2:16
14:30 *ter*
31
20: 1
23:11, 12
1 Ki. 12:16
p 24 *l* 70
2 Ki. 3:19, 25
9:10, 21
25, 26
26, 36
37
1 Ch. 11:13, 14
2 Ch. 10:16
31: 3, 4, 19
35: 5
Neh. 2:20
8:10, 12[e]
11:36
12:44, 47
13:10
Est. 2: 9
9:19
19+ABS
22
Job 17: 5
20:29
24:18
27:13
30:19
Psa. 10: 6
15: 5
49:18
62:11
72:26
118:57
141: 6
Pro. 15:16
Pro. 20:21
Ecc. 2:10, 21
3:22
5:17
9: 6, 9
11: 2
Isa. 17:14
57: 6
Jer. 10:16
12:10−S
10
13:25
28:19
Lam. 3:24−AB
4:16
Eze. 45: 7
48: 8, 21
Dan. 4:12, 20
Amos 4: 7, 7
7: 4
Mic. 2: 4
Nah. 3: 8−S^{3}
8
Hab. 1:16
Zec. 2:12
[a] *pro* μέρος. [b] A κληρονομία [c] A διαίρεσις. [d] *pro* μέλος. [e] S^{1} μυριάς.

μερισμός.
Jos. 11:23
Ezra 6:18

μεριτεύομαι.
Job 40:25[a]
[a] S^{3} μερίζω.

μέρος.
Gen. 23: 9[a]
47:24, 24
Exo. 16:35
25:25
26: 4, 5, 19
19−AB^{1}
21
21−B
22, 25
26, 35
35
29: 7
32:15
36:11, 25
38: 3+A
14, 24
Nu. 8: 2, 3
11: 1
20:16
22:36, 41
23:13
33: 6
34: 3
Jos. 2:18
3: 8[b], 15
16
4:19
12: 2
13:27
15: 2, 5, 8
18:14[c], 14
15, 15
16, 16
19, 20
Jud. 7:11 A[d]
19 A[d]
18: 2+A
1 Sa. 6: 8
9:27
23:26[e], 26[e]
30:14
2 Sa. 13:34
1 Ki. (3) *p* 46
1 Ki. 4:24
6:22
22−B
7:16
12:31
13:33
2 Ki. 7: 5[f], 8
19:23 A[g]
23 A[h]
2 Ch. 36: 7
Ezra 4:20
Neh. 3:15−ABS
7:70
11: 1
Job 26:14
30: 1
31:12
Pro. 17: 2
29:11
Ecc. 5:18
Isa. 7:18
9: 1+AS
18: 7
37:24
Jer. 30:10 A[i]
32:17, 19
19−S^{1}
52:23
Eze. 1: 8, 17
10:11
40:47
42:20
43:16, 17
46:21
47:20, 20
48: 1[k], 1
Dan. 1: 2
2:33, 33
41, 41
42 *ter*
7: 5
11:45
Zec. 13: 8
[a] A μερίς. [b] B μέσος. [c] B^{1} ὅμος. [d] *pro* ἀρχή. [e] A μέσος. [f] AB^{1} μεσος. [g] *pro* μηρός. [h] *pro* μέσος. [i] *pro* πέραν. [k] A μέτρον.

μέσακλον.
1 Samuel 17: 7

μεσημβρία.

Gen. 18: 1
43:15, 24
Deu. 28:29
Jud. 5:10—A
2 Sa. 4: 5
1 Ki. 18:26, 27
21:16
2 Ki. 4:20
Job 11:17
Psa. 36: 6
Psa. 54:18
Cant. 1: 7
Isa. 18: 4
58:10
59:10
Jer. 6: 4
15: 8
20:16
Amos 8: 9
Zeph. 2: 4

μεσημβρινός.

Job 5:14
Psa. 90: 6
Isa. 16: 3

μεσθάιλ.

2 Kings 10:22

μεσίτης.

Job 9:33

μεσονύκτιος.

Jud. 16: 3, 3A[a]
Ruth 3: 8
Ps. 118:62
Isa. 59:10

[a] pro ἡμίσει τῆς νυκτός.

μεσοπόρφυρος.

Isaiah 3:21, 24

μέσος, τὸ μέσον.

Gen. 1: 4, 4, 6
6, 7, 7
14, 14
18, 18
2: 9
3: 3, 8
15 qtr
9:12, 12
13, 15
15, 16
16, 17
17
10:12, 12
13: 3, 3, 7
7, 8, 8
8
15:10, 17
16: 5, 14
14
17: 2, 2
7+A
7, 7
10, 10
11
19:29
20: 1, 1
23:10, 15
26:28, 28
30:36, 36
31:37, 44
41, 46
48, 49
53
32:16
35: 2
37: 7
40:20
42:23
49:14
Exo. 7: 5
8:23, 23
9: 4, 4
11: 4, 4, 7
7+A
14: 2, 2, 16
20, 20
22, 23
27, 29
15: 8, 19
16: 1, 1
22:11
24:16, 18
25:21
Exo. 26:10, 28
28, 33
33
28:28, 29
30:18, 18
31:14
36:31, 33
Lev. 10:10, 10
11:47 qtr
16:16
20:25, 25
25—A
22:32
23: 5
25:33
26:41, 46
27:12, 12
14, 14
Nu. 1:49
2:17
3:12
4: 2
4+A
18
5:21
7:89
8: 6, 14
16, 19
9: 7
14:44+A
16:21, 33
37, 45
48
17: 6
18: 6, 20
23, 24
19: 6
10+A
20
21:13, 13
25: 7
26:56
62—A
62
27: 3, 4, 4
7
30:17
17+A
17
31:27, 27
33: 8, 49
35: 5, 24
24, 34
Deu. 1: 1
16 qtr
2:15—A
16
3:16
4:12, 15
33, 34
36
5: 4, 5, 22
23, 24
26
9:10+A[a]
10: 4
11: 3, 6
14: 1
17: 8 qtr
18:18+A
19: 2
25: 1
29:11, 16
33:12
Jos. 1:11
3: 4, 8B[a]
17
4: 3, 5, 8
18+A
8: 9, 9, 22
10:13
13: 9
15:13
16: 9
17: 4, 6, 9
18:11, 11
19: 1, 9
21:41
22:25, 27
27, 28
28, 28
34
24: 7, 7
Jud. 1:29, 30
32, 33
3: 5
19+A
4: 5, 5, 17
17
21+A
5:11
15+A
16, 27
27—A
7:16+A
17 A[b]
19[c]
9:23, 23
51
10:16
11:10, 27
27
12: 4, 4
13:25, 25
15: 4, 4 A[d]
16:19+A
25
29+A
31, 31
18: 1, 7-A
20
20:42
Ruth 1:17
2:15
1 Sa. 2:10
4: 3
5: 6
7: 3, 12
12, 14
14
9:14, 18
10:10, 11
23
11:11
14: 4
42 qtr
15: 6, 6
16:13
17: 1, 1, 3
6
18:10 A
20:3, 3+A
23, 42
1 Sa. 20:42
42—B
23:26 A[e]
26 A[e]
24:13, 16
16
25:29
26:13
2 Sa. 1:25
3: 1, 1, 6, 6
6:17
7: 2
14: 6
17:11
18: 9, 9, 24
19:35
20:12
21: 7 ter
23:12, 20
24: 5
1 Ki. 3: 8, 9, 20
5:12 ter
6:10, 12
12
(13) A
18, 25
25
7:14, 15
33, 33
8:51, 64
11:20
20—A
12 p24 l10
14: 7 A
30, 30
15: 7, 7, 16
16, 19
19—B
19—B
18:42
22: 1, 1
34, 34
2 Ki. 2:11
4:13
6:20
7: 5AB[1 e]
9: 2, 24
11: 2
17 qnq
10:14, 14
19:23[e]
20: 4
23: 9
25: 4
1 Ch. 9:38
38—A
11:14
16: 1
21: 6, 16
16+A
28: 2
2 Ch. 4:17
6:13
7: 7
13: 2, 2
16: 3, 3+A
3, 3
18:33, 33
19:10, 10
22:11
23: 5, 16
Ezra 4:15
Neh. 3:31 B[f]
32
4:11, 22
5:18
6:10
8: 3 A[g]
9:11
Job 2: 1
8:17
9:33
20:13
29:17
30: 7
34: 4
Psa. 21:15, 23
22: 4
39: 9
45: 6
Psa. 47:10
54:11, 16
56: 5
67:14, 26
73: 4, 11
12
77:28
81: 2
100: 2, 7
103:10, 12
108:30
109: 2
115:10
134: 9
135:11, 14
136: 2
137: 7
Pro. 5:14
6:19
8: 2, 20
27:22
Cant. 1:13—B
2: 2, 2, 3
Isa. 2: 4
4: 4
5: 2, 3, 25
6: 5
12: 6
22:11
24:13
41:18
44: 4
51:23[h]
52:11
57: 2, 5
58:12
59: 2
2-AS[3]
61: 9-AS[3]
Jer. 6: 1
7: 5, 5
12:14, 16
21: 4
27: 8, 37
28: 6, 63
29:14
20—S[1]
32: 2, 13[i]
36:32
44: 4, 12
46: 3, 14
47: 1, 5, 6
48: 7, 8
51: 7
52: 7, 25
Lam. 1: 3, 15
17
3:44
4:13
Eze. 1: 1, 4, 4, 5
13, 13
2: 5, 6
3:15, 24
25—A
4: 3, 3
5: 2, 2, 4
5, 8, 10
12
6: 7, 13
7: 9, 4
8: 3, 3, 11
16, 16
9: 2, 4, 4
10: 2, 2, 6
6, 7, 7
10
11: 1, 7, 7
9, 11A
23
12: 2, 10
11+A
12, 24
14: 8, 9, 14
16, 18
20
16:53
17:16
18: 8, 8, 18
19: 2, 2, 6
11
Eze. 20: 8, 9, 12
12, 20
20+A
21:20, 32
22: 3, 9, 13
18, 19
26, 21
22, 22
25, 25
26 ter
27
23:39
24: 5, 7, 11
26: 5, 12
15
27:26 A[k]
27
32+A
34
28:14, 16
18
29: 3, 4, 12
12, 21
30: 7, 7
31: 3, 10
14, 14
17, 18
32:10, 21
25, 28
32
33:33
34:12, 17
20, 20
22, 24
36:23
37: 1, 21
24, 26
28
39: 7
40: 7
41: 7 A[m]
9, 10
18—A
18
42: 6, 20
20
43: 7, 7, 9
44: 9
23, 23
23+A
46:10
47:16, 16
18 qtr
22 ter
48: 8, 10
15, 21
22 ter
Dan. 3:21, 23
23, 24
25, 26
4: 7
7: 5, 8
8: 5, 6A[n]
16
17 A[o]
21
11:10[p], 45
Hos. 2: 2
13:15
Joel 2:17, 27
Amos 3: 9
5:17
6: 4—A
7: 8, 10
Obad. 4
Mic. 2:12
4: 3
5: 7, 8, 10
13, 14
7:14
Hab. 3: 2
Zeph. 2:14
3: 5, 15
Hag. 2: 5
Zec. 1: 8, 10
11
2: 4, 5, 10
11
3: 7
5: 4, 7, 8
Zec. 5: 9, 9
6: 1, 13
8: 3, 8
9: 7
Zec. 11:14, 14
13: 6
Mal. 2:14, 14
3:18 ter

[a] pro μέρος. [b] pro ἀρχή. [c] A μεσόω. [d] pro δέω (B). [e] A μέρος. [f] pro ἀναβασις. [g] pro ἥμισυς. [h] AS μεταφρ...ον. [i] S[1] πρόσωπον. [k] pro καρδία. [m] pro γεῖσος. [n] pro ἐνώπιον. [o] pro ἔχω. [p] A δύναμις.

μεσόω.

Exo. 12:29
34:22
Jud. 7:19 A[a]
Neh. 8:3B[a]S[3 b]
Jer. 15: 9

[a] pro μέσος. [b] pro ἥμισυς.

μεσσάβ.

1 Samuel 14: 1, 6, 11, 12, 15

μεστός.

Pro. 6:34—S[1]
Eze. 37: 1
Nah. 1:10

μεταβάλλω.

Exo. 7:17, 20
10:19
Lev. 13: 3, 4, 7
10, 13
16, 17
20, 25
55
Jos. 7: 8
Jos. 8:21
Job 10: 8, 16
11:19
Isa. 13: 8
29:22
60: 5
Hab. 1:11

μεταβολή.

Isa. 30:32
Isa. 47:15

μεταβόλος.

Isaiah 23: 2, 3, 3

μετάγω.

1 Ki. 8:47, 48
2 Ch. 6:37
2 Ch. 36: 3

μεταδίδωμι.

Job 31:17
Pro. 11:26

μεταίρω.

2 Ki. 16:17
25:11
Psa. 79: 9
Pro. 22:28

μετακαλέω.

Hosea 11: 1, 2

μετακινέω.

Deu. 19:14
32:30
2 Sa. 15:20—A
Ezra 9:11
Isa. 54:10

μετακίνησις.

Ezra 9:11
Zec. 13: 1

μεταλλάσσω.

Est. 2: 7, 20[a]
[a] A ἀλλάσσω.

μεταλλεύω.

Deuteronomy 8: 9

μεταμέλεια.

Hosea 11: 8

μεταμέλομαι.

Exo. 13:17
1 Sa. 15:35
1 Ch. 21:15
Ps. 105:45
109: 4
Pro. 5:11
25: 8
Jer. 20:16
Eze. 14:22
Zec. 11: 5

μετάμελος.
2 Ki. 3:27
Pro. 11: 4

μεταναστεύω.
Psa. 10: 1
51: 7
Psa. 61: 7

μετανίστημι.
2 Sa. 15:20—A
Psa. 108:10

μετανοέω.
1 Sa. 15:29, 29
Pro. 20:25
24:24, 47
Isa. 46: 8
9+S[1]
Jer. 4:28
8: 6
Jer. 18: 8, 10
38:19
Joel 2:13, 14
Amos 7: 3, 6
Jon. 3: 9, 10
4: 2
Zec. 8:14

μετάνοια.
Proverbs 14:15

μεταξύ.
Gen. 31:50—A
Jud. 5:27+A
1 Ki. 15:32 A
32 A

μεταπέμπω.
Gen. 27:45
Nu. 23: 7

μεταποιέω.
Job 34: 8[a]
[a] A ποιέω.

μεταπίπτω.
Leviticus 13: 5, 6, 7, 8

μετασκευάζω.
Amos 5: 8

μεταστρέφω.
Exo. 14: 5
Deu. 23: 5
Jud. 5:28+A
1 Sa. 10: 9
2 Ch. 36: 4
Psa. 65: 6
77:44, 57
104:25, 29
Jer. 6:12
Jer. 21: 4
Lam. 5: 2
Dan. 10: 8
Hos. 7: 8
11: 8
Joel 2:31
Amos 8:10
Zeph. 3: 9

μεταστροφή.
1 Ki. 12:15
2 Ch. 10:15

μετατίθημι.
Gen. 5:24
Deu. 27:17
1 Ki. 20:25
Psa. 45: 3
Pro. 23:10
Isa. 29:14, 14
17
Hos. 5:10

μεταφέρω.
1 Chronicles 13: 3

μετάφρενον.
Deu. 32:11
Psa. 67:14
Psa. 90: 4
Isa. 51:23 AS[a]
[a] pro μέσος.

μετέρχομαι.
1 Samuel 5: 8, 8, 9

μετέχω.
Pro. 1:18
Pro. 5:17

μετεωρίζω.
Ps. 130: 1
Eze. 10:16, 17
17, 19
Obad. 4
Mic. 4: 1

μετεωρισμός.
Psa. 41: 8
87: 8
Psa. 92: 4
Jon. 2: 4

μετέωρος.
Jud. 1:15
2 Sa. 22:28
Job 28:18
Isa. 2:12, 13
5:15
17: 6
18: 2
Isa. 30:25
57: 7
Jer. 38:37
39:17—S
Eze. 3:14+A
15
17:23

μετοικεσία.
Jud. 18:30 A[a]
2 Ki. 24:16
25:27 A[a]
1 Ch. 5:22
Jer. 50: 5 S[b]
Lam. 1: 7 A[c]
Eze. 12:11
Obad. 20, 20
Nah. 3:10
[a] pro ἀποικία. [b] pro κατοικέω. [c] pro κατοικεσία.

μετοικέω.
2 Sa. 15:19
Jer. 20: 4

μετοικία.
1 Ki. 8:47
1 Ch. 6:15
Jer. 9:11
20: 4

μετοικίζω.
1 Ch. 5: 6, 26
8: 6
Jer. 22:12
Lam. 1: 3
Hos. 10: 5
Amos 5:27

μέτοικος.
Jeremiah 20: 3

μετοχή.
Psalm 121: 3

μέτοχος.
1 Sa. 20:30
Psa. 44: 8
118:63
Pro. 29:10
Ecc. 4:10
Hos. 4:17

μετρέω.
Exo. 16:18
Nu. 35: 5
Ruth 3:15
Isa. 40:12
Dan. 5:26

μέτρησις.
1 Kings 7:24—A

μετρητής.
1 Ki. 18:32
2 Ch. 4: 5
Hag. 2:16

μετριάζω.
Nehemiah 2: 2

μέτρον.
Gen. 18: 6
Exo. 16:36
26: 2, 8
Lev. 19:35
Deu. 2: 6
25:14, 14
15
1 Ki. 6:23
7:23
46+A
48
2 Ki. 7: 1, 16
18
21:13
1 Ch. 23:29
2 Ch. 2:10, 10[a]
Neh. 3:19, 20
Neh. 3:21, 24
27, 30
Job 11: 9
28:25
38: 5
Psa. 79: 6
Pro. 20:10
Isa. 5:10
44:13
Lam. 2: 8
Eze. 4:11, 16
40: 3, 5, 10
10, 21
24, 28
29, 32
33, 35
41:17+A
Eze. 42:11, 16
17, 18
19
20 A[b]
43:13
45:10, 10
11+A
13
46:14, 22
Eze. 47: 3, 3
4+A
48: 1 A[c]
16, 30
33, 34
Amos 8: 5
Zec. 1:16
5: 6, 7[d], 8
9, 10
[a] A κάδος. [b] pro κάλαμος. [c] pro μέρος. [d] A τάλαντον.

μέτωπον.
Exo. 28:34, 34
1 Sa. 17:49, 49
2 Ch. 26:19, 20
Isa. 48: 4
Eze. 9: 4

μέχρι, -ρις.
Jos. 4:23
Job 2: 7 S[2 a]
9
4:20[b]
8: 2
18: 2
26:10
32:12
38:11
Psa. 45:10
49: 1
70:17
103:23 S[1 a]
104:19
112: 3
129: 6
Ecc. 3:11
Dan. 11:36
[a] pro ἕως. [b] AS ἕως.

μεχωνώθ.
1 Ki. 7:13, 13
14, 16
17, 20
20, 21
21, 23
24, 24
1 Ki. 7:25, 28
29, 29
2 Ki. 16:17
25:13, 16
2 Ch. 4:14, 14

μηδαμῶς.
Gen. 18:25, 25
19: 7
1 Sa. 2:30
12:23
20: 2, 9
22:15
1 Sa. 24: 7
26:11
Eze. 4:14
20:49
Jon. 1:14

μηδείς.
Gen. 19: 8+A
Exo. 34: 3 A[a]
2 Ki. 10:21—A
Ecc. 7:15 ACS[b]
Jon. 3: 7+BS
[a] pro μηδέ. [b] pro οὐδείς.

μηδέτερος, BS μηθ—
Proverbs 24:21

μηθείς.
Jonah 3: 7+A

μηκέτι.
Exo. 36: 6
Jos. 22:33
2 Ch. 16: 5
Job 40:27—BS[1]

μῆκος.
Gen. 6:15
12: 6
13:17
Exo. 25: 9, 16
22
26: 2, 8
13—A
27: 1, 9
11, 18
28:16
30: 2
36:16
37: 2, 16
38: 1+A
Deu. 3:11
Jud. 3:16
1 Ki. 6: 6, 7, 19
7:13, 39
43
2 Ch. 3: 3, 4, 8
2 Ch. 3: 8[a], 11
4: 1
6:13
24:13
Pro. 3: 2, 16
16:17
Jer. 52:22
Eze. 40: 7
7—A
8, 18
20, 21
25, 29
30A, 33
36, 42
47, 49
41: 2, 4[a]
12, 13
13
15[b]
15, 22
Eze. 42: 2, 4, 7
8, 11
43:16, 17
45: 1, 3, 5
6, 7, 7
46:22
48: 8
Eze. 48: 9—A
10+A
13, 13
18, 21
Zec. 2: 2
5: 2
[a] A εὖρος. [b] A τοῖχος.

μηκύνω.
Isa. 44:14
Eze. 12:25, 28

μῆλον.
Gen. 30:14
Pro. 25:11
Cant. 2: 3, 5
4: 3
Cant. 6: 6
7: 8
8: 5
Joel 1:12

μηλωτή.
1 Ki. 19:13, 19
2 Ki. 2: 8, 13
2 Ki. 2:14

μήν.
Gen. 7:11, 11
8: 4, 4, 5
5, 5, 13
13, 14
14
29:14
Exo. 2: 2
12: 2 *ter*
3, 6, 18
18
13: 4, 5
16: 1
19: 1
23:15
34:18, 18
40: 2, 15
Lev. 16:29
29—AB[1]
23: 5, 5, 6
24, 24
27, 32
34, 39
41
25: 9, 9
Nu. 1: 1, 18
9: 1, 3, 5
11, 22
10:11, 11
11:20, 21
20: 1
28:14 *ter*
16, 16
17—A
29: 1, 1, 7
12
33: 3, 3, 38
38
Deu. 1: 3, 3
16: 1, 1
21:13
33:14
Jos. 4:19
5:10
Jud. 11:37, 38
39
19: 2
20:47
1 Sa. 6: 1
11: 1
20:24, 27
34
27: 7
2 Sa. 2:11
5: 5
6:11
24: 8, 13
1 Ki. 4: 7, 20
5:14 *ter*
6: 1, 4, 4
5, 5
8: 2
2+A
11:16
1 Ki. 12:32, 32
33
2 Ki. 15:13—AB
22: 3
25: 1
1+A
2, 8, 8
25, 27
27
1 Ch. 12:15
13:14[a]
21:12
27: 1 *ter*
2, 3, 4
5, 7, 8
9, 10
11, 12
13, 14
15
2 Ch. 3: 2
5: 3
7:10
8:13
15:10
29: 3, 17
17, 17
30: 2, 13
15
31: 7, 7
35: 1
Ezra 3: 1, 6, 8
6:15, 19
7: 8, 9
9—AB
8:31
10: 9, 9
16
17—S[1]
Neh. 1: 1
2: 1
6:15—AB
8: 1
1+S[1]
2, 14
9: 1
Est. 2:12 *ter*
16
3: 7+S[3]
7+S[3]
7 *ter*
12
12+S[3]
13
8: 9
9 A[b]
12
9: 1, 1
15+S
17
19+S[1]
21+S[3]
22
Job 3: 6

Job 7: 3
14: 5
21:21
29: 2+A
2
39: 2
Isa. 66:23, 23
Jer. 1: 3
35: 1, 17
36:28-ABS
43: 9
46: 1[c]
1+A
2, 2
48: 1
52: 4, 4, 6
12, 12
31, 31
Lam. 3:22—AB
Eze. 1: 1, 1, 2
8: 1, 1
20: 1+A
1
24: 1, 1

Eze. 26: 1
29: 1, 1, 17
30:20, 20
31: 1, 1
32: 1, 1, 17
17
33:21, 21
40: 1, 1
45:18, 18
20, 20
21+A
21, 25
25—B
Dan. 10: 4
Amos 4: 7
8: 5
Hag. 1: 1, 1
2: 1 *ter*
10, 18
20
Zec. 1: 1, 7, 7
7: 1, 3
11: 8

[a] A ἡμέρα. [b] *pro* ἔτος. [c] A ἔτος.

μηνιαῖος.

Lev. 27: 6
Nu. 3:15, 22
28, 31
39, 40

Nu. 3:43
18:16
26:62

μῆνις.

Gen. 49. 7 | Nu. 35:21

μηνίσκος.

Jud. 8:21, 26[a] | Isa. 3:18

[a] A σιωνων.

μηνίω.

Lev. 19:18
Ps. 102: 9

Jer. 3:12

μηρία.

Lev. 3: 4, 10
15
4: 9

Lev. 6:34
Job 15:27[a]

[a] AS μηρός.

μηρός.

Gen. 24: 2, 9
32:25, 25
31, 32
32
46:26
47:29
49:10
50:23
Exo. 28:38
32:27
Nu. 5:21, 22
27
Deu. 28:57
Jud. 3:16, 21

Jud. 8:30
15: 8
19: 1, 18
2 Ki. 10:14
19:23[a]
Job 15:27 AS[b]
Psa. 44: 4
Cant. 3: 8
7: 1
Eze. 7:17
21: 7
32.23+A
47: 4
Dan. 2:32

[a] A μέρος. [b] *pro* μηρία.

μηρυκάομαι.

Lev. 11·26[a] | Deu. 14: 8[a]

[a] A ἀναμαρυκάομαι.

μηρυκισμός.

Lev. 11: 3, 4, 4, 5
6, 7, 26

Deu. 14: 6, 7, 7
8

μηρύω.

Proverbs 29:31

μήτηρ.

Gen. 2:24
3.20
20:12

Gen. 21:21
24:28, 53
53, 67

Gen. 24:67
27:11, 13
14, 14
28: 2, 2, 5
7
29: 1, 10
10—A
10
30:14
32:11
37:10
44:20[a]
48: 7
49:26
Exo. 2: 3, 8
20:12
21:15, 16
22:30
23:19
34:26
Lev. 18: 7, 7, 9
12 A[b]
13—A
13—A
19: 3—A
20: 9, 9, 14
17, 19
21: 2, 11
22:27
24:11
Nu. 6: 7
12:12
Deu. 5:16
13: 6
14:20
21:13, 18
19
22: 6, 6, 7
15
27:16, 22
33: 9
Jos. 2:13, 18
6:23
Jud. 5: 7, 28
8:19
9: 1, 1, 3
14: 2, 3, 4
5, 6, 9
16
16:17
17: 2, 2, 3
3, 4, 4
Ruth 1: 8[a]
2:11
1 Sa. 1:25
2:19
15:33
20:30
22: 3
2 Sa. 17:25
19:37
1 Ki. 1:11
2:13, 19
20, 22
3:27
11:26+A
12 *p* 24 *l* 4
l 8
14:21
31+A
15: 2, 10
13
16 *p* 28—A
17:23
22:42, 53
2 Ki. 1:18
3: 2—A
13—B
4:19
20—AB
30
8:26
9:22
11: 1
12: 1
14: 2
15: 2, 33

2 Ki. 18: 2
21: 1, 19
22: 1, 14[c]
23:31, 36
24: 8, 12
15, 18
1 Ch. 2:26
4: 9
2 Ch. 2:14
12:13
13: 2
15:16
20:31
22: 2, 3, 10
24: 1
25: 1
26: 3
27: 1
29: 1
36: 2, 5
Job 1:21
3:10
12+A
16
17:14
31:18
38: 8
42 *p* 18
Psa. 21:10, 11
26:10
49:20
50: 7
68: 9
70: 6
86: 5
108:14
112: 9
130: 2
138:13
Pro. 1: 8
4: 3
6:20
10: 1
13: 1 S[1 b]
15:20
17:21
19:26
20 20
23:22, 25
24:34, 52
69
28:24
Ecc. 5:14
Cant. 1: 6
3: 4, 11
6: 8
8: 1, 2, 5
Isa. 8: 4
45:10
49: 1
15 A[d]
50: 1, 1
66:13
Jer. 15: 8, 10
16: 3, 7
20:14
17+A
17
18 S[1 e]
22:26
27:12, 12
52: 1
Lam. 2:12, 12
5: 3
Eze. 16: 3, 44
45, 45
19: 2, 10
22: 7
23: 2
44:25
Hos. 2: 2, 5
4: 5
10:14
Amos 1:11[f]
Mic. 7: 6
Zec. 13: 3, 3

[a] A πάτηρ. [b] *pro* πάτηρ. [c] A γυνή. [d] *pro* γυνή. [e] *pro* μήτρα. [f] A μήτρα.

μήτρα.

Gen. 20:18
29:31
30:22
49:25
Exo. 13: 2, 12
12, 13
15
34:19
Nu. 3:12
8:16
12:12
18:15

Nu. 25: 8
1 Sa. 1: 5, 6
1 Ki. 3:26
Job 3:16
Psa. 21:11
57: 4
Jer. 1: 5
20:17, 17
18[a]
Eze. 20:26
Hos. 9:14
Amos 1:11 A[b]

[a] S[1] μήτηρ. [b] *pro* μήτηρ.

μητρόπολις.

Jos. 10: 2
14:15
15:13
21:11
2 Sa. 20:19

Neh. 1: 1+S[1]
Est. 9:19+ABS
Isa. 1:26

μηχανεύομαι.

2 Chronicles 26:15

μηχανή.

2 Chronicles 26:15

μιαίνω.

Gen. 34: 5, 13
27
49: 4
Exo. 20:25
Lev. 5: 3
11:24, 43
44
13: 3, 8
11, 14
15, 20
22, 25
27, 30
44, 59
15:31, 32
18:24, 24
25 AB[a]
27, 28
30
20: 3
21: 1, 3
4·AB[1]
11
22: 5, 5, 8
Nu. 5: 3, 13
14, 14
19, 20
27, 28
29
6: 7, 9, 12
19:13, 20
20
35:34
Deu. 21:23
24: 6, 6
2 Ki. 23: 8, 10
13, 16
2 Ch. 29:19

2 Ch. 36:14
Job 31:11
Psa. 78: 1
105:39—A
Ecc. 7:19
Isa. 30:22[b]
43:28
47: 6
Jer. 2: 7, 23
33
3: 1, 1, 2
7:30
Eze. 4:14
5:11
7:22, 24
9: 7
14:11
18: 6, 11
15
20: 7, 18
26, 30
31, 43
22: 3, 4, 11
23: 7, 13
17, 17
30, 38
24:13
33:26 A
36:17
18+A
37:23
44:25, 25
Hos. 5: 3
6:10
9: 4
Hag. 2:13 *ter*
14

[a] *pro* ἐκμιαίνω. [b] AS[3] ἐξαίρω.

μίανσις.

Leviticus 13:44—A

μίασμα.

Lev. 7: 8
Jer. 39:34

Eze. 33:31

μίγνυμι, -νύω.

Gen. 30:40
Exo. 30:35
2 Ki. 18:23

Ps. 105:35
Pro. 14:16
Isa. 36: 8

μικρός.

Gen. 19:11, 20
20
24:17, 43
26:10
30:30
42: 2, 32
43: 1
44:25
47: 9
Exo. 17: 4
23:30
30+A
Nu. 16: 9, 13
22:18
Deu. 1:17
7:22, 22
25:13, 14
Jos. 22:17, 19
Jud. 4:19
6:15
Ruth 2: 7
1 Sa. 2:19
5: 9
9:21
15:17
16:11
17:28 A
20: 2, 35
22:15
25:36
30: 2, 19
2 Sa. 7:19
9:12
12: 3, 8
17:20
21:25
1 Ki. 2·20
3: 7
8:64
11:17
17:13
18:44
22:31
2 Ki. 2:23
4:10
5: 2, 14
23: 2
25·26
1 Ch. 12:14
25: 8
26:13
2 Ch. 10·10
12: 7
18:30
21:17
22: 1
31:15
34:30

2 Ch. 36:18
Ezra 9: 8
Est. 1: 5+S[3]
Job 2: 9
3:19
10:20[a]
36: 2
Psa. 41: 7
72: 2
103:25
113:21
150 *p* 6
Pro. 6:10
15:16
20:10
Ecc. 9:14
Cant. 2:15
3: 4
8: 8
Isa. 7:13
9.14
10:25
11: 6
18: 5
22: 5, 24
26:16, 20
28:10, 10
13, 13
25
29:17
30:14
33: 4, 19
54: 7, 8
63:18
Jer. 6:13
28:33
29:16
38:34
49: 1, 8
51:12
Lam. 4:18
Eze. 8:15+A
17
11:16
16:20, 47
17: 6
43:14
46:22
Dan. 7: 8
11:34
Hos. 1: 4
8:10—A
Amos 6:11
8: 5
Jon. 3: 5
Zec. 4:10
13: 7—A

[a] S ὀλίγος.

μικρότης.

1 Ki. 12:10 | 1 Ki. 12 *p* 24 *l* 65

μικρύνω *vide* σμικρύνω.

μῖλαξ *vide* σμῖλαξ.

μίλτος.

Jeremiah 22:14

μιμνήσκω, μνάομαι.

Gen. 8: 1 A[a]
9:15, 16
19:29
30.22
40:13, 14
14, 20
23
42: 9
Exo. 2:24
6: 5
20: 8
32:13

Lev. 26:42 *ter*
45
Nu. 11: 5
15:39, 40
Deu. 5:15
7:18
8: 2, 18
9: 7, 27
15:15
16: 3, 12
24:11, 20
22, 24

Deu. 25:17
32: 7
Jos. 1:13
Jud. 8:34
9: 2
16:28
1 Sa. 1:11, 19
4:18
25:31
2 Sa. 19:19
2 Ki. 20: 3
2 Ch. 6:42
24:22
Neh. 1: 8
4:14
5:19
6:14
9:17[b]
13:14, 22
29, 31
Est. 2: 1
4: 8
Job 4: 7
7: 7
10: 9
21: 6
24:20 A[a]
28:18
36:24
40:27
Psa. 8: 5
9:13
15: 4
19: 4
21:28
24: 6, 7, 7
41: 5, 7
44:18
70:16
73: 2, 18
22
76: 4,7,12
12
77:35, 39
42
78: 8
82: 5
86: 4
87: 6
88:48, 51
97: 3
102:14, 18
104: 5,8,42
105: 4,7,45
108:16
110: 5
113:20
118:49, 52
55
131: 1

Ps. 135 23—S[1]
136: 1, 6, 7
142: 5
Pro. 24:75
Ecc. 5:19
9:15
11: 8
12: 1
Isa. 12: 4
17:10
26:16
38: 3
43:25, 26
44:21
46: 8, 9
47: 7
48: 1
54: 4
57.11
62: 6
63: 7, 11
64: 5, 7, 9
65:17
66: 9
Jer. 2: 2
11:19
14:10, 21
15:15
18:20
28 50
38:20, 31
40: 8
51:21
Lam. 1: 7, 9
2: 1
3:19, 20
5: 1
Eze. 3:20
6: 9
16:22, 43
60, 61
63
18:22, 24
20:43
21:23
23:27
33:13 A[a]
16 A[a]
36:31
Hos. 2:17
7: 2
8:13
9: 9
Amos 1: 9
Jon. 2: 8
Mic. 6: 5
Nah. 2: 6
Hab. 3: 2
Zec. 10: 9
Mal. 4: 6

[a] pro ἀναμιμνήσκω.
[b] BS[1] ἀναμιμνήσκω.

Psa. 17:41
20: 9
24:19
25: 5
30: 7
33:22
34:19
35: 3
37:20
43: 8, 11
44: 8
49:17
54:13
67: 2
68: 5, 15
73: 4, 23
82: 3
85:17
88:24
96:10
100: 3
104:25
105:10, 41
118:104
113, 128
163
119: 6
128: 5
138:21, 21
22
Pro. 1:22, 29
5:12
6:16
8:13, 13
36
9: 8
8+AS[2]
11:15, 16

Pro. 12: 1
13: 5, 24
14:20
15:10, 27
16: 1
17: 9
19: 7[b]
22:14
25:17
26:28
28:16
29:10[c], 24
Ecc. 2:17, 18
3: 8
8: 1
Isa. 1:14
33:15
54: 6
60:15
61: 8
66: 5
Jer. 12: 8
51: 4
Eze. 16:27, 37
23:28
38+A
35:11+A
36: 3
Dan. 4:16
Hos. 9:15
Amos 5:10, 15
21
6: 8
Mic. 3: 2
Hag. 2:14
Zec. 8:17
Mal. 1: 3
2:13, 16

[a] pro ἐπαίρω. [b] S[1] ποιέω.
[c] A ζητέω.

μίσγω.

Isa. 1:22
Hos. 4: 2

μισέω.

Gen. 26:27
29:31, 33
37: 4, 8
Exo. 18:21
20: 5
Lev. 19:17
26:17
Nu. 10:35
Deu. 1:27
4:42
5: 9
7:10, 10
15
9:28
12:31
16:22
19: 4,6,11
21:15 ter
16, 17
22:13, 16
24: 5

Deu. 30: 7
32:41, 43
33:11
Jos. 20: 5 A
Jud. 11: 7
14:16
15: 2, 2
2 Sa. 5: 8
13:15, 15
22
18:28 B[a]
19: 6, 6
22:18, 41
1 Ki. 22: 8
2 Ch. 18: 7
19: 2
Job 34:17
Psa. 5: 6
10: 5
17:18
21+AB

Eze. 16:33—A
34, 34
41

Hos. 2:12
Mic. 1: 7 ter

μισητός.

Gen. 34:30
Pro. 24:39, 58

Pro. 26:11

μίσθιος.

Lev. 19:13 A[a]
25:50

Job 7: 1[b]

[a] pro μισθωτός. [b] A μισθός.

μισθός.

Gen. 15: 1
29:15
30:18, 18
28, 32
33
31: 7, 8, 8
41
Exo. 2: 9
22:15
Lev. 19:13
Nu. 18:31
Deu. 15:18
24:16, 17
Ruth 2:12
1 Ki. 5: 6—B
2 Ch. 15: 7
Job 7: 1 A[a], 2
Ps. 120: 3

Pro. 11:18, 21
17: 8
Ecc. 4: 9
9: 5
Isa. 23:18
40:10
62:11
Jer. 22:13
38:16
Eze. 27:15, 27
33
29:18, 19
Mic. 3:11
Hag. 1: 6
Zec. 8:10, 10
11:12, 12
Mal. 3: 5

[a] pro μίσθιος.

μισθόω.

Gen. 30:16
Deu. 23: 4
Jud. 9: 4
18: 4
2 Sa. 10: 6
2 Ki. 7: 6
1 Ch. 19: 6, 7
2 Ch. 24:12

2 Ch. 25: 6
Ezra 4: 5
Neh. 6:12
13: 2
Isa. 7:20[a]
46: 6
Hos. 3: 2

[a] AS μεθύω.

μίσθωμα.

Deu. 23:18
Pro. 19:13

Eze. 16:31, 32
33

μισθωτός.

Exo. 12:45
22:15
Lev. 19:13[a]
22:10
25: 6, 40
52
Deu. 15:18

Job 7: 2
14: 6
Isa. 16:14
21:16
28: 1, 3
Jer. 26:21
Mal. 3: 5

[a] A μίσθιος.

μῖσος.

2 Sa. 13:15, 15
Psa. 24:20
108: 3, 5
138:22

Pro. 10:12
Ecc. 9: 1, 6
Jer. 24: 9
Eze. 23:29

μίτρα.

Exo. 28:33, 33
29: 6, 6
36:36, 40

Lev. 8: 9, 9
Isa. 61:10
Eze. 26:16

μνᾶ.

1 Ki. 10:17
Ezra 2:69[a], 69
Neh. 7:71

Neh. 7:71—AB[b]
Eze. 45:12

[a] A δραχμή. [b] S[3] σκεῦος.

μνάομαι vide μιμνήσκω.

μνεία.

Deu. 7:18
Job 14:13
Ps. 110: 4
Isa. 23:16
26: 8
32:10

Jer. 38:20
Eze. 21:32
25:10
Hos. 9: 7 A[a]
Zec. 13: 2

[a] pro μανία.

μνῆμα.

Exo. 14:11
Nu. 11:34, 35
19:16, 18
33:16, 17
Deu. 9:22
Jos. 24:31[a]
2 Ch. 16:14

2 Ch. 34: 4, 28
Job 10:19
Isa. 65: 4
Jer. 33:23[a]
Eze. 32:22, 24
26
37:12, 12

[a] A μνημεῖον.

μνημεῖον.

Gen. 23: 6, 6, 9
35:20, 20
49:30
50: 5, 13
Jos. 24:31 A[a]
Neh. 2: 3, 5

Isa. 22:16
16—S[1]
26:19
Jer. 33:23 A[a]
Eze. 39:11

[a] pro μνῆμα.

μνήμη.

Psa. 29: 5
96:12
144: 7
Pro. 1:12

Pro. 10: 7
Ecc. 1:11, 11
2:16
9: 5

μνημονεύω.

Exo. 13: 3
2 Sa. 14.11
2 Ki. 9:25
1 Ch. 16:12, 15
Est. 2: 1—A

Psa. 6: 6
62: 7
Pro. 8:21
Isa. 43:18

μνημόσυνον.

Exo. 3:15
12:14
13: 9
17:14
14—A
28:12, 12

Exo. 28:23
30:16
36:14
Lev. 2: 2,9,16
5:12
6:15

Lev. 23:24
Nu. 5:15, 18
26
16:40
31:54
Deu. 32:26
Jos. 4: 7
Neh. 2:20
Est. 2:23
6: 1
9:27, 28
31
10: 2
Job 2: 9

Job 18:17
Psa. 9: 7
33:17
101:13
108:15
111: 6
134:13
Isa. 23:18
57: 8
66: 3
Hos. 12: 5
14: 7
Mal. 3:16

μνησικακέω.

Gen. 50:15
Pro. 21:24
Eze. 25:12

Joel 3: 4
Zec. 7:10

μνησίκακος.

Proverbs 12:27

μνηστεύω.

Deu. 20: 7
22:23, 25
27, 28

Hos. 2:19, 19
20

μογιλάλος.

Isaiah 35: 6

μοιχαλίς.

Pro. 18:22
24:55
Eze. 16:38

Eze. 23:45, 45
Hos. 3: 1
Mal. 3: 5

μοιχάω.

Jer. 3: 8
5: 7
7: 9
9: 2

Jer. 23:14
36:23
Eze. 16:32
23:37, 37

μοιχεία.

Jer. 13:27
Hos. 2: 2

Hos. 4: 2

μοιχεύω.

Exo. 20:13
Lev. 20:10 qtr
Deu. 5:18
Jer. 3: 9

Eze. 23:43
Hos. 4:13, 14
7: 4

μοιχός.

Job 24:15
Psa. 49:18

Pro. 6:32
Isa. 57: 3

μόλιβδος, -βος.

Exo. 15:10
Nu. 31:22
Job 19:24
Jer. 6:29

Eze. 22:18, 20
27:12
Zec. 5: 7, 8

μόλις.

Proverbs 11:31

μολόχη.

Job 24:24[a]

[a] A χλόη.

μόλυνσις.

Jeremiah 51:4

μολύνω.

Gen. 37:31
Cant. 5: 3
Isa. 59: 3
65: 4
Jer. 12:10—S

Jer. 23:11
Lam. 4:14
Eze. 7:17
21: 7
Zec. 14: 2

μολυσμός.

Jeremiah 23:15

μονάζω.
Psalm 101: 8

μόνιμος.
Gen. 49:26
Jer. 38:17

μονιός.
Psalm 79:14[a]
[a] BS[1] ὄνος.

μονογενής.
Jud. 11:34
Psa. 21:21
Psa. 24:16
34:17

μονόζωνος.
2 Sa. 22:30
2 Ki. 5: 2
6:23
13:20, 21
2 Ki. 24: 2 − A
2, 2, 2
Job 29:25

μονόκερως.
Nu. 23:22
24: 8
Deu. 33:17
Job 39: 9
Psa. 21:22
28: 6
77:69
91:11

μονομαχέω.
1 Sa. 17:10
Ps. 150 p6

μόνορχις.
Leviticus 21:20

μόνος.
Gen. 2:18
3:11:17
7:23
19: 8
21:28, 29
24: 8
27:13
32:24
34:15 − A
22, 23
42:38
43:31
44:20
47:22, 26
Exo. 12:16
18:14
18 − A
21: 3, 5, 1
22:20, 27
24: 2
Lev. 16:11 + AB
Nu. 3: 9 + A
11:14, 17
12: 2
23: 9
Deu. 1: 9, 12
6:13 − B
8: 3
10:20 + A
22:25
29:14
32:12
33:28
Jos. 11:13
22:20 + AC
20 + A
Jud. 3:20
6:37, 39
40
10:16 − A
1 Sa. 7: 3, 4
21: 1
2 Sa. 10: 8
13:32, 33
17: 2
18:24, 25
26
20:21
1 Ki. 8:39
11:20 − AB
1 Ki. 12:20
14:13 A
18: 6 + A
6
7 − A
7, 22
37 + A
19:10, 14
22:31
2 Ki. 10:23
17:18
19:15, 19
2 Ch. 6:30
18:30
Neh. 9: 6
Est. 1:16
4:13
Job 1:15, 16
17, 19
2: 6
9: 8
12: 2 + A
15:19
19: 3
31:17
39 − S
Psa. 50: 6
70:16
71:18
76:15 + S[2]
82:19
85:10
135: 4, 7
148:13
Pro. 5:17
9:12
Isa. 2:11, 17
8:26
5: 8
10: 8
37:16, 20
44:24
49:21
Jer. 30: 9
39:30
Lam. 1: 1
Eze. 14:16, 18
Dan. 10: 7
8 + B
8

μονότρωπος.
Psalm 67: 7

μορφή.
Jud. 8:18 A[a]
Job 4:16
Isa. 44:13
Dan. 4:33
5: 6, 9, 10
7:28
[a] pro ὁμοίωμα.

μοσφαιθάμ.
Jud. 5:16 A[a]
[a] pro διγομία.

μοσχάριον.
Gen. 18: 7, 8
Exo. 24: 5
29: 1, 3, 36
Lev. 9: 2, 3, 8,
Isa. 11: 6
Amos 6: 4
Mal. 4: 2

μόσχος.
Gen. 12:16
20:14
21:27
24:35
Exo. 20:24
21:33
22: 1 ter
9, 10
30
29:10, 10
11 − A
12, 14
32: 4, 8, 19
20, 24
35
34:19
Lev. 1: 5
4: 3, 4, 4
4, 5, 7
7, 8, 10
11, 12
14, 15
15, 16
17, 20
20, 21
21, 21
8: 2, 14
14, 17
9: 4, 18
19
16: 3, 6, 11
11, 14
15, 18
27
17: 3
22:23, 27
28
23:18
Nu. 7: 3, 15
21, 27
33, 39
45, 51
57, 63
69, 75
81, 87
8: 8, 8, 12
15: 9, 11
24
19:17
22: 4, 40
23: 1, 2, 1
14, 29
30
28:11, 12
14, 19
20, 27
28
29: 2, 3, 8
9, 13
14, 14
17, 18
20, 21
23, 24
26, 27
29, 30
32, 33
36, 37
Deu. 9:16 + A
Deu. 9:21
14: 4
15:19
17: 1
18: 3
22: 1, 4, 10
28:31
Jos. 6:21
7:24
Jud. 3:31 + A
6: 4 A[a]
25, 25
26, 28
1 Sa. 1:24, 25
12: 3
14:34
15: 3
22:19
2 Sa. 6: 6, 13
1 Ki. 1: 9[b], 19
25
(3) p 46
4:23
10:19
18:25, 26
1 Ch. 12:40, 40
13: 9
15:26
21:23
29:21
2 Ch. 4: 3, 3[c], 4
13
5: 6
7: 5
11:15
13: 8, 9
15:11
18: 2
29:21, 22
32, 33
30:24, 24
31: 6
35: 7, 8, 9
Ezra 6:17
7:17
8:35
Neh. 5:18
9:18
Job 1: 5
42: 8
Psa. 21:13
28: 6
49: 9
50:21
68:32
105:19, 20
Pro. 15:17
Isa. 22:13
66: 3
Jer. 3:24[d]
5:17
26:15, 21
38:18
41:18
52:20
Eze. 1:10
27:21 + A
39:18, 18
Eze. 43:19, 21
22, 23
25
45:18
19 + A
22, 23
24
Eze. 46: 6, 7
11
Hos. 5: 6
8: 5, 6
10: 5
13: 2
Mic. 6: 6
[a] pro ταῦρος. [b] A βοῦς.
[c] B μοχλός. [d] A μόχθος.

μοτόω.
Hosea 6: 1

μουσικός.
Gen. 31:27
Eze. 26:13
Dan. 3: 5, 7, 10
15 − A

μοχθέω.
Ecc. 1: 3
2:11
18 AS[a]
19, 20
21, 22
3: 9
Ecc. 4: 8
5:15, 17
8:17[b]
9: 9
Isa. 62: 8
Lam. 3: 5
[a] pro κοπιάω. [b] A ποιέω.

μόχθος.
Exo. 18: 8
Lev. 25:43, 46
53
Nu. 20:14
23:21
Deu. 26: 7 − B
Neh. 9:32
Job 2: 9, 9
Ecc. 1: 3
2:10, 10
11, 18
19, 20
21, 22
24
3:13
4: 4, 6, 8
Ecc. 4: 9
5:14, 17
18
6: 7
8:15
9: 9
10:15
Isa. 55: 2
61: 8
Jer. 3:24
24 A[a]
20:18 S[1] [b]
28:35[c]
Lam. 3:64
Eze. 23:29
34: 4
[a] pro μόσχος. [b] pro πόνος.
[c] S ἐχθρός.

μοχλός.
Exo. 26:26, 27
27, 28
29, 29
35:10
38:18, 24
39:14
40:16
Nu. 3:36
4:31
Deu. 3: 5
Jud. 16: 3
1 Sa. 23: 7
1 Ki. 4:13
2 Ch. 4: 3 B[a]
8: 5
2 Ch. 14: 7
Neh. 3: 3
6 − A
13, 14
15
Ps. 106:16
147: 2
Isa. 45: 2
Jer. 28:30
30: 9
Lam. 2: 9
Eze. 38:11
Amos 1: 5
Jon. 2: 7
Nah. 3:13
[a] pro μόσχος.

μυγάλη.
Leviticus 11:30

μυελός.
Gen. 45:18
Job 21:24
Job 33:24

μυελόω, μυα–
Psalm 65:15

μυῖα.
2 Ki. 1: 2, 3, 6
16
Ecc. 10: 1
Isa. 7:18

μυκτήρ.
Nu. 11:20
2 Ki. 19:28
Job 40:21
41:11
Pro. 24:68
Cant. 7: 4
Eze. 16:12
23:25

μυκτηρίζω.
1 Ki. 18:27
2 Ki. 19:21
2 Ch. 36:16
Job 22:19
Psa. 43:14 + A
79: 7
Pro. 1:30
Pro. 11:12
12: 8
15: 5, 20
23: 9
Isa. 37:22
Jer. 20: 7
Eze. 8:17

μυκτηρισμός.
Neh. 4: 4, 5[a]
Job 34: 7
Psa. 34:16
Psa. 43:14 − S[1]
78: 4
Eze. 23:32 + A
[a] S[3] ὀνειδισμος.

μύλη.
Job 29:17
Psa. 57: 7
Pro. 24:37
Joel 1: 6

μύλος.
Exo. 11: 5
Nu. 11: 8
Deu. 24: 8
Jud. 9:53 A[a]
2 Sa. 11:21, 22
Isa. 47: 2
[a] pro ἐπιμύλιος.

μυλών.
Jeremiah 52:11

μυξωτήρ.
Zechariah 4:12

μυρεψικός.
Exo. 30:25, 35
Cant. 3: 6 S[1] [a]
Cant. 5:13
8: 2
[a] pro μυρεψός.

μυρεψός.
Exo. 30:25, 35
38:23
1 Sa. 8:13
1 Ch. 9:30
2 Ch. 16:14
Cant. 3: 6[a]
[a] S[1] μυρεψικός.

μυριάς.
Jud. 5:12 + A
Neh. 7:71 + A
Neh. 7:71 − AB
8:12 S[1] [a]
[a] pro μερίς.

μυριοπλάσιος.
Psalm 67:18

μυρμηκιάω.
Leviticus 22:22

μυρμηκολέων.
Job 4:11

μύρμηξ.
Pro. 6: 6
Pro. 24:60

μύρον.
Exo. 30:25
1 Ch. 9:30
2 Ch. 16:14
Ps. 132: 2
Pro. 27: 9
Cant. 1: 3, 3, 4
2: 5
Cant. 4:10 S[a]
14
Isa. 25: 7
39: 2
Jer. 25:10
Eze. 27:17
Amos 6: 6
[a] pro ἱμάτιον.

μυρσίνη.
Neh. 8:15
Isa. 41:19
Isa. 55:13

μύς.
Lev. 11:29
1 Sa. 5: 6

1 Sa. 6: 1, 4+A 1 Sa. 6:11, 18
5—A, 5. Isa. 66:17

μυσαρὸς.
Leviticus 18:23

μύσταξ.
2 Samuel 19:24

μυστήριον.
Dan. 2:18, 19 | Dan. 2:47, 47
27, 28 | 4: 6
29, 30 |

μωήδ.
Jeremiah 26:17

μωκάομαι.
Jeremiah 28:18

μώλωψ.
Gen. 4:23 | Isa. 1: 6
Exo. 21:25, 25 | 53: 5
Psa. 37: 6 |

μωμάομαι.
Proverbs 9: 7

μωμητός.
Deuteronomy 32: 5

μῶμος.
Lev. 21:17, 18 | Deu. 15:21, 21
21, 21 | 17: 1
23 | 19:21+AB*
22:20, 21 |
25—A | 2 Sa. 14:25
24:19, 20 | Cant. 4: 7
Nu. 19: 2 | Dan. 1: 4

μωραίνω.
2 Sa. 24:10 | Jer. 10:14
Isa. 19:11 | 28:17 A[b]
44:25[a] |
[a] ABS μωρεύω. [b] pro ματαιόω.

μωρεύω.
Isa. 44:25 ABS[a] [a] pro μωραίνω.

μωρός.
Deu. 32: 6 | Isa. 19:11
Job 16: 7 | 32: 5, 6, 6
Psa. 93: 8 | Jer. 5:21

νάβλα.
1 Sa. 10: 5 | 1 Ch. 16: 5
2 Sa. 6: 5 | 25: 1, 6
1 Ki. 10:12 | 2 Ch. 5:12
1 Ch. 13: 8 | 9:11
15:16, 20 | 20:28
28 | 29:25

ναγέβ.
Jer. 39:44 | Jer. 40:13

ναζειραῖος, ναζι—
Jud. 13: 5 A[a] | Jud. 16:17 A[b]
7 A[b] | Lam. 4: 7
[a] pro ναζίρ. [b] pro ἅγιος.

ναζίρ.
Jud. 13: 6[a] [a] A ναζειραῖος.

ναίω.
Job 22:12[a] [a] S[1] νέος.

νᾶμα.
Canticles 8: 2

ναός.
1 Sa. 1: 9 | Psa. 27: 2
3: 3[a] | 28: 9
2 Sa. 22: 7 | 44:16
1 Ki. 6: 7, 9, 17 | 64: 5
30+A[2] | 67:30
33—A | 78: 1
7: 7, 36 | 137: 2
49+A | 143:12
2 Ki. 18:16 | Isa. 66: 6
23: 4 | Jer. 7: 4, 4
24:13 | 24: 1
1 Ch. 28:11, 20 | Eze. 8:16, 16
2 Ch. 3:17 | 41: 1, 4, 15
4: 7, 8, 22 | 21, 22
8:12 | 25
15: 8 | 42:19 B[e c]
26:16, 19 | Dan. 4:26
27: 2 | 5: 2, 3
29: 7, 17 | Joel 3: 5[d]
36: 7 | Amos 8: 3
Ezra 5:14 | Jon. 2: 5[e], 8
14—B | Hab. 2:20
6: 5—B | Hag. 2: 9, 15
Psa. 5: 8 | 18
10: 4 | Zec. 8: 9
17: 7 | Mal. 3: 1
26: 4[b] |
[a] A οἶκος. [b] S[1] λαός.
[c] pro ναός. [d] A θησαυρός.
[e] B[1] λαός.

νάπη.
Nu. 21:20 A[a] | Jer. 14: 6
24: 6 | Eze. 6: 3
Deu. 3:29 | 36: 4+A
Jos. 18:16 | 6
Isa. 40:12 | [a] pro Ἰανήν.

νάρδος.
Cant. 1:12 | Cant. 4:13, 14

ναρκάω.
Gen. 32:25, 32 | Job 33:19
32 |

ναῦλον.
Jonah 1: 3—S[1]

ναῦς.
1 Sa. 5: 6[a] | 1 Ki. 22:49 A
1 Ki. 9:26, 27 | 50 A
10:11, 22 | 2 Ch. 9:21
22, 22 | Job 9:26
16 p 28—A | Pro. 24:54
p 28—A | 29:32
p 28—A | Dan. 11:40
1 Ki. 22:49 A | [a] A ἕδρα.

ναυτικός.
1 Ki. 9:27 | Jon. 1: 5

νεανίας.
Jud. 16:26[a] | 2 Sa. 10: 9[b]
17: 7[a], 11[a] | 1 Ki. 12:21
19: 3[a], 9[a] | 1 Ch. 19:10
11[a], 13[a] | Pro. 7: 7
Ruth 3:10 | 20:29
1 Sa. 20:31, 38 | Zec. 2: 4[c]
2 Sa. 6: 1 |
[a] A παιδάριον. [b] B νεανίσκος.
[c] S νεανίσκος.

νεᾶνις.
Exo. 2: 8 | Jud. 19: 6, 8, 9
Deu. 22:19, 20 | 21:12
21, 24 | Ruth 2: 5
26 | 1 Ki. 1: 2, 3, 4
26+AB* | 2 Ki. 5: 2, 4
| Psa. 67:26
27, 29 | Cant. 1: 3
Jud. 5: 8+A | 6: 7
19: 3, 4, 5 | Dan. 11: 6

νεανίσκος.
Gen. 4:23 | Isa. 3: 4
14:24 | 9:17
19: 4 | 13:18
25:27 | 20: 4
34:19 | 23: 4
41:12 | 31: 8
Exo. 10: 9 | 40:30
24: 5 | 62: 5
Nu. 11:27 | Jer. 6:11
Deu. 32:25 | 9:21
Jos. 2: 1, 1, 23 | 11 22
6:21, 22 | 15: 8
23 | 18:21
Jud. 14:10 | 27:30, 44
18: 3[a] | 28: 3, 22
15[a] | 29:20
19:19[a] | 30:15
20:15+A | 31:15
1 Sa. 9:27 | 38:13
17:55 A | Lam. 1:18
56 A | 2:21
20:22 | 5:13
2 Sa. 10: 9 B[b] | Eze. 9: 6
2 Ch. 11: 1 | 23: 6, 12
36:17 | 23
Ezra 10: 1 | 30 17
Neh. 4:22-ABS | Dan. 1: 4
Est. 3:13+S[3] | Joel 2:28
Job 29: 8 | Amos 2:11
Psa. 77:63 | 4:10
148:12 | 8:13
Pro. 20:11 | Zec. 2: 4 S[b]
Ecc. 4:15 | 9:17
11: 9 |
[a] A παιδάριον. [b] pro νεανίας.

νέβελ.
1 Sa. 1:24 | Hos. 3: 2
2 Sa. 16: 1 |

νεβρός.
Cant. 2: 9, 17 | Cant. 7: 3
4: 5 | 8:14

νεέλασσα.
Job 39:13—BS

νεεσσαράν.
1 Samuel 21:7

νεζέρ.
2 Kings 11:12

νεῖκος.
Pro. 10:12 | Eze. 3: 8 B[a]
22:10 | 8 AB[a]
29:22 | 9+A
Lam. 3:18 B[a] | Hos. 10:11
5:20 B[a] | Zeph. 3: 5[b]
[a] pro νῖκος. [b] A νῖκος.

νεκριμαῖος.
1 Kings 13:30+A

νεκρός.
Gen. 23: 3, 4, 6 | Psa. 30:13
6, 8, 11 | 87: 6, 11
13, 15 | 105:28
Lev. 21: 5 | 113:25
Nu. 19:16 | 142: 3
Deu. 14: 1 | Ecc. 9: 3, 4, 5
18:11 | Isa. 5:13
28:26 | 8:19
Jud. 4:22 | 14:19
19:28[a] | 22: 2, 2
1 Sa. 31: 8 | 26:14, 19
2 Sa. 19: 6 | 34: 3
1 Ki. 3:22+A | 37:36
2 Ki. 19:35 | Jer. 7:33
25:30 | 9:22
2 Ch. 20:24 | 19: 7

Jer. 40: 5 | Eze. 11: 6, 7
Lam. 3: 6[b] | 32:18
Eze. 9: 7 | 37: 9
[a] A θνήσκω. [b] A σκοτεινός.

νέμω.
Gen. 36:24 | Eze. 19: 7
41: 3, 18 | 34:18, 19
19+A | Hos. 4:16
Exo. 34: 3 | Jon. 3: 7
Nu. 14:33 | Mic. 7:14
1 Sa. 21: 7 | Zeph. 2: 7, 14
Cant. 4: 5 | 3:13
Jer. 27:19 |

νεομηνία, νουμηνία.
Exo. 40: 2, 15 | 2 Ch. 31: 3
Nu. 10:10 | Ezra 3: 5
28:11 | Neh. 10:33
31+A | Psa. 80: 4
29: 6 | Isa. 1:13
1 Sa. 20: 5, 18 | 14—S
2 Ki. 4:23 | Eze. 23:34
1 Ch. 23:31 | 45:17
2 Ch. 2: 4 | 46: 1, 3, 6
29:17 | Hos. 2:11

νέος.
Gen. 9:24 | Jud. 9: 5
19:31, 34 | 15: 2
35, 38 | 18: 3+A
27:15, 42 | 1 Sa. 17:14 A
29:16, 18 | 1 Ki. 16:34
26 | 1 Ch. 12:28
37: 1 | 24:31
42:13, 15 | 29: 1
20, 34 | 2 Ch. 10:14
43: 2, 4, 28 | 13: 7
32 | 15:13
44: 2, 12 | Job 13: 2+A
20, 23 | 22:12 S[1 a]
26, 26 | 24: 5
48:14, 19 | 32: 7
49:22 | Psa. 36:25
Exo. 13: 4 | 67:28
23:15 | 68:32
33:11 | 118: 9, 141
34:18, 18 | 148:12
Lev. 2:14 | 150 p 6
23:14, 16 | Pro. 1: 4
26:10 | 7:10
Nu. 14:23 | 22:15
28:26, 26 | Ecc. 10:16
Deu. 1:39 | Cant. 7:13
16: 1, 1 | Isa. 40:30
28:50 | 49:26
Jos. 5:11 | 65:20
15:17+A | Jer. 1: 6, 7
Jud. 1:13 | 14: 3
3: 9 | Eze. 16:46, 61
8:20 | Zec. 9: 9
[a] pro ναίω.

νεοσσός, νοσσός.
Lev. 5: 7, 11 | Job 5: 7
12: 6, 8 | 38:41
14:22, 30 | 39:30
15:14, 29 | Ps. 146: 9
Nu. 6:10 | Pro. 24:23, 52
Deu. 22: 6, 6 | Isa. 16: 2
32:11 | 60: 8

νεότης.
Gen. 8:21 | Job 31:18
43:32 | 36:14
48:15 | Psa. 24: 7
Lev. 22:13 | 42: 4
Nu. 22:30 | 70: 5, 17
30: 4, 17 | 87:16
1 Sa. 12: 2 | 102: 5
17:33 | 128: 1, 2
2 Sa. 19: 7 | 143:12
1 Ki. 18:12 | Pro. 2:17
Job 13:26 | 5:18
20:11 | 24:54

Ecc. 11: 8,9,10; 12: 1; Isa. 47:12, 15; 54: 6; Jer. 2: 2; 3:24, 25; 22:21 – A
Jer. 38:19; 39:30; Lam. 3:27; Eze. 23: 3,9,19; 21, 21; Zec. 13: 5; Mal. 2:14, 15

νεόφυτος, –τον.

Job 14: 9; Ps. 127: 3
Ps. 143:12; Isa. 5: 7

νεόω.

Jeremiah 4: 3

νέσσα.

Job 30:13

νεῦμα.

Isaiah 3:16

νευρά.

Judges 16: 7, 8, 9

νευροκοπέω.

Gen. 49: 6; Deu. 21: 4, 6
Jos. 11: 6, 9

νεῦρον.

Gen. 32:32, 32; 40:24; Job 10:11; 30:17
Job 40:12; Pro. 24:23; Isa. 48: 4; Eze. 37: 6, 8

νεύω.

Pro. 4:25
Pro. 21: 1

νεφέλη.

Gen. 9:13, 14; 14, 16; Exo. 13:21, 22; 14:19, 24; 16:10; 19: 9, 13; 16; 24:15, 16; 16, 18; 33: 9, 10; 34: 5; 40:28, 29; 30, 31; 31, 32; Lev. 16: 2; Nu. 9:15, 16; 17, 17; 18, 19; 20, 21; 21; 22 – A; 10:11, 12; 34; 11:25; 12: 5, 10; 14:10, 14; 14; 16:42; Deu. 1:33; 31:15, 15; Jos. 24: 7; Jud. 5: 4; 2 Sa. 22:12; 1 Ki. 8:10, 11; 18:44, 45; 2 Ch. 5:13, 14; Neh. 9:12, 19; Job 22:14[a]; 26: 8; 35: 5 S[b]; 36:27, 29; 37:10 – C; Psa. 17:12, 13
Psa. 35: 6; 56:11; 67:35; 76:18; 77:14, 23; 88: 7; 96: 2; 98: 7; 103: 3 S[1] [b]; 104:39; 107: 5; 134: 7; 146: 8; Ecc. 11: 4; Isa. 4: 5; 5: 6; 14:14 AS[b]; 18: 4; 19: 1; 44:22; 45: 8; 60: 8; Jer. 4:13; 10:13; 28:16; Lam. 3:43; Eze. 1: 4, 20; 28; 10: 3, 4; 30: 3 – 8; 18; 31: 3, 10; 14; 32: 7; 34:12, 12; 38: 9, 16; Dan. 7:13; Hos. 6: 4; 13: 3; Joel 2: 2; Nah. 1: 3; Zeph. 1:15; Zec. 2:13

[a] S νέφος. [b] pro νέφος.

νέφος.

Job 7: 9; 20: 6; 22:14 S[a]; 26: 8, 9; 30:15; 35: 5[b]; 36:28; 37:10, 15; 20, 21; 38: 1, 9, 34
Job 38:37; 40: 1; Ps. 103: 3[c]; Pro. 3:20; 8:28; 16:15; 25:14, 23; Ecc. 11: 3; 12: 2; Isa. 14:14[d]

[a] pro νεφέλη. [b] S νεφέλη. [c] S[1] νεφέλη. [d] AS νεφέλη.

νεφρός.

Exo. 29:13, 22; Lev. 3: 4, 4, 10; 10, 15; 15; 4: 9, 9; 6:34, 34; 8:16, 25; 9:10, 19; Deu. 32:14; Job 16:13
Psa. 7:10; 15: 7; 25: 2; 72:21; 138:13; Jer. 11:20; 12: 2; 17.10; 20:12; Lam. 3:13

νεχωθά.

2 Ki. 20:13
Isa. 39: 2

νέωμα.

Jeremiah 4: 3

νή.

Genesis 42: 15, 16

νήθω.

Exo. 26:31; 35:25, 25; 26
Exo. 36: 9, 32; 37; 37: 3, 5, 16

νήπιος, –ον.

1 Sa. 15: 3; 22:19; 2 Ki. 8:12; Est. 8:11 + S[3]; Job 3:16; 24:12; 31:10; 33:25; Psa. 8: 3; 16:14; 18: 8; 63: 8; 114: 6; 118:130; 136: 9; Pro. 1:32
Pro. 23:13; Isa. 11: 8; Jer. 6:11; 9:21; 50: 6 – BS; 51: 7; Lam. 1: 5; 2:11, 19; 20; 4: 4; Eze. 9: 6; 45:20 + A; Hos. 11: 1; Joel 2:16; Nah. 3:10

νηπιότης.

Eze. 16:22, 43; 60
Hos. 2:15

νῆσος.

Gen. 10: 5, 32; Psa. 71:10; 96: 1; Isa. 20: 6; 23: 2, 6; 24:15; 41: 1; 42:10, 12; 15; 45:16; 49: 1, 22; 51: 5; 60: 9
Isa. 66:19; Jer. 2:10; 27:38, 39; 29: 4; 38:10; Eze. 26:15, 18; 18 + A; 27: 3, 6, 7; 15, 35; 39: 6; Dan. 11:18; Zeph. 2:11

νηστεία.

2 Sa. 12:16; 1 Ki. 20: 9; 12 – B; 2 Ch. 20: 3
Ezra 8:21; Neh. 9: 1; Psa. 34:13; 68:11

Ps. 108:24; Isa. 1:13; 58: 3, 5, 5; 6; Jer. 43: 6, 9; Dan. 9: 3
Joel 1:14; 2:12, 15; Jon. 3: 5; Zec. 7: 5; 8:19 qtr

νηστεύω.

Exo. 38:26, 26; Jud. 20:26; 1 Sa. 7: 6; 31:13; 2 Sa. 1:12; 12:16, 21; 22, 23; 1 Ki. 20: 9
1 Ki. 20:27 – A; 1 Ch. 10:12; Ezra 8:23; Neh. 1: 4; Est. 4:16; Isa. 58: 3, 4, 4; Jer. 14:12; Zec. 7: 5, 5

νηστός.

Exodus 31: 4

νηῦς vide ναῦς.

νήχομαι.

Job 11:12

νικάω.

Psa. 50: 6; Pro. 6:25
Hab. 3:19

νίκη.

1 Ch. 29:11
Pro. 22: 9

νῖκος.

2 Sa. 2:26; Job 36: 7; Jer. 3: 5; Lam. 3:18[a]; 5:20[a]
Eze. 3: 8[a], 8[b]; Amos 1:11; 8: 7; Zeph. 3: 5 A[c]

[a] B νεῖκος. [b] AB νεῖκος. [c] pro νεῖκος.

νίπτω, νίζω.

Gen. 18: 4; 19: 2; 24:32 – A; 43:23, 30; Exo. 30:18, 19; 20, 21; 21; 38:27, 27; Lev. 15:11, 12; Deu. 21: 6
Jud. 19:21; 1 Sa. 25:41; 2 Sa. 11: 8; 2 Ch. 4: 6; Job 20:23[a]; Psa. 25: 6; 57:11; 72:13; Cant. 5: 3

[a] AS[2] ῥίπτω.

νισάν.

Neh. 2: 1; Est. 3: 7 + S[3]
Est. 3:12 + S[3]; 8: 9[a]

[a] S[3] σιουάν.

νίτρον.

Jeremiah 2:22

νιφετός.

Deuteronomy 32: 2

νοέω.

1 Sa. 4:20; 2 Sa. 12:19; Job 13: 9 A[a]; 33: 3, 23; Pro. 1: 2, 3, 6; 8: 5; 16:23; 19:25; 20:24; 23: 1
Pro. 24:33; 28: 5 S[a]; 29: 7[b]; 19; Isa. 29: 3 + S; 32: 6; 44:18; 47: 7; Jer. 2:10; 10:21[c]; 20:11, 11; 23:20
Dan. 12:10 A[a]

[a] pro συνίημι. [b] AS[2] συνίημι. [c] S[1] ἀνομέω.

νοήμων.

Pro. 1: 5; 10: 5, 19; 14:35
Pro. 17: 2, 12; 28:11; Dan. 12:10

νοητῶς.

Proverbs 23: 1

νομάς.

1 Sa. 28:24; 1 Ki. (3) p 16bis; 4:23; 1 Ch. 27:29
Job 1: 3; 20:17; 30: 1; 42:12

νομή.

Gen. 47: 4; 1 Ch. 4:39, 40; 41; Job 20:17; 27 S[1] [a]; 39: 8; Psa. 73: 1; 78:13; 94: 7; 99: 3; Pro. 24:15; Isa. 49: 9; Jer. 10:21, 25
Jer. 23: 1, 3, 10; 27: 7, 19; 45; Lam. 1: 6; Eze. 25: 5, 5[b]; 34:14, 14; 18, 18; Hos. 13: 6; Joel 1:18; Amos 1: 2; Nah. 2:11; Zeph. 2: 6; (2)15

[a] pro ἀνομία. [b] A πρ νομή.

νόμιμος.

Gen. 26: 5; Exo. 12:14 – A; 17, 24; 27:21; 28:39; 29:28; 30:21; Lev. 3:17; 6:18; 7:24, 26; 10: 9, 11; 13, 13; 14, 14; 15; 16:29, 31; 34; 17: 7; 18: 3, 26; 30[a]; 20:23; 23:14, 21
Lev. 23:31, 41; 24: 3, 9; Nu. 10: 8; 18: 8, 11; 19, 23; 19:10, 21; Pro. 3: 1; Jer. 10: 3; 33: 4[b]; Eze. 5: 6, 6, 7; 16:27; 18:19; 20:18; 43:11; 44: 5, 24; Dan. 6: 5[b]; Hos. 8:12; Mic. 6:15; 7:11; Zec. 1: 6; Mal. 3: 7

[a] A ἄνομος. [b] A νόμος.

νόμισμα.

Ezra 8:36
Neh. 7:71 – ABS

νομοθεσμός.

Proverbs 29:45 S[1] [a]

[a] pro νομοθέσμως.

νομοθέσμως.

Proverbs 29:45[a]

[a] S[1] νομοθεσμός.

νομοθετέω.

Exo. 24:12; Deu. 17:10; Psa. 24: 8, 12; 26:11
Psa. 83: 7; 118:33, 102; 104 + AS[1]

νομοθέτης.

Psalm 9:21

νόμος.

Exo. 12:43, 49
13: 9, 10
16: 4[a], 28
18:16, 20
24:12
Lev. 6: 9, 14
22, 24
31, 37
7: 1, 27
11:46
12: 7
13:59
14: 2, 32
54, 57
15: 3, 32
19:19, 37
26:46
Nu. 5:29, 30
6:13, 21
21
9: 3, 12
14, 14
15:15, 15
16, 29
19: 2, 14
31:21
Deu. 1: 5
4: 8, 44
17 11
24:10
27: 3,8,26
28:58, 61
29:20+A
21, 27
29
30:10
31: 9, 11
12, 24
26
32:44, 46
33: 4, 10
Jos. 1: 8
9 :4,5,7,7
22: 5
23: 6
24:25, 26
2 Sa. 7:19
1 Ki. 2: 3
2 Ki. 10:31
14: 6
17:13, 34
37
22: 8, 11
23:24, 25
1 Ch. 16:40
22:12
2 Ch. 6:16[b]
14: 4
15: 3
17: 9
23:18
25: 4
31: 3, 21
33: 8
34:14, 15
18+A
19
35:12+A
19, 19
26
Ezra 3: 2
7: 6, 10
12, 14
21+AB
25, 26
26
10: 3
Neh. 8: 1
2−A
3, 7, 8
9, 13
14, 18
9: 3, 13
14, 26
29, 34
10:28, 29
Neh. 10: 34[f], 36
12:44+S[3]
13: 3
Est. 1: 8, 13
15, 19
20[i]
3: 8, 8
4:16
8:11
Job 34:27
Psa. 1: 2, 2
18: 8
36:31
39: 9
58:12[e]
77: 1,5,10
88:31
93:12
104:45
118: 1, 18
29, 34
44, 51
53, 55
57[f], 61
70, 72
77, 85
92, 97
105,109
113,126
136
142[e]
150,153
163
165[a],174
129: 5 S[1 h]
Pro. 1: 8ACS[i]
3:16
4: 2
6:20, 23
9:10
13:14, 15
28: 4,4,7,9
29:18
Isa. 1:10[g]
2: 3
5:24
8:16, 20
19: 2, 2
24: 5, 16
30: 9
33: 6
42:24
51: 4, 7
Jer. 2: 8
6:19
8: 8, 9[k]
9:13
13:25+A
16:11
18:18
23:27
29:13
33: 4 A[m]
34:15 S[1 h]
38:33, 36
51:23
Lam. 2: 9
Eze. 7:26
22:26
43:12+A
Dan. 6: 5 A[m]
7:25
9:10, 11
11, 13
Hos. 4: 6
8: 1
Amos 2: 4
4: 5
Mic. 4: 2
Hab. 1: 4
Zeph. 3: 4
Hag. 2:11
Zec. 7:12
Mal. 2: 6, 7, 8
9
4: 6

[a] A ὄνομα. [b] B ὄνομα. [c] B βιβλίον. [d] AS[3] λόγος. [e] S[1] ὄνομα. [f] S[1] ἐντολή. [g] S[1] λόγος. [h] pro λόγος. [i] pro παιδεία. [k] AS λόγος. [m] pro νόμιμος.

νοσερός.

Jer. 14:15
Jer. 16: 4

νόσος.

Exo. 15:26
Deu. 7:15
28:59
29:22
2 Ch. 21:15, 19
Job 24:23
Ps. 102: 3
Hos. 5:13

νοσσεύω.

Isa. 34:15
Jer. 31:28
Eze. 31: 6

νοσσία, −ον.

Gen. 6:14
Nu. 24:21, 22
Deu. 22: 6
32:11
Job 39:27
Psa. 83: 4, 4
Pro. 16:16, 16
Pro. 27: 8
Isa. 10:14
Jer. 29:17
Obad. 4
Nah. 2:12
Hab. 2: 9

νοσσοποιέω.

Isaiah 13:22

νοσσός vide νεοσσός.

νοσφίζω.

Joshua 7: 1

νότος.

Exo. 10:13, 13
14:21
26:20, 35
27:13[a]
37: 9−A[2]
40:22
Nu. 2: 3 B[c]
10: 6 A[b]
13:30
34:15
Deu. 3:27 A[b]
Jos. 15: 1 A[b]
2 A[b]
2 A[b]
3 A[b]
4 A[b]
7 A[b]
8 B[d]
10 A[b]
18:13 A[d]
16 B[d]
19:34 AB[d]
Jud. 1: 9, 14
15, 16
21:19
1 Sa. 13: 5[e]
14: 5
27:10 ter
30: 1, 14
14−B
27
2 Sa. 24: 7−A
1 Ki. 7:12, 25
1 Ch. 9:24
26:15
17−A
26:18
2 Ch. 4: 4
2 Ch. 33:14[f]
Job 9: 9
37:16+CS[2]
38:24
39:26
Psa. 77:26
125: 4
Ecc. 1: 6
11: 3
Cant. 4:16
Jer. 13:19
17:26
Eze. 27:26
40:24, 24
27, 27
28, 44
44, 45
41:11
42:10, 10
12, 13
19, 19[g]
46: 9, 9
47: 1, 19
20
48:10, 16
17−A
33
Dan. 8: 4, 9
11: 5, 6, 9
11, 14
15, 25
25, 29
40
Zec. 6: 6
7+S[3]
14: 4, 10

[a] A ἀνατολή. [b] pro λίψ. [c] pro πρῶτος. [d] pro νῶτος. [e] B νῶτος. [f] (B γιόν). [g] B* ναός.

νουθεσία.

Proverbs 2: 2 C[a]

[a] pro νουθέτησις.

νουθετέω.

1 Sa. 3:13
Job 4: 3
23:14
30: 1
34:16
Job 36:12
37:13
38:18
39:34

νουθέτημα.

Job 5:17

νουθέτησις.

Pro. 2: 2[a]

[a] C νουθεσία.

νουμηνία vide νεομηνία.

νοῦς.

Exo. 7:23
Jos. 14: 7
Job 7:17, 20
12:11 ABS[a]
33:16
34: 3 A[a]
Job 36:19
Pro. 24:71
Isa. 10: 7, 12
40:13
41:22

[a] pro οὖς.

νυκτερινός.

Job 4:13
20: 8
33:15
Job 35:10
Psa. 90: 5
Pro. 7: 9

νυκτερίς.

Lev. 11:19
Deu. 14:17
Isa. 2:20

νυκτικόραξ.

Lev. 11:17
Deu. 14:16
1 Sa. 26:20
Ps. 101: 7

νυμφαγωγός.

Gen. 21:22, 32
26:26
Jud. 14:20 A[a]

[a] pro φίλος.

νύμφευσις.

Canticles 3:11

νύμφη.

Gen. 11:31
38:11, 13
16, 24
Lev. 18:15
20:12
Deu. 27:23[a]
Ruth 1: 6, 7, 8
22
2:20, 22
3: 1 A[b]
4:15
1 Sa. 4:19
2 Sa. 17: 3
1 Ch. 2: 4
Cant. 4: 8,9,10
Cant. 4:11, 12
5: 1
Isa. 49:18
61:10
62: 5
Jer. 2:32
7:34
16: 9
25:10
40:11
Eze. 22:11[c]
Hos. 4:13, 14
Joel 1: 8
2:16
Mic. 7: 6

[a] A πενθερά. [b] pro πενθερά. [c] A ἀδελφή.

νυμφίος.

Jud. 15: 6[a]
19: 5[a]
Neh. 13:28
Psa. 18: 6
Isa. 61:10
62: 5
Jer. 7:34
16: 9
25:10
40:11
Joel 2:16

[a] A γαμβρός.

νῦν.

Gen. 44:28[a]
47: 3+A
Jud. 11: 7−A
1 Ki. 3: 2−A
Jos. 5:15[b]
Jud. 9:38+A
Isa. 29:23+S[1]
Hos. 13: 2−AB

[a] A ἔτι. [b] A σύ.

νύξ.

Gen. 1: 5
14+A
14, 16
18
7: 4, 12
17
8:22
14:15
19: 5, 33
33, 34
35
20: 3
26:24
30:15, 16
31:24, 39
40
32:13, 21
22
40: 5
41:11
46: 2
Exo. 10:13
11: 4
12: 8, 12
29, 30
31
41−A[l]
42
13:21, 22
14:20, 20
21
24:18
34:28
40:32
Lev. 6: 9
8:35
Nu. 9:16, 21
11: 9, 32
14: 1, 14
22: 8, 19
20
Deu. 1:33
9: 9, 11
18, 25
10:10
16: 1
3+A[2]
23:10
28:66
Jos. 1: 8
2: 3
4: 3
8: 3
10: 9
Jud. 6:25, 27
40
7: 9
9:32, 34
16: 2, 2
3[a], 16A[b]
19:25
20: 5
Ruth 3: 2, 13
1 Sa. 14:34+A
36
15:11, 16
19:11, 11
24
25:16
26: 7
28: 8, 20
25
30:12
31:12
2 Sa. 2:29, 32
4: 7
7: 4
17: 1, 16
19: 7
21:10
1 Ki. 3: 5, 19
20
8:29, 29
59
1 Ki. 19: 8
2 Ki. 6:14
7:12
8:21+A
19:35
25: 4
1 Ch. 9:33
17: 3
2 Ch. 1: 7
6:20
7:12
21: 9
35:14
Neh. 1: 6
2:12
13+S[3]
15
4: 9, 22
6:10
9:12, 19
Est. 4:16
6: 1
Job 2:13
3: 3, 4[c]
6−S[1]
7, 9
5:14
7: 3
17:12
18:15[l]
24:14
27:20
30:17
34:25
36:20
Psa. 1: 2
6: 7
12: 3+AS[2]
15: 7
16: 3
18: 3, 3
21: 3
31: 4
41: 4, 9
54:11
73:16
76: 3, 7
77:14
87: 2
89: 4
91: 3
103:20
104:39
118:55
120: 6
129: 6
133: 2
135: 9
138:11
12−A
Pro. 29:33, 36
Ecc. 2:23
8:16
Cant. 3: 1, 8
5: 2
Isa. 4: 5
15: 1, 1
21: 8, 12
26: 9
27: 3
28:19
29: 7−AS
34:10
38:13
60:11, 19
62: 6
Jer. 6: 5
9: 1
14:17
29:10
38:35
43:30
52: 7
Lam. 1: 2

Lam. 2:18, 19
Dan. 2:19
4:10
5:30
7: 2+A
13
Hos. 4: 5
6+A
Hos. 7: 6
Amos 5: 8
Obad. 5
Jon. 2: 1
4:10, 10
Mic. 3: 6
Zec. 1: 8
14: 7

[a] A μεσονύκτιος. [b] pro ἡμέρα. [c] ACS[3] ἡμέρα. [d] A σῶμα.

νύσταγμα.

Job 33:15

νυσταγμός.

Ps. 131: 4
Jer. 23:31—B

νυστάζω.

2 Sa. 4: 6
Psa. 75: 7
118:28
120: 3, 4
Pro. 6:10
Pro. 24:48
Isa. 5:27
56:10
Jer. 23:31—B
Nah. 3:18

νωθροκάρδιος.

Proverbs 12: 8

νωθρός.

Proverbs 22:20

νῶτος, —τον.

Gen. 9:23
40: 8
Exo. 37:12, 13
Nu. 34:11
Jos. 15: 8[a], 10
11
18:12, 13[b]
16[a], 18
19
19:34[c]
1 Sa. 4:18
13: 5 B[d]
2 Sa. 22:41
1 Ki. 7:19
2 Ki. 17:14, 14
Neh. 9:29
Job 15:26—A
Psa. 17:41
Psa. 20:13
65:11[e]
68:24
80: 7
128: 3
Isa. 17:12
50: 6
Jer. 2:27
31:39
39:33
Eze. 1:18, 18
10:12
40:18, 40
40, 41
44, 44
42:16
46:19
Zec. 7:11

[a] B νότος. [b] A νότος. [c] AB νότος. [d] pro νότος. [e] BS[1] ἐνώπιον.

νωτοφόρος.

2 Ch. 2: 2—B
18
2 Ch. 34:13

ξανθίζω.

Leviticus 13:30, 31, 32

ξανθός.

Leviticus 13:36

ξένιος.

2 Sa. 8: 2, 6
Ezra 1: 6
Hos. 10: 6

ξενισμός.

Proverbs 15:17

ξένος.

Ruth 2:10
1 Sa. 9:13
2 Sa. 12: 4
15:19
Job 31:32
Psa. 68: 9
Ecc. 6: 2
Isa. 18: 2
Lam. 5: 2

ξεστός.

Amos 5:11[a]

[a] A ξυστός.

ξέω.

Job 7: 5 AC[a]

[a] pro ξύω.

ξηραίνω.

Gen. 8: 7, 14
Jos. 9:18
1 Ki. 13: 4
17: 7
Job 4:21[a]
8:12
12:15
14:11
18:16
Psa. 21:16
73:15—B
89: 6
101: 5, 12
105: 9
128: 6
Pro. 17:22
Isa. 19: 5, 6, 7
27:11
37:27
40: 7, 24
41:17
42:14
15—AS
Isa. 42:15—AS
44:11, 27
50: 2
51:12
Jer. 12: 4
23:10
28:30[b]
Lam. 4: 8
Eze. 17: 9, 10
10—A
24
19:12, 12
Hos. 9:16
Joel 1:10, 11[c]
12, 12
17, 20
Amos 1: 2
2: 9
4: 7
Nah. 1: 4
Zec. 10: 2[d], 11
11:17, 17

[a] A τελευτάω. [b] S ἐξαίρω. [c] S[2] καταισχύνω. [d] S[3] ἐξαίρω.

ξηρασία.

Jud. 6:37, 39
40
Neh. 9:11
Eze. 17:10+A
40:43
Nah. 1:10

ξηρός.

Gen. 1: 9, 9, 10
7:22
Exo. 4: 9, 9
14:16, 21
22, 29
15:19
Jos. 3:17, 17
4:18 A[a]
22
9:11
Job 24:19
Psa. 65: 6
Psa. 94: 5
Isa. 9:18
37:27[b]
56: 3
Eze. 17:24
20:47
37: 2, 4, 11
Dan. 2:10
Hos. 9:14
Jon. 1: 9
2:11
Hag. 2: 6, 21

[a] pro γῆ. [b] A χλωρός.

ξίφος.

Jos. 10:28[a]
30[b]
32, 33
35, 37
39
Jos. 11:11, 12
14
Job 3:14
Eze. 16:40
23:47

[a] B[1] μάχαιρα. [b] B* μάχαιρα.

ξυλάριον.

1 Kings 17:12

ξύλινος.

Lev. 11:32
15:12
26:30
27:30
Nu. 31:20
35:18
Deu. 10: 1[a]
Deu. 28:42
1 Ki. 6:20 B[b]
Ezra 6: 4
Neh. 8: 4
Jer. 35:13
Eze. 41:22, 22
Dan. 5: 4, 23

[a] A λίθινος. [b] pro ξύλον.

ξυλοκόπος.

Deu. 29:11
Jos. 9:27, 29
Jos. 9:33
33—A

ξύλον.

Gen. 1:11, 12
29
2: 9 ter
16, 17
3: 1, 2, 3
6, 8, 11
Gen. 3:12, 17
22, 24
6:14
22: 3, 6, 7
9, 9
40:19
Exo. 7:19
9:25
10: 5, 12
15, 15
15:25
25: 5, 9, 12
27
26:15, 26
27: 1, 6
30: 1, 5
31: 5
35: 7, 24
33
Lev. 1: 7, 8, 12
17
3: 5
4:12
6:12
14: 4, 6, 45
49, 51
52
19:23
23:40, 40
26: 4, 20
Nu. 15:32, 33
19: 6
Deu. 4:28
10: 3
16:21
19: 5, 5, 5
20:19, 20
21:22, 23
23
28:36, 64
29:17
Jos. 8:29 ter
10:26, 26
27
Jud. 6:26
9: 8, 9, 10
11, 12
13, 14
15, 48
1 Sa. 6:14
2 Sa. 5:11, 11
21:19
23: 7
21—A
24:22
1 Ki. 4:20
5: 6, 6, 8
17
6:14, 15
15
21+A
29[a], 31
(32)A
30+A
9:11
11—A
10:11, 12
12
14:23
15:22
17:10
18:23
2 Ki. 3:19, 25
6: 4, 6
12:11, 12
16: 4
17:10
19:18
22: 6
1 Ch. 14: 1, 1
16:32, 33
20: 5
21:23
22: 4, 4, 14
15
29: 2
2 Ch. 2: 8, 8, 9
10, 14
16
3: 5, 10
7:13
9:10, 11
16: 6
28: 4
2 Ch. 34:11
Ezra 3: 7
5: 8
6:11
Neh. 2: 8
8:15, 15
9:25
10:35, 37
Est. 5:14 ter
6: 4
7: 9
9—A
10
8: 7
9:13+S[3]
25+AS[1]
Job 24:20
30: 4
33:11[b]
41:18
Psa. 1: 3
73: 5
95:12
103:16
104:33
148: 9
Pro. 3:18
12: 4
25:20
26:20, 21
Ecc. 2: 5
6—B
10: 9
11: 3, 3
Cant. 2: 3
3: 9
4:14
Isa. 7: 2, 4
19+AS
10:15
14: 8
30:33, 33
34:13—A
37:19
40:20
44:13, 14
23
45:20
55:12
56: 3
60:17
65:22
Jer. 2:20, 27
3: 6, 9, 13
5:14
6: 6
7:18, 20
10: 3
11:19
17: 8
26:23
38:12
Lam. 4: 8
5: 4, 13
Eze. 15: 2 ter
3, 6, 6
17: 24 quq
20:28, 32
47, 47
21:10
24:10
26:12
31: 4, 5, 8
9, 14
15, 16
18
34:27
36:30
39:10
41:25
47:12
Joel 1:12, 19
2:22
Hab. 2:11, 19
Hag. 1: 8
2:19[c]
Zec. 5: 4
12: 6—S[1]

[a] B ξύλινος. [b] A κύκλωμα. [c] S[1] φύλλον.

ξυλοφορία.

Nehemiah 10:34

ξυλοφόρος.

Nehemiah 13:31

ξυλόω.

2 Ch. 3: 5
Jer. 22:14
Eze. 41:16
26 A[a]

[a] pro ζυγόω.

ξυνωρίς.

Isa. 21: 9[a]

[a] ABS[2] συνωρίς.

ξυράω, —ρέω.

Gen. 41:14
Lev. 13:33, 33
34
14: 8, 9, 9
21: 5, 5
Nu. 6: 9, 9[a]
18, 19
Deu. 21:12
Jud. 16:17, 19
Jud. 16:22
2 Sa. 10: 4
1 Ch. 19: 4
Isa. 7:20
Jer. 16: 6
31:37, 37
48: 5
Eze. 44:20
Mic. 1:16

[a] A[1]? καθαρίζω.

ξύρησις.

Isaiah 22:12

ξυρόν, —ός.

Nu. 6: 5
8: 7
Jud. 16:17 A[a]
Psa. 51: 4
Isa. 7:20
Jer. 43:23
Eze. 5: 1

[a] pro σίδηρος.

ξυστός.

1 Ch. 22: 2
Amos 5:11 A[a]

[a] pro ξεστός.

ξύω.

Job 2: 8[a]
Job 7: 5[b]

[a] A ἀποξέω. [b] AC ξέω.

ὀβελίσκος.

Job 41:21

ὀβολός.

Exo. 30:13
Lev. 27:25
Nu. 3:47
18:16
1 Sa. 2:36
Pro. 17: 6
Eze. 45:12

ὀγδοήκοντα.

Nu. 4:48[a]
1 Ki. (3) p1—A
2 Ki. 10:24[b]
2 Ch. 14: 8[c]

[a] A πεντήκοντα. [b] A ὀκτώ. [c] AB πεντήκοντα.

ὄγδοος.

1 Ki. 16:29+A
2 Ki. 22: 3[a]
1 Ch. 26: 4—AB
1 Ch. 26: 5—B
2 Ch. 23: 1[a]
Jer. 43: 9[b]

[a] A ἕβδομος. [b] A πέμπτος.

ὁδεύω.

1 Kings 6(12)A

ὁδηγέω.

Exo. 13:17
15:13
32:34
Nu. 24: 8
Deu. 1:33
Jos. 24: 3
2 Sa. 7:23
1 Ch. 17:21
Neh. 9:12
12+S[1]
19
Job 31:18
Psa. 5: 9
22: 3
24: 5, 9
26:11

Psa. 30: 4
42: 3
44: 5
59:11
60: 3
66: 5
72:24
76:21
77:14, 53
72
79: 2
Psa. 85:11
89:16
105: 9
106: 7, 30
107:11
118:35
138:10, 24
142:10
Pro. 11: 3 A
Ecc. 2: 3
Isa. 63:14

ὁδηγός.

Ezra 8: 1

ὁδοιπόρος.

Gen. 37:25
Jud. 19:17
2 Sa. 12: 4−A
Pro. 6:11

ὁδοποιέω.

Job 30:12
Psa. 67: 5
77:50
Psa. 79:10
Isa. 62:10

ὁδός.

Gen. 3:24
6:12
16: 7
18: 5, 19
19: 2
24:21, 40
42, 48
56
28:15, 20
30:36
31:23
32: 1
33:14, 16
35: 3, 19
38:16, 21
42:25, 38
44:29
45:21, 23
24
48: 7
49:17
Exo. 3:18
4:24
5: 3
8:27
12:39
13:17, 18
21
18: 8, 20
23:20
32: 8
33: 3
Lev. 26:22
Nu. 9:10, 13
10:33, 33
11:31, 31
14:25
20:17
21: 1, 4, 4
22, 22
33
22:23 ter
31, 32
34
33: 8
Deu. 1: 2, 19
22
31−A
31, 33
33, 40
2: 1, 8, 8
27
3: 1
5:33
6: 7
8: 2, 6
9:12, 16
10:12
11:19, 22
28, 30
13: 5
Deu. 14:23
17:16
19: 3, 6, 9
22: 1, 4, 6
23: 4
24:11
25:17, 18
26:17
27:18
28: 7, 7, 9
25, 25
29, 68
30:16
31:29
32: 4
Jos. 1: 8
2: 7, 16
22
3: 4, 4
5: 4, 7
9:17, 19
10:10
12: 3
21:42
22: 5
23:14
24:17
Jud. 2:17, 19
22
4: 9
5: 6[a], 6
10−A
10−A
8:11
9:21+A
25, 37
15:15+A
17: 8
18: 5, 6, 26
19: 9, 27
20:31, 32
42
45+A
21:19
Ruth 1: 7
1 Sa. 1:18, 19
3:21
4:13
6: 9, 12
12
8: 3, 5
9: 6, 8
12:23
13:15+B
17, 18
18
14: 4[b], 4
5, 5
15: 2, 18
20
17:52
1 Sa. 18:14
21: 5, 5
24: 4, 8, 20
25:12
26: 3, 13
25
27: 7 B[c]
28:22
29:10
30: 2
2 Sa. 2:24
4: 7
11:10
13:30, 34
34
15: 2, 23
16:13
18:23
22:22, 31
33
1 Ki. 1:49
2: 2, 3, 4
3:14
8:25, 32
36, 39
41, 44
48, 58
11:29, 29
33, 38
12 p24 f 6
13: 9, 10
10, 12
12, 17
24, 24
25, 26
28
15:26, 34
16: 2, 19
26
p 28−A
18: 6 ter
7, 43
19: 4, 7, 15
15
21:38
22:43, 53
53
2 Ki. 2:23
3: 8, 8, 9
20
6:19
7:15
8:18, 27
9:27
10:12
11: 6, 16
19
16: 3
17:13
18:17
19:28, 33
21:21, 22
22: 2
25: 4, 4
2 Ch. 6:16, 23
27, 30
31, 34
34, 38
7:14
11:17
17: 3, 6
18:23
20:32
21: 6
12−A
12, 13
22: 3
27: 6
28: 2
34: 2
Ezra 8:21, 22
27, 31
Neh. 9:12, 19
19
Job 3:23+A
4: 6
6:19
8:14+A
9:26
12:24
Job 13: 9+A
16:22
17: 9
19:12
21:14, 29
31
22: 3, 28
23:10, 11
24: 4, 11
13
26:14[d]
28: 4, 13
23, 26
29: 4, 6
25
31: 4, 7
33:11, 29
31+A
34: 8+A
38:25
Psa. 1: 1, 6, 6
2:12
5: 9
9:26
13: 3−A
3−A
15:11
16: 4
17:22, 31
33
18: 6
24: 4, 8, 9
10, 12
26:11
31: 8
34: 6
35: 5
36: 5, 7[e]
18, 23
34
38: 2
43:19
48:14
49:23
50:15
66: 3
73: 5 S[1 f]
76:14, 20
79:13
80:14
84:14
85:11
88:42
90:11
94:10
100: 2[g], 6
101:24
102: 7
106: 4, 7, 17
40
109: 7
118: 1, 3, 5
9, 14
15, 26
27, 29
30, 32
33, 37
59, 101
104, 128
151[h]
168
127: 1
137: 5
138: 3
24[i]
24
141: 4
142: 8
144:17
145: 9
Pro. 1:15, 19
31
2: 8, 8, 12
13, 13
16, 22
3: 6, 6, 17
17, 23
26, 31
4:10, 11
14, 14
Pro. 4:18, 19
26, 27
27
5: 6, 8
21
6: 6, 12
23
7:19
25−S[1]
27
8:13, 13
20
20 S[1 j]
22
32+AS[2]
34
9:12
15+A
15
10: 9, 17
11: 5, 20
20
12:15, 26
28, 28
13: 6 A
13, 15
14: 2, 8, 12
14
15: 9, 19
24, 28
16: 5, 17
17, 25
29, 31
17:23, 23
18:22
19:16
20:11, 24
21: 8, 16
21, 29
22: 5, 13
14, 14
19, 25
23:26
24:54, 54
55
25:10, 19[k]
26: 6, 13
13
28:10, 18
23
29:27
Ecc. 10: 3
11: 5, 9
12: 5
Isa. 2: 3
5:25
7: 3
8:11
9: 1+AS[2]
10:24, 26
26, 32
11:16 A[m]
15: 5
19:23
21:13
26: 7, 7, 8
30:11, 21
33: 8, 15
21
35: 8 ter
36: 2
37:29, 34
40: 3
4+A
14, 27
41: 3, 27
42:16, 24
43:16, 19
45:13
46:11
48:15, 17
49: 9, 11
51:10
53: 6
55: 3, 7, 8
8, 9, 9
11
56:11
57:14, 14
Isa. 57:17[n], 18
58: 2
59: 7, 8, 8
14
62:10
63:17
64: 5
65: 2
66: 3
Jer. 2:18[o], 18[p]
23, 24
25, 33
33, 36
3: 2, 13
21
4:11, 18
5: 1, 4, 5
6:16, 16
25, 27
7: 3, 5, 17
23
10: 2, 23
12: 1, 4, 16
14:16[p]
18 A[q]
16:17
17:10
18:11, 15
15
21: 8, 8
22:21−A
23:12, 14
25: 5
27: 5
31: 5, 19
33: 3, 13
35:11
38: 9, 21
39:19, 19
39
42: 4 S[3 r]
15
43: 3, 7
49: 3
52: 7, 7
24
Lam. 1: 4, 12
2:15
3: 9, 39
Eze. 3:18, 19
7: 8, 9, 3
4, 27
9: 2, 7, 10
11: 6, 21
13:22
14:22, 23
16:25[s]
27, 31
43, 47
47, 61
18:11, 23
25 ter
29 ter
30
20:43, 44
21:19, 20
20, 21
21
22:31
23:13, 31
24:14
27: 3 A[t]
33: 8, 9, 9
11, 11
17, 17
20, 20
36:17, 17
19, 31
32
42:15
43: 2, 4
44: 1, 3, 3, 4
46: 2, 8, 8
9 qtr
47: 2, 2
Dan. 5:23
Hos. 2: 6, 6
4: 9
6: 9
7: 1
Hos. 9: 8
12: 2
13: 7
14: 9
Joel 2: 7
Amos 2: 7
4:10
5:16, 17
Jon. 3: 3, 4+A
8, 10
Mic. 4: 2, 5
6:16[l]
7:10
Nah. 1: 3
2: 2, 5
3:10[u]
Hab. 3:19 S[1 v]
Zeph. 3: 6
Hag. 1: 5, 7
Zec. 1: 4, 6
3: 7
9: 3
7 S[1 w]
10: 5
Mal. 2: 8, 9
3: 1

[a] A βασιλεύς.
[b] B ἀκρωτήριον.
[c] pro ἀγρός.
[d] S[1] λόγος.
[e] BS[1] ζωή.
[f] pro εἴσοδος.
[g] B ᾠδή.
[h] A ἐντολή.
[i] B[2]S[1] εἰδέω.
[j] pro τρίβος.
[k] A ὀδούς.
[m] pro δίοδος.
[n] S[2] καρδία.
[o] A γῆ.
[p] A δίοδος.
[q] pro γῆ.
[r] pro αὐλή.
[s] A ἔξοδος.
[t] A βουλή.
[u] S[1] ὄρος.
[v] pro ᾠδή.
[w] pro ὀδούς.

ὀδούς.

Gen. 49:12
Exo. 21:24, 24
27 ter
Lev. 24:20, 20
Nu. 11:33
Deu. 19:21, 21
32:24
1 Sa. 13:21
1 Ki. 10:22+A
2 Ch. 9:17, 21
Ezra 8:17 B[a]
Job 13:14
16: 9
19:20[b]
29:17
41: 5
Psa. 3: 8
34:16
36:12
56: 5
Psa. 57: 7
111:10
123: 6
Pro. 10:26
24:37
25:19 A[c]
Cant. 4: 2
6: 5
7: 9
Jer. 38:29, 30
Lam. 2:16
3:16
Eze. 18: 2
4+A
27:15
Dan. 7: 5, 7, 19
Joel 1: 6, 6
Amos 4: 6
Mic. 3: 5
Zec. 9: 7[d]

[a] pro ᾄδω.
[b] A ὀδύνη.
[c] pro ὁδός.
[d] S[1] ὁδός.

ὀδυνάω.

Pro. 29:21
Isa. 21:10
40:29
53: 4
Lam. 1:13[a], 14
Hag. 2:14
Zec. 9: 5
12:10

[a] A ὀδύρομαι.

ὀδύνη.

Gen. 35:18
44:31 A[a]
Exo. 3: 7
Deu. 26:14
28:60
1 Sa. 15:23
Est. 9:22−S
Job 2: 9
3: 7[b], 20
4: 8
6: 2
7: 3, 4
19+ABS
15:35
18:11
19:20 A[c]
20:10, 23
24: 6
27:20
30:14, 15
16, 22
37: 8
Psa. 12: 3
30:11
40: 4
93:19
Ps. 106:39
114: 3
126: 2
Pro. 6:33
17:21, 25
19:13+A
24:74
Isa. 14: 3
19:10
23: 5
30:26
32:10
35:10
38:14
51:11
Jer. 8:18
22:23[d]
23:15
Lam. 5:17−A
Eze. 12:18
21: 6
28:21
Hos. 5:13, 13
Amos 8:10
Mic. 1:11, 12
Hab. 1:13[e]
Zec. 12:10

[a] pro λύπη.
[b] AC ὀδυνηρός.
[c] pro ὀδούς.
[d] A ὠδίν.
[e] AS[3] ὄνομαι.

ὀδυνηρός.

1 Ki. 2: 8
(3) p 1
Job 3: 7 AC[a]
Jer. 14:17
37:17
Lam. 5:17

[a] pro ὀδύνη.

ὀδυρμός.

Jeremiah 38:15

ὀδύρομαι.

Jer. 38:18
Lam. 1:13 A[a]

[a] pro ὀδυνάω.

ὄζω.

Exodus 8:14

ὅθεν.

Ps. 120: 1[a]

[a] AS πόθεν.

ὀθόνιον.

Jud. 14:13[a]
Hos. 2: 5, 9

[a] A σινδών.

οἰακίζω.

Job 37: 9[a]

[a] A οἰκεῖος.

οἶδα *vide* εἰδέω.

οἰκεῖος.

Exo. 8: 9 A[a]
11 A[a]
13 A[a]
Lev. 18: 6, 12
13 – A
17
21: 2
25:32 A[a]
49
Nu. 25: 5
27:11
1 Sa. 10:14, 15
1 Sa. 10:16
14:50
1 Ch. 4:21[b]
Job 19:15 A[a]
37: 9 A[c]
Pro. 17: 9
Isa. 3: 6
31: 9
58: 7
Jer. 18:22 B[a]
19:13 B[a]
Amos 6:10

[a] pro οἰκία. [b] AB οἰκία.
[c] pro οἰακίζω.

οἰκειότης.

Leviticus 20:19

οἰκεσία.

2 Kings 19:25 B[a]

[a] pro ἀποικεσία.

οἰκέτης.

Gen. 9:25
26 – A
27:37
44:16, 33
50:18
Exo. 5:15, 16
12:44
21:26, 27
32:13
Lev. 25:39, 42
42, 55
Nu. 32: 5[a]
Deu. 5:15
6:21
15:15, 17
Deu. 16:12
24:20, 22
24
34: 5
Jos. 5:14
9:14, 17
Pro. 13:13
17: 2
19:10
22: 7
24:33, 57
58[b]
29:19, 21
Isa. 36: 9

[a] A παῖς. [b] ABS[1] οἰκέτις.

οἰκέτις.

Exo. 21: 7
Lev. 19:20
Pro. 24:58 ABS[1a]

[a] pro οἰκέτης.

οἰκέω.

Gen. 4:16, 20
16: 3
19:30 A[a]
20: 1
24: 3, 13
25:27
Gen. 27:44
29:19
34:16, 21
23
35: 1
36: 7
Gen. 36: 8 A[a]
Exo. 2:15[b]
Deu. 28:30
Jos. 21:42
Jud. 9:21[b], 41
10: 1[b]
11: 3[b], 8 B[c]
26[d]
20:15[b]
21: 9, 10[b]
12[b], 21[b]
2 Sa. 15: 8, 19
19:32
1 Ki. 3:17
2 Ki. 6: 1, 2
19:36
1 Ch. 4:41
2 Ch. 34: 9
Ezra 4: 6, 17
Neh. 3:26
4:12
7: 3
13: 4
Est. 9:19 + S[3]
Psa. 16:12
83:11
Pro. 8:26
10:30
Pro. 21: 9, 19
25:24
27:10
Isa. 5: 8
6: 5
21:12
30:19
32:18 B[e]
33:16
34: 1 S[1e]
11
37:26[f], 37
Jer. 31:28
28 A[a]
42: 4 A[g]
7[h]
9 A[1i]
10, 11
15
47: 5, 10
49:14
50: 2[b]
Eze. 38:11[h]
Dan. 3:31
6:25
Hos. 10:14 A[i]
Hag. 1: 4

[a] pro κατοικέω. [b] A κατοικέω.
[c] pro κατοικέω. [d] A οἶκος.
[e] pro οἰκουμένη. [f] AS ἐνοικέω.
[g] pro οἶκος. [h] pro οἰκοδομέω.
[i] pro οἴχομαι.

οἴκημα.

Ezekiel 16:24

οἴκησις.

2 Ch. 17:12
2 Ch. 27: 4

οἰκητός.

Leviticus 25:29

οἰκήτωρ.

1 Ch. 4:41 A[a]
Pro. 2:21 + AS

[a] pro οἶκος.

οἰκία.

Gen. 17:12 + A
13
19: 3 A[a], 4
24: 2, 31
32
25:27
31:41
33:17
34:29
39: 9, 11
11, 14
43:15, 15
16 A[a]
25
44: 1, 4
50: 8, 21
Exo. 1:21
8: 9[b], 11[b]
13[b], 21
9:19
10: 6 *ter*
12: 3, 4, 13
15, 19
23, 30
46, 46
20:17
22: 7, 8
Lev. 14:34, 35
35, 36
36 AB[c]
36
36 (*a*38)
41 (*a*49)
51, 52
53, 55
25:29, 30
31, 32[b]
33, 33
Lev. 27:14, 15
Nu. 19:14 *ter*
31:10 B[d]
32:18
Deu. 5:21
6: 9, 11
8:12
11:20[e]
15:16
20: 5, 5, 6
7, 8
21:12, 13
22: 2, 8, 8
24: 3, 5, 7
12
25:14
26:11, 13
28:30
Jos. 2: 1, 3, 18
19, 19
6:22, 23
24:15[c]
Jud. 15: 6 A[a]
18:22[e]
19:15[e], 18
21 A[a]
22
22 A[a]
22
23 A[a]
23
20: 5
1 Sa. 21:15
28:24
2 Sa. 16: 2
17:18, 20
1 Ki. 13:15 + A
2 Ki. 4:35
1 Ch. 4:21 AB[f]
12:28
15: 1
Ezra 6:11
Neh. 3:10
5: 3, 4, 11
7: 3, 4
9:25
Est. 1:22
7: 8
Job 1:10, 13
10, 19
2: 9, 9
4:19
8:15
19:15[b]
20:15
24:16
30:23
Psa. 48:12
83: 4
100: 7
103:17
127: 3
Pro. 14: 9, 9, 11
25:24
Ecc. 10:18
12: 3
Isa. 3:22
5: 8, 8, 9
13:16 – S[1]
21
24:10
32:13
65:21
Jer. 5: 6
6:12
16: 8
17:22 – S[1e]
18:22[g]
19:13[g]
22:13
36: 5 AS[a]
28
39:15, 29
40: 4 AS[3a]
42: 2 S[a]
3, 7, 9
43:12[h]
44: 4 S[a]
15, 15[c]
16, 18
20, 21
45: 7, 11
14, 17
22, 26
50: 9, 12
13
52:11, 13
13, 31
Eze. 11: 3
28:26
33:30
Dan. 5:17
Joel 2: 9
Amos 6: 9, 10
Mic. 2: 9
Zeph. 1:13
Zec. 5:11
14: 2

[a] pro οἶκος. [b] A οἰκεῖος.
[c] pro ἀφή. [d] pro κατοικία.
[e] A οἶκος. [f] pro οἰκεῖος.
[g] B οἰκεῖος. [h] AS οἶκος.

οἰκίζω.

Job 22: 8[a]

[a] A κομίζω.

οἰκογενής.

Gen. 14:14
15: 2, 3
17:12, 13
23, 27
Lev. 22:11
Ecc. 2: 7
Jer. 2:14

οἰκοδομέω.

Gen. 2:22
4:17
8:20
10:11
11: 4, 5, 8
12: 7, 8
13:18
22: 9
26:25
35: 7
Exo. 1:11
17:15
20:25
24: 4
32: 5
Nu. 13:23
21:27
23: 1, 14
29
32:16, 24
34, 37
38
Deu. 6:10
8:12
20: 5, 20
22: 8
25: 9
27: 5, 6
28:30
Jos. 6:26
9: 3
19:50
21:42
22:10, 11
16, 19
23, 26
29
Jos. 24:13
Jud. 1:26
6:24, 26
28
18:28
21: 4, 23
Ruth 4:11
1 Sa. 2:35
7:17
14:35, 35
2 Sa. 5: 9, 11
7: 5, 7
11, 13
27
24:21, 25
1 Ki. (3) 1 – AB
p 1 *sep*
36
p 46 + A
p 46
3: 2
4:30 – A
5: 3, 5
5
6: 5 + A
6 + A
6, 7
11 *ter*
(12) A
13, 14
(14) A
15, 16
33
33 – A
7:38, 39
49 + A
8: 1 – A
1 Ki. 8:13 A
16, 17
18, 19
19, 20
27, 43
44, 48
53, 53
65
9: 1, 3, 9
10
11 A[a]
17 A
24 A
25 A
10: 4
p 22 *bis*
11: 5, 27
38, 38
12 p 24 l 9
l l 1, 23
25, 25
14:23
15:17, 21
22, 22
23 – B
16:24, 24
32, 34
18:32
21:12
22:39
2 Ki. 14:22
15:35
16:11, 18
17: 9
21: 3, 4, 5
23:13
25: 1
1 Ch. 6:10, 32
7:24
8:12
11: 8
14: 1
17: 4, 6, 10
12, 25
21:22, 26
22: 2, 5, 6
7, 8, 10
11, 19
19
28: 2, 3
6[b], 10
29:16
2 Ch. 2: 1, 3, 4
5, 6, 6
9, 12
3: 1, 2, 3
6: 2, 5, 7
8, 9, 9
10, 18
33, 34
38
8: 1, 2 – A
4, 4, 5
6, 11
12
9: 3
11: 5, 6
14: 7
16: 1, 5, 6, 6
17:12
20: 8
26: 2, 6, 9
10
27: 3, 3
4 + A
32: 5, 29
33: 3, 4, 5
14, 15
19
35: 3
36:23
Ezra 1: 2, 3 – B
5
3: 2, 10
4: 1, 2, 3
3, 4, 12
13 B[c]
16, 21
Ezra 5: 2, 3, 4
8, 9, 11
11, 11
13, 16
17
6: 3 – B
7, 8, 14
14 B[c]
Neh. 2:18, 20
3: 1, 3, 13
4: 1, 2, 10
17, 18
6: 1, 6
7: 1, 4
12:29
Job 12:14
Psa. 27: 5
50:20
68:36
77:69
88: 3, 5
95: 1
101:17
117:22
121: 3
126: 1, 1
146: 2
Pro. 9: 1
14: 1
24: 3
Ecc. 2: 4
3: 3
9:14
Cant. 4: 4
8: 9
Isa. 5: 2
9:10
10: 9
25: 2
44:26, 28
45:13
49:17
54:14
58:12
60:10
61: 4
65:21, 22
66: 1
Jer. 7:31
12:16
19: 5
22:13, 14
30: 5, 28
37:18
38: 4, 4, 28
38
39:31, 35
40: 7
42: 7, 9[d]
49:10
51:34
Eze. 4: 2
11: 3
13:10
16:24, 25
31
21, 22
26:14
27: 5
28:26
36:10, 33
36
39:15
Dan. 4:27
9:25, 25
Hos. 8:14
10: 1
Amos 5:11
9: 6, 14
Mic. 3:10
Hab. 2:12
Zeph. 1:13
Hag. 1: 2, 8
Zec. 5:11
6:12, 15
8: 9
9: 3
Mal. 1: 4

[a] pro δίδωμι. [b] B κληρονομέω.
[c] pro ἀνοικοδομέω. [d] A[1] οἰκέω.

οἰκοδομή.

1 Ch.26:27
29: 1+A
Eze. 16:61
Eze. 17:17
40: 2

οἰκοδόμος.

2 Ki.12:11
22: 6
1 Ch.14: 1
22:15
29: 6[a]
2 Ch.34:11
Neh. 4:18
Isa. 58:12
Eze. 40: 3

[a] A οἰκονόμος.

οἰκονομέω.

Psalm 111: 5

οἰκονομία.

Isaiah 22:19, 21

οἰκονόμος.

1 Ki. 4: 6, 6
16: 9
18: 3
2 Ki.18:18, 37
19: 2
1 Ch.29: 6 A[a]
Est. 1: 8
8: 9
Isa. 36: 3, 22
11+S[1]
37: 2

[a] *pro* οἰκοδόμος.

οἰκόπεδον.

Ps. 101: 7
Ps. 108:10

οἶκος.

Gen. 7: 1
9:21, 27
12: 1
15—A
17
17:23, 27
18:19
19: 2, 3[a]
10, 10
11
20:13, 18
24: 7, 27
28, 38
40, 67
27:15
28: 2, 17
19, 21
22
29:13
30:30
31:14
30—A
33 *qnq*
35, 37
37
34:19, 26
30
35: 2
36: 6
38:11, 11
39: 2, 4, 5
5, 5, 8
16
41:10, 40
42:33—A
43:16[a], 17
18, 18
25
44: 8
45: 2,8,16
46:27, 31
47:12, 14
24
50: 7
Exo. 6:14, 17
19
7:23
8: 3,3,21
24, 24
9:20
12: 3,7,22
Exo. 12:27, 27
13: 3, 14
16:29
29 A[b]
19: 3
20: 2, 22
23:19
34:26
Lev. 9: 7
10: 6, 14
14: 8
16: 6
11+AB
11, 17
24
22:13
26:45
Nu. 1: 2,4,20
22, 24
26, 28
30, 32
34, 36
38, 40
42, 44
2: 2, 32
34
3:15, 20
24, 30
35
4: 2
4+A
22, 29
34, 38
40, 42
44, 46
7: 2
9:15
12: 7
14:12
16:30, 32
17: 2, 2, 3
6, 8
18: 1, 11
13, 31
19:18
20:29
22:18
24: 5, 13
25:14, 15
26: 2
30: 4, 11
Nu. 30:17
34:14
36: 1
Deu. 3:29
4:46
5: 6, 30
6: 7, 12
22
7: 8, 26
8:14
11: 6, 19
20 A[c]
12: 7
13:10
14:25[d]
15:20
16: 7
19: 1
22:21—B
21
23: 1 A[2e]
18
25: 9, 10
26:15
34: 6
Jos. 2:12, 13
13[f], 18
6:17, 25
7:14, 14
13:17
20: 6 A
22: 4, 6, 7
8, 14
14
24:15 A[c]
Jud. 1:23+A
35
2: 1
6+A
4:17
6: 8—A
15, 27
8:27, 29
35
9: 1, 4, 5
6, 16
18, 19
20, 20
23, 27
46+A
10: 9+A
11: 2, 7
26 A[g]
31, 34
12: 1
14:15, 19
15: 6—B[a]
16:21, 25
25, 26
27
29—A
29, 30
31
17: 4, 5[h]
5,8,12
18: 2,3,13
14, 15
15, 18
19
19—A
22
22 A[c]
22, 25
26, 28
31
19: 2, 3
15 A[c]
18
21[a],22[a]
23[a], 26
27
27—A
29+A
20: 8
Ruth 1: 8, 9
4:11, 11
12, 12
1 Sa. 1: 7, 19
21, 24
2:11+A
1 Sa. 2:27, 27
28, 28
30, 30
31, 32
32+A
33, 35
36
3: 3[i]
12, 13
14, 14
15
5: 2, 3, 5
5
6: 7, 10
7: 1, 2, 3
17
9:18, 20
10:26
15:34
17:25 A
18: 2 A
10 A
19: 9, 11
20:15, 15
22: 1, 14
15, 16
22
23:18
24:22
25: 1,6,17
28, 35
36
27: 3
2 Sa. 1:12
2: 3, 4, 7
10, 11
3: 1 *qtr*
6 *ter*
8,8,10
12, 19
29, 29
4: 5, 6, 7
11
5: 8,9,11
6: 3
3+A
10, 11
11, 12
12, 15
19, 20
21
7: 1, 2, 5
6,7,11
13, 16
18, 19
25
25+A
27, 29
29
9: 1, 2, 3
4, 5, 9
9 A[k]
12
11: 2, 4, 8
8
9+A
9, 10
10, 11
13, 27
12: 8,8,10
11, 15
17, 20
20
13: 7, 7, 8
17, 20
14: 8,9,24
24, 31
15:16, 16
17, 35
16: 3, 5, 8
21
17:23, 23
23 A[m]
19: 5, 11
11—AB
12, 17
18, 20
28[n], 30
33 A[o]
41
2 Sa. 20: 3 *ter*
21: 1, 4
22—A
23: 5
24:17
1 Ki. 1:53
2:24, 27
31, 33
34
(3)1—B, 1
p 1 *ter*
36
p 46+A
p 46
3: 2, 17
17
18+A
18
4: 7, 12
30—A
30—A
5: 3, 5, 5
9, 11
14
6: 2, 4, 5
6+A
6
7+A
7 *ter*
8, 9
9+A
10 *ter*
11
11—A
(12)A
12, 13
13, 14
(14)A
15 *ter*
16+A
17+A
18
(18)A
19+A
20, 20
25, 25
27, 28
33—A
7: 3, 12
25
25—B
25, 26
31 *ter*
34, 36
36+A
37, 37
38
38+A
39, 40
45
45+3
45
49+A
49+A
49—A
8: 1—A
1—A
6, 10
11
13A, 16
17, 18
19, 19
20, 27
29, 31
33, 38
43
44, 48
53 *ter*
63, 64
65
9: 1, 1, 3
7, 8, 8
9,9,10
10, 10
21 A
25 A
10: 4,5,12
12, 17
21
p 22 *bis*
1 Ki.11:18, 28
38
12:16, 19
20—B
21, 23
24
p 24 *l* 9
ll 11,79
l 81
26, 27
30—AB
31
13: 2, 7, 8
18, 19
32, 34
14: 4 A,8 A
10 A
10 A
12 A
13 A
14 A
17 A
26, 26
27, 28
15:15
18—B
18
20—B
27, 29
16: 3 *ter*
7—A
7, 9
11
12+A
12, 18
18, 32[p]
17:17, 23
18:18
20: 2
4+A
22 *ter*
29+A
21: 6, 6
30
31+A
43+A
22:17, 30
53—A
2 Ki. 1:18, 18
4: 2
2—B
13, 32
33
5: 9, 18
18
18—A
24
6:32
7: 9, 11
8: 1, 2, 3
5, 18
27, 27
27+A
9: 6, 7, 8
8, 9, 9
9
10: 3,5,10
11, 21
21
22—A
23, 25
26+A
27+A
30
11: 3, 4, 5
6,7,10
11
11—A
11, 13
15, 16
18, 18
19, 19
20
12 *passim*
13: 6
14:10, 14
14
15: 5,5,25
35
16: 8,8,14
2 Ki.16:14, 18
18
17: 1, 21
29, 32
32
18:15, 15
19: 1, 14
30, 37
20: 1, 5, 8
13 *ter*
15 *ter*
17, 18
21: 4, 5
7+A
7,7,13
18, 23
22: 3, 4, 5
5, 5, 6
8, 9, 9
9
23: 2, 2, 6
7, 7, 8
11, 12
13, 19
24, 27
24:13, 13
25: 9 *qtr*
13, 13
16, 27
30
1 Ch. 2:10, 54
55
4:21, 31
38
41[q]
5:13, 15
24, 24
6:10, 31
32+AB
32, 48
48
7: 2, 4, 7
9, 23
9: 9, 11
13, 13
19, 28
23, 26
10: 6, 10
10
12:29, 30[r]
13: 7, 13
14
14: 1
15:25
16:43, 43
17: 1, 1, 4
5, 6
10—ABS
12, 14
16, 17
23, 24
25, 27
21:17
22: 1, 2, 5
6, 7, 8
10, 11
14, 19
23: 4, 11
24, 24
28
28—B
32
24: 3, 4, 4
6, 19
30
25: 6
6—AB
26: 6, 12
13, 15
20, 22
27
28: 2, 3, 4
4, 4, 6
10, 11
11, 12
12—B
13
13—B
20 *qtr*
21
1 Ch.29: 2, 3, 3
3, 7, 8
16, 19
2 Ch. 2: 1, 1, 3
4, 5, 6
6,9,12
12
3: 1, 3, 4
4, 5, 6
7, 8
8—AB
10, 11
12 A
13, 15[s]
4:10, 11
16, 17
19, 22
22, 22
5: 1—B
7, 13
14
6: 2, 5, 7
8, 9, 9
10, 18
20, 22
24, 29
33, 34
38
7: 1, 2, 2
3, 5, 7
11 *qtr*
12, 16
20, 21
21
8: 1,1,11
16
9: 3,4,11
11, 16
20
10:16, 19
11: 4
12: 9,9,11
15:18
16: 2, 2
17:14
18: 1, 16
26
19: 1, 11
20: 5, 9, 9
28
21: 6,7,13
17
22: 3, 4
7—A
8,9,10
12
23: 1, 3, 3
5—A[l]
5, 6, 7
9, 10
10, 12
14, 14
15, 17
18, 18
19, 20
20
24: 4, 5, 7
7, 8
12, 12
12—A
13, 14
14, 16
18—AB
21
25: 5,5,19
24, 24
26:19, 21
21
27: 3
28: 7
18—A
18—A
21, 21
24, 24
29: 3, 5
15—B
16 *ter*
17, 18
20, 25
31

2 Ch.29:31—A
35
30: 1, 15
31: 2, 4
10, 10
11, 13
16, 17
21
32:21
33: 4, 5, 7
7, 15
15, 20
24
34: 8, 8, 9
10 *ter*
11, 14
15, 17
30, 30
32
35: 2, 3, 4
5, 5, 5
8, 12
19—AB
19, 19
36: 7, 10
14, 17
18
18—AB
19, 23
Ezra 1: 2
3—B
4, 5, 7
7
2:36, 59
68, 68
3: 6, 8
8—B
9, 10
11, 12
12
4: 1, 3
24—A
5: 2, 3, 8
9—B
11, 12
13
14—B
14, 15
16, 17
17
6: 3
3—B
4, 5, 5
5
7—A
7, 8, 11
12, 15
16, 17
22
7:15, 16
17, 19
20, 20
23, 24
27
8:17, 25
29, 30
33, 36
9: 9
10: 1, 6, 9
16
Neh. 1: 6
2: 3
8+S[3]
8
3:23, 23
25, 28
29
29 B[t]
4:14, 16
5:13
6:10, 10
11
7:39, 61
8:16
16 A[t]
10:32, 33
34, 34
35, 36
36
37—A

Neh.10:38, 38
39
11:11, 12
16A, 22
12:37
40 S[3]
13: 4, 7, 8
9, 11
14
Est. 1: 5
4:14
6: 4+S[3]
7: 8+S[3]
Job 3:15
5:24
7:10
8:14
12: 6
15:28, 34
17:13
18:19, 21
20:19, 26
28
21: 9, 21
28
22:18
24:12
27:18
29: 4
30: 6
Psa. 5: 8
22: 6
25: 8
26: 4
29: 1
30: 3
35: 9
41: 5
44:11
48:17
18+S[2]
49: 9
51: 2, 10
54:15
58: 1
64: 5
65:13
67: 7, 13
68:10
73:20
83: 5, 11
91:14
92: 5
95: 1
97: 3
100: 2
104:21
111: 3
112: 9
113: 1, 17
18, 20
20
115:10
117: 2, 3, 26
118:139+
AS[1]
121: 1, 5, 9
126: 1
131: 3
133: 1, 1
134: 2, 2, 19
19, 20
150 *p*6
Pro. 1:13
2:18
3:33
5: 8, 10
7: 6, 8, 11
17, 19
20, 27
9: 1, 14
11:29
12: 7
14: 1
15: 6—S[1]
25
17: 1, 13
16
21: 9[m]
23: 5, 27

Pro. 24: 3, 42
61
27:10, 15
15
29:33, 39
45
Ecc. 2: 4
4:14, 17
7: 3, 3, 5
5
12: 5
Cant. 1:17
2: 4
3: 4
8: 2
Isa. 2: 2, 3, 5
6
3: 7, 14
5: 7
6: 1, 4, 11
7: 2, 13
17
8:14, 17
18—A
13:10 S[1 v]
22
14: 1
2+S
18
22: 8, 9, 10
18
22—B
23, 24
24:12
29:22
30:29 A[w]
31: 2
32:14, 14
37: 1
14-AS[3]
38
38: 1, 8, 20
22
39: 2 *ter*
4 *ter*
6, 7
42: 7, 22
44:13—S[1]
28
46: 3
48: 1
56: 5, 7, 7
7
58: 1, 7
60: 7
62: 7 S[1 x]
63: 7, 15
64:11
66: 1, 20
Jer. 2: 4, 4
3: 4, 18
18, 20
5: 7, 11
11, 15
20
20-ABS
27
7:10, 11
14, 30
9:26
10: 1
11:10, 10
15, 17
17
12: 6, 7
13:11, 11
16:15
17:22 A[c]
26
18: 2, 3, 6
19:13, 13
14
20: 1, 2, 2
6
21:11, 12
22: 1, 2, 4
5, 6
14
30+A
23:11, 34

Jer. 23: 7[a]
27:16 A[aa]
28:33, 51
31:13, 22
23—S[1]
23
33: 2, 2, 6
7, 9, 9
10, 10
12, 18
34:13
35: 1, 3, 5
6
36: 5[bb]
26
38:31, 31
33
39: 2—S[1]
34
40: 4
4—S[1 cc]
11
41:13, 15
42: 2[dd], 2
4, 4[ee]
4
43: 3, 5, 6
8, 9
10 *ter*
12 AS[c]
12, 20
21, 22
44: 4[gg]
15 A[e]
45:14
48: 5
52:13, 13
17
17—A
20
Lam. 1:20
2: 7
5: 2
Eze. 2: 3, 5, 6
7, 8
3: 4, 5, 7
7, 9, 17
24, 26
27
4: 4, 5, 6
5: 4
6:11
7:24+A
8: 1
6+A
10, 11
12, 14
15+A
16, 17
9: 3, 6, 7
9
10: 3, 4, 4
18, 19
11: 1, 5
15
12: 2, 3 A[b]
3, 6, 9
9—A
10, 23
23, 27
13: 5, 9
14: 4, 5, 6
7, 11
16:41
17: 2, 12
18: 6, 15
25, 29
29, 30
31
20: 1, 3—B
5, 5
13
13+A
27, 30
31, 39
40
22: 6, 18
23:39, 47
24: 3, 21
25: 3, 8, 9

Eze. 25:12
26:12
27: 6, 14
28:24
29: 6, 16
21
33: 7, 10
11, 20
34:30
35: 5
36:10, 17
21, 22
22, 32
37
37:11, 21
38: 6
39:13, 22
23, 25
29
40: 4, 5, 45
47, 48
41: 5, 6
6+A
6, 7A[ff]
7, 8, 9
10, 13
14, 15
16
17 A[ff]
19, 26
42:15, 15
20
43: 4, 5, 6
7, 7, 10
10, 11
12
12+A
21
44: 4, 4, 5
5, 6, 6
6, 9, 11
11
12—A
14, 15
30
45: 4, 5, 6
8
9+A
17, 17
19, 20
22
46:24, 24
47: 1
1+A
1
48:11, 21
Dan. 1: 2 *ter*
4—A
2: 5, 17
3:29
4: 1, 27
5: 5, 10
23
6:10, 18
Hos. 1: 4, 4, 6
4:15
5: 1, 1, 8
12, 14

Hos. 6:10
8: 1
9: 4, 8, 15
10: 5, 14
15
11:11, 12
12: 4
Joel 1: 9, 13
14, 16
3:18
Amos 1: 4
2: 8
3: 1, 13
15 *qtr*
5: 1, 3, 4
6, 6, 11
19, 25
6: 1, 10
11, 11
14
7: 9, 10
13, 16
9: 8, 9
Obad. 17
18 *qtr*
Mic. 1: 2, 5
5+A
5, 10
11, 14
2: 2, 2, 7
3: 1, 1, 9
9, 12
4: 2
5: 2
6: 4, 10
16
7: 6
Nah. 1:14
Hab. 2: 9
9 S[1 gg]
10
Zeph. 1: 8, 9, 13
2: 7, 7
Hag. 1: 2, 4, 4
8, 9, 9
9, 14
2: 3, 7, 9
Zec. 1:16
3: 7
4: 9
5: 4 *ter*
6:10, 12
14, 15
7: 3
8: 9, 13
13, 15
19
9: 8
10: 3, 6, 6
11:13
12: 4, 7, 8
8, 10
12, 12
13
13: 1, 6
14:20, 21
Mal. 3:10

[a] A οἰκία. [b] *pro* τόπος.
[c] *pro* οἰκία. [d] B υἱός.
[e] *pro* ἐκκλησία. [f] A ἀδελφή.
[g] *pro* οἰκέω. [h] A ἀνήρ.
[i] *pro* ναός. [k] *pro* υἱός.
[m] *pro* τάφος. [n] A πάροικος.
[o] *pro* γῆρας. [p] A ἐνώπιον.
[q] A οἰκήτωρ. [r] S κατοικέω.
[s] B τοῖχος. [t] *pro* πύλη.
[u] S[1] κοινός. [v] *pro* κόσμος.
[w] *pro* ὄρος. [x] *pro* ὅμοιος.
[y] A τόπος. [z] S λαός.
[aa] *pro* γῆ. [bb] AS οἰκία.
[cc] AS[3] οἰκία. [dd] S οἰκία.
[ee] A οἰκέω. [ff] *pro* τοῖχος.
[gg] *pro* ὕψος.

οἰκουμένη.

Exo. 16:35
2 Sa. 22:16
Psa. 9: 9
Psa. 17:16
18: 5
23: 1

Psa. 32: 8
48: 2
49:12
66: 5+S[1]
71: 8
76:19
88:12
89: 2
92: 1
95:10, 13
96: 4
97: 7, 9
Pro. 8:31
Isa. 10:14, 23
13: 5, 9, 11
14:17, 26
26+AS
23:17
24: 1, 4
27: 6
34: 1[a]
37:16, 18
62: 4
Jer. 10:12
28:15
Lam. 4:12

[a] S[1] οἰκέω.

οἰκτείρημα.

Jeremiah 38: 3

οἰκτείρω.

Exo. 33:19, 19
Jud. 5:30—A
1 Ki. 8:50
2 Ki. 13:23
Psa. 4: 2
36:21
58: 6
59: 3
66: 2
76:10
101:14, 14
15
102:13, 13
Ps. 111: 5[a]
122: 2
134:14 S[1 b]
Pro. 12:10
13: 9, 11
21:26
Isa. 27:11
30:18
Jer. 13:14
21: 7
Lam. 3:31
Mic. 7:19

[a] S οἰκτιρμός. [b] *pro* ὅτι κρινεῖ.

οἰκτιρμός.

Jud. 5:30—A
2 Sa. 24:14
1 Ki. 8:50
1 Ch. 21:13
2 Ch. 30: 9
Neh. 1:11
9:19, 27
28, 31
Psa. 24: 6
39:12
50: 3
68:17
76:10
78: 8
102: 4
105:46
Ps. 111: 5 S[a]
118:77, 156
144: 9
Isa. 63:15
Lam. 3:22—AB
22—AB
Dan. 1: 9
2:18
4:24
9: 9, 18
18
Hos. 2:19
Zec. 1:16
7: 9
12:10

[a] *pro* οἰκτείρω.

οἰκτίρμων.

Exo. 34: 6
Deu. 4:31
2 Ch. 30: 9
Neh. 9:17, 31
Psa. 77:38
85:15
102: 8
Ps. 108:12
110: 4
111: 4
144: 8
Lam. 4:10
Joel 2:13
Jon. 4: 2

οἶκτος.

Jeremiah 9:19 S[2 a], 20[b]

[a] *pro* οἰκτρός. [b] AS[1] οἰκτρός.

οἰκτρός.

Jer. 6:26
9:19[a]
Jer. 9:20 AS[1 b]

[a] S[2] οἶκτος. [b] *pro* οἶκτος.

οἶμαι *vide* οἴομαι.

οἴμοι, οἴμμοι.

Jud. 11:35 A[a]
1 Ki. 17:20 B[b]
Job 10:15
Ps. 119: 5
Jer. 4:31
15:10
22:18—A
Jer. 51:33, 33
Lam. 1:21 A[c]
21 A[d]
Eze. 9: 8
11:13, 13
Joel 1:15 *ter*
Mic. 7: 1, 1

[a] A οἴμμοι *pro* ἆ ἆ.
[b] B οἴμμοι *pro* οἴ μοι.
[c] *pro* ὅμοιος. [d] *pro* ἐμοί.

οἰνόομαι.
Ezekiel 23:42+A

οἰνοποτέω.
Proverbs 24:72

οἰνοπότης.
Proverbs 23:20

οἶνος.
Gen. 9:21, 24; 14:18; 19:32, 33; 34, 35; 27:25, 28; 37; 49:11, 12
Exo. 23:25—A^1; 29:40; 32:18
Lev. 10: 9; 23:13
Nu. 6: 3; 3+AB; 3,4,20; 15: 5,7,10; 18:12; 28:14
Deu. 7:13; 11:14; 12:17; 14:22; 25—B; 15:14[a]; 18: 4; 28:39, 51; 29: 6; 32:14, 33; 38; 33:28
Jos. 9:10, 19
Jud. 9:13; 13: 4,7,14; 14; 19:19
1 Sa. 1:11, 14; 15, 24; 10: 3; 16:20; 25:11, 18; 37
2 Sa. 13:28; 16: 1, 2
2 Ki. 18:32
1 Ch. 9:29; 12:40; 27:27
2 Ch. 2:10, 15; 11:11; 31: 5; 32:28
Ezra 6: 9; 7:22
Neh. 2: 1, 1; 5:11, 15; 18; 10:37, 39; 13: 5—S^1; 12, 15
Est. 1: 7; 5: 6+S^3; 7: 2+S^3; 8+S^3
Job 1:13
Psa. 4: 8; 59: 5; 68:13; 74: 9; 77:65; 103:15
Pro. 3:10; 4:17; 9: 2, 5; 12:11; 20: 1; 21:17; 23:30, 31; 24:72, 74; 27: 9
Ecc. 2: 3; 9: 7; 10:19
Cant. 1: 2, 4; 2: 4; 4:10; 5: 1; 7: 9; 8: 2
Isa. 1:22; 5:11, 12; 22; 16:10; 22:13; 24: 7,9,11; 25: 6; 28: 1, 7, 7; 29: 9; 36:17; 49:26; 51:21; 55: 1; 62: 8
Jer. 13:12, 12; 23: 9; 28: 7; 31:33; 32: 1; 38:12; 42: 2, 5, 5; 6, 6, 8; 14; 47:10, 12
Lam. 2:12
Eze. 16:49+A; 27:18, 18; 44:21
Dan. 1: 5,8,16; 5: 1, 2, 4; 23; 10: 3
Hos. 2: 8,9,22; 3: 2; 4:11; 7: 5, 14; 9: 2, 4; 14: 7
Joel 1: 5,5,10; 2:19, 24; 3: 3
Amos 2: 8, 12; 5:11; 6: 6; 9:14
Obad. 16-BS^1
Mic. 2:11; 6:15
Zeph. 1:13
Hag. 1:11; 2:12
Zec. 9:15, 17; 10: 7

[a] A ληνός.

οἰνοφλυγέω.
Deuteronomy 21:20

οἰνοχοέω.
Genesis 40:13

οἰνοχόη.
Ecclesiastes 2: 8

οἰνοχόος.
Gen. 40:20[a]
1 Ki. 10: 5
2 Ch. 9: 4
Neh. 1:11[b]
Ecc. 2: 8

[a] A ἀρχιοινοχόος.
[b] BS^1 εὐνοῦχος.

οἴομαι.
Gen. 37: 7; 40:16; 41: 1, 17
Est. 9:12
Job 11: 2; 34:12; 34:17+A; 37:22; 38: 2; 40: 3; 42: 3
Isa. 57: 8

οἶος.
Gen. 41:19; 41:15
1 Ki. 18:13
Est. 2: 1
Job 33:27
Dan. 9:12; 12: 1

οἰφί, —φεί.
Lev. 5:11; 6:20
Nu. 5:15; 15: 4; 28: 5
Jud. 6:19
Ruth 2:17
1 Sa. 1:24; 17:17 A; 25:18
Eze. 45:13

οἴχομαι.
Gen. 12: 4; 25:34; 31:19
2 Ch. 8:17, 18; 21: 9
Job 14:10, 20; 19:10; 30:15
Jer. 9:10; 10:20 S^1[a]; 16:11; 27: 6; 29: 8; 31:11; 35:11; 48:10, 12; 15, 17; 52: 7 A[b]
Hos. 10:14[c]

[a] pro ὄλλυμι.
[b] pro πορεύω.
[c] A οἰκέω.

οἰωνίζομαι.
Gen. 30:27; 44: 5, 15
Lev. 19:26
Deu. 18:10
1 Ki. 21:33
2 Ki. 17:17—A; 21: 6
2 Ch. 33: 6

οἰώνισμα.
1 Sa. 15:23
Jer. 14:14; 34: 7

οἰωνισμός.
Gen. 44: 5, 15
Nu. 23:23

οἰωνός.
Numbers 24: 1

ὀκλάζω.
1 Ki. 8:54
1 Ki. 19:18

ὀκνέω.
Nu. 22:16
Jud. 18: 9

ὀκνηρία.
Ecclesiastes 10:18

ὀκνηρός.
Pro. 6: 6, 9; 11:16; 18: 8; 20: 4; 21:25; 22:13; 26:13, 14; 26:15, 16; 29:45

ὀκτακόσιοι.
Gen. 5:26[a]
2 Sa. 23: 8[b]
Neh. 7:13[c]; 11:12-BS^1

[a] A^2 782 pro 802
[b] B^* τριακόσιοι.
[c] S^1 ἐννακόσιοι.

ὀκτάπηχυς.
1 Kings 7:47

ὀκτώ.
1 Sa. 4:15+A
2 Ki. 8:17[a]; 15:13+A
1 Ch. 24: 4—B
2 Ch. 21:20—A
Job 42:16+ ACS^2

[a] AB τεσσαράκοντα.

ὀλεθρεύω vide ὀλοθ—

ὀλέθριος.
1 Kings 21:42

ὄλεθρος.
1 Ki. 13:34
Pro. 1:26; 27—C; 21: 7
Jer. 28:55; 31: 3,8,32; 32:16
Eze. 6:14; 14:16
Hos. 9: 6
Obad. 13

ὀλέκω.
Job 10:16; 17: 1; 32:18

ὀλιγόβιος.
Job 11: 3
Job 14: 1

ὀλίγος.
Gen. 29:20—A
Exo. 16:18 A^2[a]
Lev. 25:52
Nu. 11:32; 13:19; 26:56
Deu. 4:27; 28:38
Jos. 7: 3
1 Sa. 14: 6
1 Ki. 17:10, 12
2 Ki. 10:18; 14:26 B[b]
2 Ch. 14:11; 24:24; 29:34
Neh. 2:12; 7: 4
Job 8: 7; 10:20; 20 S[c]; 14:21; 15:11
Psa. 16:14 AB^*S^d; 36:10, 16; 72: 2; 108: 8
Pro. 5:14; 6:10 ter; 15:29; 24:48 ter
Ecc. 5: 1, 11; 6:11 S[e]; 9:14; 10: 1[f]
Isa. 10: 7; 21:17; 24: 6
Jer. 49: 2; 51:28
Eze. 5: 3
Dan. 11:23
Hag. 1: 6, 9
Zec. 1:15

[a] pro ἐλασσων.
[b] pro ὀλιγοστός.
[c] pro μικρός.
[d] pro ἀπολύω.
[e] pro λόγος.
[f] B ὁ λόγος.

ὀλιγοστός.
Gen. 34:30
Exo. 12: 4
Lev. 26:22
Deu. 7: 7
2 Ki. 14:26[a]
1 Ch. 16:19
Ps. 104:12
Isa. 16:14; 41:14; 60:22
Jer. 10:24
Eze. 29:15
Amos 7: 2, 5
Obad. 2
Mic. 5: 2

[a] B ὀλίγους τοῦς.

ὀλιγότης.
Psalm 101:24

ὀλιγοψυχέω.
Nu. 21: 4
Jud. 8: 4+A; 10:16 A[a]; 16:16
Psa. 76: 4
Jon. 4: 8
Hab. 2:13

[a] pro ὠλιγώθη ψυχή.

ὀλιγοψυχία.
Exo. 6: 9
Psa. 54: 9

ὀλιγόψυχος.
Pro. 14:29; 18:14
Isa. 25: 5; 35: 4; 54: 6—A^1; 57:15

ὀλιγόω.
Jud. 10:16[a]
2 Ki. 4: 3
Neh. 9:32
Psa. 11: 2; 106:39
Pro. 10:27
Ecc. 12: 3
Joel 1:10, 12
Nah. 1: 4
Hab. 3:12

[a] A ὀλιγοψυχέω.

ὀλιγωρέω.
Proverbs 3:11

ὀλισθάνω.
Proverbs 14:19

ὀλίσθημα.
Psa. 34: 6; 55:14; 114: 8
Jer. 23:12; 45:22
Dan. 11:21, 32; 34

ὁλκή.
Gen. 24:22, 22
Nu. 7:13, 19; 25, 31; 37, 43; 49, 55; 61, 67; 7:73, 79
2 Sa. 21:16
1 Ch. 21:25; 28:14, 15
2 Ch. 3: 9, 9; 4:18

ὄλλυμι, —ύω.
Job 4:11; 8:13 A[a]; 18:11; 20:10[b]; 34:17
Pro. 1:32; 2:22; 9:18; 10:28 AS[a]; 11: 7, 7; 13: 2; 15: 6 AS^2[a]; 16: 2; 25:19
Jer. 10:20[c]; 29:11; 30: 3; 31: 1, 15; 18, 20; 38: 2, 2

[a] pro ἀπόλλυμι.
[b] A θλάω.
[c] S^1 οἴχομαι.

ὀλόθρευσις, ὀλέ—
Joshua 17:13 A[a]

[a] pro ἐξολοθρεύω.

ὀλοθρεύω, ὀλεθ—
Exo. 12:23; 22:20 B[a]
Nu. 4:18[b]
Deu. 20:20[b]
Jos. 3:10, 10; 7:25
Jud. 6:25[c], 28[c]; 6:30[d]
Jer. 2:30; 5: 6; 22: 7; 32:22
Hag. 2:22-S^1[e]

[a] pro ἐξολοθρεύω.
[b] A ἐξολοθρεύω.
[c] A ἐκκόπτω.
[d] A κόπτω.
[e] AS^2 ἐξολοθρεύω.

ὁλοκάρπωμα.
Lev. 5:10[a]; 16:24 AB[b]; 16:24
Nu. 15: 3[c]

[a] B ὁλοκαύτωμα.
[b] pro ὁλοκαύτωμα.
[c] A ὁλοκαύτωμα.

ὁλοκάρπωσις.

Gen. 8:20
22: 2,3,6
7,8,13
Lev. 4:34[a]
Lev. 9: 3
1 Sa. 6:14 A[b]
Isa. 40:16
43:23

[a] A ὁλοκαύτωσις.
[b] *pro* ὁλοκαύτωσις.

ὁλόκαυτος.

Leviticus 6:23

ὁλοκαύτωμα.

Exo. 10:25
18:12
20:24
24: 5
29:18
30:20, 28
32: 6
Lev. 1: 3,6,10
3: 2,5
4:7,24,25
25, 29
30, 33
35
5: 7
10 B[a]
12
6:25, 32
58
7:27
8:18, 21
28
9: 2,7,12
13, 14
16, 17
22, 24
10:19
12: 6, 8
14:13, 19
20, 22
31
15:15, 30
16: 3, 5
24[b]
17: 4, 8
22:18
23: 8, 12
18, 25
27, 36
36, 37
Nu. 6.11
14 A[c]
16
7:15, 21
27, 33
39, 45
51, 57
63, 69
75, 81
8:12
10:10
15: 3[d]
3 A[a]
6
8 AB[c]
24
23: 6
28: 6, 10
11, 14
19, 23
24, 27
31
31 + A
29: 2, 6, 6
8, 13
36, 39
Deu. 12: 6, 11
13, 14
27
27: 6
Jos. 9: 4
22:23
Jud. 6:26
28 + A
11:31
13:16, 23
20:26 A[c]
21: 4 A[c]
1 Sa. 15:22
2 Sa. 6:17
24:22, 24
1 Ki. 9:25 A
18:29, 33
34, 38
2 Ki. 3:27
5:17
10:24
1 Ch. 6:49
16: 1,2,40
40
21:26, 29
23:31
29:21
2 Ch. 2: 4
4: 6
7: 1, 7, 7
8:12
9: 4
13:11
23:18
24:14
29: 7
30:15
35:14, 16
Ezra 8:35
Neh. 10:33
Psa. 19: 4
39: 7
49: 8
50:18, 21
65:13, 15
Isa. 1:11
56: 7
Jer. 6:20
7:21, 22
14:12
17:26
Eze. 40:40, 42
42
43:18, 24
27
44:11
45:15, 17
17, 23
25
46: 2,4,12
12, 13
15
Hos. 6: 6
Amos 5:22
Mic. 6: 6

[a] *pro* ὁλοκάρπωμα.
[b] AB ὁλοκάρπωμα.
[c] *pro* ὁλοκαύτωσις.
[d] A κάρπωμα.

ὁλοκαύτωσις.

Exo. 29:25
Lev. 4:34 A[a]
34
6: 9,9,10
Lev. 6:12, 38
Nu. 6:14[b]
7:87
15: 5, 8[c]
Nu. 23:17
28: 3, 10
15, 23
29:11, 16
19, 22
25, 28
31, 34
38
Jud. 20:26[c]
21: 4[b]
1 Sa. 6:14[d], 15
7: 9, 10
10: 8
13: 9,9,10
12
15:13
2 Sa. 6:18
24:25
1 Ki. (3) *p*1
3: 4, 15
8:64, 64
10: 5
2 Ki. 10:25
2 Ki. 16:13
15 *qlr*
1 Ch. 21:23, 24
26, 26
22: 1
2 Ch. 1: 6
24:14
29:18, 24
27, 27
28, 31
32, 32
34, 35
35
31: 2, 3
3 – A[1]
35:12
Ezra 3: 2, 3, 4
5, 6
6: 9
8:35
Eze. 40:38 + A
39 + A

[a] *pro* ὁλοκάρπωσις.
[b] A ὁλοκαύτωμα
[c] AB ὁλοκαύτωμα.
[d] A ὁλοκάρπωσις.

ὁλοκληρία.

Isaiah 1: 6 – ABS

ὁλόκληρος.

Lev. 23:15
Deu. 16: 9 + A
27: 6
Jos. 9: 4
1 Ch. 24: 7 A[a]
25: 9 A[a]
Eze. 15: 5
Zec. 11:16

[a] *pro* ὁ κλῆρος.

ὀλολυγμός.

Isa. 15: 8
Zeph. 1:10

ὀλολύζω.

Isa. 10:10
13: 6
14:31
15: 2, 3
16: 7, 7
23: 1,6,14
24:11
52: 5
Isa. 65:14
Jer. 2:23
31:20, 31
Eze. 21:12
Hos. 7:14
Amos 8: 3
Zec. 11: 2, 2

ὁλοπόρφυρος.

Numbers 4: 7, 13

ὁλόρριζος.

Job 4: 7
Pro. 15: 6

ὅλος.

Gen. 18:26 – A
Exo. 22:11 A[a]
Lev. 4:21 – AB[1]
Jud. 7:18 – A
22 A[b]
16:16 A[b]
20:37 + A
1 Ki. 2: 4 + A
7:38 + A
49 – A
11:13 + A
1 Ki. 15:29 – B[c]
16:12 + A
2 Ch. 1: 5 + A
Est. 9:22 – A
Psa. 55: 5 – S
Isa. 13: 5 AS[b]
9 + S
24:10 + S
45: 9 – AS[2]
Eze. 11:19 + A
Dan. 6: 1[d]

[a] *pro* καθόλου.
[b] *pro* πᾶς.
[c] A σύμπας.
[d] A πᾶς.

ὁλοσχερής.

Ezekiel 22:30 A[a]

[a] *pro* ὁλοσχερῶς.

ὁλοσχερῶς.

Eze. 22:30[a]

[a] A ὁλοσχερής.

ὄλυνθος.

Canticles 2:13

ὀλύρα.

Exo. 9.32
Eze. 4: 9

ὀλυρίτης.

1 Kings 19: 6

ὅλως.

Job 34: 8 + CS[a]

ὁμαλίζω.

Isa. 28:25
Isa. 45: 2

ὁμαλισμός.

Micah 7:12

ὄμβρημα.

Psalm 77:44

ὄμβρος.

Deuteronomy 32: 2

ὁμείρω.

Job 3:21 ABCS[a]

[a] *pro* ἱμείρω.

ὅμηρος.

Isaiah 18: 2

ὁμιλέω.

Pro. 5:19
15:12
Pro. 23:31, 31

ὁμιλία.

Exo. 21:10
Pro. 7:21

ὁμίχλη.

Job 24:20
38: 9
Ps. 147: 5
Isa. 29:18
Joel 2: 2
Amos 4:13
Zeph. 1:15

ὄμμα.

Pro. 6: 4
7: 2
9:18 A[a]
Pro. 10:26
23: 5

[a] *pro* ὄνομα.

ὄμνυμι, –νύω.

Gen. 21:23, 24
31
22:16
24: 7, 9
25:33, 33
26: 3, 31
31:54
47:31, 31
50:24
Exo. 13: 5, 11
22: 8
32:13
33: 1
Lev. 6: 3, 5
19:12
Nu. 11:12
14:16, 23
30: 3
32:10, 11
Deu. 1: 8, 34
35
2:14
4:21, 31
6:10, 13
18, 23
7: 8, 12
13
8: 1, 18
9: 5, 27
Deu. 10:11, 20
11: 9, 21
13:17
19: 8
26: 3, 15
28: 9, 11
29:13
30:20
31: 7, 20
21, 23
32:40
34: 4
Jos. 1: 6
2:12
5: 6
9:21, 24
25, 26
14: 9
21:43, 44
Jud. 2: 1, 15
8:19 + A
15:12
18 A[a]
21: 1,7,18
1 Sa. 3:14
19: 6
20:17, 42
24:22, 23
28:10
1 Sa. 30:15
2 Sa. 3: 9, 35
19: 7, 23
21: 2, 17
1 Ki. 1:13, 17
29, 30
51
2: 8, 23
(3) *p*1
2 Ki. 25:24
2 Ch. 15:14, 15
Ezra 10: 5
Psa. 14: 4
23: 4
62:12
88: 4, 36
50
94:11
101: 9
109: 4
118:106
131: 2, 11
Pro. 24:32
Ecc. 9: 2
Isa. 19:17 S[1 b]
18
45:23
23[c]
Isa. 48: 1
54: 9
62: 8
65:16, 16
Jer. 4: 2
5: 2, 7
7: 9
11: 5
12:16, 16
22: 5
28:14
29:14
30:22
45:16
47: 9
51:26
Eze. 6: 9
16: 8
20: 6 A[d]
Dan. 12: 7
Hos. 4:15
Amos 4: 2
6: 8
8: 7, 14
Mic. 7:20
Zeph. 1: 5 – A, 5
Zec. 5: 4
Mal. 3: 5

[a] *pro* εἶπον.
[b] *pro* ὀνομάζω.
[c] AS[3] ἐξομολογέομαι.
[d] *pro* ἑτοιμάζω.

ὁμοθυμαδόν.

Exo. 19: 8
Nu. 24:24
27:21
Job 2:11
3:18
6: 2
9:32
16:10
17:16
19:12
Job 21:26
24: 4, 17
31:38
34:15
38:33
40: 8
Jer. 5: 5
26:21
Lam. 2: 8

ὅμοιος.

Gen. 2:20
Exo. 15:11, 11
Lev. 11:14, 15
16 – AB
16 – A
19
22 *qlr*
Deu. 14:13
14 + A[2]
14 + A
16 – A
17
33:29
Jud. 8:18 + A
18 + A
1 Sa. 10:24
2 Sa. 9: 8
1 Ki. 3:12, 13
2 Ki. 8: 7, 7
18: 5
23:25, 25
1 Ch. 17:20
2 Ch. 1:12
6:14
35:18, 19
19
Neh. 13:26
Job 1: 8 + A
2: 3 + A
34:20 S[1 a]
Job 35: 8
37:22
41:24
Psa. 34:10
49:21
70:19
85: 8
88: 9
113:16
134:18
Pro. 19:12
20: 4, 8
27:19
19 + CS[1]
Cant. 2: 9
7: 1
Isa. 13: 4 – S[1]
14:14
23: 2
62: 7[b]
Lam. 1:21[c]
Eze. 5: 9
16:32
31: 8, 8
Dan. 1:19
3:25
7: 5
Joel 2: 2

[a] *pro* ὁμοῦ.
[b] S[1] οἶκος.
[c] A οἶμοι.

ὁμοιότης.

Genesis 1:11, 11 + A, 12

ὁμοιόω.

Gen. 34:15, 22
23
Psa. 27: 1
39: 6
48:13, 21
Psa. 82: 2
88: 7
101: 7
142: 7
143: 4

Cant. 1: 9
2:17
7: 7
8:14
Isa. 1: 9
40:18, 18
25
Isa. 46: 5
Lam. 2:13
Eze. 31: 2,8,18
32: 2
Hos. 4: 5,6
12:10
Zeph. 1:11

ὁμοίωμα.

Exo. 20: 4
Deu. 4:12, 15
16, 16
17, 17
18, 18
23, 25
5: 8
Jos. 22:28
Jud. 8:18[a]
1 Sa. 6: 5+A
5
2 Ki. 16:10
2 Ch. 4: 3
Ps. 105:20
Ps. 143:12
Cant. 1:11
Isa. 40:18, 19
Eze. 1: 4 A[b]
5, 5
16—A[1]
22, 26
26, 26
2: 1
8: 2, 3
10: 1, 8
10, 21
22 A[c]
23:15

[a] A μορφή. [b] *pro* ὅρασις. [c] *pro* ὁμοίωσις.

ὁμοίως.

1 Ch. 28:16
Est. 1:18
Job 1:16
Psa. 67: 7
Pro. 1:27
Pro. 4:18
19:29
Eze. 14:10
45:11

ὁμοίωσις.

Gen. 1:26
Psa. 57: 5
Eze. 1:10
8:10+A
Eze. 10:22[a]
28:12
Dan. 10:16

[a] A ὁμοίωμα.

ὁμολογέω.

Job 40: 9
Jer. 51:25

ὁμολογία.

Lev. 22:18
Deu. 12: 6—A
17
Jer. 51:25, 25
Eze. 46:12
Amos 4: 5

ὁμολόγως.

Hosea 14: 4

ὁμομήτριος.

Genesis 43:15, 28

ὁμονοέω.

Leviticus 20: 5

ὁμόνοια.

Psa. 54:15
Psa. 82: 6

ὁμοπάτριος.

Leviticus 18:11

ὁμορέω.

1 Ch. 12:40
Jer. 27:40
Eze. 16:26

ὅμορος.

Nu. 35: 5
2 Ch. 21:16

ὁμοῦ

Ezra 2:64—B
Job 34:29[a]

[a] S[1] ὅμοιος.

ὀμόω *vide* ὄμνυμι.

ὀμφακίζω.

Isaiah 18: 5

ὀμφαλός.

Jud. 9:37
Job 40:11
Cant. 7: 2
Eze. 38:12

ὄμφαξ.

Job 15:33
Pro. 10:26
Isa. 18: 5
Jer. 38:29, 30
Eze. 18: 2
4+A

ὄναγρος.

Ps. 103:11
Jer. 14: 6 S[a]
Dan. 5:21

[a] *pro* ὄνοι ἄγριοι.

ὀνειδίζω.

Jud. 5:18
8:15
1 Sa. 17:10
25 A
26 A
36, 45
2 Sa. 21:21
23: 9
2 Ki. 19: 4, 16
22, 23
1 Ch. 20: 7
2 Ch. 32:17
Neh. 6:13
Psa. 34: 7
41:11
43:17
54:13
Psa. 68:10
73:10, 18
78:12
88:52, 52
101: 9
118:42
Pro. 20: 4
25: 8, 10
Isa. 27: 8
37: 4, 4, 6
17, 23
24
43:12
51: 4
65: 7
Jer. 15: 9
Zeph. 2: 8, 10

ὀνείδισμα.

Ezekiel 36: 3

ὀνειδισμός.

Jos. 5: 9
1 Sa. 17:26 A
25:39
Neh. 1: 3
4: 5
5 S[3 a]
5: 9
Psa. 14: 3
68: 8, 10
11, 20
21
73:22
78:12
88:51
118:39[b]
Isa. 4: 1
37: 3
43:28
47: 3
51: 7
Jer. 6:10
12:13
15:15
Jer. 20: 8
23:40
24: 9
25: 9
28:51
29:14
38:19
49:18
51: 8, 12
Lam. 3:29, 60
5: 1
Eze. 21:28
22: 4[c]
34:29
36: 6, 15
30
Dan. 9:16
11:18, 18
12: 2
Hos. 12:14
Joel 2:19
Zeph. 2: 8
3:18

[a] *pro* μυκτηρισμός. [b] S[1] ὄνειδος. [c] AB ὄνειδος.

ὄνειδος.

Gen. 30:23
34:14
Lev. 20:17
1 Sa. 11: 2
17:36
2 Sa. 13:13
Neh. 2:17
Job 19: 5, 7
Psa. 21: 7
30:12
38: 9
43:14
56: 4
77:66
78: 4
88:42
108:25
118:22
Ps. 118:39 S[1 a]
122: 4
150 *p* 6
Pro. 3:31
6:33
18: 3, 13
19: 6[b]
26: 6
Isa. 25: 8
30: 3, 5
6+AS
54: 4
59:18
Eze. 16:57
22: 4 AB[a]
Joel 2:17
Mic. 2: 6
6:16

[a] *pro* ὀνειδισμός. [b] A ἄδικος.

ὄνησις.

Zechariah 8:10

ὀνοκένταυρος.

Isa. 13:22
34:11, 14
Isa. 34:14

ὄνομα.

Gen. 2:11, 13
19, 20
3:20
4:17, 19
19, 21
25, 26
26
5: 2,3,29
10:25, 25
11: 4,9,29
29
12: 2, 8
13: 4
16: 1, 11
13, 15
17: 5,5,15
15, 19
19:22, 37
38
21: 3, 23
31, 33
22:14, 24
24:29
25: 1, 13
13, 16
25, 26
30
26:18, 18
20, 21
22, 25
33+A
33
27:36
28:19, 19
29:13, 16
16, 32
33, 34
35
30: 6,8,11
13, 18
20, 21
24
31:18
32: 2, 27
28, 28
29, 29
30
33:17
35: 7, 8
10, 10
10—A
15, 18
18—A
36:10, 32
35, 39
39, 40
38: 1, 2, 3
4, 5, 6
29, 30
41:45, 51
52
46: 8
48: 6, 16
16
50:11
Exo. 1: 1, 15
15
2:10, 22
3:13, 15
5:23
6: 3, 16
9:16
15: 3, 23
16: 4 A[a]
31
17: 7, 15
18: 3, 4
20: 7,7,24
23:13, 21
Exo. 28: 9, 10
10
11—B
12, 21
21, 21
23
31: 2
33:19
34: 5, 14
35:30
36:13, 21
21, 21
Lev. 18:21
19:12, 12
20: 3
21: 6, 9
22: 2, 32
24:11, 11
16, 16
Nu. 1: 2,5,17
18, 20
22, 24
26, 28
30, 32
34, 36
38, 40
42
3: 2,3,17
18, 40
43
4:27, 32
6:27
11: 3, 26
26, 34
13: 5, 17
14:15, 21
17: 2, 3
21: 3
25:14, 15
26:30, 37
53, 55
59
27: 1, 4
32:38, 38
42
33:54
34:17, 19
Deu. 2:25
3:14
5:11, 11
6:13
7:24
9:14
10: 8, 20
12: 3,5,11
21, 26
14:24, 23
16: 2,6,11
15+A[1]
17: 8+A
10+A
12
18: 5,7,19
20, 20
22
21: 5
5 A[b]
22:14, 19
25: 6, 6, 7
10, 19
26: 2
28:10, 58
29:20
32: 3
Jos. 2: 1
5: 9
6:27
7: 9
9:15, 15
Jos. 14:15
15:15—A
17: 3
19:48
23: 7
Jud. 1:10, 11
17, 23
26, 26
2: 5
8:14—A
31
13: 2,6,17
18, 24
15:19
16: 4
17: 1
18:29 *ter*
Ruth 1: 2, 2
2—B
4, 4
2: 1, 19
4: 5, 10
10, 11
14, 17
17
1 Sa. 1: 1, 2, 2
20
7:12
8: 2, 2
9: 1, 2
12:22
14: 4, 4
49, 49
49—A
50, 50
17: 4
12 A
13 A
23 A
45
18:30 A
20:15, 42
21: 7
22:20
24:22
25: 3, 3, 5
9, 25
25—A
2 Sa. 2:16
4: 2, 2, 4
5:14, 20
6: 2, 18
7: 9, 13
23
25+A
26
8:13
9: 2, 12
12:24, 25
28
13: 1, 3
14: 7, 27
16: 5
17:25
18:18
18+A
20: 1, 21
22:50
23: 8, 18
22, 23
1 Ki. 1:47, 47
3: 2+A
4: 8
5: 3, 5, 5
7: 7, 7
8:16
16—A
17, 18
19, 20
27—A
29, 33
35
41+A
41+A
43, 43
44, 44
48
9: 3, 7
10: 1, 1
11:26+A
1 Ki. 11:36
12 *p* 24 *l* 4
l 7, 8, 27
13: 2
14:21, 21
31+A
15: 2, 10
16:24, 24
p 28—A
18:24, 24
25, 26
31, 32
20: 8
22:16, 42
2 Ki. 2:24
5:11
8:26
12: 1
14: 2, 7
15: 2, 33
17:34
18: 2
21: 1, 1[c]
7, 19
22: 1
23:27, 31
34, 36
24: 8, 17
18
1 Ch. 1:19 A
19 A
43, 46
50
50+A
2: 1, 26
29, 34
4: 3, 9
38, 41
6:17, 65
7:15, 15
16
16—B
23
8:29, 38
9:35, 44
11:24
12:23, 31
13: 6
14: 4, 11
17
16: 2,8,10
29—BS
35, 41
17: 8,8,21
24 ABS
21:19
22: 5
6+A
7, 8, 9
10, 19
23:13, 24
28: 3
29:13, 16
2 Ch. 1: 9
2: 1, 4
3:17, 17
6: 2, 5
6—B
7, 8, 9
10
10 B[a]
20, 24
26, 32
33, 33
34, 38
7:14, 16
20
9: 1
12:13, 13
13: 2
14:11
18:15
20: 8, 9
26, 31
22: 2
24: 1
25: 1
26: 3, 8
27: 1
28: 9, 15

2 Ch.29: 1
31:19
33: 4,7,18
35:19
36: 2,4,5
Ezra 2:61
5: 1,4,10
10
6:12
8:13,20
10:16
Neh. 1: 9,11
6:13
7:63
9: 5,7,10
Est. 2:5,7,14[d]
8: 8
Job 1: 1,21
18:17
19:14
30: 8
35:14B[e]
42p18q(r
Psa. 5:12
7:18
8: 2,10
9: 3,6,11
12: 6
15: 4
17:50
19: 2,6,8
21:23
22: 3
24:11
14+AB
28: 2
30: 4
32:21
33: 4
39: 5
40: 6
43: 6,9
21–A
27
44:18
47:11
48:12
51:11
53: 3,8
58:12 S²[a]
60: 6,9
62: 5,6[f]
65: 2,4
67: 5,5
68:31,37
71:14,17
17,19
73: 7,10
18,21
74: 2
75: 2
78: 6,9,9
79:19
82: 5,17[g]
19
85: 9,11
12
88:13,17
25
90:14
91: 2
95: 2,8
98: 3,6
99: 4
101:16,22
102: 1
104: 1,3
105: 8,47
108:13,21
110: 9
112: 1,2,3
113: 9
114: 4
115: 4
8–S¹
117:10,11
12,26
118:55,132
165 A[a]
121: 4
Ps. 123: 8
128: 8
129: 4
134: 1,3,13
137: 2,2
139:14
141: 8
142:11
144: 1,2,21
146: 4
148: 5,13
13
149: 3
Pro. 9:18[h]
10: 7
18:10
22: 1
24:27
27–A
32
27:16
Ecc. 6: 4,10
7: 2
Cant. 1: 3
Isa. 4: 1
7:14
8: 3
9: 6
12: 4,4,5
14:22
18: 7
19:18
24:15
25: 1
26: 8,13
29:23
30:27
33:21
40:26
41:25
42: 4,8
10–S¹
43: 1,7
44: 5,5
45: 3,4
47: 4
48: 1,1,2
2,9
11,19
49: 1
50:10
51:15
52: 5,6
54: 5
9+S¹
55:13
56: 5,6
57:15
59:19,19
60: 9
62: 2
63:12,14
16,19
64: 2,7
65: 1,15
15
66: 5,19
22
Jer. 7:10,11
12,14
30
10:16,25
11:16,19
21
12:16
14: 9,14
15,21
15:16
16:21–S³
20: 3,9,9
23: 6
13+A
25,27
26:17
27:34
28:19,57
31:17
32:15
33: 9,16
20
Jer. 34:12
36: 9,23
25
38:35
39:20,34
40: 2
41:15,16[i]
51:16,26
26
52: 1
Lam. 3:54–A
Eze. 16:14,15
20: 9,14
22,29
39,44
23: 4,4
36:20,21
22,23
39: 7,7
16,25
43: 7,7,8
48: 1,31
35,35
Dan. 1: 7
2:20,26
4: 5,5,16
5:12
9: 6,15
Dan. 9:18,19
10: 1
Hos. 1: 4,6,9
2:17,17
Joel 2:26,32
Amos 2: 7
4:13
5: 8,27
6:10
9: 6,12
Mic. 4: 5
5: 4
6: 9
Nah. 1:14
Zeph. 1: 4,4
3: 9,12
Zec. 5: 4
6:12
10:12
13: 2,3,9
14: 9
Mal. 1: 6,6
11 *ter*
14
2: 2,5
3: 5,16
4: 2

[a] *pro* νόμος. [b] *pro* στόμα.
[c] A θρόνος. [d] A ὀνομαστί.
[e] *pro* ἄνομος. [f] S² στόμα.
[g] A πρόσωπον. [h] A ὄμμα.
[i] A διαθήκη.

ὀνομάζω.

Gen. 26:18
Lev. 24:16,16
Jos. 23: 7
1 Ch. 12:31
2 Ch. 31:19
Est. 9: 4
Isa. 19:17[a]
Isa. 26:13
62: 2
Jer. 3:16
20: 9
23:36
32:15
Amos 6:10

[a] S¹ ὄμνυμι.

ὀνομαστί.

Est. 2:14 A[a] [a] *pro* ὄνομα.

ὀνομαστός.

Gen. 6: 4
Nu. 16: 2
Deu. 26:19
2 Sa. 7: 9
1 Ki. 4:27+A
1 Ch. 5:24
11:20
12:30
Isa. 56: 5
Jer. 13:11
52:25
Eze. 22: 5
23:23
24:14
39:11,13
Zeph. 3:19,20

ὄνος.

Gen. 12:16
22: 3,5
24:35
30:43
32: 5,15
34:28
42:26,27
43:17,23
44: 3,13
45:23
47:17
49:11
Exo. 13:13
21:33
22: 4
Lev. 15: 9
Nu. 22:21,22
23 *ter*
25,27
27,28
29,30
30,32
33
31:28[a],30
34,39
45
Deu. 22: 3,4,10
28:31
Jos. 9:10 A[b]
15:18
Jud. 5:10–A
6: 4
15:15,16
16
19: 3[c],10[c]
19,21[c]
28[c]
1 Sa. 8:16
9: 3,3,5
20
10: 2,2,14
16
12: 3
15: 3
22.19
25:18,20
23,42
27: 9
2 Sa. 16: 1
17:23
19:26
1 Ki. (3)40
13:13,13
23,24
27 A
28
1 Ki. 13:28–A
29
2 Ki. 4:22,24
6:25
7: 7,10
1 Ch. 5:21
12:40
27:30
Ezra 2:67
Neh. 7:69
13:15
Job 1: 3,14
6: 5
11:12
Job 24: 5
39: 5
42:12
Psa. 79:14 BS¹[d]
Pro. 26: 3
Isa. 1: 3
21: 7
30: 6
32:14,20
Jer. 14: 6[e]
22:19[f]
31: 6
Eze. 23:20
Zec. 14:15

[a] S αἴξ. [b] *pro* ὦμος.
[c] A ὑποζύγιον. [d] *pro* μονιός.
[e] S ὄναγρος. [f] S οὐ.

ὄντως.

Nu. 22:37
Jer. 3:23
Jer. 10:19

ὄνυξ.

Exo. 30:34
Lev. 11: 7
Deu. 14: 8 A[a]
Job 28:16
Eze. 17: 3,7
Dan. 4:30
7:19

[a] *pro* ὀνυχιστήρ.

ὀνυχίζω.

Lev. 11: 3,4,7
26
Deu. 14: 6,7,8
2 Sa. 19:24

ὀνύχιον.

Exo. 28:20
36:20
Eze. 28:13

ὀνυχιστήρ.

Lev. 11: 3,4,26
Deu. 14: 6,7,8[a]

[a] A ὄνυξ.

ὀξέως.

Isa. 8: 1,3
Joel 3: 4

ὄξος.

Nu. 6: 3,3
Ruth 2:14
Psa. 68:22
Pro. 25:20

ὀξυγράφος.

Psalm 44: 2

ὀξύθυμος.

Pro. 14:17
Pro. 26:20 AS²[a]

[a] *pro* δίθυμος.

ὀξύνω.

Pro. 24:23
27:17
Isa. 44:12
Eze. 21: 9,10
16
Zec. 1:21

ὀξύς.

Job 16:10
41:21
Psa. 13: 3–A
56: 5
Pro. 22:29
27: 4
Isa. 5:28
49: 2
Eze. 5: 1
Amos 2:15
Hab. 1: 8

ὀξυσθενής.

Job 39:23+A

ὀξύτης.

Jeremiah 8:16

ὀπή.

Exo. 33:22
Jud. 15:11 A[a]
Ecc. 12: 3
Cant. 5: 4
Eze. 8: 7+A
Obad. 3
Zec. 14:12

[a] *pro* τρυμαλιά.

ὠτίον.

Exo. 21: 6
Deu. 15:17

ὄπισθε, –θεν.

Gen. 18:10
Exo. 14:19
Jos. 6:13
Ruth 1:16
2: 3 A[a]
7
1 Sa. 6: 7
12:20
14:46
15:11
24: 2
2 Sa. 2:21,26
30
7: 8+A
10: 9
11:15
13:34
2 Sa. 20: 2
1 Ki. 16: 3
19:21
2 Ki. 10:29[b]
18: 6
2 Ch. 13:13,13
14
34:33
Isa. 59:13
Jer. 7:24
31: 2[c]
39:40
Eze. 2:10 A[d]
Hos. 1: 2
Joel 2: 3 A[d]
3[e]

[a] *pro* κατόπισθε. [b] B ἔμπροσθεν.
[c] S ὀπισω. [d] *pro* ὀπίσω.
[e] S³ ὀπίσω.

ὀπίσθιος.

Exo. 26:23,27
36:27
1 Ki. 7:12
2 Ch. 4: 4
Jer. 13:22
Eze. 8:16

ὀπισθίως.

1 Samuel 4:18

ὀπισθότονος.

Deuteronomy 32:24

ὀπισθοφανῶς.

Genesis 9:23,23

ὀπίσω.

Gen. 8: 8
14:14
19: 6,17
26
24: 5
31:23,36
32:18,19
20
33: 2
35: 5
41:19,27
44: 4
49:17
Exo. 14: 4,8,9
10,17
19,23
28
15:20
26:12,22
33:23
34:15,16
16–A
Lev. 17: 7
20: 6
Nu. 3:23
15:39
39+A
39
16: 8+B
25: 8
32:11,12
Deu. 4: 3
6:14
8:19
11: 4,30
13: 4
19: 6
24:22,23
25:18
28:14
31:16
Jos. 2: 5,7,8
16
3: 3
Jos. 6: 9
8: 2,4,6
14,16
17
17–A
20
10:19
14: 9
20: 5 A
24: 6
Jud. 1: 6
2:12,17
19
3:22,28
28
4:14,16
16
5:14–A
6:34
35+A
7:23
8: 5,12
27,33
9: 3,4
49–A
13:11
18:12[a]
19: 3[a]
20:40,45
Ruth 1:15
3:10
1 Sa. 6:12
7: 2
8: 3
11: 7,7
12:14,21
13: 4,7
15,15
14:12,13
22,36
37
15:31
17:13 A
14 A

1 Sa. 17:31 A
35, 52
53
20:38, 38
21: 9+A
22:20
23:25, 28
24: 9 *ter*
15 *qtr*
22
25:13, 19
42
26: 3, 18
30: 8, 21
2 Sa. 1: 7, 22
2:10, 19
20, 23
23, 24
25, 28
3:16, 26
31
11: 8
13:17, 18
15:13
17: 1, 9
18:16, 22
20: 2, 6, 7
7, 10
11, 13
13
23:10
1 Ki. 1: 6, 7
8, 14
24
33+A
40
2:28, 28
10:19
11: 2, 4
5+A
5+A
8, 10
12:20
*p*24*l*74
14: 8 A
9 A
16: 3, 21
21, 22
22−B
17:10, 11
18:18, 21
21, 37
19:20, 20
21
20:21, 26
21:19
2 Ki. 2:24
4:30
5:20, 21
21
6:19
7:14, 15
9:18
19−A
25, 27
11: 6, 15
13: 2
14:19
17:15
15−A
20:10, 11
23: 3
25: 5
1 Ch. 5:25
10: 2, 2
14:14
2 Ch. 13:19
23:14
26:17
Neh. 3:16, 17
4:16, 23
9:26
11: 8
12:32

Neh. 12:38 S[3]
13:19
Job 21:33
37: 3
39: 8
Psa. 6:11+AS
9: 4
31: 4
39:15
43:11, 19
44:15
49:17
55:10
62: 9
69: 3
77:66
113: 3, 5
128: 5
Pro. 25: 9
Ecc. 2:12
7: 1−C
15
9: 3
10:14
12: 2
Cant. 1: 4
2: 9
Isa. 28:13
30:21
38:17
42:17
44:25
45:14
57: 8
59:14
65: 2
Jer. 2: 5, 8
23, 25
3:17
7: 6, 9
8: 2
9:14, 14
22
11:10
12: 6
13:10, 26
27
15: 6
16:11, 12
17:16
18:12
25: 6, 16
26: 5
31: 2 S[b]
42:15
49:16
52: 8
Lam. 1: 8, 13
2: 3
Eze. 2:10[c]
5: 2, 12
6: 9
9: 5
12:14
20:16, 24
30
23:30, 35
29:16
33:31
Dan. 2:39
7: 6, 7
24
Hos. 2: 5, 13
5:11
11:10
13: 4
Joel 2: 3[c]
3 S[3 b]
14, 20
Amos 2: 4
Nah. 3: 5
Zec. 1: 8
2: 8

[a] A κατόπισθε. [b] *pro* ὀπισθεν.
[c] A ὄπισθεν.

ὁπλή.

Exo. 10:26
Lev. 11: 3, 4, 4
5, 6, 7
7, 26
Deu. 14: 6, 7, 7
8−A

Deu. 14: 8
Psa. 68:32
Eze. 26:11
Mic. 4:13

ὁπλίτης, ὁπλιστής.

Numbers 32:21

ὁπλοθήκη.

2 Chronicles 32:27

ὁπλομάχος.

Isaiah 13: 4, 5

ὅπλον.

1 Sa. 17: 7
1 Ki. 10:17, 17
14:26, 27
2 Ki. 10: 2
2 Ch. 21: 3
23: 9, 10
32: 5
Neh. 4:17
Psa. 5:13
34: 2
45:10
56: 5
75: 4
90: 4

Pro. 14: 7
Jer. 21: 4
26: 3, 9
28: 3, 12
29: 3
50:10
Eze. 26: 8
32:27
39: 9, 10
Joel 2: 8
Amos 4: 2
Nah. 2: 4
3: 3
Hab. 3:11

ὁπλοφόρος.

2 Chronicles 14: 8

ὅπου.

Jud. 18:10
20:22
Ruth 1:16
3: 4
2 Ch. 6:38−AB

Pro. 26:20
Ecc. 9:10
Isa. 42:22
Dan. 2:38

ὀπτάζω.

Numbers 14:14

ὀπτάνω.

1 Kings 8: 8

ὀπτασία.

Dan. 9:23
10: 1, 7, 7

Dan. 10: 8, 16
Mal. 3: 2

ὀπτάω.

Gen. 11: 3
Deu. 16: 7
1 Sa. 2:15

2 Ch. 35:13
Isa. 44:16, 19

ὅπτομαι *vide* ὁράω.

ὀπτός.

Exodus 12: 8, 9

ὀπώρα.

Jer. 31:32
Jer. 47:10, 12

ὀπωροφυλάκιον.

Psa. 78: 1
Isa. 1: 8
24:20

Jer. 33:18 A[a]
Mic. 1: 6
3:12

[a] *pro* ἄβατος.

ὅραμα.

Gen. 15: 1
46: 2
Exo. 3: 3
Nu. 12: 6
Deu. 4:34−B[1]
26: 8
28:34, 67
Job 7:14

Ecc. 6: 9
Isa. 15: 1 A[a]
21: 1, 2, 11
22: 1 A[a]
23: 1 AS[a]
30:10
Jer. 30:22
Dan. 2:19, 23
4:10
7: 2+A

Dan. 7:13
8: 2+A

[a] *pro* ῥῆμα.

ὅρασις.

Gen. 2: 9
24:63
25:11
31:49
40: 5
Lev. 13:12
Nu. 24: 4, 16
Jud. 13: 6 A[a]
6 A[a]
1 Sa. 3: 1, 15
16:12
2 Sa. 7:17
1 Ch. 17:15, 17
2 Ch. 9:29
Job 37:17
Psa. 88:20
Ecc. 11: 9
Isa. 1: 1
13: 1
19: 1
30: 6
66:24
Jer. 14:14
23:16
Lam. 2: 9
Eze. 1: 1, 4[b]
5, 13
22, 26
27+A
27 *ter*
28
2: 1
3:23
7:13+A
26
8: 2, 3
4
10:22+A

Eze. 11:24, 24
12:22, 23
24, 27
13: 7
21:29
23:16
40: 2, 3, 3
41:21
43: 3 *qtr*
10
Dan. 1:17
2:28, 31
3:25
4: 2, 6
7: 1, 15
20
8: 1, 13
15, 15
16, 17
19, 26
26, 27
9:21
24+A
24
10: 6, 6
14, 18
11:14
Hos. 12:10
Joel 2: 4, 4[c]
28
Obad. 1
Mic. 3: 6
Nah. 1: 1
2: 5
Hab. 2: 2, 3
Zec. 10: 2
13: 4

[a] *pro* εἶδος. [b] A ὁμοίωμα.
[c] A ὄψις.

ὁρατής.

Job 34:21
Job 35:13

ὁρατικός.

Proverbs 22:29

ὁρατός.

2 Sa. 23:21
1 Ch. 11:23

Job 34:26
37:20

ὁράω.

Gen. 1: 9, 9
8: 5
9:14, 16
12: 7, 7
8+A[1 f]
13:15
16:13
17: 1
18: 1, 21
22: 8, 14
26: 2, 24
28
27: 1
29: 2
31: 5, 12
13, 43
50
50−A
32:20
35: 1, 9
37:20, 29
41:15
43: 2, 4
45:28
46:29, 30
48: 3
Exo. 2: 6, 11
12, 13

Exo. 3: 2, 3, 9
16
4: 1, 5, 18
21, 23
5:19
6: 1, 3
10: 6, 28
29
12:13, 23
13: 7
14:10, 13
13
16: 7, 10
19: 4
20:18, 22
23:15, 17
24:11
25: 7, 40
31:13
32:19
33: 5, 10
23, 23
34: 3, 10
20, 23
24
Lev. 5: 1
9: 4, 6, 23
13: 3, 3, 5
6, 7, 8
10, 13
14, 15
17, 19
20, 25
27, 30
32, 34
36, 39
43, 50
51, 55
57
14: 3, 35
37, 39
44
16: 2
Nu. 1:49
13:19, 29
33, 34
14:10, 22
23, 23
15:39
16:19, 42
20: 6
22:31
23: 9, 13
13, 21
24: 3, 15
27:13
32:11
Deu. 1:28, 35
36
3:21, 25
28
4: 3, 9, 28
7:15
9:13
11: 7
16: 4, 16
16
18:16
21: 7
22: 1[a]
23:14
28:10, 67
29: 2, 3[b]
23
31:11
32:52
33: 9, 16
Jos. 8:20 A[c]
9:13 23:3
Jud. 5: 8−A
6:12[1]
26+A
7:17
9:36 A[e]
13: 3, 10
21
22 A[f]
14: 2
19:30 A[e]
30
21:21
1 Sa. 1:22
6: 9, 16
10:24
16: 1, 7, 7
7, 18
17:25 A
19: 3
20:29
22: 9
24:11
28:13, 13
2 Sa. 3:13
13:34
14:15
17:17
18:10, 11
27
22:11, 16
24: 3, 11
1 Ki. 3: 5, 16
9: 2, 2
10:7, 12−A
11: 9
18: 1, 2, 15
20:29
21:13
22:17, 25

2 Ki. 2:12
3:17−A, 17
7: 2, 13
19
9: 2
10: 3
14: 8, 11
17:13
22:20
23:17
25:19
1 Ch. 21: 9
2 Ch. 1: 7
3: 1
7: 3, 12
9:11, 29
12:15
18:24
25:17−B
21
29: 8, 25[g]
30: 7
33:18, 19
34:28
Neh. 4:11
Est. 7: 7
Job 2:13
5: 1, 3
6: 7
20+A
7: 8
8:18
10: 4, 4, 21
13: 1
15:17
17:15
19:27
22:14
23: 9
27:12 A[h]
31: 4, 26
33:28
34:29
32−S[i]
38:22
41: 1-BS[i]
25
42: 5
Psa. 8: 4
16:15, 15
17:16
35:10
36:34
39: 4
41: 3
48:10, 20
51: 8
62: 3
63: 6
83: 8
88:49
90: 8
93: 7
101:17
106:42
111:10
113:13
118:74
134:16
Pro. 20:20[j], 12
24:18, 32
26:19[j]
Ecc. 1: 8
5:10
12: 5
Cant. 2:12
6:12
7: 1
Isa. 1:12
17: 8
29:10, 15
18[k]
30:10, 20
33:11, 17
17, 20
35: 2
40: 5, 5
41:23−A
47:13
49: 7

Isa. 52: 8, 10
15
53:10
57:18
60: 2, 5
61: 9
62: 2
66: 5,8,14
18, 19
24
Jer. 1:11
12—S[1]
13—S[1]
4:21
5:12
7:11, 17
12: 4
13:20, 27
14:13
17: 6
20: 4
22:10[n], 12
23:11, 21
24: 3
28:61
29:23
30:32
37: 6
38: 3
39: 4
41: 3
51: 2
Eze. 8: 6,6,12
12, 13
15, 15
17
12: 2 A[e]

Eze. 12:12, 12
13, 27
13: 7,9,16
14:22, 23
16:37
20:43 A[2 o]
21:24
22:28
28:18
32:31
39:21
40: 4, 4
41: 6
43: 7
47: 6
Dan. 1:13, 15
3:25
8: 1, 1
Joel 2:28
Amos 7: 8, 12
8: 1 A[e]
Mic. 3: 7
5: 4
7: 9, 10
15, 16
Nah. 3: 7
Hab. 1:13
3:10
Zeph. 3:15
Zec. 1: 8
4: 2, 10
5: 2
9: 5, 8
10: 7
12:10 S[1 o]
Mal. 1: 5
3:18

[a] A[2] ὑπερoράω. [b] A εἰδέω.
[c] pro θεωρέω. [d] A εὑρίσκω.
[e] pro βλέπω. [f] pro εἰδέω.
[g] B προφήτης. [h] pro οἶδα.
[i] S ἔσονται. [j] AS φωνέω.
[k] AS[1] βλέπω. [m] S εἰδέω.
[n] A ἐφοράω. [o] pro κόπτω.

ὄργανον.

2 Sa. 6: 5, 14
1 Ch. 6:32
15:16
16: 5, 42
23: 5
2 Ch. 5:13
7: 6
23:13

2 Ch. 29:26, 27
30:21
34:12
Ps. 136: 2
150: 4, p 6
Amos 5:23
6: 5

ὀργή.

Gen. 27:45
39:19
Exo. 4:14
15: 7
32:10, 11
12
Nu. 11: 1, 10
11 A[a]
12: 9
14:34
16:22
46—A[1]
25: 4
32:14
Deu. 9:19
11:17[b]
13:17
29:20, 23
24, 28
32:19, 27
33:10[c]
Jos. 7: 1, 26
9:26
22:18, 20
Jud. 9:30 A[d]
14:19 A[d]
1 Sa. 11: 6
19:22
20:30, 34
28:18
2 Sa. 6: 7—AB
12: 5

2 Sa. 22: 9
24: 1
2 Ki. 1:18
22:13
23:26, 26
1 Ch. 13:10—B
27:24
2 Ch. 12:12
19: 2, 10
24:18
25:10, 15
28: 9,9,11
13
29: 8[e], 10
30: 8
32:25, 26
35:19
Ezra 7:23
10:14
Neh. 13:18
Est. 7: 7+S[3]
Job 3:17, 26
4: 9
5: 2
6: 2, 7[f]
9: 5, 13
22
10:17
14: 1, 13
16: 9
17: 7
18: 4

Job 19:11
20:23, 28
21:17, 30
27:13 AS[2 g]
31:11
32: 5
35:15
37: 1
39:24
40: 6
Psa. 2: 5
6: 2
7: 7, 12
9:25
17: 9, 16
20:10
26: 9
29: 6
34:20
36: 8
37: 2, 4
54: 4, 22
55: 8
57:10
58:14
68:25
25—S[1]
73: 4 S[1 h]
75: 8
76:10
77:21, 31
38, 40
49, 50
78: 6
82:16
84: 4, 4, 6
87:17
88:47
89: 7,9,11
94:11
101:11
105:23—AS[2]
109: 5
137: 7
Pro. 12:16
15: 1, 1
16:32
17:25
21:14
27: 3, 4
29: 8
Isa. 5:25[i]
7: 4
9:19
10: 4[k], 5
6, 25
13: 9, 13
26:20, 21
30:27, 27
30
34: 2
37: 3
42:25

Isa. 58:13
59:10
60:10
63: 6
Jer. 4:26
7:20
10:25 A[d]
21: 5, 12
23:19
25:16
27:13, 25
28:11
32:23
37:23, 23
24
39:31, 37
40: 5
43: 7
51: 6
Lam. 1:12
2: 1, 2, 3
6, 21
22
3:65
4:11
Eze. 5:13, 13
15+A
6:12
7: 8
12+A
14+A
19+A
13:13
20: 8
21—A
21:31, 31
22:20, 21
24—A
30[m], 31
23:25
25:14
38:19
Dan. 2:12
3:13
8:19[n]
9:16
11:36
Hos. 11: 9
13:11
14: 4
Amos 4:10
Jon. 3: 9
Mic. 5:15
7: 9, 18
Nah. 1: 6, 6
Hab. 3: 2
Zeph. 1:15, 18
2: 2—S[3]
3
3: 8
Zec. 1: 2, 15
7:12

[a] pro ὁρμή. [b] A ὀργίζω.
[c] A[2] ἑορτή. [d] pro θυμός.
[e] A θυμός. [f] AS[2] ψυχή, C ψυχή.
[g] pro κτῆμα. [h] pro ἑορτή.
[i] S θυμος. [k] AS θυμός.
[m] B γῆ. [n] A[1] ἑορτή.

ὀργιάω.

Isa. 5:20[a] [a] AS ὁρμάω.

ὀργίζω.

Gen. 31:36
40: 2
41:10
45:24
Exo. 15:14[a]
22:24
32:19, 22
Nu. 22:22
25: 3
31:14
32:10, 13
Deu. 6:15
7: 4
11:17 A[b]

Deu. 29:27
31:17
Jud. 2:14, 20
3: 8
6:39
9:30[c]
10: 7[c]
14:19[c]
19: 2 A[d]
1 Sa. 17:28 A
1 Ki. 11: 9
2 Ki. 13: 3
19:28
2 Ch. 16:10

2 Ch. 29: 8
35:19
Neh. 4: 1
Est. 1:12
Job 12: 6 A[e]
32: 2, 2, 3
Psa. 2:12
4: 5
17: 8
59: 3
73: 1
78: 5
79: 5
84: 6
98: 1
102: 9

Ps. 105, 40
111:10
123: 3
Pro. 16:30 A[f]
29: 9
Ecc. 5: 5
Isa. 5:25 S[g]
12: 1
28:28
57: 6, 16
64: 5, 9
Lam. 5:22
Hab. 3: 8
Zec. 1: 2, 15
15

[a] A φοβέω. [b] pro ὀργή.
[c] A θυμόω. [d] pro πορεύω.
[e] pro παροργίζω. [f] pro ὁρίζω.
[g] pro θυμόω.

ὀργίλος.

Psa. 17:49
Pro. 21:19

Pro. 22:24
29:22

ὀρεινός.

Gen. 14:10
Nu. 13:30
Deu. 2:37
11:11
Jos. 2:16, 22
9: 1
10: 6, 40
11: 2,7,16
21

Jos. 13: 6
15:48
16: 1
18:13
Jud. 1: 9
2 Ch. 26:10
Pro. 27:24
Jer. 40:13
Zec. 7: 7

ὄρθιος.

1 Sa. 28:14[a] [a] A ὄρθριος.

ὀρθός.

1 Ki. 21:11
Jud. 15: 5—A
Ps. 138: 9[a]
Pro. 4:11, 25
26, 27
7:18 S[b]
8: 6, 9
11: 6—S[1]
12: 6, 15
14:12
15:14

Pro. 16:13[c], 25
21: 8
23:16, 35 S[b]
24:73
Jer. 7:25 S[1 b]
25: 4 S[1 b]
38: 9
39:33 S[1 b]
Eze. 1: 7
Mic. 2: 3[a], 7
3: 9

[a] A ὄρθρος. [b] pro ὄρθρος.
[c] C ἀγαθός.

ὀρθοτομέω.

Pro. 3: 6
Pro. 11: 5

ὀρθόω.

Gen. 37: 7
Ezra 9:11

Est. 7: 9
Jer. 37:20

ὀρθρίζω.

Gen. 19: 2, 27
20: 8
Exo. 8:20
9:13
24: 4
32: 6
34: 4
Nu. 14:40
Jos. 3: 1
7:16
8:10
Jud. 6:28, 38
7: 1
9:33
19: 5, 8, 9
21: 4
1 Sa. 1:19
3:15
5: 3, 4
15:12
17:16 A

1 Sa. 17:20 A
29:10, 10[a]
11
2 Sa. 15: 2
2 Ki. 3:22
6:15
19:35
2 Ch. 20:20
29:20
36:15
Job 7:21
8: 5
Psa. 62: 2
77:34
126: 2
Cant. 7:12
Isa. 26: 9
Jer. 25: 3
Hos. 6: 1
Zeph. 3: 7

[a] A διορθρίζω.

ὀρθρινός.

Hos. 6: 4
13: 3

Hag. 2:14

ὄρθριος.

1 Sa. 28:14 A[a]
Job 29: 7

[a] pro ὄρθιος.

ὄρθρος.

Gen. 19:15
32:26
Exo. 19:16
Jos. 6:15
Jud. 16: 2—A
19:25 A[a]
26[b]
1 Sa. 9:26
Neh. 4:21
Est. 5:14
Psa. 56: 9
62: 7
107: 3
118:148
138: 9 A[c]

Pro. 7:18[d]
23:35[d]
Cant. 6: 9
Jer. 7:25[d]
25: 4[d]
33: 5
39:33[d]
42:14
51: 4
Hos. 6: 3
11: 1
Joel 2: 2
Amos 4:13
Mic. 2: 3 A[c]

[a] pro πρωί. [b] A πρωΐ.
[c] pro ὀρθός. [d] S ὀρθός.

ὀρθῶς.

Gen. 4: 7, 7
40:16
Exo. 18:18
Nu. 27: 7
Deu. 5:28

Deu. 18:17
1 Sa. 16:17
Pro. 14: 2
16: 5
Eze. 22:30

ὁρίζω.

Nu. 30: 3, 4, 5
5, 6, 7
8,9,12
34: 6
Jos. 13: 7, 27
15:12

Jos. 18:20
23: 4
Pro. 16:30[a]
18:18
Eze. 47:20[b]

[a] A ὀργίζω. [b] A διορίζω.

ὅριον.

Gen. 10:19
23:17
47:21
Exo. 8: 2
10: 4, 14
13: 7
23:18, 31
34:24
Nu. 20:16, 17
21, 23
21:13, 13
15, 22
23, 24
22:36, 36
32:33
33:14
34: 2 to 12
35:26, 27
Deu. 2: 4, 18
3:14, 16
16, 17
11:24
12:20
16: 4
19: 3,8,14
27:17
28:40
32: 8
Jos. 1: 4
11:16 A[a]
12: 2, 5, 5
13: 2, 3, 4
10, 11
16, 23
23, 25
26, 30
31+A[2]
15: 1, 1
1 A[b], 2
4 to 10

Jos. 15:11, 11
11[c], 11
12, 12
21
16: 1, 2, 3
3, 5, 5
6, 8
17: 1, 7, 7
8, 9—A
9, 10
18: 5
11 to 16
19—A
19, 19
20
19:10, 10
12
12+A
14, 18
22, 22
25, 27
29, 29
33, 34
41, 46
47, 49
21:20 A[d]
40, 42
22:11, 25
24:31
Jud. 1:18 ter
36
2: 9[e]
7:24 A[a]
11:18, 18
20
22+A
26[c], 26[e]
19:29[f]
20: 6
1 Sa. 5: 3

1 Sa. 6: 9, 12
7:13, 14
11: 3, 7
27: 1
2 Sa. 21: 5
1 Ki. 1: 3
3 *p* 46
4(21)+A
9:13
10:26
2 Ki. 3:21
10:32+A
32
14:25
15:16
18: 8
1 Ch. 4:10
6:54, 66
7:29
13: 5
21: 4+A
2 Ch. 9:26
11:13, 23
Job 24: 2
38:10, 20
42 *p* 18
Psa. 73:17
103: 9
104:31, 33
147: 3
Pro. 15:25
22:28
23:10
Isa. 9: 7
10:13
14:25 S[2] [a]

Isa. 15: 8[c]
19:19
28:25
54:10 S[e]
57: 9
60:18
Jer. 5:22
15:13
Eze. 29:10
40:12+A
43:12
45: 1, 7, 7
47:13, 15
16 *ter*
17, 17
17+A
17+A
48: 1, 2, 3
4, 5, 6
7, 8
12[g], 13
21, 21
22, 22
24, 25
26, 27
28, 28
Hos. 5:10
Joel 3: 6
Amos 1:13
6: 2, 2
Obad. 7
Mic. 5: 6
Zeph. 2: 8
Hag. 2:22+A
Zec. 9: 2
Mal. 1: 3, 4, 5

[a] *pro* ὅρος. [b] *pro* ἔρημος. [c] A ὅρος. [d] *pro* ἱερεύς. [e] A θυγάτηρ. [f] A φυλή. [g] A ἀπαρχή.

ὁρισμός.

Exo. 8:12
Nu. 30: 3, 4, 5
5, 6, 8
9, 11
12, 13

Nu. 30:15
Dan. 6: 7, 8, 12
13+A
15

ὁρκίζω.

Gen. 24:37
50: 5, 6
16, 25
Exo. 13:19
Nu. 5:19, 21
Jos. 6:26
1 Sa. 14:27, 28
28
1 Ki.(3)37, 42
22:16[a]

2 Ki. 11: 4 A[b]
2 Ch. 18:15
36:13
Ezra 10: 5
Neh. 5:12
13:25[c]
Cant. 2: 7
3: 5
5: 8, 9
8: 4

[a] B ἐξορκίζω. [b] *pro* ὁρκόω. [c] A ἐνορκίζω.

ὁρκισμός.

Gen. 21:31, 32[a]
24:41

Lev. 5: 1

[a] A ὅρκος.

ὅρκος.

Gen. 21:14
32 A[a]
33
22:19, 19
24: 8
26: 3, 23
33, 33
28:10
46: 1, 5
Exo. 13:19
22:11
Lev. 5: 4
Nu. 5:21[b]
30: 3, 11
14
Deu. 7: 8
Jos. 2:17, 19

Jos. 2:20
9:26
Jud. 21: 5
1 Sa. 14:26
2 Sa. 21: 7
1 Ki.(3)43
1 Ch. 16:16
2 Ch. 15:15
Neh. 10:29
Ps. 104: 9
Pro. 29:24
Ecc. 8: 2
9: 2
Jer. 11: 5
Dan. 9:11
Amos 5: 5
Zec. 8:17

[a] *pro* ὁρκισμός. [b] B λόγος.

ὁρκόω.

2 Ki. 11: 4[a]

[a] A ὁρκίζω.

ὁρκωμοσία.

Ezekiel 17:18, 19

ὁρμάω.

Gen. 31:21
Nu. 16:42
Jos. 4:18
6: 5
Jud. 20:37 A[a]

1 Sa. 15:19
Isa. 5:29 AS[b]
Jer. 4:28
Nah. 3:16
Hab. 1: 8

[a] *pro* κινέω. [b] *pro* ὀργιάω.

ὁρμή.

Nu. 11:11[a], 17
Pro. 3:25
21: 1

Jer. 29: 3
Eze. 3:14
Dan. 8: 6

[a] A ὀργή.

ὅρμημα.

Exo. 32:22
Deu. 28:49
Psa. 45: 5

Hos. 5:10
Amos 1:11
Hab. 3: 8–S[1]

ὁρμίσκος.

Gen. 38:18, 25
Jud. 8:26+A
Pro. 25:11

Cant. 1:10
7: 1

ὅρμος.

Gen. 49:13

Eze. 27:11

ὄρνεον.

Gen. 6:20
7:14–A
9: 2 A[a]
10
15:10, 11
40:19
Deu. 4:17
14:11
22: 6
32:24
Job 40:24
Pro. 6: 5
7:23
9:12–S

Pro. 26: 2
27: 8
Ecc. 9:12
Isa. 31: 5
34:11
35: 7
Eze. 17:23[b]
39: 4, 17
Dan. 4: 9, 11
18, 30
Hos. 9:11
11:11
Amos 3: 5

[a] *pro* πετεινός. [b] A θηρίον.

ὀρνίθιον.

Lev. 14: 4, 5, 6
6, 6, 7
49, 50

Lev. 14:51, 51
52, 52
53

ὀρνιθοσκοπέω.

Leviticus 19:26

ὄρνις.

1 Ki.(3) *p* 46

1 Ki. 4:23+AB

ὅρος.

Exo. 9: 5

Neh. 2: 6

ὄρος.

Gen. 7:19, 20
8: 4, 5
10:30
12: 8
14: 6
19:17, 19
30
22: 2, 14
31:21, 23
25, 25
54, 54
36: 8, 9
49:26
Exo. 3: 1, 12

Exo. 4:27
15:17
18: 5
19: 2, 3, 3[a]
11, 12
12, 13
13, 14
16, 17
18, 20
20, 20
23, 23
20:18
24: 4, 12
13, 15

Exo. 24:15, 16
17, 18
18
25: 8, 40
26:30
27: 8
31:18
32: 1, 12
15, 19
33: 6
34: 1, 2, 2
3, 3, 4
29, 29
32
Lev. 7:28
19:26
25: 1
26:46
27:34
Nu. 3: 1
10:33
13:18
14:40, 44
45
20:19, 19
22, 23
25, 27
28, 28
21: 4
23: 7, 9
27:12, 12
13
28: 6
33:32, 33
37
38+A
39, 41
47, 48
34: 7
7–A
8, 8
Deu. 1: 2, 6, 7
7, 19
20, 24
31–A
41, 43
44
2: 1, 3, 5
36
3:12, 25
4:11, 11
12+A
15, 48
5: 4–A
5, 22
23
8: 7, 9
9: 9, 9
10, 15
15, 21
10: 1, 3, 4
5, 10
11:29, 29
12: 2
27: 4, 12
13
32:22, 49
49, 50
50
33: 2
13 A[b]
15
34: 1
Jos. 2:23
8:24
9: 3, 6, 6
11: 3, 16[c]
17
17–A
17
21 A[d]
21
12: 1, 5, 7
8
13: 5, 11
19
14:12
15: 8, 9, 9
10
11 A[e]

Jos. 17:15, 16
18:12
14 B[1 f]
14
16+A
19:47, 50
20: 7 *ter*
21:11, 42
24: 4, 31
31, 33
Jud. 1:19, 34
35
2: 9 A[r], 9
9
3: 3, 27
27
4: 5, 6, 12
14
5: 5
6: 2
26+A
7: 3
24[c]
9: 7, 25
36, 36
48
10: 1
11:37, 38
12:15
16: 3
17: 1, 8
18: 2, 13
19: 1, 16
18
1 Sa. 1: 1
9: 4
10: 2
13: 2
14:22, 23
17: 3, 3
23:14
14+A
15, 26
26
25:20
26:13, 20
31: 1, 8
2 Sa. 1: 6, 21
13:34, 34
16:13
20:21
21: 9
1 Ki.(3) *p* 1
4: 8
5:15
11: 7+A
43–A
12 *p* 24 *l* 7
ll 10, 22
l 48
25
16:24 *qnq*
18:19, 20
19: 8, 11
11
21:23, 28
22:17
2 Ki. 1: 9
2:16, 25
4.25
25–AB
27
5:22
6:17
17: 6
18:11
19:23, 31
23:13
1 Ch. 4:42
5:23
6:67
10: 1, 8
12: 8
2 Ch. 2: 2
3: 1
13: 4, 4
15: 8
18:16
19: 4
20:10, 22

2 Ch. 20:23
27: 4
30:10
33:15
Neh. 8:15
9:13
Job 5: 6
9: 5
14:18
18: 4[h]
24: 8
28: 9
29: 6
39: 8
40:15
Psa. 2: 6
3: 5
10: 1
14: 1
17: 8
23: 3
35: 7
41: 7
42: 3
45: 3, 4
47: 2, 3, 12
49:10
64: 7, 13[i]
67:16 *qtr*
17, 17
71: 3, 16
73: 2
74: 7–B
75: 5
77:54, 54
68
79:11
82:15
86: 1
89: 2
94: 4
96: 5
97: 8
98: 9
103: 6, 8, 10
13, 18
32
113: 4, 6
120: 1
124: 1, 2
132: 3
143: 5
146: 8
148: 9
Pro. 8:25
Cant. 2: 8, 9, 17
4: 6, 8
8:14
Isa. 2: 2, 2, 3
14
4: 5
5:25
7:25
8:18
9:11
10:12, 18
32
11: 9
13: 2
4–S[1]
14:13, 13
19, 25[k]
15: 8 A[e]
16: 1
18: 3, 7
22: 5
25: 6, 7, 10
27:13
28: 1, 4, 21
29: 8, 17
17+AS[3]
30:17, 25
29[m]
31: 4 *ter*
34: 3
37:24, 32
40: 4, 9, 12
41:15, 18
42:11

Isa. 42:15–AS
44:23
45: 2
49:11, 13
52: 7
54:10[n]
55:12
56: 7
57: 7, 13
63:18
64: 1, 3
65: 7, 9, 11
25
Jer. 3: 6, 23
4:15, 24
9:10
13:16
16:16
17:26
26:18
27: 6, 6, 19
28:25, 25
35:18
38: 5, 6
6+A
12, 23
39:44
Lam. 4:19
19 A[o]
5:18
Eze. 6: 2, 3, 3
13+A
7:16
11:10
11 A, 23
17:22, 23
18: 6, 11
15
19: 9
20:40, 40
22: 9
28:14, 16
31:12
32: 5, 6
33:28
34: 6, 13
14
14+A
14
26
35: 2, 3, 7
12, 15
36: 1, 1, 4
4, 6, 8
37:22
38:20
39: 2, 4, 17
40: 2
43:12
48:10
Dan. 2:34, 35
45
9:16, 20
11:45
45+A
Hos. 4:13
10: 8
Joel 2: 1, 2, 5
32
3:17, 18
Amos 3: 9
4: 1, 3
6: 1
9:13
Obad. 8, 9, 16
17, 19
19, 21
21
Jon. 2: 6
Mic. 1: 4
2: 9
3:12
4: 1, 1, 2
7
6: 1, 2[p]
7:12, 12
Nah. 1: 5, 14
3:10 S[1 q]
18
Hab. 3: 3, 6

Zeph. 3:11
Hag. 1: 8, 11
Zec. 1: 8, 10
11
4: 7
6: 1 *ter*
Zec. 8: 3
3 – S[1]
14: 4
4 – A
4, 5, 5

[a] B οὐρανός. [b] *pro* ὥρα.
[c] A ὅριον. [d] *pro* γένος.
[e] *pro* ὅριον. [f] *pro* μέρος.
[h] A γῆ. [i] S[2] ὡραῖος.
[k] S[2] ὅριον. [m] A οἶκος.
[n] S ὅμιον. [o] *pro* ἔρημος.
[p] A βουνός. B λαός. [q] *pro* ὁδός.

ὀροφόω.

1 Kings 7:14 + A

ὀρόφωμα.

2 Ch. 3: 7
Eze. 41:26

ὀρτυγομήτρα.

Exo. 16:13
Nu. 11:31, 32
Ps. 104:40

ὄρυξ.

Deuteronomy 14: 5

ὀρύσσω.

Gen. 21:30
26:15, 18
18, 19
21, 22
25, 32
50: 5
Exo. 7:24
Nu. 21:18
Deu. 23:13
2 Ch. 16:14
Psa. 7:16
21:17
56: 7
Psa. 93:13
Pro. 16:27
27 A[a]
26:27
29:22 AS[b]
Ecc. 10: 8
Isa. 5: 2
51: 1
Jer. 2:13
18: 7
Eze. 8: 8, 8
12:12 A[c]
Zec. 3: 9

[a] *pro* θησαυρίζω.
[b] *pro* ἐγείρω. [c] *pro* διορύσσω.

ὀρφανία.

Isaiah 47: 8

ὀρφανός.

Exo. 22:22, 24
Deu. 10:18
14:28
16:11, 14
24:19, 21
22, 23
26:12, 13
27:19
Job 6:27
22: 9
24: 3, 9, 19
29:12
31:17, 21
Psa. 9:35, 39
67: 6
81: 3
93: 6
Ps. 108: 9, 12
145: 9
Pro. 23:10
Isa. 1:17, 23
9:17
10: 2
Jer. 5:28
7: 6
22: 3
29:12
Lam. 5: 3
Eze. 22: 7
Hos. 14: 3
Mic. 2: 2
Zec. 7:10
Mal. 3: 5

ὀρχέομαι.

2 Sa. 6:16, 20
21 – A
21
1 Ch. 15:29
Ecc. 3: 4
Isa. 13:21

ὅσιος.

Deu. 29:19
32: 4
33: 8
2 Sa. 22:26
Psa. 4: 4
11: 2
15:10
17:26
29: 5
Psa. 30:24
31: 6
36:28
42: 1
49: 5
51:11
67:36[a]
78: 2
84: 9
Psa. 85: 2
96:10
115: 6
131: 9, 16
144:10, 14
17
148:14
149: 1, 5, 9
Pro. 2:11
21 – S[1]
Pro. 10:29
17:26
18: 5
20:11
21:15
22:11
29:10
Isa. 55: 3
Amos 5:10

[a] S ἅγιος.

ὁσιότης.

Deu. 9: 5
1 Sa. 14:41
1 Ki. 9: 4
Pro. 14:32

ὁσιόω.

2 Sa. 22:26
Psa. 17:26

ὁσίως.

1 Kings 8:61

ὀσμή.

Gen. 8:21
27:27 *ter*
Exo. 5:21
29:18, 25
41
Lev. 1: 9, 13
17
2: 2, 9, 12
3: 5, 11
16
4:31
6:15, 21
8:21, 28
17: 4, 6
23:13, 18
26:31
Nu. 15: 3, 5, 7
10, 13
14, 24
18:17
28: 2, 6, 8
Nu. 28:13, 24
27
29: 2, 6, 8
11, 13
36
Job 6: 7
14: 9
Cant. 1: 3, 4, 12
2:13
4:10, 11
11
7: 8, 13
Isa. 3:24
34: 3
Jer. 25:10
31:11
Eze. 6:13
16:19
20:28, 41
Dan. 3:27

ὅσος.

Nu. 2:34[a]
Jud. 9:33[b]
1 Ki. 8:40 – A
17:12
Est. 9:29
Isa. 26:20, 20
Jer. 32: 1 + A
&c., &c.

[a] A καθά. [b] A καθάπερ.

ὀστέον, ὀστοῦν.

Gen. 2:23 – A[1]
23
29:14
50:25
Exo. 12:10, 46
13:19, 19
Nu. 9:12
19:16, 18
Jos. 24:32
Jud. 9: 2
19:29 + A
1 Sa. 31:13
2 Sa. 5: 1
19:12, 13
21:12, 12
13 *ter*
14, 14
14 – AS
1 Ki. 13: 2 – A
31 *ter*
2 Ki. 13:21
23:14, 16
18 *ter*
20
1 Ch. 10:12
11: 1
2 Ch. 34: 5
Job 2: 5
4:14
7:15[a]
10:11
19:20
Job 20:11
30:17, 30
33:19, 21
Psa. 6: 3
21:15[b], 18
30:11
31: 3
33:21
34:10
37: 4
41:11
50:10
52: 6
101: 4, 6
108:18
138:15
140: 7
Pro. 3: 8, 22
14:30
16: 1
17:22
24:23
25:15
Ecc. 11: 5
Isa. 38:13
58:11
11 + AS[a]
66:14
Jer. 8: 1 *qnq*
20: 9
23: 9
Jer. 27:17
Lam. 1:13
3: 4
4: 8
Eze. 6: 5
24: 4, 5, 5
10 + A
32:27
37: 1, 3, 4
4, 5, 7
Eze. 37:11, 11
39:15
Dan. 6:24
Amos 2: 1
6:10
Mic. 3: 2
3 + A
3
Hab. 3:16

[a] A σῶμα. [b] S[1] διάβημα.

ὀστράκινος.

Lev. 6:28
11:33
14: 5, 50
15:12
Nu. 5:17
Isa. 30:14
Jer. 19: 1 – S[1]
Jer. 19:11
39:14
Lam. 4: 2
Eze. 4: 9
Dan. 2:33, 34
41, 42

ὄστρακον.

Job 2: 8
Psa. 21:16
Pro. 26:23
Isa. 30:14
Dan. 2:35, 41
43, 43
45

ὀστρακώδης.

Judges 1:35 – A

ὀσφραίνομαι.

Gen. 8:21
27:27
Exo. 30:38
Lev. 26:31
Deu. 4:28
Jud. 15:14 A[a]
Jud. 16: 9
1 Sa. 26:19
Job 39:25
Ps. 113:14
134:17 + A
Amos 5:21

[a] *pro* ἐκκαίω.

ὀσφρασία.

Hosea 14: 6

ὀσφύς.

Gen. 35:11
37:34
Exo. 12:11
28:38
Lev. 3: 9
6:33
8:25
9:19
Deu. 33:11
2 Sa. 20: 8
1 Ki. 2: 5
12:10
p 24 *l* 65
18:46
21:31, 32
2 Ki. 1: 8
4:29
9: 1
2 Ch. 6: 9
10:10
Neh. 4:18
Job 12:18
38: 3
40: 2, 11
Pro. 29:35
Isa. 5:27
11: 5
15: 4
20: 2
21: 3
32:11
Jer. 1:17
13: 1, 2, 4
11
31:37
37: 6, 6
Eze. 1:27, 27
8: 2, 2
9: 2, 3, 11
21: 6
23:15
24:17
29: 7
44:18
47: 4
Dan. 5: 6
10: 5
Amos 8:10
Nah. 2: 2, 10

ὅταν.

Jud. 13:17 + A
Isa. 7: 2 + A
Isa. 29:23 – S[1]
Amos 5:10 A[a]

[a] *pro* ἐάν.

ὁτιοῦν.

Deuteronomy 24:12

οὐαί.

Nu. 21:29
1 Sa. 4: 7, 8
1 Ki. 12 *p* 24 *l* 45
13:30
Job 31: 3
Pro. 23:29
Ecc. 4:10
10:16
Isa. 1: 4, 24
3: 9, 11
5: 8, 11
18, 20
21, 22
10: 1, 5
17:12
18: 1
24:16
28: 1
29: 1, 15
15
30: 1
31: 1
33: 1
Jer. 4:13
6: 4
10:19
13:27
22:18 + A
18 AS[a]
27:27
28: 2
Jer. 31: 1
41: 5 – S[b]
Lam. 5:16
Eze. 2:10
7:26, 26
13: 3, 18
16:23 + A
23 + A
21:27
24: 9 + A
Hos. 7:13
9:12
Amos 5:16, 16
18
6: 1
Mic. 7: 4 + AB
4
Nah. 3:17
17 + A
Hab. 2: 6, 12
19
Zeph. 2: 5
3:18

[a] *pro* ὦ. [b] A ὦ.

οὐδαμοῦ.

1 Ki. (3)36
Job 19: 7
20 A[a]
Job 21: 9
Pro. 23: 5

[a] *pro* ποῦ.

οὐδείς.

Lev. 26:17 – A
Ecc. 7:15[a]
Jer. 30: 4 S[1b]

[a] ACS μηδείς. [b] *pro* τίς.

οὐδέποτε.

Exo. 10: 6
1 Ki. 1: 6

οὐδέπω.

Exodus 9:30

οὐθείς.

1 Sa. 20:39 – A
Jer. 2: 6[a]

[a] S ἄνθρωπος.

οὐκέτι.

Jos. 8:20 – A
2 Sa. 7:10 + S
1 Ki. 22: 7 + A
Job 20: 9 + A
Isa. 38:11[a] – AS
Eze. 26:13 + A
37:22 A[a]
Hos. 2:16 A[a]
Joel 2:27 A[a]

[a] *pro* ἔτι.

οὔκουν.

2 Kings 5:23 + A

οὐλή.

Lev. 13: 2, 10
10, 19
Lev. 13:23, 28
14:56

οὖν.

Exo. 3:18
10:17
Job 17:15
19: 6

οὔπω.

Gen. 15:16
18:12
Gen. 29: 7
Isa. 7:17

οὐρά.

Deu. 28:13, 44
Job 40:12, 26
Isa. 9:14, 15
19:15

οὐραγέω.

Joshua 6: 9

οὐραγία.

Deu. 25:18
Jos. 10:19

οὐράνιος.

Deu. 28:12 A[a] | Dan. 4:23[b]

[a] *pro* οὐρανός.
[b] A ἐπουράνιος.

οὐρανός.

Gen. 1: 1, 8, 9, 9, 14, 15, 17, 20, 26, 28, 30
2: 1, 4, 4, 19, 20
6: 7, 17
7: 3, 11, 19, 23
8: 2, 2
9: 2
11: 4
14:19, 22
15: 5
19:24
21:17
22:11, 15, 17
24: 3, 7
26: 4
27:28, 39
28:12, 17
40:17, 19
49:25
Exo. 9: 8, 10, 22, 23, 29+A
10:13, 21, 22
16: 4
17:14
19: 3 B[a]
20: 4, 11, 22
24:10
31:17
32:13
Lev. 26:19
Deu. 1:10, 28
2:25
3:24
4:11, 17, 19 *ter*, 26, 32, 32, 36, 39
5: 8, 14+B[e]
8:19
9: 1, 14, 15−A
10:14 *ter*, 22
11:11, 17, 21
17: 3
25:19
26:15
28:12[b], 23, 24, 26, 62
29:20
30: 4, 4, 12, 12, 19
31:28
32: 2, 40, 43
33:13, 26, 28
Jos. 2:11
8:20, 21−A
10:11, 13
Jud. 5: 4, 20
13:20, 20+A
20:40
1 Sa. 2:10
5:12
17:44, 46
2 Sa. 18: 9
2 Sa. 21:10, 10
22: 8, 10, 14
1 Ki. 8:22, 23, 27 *ter*, 30, 32, 34 *to* 36, 39, 43, 45, 49, 53, 54, 12*p*24*l*44
14:11 A
16: 4
18:36, 38, 45
20:24
22:19
2 Ki. 1:10, 10, 12, 12, 14
2: 1, 11
7: 2, 19
14:27[c]
17:16
19:15
21: 3, 5
23: 4, 5
1 Ch. 16:26, 31
21:16, 26
27:23
29:11
2 Ch. 2: 6 *ter*, 12
6:13, 14, 18 *ter*, 21, 23, 25, 26, 27, 30, 33, 35, 39
7: 1, 13, 14
18:18
20: 6
28: 9
30:27
32:20
33: 3, 5
36:23
Ezra 1: 2
5:11, 12
6: 9, 10
7:12, 21, 23, 23
9: 6
Neh. 1: 4,5−S[1], 9, 9+S[3]
2: 4, 20
9: 6−AB, 6 *ter*, 13, 15, 23, 27, 28
Job 1: 6+A, 7, 16
2: 2
5:10
7: 9
9: 6,8,13
11: 8
12: 7
14:12
15:15
16:19
18: 4, 19
20: 6, 27
22:14, 26
26:11, 13
28:21, 24
34:13
35: 5, 11
Job 37: 2−A
38:18, 24, 29, 33, 33, 37
41: 2
42:15
Psa. 2: 4
8: 2, 4, 9
10: 4
13: 2
17:10, 14
18: 2, 7, 7
19: 7
32: 6, 13
35: 6
49: 4,6,11
52: 3
56: 4,6,11, 12
67: 9, 34, 34
68:35
72: 9, 25
75: 9
77:23, 24, 26
78: 2
79:15
84:12
88: 3,6,12, 30, 38
90: 1
95: 5, 11
96: 6
101:20, 26
102:11, 19
103: 2, 12
104:40
106:26
107: 5, 6
112: 4, 6
113:11, 11+S[1], 23, 24, 24
118:89
120: 2
122: 1
123: 8
133: 3
134: 6
135: 5, 26
138: 8
143: 5
145:6 146:8
148: 1, 4, 4, 4, 13
Pro. 3:19
8:26, 27, 28
24:27
25: 3
Ecc. 1:13[d]
3: 1[d]
5: 1
10:20
Isa. 1: 2
5:30+S
8:21
13: 5, 10, 10, 13
14:12, 13, 13
18: 6, 6
24:18, 21
34: 4−AS, 4, 5
37:16
38:14
40:12, 22
42: 5
44:23, 24
45: 8, 12, 18
47:13
48:13
49:13
Isa. 50: 3
51: 6,6,13, 16
55: 9, 10
63:15
64: 1
65:17
66: 1, 22
Jer. 2:12
4:23, 25, 28
7:18, 33
8: 2, 7
9:10
10: 2, 11, 11, 12, 13
14:22
15: 3
16: 4
19: 7, 13
23:24
25:15
28: 9, 15, 16, 53
38:37
39:17
41:20
51:17, 18, 19, 25−S[1]
Lam. 2: 1
3:40, 49, 65
4:19
Eze. 1: 1
8: 3
29: 5
31: 6, 13
32: 4−B,7, 7+A,8
34: 5+A
37: 9+A
38:20
Dan. 2:18, 19, 28, 37, 38, 44
3:17
4: 8,9,10, 12, 17, 18, 19, 20, 20, 22, 28, 30, 31, 32, 34
5:21, 23
6:27
7: 2, 13, 27
8: 8, 10, 10
9: 3+A, 4+A, 12
11: 4
12: 7
Hos. 2:12, 18, 21, 21 A[e]
4: 3
7:12
13: 4, 4
Joel 2:10, 30
3:16
Amos 9: 2, 6
Jon. 1: 9
Nah. 3:16−S[1]
Hab. 3: 3
Zeph. 1: 3, 5
Hag. 1:10
2: 6, 21
Zec. 2: 6
5: 9
6: 5
8:12
12: 1
Mal. 3:10

[a] *pro* ὄρος.
[b] A οὐράνιος.
[c] B Ἰσραήλ.
[d] S[2] ἥλιος.
[e] *pro* αὐτός.

οὐρέω.

1 Sa. 25:22, 34
1 Ki. 12*p*24*l*42
14:10 A
1 Ki. 16:11+A
20:21
2 Ki. 9: 8

οὔριος.

Isaiah 59: 5

οὖρον.

2 Ki. 18:27 | Isa. 36:12

οὖς.

Gen. 20: 8
23:13, 16
35: 4
50: 4
Exo. 10: 2
11: 2
17:14
21: 6
24: 7
29:20, 20
32: 2, 3
Lev. 8:23, 24
14:14, 17, 25, 28
Nu. 14:28−A
Deu. 5: 1
15:17 A[a]
29: 4
31:11, 28
32: 1, 14
Jos. 9: 8
20: 4 A
Jud. 7: 3
9: 2, 3
17: 2
Ruth 4: 4
1 Sa. 3:11, 17
8:21
11: 4
15:14
18:23
25:24
2 Sa. 3:19, 19
7:22
18:12
22: 7
1 Ki. 8:52, 12*p*24*l*15, *l*60
2 Ki. 18:26
19:16, 28
21:12
23: 2[b]
1 Ch. 17:20, 25
28: 8−B
2 Ch. 6:40
7:15
34:30
Neh. 1: 6, 11−S[3]
8: 3
13: 1
Job 4:12
12:11[c]
13: 1
15:21
29:11[d]
33: 8
34: 3[e]
39:14 AS[f]
42: 5
Psa. 9:38
16: 6
17: 7
30: 3
33:16
43: 2
44:11
48: 5
57: 5
Psa. 70: 2
77: 1
85: 1
87: 3
91:12
93: 9
101: 3
113:14
114: 2
129: 2
134:17
Pro. 2: 2
4:20
5: 1, 13
18:15
20:12
21:13
22:17
23: 9, 12
25:12
28: 9
Ecc. 1: 8
12: 9
Isa. 5: 9
6:10, 10
22:14
30:21
32: 3
33:15
35: 5
36:11
37:17−AS
42:20
43: 8
48: 8
49:20
50: 5
55: 3[g]
59: 1
Jer. 5:21
6:10
7:24, 26
9:20
17:22
19: 3
25: 4
33:11, 15−B
35: 7, 7
36:29
41:14
42:15
43: 6,6,10, 13, 14, 15, 21, 21
51: 5
Lam. 3:55−A
Eze. 3:10
8:18+A
9: 1
12: 2
16:12
23:25
24:26
40: 4
44: 5
Dan. 9:18
Mic. 7:16
Zec. 7:11

[a] *pro* ὠτίον.
[b] B ἐνώπιον.
[c] ABS νοῦς.
[d] C ὠτίον.
[e] A νοῦς.
[f] *pro* ᾠόν.
[g] A ὠτίον.

ὀφείλημα.

Deuteronomy 24:12, 12

ὀφείλω, ὄφελον.

Exo. 16: 3
Nu. 14: 2; 20:3
Deu. 15: 2
2 Ki. 5: 3
Job 6:20
14:13
Job 30:24
Ps. 118: 5
Pro. 14: 9
Isa. 24: 2, 2
Eze. 18: 7

ὄφελος.

Job 15: 3

ὀφθαλμός.

Gen. 3: 5, 6, 7
13:10, 14
18: 2
21:19
22: 4, 13
24:63, 64
27: 1
29:17
31:10, 12, 40
32: 1+A
33: 1−A[2], 8+A
37:25
39: 7
43:28
45:12, 12, 20
46: 4
48:10
49:12
Exo. 13: 9, 16
14:10−A[1]
21:24, 24, 26, 26, 26
23: 8
Lev. 4:13
5: 4
20: 4
21:20
24:20, 20
26:16
Nu. 5:13
11: 6
14:14, 14
15:24, 39
16:14
22:31
24: 2, 4, 16
33:55
Deu. 1:30+A[2]
3:21, 27, 27
4: 3, 9
6: 8
7:16, 19
10:21
11: 7, 12, 18
13: 8
14: 1
15: 9
16:19
19:13, 21 *ter*
21: 7
25:12
28:32, 34, 54, 56, 65, 66, 67
29: 3, 4
32:10
34: 4, 7
Jos. 5:13
23:13
24: 7
Jud. 6:17, 21
10:15[a]
11:35+A
14: 3, 7[a]
16:21, 28
17: 6
19:17, 24
21:25 A[b]
Ruth 2: 2,9,10, 13
1 Sa. 1:18, 23
2:29, 33
3: 2
4:15
6:13
8: 6[a]
11: 2
12:16
14:27, 29
16:12, 22
17:42
18: 5 A, 5 A, 8, 20, 23, 26
20: 3[a], 29
24: 5, 11
25: 8
26:21, 24
27: 5
29: 6, 6, 7, 9
2 Sa. 3:19, 19
6:20, 22
10:12
11:25, 27
12: 9, 11
13: 2, 5, 6, 8, 34
14:22
15:25, 26
16: 4, 22
17: 4, 4
18: 4, 24
19: 6, 18, 27, 37, 38
20: 6
22:25, 28
24: 3, 22
1 Ki. 1:20, 48
8:29, 52
9: 3
10: 7
12*p*24*l*33
14: 4 A, 8 A
21: 6, 38, 41
22:43[a]
2 Ki. 1:13, 14
3: 2, 18
4:34, 34, 35
6:17, 17, 20, 20
7: 2, 19
9:30
10: 5, 30
13: 2, 11

2 Ki. 14: 3
15: 3, 9, 18
24, 28
34
16: 2
17: 2, 17
18: 3
19: 16, 22
20: 3[a]
21: 2, 6, 9
15, 16
20
22: 2, 20
23: 16, 32
37[a]
24: 9
19 A[b]
25: 7, 7
1 Ch. 13: 4
19: 13 − BS
21: 3, 16
2 Ch. 6: 20, 40
7: 15, 16
9: 6
16: 9
20: 12
29: 8
32: 23
34: 28
Ezra 3: 12
5: 5
7: 28
9: 8
Neh. 1: 6
6: 16
Est. 8: 5 + S[3]
Job 3: 10
4: 16
7: 7, 8, 8
10: 18
11: 20
13: 1
15: 12
16: 10, 20
17: 5, 7
19: 27
20: 9
21: 8, 20
22: 29
24: 15, 15
27: 19
28: 7, 10
29: 11, 15
31: 1[c], 7
16
36: 7
39: 29
40: 19
41: 9
42: 5
Psa. 5: 6
6: 8
9: 29
10: 4
12: 4
13: 3 − A
16: 2 − S[1]
8, 11
17: 25, 28
18: 9
24: 15
25: 3
30: 10, 23
31: 8
32: 18
33: 16
34: 19, 21
35: 2
37: 11
53: 9
55: 14 + B[a]S[2]
65: 7
68: 4, 24
76: 5 + S[2]
78: 10
87: 10
89: 4
90: 8
91: 12
Psa. 93: 9
100: 3, 5, 6
7
113: 13
114: 8
117: 23
118: 18, 37
82, 123
135, 148
120: 1
122: 1, 2, 2
2
130: 1
131: 4
134: 16
138: 16
140: 8
144: 15
Pro. 4: 25
5: 21
6: 13, 17
25
10: 10
15: 3, 15
16: 1, 30
17: 24
20: 8, 20
12, 13
22: 12
23: 26, 29
31, 33
24: 36, 52
25: 7
27: 20, 20
28: 27
Ecc. 1: 8
2: 10, 14
4: 8
5: 10
6: 9
8: 16
11: 7, 9
Cant. 1: 15
4: 1, 9
5: 12
6: 4
7: 4
8: 10
Isa. 1: 15, 16
2: 11
3: 16
5: 15
6: 5, 10
10
10: 12
13: 18
17: 7
28: 22 + S[1]
29: 10, 18
30: 20
33: 15, 17
20
35: 5
37: 17 − AS
23
38: 14
40: 26
42: 7
43: 8
44: 18
49: 18
51: 6
52: 8, 8
59: 10
60: 4
64: 4
Jer. 3: 2
4: 30
5: 3, 21
9: 1, 18
13: 17, 20
14: 6, 17
16: 9, 17
17
19: 10
20: 4
22: 17
24: 6
28: 24
34: 4
Jer. 35: 1, 5, 5
10, 11
36: 21
38: 16
39: 4, 4
12 *ter*
13, 19
30
41: 3, 3, 15
45: 26
47: 4, 5
49: 2
50: 9
52: 10, 11
Lam. 1: 16
2: 4, 11
18
3: 47, 48
50, 62
4: 17
5: 17
Eze. 1: 18
4: 12
5: 11
6: 9
7: 9, 4, 13
8: 5, 5, 18
9: 5, 10
10: 12
12: 2, 4, 12
16: 5
18: 6, 12
15
20: 7, 8, 14
17, 22
24, 41
Eze. 21: 6
22: 16[a], 26
23: 16, 27
40
24: 16, 21
25
33: 25 A
36: 23, 34
40: 4
44: 5
Dan. 4: 31
7: 8, 8, 20
8: 3, 5, 21
9: 18
10: 5, 6
Hos. 13: 14
Joel 1: 16
Amos 9: 3, 4[d]
8
Jon. 2: 5
Mic. 4: 11
7: 10
Hab. 1: 13
Zeph. 3: 7
Zec. 1: 18
2: 1, 8
3: 9
4: 10
5: 1, 5, 9
6: 1
9: 8
11: 17, 17
12: 4
14: 12
Mal. 1: 5

[a] A ἐνώπιον. [b] *pro* ἐνώπιον. [c] S[1] ἀδελφός. [d] A πρόσωπον.

ὀφθαλμοφανῶς.

Esther 8: 13

ὀφιομάχης.

Leviticus 11: 22

ὄφις.

Gen. 3: 1, 1, 2
4, 13
14
49: 17
Exo. 4: 3, 17
7: 15
Nu. 21: 6, 7, 8
8, 9, 9
9
Deu. 8: 15
2 Ki. 18: 4
Job 20: 16
Psa. 57: 5
139: 4
Pro. 23: 32
24: 54
Ecc. 10: 8, 11
Isa. 14: 29, 29
27: 1, 1
65: 25
Jer. 8: 17
26: 22
Amos 5: 19
Mic. 7: 17

ὀφρύς.

Leviticus 14: 9

ὀχλαγωγέω.

Amos 7: 16

ὀχληρία.

Ecclesiastes 7: 26

ὄχλος.

Nu. 20: 20
Jos. 6: 13, 13
2 Sa. 15: 22
1 Ki. 21: 13
2 Ch. 20: 15
Ezra 3: 12
Neh. 4: 10 BS[1 a]
6: 13
Isa. 43: 17
Jer. 31: 42
39: 8
Jer. 39: 24
45: 1 S[1 b]
Eze. 16: 40
17: 17
23: 24, 46
47
Dan. 10: 6
11: 10, 11
11, 12
13

[a] *pro* ὁ χοῦς. [b] *pro* λαός.

ὀχυρός.

Exo. 1: 11
Nu. 13: 29
Nu. 32: 36
Deu. 3: 5
28: 52
Jos. 10: 20
14: 12
2 Sa. 20: 6
2 Ki. 3: 19
10: 2
17: 9
18: 8, 13
19: 25
2 Ch. 8: 4, 5
6 − A[1]
11: 23
12: 4
17: 2, 12
19
19: 5
Psa. 70: 3
Pro. 10: 15
18: 11, 19
Pro. 21: 22
Isa. 17: 3
25: 2
26: 1 S[a]
5
27: 3[b]
30: 13 − A
33: 16 A[a]
36: 1
37: 26, 26
Jer. 1: 18, 18[c]
4: 5 A[d]
5: 17
8: 14
15: 20
41: 7
Eze. 36: 35
Dan. 11: 15
Mic. 7: 12
Zeph. 1: 16[e]

[a] *pro* ἰσχυρός. [b] AS ἰσχυρός. [c] S ἰσχυρός. [d] *pro* τειχήρης. [e] A ἰσχυρός.

ὀχυρόω.

Jos. 6: 1
2 Ch. 11: 11
Jer. 28: 53

ὀχύρωμα.

Gen. 39: 20, 20
40: 14
41: 14
Jos. 19: 29 + A
Jud. 6: 2 A[a]
9: 46 A[b]
49 A[b]
49 A[b]
2 Sa. 22: 2
2 Ki. 8: 12
Job 19: 6
Psa. 88: 41
Pro. 10: 29
12: 11, 12
21: 22
Pro. 24: 63
Isa. 22: 10
23: 14
24: 22
34: 13
Jer. 29: 23
31: 7, 18
41
Lam. 2: 2, 5
Dan. 11: 39, 43
Amos 5: 9
Mic. 5: 11
Nah. 3: 12, 14
Hab. 1: 10
Zec. 9: 3, 12

[a] *pro* κρεμαστός. [b] *pro* συνέλευσις.

ὀψέ.

Gen. 24: 11
Exo. 30: 8
Isa. 5: 11
Jer. 2: 23

ὀψίζω.

1 Samuel 17: 16 A

ὄψιμος.

Exo. 9: 32
Deu. 11: 14
Pro. 16: 15
Jer. 5: 24
Hos. 6: 3
Joel 2: 23
Zec. 10: 1

ὄψις.

Gen. 24: 16
26: 7
29: 17
39: 6
41: 21
Exo. 10: 5, 15
34: 29, 30
Lev. 13: 3, 4, 20
25, 30
31, 32
34, 43
55
14: 37
19: 27
21: 5
Nu. 22: 5, 11
1 Sa. 16: 7[a]
1 Ki. 1: 6 − A
Est. 2: 7 + S[3]
Cant. 2: 14, 14
Jer. 3: 3
Eze. 1: 13, 27
10: 9, 9, 10
23: 15
41: 21
Dan. 1: 4
2: 31 A[b]
3: 19
Joel 2: 4 A[c]

[a] A πρόσωπον. [b] *pro* πρόσοψις. [c] *pro* ὅρασις.

ὄψον.

Numbers 11: 22

παγετός.

Gen. 31: 40
Jer. 43: 30

παγιδεύω.

1 Sa. 28: 9
Ecc. 9: 12

παγίς.

Jos. 23: 13
Job 18: 8, 9
22: 10
Psa. 9: 16, 30
10: 6
17: 6
24: 15
30: 5
34: 7, 8, 8
56: 7
63: 6
65: 11
68: 23
90: 3
118: 110
123: 7, 7
139: 6, 6
140: 9
141: 4
Pro. 6: 2, 5
7: 23
Pro. 11: 9
12: 13
13: 14
14: 27
18: 7
20: 25
21: 6
22: 5
29: 6
Ecc. 9: 12
Isa. 8: 14
24: 17, 18
42: 22
Jer. 5: 26, 27
18: 22
31: 43, 44
Eze. 29: 4
Hos. 5: 1
9: 8
Amos 3: 5

πάγος.

Exo. 16: 14
Job 37: 9
Nah. 3: 17
Zec. 14: 6

παθεινός.

Job 29: 25[a]

[a] A συμπαθής.

πάθος.

Job 30: 31 BS[a]
Pro. 25: 20

[a] *pro* πένθος.

παιγνία.

Jud. 16: 27[a]
Jer. 29: 17

[a] A ἐμπαίζω.

παίγνιον.

Habakkuk 1: 10

παιδάριον.

Gen. 22: 5[a], 12
33: 14
37: 30
42: 22
43: 7
44: 30 A[b]
31 A[b]
Jud. 7: 10, 11
8: 14, 20
9: 54, 54
13: 5, 7
8 A[b]
12 A[b]
24
16: 26 A[c]
17: 7 A[c]
11 A[c]
12 + A
18: 3 A[d]
15 A[d]
19: 3 A[e]
9 A[c]
11 A[c]
13 A[c]
19 A[d]
Ruth 2: 5, 6, 9
9, 15
21 AB[e]
1 Sa. 1: 14, 22
24, 24
1 Sa. 1: 25, 27
2: 11, 13
15, 17
18, 21
26
3: 1, 8
4: 17, 21
9: 3, 5, 6
7, 8, 10
22
10: 14
14: 1, 6
16: 11, 18
17: 33[a], 42
58 A
20: 21, 21
35, 36
36, 37
38, 38
39
40 − A
40, 41
21: 2, 4[a]
5 AB[b], 7
25: 5, 5, 8
8, 9
12, 14
19, 25
27
26: 22

1 Sa. 30:13, 17
2 Sa. 1: 5—A
6, 13
15
2:14, 21
4:12
9: 9
12:15 A[b]
16
18qtr
19, 19
21, 21
22, 22
23+A
13:17, 28
29, 32[a]
34
14:21
16: 1, 2
17:18
18: 5, 12
15, 29
32, 32
19:17
20:11
1 Ki. 3: 7
11:17, 29
12: 8, 10
14
p24l24
ll25,26
ll35,41
ll45,47
l68
14:12 A
17 A
16p28—A

1 Ki. 17:21, 21
22+A
22
18:43, 43
44
19: 3
21:14, 15[f]
17, 19
2 Ki. 2:23
4:12, 14
18, 19
22, 24
25, 26
29, 30
31, 31
32, 34
34, 35
35, 38
41
5:14, 20
22, 23
6:15, 17
8: 4
9: 4
19: 6
1 Ch. 22: 5
2 Ch. 10: 8, 10
34: 3
Neh. 13:19—ABS[1]
Jer. 31:11
Lam. 2:21
Dan. 1:10, 13
13 A[g]
15, 17
Joel 3: 3
Zec. 8: 5

[a] A παιδιον. [b] pro παιδίον. [c] pro νεανίας. [d] pro νεανίσκος. [e] pro κοράσιον. [f] A παῖς. [g] pro παῖς.

παιδεία.

Deu. 11: 2
Ezra 7:26
Job 20: 3
37:12
Psa. 2:12
17:36
36—S[1]
49:17
118:66
Pro. 1: 2,7,8[a]
29 A[b]
3:11
4: 1, 13
5:12
6:23
8:10
33 S[2]
10:17, 17
12: 1
13:18
15: 5, 10
16: 1,1,17

Pro. 16:22
17: 8
19:20, 27
22:15
23:12
24:31 A[c]
47
25: 1[d]
Isa. 26:16
50: 4[e], 5
53: 5
Jer. 2:30
5: 3
7:28
17:23—A
37:14
39:33
42:13
Eze. 13: 9
Amos 3: 7
Hab. 1:12
Zeph. 3: 2, 7

[a] ACS νόμος. [b] pro σοφία. [c] pro πενία. [d] AS[2] παροιμία. [e] A σοφία.

παιδευτής.

Hosea 5: 2

παιδεύω.

Lev. 26:18, 23
28
Deu. 4:36
8: 5, 5
21:18
22:18
32:10
1 Sa. 26:10 B[a]
2 Sa. 22:48
Ki. 12:11, 11
14, 14
1 Ch. 10:11 ter
14, 14
Est. 2: 7

Psa. 2:10
6: 2
15: 7
37: 2
38:12
89:10, 12[c]
93:10, 12
104:22
117:18, 18
140: 5
Pro. 3:12 AS[b]
5:13
9: 7
10: 5

Pro. 13:24
19:18
22: 3
23:13
24:69
28:17
29:17, 19
Isa. 28:26
46: 3

Jer. 2:19
6: 8
10:24
26:28
38:18, 18
Eze. 23:48
28: 3
Hos. 7:12, 15
10:10, 10

[a] pro παίω. [b] pro ἐλέγχω. [c] A πεδάω.

παιδιόθεν.

Genesis 47: 3+A

παιδίον.

Gen. 17:12
21: 7,9,12
14, 15
16, 16
17, 17
18, 19
20
22: 5 A[a]
25:22
30:26
31:17, 28
32:15, 22
33: 1, 2, 5
5, 6A[b]
13
44:20, 22
30[c]
31[c], 32
33, 33
34
45:19
48:16
50:23
Exo. 2: 3, 6, 6
7, 8, 9
9, 10
4:20, 25
26—B
21: 4,5,22
22:24
Lev. 22:28
25:54
Nu. 3: 4
14: 3, 31
Deu. 1:38+A
39
3: 6
11: 2
22: 7

Deu. 25: 6
Jos. 1:14
9: 8
Jud. 13: 8[c]
12[c]
19:19 B[d]
Ruth 4:16
1 Sa. 1: 2, 2, 5
6, 6
17:33 A[a]
21: 4 A[a]
21: 5[e]
2 Sa. 6:23
12:15[e]
13:32 A[a]
1 Ki. 3:25, 26
27
2 Ch. 20:13
Job 1:19
21:11
39: 3
40:24
Isa. 3: 5
7:16
8: 4, 18
9: 6
10:19
11: 6, 7, 8
21:15 A[f]
34:15
38:19
46: 3
49:15
53: 2
66: 8, 12
Jer. 38:20
Lam. 4:10
Eze. 3:23 A[g]

[a] pro παιδάριον. [b] pro τέκνον. [c] A παιδάριον. [d] pro παῖς. [e] AB παιδάριον. [f] pro πόλεμος. [g] pro πεδίον.

παιδίσκη.

Gen. 12:16
16: 1, 2, 3
5, 6, 8
20:14, 17
21:10, 10
12, 13
24:35
25:12
29:24, 24
29, 29
30: 3, 4, 5
7,9,10
12, 18
43
31:33
32: 5, 22
33: 1, 2, 6
34: 4 A[a]
35:25, 26
Exo. 20:10, 17
21:20, 32
23:12
Lev. 25: 6, 44
Deu. 5:14, 14
21

Deu. 12:12, 18
15:17
16:11, 14
28:68
Jud. 9:18
19:19[b]
Ruth 2:13
4:12
1 Sa. 25:41
2 Sa. 6:20, 22
17:17
2 Ki. 5:26
Ezra 2:65
Neh. 7:67
Est. 7: 4
Psa. 85:16
115: 7
122: 2
Ecc. 2: 7
Jer. 41: 9
10—A
11, 16
16
Amos 2: 7

[a] pro παῖς. [b] A δούλη.

παίζω.

Gen. 21: 9
26: 8
Exo. 32: 6
Jud. 16:25, 25[a]
1 Sa. 18: 7+A
2 Sa. 2:14
6: 5, 21
1 Ch. 13: 8

1 Ch. 15:29
Job 40:24[a]
Pro. 26:19
Isa. 3:16
Jer. 15:17
37:19
38: 4
Zec. 8: 5

[a] A ἐμπαίζω.

παῖς.

Gen. 9:25, 26
27
12:16
14:15
18: 3, 5, 7
17
19: 2, 19
20: 8, 14
21:25
22: 3,5,19
24: 2, 5, 9
10, 14
17, 28
34, 35
52, 53
57, 59
61, 65
65, 66
26:15, 18
19, 25
32
30:43
32: 4,5[a],5
10, 16
16, 18
20
33: 5,8,14
34: 4[b], 12
39:14, 17
19
40:20, 20
41:10, 12
37, 38
42:10, 11
13
43:17, 27
44: 7, 9, 9
10, 16
17, 18
18, 19
21, 23
24, 27
30, 31
31, 32
33
46:34, 34
47: 3, 4
4+A
19, 21
25
50: 2, 7
Exo. 5:16
11: 8
20:10, 17
21: 2,5,20
32
Lev. 25: 6, 44
55
Nu. 14:24
22:22
31:49
32: 4, 5 A[c]
25, 27
Deu. 5:14, 14
21
12:12, 18
16:11, 14
22:15, 15
16, 23
25, 28
23:15
28:68
Jos. 1:7,13 7:7
9:15, 30
10: 6
11:12, 15

Jos. 12: 6
13: 8
14: 7[d]
18: 7
22: 2, 6
Jud. 3:24
16:26+A
19:19[e]
Ruth 2: 6
1 Sa. 16:15, 17
18:22, 22
23, 24
26
19: 1
21:11, 14
22: 6,7,17
25: 8+A
10, 40
41, 42
28: 7,7,23
25
29:10
2 Sa. 2:12, 13
15, 15
17, 30
31
3:22
34 A[f]
38
8: 7
9: 2
10: 2, 3, 4
11: 1, 24
24
12:19, 19
21
13:24, 31
36
14:30, 30
31
15:14, 15
15, 17
18, 22
34, 34
16: 6, 11
17:20
18: 7, 9
19: 6, 10
26
20: 6
21:15
24:20
1 Ki. 1: 2, 9
3:15
5: 1
9:27, 27
10: 5,8,13
p22
11:17
14: 3 A[g]
26
15:18
16: 9+A
p28—A
21: 6,6,12
15 A
23, 31
22: 3
2 Ki. 2:16, 24
3:11
5:13, 26
6: 8, 11
12
7:12, 13
9:11, 28
10: 5

2 Ki. 18:26
19: 5
21:23
23:30
24:11, 12
1 Ch. 2:34, 35
6:49
16:13
17: 4 AS[b]
17, 23
24, 25
25, 27
18: 2, 6, 7
13
19: 2, 3, 4
19
20: 3 B[i], 8
21: 3, 8
22:17 AB[i]
2 Ch. 1: 3
2: 8,8,10
13AB[*k]
15
6:14,15,16
17, 19
19, 20
21, 27
8: 9, 18
18, 18
9: 4,7,10
10, 21
10: 7
12: 8
13: 6
24: 9, 25
25: 3
32: 9, 16
16
33:24
34:16, 20
35:23, 24
36: 5
Ezra 4:11
Neh. 1: 7,9,10
11, 11
2: 5
6: 5
9:10
Est. 2:7 6:9-A
7: 4

Job 1: 8[m],15
17
4:18
29: 5
42: 8 A[n]
Psa. 17: 1
69:18
85:16
112: 1
Pro. 1: 4
4: 1
19:14, 28
20: 7
29:15, 21
Ecc. 4:13
Isa. 20: 3
22:20
24: 2
36:11
37: 5, 35
41: 8, 9
42: 1, 19
23+S[1]
43:10
44: 1,2,21
21, 26
45: 4
49: 6
50:10
52:13
Jer. 21: 7
22: 3+S[3]
4
26:28
32: 5
33: 5
41: 9, 10
11, 16
16
42:15[i]
43:24, 31
44: 2, 18
47: 9
51: 4[d]
52: 8
Eze. 46:17
Dan. 1:12, 13
2: 4, 7
3:28
10:17

[a] A βοῦς. [b] A παιδίσκη. [c] pro οἰκέτης. [d] A δοῦλος. [e] A δουλος, B παιδίον. [f] pro πούς. [g] pro παιδάριον. [h] pro δοῦλος. [i] pro πας. [k] pro πατήρ. [m] A θεράπων. [n] pro θεράπων. [o] A παιδάριον.

παίω.

Exo. 12:13
Nu. 22:28
Jos. 20: 9
Jud. 14:19 A[a]
1 Sa. 8:13 A[b]
13: 4
26:10[c]
2 Sa. 6: 7
14: 6, 7
20:10
1 Ki. 16:16
2 Ki. 9:15

2 Ki. 25:21
Job 2: 7
4:19
5:18[d]
10: 8
16:10
Isa. 14: 6, 29
Jer. 5: 6
14:19
37:14
Lam. 3:29
Dan. 8: 7

[a] pro πατάσσω. [b] pro πέσσω. [c] B παιδεύω. [d] A πατάσσω.

παλάθη.

1 Sa. 25:18
30:12
2 Ki. 4:42

2 Ki. 20: 7
1 Ch. 12:40
Isa. 38:21

πάλαι.

Isa. 37:26
Isa. 48: 5, 7

παλαιός.

Lev. 25:22 ter
26:10 qtr
Jos. 9:10, 10

Jos. 9:11
1 Sa. 7:12
Job 15:10

Psa. 38: 6[a]
Cant. 7:13
Jer. 45:11, 11
Dan. 7: 9, 13
22

[a] AB[2]S[2] παλαιστή.

παλαιόω.

Lev. 13:11
Deu. 8: 4—A
29: 5
Jos. 9:11, 19
Neh. 9:21
Job 9: 5
13:28
14:12 A[a]
18
21: 7
32:15
Psa. 6: 8
17:46
31: 3
48:15
101:27
Isa. 50: 9
51: 6
65:22
Lam. 3: 4
Eze. 47:12
Dan. 7:25

[a] pro συρράπτω.

παλαιστή.

Exo. 25:23
1 Ki. 7:11
2 Ch. 4: 5
Psa. 38: 6AB[2]S[2a]
Eze. 40: 5, 43
43:13

[a] pro παλαιός.

παλαίω.

Gen. 32:24, 25
Jud. 20:33 A[a]

[a] pro ἐπέρχομαι.

παλαίωμα.

Job 36:28
Job 37:17, 20

παλαίωσις.

Nahum 1:14

πάλιν.

Gen. 8:10, 12
24:20[a]
26:18
29:33
30:31
41:22
42:24
43: 1
Exo. 3:15
4: 6, 7, 7
Lev. 14:43
Nu. 35:32
Deu. 30: 3
Jos. 6:14
Jud. 2:19
19: 3+A
7+A
20:39[b]
2 Ch. 19: 4
Neh. 9:28
Est. 4:15+A
Job 5:18
Job 6:29
7: 4
10: 9, 16
14: 7+ ACS[2]
14
32:18
33:19
42:18
Psa. 70:20
21—S
Isa. 6:13
7: 4
8: 9
9—S[1]
23:16
25: 8
28:25
30:18
Jer. 18: 4
43:15, 28
Dan. 2:10+A

[a] A ὕδωρ. [b] A πλήν.

παλλακή.

Gen. 25: 6
35:21
36:12
46:20
Jud. 8:31
19: 1, 2, 9
10, 24
25, 27
29
20: 4[a],5,6
2 Sa. 3: 7, 7
5:13
15:16
16:21
2 Sa. 16:22—A
19: 5
20: 3[b]
21:11
1 Ki. 11: 1
1 Ch. 1:32
36+A
— 2:46, 48
3: 9
7:14
2 Ch. 11:21, 21
Neh. 2: 6
Cant. 6: 7, 8
Dan. 5: 2,3,23

[a] A γυνή. [b] A παλλακίς.

παλλακίς.

Gen. 22:24
2 Sa. 20: 3 A[a]
Job 19:17

[a] pro παλλακή.

πάλλω.

Ezra 9: 3, 5

παμβότανον.

Job 5:25

πανδημεί.

Deuteronomy 13:16

πανηγυρίζω.

Isaiah 66:10

πανήγυρις.

Eze. 46:11
Hos. 2:11
Hos. 9: 5
Amos 5:21

πάνθηρ.

Hos. 5:14
Hos. 13: 7

πανοικία, —κεία, —κί.

Gen. 50: 8, 22
Exo. 1: 1
Jud. 18:21 A[a]

[a] pro τέκνον.

πανοπλία.

2 Sa. 2:21
Job 39:20

πανουργεύομαι.

1 Samuel 23:22

πανουργία.

Nu. 24:22
Jos. 9:10
Pro. 1: 4
8: 5

πανοῦργος.

Job 5:12
Pro. 12:16
13: 1, 16
14: 8, 15
18, 24
15: 5
Pro. 19:25
21:11
22: 3
27:12
28: 2

πανταχῆ.

Isaiah 24:11

πανταχοῦ.

Isaiah 42:22

παντοδαπός.

Job 40:16

πάντοθεν.

2 Sa. 24:14
Jer. 20: 9
Jer. 31:31

παντοκράτωρ.

2 Sa. 5:10
7: 8
25+A
25, 27
1 Ki. 19:10, 14
1 Ch. 11: 9
17: 7, 24
29:12
Job 5: 8A[a],17
8: 5
11: 7
15:25
22:17, 25
23:16
27: 2, 11
13
32: 9
33: 4
34:10, 12
35:13
37:21
Jer. 3:19
5:14
15:16
23:16—S
27:34
28: 5, 57
29:19
32:13
37: 3+AS
38:35
39:14, 19
40:11
51: 7
Hos. 12: 5
Amos 3:13
4:13
5: 8+A
14, 15
16, 27
9: 5,6,15
Mic. 4: 4
Nah. 2:13
3: 5
Hab. 2:13
Zeph. 2:10
Hag. 1: 2, 5
6+A
7,9,14
2: 4, 6, 7
8, 9, 9
11, 23
23
Zec. 1: 3
3 S[1b]
3 A[b], 4
6, 12
13, 14
16+A
16, 17
2: 8,9,11
3: 7,9,10
4: 6, 9
5: 4
6: 12, 15
7: 3,9,12
12, 13
8: 1, 2, 3
4, 6, 6
7, 9, 9
11, 14
Zec. 8: 14, 17
18, 19
20, 21
22—S[1]
23
9: 14, 15
10: 3
5+A
11: 4
6+A
12: 4, 5
13: 7
14: 16, 17
20—S[3]
21, 21
Mal. 1: 4, 6, 8
9, 10
11, 13
13, 14
2: 2, 4, 7
8, 12
16+A
16
3: 1, 5, 7
10, 11
12, 14
17
4: 1, 3

[a] pro πάντων δεσπότην.
[b] pro δύναμις.

πάπυρος.

Job 8:11
40:16
Isa. 19: 6

παραβαίνω.

Exo. 32: 8
Lev. 26:40
Nu. 5:12, 19
20, 29
14:41
22:18
24:13
27:14
Deu. 1:43
9:12, 16
11:16
17:20
28:14
Jos. 7:11, 15
11:15
23:16
1 Sa. 12:21
15:24
2 Ki. 18:12
Job 11: 6 A[a]
14:17
Ps. 118:119
Isa. 24: 5 A[b]
66:24
Jer. 5:28
Eze. 16:59
17:15, 16
18, 19
44: 7
Dan. 9:11
Hos. 6: 7
8: 1

[a] pro ἀποβαίνω.
[b] pro παρέρχομαι.

παραβάλλω.

Ruth 2:16, 16
Pro. 2: 2, 2
4:20
Pro. 5: 1, 13
22:17

παραβαπτός.

Eze. 23:15[a]

[a] A βαπτός.

παράβασις.

2 Ki. 2:24+A
Psa. 100: 3[a]

[a] S[1] παρὰ βασιλεῖς.

παραβιάζομαι, —βιάω.

Gen. 19: 3 A[a]
9
Deu. 1:43
1 Sa. 28:23
2 Ki. 2:17
5:16
Amos 6:10
Jon. 1:13[b]

[a] pro καταβιάζω. [b] B[1] βιάζω.

παραβιβάζω.

2 Sa. 12:13
24:10
Dan. 11:20

παραβλέπω.

Job 20: 9
28: 7
Cant. 1: 6

παραβολή.

Nu. 23: 7, 18
24: 3, 15
20, 21
23
Deu. 28:37
1 Sa. 10:12
24:14
2 Sa. 23: 3
1 Ki. 4:28
2 Ch. 7:20
Psa. 43:15—S[1]
48: 5
68:12
77: 2
Pro. 1: 6
Ecc. 1:17
12: 9
Jer. 24: 9
Eze. 12:22, 23
23
16:44
17: 2
18: 2, 3
19:14
20:49
24: 3
Mic. 2: 4
Hab. 2: 6

παραγγέλλω.

Jos. 6: 7
Jud. 4:10 A[a]
1 Sa. 10:17
15: 4
23: 8
1 Ki. 12: 6 AB[b]
1 Ki. 15:22
2 Ch. 36:22
Ezra 1: 1
Jer. 26:14
27:29
28:27

[a] pro βοάω.
[b] pro ἀπαγγέλλω.

παράγγελμα.

1 Samuel 22:14

παραγίνομαι.

Gen. 14:13
26:32
32:20
35: 9
45:19
50:10, 16
Exo. 2:16, 17
18, 18
8:24
16:35
18: 6, 12
15
19: 9
20:20
36: 4
Lev. 14:48
Nu. 9: 6
10:21
14:36
20: 5, 22
21: 7
Deu. 18: 6
Jos. 5:14
9:14, 18
10: 9[a]
11: 5
18: 8
21:45
22:15
24:11
Jud. 5:28+A
6: 5, 5A[b]
8:15
9:31 A[b]
37 A[b]
11:18 A[b]
13: 9 A[b]
18: 2 A[b]
7 A[b]
8 A[b]
19:10 A[b]
20:34 A[b]
21: 2 A[b]
Ruth 1:19, 22
1 Sa. 8: 4
9: 6
13: 8, 10
11, 15
1 Sa. 15:13
19:18
20:21, 24
27, 29
22: 9, 11
25:19, 34
36
30:21
2 Sa. 1: 3
3:13, 22
25
5: 1, 18
6: 6, 16
8: 5
9: 6
10: 2, 14
16, 17
11: 7, 22
13:34
14:29, 30
15: 6, 13
20
18:31
19:24, 30
41
20:15
23:16
24: 6, 8
1 Ki. 3:15
4:30
10: 7
12:12
13: 1
21:27
2 Ki. 9:17
10:21
2 Ch. 24:24
Est. 5: 5
6:14
Job 1: 7
2:11, 11
Ecc. 5: 2, 15
Isa. 56: 1
62:11
63: 1
Jer. 29:15
46: 1

[a] A ἐπιπαραγίνομαι.
[b] pro ἔρχομαι.

παράγω.

1 Sa. 16: 9, 10
20:36
2 Sa. 15:18
1 Ki. 6:10+A
Ezra 1: 9 B[a]
9: 2

Neh. 2: 7
Ps. 128: 8
143: 4
Ecc. 11:10[b]
Isa. 5:27 S[1c]

[a] pro παραλλάσσω. [b] S[1] ἀπάγω. [c] pro ῥήγνυμι.

παράδειγμα.

Exo. 25: 8, 8
1 Ch. 28:11, 12
18, 19
20, 20
Jer. 8: 2
9:22
16: 4
Nah. 3: 6

παραδειγματίζω.

Nu. 25: 4
Jer. 13:22
Eze. 28:17

παραδείκνυμι.

Exo. 27: 8
Eze. 22: 2
Hos. 13: 4

παράδεισος.

Gen. 2: 8, 9, 10
15, 16
3: 1, 2, 3
8, 8, 10
23, 24
13:10
Nu. 24: 6
2 Ch. 33:20
Neh. 2: 8
Ecc. 2: 5
Cant. 4:13
Isa. 1:30
51: 3—A
3—S[3]
Jer. 36: 5
Eze. 28:13
31: 8, 8, 9
Joel 2: 3

παραδέχομαι.

Exo. 23: 1
Pro. 3:12

παραδίδωμι.

Gen. 14:20
27:20
Exo. 21:13
23:31
Lev. 26:25
Nu. 21: 2, 3, 34
32: 4
Deu. 1: 8, 21
27
2:24, 30
31, 33
36
3: 2, 3
7: 2, 23
24
19:12
20:13, 20
21:10
23:14, 15
28: 7
31: 5
32:30
Jos. 2:14, 24
6: 2, 16
7: 7
8:18
10: 8, 12
19, 30
32, 35
11: 6, 8
19 A[a]
21:44
24: 8
10—A
11, 33
Jud. 1: 4[b]
2:14, 23
3:10, 28
4: 7, 14
6: 1 A[c]
13 A[c]
7: 2
7 A[c], 9
14, 15
8: 3
11: 9, 21
30 A[c]
30 A[c]
32
12: 3 A[c]
Jud. 13: 1
15:12 A[c]
12+A
13
16:23 A[c]
24
18:10 A[c]
20:28 A[c]
1 Sa. 11:12
14:10, 12
37
17:44 A[c]
47
23: 4, 12A
12A, 14
24: 5, 11
26:23
28:19
30:15, 23
23
2 Sa. 5:19 *ter*
1 Ki. 8:46
14:16 A
2 Ki. 3:13[b], 18
18:30
19:10
21:14
1 Ch. 12:17
2 Ch. 6:36
13:16
16: 8
24:24
25:20
28: 5, 5, 9
30: 7
32:11
35:12
36:17
Ezra 7:19
9: 7
Neh. 5: 8-ABS
Est. 2: 3, 13
Job 2: 6
9:24
16:11
24:14
Psa. 9:35
26:12
40: 3
62:11—S[1]
Psa. 73:19
77:18, 61
87: 9
105:41
117:18
118:121
139: 9
Pro. 6: 1
11: 8
24:23, 33
27:23
Isa. 19: 4
23: 7
25: 5, 7
33: 1, 6, 23
34: 2
36:15
37:10
38:13, 13
47: 3
53: 6, 12
12
64: 7
65:12
Jer. 2:24
15: 4
21:10
22:25—S
26 A[d]
Jer. 24: 8
26:24, 28
27: 2
33:24
39: 4—S[1]
28, 36
43
41: 2
44:17
45: 3, 3
16 A[c]
18 A[c]
20
23 A[e]
46:17 A[c]
Eze. 7:21
11: 9
16:27, 39
21:15, 27
29, 31
23: 9, 28
25: 4
31:11
39:23
Dan. 8:28
11: 6, 11
Hos. 8:10
Mic. 6:14, 16
Zec. 11: 6

[a] pro λαμβάνω. [b] A δίδωμι. [c] pro δίδωμι. [d] pro ἀπορρίπτω. [e] pro συλλαμβάνω.

παραδοξάζω.

Exo. 8:22
9: 4
Exo. 11: 7
Deu. 28:59

παράδοσις.

Ezra 7:26[a]
Jer. 30: 4—S[1]
Jer. 41: 2

[a] A δεσμός.

παραδρομή.

Canticles 7: 5

παραζηλόω.

Deu. 32:21, 21
1 Ki. 14:22
Psa. 36: 1, 7, 8
77:58

παραζώνη.

2 Samuel 18:11

παραθαλάσσιος.

2 Ch. 8:17
Jer. 29: 7
Eze. 25: 9
16 A[a]

[a] pro παράλιος.

παράθεμα.

Exo. 38:24[a], 24
Exo. 39:10

[a] A περίθεμα.

παραθερμαίνω.

Deuteronomy 19: 6

παράθεσις.

2 Ki. 6:23
2 Ch. 11:11
Pro. 6: 8
15:17

παραθήκη.

Leviticus 6: 2, 4

παραθλίβω.

2 Kings 6:32

παραιρέω.

Numbers 11:25

παραιτέομαι.

1 Sa. 20: 6, 6, 28
Est. 4: 8
Est. 7: 7

παρακάθημαι.

Est. 1:14
Job 2:13 A[a]

[a] pro παρακαθίζω.

παρακαθίζω.

Job 2:13[a]

[a] A παρακάθημαι.

παρακαλέω.

Gen. 24:67
37:35, 35
38:12
50:21
Exo. 15:13
Deu. 3:28
13: 6
32:36
Jud. 2:18
21: 6, 15
Ruth 2:13
1 Sa. 15:11
22: 4
2 Sa. 10: 2, 3
12:24
13:39
24:16
1 Ch. 7:22
19: 2, 2, 3
Job 2:11+A
11
4: 3
7:13
21:34
29:25
42:11
Psa. 22: 4
68:21
70:21
76: 3
85:17
89:13
118:50, 52
76
82—A
125: 1
Ps. 134:14
Pro. 1:11
8: 4
Ecc. 4: 1
1—C
Isa. 10:32, 32
13: 2
21: 2
22: 4
33: 7
35: 4
38:16
40: 1, 1, 2
11
41:27
49:10, 13
51: 3, 3, 12
18, 19
54:11
57: 5
18—S[3]
61: 2
66:12, 13
13, 13
Jer. 3:19 S[1a]
38:15 AB[b]
Lam. 1: 2, 9, 16
17, 21
2:13
Eze. 14:23
24:17, 22
23
31:16
32:31
Zec. 10: 2

[a] pro καλέω. [b] pro πάνω.

παρακαλύπτω.

Isa. 44: 8
Eze. 22:26

παρακαταθήκη.

Exodus 22: 8, 11

παρακατατίθημι.

Jer. 47: 7
Jer. 48:10

παρακελεύομαι.

Proverbs 9:16

παράκλησις.

Job 21: 2
Psa. 93:19
Isa. 28:29
30: 7
57:18
Isa. 66:11
Jer. 16: 7, 7
38: 9
Hos. 13:14
Nah. 3: 7

παρακλητικός.

Zechariah 1:13

παράκλητωρ.

Job 16: 2

παράκοιτος.

Daniel 5: 2, 3, 23

παρακούω.

Est. 3: 3, 8
4:14+S[3]
14
Est. 7: 4
Isa. 65:12

παρακρούω.

Genesis 31: 7

παρακύπτω.

Gen. 26: 8
Jud. 5:28[a]
1 Ki. 6: 8
1 Ch. 15:29
Pro. 7: 6
Cant. 2: 9

[a] A διακύπτω.

παραλαλέω.

Psa. 43:17[a]

[a] AS[2] καταλαλέω.

παραλαμβάνω.

Gen. 22: 3
31:23
45:18 A[a]
47: 2
Nu. 22:41
23:14, 20
27, 28
Jos. 4: 2
Jud. 9:43 A[b]
11: 5 A[b]
1 Sa. 17:31 A
57 A
2 Ch. 25:11
Cant. 8: 2
Jer. 30: 1, 1, 2
39: 7
8+A
Lam. 3: 2
Dan. 5:31
7:18

[a] pro ἀναλαμβάνω. [b] pro λαμβάνω.

παράλιος.

Gen. 49:13
Deu. 1: 7
33:19
Jos. 9: 1
11: 3, 3
Jud. 5:17[a]
Job 6: 3
Isa. 9: 1
Eze. 25:16[b]

[a] A παρ' αἰγιαλόν. [b] A παραθαλάσσιος.

παραλλαγή.

2 Kings 9:20

παράλλαξις.

Daniel 12:11

παραλλάσσω.

1 Ki. 4:20
Ezra 1: 9[a]
Pro. 4:15
Dan. 6:15

[a] B παράγω.

παραλογίζομαι.

Gen. 29:25
31:41
Jos. 9:28
Jud. 16:10 A[a]
13 A[a]
15 A[a]
1 Sa. 19:17
28:12
2 Sa. 19:26
21: 5
Lam. 1:19

[a] pro πλανάω.

παράλυσις.

Ezekiel 21:10

παραλύω.

Gen. 4:15
19:11
Lev. 13:45
Deu. 32:36
2 Sa. 8: 4
1 Ch. 18: 4
Isa. 23: 9
35: 3
Jer. 6:24
26:15
27:15, 36
43
Eze. 7:27
21: 7
25: 9

παραμένω.

Gen. 44:33
Pro. 12: 7
Dan. 11:17

παραναλίσκω.

Numbers 17:12

παρανομέω.

Job 34:18
Psa. 25: 4
70: 4
Psa. 74: 5, 5
118:51

παρανομία.

Psa. 36: 7
Pro. 5:22
Pro. 10:26
26: 7

παράνομος.

Deu. 13:13
Jud. 19:22
20:13[a]
2 Sa. 16: 7
20: 1
23: 5
1 Ki. 20:10
13—B
2 Ch. 13: 7
Job 17: 8
20: 5[a]
27: 7[b]
Psa. 5: 6
35: 2
36:38
40: 9
85:14
100: 3
118:85, 113
Pro. 1:18
Pro. 2:22
3:32
4:14, 17
6:12
10: 5
11: 6, 30
12: 2
13: 2
14: 9[c]
16:20
17: 4
19:11
21:24
22:12, 14
23:28
25:19
26: 3
28:17
29: 4, 12
18

[a] A ἀσεβής. [b] S ἄνομος.
[c] A ἄφρων.

παρανόμως.

Job 34:20[a]
Pro. 21:27

[a] A ἄνομος.

παραξιφίς.

2 Samuel 5: 8

παράπαν.

1 Ki. 11:10
Jer. 7: 4
Eze. 24: 9, 14
15, 22
Eze. 41: 6
46:20
Zeph. 3: 6

παραπέτασμα.

Amos 2: 8

παραπικραίνω.

Deu. 31:27
32:16[a]
1 Ki. 13:21, 26
Psa. 5:11
65: 7
67: 7
77: 8, 17
40, 56
104:28
105: 7, 33
43
106:11
Jer. 39:29
32 AS[b]
51: 3, 8
Lam. 1:18, 20
20
Eze. 2: 3, 3, 5
6, 7, 8
8
3: 9, 26
27
12: 2, 3, 9
25, 27
17:12
20:13+A
21
24: 3, 14
44: 6
Hos. 10: 5

[a] A ἐκπικραίνω.
[b] pro πικραίνω.

παραπικρασμός.

Psalm 94: 8

παραπίπτω.

Est. 6:10
Eze. 14:13
15: 8
Eze. 18:24
20:27
22: 4

παράπληκτος.

Deuteronomy 28:34

παραπληξία.

Deuteronomy 28:28

παραπορεύομαι.

Gen. 37:28
Exo. 2: 5
Exo. 30:13, 14
39: 3
Deu. 2: 4, 13
14, 18
Jos. 6: 7, 9
9: 6
15: 6
Jud. 9:25[a]
19:18[b]
Ruth 4: 1
1 Sa. 20: 2, 2
2 Sa. 15:18—A
23, 23
24:20
1 Ki. 13:25
21:39
2 Ch. 24:20
Job 21:29[c]
Psa. 79:13
88:42 A[d]
Pro. 7: 8
10:25—S[1]
Isa. 51:23
Jer. 18:16 A[e]
19: 8[f]
29:18
Lam. 1:12
2:15
4:18 A[g]
Zeph. 2: 2
(2)15 A[e]

[a] A διαπορεύω. [b] A διαβαίνω.
[c] C πορεύω. [d] pro διοδεύω.
[e] pro διαπορεύω. [f] S[1] πορεύω.
[g] pro πορεύω.

παράπτωμα.

Job 35:15
36: 9—S[1]
Psa. 18:13
21: 2
Eze. 3:20
14:11, 13
15: 8
Eze. 18:22[a], 26
26, 26
20:27
Dan. 4:24
6: 4, 22
Zec. 9: 5[b]

[a] A ἀδικία. [b] A ἐλπίς.

παράπτωσις.

Jeremiah 22:21

παραρρέω, —ρύω.

Pro. 3:21
Isa. 44: 4

παραρρίπτω.

1 Sa. 2:36
Psa. 83:11
Mal. 2: 9 S[3 a]

[a] pro ἀπορρίπτω.

παράρυμα.

Exodus 35:10

παρασιωπάω.

Gen. 24:21
34: 5
Nu. 30: 5, 8, 12
15
1 Sa. 7: 8
23: 9
Psa. 27: 1, 1
34:22
Psa. 38:13
49: 3
108: 1
Pro. 12: 2
Hos. 10:11, 13
Amos 6:12
Hab. 1:13

παρασκευάζω.

1 Sa. 24: 4
Pro. 15:18
21: 2
24:42
29: 5
Isa. 26: 7
Jer. 6: 4
12: 5
26: 9[a]
27:42
28:11

[a] A κατασκευάζω.

παρασκευή.

Exo. 35:24[a]
Exo. 39:22 A[b]

[a] AB κατασκευή.
[b] pro ἀποσκευή.

παραστήκω.

Nu. 7: 2 A[a]
Jud. 3:19 A[b]
1 Ki. 10: 8 A[a]

[a] pro παρίστημι.
[b] pro ἐφίστημι.

παρασυμβάλλω.

Psalm 48:13, 21

παρασφαλίζω.

Nehemiah 3: 8—ABS

παράταξις.

Nu. 31: 5, 14
21, 27
28
Jud. 6:26
8:13[b]
13[a]
18:11[c]
16[c]
20:14[d], 17[e]
18[d]
20[b], 22[b]
23[b], 28[b]
34[b]
39[b]
39[b], 42[b]
21:22[b]
1 Sa. 4: 2, 12
16
17: 4, 8, 10
20 A
21 A
21 A
1 Sa. 17:22 A
23 A
26 A
36, 45
48+A
1 Ch. 5:18
7:40
12: 8, 24[f]
25, 33
38
2 Ch. 20:15
26:11
11—AB
Neh. 11:14
Ps. 143: 1
Isa. 22: 6
36: 5
Jer. 6:23 S[1 g]
Eze. 17:21
24:10
Zec. 14: 3

[a] A ἀνάβασις. [b] A πόλεμος.
[c] A πολεμικός. [d] A πολεμέω.
[e] A πολεμιστής. [f] S πρᾶξις.
[g] pro παρατάσσω.

παρατάσσω.

Gen. 14: 8
Exo. 17: 9, 10
Nu. 1:45
21:23, 23
26: 2
31: 3, 4, 7
Jos. 24: 8+A
9
Jud. 1: 3[a], 5[a]
5:19
20[a], 20[a]
8: 1[a]
9:17[a]
38[a], 39[a]
45[a], 52[b]
10: 9[b], 18[a]
11: 4[a], 6[a]
8[a], 9[a]
12[a], 20[a]
27[a], 32[a]
12: 1[a], 3[a]
4[a]
20:20 A[c]
22 A[c]
22 A[c]
Jud. 20:30 A[c]
1 Sa. 4: 2
17: 2, 8
21 A
2 Sa. 10: 8, 9, 10
17
1 Ch. 7: 4
12:33, 38
19: 9, 10
11, 14
17, 17
2 Ch. 13: 3, 3
14:10
Neh. 4: 8, 14
Psa. 26: 3
139: 3
Jer. 6:23[d]
27: 9, 14
Joel 2: 5
Zec. 1: 6
8:15
10: 5
14: 3, 14
Mal. 1: 4

[a] A πολεμέω. [b] A ἐκπολεμέω.
[c] pro συνάπτω. [d] S[1] παράταξις.

παρατείνω.

Gen. 40:13
Nu. 23:28
2 Sa. 2:29
Psa. 35:11
Eze. 27:13

παρατηρέω.

Psa. 36:12
129: 3
Dan. 6:11

παρατίθημι.

Gen. 18: 8
24:33
30:38
43:30, 31
Exo. 19: 7
21: 1
Lev. 6: 4, 10
Deu. 4:44
1 Sa. 9:24, 24
1 Sa. 21: 6
28:22
2 Sa. 12:20
2 Ki. 5:24
6:22, 23
2 Ch. 16:10
Psa. 30: 6
Pro. 23: 1

παρατρέχω.

1 Sa. 22:17
2 Sa. 15: 1
1 Ki. 1: 5
14:27, 28
28
2 Ki. 10:25, 25
11: 6, 11
19
2 Ch. 12:10, 11
11

παραυτίκα.

Psalm 69: 4

παραφέρω.

Jud. 6: 5+A
1 Sa. 21:13
Ezra 10: 7

παραφορά.

Ecc. 2:12[a]
Ecc. 7:26 A[b]

[a] AS περιφορά. [b] pro περιφορά.

παραφρονέω.

Zechariah 7:11

παραφρόνησις.

Zechariah 12: 4

παραφυάς.

Psa. 79:12
Eze. 17:22+A
31: 3
Eze. 31: 5+A
6, 8

παραχρῆμα.

Nu. 6: 9
12: 4
2 Sa. 3:12
Job 39:30
Job 40: 7
Psa. 39:16
Isa. 29: 5
30:13, 13

πάρδαλις.

Cant. 4: 8
Isa. 11: 6
Jer. 5: 6
13:23
Dan. 7: 6
Hos. 13: 7
Hab. 1: 8

παρεδρεύω.

Pro. 1:21
Pro. 8: 3

παρείδω.

Lev. 6: 2, 2
Nu. 5: 6, 6, 12
Ps. 137: 8[a]
Pro. 4: 4

[a] B πάρειμι.

πάρειμι.

Nu. 22:20
Deu. 32:35
Jud. 19: 3 A[a]
1 Sa. 9: 6
2 Sa. 5:23[b]
13:35
15:18—A
1 Ch. 14:14
Est. 9: 1
Job 1: 7
2: 2
31:21 AS[c]
Ps. 137: 8 B[d]
138: 8
Pro. 1:27
7:19
Isa. 8: 1
30:13
52: 6
58: 9
63: 4
Lam. 4:19
Joel 2: 1
Hab. 3: 2

[a] pro εὐφραίνω. [b] A περιπίπτω.
[c] pro περίειμι. [d] pro παρείδω.

παρεκτείνω.

Pro. 23: 4
Eze. 47:19

παρέλκυσις.

Job 23: 3

παρεμβάλλω.

Gen. 32: 1
33:18
Exo. 14: 9
15:27
17: 1
18: 5
19: 2
Nu. 1:50, 51
52, 53
2: 2, 2, 3
5, 7, 12
14, 17
20, 22
Nu. 2:27, 29
34
3:23, 29
35, 38
9:17, 18
18, 20
22
10: 5, 6, 6, 6
13: 1
21:10, 11
12, 13
22: 1
31:19

Nu. 33: 5, 6, 7
7to36
36, 37
41to49
Deu. 23: 9
Jos. 4: 3
11: 5
Jud. 1:23
6: 3, 33
7: 1
12 A[a]
9:50[b]
10:17, 17
11:18, 20
15: 9
18:12
19:21 + A
20:19
1 Sa. 4: 1, 1
11: 1
13: 5, 16

1 Sa. 17: 1, 2
23:26
26: 3, 5
28: 4, 4
29: 1
2 Sa. 11:11
12:28
17:12, 26
23:13
24: 5
1 Ki. 21:27, 29
2 Ki. 6: 8
25: 1
1 Ch. 9:26
11:15 + A
19: 7, 9
2 Ch. 32: 1
Ezra 8:15
Neh. 11:30
Psa. 33: 8
Jer. 27:29

[a] pro βάλλω. [b] A περικαθίζω.

παρεμβολή.

Gen. 32: 1, 2, 2
7, 8, 8
10, 21
33: 8
50: 9
Exo. 14:19
20 — B
20, 24
24
16:13, 13
17: 1
19:16, 17
20:14
32:17, 19
26, 27
33: 7 ter
8 — A
11
36: 6
Lev. 4:12, 21
6:11
8:17
9:11
10: 4, 5
13:46
14: 3, 8
16:26, 27
28
17: 3, 3
24:10, 14
23
Nu. 2: 3, 9[a]
10, 16
17, 17
18, 24
25, 31
32
4: 5, 15
5: 2[b], 3
3, 4
10: 2, 5, 6
6, 6, 14
18, 22
25, 25
34
11: 1, 9, 26
26, 27
30, 31
31, 32
12:14, 15
14:44, 45
15:36, 36
16:46
19: 3, 7, 9
31:12, 13
19, 24
Deu. 2:14, 15
23:10 — B
10, 11
12 — B[1]
14, 14
29:11
Jos. 1:11
3: 2

Jos. 4: 8
5: 8
6:11, 14
18, 23
7:22
8:22
9:12
10: 6
Jud. 4:15, 16
16
7: 1, 8, 9
10, 11
11, 13
14, 15
15, 17
18, 19
21, 21
22, 22
8:10
10 — A
11, 11
12
13:25
18:12
21: 8, 12
1 Sa. 4: 3, 5, 6
6, 7, 16
11:11
14:15, 16
19, 21
17: 1, 17A
46, 53
26: 6
28: 1, 5, 19
29: 1, 4, 6
2 Sa. 1: 2, 3
2: 8, 29
23:16
1 Ki. 2: 8
(3) p 1
16:15, 16
16
22:36 + A
2 Ki. 3: 9, 24
5:15
6:24
7: 4, 5, 5
6, 7, 8
10, 12
16
19:35
1 Ch. 9:18, 19
11:15, 18
14:15, 16
2 Ch. 32:21
Psa. 26: 3
77:28
105:16
Cant. 7: 1
Isa. 8: 8
21: 8
37:36
Eze. 1:24 + A
4: 2

Eze. 43: 2
Joel 2:11

Amos 4:10
Zec. 14:15

[a] A φυλή. [b] A συναγωγή.

παρενοχλέω.

Jud. 14:17
16:16 A[a]
1 Sa. 28:15
Job 16: 3

Psa. 34:13
Jer. 26:27
Dan. 6:18
Mic. 6: 3

[a] pro στενοχωρέω.

πάρεξ.

Jud. 8:26[a]
Ruth 4: 4
1 Sa. 20:39 — A
21: 9
1 Ki. 3:18
12:20
Ezra 1: 6
Neh. 7:67
Psa. 17:32 S[b]

Ecc. 2:25
Isa. 43:11
45:21 A[a] [b]
21
22 + A
Eze. 15: 4
42:14
Hos. 13: 4

[a] A πλήν. [b] pro πλήν.

παρεξίστημι.

Hosea 9: 7

παρέξω.

Lev. 8:17 A[a] [a] pro ἔξω.

παρεπίδημος.

Gen. 23: 4
Psa. 38:13

παρέρχομαι.

Gen. 18: 3, 5
30:32
32:31
33: 3 A[a]
41:53
50: 4
Exo. 3: 3
12:23, 23
15:16, 16
23: 5
33:19, 22
22
34: 6
Nu. 13:33
20:17, 17
19, 19[b]
21
21:22, 22
23
32:21, 27
34: 4, 4
Deu. 2: 8, 8
13 + AB
14, 24
27
27 B[c]
28, 29
30
17: 2
26:13
29:12, 16
16
Jos. 4:23
6: 8
15:10, 10
11
16: 2, 6A[d]
6, 8 A[e]
18:14[e], 17
24:17
Jud. 3:26
9:26 — A
11:17, 19
20, 29[f]
29[f], 32[f]
12: 1[g], 1[h]
3[f]
18:13
19:12, 14
1 Sa. 16: 8
2 Sa. 2:15

2 Sa. 15:22
23 A[h]
24
16: 1
17:20
18: 9
20:13
23: 4
1 Ki. 18:29
19:11
22:24 + A
2 Ki. 3:10[i]
13 + A
6: 9
2 Ch. 8:15
9: 2
18:23 — B
25: 7 A[c]
Neh. 2:14, 14
9:11
Job 6:15
9:11
11:16
14:16
17:11
23:12
28: 8[g]
30:15 + A
Psa. 36:36
56: 2
89: 5, 6
103: 9
140:10
148: 6
Pro. 8:29 + AS[2]
22: 3
27:12 C[k]
13
Cant. 2:11
3: 4
5: 6
Isa. 10:29, 29
24: 5[m]
26:20
28:15, 17
19, 10
33:22
34:16
35: 8
51:23

Jer. 8:20
40:13
41:18
48: 8
Dan. 2: 9
4:28

Dan. 6:12
7:14
11:10, 40
Amos 7: 8
8: 2

[a] pro προέρχομαι. [b] A πορεύω. [c] pro παρεύω. [d] pro περιέρχομαι. [e] A διέρχομαι. [f] A διαβαίνω. [g] A ἔρχομαι. [h] pro διαβαίνω. [i] A κατέχω. [k] pro ἐπέρχομαι. [m] A παραβαίνω.

παρέχω.

2 Ki. 12: 4 + A
Job 34:29

Psa. 29: 8
Isa. 7:13, 13

παρθενεία, —νία, ἡ.

Jeremiah 3: 4

παρθένια, τά.

Deu. 22:14, 15
17, 17

Deu. 22:20
Jud. 11:37, 38

παρθενικός.

Est. 2: 3[a]
Joel 1: 8

[a] S[1] παρθένιος.

παρθένιος.

Esther 2: 3 S[1] [a]

[a] pro παρθενικός.

παρθένος.

Gen. 24:14, 16
16, 43
55
34: 3, 3
Exo. 22:16, 17
Lev. 21: 3, 13
14
Deu. 22:19, 23
28
32:25
Jud. 19:24
21:11 — A
12
2 Sa. 13: 2, 18
1 Ki. 1: 2
2 Ki. 19:21
2 Ch. 36:17
Est. 2:17
Job 31: 1
Psa. 44:15
77:63
148:12

Isa. 7:14
23: 4
37:22
47: 1
1 + S[1]
62: 5
Jer. 2:32
18:13
26:11
28:22
38: 4, 13
21 — S[1]
Lam. 1: 4, 15
18
2:10, 13
21
5:11
Eze. 9: 6
44:22
Amos 5: 2
8:13
Zec. 9:17

παρίημι.

Exo. 14:12
Nu. 13:21
Deu. 32:36
1 Sa. 2: 5
2 Sa. 4: 1

Pro. 9:15
15:10
Jer. 4:31
20: 9
Zeph. 3:16

πάριος, —νος.

1 Ch. 29: 2
Est. 1: 6

Est. 1: 6 — S[1]

παρίστημι.

Gen. 18: 8
40: 4
45: 1, 1
Exo. 9:31
18:13, 14
23
19:17
24:13
34: 5
Nu. 1: 5
7: 2[a]
11:28
16: 9

Nu. 23: 3, 3
15
Deu. 1:38
10: 8
17:12
18: 5, 7
21: 5
Jud. 20:28
1 Sa. 2:22 + A
4:20
5: 2
10:21, 22
22: 6, 7

1 Sa. 25:27
1 Ki. 1: 2
10: 8[a]
12: 6, 8, 10
32
17: 1
18:15
2 Ki. 3:14
5:16, 25
8:11
2 Ch. 6: 3
9: 7
18:18[b]
Est. 3: 9 + S[3]
4: 5
7 + S[3]
8: 4
Job 1: 6
2: 1
1 — S[1]

Job 37:19
Psa. 2: 2
5: 4
35: 5
44:10
49:21
77:13 S[2] [c]
108:31
Pro. 22:29, 29
Isa. 5:29
60:10
Jer. 15:11
39:12[d]
42:19
Dan. 6: 6
7:10
Hos. 9:13
Joel 3:13
Zec. 4:14
6: 5

[a] A παραστήκω. [b] B ἵστημι. [c] pro ἵστημι. [d] AS ἵστημι.

παροδεύω.

Eze. 36:34[a] [a] A διοδεύω.

πάροδος.

Gen. 38:14
2 Sa. 12: 4

2 Ki. 25:24
Eze. 16:15, 25

παροικεσία.

Ezekiel 20:38

παροικέω.

Gen. 12:10
17: 8
19: 9
20: 1
21:23, 34
24:37
26: 3
32: 4
35:27
(37) 1
47: 4, 9, 9
Exo. 6: 4, 4
12:40 A[a]
20:10
Nu. 20:15
Deu. 18: 6
26: 5
Jos. 24: 2[b]
Jud. 5:17
17 A[c]
17: 7, 8, 9
11
19: 1, 16
Ruth 1: 1
2 Sa. 4: 3
2 Ki. 8: 1, 1, 2

1 Ch. 16:19
29:15[b]
2 Ch. 15: 9
Ezra 1: 4
Psa. 5: 5
14: 1
30:14
55: 7
60: 5
93:17
104:23
119: 6
Pro. 3:29
Isa. 16: 4
52: 4
54:15 — AS
Jer. 6:25
27:31 S[a]
40[d]
51:14
28 S[e]
28 AS[a]
Lam. 4:15
Eze. 21:12
47:22[f]
Hos. 10: 5

[a] pro κατοικέω. [b] B κατοικέω. [c] pro καθίζω. [d] A κατοικέω. [e] pro καθίστημι. [f] A προσοικέω

παροίκησις.

Gen. 28: 4
36: 7

Exo. 12:40 A[a]

[a] pro κατοίκησις.

παροικία.

Ezra 8:35
Psa. 33: 5[a]
54:16
118:54

Ps. 119: 5
Lam. 2:22
Hab. 3:16
Zec. 9:12

[a] AS[2] θλίψις.

πάροικος.

Gen. 15:13
23: 4
Exo. 2:22
12:45
18: 3

Lev. 22:10
25: 6, 23
35, 40
45, 47
47

Nu. 35:15
Deu. 5:14
14:20
23: 7
2 Sa. 1:13
19:28 A[a]
1 Ch. 5:10
29:15
Psa. 38:13
104:12
118:19
Jer. 14: 8
29:19
30: 5 A[b]
Zeph. 2: 5

[a] *pro* πᾶς ὁ οἶκος.
[b] *pro* περίοικος.

παροιμία.

Pro. 1: 1
Pro. 25: 1 AS^2[a]

[a] *pro* παιδεία.

παροινέω.

Isaiah 41:12

παροιστράω, –έω.

Eze. 2: 6
Hos. 4:16, 16

παροξύνω.

Nu. 14:11, 23
15:30
16:30
20:24
Deu. 1:34
9: 7,8,18
19, 22
31:20
32:16, 19
21[a], 41
2 Sa. 12:14 AB[b]
14 AB[b]
Ezra 9:14
Psa. 9:25, 34[c]
73:10, 18
77:41
105:29
106:11
Pro. 6: 3
Pro. 14:31
17: 5
20: 2
27:17
Isa. 5:24, 25
14:16
23:11
37:23
47: 6
60:14
63:10
65: 3
Jer. 22:15
27:34
Lam. 2: 6
Hos. 8: 5
Zec. 10: 3
Mal. 2:17, 17

[a] A παροργίζω. [b] *pro* παροργίζω
[c] S παροργίζω.

παροξυσμός.

Deu. 29:28
Jer. 39:37

παροράω, –όπτομαι.

1 Ki. 10: 3
Job 11:11
Ecc. 12:14
Isa. 57:11
Nah. 3:11 S^3[a]

[a] *pro* ὑπεροράω.

παροργίζω.

Deu. 4:25
31:29
32:21 A[a]
21
Jud. 2:12
17 + A
2 Sa. 12:14[b]
14[b]
1 Ki. 14: 9 A
15 A
15:30
16: 2,7,13
26, 33
20:20, 22
22:54
2 Ki. 17:11, 17
21: 6, 15
22:17
23:19, 26
2 Ch. 28:25
2 Ch. 33: 6
34:25
35:19
Ezra 5:12
Job 12: 6[c]
Psa. 9:34 S[a]
77:40, 58
105:16, 32
Isa. 1: 4
Jer. 7:18, 19
8:19
11:17
25: 6
Eze. 8:17 + A
16:26, 54
20:27
32: 9
Hos. 12:14
Mic. 2: 7
Zec. 8:14

[a] *pro* παροξύνω. [b] AB παροξύνω.
[c] A γὰρ ὀργίζω.

παρόργισμα.

1 Ki. 16:33 – A
20:22
2 Ch. 35:19[a]

[a] B πρόσταγμα.

παροργισμός.

1 Ki. 15:30
2 Ki. 19: 3
23:26
Neh. 9:18, 26
Jer. 21: 5 + A

παρουσία.

Neh. 2: 6 A[a]
[a] *pro* πορεία.

παρρησία.

Lev. 26:13
Job 27:10
Pro. 1:20
Pro. 10:10
13: 5

παρρησιάζομαι.

Job 22:26[a]
Psa. 11: 6
Psa. 93: 1
Pro. 20: 9

[a] A ἐμπαρρησιάζομαι.

παρωμίς.

Exodus 28:14

πᾶς, πᾶσα, πᾶν.

Var. Lec. tantum.

Gen. 18:24 – A
23:11 – A
13 + A
17^2 – A
31:23 + A
34:30 – A
36: 6^3 – A
6^5 – A
41:55 + A
47:15^1 – A
50:14 + A
Exo. 9: 7 – A^2
11: 3 + B
12:14 – A
30 + A
13:15 + B
18: 8^2 – A
26: 2 – A
29:12 – A
30: 8 – A^1
34:19 – A^2
35: 9^2 – A
39:21^2 – A
Lev. 3: 9 – AB
9 – AB
15 – A
4: 2 – AB
6:15 – AB
Nu. 2:34 – A
5: 6 – AB
6:12 + A
8: 7 – A
16:33 + A
18:15 + A
19:13 + A
22:17 + A
25: 4 – A
30: 6 – A
33:53 – A
Deu. 3:28 – A
7:12 + A
12:19 – A
13:18 + A
15:21 + A
16:18 + A
17: 7 + A
20:14^1 – B
14^2 – B
26:17 – A
18 + A
27:15 – B
21^1 – A
28: 9 – A
45 + A
52 + A
52 + A
57 + A
61^2 – A
29: 2 + A
30:10 + A
Deu. 31: 9 + A
32:43^1 – B
34:11^2 – A
12 + A
Jos. 2:13^1 – A
6: 3 + A
17^2 – B
22 + A
23 + A
25 – A
8:15 + A
27 – A
9: 1 + A
12 + A
10:39 + A
23: 3 + A
Jud. 6:17 – A
7: 6 + A
9: 2^1 – A
14 – A
15:10 + A
16:18 + A
18 + A
31 + A
20: 1 + A
17 + A
21: 2 + A
10 + A
Ruth 2:11 + A
1 Sa. 1: 4 + A
2:23 – A
36 + A
5: 8 + A
11 + A
8: 4 + A
9:20 + A
11: 2 + A
14:34 + AB
15: 6 + A
13 – B
22: 1 + A
25:12 + A
17 + A
2 Sa. 3:19 + AB
6:11 – A
8:15^1 – AB
16:13 – AB
17:12 + A
16 – A
18: 7 + A
1 Ki. 1: 9 – B
9 – B
7:37 + A
8: 4 + A
30 + A
40 + A
66 + A
12:20 – A
14:26^1 – A
15: 3 + A
1 Ki. 15:23 + A
33 + A
16:14 + A
27^2 – AB
18:5 + A
19: 1 + A
21: 6 – AB
13 + A
21 – A
2 Ki. 4: 4 + A
9 – A
8: 6^2 – B
10:19^3 – A
15: 9 – AB
16:15^1 – A
18: 4 + A
5 + A
19: 4 – A
21:24 + A
23: 2^2 – B
24:14 + A
1 Ch. 20: 3^1[a]
22:17[b]
28: 1^2 – B
29:16^1 – A
2 Ch. 5: 2^1 – AB
6:29^3 – B
8: 6 + A
9:14^2 – AB
18:22 + A
21:18 – A
26: 5 + B
28: 3 + A
29:30 + A
34:12^2 – A
Ezra 10: 9^2 – S^1
Neh. 4:12 – S^1
6:16^1 – B
8:11 – BS^1
9: 6^2 – S
38 + AS^1
10:31^1 – S^1
Est. 9:19 – A
Job 2: 4 + A
14:16 + C
25: 6 + A
30: 4 – A
33:29 – C
Psa. 9:11 + A
11: 9 + A
14: 4 + A
17:40 – S^1
21:26 + A
24:3 + AB^2
33:10 – S^1
35:13 – S^1
46: 9 + A
74: 2 – S^1
83: 5 + AB
84: 3 – B
90:11 – B
94: 4 + S^1
97: 7 + AS^2
98: 3 + B
104:33 – S^1
35 + AS^2
108:11 + S^1
115: 3 – S^1
118:64 + S^1
134: 6^2 – AS^1
18 + AS^1
137: 1 – AS
138: 2 + BS^1
Pro. 24:27 – BS
31 + A
Ecc. 2:11 + S
3:10 – ACS
4: 3 AS^2
5:16 – S^1
6: 6 – B
Isa. 19: 7^2 – B^1
21: 9 – S^1
23: 9^1 – A
24: 1 + S^1
26:10 – AS^2
15 + AS
18 – AS
30:18 + A
31: 4 + S^1
36:20 – S
38:13 – AS
40: 4^3 – A
41:20 + AS^3
44:24[c]
53: 3 + AS
56:10 + AB[a]S
65: 3 – S^1
Jer. 7:20 + A
23 – S
33 + A
9:26 + A
15:10 – A
17:20^1 – A
18: 8 + A
19: 8^2[d]
15 – S
31:24 – S^1
32: 6 + A
8 + A
12 + S
15 – ABS
16 + A
33: 2 – S
34: 5 + A
35:11^1 – S
43:17 – S
21 – A
48:13 + A
49: 8 + A
50: 6 + A
Lam. 2: 5 + A
3:51 – A
Eze. 4: 6 + A
12:16 – A
16:30 – A
18:25 – B
20:47^1 – B
21:15 + A
22:18 – A
19 + A
27:35 – A
29: 9 + A
30: 8 + A
31:17 + A
18 + A
35: 8 + A
37:22 + A
39: 7 + A
14 + A
15 + A
Dan. 1:20^3 – A
5: 8 – A
Joel 2:27 + A
Amos 9:12^2 – AB
Jon. 3: 7 + S^1
Mic. 5:12 + A
Zeph. 1: 9 + AS
Mal. 3:15 – A
&c., &c.

[a] B παῖς. [b] AB παῖς.
[c] A οὗτος. [d] S^1 οὗτος.

πάσσαλος.

Exo. 27:19
37, 18
38:21 – B
21
39: 9,9,21
Nu. 3:37
4:32
Deu. 23:13
Jud. 4:21, 21
22
5:26
10:13, 14
14
Isa. 33:20
54: 2
Eze. 15: 3

πάσσω.

Exo. 9: 8, 10
2 Sa. 16:13
Est. 1: 6[a]
Ps. 147: 5

[a] S^1 πλάσσω.

παστός.

Psa. 18: 6
Joel 2:16

παστοφόριον.

1 Ch. 9:26
23:28
26:16, 18
28:12
2 Ch. 31:11
Isa. 22:15
Jer. 42: 4
Eze. 40:17[a], 17
38

[a] A γαζοφυλάκιον.

πάσχα.

Exo. 12:11, 21
27, 43
48
34:25
Lev. 23: 5
Nu. 9: 2, 4, 6
10, 12
13, 14
14
Nu. 28:16 – A
33: 3
Deu. 16:1,2,5,6
Jos. 5:10
2 Ki. 23:21, 22
23
Ezra 6:19, 20
21
Eze. 45:21

πάσχω.

Est. 9:26
Job 41: 8 S^1[a]
Eze. 16: 5
Amos 6: 6
Zec. 11: 5

[a] *pro* ἀποσπάω.

πατάσσω.

Gen. 8:21
14:15
19:11
32:11
37:21
Exo. 2:12
3:20
7:20, 25
8:16, 17
9:15, 25
25
12:12, 23
23, 27
29
17: 5, 6
21:12, 18
19, 20
22, 26
32:35
Lev. 24:17, 18
21
26:24
Nu. 3:13
8:17
11:33
14:12
20:11
21:24, 35
22: 6, 11
23, 32
25:17
33: 4
35:11, 15
16, 17
18, 21
21
21 A[a]
24, 30
Deu. 1: 4
2:33
3: 3
4:46
7: 2
19: 4,6,11
20:13
21: 1
27:25
28:22, 27
28, 35
29: 7
Deu. 32:39
Jos. 8:21, 22
24
10:33, 37
39, 40
42[b]
12: 6
13:12, 21
19:48
20: 3, 5 A
24: 5
Jud. 1: 4 AB[a][c]
5 A[c], 8
10, 12
17 A[c]
25
3:13, 29
31
5:26^1
6:16
7:13
8:11
9:43, 44
11:21, 33
12: 4
14:19[e]
15: 8, 15
16
18:27
20:31[f]
35[e], 37
39[f], 45
48
21:10
1 Sa. 2:14
4: 8
5: 3, 9, 9
6:19, 19
7:11
13: 3
14:13, 14
31, 48[b]
15: 3, 7
17: 9, 9
25 A
26 A
35, 35
36, 49
50 A

1 Sa. 17:57 A
18: 6 A, 7
11A, 27
19: 5,8,10
10
21: 9, 11
22:19
23: 2, 2
2 B[i], 5
24: 6
25:38
26: 8
29: 5
30: 1, 17
2 Sa. 1:15
2:22, 31
3:27
5:25
8: 1, 2, 3
5, 9
10 AB[k]
10, 13
10:18
11:21, 22
12: 9
13:28, 30
15:14
17: 2
18:11, 15
21: 2, 12
16, 17
18, 19
21
23:10, 12
20—A
20, 21
24:10
1 Ki. 15:20
27 A[m]
29
16: 7, 10
11
20:27
21:20, 21
29, 35
35, 36
36
37—A
37—A
37
22:24, 34
2 Ki. 2: 8, 14
14
3:19, 23
24, 25
6:18, 18
21, 21
22
8:21, 28
29
9:24, 27
10: 9, 11
17, 25
25
27 B[n]
32
12:20, 21
13:17, 18
18, 19
19, 19
25
14: 5, 5, 6
7, 10
15:10, 14
16, 16
25, 30
18: 8
19:35, 37
21:24
25:25
1 Ch. 1:46
4:41, 43
10: 2
11:14, 22

1 Ch. 11:22, 23
13:10
14:11, 15
16
18: 1, 2, 3
5,9,10
12
20: 1, 4, 5
7
21: 7
2 Ch. 6:36
13:15, 17
20
14:12
16: 4
18:23, 33
21: 9, 14
18
22: 5, 6
25:11, 13
14, 19
28: 5,5,17
20 A[o]
33:24, 25
Neh. 13:25
Job 1:15 A[a]
5:18 A[p]
Psa. 3: 8
59: 2
68:27
77:20, 51
66
104:33, 36
134: 8, 10[q]
135:10, 17
Pro. 23:13, 14
Cant. 5: 7
Isa. 5:25
10:24
11: 4, 15
14: 6
19:22
27: 7
30:31
37:38
49:10
57:17
60:10
Jer. 2:30
18:18
20: 2
21: 6
25:13 A[r]
26: 2
30: 6
33:23
36:21
40: 5
44:10, 15
47:14, 15
15
48: 2, 4, 9
18
50:11
52:27
Eze. 11: 7[s]
22:13[t]
Dan. 2:34, 35
Hos. 6: 1
Amos 3:15
4: 9
6:11
9: 1
Jon. 4: 7, 8
Mic. 5: 1
6:13
Hag. 2:17
Zec. 9: 4[u]
10:11
12: 4, 4[v]
13: 7
14:18
Mal. 4: 5

[a] pro ἀποκτείνω. [b] A λαμβάνω
[c] pro κόπτω. [d] A συνθλάω.
[e] A παίω. [f] A τύπτω.
[g] A τροπόω. [h] B ποιέω.
[i] pro σώζω. [k] pro πολεμέω
[m] pro χαράσσω. [n] pro τάσσω.

[o] pro θλίβω. [p] pro παίω.
[q] S[1] ἀποκτείνω. [r] pro ἐπάγω.
[s] A φονεύω. [t] B ἐπάγω.
[u] AS[1] κατάγνυμι. [v] S[1] κατάγνυμι

πατέω.

Deu. 11:24
Jud. 9:27[a]
Neh. 13:15
Job 22:15[b]
28: 8[c]
Isa. 1:12
16:10
25:10

Isa. 26: 6
32:20
42: 5, 16
Jer. 31:33
Lam. 1:15
Joel 3:13
Amos 2: 7
Zec. 10: 5

[a] A καταπατέω. [b] A[1] ἐπανίστημι
[c] S καταπατέω.

πάτημα.

2 Ki. 19:26
Eze. 34:19

πατήρ.

Gen. 2:24
4:20
9:18, 22
22, 23
23
10:21
11:28, 29
29
12: 1
15:15
17: 4, 5
19:31, 32
32, 33
33, 34
34, 35
35, 36
37, 37
38
20:12, 13
22: 7,7,21
24: 7, 23
38, 40
26: 3,5,15
15, 18
18, 18
24, 24
27: 5, 6, 9
10, 10
12, 14
18, 18
19, 22
26, 29
30, 31
31, 31
32, 34
34, 36
36, 38
38, 38
39, 41
41
28: 2, 4, 7
8, 13
21
29: 6+A
6+A
9,9,12
12
31: 1, 1, 3
5, 5, 6
7,9,14
16, 18
19, 29
30, 35
42, 54
32: 9, 9
33:19
34: 4,6,11
13, 19
35:18, 21
27
36: 9, 24
43
(37) 1
37: 1—A
1, 1, 4

Gen. 37: 9, 10
11, 12
22, 32
35
38:11, 11
41:51
42:13, 29
32, 32
35, 36
37
43: 1, 6, 7
10, 22
26, 27
44:17, 19
20
20 A[a]
20, 22
22:24
25, 27
30, 31
32, 32
34, 34
45: 3, 8, 9
13, 13
18, 19
23, 23
25, 27
46: 1, 3, 5
8—A
29, 31
34
47: 1, 3, 5
6, 7, 9
11, 12
12, 30
48: 1,9,15
16, 17
17, 18
18:21
49: 2, 4, 8
24, 26
28
28+B
29
50: 1, 2, 5
5, 6, 7
10, 14
15, 16
17, 22
24—A
Exo. 1: 1
2:16, 16
18
3: 6, 13
15, 16
4: 5
6:20
10: 6
12:40+A
13: 5, 11
15: 2
18: 4
20: 5, 12
21:15, 16
22:17, 17[b]

Exo. 34: 7
40:13
Lev. 10: 4
16:32
18: 7, 8, 8
9, 11
12, 12[c]
14
19: 3
20: 9,9,11
11, 17
19
21: 2,9,11
22:13
25:49, 49
26:39—AB
40
Nu. 3: 4
6: 7
11:12
12:14
14:12, 18
23
18: 1[d], 2
20:15, 15
27: 3, 4, 4
7,7,10
11
30: 4, 5, 5
6,6,17
17
32: 8, 14
36: 3, 6, 8
12
Deu. 1: 8, 11
21, 35
4: 1, 31
37
5: 3,9,16
6: 3, 10
18, 23
7: 8, 12
13
8: 1,3,16
18
9: 5
10:11, 15
22
11: 9, 21
12: 1
13: 6,6,17
19: 8, 8
14[e]
21:13, 18
19
22:15, 16
19, 21
21, 29
30, 30
24:18, 18
26: 3, 5
7+A
15
27: 3,3,16
20, 20
22
28: 9, 11
36, 64
29:13, 25
25
30: 5, 5, 9
20
31: 7, 16
20, 21
32: 6,7,17
33: 9
Jos. 1: 6, 11
2:12, 13
18, 18
5: 6
6:23
15:18
17: 1, 4
18: 3+A
21:43, 44
22:28
24: 2,2,2,3
6—A
6, 14
15, 17

Jos. 24:33
Jud. 1:14
2: 1, 10
12, 17
19, 20
22—A
3: 4
6:11, 13
15, 24
25, 25
27
8:32
32+A
9: 1—A
5, 17
18, 28
56
11: 2,7,36
37, 37
39
14: 2, 3, 3
4, 5, 6
9, 10
15, 16
19
15: 1, 2, 6
6+A
16:31, 31
17:10
18:19, 29
19: 2, 3, 3
4, 5, 6
8, 9
21:22
Ruth 1: 8 A[a]
2:11
4:17, 17
1 Sa. 1:24
2:25, 27
28, 28
30, 31
9: 3,5,20
10: 2, 12
12: 6, 7, 8
8
13:23+B
14: 1, 27
28, 29
51, 51
17:15 A
25 A
34
18: 2 A
18 A
19: 2+A
3, 3, 4
20: 1, 2, 2
3
3+A
6, 8, 9
10, 12
13
32+A
33, 34
22: 1,3,11
15, 16
22
23:17, 17
24:12+A
22
2 Sa. 2:32
3: 7,8,29
6:21
7:12, 14
9: 7, 7-A
7
10: 2, 2, 3
13: 5
14: 9
15: 7, 34
34
16: 3, 19
21, 21
22
17: 8,8,10
23
19:28, 37
21:14
24:17
1 Ki. 1: 6, 21

1 Ki. 2:10, 12
24, 26
26, 31
32
(3)44
3: 3, 6, 7
14
5: 1, 3, 5
6(12) A
7: 2, 37
8: 1+A
15, 17
18, 20
21, 24
25, 26
34, 40
48, 53
57, 58
9: 4, 5, 9
11: 3, 8
10—A
12, 17
21, 27
33, 43
43
44—A
12: 4, 4, 6
9, 10
10, 11
11, 14
14
p24ll 1,2
ll 6, 53
ll 66, 66
13:11, 12
22
14:15 A
20A, 22
31, 31
15: 3, 3, 8
8—A
11, 12
15, 19
19
24—B
24
24—B
26
16: 6, 28
p28—A
p28—A
p28—A
p28—AB
18:18
19: 4, 20
20: 3
4+A
6
21:34 ter
22:40, 43
47A, 51
51—B
51, 53
2 Ki. 1:18
2:12, 12
3: 2
2—A
13
4:18, 19
5:13+A
6:21
8:24
24—A
24
9:25
28+A
10: 3, 35
12:18, 21
13: 9
9+A
13
13 B[f]
14, 14
25
14: 3—A
3, 5, 6
6
16—A
20, 21
22, 29

2 Ki. 14:29+AB
15: 3, 7
7—A
9, 22
34, 38
38—A
38
16: 2, 20
20+A
17:13, 14
15+A
41
18: 3
19:12
20: 5, 17
21
21: 3, 8
15—A
18, 20
21, 21
22
22: 2, 13
20
23:30, 32
34, 37
24: 6, 9
1 Ch. 2:17, 21
23, 24
42, 42
44, 45
49 ter
50, 51
51, 51
52, 55
4: 4 ter
5, 11
11, 12
14, 17
18 ter
19+AB
19+AB
19, 21
21
5: 1, 25
7:14, 22
31
8:29
9:19, 19
35
12:17
16:28 S[g]
17:11, 13
19: 2, 2, 3
21:17
22:10
24: 2, 19
25: 3, 6
26:10
26: 4, 4
4—B
6, 9
29:10, 15
18, 20
23, 24
2 Ch. 1: 8, 9
2: 3, 7
13[h], 14
14, 17
3: 1
5: 1
6: 4, 7, 8
10, 15
16—B
25, 31
38
7:17, 18
22
8:14—AB
9:31
10: 4, 4, 6
9, 10
10, 11
11, 14
14
11:16
12:16
13:11, 12
18
14: 1, 4
15:12, 18

2 Ch. 16: 3, 3
13
17: 2, 3, 4
4
19: 4
20: 6, 32
33
21: 1
1+A
3, 10
12
12−A
13, 19
22: 4
24: 18, 22
24
25: 3, 4, 4
28
26: 1, 2, 4
23, 23
27: 2, 9
28: 1, 6, 9
25, 27
29: 2, 5, 6
9
30: 7, 7
8−AB
19, 22
32: 13, 14
15, 33
33: 3, 8, 12
20, 22
22, 23
34: 2, 3, 21
28, 32
33
35: 24
36: 1, 2, 4
5, 8, 8
10, 15
Ezra 4: 15
5: 12
7: 27
8: 28
9: 7
10: 11
Neh. 1: 6
2: 3, 5
9: 2, 9
16−S[1]
23, 32
34, 36
13: 18
Est. 2: 7
15−S[1]
4: 14
Job 8: 8
15: 10, 18
17: 14
29: 16
30: 1
31: 18
38: 28
42: 15−A
p 18
Psa. 21: 5
26: 10
38: 13
43: 2
44: 11, 17
48: 20
67: 6
77: 3, 5, 8
12, 57
88: 27
94: 9
102: 13
105: 6, 7
108: 14
150 p 6 bis
Pro. 1: 8
4: 1, 3
6: 20
10: 1
13: 1[1]
15: 5, 20
17: 6, 21
25
19: 13, 14
20, 26

Pro. 19: 27
20: 20
22: 28
23: 10+A
22, 24
25
24: 34, 52
28: 7, 24
29: 3
Isa. 3: 6
7: 17 8: 4
9: 6+AS[2]
14: 21
17: 11
22: 21, 23
24
33: 22+A[2]
37: 12
38: 5, 8
39: 6
43: 27
45: 10
51: 2
58: 14
63: 16, 16
64: 8, 11
65: 7
Jer. 2: 5, 27
3: 4, 18
19−S[1]
24, 25
6: 21
7: 7, 14
18, 22
25, 26
9: 14, 16
11: 4, 5
10, 10
12: 6
13: 14
14: 20
16: 3, 7, 11
12, 13
15, 19
17: 22, 23
18: 23+AS
19: 4
20: 15
22: 11, 15
23: 27, 39
25: 5
27: 7
29: 3
37: 3
38: 9, 20
32
39: 7, 8, 9
12, 18
22
32+A
41: 5, 13
42: 6, 8, 10
15, 16
18, 18
51: 9, 10
17, 21
Lam. 5: 3, 7
Eze. 2: 3
5: 10, 10
16: 3, 45
18: 2, 4, 11
14, 17
18, 19
20, 20
20: 4, 18
24, 27
30, 36
42[h]
22: 7, 10, 11
28: 26
36: 28
37: 25
44: 25
47: 14
Dan. 2: 23
5: 2, 11
11
11+A
13, 18
9: 6, 8, 16

Dan. 11: 24 ter
37, 38
Hos. 9: 10
Joel 1: 2
Amos 2: 4, 7
Mic. 7: 6, 20
Zec. 1: 2, 4, 5

Zec. 1: 6
8: 14
13: 3, 3
Mal. 1: 6, 6
2: 10, 10
3: 7
4: 5

[a] *pro* μήτηρ. [b] A αὐτῷ
[c] A μήτηρ. [d] B πατριά.
[e] A πρότερος. [f] *pro* θρόνος.
[g] *pro* πατριά. [h] AB[1] παῖς.
[i] S[1] μήτηρ. [k] A αὐτοῖς.

πατητός.

Isaiah 63: 2

πάτος.

Jeremiah 7: 19+S[1]

πατράδελφος.

Jud. 10: 1
2 Sa. 23: 9, 24
1 Ch. 27: 32

πάτρυρχος.

Isaiah 37: 38

πατριά.

Exo. 6: 14, 15
17, 19
25
12: 3
Lev. 25: 10[a]
Nu. 1: 2, 4, 16
18, 20
22, 24
26, 28
30, 32
34, 36
38, 40
42, 44
47
2: 2, 32
34
3: 15, 20
24, 30
35
4: 2
4+A
22, 29
34, 38
40, 42
44, 46
7: 2
13: 3
17: 2, 2, 3, 6
18: 1 B[b]
25: 14, 15
26: 2, 55
31: 26
32: 28
33: 54
34: 14
36: 1+A
1, 4, 7
Deu. 18: 8
29: 18
Jos. 14: 1
19: 51
21: 1
22: 14, 14
32+A
2 Sa. 14: 7
1 Ki. 4: 6
1 Ch. 2: 55
4: 27, 38
5: 7 A[c]
13, 15
24, 24
6: 19, 19
48, 54
60, 61
62, 63

1 Ch. 6: 66, 70
71−A
7: 2, 4[d]
5, 7[e]
9, 11
40
8: 6, 10
13, 28
9: 9, 9, 13
33, 34
11: 20+A
25
12: 30
15: 12
16: 28[f]
23: 9, 11
24, 24
24: 3, 4, 4
6, 6, 30
31
31 A[g]
26: 13, 21
26, 31
32
27: 1
29: 6
2 Ch. 1: 2
5: 2
17: 14
23: 2
25: 5
31: 17
35: 4, 5, 5
12
Ezra 1: 5
2: 59, 68
3: 12
4: 2, 3
8: 1, 29
10: 16
Neh. 7: 61, 70
71
8: 13
10: 34
11: 13
12: 12, 22
23
Est. 9: 27
Psa. 21: 28
95: 7
106: 41
Jer. 2: 4
3: 14
25: 9
Eze. 45: 15

[a] AB πατρίς. [b] *pro* πατήρ.
[c] *pro* πατρίς. [d] AB πατρικός.
[e] B πατρικός. [f] S πατήρ.
[g] *pro* πατριάρχης.

πατριάρχης.

1 Ch. 24: 31[a]
27: 22
2 Ch. 19: 8
2 Ch. 23: 20
26: 12

[a] A πατριά.

πατρικός.

Gen. 50: 8
Lev. 22: 13
25: 41
Nu. 36: 8
Jos. 6: 25
1 Ch. 7: 4 AB[a]
7 B[a]
12: 28
26: 6

[a] *pro* πατριά.

πάτριος.

Isaiah 8: 21

πατρίς.

Lev. 25: 10 AB[a]
1 Ch. 5: 7[b]
Est. 2: 10, 20
4: 8+AS[3]
Est. 8: 6
Jer. 22: 10
26: 16−A
Eze. 23: 15

[a] *pro* πατριά. [b] A πατριά.

πατρῷος.

Ezra 7: 5 B[a]
Pro. 27: 10

[a] *pro* πρῶτος.

παῦσις.

Jeremiah 31: 2

παύω.

Gen. 11: 8
18: 33
24: 14, 18
22
27: 30
Exo. 9: 28, 29
33, 34
31: 17
32, 12
Nu. 16: 31
17: 10
25: 8
Deu. 20: 9
32: 26[a]
Jos. 7: 26
8: 24
Jud. 15: 17[b]
2 Sa. 15: 24
1 Ch. 21: 22
Est. 5: 1
Job 3: 17 A[c]
6: 7, 26
14: 13
18: 2
29: 9
32: 1
37: 18
Job 38: 1
Psa. 33: 14
36: 8
Pro. 18: 18
24: 24
Isa. 1: 16, 24
10: 25
16: 10
24: 8
8+ABS
8, 11, 13
26: 10
32: 10
33: 8
38: 20
57: 10
58: 12
Jer. 28: 63
31: 2
11 S[1 d]
32: 23
33: 3, 8, 13
19
38: 15[e], 36
36
50: 1
51: 10

[a] A καταπαύω. [b] A συντελέω.
[c] *pro* ἐκκαίω. [d] *pro* ἀναπαύω.
[e] AB* παρακαλέω.

πάχνη.

Job 38: 24, 29
Psa. 77: 47
Ps. 118: 83

πάχος.

Nu. 24: 8
1 Ki. 7: 3
9−A
11, 33
43
2 Ch. 4: 5, 17
Job 15: 26
Ps. 140: 7
Jer. 52: 21[a]

[a] S πλάτος.

παχύνω.

Deu. 32: 15
2 Sa. 22: 12
Ecc. 12: 3
Isa. 6: 10
34: 6

πηχύς.

1 Ki. 12: 10
p 24 l 65
2 Ch. 10: 10
Ps. 143: 14
Isa. 28: 1
Eze. 34: 3

πεδάω, −δέω.

Job 36: 8
Psa. 67: 7
68: 34
78: 11
89: 12 A[a]
Ps. 101: 21
106: 10
145: 7
Dan. 3: 20, 23
24

[a] *pro* παιδεύω.

πεδεινός *vide* πεδινός.

πέδη.

Jud. 16: 21
2 Sa. 3: 34
2 Ki. 25: 7
2 Ch. 33: 11
2 Ch. 36: 6
Ps. 104: 18
149: 8
Jer. 52: 11

πέδιλον.

Hab. 3: 5 A[a] [a] *pro* πεδίον.

πεδινός, πεδεινός.

Deu. 4: 43
11: 11
Jos. 9: 1
10: 40
11: 16
16 A[a]
15: 33
Jud. 1: 9
1 Ki. 10, 27
1 Ch. 27: 28
2 Ch. 1: 15
9: 27
26: 10
28: 18
Isa. 13: 2
32: 19
Jer. 17: 26
21: 13
31: 8
Zec. 7: 7

[a] *pro* ταπεινός.

πεδίον.

Gen. 4: 8, 8
11: 2
14: 17
24: 63, 65
25: 29
27: 3, 5
29: 2
31: 4
34: 5, 7, 28
35: 27
36: 35
37: 7, 15
41: 48
Exo. 1: 14
9: 3, 19
19, 21
25, 25
10: 15
16: 25
22: 6
Lev. 14: 7, 53
17: 5
25: 12
26: 4
Nu. 19: 16
21: 20
22: 4, 23
Deu. 1: 7
8: 7
21: 1
22: 25
28: 38
Jos. 5: 10
8: 24
11: 2, 8, 17
12: 7, 8
17: 5
20: 8
Jud. 9: 42 A[a]
1 Sa. 14: 14
20: 5
2 Sa. 17: 8−A
1 Ki. 11: 29
16: 4
18: 5 A[b]
20: 24
1 Ch. 1: 46
6: 56
8: 8
19: 9
2 Ch. 26: 23
35: 22
Neh. 6: 2
Job 39: 10, 21[c]
21
42 p 18
Psa. 8: 8
64: 12
77: 12, 43
95: 12
103: 8, 16[1]
131: 6[e]
Pro. 27: 24, 24
Cant. 2: 1
Isa. 10: 8
40: 4−AS[2]
41: 18
63: 14
Jer. 9: 22
14: 18
30: 4
Eze. 3: 22, 23[f]
7: 15
8: 4
16: 5
17: 5, 8
24[g]
26: 6, 8, 10
29: 5
31: 4, 5, 6
12, 15
32: 4
33: 27
34: 8[g], 27
35: 8
37: 1, 2
38: 20
39: 4, 5, 10
17[g]
Dan. 3: 1
Hos. 12: 12
Joel 1: 10, 20

Joel 2 : 3, 22 | Obad. 19
22 | Mic. 4:10
3:19 | Hab. 3: 5b, 17
Amos 1: 5 | Zec. 12:11

a pro ἀγρός. b pro γῆ.
c S² ποῦς. d S¹ κύριος.
e AS¹ δασος. f A παιδίον.
g A ἀγρός. h A πέδιλον.

πεζός.

Exo. 12:37 | 2 Sa. 15:17
Nu. 11:21 | 1 Ki. 21:10, 29
Jud. 5:15+A | 2 Ki. 13: 7
20: 2 | 1 Ch. 18: 4–BS
2 Sa. 8: 4 | 19:18
10: 6

πείθω.

Lev. 25:18, 19 | Pro. 28:1, 25, 26
Deu. 28:52 | 29:25, 25
33:12, 28 | Isa. 8:14, 17
Jud. 8:11 | 10:20, 20
9:15 Aa | 12: 2
26 Ab | 14: 6
18:10 Ac | 17: 7, 8
27 | 8+S
Ruth 2:12 | 20: 5, 6
1 Sa. 12:11 | 22:24
24: 8 | 28:17
2 Sa. 22: 3, 31 | 30: 3, 12
1 Ki. (3) p 16 | 15, 32
4(25) A | 31: 1, 1
2 Ki. 18:19, 20 | 32: 3, 11
21, 21 | 17, 18
22 | 19
19:10 | 33: 2
2 Ch. 14:11 | 36: 4, 5, 6
16: 7, 7, 8 | 6, 7, 9
32:10, 15 | 37:10
Est. 4: 4d | 42:17
Job 6:13, 20 | 47: 8
11:18 | 50:10
12: 6 | 58:14
27: 8 | 59: 4
31:24, 24 | Jer. 5:17
39:11 | 7: 4, 8, 14
40:18 | 9: 4
Psa. 2:13 | 12: 5
10: 1 | 17: 7
24: 2 | 23: 6
48: 7 | 26:25
56: 2 | 27:38+A
96: 7 S¹e | 29:12
113:16 | 30: 4
117: 8, 8 | 31: 7, 11
121: 1 | 13
134:18 | 35:15
145: 3 | 36: 8 Sf
Pro. 3: 5, 23 | 31
29 | 39:37
10: 9 | 46:18
11:28 | Eze. 33:13
14:16, 32 | Dan. 3:28
16:20 | Amos 6: 1
21:22 | Hab. 2:18
26:25 | Zeph. 3: 2g

a pro ὑφίστημι. b pro ἐλπίζω.
c pro ἐλπίς. d AS³ τίθημι.
e pro προσκυνέω.
f pro ἀναπείθω. g S¹ ἐπιποθέω.

πεινάω, –νέω.

Gen. 41:55 | Pro. 25:21
Deu. 25:18 | 28:15
Jud. 8: 4, 5Aa | Isa. 5:27–A
1 Sa. 2: 5b | 8:21
2 Sa. 17:29 | 9:20
2 Ki. 7:12 | 28:12
Job 22: 7 | 32: 6
24:10 | 6 S¹c
Psa. 33:11 | 40:28, 29
49:12 | 30, 31
106: 5, 9, 36 | 44:12
145: 7 | 46: 2
Pro. 6:30 | 49:10
18: 8 | 58: 7, 10
19:15 | 65:13

Jer. 38:12, 25 | Eze. 18: 7, 16
40:14–S¹

a pro ἐκλείπω. b B ἀσθενέω.
c pro διψάω.

πεῖρα.

Deu. 28:56 | Deu. 33: 8

πειράζω.

Gen. 22: 1 | 1 Sa. 17:39
Exo. 15:25 | 1 Ki. 10: 1
16: 4 | 2 Ch. 9: 1
17: 2, 7 | 32:31
20:20 | Psa. 25: 2–S¹
Nu. 14:22 | 34:16
Deu. 4:34 | 77:41, 56
8: 2a | 94: 9
13: 3 | 105:14
33: 8 | Ecc. 2: 1
Jud. 2:22 | 7:24
3: 1, 4 | Isa. 7:12
6:39 | Dan. 1:12, 14

a B ἐκπειράζω.

πειρασμός.

Exo. 17: 7 | Ecc. 3:10 Aa
Deu. 4:34 | 4: 8 Ab
6:16 | 8 Aa
7:19 | 5: 2
9:22 | 13 Sa
29: 3 | 8:10 Aa
Psa. 94: 8

a pro περισπασμός.
b pro περασμός.

πειρατεύω.

Genesis 49:19, 19

πειρατήριον.

Gen. 49:19 | Job 16: 9 Aa
Job 7: 1 | 19:12
10:17 | Psa. 17:30

a pro πειρατής.

πειρατής.

Job 16: 9a | Hos. 6: 9
25: 3

a A πειρατήριον.

πειράω.

Pro. 26:18 S²a a pro ἰάομαι.

πέλας.

Proverbs 27: 2

πέλειος.

Pro. 23:29 AS¹a a pro πελιδνός

πελεκάν.

Lev. 11:18 | Ps. 101: 7
Deu. 14:17

πελεκάω.

1 Kings 6: 3

πελεκητός.

1 Ki. 10:11, 12a | 1 Ki. 10:22–A
12 Bb

a A ἀπελέκητος.
b pro ἀπελέκητος.

πέλεκυς.

1 Ki. 6:11 | Jer. 22: 7
Psa. 73: 6 | 23:20 Aa

a pro πέλυξ.

πελιδνός.

Proverbs 23:29a a AS¹ πέλειος.

πελιόω.

Lamentations 5:10

πελταστής.

2 Ch. 14: 8 | 2 Ch. 17:17

πέλτη.

Eze. 23:24 | Eze. 38: 4, 5
27:10 | 39: 9

πέλυξ.

Jer. 23:20a | Eze. 9: 2

a A πέλεκυς.

πέμμα.

Eze. 45:24 ter | Eze. 46:11, 11
46: 5, 5, 7 | Hos. 3: 1
7, 7, 11

πέμπτος.

Lev. 6: 5 A¹Ba | 1 Ch. 26: 4–B
Jud. 19: 8b | Neh. 6: 5+S³
1 Ch. 26: 3–B

a pro ἐπίπεμπτος. b A τρίτος.

πέμπω.

Gen. 27:42 | Ezra 5:17
1 Sa. 28:24 Aa | Neh. 2: 5
Ezra 4:14 | Est. 8: 5

a pro πέπτω.

πενέω.

1 Ch. 11: 2 S²a a pro ποιμαίνω.

πένης.

Exo. 23: 3, 6 | Ps. 108:31
Lev. 14:21 | 111: 9
Deu. 15:11 | 112: 7
24:16, 17 | 139:13
1 Sa. 2: 8 | Pro. 14:21, 31
2 Sa. 12: 1, 3, 4 | 22:16, 22
Job 34:28 | 23: 4
Psa. 9:10, 13 | 24:37, 77
19, 29 | 28:11
31, 33 | 29:38
38 | Ecc. 4:13, 14
10: 4 | 5: 7
11: 6 | 6: 8
21:27 | 9:15, 15
34:10 | 16
36:14 | Isa. 10: 2
39:18 | Jer. 20:13
40: 1 | 22:16
48: 3 | Eze. 16:49
68:34 | 18:12
69: 6 | 22:29
71: 4, 12 | Dan. 4:24
13, 13 | Amos 2: 6
73:19, 21 | 4: 1
81: 3, 4 | 5:12
85: 1 | 8: 4, 6a
106:41 | Zec. 7:10
108:16, 22

a AB ταπεινός.

πενθερά.

Deu. 27:23 Aa | Ruth 2:21
Ruth 1:14 | 3: 1, 1b, 6
2:11, 18 | 16, 17
19, 19 | Mic. 7: 6

a pro νύμφη. b A νύμφη.

πενθερός.

Gen. 38:13, 25 | 1 Sa. 4:19, 21
Jud. 1:16 Aa | 22+A

a pro γαμβρός.

πενθέω.

Gen. 23: 2 | Gen. 37:34, 35
Gen. 50: 3 | Isa. 33: 9
Nu. 14:39 | 61: 2, 3, 3
1 Sa. 6:19 | 66:10
15:35 | Jer. 4:28
16: 1 | 12: 4
2 Sa. 13:37 | 14: 2
14: 2, 2 | 16: 5
19: 1 | 23:10
1 Ch. 7:22 | 38:21
2 Ch. 35:24 | Lam. 1: 4
Ezra 10: 6 | 2: 8
Neh. 1: 4 | Eze. 7:27+A
8: 9 | 31:15
Job 14:22 | Dan. 10: 2
Psa. 34:14 | Hos. 4: 3
77:63 | 10: 5
Isa. 3:26 | Joel 1: 9, 10
16: 8 | Amos 1: 2
19: 8 | 8: 8
24: 4, 4, 7 | 9: 5
7

πενθικός.

Exo. 33: 4 | 2 Sa. 14: 2

πένθος.

Gen. 27:41 | Ecc. 7: 3, 5
35: 8 | Isa. 16: 3
50: 4, 10 | 17:14
11 ter | 60:20
Deu. 34: 8 | Jer. 6:26
2 Sa. 11:27 | 16: 7
19: 2 | 38:13
Est. 4: 3 | Lam. 5:15
9:22–S | Eze. 24:17
Job 30:31a | Hos. 9: 4
Pro. 10: 6 | Amos 5:16
14:13 | 8:10, 10
Ecc. 5:16 | Mic. 1: 8

a BS παθος.

πενία.

Job 36: 8 | Pro. 24:31a, 49
Pro. 6:11 | 75
10: 4, 15 | 28:19
13:18

a A παιδεία.

πενιχρός.

Exo. 22:25 | Pro. 29: 7
Pro. 28:15

πένομαι.

Exo. 30:15 | Deu. 24:14
Lev. 25:25, 35 | Pro. 24:32

πενταετής.

Leviticus 27: 5, 6

πεντάκις.

1 Ki. 22:16 B¹a | 2 Ki. 13:19

a pro ποσάκις.

πεντακόσιοι.

Exo. 39: 7a | 2 Ch. 29:33+B*

a A 2400 pro 1500.

πεντάπηχυς.

1 Chronicles 11:23

πενταπλασίως.

Genesis 43:33

πενταπλοῦς.

1 Kings 6:29+A

πέντε.

Nu. 4: 3–A | Nu. 26:50+A
7:35¹–A | 31:32a

Deu. 10:22+A
1 Sa. 6: 4+A
1 Ki. 6: 6[b]
10[c]
22−B
7: 4−B
9+A
25²−B
40+A
1 Ki. 16 p 28−A
2 Ki. 7:13[d]
2 Ch. 28: 1−AB
Neh. 7:13−ABS
20[e]
Eze. 8:16+A
40:14+A
42: 1[f]

[a] A πεντακισχίλιοι.
[b] A 30 *pro* 25. [c] A ἕξ.
[d] A πᾶς. [e] A τέσσαρες.
[f] A δεκαπεντε.

πεντεκαίδεκα.

Exo. 37:12−B
Exo. 37:13[a]

[a] B ἑκατὸν πεντήκοντα.

πεντεκαιδέκατος.

Nu. 28:17−A
Est. 9:19+AS
Eze. 20: 1[a]

[a] A πέμπτῳ μηνὶ, δεκάτῃ.

πεντήκοντα.

Exo. 30:23²−A¹
Nu. 26:38[a]
1 Ki. 7:43²[b]
10:29−A
18:19+A
2 Ki. 1:13²−B
14+A
2 Ki. 6:25+A
1 Ch. 8:40[c]
Neh. 7:10[d]
Eze. 40:15[e]
48:17²−A
17³−A
17⁴−A

[a] A ἑξήκοντα. [b] A τριάκοντα.
[c] A ἐνενήκοντα. [d] A ἑβδομήκοντα
[e] A ὀκτώ.

πεντηκονταέξ.

Neh. 7:26−B
Neh. 7:33+AS

πεντηκονταέτης.

Nu. 4:23, 30
35, 39
Nu. 4:43, 47
8:25

πεντηκονταπέντα.

2 Ch. 33: 1[a] [a] A πεντήκοντα.

πεντηκόνταρχος.

Exo. 18:21, 25
Deu. 1:15−B
2 Ki. 1: 9, 9, 10
11, 11
2 Ki. 1:13+A
13, 14
Isa. 3: 3

πεντηκοστός.

Lev. 25:10, 11
2 Ki. 15:23, 27

πέπειρος.

Genesis 40:10

πεποίθησις.

2 Kings 18:19

πεποιθότως.

Zechariah 14:11−S¹

πέπτω.

Gen. 19: 3
Exo. 12:39
Lev. 2: 4
6:17
23:17
Lev. 26:26
1 Sa. 28:24[a]
Isa. 44:15, 16
19
Eze. 46:20

[a] A πέμπω.

πέπων.

Numbers 11: 5

πέρα.

Ezra 7:21, 25
Psa. 2: 8 A[a]
Psa. 21:28 A[a]

[a] *pro* πέρας.

περαίνω.

1 Sa. 12:21
Hab. 2: 5

πέραν.

Gen. 50:10, 11
Nu. 21:11, 13
27:12
32:19, 19
32
33:44
34:15
35:14
Deu. 1: 1, 5
3: 8, 20
25
4:41, 46
47, 49
11:30
30:13, 13
31: 4
Jos. 1:15
2:10
5: 1
10−A
9: 1, 10
12: 1, 7
13: 8, 14
27, 32
32
14: 3
17: 5
18: 7
20: 8
21:36
22: 4
7−A
11
24: 2, 3, 8
14, 15
Jud. 5:17
Jud. 7:25
10: 8
11:18, 20
1 Sa. 13:23
14: 1
26:13
30:10
31: 7−A
7
2 Sa. 10:16
1 Ki. (3) p 16*bis*
4:24
24+A
7:16+A
10:15
14:15 A
1 Ch. 6:78
12:37
19:16
26:30
2 Ch. 20: 2
Ezra 4:10, 11
17, 20[a]
5: 3, 6, 6
6: 6, 6, 8
13
8:36
Neh. 2: 7
9
3: 7−ABS
Isa. 7:20
9: 1
Jer. 30:10[b]
32: 8
48:10
52: 8

[a] AB ἑσπέρα. [b] A μέρος.

πέρας.

2 Sa. 16:13 B[a]
Job 28: 3
Psa. 2: 8[b]
7: 7
18: 5
21:28[b]
38: 5
45:10
47:11
58:14
60: 3
64: 6, 9[c]
66: 8
68:35 S¹[d]
71: 8
94: 4
97: 3
118:96
144: 3
Jer. 18: 7, 9
22:20
28:13
Eze. 7: 2, 2, 6
3, 10
21:25, 29
30: 3
Dan. 4: 8, 19
7:28
8:17, 19
11:27, 35
40
12: 6, 9
Amos 8: 2
Nah. 2: 9
3: 3, 9
Hab. 2: 3
Zeph. 3:10

[a] *pro* πλευρά. [b] A πέρα.
[c] S¹ γῆ. [d] *pro* ἕρπω.

περασμός.

Ecc. 4: 8[a], 16
Ecc. 12:12

[a] A πειρασμός.

περάτης.

Genesis 14:13

πέρδιξ.

Jeremiah 17:11

περιάγω.

Isa. 28:27
Eze. 37: 2
46:21
Eze. 47: 2
Amos 2:10

περιαιρέω.

Gen. 38:14, 19[a]
41:42
Exo. 8: 8, 11
31
Exo. 10:17
32: 2, 3, 24
33: 6
34:34
Lev. 3: 4, 9, 10
15
4: 8, 9, 10
31, 31
35, 35
6:34
Nu. 17: 5
30:13 *ter*
14, 16
16
Deu. 7:15
21:13
Jos. 24:14, 23
1 Sa. 1:14
1 Sa. 7: 3, 4
28: 3
2 Sa. 3:10
14:20 A[b]
1 Ch. 21: 8
2 Ch. 32:12
33:15
34:33
Est. 3:10
Ps. 118:22, 39
43
Pro. 4:24
27:22
Jer. 4: 1
4 AS¹[c]
Jon. 3: 6
Zeph. 3:11, 15
Zec. 10:11

[a] A περιβάλλω. [b] *pro* περιέρχομαι. [c] *pro* περιτέμνω.

περιαργυρόω.

Exo. 27:11
37:15, 15
17
17+AB
Exo. 37:18−AB
38:18, 20
Psa. 67:14
Isa. 30:22

περιβάλλω.

Gen. 24:65
28:20
38:14
19 A[a]
Lev. 13:45
Deu. 22:12
Jud. 4:18[b]
19[b]
Ruth 3: 9
1 Sa. 28: 8
1 Ki. 1: 1
11:29
12 p 24 l 53
20:16
27−A
2 Ki. 8:15
19: 1, 2
1 Ch. 21:16
2 Ch. 28:15
Est. 5: 1
6: 8
Job 23: 9
24: 8
Psa. 44:10, 14
47:13 B¹[c]
Psa. 70:13
72: 6
108:19, 29
146: 8
Pro. 28: 4
29: 5
Ecc. 4: 5[d]
Cant. 1: 7
Isa. 4: 1
37: 1, 2
58: 7
59: 6, 17
Jer. 4:30
Lam. 4: 5[e]
Eze. 4: 2
16:10, 18
18: 7, 16
27: 7
32: 3
34: 3
Jon. 3: 6, 8
Mic. 7:10
Hag. 1: 6
Zec. 3: 5

[a] *pro* περιαιρέω. [b] A συγκαλύπτω. [c] *pro* περιλαμβάνω.
[d] AS περιλαμβάνω.
[e] A περιλαμβάνω.

περιβιόω.

Exodus 22:18 A[a]

[a] *pro* περιποιέω.

περίβλεπτος.

Proverbs 29:41

περιβλέπω.

Gen. 19:17
Exo. 2:12
Jos. 8:20
1 Ki. 21:40
Job 7: 8

περίβλημα.

Numbers 31:20

περιβόλαιον.

Exo. 22:27
Deu. 22:12
Jud. 8:26 A[a]
Job 26: 6
Ps. 101:27
103: 6
Isa. 50: 3
59:17
Jer. 15:12
Eze. 13:21 A[b]
16:13
27: 7

[a] *pro* ἱμάτιον.
[b] *pro* ἐπιβόλαιον.

περιβολή.

Genesis 49:11

περίβολος.

Isa. 54:12
Eze. 40: 5
Eze. 42:20

περιβώμιος.

2 Chronicles 34: 3−AB

περιγίνομαι.

1 Chronicles 28:19

περίγλυφος.

1 Kings 6:27+A

περιδειπνέω, −νίζω.

2 Samuel 3:35

περιδέξιον.

Exo. 35:22
Nu. 31:50
Isa. 3:20−S¹

περιδέω.

Job 12:18[a] [a] A περιζωννύω.

περίειμι.

Job 27: 3, 15
Job 31:21[a]

[a] AS πάρειμι.

περιέρχομαι.

Jos. 6: 7, 11
15
15:10
16: 6[a]
19: 13, 14
2 Sa. 14:20[b]
Job 1: 6+A
7
2: 9+AS²
Jer. 38:22
Eze. 3:15

[a] A παρέρχομαι. [b] A περιαιρέω.

περιέχω.

2 Sa. 22: 5
1 Ki. 6:15, 19
19, 20
26, 28
(32) A
32
2 Ch. 4: 3
5: 9 A[a]
Job 2: 9+A
30:18
Psa. 16: 9
17: 5
21:13, 17
31: 7
39:13
87:18
114: 3
Jer. 20: 5
Eze. 6:12
16:57

[a] *pro* ὑπερέχω.

περίζωμα.

Gen. 3: 7
Ruth 3:15
Pro. 29:42
Jer. 13: 1, 2, 4
6, 7
10, 11

περιζώννυμι, −νύω.

Exo. 12:11
Jud. 3:16
18:11 A[a]
16 A[b]
17+A
1 Sa. 2: 4, 18
17:39+A
25:13+A
13+A
2 Sa. 3:31
20: 8
8 AB[a]
21:16
1 Ki. 21:32
2 Ki. 1: 8
3:21
1 Ch. 15:27
Job 12:18 A[c]
Psa. 17:33, 40
Psa. 29:12
44: 4
64: 7, 13
92: 1
108:19[d]
Isa. 3:24
15: 3
32:11
Jer. 1:17
4: 8
6:26
30: 3
Lam. 2:10
Eze. 7:18
9:11 A[a]
27:31 A
44:18
Dan. 10: 5
Joel 1: 8, 13

[a] *pro* ζώννυμι.
[b] *pro* αναζώννυμι.
[c] *pro* περιδέω. [d] S¹ ζώννυμι.

περίθεμα.
Exo. 38:24 A[a]
Nu. 16:38, 39
Jud. 8:26—A
[a] pro παράθεμα.

περιΐστημι.
Jos. 6: 3
1 Sa. 4:15
2 Sa. 13:31

περικαθαίρω.
Deu. 18:10
Jos. 5: 4

περικαθαρίζω.
Lev. 19:23
Deu. 30: 6
Isa. 6: 7

περικάθαρμα.
Proverbs 21:18

περικάθημαι.
Jud. 9:31[a]
1 Ki. 15:27
2 Ki. 6:25
[a] A πολιορκέω.

περικαθίζω.
Deu. 20:12, 19
Jos. 10: 5, 31
34, 36
38
Jud. 9:50 A[a]
1 Ki. 15:27
16:17
21: 1, 1
2 Ki. 6:24
1 Ch. 20: 1
[a] pro παρεμβάλλω.

περικαλύπτω.
Exo. 28:20
Nu. 32:38 A[a]
1 Sa. 28: 8 A[b]
1 Ki. 7: 5, 28
8: 7
[a] pro περικυκλόω.
[b] pro συγκαλύπτω.

περικείρω.
Jer. 9:26
Jer. 32: 9

περικεφαλαία.
1 Sa. 17: 5, 38
49
2 Ch. 26:14
Isa. 59:17
Jer. 26: 4
Eze. 23:24+A
27:10
38: 4, 5

περικνημίς.
Daniel 3:21

περικοσμέω.
Psalm 143:12

περίκυκλος.
Exo. 28:29
Deu. 6:14
Jos. 19: 8 A[a]
Jud. 2:12
2 Ki. 6:17
17:15[b]
23: 5
Psa. 88: 8
Isa. 4: 5
Eze. 28:23, 24[c]
32:22, 24
26
34:26[c]
36: 4, 7
37:21
39:17
Dan. 9:16
[a] pro κύκλος. [b] A περικυκλόω.
[c] A κύκλος.

περικυκλόω.
Gen. 19: 4
Exo. 36:20
Nu. 21: 4
32:38[a]
Jos. 6:13—A
7: 9
Jud. 19:22 A[b]
20: 5 A[b]
2 Ki. 6:14
17:15 A[c]
2 Ch. 33:14+AB[a]
Job 30: 4
Psa. 16:11
17: 6
21:13
Pro. 26:28
Jer. 38:39
Jer. 52:21
[a] A περικαλύπτω.
[b] pro κυκλόω. [c] pro περίκυκλος

περιλαμβάνω.
Gen. 29:13
33: 4
48:10
Jud. 16:29
2 Ki. 4:16
Psa. 47:13[a]
Pro. 4: 8
Ecc. 3: 5
4: 5 AS[b]
Cant. 2: 6
8: 3
Isa. 31: 9
Lam. 4: 5 A[b]
[a] B[1] περιβάλλω.
[b] pro περιβάλλω.

περιλείπω.
2 Ch. 34:21 A[a]
Hag. 2: 3+S[2]
[a] pro καταλείπω.

περίλημμα.
Ecclesiastes 3: 5 AC[a]
[a] pro περίληψις.

περίληψις.
Ecclesiastes 3: 5[a]
[a] AC περίλημμα.

περίλοιπος.
Psa. 20:13
Amos 5:15

περίλυπος.
Gen. 4: 6
Psa. 41: 6, 12
Psa. 42: 5

περιμένω.
Genesis 49:18

περίμετρος.
1 Kings 7: 3

περιοδεύω.
2 Sa. 24: 8
Zec. 1:10, 11
Zec. 6: 7—S[1]
7, 7

περίοδος.
Joshua 6:16

περιοικοδομέω.
Job 19: 8
Jer. 52: 4
Eze. 26: 8
39:11

περίοικος.
Gen. 19:25 A[a]
29
Deu. 1: 7
Jud. 1:27[b]
27—A
Jud. 1:27—A
27—A
1 Ki. 7:33
Jer. 30: 5[c]
[a] pro περίχωρος.
[b] A περισπόρια. [c] A πάροικος.

περιονυχίζω.
Deuteronomy 21:12

περιουσιασμός.
Psa. 134: 4
Ecc. 2: 8

περιούσιος.
Exo. 19: 5
23:22
Deu. 7: 6
Deu. 14: 2
26:18

περιοχή.
1 Sa. 22: 4, 5
2 Sa. 5: 7, 9, 17
23:14
2 Ki. 19:24
2 Ki. 24:10
25: 2
1 Ch. 11: 5, 7, 16
2 Ch. 32:10
Psa. 30:22
59:11
107:11
140: 3
Jer. 19: 9
28:30
Eze. 4: 2
12:13
17:20
Obad. 1
Nah. 3:14
Zec. 12: 2

περιπατέω.
Gen. 3: 8, 10
Exo. 21:19
Jud. 21:24
1 Sa. 17:39
2 Sa. 11: 2
2 Ki. 20: 3
Est. 2:11
Job 9: 8
20:25
38:16
Psa. 11: 9
103: 3
Ps. 113:15
134·17+A
Pro. 6:22, 28
8:20
23:31
Ecc. 4:15
11: 9
Isa. 8: 7
59: 9
Dan. 3:23, 25
4:26

περίπατος.
Job 41:23
Pro. 23:31
Eze. 42: 4, 5, 10
11, 12

περιπιλέω.
1 Kings 6:19+A

περιπίπτω.
Ruth 2: 3
2 Sa. 1: 6
2 Sa. 5:23 A[a]
Pro. 11: 5—S[1]
[a] pro πάρειμι.

περιπλέκω.
2 Sa. 18: 9[a]
Psa. 49:19
118:61
Eze. 17: 7
Nah. 1:10
[a] AB κρεμάω.

περιποιέω.
Gen. 12:12
31:18
36: 6
Exo. 1:16
22:18[a]
32:14—A
Nu. 22:33
Jos. 6:17
9:26
Jud. 21:11—A
1 Sa. 15: 3, 9, 15
25:39
2 Sa. 12: 3
1 Ki. 18: 5
1 Ch. 29: 3
Job 27:17
Psa. 78:11
Pro. 6:32
7: 4
22: 9
Isa. 31: 5
43:21
Jer. 31:36
Eze. 13:18, 19
26: 8 A[b]
[a] A περιβιόω. [b] pro ποιέω.

περιποίησις.
2 Ch. 14:13
Hag. 2: 9
Mal. 3:17

περιπόλιος.
1 Ch. 6:71[a]
1 Ch. 6:71[b]
[a] A[2] περισπόρια. [b] A[2]B περισπόρια

περιπορεύω.
Jos. 15: 3 A[a]
[a] pro ἐκπορεύω.

περιπόρφυρος.
Isaiah 3:21

περίπτερος.
Cant. 8: 6, 6
Amos 3:15

περίπτωμα.
Ruth 2: 3
2 Sa. 1: 6

περιρραίνω, —ραντίζω.
Lev. 14: 7, 51
Nu. 8: 7
19:13, 18
Nu. 19:19, 20
21
Eze. 43:20+A

περισιαλόω.
Exodus 36:13

περισκελής.
Exo. 28:38
36:36
Lev. 6:10
Lev. 16: 4
Eze. 44:18

περισπασμός.
Ecc. 1:13
2:23, 26
3:10[a]
Ecc. 4: 8[a]
5:13[b]
8:16[a]
[a] A πειρασμός. [b] S πειρασμός.

περισπάω.
2 Sa. 6: 6
Ecc. 1:13
Ecc. 3:10
5:19

περισπόρια.
Jos. 21: 2—A
3, 8, 11
19+A
34, 34
35+A
35, 36
36, 37
37, 38
38, 39
39, 41
42
Jud. 1:18
27 A[a]
1 Ch. 6:55, 57
57, 57
58, 58
59, 59
59+A
60, 60
60+A
60
60+A
1 Ch. 6:64, 67
67
68, 68
69, 69
70
70—B
71 A[2 b]
71 A[2]B[b]
72 ter
73—B
74, 74
75, 75
76 ter
77+A
77+A
77, 77
78
78—B
79, 79
80, 80
81, 81
[a] pro περίοικος.
[b] pro περιπόλιος.

περίσσεια.
Ecc. 1: 3
2:11 S[a]
11, 13
13
3: 9
Ecc. 3:19 S[2 b]
5: 8, 15
6: 8
7:12, 13
10:10, 11
[a] pro προαίρεσις.
[b] pro περισσεύω.

περίσσευμα.
Ecclesiastes 2:15

περισσεύω.
1 Sa. 2:33, 36
Ecc. 3:19[a]
[a] S[2] περίσσεια.

περισσός.
Exo. 10: 5
Nu. 4:26
Jud. 21: 7—A
16[a]
1 Sa. 30: 9
10+B
1 Ki. 14:19 A
22:47 A
2 Ki. 25:11
Pro. 14:23
Ecc. 2:15
7: 1, 17
12: 9, 12
Eze. 48:15, 18
21, 23
Dan. 3:22
4:33
5:12, 14
6: 3
[a] A ἐπίλοιπος.

περισσῶς.
Psa. 30:24
Dan. 7: 7, 7, 19
Dan. 8: 9

περίστασις.
Eze. 26: 8[a]
[a] A βιλόστασις.

περιστέλλω.
Isa. 58: 8
Eze. 20: 5

περιστερά.
Gen. 8: 8,9,10, 11, 12; 15: 9
Lev. 1:14; 5: 7, 11; 12: 6, 8; 14:22, 30; 15:14, 29
Nu. 6:10
2 Ki. 6:25
Psa. 54: 7; 67:14
Cant. 1:15; 2:10, 13; 2:14; 4: 1; 5: 2, 12; 6: 8
Isa. 38:14; 59:11; 60: 8
Jer. 31:28
Eze. 7:16+A
Hos. 7:11; 11:11
Nah. 2: 7
Zeph. 3: 1

περιστήθιος.
Exodus 28: 4

περιστολή.
Exodus 33: 6

περιστόμιος.
Exo. 28:28, 28; 36:31, 31
Job 15:27; 30:18
Eze. 39:11

περιστρέφω.
Gen. 37: 7
Nu. 36: 7, 9

περίστυλος.
Eze. 40:17, 17, 18
Eze. 42: 3, 5, 5, 5

περισύρω.
Genesis 30:37

περισχίζω.
Eze. 47:15
Eze. 48: 1

περισώζω.
1 Sa. 30:17 A[a]
[a] pro σώζω.

περιτειχίζω.
Hosea 10:14

περίτειχος.
2 Ki. 25: 1
Isa. 26: 1
Dan. 9:25 A[a]
[a] pro τεῖχος.

περιτέμνω.
Gen. 17:10, 11, 12, 13, 14, 23, 24, 25, 26, 27+A; 21: 4; 34:15, 17, 22, 22, 24
Exo. 4:25
Exo. 12:44, 48
Lev. 12: 3
Deu. 10:16
Jos. 5: 2, 3, 5, 7, 8; 21:42; 24:31
Est. 8:17
Jer. 4: 4[a], 4; 9:25
[a] AS[1] περιαιρέω.

περιτίθημι.
Gen. 24:47; 27:16; 41:42, 42
Exo. 29: 9; 34:35; 40: 6
Lev. 8:13; 16: 4−A
Nu. 27: 7, 8
Ruth 3: 3
Est. 1:11, 20; 5:11
Job 4: 4; 13:26; 31:36; 38:10; 39:19, 20; 40:20
Pro. 7: 3; 12: 9
Isa. 5: 2; 49:18; 59:17; 61:10
Jer. 13: 1, 2; 28: 3
Jer. 34: 1
Eze. 16:11; 27: 3, 4, 7
Dan. 5:29
Hos. 2:13

περιτομή.
Gen. 17:13
Exo. 4:25
Exo. 4:26−B
Jer. 11:16

περιτρέχω.
Jer. 5: 1
Amos 8:12

περιφέρεια.
Ecc. 9: 3
Ecc. 10:13

περιφερής.
Ezekiel 41:10

περιφέρω.
Jos. 24:33
Pro. 10:24
Ecc. 7: 7

περιφορά.
Ecc. 2: 2, 12 AS[a]
Ecc. 7:26[b]
[a] pro παραφορά. [b] A παραφορά.

περιφράσσω.
1 Ki. 10 p 22
Job 1:10

περιχαλκόω.
Exodus 27: 6

περιχαρακόω.
Pro. 4: 8
Jer. 52: 4

περιχαρής.
Job 3:22
Job 29:22

περιχέω, −χύω.
2 Ch. 29:22−B
Jon. 2: 6

περιχρυσόω.
1 Ki. 10:18
Isa. 30:22
Isa. 40:19

περίχωρος.
Gen. 13:10, 11, 12; 19:17, 25[a], 28
Deu. 3: 4, 13, 14; 34: 3
1 Ch. 5:16
2 Ch. 4:17; 16: 4
Neh. 3: 9, 12, 14, 16, 17, 17, 18; 12:28
Est. 9:12[b]
[a] A περίοικος. [b] A χώρα.

περκάζω.
Amos 9:13

πέσσω.
Exo. 16:23, 23
1 Sa. 8:13[a]
Jer. 44:21
[a] A παίω.

πέταλον.
Exo. 28:32; 29: 6; 36:10, 38
Lev. 8: 9
1 Ki. 6(18)A, (32)A, 32

πεταλόω.
1 Kings 6(22)A

πέταμαι vide **πέτομαι**

πετάννυμι.
Job 26:11[a]
[a] A ἐφίστημι.

πέταυρον.
Proverbs 9:18

πετεινός.
Gen. 1:20, 21, 22, 26, 28, 30; 2:19, 20; 6: 7, 20; 7: 3, 3, 8, 8, 14, 21, 23; 8: 1, 17, 19, 20; 9: 2[a]; 40:17
Lev. 1:14; 7:16; 11:13, 20, 21, 23, 46; 17:13; 20:25, 25
Deu. 14:18, 19; 28:26
1 Sa. 17:44, 46
2 Sa. 21:10
1 Ki. 4:29; 12 p 24 l 44; 14:11 A; 16: 4; 20:24
Job 12: 7; 28: 7, 21; 35:11
Psa. 8: 9
Psa. 49:11; 77:27; 78: 2; 103:12; 148:10
Ecc. 10:20
Isa. 16: 2; 18: 6, 6; 46:11
Jer. 4:25; 5:27; 7:33; 9:10; 12: 4; 15: 3; 16: 4; 19: 7; 41:20
Eze. 17:23; 29: 5; 31: 6, 13; 32: 4; 34: 5+A; 38:20; 39: 4, 17; 44:31
Dan. 2:38; 7: 6
Hos. 2:12, 18; 4: 3; 7:12
Zeph. 1: 3
[a] A ὄρνεον.

πέτομαι, πέταμαι.
Gen. 1:20
Deu. 4:17
2 Sa. 22:11
Job 5: 7; 9:26
Psa. 17:11, 11; 54: 7; 90: 5
Pro. 9:12−S; 24:54; 26: 2
Isa. 6: 2; 11:14; 14:29; 30: 6; 31: 5; 60: 8
Eze. 32:10
Dan. 9:21
Hab. 1: 8
Zec. 5: 1, 2

πέτρα.
Exo. 17: 6, 6; 33:21, 22
Nu. 20: 8, 8, 10, 10, 11; 24:21
Deu. 8:15; 32:13, 13
Jos. 5: 2
Jud. 1:36; 6:20, 21; 13:19; 15: 8[a], 11, 13; 20:45, 47, 47; 21:13
1 Sa. 13: 6; 14: 4+B, 4, 4; 23:25, 28
2 Sa. 21:10; 22: 2
1 Ki. 19:11
2 Ki. 14: 7
1 Ch. 11:15
2 Ch. 26: 7
Neh. 9:15
Job 14: 8, 18; 19:24; 22:24, 24−AS[1]; 24: 8−S[1]; 30: 6; 39: 1, 28; 40:13 A[b]
Psa. 26: 5; 39: 3; 60: 3; 77:15, 16, 20; 80:17; 103:12, 18; 104:41; 113: 8; 136: 9; 140: 6
Pro. 24:54, 61
Cant. 2:14
Isa. 2:10, 19, 21, 21; 5:28; 7:19; 8:14; 16: 1; 22:16; 31: 9; 33:16; 42:11; 48:21, 21; 50: 7; 51: 1; 57: 5
Jer. 4:29−S[1]
Jer. 5: 3; 13: 4; 16:16; 18:14; 23:29; 28:25; 29:17; 31:28, 28
Eze. 3: 9
Amos 6:12
Obad. 3
Nah. 1: 6
Hab. 2: 1
[a] A σπήλαιον. [b] pro πλευρά.

πέτρινος.
Jos. 5: 2−A, 3
Jos. 21:42; 24:31

πετροβόλος.
1 Sa. 14:14−B
Job 41:19
Eze. 13:11, 13

πεύκη.
1 Ki. 5:10−B
Isa. 60:13

πεύκινος.
1 Ki. 5: 8; 6:15, 31; 9:11−A
2 Ch. 2: 8; 9:10, 11

πέψις.
Hosea 7: 4

πηγή.
Gen. 2: 6; 7:11; 8: 2; 14: 7; 16: 7, 7; 24:13, 16, 29, 30, 42, 43, 45
Exo. 15:27
Lev. 11:36; 12: 7; 20.18
Nu. 33: 9; 34:11
Deu. 8: 7, 15; 33:13
Jos. 15: 7, 7, 9; 17: 7[a]; 18:15, 16, 17; 19:29−A, 37; 21:29
Jud. 7: 1[a]; 15:19[b]
2 Sa. 17:17
1 Ki. 1: 9+A; 18: 5
2 Ki. 3:19, 25
2 Ch. 32: 3, 4
Neh. 2:13; 3:15−ABS
Job 38:16[c]
Psa. 17:16; 35:10; 41: 2; 67:27; 73:15; 103:10; 113: 8
Pro. 4:21; 5:15, 16, 18; 6:11; 8:24, 28; 9:18; 10:11; 13:14; 14:27; 16:22; 18: 4; 25:26
Ecc. 12: 6[d]
Cant. 4:12, 15
Isa. 12: 3; 35: 7; 41:18; 49:10; 58:11
Jer. 2:13; 9: 1; 17:13; 28:36[e]
Eze. 25: 9−B
Hos. 13:15
Joel 3:18
[a] A τὴν γῆν. [b] A πληγή. [c] AC γῆ. [d] S τὴν γῆν. [e] AS γῆ.

πῆγμα.
Joshua 3:16

πήγνυμι, πηγνύω.
Gen. 26:25; 31:25; 35:16
Exo. 15: 8, 8; 33: 7; 38:26
Nu. 24: 6
Jos. 18: 1
Jud. 4:11, 21[a]; 16:14[b]
2 Sa. 6:17; 16:22; 21:10
1 Ch. 16: 1

2 Ch. 1: 4—AB
Ezra 6:11 A[c]
Job 6:16
10:10 A[d]
38: 6
41:15
Psa. 31: 4 A[e]
Isa. 38:12
42: 5[f]
54: 2
Jer. 6: 3
Lam. 4: 8
Dan. 11:45

[a] A τίθημι. [b] A κατακρούω. [c] pro πλήσσω. [d] pro τυρόω. [e] pro ἐμπήγνυμι. [f] A[1] ? γῆν.

πηδάω.

Lev. 11:21
Cant. 2: 8

πηλίκος.

Zechariah 2: 2, 2

πήλινος.

Job 4:19
Job 13:12

πηλός.

Gen. 11: 3
Exo. 1:14
2 Sa. 22:43
Job 4:19
10: 9
27:16
30:19
33: 6
6+ AC[2]S[2]
38:14
41:21
Psa. 17:43
Psa. 39: 3
68:15
Isa. 14:23
29:16
41:25, 25
45: 9, 9
64: 8
Jer. 18: 6
Mic. 7:10
Nah. 3:14[a]
Zec. 9: 3
10: 5

[a] S πόλεμος.

πηρόω.

Job 17: 7 AS[2a]

[a] pro πωρόω.

πῆχυς.

Gen. 6:15 ter
16
7:20
Exo. 25: 9 ter
16, 16
22 ter
26: 2
2—A[1]
8, 9, 13
13, 16
16
27: 1 ter
9, 11
12, 13
14, 15
16, 18
30: 2 ter
37: 2, 2
10—A[2]
11
12—B
13
16, 16
38: 1+A
1+A
1+A
Nu. 35: 4, 5, 5
5, 5
Deu. 3:11 ter
Jos. 3: 4
1 Sa. 17: 4
1 Ki. 6: 6 ter
7
7+A
10 ter
14, 16
17, 19
19, 19
21, 22
22-8, 22
23+A
24
7: 3, 3, 4
1 Ki. 7: 4—B
8, 10
10, 10
11, 13
13, 13
17+A
17+A
17+A
18
18+A
21
24—B
30, 30
30—B
43+A
2 Ki. 14:13
25:17, 17
2 Ch. 3: 3
3—A[2]
3, 4
4—A[1]
8, 8, 11
11, 11
12 A
12 A
13, 15
15
4: 1, 1
1—A
2 ter
3
6:13 ter
25:23
Ezra 6: 3
3—B
Neh. 3:13
Est. 5:14
7: 9
Pro. 20:37
Jer. 52:21, 21
22 ter
Eze. 40 passim
12+A
Eze. 40:12+A
27+A
30 A
30 A
41 passim
42: 2
2+A
4, 4, 7
8, 8, 17
20
43:13, 13
Eze. 43:13+A
13, 13
14 qtr
15, 15
16, 16
17 qtr
45: 2
46:22, 22
Dan. 3: 1, 1
Zec. 5: 2, 2

πιάζω.

Canticles 2:15

πιαίνω.

Psa. 19: 4
64:13
Pro. 16: 1
Isa. 58:11
11+AS[3]
Eze. 17: 8, 10

πιέζω.

Micah 6:15

πίθηκος.

1 Ki. 10:22+A
2 Ch. 9:21

πίθος.

Proverbs 23:27

πικραίνω.

Exo. 16:20
Ruth 1:13, 20
Job 27: 2[a]
Isa. 14: 9
Jer. 39:32[b]
40: 9—A
44:15
Lam. 1: 4

[a] A πικρόω. [b] AS παραπικραίνω.

πικρασμός.

Ezekiel 27:31 A

πικρία.

Exo. 15:23
Deu. 29:18
32:32
Ruth 1:20 A[a]
Job 3:20 7:11
9:18
10: 1
21:25
Psa. 9:28
13: 3—A
Isa. 28:21
21 AS[b]
28
37:29
38:16+S[2]
Jer. 2:21
15:17
Lam. 3:15, 20
Eze. 28:24
Amos 6:12

[a] pro πικρός. [b] pro σαπρία.

πικρίς.

Exo. 12: 8
Nu. 9:11

πικρός.

Gen. 27:34
Exo. 15:23
Jud. 18:25
Ruth 1:20[a]
1 Sa. 15:32
2 Sa. 2:26
2 Ki. 14:26
Est. 4: 1+S[3]
Psa. 63: 4
Pro. 5: 4
27: 7
Ecc. 7:27
Isa. 5:20, 20
24: 9
Jer. 2:19
4:18
20: 8
23:15
Eze. 27:30, 31 A
Hab. 1: 6
Zeph. 1:14

[a] A πικρία.

πικρόω.

Job 27: 2 A[a]

[a] pro πικραίνω.

πικρῶς.

Isa. 22: 4
33: 7
Jer. 27:21

πίμπλημι, πλήθω.

Gen. 6:11, 13
21:19
Gen. 24:16
20:15
Gen. 44: 1
Exo. 2:16
8:21
10: 6
16:12, 32
40:28
29 AB[a]
Lev. 9:17
16:12
19:20[h]
Deu. 13:17+A
Jos. 9:19
1 Sa. 16: 1
1 Ki. 8:10, 11
18:35
21:27
2 Ki. 3:17, 20
4: 5
9:24
10:21
21:16
23:14
24: 4
2 Ch. 7: 1, 2
16:14[c]
36: 5[d]
Ezra 9:11[e]
Job 3:15
31:31[b]
Psa. 16:14
25:10
37: 8
64: 5, 12
79:10[f]
87: 4
103:28[d]
122: 3[g], 4[g]
125: 2
Pro. 1:13, 31
3:10
5:10
12:14, 21
14:14
15: 4
Pro. 18:20
20 S[a]
24:32, 57
25:16[h]
17
28:19, 19
Ecc. 1: 8[i]
5: 9
6: 3[i]
9: 5 AS[k]
11: 3[m]
Cant. 5: 2
Isa. 6: 4 AS[a]
13:21 A[a]
15: 9
22: 7[n]
27: 6 B[a]
40: 2
Jer. 6:11
19: 4
26:10 BS[a]
12
27:19[b]
28: 5 34
31: 5
51:17
Eze. 3: 3
8:17
9: 7[c], 9, 9
10: 2, 3, 4
4
23:33
28:16[o]
30:11
32: 4
43:26
Dan. 3:19
Joel 2:24[b]
Mic. 6:12[b]
Nah. 2:12
Hab. 2:14 S[2a]
Hag. 2: 7[c]
Zec. 8: 5
9:13, 15

[a] pro ἐμπίπλημι. [b] A ἐμπίπλημι. [c] A πληρόω. [d] B ἐμπίπλημι. [e] S[1] πλανάω. [f] S[2] πληρόω. [g] S πληθύνω. [h] S ἐμπίπλημι. [i] ACS ἐμπίπλημι. [k] pro ἐπιλανθάνω. [m] ACS πληρόω. [n] S[2] ἐμπίπλημι. [o] A πληθύνω.

πίνινος, πίννινος.

Esther 1: 6

πίνω.

Gen. 9:21
24:14 ter
18, 18
19, 22
44, 46
46, 54
25:34
26:30
27:25
30:38, 38
31:46+A
54
43:33
44: 5
Exo. 7:18, 21
24, 24
15:23, 23
24
17: 1, 2, 6
24:11
32: 6
34:28
Lev. 10: 9
11:34
Nu. 6: 3, 3, 20
20: 5, 11
17, 19
21:16, 22
23:24
33:14
Deu. 2: 6, 28
Deu. 9: 9, 18
11:11
28:39
29: 6
32:14, 38
Jud. 7: 5, 6
9:27[a]
13: 4, 7, 14
15:19
19: 4, 6
8+A
21
Ruth 2: 9
3: 3
7—B
1 Sa. 1: 9+A
11, 15
18
30:12
16—A
2 Sa. 11:11, 13
12: 3, 21
16: 2
19:35
23:16
16 A[b]
17, 17
1 Ki. 1:25
(3) p 46 bis
4(20) A
(25) A
1 Ki. 8:65
13: 8, 9, 16
17, 18
19, 22
22, 23
16: 9
17: 4, 6, 10
18:41, 42
19: 6, 8
21:12, 16
2 Ki. 3:17
6:22, 23
7: 8
9:34
18:27, 31
31
19:24
1 Ch. 11:18, 19
19
12:39—S
29:22
2 Ch. 31:10
Ezra 10: 6
Neh. 8:10, 12
Est. 1: 7
4:16
Job 1: 4, 13
18
8:12
12+A
15:16
34: 7
42:11
Psa. 40:13
68:13
74: 9
77:44
109: 7
Pro. 5:15
9: 5, 18
23: 7
24:72, 73
74
Ecc. 2:24, 25
3:12 S[1c]
13
5:17
8:15
9: 7
Cant. 5: 1, 1
Isa. 5:12, 22
7:22[d]
9: 1
19: 5
21: 5
22:13, 13
Isa. 23:18
24: 9, 9
25: 6, 6
29: 8, 8
36:12, 16
44:12
48:21
49:26
51:17
17 A[e]
22
55: 1 AS[f]
62: 8, 9
65:13
Jer. 2:18, 18
16: 8
22:15
28: 7
29:13, 13
13+A
13+A
32: 2—BS
13, 14
14, 14
42: 5, 6, 6
8, 14
14
Lam. 5: 4—AB
Eze. 4:11, 11
16
12:18, 19
23:32, 34
25: 4
31:14, 16
34:18, 19
39:17, 18
19
44:21
Dan. 1:12
5: 2, 2, 3
4, 23
Joel 1: 5
3: 3
Amos 2: 8
4: 1, 8
5:11
6: 6
9:14
Obad. 16, 16
16 BS[l]
Jon. 3: 7
Mic. 6:15
Hab. 2:16
Zeph. 1:13
Hag. 1: 6
Zec. 7: 6, 6

[a] B εἶπον. [b] pro σπένδω. [c] pro ποιέω. [d] ABS ποιέω. [e] pro ἐκπίνω. [f] pro φάγω.

πιότης.

Gen. 27:28, 39
Jud. 9: 9
1 Ki. 18: 3, 5
Job 36:16
Psa. 35: 9
62: 6
Psa. 64:12
103:28 A[a]
Pro. 15: +S[1b]
Eze. 25: 4
Zec. 4:14

[a] pro χρηστότης. [b] pro πνεῦμα.

πιπράσκω.

Gen. 31:15
Exo. 22: 3
Lev. 25:23, 34
39, 42
47, 48
27:27
Deu. 15:12
21:14
28:68
1 Sa. 23: 7
1 Ki. 20:20
1 Ki. 20:25+A
25
2 Ki. 17:17
Est. 7: 4
4+S[3]
Ps. 104 17
Isa. 48:10
50: 1, 1
52: 3
Jer. 41:14
Eze. 48:14

πίπτω.

Gen. 17: 3, 17
41:14
49:17
Exo. 9:19
19:21
23: 5

Exo. 32:28
Lev. 9:24
11:33
35AB[1][a]
26: 7,8,17
36
Nu. 14: 3,5,29
32, 42
43
16: 4, 22
45
20: 6
Deu. 2:16[b]
21: 1
22: 4, 8, 8
Jos. 5:14
6: 5, 20
7: 6, 10
8:25
11: 7 A[a]
17: 5
23.14
Jud. 3:25
4:16
22 A[c]
5:27
27−A
27
7:13, 13
8:10
9:40
12: 6
13:20
16:30
19:26, 27
20:22[d]
39[e], 44
46
Ruth 2:10
3:18
1 Sa. 2:33
3:19
4:10, 18
5: 3, 4, 4
14:45
17:49, 52
18:10 A
19:24
20:41
21:13
25:23
24+A
26:12 AB[h]
20
28:19, 20
31: 1, 5, 8
2 Sa. 1: 2, 4
7+A
10, 19
21+A
25, 27
2:16, 23
23
3:29, 34
38
4: 4
9: 6
11:17
14: 4, 11
22, 33
17:12
19:18
20: 8
21: 9, 22
22:39
1 Ki. 1:52
18: 7, 38
39
21:25, 30
22:20
2 Ki. 1: 2
2:13, 14
4:37[f]
6: 6
10:10[g]
14:10
1 Ch. 5:10, 22
10: 1
4 AS[a]
5, 8

1 Ch. 20: 8
21:14, 16
26:14
2 Ch. 6:13
7: 3
13:17
14:13
18:19
20:18, 24
25:19
29:30
Neh. 6:16 A[a]
Est. 3: 7
6:13, 13
7: 8+A
Job 1:16, 19
20
12: 5
14:10, 18
18 A[h]
15:24
16: 9
24:23
33:18, 24
Psa. 9:31
15: 6 S[a]
17:39
19: 9
26: 2
34: 8
35:13
36:24
44: 6
57: 9[i]
77:28 S[1][a]
64
81: 7
90: 7
117:13
139:11
140:10
Pro. 11:14, 28
23: 5 BS[1][j]
24:16, 17
25:26
29:16
Ecc. 4:10, 10
11: 3, 3
Isa. 2:17
3:25, 25
8:15
9:10
10: 4+AS[a]
34−A
34
13:15
16: 9
21: 9
9−AS
15
22:25
23:13
24:20, 23
25: 2
26:18−ABS[1]
18, 19
27: 3
28:13
30:13, 25
31: 8
34: 4, 4
37: 7
46: 1
49:19[k]
59:10
65:12
Jer. 6:15
8: 4
11:22 A[m]
16: 4
18: 4[n], 21
20: 4
23:12
26: 6, 12
16
27:15, 30
32
28: 4,8,10
52

Jer. 30:15
15−A
31:32 A[a]
32:13, 20
34:6+AS[1]
43: 7
44:20
46:18
49: 2
51:12
Lam. 1: 7
5:16
Eze. 2: 1
3:23
5:12
6: 7, 11
12[o]
9: 8
11: 5, 10
13
13:10−A
11, 11
12, 14
14, 15
17:21
22:28
23: 3
21+A
24: 6[p], 21
25:13
26: 6 A[q]
27:27, 35
28:23
29: 5
30: 4 A[r]
5, 6, 6

Eze. 30:17, 25
31:12
32:19, 22
23+A
24:27
33:27
35: 8
38: 9 A[s]
20, 20
39: 4,5,23
43: 3
44: 4
47:14
Dan. 2:46
3: 5
6−AB
7, 11
15, 23
8:10, 17
18
11:19, 26
Hos. 7: 7, 16
10: 8
14:1
Joel 2: 8
Amos 3: 5, 14
5: 2
7:17
8: 3, 14
9: 9, 11
11
Jon. 1: 7
Mic. 5: 7
7: 8
Nah. 3:12
Zec. 11: 2

[a] pro ἐπιπίπτω. [b] B διαπίπτω. [c] pro ῥίπτω. [d] A προκόπτω. [e] A τροπόω. [f] A ἐπιπίπτω. [g] A ποιέω. [h] pro διαπίπτω. [i] BS[1] ἐπιπίπτω. [j] pro φαίνω. [k] S[1] καταπίπτω. [m] pro ἀποθνήσκω. [n] S διαπίπτω. [o] A τελευτάω. [p] B ἐπιπίπτω. [q] pro ἀναιρέω. [r] pro συμπίπτω. [s] pro εἰμί.

πίσσα.

Isaiah 34: 9, 9

πιστεύω.

Gen. 15: 6
42:20
45:26
Exo. 4: 1, 5, 8
8,9,31
14:31
19: 9
Nu. 14:11
20:12
Deu. 9:23
28:66
1 Sa. 3:21
27:12
1 Ki. 10: 7
2 Ki. 17:14+A
2 Ch. 9: 6
24: 5 AB[a]
32:15
Job 4:18
9:16
15:15, 22
31

Job 24:22
29:24
39:12, 24
Psa. 26:13
77:22, 32
105:12, 24
115: 1
118:66
Pro. 14:15
24:24
Isa. 7: 9
28:16
43:10
53: 1
Jer. 12: 6
25: 8
47:14
Lam. 4:12
Dan. 6:23
Jon. 3: 5[b]
Hab. 1: 5

[a] pro σπεύδω. [b] BS[1] ἐμπιστεύω.

πίστις.

Deu. 32:20
1 Sa. 21: 2
26:23
2 Ki. 12:15
22: 7
1 Ch. 9:22, 26
31
2 Ch. 31:12, 15
18
34:12
Neh. 9:38

Psa. 32: 4
Pro. 3: 3
12:17, 22
14:22, 22
15:27, 28
Cant. 4: 8
Jer. 5: 1, 3
7:28
9: 3
15:18
35: 9
39:41
40: 6
Lam. 3:23−AB

Hos. 2:20
Hab. 2: 4

πιστός.

Nu. 12: 7
Deu. 7: 9
28:59
32: 4
1 Sa. 2:35, 35
3:20
22:14
25:28−A
2 Sa. 20:18
23: 1, 1
1 Ki. 11:38
Neh. 9: 8
13:13
Job 12:20
17: 9
Psa. 18: 8
88:29, 38
100: 6
110: 7
144:14

Pro. 2:12
11:13, 21
13:17 S[1][a]
14: 5, 25
17: 6
7−S
7 S[2][b]
20: 6
25:13
Isa. 1:21, 26
8: 2
22:23, 25
33:16
49: 7
55: 3
Jer. 49: 5
Dan. 2:45
6: 4
Hos. 5: 9

[a] pro σοφός. [b] pro ψευδής.

πιστόω.

2 Sa. 7:16, 25
1 Ki. 1:36
8:26
1 Ch. 17:14, 23
24−ABS

2 Ch. 1: 9
6:17
Psa. 77: 8, 37
92: 5

πιστῶς.

2 Kings 16: 2

πίτυς.

Isa. 41:14−ABS[a]
Eze. 31: 8

Zec. 11: 2

[a] Ti. πίτην.

πίων.

Gen. 46:20[a]
49:15, 20
Nu. 13:21
Psa. 21:13, 30
67:16, 16
77:31[b]
91:11, 15

Isa. 5: 1
17: 4[c]
30:23
Eze. 34:14
Dan. 11:24[d]
Mic. 6: 7

[a] AB[a] πλείων. [b] BS πλείων. [c] A[2]S πλείων. [d] A πλείων.

πλαγιάζω.

Isa. 29:21

Eze. 14: 5[a]

[a] A διαστρέφω.

πλάγιος, -ον.

Gen. 6:16
Exo. 25:31
26:13
Lev. 1:11
26:21, 23
24, 27
28, 40
41

Nu. 3:29, 35
Deu. 31:26
Ruth 2:14
1 Sa. 20:25
2 Sa. 2:16 A[a]
3:27
16:13

[a] pro πλευρά.

πλανάω.

Gen. 21:14
37:15
Exo. 14: 3
23: 4
Deu. 4:19
11:28
13: 5
22: 1
27:18
30:17
Jud. 16:10[a]
13[a], 15[a]

2 Ki. 4:28
21: 9
2 Ch. 33: 9
Ezra 9:11 S[1][b]
Job 2: 9[c]
5: 2
6:24
12:23, 24
25
19: 4, 4
38:41
Psa. 57: 4
94:10
106: 9, 40
118:110
176
Pro. 1:10
7:25+AS[2]
9:12
10:17
12:26
13: 9
14:22
16:10
21:16
28:10
29:15
Isa. 3:12
9:16, 16
13:14
16: 8
17:11
19:13, 14
14
21: 4, 15
22: 5, 5
28: 7 AS[d]
7, 7
29:24

Isa. 30:20, 20
21
35: 8
41:10, 29
44: 8−AS
20
46: 5, 8
47:15
53: 6, 6
63:17
64: 5
Jer. 23:13, 32
27:17
38: 9
Eze. 13:10
14: 9,9,11
33:12
34: 4, 16
44:10
10+A
13, 15
48:11, 11
Hos. 2:14
4:12
8: 6
Amos 2: 4
Mic. 3: 5

[a] A παραλογίζομαι. [b] pro πίμπλημι. [c] AS[2] πλανῆτις. [d] pro πλημμελέω.

πλάνη.

Pro. 14: 8
Jer. 23:17

Eze. 33:10

πλάνησις.

Isa. 19:14
22: 5−S[1]
30:10, 28
28

Isa. 32: 6
Jer. 4:11
Eze. 44:13
48:11

πλανήτης.

Hosea 9:17

πλανῆτις.

Job 2: 9 AS[2][a]

[a] pro πλανάω.

πλάνος.

Job 19: 4

Jer. 23:32

πλάξ.

Exo. 31:18, 18
32:15, 15
16, 16
19
34: 1, 1, 1
4, 4, 28
29
Deu. 4:13
5:22

Deu. 9: 9,9,10
11, 11
15, 17
10: 1, 2, 2
3, 3, 4
5
1 Ki. 8: 9, 9
2 Ch. 5:10

πλάσμα.

Job 40:14
Ps. 102:14
Isa. 29:16

Isa. 45:10−AS[2]
Hab. 2:18

πλάσσω.

Gen. 2: 7,8,15
19
Exo. 32: 4
Deu. 32: 6−B[a]
1 Ki. 12:33
2 Ki. 19:25
Est. 1: 6 S[1][b]
Job 10: 8, 9
34:15
38:14
Psa. 32:15
73:17 S[2][c]
89: 2
93: 9, 20
94: 5

Ps. 103:26
118:73
138: 5, 16
Pro. 8:25+S
24:12
Isa. 27:11
29:16, 16
43: 1, 7
44: 2,9,10
21, 24
45:10−AS[2]
18−AS
49: 5
8−AS
53:11

Jer. 1: 5
10:16
18:11
19: 1
28:19
Jer. 40: 2
Hab. 1:12
2:18, 18
Zec. 12: 1

[a] A κτίζω. [b] pro πάσσω.
[c] pro ποιέω.

πλάτανος.

Genesis 30:37

πλατεῖα.

Gen. 19: 2
Jud. 19:15, 17
20
2 Sa. 21:12
2 Ch. 32: 6
Ezra 10: 9
Neh. 8:16
Est. 4: 1
5+AS^{3}
6: 9, 11
Job 29: 7
Psa. 17:43
54:12
143:14 S^{2}[a]
Pro. 1:20
5:16
7: 6, 12
9:14
22:13
Pro. 26:13
Cant. 3: 2
Isa. 15: 3
3−BS
Jer. 5: 1
9:21
27:30
30:15
31:38
Lam. 2:11, 12
4:18
Eze. 7:19
16:24, 31
26:11
28:23
Dan. 9:25
Amos 5:16
Nah. 2: 5
Zec. 8: 4, 5, 5

[a] pro ἔπαυλις.

πλάτος.

Gen. 6:15
13:17
32:25, 25
32, 32
Exo. 25: 9, 16
26:16
38: 1+A
1 Ki. 2:35
6: 6,7,10
10+A
10, 19
7:13, 39
43
2 Ch. 3: 4, 8
Ezra 6: 3−B
Neh. 3: 8
8: 1
12:38 S^{3}
Pro. 3: 3+A
Pro. 7 :3
22:20
Isa. 8: 8
Jer. 52:21 S[a]
Eze. 40: 5, 7, 7
8, 11
13, 19
20
30 A
42, 48
41: 1, 11
12
42: 2, 4
43:16+A
48:10+A
15
Hab. 1: 6
Zec. 2: 2
5: 2

[a] pro πάχος.

πλατύνω.

Gen. 9:27
26:22
28:14
Exo. 34:24[a]
Deu. 6:12+A
11:16
32:15
1 Sa. 2: 1
Psa. 4: 2
17:37
Psa. 34:21
80:11
118:32
Pro. 24:43
Isa. 5:14
54: 2
Jer. 2:24
28:58
Eze. 31: 5
Hab. 2: 5

[a] A ἐμπλατύνω.

πλατύς.

Gen. 34:10, 21
Jud. 18:10[a]
1 Ch. 4:40
Neh. 4:19
7: 4
Neh. 9:35
Ps. 118:96
Isa. 33:21
Eze. 23:32

[a] A εὐρύχωρος.

πλατυσμός.

2 Sa. 22:20, 37
Psa. 17:20
Ps. 117: 5
118:45

πλειάς.

Job 9: 9
Job 38:31

πλεῖον vide πλείων.

πλειστάκις.

Ecclesiastes 7:23

πλεῖστος.

Jos. 5: 6
1 Ch. 12:29
2 Ch. 25: 9
2 Ch. 30:18
Isa. 7:22
9: 3

πλείων, πλεῖον, πλέον.

Gen. 46:29AB*[a]
Exo. 1:12
23: 2, 2
Lev. 15:25
25:16, 51
Nu. 9:19
20:15
22:15
26:54
33:54
Deu. 20: 1, 19
25: 3
Jos. 10:11
11:18
22: 3
23: 1
24: 7
Jud. 16:30
20:40−A
1 Sa. 9: 7
2 Ki. 6:16
1 Ch. 4:40
24: 4
2 Ch. 32: 7
Psa. 50: 4
61: 3
77:31 BS[a]
89:10
122: 4
Pro. 11:24
16:21
Isa. 16: 2
17: 4 A^{2} S[a]
22: 9
57: 8
Jer. 2:12
39:14
43:32
Eze. 29:15
33:24
38: 8
Dan. 11:24 A[a]
Amos 6: 2
Jon. 4:11
Mal. 3:14

[a] pro πίων.

πλέκω.

Exo. 28:14
Isa. 28: 5

πλέον vide πλείων.

πλεονάζω.

Exo. 16:18, 23
26:12
12−B
Nu. 3:46, 48
49, 51
9:22
26:54
2 Sa. 18: 8
1 Ch. 4:27
1 Ch. 5:23
2 Ch. 24:11
31: 5
Psa. 49:19
70:21
Pro. 15: 6
Jer. 37:19
Eze. 23:32

πλεονάκις.

Ps. 105:43
128: 1, 2
Isa. 42:20

πλεόνασμα.

Numbers 31:32

πλεονασμός.

Lev. 25:37
Pro. 28: 8
Eze. 18: 8, 13
Eze. 18:17
22:12

πλεόναστος.

Deuteronomy 30: 5

πλεονεκτέω.

Jud. 4:11[a]
Eze. 22:27
Hab. 2: 9

[a] A ἀναπαύω.

πλεονεξία.

Jud. 5:19 A[a]
Ps. 118:36
Isa. 28: 8
Jer. 22:17
Eze. 22:27
Hab. 2: 9

[a] pro δῶρον.

πλευρά, −ρόν.

Gen. 2:21, 22
Exo. 27: 7
Exo. 30: 4
Nu. 33:55
2 Sa. 2:16[a]
13:34
16:13[b]
21:14
1 Ki. 6:10+A
10, 12
15, 16
16+B
7: 9, 40
8:19
Job 40:13, 13[c]
Psa. 47: 3
Pro. 22: 7
Isa. 11: 5
Eze. 4: 4, 6, 8
8, 9
34:21
41: 5, 6,
6, 6,
8, 9,
26
Dan. 7: 5

[a] A πλάγιος. [b] B πέρας.
[c] A πέτρα.

πλέω.

Isa. 42:10
Jon. 1: 3−S^{1}

πληγή.

Exo. 11: 1
12:13
33: 5
Lev. 26:21
Nu. 11:33
14:37
25: 8,9,18
26: 1
31:16
Deu. 25: 2, 3
28:59 *ter*
61
29:22
Jos. 22:17
Jud. 11:33
15: 8
19 A[a]
1 Sa. 4: 8, 10
17
6:19
14:14, 30
19: 8
23: 5
1 Ki. 21:21
22:35
2 Ki. 8:29
9:15
1 Ch. 21:23
2 Ch. 6:28
13:17
21:14
22: 6
28: 5
Job 2:13
42:16
Psa. 63: 8
Pro. 20:30
22: 8
29:15
Isa. 1: 6
10:24[b], 26
14: 6, 6
19:22
30:26, 31
53: 3, 4, 10
Jer. 10:18, 19
14:17
15:18
19: 8
27:13
37:12, 14
17
Mic. 1: 9, 11
Nah. 3:19
Zec. 13: 6

[a] pro πηγή. [b] S^{1} πλήν.

πλῆθος.

Gen. 16:10
17: 4
27:28
30:30
32:12
36: 7
48:16, 19
Exo. 1: 9
8:24
12: 6
15: 7
19:21
22 A[a]
23: 2
32:13
36: 5
Lev. 25:36
Nu. 32: 1, 1
Deu. 1:10
10:22
26: 5
28:47, 62
Jos. 11: 4
Jud. 4: 7
6: 5
7:12, 12
1 Sa. 1:16
13: 5
2 Sa. 17:11
18:29
1 Ki. 1:19, 25
(3) *p* 46
3: 8+A
4(20)A
7:32
34+A
8: 5+A
10:10, 27
2 Ki. 7:13
19:23
1 Ch. 4:38
12:40
22: 3, 4, 5, 8
14, 15
29:16, 21
2 Ch. 1:15
2: 9
4:18
5: 6
9: 1, 6, 9
27
11:12, 23
23
12: 3
13: 8
14:11
16: 8
20: 2, 12
21
30: 5, 17
24
31: 5
10−AB
10, 18
32:29
Neh. 5:18
9:25
13:22
Est. 5:11+S^{3}
Job 31:34[b]
33:19
35: 9
Psa. 5: 8, 11
9:25
30:20
32:16, 17
Psa. 36:11
43:13
48: 7
50: 3
51: 9
63: 3
65: 3
68:14, 17
71: 7
76:18
93:19
105: 7, 45
144: 7
146: 4
150: 2
Pro. 5:23
Ecc. 1:18, 18
5: 2, 2, 6
9, 10
6: 3
11: 1
Isa. 1:11
5:13
17:12
21:15[a]
28: 2
29: 5−AS
31: 1, 4
37:24
51:10
60: 5 S^{1}[c]
63: 7, 15
Jer. 10:13
13:22
26:16
28:13
28:27−S^{1}
Jer. 30:10
37:16
Lam. 1: 3, 5
3:31
Eze. 7:12+A
13+A
14+A
19:11
23:42
26:10, 13
27:12, 16
18, 25
33
28:10, 16
17, 18
29:19+A
30: 4+A
10, 15
31: 2, 6, 7
9, 15
18
32: 6, 32
39: 4, 12
47:10
Dan. 2:35
Hos. 4: 7
8:12
9: 7
10: 1, 13
Mic. 4:13
Nah. 2:13
3: 3, 3
Zec. 2: 4
8: 4
9:10
14:14

[a] pro κύριος. [b] A λαός.
[c] pro πλοῦτος.

πληθύνω.

Gen. 1:22, 22
28
3:16, 16
6: 5
7:17 A[a]
18
8:17
9: 1, 7
7 A[b]
16:10, 10
17: 2, 20
18:20
22:17, 17
26: 4, 24
28: 3
34:12
35:11
38:12
47:27
48: 4, 16
Exo. 1: 7, 7, 10
20
7: 3
11: 9−A
9
32:13
Lev. 25:16
26: 9
Nu. 33:54
Deu. 1:10
6: 3
7:13, 22
8:13 *ter*
13:17
17:16, 16
17, 17
28:11
63−B
Jos. 24: 3
Jud. 9:29
16:24
1 Sa. 1:12
7: 2
14:19
25:10
2 Sa. 14:11
22:36
1 Ki. (3) 1
1 Ki. 3:14
4:26
2 Ki. 21: 6
1 Ch. 4:10, 38
7: 4
8:40
23:11
27:23
2 Ch. 33: 6[c], 23
36:14
Ezra 4:22
9: 6
10:13
Neh. 9:23
Job 39: 4
Psa. 3: 2
4: 8
15: 4
17:15
24:17, 19
35: 8
37:20
39: 6, 13
48:17
64:10, 11
14
68: 5
77:38
91:13, 15
105:29
106:38
118:69
122: 3 S^{1}[d]
4 S[d]
138:18
143:13
Pro. 4:10
13:11
28: 8, 28
Ecc. 5:10
6:11
10:14
Isa. 1:15
6:12
14: 2
51: 2−B
57: 9
Jer. 2:22

Jer. 3:16
5: 6
15: 8
23: 3
26:11, 23
36: 6
37:14, 16
Lam. 1: 1, 1
2: 5, 22
Eze. 11: 6
16: 7,7,25
29, 51
19: 2
21:15
22:25
23:19
24:10
27:15
28: 5
Eze. 28:16 A[d]
36:10, 11
30, 30
37
Dan. 3:31
6:25
11:39
12: 4
Hos. 2: 8
8:11, 14
9: 7
10: 1
12: 1, 10
Joel 3:13
Amos 4: 4, 9
Nah. 3:16—S[1]
Hab. 2: 6
Zec. 10: 8

[a] pro ἐπιπληθύνω.
[b] pro κατακυριεύω.
[c] A ποιέω. [d] pro πίμπλημι.

πλήθω vide πίμπλημι

πλημμέλεια.

Lev. 5:15, 16
18, 19[a]
6: 6, 17
31, 32
35, 37
7:27
14:12, 13
14, 17
24, 25
25, 28
19:21, 21
22
22:16
Nu. 5: 7
6:12
Nu. 18: 9
Jos. 7: 1
22:16, 20
31
1 Sa. 24:14
2 Sa. 14:13
2 Ki. 12:16
2 Ch. 33:23
Ezra 9: 6,7,13
15
10:10
19—S[1]
Psa. 67:22
68: 6

[a] AB πλημμέλησις.

πλημμελέω.

Lev. 4:13, 22
27
5: 3,6,15
17, 19
6: 4, 6, 7
14:21
Nu. 5: 6+B[1]
6, 7
Jos. 7: 1
Jos. 22:16, 20
22, 31
Jud. 21:22
Psa. 33:22, 23
118:67
Isa. 28: 7[a]
Jer. 2: 3
16:18

[a] AS πλανάω.

πλημμέλημα.

Nu. 5: 8, 8
Ezra 10:19 S[2a]
Jer. 2: 5

[a] pro πλημμέλησις.

πλημμέλησις.

Lev. 5:19 AB[a]
Ezra 10:10—S[1b]

[a] pro πλημμέλεια.
[b] S[2] πλημμέλημα.

πλήμμυρα.

Job 40:18

πλήν.

Lev. 11: 4—A
Deu. 5:7 A[a]
17:16 A[b]
Jud. 7:19+A
8:26 A[c]
26 A[d]
11:34+A
14:16—A
16:28+A
20:39 A[c]
1 Sa. 21: 4—B
1 Ki. 3: 2—B
16 p 28—A
Psa. 17:32[1 f]
Ecc. 2:24+S[2]
Isa. 10:21 S[1 g]
45:21[h]
22+A[2]
64: 4—A[1]
Jer. 2:24+S[1]

[a] pro πρόσωπον. [b] pro διότι.
[c] pro παρέξ. [d] pro ἐκτός.
[e] pro πάλιν. [f] S πάρεξ.
[g] pro πληγή. [h] A[2] παρέξ.

πλήρης, -ες.

Gen. 25: 8
27:27
35:29
41:7,22,24
Exo. 9: 8
16:33
Lev. 2: 2
5:12
16:12
Nu. 7:13, 14
19, 20
25, 26
31, 32
37, 38
43, 44
49, 50
55, 56
61, 62
67, 68
73, 74
79, 80
86
22:18
24:13
Deu. 6:11
Jud. 6:38
16:27
Ruth 1:21
2:12
1 Sa. 2: 5
2 Sa. 23: 7, 11
2 Ki. 4:39
6:17
7:15
20: 3
1 Ch. 11:13
23: 1
29: 9, 28
2 Ch. 15:17
16: 9
2 Ch. 19: 9
24:15
25: 2
Ezra 4:20
Neh. 9:25
Job 7: 4
10:15
14: 1
21:24
32:18
36:16
39: 2
42:17
Psa. 32: 5
47:11
72:10
74: 9
118:64
143:13
Pro. 17:1+ACS
Cant. 5: 5, 13
Isa. 1: 4, 11
15, 21
6: 1, 3
30:27
51:20
63: 3
Jer. 5:27, 27
6:11
Eze. 1:18
7:23, 23
10:12
17: 3
26: 2
36:38
43: 5
44: 4
Joel 3:13
Nah. 3: 1
Hab. 3: 3

πληροφορέω.

Ecclesiastes 8: 11

πληρόω.

Gen. 1:22, 28
9: 1, 7
25:24
29:21
50: 3
Exo. 32:29
Lev. 8:33
12: 4
25:29, 30
Nu. 6: 5, 13
7:88
Jos. 3:15
Jud. 17: 5[a], 12[a]
1 Sa. 18:27+A
27+A
20: 3 A[b]
2 Sa. 7:12
1 Ki. 1:14
2:27
7: 2
8:15, 24
13:33
2 Ki. 4: 4
1 Ch. 12:15
17:11
29: 5
2 Ch. 6: 4, 15
13: 9
16:14 A[c]
24:10
29:31
36:21, 22
Job 20:22[d], 23[e]
Psa. 15:11
19: 5, 6
64:10
70: 8
Psa. 71:19—S[1]
73:20
79:10 S[2 c]
80:11
82:17
103:24
109: 6
126: 5
128: 7
Ecc. 1: 8[f]
6: 7
9: 3
11: 3 AOS[c]
Cant. 5:14
Isa. 8: 8—A
13: 3
40: 4
65:11
Jer. 13:12, 12
13
23:24
25:12[g]
28:11, 14
32:20
36:10
40: 5
41:14
51:25
Lam. 4:19
Eze. 7:19
9: 7 A[c]
Dan. 2:35
5:26
8:23
Zeph. 1: 9
Hag. 2: 7 A[c]

[a] A ἐμπίπλημι. [b] pro ἐμπλήθω
[c] pro πίμπλημι. [d] C εἰρηνεύω.
[e] C κληρόω. [f] S ἐμπίπλημι.
[g] A συμπληρόω.

πλήρωμα.

1 Ch. 16:32
Psa. 23: 1
49:12
88:12
95:11
97: 7
Ecc. 4: 6, 6
Cant. 5:12, 12
Jer. 8:16
29: 2
Eze. 12:19
19: 7
30:12

πλήρωσις.

Exo. 35:27
Deu. 33:16
1 Ch. 29: 2
Jer. 4:12
Jer. 5:24
Eze. 5: 2
32:15
Dan. 10: 3

πλησίος, -ον.

Gen. 11: 3, 7
26:31
Exo. 2:13
11: 2
2+A
12: 4
20:16, 17
17, 17
21:14, 18
35
22: 7, 8, 9
10, 11
12 A[a]
14, 26
32:27—B
34: 3
Lev. 6: 2, 2
18:20
19:11, 13
15, 16
17, 18
20:10
24:19
25:14 ter
15—A
17
Nu. 33:37
38+A
Deu. 1: 1
4:42
5:20, 21
21, 21
10:18 A[b]
11:30
15: 2
19: 4, 5, 5
11, 14
19 A[c]
21+AB[e]
22:24, 26
24: 1, 1, 2
12
27:17, 24
Jos. 9: 6, 6
12: 9
15:46
19:46
20: 5 A
Jud. 4:11 A[d]
6:29
7:13, 14
22
10:18
Ruth 3:14
4: 7
1 Sa. 10:11
14:20
15:28
20:41, 41
28:16, 17
30:26
2 Sa. 2:16, 16
5:23
2 Sa. 12:11
1 Ki. 8:31
12 p 24 l 69
21:35
2 Ki. 3:23
7: 3, 9
1 Ch. 14:14
2 Ch. 6:22
Est. 9:19
19+ABS
Job 16:21—S[2]
Psa. 11: 3
14: 3, 4
23: 4
27: 3
34:14
37:12
44:15
87:19+AS[2]
100: 5
121: 8
Pro. 9:12
26:27
Cant. 1: 9, 15
2: 2, 10
13
4: 1, 7
5: 1, 2, 16
6: 3
Isa. 3: 5
5: 8
19: 2
41: 6
Jer. 5: 8
6:21
7: 5
9: 4, 8, 20
19: 9
22: 8, 13
23:27
30—B
35
24: 1 B[1 e]
26:16
38:34 A[f]
41:13, 17
43:16
Eze. 18: 6, 8, 11
15
22:11
33:26 A
40: 9
41:16, 17
Jon. 1: 7
Mic. 7: 2
Hab. 2:15
Zec. 3: 8, 10
8:10, 16
17
11: 6, 9
14:13, 13
Mal. 3:16
4: 5

[a] pro κύριος.
[b] pro προσήλυτος.
[c] pro ἀδελφός. [d] pro Χαβέρ.
[e] pro πλούσιος.
[f] pro ἀδελφός.

πλησμονή.

Gen. 41:30
Exo. 16: 3, 8
Lev. 25:19
26: 5
Deu. 33:23
Psa. 77:25
105:15
Pro. 3:10
26:16
27: 7
Isa. 1:14
Isa. 30:23
55: 2
56:11
65:15
Jer. 14:22
Lam. 5: 6
Eze. 16:49
39:19
Hos. 13: 6
Hab. 2:16
Hag. 1: 6

πλήσσω.

Exo. 9:31, 32
16: 3
22: 2
Nu. 25:14, 14
15, 18
Jud. 20:36[a]
1 Sa. 4: 2
5:12
11:11 A[b]
2 Sa. 1:12
4: 4
9: 3
11:15
208[a c]
2 Sa. 11:22
1 Ki. 14:14 A
15 A
2 Ch. 29: 9
Ezra 6:11[d]
Ps. 101: 5
Pro. 7:23
23:32
Isa. 1: 5
9:13
27: 7
Jer. 30: 6
Zec. 13: 6

[a] A τροπόω. [b] pro τύπτω.
[c] pro τοξεύω. [d] A πήγνυμι.

πλινθεία.

Exo. 1:14
5: 8[a], 14
Exo. 5:18, 19

[a] A πλινθουργία.

πλινθεύω.

Genesis 11: 3

πλινθίον.

2 Sa. 12:31
1 Ki. (3) p 46

πλίνθος.

Gen. 11: 3, 3
Exo. 5:16
24:10
Isa. 9:10
24:23
Isa. 65: 3
Eze. 4: 1
Mic. 7:11
Nah. 3:14

πλινθουργία.

Exodus 5: 7, 8 A[a]

[a] pro πλινθεία.

πλοῖον.

Gen. 49:13
Deu. 28:68
Jud. 5:17
2 Ch. 8:18
9:21
20:36—A
36, 37
Job 40:26
Psa. 47: 8
103:26
106:23
Isa. 2:16, 16
Isa. 11:14
18: 1
23: 1, 10
14
33:21
43:14[a]
60: 9
Eze. 27: 9, 25
29
Jon. 1: 3, 4, 5
5

[a] AS[2] κλοιός.

πλοκή.

Exo. 28:14
1 Ki. 6(18) A
Eze. 7:10+A

πλόκιος.

Canticles 7: 5

πλούσιος.

Gen. 13: 2
Ruth 3:10
1 Sa. 2:10
2 Sa. 12: 1, 2, 4

Est. 1:20
Job 27:19
Psa. 9:29
33:11
44:13
48: 3
Pro. 10:15
14:20
18:11
19:22
Pro. 22: 2,7,16
23: 4
28: 6, 11
Ecc. 10: 6, 20
Isa. 5:14
32: 9, 13
33:20
53: 9
Jer. 9:23
24: 1[a]

[a] B[1] πλησίος.

πλουτέω.

Gen. 30:43
Exo. 30:15
Psa. 48:17
Pro. 28:22
29:46
Ecc. 5:11
Jer. 5:27
Eze. 27:33
Dan. 11: 2
Hos. 12: 8
Zec. 11: 5

πλουτίζω.

Gen. 14:23
1 Sa. 2: 7
17:25 A
Job 15:29
Psa. 64:10
Pro. 10: 4
22—A
13: 7

πλοῦτος.

Gen. 31:16
Deu. 33:19
1 Sa. 2:10
17:25 A
1 Ki. 3:11, 13
10:23
1 Ch. 29:12, 28
2 Ch. 1:11, 12
9:22
17: 5
18: 1
32:27
Est. 1: 4, 4
5:11
10: 2
Job 20:15, 18
21: 7
27:18+A
31:25
Psa. 36: 3, 16
48: 7, 11
51: 9
61:11
72:12
75: 6
111: 3
118:14
Pro. 3:16
8:18
11:16, 16
Pro. 11:28
13: 7,8,22
23
19: 4
21:17
22: 1, 4
24: 4, 31
71
28: 8
29: 3
32AS²[a]
47
Ecc. 4: 8
5:12, 13
18
6: 2
9:11
Isa. 16:14
24:8+ABS
29: 2, 5, 7
8
30: 6
32:14, 18
60: 5[b], 10
61: 6
Jer. 9:23
17:11
Eze. 26:12 A[c]
Dan. 11: 2, 2
Mic. 6:12

[a] *pro* βίος. [b] S[1] πλῆθος.
[c] *pro* ὑπάρχω.

πλύνω.

Gen. 49:11
Exo. 19:10, 14
29:17
Lev. 1: 9, 13
6:27
8:21
9:14
11:25, 28
40, 40
13: 6, 34
54, 55
56[a], 58
58
14: 8,9,47
47
15: 5, 6, 7
Lev. 15: 8, 10
11, 13
17, 21
22, 27
16:26, 28
17:15, 16
Nu. 8: 7, 21
19: 7,8,10
19, 21
31:24
2 Sa. 19:24 A[b]
2 Ch. 4: 6
Psa. 50: 4, 9
Eze. 40:38+A
Mal. 3: 2

[a] A καίω. [b] *pro* ἀποπλύνω.

πλωτός.

Job 40:26

πνεῦμα.

Gen. 1: 2
6: 3, 17
Gen. 7:15
8: 1
Gen. 41:38
45:27
Exo. 15: 8, 10
28: 3
31: 3
35:31
Nu. 5:14, 14
30
11:17, 25
25, 26
29, 31
14:24
16:22
23: 6
24: 2
27:16, 18
Deu. 2:30
34: 9
Jos. 2:11
Jud. 3:10
6:34
8: 3
9:23
11:29
13:25
14: 6, 19
15:14, 19
1 Sa. 10: 6, 10
11: 6—A
16:13, 14
14, 15
16, 23
23
18:10 A
19: 9, 20
23
30:12
2 Sa. 13:21
22:16
23: 2
1 Ki. 17:17
18:12, 45
19:11 *ter*
20: 4-A, 5
22:21, 22
23, 24
2 Ki. 2: 9, 15
16
3:17—A
19: 7
1 Ch. 5:26, 26
12:18
28:12
2 Ch. 15: 1
18:20, 21
22
23+B
23+B
23
20:14
24:20
36:22
Ezra 1: 1, 5
Neh. 9:20, 30
Job 1:19
4: 9, 15
7: 7
11+AS²
15
8: 2
10:12
12:10
13:25
15: 2
16: 3
17: 1
20: 3
27: 3
30:15
32: 9, 18
33: 4
34:14
41: 7
Psa. 10: 6
17:16
30: 6
32: 6
33:19
47: 8
50:12, 13
Psa. 50:14, 19
75:13
76: 4, 7
77: 8, 39
102:16
103: 4, 29
30
105:33
106:25
118:131
134:17
138: 7
141: 4
142: 4,7,10
145: 4
147: 7
148: 8
Pro. 15: 4[a]
Ecc. 1: 6,6,14
17
2:11, 17
26
3:19, 21
21
4: 4,6,16
6: 9
7: 9, 10
8: 8, 8
10: 4
11: 5
12: 7
Isa. 4: 4
4—A
7: 2
11: 2 *qtr*
3,4,15
19: 3, 14
25: 4
26: 9, 18
27: 8, 8
28: 6
29:10, 24
30: 1, 28
32:15
33:11
34:16
37: 7
38:12
42: 1, 5
44: 3
48:16
57:16
59:21
61: 1, 3
63:10, 11
14
65:14
Jer. 4:11, 12
10:14
28:11, 17
30:10
Lam. 4:20
Eze. 1: 4, 12
20, 20
21
2: 2
3:12, 14
14, 24
5: 2
8: 3
10:17
11: 1, 5, 5
19, 24
24
13:11
18:31
20:31
21: 7
27:26
36:26, 27
37: 1, 5, 6
8, 9, 9
9[b]
9+A
10, 14
43: 5
Dan. 2: 1,3,35
4: 5,6,15
5: 4+AB²
11, 12
Dan. 5:14, 20
6: 3
7:15
10:17[c]
Hos. 4:12, 19
5: 4
12: 1
Joel 2:28, 29
Amos 4:13
Jon. 1: 4
4: 8
Mic. 2: 7, 11
3: 8
Hab. 1:11
2:19
Hag. 1:14 *ter*
2: 5
Zec. 1: 6
4: 6
5: 9
7:12
12: 1, 10
13: 2
Mal. 2:15, 15
16

[a] S[1] πιότης, S[2] καρπός.
[b] A ἄνεμος. [c] A πνοή.

πνευματοφορέομαι.

Jeremiah 2:24

πνευματοφόρος.

Hos. 9: 7
Zeph. 3: 4

πνεύμων.

1 Ki. 22:34
2 Ch. 18:33

πνέω.

Ps. 147: 7
Isa. 40:24

πνίγω.

1 Samuel 16:14, 15

πνοή.

Gen. 2: 7
7:22
2 Sa. 22:16
1 Ki. 15:29
Neh. 6: 1
Job 26: 4
27: 3
32: 9
33: 4
37: 9
Ps. 150: 6
Pro. 1:23
11:13
20:27
24:12
Isa. 38:16
42: 5
57:16
Eze. 13:13
Dan. 5:23
10:17 A[a]

[a] *pro* πνεῦμα.

πόα, ποία.

Pro. 27:24
Jer. 2:22
Mal. 3: 2

ποδήρης.

Exo. 25: 6
28: 4, 27
29: 5
Exo. 35: 8
Eze. 9: 2,3,11
Zec. 3: 4

ποδιστῆρες.

2 Chronicles 4:16

ποθεινός.

Proverbs 6: 8

πόθεν.

Gen. 16: 8
29: 4
42: 7
Nu. 11:13
Jos. 9:14, 14
Jud. 13: 6
17: 9
19:17
1 Sa. 25:11
30:13
2 Sa. 1: 3, 13
2 Ki. 5:25
6:27
20:14
Job 1: 7
2: 2
28:12, 20
38:24
Ps. 120: 1 AS[a]
Pro. 22:27
Isa. 39: 3
41:24, 24
28
Jer. 15:18
31: 9—A
43:17 AS[b]
Jon. 1: 8
Nah. 3: 7

[a] *pro* ὅθεν. [b] *pro* ποῦ.

ποθέω.

Proverbs 7:15

ποιέω.

Gen. 1: 1,7,11
12, 16
21, 25
26, 27
27, 27
31
2: 2, 2, 3
4, 18
3: 1, 7
13, 14
21
4:10
5: 1, 1, 2
2
6: 6, 7, 7
14, 14
15, 16
16, 16
22, 22
7: 4, 5
8: 6
13—A²
21
9: 6, 24
11: 4, 6, 6
12: 2, 18
13: 4, 16
14: 2
18: 5, 6, 7
8, 17
19, 25
25
19: 3,8,19
22
20: 5, 6, 9
9,9,10
13
21: 1, 6, 8
13, 18
22, 23
23, 26
22:12, 16
24:12, 14
44, 49
66
26:10, 29
30
27: 4, 7, 9
14, 17
19, 31
37 *ter*
45
28:15
29:22, 25
28
30:30, 31
31: 1, 12
16, 26
43, 46
32: 9, 10
12, 16
33: 2 A[a]
17, 17
34: 7, 14
19, 30
35: 1, 3
37: 3
38:10
39: 3,9,11
19, 22
22—A
23
40:14, 15
20
41:25, 28
32, 34
47, 51
55
42:18, 20
28
43:10, 16
44: 5,7,15
17
45: 8,9,17
21
46: 3
47:29, 30
48: 4, 20
Gen. 50:10, 12
Exo. 1:17, 18
20, 21
3:20
4:11, 15
17, 21
30
5: 8, 15
16
6: 1
7: 6,6,10
11, 20
22
8: 7, 13
18, 24
31
9: 5, 6
10: 2, 25
11:10
12:12, 16
16, 16
17, 28
28, 35
39, 47
48, 48
50, 50
13: 5, 8
14: 4,5,11
13, 21
31
15:11, 26
16:17
17: 4,6,10
18: 1, 8, 9
14, 14
18
18—A
20, 23
24, 25
19: 4, 8
20: 4, 6, 9
10, 11
23, 23
24, 25
21: 9, 11
31
22:30
23:11, 11
12
15—A
16, 22
22, 24
33
24: 3, 7
25: 7, 8, 8
9, 10
12, 16
17, 18
18, 22
23, 23
24, 25
27, 28
28, 30
30, 37
38—A
40
26: 1, 1, 4
4, 5, 5
6, 7, 7
10, 10
11, 14
15
16—A
17, 18
19, 22
23, 24
26, 29
31, 31
36, 37
27: 1, 2, 3
3, 4, 4
6, 8, 8
9
28: 2, 3, 4
4,6,13
14, 15
15, 16
22, 27

Exo. 28: 29, 32
35, 35
36, 36
38
29: 1, 2, 35
36, 38
39, 39
41, 41
30: 1, 2, 3
4, 4, 5
18, 25
32, 33
35, 37
38
31: 6 AB[b]
11, 14
15, 15
16, 17
32: 1, 4, 8
10
14+A
20, 21
23, 28
31, 35
33: 5, 17
34: 7+A
10, 10
17, 22
35: 1, 2, 2
29, 29
32, 33
35, 35
36: 1, 1, 3
4, 5, 7
8, 9, 10
12, 13
15, 16
22, 23
27, 28
30, 32
33, 35
38
37: 1, 3, 5
7, 20
38: 1
3+A
5
6+A
9, 11, 12
13, 18
19, 20
21, 22
23, 24
25, 26
27, 23
39: 6, 8, 11
11, 12
13, 22
23
40: 14, 14
Lev. 2: 7, 8, 11
4: 2, 2, 13
13
20 *ter*
22, 22
27, 27
5: 4, 10
17, 17
6: 3, 7, 21
22, 39
39
7: 14
8: 4, 5, 34
34, 36
9: 6, 7, 7
16, 22
10: 7
11: 32
13: 51
14: 19, 30
15: 15, 30
31
16: 15, 15
16, 24
29, 34
17: 4, 8, 9
18: 3, 3, 4
5, 5, 26
27, 29
29, 30

Lev. 19: 4, 15
27, 28
28, 35
37
20: 8, 13
22, 23
22: 23[c], 24
31
23: 3, 3, 7
8, 12
19, 21
25, 28
30, 31
35, 36
24: 5, 19
23
25: 18, 18
21
26: 1, 3, 14
15, 16
22
Nu. 1: 54, 54
2: 34
4: 3, 19
23, 26
35, 39
5: 4, 4, 6
7[a], 30
6: 11, 16
17, 17
8: 3, 4, 7
12, 20
20, 22
26
9: 2, 3, 3
4, 5, 6
10, 11
12, 13
14, 14
10: 2, 2, 29
32
11: 8, 15
14: 11, 12
22, 28
35
15: 3, 3, 5
5, 6
6−A
8
8+A[2]
11, 12
12, 13
14 *ter*
22, 24
29, 30
34, 38
39, 40
16: 6, 28
38
17: 11, 11
20: 27
21: 8, 9, 34
34
22: 2, 17
18, 20
28, 30
23: 2, 11
19, 26
30
24: 13, 14
18
27: 22
28: 4, 4, 5
8, 8, 15
17+A
18
20+A
21, 24
24, 25
26, 31
29: 1, 2, 7
12, 35
39
30: 3
31: 31
32: 8, 13
20, 23
24, 25
31
33: 4, 56

Nu. 33: 36
36: 10
Deu. 1: 14, 18
30, 44
2: 12, 22
29
3: 2, 2, 6
21, 21
24, 24
4: 1, 3, 5
6, 13
14, 16
23, 25
25, 34
36 A[e]
5: 1, 8, 10
13, 14
14+B[e]
27, 31
32
6: 1, 3, 18
24, 25
7: 5, 11
12, 18
19
8: 1, 16
17, 18
9: 12, 14
16
16−AB
18, 21
10: 1, 3, 5
18, 21
22
11: 3, 4, 5
6, 7
22, 32
12: 1, 4, 8, 8
14, 25
27, 28
28, 30
30, 31
31, 32
13: 11, 18
14: 28
15: 1, 3
5−A
11−A
15, 17
18
16: 1, 8, 8
10, 12
13, 18[f]
21
17: 2
5+A
10, 10
11, 12
19
18: 9, 12
19: 9, 19
19, 20
20: 12, 15
18, 18
20
21: 9
22: 3
3−B
3, 5, 8
8, 12
21
26+AB
23: 23
24: 10, 10
11, 20
22, 24
25: 9
16−A[2]
16−A[1]
17
26: 1[k]
16, 16
19
27: 10, 15
26
28: 1
13+A
15+A
20+A
58, 63

Deu. 20: 2, 9
9+A
9
24, 29
30: 5, 5, 8
10+A
12
13−A
13, 14
31: 4, 4, 5
12, 18
21, 29
32: 6, 15
27, 39
46
33: 21
34: 9, 11
12
Jos. 1: 7, 8, 16
2: 10, 12
12, 14
3: 5
4: 8, 23
5: 2, 3
10
6: 14, 18
26
7: 9, 15
19, 20
8: 2, 2, 8
9: 9, 10
15, 16
21, 26
30, 31
32
10: 1, 1, 25
28, 28
30, 30
32, 35
37, 39
39
39+A
11: 9, 15
18
14: 5
17: 13
22: 5
5−A
23, 24
26, 28
23: 3, 6, 8
12
24: 5, 7, 20
29
Jud. 1: 7, 24
28[a]
2: 2, 7, 10
11, 17
3: 7, 12
12, 16
4: 1
6: 1, 2
17, 19
20, 27
27, 27
29, 29
40
7: 17 *ter*
8: 1, 2, 3
27, 35
35
9: 16 *ter*
19, 27
33, 48
48, 56
10: 6, 15
11: 10, 27
36, 36
37, 39
13: 1, 8, 15
16, 19
23+A
14: 6, 10
10
15: 3, 6, 7
7 A[k]
10, 10
11, 11
11
16: 20+A

Jud. 16: 26+A
26+A
17: 3, 4, 5
6, 8
18: 3, 4, 14
18, 24
27, 31
19: 21−A
23, 24
24
20: 6, 9
10−A
10−A
10
32−A
21: 7, 11
11−A
15, 16
22−A
23, 25
Ruth 1: 8, 8, 17
2: 11, 19
19, 19
3: 4, 5, 6
11, 16
4: 11
1 Sa. 1: 7, 23
24
2: 10, 10
14, 19
22, 23
24, 35
3: 11, 17
18
5: 8, 9
6: 2
5+A
7, 9, 10
8: 8, 8, 12
10: 2, 7, 8
11: 7, 10
13
12: 6, 7, 16
17, 20
13: 9, 11
19
14: 6, 7
15[a], 36
40, 43
44, 45
45, 48
48 B[a]
15: 2, 6, 19
16: 3, 4
17: 25 A
26 A
27 A
29 A
19: 5, 18
20: 1, 2, 4
8, 13
14, 32
22: 3
24: 5, 7, 19
20
25: 17, 18
22
28−A
28, 30
26: 16, 25
25
27: 11
28: 2, 9
15, 17
18, 18
29: 7, 8
30: 23
31: 11
2 Sa. 2: 5, 6, 6
6
3: 8, 9, 9
18, 20
24, 25
35, 36
39
5: 25
7: 3, 9, 21
21, 23
25+A
8: 8, 13

2 Sa. 8: 15
9: 1, 3, 7
7, 11
10: 2, 2, 12
11: 11, 27
12: 4, 4, 5
6, 7, 9
12, 12
18, 21
31
13: 2, 5, 7
10, 12
12, 16
27, 29
14: 15, 20
21, 22
15: 1, 6, 20
26
16: 10, 20
17: 6
18: 4, 13
19: 13, 18
24
27+AB
27, 37
38, 38
21: 3, 4, 11
14
22: 51
23: 10, 12
17, 17
22
24: 10, 12
17
1 Ki. 1: 5, 6, 30
2: 3, 5, 5
6, 7, 9
23, 24
31
(3) 1
p 1 *ter*
38, 44
p 46+A
3: 6, 12
15, 15
28
5: 8, 9, 16
6: 8
10+A
(12)A
16, 19
21, 29
30+A
7: 2, 2, 4
5, 6, 10
13, 23
24, 26
26, 26
31, 31
32, 34
37
43+A
44+A
8: 18, 30
32, 39
43, 45
49+A
59, 64
65, 66
9: 1, 3, 4
8, 23A
26
10: 9, 12
16, 18
11: 7, 8
10, 12
22−A
33, 33
38, 38
41
12: 21
p 24 *t* 5
28, 31
31, 32
32, 32
32, 33
33
13: 11, 33
14: 4 A
8 A

1 Ki. 14: 9 A
9 A
15 A
22, 22
24, 26
27, 29
15: 3, 5, 7
11, 12
13, 23
26, 31
34
16: 5, 7, 14
19, 19
19+A
25, 27
27+A
p 28−A
p 28−A
p 28−A
30, 33
33
17: 5, 12
13 *ter*
15
18: 13, 23
25, 26
26, 29
32, 33
34−A
36
19: 1, 2, 20
20: 7
11−B
20, 25
26
21: 9, 9
10, 22
24, 25
22: 11, 22
30, 39
43, 46
49A, 53
2 Ki. 1: 18 *ter*
2: 9
3: 2
2−A
16
4: 2, 10
13, 14
5: 13, 17
6: 2, 15
31
7: 2, 6, 9
12, 19
8: 2, 4, 12
13, 18
18, 23
27
10: 5, 5
10 AP
10, 19
21−A
24, 25
30, 30
34
11: 5, 9
12: 2, 11
11, 13
14, 15
15, 19
13: 2, 8
11, 12
12
14: 3 *ter*
15, 18
24, 28
15: 3, 3, 6
9, 9, 18
21, 24
26, 28
31, 34
34, 36
16: 2
11+A
16, 19
17: 2, 8, 11
12, 15
16
16−A
17, 19

2 Ki. 17: 22, 29
29, 30
30−A
30, 31
32 *ter*
34, 34
37, 40
41, 41
18: 3, 3, 4
7, 12
31
19: 11, 15
25+A
30, 31
20: 3, 9, 20
21: 2, 3, 3
6, 6
7+A
8+A
9, 11
11, 15
16, 17
20, 20
25
22: 2, 5, 5
7, 9, 13
23: 4, 12
12, 15
19, 19
19, 21
28, 32
32, 37
37
24: 3, 5, 9
9, 13
16, 19
19
25: 16
1 Ch. 4: 10
5: 10, 19
10: 11
11: 14, 19
19, 24
12: 32
13: 4
14: 16
15: 1, 1, 19
16: 9, 12
26
17: 2, 8, 19
23 ABS
18: 8, 14
19: 2, 2, 13
20: 3
21: 8, 10
17, 23
29
22: 8, 12
13, 15
16
23: 5, 24
26: 8, 10
28: 10, 20
29: 19
2 Ch. 1: 3, 5, 8
2: 3, 7, 12
14, 18
3: 8, 10
14, 15
16, 16
4: 1, 2, 4
6, 7, 8
8, 9, 11
11, 11
14, 14
16, 18
19, 22
6: 8, 13
23, 33
35, 39
7: 7, 7
7 A[r]
8, 9, 9
10
11 B[*e]
11, 17
21
9: 8, 11
15, 17
11: 1, 15

2 Ch.12: 9, 10
14
13: 8, 9
14: 2, 4, 7
16:14
18:10, 21
23 A[h]
19: 6, 7, 9
10, 11
20:12, 32
36
36—A
36
21: 6, 6
11, 19
22: 4
23: 4, 8
24: 2,7,11
12, 13
13, 14
16, 22
24
25: 2,9,16
26: 4,4,11
13, 15
27: 2, 2
28: 1, 2
24, 25
29: 2, 2, 6
30: 1, 2, 3
5,5,12
13, 21
23, 23
31:20, 20
21
32:13, 15
27
33: 2, 3, 6
6 A[u],6
7, 8, 9
22 *ter*
34: 2, 10
10, 10
13, 16
17, 21
31—AB
32, 33
35: 1, 6
16, 17
18, 18
19—AB
21 A[v]
36: 2, 2, 5
5, 5, 8
9, 12
Ezra 3: 4
8—B
9
4:22
6: 8, 11
13, 16
19, 22
7:10
18 *bis*
26
10: 3 S^3[a]
4,5,11
12, 16
37
Neh. 1: 9
2:12, 16
16, 19
4: 8-ABS
16, 17
21
5: 9, 12
12, 13
15, 19
6: 2, 3, 9
13
8:12, 15
16, 17
17, 18
9: 6, 10
17, 18
18, 24
26, 28
29, 31
33, 34
10:29

Neh.10:32 B[w]
11:12
12:27
13: 6, 7-9
7, 10
14, 17
18, 20
27
Est. 1: 3, 5, 8
9, 13
15, 15
20, 21
2: 1+A
4, 18
18, 20
3: 2, 7
9+S^3
4:17
5: 4, 5
8+S^3
8—S^1
8, 11
12+S^3
6: 3, 3, 6
10
7: 5
8: 3
9: 1+S^3
29
30+S^1
Job 1: 4, 5
10, 17
5: 9, 11
12, 18
27 A[x]
7:18, 21
8: 3
9: 9, 10
12, 17
10: 8, 14[y]
11: 7,8,10
14
12: 9
13: 9
14: 3, 3, 9
13
15:27
16: 7
17: 2
19: 2, 3
21:31
22: 4, 17
23
23: 9, 13
24:13
21—A
25: 2
26:14
28:24
25+AC^1
26
29: 4
30:24
31: 3, 14
14, 14
33: 4
34: 8 A[z]
11, 12
13, 13
22
35: 3 ACS^2
6, 10
37: 4, 14
40:14, 15
41:17, 24
42: 8, 9
Psa. 1: 3
7: 4
9: 5, 16
17
10: 3
13: 1, 3
14: 3, 5
17:51
21:32
30:24
33:15, 17
36: 1, 3, 5
7, 27
38:10

Psa. 39: 6, 9
49:21
50: 6
51: 4,11[aa]
52: 2, 4
55: 5, 12
59:14
65:15[bb]
16
70:19
71:18
73:17,17[cc]
76:15
77: 4, 12
82:10
85: 9, 10
17
87:11
94: 5, 6
95: 5
97: 1
98: 4
99: 3
100: 3, 7
102: 6, 10
18, 20
21
103: 4, 19
21, 32
104: 5
105: 2, 3
19, 21
106:23, 37
107:14
108:16, 21
27
110: 4,8,10
113:11, 16
23
117: 6, 15
16—S^1
24
118:65
73—S^1
84, 112
121, 124
126
120: 2
123: 8
125: 2, 3
133: 3
134: 6,7,18
135: 4, 5, 7
138:15
139:13
142: 8, 10
144:19
145: 6, 7
147: 9
148: 8
149: 2, 7, 9
150 *p* 6
Pro. 1: 7, 25
2:16
3:27
27 A[dd]
28
4:26, 27
5: 7, 8
6: 3, 8, 8
7:10
8:23, 24
26, 28
29
10:16
11:17, 18
24
12:22
13: 6 A
23
14:27, 31
16: 5, 12
17: 5, 16
22, 28
19: 7 S^1[ee]
20:11
21: 3, 15
25
22: 2, 16
24:31, 49

Pro. 24:61, 72
25:22
26: 6, 28
29:13, 31
40, 42
47
Ecc. 1: 9,9,14
2: 2, 3, 5
6,8,11
11, 12
17
3: 9, 11
11,12[ff]
14, 14
4: 3, 17
7: 1—C
15, 21
30
8: 3, 4, 9
10, 11
11, 12
14, 16
17
17 A[gg]
9: 3,6,10
10
10:19
11: 5
12:12
Cant. 1:11
3: 9, 10
8: 8
Isa. 1:17, 24
2: 8—B
20
5: 2, 2
4 *qtr*
5, 7, 7
10, 10
19
7:22 ABS[hh]
8: 1, 2
9: 1, 7
10: 3,6,11
11, 12
13, 23
12: 5
16: 3
17: 7, 8
19:10, 15
21
20: 2
22:11, 11
13, 16
23:16
25: 1, 6
26:10, 18
27: 4, 5
5—B
11
28: 2, 15
21, 22
29:15 *ter*
16, 16
21
30: 1, 22
30
31: 7
32: 6, 10
33: 1, 13
23
37:11, 16
26, 31
32
38: 3,7,19
39: 7
40: 3, 19
23
41: 4, 15
18, 20
23, 29
42: 5
9+S^1
16
16—S
16
43: 1, 3, 7
13, 19
19, 22
23

Isa. 44: 2, 7, 9
13, 17
19, 28
45: 7 *ter*
9, 11
12, 18
18, 18
21
46: 4,6,10
11 S^1[ii]
11
48: 3, 5, 5
6, 11
14
49:20
51:13, 13
52: 7
53: 9
54: 5
56: 1, 2, 2
57: 9, 16
58: 2, 13
62: 7, 11
63:12, 14
64: 3, 4
5[kk]
65: 8, 12
18
23 A[nn]
66: 2, 4, 9
22
Jer. 1:12—S^1
2:13, 16
23, 28
3: 5—S
6, 16
4:18, 22
27, 30
5: 1, 10
18, 19
31
6: 8, 13
26
7: 5,5,10
12, 13
14, 14
17, 18
29, 30
8: 6
9: 7, 24
10:11, 12
13, 24
11: 4, 6, 8
15, 17
12: 2—S
5
13:23
14: 7, 22
15: 4
16: 6, 20
17: 8, 11
22, 24
18: 3, 4, 4
4, 6, 8
10, 10
11, 12
13, 23
19:12—S^1
21: 2
22: 3, 4, 4
5, 8, 15
17
23: 5, 20
26:19, 28
28
27: 2, 15
15, 21
29, 29
28:12—S^1
15, 16
24
29: 9
31:10, 30
33
33: 3, 13
14, 19
34: 1, 4
35: 6, 13
15
36:22, 22

Jer. 36:23, 31
32
37:16, 24
38: 7, 13
21, 37
39:17, 18
20, 20
23
23—S^1
30, 32
35
40: 2
6-BS^1
9, 9
41:15, 18
18
42:10—A
15, 18
43: 3—A
8
44:15
45: 9, 12
16
47: 3, 16
48: 9, 11
49: 3, 5
10, 20
51: 3, 4, 7
9, 17
17, 17
19, 22
25—S^1
25 *ter*
52:20
Lam. 1:21, 22
2: 6, 17
20
Eze. 3:20
20+A
4: 9, 15
5: 7, 7, 8
9, 9, 9
10, 15
6: 9+A
10+A
7:20, 23
27
8: 6, 6, 9
12, 13
15+A
15+A
17, 17
18
9:11
11: 9, 13
20
21+A
12: 3, 7, 9
11, 11
25, 25
28
13:18
14:23, 23
15: 3
16: 5, 16
17, 24
30, 31
41, 43
47, 48
48, 50
51, 54
59, 59
63
17: 6,8,15
17, 18
23, 24
18: 5, 8, 9
10, 12
13, 14
14, 17
18, 19
19, 21
21, 22
22, 24
24, 24
26, 26
27, 27
28
31 A[oo]
31

Eze. 18:31+A
20: 9, 11
13+A
13+A
13, 14
17, 19
21, 21
22, 24
44
22: 3, 4, 9
13, 14
14
23:10, 21
25, 29
30, 38
38+A
39
43+A
44, 48
24:14, 18
19, 22
22, 24
24
25:11, 12
14, 15
17
26: 8[pp]
27: 5, 6, 6
28: 4
4+A
22, 26
29: 3,9,15
20+A
30:14, 19
31:11
33:13
13+A
13, 14
15
16 A[qq]
18, 19
26A, 29
29, 31
32
35: 4, 11
11+A
14—A
36:11, 22
27, 27
32, 36
37
37:14, 24
38:12
39:21, 24
43: 8, 11
11, 25
25, 27
44:14
45: 9, 17
20, 22
23, 24
25
46: 2, 12
12, 12
13, 13
14, 15
15

Dan. 1:13
3: 1, 15
32
4:32, 32
5: 1
6:10, 22
27
7:21
8: 4, 12
24, 27
9:14, 15
19+A
11: 3, 6, 7
16, 17
23, 24
24, 28
30, 32
36, 39
Hos. 2: 8
6: 4, 4, 9
8: 4, 6, 7
7, 14
9: 5
10: 3, 15
11: 9
13: 2
Joel 2:21, 26
Amos 2: 4, 8
3: 6, 7
4:12, 12
13
5: 7,8,26
7:10
8: 5, 5
9:12
14[rr]
Obad. 15
Jon. 1: 5,9,10
11, 14
3:10, 10
4: 5
Mic. 1: 8
5:15
6: 3, 8
7: 9[ss]
Nah. 1: 8, 9
11+A
Hab. 1:14
2:18
3:17
Zeph. 1:19
3: 5, 13
19, 20
Hag. 1:14
2: 4
Zec. 1: 6,6,21
6:11
7: 3, 9
8:11, 15
16
10: 1
Mal. 2:12, 13
15, 17
3:15—S^3
17
4: 1, 3

[a] *pro* τίθημι. [b] *pro* πονέω.
[c] A^2 ἀποτίθημι. [d] A ἁμαρτάνω.
[e] *pro* γίνομαι. [f] A καθίστημι.
[g] B ἐπακούω. [h] A τίθημι.
[i] A ἐπιτελέω. [k] *pro* κοπάζω.
[n] A πονέω. [o] *pro* πατάσσω.
[p] *pro* πίπτω. [q] A ἀφίστημι.
[r] *pro* ἐκποιέω. [s] *pro* ἐθέλω.
[t] *pro* ἐγγίζω. [u] *pro* πληθύνω.
[v] *pro* πολεμέω. [w] *pro* ἵστημι.
[x] *pro* πράσσω. [y] A ἐάω.
[z] *pro* μεταποιέω. [aa] S^1 ἐπακούω
[bb] B^2S^2 ἀναφέρω. [cc] S^2 πλάσσω.
[dd] *pro* βοηθέω. [ee] *pro* μισέω.
[ff] S^1 πίνω. [gg] *pro* μοχθέω.
[hh] *pro* πίνω. [ii] *pro* ἄγω.
[kk] S ὑπομένω.
[nn] *vide* τεκνοποιέω.
[oo] *pro* ἀσεβέω.
[pp] A περιποιέω.
[qq] *pro* ἁμαρτάνω.
[rr] A καταφυτεύω, B φυτεύω.
[ss] A ἀποφέρω.

ποίημα.

Jud. 13:12[a]
1 Sa. 8: 8–A
10: 4
1 Ki. 7:17+A
Ezra 9:13
Neh. 6:14
Psa. 63:10
91: 5
142: 5
Ecc. 1:14–S[1]
2: 4, 11
17
Ecc. 3:11, 17
22
4: 3, 4
5: 5
7:14
8: 9, 14
14, 17
17
9: 7, 10
11: 5
12:14
Isa. 29:16

[a] A ἔργον.

ποίησις.

Exo. 28: 8
32:35
36:12 AB[1]
Lev. 8: 7
2 Ki. 16:10
Psa. 18: 2
Eze. 43:18
Dan. 9:14

ποικιλία.

Exo. 27:16
35:35
36:15
Jud. 5:30
Eze. 27: 7

ποικίλλω.

Psalm 44:10, 14

ποίκιλμα.

Jer. 13:23
Eze. 23:15
Eze. 27:16

ποικίλος.

Gen. 30:37, 39
40
31: 8, 8, 10
12
37: 3, 23
32
Jos. 7:21
Jud. 5:30 A[a]
1 Ch. 29: 2
Eze. 16:10, 13
18
26:16
Zec. 1: 8
6: 3, 6

[a] pro ποικιλτός.

ποικιλτής.

Exo. 26:36
28: 6, 15
35
Exo. 36:37
37:16

ποικιλτικός.

Exo. 37:21[a]
Job 38:36

[a] A ποικιλτός.

ποικιλτός.

Exo. 35:35
37:21 A[a]
Jud. 5:30[b]

[a] pro ποικιλτικός. [b] A ποικίλος

ποικίλως.

Esther 1: 6

ποιμαίνω.

Gen. 30:31, 36
37: 1, 13
Exo. 2:16
3: 1
1 Sa. 16:11
17:15A, 34
25:16
2 Sa. 5: 2
7: 7
1 Ch. 11: 2[a]
17: 6
Psa. 2: 9
22: 1
27: 9
36: 3
47, 15–S
48:15
77:71, 72
79: 2
Ps. 150 p 6
Pro. 9:12
22:11
28: 7
29: 3
Cant. 1: 7, 8
2:16
6: 1, 2
Isa. 40:11
61: 5
Jer. 3:15, 15[b]
6: 3, 18
22:22
23: 1 S[c], 2
4
Eze. 34:10, 23
Hos. 13: 5
Mic. 5: 4, 6
7:14
Zec. 11: 4, 7, 7
9, 15
Zec. 11:17

[a] S[2] πενέω. [b] A ποιμήν.
[c] pro ποιμήν.

ποιμενικός.

1 Sa. 17:40
Zec. 11:15

ποιμήν.

Gen. 4: 2
13: 7, 7, 8
8
26:20, 20
29: 8
38:12, 20
43:31+A
46:32, 34
47: 3
Exo. 2:17, 19
Nu. 27:17
1 Sa. 25: 7
2 Sa. 24:17+A
1 Ki. 22:17
2 Ki. 10:12
2 Ch. 18:16
Job 1:16
24: 2
Ecc. 12:11
Cant. 1: 8
Isa. 13:20
32:14
40:11
63:11
Jer. 2: 8
3: 1
3–S
15
15 A[a]
Jer. 6: 3
10:21
12:10
22:22
23: 1[b], 4
27: 6, 44
28:23
29:20
32:20, 21
22
40:12
50:12
Eze. 34: 2 qnq
5, 7, 8
8, 8, 9
10, 10
12, 23
23
37:24
Amos 1: 2
3:12
Mic. 5: 5
Nah. 3:18
Zec. 10: 3
11: 3, 5, 8
16
13: 7, 7
7+AS[2]

[a] pro ποιμαίνω, [b] S ποιμαίνω.

ποίμνη.

Gen. 32:16, 16
Zec. 13: 7+A

ποίμνιον.

Gen. 29: 2, 2, 3
30:40
31: 4
32:16, 19
Deu. 7:13
28: 4, 18
51
Jud. 6: 4
1 Sa. 8:17
14:32
15: 9, 14
15, 21
16:11, 19
17:34
24: 4
25: 2, 2, 2
4, 16
27: 9
30:20
2 Sa. 12: 2, 4
1 Ki. 21:27
22:17
1 Ch. 17: 7
2 Ch. 32:28
Neh. 10:36
Job 24: 2
Psa. 49: 9
77:52, 70
Pro. 27:23
Ecc. 2: 7
Cant. 1: 8
Isa. 17: 2
27:10, 10
10–ABS
35: 7 S[a]
40:11
65:10
Jer. 6: 3, 18
13:17, 20
28:23
38:10, 24
Eze. 13: 5
34:12, 31
Joel 1:18
Amos 6: 4
Mic. 2:12
4: 8
5: 4, 8
Zeph. 2: 6, 14
Zec. 10: 3
Mal. 1:14

[a] pro κάλαμος.

ποῖος.

Deu. 4: 7, 8
Jud. 9: 2+A
1 Sa. 9:18
2 Sa. 15: 2
1 Ki. 13:12
22:24
2 Ki. 3: 8
2 Ch. 18:23
Est. 7: 5+S[3]
Job 28:12, 20
Job 38:19, 19
Ecc. 2: 3
11: 6
Isa. 45: 9
50: 1
66: 1, 1
Jer. 5: 7
6:16
Jon. 1: 8, 8

πόκος.

Jud. 6:37, 37
38, 38
39, 39
Jud. 6:40
2 Ki. 3: 4
Psa. 71: 6

πολεμέω.

Exo. 14:14, 25
17: 8[a], 16
Nu. 21: 1 26
Deu. 1:41, 42
3:22
Jos. 11: 5, 23
19:48
24:11
Jud. 1: 1
3 A[b]
5 A[b]
8, 9
5: 8–A
14+A
19
20 A[b]
20 A[b]
8: 1 A[b]
9:17 A[b]
38 A[b]
39 A[b]
45 A[b]
10:18 A[b]
11: 4 A[b]
5+A
6 A[b]
8 A[b]
9 A[b]
12 A[b]
20 A[b]
25, 25
27 A[b]
32 A[b]
12: 1 A[b]
3 A[b]
4 A[b]
20:14 A[c]
18 A[c]
1 Sa. 4: 9, 10
8:20
12: 9
14:47
15:18
17: 9
19 A
32, 33
18:17 A
19: 8
23: 1, 5
25:28
28: 1, 15
29: 8, 11
31: 1
2 Sa. 2:28
8:10[d]
10:17
11:17, 20
22
12:26, 27
29
21:15
1 Ki. 12:21, 24
p 24 l 77
l 80
14:19 A
1 Ki. 16 p 28–A
21: 1, 23
25
22:31, 32
46+A
2 Ki. 3:21
6: 8
8:29
9:15
10: 3
12:17
14:15, 28
16: 5
19: 8, 9
1 Ch. 7:11, 40
10: 1
11: 8+ABS
18:10
19: 7, 10
17
2 Ch. 11: 1, 4
12:15
13:12
15: 6
17:10
18:30, 31
20:17, 22
29
22: 6
26: 6
32: 2, 8
35:21[e], 22
22
Neh. 4:20
Est. 8:13
9:24
Job 11:19
Psa. 34: 1, 1
55: 2, 3
108: 3
119: 7
128: 1, 2
Isa. 2: 4
7: 1
19: 2
2+S[1]
20: 1
29: 1
30:32
36:10
63:10
Jer. 1:19
15:20
21: 4, 5
28:30
31:27
39:24, 29
41: 1, 7, 22
44: 8, 10
45: 4[f]
48:12
51:12 S[g]
Dan. 10:20
11:11
Mic. 4: 3

[a] A πορεύω.
[b] pro παρατάσσω.
[c] pro παράταξις.
[d] AB πατασσω. [e] A ποιέω.
[f] A πολεμιστής.
[g] pro ἀπόλλυμι.

πολεμικός.

Deu. 1:41
Jud. 18:11 A[a]
16 A[a]
17+A
1 Sa. 8:12
2 Sa. 1:27
1 Ch. 12:33, 37
2 Ch. 26:13
Jer. 21: 4
31:14
Eze. 32:27
Zec. 9:10

[a] pro παράταξις.

πολέμιος.

1 Ch. 18:10
Ezra 8:31
Est. 9:16
Isa. 27: 4

πολεμιστής.

Nu. 31:27, 28
32, 42
49, 53
Deu. 2:14, 16
Jos. 8: 1, 3, 11
10: 7
11: 7
17: 1
Jud. 20:17 A[a]
1 Sa. 13:15
16:18
17:33
30:22
2 Sa. 17: 8
1 Ki. 10 p 22
2 Ki. 25:19
1 Ch. 12:38
28: 3
2 Ch. 8: 9
13: 3, 3
14: 8
17:13
28:14
32:21
Isa. 3: 2
Jer. 27:30
28:32
30:15
45: 4 A[b]
52: 7, 25
Eze. 27:10, 27
39:20
Joel 2: 7
3: 9
Zec. 13: 7 S[1] [c]

[a] pro παράταξις.
[b] pro πολεμέω. [c] pro πολίτης.

πόλεμος.

Gen. 14: 2, 8
Exo. 1:10
13:17
15: 3
32:17
Lev. 26: 5
7+AB[a]
36, 37
Nu. 10: 9
14: 3
20:18
21:14, 33
31:14, 21
36
32: 6, 20
27, 29
30
Deu. 2: 5, 9, 19
24, 32
3: 1
4:34
20: 1, 2, 3
5, 6, 7
12, 20
21:10
23: 9+A[2]
24: 7
29: 7
Jos. 4:13
8:14
10:11, 24
11:18, 19
20
14:11, 15
22:33
Jud. 3: 1, 2, 10
8:13 A[a]
20:20 A[a]
20+A
22 A[a]
23 A[a]
28 A[a]
34 A[a]
39 A[a]
39 A[a]
42 A[a]
21:22 A[a]
1 Sa. 4: 1, 1, 2
2
7:10
8:20
13: 5, 22
14:20, 22
23, 23
52
17: 1, 2, 8
13 A
13 A
20 A
28 A
1 Sa. 17:47
18: 5 A
17 A
19: 8
23: 8
25:28
26:10
28: 1
29: 4, 9
30:24
31: 3
2 Sa. 1: 4–A
25
2:17
3: 1, 6, 30
5:24
10: 8, 9, 13
11: 7, 15
18, 19
22, 25
18: 6, 8
19: 3, 10
21:15, 17
18, 19
20
22:35, 40
23: 9
1 Ki. 2: 5
5: 3
8:44
12:21
14:30
15: 6 A, 7
16
32 A
21:14, 18
26, 29
39
22: 1, 4, 6
15, 30
30, 34
35
2 Ki. 3: 7, 26
8:28
9:16
13:25
14: 7
16: 5
18:20
24:16
25: 4
1 Ch. 5:10, 18
19, 20
22
7: 4
10: 3
11:13
12: 1, 8
19, 33
35, 36

1 Ch. 14:15
18: 8 B[b]
19: 9, 14
17-ABS
20: 4, 5, 6
22: 8
26:27 A[b]
2 Ch. 6:34
11: 1
13: 2
3+A
3, 14
14: 6, 10
15:10
16: 9
17:18
18: 3,5,14
29, 29
33, 34
20: 1
22: 5
25: 5, 13
26:11
11-AB
12, 13
27: 7
28:12
32: 6, 8
35:21
Job 5:15, 20
22:10
33:18
38:23
39:25
40:27
Psa. 17:35, 40
23: 8
26: 3
45:10
67:31
75: 4
77: 9
88:44
Ps. 139: 3, 8
143: 1
Pro. 21:31
24: 6
Ecc. 3: 8
8: 3
9:11, 18
Cant. 3: 8
Isa. 14:21
21:15[c]
22: 2
42:13, 25
46: 2
Jer. 4:19
6: 4, 23
18:21
26: 3
27:22, 42
28:20
29:15
30: 2
35: 8
48:16
49:14
Eze. 7:14+A
15
17:17
Dan. 7:21
9:26
11:20, 25
Hos. 1: 7
2:18
10: 9, 14
Joel 2: 5
3: 9
Amos 1:14
Obad. 1
Mic. 2: 8
3: 5
Nah. 3:14 S[d]
Zec. 10: 3, 5
14: 2, 3

[a] pro παράταξις. [b] pro πόλις. [c] A παιδίον. [d] pro πηλός.

πολιορκέω.

Jos. 10:29, 31
34 AB[a]
Jud. 2:18
9:31 A[b]
2 Sa. 20:15
2 Ki. 16: 5
17: 4, 5
18: 9
24:11
Job 17: 7
Isa. 1: 8
7: 1
9:21
27: 3
37: 8, 9
Jer. 19: 9
46: 1
Dan. 1: 1

[a] pro ἐκπολιορκέω.
[b] pro περικάθημαι.

πολιορκία.

Pro. 1:27
Jer. 19: 9

πολιός.

Lev. 19:32
Jud. 8:32 A[a]
Ruth 4:15
1 Ki. 2: 6, 9
1 Ki. (3) p 1
Pro. 20:29
Isa. 47: 2
Hos. 7: 9

[a] pro πόλις.

πόλις.

Gen. 4:17, 17
10:11, 12
11: 4, 5, 8
13:12
14: 5
18:24, 26
26-A
28
19: 4, 12
14, 15
20, 21
22, 25
25, 29
29
20: 2
22:17
Gen. 23: 2, 10
18
24:10, 11
13, 43
60
26:33
28:19
33:18, 18
34:20, 20
24, 25
27, 28
29
35: 5, 27
36:32, 35
39
41:35, 48
Gen. 41:48
44: 4, 13
46:28, 29
Exo. 1:11
9:29, 33
Lev. 14:40, 41
45, 53
25:29, 30
32, 32
33, 33
34
26:25, 31
33
Nu. 13:20, 29
20:16
21: 2,3,25
25, 26
27, 28
31
22:36, 39
24:19
31:10
32:16, 17
24, 26
33, 33
36
36 A[a]
38
35: 2, 2, 3
4, 4, 5
5, 5, 6
6, 6, 7
7, 8, 8
11, 12
13, 13
14, 14
15, 25
26, 27
28, 32
Deu. 1:22, 28
2:34, 34
35, 36
36, 37
3: 4 ter
5, 5, 6
7, 10
10, 12
19
4:41, 42
6:10
9: 1
12: 5[b]
14 A[c]
15, 17
18, 21
13:12
13 A[d]
15 A[d]
16
14:29, 26
27, 28
15: 7, 22
16: 5
11+A
14, 18
17: 2, 8
18: 6
19: 1, 2, 5
7, 9
11, 12
20:10
11+A
14, 15
15
16+A
19, 20
21: 2, 3, 3
4, 6, 19
19 A[e]
20, 21
22:17, 18
21+A
23, 24
24
24:16
25: 8
26:12
28: 3, 16
52, 52
55, 57
Deu. 31:12
34: 3
Jos. 2:14, 18
4:13
6: 5, 5, 7
11+A
13-A
15, 16
17, 20
21, 23
24, 26
7: 3
8: 2, 4, 4
5, 6, 7
11, 12
14, 16
17-A
18, 18
19, 19
20
21-A
21-A
22, 27
28
9:23 ter
10: 2, 19
20
11:12, 13
19, 21
13: 9, 10
16, 17
21, 23
25
28-B
28-A
30, 31
14: 4, 12
15
15: 9, 10
10, 13
15, 16
21, 21
25, 32
36, 41
44, 49
51, 54
54, 57
59, 59
60, 60
62, 62
16: 9, 9
10+A
17: 9, 12
18: 9, 14
21, 24
28+AB
28
19: 6, 7, 8
13, 16
23
29+A
30+A
31-A
35
38+A
41, 47
50, 50
20: 2, 3
4A, 4A
4A, 6A
6A, 6A
7, 9
21: 2, 3, 4
5, 6, 7
8, 9, 12
13, 16
18, 19
19+A
20, 21
22, 24
25, 26
27, 27
29, 31
32, 32
33, 33
35, 36
37, 38
39, 40
40, 41
41, 41
Jos. 21:42 quq
24:12 A[f]
13, 33
Jud. 1: 8, 11
12, 16
17, 20
23, 24
24, 25
25, 26
27
3:13
5: 8-A
11
6:27, 28
30
8:16
16-A
17, 27
32[g]
9:30, 31
33, 35
40 A[h]
43, 44
45 ter
51, 51
10: 4
11:26, 33
12: 7
14:18
16: 2, 3
17: 8
18:27, 28
29, 29
19:11, 12
15, 17
22
20:11, 14
15
21+A
31, 32
37, 38
40, 40
42, 48
48, 48
21:23
Ruth 1:19
2:18
3:15
4: 2
1 Sa. 1: 3
4:13, 13
5: 6, 9, 9
11, 12
6:18, 18
7:14
8:22
9: 6, 10
11, 12
13, 13
14, 14
18, 25
27
10: 5
11: 9
14:23
15: 5
16: 4
18: 6
20: 6, 9
28, 29
40, 43
21:13
22: 5, 19
23: 7, 10
27: 5, 5
28: 3
30: 3, 29
29
31: 7
2 Sa. 2: 1, 3
5: 7, 9, 9
6:10, 12
16
8: 8, 11
10: 3, 12
14
11:16, 17
20, 22
25
12: 1, 26
2 Sa. 12:27, 28
28, 30
31
15: 2, 12
14
18 A[i]
24, 25
27, 31
37
37+A
17:13, 13
17, 23
18: 3
19: 3, 37
20: 6, 15
19, 21
22, 22
24: 5, 7
1 Ki. 1:41, 45
2:10
(3) 1
p 1 ter
p 16+A
3:25
4:30-A
8: 1, 16
37, 44
48
9: 9, 11
12, 13
16 A
24 A
10 p 22 ter
26
11:13, 18
27, 32
36, 43
43-A
12:17 A
p 24 l 2
ll 12, 34
l 40[k]
l 43
13:25, 29
14:11 A
12 A
21, 31
15: 8, 20
23-B
24
16: 4, 18
p 28-A
17:10
20: 8+A
11-B
11-B
13, 24
21: 2, 12
14 A[m]
19, 30
34
22:26, 36
39, 51
2 Ki. 2:19, 19
23
3:19
19+A
25
6:14, 15
19
7: 3, 4, 4
10, 12[n]
12
8: 3-A
24
9:15, 28
31
10: 2, 5, 6
8 A[h]
8+B*
25
11:20
12:21
13:25, 25
14:20
15: 7, 38
16:20
17: 9, 9
24, 24
26, 29
2 Ki. 17:32
18: 8, 13
30
19:13-B
25, 32
33, 34
20: 6, 6, 20
23: 5, 8, 8[o]
8, 16
17, 19
27
24:10, 11
25: 2, 3, 4
4, 11
19 ter
1 Ch. 1:43, 46
50
2:22, 23
53-A
4:12, 31
32, 33
6:56, 57
60, 60
61, 62
63, 64
65, 66
67
9: 2
10: 7
11: 5, 7, 8
8+ABS
13: 2, 5, 6
13
15: 1, 29
16:42 S[1 b]
18: 8[p]
19: 3, 7, 9
13-BS
15
20: 2
3+A
26:27[q]
2 Ch. 1: 4, 14
5: 2
6: 5, 28
34, 38
8: 2, 4, 5
6-A[l]
6, 6
11, 11
9:25, 31
10:17
11: 5, 10
12
12-A
23
12: 4, 13
16
13:19
14: 1, 5, 6
7, 14
15: 6, 6, 8
16: 4, 14
17: 2 ter
7, 9, 12
19
18:25
19: 5 ter
10-B
20: 4
21: 1, 3
11, 20
23: 2, 21
24: 5, 16
25
25:13, 28
26: 6
27: 4+AB
9
28:15, 18
25, 25
27
29:20
30:10, 10
31: 1, 1, 6
19 ter
32: 1, 3, 4
5, 18
28, 29
30
2 Ch. 33:14, 14
15
34: 6, 8[r]
35:19
Ezra 2: 1, 70
70
3: 1
4:10, 12
13, 15
15, 15
16, 19
21
5: 4
6: 2
10:14 ter
Neh. 1: 3+BS
2: 3, 5, 8
3:15
4: 2
7: 4, 6, 72
8: 1, 15
16
9:25
10:37
11: 1, 1, 3
3, 9
17+S[3]
20 S[3]
12:37, 44
13:18
Est. 1: 2, 5
2: 3, 5, 8
3:15
4: 1
5+S[3]
5+S[3]
6: 9, 11
8:11
(9) 17
9: 6-S[1]
11+S[3]
12-S[1]
14-S[1]
18-S[1]
27
Job 2: 8
11 A[m]
6:10, 20
15:28
24:12
29: 7
39: 7
42 p 18
p 18
Psa. 9: 7
30:22
45: 5
47: 2, 3, 9
9
54:10[s]
58: 7, 15
59:11
68:36
71:16
72:20
86: 3
100: 8
106: 4, 7, 36
107:11
121: 3
126: 1
138:20
Pro. 1:21
6:14
10:15
11:10
11+
AB*S[2]
16:32
18:11, 19
21:22
25:28
29: 8
Ecc. 7:20
8:10
9:14, 15
10:15, 16
Cant. 3: 2, 3
5: 7
Isa. 1: 7, 8+B

Isa. 1: 8, 21
22+A
26
6:11
10: 6, 14
28, 29
14:17−A
31, 31
17: 1, 9
18: 4
19: 2,2,18
18, 18
22: 2, 8, 9
10
23:16
24:10, 12
25: 2, 2, 2
3, 4
26: 1, 5
27: 3, 3
29: 1
30:13
32:13, 14
18
33:20
20+B[1]
20
34:13
36: 1, 15
19
37:13, 26
33
34−AS
35
38: 6−AS
6
40: 9
41:26
45: 1, 13
48: 2
52: 1
54: 3
60:14
61: 4
62:12
64:10
66: 6−S[1]
20
Jer. 1:15, 18
2:15, 28
3:14
4: 5, 7
7+S[1]
16, 26
29
5: 6, 17
6: 6
7:17−A
34
8:14, 16
9:11
10:22
11: 6, 9A[i]
12, 13
13:19
14:18
17:24, 25
25, 26
19: 8, 11
12, 15
15
15+AS
20: 5, 16
21: 4, 6, 7
9, 10
22: 6, 8, 8
23:39
24: 8A[d]
28:31, 43
29: 2, 14
30: 1, 14
31: 8
8+A
9, 15
24, 28
32, 34
32: 4, 15
33: 6,9,11
12, 15
37:18

Jer. 38:21, 23
24−S
24AS[d]
38
39: 3−S[1]
24, 24
25, 28
29[a], 29
31, 36
44, 44
44−B
44
40: 4−S[1]
10, 12
13
13−A
13, 13
41: 1, 2, 7
7,7,22
43: 6
44: 4, 8[n]
10, 21
45: 2, 3, 4
9, 17
18, 23
28+A
46: 2, 16[n]
47:10
48: 7
51: 2, 9A[d]
17, 21
52: 5, 6, 7
7S[1h]
7, 13
25+A
25, 25
Lam. 1: 1, 19
2:11, 12
15
3:50
5:11
Eze. 4: 1, 3
5: 2
6: 6
7:15, 23
9: 1, 5, 9
10: 2
11: 2, 6
23, 23
12:20
16: 7, 7
17: 4
19: 7
21:20
22: 2, 3
24: 6
9+A
25: 5
9+A
9, 9
26:10, 17
19, 19
29:12, 12
30: 7, 7
17A[u]
33:21
35: 4, 9
36: 4, 10
33, 35
38
38:11A[d]
39: 9, 16
40: 1, 2
43: 3
45: 5, 6, 7
7
48:15, 15
17, 18
19, 20
21, 22
30, 31
35
Dan. 9:16, 18
19, 24
26
11:15
Hos. 6: 8
8:14, 14
11: 6, 9
13:10

Joel 2: 9
3:17+S[e]
Amos 2: 2
3: 6, 6
4: 6, 6A[e]
7, 7
8+A
8−A[1]
8
5: 3
6: 8
7:17
9:14
Obad. 20
Jon. 1: 2
3: 2, 3, 4
4: 5, 5, 5
11

Mic. 1:11
4:10
5:11, 14
6: 9, 9
7:12, 12
Nah. 2: 6[r]
3: 1
Hab. 2: 8, 12
12, 17
Zeph. 1:16
(2)15
3: 1, 6
Zec. 1:12, 17
7: 7
8: 3,5,20
21+S[1]
21, 21
14: 2, 2, 2

[a] *pro* ἔπαυλις. [b] A φυλή. [c] *pro* φυλή. [d] *pro* γῆ. [e] *pro* τόπος. [f] *pro* βασιλεύς. [g] A πολιός. [h] *pro* πύλη. [i] *pro* πούς. [k] B πύλη. [m] *pro* χώρα. [n] A γῆ. [o] AB[2] πύλη. [p] B πόλεμος. [q] A πόλεμος. [r] A δύναμις. [s] S[1] γῆ. [t] *pro* ἀνήρ. [u] *pro* γυνή. [v] S[1] ποταμός.

πολίτης.

Gen. 23:11
Pro. 11: 9, 12
24:43

Jer. 36:23
38:34[a]
Zec. 13: 7[b]

[a] A ἀδελφός. [b] S[1] πολεμιστής.

πολλάκις.

Job 4: 2
Job 31:31

πολλαχῶς.

Ezekiel 16:26

πολλοστός.

2 Sa. 23:20
Pro. 5:19

πολυάνδριον.

Jer. 2:23
19: 2, 6, 6
Eze. 39:11, 12
15, 16

πολυδυνάμεως.

2 Samuel 23:36[a]

[a] A πολλὺς δυνάμεως.

πολυέλεος.

Exo. 34: 6
Nu. 14:18
Neh. 9:17
Psa. 85: 5, 15
Ps. 102: 8
144: 8
Joel 2:13
Jon. 4: 2

πολυήμερος.

Deu. 6:24 A[a]
22: 7
Deu. 25:15
30:18

[a] *pro* εὖ.

πολυημερεύω.

Deuteronomy 11:21 A[a]

[a] *pro* μακροημερεύω.

πολυλογία.

Proverbs 10:19

πολυοδία.

Isaiah 57:10

πολυοχλία.

Job 31:34
Job 39: 7

πολυπλασιάζω.

Deu. 4: 1−A
8: 1
Deu. 11: 8

πολυπληθέω.

Exo. 5: 5
Lev. 11:42
Deu. 7: 7

πολύπλοκος.

Job 5:13[a]

[a] S[1] πολύτροπος.

πολυρρήμων.

Job 8: 2

πολύς.

Gen. 6: 1
13: 6
15: 1, 14
17: 5
18:18
21:34
24:25
26:14
29: 7
30:43
33: 9
36: 7
37:34[a]
41:29, 49
48:16
50:20
Exo. 2:11, 23
3: 8
4:18
9:18, 24
10: 4, 14
12:38, 38
16:17, 18
23:29
32:13
Nu. 13:19
14:12
20:11
21: 6
22: 3
24: 7
26:56
32: 1+A
35: 8, 8
Deu. 1: 28, 46
2: 1, 10
21
3: 5, 19
7: 1+A
1, 17
8: 7
9: 2, 14
15: 6, 6
26: 5
28:12, 12
38
30:16
31:17
21+A
33: 6
Jos. 9:19
11: 4
13: 1
17:14, 15
17
22: 8 *ter*
24: 4
Jud. 7:, 2, 4
8:24+A
30
9:40
1 Sa. 2: 5
14: 6
26:13, 21
2 Sa. 1: 4
3: 1, 22
8: 8
12: 2, 30
13:34
14: 2
15:12
22:17
24:14, 16
1 Ki. 2:35
(3) *p* 46

1 Ki. 3: 8, 11
4(20)A
25
5: 7
10: 2, 10
11
11: 1+A
18: 1, 25
19: 7
2 Ki. 9:22
10:18
12:10
21:16
1 Ch. 4:27
5: 9, 22
7:22
11:22
18: 8
20: 2
21:13
22: 3, 8
28: 5
29: 2
2 Ch. 1: 9, 11
9: 9
11:23
13: 8
8A[2b]
14:11, 11
13, 14
15
15: 3, 9
16: 8
17: 5, 13
18: 1, 2
20: 2, 12
15, 25
25
21: 3
24:11, 24
25:13
26:10, 10
27: 3
28: 5,8,13
29:35
30:13, 13
32: 4, 4, 5
23, 27
29
Ezra 3:12
5:11
10: 1, 13
Neh. 2: 2
4: 1, 10
19
5: 2
6:17, 18
7: 2
9:10[c], 28
30, 31
35
37-ABS
13:26
Est. 1: 7
2: 8−S[1]
(9)17
Job 1: 3, 10
2: 9
3:15
4: 3
5:25
9:17
11: 2,3,19
12:12, 12[d]
14:21

Job 16: 2
18:11
20:10
22: 5
23: 6
24: 7, 24
26: 2
27:14
29:18
30:18
31:21, 25
32: 8
34:37
35: 6, 9
36:26
37:18
38:21
39:11
Psa. 3: 2, 3
4: 7
17:17
18:11, 12
21:13, 17
24:11
28: 3
30:14, 20
31: 6, 10
32:10
33:20
34:19
35: 7
36:16
39: 4,6,11
54:19
55: 3
67:12
70: 7, 20
76:20
77:15
88:51
92: 4
96: 1
106:23
108:30
109: 6
118:156
157,162
165
119: 6
122: 3
129: 7
134:10
137: 3+S[1]
143: 7
Pro. 4:10
5:20
6: 8, 35
7:20, 21
26
8: 6S[1e]
18
19+A
9:11, 18
11:14
13: 7, 23
14: 4, 17
20, 28
29
15: 6
6−S[1]
29
17: 1
19: 4, 6
7[f]
19−BS
21
22: 1, 16
23:34
25:27
26:10, 20
28:12, 20
27
29:16, 16
26, 47
47
Ecc. 1:17
2: 7−S[1]
5: 6, 11
16, 19[f]
6: 1,3,11

Ecc. 7:17, 18
23, 30
8: 6
9:18
11: 8, 8
12:10, 12
12
Cant. 7: 4
8: 7
Isa. 2: 3
4+S
4, 6
5: 9
8: 7, 15
11: 9
13: 4
4−S[1]
20
14:11, 19
16:14
17:12, 12
13 *ter*
21: 7
23: 3, 16
24:22
27:10
11+S
28: 2
30:17, 25
27+AS
33
31: 1
33:23
34:10−AS[5]
36: 2
40:26[h]
43: 4+AS
47:12
49: 1
52:14, 15
53:11, 12
12
54: 1, 13
55: 7
57: 9
59:12
66:16
Jer. 3: 1, 3
12:10
13: 6, 10
14: 7
16:16, 16[i]
20:10
23:14[k]
27:29, 41
28:13, 55
35: 8
38: 8
42: 7
44:16
47:12
48:12
49: 2
Lam. 1:22
3:23−AB
Eze. 1:24
3: 6
9: 9
12:27
16:41
17: 5, 7, 8
9, 15
17
19:10
22: 5
24:12, 14
26: 3, 7
19
27: 3, 26
28: 5
31: 5, 7
32: 3, 9
10−A
13
37: 2, 10[e]
38: 4, 6, 8
9, 12
15, 15
22, 23

Eze. 39:27+A
43: 2
47: 7,9,10
Dan. 2: 6
12+B[a]
48
4: 7,9,18
5: 9+A
6:14, 23
7: 5, 28
8:25, 25
26
9:18, 27
27+AB[2]
11: 3,5,10
11, 13
13, 14
18, 26
28, 33
34, 39
40, 41
44, 44
12: 2, 3, 4
10
Hos. 3: 3, 4
Joel 2: 2,5,11
Amos 3: 9, 15
5:12
7: 4
8: 3
Jon. 4:11
Mic. 4: 2, 3
11, 13
5: 7, 8
Nah. 1:12
Hab. 2: 8, 10
13
14+A
3:15
Zeph. 3:12 A[m]
Hag. 1: 6, 9
Zec. 2:11
8:20, 20
21+S[1]
22, 22
10: 8
Mal. 2: 6, 8

[a] A τινάς. [b] pro χρύσεος.
[c] A μέγας. [d] A μακρός.
[e] pro σεμνός. [f] B[1] ἄλλος.
[g] C μέν. [h] S[1] πᾶς.
[i] A σοφός. [k] A πονηρός.
[m] pro πραΰς.

πολυτελής.

1 Ch. 29: 2
Job 31:24
Pro. 1:13
3:15
Pro. 8:11
25:12
29:28
Isa. 28:16

πολυτόκος.

Psalm 143:13

πολύτροπος.

Job 5:13 S[1a] [a] pro πολύπλοκος

πολυχρονίζω.

Deuteronomy 4:26

πολυχρόνιος.

Gen. 20: 8 | Job 32:10

πολυωρέω.

Deu. 30: 9 A[a]
Psa. 11: 9
Ps. 137: 3
[a] pro εὐλογέω.

πόμα.

Ps. 101:10 | Dan. 1:16

πονέω.

Gen. 49:15
Exo. 31: 6[a]
1 Sa. 14:15 A[b]
22: 8
23:21
1 Ki. 15:23
1 Ch. 10: 3
2 Ch. 18:33
2 Ch. 35:23
Pro. 16:26
23:35
Isa. 19:10
Jer. 5: 3−S[1]
28:29
Lam. 4: 6
Hos. 9:16

[a] AB ποιέω. [b] pro ποιέω.

πονηρεύομαι.

Gen. 19: 7
37:18[a]
Exo. 22: 8, 11
Deu. 15: 9
19:19
Jud. 19:23 A[b]
1 Ki. 14: 9 A
16:25
30−A
1 Ch. 16:22
Psa. 5: 5
14: 4
21:17
Psa. 25: 5
36: 1, 8, 9
63: 3
73: 3
91:12
93:16
104:15
118:115
Ecc. 7:23
Jer. 2:33
16:12[c]
20:13−A
45: 9
Jer. 49:20
Mic. 3: 4

[a] A πορεύω. [b] pro κακοποιέω.
[c] S[1] πορεύω.

πονηρία.

Exo. 10:10
32:12
Deu. 31:21
Jud. 9:56[a]
57[a]
11:27
15: 3[b]
20: 3[a]
12[a]
13[a]
41[a]
Neh. 1: 3
2: 2, 17
6: 2
13: 7, 27
Psa. 7:10
27: 4
54:16
72: 8
93:23
140: 4[c]
Pro. 26:25
Ecc. 2:21
6: 1
10: 5
11:10
Isa. 1:16, 16
7:16−S[1]
10: 1, 1
47:10
59: 7
Jer. 4: 4
6:29
9: 7−S
10:23 S[1d]
13:27 S[e]
23:11
24: 2, 3, 8
31:16
39:32
40: 5
51: 3, 22
Dan. 11:27
Hag. 2:14 S[a f]

[a] A κακία. [b] A κακός.
[c] S πονηρός. [d] pro πορεία.
[e] pro πορνεία. [f] pro πόνος.

πονηρός.

Gen. 2: 9, 17
3: 5, 22
6: 5
8:21
12:17
13:13
28: 8
31:24, 29
34:30
35:21
37: 1, 20
33
38: 7, 10
39: 9
41:19
44: 4, 5
47: 9
50:17, 20
Exo. 33: 4
Lev. 26: 6
27:10, 10
12, 14
33
33−AB
Nu. 11: 1, 10
13:20
14:27, 35
36, 37
20: 5
24:13
32:13
Deu. 4:25
6:22
7:15
9:18
13: 5, 11
15:21
17: 1, 2
5+A
7, 12
19:19, 20
21:21
22:14, 19
21, 22
24
23: 9
24: 9
28:20, 35
59, 60
31:29
Jos. 23:15
Jud. 2:11
3: 7, 12
12
4: 1
6: 1
Jud. 9:23
10: 6
13: 1
1 Sa. 2:23+A
3:21
8: 6
15:19
16:14, 15
16, 23
23
18: 8
10 A
19: 9
25: 3, 21
30:22
2 Sa. 3:39
4:11
11:25, 27
12: 9
13:22
14:17
19:35+B
1 Ki. 5: 4
11: 8
12 p 24 l 6
14:22
15:26, 34
16:19, 25
30
20:20, 25
22:53
2 Ki. 1:18
2:19
3: 2
4:41
8:18, 27
13: 2, 11
14:24
15: 9, 18
24, 28
17: 2, 13
17
21: 2, 6, 9
11, 15
16, 20
23:32, 37
24: 9, 19
1 Ch. 2: 3
21: 7
2 Ch. 7:14
12:14
21: 6, 15
19
22: 4
29: 6
33: 2, 6, 9
2 Ch. 33:22
36: 2, 5, 9
12
Ezra 4:12
9:13
Neh. 2: 2,3,10
4: 1, 7
6:13
9:28, 35
13: 8, 17
Est. 7: 6
Job 1: 1, 8
2: 7
12: 6
21:30
34:17
35:12
37:15
Psa. 9:36
33:22
34:12
36:19
40: 2
48: 6
50: 6
63: 6
77:49
93:13
96:10
100: 4
108:20
111: 7
118:101
139: 2
140: 4 S[a]
143:10
Pro. 3:15
7: 5
8:13
11:15
20: 8
22: 3
24:20
Ecc. 1:13
2:17
4: 3, 8
5:13[b], 15
6: 2
8: 3,5,11
11, 12
9: 3,3,12
10:13
11: 2
12:14
Isa. 1: 4
3: 9, 11
5:20, 20
7: 5, 15
9:17
14:29
Isa. 25: 4
28:19
30: 4
31: 2
32: 7
35: 9
53: 9
56:11
65:12
66: 4
Jer. 2:13
3: 5, 17
7:30
11:19
12:14[c]
15:21
16:12
17:17−S[1]
18
18:10, 11
12
23: 2, 10
14 A[d]
14, 22
24: 2,3,3,8
25: 5, 5
30:12
33: 3, 3
39:30
42:15
43: 3, 7
45: 4
51:29
Eze. 5:17
7:24+A
8: 9+A
11: 2
21+A
13:22
14:15, 21
21
18:23
30:12+A
33:11+A
11+A
34:25
36 31
38:10
Hos. 3: 1
7:15
12: 1
Amos 5:13, 14
15
Jon. 3: 8, 10
Mic. 2: 3, 9
3: 2
Nah. 1:11
Hab. 1:13
Zec. 1: 4, 4
Mal. 2:17

[a] pro πονηρία. [b] A αὐτός.
[c] A σκληρός. [d] pro πολύς.

πόνος.

Gen. 34:25
41:51
Exo. 2:11
Nu. 23:21
Deu. 28:33
1 Sa. 15:23
1 Ki. 8:37
1 Ch. 10: 3
2 Ch. 6:28
Job 2: 9
3:10[a]
4: 5
5: 6
15: 2,35 A[b]
20:14+A
Psa. 7:15, 17
9:28, 35[a]
51:11[c]
77:46, 51[d]
89:10
104:36, 44
108:11
Ps. 127: 2
Pro. 3: 9
5:10
6: 8
16:26
24: 2, 75
Isa. 1: 5
40: 4
53: 4, 10
59: 4
65:14, 22
66: 7
Jer. 4:14, 15
6: 7
14:18
20: 5, 18[e]
Eze. 23:29
Hos. 12: 8
Obad. 13
Hab. 1: 3, 13
Hag. 1:11
2:14[f]

[a] A κόπος. [b] pro δόλος.
[c] S[1] κόπος. [d] S[1] πρωτοτόκος.
[e] S[1] μόχθος. [f] S[2] πονηρία.

ποντοπορέω.

Proverbs 24:54

πόντος.

Exodus 15: 5

πορεία.

Nu. 33: 2
Neh. 2: 6[a]
Psa. 67:25, 25
Pro. 2: 7
4:27
26: 7
Isa. 3:16
Isa. 8:11
Jer. 10:23[b]
18:15
Jon. 3: 3, 4
Nah. 1: 8
2: 6
Hab. 3: 6, 10

[a] A παρουσία. [b] S[1] πονηρία.

πορεῖον.

Gen. 45:17 A[a] | Est. (9)14+S[3]
[a] pro φορεῖον.

πόρευσις.

Gen. 33:14 | Zec. 8:21+S[2]

πορεύω.

Gen. 2:14 A[a]
3:14
8: 3
5+A
9:23
11:31
12: 4, 5, 9
13: 3
16: 8
21:19
22: 2, 3, 6
8, 13
19
24: 4, 5, 8
10, 38
39, 42
58, 58
61
62 A[b]
65
25:22, 32
26: 1, 26
27: 5,9,13
14
28: 5, 7, 9
10, 15
20
29: 1
30:14
31:30
32:17
33:12
35: 3, 21
36: 6
37:12, 14
17, 17
18 A[c]
25, 30
41:55
42:38
43: 1, 4, 7
45:24, 28
Exo. 2: 8
3:11, 18
19
4:12, 18
18, 21
27, 27
29
5: 3, 7
8 A[d]
11, 17
18[e], 23
8:27, 28
10: 8, 8, 9
11, 26
12:32
14:19, 29
15:19, 22
16: 4
Exo. 17: 5, 8 A[f]
18:20
23:23
33: 1 AB[g]
15 B[g]
Lev. 11:20, 21
27, 27
42, 42
18: 3, 4
19:16
20:23
26: 3, 21
23, 24
27, 28
40, 41
Nu. 10:30, 32
13:27
14:14[h], 38
16:25
20:17
19 A[i]
21:22, 22
22: 7, 12
13, 14
21, 22
23:35
39
23: 3, 3, 3
15
24: 1
32: 6, 39
41, 42
33: 8
Deu. 1:19, 31
33 A[a]
33
2:27[k]
4: 3
5:33
6: 7, 14
8: 6, 19
10:12
11:19, 22
28
13: 2, 4, 5
6 A[m]
13
14:24
19: 9
20: 3[n], 5
6, 7, 8
26: 2, 17
28: 9, 14
29:18, 19
26
30:16
31:14
Jos. 1: 9, 16
2: 1,5,22
3: 3, 4, 4

Jos. 3: 6
4:18
6: 9+A
8: 7,9,11
9:17
10: 9 A[o]
14:10
15: 4 A[p]
16: 8[q]
17: 7
18: 8 *ter*
9
19: 8
27+A
48, 49
51
22: 5, 6, 9
23:16
24:17
28−A
Jud. 1: 3, 3
10
11 A[r]
16+A
17, 26[e]
2:12, 15[s]
17, 19
22
3:13
17−A
4: 8 *qtr*
9 *qtr*
24, 24
5: 6, 6
10−A
6:14, 21[e]
7: 4 *qtr*
7[t]
8: 1[u], 20
9: 1, 4, 6
7, 8, 8
9, 11
13, 21
49, 50
55[e]
10:14[v]
11: 5, 8[x]
11
13−A
16, 18[y]
37, 38
38, 40[y]
12: 1 A[z], 1
13:11
14: 3, 9 *ter*
15: 4
16: 1
17: 8,9,11
18: 2, 5, 6
6, 7, 9
14, 17
24[e], 26
19: 2[e]
3 A[aa]
5[e], 5
7[e], 8[e]
9[e], 9[e]
14[e], 17
18, 18[e]
27[e], 28[e]
20:37+A
21:10, 20[y]
21[e]
23−A
Ruth 1: 1, 7, 8
11+A
11, 16
16, 18
19, 21
2: 2, 2, 3
8, 8, 9
9, 11
22 AB[bb]
3:10
1 Sa. 1:14, 17
18, 19
2:26
3: 6, 8, 9
21, 21
6: 9, 12

1 Sa. 6:12
7:16
8: 3, 5
9: 3, 6, 6
7, 9, 9
10, 10
10: 2, 14
26
11:14, 15
12:14
14: 3, 17
19, 19
26
15: 3, 12
18, 20
16: 2
17:13 A
13 A
13 A
14 A
32, 33
36, 37
39, 41A
41A, 45
48
18:27
19:18, 22
23, 23
23+A
20: 5 A[cc]
11, 22
28, 40
42
22: 5, 5
23: 2
2−A
3, 3A[o]
5, 13
13, 16
22, 23
24, 25
26, 26
28
24: 3
25:42
26: 2+A
5 A[o]
19
27: 2−B
28: 7, 8, 22
29: 7, 10
10
30: 9, 21
22
31:12
2 Sa. 2:19, 20
32
3: 1, 1, 16
16, 19
21, 21
31
4: 5
5:10 A[b]
10
6: 2
4−A
12
7: 5, 9
8: 3, 6, 14
11:22
12:23, 29
13: 7, 8
15, 19
19, 24
25, 25
26, 26
34, 37
38
14:21−B
23, 30
15: 7, 9
11, 11
12, 14
18, 19
20 *ter*
30
37 A[o]
16:13 *ter*
17:11, 17
17, 18

2 Sa. 17:21
18:22, 24
23[dd]
25, 33
19:15, 25
26
20: 5
21:12
15[ee]
23:17
24:12
1 Ki. 2: 2, 3, 4
8, 29
31
(3) *p*1
40, 40
41, 42
3: 3, 4
14, 14
8:23, 25
25, 36
58, 61
9: 4, 4, 6
12
11: 5+A
8, 10
15
24 A
33, 38
12: 1, 24
*p*24*l*6
*ll*24, 26
*ll*34, 48
*ll*74, 82
28, 30
13: 9, 12
14−A
17, 28
14: 2A, 4A
7A, 8A
9 A
12 A
17 A
15: 3, 20
34
16: 2, 18[ff]
19, 26
*p*28−A
*p*28−A
*p*28+B
*p*28−A
31, 31
17: 3
5+A
9, 10
11, 15
18: 1, 2, 6
6, 8
11, 14
16, 16
18, 21
21, 45
19: 4, 8, 15
20+A
21
20:26, 27
27
21:38
22: 6, 13
43
49 A
49 A
50 A
53
2 Ki. 1: 2
3 A[gg]
3, 4, 6
2: 1, 6, 11
14, 16
18, 25
3: 7, 7, 9
4:23, 24
25
25−AB
30, 35
5: 5+A
5, 10
19
12 A[hh]
24+A

2 Ki. 5:25, 26
6: 2, 3, 4
7: 8, 8, 15
8: 2+AB
9, 18
27, 28
9: 4, 15
16, 18
35
10:12, 15
25, 31
12:17 A[r]
13: 2, 6
11, 21
16: 3, 10
17: 8, 15
19, 22
27
19:36
20: 9
21:21, 21
22
22: 2, 14
23: 3, 29
25: 4
1 Ch. 4:39, 42
6:15
11: 4, 9, 9
12:18, 20
14:14
15:25
16:20, 43
17: 4, 8
18: 3, 6
13
21: 2, 10
30
2 Ch. 1: 3, 16
2: 9
6:14, 16
16, 27
7:17, 19
9:21
10: 5, 16
11: 4, 14
17
17: 3, 4, 12
18: 3, 5, 12
14[ff]
20:32, 36
36−A
37
21: 6
12−A
13, 20
22: 3, 5, 5
25: 7[q], 11
13[kk]
28: 2
30: 6
33:14 A[p]
34: 2, 21
22, 31
35:20
Ezra 4:23
5: 8, 15
7:13, 13
10: 6, 6
Neh. 2:16
6:17
8:10
9:12, 19
10:29
12:32
38 S[3]
Est. 4:10, 13
9: 3+S[3]
Job 10:21
16:22
21:20 C[nn]
23: 8
24:13
29: 3, 20
30:28
31: 5
34: 8
38:35
42: 8, 9
Psa. 1: 1
14: 2

Psa. 22: 4
25: 1, 11
31: 8
37: 7
41:10
42: 2
54:15
77:10, 39
80:13, 14
83: 8, 12
84:14 S[1 a]
85:11
88:16, 31
100: 6
104:41
106: 7
118: 1, 3, 45
121: 1
125: 6, 6
127: 1
130: 1
137: 7
138: 7
141: 4
142: 8
Pro. 1:15
2:13, 19
20
3:23
4:12
6: 8, 12
7:19
10: 9, 9
14: 2
15:21
24:42, 64
28: 6, 18
18, 26
Ecc. 1: 4, 6, 6
7, 7, 7
2:14
3:20+
ACS[2]
4:17
5:14, 14
6: 4, 6, 8
9
7: 3, 3
8: 3
10+S[2]
10
9:10
10: 3, 7, 15
12: 5
Cant. 2:11
4: 6
7: 9
Isa. 2: 3, 3, 5
3:16
6: 8, 9
8: 6
9: 2[oo]
18: 2
19:23
20: 2, 2, 3
22:15
28:13
30: 2, 21
33:15, 21
21
35: 8, 9
38: 3, 5
10+S[2]
41: 2
42:24
44: 3
45: 2, 16
46: 7
48:17
50:10, 11
52:12
12 A[a]
55: 1
57:17
59:11
60: 3, 14
62:10
63: 2
Jer. 1: 7
2: 5, 8, 20

Jer. 2:23, 25
3: 6, 8
12, 17
5: 5
6:16, 28
7: 6, 9, 12
23, 24
8: 2
9: 4, 14
10: 2 A[pp]
9, 23
11:10[qq]
12
13: 5−S[1]
7, 10
14:18
15: 6
16: 5
12 S[1 c]
12
18:12
19: 8 S[1 nn]
20: 6
22: 1
23:14, 17
17
25: 6
26:22
27: 4
28:50, 50
33: 4
38:21
39:23
42: 2 A[m]
13, 15
44:12
46:16
47: 5, 5
15
48: 6, 17
49: 3
51: 3, 23
52: 7[rr]
Lam. 1: 5, 6, 18
2:21
4: 9
18[ss]
Eze. 1: 9, 12
12, 12
17, 17
19, 19
20, 20
21, 21
24
24+A
2:10
3:14
5: 6, 7
7:14+A
9: 5
10:11 *qnq*
16, 16
22
11:20, 21
12:11
16:47
18: 9, 11
17
20:13, 13
16, 16
18, 19
21
23:31
25: 3
30:17−A
32:14
36:27
37:24
Dan. 4:34
9:10
Hos. 1: 3
2: 5[tt], 7
13
3: 1
5: 6, 11
13, 14
15
6: 1, 4
7:11, 12
9: 6

Hos. 11:10
13: 3, 4
14: 6, 9
Joel 2: 7, 8
Amos 1:15
3: 3
5: 3 AP
3 AP
9: 4
Jon. 1: 2
8+S[3]
11[uu]
13[uu]
3: 2, 3
Mic. 1: 8
2: 3, 7, 10
4: 2, 2, 5

Mic. 4: 5
6: 8, 16
Nah. 2:11
3:10
Hab. 1: 6
3: 5, 11
Zeph. 1:17
Zec. 2: 2
3: 7
6: 7−S[1]
7
8:21, 21
23
9:14
Mal. 2: 6
3:14

[a] *pro* προπορεύω.
[b] *pro* διαπορεύω.
[c] *pro* πονηρεύομαι.
[d] *pro* ἐγείρω. [e] A ἀπέρχομαι.
[f] *pro* πολεμέω. [g] *pro* συμπορεύω. [h] B συμπορεύω.
[i] *pro* παρέρχομαι.
[k] B παρέρχομαι. [m] *pro* βαδίζω.
[n] A προσπορεύω. [o] *pro* εἰσπορεύω. [p] *pro* ἐκπορεύω.
[q] A παρέρχομαι. [r] *pro* ἀναβαίνω
[s] A πορνεύω, B ἐκπορεύω.
[t] A ἀποτρέχω.
[u] A ἐκπορεύω. [v] A βαδίζω.
[x] A συμπορεύω. [y] A διέρχομαι.
[z] A ὀργίζω. [aa] *pro* εἰσφέρω.
[bb] *pro* ἐξέρχομαι [cc] *pro* κρύπτω
[dd] A γίνομαι. [ee] A ἐκλύω.
[ff] A εἰσπορεύω. [gg] *pro* δεῦρο.
[hh] *pro* λούω. [kk] B εὑρίσκω.
[nn] *pro* παραπορεύομαι.
[oo] A κάθημαι. [pp] *pro* μανθάνω.
[qq] AS βαδιζω. [rr] A οἴχομαι.
[ss] A παραπορεύομαι.
[tt] A ἀκολουθέω. [uu] A ἐπωρύω.

πορνεία.

Gen. 38:24
Nu. 14:33
2 Ki. 9:22
Isa. 47:10
57: 9
Jer. 2:20
3: 2, 9
13:27[a]
Eze. 16:15, 22
25, 33
34, 36
41
23: 7, 8, 8

Eze. 23:11, 11
14, 17
18, 19
27, 29
29, 35
43: 7, 9
Hos. 1: 2, 2
2: 2, 4
4:11, 12
5: 4
6:10
Mic. 1: 7, 7
Nah. 3: 3, 4

[a] S πονηρία.

πορνεῖον.

Ezekiel 16:25, 31, 39

πορνεύω.

Deu. 23:17
Jud. 2:15 A[a]
1 Ch. 5:25
Psa. 72:27
105:39−A
Jer. 3: 6, 7, 8
Eze. 6: 9 B[b]
16:15, 34

Eze. 23: 3+A
19
Hos. 3: 3
4:10, 14
17
9: 1
Amos 7:17

[a] *pro* πορεύω.
[b] *pro* ἐκπορνεύω.

πόρνη.

Gen. 34:31
38:15, 21
21, 22
Lev. 21: 7, 14
Deu. 23: 2-AB[1]
17, 18
Jos. 2: 1
6:17, 23
25
Jud. 11: 1
16: 1
1 Ki. 3:16

1 Ki. 12 *p*24*l*8
20:19
22:38
Pro. 5: 3
6:26
29: 3
Isa. 1:21
23:15, 16
57: 3
Jer. 3: 3
5: 7
Eze. 16:30, 31

Eze. 16:35
23:43, 44
Hos. 4:14, 14
Joel 3: 3
Nah. 3: 4

πορνικός.

Pro. 7:10
Eze. 16:24

πορνοκόπος.

Proverbs 23:21

πόρος.

1 Ki. 10:28 A[a]

[a] pro ἔμπορος.

πόρρω.

2 Ch. 26:15
Job 5: 4
11:14
22:18, 23
Isa. 17:13
22: 3
Isa. 29:13
65: 5
66:19
Jer. 12: 2
31:24
32:12

πόρρωθεν.

2 Ki. 20:14
Job 2:12
39:25, 29
Isa. 10: 3
13: 5
33:13, 17
39: 3
Isa. 43: 6
46:11
49:12
Jer. 5:15
23:23
38: 3

πορφύρα.

Exo. 25: 4
26: 1, 31
36
27:16
28: 5, 8
15, 29
31: 4
35: 6
23+A
25
36: 9, 10
12, 15
Exo. 36:32, 37
37: 3, 5, 16
39:13
2 Ch. 2: 7, 14
3:14
Pro. 29:40
Cant. 7: 5
Jer. 10: 9
Eze. 27: 7
24+A
Dan. 5: 7, 16
29

πορφύρεος.

Nu. 4:14
Jud. 8:26 A[a]
Est. 1: 6
Est. (9)15
Cant. 3:10

[a] pro πορφυρίς.

πορφυρίς.

Jud. 8:26[a]

[a] A πορφύρεος.

πορφυρίων.

Lev. 11:18
Deu. 14:16+A
Deu. 14:17−A

ποσάκις.

1 Ki. 22:16[a]
2 Ch. 18:15
Psa. 77:40

[a] A ἔτι δείς, B[1] πεντάκις.

ποσαπλῶς.

Psalm 62: 2

πόσις.

Daniel 1:10

πόσος.

Gen. 47: 8
2 Sa. 19:34
Job 13:23
Job 38:18
Ps. 118:84
Eze. 27:33

ποταμός.

Gen. 2:10, 13
14, 14
15:18, 18
31:21
36:37
Gen. 41: 1, 2, 3
3, 17
18, 19
Exo. 1:22
2: 3, 5, 5
Exo. 4: 9, 9
7:15, 17
18 ter
19A, 19
20, 20
21 ter
24
24+B[1]
24, 25
8: 3, 5, 9
11
17: 5
23:31
Nu. 13:30
22: 5
24: 6
Deu. 1: 7
7−AB[1]
11:24, 24
Jos. 1: 4, 4
4: 7
5: 1
24: 2, 3
14, 15
Jud. 3: 8
10−A
2 Sa. 8: 3
10:16
1 Ki. (3) p 46
p 46
p 46
4(21)A
24
24+A
8:65
10:26
14:15 A
2 Ki. 5:12
17: 6
18:11
19:24
23:29
24: 7
1 Ch. 1:48
5: 9, 26
18: 3
19:16
2 Ch. 9:26
20:16−A
32: 4
35:20
Ezra 4:10, 11
17, 20
5: 3
6−B
6
6: 6, 6, 8
13
7:21, 25
8:15, 21
31, 36
Neh. 2: 7, 9
3: 7−ABS
Job 14:11
22:16
28:10, 11
Psa. 23: 2
45: 5
64:10
Psa. 65: 6
71: 8
73:15−B
77:16, 44
79:12
88:26
92: 3, 3
3+AS[2]
97: 8
104:41
106:33
136: 1
Pro. 9:18+AS[2]
18: 4
Cant. 8: 7
Isa. 7:18, 20
8: 7
11:15
18: 1, 2, 7
19: 5, 6, 6
7, 7, 8
27:12
32: 2
33:21
41:18
42:15
43: 2, 10
20
44:27
47: 2
48:18
50: 2
59:19
66:12
Jer. 2:18
13: 7
26: 2, 7, 7
8, 10
Eze. 1: 1, 2
3:15, 23
10:15, 20
22
29: 3, 3, 4
4
4+A
5, 9, 10
30:12
31: 4, 15
32: 2, 2, 14
43: 3
47: 6, 7, 9
9, 12
Dan. 7:10
10: 4
12: 5, 5, 6
7
Amos 8: 8, 8
9: 5, 5
Jon. 2: 4
Mic. 7:12
Nah. 1: 4
2: 6 S[1][a]
3: 8
Hab. 3: 8, 8, 9
Zeph. 3:10
Zec. 9:10
10:11

[a] A pro πόλις.

πότερος.

Job 4: 6, 12
7: 1, 12
13: 7, 11
15: 2[a]
Job 21:22
22: 2, 5
26: 2
31:15

[a] A τίνα ἄρα.

πότημα.

Jeremiah 28:39

ποτήριον.

Gen. 40:11 ter
13, 21
2 Sa. 12: 3
1 Ki. 7:11
2 Ch. 4: 5
Est. 1: 7
Psa. 10: 6
15: 5
22: 5
74: 9
Ps. 115: 4
Pro. 23:31
Isa. 51:17, 17
22
Jer. 16: 7
28: 7
29:13
Jer. 32: 1, 3, 14
42: 5
Lam. 2:13
4:21
Eze. 23:31, 32
33, 33
Hab. 2:16

ποτίζω.

Gen. 2: 6, 10
13:10
19:32, 33
34, 35
21:19
24:14, 17
18, 43
45, 46
46
29: 2, 3, 7
8, 10
Exo. 2:16, 17
19
32:20
Nu. 5:24, 26
20: 8
Deu. 11:10
Jud. 4:19, 19
1 Sa. 30:11
2 Sa. 23:15
1 Ch. 11:17
Job 22: 7
Psa. 35: 9
Psa. 59: 5
68:22
77:15
79: 6
103:11, 13
Pro. 25:21
Ecc. 2: 6
Cant. 8: 2
Isa. 27: 3
29:10
43:20
Jer. 8:14
9:15
16: 7
23:15
32: 1, 3
42: 2
Eze. 17: 7
32: 6
Joel 3:18
Amos 2:12
Hab. 2:15

ποτιστήριον.

Gen. 24:20
Gen. 30:38

ποτόν.

Lev. 11:34
1 Ki. 10:21+A
Ezra 3: 7
Job 8:11
15:16
Dan. 1: 5, 8

πότος.

Gen. 19: 3
40:20
Jud. 14:10, 12
17
1 Sa. 25:36, 36
2 Sa. 3:20
13:27, 27
1 Ki. 3:15
Est. 1: 5AS[3][a]
5
5+S[3]
8, 9
Est. 2:18
5: 6
6:14
7: 2
8+S[3]
9:19+S[3]
Job 1: 4, 5
Pro. 23:30
Ecc. 7: 3
Jer. 16: 8
Dan. 5:10

[a] pro γάμος.

ποῦ, που.

Gen. 3: 9
4: 9
16: 8
18: 9
19: 5
22: 7
32:17
37:16, 30
38:21
Exo. 2:20
Deu. 1:28
32:37
Jos. 2: 5
8:20
Jud. 6:13
8:18
9:38
19:17
Ruth 2:19, 19
1 Sa. 10:14
19:22
26:16
2 Sa. 2: 1
13:13
16: 3
17:20
2 Ki. 2:14
6: 6, 13
18:34, 34
2 Ki. 19:13, 13
Job 17:15
19:29[a]
20: 7
21:28, 28
35:10
38: 4
Psa. 41: 4, 11
78:10
88:50
113:10
138: 7, 7
Pro. 20:39
Cant. 5:17, 17
Isa. 10: 3
19:12
33:18 ter
36:19, 19
37:13 ter
49:21
51:13
63:11, 11
15, 15
Jer. 2: 6, 8, 28
3: 2
6:14
13:20
15: 2
17:15
Jer. 43:17[b], 19
44:19
Lam. 2:12
Eze. 13:12
Hos. 13:10, 14
14
Joel 2:17
Mic. 7:10
Nah. 2:11
Zec. 1: 5
2: 2
5:10
Mal. 1: 6
2:17

[a] A οὐδαμοῦ.
[b] AS πόθεν.

πούς.

Gen. 8: 9
18: 4
19: 2
24:32, 32
29: 1
30:30
33:14
43:23
49:10, 33
Exo. 3: 5
4:25
12: 9, 11
21:24, 24
24:10
25:25
29:17, 20
20
30:19, 21
38:27
Lev. 1: 9, 13
8:21, 23
24
9:14
11:21, 23
42
13:12
14:14, 17
25, 28
21:19
Nu. 16:31+A
22:25
Deu. 2: 5, 28
8: 4
11:10, 24
19:21, 21
25: 9
28:35, 56
65
29: 5
32:35
33:24
Jos. 1: 3
3:13, 15
4: 9, 18
5:15
9:11
10:24, 24
Jud. 1: 6, 7
3:24−A
4:10, 15
17
5:15, 27
27, 28[a]
8: 5
19:21
20:43−A
Ruth 3: 4, 7, 8
14
1 Sa. 14:13
23:22
25:24, 41
2 Sa. 2:18
3:34[b]
4: 4, 12
9: 3, 13
11: 8
14:25
15:16, 18[c]
19:24
21:20
22:10, 34
39
1 Ki. 2: 5
5: 3
14: 6 A
12 A
15:23
18:41
2 Ki. 3: 9
2 Ki. 4:27, 37
6:32
9:35
13:21
19:24
21: 8
1 Ch. 28: 2
2 Ch. 3:13
16:12
33: 8
Neh. 9:21[d]
Est. 8: 3
Job 2: 7
13:27, 27
18:8, 11, 13
29:15
30:12
31: 5, 7
33:11
39:15
21 S[2][e]
Psa. 8: 7
9:16
13: 3−A
17:10, 34
39
21:17
24:15
25:12
30: 9
35:12
37:17
39: 3
46: 4
55:14
56: 7[f]
65: 6, 9
67:24
72: 2
90:12
93:18
98: 5
104:18
109: 1
113:15
114: 8
118:59, 101
105
120: 3
121: 2
131: 7
134:17+A
139: 6
Pro. 1:15
16 AS[2]
3: 6+S[2]
23, 26
4:26, 27
5: 5
6:13, 18
28
7:11
25:17, 19
29: 5
Ecc. 4:17
Cant. 5: 3
Isa. 1: 6
3:12, 16
16
5:28
6: 2
7:20
20: 2
26: 6
28: 3
41: 2, 3
49:23
52: 7
57: 6 S[1][g]

Isa. 58:13, 13
59: 7
60: 1
Jer. 2:25
12: 5
13:16
14:10
20: 3
45:22
Lam. 1: 9, 13
2: 1
3:33
Eze. 1: 7
2: 1, 2
3:24
6:11
24:17, 23
Eze. 25: 6
29:11—A
11—A
32: 2, 13
34:18, 18
19, 19
37:10
43: 7
Dan. 2:33, 34
41, 42
7: 4,7,19
8:18
Amos 2:15
Nah. 1: 3, 14
Hab. 3: 5, 19
Zec. 14: 4, 12
Mal. 4: 3

[a] A *ἴχνος.* [b] A *παῖς.*
[c] A *πόλις.* [d] AS *ὑπόδημα.*
[e] *pro πεδίον.* [f] S *ψυχή.*
[g] *pro σπονδή.*

πρᾶγμα.

Gen. 19:22
21:26 A[a]
21:50[b]
41:15
Exo. 1:18
Lev. 5: 2
6: 5
7:11
Nu. 20:19
22: 8
31:23
Deu. 17: 5+A
10[c]
22:26
23: 9 A[a]
14, 19
24: 3, 7
Jos. 9:30
Jud. 6:29 A[a]
29 A[a]
19:19
1 Ki. 10*p* 22
11:27
1 Ch. 21: 7, 8
2 Ch. 23:19
Est. 2: 4[d]
3:15
7: 5
Job 1: 1, 8
Psa. 63: 4
90: 6
100: 3
Pro. 11:13
13:13
16:20
25: 2[b]
Ecc. 3: 1, 17
5: 7
8: 6
Isa. 25: 1
28:22
Jer. 47:10
51: 4, 22
Dan. 6:17
Amos 3: 7

[a] *pro ῥῆμα.* [b] A *πρόσταγμα.*
[c] A *ῥῆμα.* [d] B[1] *πρόσταγμα.*

πραγματεία.

1 Ki. 7:19
9: 1
10*p* 22 *bis*
1 Ch. 28:21
Psa. 70:15[a]

[a] 8[a]S *γραμματεία.*

πραγματεύομαι.

1 Kings 10*p* 22

πράκτωρ.

Isaiah 3:12

πρᾶξις.

1 Ch. 12:24 S[a]
2 Ch. 12:15
13:22
27: 7
2 Ch. 28:26
Job 24: 5 AS[2 b]
Pro. 13:13

[a] *pro παράταξις.* [b] *pro τάξις.*

πραότης.

Psa. 89:19 A[a]
Psa. 131: 1

[a] *pro πραΰτης.*

πράσινος.

Genesis 2:12

πρᾶσις.

Gen. 42: 1
Lev. 25:14, 25
27, 28
42, 50
51
Deu. 18: 8
Deu. 21:14
2 Ki. 12: 5, 7
Neh. 10:31
13:15, 16
20
Eze. 27:17

πράσον.

Numbers 11: 5

πράσσω.

Gen. 31:28
Jos. 1: 7
Job 5:27[a]
7:20
24:20
27: 6
34:21
35: 6
36:21, 23
Pro. 10:23
13:10, 16
14:17
21: 7
24:55, 55
25:28
26:19
Isa. 57:10
Dan. 11:20

[a] A *ποιέω.*

πραΰθυμος.

Pro. 14:30
Pro. 16:19[a]

[a] A *πράθυμος.*

πραΰνω.

Psa. 93:13
Pro. 18:14

πραΰς.

Nu. 12: 3
Job 24: 4
36:15
Psa. 24: 9, 9
33: 3
36:11
75:10
Ps. 146: 6
149: 4
Isa. 26: 6
Joel 3:11
Zeph. 3:12[a]
Zec. 9: 9

[a] A *πολύς.*

πραΰτης.

Psa. 44: 5
Psa. 89:10[a]

[a] A *πραότης.*

πρέπει.

Psa. 32: 1
64: 2
Psa. 92: 5

πρεσβεῖον.

Gen. 43:32
Psa. 70:18

πρέσβυς, –βύτερος.

Gen. 18:11, 12
19: 4, 31
31, 33
34, 37
24: 1, 2
27: 1, 15
42
29:26
35:29
43:26 A[a]
44:12, 20
50: 7, 7
Exo. 10: 9[b]
17: 5
18:12
19: 7
24: 1, 9 A[c]
14
34:30[d]
32 A[1 e]
Lev. 4:15
19:32
Nu. 11:16, 16
24, 25
30
16:25
21:21
22: 5
Deu. 2:26
28:50 A[a]
31: 9
28—B
32: 7
25 A[a]
Jos. 6:21 A[a]
7: 6, 23
8:10
9: 6, 17
Jos. 13: 1
20: 4 A
23: 1
24: 1, 20
Jud. 2: 7
8:14, 16
11: 5, 7, 8
9, 10
11
21:16
Ruth 4: 2, 4, 9
11
1 Sa. 4: 3
15:30
16: 4
17:12 A
30:26
2 Sa. 3:17
5: 3
12:17
17: 4, 15
19:11, 32
1 Ki. 1: 1
8: 1
3+A
12: 6,8,13
p 24 *l* 18
ll 33,58
l 61
13:29+A
14: 4 A
20: 8
11—B
21: 7, 8
2 Ki. 6:32, 32
10: 1, 5
19: 2
23: 1
1 Ch. 11: 3
15:25
21:16
2 Ch. 5: 2, 4
10: 6,8,13
15:13
22: 1
32: 3
34:29
36:17
Ezra 3:12
5: 9
6: 7,8,14
10: 8, 14
Job 1:13, 18
12:20
15:10 A[1 f]
29:21+
AC[2]
32: 4, 7
42:17[g]
Psa. 67:32
104:22
106:32
118:100
148:12 S[a]
Pro. 20:29
29:41 AS[2 h]
Ecc. 4:13
Isa. 3: 2, 14
Isa. 13: 8
21: 2
24:23
37: 2, 6
39: 1
47: 6
57: 9
63: 9
Jer. 6:11
19: 1
1+A
33:17
36: 1
39: 8
Lam. 1:19
2:10
5:12
Eze. 7:26
8: 1, 11
12
9: 6, 6
14: 1
16:46, 61
20: 1, 3
23: 4
27: 9
Hos. 5:13
Joel 1: 2, 14
2:16, 28
Zec. 8: 4, 4

[a] *pro πρεσβύτης.*
[b] A *πρεσβύτης.* [c] *pro γερουσία.*
[1] A *υἱός.* [e] *pro υἱός.*
[f] *pro βαρύς.* [g] S *πρεσβύτης.*
[h] *pro γεράντων κατοίκων.*

πρεσβύτης.

Gen. 25: 8
43:26[a]
Exo. 10: 9 A[b]
Nu. 10:31
Deu. 28:50[a]
32:25[a]
Jos. 6:21[a]
Jud. 19:16, 17
20, 22
1 Sa. 2:22, 32
32+A
3:21
4:18
1 Ki. 1:15
13:11, 25
2 Ki. 4:14
1 Ch. 23: 1
2 Ch. 32:31
Job 15:10
29: 8
42:17 S[b]
Ps. 148:12[c]
Isa. 3: 5
9:14
20: 4
65:20
Jer. 38:13
Lam. 2:21
4:16 A[d]
5:14

[a] A *πρέσβυς.* [b] *pro πρέσβυς.*
[c] S *πρέσβυς.* [d] *pro προφήτης.*

πρίηθω.

Numbers 5:21, 22, 27

πρίαμαι.

Gen. 42: 2,3,10
43: 1, 19
Pro. 20:34

πρίν.

Gen. 27: 4
29:26
Jos. 2: 8
Jud. 14:18 A[a]
1 Sa. 2:15
Isa. 7:16
8: 4
17:14
Isa. 23: 7
28: 4, 24
46:10
66: 7, 7
Eze. 33:22
Joel 2:31
Mal. 4: 4

[a] *pro πρό.*

πριστηροειδής.

Isaiah 41:15

πρίω, –ίζω.

Amos 1: 3

πρίων.

2 Sa. 12:31
1 Ch. 20: 3
Isa. 10:15
Amos 1: 3

προάγω.

1 Sa. 17:16 A
Est. 2:21
Pro. 4:27
6: 8

προαίρεσις.

Jud. 5: 2 A[a]
Ecc. 1:14, 17
2:11[b], 17
22, 26
Ecc. 4: 4,6,16
6: 9
Jer. 8: 5
14:14

[a] *pro ἑκουσιάζομαι.*
[b] S *περίσσεια.*

προαιρέω.

Gen. 34: 8
Deu. 7: 6, 7
10:15
Pro. 1:29
Pro. 17:27 S[1 a]
21:25
Isa. 7:15

[a] *pro προίημι.*

προανατάσσω.

Psalm 136: 6

προανατέλλω.

Ezekiel 17: 9

προαπαγγέλλω.

Ezekiel 33: 9

προάστειον.

Numbers 35: 2, 7

προβαίνω.

Gen. 18:11
24: 1
26:13
Exo. 19:19
Jos. 13: 1, 1
Jos. 23: 1, 2
Jud. 19:11[a]
1 Ki. 1: 1
Job 2: 9

[a] A *κλίνω.*

προβάλλω.

Jud. 14:12, 13
16
Pro. 22:21
Pro. 26:18
Jer. 26: 4 AS[a]

[a] *pro προσβάλλω.*

προβατικός.

Neh. 3: 1, 32
Neh. 12:39

πρόβατον.

Gen. 4: 2, 4
12:16
13: 5
20:14
21:27, 28
29
22: 7, 8
24:35
26:14
27: 9
29: 2, 3, 6
6+A
7, 8, 9
9
10—A
10
30:31, 32
32, 36
38, 38
39—A
39, 40
40, 41
41, 42
31: 8,8,10
10, 12
19, 38
38, 41
32: 5,7,14
33:13
34:28
37: 1, 12
14
Gen. 38:12, 13
17
43:31+A
45:10
46:34
47: 3, 17
50: 8
Exo. 2:16, 16
17, 19
3: 1, 1
9: 3
10: 9, 24
12: 3, 3, 4
4,5,21
32, 38
13:13
20:24
22: 1, 1, 1
4, 9
10, 30
34: 3, 19
20—A[1]
Lev. 1: 2, 10
3: 6
4:32, 35
5: 6, 7
15, 18
6: 6
7:13
14:10
17: 3
22:19, 21

Lev. 22:23, 27
28
23:12
27:26, 32
Nu. 11:22
15: 3, 11
18:17
22:40
27:17
31:28, 30
32, 36
37, 43
32:16, 36
Deu. 7:13
8:13
12: 6
17—B
21
14: 4, 22
25—B
15:14, 19
19
16: 2
17: 1
18: 3, 4
22: 1
28: 4, 18
31, 51
32:14
Jos. 6:21+A
7:24
1 Sa. 14:34
15: 3
13 A[a]
17:15 A
20 A
28 A
34
22:19
25:11, 18
2 Sa. 7: 8
17:29
24:17
1 Ki. 1: 9, 19
25
(3) *p* 46
4:23
8: 5
63—B
2 Ki. 5:26
1 Ch. 5:21
12:40
21:17
27:31
2 Ch. 5: 6
14:15
15:11
17:11
18: 2, 16
29:33
30:24, 24
31: 6
32:29
35: 7, 8
9—B
Ezra 10:19—S[1]
Neh. 5:18
Job 1: 3, 16
21:11
42:12

Psa. 8: 8
43:12, 23
48:15
64:14
73: 1
76:21
77:52, 70
78:13
79: 1
94: 7
99: 3
106:41
113: 4
6—S[1]
118:176
143:13
150 *p* 6 *bis*
Pro. 27:24
Isa. 7:21, 25
13:14
22:13
43:23
53: 6, 7
60: 7
61: 5
63:11
Jer. 3:24
5:17
10:20
13:20
23: 1, 2
27: 6, 8
17, 45
29:21
30: 7
32:20, 21
22
38:12
40:12, 13
Eze. 25: 5
34: 2, 3, 5
6
6+A
8 *qtr*
10 *ter*
11, 12
12, 15
17 *ter*
19, 20
20, 22
31, 31
36:37, 38
38, 38
43:23, 25
45:15, 15
Hos. 5: 6
Joel 1:18
Amos 7:15[b]
Jon. 3: 7
Mic. 2:12
5: 8
7:14
Hab. 3:17
Zeph. 2: 6
Zec. 9:16
10: 2
11: 4, 7, 7
11, 17
13: 7

[a] *pro* πρῶτος. [b] B προφήτης.

προβιβάζω.

Exo. 35:34 | Deu. 6: 7

προβλέπω.

Psalm 36:13

πρόβλημα.

Jud. 14:12
12+A
13, 14
15, 16
18, 19

Psa. 48: 5
77: 2
Dan. 8:23
Hab. 2: 6

πρόβλητος.

Jeremiah 10: 9 S[a]

[a] *pro* προσβλητός.

προδίδωμι.

2 Ki. 6:11
Isa. 40:14+AS[1]

Eze. 16:34 A[a]

[a] *pro* προσδίδωμι.

πρόδρομος.

Nu. 13:21 | Isa. 28: 4

προειδέω.

Gen. 37:18 | Psa. 139: 3

προεκφέρω.

Genesis 38:28

προέρχομαι.

Gen. 33: 3[a]
14[b]

Pro. 8:24

[a] A παρέρχομαι.
[b] A[1] προσέρχομαι.

προετοιμάζω.

Isaiah 28:24[a]

[a] S[1] ἑτοιμάζω.

προέχω.

Job 27: 6 A[a] | Psa. 21: 2

[a] *pro* προσέχω.

προηγέομαι.

Deu. 20: 9 | Pro. 17:14

προθερίζω.

Judges 15: 5+A

πρόθεσις.

Exo. 39:18
18 A[2 a]
40: 4, 21
1 Sa. 21: 6
1 Ch. 9:32
23:29

1 Ch. 28:16
2 Ch. 2: 4
4:19
13:11
29:18

[a] *pro* πρόκειμαι

προθυμέω, —μόω.

1 Ch. 29: 5, 6, 9
9, 14

1 Ch. 29:17, 17
2 Ch. 17:16

πρόθυμος.

1 Ch. 28:21
2 Ch. 29:31

Pro. 16:19 A[a]
Hab. 1: 8[b]

[a] *pro* πραΰθυμος. [b] S πρόϊμος.

προθύμως.

2 Chronicles 29:31

πρόθυρον.

Gen. 19: 6—A
Jud. 19:27
1 Sa. 5: 4
1 Ki. 7:36
14:17 A
Isa. 66:17
Jer. 1:15
19: 2
33:10
43:10

Jer. 50: 9
Eze. 8: 3, 7, 14
16
10:19
11: 1
43: 8, 8
46: 2, 3, 3
47: 1
Zec. 12: 2

προΐημι.

Exo. 3:19
Job 7:19
27: 6
Pro. 1:23

Pro. 5: 9
8: 4
17:27[a]
24:67

[a] S[1] προαιρέω.

πρόϊμος.

Habakkuk 1:8 S[a]

[a] *pro* πρόθυμος.

προΐστημι.

2 Sa. 13:17
Pro. 23: 5
26:17

Isa. 43:24
Amos 6:10

προκαταλαμβάνω.

Jud. 1:12, 13
3:28
7:24
9:50 A[a]
12: 5
20:39—A
2 Sa. 5: 7[b]
8: 4
12:28, 28
1 Ki. 4:30—A

1 Ki. 11:14—A
16:18
2 Ki. 12:17
1 Ch. 11: 5
18: 4
2 Ch. 13:19
17: 2
32: 1, 18
Psa. 76: 5
78: 8

[a] *pro* καταλαμβάνω.
[b] AB καταλαμβάνω.

πρόκειμαι.

Exo. 10:10 A[a]
38: 9
39:18[b]

Lev. 24: 7
Nu. 4: 7
Est. 1: 7, 8

[a] *pro* πρόσκειμαι.
[b] A[2] πρόθεσις.

προκόπτω.

Jud. 20:32 A[a] | Isa. 3: 5[b]

[a] *pro* πίπτω.
[b] ABS προσκόπτω.

προλέγω.

Isaiah 41:26

προλήνιον.

Isaiah 5: 2

προλόβος.

Leviticus 1:16

προμαχών.

Jer. 5:10
40: 4

Eze. 4: 2

προνοέω.

Job 20: 9 C[a]
24:15[b]

Pro. 3: 4

[a] *pro* προσνοέω.
[b] ABS[2] προσνοέω, S[1] προστίθημι.

προνομεύω.

Nu. 24:17
31: 9, 9
32, 53
Deu. 2:35
3: 7
12 B[a]
20:14
21:10
Jos. 8: 2, 27
11:14
Jud. 2:14
14 A[b]
14 A[c]
16
Pro. 11: 3 A

Isa. 8: 3
10:13
11:14
13:16
17:14
24: 3
42:22, 24
Jer. 27:10
37:16
Eze. 26:12
29:19
30:24
38:12, 13
39:10, 10

[a] *pro* κληρονομέω.
[b] *pro* καταπρονομεύω.
[c] *pro* ἐχθρός.

προνομή.

Nu. 31:11, 12
32
Deu. 20:14
21:10, 11

Jos. 7:21
8: 2
22: 8
1 Ki. 10 *p* 22

2 Ki. 21:14
Est. 8:11+S[3]
Pro. 12:24
Isa. 6:13
8: 1
10: 2, 6
24: 3
33:23, 23
42:22
Jer. 2:14
15:13
27:10

Jer. 30:10
37:16
Eze. 25: 5 A[a]
26: 5
29:19
30:24
34: 8, 22
28
36: 4, 5
38:12, 13
Dan. 11:24

[a] *pro* νομή.

προοίμιον.

Job 25: 2
27: 1

Job 29: 1

προοράω.

Psalm 15: 8

πρόπαππος.

Exodus 10: 6

προπέτεια.

2 Samuel 6: 7+A

προπετής.

Pro. 10:14 | Pro. 13: 3

προπορεύω.

Gen. 2:14[a]
32:16, 17
19, 20
21
Exo. 14:19
17: 6
32: 1, 23
34
33: 1[b], 14
Nu. 10:33
Deu. 1:30, 33[a]
3:18
9: 3
20: 4

Deu. 31: 3, 3, 6
Jos. 3: 6
6:13
10:13, 24[c]
1 Sa. 17: 7[c]
25:19
Psa. 84:14[d]
88:15
96: 3
Pro. 4:18
24:49
Isa. 52:12[a]
58: 8

[a] A πορεύω. [b] AB πορεύω.
[c] A προσπορεύομαι. [d] S[1] πορεύω.

προπύλαιος.

Zephaniah 1: 9 S[2 a]

[a] *pro* πρόπυλον.

πρόπυλον.

Amos 9: 1 | Zeph. 1: 9[a]

[a] S[2] προπύλαιος.

προσάββατον

Psa. 91: 1 S[a] | Psa. 92: 1[b]

[a] *pro* σάββατον. [b] A σάββατον

προσαγορεύω.

Deu. 23: 6 | Ezra 10: 1 B[1 a]

[a] *pro* ἐξαγορεύω.

προσάγω.

Gen. 27:25
48: 9
Exo. 3: 4
14:10
19: 4
21: 6, 6
28: 1
29: 4, 8, 10
40:10, 12
Lev. 1: 2[a], 3
10
3: 1, 1, 3
7, 7, 12
4: 3, 4
14, 14

Lev. 5: 8
6:14, 38
7: 4, 6
15, 25
8:13, 14
18, 22
24
10:19
14: 2, 12
16: 1, 6, 9
11, 20
21 A[b]
19:21
22:20, 22
24

Lev. 23: 8, 18
25, 27
36, 36
Nu. 5:16
6:12, 14
7: 3[a]
8: 9, 10
15:27, 33
16: 5, 5, 9
10, 17
18: 2
25: 6
27: 5
28: 3, 9, 11
19, 27
29:13, 36
Deu. 2:19
Jos. 3: 9
4: 5
7:14 *ter*
16, 17
17
8: 5, 23
Jud. 3:13 A[c]
1 Sa. 1:24, 24
25
7:10
9:18
10:20, 21
21
13: 6, 9
14:18, 34
34 38

1 Sa. 15:32
22:17
23: 9
28:25
30: 7
8+A
21
2 Sa. 3:34
11:21, 22
22
13:11
1 Ki. 18:21, 30
30
21:29
2 Ki. 16:14
2 Ch. 29:23, 31
35:12
Psa. 71:10
Pro. 19:24 ACS[d]
24:15
Isa. 34: 1
48:16
57: 3
Jer. 26: 3
Eze. 37: 7
42:14
44:13, 15
Dan. 7:13 AB[d]
Joel 3: 9
Mal. 1: 7, 8, 8
8, 11
2:12
3: 3, 5

[a] A προσφέρω. [b] *pro* ἐπιτίθημι. [c] *pro* συνάγω. [d] *pro* προσφέρω

προσαιτέω.

Job 27:14

προσαλλήλων.

Ezekiel 37:17

προσαναβαίνω.

Exo. 19:23
Jos. 11:17
15: 3, 6, 7

Jos. 18:12
19:12

προσανάβασις.

Joshua 15: 3, 7 A[a]

[a] *pro* πρόσβασις.

προσαποθνήσκω.

Exodus 21:29

προσβάλλω.

Jer. 26: 4[a] Dan. 7: 2

[a] AS προβάλλω.

πρόσβασις.

Joshua 15: 7[a]

[a] A προσανάβασις.

προσβλητός.

Jeremiah 10: 9[a]

[a] S πρόβλητος.

προσγεννάω.

Leviticus 20: 2 A[a]

[a] *pro* γίνομαι.

προσγίνομαι.

Lev. 18:26 Nu. 15:14

προσδεκτός.

Pro. 11:20 Pro. 16:15

προσδέομαι.

Proverbs 12: 9

προσδέχομαι.

Gen. 32:20
Exo. 10:17
22:11
36: 3
Lev. 22:23 A[a] B[1a]
26:13, 43
Ruth 1:13
1 Ch. 12:18[b]
2 Ch. 36:21
Est. 9:23, 27
Job 2: 9, 9
20:23
23+A
33:20
Psa. 6:10
54: 9

Ps. 103:11
Pro. 15:15
Isa. 28:10
42: 1
45: 4
55:12
Eze. 20:40, 41
32:10
43:27
Hos. 8:13
Amos 5:22
Mic. 6: 7
Zeph. 3:10−A
Mal. 1: 8, 10
13

[a] *pro* δέχομαι. [b] S[1] προστάσσω.

προσδίδωμι.

Gen. 29:33 Eze. 16:33, 34[a]

[a] A προδίδωμι, B[1] δίδωμι.

προσδοκάω.

Deu. 32: 2
Psa. 68:21
103:27

Ps. 118:166
Lam. 2:16

προσδοκία.

Gen. 49:10
Ps. 118:116

Isa. 66: 9

προσεγγίζω.

Gen. 33: 6, 7, 7
Lev. 2: 8
15: 8 A[a]
21:21 AB[1b]
Nu. 8:19
Deu. 20: 2
Jos. 3: 4
Jud. 6:25 A[c]

Jud. 6:19[d]
20:23 A[b]
2 Sa. 20:17[e]
1 Ki. 4(21) A
2 Ki. 4: 5
Ps. 118:150
Eze. 18: 6

[a] *pro* προσπελάζω. [b] *pro* ἐγγίζω. [c] *pro* προσφέρω. [d] A προσκυνέω. [e] A ἐγγίζω.

προσειδέω.

Job 6:15 Job 19:14 S[a]

[a] *pro* προσποιέω.

προσεῖπον.

Jud. 17: 2[a] Pro. 7:13[b]

[a] A εἶπον. [b] S[1] εἶπον.

προσεκκαίω.

Numbers 21:30

προσεμπρήθω.

Exodus 22: 6

προσεπαπατάω.

Job 36:16[a]

[a] S[2] προσέτι ἠπάτησεν.

προσέρχομαι.

Gen. 29:10
33:14 A[1a]
42:24
43:18
Exo. 12:48, 48
49[b]
16: 9
19:15
22: 8
34:32
Lev. 9: 5, 7, 8
10: 4, 5

Lev. 18: 6
19 AB[c]
19:33
20:16
21:17, 18
21, 23
22: 3
Nu. 9: 6, 14
10: 4
16:40
18: 3, 4, 22
27: 1

Nu. 31:48
32: 2, 16
36: 1
Deu. 1:22
2:37
4:11
5:23, 27
20:10
21: 5
22:14
25: 1, 9, 11
32:44 A[c]
Jos. 5:13
10:24
14: 6
21: 1
Jud. 20:24
Ruth 2:14
1 Sa. 4:16
7:13[d]
14:36
15:32

1 Sa. 17:40
2 Sa. 1:15
10:13
1 Ki. 21:13, 22
28
22:24
2 Ki. 16:12+A
2 Ch. 24:27
Est. 1:14
Psa. 33: 6
63: 7
90:10
Isa. 8: 3
54:15
Jer. 7:16−A
49: 1
Eze. 44:16
Dan. 3: 8, 26
6:12
7:16
Jon. 1: 6

[a] *pro* προέρχομαι. [b] A πρόσκειμαι. [c] *pro* εἰσέρχομαι. [d] A ἐπέρχομαι.

προσέτι.

2 Samuel 16:11

προσευχή.

2 Sa. 7:27
1 Ki. 8:28+A
28−B
29, 38
45
49+A
54
9: 3, 3
2 Ki. 19: 4
20: 5
2 Ch. 6:19, 19
20, 29
35, 39
7:12, 15
30:27
33:18, 19
Neh. 1: 6, 11
11
11:17+S[3]
Psa. 4: 2
6:10
16: 1, 1
34:13
38:13
41: 9
53: 4
54: 2
60: 2, 6[a]

Psa. 63: 2[b]
64: 3
65:19[c], 20
68:14
79: 5
83: 9
85: 1−A
6
87: 3, 14
15[d]
89: 1
101: 1, 2, 18
108: 7
129: 2 A[e]
140: 2, 5
141: 1
142: 1
Pro. 28: 9
Isa. 38: 5, 9
56: 7, 7
60: 7
Jer. 11:14
Lam. 3: 8, 43
Dan. 9: 3, 17
21
Jon. 2: 8[f]
Hab. 3: 1, 16

[a] S[2] εὐχή. [b] S φωνή. [c] S[2] δέησις. [d] AS ψυχή. [e] *pro* φωνή. [f] BS[1] εὐχή.

προσεύχομαι.

Gen. 20: 7, 17
Exo. 10:17
Jud. 13: 8[a]
1 Sa. 1:10, 12
26, 27
2: 1+A
25, 25
7: 5
8: 6
12:19, 23
14:45
2 Sa. 7:27
1 Ki. 8:28, 29
30, 33
35, 42
44, 48
54
13: 6+A
2 Ki. 4:33
6:17, 18
19:15+A
20
1 Ch. 17:25
2 Ch. 6:19, 20

2 Ch. 6:21, 24
26, 32
34, 38
7: 1, 14
30:18
32:20, 24
33:13
Ezra 6:10
10: 1, 1
Neh. 1: 4, 6
2: 4
4: 9
Est. 5: 1
Psa. 5: 3
31: 6
71:15
108: 4
Isa. 16:12
37:15, 21
38: 2
44:17
45:14, 20
Jer. 7:16
11:14

Jer. 14:11
36: 7, 12
39:16
44: 3
49: 2, 4, 20

Dan. 6:10
9: 4, 20
21+A
Jon. 2: 2
4: 2

[a] A δέω (A).

προσεχόντως.

Proverbs 29:43

προσέχω.

Gen. 4: 5
24: 6
34: 3
Exo. 9:21
10:28
19:12
23:21
34:11, 12
Lev. 22: 2
Nu. 16:15
Deu. 1:45
4: 9, 23
6:12
8:11
11:16
12:13, 19
23, 30
15: 9
24:10
32: 2, 46
1 Ki. 7:16
2 Ch. 25:16
35:21
Ezra 7:23
Neh. 1: 6, 11
9:34
Job 1: 8
2: 3
7:17
10: 3
13: 6
27: 6[a]
29:21
33:31 A[b]
Psa. 5: 3
9:38
16: 1
21:20
34:23
37:23

Psa. 30: 2, 14[c]
54: 3
58: 6
60: 2
65:19
68:19
69: 2
70:12−B
76: 2
77: 1
79: 2
80:12
85: 6
129: 2
140: 1
141: 2 A[d], 7
Pro. 1:24
25 AS[e]
30
4: 1, 20
5: 1, 3
7:24
17: 4
Ecc. 4:13
Cant. 8:13
Isa. 1:10, 23
28:23
32: 4[f]
49: 1
55: 3
58: 3 A[g]
Jer. 6:19
7:24, 26
25: 4
Dan. 9:19
Hos. 5: 1
Mic. 1: 2
Zec. 1: 4
7:11
Mal. 3:16

[a] A προέχω. [b] *pro* ἐνωτίζομαι. [c] A σπεύδω. [d] *pro* δέω (A). [e] *pro* ἀπειθέω. [f] B προσήκω. [g] *pro* γινώσκω.

προσήκω.

Isaiah 32: 4 B[a]

[a] *pro* προσέχω.

προσηλυτεύω.

Ezekiel 14: 7[a]

[a] A πρόσκειμαι.

προσήλυτος.

Exo. 12:48, 49
20:10
22:21, 21
23: 9 *ter*
12
Lev. 16:29
17: 3, 8, 10
12, 13
15
18:26
19:10, 33
34, 34
20: 2
22:18
23:22
24:16, 22
25:23, 35
47 *ter*
Nu. 9:14, 14
15:14, 15

Nu. 15:15, 16
26, 29
30
19:10
35:15
Deu. 1:16
5:14
10:18, 18[a]
19, 19
12:18
14:28
16:11, 14
24:16, 19
21, 22
23
26:11, 12
13
27:19
28:43
29:11

Deu. 31:12
Jos. 9: 6, 8
20: 9
1 Ch. 22: 2
2 Ch. 2:17
15: 9
30:25
Psa. 93: 6
145: 9
Isa. 54:15
Jer. 7: 6
22: 3
Eze. 14: 7
22: 7, 29
47:22, 23
23
Zec. 7:10
Mal. 3: 5

[a] A πλησίος.

προσηνής.

Proverbs 25:25

πρόσθεμα.

Lev. 10:25
Eze. 41: 7

πρόσθεσις.

Ezekiel 47:13

προσθλίβω.

Numbers 22:25

προσκαθίστημι.

Judges 14:11+A

προσκαίω.

Eze. 24:11[a]

[a] A ἐκκαίω.

προσκαλέω.

Gen. 28: 1
Exo. 3:18
5: 3
1 Sa. 26:14
Est. 4: 5
8: 1
Job 17:1+ACS[a]
Job 19:17
Psa. 49: 4
Pro. 9:15
Joel 2:32
Amos 5: 8
9: 6

[a] pro ἐπικαλέω.

προσκαρτερέω.

Numbers 13:21

προσκαταβαίνω.

Ezekiel 31:14

προσκαταλείπω.

Exodus 30: 7

πρόσκαυμα.

Joel 2: 6
Nah. 2:10

πρόσκειμαι.

Exo. 10:10[a]
12:49 A[b]
Lev. 16:29
17: 3,8,10
12, 13
22:18
25: 6
Nu. 15:15, 16
26[c], 29
19:10
21:15
Deu. 1:36
4: 4
Jos. 20: 9
22: 5
1 Ki. 7:16+A
Job 26: 2
Isa. 56: 3, 6
Eze. 14: 7 A[d]
37:16
16 A[e]
19

[a] A πρόκειμαι. [b] pro προσέρχομαι. [c] A προσπορεύομαι. [d] pro προσηλυτεύω. [e] pro προστίθημι.

προσκεφάλαιον.

Ezekiel 13:18, 20

προσκεφαλή.

1 Samuel 26:11, 12

προσκολλάω.

Gen. 2:24
Lev. 19:31
Nu. 36: 7, 9
Deu. 11:22
Deu. 13:17
28:21
Jos. 23: 8
Jud. 20:45 A[a]
Ruth 2:21[b], 23
2 Sa. 23:10
Job 41: 8
Psa. 72:28
Eze. 29: 4
Dan. 2:43

[a] pro καταβαίνω. [b] B κολλάω.

πρόσκομμα.

Exo. 23:33
34:12
Isa. 8:14
Isa. 29:21
Jer. 3: 3

προσκόπτω.

Psa. 90:12
Pro. 3: 6+S[2]
23
Pro. 4:19
Isa. 3: 5ABS[a]
Jer. 13:16

[a] pro προκόπτω.

προσκρούω.

Job 40:18

προσκυνέω.

Gen. 18: 2
19: 1
22: 5
23: 7, 12
24:26, 48
52
27:29, 29
33: 3, 6, 7
7
37: 7,9,10
42: 6
43:26, 27
47:31
48:12
49: 8
Exo. 4:31
11: 8
12:27
18: 7
20: 5
23:24
24: 1
32: 8
33:10
34: 8, 14
Lev. 26: 1
Nu. 22:31
25: 2
Deu. 4:19
5: 9
6:13 A[a]
8:19
10:20 A[a]
11:16
17: 3
26:10
29:26+A
30:17
32:43
Jos. 23: 7, 16
Jud. 2: 2, 12
17, 19
6:10 A[b]
7:15
Ruth 2:10
10+A
1 Sa. 1: 3, 19
2:36
15:25, 30
31
20:41
24: 9
25:23, 41
28:14
2 Sa. 1: 2
9: 6, 8
12:20
14: 4, 22
33
15: 5, 32
16: 4
18:21, 28
24:20
1 Ki. 1:16, 23
1 Ki. 1:31, 47
53
2:13
9: 6, 9
16:31
19:18
22:54
2 Ki. 2:15
4:37
5:18, 18
18—A
17:16, 35
36
18:22
19:37
21: 3, 21
1 Ch. 16:29
21:21
29:20
2 Ch. 7: 3, 19
22
20:18
24:17
25:14
29:28, 29
30
32:12
33: 3
Neh. 8: 6
9: 3, 6
Est. 3: 2, 2, 5
Job 1:20
Psa. 5: 8
21:28, 30
28: 2
44:13
65: 4
71:11
80:10
85: 9
94: 6
95: 9
96: 7[c], 7
98: 5, 9
105:19
131: 7
137: 2
Isa. 2: 8, 20
27:13
37:38
44:15, 17
19
45:14
46: 6
49: 7, 23
66:23
Jer. 1:16
8: 2
13:10
16:11—A
22: 9
25: 6
33: 2
Eze. 8:16
Eze. 46: 3, 3, 9
Dan. 2:46
3: 5, 6, 7
11, 12
14, 15
15, 18
27+AB[2]
Dan. 3:28—A
Mic. 5:13
Zeph. 1: 5
5—A
2:11
Zec. 14:16, 17

[a] pro φοβέω. [b] pro προσεγγίζω. [c] S[1] πείθω.

προσλαλέω.

Exo. 4:16AB[2a]

[a] pro λαλεω.

προσλαμβάνω.

1 Sa. 12:22
Psa. 17:17
26:10
Psa. 64: 5
72:24

προσλογίζομαι.

Lev. 27:18
Jos. 13: 3
Psa. 87: 5

προσμένω.

Jud. 3:25 A[a]

[a] pro ὑπομένω.

προσμίγνυμι.

Proverbs 14:13

προσνοέω.

Nu. 23: 9
Jud. 3:26
Job 20: 9[a]
Job 24:15ABS[2b]
Isa. 63: 5
Dan. 7: 8

[a] C προνοέω. [b] pro προνοέω.

πρόσοδος.

Pro. 28:16[a]

[a] S[3] χρῆμα.

προσόζω.

Psalm 37: 6

προσοίγω.

Genesis 19: 6

προσοικέω.

Ezekiel 47:22 A[a]

[a] pro παροικέω.

προσοχθίζω.

Gen. 27:46
Lev. 18:25, 28
28
20:22
26:15, 30
43, 44
Nu. 21: 5
22: 3
Deu. 7:26
2 Sa. 1:21
1 Ch. 21: 6 A[a]
Psa. 21:25
35: 5
94:10
Eze. 36:31

[a] pro κατισχύω.

προσόχθισμα.

Deu. 7:26
1 Ki. 11:33
16:32
18:29
2 Ki. 23:13, 13
24
Eze. 5:11+A
37:23+A

πρόσοψις.

Daniel 2:31[a]

[a] A ὄψις.

προσπαίζω.

Job 21:11

προσπίπτω.

Gen. 33: 4
Exo. 4:25
Est. 8: 3
9: 4[a]
Psa. 21:30
71: 9
94: 6
Pro. 25: 8, 20

[a] S[3] ἐπιπίπτω.

προσποιέω.

1 Sa. 21:13
Job 19:14[a]

[a] S προσειδέω.

προσπορεύομαι.

Exo. 24:14
28:39
30:20
36: 2
38:27
Lev. 10: 9
19:34
Nu. 1:51
3:38 A[a]
4:19, 19[b]
Nu. 15:26 A[c]
18: 7
Deu. 20: 3 A[d]
Jos. 9: 8
10:24 A[e]
1 Sa. 17: 7 A[e]
2 Ch. 13: 9
Ezra 7:17
Neh. 10:28
Pro. 16: 1+AS[2]

[a] pro ἅπτω. [b] A εἰσπορεύω. [c] pro πρόσκειμαι. [d] pro πορεύω. [e] pro προπορεύω.

προσραίνω.

Lev. 4: 6
Lev. 8:30

προσσιελίζω.

Leviticus 15: 8[a]

[a] A προσεγγίζω.

πρόσταγμα.

Gen. 24:50 A[a]
26: 5
47:26
Exo. 18:16, 20
20: 6
Lev. 4: 2
18: 4, 5
26—A
30
19:37
20: 8, 22
24:12
26: 3, 14
43, 46
Nu. 9:18, 18
20, 23
23
33:38
36: 5
Deu. 5:10
11:32
12: 1
15: 2
19: 4
Jos. 8:27
14:14
15:13
17: 4
19:50
21: 3, 42
22: 9
Jud. 11:30
1 Sa. 30:25
1 Ki. 3: 3, 14
6(12)A
8:58, 61
9: 4, 6
11:11, 38
1 Ch. 16:17
22:13
26:32[b]
29:19
2 Ch. 7:17—A
19
8:10 A[c]
19:10
29:15, 25
30: 6, 12
31:21
2 Ch. 33: 8
34:31
35:19 B[d]
25
Ezra 7:10, 11
Neh. 1: 7
9:13, 14
10:29 -ABS[1]
Est. 2: 48[1a]
8, 20
4: 3+S[3]
(9)14[e]
17—A
9: 4
Job 4: 9
26:10, 13
39:27
Psa. 2: 7
7: 7
80: 5
93:20
98: 7
104:10
148: 6
Pro. 14:27
25: 2 A[a]
Isa. 24: 5
26: 9
56: 4 S[1f]
Jer. 5:22, 24
39:23
51:10, 23
Eze. 11:20
18: 9, 17
20:11, 13
13+A
16, 19
21, 24
25
33:15
37:24
43:11, 11
18
44: 5, 24
45:14
46:14
Amos 2: 4
Zec. 3: 7
Mal. 4: 6

[a] pro πρâγμα. [b] A λόγος. [c] pro προστάτης. [d] pro παρόργισμα. [e] A ἔκθεμα. [f] pro σάββατον.

προστάς.

Judges 3:23

προστάσσω.

Gen. 47:11
50: 2
Exo. 36: 6
Lev. 10: 1
14: 4, 5
36, 10
Nu. 5: 2
Deu. 17: 3
18:20
27: 1
Jos. 5:14

1 Ch. 12:18 S[1][a]
2 Ch. 31: 5, 13
Est. 1:15, 19
2:23
3: 2[b]
12 A[c]
14
Isa. 36:21
55: 4
Jon. 2: 1, 11
4: 6, 7, 8

[a] pro προσδέχομαι. [b] A ἐπιτασσω. [c] pro ἐπιτάσσω.

προστάτης.

1 Ch. 27:31
29: 6

2 Ch. 8:10[a]
24:11, 11

[a] A πρόσταγμα.

προστίθημι.

Gen. 4: 2, 12
8:12, 21
21
18:29
25: 1,8,17
30:24
35:29
37: 8
38: 5, 26
41:23
49:29, 33
Exo. 1:10
5: 7
8:29
9:28, 34
10:28
11: 6
14:13
23: 2
30:15
40:21[a]
Lev. 5:16
6: 5
19:14[b]
22:14
24: 8[c]
26:18, 21
27:13, 15
19, 27
31
Nu. 5: 7
11:25
16:39
18: 2, 4
20:24, 26
22:15, 19
25, 26
27:13, 13
31: 2
32:14, 15
36: 3, 4
Deu. 1:11
3:26
4: 2
5:22, 25
12:32
13: 4, 11
17:16
18:16
19: 9, 20
20: 8
23:15
25: 3, 3
28:68
32:50, 50
Jos. 7:12
14: 8, 9
23:12[f], 13
Jud. 2: 3 A[e]
10, 21
3:12
4: 1
8:28
9:37
10: 6, 13
11:14—A

Jud. 13: 1, 21
18:25
20:22, 23
28
Ruth 1:17
1 Sa. 3: 6, 8
17—B
21
7:13
9: 8
12:19, 25
14:44
15: 6, 35
18:29
19: 8, 21
20:13, 17
23: 4
25:22
26:10
27: 1, 4
2 Sa. 2:22, 28
3: 9, 35
5:22
7:10, 20
12: 8
14:10
18:22
19:13
24: 1,3,25
1 Ki. 2:23
10: 7
12:11, 14
16:33
19: 2
21:10
2 Ki. 1:11, 13
6:23, 31
19:30
20: 6
21: 8
22:20
24: 7
1 Ch. 14:13
17: 9, 18
21: 3
22:14, 15
2 Ch. 9: 6
10:11, 14
15: 9
28:13[e], 22
33: 8
34:28, 28
Ezra 10:10
Neh. 13:18
Est. 8: 3
9:27[b]
Job 13: 9
20: 9
24:15 S[1][f]
27: 1, 19
29: 1, 22
32:13
34:32, 37
36: 1
39:35
42:10 A[g]

Psa. 9:39
40: 9
60: 7
61:11
68:27, 28
70:14
76: 8
77:17
85:14 S[h]
88:23—A[1]S[1]
113:22
119: 3
Pro. 3: 2
9: 9, 11
18
10:22, 27
19: 4, 19
24:29
Ecc. 1:16[i]
18[b], 18
2: 9, 26
3:14
Isa. 1: 5, 13
7:10
8: 5
10:20
11:11
14: 1, 1
23:12
26:15, 15

Isa. 29:14
30: 1
38: 5
47: 1
50: 4
51:22
52: 1
Jer. 43:32
51:33
Lam. 4:15, 16
22
Eze. 23: 5 A[k]
14
36:12
37:16[m]
Dan. 4:33
10:18
11:34
Hos. 1: 6
9:15
13: 2
Joel 2: 2
Amos 3:15
5: 2
7: 8, 13
8: 2
Jon. 2: 5
Nah. 1:14
Zeph. 3:11
Zec. 14:17

[a] B προτίθημι. [b] A προτίθημι. [c] AB προτίθημι. [d] A ὑπολείπω. [e] pro ἐξαίρω. [f] pro προνοέω. [g] pro δίδωμι. [h] pro προτίθημι. [i] S προτίθημι. [k] pro ἐπιτίθημι. [m] A πρόσκειμαι.

προστρέχω.

Gen. 18: 2
33: 4

Nu. 11:27
Pro. 18:10

προσυμπλέκω.

Daniel 11:10 A[a]

[a] pro συμπροσπλέκω.

πρόσφυτος.

Nu. 6: 3
Deu. 32:17

Psa. 80:10
Ecc. 1: 9

προσφύτως.

Deu. 24: 7

Eze. 11: 3

προσφέρω.

Gen. 4: 7
27:25, 31
43:25
Exo. 29: 3
32: 6
34:26 B[a]
36: 3, 6
Lev. 1: 2 A[b]
2, 3
5, 13
14, 14
15
2: 1, 4, 8
8, 11
11, 12
13, 14
14
3: 6, 9
4:23, 32
32
6:20, 33
38, 39
7: 1, 2, 2
3,8,19
20, 20
23, 28
8: 6
9: 2,9,12
13, 15
16, 17
18

Lev. 10: 1, 15
12: 6, 7
14:23
16: 9
17: 4
21: 6,8,17
21, 21
22:15 A[c]
18, 18
21, 25
23:14, 15
16, 17
20, 37
27: 9, 11
Nu. 3: 4
5: 9, 15[d]
25
6:13, 16
20
7: 2
3 A[b]
10, 10
11, 12
13, 18
19
9: 7, 13
15: 4, 4, 7
9, 13
16:35, 38
39, 39
18:15

Nu. 26:61
28: 2, 26
29: 8
31:50
Deu. 17: 1 A[e]
23:18
Jud. 3:17, 18
5:25[f]
2 Sa. 17:29
1 Ki. (3) p 46
3:24
2 Ki. 16:15
1 Ch. 16: 1
2 Ch. 29: 7
Ezra 6:10, 17

Ezra 7:17
8:35
Job 1: 5
Psa. 71:10
Pro. 6: 8[d]
19:24[g]
21:27
Jer. 14:12
Eze. 43:23, 24
44: 7, 15
27
46: 4
Dan. 7:13[h]
Amos 5:25
Mal. 1:13 S[2][i]

[a] pro ἕψω. [b] pro προσάγω. [c] pro ἀφαιρέω. [d] A φέρω. [e] pro θύω. [f] A προσεγγίζω. [g] ACS προσάγω [h] AB προσάγω. [i] pro φέρω.

προσφορά.

1 Ki. 7:34

Psa. 39: 7

προσχαίρω.

Proverbs 8:30

προσχέω.

Exo. 24: 6
29:16, 21
Lev. 1: 5, 11
3: 2,8,13
6:32
7: 4
8:19, 24
9:12, 18

Lev. 17: 6
Nu. 18:17
Deu. 12:27—B
2 Ki. 16:13
15 AB[a]
2 Ch. 29:22, 22
35:11
Eze. 43:18

[a] pro ἐκχέω.

πρόσχωμα.

2 Sa. 20:15[a]
2 Ki. 19:32

Dan. 11:15

[a] A πρόχωμα.

προσχωρέω.

1 Ch. 12:19, 20

Jer. 21: 9

πρόσωπον.

Gen. 2: 6, 7
3: 8, 19
4: 5,6,14
14, 16
6: 7
7: 4, 23
8: 9, 13
9:23
11: 4, 8, 9
16: 6,8,12
17: 3, 17
18:16
19: 1, 21
28, 28
20:16
23: 8, 17
25:18, 18
27:30
31: 2, 5
32:20 *ter*
21, 30
30
33:10, 10
18
35: 1, 7
36: 6
38:15
40: 7
41:46, 56
42: 6
43: 2, 4
25, 30
44:23, 26
29
46:30
48:11, 12
50: 1[a]

Exo. 2:15
3: 6
10:11, 28
29
14:19, 25
16:14
23:18, 20
25:19, 19
37
26: 9
28:25, 33
32:34
33: 2[b], 20
20, 23
34: 6, 11
24, 29
30, 33
35, 35
36:26
28—B
38: 8+A
Lev. 8: 9
9:24
10: 4, 18
13:41
16: 2, 14
15
17:10
18:24
19:15, 15
32, 32
20: 3, 5, 6
26:10, 17
Nu. 3:38
6:25, 26
8: 2, 3
12:14

Nu. 14: 5, 42
16: 4, 22
43, 45
46
17: 9
19: 4, 16
20: 6, 6
21:11, 20
22: 3, 31
24: 1
27:17, 17
32:21
33:52, 55
Deu. 1:17, 17
21, 30
2:12, 21
22, 25
25
31—A
33
3:18, 28
4:38
5: 4, 4, 5
7[c]
6:15, 19
7: 1,6,10
10, 19
21, 22
24
8:20
9: 2, 3, 3
4
4+A
5
10:17
11: 4, 23
25, 25
12:29, 30
14: 2
16:19
18:12—B
20: 3, 19
22: 6
23:14[d]
25: 9
28: 7,7,25
50, 50
60
30: 1, 15
19
31: 3, 3, 3
6,7,17
18
19—A
21
32:20, 49
33:27
34: 1, 10
10
Jos. 2:10, 11
3:10
4: 5, 7
5: 1, 14
6: 5
7: 4, 6
10, 12
12 A[d][e]
8: 5, 6
10, 15
9:30, 30
10:10, 11
12
11: 6
13: 3, 6
16, 25
15: 8
17: 7
18:14, 16
19:11
20: 6 A
23: 3, 5, 5
9, 13
24: 8, 12
18
Jud. 2: 3, 14
18, 21
4:19+A
5: 5, 5
6: 2, 6
7—A

Jud. 6: 9, 11
22, 22
8:28 A[f]
9:21
39 A[f]
40
11: 3, 23
24—A
33
13:20
16: 3
18:23
20: 2—A
35 A[f]
Ruth 2:10
10+A
1 Sa. 1:14, 18
22
2:11
4:17
5: 3, 4
7: 7
8:18
9:12
13:12
14:13, 25
15: 7, 27
16: 7 A[g]
7, 8
17:24 A
49
18:11 A
12, 15
16
19: 8, 10
20:15, 41
21: 6[h], 6
10, 12
13[i]
22: 4
23: 5, 26
24: 3, 9
25:10, 23
35, 41
26: 1,3,20
28:14
30:16
31: 1
2 Sa. 1: 2+A
2:22, 24
3:13, 13
7: 9, 15
23
9: 6
10: 9, 13
14, 18
11:11
14: 4,7,20
22, 24
24, 28
32, 33
33
15:14, 18
23
17:11, 19
18: 8, 28
19: 4, 5, 8
18
21: 1
23:11
24:20
1 Ki. 1:23, 23
31, 50
2: 7, 15
16, 17
20, 29
3:15, 15
28
5: 3
6: 7
7+A
7, 18
19+A
19
33—A
7:22, 35
43, 43
49+A
8: 8, 11
14, 22

1 Ki. 8:27, 31
40+A
54, 64
9: 7
25 A
10:24
11: 7+A
43
12: 2A, 8
10, 30
13: 6, 6
11, 34
14: 9 A
24
17: 3, 5
14+A
18: 1, 7
39, 42
19:13
20: 4, 26
27, 29
2 Ki. 1:15
3:14, 24
4:29, 31
44+A
5: 1, 15A[f]
27
6:32
8:11, 15
9: 7, 14
32, 37
10: 4
11: 2, 18
12:17
13: 4, 14
23
14: 8, 11
12
16: 3, 14
18
17: 8, 11
18, 20
23
18:24
19: 6+A
15+A
21: 2, 9
13
22:19
23:13, 27
24: 3, 20
25:19, 26
1 Ch. 5:25
10: 1
11:13
12: 1, 8, 8
16: 4, 11
27, 29
30, 33
17: 8, 21
25
19:10, 15
15, 18
19
21:12, 16
21, 30
28: 8
29:11
2 Ch. 1:13
3: 4, 4, 8
13, 17
4:20
5: 9, 14
6: 3, 16
31, 36
42
7: 3, 14
20
9:23
10: 2
12: 5
13: 7, 8
16
19: 7, 11
20: 3, 5, 7
15, 18
22:11
25:17−B
22
28: 3

2 Ch. 29: 6
30: 9
32: 2, 7, 7
21
33: 2, 9
12, 12
34: 4, 4, 27
35:19, 22
36: 5, 12
Ezra 7:14
9: 6, 7
10: 6
Neh. 1:11+S[3]
2: 2, 3
4: 9, 14
5:15
8: 6
10:33
Est. 4: 5+S[3]
7: 8
(9)15+S[3]
9: 2+S[3]
Job 1:11
12+A
2: 5
4:15
6:28
9:24, 27
11:15
13:10, 20
14:20
15:27
16: 8
17:12
18:17
19: 8[k]
21:31
22: 8
23:15, 17
24:15[m], 18
26: 9−S[1]
10
29:24
30:10, 11
32:22
33:26
34:19, 19
29
38:30
40: 8
41: 4, 5
42: 8
Psa. 1: 4
3: 1
4: 7
9: 4, 26
32
10: 7
12: 2
15:11
16: 2, 9, 15
17: 9[n], 43
20: 7, 10
13
21:25
23: 6
26: 8, 8, 9
29: 8
30: 17, 21
23−S[1]
33: 1, 6, 17
34: 5
37: 4, 4, 6
41: 3, 6, 12
42: 5
43: 4, 16
17[o], 25
44:13
45: 6[p]
49:21
50:11, 13
54:22
56: 1, 7
59: 6
60: 4
66: 2
67: 2, 3, 3
6, 9
9−S[1]
68: 8, 18

Psa. 68:30
77:55
79: 4, 8
17, 20
81: 2
82:14, 17
17 A[q]
83:10
87:15
88:15, 16
24
89: 8
94: 2
95: 9, 13
96: 5, 5
97: 8+AS[2]
101: 3, 11
103:15, 20
30
104: 4
113: 7, 7
118:58, 135
131:10
138: 7
139:14
142: 7
147: 6
Pro. 2: 6
4: 3
7:13, 15
8:30
15:13
17:24
18: 5
19: 6
21:29
22:26
24:38−S
25: 5, 7, 23
27:17, 19
19
28:21
29: 5, 26
Ecc. 2:26, 26
3:14
5: 1, 5
7: 4, 27
8: 1, 1, 3
12, 13
9: 1
10: 5, 10
11: 1
Cant. 7: 4
Isa. 2:10, 19
21
3: 9, 15
19
6: 2
7:16
8:17
9:14
13: 8
16: 4
17: 9
19: 1, 16
23:17−AS
24: 1
25: 8
28:25
29:22
30:28
31: 8
34:15
36: 9
38: 2
40:23
50: 6, 7
51:13
52:12 S[r]
53: 3
54: 8
57: 1, 14
17
59: 2
62:11
63:12
64: 2−BS
2, 7
Jer. 1: 8
13−S[1]

Jer. 1:13−S[1]
14
15+A
17
2:27
3:12
4: 1, 4
26, 26
5: 3, 22
6: 7
7:12, 15
19
8: 2
9: 7, 13
22, 26
10: 2
13:17, 26
14:16
15: 1, 17
19
16: 4
17+S[1]
17:16
18:17, 20
23
21: 8, 10
22:25
23: 9, 9, 10
24: 1
26:16
27: 5, 8
16, 44
28:51, 64
29:20
30: 5, 10
31:44
32: 2, 9
12, 13
13 S[1 s]
19, 23
24
33: 4, 19
35:16
37: 6, 20
38:36, 36
39:24, 31
33
40: 5
41:15−S[1]
18
42: 5, 11
11−AS[1]
19
43: 7, 9, 22
44:11, 20
45: 9
46:17
47: 9, 10
48: 9, 18
18
49: 2, 11
11, 15
16, 16
17
51: 3, 10
11, 22
23
52:12, 25
33
Lam. 1: 5[t]
6[u], 22
2: 3−S[1]
19
3:34
4:16, 16
20
5: 9, 10
Eze. 1: 6, 8
8+A
9
10qnq
12
23+A
2: 1, 6, 6
3: 8, 8, 9
20, 23
4: 1, 3, 7
6: 2
5+A
9

Eze. 7:18, 22
8:11, 16
9: 8
10:14A, 14A
14A, 14A
14A, 14A
14A, 14A
21, 22
22, 22
11:18
12: 6, 12
13:17
14: 1, 3, 4
6−A
7, 8, 15
15: 7, 7
16: 5, 18
19, 63
20: 1, 35
35, 43
46, 47
21: 2, 16
22:30
23:25, 41
25: 2
27:35
28:21
29: 2, 5
32:10
33:27
34: 6
35: 2
36:17, 31
37: 2
38: 2, 20
20
39: 5, 14
23, 24
29
40:12
41: 4, 12
14, 15
18, 19
19, 21
22, 25
42: 2+A
10 *ter*
11, 13
17, 18
19 A[v]
43: 3
44: 4, 12
15
45: 7, 7
47: 1
48:21+A
21+A

Dan. 1:10
2:15, 31
46
3:19
5:19, 24
6:26, 26
7: 8
8: 5, 17
18, 23
9: 3, 7, 8
10, 13
17
10: 6, 9, 15
11:16, 17
18, 19
20, 22
Hos. 2: 2
5: 5, 15
7: 2, 10
10: 7, 15
11: 2
Joel 2: 3, 6, 6
10, 11
20
Amos 2: 9
5: 8, 19
9: 4
4 A[w]
6, 8
Jon. 1: 3, 3, 10
Mic. 1: 4
2:13, 13
3: 4
6: 4
Nah. 1: 5, 6
2: 2, 10
3: 5
Hab. 1: 9
2:20
3: 5
Zeph. 1: 2, 3, 7
2: 7
Hag. 1:12
2:14
Zec. 2:13
3: 1, 3, 4
8, 9
4: 7
5: 3
8:21, 21
22, 22
14: 5 S[3 x]
20
Mal. 1: 8, 8, 9
2: 3−S[1]
5, 9
3: 1, 14

[a] A τράχηλος. [b] A πρότερον. [c] A πλήν. [d] A χείρ. [e] *pro* έναντι. [f] *pro* ἐνώπιον. [g] *pro* ὄψις. [h] A προφήτης. [i] A τρόπος. [k] A ἀτραπός. [m] A πρός με ποῦ. [n] B ἐναντίον. [o] S[1] φόβος. [p] AS[2] πρωῒ πρωΐ. [q] *pro* ὄνομα. [r] *pro* πρότερος. [s] *pro* μέσος. [t] S ἐνώπιον. [u] A ἐνώπιον. [v] *pro* κατέναντι. [w] *pro* ὀφθαλμός. [x] *pro* ἡμέρα.

Nu. 10:33
14:14
21:26
32:17, 30
Deu. 1:22, 33
2:10, 12
20
4:32, 32
9:18
19:14 A[b]
24: 6
Jos. 1:14
3:14
10:14
11:10
14:15
15:15
24:12
Jud. 1:10[c]
18:29
2 Sa. 19:20
1 Ki. 13: 6

1 Ch. 9: 2
15:13
29:29
Neh. 13: 5
Job 42: 5
Ecc. 7:11
Isa. 1:26
41:22
46: 9, 10
48: 3, 7
52: 4, 12[d]
61: 4
65:17
Jer. 11:10
35: 8, 8
37:20
40: 7, 11
41: 5
Dan. 7:20 A[e]
11:13
Hos. 2: 7

[a] *pro* πρόσωπον. [b] *pro* πατήρ. [c] A ἔμπροσθεν. [d] S πρόσωπον. [e] *pro* πρῶτος.

προτίθημι.

Exo. 29:23
40: 4
21 B[a]
Lev. 19:14 A[a]
24: 8 AB[a]
2 Ch. 28:13 A[a]
Est. 9:27 A[a]

Psa. 53: 5
85:14[b]
100: 3
Pro. 29:24
Ecc. 1:16 S[a]
18 A[a]

[a] *pro* προστίθημι.
[b] S προστίθημι.

προτομή.

1 Kings 10:19

προτρέχω.

1 Sa. 8:11
Job 41:13 A[a]

[a] *pro* τρέχω.

προυπάρχω.

Job 42 *p* 18

προφασίζομαι.

2 Ki. 5: 7
Ps. 140: 4
Pro. 22:13

πρόφασις.

Ps. 140: 4
Pro. 18: 1
Dan. 6: 4, 4, 5
Hos. 10: 4

προφασιστικός.

Deuteronomy 22:14, 17

προφέρω.

Proverbs 10:13−B

προφητεία.

2 Ch. 15: 8
32:32
Ezra 5: 1
Ezra 6:14
Neh. 6:12
Jer. 23:31−B

προφητεύω.

Nu. 11:25, 26
27
1 Sa. 10: 5, 6, 10
11+A
13
18:10 A
19:20+A
20, 21
21, 23
24
1 Ki. 18:29
22:10, 12
18
2 Ch. 18: 7, 9

2 Ch. 18:11, 17
20:37
Ezra 5: 1
Jer. 2: 8
5:31
11:21
14:13, 14
14, 15
16
19:14
20: 1, 6
23:13, 21
25, 26
26, 32

προτείχισμα.

2 Sa. 20:15
1 Ki. 20:23
2 Ch. 32: 5
Cant. 2:14
Jer. 52: 7

Lam. 2: 8
Eze. 40: 5
42:20
48:15

προτέρημα.

Judges 4: 9

πρότερος, −ρον.

Gen. 13: 3
26: 1
28:19
38:28
40:13
Exo. 10:14
23:28

Exo. 33: 2 A[a]
19
Lev. 4:21
5: 8
18:27
26:45
Nu. 6:12

Jer. 25:18
32: 1+A
16
33: 9, 11
12, 20
20
34: 8, 11
12, 12
13, 13
35: 6, 8, 9
36: 9, 26
27, 31
39: 3—S¹
44:19
Eze. 4: 7
6: 2
11: 4,4,13
12:27
13: 2
2+A
2+A
2,3,16
17, 17
Eze. 20:46
21: 2, 2, 9
14, 28
25: 2
28:21
29: 2
30: 2
34: 2, 2
35: 2
36: 1, 3, 6
37: 4, 7, 7
9, 9
10, 12
38: 2, 14
39: 1
Joel 2:28
Amos 2:12
3: 8
7:12, 13
15, 16
Zec. 13: 3
3+A
3, 4

προφήτης.

Gen. 20: 7
Exo. 7: 1
Nu. 11:29
12: 6
Deu. 13: 1, 3, 5
18:15, 18
19, 20
20, 22
22
34:10
Jud. 6: 8
1 Sa. 3:20, 21
9: 9
10: 5
10+A
10, 11
11, 12
19:20, 24
21: 6 A[a]
22: 5
28: 6, 15
2 Sa. 7: 2
12: 1, 25
24:11
1 Ki. 1: 8, 10
22
23+B
23, 32
34, 38
44, 45
11:29
13:11, 18
20
23+A
25, 29
30
14: 2 A
18 A
16: 7+A
12
17: 1
18: 4, 4, 13
13
19+A
19, 19
20, 22
22, 82
25 29
40
19: 1, 10
14, 16
21:13, 22
35, 38
41
22: 6,7,10
12, 13
22, 23
2 Ki. 2:3, 3+A
5,7,15
3:11, 13
13-B
4: 1, 38
38
5: 3, 8
2 Ki. 5:13, 22
6: 1, 12
9: 1, 1, 4
7
10:19
21—A
21—A
14:25
17:13, 13
23
19: 2
20: 1, 11
14
21:10
23: 2, 18
24: 2
1 Ch. 10:13
16:22
17: 1
26:28
29:29
2 Ch. 9:29
12: 5, 15
13:22
15: 8
16: 7, 10
18: 5, 6, 9
11, 12
21, 22
19: 2
20:20
21:12
24:19
25:15, 16
26:22
28: 9
29:25 B[b]
25, 25
30
32:20, 32
35:15, 18
36: 5, 12
15—B
16
Ezra 5: 1, 2
6:14
9:11
Neh. 6: 7, 14
14[c]
9:26, 30
32
Psa. 50: 2
73: 9
104:15
Isa. 3: 2
9:15
28: 7
29:10
30:10
37: 2
38: 1
21+S¹
39: 3
Jer. 1: 5
Jer. 2: 8, 26
30
4: 9—A
5:13, 31
7:25
8: 1
13:13
14:13, 14
15, 15
18
18:18
23: 6, 11
13, 14
15, 16
21, 25
26, 28
30—B
31—B
32, 33
34
25: 4
28:59
33: 5
34:12, 13
15
35: 8, 9, 9
36:15
39:32
42:15
44:19
49: 2
50: 6
51: 4, 31
Lam. 2: 9, 14
20
Lam. 4:13, 16[d]
Eze. 2: 5
7:26
13: 2
2+A
4,9,16
14: 4, 7, 9
9, 10
22:28
33:33
38:17
Dan. 9: 2, 6
10, 24
Hos. 4: 5
6: 5
9: 7, 8
12:10, 10
13, 13
Amos 2:11, 12
3: 7
7:14, 14
15 B[e]
Mic. 3: 5,6,11
Hab. 1: 1
3: 1
Zeph. 3: 4
Hag. 1: 1,3,12
2: 1, 10
20
Zec. 1: 1, 4, 5
6, 7
7: 3,7,12
8: 9
13: 4, 5

[a] pro πρόσωπον. [b] pro ὁράω.
[c] SS¹ ἱερεύς. [d] A πρεσβύτης.
[e] pro πρόβατον.

προφῆτις.

Exo. 15:20
Jud. 4: 4
2 Ki. 22:14
2 Ch. 34:22
Isa. 8: 3

προφθάνω.

1 Sa. 20:25
2 Sa. 22: 6, 19
2 Ki. 19:32
Job 30:27
Psa. 16:13
17: 6, 19
20: 4
Psa. 58:11
67:26, 32
87:14
94: 2
118:147
148
Jon. 4: 2

προφυλακή.

Exo. 12:42, 42
Nu. 32:17
Neh. 4:22, 23
7: 3
Eze. 23:24 A[a]
26: 8
38: 7

[a] pro φυλακή.

προφύλαξ.

Neh. 4: 9
7: 3
Nah. 2: 6

προφυλάσσω.

2 Samuel 22:24

προχειρέω.

Exodus 4:13 A[a]

[a] pro προχειρίζω.

προχειρίζω.

Exo. 4:13[a]
Jos. 3:12

[a] A προχειρίω.

πρόχειρος.

Proverbs 11: 4

πρόχωμα.

2 Samuel 20:15 A[a]

[a] pro πρόσχωμα.

προχώρημα.

Ezekiel 32: 6[a] [a] A χώρημα.

πρώην.

Joshua 8: 5

πρωΐ.

Gen. 1: 5, 8
13, 19
23, 31
19:27
20: 8
21:14
22: 3
24:54
26:31
28:18
29:25
31:55
32:24
40: 6
41: 8
44: 3
Exo. 7:15
8:20
9:13
10:13
12:10, 10
22
46+A
16: 7,8,12
13, 19
20, 21
21—S
23, 24
18:14 A[a]
23:18
24: 4—A
27:21
29:34, 39
30: 7, 7
34: 2
4+A
25
36: 3
3+A
Lev. 6: 9, 12
12, 20
7: 5
19:13
22:30
24: 3, 4
Nu. 9:12, 15
21, 21
14:40
22:13, 21
41
28: 4
Deu. 16: 4, 7
28:67, 67
Jos. 3: 1
6:12
7:14
8:10
Jud. 6:28, 31
9:33
35+A
16: 2+A
19: 5,8,25
25[b]
26 A[c]
27
20:19—A
Ruth 3:13, 13
14
1 Sa. 1:19
3:15, 15
5: 4
1 Sa. 9:19
11: 5
15:12
17:20 A
19: 2, 11
20:35
25:22, 34
36, 37
29:10
11+A
2 Sa. 11:14
13: 4, 4
17:22
23: 4
24:11
1 Ki. 3:21, 21
17:6 22:35
2 Ki. 3:20, 22
7: 9
10: 8, 9[d]
16:15
19:35
1 Ch. 9:27, 27
16:40
23:30
2 Ch. 2: 4
13:11
20:20
35:12
Ezra 3: 3
Job 1: 5
7: 4, 18
24:17
Psa. 5: 4, 4
29: 6
45: 6 AS²[e]
48:15
54:18
58:17
87:14
89: 5,6,14
91: 3
142: 8
Pro. 27:14
Ecc. 10:16[f]
11: 6[f]
Isa. 5:11
14:12
17:11, 14
21:12
28:19, 19
37:36
38:13
50: 4
4+S³
Jer. 20:16
21:12
31:33
Eze. 12: 8
24:18, 18
33:22
46:13, 14
15
Dan. 6:19
8:14
Hos. 7: 6
Amos 4: 4
5: 8
8: 4
Zeph. 3: 3, 5, 5

[a] pro πρωΐθεν. [b] A ὄρθρος.
[c] pro ὄρθρος. [d] A πρωία.
[e] π. π. pro πρόσωπον.
[f] ACS πρωΐα.

πρωΐα.

2 Sa. 23: 4
2 Ki. 10: 9 A[a]
Psa. 64: 9
72:14
Ps. 100: 8
129: 6
6+A
Ecc. 10:16 ACS[a]
Ecc. 11: 6 ACS[a]
Lam. 3:22—AB
23—AB
Dan. 8:26[b]

[a] pro πρωΐ. [b] A πρωϊνός.

πρωΐθεν.

Exo. 18:13, 14[a]
Ruth 2: 7
24:15
2 Sa. 24:15
1 Ki. 18:26
Job 4:20

[a] A πρωΐ.

πρώϊμος.

Deu. 11:14
Isa. 58: 8
Jer. 5:24
24: 2
Hos. 6: 3
9:10
Joel 2:23
Zec. 10: 1

πρωϊνός.

Gen. 49:27
Exo. 29:41
Lev. 9:17
Nu. 28:23
1 Sa. 11:11 A[a]
2 Ki. 16:15
2 Ch. 31: 3—A¹
Job 38:12
Dan. 8:26 A[b]
Hos. 6: 4
13: 3

[a] pro ἑωθινός. [b] pro πρωΐα.

πρωΐόθεν.

2 Samuel 2:27

πρωρεύς.

Eze. 27:29
Jon. 1: 6

πρωτεύω.

Esther 5:11[a] [a] A πρῶτος.

πρωτοβαθρέω.

Esther 3: 1

πρωτοβολέω.

Ezekiel 47:12

πρωτογενής.

Exo. 13: 2
Pro. 24:70

πρωτογέννημα.

Exo. 23:16, 19
34:26
Lev. 2:14, 14
23:17, 19
20
Nu. 18:13
2 Ki. 4:42
Neh. 10:35, 35
Eze. 44:30
48:14

πρωτόγονος.

Micah 7: 1

πρωτολογία.

Proverbs 18:17

πρῶτος.

Gen. 8: 5, 13
32:17, 19
33: 2
41:20
Exo. 4: 8
12: 2, 15
15, 16
18
34: 1, 1, 4
40: 2, 15
Lev. 9:15
23: 5, 7
11, 35
39, 40
Nu. 2: 3[a], 9
7:12
9: 1, 3
10:13, 14
20: 1
28:16, 18
Nu. 20:13
33: 3, 3
Deu. 10: 1, 2, 3
4
13: 9
16: 4
17: 7
Jos. 4:19
9: 6
15:21+A
18:11
Jud. 20:22, 32[b]
39[b]
Ruth 3:10
1 Sa. 2:16
9:22
14:12+A
14
15:13[c], 21
17:30 A

2 Sa. 13:15−A
16:23
18:27
19:43
20:18
21: 9
24:25
1 Ki. 2:35
(3) 1
17:13
18:25
21: 9−A
17
2 Ki. 1:14
23:18
1 Ch. 11: 6, 6
11[d]
12:15
18:17
24: 7
25: 9
27: 2, 2, 3
33
29:21
2 Ch. 3: 3−A^2
9:29
12:15
16:11
17: 3
20:34
25:26
26:22
27: 5
28:26
29: 3, 17[e]
17, 17
35: 1, 27
36:22
Ezra 1: 1
3:12
5:13
6: 3, 19
7: 5[f], 8
9−AB
9−AB
8:31
10:17−S^1
Neh. 5:13
7: 5
8:18
Neh. 12:46
Est. 1:14
3: 7+S^3
12
5:11 A[g]
8: 9[h]
Job 8: 7, 8
15: 7
18:20
23: 8
42:11[i], 14
p 18
Psa. 70: 1
Pro. 20:21
26:18
Ecc. 1:11
Cant. 4:14
Isa. 9: 1
11:14, 14
28:25+A
41: 4
43:18, 26
27
44: 6
48:12
60: 9
65:16
Jer. 27:17
52:24[k]
Eze. 26: 1+A
27:17, 22
29:17
30:20
32:17
40: 1
45:18, 21
Dan. 7: 1[m], 4
20[n]
8:21
9: 1
10: 4
12−A
13+A
11: 1, 29
Joel 2:20
Amos 6: 6
Mic. 4: 8
Hag. 2: 9
Zec. 6: 2
14: 8, 10

[a] B νότος. [b] A ἔμπροσθεν.
[c] A πρόβατον. [d] A πρωτότοκος.
[e] B τρίτος. [f] B πατρῷος.
[g] pro πρωτεύω. [h] S^3 τρίτος.
[i] A πρὸ τούτου. [k] S^1 δεύτερος.
[m] B^1 τρίτος. [n] A πρότερος.

πρωτοστάτης.

Job 15:24

πρωτοτοκεῖα.

Gen. 25:32 A[a]
33 A[a]
34 A[a]
Gen. 27:36 A[a]
Deu. 21:17

[a] pro πρωτοτόκια.

πρωτοτοκεύω.

Deuteronomy 21:16

πρωτοτοκέω.

1 Sa. 6: 7, 10
Jer. 4:31

πρωτοτόκια.

Gen. 25:31, 32[a]
33[a], 34[a]
Gen. 27:36[a]
1 Ch. 5: 1

[a] A πρωτοτοκεῖα.

πρωτότοκος.

Gen. 4: 4
10:15
22:21
25:13, 25
27:19, 32
35:23
Gen. 36:15
38: 6, 7
41:51
43:32
46: 8
48:18
Gen. 49: 3
Exo. 4:22, 23
6:14
11: 5 *qtr*
12:12
29 *qtr*
13: 2, 13
15 *ter*
15+B
15
22:29
34:19, 19
20, 20
Lev. 27:26
Nu. 1:20
3: 2, 12
13 *ter*
40, 41
41, 42
43, 45
46, 50
8:16, 17
17, 18
18:15, 15
17 *ter*
26: 5
33: 4
Deu. 12: 6, 17
14:22
15:19 *ter*
21:15, 16
17
33:17
Jos. 6:26, 26
17: 1, 1
Jud. 8:20
1 Sa. 8: 2
1 Sa. 14:49
17:13 A
2 Sa. 3: 2
13:21
19:43
1 Ki. 16:34
2 Ki. 3:27
1 Ch. 1:13 A
29
2: 3, 13
25, 25
27, 42
50
3: 1, 15
4: 4
5: 1, 1, 3
12
6:28
8: 1, 30
38, 39
9: 5, 31
36, 44
11:11 A[a]
26: 2, 4, 6
10
2 Ch. 21: 3
Neh. 10:36, 36
Psa. 77:51
51 S^1[b]
88:28
104:36
134: 8
135:10
Jer. 38: 9
Eze. 44:30
Mic. 6: 7
Zec. 12:10

[a] pro πρῶτος. [b] pro πόνος.

πταῖσμα.

1 Samuel 6: 4

πταίω.

Deu. 7:25
1 Sa. 4: 2, 3, 10
7:10−A
2 Sa. 2:17
10:15, 19
2 Sa. 18: 7
1 Ki. 8:33
2 Ki. 14:12
19:26 B[a]
1 Ch. 19:19

[a] pro πτήσσω.

πταρμός.

Job 41: 9

πτέρνα.

Gen. 3:15
25:26
49:17
Jos. 23:13
Jud. 5:22
Psa. 48: 6
55: 7
Cant. 1: 8
Jer. 9: 4
13:22

πτερνίζω.

Gen. 27:36
Jer. 9: 4
Hos. 12: 3
Mal. 3: 8, 8, 8
9

πτερνισμός.

2 Ki. 10:19
Psa. 40:10

πτερόν.

Lev. 1:16
Dan. 7: 4+AB^2
Dan. 7: 4, 4, 6

πτεροφυέω.

Isaiah 40:31

πτερύγιον.

Exo. 36:27
Lev. 11: 9−A
10, 12
Nu. 15:38, 38
Deu. 14: 9, 10
Ruth 3: 9
1 Sa. 15:27
24: 5, 6, 12
12
1 Ki. 6:23
22−B
22
1 Ki. 6:22−B
Dan. 9:27+AB^2

πτέρυξ.

Exo. 19: 4
25:19, 19
38: 8
Lev. 1:17
Deu. 32:11
Ruth 2:12
2 Sa. 22:11
1 Ki. 6:25 *ser*
8: 6, 7
1 Ch. 28:18
2 Ch. 3:11 *qtr*
12 A
12 A
12 A
13
5: 7, 8
Job 37: 2
38:13
39:13, 26
Psa. 16: 8
17:11
35: 8
54: 7
56: 2
60: 5
62: 8
67:14
90: 4
Ps. 103: 3
138: 9
Pro. 23: 5
Ecc. 10:20
Isa. 6: 2, 2
11:12
18: 1
24:16
Jer. 29:23
Eze. 1: 6, 7, 8
8+A
11, 22
23, 24
24
25+A
3:13
7: 2
10: 5, 8, 12
16, 19
21, 21
11:22
16: 8
29: 4
Hos. 4:19
Zec. 5: 9, 9
9+AS
Mal. 4: 2

πτερύσσομαι.

Eze. 1:23
Eze. 3:13

πτερωτός.

Gen. 1:21
Deu. 4:17
Psa. 77:27
Ps. 148:10
Pro. 1:17
Eze. 1: 7

πτήσσω.

Deu. 1:29
2 Ki. 10:26[a]
Job 38:17, 30[b]

[a] B πταίω. [b] AS τήκω.

πτίλλος.

Leviticus 21:20

πτοέω.

Exo. 19:16
Deu. 31: 6
Jos. 7: 5
1 Ch. 22:13
28:20
2 Ch. 20:15, 17
32: 7
Job 11:16
23:15
32:15
Pro. 13: 3
Isa. 31: 4
Jer. 1:17
4:25
8: 9
17:13+S^1
Jer. 17:13+S^1
18 A[a]
18
18−A
21:13
23: 4
25:16
26: 5, 27
28:56
Eze. 2: 5, 7
3: 9
34:28 A[b]
Amos 3: 6
Obad. 9
Hab. 2:17
3: 7, 16

[a] pro καταισχύνω. [b] pro φάγω.

πτόησις.

Proverbs 3:25

πτύελος.

Job 7:19
Job 30:10

πτύξις.

Job 41: 4

πτυχή.

1 Kings 6:31, 31

πτύω.

Numbers 12:14

πτῶμα.

Jud. 14: 8
Job 15:23[a]
16:14−S^1
14
18:12
20: 5
31:29
33:17
Job 37:15
Ps. 109: 6
Pro. 16:18
Isa. 8:14
30:13, 14
51:19
Eze. 6: 5+A

[a] S πτῶσις.

πτῶσις.

Exo. 30:12
Jud. 20:30[a]
Job 15:23 S[b]
Ps. 105:29
Isa. 17: 1
51:17, 22
Jer. 6:15
29:22
Eze. 26:15, 18
27:27
31:13, 16
32:10, 10
Nah. 3: 3
Zec. 14:12−S^1
15, 15
18

[a] A τροπόω. [b] pro πτῶμα.

πτωχεία.

Deu. 8: 9
1 Ch. 22:14
Job 26: 6 S^1[a]
30:27
36:21
Psa. 30:11
Psa. 43:25
87:10
106:10, 41
Isa. 48:10
Lam. 3: 1, 19

[a] pro ἀπώλεια.

πτωχεύω.

Jud. 6: 6
14:15 A[a]
Psa. 33:11
Psa. 78: 8
Pro. 23:21

[a] pro ἐκβιάζω.

πτωχίζω.

1 Samuel 2: 7

πτωχός.

Exo. 23:11
Lev. 19:10, 15
23:22
Deu. 24:21+A
Ruth 3:10
1 Sa. 2: 8
2 Sa. 22:28
2 Ki. 24:14
25:12
Est. 1:20
9:22
Job 22: 8+ACS²
29:12
34:28
36: 6
Psa. 9:19, 23
30, 30
35
11: 6
13: 6
21:25
24:16
33: 7
34:10, 10
36:14
39:18
40: 1
67:11
68:30, 33
69: 6
71: 2, 4
12, 13
73:21
81: 3, 4
85: 1
87:16
Ps. 101: 1
18 S^1[a]
108:16, 22
112: 7
131:15
139:13
Pro. 13: 8
14:20, 21
31
17: 5
19: 4, 7
17, 22
22: 2, 7, 9
9, 22
28: 3, 6, 8
15, 27
29: 7, 14
38
Isa. 3:14, 15
10: 2
14:30, 30
24: 6
25: 3
29:19
41:17
58: 7
61: 1[b]
Jer. 5: 4
Eze. 16:49
18:12
22:29
Amos 2: 7
4: 1
5:11
8: 4, 6
Hab. 3:14

[a] pro ταπεινός. [b] S^1 ταπεινός.

πύγαργος.

Deuteronomy 14: 5[a]
([a] A πύδαργος.)

πυγμή.

Exo. 21:18
Isa. 58: 4

πυθμήν.

Gen. 40:10, 12
41: 5, 22
Pro. 14:12
16:25

πυκάζω.

Job 15:32
Ps. 117:27
Hos. 14: 8

πυκνός, πυκινός.

1 Ki. 6(32) A
Eze. 31: 3+A

πύλη.

Gen. 19: 1
28:17
34:20, 24
38:14
Exo. 27:16
32:26, 27
27
37:13
14 A[a]
16
38:20
39: 9 B[b]
9, 20
Nu. 3:26
4:32
Deu. 3: 5
6: 9
11:20
12:12
17: 5+A
21:19
22:15, 24
25: 7
Jos. 2: 5, 7
6:26, 26
7: 5
Jud. 9:35
40[c], 41
16: 2, 3
18:16[d]
Ruth 4: 1, 11
1 Sa. 4:13, 18
17:52, 52
21:13
2 Sa. 3:27
10: 8
11:23
15: 2
18: 4, 24
24, 26
33
19: 8, 8
8—AB
23:15, 16
1 Ki. 12 *p* 24 *l*
40 B[e]
22:10
2 Ki. 7: 1, 10
17, 17
18, 20
10: 8[e]
11: 6, 6, 19
14:13, 13
15:35
23: 8, 8
8 AB[2r]
8
25: 4
1 Ch. 9:18, 18
22, 22
23, 24
26
11:17, 18
16:42[f]
22: 3
26: 1[g], 12
16, 18
2 Ch. 8: 6, 14
14
14: 7
18: 9
2 Ch. 23: 4, 5, 15
19, 20
24: 8
25:23, 23
26: 9, 9
27: 3
31: 2—A
32: 6
33:14, 14
34: 9
35:15, 15
Ezra 2:42 B[h]
Neh. 1: 3
2: 3, 8, 13
13, 13
14, 15
17
3: 1, 3, 6
13, 13
14
15-ABS
26, 28
29[i]
31, 32
6: 1
7: 3
8: 1, 16[k]
11:19+S[3]
12:31+S[1]
37, 37
(39) S[3]
39
39+S[3]
39
40 S[3]
13:19 *ter*
22
Est. 4: 2[m]
2 S[3 b]
5+S[3]
Job 3:10
38: 8, 10
17
41: 5
Psa. 9:14, 15
23: 7, 7, 9
9
68:13
72:28
86: 2
99: 4
106:16, 18
117:19, 20
126: 5
147: 2
Pro. 1:21, 21
8: 3
12:13
22:22
24: 7
29:41[n], 49
Cant. 7: 4
Isa. 14:31
22: 7, 8
26: 2
29:21
38:10
54:12
60:11, 18
62:10
Jer. 1:15
Jer. 14: 2
15: 7
17:19, 19
20
21—S[1]
24, 25
27, 27
19: 2
3—S
20: 2
22: 2, 4, 19
28:58
33:10
38:38, 40
43:10—A
44:13
45: 7[m]
46: 3
50: 9
51: 6
52: 7[f]
7 A[o]
Lam. 1: 4
2: 9
4:12
5:14
Eze. 8: 3, 5, 14
9: 2
10:19
11: 1, 1
21:15, 22
26:10
40 *passim*
9+A
Eze. 40:15+A
39+A
42: 1, 3
15, 16
43: 1
2+A
4
44: 1, 2, 3
4, 11
17, 17
45:19
46: 1, 2, 2
3 *ter*
8, 8
9 *qnq*
12, 19
47: 2, 2
48:31 *qnq*
32 *qtr*
33 *qtr*
34 *qtr*
Amos 5:10, 12
15
Obad. 11, 13
Mic. 1: 9, 12
2:13
5: 1 BP
Nah. 2: 6
3:13
Zeph. 1:10
Hag. 2:14
Zec. 8:16
14:10 *ter*

[a] *pro* αὐλαία. [b] *pro* αὐλή.
[c] A πόλις. [d] A πυλών.
[e] *pro* πόλις. [f] S[1] πόλις.
[g] B φυλή. [h] *pro* πυλωρός.
[i] B οἶκος. [k] A οἶκος.
[m] A αὐλή. [n] S ῥύμη.
[o] *pro* τεῖχος. [p] *pro* φυλή.

πυλών.

Gen. 43:18
Jud. 18:16 A[a]
17+A
19:26+A
1 Ki. 6:12
30+A
14:27
17:10
2 Ki. 11: 5
1 Ch. 10: 9
26:13, 13
2 Ch. 3: 7
12:10
Eze. 33:30
40: 9, 11
11
41: 2, 2
Zeph. 2:14

[a] *pro* πύλη.

πυλωρός.

1 Ch. 9:17, 21
15:18, 23
24
16:38
23: 5
26:19
2 Ch. 8:14
23:19
31:14
34:13
35:15
Ezra 2:42[a], 70
Ezra 7: 7, 24
10:24
Neh. 7: 1, 45
72
10:28, 39
11:19
12:25+S[3]
25, 30
45, 47
13: 5
Job 38:17

[a] B πύλη.

πυνθάνομαι.

Gen. 25:22
2 Ch. 31: 9
32:31
Est. 6: 4
Dan. 2:15+A

πυξίον.

Exo. 24:12
Cant. 5:14
Isa. 30: 8
Hab. 2: 2

πύξος.

Isaiah 41:19

πῦρ.

Gen. 11: 3
15:17
19:24
Gen. 22: 6, 7
Exo. 3: 2, 2
9:23, 24
Exo. 9:28—A[1]
12: 8, 9, 10
13:21, 22
14:24
19:18
22: 6, 6
24:17
29:14, 34
32:20, 24
34:13
35: 3
40:32
Lev. 1: 7, 7, 8
12, 17
3: 5
4:12
6: 9, 10
12, 13
30
7: 7, 9
8:17—A
32
9:11, 24
10: 1, 1, 2
13:24, 52
55, 57
16: 1, 12
13, 27
19: 6
20:14
21: 9
Nu. 3: 4
6:18
9:15, 16
11: 1, 2
3+A
14:14
16: 7
18—A[2]
35, 37
46
21:28, 30
26:10, 61
31:10, 23
23
Deu. 1:33
4:11, 12
15, 24
33, 36
36
5: 4, 5, 22
23, 23
24, 25
26
7: 5, 25
9: 3
10+A[2]
15, 21
10: 4
12: 3, 31
13:16
18:10, 16
32:22
Jos. 6:24 A[a]
7:15
8:19, 28
11: 6, 9, 11
16:10
Jud. 1: 8
6:21
9:15, 20
20, 49
52
12: 1
14:15
15: 5, 6, 14
16: 9
18:27—A
20:48
1 Sa. 2:28
30: 1, 3, 14
2 Sa. 14:30, 30
31
22: 9, 13
23: 7
1 Ki. 9:16 A
15:13
16:18+A
18:23, 23
24, 25
1 Ki. 18:36—A
38, 38
19:12 *ter*
2 Ki. 1:10, 10
12, 12
14
2:11, 11
6:17
8:12
16: 3
17:17, 31
19:18
21: 6
23:10, 11
25: 9+A
1 Ch. 14:12
21:26
2 Ch. 7: 1, 3
28: 3
33: 6
35:13
36:19
Neh. 1: 3
2: 3, 13, 17
9:12, 19
Job 1:16
15:34
20:26
22:20
28: 5
31:12
41:10, 11[b]
Psa. 10: 6
17: 9, 13
20:10, 10
28: 7
38: 4
45:10
49: 3
57: 9
65:12
67: 3
73: 7
77:14[c], 21
48, 63
78: 5
79:17
82:14 S[1 d]
15
88:47
96: 3
103: 4
104:32, 39
105:18
117:12
139:11
148: 8
Pro. 6:27
16:27
24:51
25:22—A
26:20, 21
Cant. 8: 6
6+S[2]
Isa. 1:31+AS
4: 5
5:24
6: 6+A
9:18, 18
19
10:16, 17
17
26:11
29: 6
30:14, 27
33
33:11, 14
37:19
43: 2
44:16, 16
19
47:14, 14
50:11
11+S
11[e]
64: 2, 2
65: 5
66:15, 15
16, 24
Jer. 4: 4
Jer. 4:26—BS
5:14
6:23, 29[f]
7:18, 31
11:16
15:14
17:27
19: 5
20: 9
21:10, 12
14
22: 7
23:29
27:32, 42
28:32
30: 2, 16
36:22
39:29
41: 2, 22
43:22, 23
23
44: 8, 10
45:17, 18
50:12, 13
52:13
Lam. 1:13
2: 3, 4
4:11
Eze. 1: 4, 4
13 *ter*
27+A
27
5: 2, 4, 4
4
8: 2
10: 2, 6, 7
15: 4, 4, 5
6, 7, 7
16:41
19:12, 14
20:31+A
47
21:31, 32
22:20, 21
31
23:25
24:10
Eze. 28:18
30: 8, 14
16
36: 5
38:19, 22
39: 6, 9, 10
Dan. 3: 6, 11
15, 17
20, 21
22+A
23+A
24, 25
26, 26
27, 27
28
7: 9, 9
10, 11
10: 6
Hos. 7: 6
7+A
7+A
8:14
Joel 1:19, 20
2: 3, 5, 30
Amos 1: 4, 7, 10
12, 14
2: 2, 5
4:10, 11
5: 6
7: 4
Obad. 18
Mic. 1: 4, 7
6:10
Nah. 2: 4, 5
3:13, 15
Hab. 2:13
Zeph. 1:18
3: 8
Zec. 2: 5
3: 2
9: 4
11: 1
12: 6
6—S[1]
13: 9
Mal. 3: 2

[a] *pro* πυρισμός. [b] A φλόξ.
[c] S[1] φῶς. [d] *pro* ἄνεμος.
[e] S[1] πρός. [f] A γῆ.

πυργόβαρις.

Psalm 121: 7

πύργος.

Gen. 11: 4, 5, 8
35:16
Jud. 8: 9, 17
9:46, 47
49, 51
51, 52
52
20:38 A[a]
40 A[a]
2 Ki. 9:17
17: 9
18: 8
1 Ch. 27:25
2 Ch. 14: 7
26: 9, 10
15
27: 4
32: 5
Neh. 3: 1, 1, 11
19, 25
Neh. 3:26, 27
12:38 S[3]
39
39+S[3]
Psa. 47:13
60: 4
Cant. 4: 4
7: 4, 4
8:10
Isa. 2:15
5: 2
9:10
10: 9
29: 3
30:25
Jer. 38:38
Eze. 26: 4, 9
27:11
Mic. 4: 8
Zec. 14:10

[a] *pro* σύσσημον.

πυρεῖον.

Exo. 27: 3
38:22, 23
24
Lev. 10: 1
16:12
Nu. 4:14
16: 6
Nu. 16:17 *qtr*
18, 37
37, 39
46
2 Ki. 25:15
2 Ch. 4:11, 21

πυρετός.

Deuteronomy 28:22

πυρίκαυστος.

Isa. 1: 7
22+A
Isa. 9: 5
64:11

πύρινος.

Ezekiel 28:14, 16

πυρισμός.

Jos. 6:24[a]

[a] A πῦρ.

πυρός.

Gen. 30:14
Exo. 9:32
29: 2
34:22
Deu. 8: 8
32:14
Jos. 3:15
Jud. 6:11 A[a]
15: 1
Ruth 2:23
1 Sa. 6:13
12:17
2 Sa. 4: 6
17:28
24:15
1 Ki. 5:11
1 Ch. 21:20
2 Ch. 2:10—B
27: 5
Ezra 6: 9
7:22
Neh. 13:12
Job 31:40
Psa. 80:17
147: 3
Isa. 28:25
Jer. 12:13
48: 8
Eze. 4: 9
45:13
Joel 1:11

[a] pro σῖτος.

πυροφόρος.

Obadiah 18[a]

[a] AS* πυρφόρος.

πυρόω.

2 Sa. 22:31
Job 22:25
Psa. 11: 7
16: 3
17:31
25: 2
65:10, 10
104:19
118:140
Pro. 10:20
24:28
Ecc. 12:11ACS[a]
Isa. 1:25
Jer. 9: 7
Lam. 4: 7[b]
Dan. 11:35
12:10
Zec. 13: 9, 9

[a] pro φυτεύω. [b] A τυρόω.

πυρράκης.

Gen. 25:25
1 Sa. 16:12
1 Sa. 17:42

πυρρίζω.

Lev. 13:19, 42
43, 49
Lev. 14:37—AB[1]

πυρρός.

Gen. 25:30
Nu. 19: 2
2 Ki. 3:22
Cant. 5:10
Zec. 1: 8, 8
6: 2

πυρσεύω.

Job 20:10[a]
Pro. 16:28

[a] A ψηλαφάω.

πυρφόρος.

Job 41:20
Obad. 18AS*[a]

[a] pro πυροφόρος.

πύρωσις.

Pro. 27:21
Amos 4: 9

πυρωτής.

Nehemiah 3: 8—ABS

πώγων.

Lev. 13:29, 30
Lev. 14: 9
Lev. 19:27
21: 5
1 Sa. 21:13
2 Sa. 10: 4, 5
20: 9
1 Ch. 19: 5
Ezra 9: 3
Ps. 132: 2, 2
Isa. 7:20
Jer. 31:37
48: 5
Eze. 5: 1

πωλέω.

Gen. 41:56
42: 6
Exo. 21: 8
Neh. 5: 8, 8
13:16
Isa. 24: 2
Eze. 7:12, 13
Joel 3: 3
Nah. 3: 4
Zec. 11: 5

πῶλος.

Gen. 32:15
49:11, 11
Jud. 10: 4
Jud. 12:14
Pro. 5:19
Zec. 9: 9

πώποτε.

1 Samuel 25:28

πωρόω.

Job 17: 7[a]

[a] AS[2] πηρόω.

πῶς.

Deu. 28:67, 67
1 Ch. 13:12
Job 11: 5
Pro. 20:24
Dan. 10:17
&c., &c.

πως.

Job 20:23

ῥαβδίζω.

Jud. 6:11
Ruth 2:17

ῥαβδίον.

Ezekiel 21:21 A[a]

[a] pro ῥάβδος.

ῥάβδος.

Gen. 30:37, 37
38 ter
39—A
41, 41
32:10
38:18, 25
47:31
Exo. 4: 2, 4
17, 20
7: 9, 10
12 ter
15, 17
19, 20
8: 5, 16
17
10:13
14:16
17: 5, 9
21:19, 20
Lev. 27:32
Nu. 17: 2, 2, 2
2, 3, 3
5, 6, 6
6, 6, 6
7, 8, 9
9, 10
20: 8, 9, 11
22:23, 27
Jud. 5:14—A
6:21
1 Sa. 17:43
2 Sa. 7:14
23:21—A[a]
1 Ki. 8: 1+A
2 Ki. 18:21
1 Ch. 11:23
Est. 4:11
5: 2
Est. 8: 4
Job 9:34
Psa. 2: 9
22: 4
44: 7, 7
73: 2
88:33
109: 2
124: 3
Pro. 10:13
22:15
23:13, 14
26: 3
Isa. 9: 4, 4
10: 5, 15
24
11: 1
28:27
30: 6
Jer. 31:17
Lam. 3: 1
Eze. 7:10
19:11, 12
14, 14
20:37
21:21[b]
29: 6
37:16 ter
17, 19
20
39: 9
Hos. 4:12
Mic. 5: 1
7:14
Nah. 1:13
Zec. 8: 4
11: 7, 10
14

[a] B δόρυ. [b] A ῥαβδίον.

ῥαγάς.

Isaiah 7:19

ῥάγμα.

Amos 6:11

ῥάδαμνος.

Job 8:16
14: 7
Job 15:32
40:17[a]

[a] S[1] ῥάμνος.

ῥαθυμέω.

Genesis 42: 1

ῥαίνω.

Exo. 29:21
Lev. 4:17
5: 9
8:11
14:16, 27
Lev. 16:14, 14
15, 19
Nu. 19: 4
Isa. 45: 8
Eze. 36:25

ῥάκος.

Isa. 64: 6
Jer. 45:11

ῥακώδης.

Proverbs 23:21

ῥάμμα.

Judges 16:12 A[a]

[a] pro σπαρτίον.

ῥάμνος.

Jud. 9:14, 15
15+A
Job 40:17 S[1][a]
Psa. 57:10

[a] pro ῥάδαμνος.

ῥαντίζω.

Lev. 6:27
2 Ki. 9:33
Psa. 50: 9

ῥαντισμός.

Nu. 19: 9, 13
20, 21
Nu. 19:21
Zec. 13: 1AS[2][a]

[a] pro χωρισμός.

ῥαντός.

Gen. 30:32[a], 33
35, 35
Gen. 30:39
31:10, 12

[a] A λευκός.

ῥαπίζω.

Jud. 16:25—A
Hos. 11: 4

ῥάπισμα.

Isaiah 50: 6

ῥαπτός.

Ezekiel 16:16

ῥάπτω.

Gen. 3: 7
Job 16:15[a]
Ecc. 3: 7

[a] AS[2] ῥίπτω.

ῥασίμ.

2 Kings 11: 4, 19

ῥάσσω.

Isa. 9:11
13:16—S[1]
Jer. 23:33, 39
Dan. 8:11[a]

[a] A ταράσσω.

ῥαφιδευτής.

Exodus 27:16

ῥαφιδευτός.

Exodus 37:21

ῥάχις.

1 Sa. 5: 4
5+A
Job 40:13

ῥέγχω.

Jonah 1: 5, 6

ῥεμβεύω, —βω.

Pro. 7:12
Isa. 23:16

ῥέω vide ἐρῶ.

ῥέω, ῥυέω.

Exo. 3: 8, 17
13: 5
33: 3
Lev. 15: 3, 19
25, 25
20:24
Nu. 13:28
14: 8
16:13, 14
Deu. 6: 3
11: 9
26: 9, 10
15
27: 3
31:20
Jos. 5: 6
Job 36:28
38:30
Psa. 61:11
77:20
104:41
147: 7
Pro. 3:20
Cant. 4:16
Isa. 18:21
Jer. 9:18
11: 5
39:22
Eze. 20: 6, 15
Joel 3:18, 18
Zec. 14:12

ῥῆγμα.

1 Ki. 11:30, 31
31 A[a]
12p24l51
1 Ki. 12p24l52
2 Ki. 2:12

[a] pro σκῆπτρον.

ῥήγνυμι, ῥήσσω.

Gen. 7:11
Exo. 14:16
28:28
Nu. 16:31
Jos. 9:19
Jud. 15:19[a]
1 Ki. 1:40
11:31
12p24l51
13: 3, 5
14: 8 A
2 Ki. 22:11 A[b]
25: 4
Neh. 9:11
Job 1:20[e]
2:12
6: 5
15:13
17:11
Job 26: 8
28:10BCS[b]
31:37
32:19—S[1d]
Ps. 140: 7S[2b]
Pro. 3:20
Ecc. 3: 7
Isa. 5:27[c]
33:23
35: 6
49:13
52: 9
54: 1
58: 8
59: 5
Jer. 46: 2
Eze. 13:11, 13
38:20
Hab. 3: 9

[a] A ἀνοίγω. [b] pro διαρρήγνυμι. [c] ABS διαρρήγνυμι. [d] A καταρρηγνυμι. [e] S[1] παράγω

ῥῆμα.

Gen. 15: 1, 1
18:14, 25
19:21
20: 8
21:11
12+A
26[a]
22: 1, 16
20
24: 9, 28
30, 33
52, 66
27:34, 42
29:12
30:31, 34
31: 1
32:19
34:14—A
Gen. 34:19
37: 8, 11
38:10+A
39: 7, 9
17, 19
40: 1
41:28, 32
37
42:16, 20
44: 2, 6, 7
7, 17
18, 24
47:30
48: 1
Exo. 2:14, 15
4:15, 28[b]
30
9: 5, 6

Exo. 9:20, 21
12:24
14:12
16:16, 23
32
17: 1
18:18
18—A
22, 23
26, 26
19: 6, 9
23: 7,8,22
24: 3, 4
33: 4
34: 1, 27
28
35: 4
Lev. 4:13
8: 5
9: 6
10: 7
17: 2
Nu. 11:14, 24
13:27
14:20, 36
39, 41
15:31
22: 7, 18
20, 35
38
23: 3, 5
16, 26
24:13
27:14
30: 2, 3
31:16, 16
32:20
33: 2
36: 6
Deu. 1:14, 17
23, 26
43
2: 7
4: 1 A[c], 2
10, 12
13, 32
36
5: 5[d], 22
6: 6
8: 3
9:23
10: 2
11:18
12:32
13:11
15: 9, 10
11, 15
17: 1, 4, 8
8
10 A[e]
11
18:18, 20
21
22+A
22
19: 7, 15
20
23: 9[s]
24:20, 22
24
28:58
29:19, 29
30: 1, 14
31: 9, 19
32: 1, 2, 2
51
34: 5
Jos. 1:13, 18
2:21
3: 9
8: 8
9: 7, 8
14: 6, 10
12
21:45
22:24
23:15, 15
24:26
Jud. 5:29 A[f]
6:29[a], 29[t]

Jud. 8: 1
11:10
37 A[f]
13:12 A[f]
17
18: 7 A[f]
10
19:24
30+A
20: 9
Ruth 3:18, 18
1 Sa. 2:23
23+A
3: 1,7,11
17, 17
4:16
8: 6, 10
9:10, 21
27
10: 2, 16
11: 5
6—A
12:16
14:12, 42
15:10, 23
24, 26
17:11, 23A
27 A
29 A
30 A
30 A
18: 8
20+A
23, 24
26
19: 7
20: 2
2+A^2
2, 23
21: 2, 2, 8
12
22:15
24: 7, 17
25: 9, 12
36, 37
26:16, 19
28:18
2 Sa. 2: 6
3:11
7: 4, 25
11:11, 22
25, 27
12: 6, 12
14, 21
13:20, 33
14: 3, 12
15, 15
18, 20
15: 6, 11
28, 35
36
17: 6, 19
19:10
22:31
24:10+A
13
1 Ki. 1:27
2:27
(3)38
42+A
3:10, 11
12
8:20, 26
59
11:41 B[f]
41
12:15, 24
24
*p*24 *l*28
*l*45, 58
*l*59, 67
*l*77, 82
*l*83
13: 3[c], 18
21, 26
26+A
32, 33
34
14: 5 A
13 A

1 Ki. 14:18 A
19 A
19 A
15: 5+A
29—A
16:12, 34
17: 2[h]
5—A
8, 13
15+A
16
17+A
24
18: 1, 24
19: 9
20: 1+A
28
21: 9, 24
22:19, 38
2 Ki. 1:16+A
17
2:22
3:12
4:41, 44
5:14, 17
6:18
7: 2, 16
19
8: 2, 13
9:25 A[i]
26
10:10, 17
14:25
17:12
20: 4, 17
22: 9
23: 1, 16
24:13
1 Ch. 11:19
21: 4—B
2 Ch. 6:17
11: 4
36:22
Ezra 5: 7[k], 11
6: 9, 11
7: 1
10: 4, 5, 9
12, 13
14, 16
Neh. 2:19
5:12
13[m]
6: 4—A
11:24 S^3[n]
Est. 1:12+S^3
17
5:14
Job 2: 9
4: 2,4,12
6: 3, 6
10, 25
25+A
26, 26
8:10+A
10
9:14
10: 1
11: 3
12:11
13:17
15: 3, 4, 5
5, 13
16: 3, 4[h]
19: 4, 4
23
22:22
23: 5AS^2[o]
12
24:25
26: 4

Job 27: 3 A^2[p]
29:22
32: 1, 11
12—S^1
14, 18
33: 1, 3, 8
13
34:16, 34
35, 37
35:16
36: 4
38: 2
42: 3, 7
Psa. 5: 2
16: 6
18: 3, 5
35: 4
51: 6
53: 4
55:11
67:12
76: 9+S^2
77: 1
137: 1—A
4
140: 6
Pro. 3: 1
4: 5 A
7:24[q]
8: 8[r]
17:27
Ecc. 1: 1
8: 1, 5
Isa. 8:20
14:28
15: 1[s]
16:13
17: 1
22: 1[s]
23: 1[t]
29:11
38: 7
40: 8
42:16
44:26
55:11
58: 9
59:21
66: 5
Jer. 1: 1
5:14
6:10
7:23
9: 8
16:10
18:20
23:33 S^1[i]
33: 2
42:14
45:14
49: 4
Lam. 2:17
Eze. 33:31, 32
38:10
Dan. 1:20
2: 8, 9
10, 10
15, 17
3:16, 22
28
4:14[h]
5:26
6:14
7:28
9:23
10: 9+A
Hos. 6: 5
10: 4
Zec. 1:13

[a] A πρᾶγμα. [b] A σημεῖον. [c] *pro* κρῖμα. [d] A ἐνώπιον. [e] *pro* πρᾶγμα. [f] *pro* λόγος. [g] A τέρας. [h] A λόγος. [i] *pro* λῆμμα. [k] AB ῥήσεις. [m] S^3 λόγος. [n] *pro* χρῆμα. [o] *pro* ἴαμα. [p] *pro* ῥίς. [q] A ῥῆσις. [r] A κρῖμα. [s] A ὅραμα. [t] AS ὅραμα.

ῥῆσις.

Ezra 5: 7 AB[a]
Pro. 1: 6, 23
2: 1
4: 4, 20
7:24 A[a]

Pro. 15:26
19:27
24:70
27:25

[a] *pro* ῥῆμα.

ῥήσσω *vide* ῥήγνυμι.

ῥητίνη.

Gen. 37:25
43:10
Jer. 8:22

Jer. 26:11
28: 8
Eze. 27:17

ῥητός.

Exo. 9: 4

Exo. 22: 9

ῥῖγος.

Deuteronomy 28:22

ῥίζα.

Deu. 29:18
2 Ki. 19:30
Job 5: 3
8:12—S^1
13:27
14: 8
18:16
19:28
28: 9
29:19
30: 4
31:12
Psa. 79:10
Pro. 12: 3, 12
Isa. 5:24
11: 1,1,10

Isa. 37:31
40:24
53: 2
Jer. 17: 8
Eze. 16: 3
17: 6, 7, 9
9
31: 7
Dan. 2:41
4:12, 20
23—A
11: 7, 20
Hos. 9:16
14: 5
Amos 2: 9
Mal. 4: 1

ῥιζόω.

Isa. 40:24

Jer. 12: 2

ῥίζωμα.

Job 36:30

Psa. 51: 7

ῥίν, ῥίς.

Job 27: 3[a]
40:19, 20
Ps. 113:14
134:17+A

Pro. 11:22
Cant. 7: 8
Isa. 37:29

[a] A^2 ῥῆμα.

ῥιπιστός.

Jeremiah 22:14

ῥίπτω.

Gen. 21:15
37:20, 24
Exo. 1:22
4: 3, 3
7: 9, 10
12
15: 1, 4, 21
32:19, 24
Deu. 9:17, 21
Jos. 8:29
10:27
Jud. 4:22[a]
8:25 A[b]
9:17 A[c]
53
15:15 A[c]
17
2 Sa. 11:21, 22
18:17
20:21
1 Ki. 13:24, 25
28
14: 9 A
2 Ki. 2:16, 21

2 Ki. 3:25
6: 6
7:15
9:25, 26
10:25
13:21
23: 6, 12
2 Ch. 30:14
34: 4
Neh. 9:11, 26
13: 8
Job 16:11
15AS^2[d]
20:23AS^2[e]
Psa. 87: 6-AS^2
Isa. 14:19
22:18
33:12
34: 3
Jer. 14:16
22:19
27:30
28:63[f]
33:23

Jer. 43:23, 30
45: 6, 11
26
48: 9
Eze. 5: 4
7:19

Eze. 19:12
28:17
Dan. 8: 7, 12
9:18, 20
Joel 1: 7
Zec. 5: 8, 8

[a] A πίπτω. [b] *pro* βάλλω. [c] *pro* ἐκρίπτω. [d] *pro* ῥάπτω. [e] *pro* νίπτω. [f] S ἐπιρρίπτω.

ῥίς *vide* ῥίν.

ῥοά.

Exo. 28:29
36:32
Nu. 13:24
20: 5
Deu. 8: 8
1 Sa. 14: 2
1 Ki. 7: 6
9+A
28, 28
2 Ki. 25:17—B
Cant. 4: 3

Cant. 4:13—A^2BS^1
6: 6, 10
7:12
8: 2
Jer. 52:22, 22
23, 23
Eze. 19:10
Joel 1:12
Hag. 2:19

ῥόδον.

Esther 1: 6

ῥοιζέω.

2 Ki. 13:17 A[a]
17 A[a]

Cant. 4:15

[a] *pro* τοξεύω.

ῥοῖζος.

Ezekiel 47: 5+A

ῥοΐσκος.

Exo. 28:29, 29
30
36:32, 33

Exo. 36:34
2 Ch. 3:16
4:13

ῥομφαία.

Gen. 3:24
Exo. 5:21
32:27
Nu. 22:23
31: 8
Jos. 5:13
6:21
8:24[a]
24:12
Jud. 1: 8[b], 25
4:15, 16
7:14, 22[b]
8:10, 20[b]
9:54[b]
18:27
19:29[b]
20: 2, 15
17, 25
35, 37
46, 48
21:10
1 Sa. 2:33
13:19, 22
14:20
15: 8, 33
17:39, 45
47, 50A
51
18: 4 A
21: 8, 8, 9
22:10, 13
19
19+A
25:13
31: 4, 4, 5
2 Sa. 1:12, 22
2:26
3:29
12: 9,9,10
23: 8—A
24: 9

1 Ki. 1:51
2: 8, 32
(3) *p* 1
19: 1, 10
14, 17
17—A
2 Ki. 3:23, 26
6:22
8:12
10:25
11:15, 20
19: 7
1 Ch. 10: 4, 4, 5
11:11, 20
21:12, 16
27, 30
2 Ch. 20: 9
21: 4
32:21
36:17
Ezra 9: 7
Neh. 4:13, 18
Psa. 7:13
9: 7
16:13
21:21
34: 3
36:14, 15
43: 4, 7
44: 4
58: 8
62:11—S^1
63: 4
75: 4
77:62, 64
88:44
143:10
149: 6
Cant. 3: 8, 8
Isa. 66:16
Jer. 5:17

Jer. 6:25
14:18 A[c]
45: 2
46:18
49:16, 17
22
50:11
11 − S[1]
51:12, 13
18, 27
28
Lam. 2:21
4: 9
5: 9
Eze. 5: 1, 2
12, 17
6: 3, 8
11, 12
7:15, 15
11: 8,8,10
12:14, 16
14:17, 17
21
17:21
21: 9,9,11
12, 14
14, 14
15, 20
20, 28
28
23:10, 25
Eze. 24:21
25:13
29: 8
10 − A
30:24, 25
32:10, 11
33: 2 − A
3, 4, 6
6, 26A
Dan. 11:33
Hos. 1: 7
2:18
7:16
11: 6
14:a1
Joel 3:10
Amos 1:11
4:10
7: 9, 11
17
9: 1,4,10
Mic. 4: 3, 3
5: 6
6:14
Nah. 2:13
3: 3, 15
Zeph. 2:12
Hag. 1:11
2:22
Zec. 9:13
13: 7

[a] B[a] μάχαιρα. [b] A μάχαιρα.
[c] *pro* μάχαιρα.

ῥόπαλον.

Proverbs 25:18

ῥοπή.

Jos. 13:22
Pro. 16:11
Isa. 40:15

ῥοών.

Zechariah 12:11

ῥύαξ.

Ezekiel 40:40

ῥυέω *vide* ῥέω.

ῥυθμίζω.

Isaiah 44:13

ῥυθμός.

Exo. 28:15
2 Ki. 16:10
Cant. 7: 1

ῥύμη.

Pro. 29:41 S[a]
Isa. 15: 3

[a] *pro* πύλη.

ῥύομαι.

Gen. 48:16
Exo. 2:17, 19
5:23
6: 6
12:27
14:30
Jos. 22:22, 31
Jud. 6: 9 − A
8:34
9:17[a]
11:26
18:28[a]
2 Sa. 12: 7
14:16
19: 9, 9A[b]
22:18, 44
49
2 Ki. 18:32, 33
33
19:11
23:18[c]
Ezra 8:31
Neh. 9:28
Est. 4: 8
Job 5:20
20 A[d]
6:23
22:30
33:17, 30
Psa. 6: 5
7: 2
16:13
17: 1, 18
20
21 + ABS
30, 44
49
21: 5,9,21
24:20
30: 2, 16
32:19
Psa. 33: 5, 8
18, 20
34:10
36:40 − S[1]
38: 9[e]
39:14
40: 2
42: 1
49:22
50:16
53: 9
55:14
56: 5
58: 3
59: 7
68:15, 19
70: 2,4,11
71:12
78: 9
80: 8
81: 4
85:13
88:49
90: 3, 14
96:10
105:43
106: 6, 20
107: 7
108:21
114: 4
118:170[f]
119: 2
123: 7, 7
139: 2, 5 A[g]
141: 7
143: 7, 11
Pro. 2:12
6:31
10: 2
11: 4 + A
6 − S[1]
Pro. 12: 6
13:17
14:25
22:23
23:14
24:11
Isa. 1:17
5:29
25: 4
25: 5 + S[1]
36:14, 15
18, 18
19, 20
20
37:11 − AS
12
38: 6[h]
44: 6
47: 4
48:17, 20
49: 7, 25
26
50: 2
51:10
52: 9
54: 5, 8
59:20
63: 5, 16
Eze. 3:19, 21
13:21, 23
14:18, 20
33: 9 A[g]
37:23
Dan. 3:17, 29
6:27
8:11
11:45
Hos. 13:14
Mic. 4:10
5: 6

[a] A ἐξαιρέω. [b] *pro* ἐξαιρέω.
[c] A εὑρίσκω. [d] *pro* λύω.
[e] S[1] καθαριζω. [f] A ζάω.
[g] *pro* ἐξαιρέω. [h] AS σώζω.

ῥυπαρός.

Zechariah 3: 3, 4

ῥύπον.

Job 11:15

ῥύπος.

Job 9:31
14: 4
Isa. 4: 4

ῥύσις.

Lev. 15: 2
2 − A
3 *qtr*
13, 15
19, 25
25, 26
Lev. 15:28, 30
33
20:18
Deu. 23:10
Job 38:25

ῥύστης.

Psa. 17: 3, 49
69: 6
Psa. 143: 2

ῥώμη.

Proverbs 6: 8

ῥώξ.

Lev. 19:10
Isa. 17: 6
Isa. 65: 8

ῥωποπώλης.

1 Ki. 10:15 + A
Neh. 3:31[a], 32[a]

[a] BS[a] ῥοβοπώλης.

σαβαείν.

Daniel 11:45

σαβάτ.

Zechariah 1: 7

σαβαχά.

2 Kings 25:17, 17

σαβαώθ, σαββαώθ.

1 Sa. 1: 3, 11
15: 2
17:45
Isa. 1: 9, 24
2:12
3: 1
5: 7, 9
16, 24
6: 3, 5
7: 7
8:18
9: 7
10:16, 24
33
13: 4, 13
14:22, 24
17: 3
18: 7, 7
19: 4, 12
16
17 − BS
18 − ABS
Isa. 19:25
21: 6 + S[a]
10
22: 5, 12
14, 15
17, 25
23: 9
25: 6
28: 5, 22
29
29: 6
31: 4
5 − A
37:16, 32
39: 5
44: 6
45:13, 14
47: 4
48: 2
51:15
54: 5
Zec. 13: 2 − A

vide κύριος.

σαββατίζω.

Exo. 16:30
Lev. 23:32
26:34, 35
Lev. 26:35
2 Ch. 36:21
21 − B

σάββατον.

Exo. 16:23, 25
26
29 − B
20: 8, 10
31:13, 14
15
15 A[a]
16
35: 2, 3
Lev. 16:31, 31
19: 3, 30
23: 3,3,15
32 *ter*
38
24: 8
25: 2, 4, 4
6
26: 2, 34
34, 35
43
Nu. 15:32
33 − A
28: 9, 10
10
Deu. 5:12, 14
15
2 Ki. 4:23
11: 5
7 − A
9
9 − B
1 Ch. 9:32, 32
23:31
2 Ch. 2: 4
8:13
23: 4, 8, 8
31: 3
34:21
Neh. 9:14
10:31, 31
33
13:15, 15
16, 17
18, 19
19, 19
21, 22
Psa. 23: 1 − S
37: 1
47: 1 − A
91: 1[b]
92: 1 A[c]
93: 1
Isa. 1:13
56: 2, 4[d]
6
58:13, 13
66:23, 23
Jer. 17:21
22 − S[1]
22, 24
24 − S[1]
27, 27
Lam. 2: 6
Eze. 20:12, 13
16, 20
21, 24
22: 8, 26
26 + A
23:38
44:24
45:17
46: 1, 3, 4
12
Hos. 2:11
Amos 6: 3
8: 5

[a] *pro* ἕβδομος. [b] S προσάββατον
[c] *pro* προσάββατον.
[d] S[1] πρόσταγμα.

σαβεί.

Dan. 11:16[a] [a] A σαββείρ.

σαβέκ.

Genesis 22:13

σαγήνη.

Ecc. 7:27
Isa. 19: 8
Eze. 26: 5, 14
Eze. 47:10
Hab. 1:15, 16

σάγμα.

Genesis 31:34

σαδδαΐ

vide θεός *et* κύριος.

σαδημώθ.

2 Kings 23: 4

σαδηρώθ.

2 Kings 11: 8, 15

σαθρός.

Job 41:18

σαθρόω.

Judges 10: 8 A[a]

[a] *pro* θλίβω.

σάκκος.

Gen. 37:34
42:25, 35
35
Lev. 11:32
Jos. 9:10
2 Sa. 3:31
21:10
1 Ki. 20:16, 27
27 − A
21:31, 32
2 Ki. 6:30
19: 1, 2
1 Ch. 21:16
Neh. 9: 1
Est. 4: 1, 2, 3
4
Job 16:15
Psa. 29:12
34:13
68:12
Isa. 3:24
15: 3
20: 2
22:12
32:11 + AS
37: 1, 2
50: 3
58: 5
Jer. 4: 8
6:26
30: 3
31:37
Lam. 2:10
Eze. 7:18
27:31 A
Dan. 9: 3
Joel 1: 8, 13
Amos 8:10
Jon. 3: 5, 6, 8

σαλεύω.

Jud. 5: 5
2 Sa. 22:37
2 Ki. 17:20
21: 8
1 Ch. 16:30
2 Ch. 33: 8
Job 9: 6
28: 4 − ABCS
41:14
Psa. 9:27
12: 5
14: 5
15: 8
16: 5
17: 8, 8
20: 8
25: 1[a]
29: 7
32: 8
35:12
37:17
45: 6, 7
47: 6
59: 4
61: 3
72: 2
76:19
81: 5
Psa. 92: 1
93:18
95: 9, 10
11
96: 4
97: 7
98: 1
106:27
108:10, 25
111: 6
113: 7
124: 1
Pro. 3:26
Ecc. 12: 3
Isa. 7: 2
40:20
Jer. 23: 9
28: 7
Lam. 4:14, 15
Dan. 4:11
Amos 8:12
9: 5
Mic. 1: 4
Nah. 1: 5
3:12
Hab. 2:16[b]
3: 6
Zec. 12: 2

[a] AS ἀσθενέω. [b] S[3] διασαλεύω

σάλος.

Psa. 54:23
65: 9
Psa. 88:10
120: 3

Lam. 1: 8
Jon. 1:15
Zec. 9:14

σάλπιγξ.

Exo. 19:13, 16
19
20:18
Lev. 23:24
25: 9, 9
Nu. 10: 2, 8, 9
10
31: 6
Jos. 6: 4, 8
13, 13
20, 20
1 Sa. 13: 3
2 Sa. 2:28
6:15
2 Ki. 11:14, 14
12:13
1 Ch. 13: 8
15:24, 28
16: 6, 42
2 Ch. 5:12, 13
7: 6
13:12, 14
15:14
20:28
23:13, 13
29:26, 27
28
Ezra 3:10
Neh. 8:15
12:35[a]
41 S[3]
Job 39:24, 25
Psa. 46: 6
80: 4
97: 6, 6
150: 3
Isa. 18: 3
27:13
58: 1
Jer. 4: 5, 19
21
6: 1, 17
28:27
49:14
Eze. 7:14
33: 3, 4, 5
6
Dan. 3: 5, 7
10, 15
Hos. 5: 8
Joel 2: 1, 15
Amos 2: 2
3: 6
Zeph. 1:16
Zec. 9:14

[a] A σαλπίζω.

σαλπίζω.

Nu. 10: 3, 4, 5
6, 6, 6
6, 7, 8
9A[a]
10
Jos. 6: 4, 9, 13
16, 20
Jud. 3:27
6:34
7:18, 18
19, 20
20, 22
1 Sa. 13: 3
2 Sa. 2:28
18:16
20: 1, 22
1 Ki. 1:34, 39
2 Ki. 9:13
2 Ki. 11:14
1 Ch. 15:24
2 Ch. 5:12, 13
7: 6
13:14
23:13
29:28
Neh. 4:18
12:35 A[b]
Psa. 80: 4
Isa. 27:13
44:23
Jer. 28:27 – S[1]
Eze. 7:14
33: 3
Hos. 5: 8
Joel 2: 1, 15
Zec. 9:14

[a] pro σημαίνω. [b] pro σάλπιγξ

σαμβύκη.

Daniel 3: 5, 7, 10, 15

σανδάλιον.

Jos. 9:11
Isa. 20: 2

σανιδωτός.

Exodus 27: 8

σανίς.

2 Ki. 12: 9[a]
Cant. 8: 9
Eze. 27: 5

[a] AB τρώγλη.

σαπρία.

Job 2: 9
7: 5
8:16
17:14
Job 21:26
25: 6
Isa. 28:21[a]
Joel 2:20

[a] AS πικρία.

σαπρίζω.

Ecclesiastes 10: 1

σάπφειρος.

Exo. 24:10
28:18
Exo. 39:18
Job 28: 6, 16
Cant. 5:14
Isa. 54:11
Lam. 4: 7
Eze. 1:26
Eze. 9: 2
10: 1
28:13

σαράβαρα.

Daniel 3:21, 27

σάρδιον.

Exo. 28:17
36:17
Pro. 25:11, 12
Eze. 28:13

σάρδιος.

Exo. 25: 6
Exo. 35: 8

σάρκινος.

2 Ch. 32: 8
Pro. 24:23
Eze. 11:19
36:26

σάρξ.

Gen. 2:21, 23
23, 24
6: 3, 12
17, 19
7:15, 16
21
8:17, 21
9:11, 15
15, 16
17
17:11, 13
14, 24
25
29:14
34:24
37:27
40:19
41: 2 3, 4
4 – A
18, 19
Exo. 4: 7
30:32
Lev. 4:11
12: 3
13:10, 18
24, 38
39, 39
43
17:11, 14
14, 14
18: 6
21: 5
25:49
49 + A
26:29, 29
Nu. 12:12
16:22
18:15
27:16
Deu. 5:26
28:55
Jud. 8: 7
9: 2
1 Sa. 17:44
2 Sa. 5: 1
19:12, 13
2 Ki. 4:34
5:10, 14
14
6:30
9:36
1 Ch. 11: 1
Neh. 5: 5, 5
Job 2: 5
4:15
6:12
13:14
14:22
16:18
19:20, 22
21: 6
31:31
Job 33:21, 25
34:15
41:14
Psa. 15: 9
26: 2
27: 7
37: 4, 8
55: 5
62: 2
64: 3
72:26
77:27, 39
78: 2
83: 3
101: 6
108:24
118:120
135:25
144:21
Pro. 3:22
4:22
5:11
26:10
Ecc. 2: 3
4: 5
5: 5
11:10
12:12
Isa. 9:20
10:18
31: 3
40: 5, 6
49:26, 26
66:16, 23
24
Jer. 9:26
12:12
17: 5
19: 9, 9, 9
32:17
39:27
51:35
Lam. 3: 4
Eze. 11:19
20:48
21: 4, 5, 7
23:20
32: 5
36:26
37: 6, 8
44: 7, 7, 9
Dan. 1:15
2:11
4: 9
7: 5
Hos. 9:12
Joel 2:28
Mic. 3: 2, 3, 3
Zeph. 1:17
Zec. 2:13
11: 9
14:12

Σατάν.

1 Ki. 11:14, 14 – A, 23 A

Σατανᾶς.

Job 2: 3 A[a] [a] pro διάβολος.

σάτον.

Haggai 2:16, 16

σατραπεία.

Jos. 13: 3
Jud. 3: 3
Jud. 16:18 A[a]
Est. 8: 9ABS[b]

[a] pro ἄρχων. [b] pro σατράπης.

σατράπης.

Jud. 5: 3
16: 5 A[a]
8 A[a]
18 A[a]
23 A[a]
27 A[a]
30 A[a]
1 Sa. 5: 8, 11
6: 4, 12
16, 18
7: 7
29: 2, 3, 6
1 Sa. 29: 7, 9
1 Ki. 10:15
21:24
2 Ch. 9:14
Est. 1: 3
8: 9, 9[b]
9: 3
Dan. 2:48
3:27
6: 1, 2, 4
6, 7

[a] pro ἄρχων. [b] ABS σατραπεία.

σαύρα.

Leviticus 11:30

σαφώθ.

2 Samuel 17:29

σαφῶς.

Deu. 13:14
27: 8
Hab. 2: 2

σαών.

Jeremiah 26:17

σβέννυμι, –ύω.

Lev. 6: 9, 12
13
2 Sa. 14: 7
21:17
2 Ki. 22:17
2 Ch. 29: 7
34:25
Job 4:10
16:15
18: 5, 6
21:17
30: 8
34:26
40: 7
Pro. 10: 7
13: 9
20:20
Pro. 24:20
Cant. 8: 7
Isa. 1:31
34:10
42: 3
+ S[1] [a]
43:17, 17
66:24
Jer. 4: 4
7:20
20 + A
17:27
21:12
Eze. 20:47, 48
32: 7
Amos 5: 6

[a] pro θραύω.

σέβομαι.

Jos. 4:24
22:25
24:33
Job 1: 9
Isa. 29:13
66:14 AS[a]
Jon. 1: 9[b]

[a] pro φοβέω. [b] S[3] φοβέω.

σειρά.

Jud. 16:13, 14[a]
19[a]
Pro. 5:22

[a] A βόστρυχος.

σειρήν.

Job 30:29
Isa. 13:21
34:13
Isa. 43:20
Jer. 27:39
Mic. 1: 8

σειρομάστης, σιρ–

Nu. 25: 7
Jud. 5: 8 + A
Jud. 5: 8 A[a]
1 Ki. 18:28
2 Ki. 11:10
Joel 3:10

[a] pro λόγχη.

σεισμός.

Job 41:20
Isa. 15: 5
29: 6
Jer. 10:22
23:19
29: 3
Eze. 3:12, 13
37: 7
38:19
Amos 1: 1
Nah. 3: 2
Zec. 14: 5ABS[a]

[a] pro συσσεισμός.

σείω.

Jud. 5: 4
2 Sa. 22: 8
Job 9: 6, 28
Psa. 67: 9
Pro. 24:56
Isa. 10:14
13:13
14:16
17: 4
19: 1
24:18, 20
28: 7
33:20
Jer. 8:16
Jer. 27:46
28:29
29:22 A[a]
Eze. 26:10, 15
31:16
38:20
Joel 2:10
3:16
Amos 1:14
9: 1
Nah. 1: 5
Hab. 2:16
3:14
Hag. 2: 6, 21

[a] pro φοβέω.

σελήνη.

Gen. 37: 9
Deu. 4:19
17: 3
Jos. 10:12, 13
2 Ki. 23: 5
Job 25: 5
31:26
Psa. 8: 4
71: 5, 7
73:16 – S[2]
88:38
103:19
120: 6
135: 9
Ps. 148: 3
Ecc. 12: 2
Cant. 6: 9
Isa. 13:10
24:23 + S[1]
30:26
60:19, 20
Jer. 8: 2
38:35
Eze. 32: 7
Joel 2:10, 31
3:15
Hab. 3:11

σελίς.

Jeremiah 43:23

σεμίδαλις.

Gen. 18: 6
Exo. 29: 2, 40
Lev. 2: 1, 2, 4
5
7 – A
5:11, 13
6:15, 20
7: 2, 2
9: 4
14:10, 21
23:13, 17
24: 5
Nu. 6:15
7:13, 19
25, 31
37, 43
49, 55
61, 67
Nu. 7:73, 79
8: 8
15: 4, 6, 9
28: 5, 9, 12
12, 13
20, 28
29: 3, 9, 14
1 Sa. 1:24
1 Ki. (3) p 46
4:22
2 Ki. 7: 1, 16
18
1 Ch. 9:29
23:29
Isa. 1:13
66: 3
Eze. 16:13, 19
46:14

σεμνός.

Jud. 11:35 + A
Pro. 6: 8
Pro. 8: 6[a]
15:26

[a] S[1] πολύς.

σεραφίμ.

Isaiah 6: 2, 6

σερσερώθ.

2 Chronicles 3:16

σευτλίον.

Isaiah 51:20

σεφηλά.

2 Ch. 26:10
Jer. 39:44
Jer. 40:13—A
Obad. 19

σημαία.

Nu. 2: 2
Isa. 30:17

σημαίνω.

Exo. 18:20
Nu. 10: 9[a]
Jos. 6: 8
Jud. 7:21
2 Ch. 13:12
Ezra 3:11
Neh. 8:15
Est. 2:22
Job 39:24, 25
Pro. 6:13
Jer. 4: 5
6: 1
Eze. 33: 3, 6
Zec. 10: 8

[a] A σαλπίζω.

σημασία.

Lev. 13: 2, 6, 7
8
14:56
23:10, 11
12, 13
25:15—A
Nu. 10: 5, 6, 6
Nu. 10: 6, 6, 7
29: 1
31: 6
1 Ch. 15:28
2 Ch. 13:12
Ezra 3:12, 13

σημεῖον.

Gen. 1:14
4:15
9:12, 13
17
17:11
Exo. 3:12
4: 8, 8, 9
17
28 A[a]
30
7: 3, 9
8:23+A
10: 1, 2
11: 9, 10
12:13
13: 9, 16
31:13, 17
Nu. 14:11[b], 22
16:38
17:10
21: 8, 9
26:10
Deu. 4:34
6: 8, 22
7:19
11: 3, 18
13: 1, 2
26: 8
28:46
29: 3
34:11
Jos. 2:18
4: 6
24: 5—B
Jud. 6:17 A[c]
20:38[d]
1 Sa. 2:34
10: 2, 7, 9
1 Sa. 14:10
2 Ki. 19:29
20: 8, 9
2 Ch. 32:24
Neh. 9:10
Job 21:29
Psa. 64: 9
73: 4, 4, 9
77:43
85:17
104:27
134: 9
Isa. 7:11, 14
8:18
11:12
13: 2
18: 3
19:20
20: 3
33:23
37:30
38: 7, 22
41:25
55:13
66:19
Jer. 6: 1
10: 2[e]
28:12, 27
31: 9
39:20, 21
51:29
Eze. 4: 3
9: 4, 6
20:12, 20
39:15
Dan. 3:32
6:27
Joel 2:30+S[3]

[a] pro ῥῆμα. [b] A θαυμάσιος. [c] pro σήμερον. [d] A συνταγή. [e] S[1] θηρίον.

σημειόω.

Psalm 4: 7

σημείωσις.

Psalm 59: 6

σήμερον.

Gen. 4:14
19:37, 38
21:26
22:14
24:12, 42
25:31, 33
26:33
Gen. 30:16, 32
31:43, 46
35: 4
20+A
40: 7
41: 9, 41
42:13, 32
Gen. 47:23
50:20
Exo. 2:18
5: 7+A
14
13: 4
14:13, 13
16:25, 25
19:10
32:29
Lev. 9: 4
10:19, 19
Nu. 22:30[a]
Deu. 1:10, 39
2:18
4: 1, 2, 4
8, 26
38, 39
40
5: 3
6: 2, 6, 24
7:11
8: 1, 11
18, 19
9: 1, 3
6—A
10:13
11: 2, 4, 7
8, 13
22, 26
27, 28
32
12: 8, 11
14, 32
13:18
15: 5
19: 9
20: 3
26: 3, 17
18
27: 1, 4, 10
28: 1, 13
14, 15
29:10, 12
15, 15
30: 2, 8, 11
15, 16
18, 19
31: 2, 21
27
32:46
Jos. 4: 9
5: 9
6:25
7:19, 25
9:33
10:27
13:13[a]
14:10, 11
14 A[b]
22: 3, 16
18
18—A[b]
29, 31
24:15, 27
31
Jud. 6:17[c]
9:18
11:27
19: 9+A
21: 3, 6
Ruth 2:19, 19
3:18
4: 9, 10
14
1 Sa. 4: 3, 7, 16
9:12, 19
20, 27
1 Sa. 10: 2, 19
11:13
12: 5, 17
14:28, 30
38, 41
44, 45
15:28
16: 5
17:10, 36
45, 46
18:22+A
20:27
21: 2, 5
22:15
24:11, 12
19, 19
20
25:10
32—B
33, 34
26: 8, 19
21
23—A
24
27:10
29: 6
30:13, 25
2 Sa. 3: 8, 8, 39
6: 8 A[b]
20, 20
11:12
14:22
15:20
20—A
16: 3
18:31
19: 5, 5, 6
6, 6, 7
20, 22
22, 22
35
1 Ki. 1:25, 48
51
2:24, 31
5: 7
8:15, 28
56
18:15, 36
21:13
22: 5
2 Ki. 2: 3, 5
4:23
6:28, 31
1 Ch. 29: 5
2 Ch. 6:19
10: 7
18: 4
35:21, 25
Neh. 1: 6, 11
4: 2—ABS
5:11
9:36
Est. 1:18
5: 4, 4
Psa. 2: 7
94: 8
Pro. 7:14
Isa. 10:32
37: 3
38:19
58: 4
Jer. 1:10, 18
41:15
Eze. 2: 3
8: 9+A
20:29, 31
24: 2

[a] A ταύτης. [b] pro ταύτης. [c] A σημεῖον.

σήπω.

Job 16: 7
19:20
33:21
Job 40: 7
Psa. 37: 6
Eze. 17: 9

σής.

Job 4:19
Job 27:18
Job 27:20 S[1 a]
32:22
Pro. 14:30
Isa. 33: 1
Isa. 50: 9
51: 8
Mic. 7: 4

[a] pro ὕδωρ.

σητόβρωτος.

Job 13:28

σῆψις.

Isaiah 14:11

σθένος.

Job 4:10
16:15
Job 26:14

σιαγόνιον.

Deuteronomy 18: 3

σιαγών.

Jud. 15:14, 15
16, 16
17, 17
19, 19
1 Ki. 22:24
2 Ch. 18:23
Job 21: 5[a]
Psa. 31: 9
Cant. 1:10
5:13
Isa. 50: 6
Lam. 1: 2
3:29
Eze. 29: 4
Hos. 11: 4
Mic. 5: 1

[a] A στόμα.

σιγάω.

Exo. 14:14
Jud. 18: 9+A
Psa. 31: 3
38: 3
40:21
82: 2
Ps. 106:29
Ecc. 3: 7
Isa. 32: 5
Lam. 3:48[a]
Amos 6:10

[a] A σιωπάω.

σιγηρός.

Proverbs 18:18[a]

[a] S[2] κλῆρος.

σιδήρεος.

Lev. 26:19
Deu. 3:11
4:20
28:23, 48
Jud. 4: 3, 13
2 Sa. 12:31
31—B
1 Ki. 22:11
1 Ch. 20: 3
2 Ch. 18:10
Job 19:24[a]
Psa. 2: 9
106:16
149: 8
Isa. 45: 2
48: 4
Jer. 11: 4
35:13, 14
Eze. 4: 3, 3
Dan. 2:33, 33
34, 41
41, 41
42
4:12, 20
5: 4, 23
7: 7, 19
Amos 1: 3
Mic. 4:13

[a] S σιδήριον.

σιδήριον.

Deu. 19: 5
2 Ki. 6: 5, 6[a]
Job 19:24 S[b]
Ecc. 10:10

[a] A σίδηρος. [b] pro σιδήρεος.

σίδηρος.

Gen. 4:22
Nu. 31:22
35:16
Deu. 8: 9
20:19
27: 5
33:25
Jos. 6:19, 24
9: 4
17:16
22: 8—A
Jud. 13: 5
16:17[a]
1 Sa. 1:11
13:19
1 Sa. 17: 5, 7
2 Sa. 23: 7
1 Ki. 6:11
8:51
2 Ki. 6: 6 A[b]
1 Ch. 22: 3, 14
16
29: 2, 7
2 Ch. 2: 7, 14
24:12—A
Job 5:20
15:22
20:24
28: 2
39:22
Job 40:13
41:18
Ps. 104:18
106:10
Pro. 27:17, 17
Isa. 44:12
60:17, 17
Jer. 6:28
15:12
Eze. 22:18, 20
27:12, 19
Dan. 2:35, 40
40, 43
43, 45

[a] A ξυρόν. [b] pro σιδήριον.

σίελον, -ος.

1 Sa. 21:13
Isa. 40:15

σίκερα.

Lev. 10: 9
Nu. 6: 3, 3
28: 7
Deu. 14:25—B
29: 6
Jud. 13: 4 A[a]
Jud. 13: 7 A[a]
14 A[a], +B
Isa. 5:11, 22
24: 9
28: 7, 7
29: 9

[a] pro μέθυσμα.

σίκιμα.

Genesis 48:22

σίκλος.

Exo. 30:23, 24
39: 1, 1, 2
2, 2, 6
7
Lev. 5:15, 15
Nu. 3:47, 47
50—A
50
7:13, 13
19, 19
25, 25
31, 31
37, 37
43, 43
49, 49
55, 55
61, 61
67, 67
73, 73
79, 79
85 ter
85—AB
85
Nu. 7:86+A
18:16, 16
31:52
Deu. 22:19
Jud. 8:26+A
1 Sa. 9: 8
13:21
17: 5, 7
2 Sa. 14:26, 26
18:12
21:16
24:24
2 Ki. 6:25+B[a]
7: 1, 1
16, 16
18, 18
15:20
1 Ch. 21:25
2 Ch. 3: 9
Isa. 7:23
Jer. 39: 9
Eze. 4:10
45:12 ter

σικυήρατον.

Isa. 1: 8[a]

[a] S[1] συκ-

σίκυος.

Nu. 11: 5
Nu. 13:24 B[a]

[a] pro συκῆ.

σινδών.

Jud. 14:12
13 A[a]
Pro. 29:42

[a] pro ὀθόνιον.

σιουάν.

Esther 8: 9 S[3 a]

[a] pro νισάν.

σισόη.

Leviticus 19:27

σιτευτός.

Jud. 6:25 A[a]
28 A[b]
1 Ki. 4:23
Jer. 26:21

[a] pro ταῦρος. [b] pro δεύτερος.

σιτέω.

Proverbs 4:17

σιτίον.

Proverbs 24:57

σιτοβολών.
Genesis 41:56

σιτοδεία.
Lev. 26:26 | Neh. 9:15AS3[a]
[a] pro σιτοδοτία.

σιτοδοσία.
Genesis 42:19, 33

σιτοδοτία.
Nehemiah 9:15[a]
[a] AS3 σιτοδεία.

σιτομετρέω.
Genesis 47:12, 14

σιτοποιός.
Genesis 40:17, 20[a]
[a] A ἀρχισιτοποιός.

σῖτος, -ον.
Gen. 27:28, 37
41:35, 49
42: 2, 3
25, 26
43: 1
44: 2
47:12, 13
14
Nu. 18:12, 27
Deu. 7:13
11:14
12:17
14:22
15:14
18: 4
28:51
33:28
Jos. 5:11, 12
Jud. 6:11[a]
2 Ki. 18:32
1 Ch. 21:23
2 Ch. 2:10, 15
31: 5
32:28
Neh. 5: 2, 3
10, 11
10:37, 39
13: 5
Job 3:24
5:26
Job 6: 5, 7
12:11
15:23
30: 4
33:20
38:41
39:20
Psa. 4: 8
64:14
Pro. 3:10
4:17
11:26
20: 4
29:45
Cant. 7: 2
Isa. 36:17
62: 8
Jer. 23:28
38:12
Lam. 2:12
Eze. 27:17
36:29
Hos. 2: 8, 9, 22
7:14
9: 1
14: 7
Joel 1:10, 17
2:19, 24
Hag. 1:11
Zec. 9:17
[a] A πυρός.

σιών.
Isa. 25: 5
32: 2
Jer. 38:21

σιώνων.
Jud. 8.26A[a]   [a] pro μηνίσκος.

σιωπάω.
Nu. 30:15, 15
Deu. 27: 9
Jud. 3:19—A
18: 9 A[a]
1 Ki. 22: 3
2 Ki. 2: 3, 5
7: 9
2 Ch. 25:16
Neh. 8:11
Job 16:6 18:3
29:21
30:27
Job 41: 3
Isa. 36:21
42:14, 14
62: 1, 6
64:12
65: 6
Jer. 4:19
45:27 A[b]
Lam. 2:10, 18
3:28
48 A[c]
Amos 5:13
[a] pro ἡσυχάζω. [b] pro ἀποσιωπάω. [c] pro σιγάω.

σιωπή.
Amos 8: 3

σιώπησις.
Cant. 4: 1, 3 | Cant. 6: 6

σκάλλω.
Psalm 76: 7

σκαμβός.
Psalm 100: 3

σκάνδαλον.
Lev. 19:14
Jos. 23:13
Jud. 2: 3
8:27 A[a]
1 Sa. 18:21
25:31
Psa. 48:14
Psa. 49:20
68:23
105:36
118:165
139: 6
140: 9
Hos. 4:17
[a] pro σκῶλον.

σκάπτω.
Isaiah 5: 6

σκελίζω.
Jeremiah 10:18

σκέλος.
Lev. 11:21
1 Sa. 17: 6
2 Sa. 22:37
Pro. 26: 7
Eze. 1: 7
Eze. 16:25
24: 4
Dan. 10: 6
Amos 3:12

σκεπάζω.
Exo. 2: 2
12:13, 27
33:22
40: 3, 19
Nu. 9:20
Deu. 13: 8
32:11
33:27
1 Sa. 23:26
26: 1, 24
Neh. 3:14
Psa. 16: 8
Psa. 26: 5
30:21
60: 5
63: 3
90:14
Isa. 4: 5
28:15
30: 2
49: 2 S1[a]
2AS3[a]
51:16
Zeph. 2: 3
[a] pro κρύπτω.

σκέπαρνον.
1 Ch. 20: 3 | Isa. 44:12

σκεπαστής.
Exo. 15: 2
Deu. 32:38
Psa. 70: 6

σκέπη.
Gen. 19: 8[a]
Exo. 26: 7[b]
Jud. 5: 8+A
9:15A[c]
1 Sa. 23:20
Est. 4:14
Job 21:28
24: 8
37: 7
Psa. 16: 8
35: 8
60: 5
62: 8
90: 1
Ps. 104:39
120: 5
Cant. 2:14
Isa. 4: 6
16: 3, 4
25: 4, 4
28: 2—S1
30: 3
49: 2
51:16 S2[c]
Eze. 31: 3+A
12, 17
Hos. 4:13
14: 7
[a] A στέγη. [b] A σκέπω.
[c] pro σκιά.

σκεπηνός.
Nehemiah 4:13

σκέπτομαι.
Gen. 41:33
Exo. 18:21
Zec. 11:13

σκέπω.
Exo. 26: 7 A[a]   Job 26: 9 A[b]
[a] pro σκέπη. [b] pro ἐκπετάζω.

σκευασία.
Ecclesiastes 10: 1[a]
[a] S1 σκεύασις.

σκεύασις.
Ecclesiastes 10: 1 S1[a]
[a] pro σκευασία.

σκευαστός.
Isaiah 54:17—S1[a]
[a] AS3 φθαρτός.

σκεῦος.
Gen. 24:53
27: 3
31:37, 37
45:20
Exo. 3:22
11: 2
12:35
22: 7
25: 8, 39
27: 3
30:27, 27
28, 28
31: 8, 8
35:15, 16
17, 22
38:12, 23
39:10, 12
14, 15
18, 21
40: 7, 8
Lev. 6:28, 28
8:11
11:32, 32
33
13:49, 52
53, 57
58, 59
14:50
15: 4, 6, 12
12, 22
23, 26
Nu. 1:50, 50
3: 8, 31
36
4:10, 12
14, 14
15, 26
32, 32
7: 1, 1, 85
18: 3
19:15, 17
18
31: 6, 20
20, 50
51
35:16, 18
20, 22
Deu. 1:41
22: 5
Jos. 7:11
Jud. 9:54
18:11, 16
17+A
Ruth 2: 9
1 Sa. 6: 8, 15
8:12, 12
10:22
13:20, 21
14: 1, 6, 7
12, 12
13, 13
14, 17
16:21
17:22 A
54
20:40—A
21: 5, 8
25:13
1 Sa. 30:24
31: 4, 4, 5
6, 9, 10
2 Sa. 1:27
8: 8, 10
10, 10
17:28—A
18:15
23:37
24:22
1 Ki. 6:11
7:31, 34
34+A
37—B
8: 4
10:21, 21
25+A
25
15:15
19:21
2 Ki. 4: 3, 3, 4
5, 6, 6
7:15
11: 8, 11
12:13, 13
14:14
20:13
23: 4
24:13
25:14, 16
1 Ch. 9:28, 29
29
10: 4, 4, 5
9, 10
11:39
12:33, 37
18: 8, 10
22:19
23:26
28:13
2 Ch. 4:11, 16
18, 19
5: 1, 5
9:20, 20
24, 24
15:18
20:25
23: 7
7—A
24:14, 14
25:24
28:24
29:18, 18
19
32:27
36: 7, 10
18, 19
Ezra 1: 6, 7, 10
11
5:14, 15
6: 5
7:19
8:25, 26
27, 28
30, 33
Neh. 7:71 S3[a]
10:39
12:36+S3
Neh. 13: 5, 8, 9
Job 28:17
Psa. 2: 9
7:14
30:13
70:22—S1
Ecc. 9:18
Isa. 10:29
39: 2
52:11
54:16 17
65: 4
Jer. 22:28
26:19
27:25
28:20
30: 7
31:12
34:13, 16
Jer. 35: 3, 6
52:18
Eze. 9: 1
12: 3, 4, 4
7
15: 3
16:17, 39
23:26
27:13
40:42—A
Dan. 1: 2, 2
5: 2, 3, 23
11: 8
Hos. 8: 8
13:15
Jon. 1: 5
Nah. 2: 9
Zec. 11:15
[a] pro μνᾶ.

σκηνή.
Gen. 4:20
12: 8
13: 3
4 A[a]
5[b]
18: 1, 2, 6
9, 10
25:16
26:25
31:25
33:17 *ter*
19
35:16
Exo. 18: 7
25: 8
26: 1, 6, 7
9, 12
12—B
12, 13
13, 14
15, 17
18, 22
23, 26
27, 27
30, 35
35
36—AB1
27: 9, 21
28:39
29: 4, 10
10
11—A
30, 32
42, 44
30:16, 18
20, 21
26
26—AB
27+B
36
31: 7, 7
33: 7 *ter*
8 *ter*
9, 9, 10
10, 11
35:10, 21
37: 1, 5
14[c], 19
38:19
20—A1[d]
20
21—B
26, 27
39: 4, 8
9 A[e]
9, 10
14, 20
21, 21
40: 2, 5, 6
6[e], 7
10, 15
16, 17
17, 19
20
20+AB
20, 22
Exo. 40:22, 24
26
27—A2
28, 28
29, 29
30, 32
Lev. 1: 1, 3, 5
3: 2, 8, 13
4: 4, 5, 7
7, 14
16, 18
18
6:16, 26
30
8: 3, 4, 11
31, 33
35
9: 5, 23
10: 7, 9
12: 6
14:11, 23
15:14, 29
31
16: 7, 16
17, 20
23, 33
17: 4, 4, 4
5, 6, 9
19:21
23:34, 42
42, 43
24: 3
26:11[f]
Nu. 1: 1, 50
50, 50
51, 51
53, 53
2: 2, 17
3: 7, 7, 8
8, 10
23, 25
25, 25
26, 29
35, 36
38
4: 3, 4
5 A[g]
15, 16
23, 25
25, 25
26, 28
30, 31
31, 31
33, 35
37, 39
41, 43
47
5:17
6:10, 13
18
7: 1, 3, 5
89
8: 9, 15
19, 22
24, 26
9:15, 15

Nu. 9:15[h], 17
18, 19
20
10: 3, 11
17, 17
21
11:16, 24
26
12: 4, 4, 5
10
14:10
16: 9, 9[i]
18, 19
26, 27
27[k], 30
42, 43
50
17: 4, 7, 8
13
18: 2, 3, 4
4, 6, 21
22, 23
31
19: 4, 13
20: 6
24: 5, 6
25: 6
27: 2
31:30, 47
54
Deu. 1:27
11: 6
16:13
31:14*ter*
15, 15
Jos. 7:21, 22
22[h], 23
24
18: 1
19:51
22:19[m], 20
24:25
Jud. 4:11, 17
18, 20
21
5:24
6: 5
7: 8[k], 13
13
8:11
1 Sa. 2:22+A
2 Sa. 6:17
7: 2, 6
11:11
16:22
22:12
1 Ki. 1:39
2:29, 30
18: 5[b]

1 Ki. 21:12
2 Ki. 7: 7, 8, 8
10
10:14+B[e]
1 Ch. 5:10
6:32, 48
9:19, 21
23
15: 1
16: 1, 39
17: 5
21:29
23:26, 32
2 Ch. 1: 3, 4, 5
6, 13
5: 5, 5
8:13
14:15
24: 6
29: 6
Ezra 3: 4
8:29
Neh. 8:14, 15
16, 17
17
Job 5:24
8:14
18:15
36:29
Psa. 17:12
26: 5, 5, 6
28: 1
30:21
41: 5
59: 8
77:60
107: 8[n]
117:15
Pro. 14:11
Isa. 1: 8
16: 5
22:16
33:20, 20
38:12
40:22
54: 2
Jer. 4:20
6: 3
10:20, 20
30: 7
42: 7, 10
Lam. 2: 4
Dan. 11:45
Hos. 12: 9
Amos 5:26
9:11
Jon. 4: 5
Hab. 3: 7

[a] *pro* ἀρχή.
[b] A κτῆνος.
[c] A αὐλή.
[d] A[2] στῦλος.
[e] *pro* αὐλή.
[f] AB διαθήκη.
[g] *pro* κιβωτός.
[h] A γῆ.
[i] A συναγωγή.
[k] A σκήνωμα.
[m] A κιβωτός.
[n] S σκήνωμα.

2 Ki. 14:12
1 Ch. 5:20
2 Ch. 7:10
10:16, 16
11:14
21: 9
25:22
Job 21:28
39: 6
Psa. 14: 1
18: 6
25: 8
42: 3
45: 5
48:12
51: 7
60: 5
68:26
73: 7
77:28, 51

Psa. 77:55, 60
67
82: 7
83: 2, 11
86: 2
90:10
105:25
107: 8 S[a]
119: 5
131: 3, 5, 7
Cant. 1: 5, 8
Jer. 9:19
28:30
Lam. 2: 6
Eze. 25: 4
Hos. 9: 6
Hab. 1: 6
3: 7
Zec. 12: 7
Mal. 2:12

[a] *pro* σκηνή.

σκηνοπηγία.

Deu. 16:16
31:10

Zec. 14:16, 18
19

σκηνόω.

Gen. 13:12
Jud. 5:17[a]
17[a]

Jud. 8:11[b]
1 Ki. 8:12 A

[a] A κατασκηνόω. [b] A κατοικέω.

σκήνωμα.

Nu. 16:27 A[a]
Deu. 33:18
Jos. 3:14
Jud. 7: 8 A[a]
19: 9
20: 8
1 Sa. 4:10
13: 2
17:54
2 Sa. 7:23

2 Sa. 18:17
19: 8
20: 1, 22
1 Ki. 2:28
8: 4, 4, 66
12:16, 16
p 24 *l* 70
l 73
2 Ki. 8:21
13: 5

σκῆπτρον.

Jud. 5:14+A
1 Sa. 2:28
9:21, 21
10:19, 20
20, 21
14:27
27 B[a]
43
15:17
1 Ki. 8:16

1 Ki. 11:13, 31[b]
32, 35
36
12:20, 21
p 24 *l* 23
ll 73, 75
Ezra 9:13+S[3]
Eze. 30:18
Hab. 3: 9
Zec. 10:11

[a] *pro* κηρίον. [b] A ῥῆγμα.

σκιά.

Jud. 9:15[a], 36
2 Ki. 20: 9, 10
10, 11
1 Ch. 29:15
Job 3: 5
7: 2
8: 9
12:22
14: 2
15:29
16:16
24:17, 17
28: 3
Psa. 22: 4
43:20
56: 2
79:11
87: 7
101:12
106:10, 14

Ps. 108:23
143: 4
Ecc. 7: 1−C
12, 12
8:13
Cant. 2: 3, 17
4: 6
Isa. 4: 6
9: 2
38: 8, 8
51:16−A[b]
Jer. 6: 4
13:16
Lam. 4:20
Eze. 17:23
31: 6
Amos 5: 8
Jon. 4:5+ABS
6

[a] A σκέπη. [b] S[2] σκέπη.

σκιάδιον.

Isaiah 66:20

σκιάζω.

Exo. 38: 8
Nu. 9:18
22−A
10:34
24: 6
Deu. 33:12

2 Sa. 20: 6
1 Ch. 28:18
Job 36:28
40:17
Isa. 4: 5
Jon. 4: 6

σκιρτάω.

Gen. 25:22
Ps. 113: 4, 6
Jer. 27:11

Joel 1:17
Mal. 4: 2

σκληροκαρδία.

Deu. 10:16 | Jer. 4: 4

σκληροκάρδιος.

Pro. 17:20 | Eze. 3: 7

σκληροπρόσωπος.

Ezekiel 2: 4+A

σκληρός.

Gen. 21:11, 12
42: 7, 30
45: 5
49: 3, 3
Exo. 1:14
6: 9
Nu. 16:26
Deu. 1:17
15:18
26: 6
31:27
Jud. 2:19
1 Sa. 1:15
5: 7
25: 3
2 Sa. 2:17
3:39
1 Ki. 12: 4, 13
p 24 *l* 37
14: 6 A
2 Ch. 10: 4, 13

Job 9: 4
22:21
Psa. 16: 4
59: 5
Pro. 17:27
27:16
28:14
29:19[a]
Ecc. 7:18
Cant. 8: 6
Isa. 5:30
8:12, 12
21
14: 3
19: 4, 4
21: 2
27: 8
28: 2
48: 4
Jer. 12:14 A[b]
Zeph. 1:14

[a] S[1] σκληροτράχηλος.
[b] *pro* πονηρός.

σκληρότης.

Deu. 9:27
2 Sa. 22: 6

Isa. 4: 6
28:27

σκληροτράχηλος.

Exo. 33: 3, 5
34: 9
Deu. 9: 6, 13

Pro. 29: 1
19 S[1][a]

[a] *pro* σκληρός.

σκληρύνω.

Gen. 49: 7
Exo. 4:21
7: 3, 22
8:19
9:12, 35
10: 1[a], 20
27
11:10
13:15
14: 4, 8, 17
Deu. 2:30
10:16
Jud. 4:24
2 Sa. 19:43

2 Ki. 2:10
17:14
2 Ch. 10: 4
30: 8
36:13
Neh. 9:16, 17
29
Psa. 89: 6
94: 8
Isa. 63:17
Jer. 7:26
17:23
19:15

[a] A βαρύνω.

σκληρῶς.

Gen. 35:17
1 Sa. 20: 7, 10

Isa. 22: 3

σκνίψ.

Exo. 8:16, 17
17, 18

Exo. 8:18
Ps. 104:31

σκολιάζω.

Pro. 10: 8
14: 2

Pro. 17:16

σκολιός.

Deu. 32: 5
Job 4:18
9: 7+BS
20
Psa. 77: 8
Pro. 2:15
4:24
8: 8
16:26, 28

Pro. 21: 8, 8
22: 5, 14
23:33
28:18
Isa. 27: 1
40: 4
42:16
Hos. 9: 8

σκολιότης.

Ezekiel 16: 5

σκολιῶς.

Jeremiah 6:28

σκόλοψ.

Nu. 33:55
Eze. 28:24

Hos. 2: 6

σκόπελον.

2 Kings 23:17

σκοπεύω.

Exo. 33: 8
1 Sa. 4:13
Job 39:29
Pro. 5:21

Pro. 15: 3
Cant. 7: 4
Nah. 2: 2

σκοπιά.

Nu. 23:14
33:52
Jud. 10:17[a]
11:29
29+A
1 Ki. 15:22

2 Ch. 20:24
Isa. 21: 8
41: 9
Hos. 5: 1
Mic. 7: 4

[a] A Μασσηφά.

σκοπός.

Lev. 26: 1
1 Sa. 14:16
2 Sa. 13:34, 34
18:24, 25
26, 26
27
2 Ki. 9:17, 18
20
Job 16:12

Isa. 21: 6
Jer. 6:17
Lam. 3:12
Eze. 3:17
33: 2, 6, 6
7
Hos. 9: 8, 10
Nah. 3:12[a]

[a] B[2] καρπός.

σκόρδον.

Numbers 11: 5

σκορπίζω.

2 Sa. 22:15
Neh. 4:19
Job 39:15
Psa. 17:15
111: 9

Ps. 143: 6
Eze. 5:12[a]
Hab. 3:10
Zec. 11:10[b]
Mal. 2: 3

[a] A διασπείρω.
[b] A διασκορπίζω.

σκορπίος.

Deu. 8:15
1 Ki. 12:11, 14
p 24 *l* 67

2 Ch. 10:11, 14
Eze. 2: 6

σκοτάζω.

Ps. 104:28
Ecc. 12: 3
Lam. 4: 8

Lam. 5:17
Eze. 31:15−A
Mic. 6:14 AB[a]

[a] *pro* συσκοτάζω.

σκοτεινός.

Gen. 15:12
2 Ki. 5:24
Job 10:21
15:24
21:11 AS[2][a]
Psa. 17:12
87: 7
142: 3

Pro. 1: 6
4:19
Isa. 45: 3, 19
48:16+AS[1]
Jer. 13:16
Lam. 3: 6
6 A[b]

[a] *pro* στενός. [b] *pro* πικρός.

σκοτία.

Job 28: 3
Isa. 16: 3

Mic. 3: 6

σκοτίζω.

Psa. 68:24
73:20 B[2]S[a]
138:12

Ecc. 12: 2
Isa. 13:10

[a] *pro* σκοτόω.

σκοτομήνη.

Psalm 10: 2[a]

[a] A σκοτόω.

σκότος.

Gen. 1: 2, 4, 5
18
Exo. 10:21, 21
22
14:20
Deu. 4:11
5:22
28:29
Jos. 2: 5
2 Sa. 1: 9
22:12, 12
29
2 Ki. 7: 5:7
Job 3: 4, 5
6—S[1]
5:14
10:21
12:22, 25
15:22, 30
17:12
18: 6, 18
19: 8
20:26
22:11
23:17
24:14, 15
16
26:10
28: 3
29: 3
37:14
38:19
Psa. 17:12, 29
34: 6
54: 6
81: 5
87:13
90: 6

Ps. 103:20
104:28
106:10, 14
111: 4
138:11, 12
12
Pro. 2:13
7: 9
20:20
Ecc. 2:13, 14
5:16
6: 4, 4
11: 8
Isa. 5:20, 20
30
8:22—S
22
9: 2
29:15, 18
42: 7, 16
45: 7
47: 1+AS
5
49: 9
50: 3, 10
58:10, 10
59: 9
60: 2
Jer. 13:16
28:34
Lam. 3: 2
Eze. 32: 8
Dan. 2:22
Joel 2: 2, 31[a]
Amos 5:18, 20
Mic. 7: 8
Nah. 1: 8
Zeph. 1:15

[a] S κότος.

σκοτόω.

Jud. 4:21—A
Job 3: 9
30:30[a]
Psa. 10: 2 A[b]

Psa. 73:20[c]
Ecc. 10:15 A[d]
Jer. 8:21
14: 2

[a] A μελανόω. [b] pro σκοτομήνη
[c] C[2]S σκοτίζω. [d] pro κακόω.

σκυθρωπάζω.

Psa. 34:14
37: 7
41:10
42: 2

Pro. 15:13
Jer. 10: 8
27:13

σκυθρωπός.

Gen. 40: 7
Neh. 2: 1+S[3]

Dan. 1:10

σκυλεύω.

Exo. 3:22[a]
12:36
1 Ch. 10: 8
2 Ch. 14:13, 14
20:25 *ter*
25:13
28: 8
Isa. 8: 3

Eze. 26:12
29:19
30:24
38:12, 13
13
39:10, 10
Hab. 2: 8, 8
Zec. 2: 8

[a] A συσκευάζω.

σκῦλον.

Exo. 15: 9
Nu. 31:11, 12
26, 27
Deu. 2:35
3: 7
7:16
13:16, 16
Jos. 8:27
11:14

Jud. 5:30 *qtr*
8:24, 25
1 Sa. 14:30, 32
15:13, 19
21
23: 3
30:16, 19
20, 20
20, 22
1 Sa. 30:26, 26
2 Sa. 3:22
8:12
12:30
2 Ki. 3:23
1 Ch. 20: 2
2 Ch. 14:13, 14
15:11—B
20:25 *ter*
24:23
25:13
28: 8, 8
14, 15
Est. 8:11+S[3]
Psa. 67:13
118:162
Pro. 1:13

Pro. 16:19
29:29
Isa. 8: 1, 4
9: 3
10: 6
33: 4
49:24, 25
53:12
Jer. 21: 9
Eze. 7:21
29:19
30:24
38:12, 13
13
Dan. 11:24
Zec. 2: 9
14: 1

σκύμνος.

Gen. 49: 9, 9
Nu. 23:24
24: 9
Deu. 33:22
Jud. 14: 5
Job 4:11
Psa. 16:12
56: 5
103:21
Pro. 24:65
Isa. 5:29
30: 6

Isa. 31: 4
Jer. 28:38
Lam. 4: 3
Eze. 19: 2, 2, 3
5
Hos. 13: 8
Joel 1: 6
Amos 3: 4
Mic. 5: 8
Nah. 2:11, 11
12

σκυτάλη.

Exo. 30: 4, 5
2 Sa. 3:29

1 Ki. 12 *p* 24 *l* 9

σκώληξ.

Exo. 16:20, 24
Deu. 28:39
Job 2: 9
7: 5
25: 6
Psa. 21: 7

Pro. 12: 4
25:20
Isa. 14:11
66:24
Jon. 4: 7

σκῶλον.

Exo. 10: 7
Deu. 7:16
Jud. 8:27[a]

Jud. 11:35+A
2 Ch. 28:23
Isa. 57:14

[a] A σκάνδαλον.

σμαραγδίτης.

Esther 1: 6[a]

[a] A σμάραγδος.

σμάραγδος.

Exo. 28: 9, 17
35:13, 27
36:13, 17

Est. 1: 6 A[a]
Eze. 28:13

[a] pro σμαραγδίτης.

σμῆγμα.

Esther 2: 3, 9, 12

σμικρύνω.

1 Ch. 16:19
17:17
Psa. 88:46

Ps. 106:38
Jer. 36: 6
Hos. 4: 3[a]

[a] B μικρύνω.

σμῖλαξ.

Jer. 26:14

Nah. 1:10[a]

[a] A μῖλαξ, S[1] μῖλας.

σμυρίτης, ABS σμι—

Job 41: 6

σμύρνα.

Exo. 30:23
Psa. 44: 9
Cant. 3: 6

Cant. 4: 6, 14
5: 1[a], 5
5, 13

[a] S σταφυλή.

σμύρνινος.

Esther 2:12

σοάμ.

1 Chronicles 29: 2

σορός.

Gen. 50:26

Job 21:32 A[a]

[a] pro σωρός.

σοφία.

Exo. 28: 3—AB
31: 3
35:26, 31
33, 35
36: 1, 2
Deu. 4: 6
2 Sa. 14:20
20:22
1 Ki. 2: 6, 35
4:25
26+A
30, 30
5:12
10: 7+A
1 Ch. 22:12
28:21
2 Ch. 1:10, 11
12
9: 3, 5, 6
7, 22
23
Ezra 7:25
Job 4:21
8:10+A
11: 6
20+A
12: 2, 12
13
13: 5
15: 8
26: 3
28:12, 18
20, 28
32: 8, 13
33:33+ACS
38:36
36+A
37
39:17
Psa. 36:30
48: 4
50: 8
89:12
103:24
106:27
110:10
Pro. 1: 2, 7, 7
20, 29[a]
2: 2, 3, 6
10
3: 5, 13
19
4: 4+S[2]

Pro. 4: 5A, 11
5: 1
6: 8
7: 4
8: 1, 11
12, 33A
9: 1, 10
10:13—B
23, 31
11: 2
14: 6, 8, 33
16: 1, 16
17:16
28—A
28
18: 2
20:29
21:30
22: 4
24: 3, 7, 14
26, 73
28:26
29: 3, 15
Ecc. 1:13, 16
16, 17
18
2: 3, 9, 12
13, 21
26
7:11, 12
13, 13
13+S
20, 24
26
8: 1, 16
9:10, 13
15, 16
16, 18
10: 1, 10
Isa. 10:13
11: 2
29:14
33: 6
50: 4 A[b]
Jer. 8: 9
9:23
10:12
28:15
29: 8, 8
Dan. 1: 4, 17
20
2:20, 21
23, 30
5:14

[a] A παιδεία. [b] pro παιδεία.

σοφίζω.

1 Sa. 3: 8
1 Ki. 4:27, 27
Psa. 18: 8
104:22
118:98

Pro. 8:33 AS[2]
16:17
Ecc. 2:15, 19
7:17, 24

σοφιστής.

Exodus 7:11

σοφός.

Gen. 41: 8
Exo. 28: 3
35: 9, 25
36: 1, 4, 8
Deu. 1:13, 15
4: 6

Deu. 16:19
32: 6
Jud. 5:29
1 Sa. 16:18[a]
2 Sa. 13: 3
14: 2, 20
2 Sa. 20:16
1 Ki. 2: 9
(3) *p* 46
3:12
1 Ch. 22:15
2 Ch. 2: 7, 7
12, 13
14, 14
Job 5:13
9: 4
15: 2, 18
21:22 AC[b]
32:10
33:31+A
34: 2, 34[c]
37:23
Psa. 48:11
57: 6
106:43
Pro. 1: 5, 5, 6
3:35
6: 6
9: 8, 9, 9
12, 12
10: 1, 5, 8
14
12:15, 18
13:10, 13
14, 17[d]
20, 20
14: 1, 3, 7
16, 24
15: 2, 7
12, 20
16:14, 21
23
17:24
18:15
19:20
20: 1+AS[2]
26
21:11, 20
22
22:17

Pro. 23:15, 19
24
24: 5, 7, 7
38
41 ACS[2e]
59, 59
25:12
26: 5, 12
16
27:11
28:11
29: 8, 9, 11
45 BS[1f]
Ecc. 2:14, 16
16, 19
4:13
6: 8
7: 5, 6, 8
20
8: 1, 5, 17
9: 1, 11
15, 17
10: 2, 12
12: 9, 11
Isa. 3: 3
19:11, 12
29:14
31: 2 ABS[f]
Jer. 4:22
8: 8, 9
9:17, 23
16:16 A[g]
28:57
Eze. 27: 8, 9
28: 3, 3
Dan. 2:12, 13
14, 18
21, 24
24, 27
48
4: 3, 15
5: 7, 8, 15
Hos. 14: 9
Obad. 8

[a] A συνετός. [b] pro φόνος.
[c] A φρόνιμος [d] S[1] πιστός.
[e] pro ἀγαθός. [f] pro σοφῶς
[g] pro πολύς.

σοφόω.

Psalm 145: 8

σοφῶς.

Pro. 29:45[a]
Isa. 31: 2[b]

Isa. 40:20

[a] BS[1] σοφός. [b] ABS σοφός.

σπάδων.

Gen. 37:36

Isa. 39: 7

σπάλαξ.

Leviticus 11:30 A[2a]

[a] pro ἀσπάλαξ.

σπανίζω.

2 Ki. 14:26

Job 14:11

σπάνιος.

Proverbs 25:17

σπαράσσω.

2 Sa. 22: 8[a]

Jer. 4:19—S[1]

[a] A ταράσσω.

σπάργανον.

Ezekiel 16: 4

σπαργανόω.

Job 38: 9

Eze. 16: 4

σπαρτίον.

Gen. 14:23
Jos. 2:18
Jud. 16:12[a]
Job 38: 5
Ecc. 4:12
Cant. 4: 3
6: 5
Isa. 34:11
Jer. 52:21
Eze. 40: 3

[a] A ῥάμμα.

σπαταλάω.

Ezekiel 16:49

σπάω.

Nu. 22:23, 31
Jos. 5:13
Jud. 8:10, 20
9:54
16:12 A[a]
20: 2 A[b]
15 A[b]
17 A[b]
25 A[b]
35 A[b]
46 A[b]
1 Sa. 31: 4
2 Sa. 23: 8–A
24: 9
2 Ki. 3:26
1 Ch. 10: 4
11:11, 20
21: 5
5–B
16
Psa. 36:14
150 p 6
Eze. 21:28, 28
26:15

[a] pro διασπάω. [b] pro ἕλκω.

σπείρω.

Gen. 1:11, 12
29
26:12
47:19, 23
Exo. 23:10, 16
32:20
Lev. 11:37
25: 3, 4, 11
20, 22
26:16
Nu. 16:37
20: 5
Deu. 11:10
21: 4
22: 9
29:23
Jud. 6: 3
9:45
Job 4: 8
31: 8
Ps. 106:37
125: 5
Pro. 11:21, 24
22: 8
Ecc. 11: 4, 6
Isa. 5:10
17:11[a]
19: 7
28:25
25–A
32:20
37:30, 30
40:24
55:10
Jer. 4: 3
12:13
37:17
38:27
42: 7
Eze. 36: 9–A
Hos. 2:23
8: 7
10:12
Mic. 6:15
Nah. 1:14
Zeph. 3:10 +S[2]
Hag. 1: 6
Zec. 10: 9

[a] A φυτεύω.

σπένδω.

Gen. 35:14
Exo. 25:28
30: 9
38:12
Nu. 4: 7
28: 7
2 Sa. 23:16[a]
1 Ki. 21:33
2 Ki. 16:13+A
1 Ch. 11:18
Jer. 7:18
19:13
39:29
51:17, 19
19, 25
Eze. 20:28
Dan. 2:46
Hos. 9: 4

[a] A πίνω.

σπέρμα.

Gen. 1:11, 11
12, 12
29, 29
3:15, 15
4:25
7: 3
8:22
9: 9
12: 7
13:15, 16
16, 17
15: 3, 5
13, 18
16:10
17: 7, 7, 8
9, 10
12, 19
19:32, 34
Gen. 21:12, 13
23
22:17, 17
18
24: 7, 60
26: 3, 4, 4
4, 24
28: 4, 13
14, 14
32:12
35:12
38: 8, 9, 9
46: 6, 7
47:19, 23
24
48: 4, 11
19
Exo. 16:31
Exo. 28:39
32:13
13+A
33: 1
Lev. 11:37, 38
15:16, 17
18, 32
18:20, 21
19:20
20: 2, 3, 4
21:15, 21
22: 3, 4, 4
13
26:16
27:30
Nu. 5:13, 28
11: 7
14:24
16:40
18:19
21:30
23:10 ter
24: 7, 20
25:13
Deu. 1: 8
3: 3
4:37
10:15
11: 9
14:21
22: 9
25: 5
28:38, 46
59
30: 6
6+A[2]
19
31:21
34: 4
Jos. 24: 3
Ruth 4:12
1 Sa. 1:11
2:20, 31
31
8:15
20:42
42–B
24:22
2 Sa. 4: 8
7:12
22:51
1 Ki. 1:48
2:33, 33
(3) p 1
11:14, 39A
18:32
2 Ki. 5:27
11: 1
14:27
17:20
25:25
1 Ch. 16:13
17:11
2 Ch. 20: 7
22:10
Ezra 2:59
Ezra 9: 2
Neh. 7:61
9: 8
Est. 9:27
Job 5:24+A
25
Psa. 17:51
20:11
21:24, 24
31
24:13
36:25, 26
28
68:37
88: 5, 30
37
101:29
104: 6
105:27
111: 2
125: 6
Pro. 11:18
Ecc. 11: 6
Isa. 1: 4, 9
14:20, 22
29, 30
15: 9
17: 5, 10
23: 3
30:23
31: 9
33: 2
37:31
41: 8
43: 5
44: 3
45:19, 25
48:14, 19
53:10
54: 3
55:10
57: 3, 4
58: 7
59:21
61: 9, 9, 11
65: 9, 23
66:22
Jer. 7:15
22:30
23: 8
26:27
27:16
38:27, 27
42: 7, 9
Eze. 17: 5, 13
20: 5
31:17
43:19
44:22
Dan. 1: 3, 12
16
2:43
9: 1
11: 6, 31
Mal. 2:15

σπερματίζω.

Exo. 9:31
Lev. 12: 2

σπερματισμός.

Leviticus 18:23

σπεύδω.

Gen. 18: 6, 6
19 22
24:18, 20
46
41:11
45: 9
Exo. 15:15
34: 8
Jos. 4:10
8:14, 19
Jud. 5:22–A
20:41
1 Sa. 4:14, 16
1 Sa. 20:38
23:27
25:18, 23
34
28:20, 21
24
2 Sa. 4: 4
17:16
1 Ki. 18: 7
21:41
2 Ki. 9:13
16 A[a]
2 Ch. 10:18
2 Ch. 24: 5, 5[b]
26:20
Est. 2: 9
3:15
(9) 14
Psa. 39:14 A[c]
69: 2+
8 ▪ S[2]
Pro. 7:23
Pro. 28:22
Ecc. 5: 1
7:10
Isa. 16: 5
Jer. 4: 6
38:20
Eze. 30: 9
Mic. 4: 1
Nah. 2: 6

[a] pro ἱππεύω. [b] AB πιστεύω.
[c] pro προσέχω.

σπήλαιον.

Gen. 19:30
23: 9, 11
17, 17
19, 20
25: 9, 10
49:29, 30
30, 32
50:13, 13
Jos. 10:16, 17
18, 22
22, 23
27, 27
Jud. 6: 2
15: 8 A[a]
1 Sa. 13: 6
22: 1
24: 4, 4
8+A
9, 11
2 Sa. 23:13
1 Ki. 18: 4, 13
19: 9, 13
1 Ch. 11:15
Psa. 56: 1
141: 1
Isa. 2:19
7:19
32:14
33:16
65: 4
Jer. 4:29
7:11
12: 9
9–A
27:26–S
Eze. 33:27
Hab. 2:15

[a] pro πέτρα.

σπιθαμή.

Exo. 28:16, 16
36:16, 16
Jud. 3:16
1 Sa. 17: 4
Isa. 40:12
Eze. 43:13

σπινθήρ.

Isa. 1:31
Eze. 1: 7

σπλαγχνίζω.

Proverbs 17: 5 A[a]

[a] pro ἐπισπλαγχνίζομαι.

σπλάγχνον.

Pro. 12:10
26:22[a]
Jer. 28:13

[a] S[2] κοιλία.

σποδιά.

Lev. 4:12, 12
Nu. 19:10[a], 17

[a] A σποδός.

σποδοειδής.

Gen. 30:39
Gen. 31:10, 12

σποδός.

Gen. 18:27
Lev. 1:16
Nu. 19: 9
10 A[a]
2 Sa. 13:19
Neh. 9: 1–ABS
Est. 4: 1, 2, 3
Job 13:12
30:19
42: 6
Ps. 101:10
Ps. 147: 5
Isa. 44:20
58: 5
61: 3
Jer. 6:26
Lam. 3:16
Eze. 27:30
28:18
Dan. 9: 3+A
Jon. 3: 6
Mal. 4: 3

[a] pro σποδιά.

σπονδεῖον.

Exo. 25:28
38:12
Nu. 4: 7
1 Ch. 28:17

σπονδή.

Gen. 35:14
Exo. 29:40, 41
30: 9
Lev. 23:13, 18
37
Nu. 6:15, 17
Nu. 7:87
15: 5, 7, 10
24
28: 7, 7, 8
9, 10
14, 15
24, 31
29: 6, 6, 11
16, 18
19
21–A
22, 24
25, 27
28, 30
31, 33
34, 37
38, 39
Deu. 32:38
2 Ki. 16:13, 15
1 Ch. 29:21
2 Ch. 29:35
Ezra 7:17
Isa. 57: 6[a]
Jer. 7:18
19:13
39:29
51:17, 19
19, 25
Eze. 20:28
45:17
Dan. 9:27
Joel 1: 9, 13
2:14

[a] S[1] ποῦς.

σπορά.

2 Kings 19:29

σπόριμος.

Gen. 1:29, 29
Lev. 11:37–A[1]

σπόρος.

Exo. 34:21
Lev. 26: 5, 20
27:16
Deu. 11:10
Job 21: 8
Job 39:12
Isa. 28:24
32:10+
A[2] S
Amos 9:13

σπουδάζω.

Gen. 19:15[a]
Job 4: 5
21: 6
22:10
Job 23:14, 16
31: 5
Ecc. 8: 2
Isa. 21: 3

[a] A ἐπισπουδάζω.

σπουδαῖος.

Ezekiel 41:25

σπουδή.

Exo. 12:11, 33
Deu. 16: 3
Jud. 5:22–A
1 Sa. 21: 8[a]
Ezra 4:23
Psa. 77:33
Jer. 8:15
15: 8
Lam. 4: 6
Eze. 7:11
Dan. 2:25
3:24
6:19
9:27+
A[1]
11:44
Zeph. 1:19

[a] A κατασπεύδω.

σταγών.

Job 36:27
Psa. 64:11
71: 6
Pro. 27:15
Isa. 40:15
Mic. 2:11

στάζω.

Exo. 9:33
Jud. 5: 4[a], 4
6:38[b]
2 Sa. 21:10
2 Ch. 12: 7
Job 16:20
Psa. 67: 9
71: 6
Ecc. 10:18[c]
Cant. 5: 5, 13
Jer. 49:18, 18
51: 6

[a] A ἐξίστημι. [b] A ἀπορρέω.
[c] A στενάζω.

σταθμάω.

1 Kings 6:21

στάθμιον.

Lev. 19:35, 36
27:25
Deu. 25:13, 13
15
2 Ki. 21:13[a]
Pro. 11: 1
Pro. 16:11
20:10, 23
Eze. 5: 1
45:12
Amos 8: 5
Mic. 6:11

[a] A σταθμός.

σταθμός.

Gen. 43:20
Exo. 12: 7, 22
23
21: 6
Lev. 26:26
27: 3
Nu. 33: 1, 2, 2
Deu. 15:17 + A[a]
Jud. 8:26
16: 3
1 Sa. 17: 5
2 Sa. 12:30
21:16
1 Ki. 7:32, 32
34 + A
10:14
2 Ki. 12: 9
21:13 A[a]
22: 4
2 Ki. 23: 4 − A
25:16, 18
1 Ch. 20: 2
22: 3, 14
28:14, 16
17, 17
18
2 Ch. 9:13
Ezra 8:30, 34
34
Job 28:25
Pro. 8:34
Isa. 28:17
40:12
46: 6
57: 8
Jer. 9: 2
52:20
Eze. 4:10, 16

[a] pro στάθμιον.

σταῖς.

Exo. 12:34, 39
2 Sa. 13: 8[a]
Jer. 7:18

[a] A στέαρ.

στακτή.

Gen. 37:25
43:10
Exo. 30:34
1 Ki. 10:25
2 Ch. 9:24
Psa. 44: 9
Cant. 1:13
Isa. 39: 2
Eze. 27:16

σταλάζω.

Micah 2:11

στάμνος.

Exo. 16:33
1 Ki. 12p24l31
l32
1 Ki. 12p24l39
14: 3 A

στάσις.

Deu. 28:65
Jos. 10:13
Jud. 9: 6
1 Ki. 10: 5
1 Ch. 28: 2
2 Ch. 9: 4
23:13
24:13
30:16
35:10, 15
Neh. 8: 7
9: 3, 6
13:11
Pro. 17:14
Isa. 22:19
Eze. 1:28
Dan. 6: 7, 15
8:17
10:11
Nah. 3:11

σταυρόω.

Esther 7: 9

σταφίς.

Nu. 6: 3
1 Sa. 25:18
30:12 + A
2 Sa. 16: 1
1 Ki. 14: 3 A
1 Ch. 12:40
Hos. 3: 1

σταφυλή.

Gen. 40:10, 11
49:11
Lev. 25: 5
Nu. 6: 3, 3
13:21, 24
Deu. 24: 2
32:14, 32
32
1 Ki. 12p24l30
1 Ki. 12p24l32
l38
Neh. 13:15
Cant. 5: 15[a]
Isa. 5: 2, 4
Jer. 8:13
Eze. 36: 8
Hos. 9:10
Amos 9:13

[a] pro σμύρνα.

στάχυς.

Gen. 41: 5, 6, 7
7, 22
23, 24
24, 26
27
Exo. 22: 6
Deu. 24: 1
Jud. 12: 6[a]
15: 5[b], 5
Ruth 2: 2
Job 24:24
Isa. 17: 5, 5

[a] A σύνθημα. [b] A δράγμα.

στέαρ.

Gen. 4: 4
Exo. 23:18
29:13, 13
22 ter
Lev. 1: 8, 12
3: 3, 3, 4
9
9 − AB
9, 10
14
14 − A[1]
15, 16
17
4: 8, 8, 8
9, 19
26, 26
31, 31
35, 35
6:12, 33
33, 33
34
7:13, 14
15, 20
21, 23
8:16, 16
20, 25
25, 25
26
9:10, 19
19, 19
20, 20
Lev. 9:24
10:15
16:25
17: 6
Nu. 18:17
Deu. 32:14, 14
38
Jud. 3:22
1 Sa. 2:15, 16
15:22
2 Sa. 1:22
13: 8 A[a]
1 Ki. 8:64
2 Ch. 7: 7, 7
29:35
35:14
Job 15:27
21:24
Psa. 16:10
62: 6
72: 7
80:17
147: 3
Isa. 1:11
34: 6, 6, 7
43:24
55: 1
Eze. 39:19
44:15
Hos. 7: 4

[a] pro σταῖς.

στεατόω.

Ezekiel 39:18

στεγάζω.

2 Ch. 34:11
Neh. 2: 8
3: 3, 3[a]
Neh. 3: 6
15 − ABS
Ps. 103: 3

[a] A ἵστημι.

στέγη.

Gen. 8:13
19: 8 A[a]
Eze. 40:43

[a] pro σκέπη.

στεγνός.

Proverbs 29:45

στεῖρα.

Gen. 11:30
25:21
29:31
Exo. 23:26
Deu. 7:14
Jud. 13: 2, 3
1 Sa. 2: 5
Job 24:21
Ps. 112: 9
Isa. 54: 1
66: 9

στέλεχος.

Gen. 49:21
Exo. 15:27
Nu. 33: 9
Job 14: 8
29:18
Cant. 3: 6
Jer. 17: 8
Eze. 19:11
31:12, 13

στέλλω.

Pro. 29:43
Mal. 2: 5

στέμφυλον.

Numbers 6: 4

στεναγμός.

Gen. 3:16
Exo. 2:24
6: 5
Jud. 2:18
Job 3:24
23: 2[a]
Psa. 6: 7
11: 6
30:11
37: 9, 10
Psa. 78:11
101: 6, 21
Isa. 35:10
51:11
Jer. 4:31
51:33
Lam. 1:22
Eze. 24:17
Mal. 2:13

[a] A στενάζω.

στενάζω.

Job 9:27
18:20
23: 2 A[a]
24:12
30:25
31:38
Ecc. 10:18 A[b]
Isa. 19: 8, 8
21: 2
24: 7
Isa. 30:15
46: 8
59:10
Jer. 38:19
Lam. 1: 8, 21
Eze. 21: 6, 7
26:15, 16
28:19[c]
Nah. 3: 7

[a] pro στεναγμός.
[b] pro στάζω. [c] A στυγνάζω.

στενακτός.

Ezekiel 5:15

στενός.

Nu. 22:26
1 Sa. 23:14, 19
24: 1, 23
2 Sa. 24:14
2 Ki. 6: 1
1 Ch. 21:13
Job 18:11
Job 24:11[a]
Pro. 23:27
Isa. 8:22
30:20
49:20
Jer. 37: 7
Zec. 10:11

[a] AS[2] σκοτεινός.

στενοχωρέω.

Jos. 17:15
Jud. 16:16[a]
Isa. 28:20
49:19

[a] A παρενοχλέω.

στενοχωρία.

Deu. 28:53, 55
57
Isa. 8:22, 22
30: 6

στένω.

Gen. 4:12, 14
Job 10: 1
30:28
Pro. 28:28
29: 2

στενῶς.

1 Samuel 13: 6

στερεοκάρδιος.

Ezekiel 2: 4 + A

στερεός.

Exo. 38:14, 16
Lev. 14:42 AB[a]
Nu. 8: 4, 4
Deu. 32:13
1 Sa. 4: 8
Psa. 34:10
Isa. 2:21
5:28
Isa. 17: 5
50: 7
51: 1
Jer. 15:18
20:13 + AS
37:14
38:11

[a] pro ἕτερος.

στερεόω.

1 Sa. 2: 1
6:18
Job 37:17 A[a]
Psa. 17:18
32: 6
74: 4
92: 1
135: 6
Isa. 42: 5
44:24
Isa. 45:12
48:13
51: 6
Jer. 5: 3
10: 4
52: 6
Lam. 2: 4
Eze. 4: 7
Hos. 13: 4
Amos 4:13

[a] pro στερέωσις.

στερέω.

Gen. 30: 2
48:11
Nu. 24:11
Job 22: 7
Psa. 20: 3
77:30
83:12 S[2a]

[a] pro ὑστερέω.

στερέωμα.

Gen. 1: 6, 7, 7
7, 8
14, 15
17, 20
Exo. 24:10
Deu. 33:26
Est. 9:29
30 + S[1]
Psa. 17: 3
18: 2
Psa. 70: 3
72: 4
150: 1
Eze. 1:22, 23
25
26 + A
10: 1
13: 5
Dan. 12: 3

στερέωσις.

Job 37:17[a]

[a] A στερεόω.

στερίσκω.

Ecclesiastes 4: 8

στεφάνη.

Exo. 25:23, 24
25
27: 3
Exo. 30: 3, 4
Deu. 22: 8
Jer. 52:18

στέφανος.

2 Sa. 12:30
1 Ch. 20: 2
Est. (9)15
Job 19: 9
31:36
Psa. 20: 4
64:12
Pro. 1: 9
4: 9, 9
12: 4
14:24
16:31
17: 6
Cant. 3:11
Isa. 22:17, 21
28: 1, 3, 5
62: 3
Jer. 13:18
Lam. 2:15
5:16
Eze. 16:12
21:26
23:42
28:12
Zec. 6:11, 14

στεφανόω.

Psa. 5:13
8: 6
Ps. 102: 4
Cant. 3:11

στηθοδεσμίς.

Jeremiah 2:32

στῆθος.

Gen. 3:14
Exo. 28:23, 26
26
Job 39:20
Pro. 6:10
24:48
Dan. 2:32

στηθύνιον.

Exo. 29:26, 27
Lev. 7:20, 21
24
8:29
Lev. 9:20, 21
10:14, 15
Nu. 6:20
18:18

στήκω.

Exo. 14:13 A[a]
Jud. 16:26 + B
1 Ki. 8:11[b]

[a] pro ἵστημι. [b] A ἵστημι.

στήλη.

Gen. 19:26
28:18, 22
31:13, 45
48, 48
51 − A
52
35:14, 14
20, 20
Exo. 23:24
34:13
Lev. 26: 1, 30
Nu. 21:28
22:41
33:52
Deu. 7: 5
12: 3
16:22
2 Sa. 18:18 − A
2 Sa. 18:18[a]
18 + A
18
1 Ki. 14:23
2 Ki. 1:18
3: 2 − A
10:26[b], 27
17:10
18: 4
23:14
2 Ch. 14: 3
31: 1
33: 3
Isa. 19:19
Eze. 8: 3
Hos. 10: 1, 2
Mic. 5:13

[a] A στήλωσις. [b] AB στολή.

στηλογραφία.

Psa. 15: 1
55: 1
56: 1
Psa. 57: 1
58: 1
59: 1

στηλόω.

Jud. 18:16 A[a]
17+A
1 Sa. 17:16 A
2 Sa. 1:19
8:14+A
18:17, 18
2 Sa. 18:30
23:12
1 Ki. 9:23 A
22:48 A
2 Ki. 17:10
Lam. 3:12

[a] pro ἵστημι.

στήλωσις.

2 Samuel 18:18 A[a]

[a] pro στήλη.

στήμων.

Lev. 13:48, 49
51, 52
53, 55
Lev. 13:56, 57
58, 59

στήριγμα.

2 Sa. 20:19
2 Ki. 25:11
Ezra 9: 8[a]
Psa. 71:16
104:16
Eze. 4:16
5:16
7:11
14:13

[a] (B[1] σωτηρισμα.)

στηρίζω.

Gen. 27:37
28:12
Exo. 17:12, 12
Lev. 13:55
Jud. 19: 5, 8
1 Sa. 20:19
2 Ki. 18:16, 21
Job 20: 7 AC[a]
Psa. 50:14
103:15
110: 8
111: 8
Pro. 15:25[b]
16:30
27:20
Cant. 2: 5
Isa. 22:25
Isa. 50:16
Jer. 3:12
17: 5
21:10
24: 6
Eze. 6: 2
13:17
14: 8
15: 7 A[c], 7
20:46
21: 2
25: 2
28:21
29: 2
38: 2
Amos 9: 4

[a] pro καταστηρίζω.
[b] S[1] ἵστημι.
[c] pro δίδωμι.

στιβαρός.

Ezekiel 3: 6

στιβαρῶς.

Habakkuk 2: 6

στίβι, A στίμη.

Jeremiah 4:30

στιβίζω.

2 Ki. 9:30 AB[2] [a] Eze. 23:40

[a] pro στιμμίζω.

στίγμα.

Canticles 1:11

στιγμή.

Isaiah 29: 5

στικτός.

Leviticus 19:28

στιλβόω.

Psalm 7:13

στίλβω.

1 Ki. 7:32+A
Ezra 8:27
Eze. 21:28
Eze. 40: 3
Dan. 10: 6
Nah. 3: 3

στίλβωσις.

Ezekiel 21:10, 15

στιμμίζω.

2 Ki. 9:30[a]

[a] AB[2] στιβίζω.

στιππύϊνος.

Lev. 13:47 A[a]

[a] pro στυπ-

στιππύον.

Jud. 15:14 AB[a] Isa. 1:31

[a] pro στυππίον.

στιχίζω.

Ezekiel 42: 3 A[a]

[a] pro στοιχίζω.

στίχος.

Exo. 28:17, 17
18, 19
20, 20
36:17, 17
18, 19
20
1 Ki. 6:33, 33
1 Ki. 7: 6, 6, 6
9+A
11+A
28, 39
40, 49
49

στοά.

1 Ki. 6:30
Eze. 40:18
Eze. 42: 3, 6

στοιβάζω.

Lev. 1: 7 AB[2] [a]
6:12
Jos. 2: 6
1 Ki. 18:33, 33
Cant. 2: 5

[a] pro ἐπιστοιβάζω.

στοιβή.

Jud. 15: 5 A[a]
Ruth 3: 7
Isa. 55:13

[a] A στυ- pro ἅλως.

στοιχέω.

Ecclesiastes 11: 6

στοιχίζω.

Ezekiel 42: 3[a]

[a] A στιχίζω.

στολή.

Gen. 27:15
35: 2
41:14, 42
45:22, 22
49:11
Exo. 28: 2, 3, 4
4
29: 5
21−A
21 ter
29
31:10, 10
33: 5
35:18, 18
21
36: 8
39:13, 14
19, 19
40:11
Lev. 6:11, 11
8: 2, 30
30
30−AB[1]
30−AB[1]
Lev. 16:23, 24
32, 32
Nu. 20:26
Deu. 22: 5
Jud. 14:12, 13
19
17:10[a]
2 Sa. 6:14
2 Ki. 5: 5, 22
23
10:26 AB[b]
1 Ch. 15:27, 27
2 Ch. 5:12
18: 9
23:13
Est. 6: 8, 11
(9)15
Job 2:12
9:31
30:13, 18
37:16
Isa. 9: 5
22:17, 21
63: 1
Jer. 52:33
Eze. 10: 2, 6, 7
44:17, 19
Eze. 44:19, 19
Jon. 3: 6

[a] A ζεῦγος.
[b] pro στήλη.

στολίζω.

Ezra 3:10
Est. 4: 4
6: 9
Est. 6:11−A
(9)15

στολισμός.

2 Ch. 9: 4
Eze. 42:14

στολιστής.

2 Kings 10:22

στόμα.

Gen. 4:11
8:11
24:57
29: 2, 3, 3
8, 10
34:26
41:40
42:27
44: 1
45:12
Exo. 4:11, 12
15, 15
15, 16
13: 9
23:13
Lev. 13:45
Nu. 4:27
12: 8, 8
16:30
22:28, 38[a]
23: 5, 12
16
26:10
27:21, 21
30: 3
32:24
33: 7
Deu. 8: 3
11: 6
18:18
19:15, 15
21: 5[b]
23:23
30:14
31:19, 21
21−8
32: 2
Jos. 1: 8
6:21
8:24
10:18, 28
30, 32
33, 35
37, 39
11:11+A
12, 14
19:48
Jud. 1: 8, 25
4:15, 16
7: 6−A
9:38
11:35, 36
36
14: 8
9 A[c]
9[i]
18:19, 27
20:37, 48
21:10
1 Sa. 1:12, 23
2: 1, 3, 23
12:14, 15
14:26, 27
15: 8
17:35
22:19
19+A
2 Sa. 1:16
13:32
14: 3, 13
2 Sa. 14:19
15:14
17: 5
18:25
22: 9
1 Ki. 7:17+A
17+A
17+A
8:15, 24
17: 1, 24
19:18
21:33
22:13, 22
23
2 Ki. 4:34, 34
10:21, 21
25
21:16, 16
23:35
1 Ch. 16:12
2 Ch. 6: 4, 15
18:12, 21
22
35:22
36: 4−A
12, 21
22
Ezra 1: 1
8:17
9:11, 11
Neh. 2:13
9:20
Est. 7: 8+S[a]
Job 1:15+A
3: 1
5:16
6: 4 S[e]
7:11
11+AS[2]
8: 2, 21
9:20
13: 6
15: 5, 6, 13
16: 5
19:16
20:12
21: 5 A[f]
22:22
23: 4
27: 4 A[g]
29: 9, 13
31:27
32: 5
33: 2
35:16
36:16
37: 1
39:34
40:18
41:10, 12
Psa. 5:10
8: 3
9:28
13: 3−A
16: 4, 10
18:15
21:14, 22
31: 2
32: 6
33: 2
Psa. 34:21
35: 4
36:30
37:14, 15
38: 2, 10
39: 4
48: 4, 14
49:16, 19
50:17
53: 4
57: 7
58: 8, 13
61: 5
62: 6 S[2] [h]
12
65:14, 17
68:16
70: 8, 15
72: 9
77: 1, 2
30, 36
80:11
88: 2
104: 5
106:42
108: 2, 2, 30
113:13
118:13, 43
72, 88
103, 108
131
125: 2
134:16, 17
137: 1−A
4
140: 3
143: 8, 11
144:21
Pro. 3:16
4: 4, 5 A
24
6: 2
7:24
8: 8
29+AS[2]
10: 6, 11
14, 31
32
11: 2, 9, 11
12: 6, 8, 14
13: 3
14: 3
15: 2, 14
28
16:10, 17
23, 26
18: 6, 7, 20
19:24, 28
21:20, 23
22:14
23:33
24: 7, 76
77
26: 7, 15
28
27: 2, 21
29:43, 45
Ecc. 5: 1, 5[i]
6: 7
8: 2
10:12, 13
13−8
Cant. 1: 2
Isa. 1:20
Isa. 5:14
6: 7
9:12, 17
11: 4
24: 3
25: 8
26:21 A[k]
29:13−AS
45:23
48: 3
49: 2
51:16
52:15
53: 7, 7, 9
55:11
57: 4
58:13, 14
59:21[m], 21
21
Jer. 1: 9, 9
4: 1−A
5:14
7:28
9: 8, 12
20
12: 2
15:19
21: 7
23:16
28:44
31:28
39: 4, 4
41: 3+A
3+A
43: 4, 18
27, 32
51:17, 25
26, 31
Lam. 1:18
2:16
3:37, 45
Eze. 2: 8, 10
3: 3, 3
17, 27
4:14
16:56, 63
21:22
24:22, 27
29:21
33: 7, 22
22, 31
34:10
35:13
Dan. 4:28
6:17, 18
20, 22
7: 5, 8, 20
10: 3
16−A
Hos. 2:17
6: 5
Joel 1: 5
Amos 3:12
Mic. 3: 5
4: 4
6:12
7:16
Nah. 3:12
Zeph. 3:13
Zec. 5: 8
8: 9
9: 7
14:12
Mal. 2: 6, 7

[a] A καρδία.
[b] A ὄνομα.
[c] pro χείρ.
[d] A ἕξις.
[e] pro σῶμα.
[f] pro σιαγών.
[g] pro χεῖλος.
[h] pro ὄνομα.
[i] A[1] αἷμα.
[k] pro αἷμα.
[m] S[1] καρδία.

στόμις.

Proverbs 24:37 AS[a]

[a] pro τομίς.

στοχάζομαι.

Deuteronomy 19: 3

στοχαστής.
Isaiah 3: 2

στραγγαλιά.
Psa. 124: 5
Isa. 58: 6

στραγγαλίς.
Judges 8:26—A

στραγγαλιώδης.
Proverbs 8: 8

στραγγίζω.
Leviticus 1:15

στρατεία.
Exo. 14: 4 A[a] 17 A[a]
Jud. 8: 6 A[b]
1 Ki. 4: 4 A[b]

[a] pro στρατιά. [b] pro δύναμις.

στρατεύω.
Jud. 19: 8
2 Sa. 15:28
Pro. 24:62[a]
Isa. 29: 7

[a] AS ἐκστρατεύω.

στρατηγία.
1 Kings 2:35

στρατηγός.
1 Sa. 29: 3, 4
1 Ch. 11: 6
12:19
2 Ch. 32:21
Neh. 2:16—B[a]
4:14-BS[1]
12: 40 S[3]
13:11—ABS[1].
Est. 3:12
Job 15:24
Jer. 28:23, 28
57—A
Eze. 23: 6, 12
23
32:30
Dan. 3: 2, 3, 27
6: 7

[a] S[1] βασιλεύς.

στρατιά.
Exo. 14: 4[a], 9
17[a]
Nu. 10:28
Deu. 20: 9
2 Sa. 3:23
8:16
1 Ki. 11:15[b], 21
16:16
21:39
22:19
1 Ch. 12:14, 21
23
1 Ch. 18:15
19: 8
20: 1
28: 1—B
2 Ch. 32: 9
33: 3, 5
Neh. 9: 6
Jer. 7:18
8: 2
19:13
Hos. 13: 4
Zeph. 1: 5

[a] A στρατεία. [b] A δύναμις.

στρατιώτης.
2 Samuel 23: 8[a]

[a] AB[a] τραυματίας.

στρατοκήρυξ.
1 Kings 22:36

στρατοπεδεία.
Joshua 4: 3

στρατοπεδεύω.
Gen. 12: 9
Exo. 13:20
14: 2, 2, 10
Nu. 24: 2
Deu. 1:40
Pro. 4:15

στρατόπεδον.
Jer. 41: 1
Jer. 48:12

στρεβλός.
2 Sa. 22:27
Psa. 17:27
Psa. 77:57

στρεβλόω.
2 Samuel 22:27[a]

[a] A διαστρέφω.

στρέμμα.
Jud. 16: 9[a]
2 Ki. 15:30 B[b]

[a] A κλῶσμα. [b] pro σύστρεμμα.

στρεπτόν.
Deu. 22:12
1 Ki. 7:27, 27
1 Ki. 7:28

στρεπτός.
Exo. 25:10, 23
24
Exo. 30: 3, 4

στρέφω.
Gen. 3:24
Exo. 4:17
7:15
Jud. 7:13 A[a]
1 Sa. 10: 6
14:47
1 Ki. 2:15
6:31
18:37
Neh. 13: 2 BS[b]
Est. 4: 8 A[c]
9:22[d]
Job 28: 5
34:25
41:16
Psa. 29:12
31: 4
40: 4
Psa. 77: 9
113: 3, 5[e], 8
Pro. 12: 7
26:14
Isa. 34: 9
38: 8
63:10
Jer. 2:21, 27[f]
20: 3 S[1 b]
31:39
37: 6, 23
38:13[g]
41:13 A[b]
Lam. 1:20
5:15
Eze. 4: 8
Dan. 10:16

[a] pro κυλίω. [b] pro ἐπιστρέφω. [c] pro τρέφω. [d] AS γράφω. [e] S[1] ἀναχωρέω. [f] S ἐπιστρέφω. [g] S[1] ἐπιστρέφω.

στρῆνος.
2 Kings 19:28

στριφνός.
Job 20:18[a]

[a] AS[2] στρύχνος.

στροβέω.
Job 9:34
13:11
Job 15:24
33: 7

στρογγύλος.
1 Ki. 7:10
17+A
1 Ki. 7:21
2 Ch. 4: 2

στρογγυλόω.
1 Kings 7:17+A

στρογγύλωσις.
1 Samuel 17:20 A

στρουθίον.
Job 40:24
Psa. 10: 1
83: 4
101: 8
103:17
Ps. 123: 7
Ecc. 12: 4
Jer. 8: 7
Lam. 3:51
4: 3

στρουθός.
Lev. 11:15
Deu. 14:14
Job 30:29
Pro. 26: 2
Isa. 34:13
43:20
Jer. 10:22
30:11

στροφεύς.
1 Ki. 6:31
1 Ch. 22: 3

στροφή.
Proverbs 1: 3

στρόφιγξ.
Proverbs 26:14

στροφωτός.
Ezekiel 41:24

στρυνφαλίς.
1 Samuel 17:18 A

στρύχνος.
Job 20:18 AS[2 a]

[a] pro στριφνός.

στρῶμα.
Proverbs 22:27

στρωμνή.
Gen. 49: 4
Est. 1: 6
Job 17:13
41:21
Psa. 6: 7
Psa. 62: 7
131: 3
Eze. 27: 7
Amos 6: 4

στρώννυμι, -νύω.
Est. 4: 3[a]
Job 17:13
26:12
Pro. 7:16
15:19
Isa. 14:11
Eze. 23:41
27:30[b]
28: 7

[a] S[3] ὑποστρώννυμι. [b] A ὑποστρώννυμι.

στυγνάζω.
Eze. 27:35
28:19 A[a]
Eze. 32:10

[a] pro στενάζω.

στυγνός.
Isaiah 57:17

στῦλος.
Exo. 13:21, 21
22, 22
14:19, 24
19: 9
26:15, 16
16, 17
17, 18
18, 19
19
19—AB[1]
20, 21
21—B
22, 23
25 ter
26, 27
27, 28
29, 32
33, 37
27:10, 11, 11
12, 13
14, 15
16, 17
33: 9, 10
35:10, 12
37: 4, 6, 8
9, 10
12, 13
15 ter
17
38:18, 18
18, 19 A[a]
20 A[2 b]
20, 20
39: 6, 14
20
40:16
Nu. 3:36, 37
4:31, 31
32, 32
12: 5
14:14, 14
Deu. 31:15+A
15
Jud. 16:25 A[c]
26 A[c]
29 A[c]
20:40
2 Sa. 8: 8
1 Ki. (3) p 1
7: 3—B
3, 3, 3
4, 5, 7
7, 7
7+A
8, 9
27 qtr
28, 31
39, 39
40, 40
43, 43
2 Ki. 11:14
23: 3
25:13, 16
17, 17
1 Ch. 18: 8
2 Ch. 3:15, 16
17
4:12, 12
12, 13
34:31
Neh. 9:12, 12
19, 19
Est. 1: 6
Job 9: 6
26:11
38: 6 A[a]
Psa. 74: 4
98: 7
Pro. 9: 1
Cant. 3:10
5:15
Jer. 50:13
52:17, 20
21, 21
22
Eze. 40:49
42: 6, 6

[a] pro κρίκος. [b] pro σκηνή. [c] pro κίων.

στυππίον.
Jud. 15:14[a]
Jud. 16: 9[b]

[a] AB στιππύον. [b] A ἀποτίναγμα

στυππύϊνος.
Lev. 13:47[a]
Lev. 13:59—A

[a] A στιππύϊνος.

στυράκινος.
Genesis 30:37

συγγένεια.
Gen. 12: 1
50: 8
Exo. 6:14, 16
19
12:21
Lev. 20: 5, 20
Nu. 1: 2, 20
22, 24
26, 28
30, 32
34, 36
38, 40
42
3:15+A
4:44 A[a]
Jos. 6:23
Jud. 1:25
9: 1
13: 2—A
17: 7+A
9+A
18: 2 A[a]
11 A[a]
19 A[a]
21:24
Ruth 2: 1, 3
1 Sa. 18:18 A
2 Sa. 16: 5
Job 32: 2
Psa. 73: 8
Isa. 38:12

[a] pro δῆμος.

συγγενής.
Lev. 18:14
20:20
25:45
2 Sa. 3:39
Eze. 22: 6

συγγίνομαι.
Gen. 19: 5
Gen. 39:10

συγγραφή.
Job 31:35
Isa. 58: 6

συγκάθημαι.
Psalm 100: 6

συγκαθίζω.
Gen. 15:11
Exo. 18:13
Nu. 22:27
Jer. 16: 8[a]

[a] A καθίζω.

συγκαθυφαίνω.
Isaiah 3:23

συγκαίω.
Gen. 31:40
1 Ki. 7:35 A[a]
Job 16:16
Ps. 120: 6[b]
Pro. 24:23[c]
Isa. 5:11, 24
9:19
Jon. 4: 8

[a] pro συγκλείω. [b] S[1] ἐκκαίω. [c] S ἐκκαίω.

συγκαλέω.
Exo. 7:11
Jos. 9:28
10:24
22: 1
23: 2
24: 1
Pro. 9: 3
Isa. 62:12 S[1 a]
Jer. 1:15
Lam. 2: 3 B[b]
Zec. 3:10

[a] pro καλέω. [b] pro συγκλάω.

συγκάλυμμα.
Deu. 22:30
Deu. 27:20

συγκαλύπτω.

Gen. 9:23; Exo. 26:13; Nu. 4:14; Jud. 4:18 A[a], 19 A[a], 21+A; 1 Sa. 28: 8[b]; 1 Ki. 20: 4, 22:30, 30

2 Ki. 4:35 A[c]; 2 Ch. 4:12, 13, 5: 8, 18:29; Job 9:24; Psa. 68:11 S[2 c]; Pro. 26:26 S[1 d]; Eze. 12: 6, 12

[a] pro περιβάλλω. [b] A περικαλύπτω. [c] pro συγκάμπτω. [d] pro ἐκκαλύπτω.

συγκάμπτω.

Jud. 5:27 A[a]; 2 Ki. 4:35[b] | Psa. 68:11[c], 24

[a] pro κατακυλίνδω. [b] A συγκαλύπτω. [c] S[2] συγκαλύπτω.

συγκαταβαίνω.

Psalm 48:18

συγκατακληρονομέομαι.

Numbers 32:30

συγκαταμίγνυμι.

Joshua 23:12

συγκατατίθημι.

Exodus 23: 1, 32

συγκαταφάγω.

Isaiah 9:18

συγκαταφέρω.

Isaiah 30:30

σύγκειμαι.

1 Samuel 22: 8

συγκερατίζομαι.

Daniel 11:40

συγκλασμός.

Joel 1: 7

συγκλάω.

Psa. 45:10, 74:10[a], 106:16 S[b]; Isa. 45: 2

Jer. 27:23 AS[c]; Lam. 2: 3[d]; Eze. 29: 7

[a] B[2] συνθλάω. [b] pro συνθλάω. [c] pro κλάω. [d] B συγκαλιω.

σύγκλεισμα.

1 Ki. 7:15, 21, 22 | 2 Ki. 16:17

συγκλεισμός.

2 Sa. 5:24, 22:46; Job 28:15; Eze. 4: 3, 7, 8

Eze. 5: 2; Hos. 13: 8; Mic. 7:17

συγκλειστός.

1 Kings 7:14, 14, 36

συγκλείω.

Gen. 16: 2, 20:18-A, 18; Exo. 14: 3; Jos. 6: 1, 20: 5 A; 1 Sa. 1: 6[a]

1 Ki. 6:19, 7:35[b], 10:21, 11:27, 12 p 24 l 12; 2 Ki. 24:14, 16

Job 3:10, 23; Psa. 16:10, 30: 9, 34: 3, 77:50, 62; Pro. 4:12; Cant. 8: 7 A[c]; Isa. 45: 1

Jer. 13:19, 21: 4, 9; Eze. 4: 3, 33:22 A[d]; Amos 1: 6, 9; Obad. 14; Mic. 3: 3 A[e]; Mal. 1:10

[a] A συναποκλείω. [b] A συγκαίω. [c] pro συγκλύζομαι. [d] pro συνέχω. [e] pro συνθλάω.

σύγκλητος.

Numbers 16: 2

συγκλύζομαι.

Cant. 8: 7[a] | Isa. 43: 2

[a] A συγκλείω.

σύγκοιτος.

Micah 7: 5

συγκομίζω.

Job 5:26

συγκόπτω.

Gen. 34:30; Exo. 30:36; Deu. 9:21[a]; 2 Ki. 10:32, 16:17-A, 18:16

2 Ki. 24:13; Psa. 88:24, 128: 4; Isa. 2: 4; Jer. 31:12; Joel 3:10

[a] A συντρίβω.

σύγκρασις.

Ezekiel 22:19

σύγκριμα.

Jud. 18: 9+A; Dan. 2:25, 4:14, 15

Dan. 4:15, 21, 5:26

συγκρίνω.

Gen. 40: 8, 16, 22, 41:12, 13

Gen. 41:15, 15; Nu. 15:34; Dan. 5:12, 16

σύγκρισις.

Gen. 40:12, 18; Nu. 9: 3, 29: 6, 11, 18, 21, 24, 27, 30, 33, 37; Jud. 7:15, 18: 7 A[a]; Dan. 2: 4, 5, 6, 6, 7, 9

Dan. 2:16, 24, 26, 30, 36, 45, 4: 3, 4, 6, 16+A, 16, 21, 5: 7, 8, 12, 15, 16, 17, 7:16

[a] pro κρίσις.

συγκροτέω.

Nu. 24:10 | Dan. 5: 6

συγκύπτω.

Job 9:27

συγκυρέω.

Nu. 21:25, 35: 4 | Deu. 2:37, 3: 4+B[1]

συγχαίρω.

Genesis 21: 6

συγχέω, -χύω.

Gen. 11: 7, 9; 1 Sa. 7:10-A; 1 Ki. 20: 4+A, 21:43; 2 Ki. 14:26 A[a]; Job 30:17[b]

Joel 2: 1[c], 10; Amos 3:15; Jon. 4: 1; Mic. 7:17; Nah. 2: 5

[a] pro συνέχω. [b] A συνθλάω. [c] A συνάγω.

σύγχυσις.

Gen. 11: 9; 1 Sa. 5: 6[a] | 1 Sa. 5:11, 14:20

[a] A χύσις.

συγχύω vide συγχέω.

συζεύγνυμι.

Eze. 1:11 | Eze. 1:23+A

συζητέω.

Nehemiah 2: 4 AB[a]

[a] pro σὺ ζητεῖς.

συζωννύω.

Leviticus 8: 7

συκάμινον.

Amos 7:14

συκάμινος.

1 Ki. 10:27; 1 Ch. 27:28; 2 Ch. 1:15

2 Ch. 9:27; Psa. 77:47; Isa. 9:10

συκέη, συκῆ.

Gen. 3: 7; Nu. 13:24[a], 20: 5; Deu. 8: 8; Jud. 9:10, 11; 1 Ki. (3) p 46, 4(25) A; 2 Ki. 18:31; Neh. 2:13; Ps. 104:33; Pro. 27:18; Cant. 2:13

Isa. 34: 4, 36:16; Jer. 8:13; Hos. 2:12, 9:10; Joel 1: 7, 12, 2:22; Mic. 4: 4; Nah. 3:12; Hab. 3:17; Hag. 2:19; Zec. 3:10

[a] B σίκυος.

συκεών, συκών.

Jer. 5:17 | Amos 4: 9

σῦκον.

2 Ki. 20: 7; Neh. 13:15; Isa. 28: 4, 38:21; Jer. 8:13

Jer. 24: 1, 2, 2, 2, 3-S, 3, 5, 8

συκοφαντέω.

Gen. 43:17; Lev. 19:11; Job 35: 9; Ps. 118:122; Pro. 14:31

Pro. 22:16, 28: 2; Ecc. 4: 1, 1-C

συκοφάντης.

Psa. 71: 4 | Pro. 28:16

συκοφαντία.

Ps. 118:134; Ecc. 4: 1, 5: 7

Ecc. 7: 8; Amos 2: 8

συκών vide συκεών.

συλλαλέω.

Exo. 34:35; 1 Ki. 12:14+A; Pro. 6:22

Isa. 7: 6; Jer. 18:20

συλλαμβάνω.

Gen. 4: 1, 17, 25, 16: 4, 19:36, 21: 2, 25:21[a], 29:32, 33, 34, 35, 30: 5, 7, 10, 12, 17, 19, 23, 38: 3, 4; Exo. 12: 4; Nu. 5:13; Deu. 21:19; Jos. 8:23; Jud. 7:25, 8:14, 13: 3[b], 15: 4; 1 Sa. 1:20, 2:21+A, 4:19, 15: 8, 23:26; 2 Sa. 12:24; 1 Ki. 13: 4, 18:40, 40, 21:18, 18; 2 Ki. 7:12, 10:14, 14+A, 14: 7, 13[a], 16: 9, 17: 6

2 Ki. 18:10, 13, 25: 6; Job 22:16, 39:13; Psa. 7:15, 9:16, 17, 23, 34: 8, 50: 7, 58:13; Ecc. 7:27; Cant. 3: 4, 8: 2; Isa. 36: 1 A[c]; Jer. 5:26, 6:11, 29:17, 31: 7, 41, 44, 33: 8, 23+A, 39:24, 41: 2, 3, 43:26, 44: 8, 13, 14, 45: 3, 23[d], 28, 52: 9; Lam. 4:20; Eze. 12:13, 19: 4, 8; Dan. 11:15, 18; Hos. 1: 3, 6, 8; Amos 3: 5

[a] A λαμβάνω. [b] A τίκτω. [c] pro λαμβάνω. [d] A παραδίδωμι.

συλλέγω.

Gen. 31:46, 46; Exo. 5:11, 16: 4, 16, 17, 18, 21, 22, 26, 27; Lev. 19: 9, 10, 23:22; Nu. 11: 8, 15:32, 33; Deu. 24: 1[a]; Jud. 1: 7, 11: 3 A[b]

Ruth 2: 3, 7, 8, 15, 15, 16, 17, 17, 18, 19, 23; 1 Ki. 10:26+A, 17:10, 12; 2 Ki. 4:39, 39; Ps. 103:28, 128: 7; Cant. 6: 1; Jer. 7:18

[a] A[2] συνάγω. [b] pro συστρέφω.

σύλληψις.

Job 18:10; Jer. 18:22, 20:17

Jer. 41: 3; Hos. 9:11

συλλογή.

1 Samuel 17:40

συλλογίζομαι.

Lev. 25:27, 50, 52 | Nu. 23: 9; Isa. 43:18

συλλογισμός.

Exodus 30:12

συλλοιδορέω.

Jer. 36:27[a] [a] S λοιδορέω.

συλλοχισμός.

1 Chronicles 9: 1

συλλυπέω.

Psa. 68:21
Isa. 51:19

συμβαίνω.

Gen. 41:13
42: 4, 29
38
44:29
Exo. 1:10
3:16
24:14
Lev. 10:19
Deu. 18:22

Jos. 2:23
Est. 2:11
6:13
Job 1:22
2:10
42:11
Isa. 3:11
41:22
Jer. 39:23

συμβάλλω.

Gen. 30: 8 A[a]
2 Ch. 25:19

Isa. 46: 6
Jer. 50: 3

[a] *pro* συναντιλαμβανομαι.

συμβαστάζω.

Job 28:16, 19

συμβιβάζω.

Exo. 4:12, 15
18:16
Lev. 10:11
Deu. 4: 9

Jud. 13: 8[a]
Psa. 31: 8
Isa. 40:13, 14
Dan. 9:22

[a] A φωτίζω.

σύμβλημα.

Isaiah 41: 7

σύμβλησις.

Exo. 26:24[a] [a] A συμβολή.

συμβοηθός.

1 Kings 21:16

συμβολή.

Exo. 26: 4, 4, 5
10
24 A[a]
28:28

Exo. 36:23
28—B
Pro. 23:20
Isa. 23:18

[a] *pro* σύμβλησις.

συμβολοκοπέω.

Deuteronomy 21:20

σύμβολον.

Hosea 4:12

σύμβολος.

2 Samuel 8:18 A[a]

[a] *pro* σύμβουλος.

συμβόσκω.

Isaiah 11: 6

συμβουλεύω.

Exo. 18:19—A
Nu. 24:14
Jos. 15:18
2 Sa. 17:11—A
11, 15
15
1 Ki. 1:12
12: 8, 8
9[a], 13

1 Ki. 12 *p* 24 *l* 58
l 68
2 Ch. 10: 8, 8
Job 26: 3[b]
Isa. 33:18, 19
40:14
Jer. 43:16
45:15
Dan. 6: 7

[a] A βουλεύω. [b] S[1] βουλεύω.

συμβουλία.

1 Ki. 1:12
2 Ch. 25:16

Ps. 118:24
Pro. 12:15

σύμβουλος.

2 Sa. 8:18[a]
15:12
1 Ki. (3) *p* 46
1 Ch. 27:32, 33
2 Ch. 22: 3, 4
25:16
Ezra 7:14, 15
28
8:25
Job 15: 8—ABCS

Isa. 1:26
3: 3
9: 6+AS[2]
19:11
40:13
Eze. 27:27

[a] A σύμβολος.

συμμαχέω.

Jos. 1:14
1 Ch. 12:21

συμμαχία.

Isaiah 16: 4

συμμένω.

Proverbs 20: 1+A

συμμερίζω.

Proverbs 20:24 S[2a]

[a] *pro* μερίζω.

σύμμετρος.

Jeremiah 22:14

συμμιγής.

Daniel 2:43

συμμίγνυμι.

Exo. 14:20
Pro. 11:15
20: 1+S[2]

Dan. 11: 6[a]
Hos. 7: 8[b]

[a] A ἀποσυμμίγνυμι.
[b] A συναναμίγνυμι.

σύμμικτος.

Jer. 27:37
32: 6, 10
Eze. 27:16, 17
19, 25

Eze. 27:27 *ter*
33, 34
Nah. 3:17

σύμμιξις.

2 Ki. 14:14
2 Ch. 25:24

συμπαθής.

Job 29:25 A[a] [a] *pro* παθεινός.

συμπαραγίνομαι.

Psalm 82: 9

συμπαραλαμβάνω.

Gen. 19:17
Job 1: 4

συμπαραμένω.

Psalm 71: 5

συμπάρειμι.

Proverbs 8:27

συμπαρίστημι.

Psalm 93:16

σύμπας.

1 Sa. 2:22+A
1 Ki. 8: 1+A
9: 9+A
15:18—B
29 A[a]
21:15+A
Est. 4: 7+S[3]
Job 2: 2[b]
25: 2
Psa. 38: 6
103:28[c]
118:91
144: 9 S[2d]
Eze. 27:13
Nah. 1: 5

Ecc. 1:14
2:18
3:11, 11[e]
4: 1[e], 2[e]
4, 4, 15
7:16[f]
8: 9, 17
17, 17
9:11[g]
11: 5
12:14
Isa. 11: 9
Eze. 7:14
Hab. 2:14+A

[a] *pro* ὅλος. [b] A γῆ.
[c] S πᾶς. [d] *pro* ὑπομένω.
[e] AS σύν. [f] B πᾶς.
[g] ACS πᾶς.

συμπατέω.

2 Ki. 7:17, 20
9:33
14: 9
Dan. 7: 7, 19

Dan. 7:23
8: 7, 10
13
Nah. 3:14

συμπεραίνω.

Habakkuk 2:10

συμπεριλαμβάνω.

Ezekiel 5: 3

συμπεριφέρω.

Pro. 5:19
Pro. 11:29

συμπίνω.

Esther 7: 1

συμπίπτω.

Gen. 4: 5, 6
1 Sa. 1:18
17:32
2 Sa. 5:18, 22
1 Ch. 14: 9, 13

Job 4:14 A[1a]
Isa. 3: 5, 8
34: 7
64:11
Eze. 30: 4[b], 4

[a] *pro* διασείω. [b] A πίπτω.

σύμπλεκτος.

Exodus 36:31

συμπλέκω.

Exo. 28:22
36:11, 22
29
Job 40:12
Psa. 57: 3
Pro. 20: 1, 3

Lam. 1:14
Eze. 24:17
Hos. 4:14
Nah. 2: 5
Zec. 14:13

συμπληρόω.

Jer. 25:12 A[a] [a] *pro* πληρόω.

συμπλήρωσις.

2 Ch. 36:21
Dan. 9: 2

συμπλοκή.

1 Ki. 16: *p* 28—A

συμποδίζω.

Gen. 22: 9
Psa. 17:40
19: 9
77:31

Pro. 20:11
Hos. 11: 3
Zec. 13: 3

συμπολεμέω.

Deu. 32:23[a]
Jos. 10:14 AB[b]

Jos. 10:42

[a] A συντελέω.
[b] *pro* συνεκπολεμέω.

συμπορεύομαι.

Gen. 13: 5
14:24
18:16
Exo. 33:15[a], 16
34: 9
Nu. 14:14 B[b]
16:25
22:35

Deu. 31: 8[c], 11
Jos. 10:24
Jud. 11: 8 A[b]
40 A[b]
13:25 A[d]
Job 1: 4
Pro. 13:20, 20[e]
Eze. 33:31

[a] B πορεύω. [b] *pro* πορεύω.
[c] A συμπροπορεύομαι.
[d] *pro* συνεκπορεύομαι.
[e] A συρρέμβομαι.

συμπορπάω.

Exodus 36:13

συμπόσιον.

Esther 7: 7

συμπροπέμπω.

Gen. 12:20
Gen. 18:16

συμπροπορεύομαι.

Deuteronomy 31: 8 A[a]

[a] *pro* συμπορεύομαι.

συμπρόσειμι.

Psa. 93:20
Ecc. 8:15

συμπροσπλέκω.

Daniel 11:10[a]

[a] A προσυμπλέκω.

σύμπτωμα.

1 Sa. 6: 9
20:26

Psa. 90: 6
Pro. 27: 9

συμφάγω.

Exo. 18:12[a]
2 Sa. 12:17

[a] A φάγω.

συμφέρον, —οντος.

Deu. 23: 6
Pro. 29:37

συμφέρω.

Est. 3: 8
Pro. 19:10

Jer. 33:14

συμφλέγω.

Isaiah 42:25

συμφοράζω.

Isaiah 13: 8

συμφράσσω.

Isa. 27:12[a] [a] S συνταράσσω.

συμφρύγω.

Job 30:30+A
Ps. 101: 4

Eze. 24:10+A
11 A[a]

[a] *pro* θερμαίνω.

συμφύρω.

Eze. 22: 6[a]
Hos. 4:14

[a] A συναναφύρω, B[*] ἐμφύρω.

σύμφυτος.

Est. 7: 7+S[3]
8+S[3]

Amos 9:13
Zec. 11: 2

συμφωνέω.

Gen. 14: 3
2 Ki. 12: 8

Ecc. 7:15 C[a]
Isa. 7: 2

[a] *pro* συμφώνως.

συμφωνία.

Dan. 3: 5+A
7+A

Dan. 3:10+A
15

σύμφωνος.

Ecclesiastes 7:15 AS[a]

[a] *pro* συμφώνως.

συμφώνως.

Ecclesiastes 7:15[a]

[a] AS σύμφωνος, C συμφωνέω.

συμψάω.

Jer. 22:19
29:21[a]
Jer. 31.33

[a] A συμψηφίζω, S συνίημι.

συμψηφίζω.

Jeremiah 29:21 A[a]

[a] pro συμψάω.

σύναγμα.

Ecclesiastes 12:11 ℵS[1] [a]

[a] pro σύνθεμα.

συνάγω.

Gen. 1: 9, 9
6:21
29: 3, 7, 8
22
34:30
37:35
41:35, 35
35 A[a]
48, 49
47:14
49: 1, 2[b]
Exo. 3:16
4:29
5: 7, 12
8: 5 A[c]
14
9:19, 20
16: 5[d], 16
23:10[e]
Lev. 25: 3, 20
Nu. 1:18[f]
8: 9
10: 3, 7
11:16, 22
24, 32
32
19: 9, 10
21:16—A
23
Deu. 13:16
16:13
19: 5
22: 2
24: 1 A[2] [g]
30: 3, 4
32:23, 34
33: 5, 21
Jos. 2:18
7:14
10: 6
24: 1
Jud. 3:13[h]
6:33
7:22 + A
9: 6, 47
10:17[i]
11:20
12: 1 A[k]
16:23
19:15, 18
20:11, 14
Ruth 2: 2, 7
1 Sa. 5: 8, 11
7: 6
13: 5, 11
14:19, 52
17: 1, 1, 2
22: 2
2 Sa. 3:34
6: 1
10:15, 16
17
11:27
12:28[m], 29
14:14
17:11, 11
13
21:13
23: 9, 11
1 Ki. 7:10
12 p 24 l 23
18:20 A[n]

2 Ki. 5:11 A[o]
19:25[m]
22: 4, 20
23: 1
1 Ch. 11:13
13: 2
15: 3 AP, 4
19: 7, 17
22: 2
23: 2
2 Ch. 1:14
2: 2
10 A[q]
17
10: 6
11:13
12: 5
13: 7
15:10
18: 5
20: 4
23: 2
24: 5, 5, 11
25: 5
29:15, 20
30: 3, 13
32: 4, 6
34: 9, 29
Ezra 3: 1
7:28
8:15, 20
9: 4
10: 1
7 S[3] [r]
9
Neh. 1: 9
4: 8, 20
5:16
6: 2, 10
7: 5
8: 1, 13
9: 1
12:25, 28[s]
44
13:11
Est. 2: 8
9:15, 16
18
Job 5: 5[t]
20:13, 15
27:16
Psa 2: 2
15: 4
30:14[u]
32: 7
34:15, 15
38: 7
40: 7
46:10
47: 5
49: 5
101:23[v]
103:22
106: 3
Pro. 9:12
10:10
11:24
13:11
24:27
27:24
28: 8
29:32

Ecc. 2: 8, 26
3: 5
Isa. 11:12, 12
13: 4, 14
15
17: 5, 5
18: 6
23:18
24:22
27:12
28:20
29: 1, 7
33: 4, 4
34:16
35:10
39: 6
40:11
43: 5, 9, 9
44:11
45:20
48:14
49: 5, 5
18
52:12 S[1] [n]
15 A[w]
56: 8, 8
60: 4, 7, 22
62: 9
9 — S[1]
66:18
Jer. 3:17
4: 5
7:21
8:13, 14
15
9:22
10:17
12: 9
17:11
21: 4-ABS
23: 7 S[1] [x]
8
27: 7
28:44
29:15
30: 5

Jer. 37:21
38: 8, 10
39:37
47:10
10 + A
12, 15
Eze. 11:17
13: 5
16:31, 37
22:20
28:25
29: 5, 13
34:12 A[y]
13
37:21
38: 4, 7, 8
12, 13
39: 2
2 A[z]
17, 17
27
Dan. 3: 2, 3
3 + A
27
11:10, 40
Hos. 1:11
10:10
Joel 1 14
2: 1 A[z]
16, 16
3: 2, 11
Amos 3: 9
Mic. 1: 7
2:12, 12
4: 6, 12
5: 7
7: 1
Hab. 1: 9, 15
2:16
Zeph. 2: 1
3:19
Hag. 1: 6, 6
Zec. 2: 6
9: 3-BS[1]
14:14

[a] pro φυλάσσω. [b] A ἀθροίζω. [c] pro ἀνάγω. [d] A εἰσφέρω. [e] A[1] εἰσάγω. [f] A ἐξεκκλησιάζω. [g] pro συλλέγω. [h] A προστάγω. [i] A ἐξέρχομαι. [k] pro βράω. [m] A ἄγω. [n] pro ἐπισυνάγω. [o] pro ἀποσυνάγω. [p] pro ἐξεκκλησιάζω. [q] pro ἄγω. [r] pro συναθροίζω. [s] S[1] ἄγω. [t] A θερίζω. [u] AS ἐπισυνάγω. [v] AS[2] ἐπισυνάγω. [w] pro συνέχω. [x] pro ἀνάγω. [y] pro ἀπελαύνω. [z] pro συγχέω.

συναγωγή.

Gen. 1: 9, 9
28: 3
35:11
48: 4
Exo. 12: 3, 6
19, 47
16: 1, 2, 3
6, 9
10, 22
17: 1
23:16
34:22, 31
35: 1, 4, 20
38:22
39: 2
Lev. 4:13, 13
14, 15
21
8: 3, 4, 5
9: 5
10: 3, 6, 17
11:36
16: 5, 17
33
19: 2
22:18
24:14, 16

Nu. 1: 2, 16
18
5: 2 A[a]
8: 9, 20
10: 2, 3, 7
13:27, 27
14: 1, 2, 5
7, 10
27, 35
36
15:14, 24
24, 25
26, 33
35, 36
36
16: 2, 3, 3
5, 6, 9
9 A[b]
11, 16
19, 19
21, 22
24, 24
26, 33
42, 45
47
19: 9, 20
20: 1, 2, 4

Nu. 20: 6, 8, 8
10, 11
12, 22
25, 27
29
22: 4
25: 6, 7
26: 2, 9, 9
10
27: 2, 3, 3
14, 16
17, 19
21, 22
31:13, 16
26, 27
43
32: 2, 15
35:12, 24
25, 25
Deu. 5:22
33: 4
Jos. 9:21
24 + A
24, 25
27, 33
18: 1
20: 3, 4 A
6 A, 9
22:16, 17
20, 30
Jud. 14: 8[c]
20: 1
21:10, 13
16
1 Ki. 8: 5 + A
12:20, 21

2 Ch. 5: 6
Ezra 10: 14 BS[1] [d]
Job 8:17
Psa. 7: 8
15: 4
21:17
39:11
61: 9 — S[1]
67:31
73: 2
81: 1
85:14
105:17, 18
110: 1
Pro. 5:14
21:16
Isa. 19: 6
22: 6
24:22 — A
37:25
56: 8
Jer. 6:11
27: 9
33:17
38: 4, 13
51:15
Eze. 26: 7
27:27, 34
32:2?, 22
37:10
38: 4, 7
13, 15
Obad. 13
Zeph. 3: 8
Zec. 9:12

[a] pro παρεμβολή. [b] pro σκηνή. [c] A συστροφή. [d] pro συνταγή.

συνᾴδω.

Hos. 7: 2, 2 A[a]

[a] pro ᾄδω.

συναθροίζω.

Exo. 35: 1
Nu. 16:11
20: 2 A[a]
Deu. 1:41
Jos. 22:12
Jud. 12: 4 A[b]
1 Sa. 4: 1
7: 7
8: 4
25: 1
28: 1, 4, 4
29: 1
2 Sa. 2:25, 30

2 Sa. 3:21
1 Ki. 11:14
12 p 24 l 48
l 76
18:19
21: 1
22: 6
2 Ki. 10:18[c]
Ezra 10: 7—ABS[1] [d]
Jer. 20:10
Joel 3:11
Amos 4: 8

[a] pro ἀθροίζω. [b] pro συστρέφω. [c] AB ζηλόω. [d] S[3] συνάγω.

συναίρω.

Exodus 23: 5[a]

[a] A ἐγείρω, B* συνεγείρω.

συνάλλαγμα.

Isaiah 58: 6

συναναβαίνω.

Gen. 50: 7, 9, 14
Exo. 12:38
24: 2
33: 3

Nu. 13:32
Jos. 14: 8 A[a]
Jud. 6: 3[b]
2 Ch. 18: 2

[a] pro ἀναβαίνω. [b] A ἀναβαίνω.

συναναμίγνυμι.

Eze. 20:18
Hos. 7: 8 A[a]

[a] pro συμμίγνυμι.

συνανάμιξις.

Daniel 11:23

συναναπαύομαι.

Isaiah 11: 6

συναναστρέφω.

Genesis 30: 8

συναναφέρω.

Gen. 50:25
Exo. 13:19
2 Sa. 6:18

συναναφύρω.

Ezekiel 22: 6 A[a]

[a] pro συμφύρω.

συναντάω.

Gen. 32: 1, 17
46:28
Exo. 4:24, 27
5: 3, 20
7:15
23: 4
Nu. 23:16
35:19, 21
Deu. 22: 6
23: 4
31:29 — B
Jos. 2:16
11:20
Jud. 8:21[a]
15:12[a]
18:25[a]
20:41[b]
2 Sa. 2:13
18: 9
Neh. 12:38 S[3]
13: 2
Job 3:12, 25

Job 4:12 A[c]
14
5:14
27:20
30:26
39:22
41:17
Psa. 84:11
Pro. 7:10
9:18
12:13, 23
17:20
20:30
22: 2
24: 8
Ecc. 2:14, 15
9:11
Isa. 8:14
14: 9
21:14
34:14, 15
64: 5

[a] A ἀπαντάω. [b] A ἅπτω. [c] pro ἀπαντάω.

συναντή.

1 Ki. 18:16[a]
2 Ki. 2:15[a]
2 Ki. 5:26[a]

[a] A συνάντησις.

συνάντημα.

Exo. 9:14
1 Ki. 8:37
Ecc. 2:14, 15
Ecc. 3:19 ter
9: 2, 3

συνάντησις.

Gen. 14:17
18: 2
19: 1
24:17, 65
29:13
30:16
32: 6
33: 4
46:29
Exo. 4:14, 27
5:20
18: 7
19:17
Nu. 20:18, 20
21:33
22:34, 36
23: 3
24: 1
31:13
Deu. 1:44
2:32
3: 1
29: 7
Jos. 8: 5, 14
22
9:17
Jud. 4:18[a]
22[b]
6:35[a]

Jud. 7:24 — A
11:31[a]
14: 5[a]
15:14
19: 3[a]
20:25[a]
31[a]
1 Sa. 17:48
18: 6
23:28
25:20
2 Sa. 2:23
5:23
1 Ki. 12 p 24 l 41
18: 7
16 A[c]
16
2 Ki. 1: 3, 6, 7
2:15 A[c]
5:26 A[c]
2 Ch. 14:10
35:20
Psa. 58: 5
150 p 6
Pro. 7:15[d]
Isa. 7: 3
21:14
Zec. 2: 3[a]

[a] A ἀπάντησις. [b] A ἀπάντη. [c] pro συναντή. [d] B[1] ὑπάντησις

συναντιλαμβάνομαι.
Gen. 30: 8[a]
Exo. 18:22
Nu. 11:17
Psa. 88:22
[a] A συμβάλλω.

συναπάγω.
Exodus 14: 6

συναποκλείω.
1 Samuel 1: 5 A[a], 6 A[b]
[a] pro ἀποκλείω.
[b] pro συγκλείω.

συναπόλλυμι.
Gen. 18:23
19:15
Nu. 16:26
Deu. 29:19
Psa. 25: 9
27: 3

συναποστέλλω.
Exodus 33: 2, 12

συνάπτω.
Exo. 26: 6, 9, 10
11, 11
29: 5—6
Deu. 2: 5, 9
19, 24
Jos. 17:10
19:11, 22
26, 27
34, 34
Jud. 20:20[a]
22[a]
22[a]
30[a]
Jud. 20:33—A
1 Sa. 14:22
31: 2
2 Sa. 1: 6
1 Ki. 16:20
21:14
2 Ki. 10:34
Neh. 3:19
Isa. 5: 8
15: 8
16: 8
Eze. 37:17
Dan. 11:23
[a] A παρατάσσω.

συναριθμέω.
Exodus 12: 4

συναρπάζω.
Proverbs 6:25

συναυλίζω.
Proverbs 22:24

σύναψις.
1 Ki. 16:20
2 Ki. 10:34

συνδειπνέω.
Gen. 43:31
Pro. 23: 6

σύνδεσμος.
1 Ki. 6:14[a]
14:24
2 Ki. 11:14, 14
12:20
Job 41: 6
Isa. 58: 6, 9
Jer. 11: 9
Dan. 5: 6, 12
[a] A ἔνδεσμος.

συνδέω.
Exo. 14:25
28:20
36:20
Jud. 15: 4 A[a]
1 Sa. 18: 1 A
Job 17: 3
Eze. 3:25
Zeph. 2: 1
[a] pro ἐπιστρέφω.

συνδοιάζω.
Psalm 140: 4[a]
[a] S[1] ἐνδνάζω, A[2]S[2] συνδυάζω.

σύνδουλος.
Ezra 4: 7, 9
17, 23
Ezra 5: 3, 6
6: 6, 13

συνδυάζω.
Ps. 140: 4 A[2] S[2] pro συνδοιάζω

σύνεγγυς.
Deuteronomy 3:29

συνεγείρω.
Exo. 23: 5 B[a][a] Isa. 14: 9
[a] pro συναίρω.

συνεδριάζω.
Proverbs 3:32

συνέδριον.
Psa. 25: 4
Pro. 11:13
15:22
22:10, 10
24: 8
Pro. 26:26
27:22
29:41
Jer. 15:17

σύνεδρος.
Judges 5:10—A

συνείδησις.
Ecclesiastes 10:20

σύνειμι.
Psa. 57:108[1] S[a]
Pro. 5:19
Jer. 3:20
[a] pro συνίημι.

συνεισέρχομαι.
Exo. 21: 3
Est. 2:13
Job 22: 4

συνεκπολεμέω.
Deu. 1:30
20: 4
Jos. 10:14[a]
[a] AB συμπολεμέω.

συνεκπορεύομαι.
Jud. 11: 3 A[a]
Jud. 13:25[b]
[a] pro ἐξέρχομαι.
[b] A συμπορεύομαι.

συνεκτρέφω.
2 Chronicles 10: 8

συνέλευσις.
Judges 9:46[a], 49[a], 49[a]
[a] A ὀχύρωμα.

συνελκύω.
Psalm 27: 3

συνεξέρχομαι.
Proverbs 22:10

συνεπακολουθέω.
Numbers 32:11, 12

συνεπισκέπτομαι.
Nu. 1:47 A[a]
49
Nu. 2:33
26:62
[a] pro ἐπισκέπτομαι.

συνεπίσταμαι.
Job 9:35
Job 19:27

συνεπισχύω.
2 Chronicles 32: 3

συνεπιτίθημι.
Nu. 12:11
Deu. 32:27
Psa. 3: 7 AS[a]
Obad. 13
Zec. 1:15, 15
[a] pro ἐπιτίθημι

συνέρχομαι.
Exo. 32:26
Jos. 9: 2
11: 5
Job 6:29
40:26
Pro. 5:20 B[a]
Pro. 23:35
29:13
Jer. 3:18
Eze. 33:30
Zec. 8:21
[a] pro συνέχω.

συνεσθίω.
Gen. 43:31
Ps. 100: 5

σύνεσις.
Exo. 31: 3, 6
35:31, 35—A
Deu. 4: 6
34: 9
1 Sa. 25: 3
1 Ki. 7: 2
1 Ch. 12:32
22:12
28:19
2 Ch. 1:10, 11
12
2:12, 13
30:22
Job 6:30
8:10+A
12:13, 16
20
15: 2
20: 3
21:22
22: 2
28:20
32:11+A
33: 3
34:35
38: 4
39:17
Psa. 31: 1[a], 9
41: 1
42: 1+A
43: 1—A
44: 1—A
48: 4
51: 1
52: 1
53: 1
Psa. 54: 1
73: 1
77: 1, 72
87: 1
88: 1
110:10
135: 5
141: 1
146: 5
Pro. 1: 7
2: 2, 3, 6
4: 4+S[2]
5 A
9: 6, 10
13:15
24: 3
Isa. 3:20 A[b]
10:13
11: 2
27:11
29:14, 24
33:19
40:14
47:10
53:11
56:11
Jer. 28:15
Dan. 1 17
2:20, 21
5:11, 12
14—B[1]
8:15
9:22
10: 1
Hos. 2:15
Obad. 7, 8
[a] A ψαλμός.
[b] pro σύνθεσις.

συνεταιρίς.
Judges 11:37, 38

συνεταῖρος.
Judges 15: 2 A[a], 6 A[a]
[a] pro φίλος.

συνετίζω.
Neh. 8: 7, 9
9:20
Psa. 15: 7
31: 8
118:27, 34
73, 125
Ps. 118:130
144, 169
Dan. 8:16
9:22
10:14

συνετός.
Gen. 41:33, 39
Exo. 31: 6
Deu. 1:13, 15
1 Sa. 16:18
18 A[a]
2 Ki. 11: 9
1 Ch. 15:22
27:32
Job 34:10, 34
Pro. 12: 8, 23
15:24
16:20, 21
17:24
23: 9
28: 7
Pro. 29:48
Ecc. 9:11
Isa. 3: 3
5:21
19:11
29:14
32: 8
Jer. 4:22
9:12[b]
18:18
27: 9, 35
29: 8
Dan. 11:33
Hos. 14:
[a] pro σοφός.
[b] A[1] συνετῶς.

συνετῶς.
Psa. 46: 8
Isa. 29:16
Jer. 9:12 A[1] [a]
[a] pro συνετός.

συνευφραίνομαι.
Proverbs 5:18

συνέχω.
Gen. 8: 2
Exo. 26: 3 A[a]
3
28: 7
36:11, 29
Deu. 11:17
1 Sa. 14: 6
21: 7
23: 8
2 Sa. 20: 3
24:21, 25
1 Ki. 6:14, 15
8:35
20:21
2 Ki. 9: 8
14:26[b]
1 Ch. 12: 1
2 Ch. 6:26
7:13
Neh. 6:10
Job 2: 9
3:24
7:11
10: 1
31:23
34:14
36: 8
38: 2
41: 8
Psa. 68:16
76:10
Pro. 5:20[c]
11:26
Isa. 52:15[d]
Jer. 2:13
23: 9
Eze. 33:22[e]
43: 8
Mic. 7:18
[a] pro ἔχω. [b] A συγχέω.
[c] B συνέρχομαι. [d] A συναγω.
[e] A συγκλείω.

συνήλικος.
Daniel 1:10

συνθέλω.
Deuteronomy 13: 8

σύνθεμα *vide* σύνθημα

σύνθεσις.
Exo. 30:32
35+A[2]
37
31:11
35:19, 28
28
38:25
Exo. 39:16
40:25
Lev. 4: 7, 18
16:12
Nu. 4:16
2 Ch. 13:11
Isa. 3:20[a]
[a] A σύνεσις.

σύνθετος.
Exodus 30: 7

συνθήκη.
2 Ki. 17:15+A
Isa. 28:15
Isa. 30: 1
Dan. 11: 6

σύνθημα, —θεμα.
Jud. 12: 6 A[a]
Ecc. 12:11[b]
[a] pro στάχυς.
[b] AS[1] σύναγμα, S[2] σύνταγμα.

συνθλάω.
Jud. 5:26 A[a]
9:53 A[b]
Job 30:17 A[c]
Psa. 57: 7
67:22
73:14 S[d]
Psa. 74:10 B[2] [e]
106:16[f]
109: 5, 6
Isa. 42: 3 A[g]
Mic. 3: 3[h]
[a] pro πατάσσω. [b] pro κλάω.
[c] pro συγχέω. [d] pro συντρίβω
[e] pro συγκλάω. [f] S συγκλάω.
[g] pro θλάω. [h] A συγκλείω.

συνθλίβω.
Ecclesiastes 12: 6 AS[a]
[a] pro συντρίβω.

συνίημι.

Exo. 35:35; 36:1; Deu. 29:9; 32:7, 29; Jos. 1:7; 8 A[a]; 8; 1 Sa. 2:10; 18:5 A; 14, 15; 30 A; 2 Sa. 12:19; 1 Ki. 2:3; 3:9, 11; 2 Ki. 18:7; 1 Ch. 25:7; 2 Ch. 20:17; 26:5; 30:22; 34:12; Ezra 8:15, 16; Neh. 8:2, 3, 8; 12; 10:28; 13:7; Job 15:9[b]; 20:2; 31:1; 32:12; 36:4, 29; 38:31; Psa. 2:10; 5:2; 13:2; 18:13; 27:5; 32:15; 35:4; 40:2; 48:13, 21; 49:22; 52:3; 57:10[c]

Psa. 63:10; 72:17; 81:5; 91:7; 93:7, 8; 100:2; 105:7; 106:43; 118:95, 99; 100, 104; 138:2; Pro. 2:5, 9; 8:9; 21:11, 12; 29; 28:5[d], 5; 29:7 AS[2e]; Isa. 1:3; 6:9, 10; 7:9; 43:10—S[3]; 52:13, 15; 59:15; Jer. 9:12, 24; 20:12; 23:5; 29:21 S[f]; Dan. 1:4, 17; 8:5, 17; 23, 27; 9:2, 13; 23, 25; 10:11, 12; 11:30, 33; 35, 37; 37; 12:3, 8; 10[b], 10; Hos. 4:14; 14:9; Amos 5:13; Mic. 4:12

[a] pro εἰδέω. [b] A νοέω. [c] B[1]S σύνειμι. [d] S νοέω. [e] pro νοεω [f] pro συμψάω.

συνίστημι.

Gen. 40:4; Exo. 7:19; 32:1; Lev. 15:3, 3; Nu. 16:3; 27:23; 32:28; 1 Sa. 17:26 A

Job 28:23; Psa. 38:2; 106:36; 117.27; 140:9; Pro. 6:14; 26:26; Jer. 5:27 S[a]

[a] pro ἐφίστημι.

συνίστωρ.

Job 16:19

συννεφέω.

Genesis 9:14

συννεφής.

Deuteronomy 33:28

σύννυμφος.

Ruth 1:15, 15

συνοδεύω.

Zechariah 8:21+S[1]

συνοδία.

Nehemiah 7:5, 5, 64

σύνοδος.

Deu. 33:14; 1 Ki. 15:13

Jer. 9:2

σύνοιδα.

Lev. 5:1

Job 27:6

συνοικέω.

Gen. 20:3; Deu. 22:13; 24:3

Deu. 25:5; Jud. 14:20 A[a]; Isa. 62:5

[a] pro γίνομαι.

συνοικίζω.

Deu. 21:13; 22:22

Isa. 62:4—AS

συνούλωσις.

Jeremiah 40:6

συνοχή.

Jud. 2:3; Job 30:3; 38:28+A

Jer. 52:5; Mic. 5:1

συνταγή.

Jud. 20:38 A[a]

Ezra 10:14[b]

[a] pro σημεῖον. [b] BS[1] συναγωγή.

σύνταγμα.

Job 15:8

Ecc. 12:11 S[2a]

[a] pro σύνθεμα.

σύνταξις.

Exo. 5:8, 11; 14, 18; 37:19; Nu. 9:14

Nu. 15:24; 1 Ki. 4:21; Jer. 52:34

συνταράσσω.

Exo. 14:24; 2 Sa. 22:8[a]; Psa. 17:15; 26:10; 41:6, 12; 42:5; 59:4; 64:8

Ps. 113:6; Isa. 10:33; 27:12 S[b]; Dan. 4:2 AB[c]; 16; 5:6, 9; 7:28; Hos. 11:8

[a] A ταράσσω. [b] pro συμφράσσω. [c] pro ταράσσω.

συντάσσω.

Gen. 18:19; 26:11; Exo. 1:17, 22; 5:6; 6:13; 9:12; 12:35; 16:16, 24; 32, 34; 19:7; 27:20; 31:6, 13; 34:4; 35:4, 9; 29; 36:1, 5, 8; 12, 14; 29, 34; 37, 40; 37:19, 20; 38:27; 39:11, 22; 23; 40:14 A[a]; 17, 19; 21, 23; 25; Lev. 8:4, 9, 13; 17, 31; 36; 9:21; 10:15, 18; 13:54

Lev. 16:34; 24:23; Nu. 1:19; 2:34[b]; 3:16, 51; 4:49; 8:3, 22; 9:5; 15:23, 23; 36[c]; 17:11; 19:2; 20:9, 27; 26:4; 27:11, 23; 30:2; 31:21, 31; 41, 47; 34:13; 35:2; 36:2, 6, 10; Deu. 4:23; 5:15; Jos. 4:3, 8; 8:27, 29; 9:30; 11:12, 15; 15; 24:31; 1 Ki. 8:5+A; Job 25:5; 37:5, 11; 38:12

Job 42:9; Pro. 24:31; Isa. 10:6; 13:3; 27:4; 37:26

Jer. 33:2, 8; 34:3; 36:23; 39:13, 35; 41:22; 44:21

[a] pro ἐντέλλω. [b] A ἐντέλλω. [c] A λαλέω.

συντέλεια.

Exo. 23:16; Deu. 11:12; Jos. 4:8; Jud. 20:40; 1 Sa. 8:3; 20:41; 1 Ki. 6:20, 23; 23+B; 2 Ki. 13:17, 19; 2 Ch. 24:23; Ezra 9:14; Neh. 9:31; Job 26:10; 30:2; Psa. 58:14, 14; 118:96; Jer. 1:3+S; 4:27; 5:10, 18

Jer. 26:28; Eze. 11:13; 13:13; 20:17; 21:28; 22:12; Dan. 9:27+AB[2]; 27, 27; 11:36; 12:4, 13; 13; Amos 1:14; 8:8; 9:5; Nah. 1:3, 8, 9; Hab. 1:9, 15; 3:19; Zeph. 1:18

συντελέω.

Gen. 2:1, 2; 6:16; 17:22; 18:21; 24:15, 45; 29.27; 43:1; 44:5; 49:5; Exo. 5:13, 14; 36:2; 40:27; Lev. 16:20; 19:9—AB[1]; 23:22, 39; Nu. 4:15; 7:1; Deu. 26:12; 31:1, 24; 32:23 A[a]; 45 A[b]; 34:8; Jos. 3:17; 4:1, 10; 11; 21:42; Jud. 3:18; 15:17 A[c]; Ruth 2:23; 3:3; 1 Sa. 10:13; 13:10; 15:18; 18:1 A; 20:7, 9; 33, 34; 24:17; 25:17; 2 Sa. 6:18; 11:19; 13:36; 21:5; 22:38; 1 Ki. 1:41; (3) 1, 1; p 1; p 46+A; 4:30—A; 6:5, 7, 13; (14)A; 7:26; 38+A; 49—A; 8:1—A; 53, 54; 9:1; 22:11

2 Ki. 10:25; 1 Ch. 16:2; 27:24; 28:20; 2 Ch. 4:11, 22; 7:1, 11; 18:10; 20:23; 24:14; 29:17, 28; 29, 34; 30:22; 31:1, 7; 34:8+A; Est. 4:1; Job 1:5; 14:14; 15:4; 19:25, 27; 21:13; 33:27; 35:14; 36:11; Psa. 7:10; 76:9+S[2]; 118:87; Pro. 1:19; 8:31; 22:8, 8; Isa. 1:28; 8:8; 10:12, 22; 16:4+A; 18:5; 28:22; 22 A[d]; 32:6; 44:24; 46:10; 55:11 AS[e]; Jer. 5:3—S[1]; 6:11, 13; 13:19; 14:12, 15; 15:16; 16:4; 41:8, 15; Lam. 2:17; 3:22—AB; 22—AB; 22—AB; 4:11; Eze. 4:6, 8; 5:12, 13; 13; 6:12, 12; 7:8, 15

Eze. 11:15; 13:14, 15; 16:14; 20:8; 21—A; 22:12, 13; 31; 23:32; 42:15; 43:23; Dan. 4:30

Dan. 9:24; 11:16 A[e]; 36; 12:7; Hos. 13:2; Joel 2:8; Amos 7:2; Mic. 2:1; Nah. 2:1; Zec. 5:4; Mal. 3:9

[a] pro συμπολεμέω. [b] pro ἐκτελέω. [c] pro παύω. [d] pro συντέμνω. [e] pro τελεω.

συντέμνω.

Isa. 10:22, 23; 28:22[a]

Dan. 9:24, 26

[a] A συντελέω.

συντηρέω.

Pro. 15:4; Eze. 18:19

Dan. 7:28 A[a]

[a] pro διατηρέω.

συντίθημι.

1 Sa. 22:13; 1 Ki. 16 p 28—A.

Dan. 2:9

συντίμησις.

Lev. 27:4, 18; Nu. 18:16; 2 Ki. 12:4—A

2 Ki. 12:4; 23:35

συντόμως.

Pro. 13:23

Pro. 23:28

συντρέπω.

1 Kings 16:9

συντρέχω.

Psalm 49:18

συντριβή.

Pro. 6:15; 10:14, 15; 29; 14:28; 16:18; 17:16; 18:7, 12; Isa. 13:6; 65:14; Jer. 4:6

Jer 6:1; 27:22; 28:54; Lam. 2:13; 3:46; Eze. 21:6; Hos. 13:13; Amos 6:6; Nah. 3:19

συντρίβω.

Gen. 19:9; 49:24; Exo. 9:25; 12:10, 46; 15:3, 7; 22:10, 14; 23:24, 24; 32:19; 34:1, 13; Lev. 6:28; 11:33; 15:12; 22:22; 26:13, 19; Nu. 9:12; Deu. 1:42; 7:5; 9:17; 21 A[a]; 10:2; 12:3; 28:7; 33:20; Jos. 7:5; 10:10, 12; 12

Jud. 2:2; 7:20; 14:6[b], 6[b]; 1 Sa. 4:18; 1 Ki. 13:26+A; 28—A; 16 p 28—A; 19:11; 21:37; 22:49 A; 2 Ki. 1:18; 11:18; 18:4; 23:14, 15; 25:13; 2 Ch. 14:3, 13; 20:37; 31:1; 34:4; Neh. 2:13, 15; 4:10; Job 24:20; 29:17; 31:22; 38:11, 15; Psa. 2:9

Psa. 3: 8
9:30
28: 5, 5
33:19, 21
36:15, 17
45:10
47: 8
50:19, 19
57: 7
73:13, 14[c]
75: 4
104:16, 33
106:16
123: 7
146: 3
Pro. 6:16
17:10
24·23
25:15
26:10
Ecc. 12: 6[d], 6
Isa. 1:28
8:15
10:33
13:18
14: 5, 12
29
21: 9
28:13
38:13
42: 3, 13
45: 2
46: 1
57:15
59: 5
61: 1
Jer. 2:13, 20
5: 5
13:17
14:17
17:18
19:10, 11
11
22·20
23: 9, 9
25:14

Jer. 27:23
28: 8, 30
31: 4, 17
20, 25
38[e]
35: 2, 4
10, 11
12, 13
37: 8
50:13
52:17
Lam. 1:15
2: 7, 9
3: 4
Eze. 4:16
5:16
6: 4, 6
7:11
14:13
26: 2
27:26, 34
29: 7
30: 8, 18
21, 22
22+A
31:12
32:12
28+A
34: 4, 16
27
Dan. 2:42
8: 7, 8
22, 25
11: 4, 20
22, 26
40
Hos. 1: 5
2:18
Joel 2: 6
Amos 1: 5
Jon. 1: 4[f]
Mic. 4: 6, 7
Nah. 1:13
Zeph. 3:18
Zec. 11:16

[a] pro συγκόπτω. [b] A διασπάω.
[c] S συνθλάω. [d] AS συνθλίβω.
[e] S[1] συστρέφω. [f] AS[3] διαλύω.

σύντριμμα.

Lev. 21:19, 19
24·20, 20
Nu. 32:14[a]
2 Sa. 15:12[b]
Job 9:17
Psa. 13: 3—A
59: 4
146: 3
Pro. 20:30
23:29
Isa. 15: 5
22: 4
28:12
30:14, 26
51:19

Isa. 59: 7
60:18
Jer. 3:22—A
6:14
8:21
10:19
14:17
17:18
31: 3, 5
37:12
Lam. 2:11
3:47
4:10
Amos 9: 9

[a] AB σύστρεμμα. [b] A σύστρεμμα

συντριμμός.

2 Sa. 22: 5
Jer. 4:20
Amos 5: 9

Mic. 2: 8
Zeph. 1:10

σύντριψις.

Joshua 10:10

σύντροφος.

1 Ki. 12 p 24 // 63, 64, 68

συντροχάζω.

Ecclesiastes 12: 6

συνυφαίνω.

Exo. 28:28
Exo. 36:10, 17

συνυφή.

Exodus 36:28—B

συνωμότης.

Genesis 14:13

συνωρίς.

Isaiah 21: 9 ABS[2 a]

[a] pro ξυνωρίς.

σύριγμα, —μός, συρισμός.

Jud. 5:16
2 Ch. 29: 8
Jer. 18:16, 19:8

Jer. 25: 9
32: 4
Mic. 6:16

σύριγξ.

Daniel 3: 5, 7, 10, 15

συρίζω.

1 Ki. 9: 8
Job 27:23
Isa. 5:26
7:18
Jer. 19: 8
26:22

Jer. 27:13
29:18
Lam. 2:15, 16
Eze. 27:36
Zeph. (2)15

συρισμός vide σύριγμα.

Συριστί.

2 Ki. 18:26
Ezra 4: 7

Isa. 36:11
Dan. 2: 4

συρράπτω.

Job 14:12[a]
Eze. 13:18

[a] A παλαιόω.

συρρέμβομαι.

Proverbs 13:20 A[a]

[a] pro συμπορεύομαι.

σύρω.

Deu. 32:24
2 Sa. 17:13
Isa. 3:16

Isa. 28: 2
30·28
Mic. 7:17

συσκευάζω.

Exodus 3:22 A[a]

[a] pro σκυλεύω.

συσκήνιος.

Exodus 16:16[a]

[a] A σύσκηνος.

σύσκηνος.

Exo. 3:22
Exo. 16:16 A[a]

[a] pro συσκήνιος.

συσκιάζω.

Exo. 25:19
Nu. 4: 5

Hos. 4:13

σύσκιος.

1 Ki. 14:23
Cant. 1:16

Eze. 6:13

συσκοτάζω.

1 Ki. 18:45
Jer. 4:28
13:16
Eze. 30:18
32: 7, 8
Joel 2:1

Joel 3:15
Amos 5: 8
8: 9
Mic. 3: 6
6:14[a]

[a] AB σκοτάζω.

συσπάω.

Lamentations 5:10

συσσεισμός.

1 Ki. 19:11, 11
12
2 Ki. 2: 1, 11
1 Ch. 14:15

Jer. 23:19
Nah. 1: 3
Zec. 14: 5[a]

[a] ABS σεισμός.

συσσείω.

Job 4:14 A[a] S[a]
Psa. 28: 8, 8

Psa. 59: 4
Hag. 2: 7

[a] pro διασείω.

σύσσημος, —ον.

Jud. 20:38[a]
40[a]
Isa. 5:26

Isa. 49:22
62:10

[a] A πύργος.

σύστασις.

Genesis 49: 6

συστέλλω.

Jud. 8:28[a]
Jud. 11:33[a]

[a] A ἐντρέπω.

σύστημα, —τεμα.

Gen. 1:10
2 Sa. 23:15
1 Ch. 11:16[a]

Jer. 28:32
Eze. 31: 4

[a] A ὑπόστεμα.

συστράτευμα.

2 Kings 14:19 A[a]

[a] pro σύστρεμμα.

σύστρεμμα.

Nu. 32:14 AB[a]
2 Sa. 4: 2
15:12 A[a]
1 Ki. 11:14

2 Ki. 14:19[b]
15:30[c]
Ezra 8: 3

[a] pro σύντριμμα.
[b] A συστράτευμα. [c] B στρέμμα.

συστρέφω.

Gen. 43:29
Jud. 11: 3[a]
12: 4[b]
2 Sa. 15:31
1 Ki. 16:16
2 Ki. 9:14
10: 9
14:19
15:10, 15

2 Ki. 15:25, 30
21:23, 24
Pro. 24:27
Isa. 33:18 AS[c]
Jer. 23:19
31:38 S[1 d]
Eze. 1:13
13:20
Mic. 1: 7

[a] A συλλέγω. [b] A συναθροίζω.
[c] pro τρίφω. [d] pro συντρίβω.

συστροφή.

Jud. 14: 8 A[a]
2 Ki. 15:15
Psa. 63: 3
Jer. 4:16

Eze. 13:21
Hos. 4:19
13:12
Amos 7:10

[a] pro συναγωγή

συσφίγγω.

Exo. 36:29
Lev. 8: 7

Deu. 15: 7
1 Ki. 18:46

σφαγή.

Job 10:16
21:20
27:14
Psa. 43:23
Pro. 7:22

Isa. 34: 2, 6
53: 7
65:12
Jer. 12: 3
15: 3

Jer. 19: 6
27:27
28:40
31:15

Jer. 32:20
Eze. 21:15
Obad. 10
Zec. 11: 4, 7

σφάγιον.

Lev. 22:23
Eze. 21:10, 15

Eze. 21:28
Amos 5:25

σφάζω vide σφάττω.

σφαιρωτήρ.

Gen. 14:23 A[a]
Exo. 25:30, 32

Exo. 25:33, 34
34, 36

[a] pro σφυρωτήρ.

σφακελίζω.

Lev. 26:16
Deu. 28:32

σφαλερός.

Proverbs 5: 6

σφάλλω.

Deu. 32:35
2 Sa. 22:46
Job 18: 7

Job 21:10
Amos 5: 2

σφάλμα.

Proverbs 29:25

σφάττω, σφάζω.

Gen. 22:10
37:31
43:15
Exo. 12: 6
22: 1
29:11—A
16, 20
34:25
Lev. 1: 5, 11
3: 2, 8, 13
4: 4, 15
24, 24
29, 29
33, 33
6:25, 25
32, 32
8:15, 19
23
9: 8, 12
15, 18
14: 5, 6, 13
13, 19
25, 50
51
16:11, 15
17: 3, 3, 4
5
22:28

Nu. 11:22
32 B[a]
19: 3
Deu. 28:31
Jud. 12: 6 A[b]
1 Sa. 1·24, 25
14:32, 34
34
15:33
1 Ki. 18:40
2 Ki. 10: 7, 14
25: 7
Ezra 6:20
Psa. 36:14
Pro. 9: 2
Isa. 14 21
22:13
57: 5
Jer. 19: 7
48: 7
52:10, 10
Eze. 16:21
21:10, 10
23:39
34: 3
40:39, 41
42
44:11

[a] pro ψύχω. [b] pro θύω.

σφενδονάω, —νέω.

1 Sa. 17:49
1 Sa. 25:29

σφενδόνη.

1 Sa. 17:40
50 A
25:29

2 Ch. 26:14
Pro. 26: 8
Zec. 9:15

σφενδονήτης, —ήστης

Jud. 20:16
2 Ki. 3:25

1 Ch. 12: 2

σφηκιά.

Exo. 23:28
Deu. 7:20

Jos. 24:12

σφηνόω.

Jud. 3:23, 24[a]
Neh. 7: 3

[a] A ἀποκλείω.

σφίγγω.

2 Ki.12:10 | Pro. 5:22

σφόδρα.

Gen. 7:19[2a]
17: 6−A
29:17−A
Exo. 9:24+A
Deu. 9:20+A
28:56+A
Jos. 3:16−A[1]
6:18−A
22: 8+A
Ruth 1:13+A
1 Sa. 17:24 A
18:30 A
2 Sa. 12: 5+A

2 Sa. 13:36−B
1 Ki. 3: 1−AB
7:34+A
34+A
2 Ki.10: 4+A
Est. 2: 7+S[3]
Psa. 6:11[1]−S[2]
36:23+A
111: 1−A[1]
118:156+S[1]
Jer. 31:20 A[b]
Eze. 16:13+A
47: 7−A

[a] A σφοδρῶς. [b] pro λίαν.

σφοδρός.

Exo. 10:19
15:10

Neh. 9:11

σφοδρῶς.

Gen. 7:19 A[a] | Jos. 3:16−A[1]

[a] pro σφόδρα.

σφόνδυλος.

Leviticus 5: 8

σφραγίζω.

Deu. 32:34
1 Ki.20: 8
2 Ki.22: 4
Neh.10: 1
Est. 3:10
8: 8,8,10
Job 14:17
24:16
Cant. 4:12

Isa. 8:16
29:11,11
Jer. 39:10[a],11
25,44
Dan. 6:17
8:26
9:24,24
12: 4,9

[a] AS διασφραγίζω.

σφραγίς.

Exo. 28:11,21
32
35:22
36:13,21

Exo. 36:39
1 Ki.20: 8
Cant. 8: 6,6
Hag. 2:23

σφῦρα.

Jud. 4:21
5:26[a]
1 Ki. 6:11
Job 41:20

Isa. 41: 7
Jer. 10: 4
27:23

[a] A ἀποτομή.

σφυροκοπέω.

Judges 5:26[a]

[a] A ἀποτέμνω.

σφυροκόπος.

Genesis 4:22

σφυρωτήρ.

Genesis 14:23[a]

[a] A σφαιρωτήρ.

σχάζω, σχάω.

Amos 3: 5[a]

[a] (A[1] χασθήσεται.)

σχεδία.

1 Ki. 5: 9 | 2 Ch. 2:16

σχῆμα.

Isaiah 3:17

σχίδαξ.

1 Kings 18:33,33,34,38

σχίζα.

1 Sa. 20:20,21
21,22
36,36

1 Sa. 20:37,38
38,38

σχίζω.

Gen. 22: 3
Exo. 14:21[a]
1 Sa. 6:14
Ecc. 10: 9

Isa. 36:22
37: 1
48:21
Zec. 14: 4−A

[a] A διασχίζω.

σχισμή.

Isa. 2:18,21 | Jon. 2: 6

σχιστός.

Isaiah 19: 9

σχοινίον.

2 Sa. 8: 2
17:13
1 Ki.21:31,32
Est. 1: 6
Job 18:10
36: 8
40:12+A
Psa. 15: 6
77:55
118:61
139: 6

Ecc. 12: 6
Isa. 3:23
5:18
33:20,23
Jer. 45:11,12
13
Eze. 27:24
Amos 2: 8
7:17
Mic. 2: 4,5
Zec. 2: 1

σχοίνισμα.

Deu. 32: 9
Jos. 17:14
19:29+A
2 Sa. 8: 2
2−A
1 Ki. 4:13

1 Ch.16:18
Ps. 104:11
Isa. 34: 2
Eze. 47:13
Zeph. 2: 5,7
Zec. 11: 7,14

σχοινισμός.

Joshua 17: 5

σχοῖνος.

Ps. 138: 3
Jer. 8: 8
18:15

Joel 3:18
Mic. 6: 5

σκολάζω.

Exo. 5: 8,17 | Psa. 45:11

σχολαστής.

Exodus 5:17

σχολή.

Gen. 33:14 | Pro. 28:19

σώζω.

Gen. 19:17 ter
20 A[a]
22
32: 8,30
47:25
Nu. 24:19
Deu. 33:29
Jos. 8:22
10:33,40[b]
Jud. 2:16,18
3: 9,31
6:14,15
31,36
37
7: 2,7
8:22
10: 1,12
13,14
12: 2,3 A[c]
13: 5
1 Sa. 4: 3
7: 8
9:16

1 Sa. 10: 1,27
11: 3
14: 6,23
39,47
17:47
19:11,12
18 A[a]
23: 2[d],5
25:26,31
33
27: 1,1
30:17[e]
2 Sa. 3:18
8: 6,14
10:11,19
14: 4,4
22: 3,4,28
1 Ki.13:31
18:40
19:17
17−A
21:20
2 Ki. 6:26,27

2 Ki. 6:27
14:27
16: 7
19:19
34+A
37[b]
20: 6
1 Ch.11:14
16:35
18: 6,13
19:12
2 Ch.14:11
16: 7
18:31
20: 9,24
32: 8,11
13,14
14,15
15,22
33: 7 A[f]
Ezra 8:22
Neh. 1: 2
9:27
Est. 4:11,13
8: 6
Job 1:15,16
17,19
6:23
18:19
20:20,24
22:29
27: 8
33:28
35:14
40: 9
Psa. 3: 8
6: 5
7: 2,3,11
11: 2
16: 7
17: 4,28
42
19: 7,10
21: 6,9,22
27: 9
29: 4
30: 3,8,17
32:16,16
17
33: 7,19
35: 7
36:40
43: 4,7,8
53: 3
54: 9
55: 8
56: 4
58: 3
59: 7
67:21
68: 2,15
69: 1
70: 2,3
71: 4,13
75:10
79: 3,4,8
20
85: 2,16
97: 1
105: 8,10
21,47
106:13,19
107: 7
108:26,31
114: 6
117:25
118:94,117
146,173
137: 7
144:19
Pro. 6: 3,5

Pro. 10:25
11:31
15:24,27
19: 7
28:26
29:25
Isa. 1:27
10:20,22
12: 2+
6*S
14:32
15: 7
19:20,20
20: 6,6
25: 9−AS
30:15
31: 5
33:22
34:15
35: 4
37:20,32
35
38: 6 AS[g]
43: 3,11
12
45:17,20
20,22
46: 2,4,7
47:13
49:24,25
51:14
59: 1
60:16
63: 9
66:19
Jer. 2:27,28
4:14
11:12−S[1]
14: 8,9
15:20
17:14−A[1]
14−A[1]
23: 6
26:27
31: 6,8,19
37: 8
38: 7
39: 4−S[1]
41: 3
45:18,23
46:17,18
18
48:15
49:11,17
51:14,28
Lam. 2:13
4:18
Eze. 14:14,16
16,18
17:15 A[a]
18
33:12
34:22
36:29
Dan.12: 1
Hos. 1: 7,7
13: 4
14: 3
Joel 2:32
Amos 2:14−A
15
Obad. 21 A[h]
Mic. 6: 9
Hab. 1: 2
3:13
Zeph. 3:17,19
Zec. 8: 7[i]
9: 9,16
10: 6
12: 7[k]
Mal. 3:15

[a] pro διασώζω. [b] A διασώζω.
[c] pro σωτήρ. [d] B πατάσσω.
[e] A περισώζω. [f] pro τίθημι.
[g] pro ῥύομαι. [h] pro ἀ ασώζω.
[i] A ἀνασώζω. [k] A δίδωμι.

σῶμα.

Gen. 15:11 | Gen. 34:29

Gen. 36: 6
47:12,18
Lev. 6:10
14: 9
15: 2,3,3
3,3,11
13,16
19,21
27
16: 4,24
26,28
17:16
19:28
22: 6
Nu. 8: 7
19: 7,8
Deu. 21:23
23:11
Jos. 8:29
1 Sa. 31:10,12
12
1 Ki.13:22,24
24,28
28,28
29−A
14: 9 A
20:27−A
2 Ki.19:35
1 Ch.10:12,12
28: 1

Neh. 9:26
37−S[1]
Est. 9:14−S[1]
Job 3:17
6: 4[a]
7: 5
15 A[b]
13:12
18:13 A[c]
19:26 AS[2d]
20:25
33:17,24
36:28
37: 4+C
40:27
41:14−S
Psa. 39: 7
Pro. 3: 8
5:11
11:17
25:20
Isa. 37:36
Eze. 1:11,23
23:35
Dan. 3:27,28
4:30
5:21
7:11
10: 6
Nah. 3: 3

[a] S στόμα. [b] pro ὀστέον.
[c] pro νύξ. [d] pro δέρμα.

σωματοποιέω.

Ezekiel 34: 4

σωρεύω.

Proverbs 25:22

σωρήκ, −ρήχ.

Isaiah 5: 2

σωρός.

Jos. 7:26
8:29
2 Sa. 18:17
2 Ch.31: 6

2 Ch.31: 6−B
7,8,9
Job 21:32[a]

[a] A σορός.

σωτήρ.

Deu. 32:15
Jud. 3: 9,15
12: 3[a]
1 Sa. 10:19
1 Ch.16:35 S[1 b]
Neh. 9:27[c]
Psa. 23: 5
24: 5
26: 1,9
61: 3,7
64: 6

Psa. 78: 9
94: 1
Pro. 29:25 S[d]
Isa. 12: 2
17:10
45:15−B
21
22+A[3]
62:11
Mic. 7: 7
Hab. 3:18

[a] A σώζω. [b] pro σωτηρία.
[c] AS σωτηρία. [d] pro δεσπότης

σωτηρία.

Gen. 26:31
28:21
41:17
49:18
Exo. 14:13
15: 2
Jud. 15:18
1 Sa. 2: 1
11: 9,13
14:45
19: 5
2 Sa. 10:11
15:14
19: 2
22: 3,3,36
47,51
23: 5,10
12
2 Ki. 5: 1

2 Ki.13: 5,17
17
1 Ch.11:14
16:23[a]
35[b]
19:12
2 Ch. 6:41
12: 7
20:17
Ezra 9: 8,13
Neh. 9:27 AS[c]
Est. 4:11
Job 2: 9
5: 4
11:20
13:16
20:20
30:15,22
Psa. 3: 3,9

Psa. 17: 3, 36
47, 51
19: 7
21: 2
27: 8
32:17
34: 3
36:39
37:23
43: 5
50:16
59:13
67:20
68:14, 30
70:15
73:12
84: 5
87: 2
88:27
107:13
117:14, 15
21, 28
118:155
131:16
139: 8
143:10

Ps. 145: 3
149: 4
Pro. 2: 7
11:14
Isa. 12: 1+S[1]
2
25: 9
26:18
33: 2, 6
38:20
45:17
46:13, 13
47:15
49: 6, 8
52: 7, 10
59:11
63: 1 S[1] [d]
8
Jer. 3:23
32:21
37: 6
38:22, 22
Dan. 11:42
Obad. 17
Hab. 3: 8, 13

[a] AS σωτήριος.
[b] S[1] σωτήρ.
[c] pro σωτήρ.
[d] pro σωτήριος.

σωτήριος, -ον.

Gen. 41:16
Exo. 20:24
24: 5
29:28
32: 6
Lev. 3: 1, 3, 6
9
4:10, 26
31, 35
6:12
7: 1, 3, 4
5, 10
11, 19
19, 22
23, 24
27
9: 4, 18
22
10:14
17: 4, 5
19: 5
22:21
23:19
Nu. 6:14, 17
18
7:17, 23
29, 35
41, 47
53, 59
65, 71
77, 83
88
10:10
15: 8
29:39
Deu. 27: 7[a]
Jos. 9: 4
22:23, 27
29
Jud. 20:26 A[b]
21: 4 A[b]
1 Ch. 16: 1, 2
23 AS[c]
21:26
2 Ch. 7: 7
29:35
30:22
31: 2

2 Ch. 33:16
Psa. 9:15
11: 6
12: 6
13: 7
19: 6
20: 2, 6
34: 9
39:11, 17
41: 6, 12
42: 5
49:23
50:14
52: 7
61: 2, 8
66: 3
69: 5
77:22
84: 8, 10
90:16
95: 2
97: 2, 3
105: 4
115: 4
118:41, 81
123, 166
174
Isa. 12: 3
26: 1
33:20
38:11
11 – AS
40: 5
51: 5, 6, 8
56: 1
59:17
60: 6, 18
61:10
62: 1
63: 1[d]
Lam. 3:26
Eze. 43:27
45:15, 17
46: 2, 12
12
Amos 5:22
Jon. 2:10

[a] A θυσιαστήριον.
[b] pro τέλειος.
[c] pro σωτηρία.
[d] S[1] σωτηρία.

σωφέρ.

1 Chronicles 15:28

τάγμα.

Nu. 2: 2, 3, 10
17 A[a]
18, 25
31, 34
10:14, 18

Nu. 10:22, 25
1 Sa. 4:10
15: 4, 4
2 Sa. 23:13

[a] pro ἡγεμονία.

ταινία.

Ezekiel 27: 5

τακτικός.

Daniel 6: 2, 4, 5, 6

τακτός.

Job 12: 5

ταλαιπωρέω.

Psa. 16: 9
37: 7
Isa. 33: 1
Jer. 4:13, 20
20
9:19

Jer. 10:20
12:12
Hos. 10: 2
Joel 1:10, 10
Mic. 2: 4
Zec. 11: 2, 3, 3

ταλαιπωρία.

Job 5:21 + A
21 + A
30: 3
Psa. 11: 6
13: 3 – A
31: 4
39: 3
68:21
87:19
139:11
Isa. 16: 4 + A
47:11
59: 7
60:18

Jer. 4:20
6: 7, 26
15: 8
20: 8
28:35, 56
Eze. 45: 9
Hos. 9: 6
Joel 1:15, 15
Amos 3:10
6: 9
Mic. 2: 4
Hab. 1: 3
2:17
Zeph. 1:15 S[3] [a]

[a] pro ἀωρία.

ταλαίπωρος.

Jud. 5:27 A[a]
Ps. 136: 8

Isa. 33: 1

[a] pro ἐξοδεύω.

τάλαντον.

Exo. 25:39
39: 1, 2, 4
5, 5, 7
2 Sa. 12:30
1 Ki. 9:14, 28
10:10, 14
16:24
21:39
2 Ki. 5: 5, 22
23 – B[b]
15:19
18:14, 14
23:33, 33
1 Ch. 19: 6
20: 2
22:14, 14

1 Ch. 29: 4, 4, 7
7, 7, 7
2 Ch. 3: 8
8:18
9: 9, 13
25: 6, 9
27: 5
36: 3, 3
Ezra 7:22
8:26, 26
Est. 1: 7
3: 9
4: 7
Zec. 5: 7
7 A[b]

[a] A διτάλαντος.
[b] pro μέτρον.

τάλας.

Isaiah 6: 5

ταμεῖον, ταμιεῖον.

Gen. 43:29
Exo. 8: 3
Deu. 28: 8
32:25
Jud. 3:24 – A
15: 1[a]
16: 9, 12
2 Sa. 13:10
1 Ki. 1:15
21:30
22:25, 25

2 Ki. 6:12
9: 2, 2
11: 2
2 Ch. 18:24, 24
22:11
Job 9: 9
37: 8
Ps. 104:30
143:13
Pro. 3:10
7:27

Pro. 20:27, 30
24: 4
26:22
Ecc. 10:20
Cant. 1: 4

Cant. 3: 4
8: 2
Isa. 26:20
42:22
Eze. 28:16

[a] A κοιτών.

ταμίας.

Isaiah 22:15[a]

[a] A γραμματεύς.

ταμιεύομαι.

Proverbs 29:11

τανύω.

Job 9: 8

τάξις.

Nu. 1:52
Jud. 5:20 A[a]
1 Ki. 7:23
Job 16: 3
24: 5[b]
28: 3
36:28

Job 37: 4 + C
38:12
Ps. 109: 4
Pro. 29:43
Dan. 9:26
27 + AB[2]
Hab. 3:11

[a] pro τρίβος.
[b] AS[2] πράξις.

ταπεινός.

Lev. 13: 3, 4
20, 21
25, 26
14:37
27: 8
Jos. 11:16[a]
Jud. 1:15
6:15 A[b]
1 Sa. 18:23
Job 5:11
12:21
Psa. 9:39
17:28
33:19
81: 3
101:18[c]
112: 6
137: 6
Pro. 3:34
11: 2
16: 1 + AS[2]
2
24:37[d]

Ecc. 10: 6
Isa. 2:11
11: 4, 4[e]
14:32
18: 7 + S
25: 4
26: 6
32: 7, 7
49:13
54:11
58: 4
61: 1 S[1] [f]
66: 2
Jer. 22:16
Eze. 17:21
21:26
29:14
Amos 2: 7
8: 6 AB[g]
Hab. 1: 6 S[1] [h]
Zeph. 2: 3
3:12

[a] A πεδινός.
[b] pro ασθενέω.
[c] S[1] πτωχός.
[d] C ἀσθενής.
[e] S ἔνδοξος.
[f] pro πτωχός.
[g] pro πενης.
[h] pro ταχινός.

ταπεινοφρονέω.

Psalm 130: 2

ταπεινοφροσύνη.

Proverbs 16:19 C[a]

[a] pro ταπείνωσις.

ταπεινόφρων.

Proverbs 29:23

ταπεινόω.

Gen. 15:13
16: 9
31:50
34: 2
Exo. 1:12
Lev. 16:29, 31
23:27, 29
32
25:39
Deu. 21:14
22:24, 29
26: 6
Jud. 4:23 A[a]
5:13 + A

Jud. 12: 2 + A
16: 5, 6, 19
19:24
20: 5
Ruth 1:21
1 Sa. 2: 7
7:13
12: 8
26: 9[b]
2 Sa. 7:10
13:12, 14
22, 32
22:28
1 Ki. 8:35

1 Ch. 4:10
17: 9, 10
20: 4
2 Ch. 6:26
13:18
28:19
32:26
33:12, 23
23
34:27, 27
Ezra 8:21
Est. 6:13
Job 22:12, 23
29
24: 9
31:10
34:25
40: 6
Psa. 9:31
17:28
34:13, 14
37: 9
38: 3
43:20, 26
50:10, 19
54:20
71: 4
73:21
74: 8
80:15
87:16
88:11
89:15
93: 5
104:18
105:42, 43
106:12, 17
114: 6
115: 1
118:67, 71
75, 107
141: 7
142: 3
146: 6
Pro. 10: 4

Pro. 13: 7
18:12
25: 7
29:23
Ecc. 10:18
19 –
ACS[2]
12: 4
Isa. 1:25 + A
2: 9, 11
12, 17
3: 8, 17
25
5:15, 15
10:33
13:11
25:11, 11
12
26: 5
29: 4
40: 4
51:21, 23
57: 9
58: 3, 5, 10
60:14
64:12
Jer. 13:18
38:37
Lam. 1: 5, 8, 12
2: 5, 5
3:31, 32
33
5:11
Eze. 17:24
21:26
22:10, 11
Dan. 4:34
5:19, 22
7:24
11:30
Hos. 2:15
5: 5
7:10
14: 8
Mal. 2:12

[a] pro τροπόω.
[b] A διαφθείρω.

ταπείνωσις.

Gen. 16:11
29:32
31:42
41:52
Deu. 26: 7
1 Sa. 1:11
9:16
2 Sa. 16:12
2 Ki. 14:26
Ezra 9: 5
Neh. 9: 9[a]
Est. 4: 8
Psa. 9:14

Psa. 21:22
24:18
30: 8
89: 3
118:50, 92
153
135:23 – S[1]
Pro. 16:19[b]
Isa. 40: 2
53: 8
Jer. 2:24
Lam. 1: 3, 7, 9

[a] S[3] κακία.
[b] C ταπεινοφροσύνη.

ταράσσω.

Gen. 19:16
40: 6
41: 8
42:28
43:29
45: 3
Deu. 2:25
Jud. 11:35 – A
Ruth 3: 8
1 Sa. 14:16
2 Sa. 18:33
22: 8
8 A[a]
8 A[b]
1 Ki. 3:26
20: 4 – A
5
1 Ch. 29:11
Est. 3:15
4: 4
7: 6
Job 8: 3
19: 6

Job 34:10, 12
36:34
Psa. 2: 5
6: 3, 4, 8
11
17: 8
29: 8
30:10, 11
37:11
38: 7
12 – AS
41: 7
45: 3, 4, 4
7
47: 6
54: 3, 5
56: 5
63: 9
64: 8
67: 6
75: 6
76: 5, 17
82:16, 18

Psa. 87:17 B[e]
89: 7
103:29
106:27
108:22
118:60
142: 4
Pro. 12:25
Ecc. 10:10
Isa. 3:12
8:12
13: 8
14:31
17:12
19: 3
24:14, 19
30:28
51:15
64: 2
Jer. 4:24
5:22
Lam. 1:20
2:11
3: 9
Eze. 26:18+A
30:16−A
32: 2, 13
34:18, 19
Dan. 4: 2, 2[d]
5: 9, 10
7:15
8:11 A[e]
11:44
Hos. 6: 8
Amos 8: 8
Hab. 3: 2, 15
16

[a] pro συνταράσσω.
[b] pro σπαράσσω.
[c] pro ἐκταράσσω.
[d] AB συνταράσσω. [e] pro ῥάσσω.

ταραχή.

Jud. 11:35−A
Psa. 30:21
Pro. 6:14
26:21
Isa. 22: 5
24:19
52:12
Jer. 14:19
Lam. 3:58
Eze. 23:46
30: 4, 9
16−A
Hos. 5:12

τάραχος.

Jud. 11:35−A
1 Sa. 5: 9
Job 24:17

ταραχώδης.

Psalm 90: 3

ταρσός.

Daniel 10:10+A

τάρταρος.

Job 40:15
41:23
Pro. 24:51+ ABCS

τάσσω.

Gen. 3:24
Exo. 8: 9, 12
29:43
Jud. 18:31 A[a]
20:30 A[b]
36 A[a]
1 Sa. 20:35
22: 7
2 Sa. 7:11
20: 5
23:23
1 Ki. 2: 5
2 Ki. 10:24, 27[c]
12:17
1 Ch. 16: 4, 7
17:10
2 Ch. 31: 2
Est. 1: 6 S[1d]
Job 14:13
30:22
31:24
36:13
Cant. 2: 4
6: 3, 9
Isa. 38: 1
Jer. 2:15
3:19
5:22
7:30
Jer. 10:22
11:13
18:16
19: 8 A[e]
Lam. 3:21
Eze. 4: 2
14: 4, 7
16:14
17: 5
19: 5
20:28
24: 7
40: 4
44: 5, 5
14 A[e]
Dan. 6:12
13+A
11:17
Hos. 2: 3, 14
Mic. 5: 1
Hab. 1:12
2: 9
3:19
Zeph. 1:14
Hag. 1: 5
2:18 AS[2f]
Zec. 7:12, 14
10: 3, 4
Mal. 1: 3

[a] pro τίθημι. [b] pro ἀναβαίνω
[c] B πατασσω. [d] pro τεινω.
[e] pro καταγω. [f] pro ὑποτάσσω

ταῦρος.

Gen. 32:15
49: 6
Exo. 21:28 ter
29, 29
Exo. 21:32, 32
35 quater
36 ter
Deu. 32:14
33:17
Jud. 6: 4[a]
25[b]
Psa. 21:13
Psa. 49:13
67:31
Isa. 1:11
5:17
11: 6
30:24
34: 7
Jer. 27:11

[a] A μόσχος. [b] A σιτευτός.

ταφέθ.

Jeremiah 7:31, 32, 32

ταφή.

Gen. 50: 3
Deu. 21:23
31: 6[a]
2 Ch. 26:23
Job 17: 1
Ecc. 6: 3[b]
Isa. 53: 9
Isa. 57: 2
Jer. 22:19
Eze. 32:22
23+A
23+A
Nah. 1:14

[a] A τελευτή. [b] S ἀφή.

τάφος.

Gen. 23: 4, 20
47:30
Jud. 8:32
16:31
1 Sa. 10: 2
2 Sa. 2:32
3:32
4:12
17:23[a]
19:37
21:14
1 Ki. 13:22, 30
31
14:13 A
2 Ki. 9:28
13:21
21:26
22:20[b]
23: 6, 16
16, 16
2 Ki. 23:30
2 Ch. 21:20
24:25
28:27
32:33
Neh. 3:16
Job 5:26
6:10
21:32
Psa. 5:10
13: 3−A
48:12
67: 7
87: 6, 12
Ecc. 8:10
Jer. 7:32+A
8: 1
20:17
Eze. 37:13, 13

[a] A οἶκος. [b] A τόπος.

τάφρος.

Micah 5: 6

ταχέως.

Jud. 9:48
2 Sa. 17:18, 21
2 Ki. 1:11
Est. 6:10+S[3]
Pro. 25: 8
Ecc. 4:12[a]
Isa. 8: 3
Jer. 27:44
Joel 3: 4

[a] B ταχύ.

ταχινός.

Pro. 1:16 AS[2]
Isa. 59: 7
Hab. 1: 6[a]

[a] S[1] ταπεινός.

τάχος.

Exo. 32: 7
Nu. 16:46
Deu. 7: 4, 22
9: 3−B
12
11:17
28:20
24−A
63−A
Jos. 8:18, 19
10: 6
Jud. 2:23
Jud. 7: 9+A
9:54 A[a]
1 Sa. 23:22
1 Ki. 22: 9
1 Ch. 12: 8
2 Ch. 18: 8
Psa. 2:13
6:11
147: 4[b]
Isa. 5:19
Eze. 29: 5

[a] pro ταχύ. [b] S[1] ταχύς.

ταχύ.

Gen. 27:20
Exo. 32: 8
Deu. 9:12
16+A
Jud. 2:17
9:54[a]
2 Sa. 17:16
Psa. 36: 2, 2
Psa. 68:18
78: 8
101: 3
137: 3
142: 7
Pro. 20:25
Ecc. 4:12 B[b]
8:11
Isa. 5:26
9: 1
14 a 1
32: 4
49:17
51: 5
58: 8
Jer. 29:20

[a] A τάχος. [b] pro ταχέως.

ταχύνω.

Gen. 18: 7
41:32
45:13
Exo. 2:18
Jud. 13:10
1 Sa. 9:12+A
17:48+A
20:38
1 Sa. 25:42+A
2 Sa. 15:14, 14
19:16
Psa. 15: 4
30: 3
105:13
Ecc. 5: 1

ταχύς.

Ezra 7: 6
Ps. 147: 4 S[1a]
Pro. 12:19
29:20[b]
Jer. 31:16
Nah. 1:14
Zeph. 1:14
Mal. 3: 5

[a] pro τάχος. [b] B τραχύς.

ταών.

1 Kings 10:22+A

τείνω.

1 Ch. 5:18[a]
8:40
2 Ch. 18:33[a]
Est. 1: 6[b]
Pro. 7:16
Jer. 27:14
28: 3, 3

[a] A ἐντείνω. [b] S[1] τάσσω.

τειχήρης.

Nu. 13:20
Deu. 9: 1
Jos. 19:35
1 Ki. 4:13
2 Ch. 11: 5, 10
2 Ch. 11:11[a]
14: 6
32: 1
33:14
Jer. 4: 5[b]

[a] A τεῖχος. [b] A ὀχυρός.

τειχίζω.

Lev. 25:29
Nu. 13:29
32:17
Deu. 1:28
1 Sa. 27: 8
2 Ch. 21: 3
Eze. 17: 4
33:27
Hos. 8:14

τειχιστής.

2 Ki. 12:12
2 Ki. 22: 6

τεῖχος.

Exo. 14:22, 22
29, 29
15: 8
Lev. 25:30, 31
Nu. 35: 4
Deu. 3: 5
28:52
Jos. 6: 5, 20
1 Sa. 25:16
31:10, 12
2 Sa. 11:20, 21
21, 22
22, 22
24
18:24
20:15, 16
21
22:30
1 Ki. (3) 1
p 1
p 46+A
4:30−A
7:10 B[1a]
10 p 22
21:30
2 Ki. 3:27
6:26, 30
2 Ki. 14:13
18:26, 27
25: 4
10−B
2 Ch. 8: 5
11:11 A[b]
14: 7
25:23
26: 6, 6, 6
27: 3
32: 5, 18
33:14
36:19
Ezra 4:12, 13
16
Neh. 1: 3
2: 8, 13
15, 15
17
3: 8, 13
15, 27
4: 1, 3, 7
10, 13
15, 17
19
5:16
6: 1, 6, 15
Neh. 7: 1
12:27, 30
31
31− ABS[1]
37
38 S[3]
38 S[3]
13:21
Job 6:10
Psa. 17:30
50:20
54:11
Pro. 1:21
25:28
28: 4
Cant. 5: 7
8: 9, 10
Isa. 2:15
8: 7
15: 1
16:11
22:10, 11
24:23
26: 1
27: 3
30:13
36:11, 12
38: 2 B[c]
49:16
Isa. 56: 5
60:10, 18
62: 6
Jer. 1:15, 18
15:20
21: 4
27:15
28:12, 33[f]
58
30:16
37:18 A[e]
52: 7[f], 14
Lam. 2: 7, 8, 8
18
Eze. 26: 4, 9
10, 12
27:11
33:30
38:11, 20
40:13 A[g]
Dan 9:25[h]
Joel 2: 7, 9
Amos 1: 7, 10
12, 14
7: 7
Nah. 2: 6
8+A
3: 8
Zec. 2: 5

[a] pro χεῖλος. [b] pro τειχήρης.
[c] pro τοῖχος. [d] AB[1]S ὕψος.
[e] pro ὕψος. [f] A πύλη.
[g] pro τοῖχος. [h] A περιτειχος.

τέκνον.

Gen. 3:16
17:16
22: 7, 8
27:13, 18
20, 21
25, 26
37, 43
30: 1
31:16, 43
32:11
33: 6[a], 7
43:28
48:19
49: 3
Exo. 10: 2, 2, 2
17: 3
20: 5
34: 7, 7, 7
Lev. 25:41, 46
Nu. 14:18, 23
16:27
Deu. 2:34
3:19
5: 9
11:19
21:17
22: 6
24:18
28:54, 55
57
29:11 A[b]
29
32: 5
33:24
Jos. 14: 9
22:24, 24
27 A[c]
27, 27
28 A[d]
Jud. 18:21[e]
1 Sa. 1: 8
2: 5, 24
3: 9, 16
4:16
6: 7, 7, 10
14:32
24:17
26:17, 21
25
30:22
1 Ki. 8:25
9: 6
1 Ki. 10 p 22
12 p 24/30
14: 3 A
15: 4
17:12, 13
15
21: 3
5−B
2 Ki. 2:24+A
1 Ch. 2:30, 32
22: 7
2 Ch. 25: 4
28: 3
30: 9
33: 6
35: 7
Ezra 8:21
Neh. 12:43
Est. 7: 4
9:25
Job 5:25
21: 8
39: 4, 16
Psa. 33:12
65: 5+B[1]
77: 4
108:13
112: 9
Pro. 7: 7
14:26
17: 6, 6, 6
24:27[f], 70
70, 70
29:46
Isa. 2: 6
13:16, 18
18
14:21
27: 6
29:23
30: 1
39: 7
44: 3
51:18
54: 1, 13
57: 4, 5
60: 4, 9
63: 8
Jer. 2:30
3:19[g]
19: 2
38:17, 29

Jer. 30:18, 39
42:14
45:23
Eze. 5:10, 10
16:21, 36
45, 45
18: 2
20:18, 21
23:37, 39
Hos. 1: 2
2: 4, 4
4: 6
Hos. 5: 7
9:12, 13
13
10: 9, 14
11: 1, 10
13:13
Joel 1: 3 *qtr*
2:23
Mic. 1:16
Zec. 9:13, 13
10: 7, 9

[a] A παιδίον. [b] *pro* ἔκγονος.
[c] *pro* γενεά. [d] *pro* υἱός.
[e] A παροικεία. [f] A[3] υἱός.
[g] B ἔθνος.

τεκνοποιέω.

Gen. 11:30
16: 2
30: 3
Isa. 65:23[a]
Jer. 12: 2
36: 6
38: 8

[a] A τέκνα ποιήσουσιν.

τεκταίνω.

Ps. 128: 3
Pro. 3:29
6:14, 18
11:27
Pro. 12:20
14:22, 22
26:24
Eze. 21:31

τεκτονικός.

Exodus 31: 5

τέκτων.

1 Sa. 13:19
2 Sa. 5:11, 11
1 Ki. 7: 2
2 Ki. 12:11
22: 6
24:14, 16
1 Ch. 4:14
14: 1
22:15
2 Ch. 24:12
2 Ch. 34:11
Ezra 3: 7
Pro. 14:22, 22
Isa. 40:19, 20
41: 7
44:12, 13
Jer. 10: 3
Hos. 8: 6
13: 2
Zec. 1:20

τελαμών.

1 Kings 21:38, 41

τέλειος.

Gen. 6: 9
Exo. 12: 5
Deu. 18:13
Jud. 20:26[a]
21: 4[a]
1 Sa. 17:40 B[b]
2 Sa. 22:26
1 Ki. 8:61
11: 3
1 Ki. 11:10 − A
15: 3, 14
1 Ch. 25: 8
28: 9
Ezra 2:63
Ps. 138:22
Cant. 5: 2
6: 8
Jer. 13:19

[a] A σωτήριος. [b] *pro* λεῖος.

τελειότης.

Jud. 9:16, 19
Pro. 11: 3 A
Jer. 2: 2 S[a]

[a] *pro* τελείωσις.

τελειόω.

Exo. 29: 9, 29
33, 35
Lev. 4: 5
8:33
16:32
21:10
Nu. 3: 3
2 Sa. 22:26
1 Ki. 7: 7 + A
14:10 A
2 Ch. 8:16 A[a]
16
Neh. 6: 3, 16
Eze. 27:11

[a] *pro* θεμελιόω.

τελείωσις.

Exo. 29:22, 26
27, 31
34
Lev. 7:27
8:22, 26
Lev. 8:28, 29
31, 33
2 Ch. 29:35
Jer. 2: 2[a]

[a] S τελειότης.

τελεσιουργέω.

Proverbs 19: 7

τελεσφόρος.

Deuteronomy 23:17

τελετή.

1 Ki. 15:12
Amos 7: 9

τελευταῖος.

Pro. 14:12, 13
16:25
Pro. 20:21

τελευτάω.

Gen. 6:17
25:32
30: 1
44:31
50: 5 + A
16, 26
Exo. 1: 6
2:23
4:18
7:18, 21
8:13
9: 4, 6, 6
7, 19
11: 5
19:12
21:16, 17[a]
34[b], 35
36
22:10
35: 2
Lev. 16: 1, 1
21:11
24:16
Nu. 3: 4
6: 6
20: 1
35:16
Deu. 17: 6
25: 5 A[c], 6
32:50
34: 5, 7
Jos. 1: 2
24:33
Jud. 2: 8
1 Ch. 29:28
2 Ch. 13:20
16:13
24:15, 15
Job 1:19
2: 9
3:11
4:21 A[d]
12: 2
14: 8, 10
21:25
27:15
34:15
42:17
Pro. 5:23
10:21
11: 7
15:10
Isa. 66:24
Jer. 11:22
Eze. 6:12 A[e]
12
7:15
12:13
17:16
18:17
Amos 7:11, 17
9:10

[a] A θανατόω. [b] A θνήσκω.
[c] *pro* θνήσκω. [d] *pro* ξηραίνω.
[e] *pro* πίπτω.

τελευτή.

Gen. 27: 2
Deu. 31:29
33: 1
34: 6 A[a]
Jos. 1: 1
Jud. 1: 1
1 Ch. 22: 5
2 Ch. 24:17
26:21
Pro. 24:14

[a] *pro* ταφή.

τελέω, τελίσκω.

Nu. 25: 3, 5
Deu. 23:17
Ruth 2:21
3:18
2 Sa. 22:39 + A
Ezra 1: 1
5:16
6:15
Ezra 7:12
9: 1
10:17
Neh. 6:15
Ps. 105:28
Isa. 55:11[a]
Dan. 11:16[b]
Hos. 4:14

[a] AS συντελέω. [b] A συντελέω.

τέλος.

Gen. 46: 4
Lev. 27:23
Nu. 17:13
31:28, 37
38, 39
40, 41
Deu. 31:24
32: 1
Jos. 3:16
8:24
10:13, 20
Jud. 11:39
2 Sa. 15: 7
2 Sa. 24: 8
2 Ki. 8: 3
18:10
19:23 + A
1 Ch. 28: 9
29:19
2 Ch. 12:12
18: 2
31: 1
Neh. 13: 6
Est. 10: 1 + AS
Job 6: 9
14:20

Job 20: 7
23: 3, 7
Psa. 4: 1
5: 1
6: 1
8: 1
9: 1, 7, 19
19 AS[2] [a]
32
10: 1
11: 1
12: 1, 2
13: 1
15:11
17: 1
36 − S[1]
18: 1
19: 1
20: 1
21: 1
29: 1 − AS
30: 1
35: 1
36: 1 + A
37: 7
38: 1
39: 1
40: 1
41: 1
42: 1 + A
43: 1, 24
44: 1 − A
45: 1 − A
46: 1
47: 1 + A
48: 1 − A
10
49: 1 + A
50: 1
51: 1, 7
52: 1
53: 1
54: 1
55: 1
56: 1
57: 1
58: 1
Psa. 59: 1
60: 1
61: 1
63: 1
64: 1
65: 1
66: 1
67: 1, 17
68: 1
69: 1
72: 6 + S[2]
73: 1, 3, 10
11, 19
74: 1
75: 1
76: 1, 9
78: 5
79: 1
80: 1
83: 1
84: 1
87: 1 − S
88:47
102: 9
108: 1
138: 1
139: 1
Ecc. 3:11
7: 3
12:13
Isa. 19:15
62: 6
Eze. 15: 4, 5
20:40
22:30
36:10
Dan. 1:15, 18
2:34
3:19
4:31
6:26
7:26
9:26
11:13
Amos 9: 8
Hab. 1: 4
3:13 + S[2]

[a] *pro* αἰών.

τέμενος.

2 Ki. 21: 6[a]
Eze. 6: 4, 6
Hos. 8:14

[a] A θελητής, (B[1] ἐλλην.)

τέμνω.

Exo. 36:10
Lev. 25: 3, 4
2 Ki. 6: 4
Isa. 5: 6
Eze. 30:22
Dan. 2:34 A[a]
45

[a] *pro* ἀποσχίζω.

τέρας.

Exo. 4:21
7: 3, 9
11: 9, 10
15:11
Deu. 4:34
6:22
7:19
11: 3
13: 1, 2
26: 8
28:46
29: 3
34:11
1 Ki. 13: 3
3 A[a]
5
1 Ch. 16:12
2 Ch. 32:31
Neh. 9:10 − AS
Psa. 45: 9
70: 7
77:43
104: 5, 27
134: 9
Isa. 8:18
20: 3
24:16
28:29
Jer. 39:20, 21
Eze. 12: 6, 11
24:24, 27
Dan. 3:32
6:27
Joel 2:30

[a] *pro* ῥῆμα.

τερατοσκόπος.

Deu. 18:11
Zec. 3: 8

τερέβινθος, -μινθος.

Gen. 14: 6
35: 4
43:10
Jos. 17: 9
24:26
Jud. 6:11[a]
19[a]
Isa. 1:30
6:13

[a] A δρῦς.

τέρετρον.

Isaiah 44:12

τέρμα.

1 Ki. 7:23 + A, 32

τερπνός.

Psa. 80: 3
Psa. 132: 1

τερπνότης.

Psa. 15:11
Psa. 26: 4

τέρπω.

Job 39:13
Psa. 34: 9
64: 9
67: 4
Ps. 119:14
Pro. 27: 9
Zeph. 3:14 S[1] [a]
Zec. 2:10

[a] *pro* κατατέρπω.

τέρψις.

1 Ki. 8:28 + AB
Zeph. 3:17

τεσσαράκοντα.

Nu. 26:50[a]
Jud. 3:11[b]
1 Ki. 4(26) + A
1 Ki. 6: 6[c]
Eze. 29:12 − A

[a] B τριάκοντα. [b] A πεντήκοντα.
[c] A ἑξήκοντα.

τεσσαρακονταπέντε.

Gen. 18:28[1] [a]
Neh. 7:13[b]
Neh. 7:69 + AS

[a] A πέντε. [b] ABS τεσσεράκοντα.

τεσσαρακοντατρεῖς.

Ezra 2:24[a]
Neh. 7:29[b]

[a] AB τεσσαρακονταδύο.
[b] B εἰκοσιεῖς.

τεσσαρακοστός.

2 Chronicles 16:13[a]

[a] B ἔννατος τριακοστός.

τέσσαρες.

Exo. 25:25 − A
34 − A
26: 2 − A[1]
38: 3 + A
Lev. 27: 5 + B[1]
Nu. 26:27 − A
1 Sa. 17: 4[a]
1 Ki. 7:18 + A
21 + B
24 − B
10:26[b]
1 Ch. 26:17 − A
Eze. 1:16 − A[1]

[a] A ἕξ. [b] A τεσσαράκοντα.

τεσσαρεσκαιδέκατος.

1 Ki. 8:65 + A
2 Ki. 25: 1 + A
Est. 9:15[a]
16 + AS

[a] S[3] τρισκαιδέκατος.

τέταρτος.

1 Ki. 15: 8 − A
9 − A
1 Ch. 26: 2 − B
1 Ch. 26: 4 − B
11 − B
Jer. 25: 1 − S[1]

τετράγωνος.

Gen. 6:14
Exo. 27: 1
28:16
30: 2
Exo. 30:16
1 Ki. 7:17 + A
42
Eze. 41:21

Eze. 43:16
17+A
Eze. 45: 2
48:20

τετράδραχμον.

Job 42:11

τετραίνω.

2 Ki.12: 9
18:21[a]
Job 40:19
Pro. 23:27
Isa. 36: 6-ABS
41:12AS[3 b]

[a] A τρυγάω. [b] *pro* ἵστημι.

τετρακισχίλιοι.

Numbers 26:27+A

τετρακόσιοι.

Exo. 39: 7+A
7 A[a]
Nu. 1:29[b]
26:21[c]
31[d],47[d]
1 Sa. 15: 4[e]
1 Ki.18:19+A
1 Ki.18:22[2]—A
1 Ch.21: 5—B
2 Ch.25:23[f]
Ezra 1:10—A[g]
2:28[h]
Neh. 7:69+AS
Dan. 8:14[i]

[a] A 2400 *pro* 1500.
[b] A[2] πεντακόσιοι.
[c] B τριακόσιοι. [d] AB ἑξακόσιοι.
[e] A δέκα. [f] A τριακόσιοι.
[g] B ἕξ *pro* 410. [h] B διακόσιοι.
[i] AB τριακόσιοι.

τετράμηνος.

Jud. 19: 2 AB[a]
Jud. 20:47 A[b]

[a] *pro* μηνῶν τέσσαρων.
[b] *pro* τέσσαρας μῆνας.

τετράπεδος, —ποδος.

2 Ch.34:11
Jer. 52: 4

τετραπλῶς.

1 Kings 6:30

τετράπους.

Gen. 1:24
34:23
Exo. 8:16, 17
18
9: 9,9,10
Lev. 7:11
18:23, 23
20:15, 15
27:27
Nu. 35: 3—A
Job 12: 7
18: 3
35:11
40:15
41:16
Isa. 30: 6
40:16

τετράς.

Hag. 2: 1, 10
18, 20
Zec. 1: 7
7: 1

τετράστιχος.

Exo. 28:17
Exo. 36:17

τεχνάζω.

Isaiah 46: 5

τέχνη.

Exo. 28:11
30:25
1 Ki. 7: 2
1 Ch.28:21

τεχνίτης.

Deu. 27:15
2 Ki.12:12+A
1 Ch.22:15
29: 5
Cant. 7: 1
Jer. 10: 9
24: 1
36: 2

τήγανον.

Lev. 2: 5
6:21, 39
2 Sa. 6:19
13: 9
1 Ch. 9:31
23:20
Eze. 4: 3

τήκω.

Exo. 15:15
16:21
Lev. 26:39
Deu. 28:65
32:24
Jos. 5: 1[a]
Jud. 15:14[b]
2 Sa. 17:10, 10
Job 6:17
7: 5
11:20
17: 5
31:16A[c]
38:30AS[d]
42: 6
Psa. 21:15
57: 9
67: 3
Psa. 74: 4
96: 5
106:26
111:10
147: 7
Isa. 24:23
34: 4—AS
64: 1, 2
Jer. 6:29
Eze. 4:17 AB[1 e]
24:10[f], 11
33:10
Mic. 1: 4
Nah. 1: 6
Hab. 3: 6
6 S[1 g]
Zec. 14:12, 12

[a] A κατατήκω. [b] A διέρχομαι.
[c] *pro* ἐκτήκω. [d] *pro* πτήσσω
[e] *pro* ἐντήκω. [f] A ἐκτήκω.
[g] *pro* διατηκω.

τηλαύγημα.

Leviticus 13:23

τηλαυγής.

Lev. 13: 2, 4
19, 24
Job 37:20
Psa. 18: 9

τηλαύγησις.

Psalm 17:13

τηρέω.

Gen. 3:15, 15
1 Sa. 15:11
Ezra 8:29
Pro. 2:11
3: 1, 21
4: 6, 23
7: 5
8:34
13: 3
16: 1, 17
Pro. 19:16
23:18, 26
24:70
25:10
Ecc. 11: 4
Cant. 3: 3
7:13
8:11, 12
Jer. 20:10

τιάρα.

Eze. 23:15+A
Dan. 3:21

τίθημι.

Gen. 1:17
2: 8, 15
3:15
4:15
9:13
15:10
17: 2, 5, 6
24: 2, 9
28:11[a]
18 A[b]
30:41, 42
31:37
32:12
33: 2[c]
40: 3
41:10, 48
48
42:17, 30
47:26
48:20
50:26
Exo. 2: 3
12: 7
15:25
23:31
26:33
35 AB[d]
35
28:12—B
24
29:12[a]
30: 6, 18
36
32:27
Exo. 33:22
34:10, 12[e]
17[e],26[f]
27
40: 3—B
5
5 A[d]
6
10 A[1 d]
20AB[2 d]
22, 24
26
Lev. 10: 1 A[d]
26: 1, 11
19, 30
31
Nu. 17: 4
21: 8
24:21, 23
Deu. 14:27
26: 4
27:15
31:26
Jos. 2:18
4: 3, 18
7:23
8:28
21:42
22:25
24:31
Jud. 1:28 A[g]
4:21
21 A[h]
6:18 AB[i]
Jud. 6:19[h]
20
37[k]
7:22
8:31[a], 33
9:24[a], 25
48[a]
11:11[m]
12: 3
15: 4
16: 3[a], 3
18:21, 31[o]
19:30
20:29, 36[n]
Ruth 4:16
1 Sa. 6: 8, 8
11, 15
8:11, 12
9:20, 22
23, 24
10:25
11: 2, 11
15:19
17:40, 54
19: 5, 13
13
21:12
22:13
25:18, 25
28: 2, 21
29:10
2 Sa. 7:10, 23
8: 6, 14
14+A
10:19+B[r]
11:16
12:31
13:20, 33
14: 3,7,19
18: 3, 3
19:19, 28
20:18
22:12, 34
23: 5
7 B[o]
1 Ki. 2:15, 19
24
5: 9
6:25+A
7:25
8: 9, 21
9: 3
10: 9, 26
11:36
12:29
13:31
14:21
18:42
19: 2
21:12, 24
32, 34
34
22:27
2 Ki. 2:20
4:10, 34
4: 1 AP
8:11
9:13
10: 7, 8
11:18
13: 7
17:29, 34
18:11
19:28
21: 4, 7, 7
24:17 A[d]
1 Ch.10:10, 10
17: 9, 21
18: 6, 13
2 Ch. 1:15
3:16 AP
16[q]
4: 6[a], 7
8, 10
5:10
6, 11, 13
9:25
24: 8
31: 6
32: 6
2 Ch.33: 7, 7[r]
35: 3
36: 7
Ezra 4:19, 21
5: 3,9,13
15, 17[s]
6: 1, 3, 3
5, 8
11, 12
7:13, 21
8:17
Neh. 5:10
7:71 BS[1p]
Est. 4: 4AS[3 t]
9:24
Job 7:20
10:12
11:13
13:14, 27
14: 5
17: 6, 12
19: 8, 23
20: 4
21: 5
22:24
24:15, 25
28: 3
29: 2, 7
31: 1, 25
32: 3
33:11
34:19, 23
36:28
37: 4+C
11 AS[u]
14
38: 5, 9
10, 14
39: 6, 34
40:23
Psa. 11: 6
12: 3
16:11
17:12, 33
35
18: 6
20: 4, 10
13
32: 7
38: 2, 6
43:14
15—S[1]
45: 9
47:14
48:15
49:18, 20
51: 9
55: 9
65: 9, 11
68:12
72:9,18,28
73: 4
77: 5
5 S[1 v]
7, 13
78: 1, 2
79: 7
80: 6
82:12, 14
83: 4, 7
84:14
87: 7, 9
88:20, 26
28, 30
41
89: 8
90: 9
103: 3,9,20
104:27, 32
106:33 35
41
108: 5
109: 1
118:110
131:11
138: 5
139: 6
140: 3
147: 3
148: 6
Pro. 2:18
8:28
29+AS[2]
22:28
23:10+A
Ecc. 7:22[w]
Cant. 1: 6
6:11
8: 6
Isa. 5:20, 20
10: 6, 29
13: 9
14:13, 17
23, 23
22:18
25: 2
26: 1
27: 4, 9
28:15, 17
29: 3, 21
37:25
41: 7, 15
19
42: 4, 15
25
46: 7
49: 2, 2
6 ASP
11
50: 2
3—S[1]
4, 7
51: 3—A
10, 16
23
54:12
57: 8
60:15
63:11
Jer. 1: 5, 15
18
2: 7
4: 7
9:11
10: 5—AS
12:11[x], 11
13:16
22: 6
25:12, 17
27: 3
28:16, 29
31: 6BS[1 y]
32: 4
35:14
39:14[z], 34
41:13BS[aa]
45:12
47: 4
49:17
Jer. 50:10
Lam. 3:11, 44
Eze. 4: 1, 3, 4
6
5: 5, 14
6:14
7:20
13:14
14: 3, 3, 4
7, 8
16:18, 19
38
17: 4
18:12, 15
19: 9
21:27
25:13
28:14
30:24 AP
32:27
35: 9
36:37 A[bb]
37: 1, 14
26
40: 2
42:13—A
43: 8
44:19, 30
Dan. 1: 8
3:10
4: 3
6:26
7: 9
Hos. 1:11
2: 3, 12
4: 7, 17
11: 8
13: 1
Joel 1: 7
Amos 5: 7
8:10
Obad. 4, 7
Mic. 1: 6, 7
2:12
4: 7, 13
13
Nah. 1:14
3: 6
Hab. 3: 4
Zeph. 2:13
3:19-BS[1]
Hag. 1: 7
2:15, 15
18, 23
Zec. 5:11
9:12 A[cc]
12: 2, 3, 6
Mal. 1: 1
2: 2, 2

[a] A ἐπιτίθημι. [b] *pro* ὑποτίθημι
[c] A ποιέω. [d] *pro* ἐπιτίθημι
[e] A διατίθημι. [f] A εἰσφέρω.
[g] *pro* ποιεω. [h] *pro* πήγνυμι.
[i] *pro* θύω. [k] A ἀπερείδω.
[m] A καθιστημι. [n] A τάσσω.
[o] *pro* καίω. [p] *pro* δίδωμι.
[q] B ἐπιτίθημι. [r] A σώζω.
[s] B γίνομαι. [t] *pro* πειθω.
[u] *vide* θεεβουλαθώθ.
[v] *pro* ἐντελλω. [w] S δίδωμι.
[x] A γινομαι. [y] *pro* εἰμί.
[z] S κατατιθημι. [aa] *pro* διατιθημι
[bb] *vide* ζητέω. [cc] *pro* καθημαι.

τιθηνέω.

Lamentations 4: 5

τιθηνός.

Nu. 11:12
Ruth 4:16
2 Sa. 4: 4
2 Ki.10: 1, 5
Isa. 49:23

τίκτω.

Gen. 3:16
4: 1, 2
17, 20
22, 25
Gen. 16: 1, 2
11, 15
15, 16
17:17[a], 19

Gen. 17:21
18:13
19:37, 38
20:17
21: 2, 3, 7
22:20, 23
24
24:15, 24
36, 47
25: 2, 12
24, 26[b]
29:32, 33
34, 34
35, 35
30: 1, 3, 5
7, 9, 10
12, 17
19, 20
21
21+A
23, 25
39, 42
31: 8, 8, 43
34: 1
35:16, 17
36: 4, 4, 5
12, 14
38: 3, 4, 5, 5
27, 28
41:50
44:27
46:15, 18
20, 20
22[a], 25
50:23
Exo. 1:16, 19
19, 22
2: 2, 22
6:23, 25
21: 4
Lev. 12: 2, 5, 7
22:27
Nu. 11:12
26:59, 59
60 A[c]
Deu. 15:19
21:15
25: 6
28:57
Jud. 8:31
11: 1 A[c], 2
13: 2, 3
3 A[d]
5, 7, 8
24
18:29[a]
Ruth 1:12
4:12, 13[b]
15, 17
1 Sa. 1:20
2: 5, 21
4:19, 19
20
2 Sa. 3: 2, 5
11:27
12:14, 15
24
14:27, 27
21: 8, 8, 20
22−A
1 Ki. 1: 6
3:17, 18
18, 21
11:20
12 p 24 l 20
13: 2
2 Ki. 4:17
19: 3
1 Ch. 1:32
36+A
2: 4, 9, 19
21, 24
29, 35
3: 1, 5
4: 6, 9, 18
7:14, 14
16, 18
21, 23
14: 3, 4
22: 9
26: 6
2 Ch. 11:19, 20
Job 38:28, 29
Psa. 7:15
21:32
47: 7
77: 6
Pro. 3:28
10:23
17:25
19:13+A
23:25
27: 1
Ecc. 3: 2
Cant. 6: 8
8: 5
Isa. 7:14
8: 3
13: 8
21: 3
23: 4
26:17, 18
37: 3, 3
42:14
51:18
54: 1
59: 4
66: 7, 7, 8
8
Jer. 6:24
8:21
13:21
14: 5
15: 9, 10
16: 3
17:11
20:14[a], 14
15
22:23, 26
26
27:12−BS
43
37: 6
Eze. 16: 4, 5
23: 4
Hos. 1: 3, 6, 8
2: 5
13:13
Mic. 4: 9, 10
5: 3, 3

[a] A γίνομαι. [b] A γεννάω.
[c] pro γεννάω.
[d] pro συλλαμβάνω.

τίλλω.

Ezra 9: 3
Isa. 18: 7

τιμάω.

Exo. 20:12
Lev. 19:32
27: 8, 8, 12
12, 14
14
Nu. 22:17, 37
24:11
Deu. 5:16
1 Sa. 15:30 A
Est. 9: 3
Isa. 58:17
Pro. 3: 9
4: 8
6: 8
7: 1
14:31
15:22
25: 2, 27
27:18, 24
Isa. 29:13
55: 2

τιμή.

Gen. 20:16
44: 2
Exo. 28: 2, 36
34:20
Lev. 5:15, 18
6: 6
27: 2, 3, 3
5, 6, 7
8, 13
15−A
16, 17
19, 23
23, 25
27
Nu. 20:19
2 Ch. 1:16
32:33
Est. 1:20
(9)16+S[1]
Job 31:39
34:19
37:21
40: 5
Psa. 8: 6
Psa. 28: 1
43:13
44:10
48: 9, 13
21
61: 5
95: 7
98: 4−S[1]
Pro. 6:26
12: 9
22: 9
26: 1
Ecc. 7: 9+BS[1]
Isa. 10:16
11:10
14:18
35: 2
55: 1
Eze. 22:25
Dan. 2: 6
4:27, 33
5:18, 20
7:14

τίμημα.

Leviticus 27:27

τίμιος.

1 Sa. 3: 1
2 Sa. 12:30
1 Ki. 6: 2
7: 2 A[a]
46, 47
48
10: 2, 10
11
1 Ch. 20: 2
29: 2
2 Ch. 3: 6
9: 1, 9, 10
32:27
Ezra 4:10
Job 28:10 AC[b]
16
Psa. 18:11
20: 4
115: 6
Pro. 3:15, 15
6:26
8:11, 19
12:27
20: 6
24: 4
29:28
Ecc. 10: 1
Isa. 60: 6+AS[1]
Jer. 15:19
Lam. 4: 2
Dan. 11:38
Hos. 11: 7

[a] pro Τύριος. [b] pro ἔντιμος.

τιμογραφέω.

2 Kings 23:35

τιμωρέω.

Jud. 5:14 A[a]
Pro. 22: 3
Eze. 5:17
14:15

[a] pro ἐκριζόω.

τιμωρία.

Pro. 19:29
24:22
Jer. 38:21

τίναγμα.

Job 28:26

τινάσσω.

Isaiah 28:27[a]

[a] AS ἐκτινάσσω.

τίνω, τίω.

Pro. 20:22
24:22, 44
Pro. 27:12

τιτάν.

2 Samuel 5:18

τιτράω vide τετραίνω

τιτρώσκω.

Nu. 31:19
Deu. 1:44
Deu. 7:21
1 Ki. 22:34

Job 6: 9
16: 6
20:24
33:23
36:14, 25
41:19
Pro. 7:26
12:18
Cant. 2: 5
5: 8
Jer. 9: 8

τίω vide τίνω.

τμητός.

Exodus 20:25

τοιγαροῦν.

Job 7:11 A[a]
22:10
24:22
Pro. 1:26, 31
Isa. 5:26

[a] pro ἀτὰρ οὖν.

τοίνυν.

Job 8:13
36:14
Isa. 3:10
Isa. 5:13
27: 4
33:23

τοιόσδε.

Ezra 5: 3

τοιοῦτος.

Deu. 4:32−A
Pro. 29:28−S
Eze. 31: 8
&c., &c.

τοῖχος.

Exo. 30: 3
Lev. 5: 9
14:37, 37
39
Nu. 22:25
25−B
Jud. 16:13, 14
14
1 Sa. 18:11 A
19:10+A
10
20:25
25:22, 34
2 Sa. 5:11+A
1 Ki. 4:29
6: 9
9+A
10, 15
15, 16
25, 25
27
12 p 24 l 43
14:10 A
16:11+A
20:21
2 Ki. 3:25
9: 8, 33
20: 2
1 Ch. 14: 1+A
29: 4
2 Ch. 3: 7, 7
2 Ch. 3:11, 12A
15 B[a]
Ezra 5: 8
Job 33:24
Psa. 61: 4
Cant. 2: 9
Isa. 5: 5
23:13
25:12
38: 2[b]
59:10
Eze. 4: 3
8: 7+A
8+A
12: 5, 7, 12
13:10, 12
14, 15
15
23:14
40:13[c]
13
41: 5 6, 6
7[d], 9
12, 13
15 A[e]
17[d], 22
43: 8
Dan. 5: 5
Amos 5:19
Hab. 2:11

[a] pro οἶκος. [b] B τεῖχος.
[c] A τεῖχος. [d] A οἶκος.
[e] pro μῆκος.

τοκάς.

1 Ki. (3) p 46
1 Ki. 4(26)A

τοκετός.

Gen. 35:16
Job 39: 1, 2

τόκος.

Exo. 22:25
Lev. 25:36[a], 37
Deu. 23:19 ter
2 Ki. 4: 7
Psa. 14: 3
54:12[b]
71:14
Pro. 29: 8
Jer. 9: 6, 6
Eze. 18: 8, 13
17
22:12
Hos. 9:11

[a] A κακός. [b] BS[1] κόπος.

τόλμα, -μη.

Job 21:27
Job 39:20

τολμάω.

Est. 1:18
7: 5
Job 15:12

τολύπη.

2 Kings 4:39

τομή.

Job 15:32
Cant. 2:12

τομίς.

Proverbs 24:37[a]

[a] AS στόμις.

τόμος.

Isaiah 8: 1

τόξευμα.

Gen. 49:23
2 Ki. 9:16
Pro. 7:23
25:18
Isa. 7:24
Isa. 13:18
21:15, 17
Jer. 27:14
28:11
Eze. 39: 3, 9

τοξεύω.

2 Sa. 11:20[a], 24
24
2 Ki. 13:17−B[b]
17−B[b]
2 Ki. 19:32
2 Ch. 35:23
Jer. 27:14

[a] B[a] πλήσσω. [b] A ῥοιζέω.

τοξικός.

Judges 5:28[a]

[a] A δικτυωτός.

τόξον.

Gen. 9:13, 14
16
21:16
27: 3
48:22
49:24
Jos. 24:12
1 Sa. 2: 4
18: 4 A
2 Sa. 1:18+A
22
22:35
1 Ki. 22:34
2 Ki. 6:22
9:24
13:15, 15
16
16+A
18
1 Ch. 5:18
8:40
10: 3, 3
12: 2, 2
2 Ch. 18:33
26:14
Neh. 4:13, 16
Job 20:24
29:20
36:30 A[a]
39:23
41:19−A
Psa. 7:13
Psa. 10: 2
17:35
36:14, 15
43: 7
45:10
57: 8
59: 6
63: 4
75: 4
77: 9, 57
Isa. 5:28
41: 2
Jer. 4:29
6:23
9: 3
25:14
26: 9
27:14, 20
42
28: 3, 56
Lam. 2: 4
3:12
Eze. 1:28
39: 3, 9
Hos. 1: 5, 7
2:18
7:16
Hab. 3: 9
Zec. 9:10 S[1] b
10, 13
10: 4

[a] pro ἠδώ. [b] pro ἅρμα.

τοξότης.

Gen. 21:20
1 Sa. 31: 3
1 Ch. 10: 3
2 Ch. 14: 8
2 Ch. 17:17
22: 5
35:23
Amos 2:15

τοπάζιον.

Exo. 28:17
36:17
Job 28:19

Ps. 118:127
Eze. 28:13

τοπάρχης.

Gen. 41:34
2 Ki. 18:24
Isa. 36: 9
Dan. 3: 2, 3

Dan. 3: 3+A
27
6: 7

τόπος.

Gen. 12: 6
13: 3, 4, 14
18:24, 26
33
19:12, 13
14, 27
20:11, 13
21:17, 17
31
22: 3, 4, 9
14
24:23, 25
31
26: 7, 7
28:11, 11
11, 16
17, 19
29: 3, 22
26
30:25
31:13, 55
32: 2, 30
33:17
35: 1, 7, 13
14, 15
36:40
38:21, 22
39:20
40: 3
50:11+A
Exo. 3: 5, 8
15:23
16:29[a]
17: 7
15+A
18:23
20:24
21:13
24:10, 11
29:31
32:34
33:21
Lev. 1:16
4:12, 24
29, 33
6:11, 16
25, 26
27
30+A
32, 36
8:31
10:13, 14
17, 18
13:19
14:13, 13
17, 28
40, 41
45
16:24
24: 9
Nu. 9:17
10:29
11: 3, 34
13:25
14:40
18:31
19: 3, 9
20: 5, 5
21: 3
22:26
23:13, 27
24:11, 14
25
32: 1, 1

Nu. 32:17
Deu. 1:31, 33
7:24
9: 7
11: 5, 24
12: 2[b], 3
5, 11
13, 14
18, 21
26
14:22, 23
24
15:20
16: 2, 6, 7
11, 15
16
17: 8, 10
18: 6
21:19[c]
23:12—B[l]
16+A
26: 2, 9
29: 7
31:11
Jos. 1: 3, 16
3: 3
4: 9
5: 3, 9
15
8:18, 19
9:33
20: 4 A
24:28, 33
Jud. 2: 5
7: 7
9:55
11:19
15:17
17: 8—A
9—A
18: 3[d], 10
12
19:13, 16
21—A
28
20:22, 33
33, 36
Ruth 1: 7
3: 4
1 Sa. 2:20
3: 2, 9
5: 3, 11
6: 2
9:22
10:25
12: 8
14:46
20:19, 25
27, 37
21: 2
22:23
23:22
23+A
28
24:23
26: 5, 25
27: 5
29: 4, 10
30:31
2 Sa. 2:16, 23
5:20
6: 8, 17
7:10
11:16

2 Sa. 15:19
20—A
21
25+A
17: 9, 12
19:39
1 Ki. 4:21
5: 9
8: 6, 7
21, 29
29, 30
30, 35
42
10:19[e]
13: 8, 16
22
20:10
21:24
2 Ki. 4:10
5:11
6: 1, 6, 8
9, 10
18:25
20:13 A[f]
22:16, 17
19
20 A[g]
20
23:14
1 Ch. 13:11
14:11
15: 1, 3
16:27
17: 9
21:22, 25
2 Ch. 3: 1
5: 7, 8
6:20, 20
21, 21
26, 32
40
7:12, 15
20:26
24:11
25:10, 10
33:19
34: 6, 24
25, 27
28
Ezra 1: 4, 4
5:15
6: 3, 5, 7
8:17, 17
9: 8
10:13 B[h]
Neh. 1: 9
2:14
4: 3, 12
13, 20
12:27
Est. 4: 3+S[3]
Job 2: 9, 9
7:10
8:18
14:18
16: 7 C[i]
18
18:21
20: 9
27:21, 23
28: 1, 1, 6
12, 20
23
34:22
36:34
38:19
Psa. 22: 2
23: 3
25: 8
36:10, 36
41: 5
43:20
67: 6
70: 3
75: 3
78: 7
83: 7
102:16, 22
103: 8
118:54

Ps. 131: 5, 7
Pro. 4:15—S[1]
9:18
15: 3
19:23
25: 6
27: 8
28:12, 28
Ecc. 1: 5, 7
3:16, 16
20
6: 6
10: 4
11: 3
Isa. 4: 5
5: 1
7:23
10:26
14: 2
18: 7
22:23, 25
30:23
33:14, 21
45:19
46: 7
48:16+AS[1]
49:20, 20
54: 2
56: 5
60:13
66: 1
Jer. 4: 7
7: 3, 6, 7
12
14 A[k]
14, 20
32
8: 3
10:20, 20
13: 7
24+A
14:13
16: 2, 3, 9
19: 3, 4, 4
6, 7
12, 13
14+A
22: 3, 11
12
24: 5, 9
27:16 A[m]
44+A
28:62
29: 9, 20
31:37
32:16
35: 3, 6
36:10
39:37
40:10, 12
43: 7 A[m]
44:10
47: 2
49:18, 22
51:35
Eze. 3:12
10:11
12: 3[n], 3
17:16
21:30
34:12
38:15
39:11
42:13
43: 7, 7
45: 4
46:19, 20
Dan. 2:35, 38
11:38
Hos. 1:10
5:15
Joel 3: 7
Amos 4: 6[n]
8: 3
Mic. 1: 3
Nah. 3:17
Zeph. 1: 4
2:11
Hag. 2: 9

Zec. 13: 1
14:10

Zec. 14:10—A
Mal. 1:11

[a] A οἶκος. [b] A ἔθνος. [c] A πόλις. [d] A ἐνταῦθα. [e] A θρόνος. [f] pro λόγος. [g] pro τάφος. [h] pro καιρός. [i] pro κατάκοπος. [k] pro οἶκος. [m] pro λαός. [n] A πόλις.

τορευτός.

Exo. 25:17 AB[2 a]
30, 36
1 Ki. 10:22—A

Cant. 5:14
7: 2
Jer. 10: 9

[a] vide χρυσοτορευτός.

τοσοῦτος.

Exo. 1:12
Nu. 15: 5

τότε.

Lev. 22: 7
Isa. 41: 7 A[a]

Dan. 2:12
&c., &c.

[a] pro ποτέ.

τραγέλαφος.

Deu. 14: 5+A
Job 39: 1

τράγος.

Gen. 30:35
31:10, 12
32:14
Nu. 7:17, 23
29, 35
41, 47
53, 59
65, 71
77, 83
88
Deu. 32:14

2 Ch. 17:11+A
Psa. 49:13
Pro. 24:66
Isa. 1:11
34: 6—AS
6
Eze. 34:17
39:18
Dan. 8: 5, 5, 8
21

τρανός.

Isaiah 35: 6

τράπεζα.

Exo. 25:22, 26
27, 29
26:35 ter
30:28
31: 8
35:15
38: 9, 11
12
39:18
40: 4, 20
Lev. 24: 6
Nu. 3:31
4: 7
Jud. 1: 7
1 Sa. 20:24, 27
29, 34
2 Sa. 9: 7, 10
11, 13
19:28
1 Ki. 2: 7
4:20
7:34
12 p 24 l 56
13:20
18:19
2 Ki. 4:10
1 Ch. 28:16, 16
2 Ch. 4: 8, 19

2 Ch. 9: 4
13:11
29:18
Neh. 5:17
Job 36:16
Psa. 22: 5
68:23
77:19, 20
127: 3
Pro. 9: 2
23: 1
Isa. 21: 5
65:11
Eze. 23:41
39:20
40:39+A
39+A
40, 40
40+A
41, 42
43
41:22
44:16
Dan. 1: 5, 8
13, 15
11:27
Mal. 1: 7, 12

τραῦμα.

Gen. 4:23
Exo. 21:25, 25
Lev. 13:31 AB[a]
31 A[a]
Nu. 19:18 A[b]
Jud. 15:19 A[c]
Job 6:21

Job 16: 6
Psa. 68:27
Pro. 27: 6
Isa. 1: 6
Jer. 10:19
Eze. 32:29

[a] pro θραῦσμα.
[b] pro τραυματίας.
[c] pro λάκκος.

τραυματίας.

Gen. 34:27
Nu. 19:16, 18[a]
23:24
31: 8, 8
Deu. 21: 1, 2, 3
6
32:42
Jud. 9:40
16:24
20:31, 39
1 Sa. 17:52
31: 1
2 Sa. 1:19—A
22, 25
23: 8 AB[a b]
18
1 Ki. 11:15
1 Ch. 5:22
10: 1, 8
11:11, 20
2 Ch. 13:17
Psa. 87: 6
88:11
Isa. 22: 2, 2
34: 3
66:16
Jer. 14:18
28: 4

Jer. 28:49—S
52
32:19
48: 9
Lam. 2:12
4: 9, 9
Eze. 6: 4, 7, 13
11: 6
21:14, 14
29
26:15
28: 8
30:11
31:17, 18
32:19, 21
22, 22
23+A
24, 25
26
28—A
29, 30
30[c]
31+A
32
35: 8
Dan. 11:26
Nah. 3: 3
Zeph. 2:12

[a] A τραῦμα. [b] pro στρατιώτης.
[c] A τραυματίζω.

τραυματίζω.

1 Sa. 31: 3
Cant. 5: 7
Isa. 53: 5
Jer. 9: 1
Eze. 28:10+A

Eze. 28:16, 23
30: 4
32:28
30 A[a]
35: 8

[a] pro τραυματιας.

τραχηλιάω.

Job 15:25

τράχηλος.

Gen. 27:16, 40
33: 4
41:42
45:14, 14
46:29
50: 1 A[a]
Lev. 16: 4+A
Deu. 10:16
28:48
31:27
33:29
Jos. 10:24, 24
Jud. 5:30
8:21, 26
2 Ch. 30: 8 A[b]
36:13
Neh. 3: 5
9:16, 17
29
Job 39:19
41:13
Pro. 1: 9
3: 3, 22
6:21
Cant. 1:10
4: 4, 9

Cant. 7: 4
Isa. 8:16
9: 4
30:28
48: 4
52: 2
58: 5
Jer. 7:26
11:10+A
17:23
19:15[c]
34: 1, 6, 9
10
35:10, 11
12, 14
37: 8
Lam. 1:14
5: 4
Eze. 16:11
21:29
Dan. 5: 7, 16
29
Hos. 10:11
Mic. 2: 3
Hab. 3:13

[a] pro πρόσωπον. [b] pro καρδία.
[c] S αὐχήν.

τραχύς.

Deu. 21: 4
2 Sa. 17: 8—A
Pro. 20:20 B[a]

Isa. 40: 4
Jer. 2:25

[a] pro ταχύς.

τρεῖς.

Exo. 10:23[1]—A
Lev. 12: 4[a]
Jos. 21:35[b]
Jud. 1:20+A

Jud. 20:15[c]
1 Sa. 31: 8—A
1 Ki. 7:35+A
15: 2[d]

2 Ki. 3:21 — AB
1 Ch. 11:20 — A
Est. 9:15 + S³
Isa. 20: 3ᵈ-AS
Dan. 7:20 + A

ᵃ A δέκα. ᵇ A τέσσαρες. ᶜ A πέντε. ᵈ A δεκαέξ, B ἕξ.

τρέμω.

Gen. 4:12, 14
1 Sa. 13:32
Ezra 10: 3 + S³
Ps. 103:32
Isa. 66: 2, 5
Jer. 4:24
Dan. 5:19
6:26

τρέπω.

Gen. 15:15
Exo. 17:13
Nu. 14:45
2 Ch. 30:11 Bᵃ

ᵃ pro ἐντρέπω.

τρέφω.

Gen. 6:19, 20
48:15
50:20ᵃ
Nu. 6: 5
Deu. 32:18
1 Ki. 18:13
Est. 4: 8ᵇ
Pro. 25:21 ASᶜ
Isa. 7:21
33:18ᵈ
58: 6 Sᵉ
Jer. 26:21
Dan. 1: 5
4: 9

ᵃ A διατρέφω. ᵇ A στρέφω. ᶜ pro ψωμίζω. ᵈ AS συστρέφω. ᵉ pro θραύω.

τρέχω.

Gen. 18: 7
24:20, 28
29
29:12, 13
Nu. 16:47
Jos. 7:22
Jud. 7:21
13:10ᵃ
13:14
1 Sa. 3: 5 — A
4:12
10:23
17:22 A
48 + A
51
20: 6, 36
36
2 Sa. 18:19, 22
22, 23
23, 23
24, 26
26
22:30
1 Ki. (3) p 46
18:16
2 Ki. 4:22, 26
2 Ki. 5:20, 21
11:13
2 Ch. 23:12
30: 6, 10
35:13
Job 15:26
16:14
41:13ᵇ
Psa. 18: 6
58: 5
61: 5
118:32
147: 4
Pro. 1:16 AS²
4:12
7:23
Cant. 1: 4
Isa. 40:31
59: 7
Jer. 8: 6
12: 5
23:21
Eze. 1:14 A
Dan. 8: 6
Joel 2: 7, 9
Zec. 2: 4

ᵃ A ἐκτρέχω. ᵇ A προτρέχω.

τριάκοντα.

Gen. 11:13 + A
Exo. 12:40ᵈ
41ᵃ
Nu. 26: 7ᵇ
1 Sa. 13: 4ᶜ
1 Ki. 7:39 — B
16 p 28 — A
1 Ch. 15: 7ᵈ
27: 6²-A¹

ᵃ B* τριακονταπέντε. ᵇ A πεντήκοντα. ᶜ A δέκα. ᵈ BS πεντήκοντα.

τριακονταδύο.

Exodus 6:20ᵃ

ᵃ A τριακονταέξ.

τριακονταέξ.

Ezra 2:66ᵃ
Neh. 7:68 + AS

ᵃ B τριάκοντα.

τριακονταεπτά.

Ezra 2:65ᵃ

ᵃ B τριάκοντα τέσσαρες.

τριακονταετής.

1 Chronicles 23: 3

τριακονταπέντε.

2 Ch. 20:31ᵃ
Neh. 7:69 + AS

ᵃ A τριάκοντα.

τριακοντατρία.

Exodus 6:18ᵃ

ᵃ AB τριάκοντα.

τριακόσιοι.

Jud. 7:22 — A
8: 4ᵃ
1 Ch. 11:20ᵇ
2 Ch. 9:16² — B
Ezra 2: 4ᶜ
8: 5 — B
Neh. 7:71 — Bᵃ

ᵃ A διακόσιοι. ᵇ A ἑξακόσιοι. ᶜ B τετρακόσιοι.

τριακοστός.

1 Ki. 16:29 + A
Jer. 52:31ᵃ

ᵃ S τριάκοντα.

τρίβολος.

Gen. 3:18
2 Sa. 12:31
Pro. 22: 5
Hos. 10: 8

τρίβος.

Gen. 49:17
Jud. 5: 6 Aᵃ
20ᵇ
1 Sa. 6:12
2 Sa. 20:12, 12
13
1 Ch. 26:18
Job 18:10
22:15
28: 7
30:12, 13
34:11
38:20
Psa. 8: 9
16: 5
17:40
22: 3
24: 4
26:11
43:19
76:20
77:50
118:35, 105
138: 3, 23
139: 6
Ps. 141: 4
Pro. 1:15
2:15, 19
20, 20
3:17
8: 2, 20ᶜ
15:21
16:17
21:54
Isa. 3:12
30:11
40: 3
42:16
43:16
49: 9, 11
58:12
59: 8
Jer. 6:16
9:10
18:15
Lam. 3: 9
Dan. 4·34
Hos. 2: 6
Joel 2: 7
Mic. 4: 2

ᵃ pro ἀτραπός. ᵇ A τάξις. ᶜ S¹ ὁδός.

τρίβω.

Nu. 11: 8
Pro. 15:19
Isa. 38:21
Jer. 7:18

τριέτης.

2 Ch. 31:16
Isa. 15: 5

τριετίζω.

Gen. 15: 9, 9, 9
1 Sa. 1:24

τριημερία.

Amos 4: 4

τριμερίζω.

Deuteronomy 19: 3

τρίμηνος.

Gen. 38:24
2 Ki. 23:31
2 Ki. 24: 8
2 Ch. 36: 2, 9

τριόδους.

1 Samuel 2:13

τριπλοῦς.

Ezekiel 42: 6

τρισκαιδέκατος.

2 Ch. 29:17ᵃ
Est. 9: 1ᵇ

ᵃ A ἐκκαιδ- ᵇ S¹ τεσσαρεσκαιδ-

τρισσεύω.

1 Sa. 20:19, 20
1 Ki. 18:34

τρισσός.

1 Ki. 10 p 22 — B
2 Ki. 11:10
Eze. 23:15, 23
42: 3

τρισσόω.

1 Kings 18:34

τρισσῶς.

1 Sa. 20:12
1 Ki. 7:41, 42
Pro. 22:20
Eze. 16:30
41:16

τριστάτης.

Exo. 14: 7
15: 4
2 Ki. 7: 2, 17
19
2 Ki. 9:25
10:25, 25
15:25

τρισχίλιοι.

Judges 16:27ᵃ

ᵃ B ἑπτακόσιοι.

τριταῖος.

1 Sa. 9:20
1 Sa. 30:13

τρίτος.

1 Sa. 20: 5 + A
2 Ki. 1:13 + A
1 Ch. 26: 2 — B
1 Ch. 26: 4 — B
2 Ch. 23: 5 — A¹

τρίχαπτος.

Ezekiel 16:10, 13

τρίχινος.

Exo. 26: 7
Zec. 13: 4

τρίχωμα.

Cant. 4: 1
6: 4
Eze. 24:17

τριώροφος, τριό-

Gen. 6:16
1 Ki. 6:12
Eze. 41: 7

τρομέω.

Esther 5: 9 + S³

τρόμος.

Gen. 9: 2
Exo. 15:15, 16
Deu. 2:25
11:25
Job 4:14
38:34ᵃ
Psa. 2:11
47: 7
Psa. 54: 6
Isa. 19:16
33:14
54:14
64: 1, 3
Jer. 15: 8
30:13
Hab. 3:16

ᵃ A δρόμος.

τροπή.

Exo. 32:18
Deu. 33:14
1 Ki. 22:35
Job 38:33
Jer. 30:10

τρόπος.

Exo. 40:25 Aᵃ
Nu. 3:16ᵇ
18: 7
Jos. 11: 9ᶜ
Jud. 6:27ᵇ
Jud. 6:36 Aᵈ
37 Aᵈ
16: 9 + A
1 Sa. 21 13 Aᵉ
25:33
Job 4: 8, 19
Psa. 41: 2
Eze. 24:18ᶠ
Eze. 42: 7
45: 6
&c., &c.

ᵃ pro καθάπερ. ᵇ A καθά. ᶜ A καθότι. ᵈ pro καθώς. ᵉ pro πρόσωπον. ᶠ A καθώς.

τροπόω.

Jos. 11: 6
Jud. 4:23ᵃ
20:35 Aᵇ
36 Aᶜ
39 Aᵈ
39 Aᵉ
2 Sa. 8: 1
1 Ki. 22:35
1 Ch. 18: 1
19:16
2 Ch. 18:34
20:22
25: 8, 8, 22
Psa. 88:24

ᵃ A ταπεινόω. ᵇ pro πατάσσω. ᶜ pro πλήσσω. ᵈ πτῶσις. ᵉ pro πίπτω.

τροφεύω.

Exodus 2: 7

τροφή.

Gen. 49:20 Aᵃ
27
Jud. 8: 5 — A
2 Ch. 11:23
Job 36:31
Psa. 64:10
103:27
110: 5
Ps. 135:25
144:15
145: 7
146: 9
Pro. 6: 8
24:69
Lam. 4: 5 ABᵃ
Dan. 4: 9, 18

ᵃ pro τρυφή.

τροφός.

Gen. 35: 8
2 Ki. 11: 2
2 Ch. 22:11
Isa. 49:23

τροφοφορέω.

Deuteronomy 1:31, 31

τροχιά.

Pro. 2:15
4:11, 26
27
Pro. 5: 6, 21
Eze. 27:19

τροχίσκος.

Ezekiel 16:12

τροχός.

2 Sa. 24:22
1 Ki. 7:16, 17
18 + A
18, 19
19
Psa. 76:19
82:14
Pro. 20:26
Ecc. 12: 6
Isa. 5:28
17:13
28:27
29: 5
41:15
Jer. 20: 3
Eze. 1:15, 16
16, 16
Eze. 1:19, 19
20, 20
21
3:13
10: 2, 6
6 + A
6, 9, 9
9, 10
10, 12
12, 13
16, 16
19
11:22
23:24
26:10
Dan. 7: 9
Nah. 3: 2

τρύβλιον.

Exo. 25:28
38:12
Nu. 4: 7
7:13, 19
25, 31
37, 43
Nu. 7:49, 55
61, 67
73, 79
84, 85
1 Ki. 7:36

τρυγάω.

Lev. 25:11
Deu. 24:23
28:30
Jud. 9:27
1 Sa. 8:12
2 Ki. 18:21 Aᵃ
Job 15:33
Psa. 79:13
Cant. 5: 1
Jer. 6: 9

Jer. 32:16
Hos. 6:10
Hos. 10:12, 13

[a] pro τετραίνω.

τρυγητής.

Jor. 29:10
Obad. 5

τρυγητός.

Lev. 26: 5, 5
Jud. 8: 2
1 Sa. 8:12
13:21
Isa. 16: 9
24:13
32:10
Jer. 31:32
Joel 1:11
3:13
Amos 4: 7
9:13
Mic. 7: 1

τρυγίας.

Psalm 74: 9

τρυγών.

Gen. 15: 9
Lev. 1:14
5: 7, 11
12: 6, 8
14:22, 30
15:14, 29
Nu. 6:10
Psa. 83: 4
Cant. 1:10
2:12
Jer. 8: 7

τρυμαλιά.

Jud. 6: 2[a]
15: 8[b]
11[c]
Jer. 13: 4
16:16
29:17

[a] A μάνδρα. [b] A χειμάρρος.
[c] A ὀπή.

τρυπάω.

Exo. 21: 6
Deu. 15:17
Job 40:21
Hag. 1: 6

τρυφάω.

Neh. 9:25[a]
Isa. 66:11

[a] A ἐντρυφάω.

τρυφερός.

Deu. 28:54, 56
Isa. 47: 1, 8
58:13
Jer. 26:29
27: 2
Mic. 1:16

τρυφερότης.

Deuteronomy 28:56

τρυφή.

Gen. 2:15—A
3:23, 24
49:20[a]
Psa. 35: 9
138:11
Pro. 4: 9
19:10
Cant. 7: 6
Jer. 28:34
Lam. 4: 5[b]
Eze. 28:13
31: 9, 16
18
34:14
36:35
Joel 2: 3
Mic. 2: 9

[a] A τροφή. [b] AB τροφή.

τρώγλη.

1 Sa. 14:11
2 Ki. 12: 9
9 AB[a]
Job 30: 6
Isa. 2:19, 21
7:19
11: 8

[a] pro σανίς.

τυγχάνω.

Deu. 19: 5
Job 3:21
7: 2
Job 17: 1
Pro. 24:58

τυλόω.

Deuteronomy 8: 4

τυμπανίζω.

1 Samuel 21:13

τυμπανίστρια.

Psalm 67:26

τύμπανον.

Gen. 31:27
Exo. 15:20, 20
Jud. 11:34
1 Sa. 10: 5
18: 6
2 Sa. 6: 5
1 Ch. 13: 8
Psa. 80: 3
149: 3
150: 4
Isa. 5:12
24: 8
30:32[a]
Jer. 38: 4

[a] AS αὐλή.

τύπος.

Exo. 25:40
Amos 5:26

τύπτω.

Exo. 2:11, 13
7:17
8: 2
21:15
Nu. 22:27
Deu. 25:11
27:24
Jud. 20:31 A[a]
39 A[a]
1 Sa. 1: 8
11:11[b]
17:36
27: 9
31: 2
2 Sa. 1: 1
2:23
4: 7
2 Sa. 5: 8
24:17
1 Ki. 18: 4
2 Ki. 3:24
6:22
14:10
1 Ch. 11: 6
2 Ch. 28:23
Pro. 10:13
23:35
25: 4[c]
26:22
Isa. 41: 7
58: 4
Eze. 7: 9
Dan. 5:19

[a] pro πατάσσω. [b] A πλήσσω.
[c] A κρύπτω.

τυραννέω.

Proverbs 28:15

τυραννίς.

Esther 1:18

τύραννος.

Est. 9: 3
Job 2:11
42 p 18
Pro. 8:16
Dan. 3: 2, 3
4:33
Hab. 1:10

τυρός.

Job 10:10

τυρόω.

Job 10:10[a]
Psa. 67:16, 17
Ps. 118:70
Lam. 4: 7 A[b]

[a] A πήγνυμι. [b] pro πυρόω.

τυφλός.

Exo. 4:11
Lev. 19:14
21:18
22:22
Deu. 15:21
27:18
28:29
2 Sa. 5: 6, 8, 8
Job 29:15
Ps. 145: 8
Isa. 29:18
35: 5
42: 7, 16
18, 19
43: 8, 8
59:10
61: 1
Zeph. 1:17
Mal. 1: 8

τυφλόω.

Isaiah 42:19

τύχη.

Gen. 30:11
Isa. 65:11

ὕαινα.

Jer. 12: 9[a]

[a] A λῃστής.

ὑακίνθινος.

Exo. 25: 5
26: 4, 14
28:27
35: 7, 23
36:30, 40
39:21
Nu. 4: 6, 6, 8
9, 10
Nu. 4:11, 11
12, 12
14, 14
25
15:38
Est. (9)15+5[3]
Isa. 3:23
Eze. 23: 6

ὑάκινθος.

Exo. 25: 4
26: 1, 31
36
27:16
28: 5, 8, 15
29, 33
31: 4
35: 6
23+A
25
36: 9, 10
12, 15
Exo. 36:29, 32
37
37: 3, 5, 16
39:13
2 Ch. 2: 7—8
14
3:14
Isa. 3:23
Jer. 10: 9
Eze. 16:10
27: 7, 24

ὕαλος.

Job 28:17

ὑβρίζω.

2 Sa. 19:43
Isa. 13: 3
Isa. 23:12
Jer. 31:29

ὕβρις.

Lev. 26:19
Job 15:26
27+A
22:12
35:12
37: 3
Pro. 1:22
8:13
11: 2
13:10
14: 3:10
16:18
19 A[a]
19:10, 18
21: 4
29:23
Isa. 2:17[b]
9: 9
10:33
13:11, 11
16: 6
Isa. 23: 7, 9
25:11
28: 1, 3
Jer. 13: 9, 9
10, 17
27:32
31:29, 29
Eze. 7:10
30: 6, 18
32:12
33:28
Hos. 5: 5
7:10
Amos 6: 8
Mic. 6:10
Nah. 2: 3, 3
Zeph. 2:10
3:11
Zec. 9: 6
10:11

[a] pro ὑβριστής. [b] AS ὕψος.

ὑβριστής.

Job 40: 6
Pro. 6:17
15:25
16:19[a]
Pro. 27:13
Isa. 2:12
16: 6
Jer. 28: 2

[a] A ὕβρις.

ὑβριστικός.

Proverbs 20: 1

ὑβρίστρια.

Jeremiah 27:31

ὑγιάζω.

Lev. 13:18, 24
37
Jos. 5: 8
2 Ki. 20: 7
Job 24:23
Eze. 47: 8, 0
11[a]
Hos. 6: 2

[a] A ἁγιάζω.

ὑγιαίνω.

Gen. 29: 6, 6
37:14
Gen. 43:26, 27
Exo. 4:18

1 Sa. 25: 6, 6
2 Sa. 14: 8
2 Sa. 20: 9
Pro. 13:13

ὑγίεια.

Gen. 42:15, 16
Est. 9:30
Pro. 6: 8
Isa. 9: 6
Eze. 47:12

ὑγιής.

Lev. 13:10, 15
15, 16
Jos. 10:21
Isa. 38:21

ὑγιῶς.

Proverbs 24:76

ὑγραίνω.

Job 24: 8

ὑγρασία.

Jer. 31:18
Eze. 7:17
Eze. 21: 7

ὑγρός.

Jud. 16: 7, 8
Job 8:16

ὑδραγωγός.

2 Ki. 18:17
20:20
Isa. 36: 2
41:18

ὑδρεύω.

Gen. 24:11, 19
20
43 AS[a]
44, 45
Jud. 5:11[b]
Ruth 2: 9
1 Sa. 7: 6
9:11
2 Sa. 23:16
1 Ch. 11:18

[a] pro ἀντλέω. [b] A εὐφραίνω.

ὑδρία.

Gen. 24:14, 15
16, 17
18, 20
43, 45
46
Jud. 7:16, 16
Jud. 7:19, 20
1 Ki. 17:12, 14
16
18:34
Ecc. 12: 6

ὑδρίσκη.

2 Kings 2:20

ὑδροφόρος.

Deu. 29:11
Jos. 9:27
29—AB
Jos. 9:33
33—A

ὕδωρ.

Gen. 1: 2, 6, 6
6, 7, 7
9, 9, 10
20, 21
22
6:17
7: 6—A
7, 10
17, 18
18, 19
20, 24
8: 1, 3, 3
5
6+A
7, 8, 9
11, 13
13
9:11, 11
15
16: 7
18: 4
21:14, 15
19, 19
25
24:11, 13
13, 17
Gen. 24:20 A[a]
32, 43
43, 43
26:18, 19
20, 32
30:38
37:24
43:23
49: 4
Exo. 2:10
4: 9, 9
7:15, 17
18, 19
19, 20
20, 21
24, 24
8: 6, 20
12: 9
14:21, 22
26, 27
27, 28
29
15: 8, 8, 10
19, 22
23+A
25, 25

Exo. 15:27, 27
17: 1, 2, 3
6
20: 4
23:25
29: 4
17 — A[1]
30:18
19 — A[1]
20
21, 21
32:20
34:28
40:10
Lev. 1: 9, 13
6:28
8: 6, 21
9:14
11: 9
9 — A
10 *ter*
12, 32
34, 36
36, 38
40 + A
40, 46
14: 5, 6, 8
9, 50
51, 52
15: 5, 6, 7
8, 10
11 — A
11, 12
13, 16
17, 18
21, 22
27
16: 4, 24
26, 28
17:15, 16
22: 6
Nu. 5:17, 17
18, 19
22, 23
24, 24
26, 27
8: 7
19: 7
8 + A
9, 13
17, 18
19, 20
21, 21
20: 2, 5, 8
8, 10
11, 13
17, 19
24
21: 5, 16
22
24: 6
27:14, 14
31:23, 23
33: 9
9 + A
9, 14
Deu. 2: 6, 28
4:18
5: 8
8: 7, 15
15
9: 9, 18
10: 7
11: 4, 11
12:16, 24
14: 9
15:23
23: 4, 11
32:51
33: 8
Jos. 3: 8, 13
13, 13
15, 16
4:18, 23
7: 5
11: 5, 7
15: 7, 9
18:15
Jud. 1:15
4:19
Jud. 5: 4, 19
25
6:38
7: 4, 5, 5
6, 24
24
15:19
1 Sa. 7: 6
9:11
26:11
12 — A
16
30:11, 12
2 Sa. 5:20
12:27
14:14
17:20, 21
21:10
22:12, 17
23:15, 16
1 Ki. 12 *p* 24 *l* 51
13: 8, 9, 16
17, 18
19, 22
22, 23
14:15 A
17: 4, 6, 10
18: 4, 5
13, 34
35, 35
36 + A
38, 44
19: 6
22:27
2 Ki. 2: 8, 8
14, 14
19, 21
21, 22
3: 9, 11
17, 19
20, 20
22, 22
25 + A
5:12
6: 5, 22
8:15
18:31
19:24
20:20
1 Ch. 11:17, 18
14:11
2 Ch. 18:26
32: 3, 4, 4
30
Ezra 10: 6
Neh. 3:26
8: 1
9:11, 15
20
12:37
13: 2
Job 5:10
8:11
11:15
12:15
14: 9, 19
19
22: 7, 11
24:18
26: 5, 8, 10
27:20[b]
28:25
29:19
34: 7
37: 9
38:30, 34
41:25
Psa. 1: 3
17:12, 16
17
21:15
22: 2
28: 3, 3
31: 6
32: 7
41: 2
45: 4[c]
57: 8
64: 8 B[d]
10
Psa. 65:12
68: 2, 15
16
73:13
76:17, 17
18, 20
77:13, 16
16, 20
78: 3
80: 8
87:18
92: 4
103: 3, 6, 10
104:29, 41
105:11, 32
106:23, 33
35
35 — S[1]
108:18
109: 7 + A
113: 8, 8
118:136
123: 4, 5
135: 6
143: 7
147: 7
148: 4
Pro. 5:15, 16
16, 18
8:24
29 + AS[2]
9:17, 18
18
18: 4
20: 5
21: 1
24:27, 51
51
25:25, 26
Ecc. 2: 6
11: 1
Cant. 4:15
5:12
12 + AS
8: 7
Isa. 1:22, 30
3: 1
5:13
8: 6, 7
11: 9
12: 3
15: 6, 9
17:12, 13
13
18: 2
19: 5, 6
21:14
22: 9, 11
23: 3
24:14
28: 2
30:14 — S[1]
20, 22
25, 28
30
32: 2, 20
33:16
35: 6, 7
36:16
37:25, 25
40:12
41:17
18 - AS[3]
43: 2, 16
20
44: 3, 4, 4
12
48:21, 21
49:10
50: 2
51:10
54: 9
Isa. 55: 1
58:11
63:12
Jer. 2:13, 13
18, 18
24
6: 7
8:14
9: 1, 15
18
10:13
13: 1
14: 3, 3
15:18
17: 8
18:14
23:15
26: 7, 8
27:38
28:13, 16
55
29: 2, 2 OS[1e]
31:34
38: 9
45: 6
48:12
Lam. 1:16
2:19
3:47, 53
5: 4[f]
Eze. 1:24
4:11, 16
17
12:18, 19
16: 4, 9
17: 5, 8
19:10, 10
24: 3
26:19
27:26, 34
30:16
31: 4, 5, 7
14, 14
15, 16
32: 2, 13
14
19 + A
34:18, 19
36:25
47: 1, 1, 2
3, 3, 4
4, 4
5 + A
5 + A
8 *ter*
9, 12
19
48:28
Dan. 1:12
12: 6, 7
Hos. 2: 5
5:10
6: 8
10: 7
11:10
Joel 1:20
3:18
Amos 4: 8
5: 8, 24
8:11, 12
9: 6
Jon. 2: 6
3: 7
Mic. 1: 4
7:12 + A
Nah. 1:12
2: 8, 8
3: 8, 8, 14
Hab. 2:14
3:10, 15
Zec. 9:10, 11
14: 8

a *pro* πάλιν. b S[1] σής.
c S[1] κυμα. d *pro* κύτος.
e *pro* μέσου τ. ὕ. f AB ἡμέρα.

ὕειος.

Psa. 16:14[a]
Isa. 65: 4
Isa. 66: 3, 17

a A υἱος.

ὑετίζω.

Job 38:26
Jer. 14:22

ὑετός.

Gen. 7: 4, 12
8: 2
Exo. 9:29, 33
34
Lev. 26: 4
Deu. 11:11, 14
17
28:12, 24
32: 2
1 Sa. 12:17, 18
2 Sa. 1:21
23: 4
1 Ki. 8:35, 36
17: 1, 7, 14
18: 1, 41
44, 45
2 Ki. 3:17
2 Ch. 6:26, 27
7:13
Job 5:10
29:23
36:27, 27
37:5 — CS[a]
5
38:25, 28
Psa. 71: 6
134: 7
Ps. 146: 8
Pro. 25:14
26: 1
28: 3
Ecc. 11: 3
12: 2
Cant. 2:11
Isa. 4: 6
5: 6
30:23
44:14
55:10
Jer. 5:24
10:13
14: 4
28:16
Eze. 1:28
13:11, 13
22:24
34:26 — A
26
38: 9, 22
40:43
Hos. 6: 3
Joel 2:23
Amos 4: 7
Zec. 10: 1, 1

υἱός.

Gen. 4:17, 25
26
5: 4, 7, 10
13, 16
19, 22
26, 28
30
6: 1, 2[a]
4, 10
18, 18
7: 7, 7, 13
13
8:16, 16
18, 18
9: 1, 8, 18
19, 24
10: 1, 1, 2
3, 4, 6
7, 7
20 *to* 23
25, 29
31, 32
11: 5, 10
11, 13
13, 15
17, 19
21, 23
25
31 *qnq*
12: 5
14:12
15: 2
16:11, 15
15
17:12, 17
19, 23
25, 26
18:10, 14
19
19:12, 37
38, 38
21: 2, 3, 5
7, 8, 9
9, 10
10, 10
11, 13
22: 2, 3, 6
9, 10
12, 13
16, 20
23
23: 3, 5
7, 10
10, 16
Gen. 23:18, 20
24: 3 *to* 8
15, 36
37, 38
40, 47
48, 51
25: 3, 4, 4
5, 6, 6
9 *to* 13
16, 19
25 + A
27: 1, 1, 5
6, 8, 15
15, 17
19 + A
20, 21
24, 27
29 *to* 32
42, 42
46
28: 5, 9
29: 1, 5, 12
13, 32
32 — A
33, 34
34, 35
30: 5, 6, 7
10, 12
14 *to* 17
19, 20
23, 24
35
31: 1, 43
43, 55
32:32
33: 2
34: 2, 5, 5
7, 8, 9
13
14 + A
18, 20
24, 25
26, 27
35: 5, 17
18
22 *to* 26
29
36 *passim*
37: 1, 1, 3
3, 4
32 *to* 35
38: 3, 4, 5
11
14 + A
Gen. 38:26
41:50
42: 1, 5
11, 32
37, 38
45: 9, 10 *ter*
11, 21
26, 28
46: 5, 7, 7
7, 7 A[b]
8 *to* 27
47: 5, 29
48: 1, 2, 5
8, 9, 13
49: 1, 2, 8
9, 22
22, 22
29, 32
33
50:12, 13
23, 23
25
Exo. 1: 1, 7, 9
12, 13
2:10, 11
11, 22
23, 25
3: 9, 10
11, 13
14, 15
16, 22
4:22, 23
25, 29
31
5: 2, 14
15, 19
6: 5, 6, 9
11 *to* 19
21, 22
24, 26
27
7: 2, 4, 5
9: 4 — A
4
6 — A[2]
7, 26
35
10: 9, 20
23
11: 7, 10
12: 3, 6
21 — A
24, 26
27, 28
31, 35
37, 40
42, 47
50, 51
13: 2, 8, 13
14, 15
18, 19
20
14: 2, 3, 5
8, 8, 10
10, 15
16, 19
22, 29
15: 1 — A[1]
19, 22
16: 1, 2, 3
6, 9, 10
12, 15
17, 31
35
17: 1, 6, 7
18: 3, 5, 6
19: 1, 3, 6
20:10, 22
21: 4, 9, 17
31
22:29
23:12, 22
24: 5, 17
25: 2, 21
27:20, 21
21
28: 1, 1, 1
4, 9
11 — B
12, 12
Exo. 28:21, 23
26, 34
36, 37
39
29: 4, 8, 9
10, 15
19, 20
21, 21
21 — A
21, 24
27, 28
28, 28
28 — A[1]
29, 30
32, 35
43, 44
45
30:12, 16
16, 19
30, 31
31: 2 + A
10, 13
16, 17
32:20, 26
28, 29
33: 5, 6, 11
34:16, 16
16 — A
20, 30 A[e]
32[1], 34
35
35: 1, 4, 19
20, 20
30
30 + A
36: 3, 13
14, 21
35
37:19
38:27
39:11, 19
22
40:10, 12
30
Lev. 1: 2, 5, 7
8, 11
2: 2, 3, 10
3: 2, 5, 8
13
4: 2
6: 8, 14
16, 20
22, 25
40
7:13, 19
21
23 *to* 26
28
8: 2, 6, 13
14, 18
22, 24
27, 30
30
30 — AB[1]
30 — AB[1]
31, 31
36
9: 1, 9, 12
18
10: 1, 4, 4
6, 9
11 *to* 14
14[2] — A[1]
15, 16
11: 2
12: 2, 6
13: 2
15: 2, 31
16: 1, 5, 16
17, 19
21, 34
17: 2, 2, 3
5, 8, 8
10, 12
13, 14
18: 2, 10
15, 17
19: 2, 18
20: 2, 2, 17
21: 1, 2, 24

Lev. 21:24
22: 2, 2, 3
15, 18
18
18+AB
32
23: 2, 10
24, 34
43, 44
24: 2, 3, 8
9, 10
10, 10
11, 15
23, 23
25: 2, 33
45, 46
49, 55
26:29, 46
27: 2, 34
Nu. 1 *passim*
2+A
5+B^{1}
2 *passim*
18^{2}−B^{1}
3 *passim*
4: 2, 2, 4
4+A, 5
15 *ter*
16, 19
22, 27
27, 28
28,29,33
33, 34
38, 41
42, 45
46+A
5: 2, 4, 4
6, 9, 12
6: 2, 23
23, 27
7 *passim*
8: 6, 9, 10
11, 13
14
16 *to* 19
19+A
20, 20
22
9: 2, 4, 5
7, 10
17, 17
18, 18
19, 22
10: 8, 12
14 *to* 23
24
24+A
25 *to* 29
11: 4
13: 3 *to* 17
25, 27
33
14: 2, 5, 7
10, 27
30, 33
38, 38
39
15: 2, 18
25, 26
29, 32
33, 38
16: 1 *sex*
2, 7, 8
10, 12
37 *to* 41
17: 2, 5, 6
9, 10
12
18: 1, 1, 2
5
6 *to* 11
14
19 *to* 24
26, 28
31+A
32
19: 2, 9, 10
20: 1, 12
13, 19
22, 24

Nu.20:25, 26
28
21: 6, 10
24, 24
29, 35
22: 1 *to* 5
10
23:18, 19
24: 3,15,17
25: 6, 6, 7
7, 8
11 *qtr*
13, 14
16
26 *passim*
27−A
65+A
27: 1 *qtr*
3, 4, 8
8, 11
12, 18
20, 21
28: 2
30: 1, 2−B
31: 2
4−AB
6, 6, 8
12, 16
30, 42
47, 54
32 *passim*
33: 1, 3, 5
38, 40
51
34: 2, 13
14, 14
17+A
19 *to* 29
35: 2, 8, 10
15, 34
36: 1 *to* 5
7, 7, 8
8, 9, 12
Deu.1: 3, 28
31, 36
36, 38
2: 4, 5, 8
9, 12
19 *ter*
22, 29
33, 37
3:11, 14
16, 18
4: 9 *ter*
10, 25
25, 25
40, 44
45, 46
5:14, 29
6: 2 *ter*
4, 7, 20
21
7: 3, 3, 4
8: 5
9: 2, 2
10: 6 *ter*
11: 6, 6, 21
12:12, 18
25, 28
31
13: 6
14: 1
25 B^{e}
16:11, 14
17:20, 20
18: 5, 5−A
6, 10
21:15, 16
16, 16
17, 18
20
22:21
23: 4, 8, 17
17
24: 9, 18
28:32, 41
53, 56
29: 1, 2, 21
22
31: 1, 9−B

Deu. 31: 9, 13
19, 19
22
23+A
23
32: 8, 14
19, 20
43 AB^{f}
43^{g}, 43
44, 46
49, 51
51
33: 1, 9−A
34: 8, 9, 9
Jos. 1: 1
2: 1, 2, 23
3: 7, 9, 12
17
4: 4, 6, 7
7, 8, 8
12 *ter*
19, 21
22
5: 1, 1, 2
3, 4, 7
9−A
10, 12
6: 6+A
16, 18
7: 1 *qnq*
12, 18
18, 24
24
8:16, 24
27
9: 4, 5
8−A
13, 23
24, 32
10: 4
10−A
11, 11
12−A
20, 21
11: 6+A
14
19+A
22
12: 1,2,6,7
13:10, 13
13, 14
23, 24
25, 28
31, 31
31−A^{2}
31^{h}
14: 1, 1, 4
5, 6, 13
13−A
15: 6, 12
13, 13
14, 14
17, 20
21, 63
16: 1, 4, 5
8+A, 9
9
17: 1, 2 *sep*
3, 3
4+A, 6
6, 7, 7
8−A
12, 13
14
16+A
17
18: 1, 2
3−A
5, 7
7+A^{2}
11−AB
11, 14
16+A
17, 20
21, 28
19: 1−A, 1
8, 9 A^{i}
9, 9, 9
16, 23
31, 39

Jos.19:47, 47
48, 49
49
20: 2, 9
21: 1, 1+A
3 *to* 10
12−A
12, 13
19, 26
20, 26
27, 34
34+A
40, 41
42, 42
45
22: 1−A, 1
9, 9
9+B
9
10 *to* 13
13^{k}−A
15, 15
21, 21
25, 25
28^{k}
30 *to* 33
23: 2
24: 4
30 *to* 33
Jud. 1: 1, 8, 9
13, 16
16, 20
21, 21
22, 34
2: 4−A
6+A
8, 8−A
11
21−A
22+A
3: 2, 5, 6
7, 8, 9
9
11 *to* 15
27, 31
4: 1, 2−A
3, 5, 6
6, 6, 11
12, 23
24
5: 1, 6, 12
6: 1, 2, 3^{m}
3, 7
8+A, 8
11, 29
30
31−A
33
7:12, 14
8:10+A
13, 18
19, 22
22−AB
22−AB
23
28−A
29 *to* 34
9: 1, 2, 5
5, 18
18, 24
26
28 *ter*
30, 31
35, 36
57
10: 1, 1, 4
6 *to* 9
9^{2}−B
10, 11
11, 15
17, 17
18
11 *passim*
5+A
12: 1 A^{n}
1, 2, 3
9, 9, 13
14 *ter*
15
13: 1, 3, 5

Jud. 13:7
24−A
14: 4+A
16, 17
17: 2, 3°
5, 11
18: 1−AB
2, 2, 16
22, 23
25, 26
27−A
30 *qtr*
19:12, 16
22, 30
30+A
20: 1,3,3,3
6−A
7, 13
13, 13
14, 14
15
17+A
18
18−A
19, 21
23
23−A
24
24−A
25−A
25−A
26
26+A
28, 28
28−A
28, 29
30−A
30−A
31, 32
32
35−A
35
36−A
38^{m}
39^{m}
42^{m}
45−A
45−A
48^{m}, 48
21: 1^{m}, 5
6, 10
13−A
14
14−A
18, 20
23, 24
Ruth 1: 1, 2, 3
5, 11
12
4:13, 15
17
1 Sa. 1: 1, 1, 1
1+A
3, 4, 20
23
2:12, 12
21, 22
22, 28
29, 34
3: 6+A
13, 13
21
4: 4, 11
15, 17
20
6:19
7: 1, 4, 6
7, 7, 8
14
8: 1, 2, 3
5, 11
9: 1 *sex*
2, 2, 3
21
10: 2, 11
18
18−A
21, 26
27
11: 5 B^{o}, 11

1 Sa. 12: 2, 8, 12
13: 4, 16
22
14: 1, 3, 3
3, 39
40, 41
42, 42
47, 47
49 *to* 52
15: 6
16: 1, 5, 10
18, 19
20
17:12 A, 12 A
13 A, 13 A
55 A, 56 A
58 A, 58 A
18:17 A
19: 1, 2
20:27, 27
30, 30
31, 31
22: 7 *to* 9
11, 11
12, 13
20, 20
23: 6, 16
25: 8, 10
17, 44
26: 5, 6, 16
19
27: 2
28:19
30: 3, 6, 7
19
31: 2, 2, 6, 7
8−A
12
2 Sa. 1: 4, 5, 12
13, 17
18
2: 5−A
7, 8, 8
10, 12
12, 13
15, 18
25, 31
3: 2, 3, 4
7, 14
15, 23
25, 28
34, 37
39
4: 1
1−AB
2, 2, 2
2−A
4 *qtr*
5, 8, 9
12
5: 4, 13
6: 3, 5
7: 6, 10
14, 14
8: 3, 7, 10
12, 12
16, 16
17, 17
18, 18
9: 3, 4, 5
6, 6, 9^{p}
10 *qtr*
11, 12
10: 1, 1, 2
2, 3, 6
6, 8, 10
11, 14
14, 19
11: 1, 21
21, 22
27
12: 3, 5, 9
14, 24
26, 31
13: 1, 1, 3
4, 21
23, 25
27, 28
29, 30
32, 32

2 Sa. 13:33, 35
36, 37
37
14: 1, 6, 11
11, 16
27, 27
15:27 *ter*
36 *ter*
16: 3, 5, 8
9, 10
11, 11
19
17:10, 10
25
27 *ter*
18: 2, 12
18, 19
20, 22
22, 27
33−B
33−A
33−A
33, 33
19: 2, 4, 4
4+A
5, 16
16, 17
18, 21
22, 24
24−A
32, 35
20: 1, 1, 1
2, 6, 7
10, 13
21, 22
23, 24
21: 2, 2, 2
6, 7, 7
7, 8, 8, 8
11, 12
12, 13
14, 17
19, 21
22:45, 46
23: 1, 9, 9
11, 18
20
20−A
22, 24
26, 27
29−A
29, 32
33, 34
34, 34
36, 36
37−A
37
1 Ki.1: 5, 7, 8
8, 9+A
11, 12
13, 17
19, 21
25, 26
30, 32
33, 36
38, 42
44
47+A
52
2: 1, 4, 5
5, 5, 7
8, 8
13−B
22, 25
28−A
29, 30
30, 32
32−AB
34−B
35
35−AB
(3) 1
p 1 *bis*
39, 46
p 46 *sep*
3: 1, 6, 19
20, 20
21, 21
22+A
22+A

1 Ki.3:22, 22
23 *qtr*
26, 26
4: 2, 3, 3
4−B
5, 5, 6
6, 8−B
9, 10
11−B
12, 13
13+A
14, 16
17+A
17
18, 19
27
5: 5, 7
6: 1, 3, 3
(13)A
7: 2
8: 1+A
9, 19
39, 62
63
10 *p* 22 *ter*
11: 2, 5
7+A
12, 13
14, 20
20
20−A
26
26−A
33, 35
36, 43
44
12:15, 16
17 A
21, 23
24
p 24 *ll* 2,3
ll 5,5−B
ll 20,28
ll 49,54
ll 79,81
31, 33
13: 2, 11
12, 13
27 A
31
14: 1 A, 5 A
5 A, 20 A
21, 21
24, 31
15: 1, 1, 8
18 *ter*
20, 24
25, 27
27−A
28−A
33, 34
16: 1, 3, 6
7−B
8, 13
19, 21
22−A
26, 28
p 28−A
p 28−A
29
29+A
30+A
31, 34
17:17 *to* 20
23
19:10, 14
16−A
16, 19
20:10
13−B
22, 22
26, 29
21 *passim*
17+A
27+A
22: 8, 9, 11
24, 26
40, 41
42, 50 A
51

1 Ki.22:52—AB
52, 53
2 Ki.1:18
18+A
18+A
2: 3, 3+A
5, 7, 15
16
3: 1, 3, 11
27
4: 1, 1, 4
5, 6, 7
14, 16
17, 28
36, 37
38, 38
5·22
6: 1, 24
28, 28
29 *ter*
31+A
32
8: 1, 5, 5
5, 7, 9
9, 12
16, 16
17
19—B
24, 25
25
26—A
28, 29
29
9: 1, 2, 2
9, 9, 14
14, 20
26
29+A
10: 1, 2, 3
6—A, 6
7, 8, 13
13, 15
23, 29
30, 35
11: 1, 2 A^{9}
2—B
2, 4, 12
21
12:21 *ter*
13: 1, 1, 2
3, 3, 5
6+A
9, 10
11, 24
24, 25
25, 25
14 *passim*
13+A
15 *passim*
16: 1, 1, 2
3+A
3, 3, 5
7, 20
17: 1, 7, 8
9, 17
21, 22
24, 31
34, 41
41—A
41
18: 1, 1, 2
4, 9, 18
18—AB
26
37, 37
19: 2, 3, 12
20, 37
37
20: 1, 12
18, 21
21: 1, 2, 6
7, 9, 18
19, 24
26
22: 1, 3, 3
12, 12
14, 14
23: 6, 10
10, 13
15, 30

2 Ki.23:31, 34
36
24: 2, 6, 8
17, 18
25: 7, 18
22, 22
23 *qtr*
25, 25
1 Ch.1 *passim*
17+A
32+A
32+A
43+A
50+AB
50—A
2 *passim*
53—A
3 *passim*
19^{2}—B
21^{4}—A^{1}
4 *passim*
19+A
26^{1}—B
26^{2}—B
26^{3}—B
36+B
5 *passim*
6 *passim*
23^{1}—B
26^{3}—A^{2}
46+A
46+A
65^{3}—AB
7 *passim*
6—AB
13^{3}—AB
17^{1}—B
21+A
25^{3}—A
26+A
27^{1}—A
35+A
8 *passim*
9 *passim*
2+B
4^{3}—AB
4^{4}—AB
5—B
14+A
43^{2}—BS
10: 2, 2, 6
7, 8, 12
14
11: 6, 11
12, 22
22, 24
26, 28
30, 31
34—BS
34, 35
35, 37
38^{r}, 38
39
41 *to* 46
12: 1,3,3,7
7+AS
14, 16
18, 24
25, 26
29, 30
32
14: 3
15: 4 *to* 10
15
17 *qtr*
16: 13, 38
40, 42
17: 9—ABS
13^{s}
18: 10, 11
12
15 *to* 17
19: 1,1,2,2
3—ABS
6, 6, 7
9, 11
12, 15
19—B
20: 1, 3, 4
5, 7

1 Ch.20:7+AB
21: 5—AB
20
22: 5, 6, 9
10, 11
17
23: 1, 6, 8
9 *to* 24
27—A
32
24: 1
1+A^{2}
2 *to* 6
20
22 *to* 31
20^{3}—AB
24^{1}—B
26+A
27+A
28—A
25: 1, 2, 2
3—A^{1}
4, 4+B
5, 5
9 *to* 31
26: 1
1+A
1, 2, 4
6 *to* 11
14, 19
19—B
21, 21
22, 25
29
30—B
32
27: 1, 3, 6
7, 10
14
20—AB
21, 32
28: 1—AB
4—B
5, 5, 5
6, 6, 8
9—B
11, 20
29: 1, 6, 19
22, 24
26, 28
2 Ch.1: 1, 5, 5
2: 4, 12
5: 2, 10
12, 12
6: 9, 16
30, 41
7: 3
8: 2, 8, 8
9
9: 29, 31
10: 2, 15
16, 18
11: 14, 18
19, 21
23
12: 13—A
16
13: 5, 7
7+A
8, 9, 10
12, 16
18, 18
21
14: 1
15: 1
16: 2, 4
17: 1, 7, 14
18: 7, 8, 10
23, 25
19: 11—B
20: 1, 1, 10
14
14—B
14, 19
19, 22
23
21: 1, 2, 2
7, 13
14
17 *ter*

2 Ch.22: 1, 1, 5
6, 6, 7
9, 10
11, 11
23: 1 *qnq*
1+B
3, 3, 11
11
24: 3, 7, 22
25, 27
27
25: 4, 4, 7
11 *to* 14
17—B
17—B
18
23—AB
24
26: 1—AB
3, 17
18, 21
23
27: 1—AB
5, 5—B
5—B, 9
28: 1—B
3, 7, 8
8, 10
12, 27
29: 9, 12
12, 12
12—A
13, 13
14, 14
21
30: 6, 21
26
31: 5+A
8, 13
18, 19
32, 20, 32
33, 33
33: 2, 7, 9
20, 23
25
34: 8, 8, 9
12, 12
20, 20
22, 22
33
35: 3, 4, 5
7, 12
13, 14
15, 17
36: 1
2—B
4, 5, 8
9+A
11—AB
20
Ezra 2 *passim*
39—B
57^{4}—A
60^{2}—A
3: 1—AB
9 *qnq*
10
4: 1
5: 2
6: 9, 10
14, 16
16, 19
20, 21
7: 1 *to* 5
7, 23
8 *passim*
5—B
5—B
33^{4}—B
9: 2, 7
12 *ter*
10: 2, 2, 6
7-ABS^{1}
15, 15
16
18—S^{1}
18, 18
20, 21
22
23+S^{3}

Ezra10: 25 *to* 31
33, 34
38, 38
43, 44
Neh.1: 1, 6, 6
2: 10
3 *passim*
4^{3}—B
4^{4}—B
4^{5}—A
8^{1}-ABS
9—ABS
15—ABS
30+S
4: 14
5: 2, 3 S^{14}
5, 5, 5
6: 10, 10
18 *ter*
7 *passim*
7 B^{u}
24^{2}—AB
26—B
26—B
27—B
33+AS
48+AS
48+AS
48+AS
48+AS
49^{3}—BS
62+AS
8: 1, 14
17, 17
9: 1, 2, 2
4, 4
4—BS^{1}
5+S^{1}
23
10: 1, 2, 9
8, 13
14, 28
30, 36
38—BS^{1}
39
39—B
11 *passim*
12^{1}—BS^{1}
12^{2}—BS^{1}
12^{3} ABS^{1}
12^{6}—A
13^{2}-ABS^{1}
13^{3}-ABS^{1}
14—ABS^{1}
15+ABS
15+S^{3}
15+S^{3}
17+S^{3} *qr*
22^{2}—ABS
22+S^{3}
24+S^{3}
12: 1, 23
23, 24
26
26—B
28
35 *sep*
45, 47
13: 2, 13
13, 16
17, 24
25, 25
28
Est. 5: 11+S^{3}
8: 5+S^{3}
9: 10
12+S^{3}
13, 14
Job 1: 2, 4, 5
13, 18
18+A
2: 9
5: 4
8: 4
14: 21
16: 21—S^{2}
17: 5
19: 17
20: 10
21: 19

Job 21: 26+A
25: 6
27: 14
28: 8
30: 8
35: 8
42: 13
15+A
16 *ter*
p 18 *qnq*
p 18+A
p 18+A
Psa. 2: 7
3: 1
4: 3
7: 1
8: 5
9: 1
10: 4
11: 2, 9
13: 2
16: 14 A^{v}
17: 45, 46
20: 11
28: 1, 1, 6
30: 20
32: 13
35: 8
41: 1
42: 1+A
43: 1
44: 1—A
3, 17
45: 1—A
46: 1—A
47: 1—A
48: 1—A, 3
49: 20
52: 3
56: 5
57: 2
61: 10, 10
65: 5
68: 9
70: 1
71: 1, 4, 19
72: 15
76: 16
77: 5, 6, 6, 9
78: 11
79: 16, 18
81: 6
82: 9
83: 1
84: 1
85: 16
86: 1
87: 1
88: 7, 20
23, 31
48
89: 3, 16
101: 21, 29
102: 7, 13
17, 17
104: 6
105: 37, 38
106: 8, 15
21, 31
108: 9, 10
113: 22, 24
115: 7
126: 3, 4
127: 3, 6, 6
131: 12, 12
136: 7
142: 1
143: 3, 7, 11
12
144: 12
145: 3
147: 2
148: 14
149: 2
150 *p* 6
Pro. 1: 1, 8, 10
15+S^{2}
2: 1, 2, 16
3: 1, 11
12, 21

Pro. 4: 3, 10
20
5: 1, 7
6: 1, 3, 20
7: 1, 1, 24
8: 4, 31
32
9: 12
10: 1, 1, 5
5, 5
11: 19
13: 1, 1, 13
22, 22
24
15: 20, 20
16: 15
17: 21, 21
25
19: 13, 18, 27
23: 15, 19
22, 24
26
24: 1, 13
21, 23
21, 27 A^{3w}
70
27: 11, 25
28: 7, 17
29: 17
Ecc. 1: 1, 13
2: 3, 8
3: 10, 18
19, 21
4: 8—S^{1}
5: 13
8: 11
9: 3, 12
10: 17
12: 12
Cant. 1: 6
2: 3
Isa. 1: 1, 2, 4
2: 1
3: 25
4: 4
7: 1, 1, 3^{r}
5, 7, 6
9, 14
8: 2, 3, 6
9: 6
11: 14
13: 1
17: 3, 9, 11
19: 11, 11
20: 2—AS
21: 16, 17
27: 12
30: 9
31: 8—AS
37: 2
6+S^{1}
21, 38
38
38: 1
39: 1
43: 6
45: 11, 25
49: 20, 22
25
51: 12, 18
20
52: 14—ABS
53: 3—A
54: 13
56: 5
57: 3
60: 4, 14
62: 5, 8
66: 20
Jer. 1: 2, 3, 3
2: 6+S
9—S^{1}
9—S^{1}
16, 29
3: 14, 21
22, 24
4: 23
5: 7, 17
6: 1, 21
7: 18, 30

Jer. 7: 31, 31
32—S^{1}
9: 26, 26
10: 20
11: 22
13: 13, 14
14: 16
15: 4
16: 2, 3, 14
17: 19
18: 21
19: 2, 5, 6
9
20: 1
21: 1, 1
22: 11
18—S
24
24: 1
25: 1—S^{1}
3
26: 25
27: 4, 4, 33
33, 40
28: 43
59—S^{1}
59
29: 3, 19
30: 1, 1, 6
11, 16
32: 7
33: 1, 20
23, 24
34: 2
35: 1
36: 3, 3, 6
6—S^{1}
25
37: 20
38: 14, 15
20
39: 7, 8, 9
12 *ter*
16
19—AS
30, 30
32, 33
35
42: 1+A
3, 3, 3
4—A
4—A
4—S
4
6—S^{1}
6, 8, 14
14, 16
16, 18
18—S
19, 19
43: 1, 4, 10
11, 11
12 *qtr*
14 *qtr*
14+A
26, 26
44: 1, 1+A
3, 3, 13
13
45: 1, 1, 1, 6
46: 14, 14
47: 3, 5
8 *qnq*
11, 11
13, 14
48: 1, 1, 10
10, 11, 15
49: 1
50: 2, 2, 3
6, 6
51: 31, 31
52: 10
Lam. 1: 16
3: 33
4: 2
Eze. 1: 2
2: 1, 3
4+A
6, 8
10, 10

Eze. 3: 3,4,10
11,17
25
4: 1,3
13,16
5: 1
6: 2
5+A
7: 2
8: 5,6,8
12,15
17
11: 2,4,15
12: 2,3,9
18,22
24,27
13: 2,17
14: 3,13
16,18
20,22
15: 2
16: 2,20
26
17: 2,12
18: 2,2,4
10,14
19,19
20,20
20: 3,4,27
31+A
40
21: 2,6,9
12,14
19,20
28,28
22: 2,18
24−A[1]
23: 2,4,7
9,10
12,15
17,23
23,25
36,47
24: 2,16
21,25
25
25: 2,2,3
4,5
10 *ter*
26: 2
27: 2,4
11,15
17,32
28: 2,12
21
29: 2,18
30: 2,5,21
31: 2,14
32: 2,18
33: 2,2,7
10
12+A
12,17
24,30
30
34: 2
35: 2

Eze. 36: 1,17
37: 3,9,11
16 *ter*
18
25+A
25+A
25+A
38: 2,14
39: 1,17
40: 4,46
42:13
43: 7,10
19
44: 5,7,9
9,13
15,25
28
46: 6+A
16,16
17,18
47: 6,13
22,22
22 A[x]
48:11,11
Dan. 1: 3,6
2:25,38
3:25
5:13,22
6:13,24
7:13
8:17
9: 1
10:16
11:10,14
41
12: 1
Hos. 1: 1,3,7
8,10
10,11
11
3: 1,4,5
4: 1
13:13
Joel 1:12
2:28
3: 6,6,6
8,8
16,19
Amos 1: 4 13
2: 4,7
11,11
3:12
4: 5
7:14,17
9: 7,7
Obad. 12,20
Mic. 5: 3,7
6: 5
7: 6
Zeph. 1: 1,1
2: 7,8,9
Zec. 1: 1,7
4:14
6:14
Mal. 1: 6
3: 3,7,17
4: 5

[a] A ἄγγελος. [b] *pro* θυγάτηρ.
[c] *pro* πρεσβύτερος.
[d] A[1] πρεσβύτερος.
[e] *pro* οἶκος. [f] *pro* ἄγγελος.
[g] AB ἄγγελος. [h] A[2] φυλή.
[i] *pro* κλῆρος. [k] A τέκνον.
[m] A ἀνήρ. [n] *pro* ἀνήρ.
[o] A κατὰ μόνας. [p] A οἶκος.
[q] *pro* ἀδελφή. [r] A ἀδελφός.
[s] S[1] λαός. [t] *pro* ἀγρός.
[u] *pro* λαός. [v] *pro* υἱός.
[w] *pro* τέκνον. [x] *pro* φυλή.

ὑλακτέω.

Isaiah 56:10

ὕλη.

Job 19:20[a]
38:40

Psa. 68: 30[1] S[b]
Isa. 10:17

[a] A ἰσχύς. [b] *pro* ἰλύς.

ὕλις.

Psalm 39: 3 ABS[a]

[a] *pro* ἰλύς.

ὑλώδης.

Job 29: 5

ὑμνέω.

Jud. 16:24[a]
1 Ch.16: 9
2 Ch.23:13
29:30,30
Neh.12:24 AS[b]
Job 38: 7+A
Psa. 21:23
64:14

Psa. 70: 8−S[1]
136: 3 S[1 b]
Pro. 1:20
8: 3
Isa. 12: 4,5
25: 1
42:10
Dan. 3:23,24

[a] A αἰνέω. [b] *pro* ὕμνος.

ὕμνησις.

Psa. 70: 6[a]

Psa. 117:14

[a] S ὑπόμνησις.

ὕμνος.

2 Ch. 7: 6
Neh.14:24[a]
46
Psa. 6: 1−A
39: 4
53: 1
54: 1
60: 1
64: 2

Psa. 66: 1
71:19
75: 1
99: 4
118:171
136: 3[b]
148:14
Isa. 42:10

[a] AS ὑμνέω. [b] S[1] ὑμνέω.

ὑμνῳδέω.

1 Chronicles 25: 6

ὑπάγω.

Exo. 14:21

Jer. 43:19 S[1 a]

[a] *pro* ὑμεῖς.

ὕπαιθρος.

Proverbs 21: 9

ὑπαίρω.

2 Chronicles 32:23 A[a]

[a] *pro* ὑπεραίρω.

ὑπακοή.

2 Samuel 22:36

ὑπακούω.

Gen. 16: 2
22:18
26: 5
27:13 A[a]
39:10
41:40
Lev. 26:14,18
21,27
Deu. 17:12
20:12
21:18,20[b]
26:14[c],17
30: 2 A[d]
Jos. 22: 2[c e]
Jud. 2:17[f]
20 A[d]
1 Sa. 30:24 B[a]
2 Sa. 22:42 AB[a]
45 AB
1 Ch.29:23[c]
2 Ch.11: 4 A[a]
24:19[b]
Est. 3: 4
4+A
Job 5: 1[e]
9: 3,14[e]
16[e]

Job 13:22
14:15
19:16
38:34[h]
Psa. 17:45[f]
Pro. 1:24
2: 2
8: 1
15:23
29 S[a]
17: 4
21:13 A[a]
22:21
28:17
29:12[i],19
Cant. 3: 1
2+AC
5: 6[f]
Isa. 11:14
29:24
50: 2[h]
10[h b]
65:12,24[k]
66: 4
Jer. 3:13[h],25
11:10 S[d]
13:10
Jer. 16:12
Dan. 3:12

Dan. 7:27
Mal. 2: 2 AB

[a] *pro* ἐπακούω. [b] A ἀκούω.
[c] B ἐπακούω. [d] *pro* εἰσακούω.
[e] A εἰσακούω. [f] A ἐπακούω.
[g] *pro* ἀκούω. [h] S ἐπακούω.
[i] BS ἐπακούω. [k] AS ἐπακούω.

ὕπανδρος.

Nu. 5:20,29

Pro. 6:24,29

ὑπάντησις.

Jud. 11:34[a]
1 Ch.14: 8 A[b]

Pro. 7:15 B[1 c]

[a] A ἀπάντησις. [b] *pro* ἀπάντησις
[c] *pro* συνάντησις.

ὕπαρξις.

2 Ch.35: 7
Ezra 10: 8
Psa. 77:48
Pro. 8:21
13:11

Pro. 18:11
19:14
Jer. 9:10
Dan.11:13,24
28

ὑπάρχω.

Gen. 12: 5
13: 6
14:16
24:50
25: 5
31:18
34:23
36: 6,7,7
39: 5
42:13,32
45:11,18
46: 6
47:18
Exo. 14:11
22. 3
32:24
Nu. 32: 4
Deu. 20:14
21:16
Jos. 4: 6
5:12
7:24
Jud. 19:19 A[a]
19 A[a]
Ruth 2:21
4: 9
1 Sa. 9: 7
1 Ch.27:31
28: 1
2 Ch.15:17
20:33
26:10
31: 3
Ezra 6: 8
Est. 3: 8,13
8: 1,7
Job 2: 3,4
15:29
17: 3
18: 7,17
20:20,29
21:10
29:12 A[a]
38:26
42 *p* 18

Psa. 30:10
38:14
54:20
58:14
68:21
71:12
72:25
102:16
103:33−A[1]
35
108:11,12
145: 2
Pro. 5:17
6: 7,31
8:18
11: 4+A
14,14
17:16,17
19: 4
29: 7,18
Ecc. 5:18
6: 2
Isa. 59:10
Jer. 4:14
5:13
7:32
26:19
27:20
Lam. 1: 2
5: 3,7
Eze. 16:49
26:12[b],21
28:19
38:11
Joel 1:18
Amos 5: 3
6:10
Obad. 16
Mic. 5: 4
7: 1,2
Hab. 3:17
Zeph. 3: 6
Hag. 2: 3
Zec. 8:10
Mal. 1:14

[a] *pro* εἰμί. [b] A πλοῦτος.

ὕπατος.

Dan. 3: 2,3

Dan. 6: 7

ὑπεναντίος.

Gen. 2[?]:17
24:60
Exo. 1:10
15: 7
23:27
32:25
Lev. 26:16
Nu. 10: 9

Deu. 32:27
Jos. 5:13
2 Ch. 1:11
20:29
26:13
Est. 8:13
Job 13:24
33:10[a]
Psa. 73:10
Isa. 1:24
26:11
59:18

Isa. 63:18+A
64: 2,2
Lam. 2: 4,4
Nah. 1: 2

[a] C ἐπεναντίος.

ὑπεξαίρω.

Genesis 30: 9

ὑπεραίρω.

2 Ch.32:23[a]
Psa. 37: 5

Psa. 71:16
Pro. 29:47

[a] A ὑπαίρω.

ὑπεράνω.

Gen. 7:20[a]
Deu. 26:19
28: 1
Neh. 12:38 S[3]
(39) S[3]
Psa. 8: 2
73: 5
148: 3
Isa. 2: 2
Eze. 1:25+A

Eze. 8: 2
10:19
11 22
43:15
Dan. 7: 6
Jon. 4: 6
Mic. 4: 1
Hag. 2:15[a]
Mal. 1: 5

[a] A ἐπάνω.

ὑπεράνωθεν.

Psa. 77:23

Eze. 1:25

ὑπέραρσις.

Ezekiel 47:11

ὑπερασπίζω.

Gen. 15: 1
Deu. 33:29
2 Ki. 19:34
20: 6
Psa. 19: 1
Pro. 2: 7
4: 9
24:28

Isa. 31:5
5−AS[3]
37:35
38: 6
Hos. 11: 8
Zec. 9:15
12: 8

ὑπερασπισμός.

2 Sa. 22:36
Psa. 17:36

Lam. 3:64

ὑπερασπιστής.

2 Sa. 22: 3,31
Psa. 17: 3,31
26: 1
27: 7,8
30: 3,5
32:20
36:39

Psa. 39:18
58:12
70: 3
83:10
113:17,18
19
143: 2

ὑπερβαίνω.

1 Sa. 5: 5,5
2 Sa. 18:23
22:30
Job 9:11
14: 5
24: 2

Job 38:11
Psa. 17:30
Pro. 9:18+AS[3]
Jer. 5:22,22
Mic. 7:18

ὑπερβαλλόντως.

Job 15:11[a]

[a] A ὑπερβάλλω.

ὑπερβάλλω.

Job 15:11 A[a]

[a] *pro* ὑπερβαλλόντως.

ὑπερδυναμόω.

Psalm 64: 4

ὑπερεῖδον.

Gen. 42:21
Lev. 20: 4
26:40,43

Lev. 26:44
Nu. 5:12
22:30

Nu. 31:16
Deu. 3:26
21:16
22: 1, 3, 4
Job 6:14
Job 31:19
Psa. 26: 9[a]
54: 2
77:59, 62
Zec. 1:12

[a] S[2] ἐγκαταλείπω.

ὑπερείδω.

Job 8:15[a] Pro. 9: 1

[a] A ὑπέρειμι.

ὑπέρειμι.

Job 8:15 A[a] [a] pro ὑπερείδω.

ὑπερεκχέω, -χύω.

Pro. 5:16
Joel 2:24 A[a]
Joel 3:13[b]

[a] pro ὑπερχέω.
[b] AS ὑπερχεω.

ὑπερέχω.

Gen. 25:23
39: 9
41:40
Exo. 26:13
Lev. 25:27[a]
Jud. 5:25[b]
1 Ki. 8: 8
2 Ch. 5: 9[c]
Dan. 7:23

[a] (AS[1] ὑπερ ἔχει). [b] A ἰσχυρός. [c] A περιέχω.

ὑπερηφανέω -νεύομαι

Neh. 9:10
16-BS[1]
Job 22:29
Psa. 9:23
Dan. 5:20

ὑπερηφανία.

Exo. 18:21
Lev. 26:19
Nu. 15:30
Deu. 17:12
1 Sa. 17:28 A
Psa. 16:10
30:19, 24
35:12
58:13
72: 6
Psa. 73: 3, 23
100: 7
Pro. 8:13
Isa. 16: 6
Jer. 31:29
Eze. 7:20
16:49, 56
Dan. 4:34
Amos 8: 7
Obad. 3

ὑπερήφανος.

Job 38:15
40: 7
Psa. 17:28
88:11
93: 2
100: 5
118:21, 51
69, 78
122
Ps. 122: 4
130: 6
Pro. 3:34
Isa. 1:25+AS
2:12
13:11
29:20
Zeph. 3: 6

ὑπέρθυρος.

Isaiah 6: 4

ὑπερισχύω.

Gen. 49:26
Jos. 17:18
2 Sa. 24: 4
1 Ki. 16:22+A
Dan. 3:22
11:23

ὑπέρκειμαι.

Pro. 29:47 Eze. 16:47

ὑπερκρατέω.

1 Kings 16:22-AB

ὑπερμεγέθης.

1 Chronicles 20: 6

ὑπερμήκης.

Numbers 13:33

ὑπέρογκος.

Exo. 18:22, 26
Deu. 30:11
2 Sa. 13: 2
Lam. 1: 9
Dan. 11:36

ὑπερόρασις.

Numbers 22:30

ὑπεροράω.

Lev. 26:37
Deu. 22: 4 A[2a]
Jos. 1: 5
Psa. 9:22
Isa. 58: 7
Eze. 7:19
Nah. 3:11[b]

[a] pro ὁράω. [b] S[3] παροράω.

ὕπερος.

Proverbs 23:31

ὑπεροχή.

1 Sa. 2: 3+A Jer. 52:22

ὑπέροψις.

Leviticus 20: 4

ὑπερτίθημι.

Proverbs 15:22

ὑπερυψόω.

Psa. 36:35
96: 9
Dan. 4:34
11:12 A[a]

[a] pro ὑψόω.

ὑπερφερής.

Daniel 2:31

ὑπερφέρω.

Daniel 7:24

ὑπερχαρής.

Esther 5: 9

ὑπερχέω, -χύω.

Lam. 3:53
Joel 2:21[a]
Joel 3:13 AS[b]

[a] A ὑπερεκχύω.
[b] pro ὑπερεκχέω.

ὑπερωμία.

1 Sa. 9: 2 1 Sa. 10:23

ὑπερῷος, -ον.

Jud. 3:20, 23
24, 25
2 Sa. 18:33
1 Ki. 17:19, 23
2 Ki. 1: 2
4:10, 11
23:12
1 Ch. 28:11, 20
2 Ch. 3: 9
Ps. 103: 3, 13
Jer. 20: 2
22:13, 14
Eze. 41: 7
42: 5
Dan. 6:10

ὑπεύθυνος.

Proverbs 1:23[a]

[a] (S[1] ὑπευθυνοντο.)

ὑπέχω.

Psa. 88:51 Lam. 5: 7

ὑπήκοος.

Deu. 20:11
Jos. 17:13
Pro. 4: 3
Pro. 13: 1
21:28

ὑπηρεσία.

Job 1: 3

ὑπηρέτης.

Pro. 14:35 Isa. 32: 5

ὕπνος.

Gen. 20: 3, 6
28:16
31:10, 11
24, 40
40: 9
41:17, 22
Nu. 12: 6
24: 4, 16
Jud. 16:14, 20
1 Sa. 20:41 A[a]
26: 7-A
1 Ki. 3: 5
20+A
Est. 6: 1
Job 14:12
Psa. 75: 6
126: 2
131: 4
Pro. 4:16
6: 4, 9
Ecc. 5:11
8:16
Isa. 29: 7[b], 8
Jer. 28:39-S[1]
38:26
Dan. 2: 1
6:18
Hos. 7: 6
Zec. 4: 1

[a] pro Ἀργάβ. [b] A ἐνύπνιον.

ὑπνόω.

Gen. 2:21
Jud. 19: 4 A[a]
1 Sa. 26:12
1 Ki. 19: 5
Job 3:13
Psa. 3: 6
4: 9
12: 4
43:24
75: 6
77:65
Ps. 120: 4[b]
Pro. 3:24
4:16
6:10
Ecc. 5:11
Jer. 14: 9
26:27-S[1]
28:39-S[1]
Eze. 34:25
Joel 1:13

[a] pro αὐλίζω. [b] S ἐξυπνόω.

ὑπνώδης.

Proverbs 23:21

ὑποβάλλω.

Daniel 3: 9+A

ὑποβλέπω.

1 Samuel 18: 9 AB

ὑπόγαιος.

Jeremiah 45:11

ὑπογράφω.

Esther 8:13

ὑπόδειγμα.

Ezekiel 42:15

ὑποδείκνυμι.

1 Ki. 10 p 22 B[a]
1 Ch. 28:18
2 Ch. 15: 3-B
20: 2
Est. 2: 9[b], 10
20
Est. 3: 4, 4
4: 7
5:11
8: 1
Jer. 38:19

[a] pro ὑπολείπω.
[b] AB ἀποδείκνυμι.

ὑποδέω.

2 Ch. 28:15 Eze. 16:10 AB[a]

[a] pro ὑποδύω.

ὑπόδημα.

Gen. 14:23
Exo. 3: 5
12:11
Deu. 8: 4-A
25: 9, 10
29: 5
33:25
Jos. 5:15
9:11, 19
Ruth 4: 7, 8
1 Sa. 12: 3
1 Ki. 2: 5
Neh. 9:21 AS[a]
Psa. 59:10
107:10
Cant. 7: 1
Isa. 5:27
11:15
Eze. 24:17, 23
Amos 2: 6
8: 6

[a] pro πούς.

ὑποδύτης.

Exo. 28:27, 29
29, 30
36:30, 31
Exo. 36:32, 33
34
Lev. 8: 7[a]

[a] A ἐπενδυτης.

ὑποδύω.

Eze. 16:10[a] [a] AB ὑποδέω.

ὑποζύγιον.

Gen. 36:24
Exo. 4:20
9: 3
20:10, 17
22: 9, 10
30
23: 4, 5, 12
34:20
Deu. 5:14
14-AB[1]
21
Jos. 6:21
Jos. 7:24
Jud. 1:14+A
14
5:10+A
19: 3 A[a]
10 A[a]
21 A[a]
28 A[a]
2 Sa. 16: 2
2 Ch. 28:15
Job 24: 3
Zec. 9: 9

[a] pro ὄνος.

ὑπόθεμα.

Exodus 25:38

ὑποκαίω.

Jer. 1:13-S[1]
Eze. 24: 5
Amos 4: 2-A

ὑποκαλύπτω.

Exo. 26:12-B Exo. 26:12[a]

[a] A ἐπικαλύπτω.

ὑποκάτω.

Deu. 28:13
Jud. 7: 8[a]
1 Ki. 6:10
2 Ch. 4: 3[a]
Job 26: 8[a]
37: 2-A
Isa. 10: 4+AS[3]
Eze. 6:13+A
24: 5
40:18
Mal. 4: 3
&c., &c.

[a] A ὑποκάτωθεν.

ὑποκάτωθεν.

1 Ki. 6:12
7:18+A
Lam. 3:65[a]
Eze. 1:23[a]
Eze. 42: 5, 6
43:14
&c., &c.

[a] A ὑποκάτω.

ὑπόκειμαι.

Job 16: 4

ὑποκρίνομαι.

Job 39:32 S[1a] [a] pro ἀποκρίνω-

ὑποκριτής.

Job 34:30 Job 36:13

ὑπολαμβάνω.

2 Ki. 20:17 A[a]
2 Ch. 25: 8
Job 2: 4
4: 1
6: 1
8: 1
9: 1
11: 1
12: 1
15: 1
16: 1
18: 1
19: 1
20: 1, 2
21: 1
22: 1
23: 1
25: 1, 3
Job 26: 1
32: 6, 17
33:31+A
34: 1
35: 1
39:33
40: 1
42: 1
Psa. 16:12
29: 2
47: 7 A[b]
10
49:21
67:17
72:16
Jer. 41: 9
Zeph. 3:12[c]

[a] pro ὑπολειπω. [b] pro ἐπιλαμβανω. [c] ABS ὑπολείπω.

ὑπόλειμμα.

1 Sa. 9:24
2 Ki. 21:14
Job 20:21
Mic. 4: 7
5: 7, 8
Mal. 2:15

ὑπολείπω.

Gen. 27:36
30:36
32:24
44:20
45: 7
47:18
50: 8
Exo. 8: 9, 11
10:12, 15
15[i], 19
24, 26
23:11
26:12—B
Lev. 23:22
Jos. 10: 8[b]
12: 4
13: 1
21:26
23:12 A[c]
12
Jud. 6: 4 A[d]
7: 3
21: 7
1 Sa. 5: 4
11:11, 11
14:36
25:22, 34
30:21[e]
2 Sa. 8: 4
9: 1, 3
17:12
1 Ki. 9:20 A
21 A
10 p 22[f]
p 22
15:29
16:11+A
17:17
18:22
1 Ki. 19:10, 14
22:47 A
2 Ki. 7:13
13: 7
17:18
19:30
20:17[g]
24:14
25:12
1 Ch. 13: 2
18: 4
Ps. 105:11
Pro. 2:21+AS
21
11:26
Isa. 4: 3
Jer. 5:10
24: 8
27:20
29:12
Eze. 6: 8+A
12+A
12:16
14:20, 22
Dan. 2:44
10: 8, 9, 17
Joel 2:14
Amos 5: 3, 3
6: 9, 9
Obad. 5 ABS[h]
Hab. 2: 8
Zeph. 3: 3[i]
12 ABS[k]
Zec. 9: 7
10:10
12:14
13: 8
Mal. 4: 1

[a] A καταλείπω. [b] A ὑφίστημι.
[c] pro προστίθημι.
[d] pro καταλειπω. [e] AB ἐκλύω.
[f] B ὑποδείκνυμι. [g] A ὑπολαμβανω
[h] pro ἐπιλειπω. [i] S[1]? ἐπιλείπω.
[k] pro ὑπολαμβάνω.

ὑπολήνιον.

Isa. 16:10
Joel 3:13
Hag. 2:16
Zec. 14:10 ABS[a]

[a] pro ἀπολήνιον.

ὑπόλοιπος.

2 Ki. 4: 7 A[a]
Isa. 11:11
Jer. 34:16 S[a]

[a] pro ἐπίλοιπος.

ὑπόλυσις.

Nahum 2:10

ὑπολύω.

Deu. 25: 9, 10
Ruth 4: 7, 8
Isa. 20: 2

ὑπομένω.

Exo. 12:39 A[a]
Nu. 22:19
Jos. 19:48
Jud. 3:25[b]
2 Ki. 6:33
Job 3: 9
6:11
7: 3
8:15
9: 4
14:14
15:31
17:13
20:26
Job 22:21
32: 4, 16
33: 5
41: 2
Psa. 24: 3, 5, 21
26:14, 14
32:20
34: 9, 34
39: 2, 2
51:11
55: 7
68: 7, 21
103:13
118:95—S[1]
Ps. 120: 5, 5
141: 8
144: 9[c]
Pro. 20:23
Isa. 25: 9—AS
40:31
49:23—AS
51: 5
59: 9
60: 9
64: 4
5 S[d]
Jer. 14:19, 22
Lam. 3:21
24—AB
25, 26
Dan. 12:12
Mic. 7: 7
Nah. 1: 7
Hab. 2: 3
Zeph. 3: 8
Zec. 6:14
Mal. 3: 2

[a] pro ἐπιμένω. [b] A προσμένω.
[c] S[2] σύμπας. [d] pro ποιεω.

ὑπομιμνήσκω.

1 Kings 4: 33[a]

[a] pro ἀναμιμνήσκω.

ὑπόμνημα.

2 Sa. 8:16
Ezra 6: 2

ὑπομνηματισμός.

Ezra 4:15

ὑπομνηματογράφος.

1 Ch. 18:15
2 Ch. 34: 8
Isa. 36: 3, 22

ὑπόμνησις.

Psalm 70: 6 S[a]

[a] pro ὕμνησις.

ὑπομονή.

1 Ch. 29:15
Ezra 10: 2
Job 14:19
Psa. 9:19
38: 8
Psa. 61: 6
70: 5
Jer. 14: 8
17:13

ὑπονοέω.

Daniel 7:25

ὑπονύσσω.

Isaiah 58: 3

ὑποπίπτω.

Proverbs 15: 1

ὑποπόδιον.

Psa. 98: 5
109: 1
Isa. 66: 1
Lam. 2: 1

ὑποπτεύω.

Psalm 118:39

ὑποπυρρίζω.

Leviticus 13:24

ὑποσκελίζω.

Psa. 16:13
36:31
139: 5
Pro. 10: 8
Pro. 26:18
29:25
Jer. 23:12

ὑποσκέλισμα.

Proverbs 24:17

ὑποσκελισμός.

Proverbs 11: 3 A

ὑπόστασις.

Deu. 1:12
11: 6
Jud. 6: 4
Ruth 1:12
1 Sa. 13:21, 23
1 Sa. 14: 4
Job 22:20
Psa. 38: 6, 8
68: 3
88:48

Ps. 138:15
Jer. 10:17
23:22
Eze. 19: 5
Eze. 26:11
43:11
Nah. 2: 7

ὑποστέλλω.

Exo. 23:21
Deu. 1:17
Job 13: 8
Hab. 2: 4
Hag. 1:10

ὑπόστημα, —τεμα.

2 Sa. 23:14
1 Ch. 11:16 A[a]
Jer. 23:18

[a] pro σύστημα.

ὑποστήριγμα.

1 Ki. (3) p 1
7:11
11+A
1 Ki. 10:12
Jer. 5:10
Dan. 11: 7

ὑποστηρίζω.

Psa. 36:17
Psa. 144:14

ὑποστρέφω.

Gen. 8: 7 A[a]
14:17
43: 9
50:14[b]
Exo. 32:31[c]
Jos. 2:23
7:12[c]
Jud. 3:19[d]
7:15[c]
14: 8[c]
Jud. 21:23[e]
2 Ki. 2:25 A[f]
3:27 A[f]
2 Ch. 25:10 A[f]
28:15 A[f]
Est. 6:12
Pro. 23: 5
24:18 S[1] [g]
Ecc. 9:11 S[f]

[a] pro ἀναστρέφω.
[b] A ἐπιστρέφω, B ἀποστρέφω.
[c] A ἐπιστρεφω. [d] A ἀναστρεφω.
[e] A ἀποστρεφω. [f] pro ἐπιστρεφω
[g] pro ἀποστρέφω.

ὑποστρώννυμι.

Est. 4: 3 S[3] [a]
Isa. 58: 5
Eze. 27:30 A[a]

[a] pro στρώννυμι.

ὑποτάσσω.

1 Ki. 10:15
1 Ch. 22:18
29:24
2 Ch. 9:14
Psa. 8: 7
17:48
36: 7
46: 4
Psa. 59:10
61: 2, 6
107:10
143: 2
Dan. 6:13
11:39
Hag. 2:18[a]

[a] AS[2] τάσσω.

ὑποτίθημι.

Gen. 28:18[a]
47:29
49:15
Exo. 17:12
Exo. 26:12
27: 5
40:18[b]
Jer. 43:25

[a] A τίθημι. [b] A ἐπιτίθημι.

ὑποτίτθιος.

Hosea 14: a 1

ὑποτομεύς.

2 Samuel 12:31—B

ὑπουργός.

Joshua 1: 1[a]

[a] A λειτουργός.

ὑπόφαυσις.

Ezekiel 41:16

ὑποφέρω.

1 Ki. 8:64—A
Job 2:10
4: 2[a]
15:35[b]
31:23
Psa. 54:13
Psa. 68: 8
Pro. 6:33
14:17
18:14
Amos 7:10
Mic. 7: 9

[a] C φερω. [b] S[1] φέρω.

ὑποφυλλίς.

Obadiah 6 S[1] [a]

[a] pro ἐπιφυλλίς.

ὑποχείριος.

Gen. 14:20
Nu. 21: 2, 3
Jos. 6: 2
9:31
Jos. 10:12
11: 8
Isa. 58: 3
Jer. 49:18

ὑποχόνδριος.

1 Samuel 31: 3

ὑπόχρεως.

1 Sa. 22: 2—A
Isa. 50: 1

ὑποχυτήρ.

Jeremiah 52:19—S

ὑποχωρέω.

Judges 20:37—A

ὕποψ.

Deuteronomy 14:16 A[a]

[a] pro ἔποψ.

ὑπτιάζω.

Job 11:13

ὕπτιος.

Job 14:19

ὑπώπιον.

Proverbs 20:30

ὗς.

Lev. 11: 7
Deu. 14: 8
2 Sa. 17: 8—A
1 Ki. 20:19
1 Ki. 22:38
Psa. 79:14 S[?][a]
Pro. 11:22

[a] pro σῦς.

ὕσσωπος.

Exo. 12:22
Lev. 14: 4, 6, 49
51, 52
Nu. 19: 6, 18
1 Ki. 4:29
Psa. 50: 9

ὑστερέω.

Nu. 9: 7, 13
Deu. 15: 8 A[a]
Neh. 9:21
Job 36:17
Psa. 22: 1
38: 5
83:12[b]
Ecc. 6: 2
9: 8
10: 3
Cant. 7: 2
Dan. 5:27
Hab. 2: 3

[a] pro ἐνδέω. [b] S[2] στερέω.

ὑστέρημα.

Jud. 18:10
19:19, 20
Ezra 6: 9
Psa. 33:10
Ecc. 1:15

ὑστεροβουλία.

Proverbs 24:71

ὕστερος, -ρον.

1 Ch.29:29
Pro. 5: 4
23:31
24:47
Jer. 27:17
36: 2
38:19, 19
47: 1+A

ὑφαίνω.

Exo. 35:35
37:21
Lev. 19:19
Jud. 16:13
14—A
1 Sa. 17: 7
2 Sa. 21:19
2 Ki.23. 7
1 Ch.11:23
20: 5
2 Ch. 2:14
3:14
Isa. 59: 5

ὑφαιρέω.

Job 21:18
27:20
Ecc. 2:10 A[a]

[a] pro ἀφαιρέω.

ὑφάντης.

Exo. 26: 1
Exo. 28:28

ὑφαντός.

Exo. 26:31
28: 6
35:35
36:10, 11
Exo. 36:15, 30
35
37: 3,5,21

ὕφασμα.

Exo. 28: 8, 17
36:17, 29
Jud. 16:14
Job 38:36

ὑφίστημι.

Nu. 22:26
Jos. 7:12
10: 8 A[a]
Jud. 9:15[b]
1 Sa. 30:10
2 Sa. 2:23
Psa. 64: 8+S[2]
129: 3
139:11
147: 6
Pro. 13: 8
Pro. 21:29
25: 6
27: 4
Eze. 22:14
Hos. 13:13
Amos 2:15
Mic. 5: 7
Nah. 1: 6
Zec. 9: 8
Mal. 3: 2

[a] pro ὑπολείπω. [b] A πείθω.

ὑψηλοκάρδιος.

Proverbs 16: 5

ὑψηλός.

Gen. 7:19, 20
12: 6
22: 2
Exo. 6: 1, 6
14: 8
32:11
Nu. 33: 3
Deu. 3: 5, 24
4:34
5:15
6:21
7:8+AB[a]
19
9:26[b], 29
11: 2, 30
12: 2
26: 8
28.52
29: 3+AB
32:27
Jud. 9:51 A[b]
1 Sa. 2: 3
9: 2
2 Sa. 22:48 A[b]
1 Ki. 3: 2, 3, 4
9: 8
11: 5
12:31, 32
13: 2, 32
33, 33
14:23, 23
1 Ki.15:14
16 p28—A
p28—A
22:44, 44
2 Ki.12: 3, 3
14: 4, 4
15: 4, 4
35, 35
16: 4
17: 9, 10
11, 29
32, 32
32, 36
18: 4, 22
21: 3
23: 5, 8, 9
15, 15
19, 20
2 Ch. 1: 3
6:32
7:21
11:15
14: 3
15:17
17: 6
20:33
21:11
27: 3
28: 4, 25
31: 1
32:12
2 Ch.33: 3, 17
19
34: 3, 4, 7
Neh. 9:25
Est. 5:14+S[3]
7: 9+S[3]
Job 5: 7
11: 8
22:12
35: 5
41:25
Psa. 17:34
88:28
92: 4
98: 2
103:18
112: 4, 5
135:12
137: 6, 6
Pro. 8: 2
9: 3
10:21
17:16
18:19
24:36
25: 3
Ecc. 5: 7, 7, 7
7: 9
Isa. 2:11, 12
13
14—AB
14, 15
15
3:16
5:25
6: 1
9: 9, 12
17, 21
10: 4, 33
33—S
34—A
Isa. 10:34
12: 5
14:13, 13
26, 27
22:16—S[1]
24: 4
26: 5, 11
28: 4
30:25
32:15
33: 5, 16
40: 9
45:14
57: 7, 15
Jer. 2:20
3: 6
16:16+A
19: 5
21: 5+S
28:58
29:17
32:16
34: 4
38:15 AS[1 c]
39:17, 21
Lam. 3:40
Eze. 6: 3,6,13
9: 2
17:22, 24
20:28, 33
34, 40
21:26
31: 3
34: 6, 14
40: 2
Dan. 8: 3, 3, 3
Hos. 5: 8
Amos 4:13[d]
Hab. 3:19
Zeph. 1:16

[a] A μέγας. [b] pro ἰσχυρός. [c] pro Ῥαμά. [d] AB ὕψος.

ὕψιστος.

Gen. 14:18, 19
20, 22
Nu. 24:16
Deu. 32: 8
2 Sa. 22:14
Job 16:19
25: 2
31: 2, 28
Psa. 7:18
9: 3
12: 6
17:14
20: 8
45: 5
7+AS[2]
46: 3
49:14
56: 3
65: 4+S[2]
70:19
72:11
76:11
77:17, 35
Psa. 77:56
81: 6
82:19
86: 5
90: 1, 9
91: 2, 9
96: 9
106:11
148: 1
Isa. 14:14
57:15, 15
Lam. 3:34, 37
Dan. 3:26—A
32
4:14, 21
22, 29
31
5:18, 21
7:18, 22
25, 25
27
Mic. 6: 6

ὕψος.

Gen. 6:15
Exo. 25: 9, 22
27: 1, 14
15, 16
18
30: 2
37:16
38: 1+A
Jud. 5:18
1 Sa. 17: 4
2 Sa. 1:19, 25
22:17, 34
1 Ki. 6: 6
7+A
14, 19
24
7: 3, 4
4—B
1 Ki. 7:10, 13
18
30—B
2 Ki.19:22, 23
25:17, 17
1 Ch.14: 2
15:16
23:17
29: 3
2 Ch. 1: 1
3: 4—A[1]
15
4: 1—A
2
6:13
17:12
20:19
32:26
Ezra 6: 3
Neh. 9: 5 S[3 a]
Job 5:11
39:18
40: 5
Psa. 7: 8
11: 9
17:17
55: 3
67:19
72: 8
74: 6
94: 4
101:20[b]
102:11
143: 7
Ecc. 10: 6
12: 5
Cant. 7: 8
Isa. 2:11
17 AS[c]
7:11
10:12
25:12
Isa. 35: 2
37:23, 24
24, 24
38:10, 14
40:26
Jer. 6: 2
28:53 AB[e] S[d]
37:18[e]
52:21
Lam. 1:13
Eze. 1:18
31: 2,7,14
40: 5, 42
41: 8, 22
43:13
Dan. 3: 1
4: 7,8,17
Amos 2: 9, 9
4:13 AB[f]
5: 7
Mic. 1: 3
Hab. 2: 9[g]
3:10

[a] pro ὑψόω. [b] S[1] ὑψοῦ. [c] pro ὕβρις. [d] pro τεῖχος. [e] A τεῖχος. [f] pro ὑψηλός. [g] S[1] οἶκος.

ὑψοῦ.

Psalm 101:20 S[1 a]

[a] pro ὕψος.

ὑψόω.

Gen. 7:17, 20
24
19:13
24:35
26:13
39:15, 18
41:52 A[a]
48:19
Exo. 15: 2
Nu. 14:17
24: 7
32:35
Deu. 8:14
17:20
Jos. 3: 7
1 Sa. 2: 1, 10
10:23
2 Sa. 22:47, 49
1 Ki.11:26+A
14: 7 A
16: 2
2 Ki. 2:13
6: 7
19:22
25:27
1 Ch.17:17
25: 5
2 Ch. 5:13
17: 6
26:16
32:25
33:14
Ezra 3:12
8:25
9: 6, 9
10: 1
Neh. 9: 5[b]
Est. 2:18
3: 1
Job 8:11
17: 4
19: 6
36: 7
39:18, 27
Psa. 3: 4
7: 7
9:14, 33
12: 3
17:47, 49
20:14
26: 5, 6
29: 2
33: 4
Psa. 36:20, 34
45:11, 11
56: 6, 12
60: 3
63: 8
65: 7, 17
74: 5,8,10
87:16
88: 4+S[1]
14, 17
18, 20
25, 43
91:11
93: 2
98: 5, 9
106:25, 32
107: 6, 8
109: 7
111: 9
117:16, 28
130: 1, 2
139: 9
144: 1
7 A[c]
148:13, 14
149: 4
Pro. 3:35
4: 8
11:11+
AB[a] S[2]
14:34
18:10, 12
Isa. 1: 2
2: 2, 11
17
3:16
4: 2
5:16
10:15
12: 4, 6
13: 2
19:13
23: 4
28:29
30:18
33:10
37:23
40: 9,9,25
51:18
52: 8, 13
58: 1
63: 9
Jer. 17:12
Jer. 29:17
31:29
38:37
Lam. 2:17
Eze. 17:24
19:11
21:22, 26
28: 2,5,17
29:15
31: 4, 5
5+A
Eze. 31:10, 14
Dan. 5:19, 20
23
11:12[1], 36
12: 7
Hos. 11: 7
13: 6
Obad. 3
Mic. 5: 9
6:12
Hab. 2:19

[a] pro αὐξάνω [b] S[3] ὕψος. [c] pro ἀγαλλιάω. [d] A ὑπερυψόω.

ὕψωμα.

Job 24:24

ὕψωσις.

Psalm 149: 6

ὕω.

Exo. 9:18
Exo. 16: 4

φάγω.

Gen. 2:16, 17
17
3: 1, 2, 3
5, 6, 6
11, 11
12, 13
14
17 *qtr*
18, 19
22
6:21
9: 4
14:24
18: 5, 8
19: 3
24:33, 33
54
25:34
26:30
27: 4, 7
10, 19
25, 25
31, 33
28:20
31:46, 54
32:32
37:25
40:19
43:15
45:18
Exo. 2:20
12: 7, 8
11, 15
19, 44
16: 8, 15
25, 32
35, 35
18:12 A[a]
24:11
32: 6
34:15, 18
28
Lev. 6:29
7: 8 *ter*
9, 10
11
14 A[b]
17
8:31, 31
10:12, 13
14, 17
17, 18
19
11: 2, 3
4—A
8, 9, 9
21, 22
39, 42
17:10, 12
12, 14
15
19:25
Lev. 21:22
22: 7, 8[c]
10, 10
11, 11
12, 13
13, 14
23:14
24: 9
25:12, 19
20, 22
22
26: 5, 10
26, 29
29
Nu. 6: 3, 4
9:11
11:13, 18
18, 18
19, 20
21—A[2]
21
18:10, 10
23:24
25: 2
Deu. 2: 6, 28
4:28
6:11
7:16
8: 9, 10
12
9: 9, 18
11:16
12: 7, 15
15, 16
17, 18
20, 20
20, 21
22, 23
24, 25
27
14: 3, 4, 6
7, 8, 9
9, 10
11, 12
18, 19
20, 20
22, 23
28
15:20, 22
22 A[d]
23
16: 3, 3, 7
8
18: 1, 8
20:14, 19
24: 2
26:12, 14
27: 7
28:31, 33
53
29: 6
31:20—A[1]

Deu. 32:15
42—B[e]
Jos. 5:11
Jud. 9:20 B[f]
27
13: 4, 7, 14
14, 16
14: 9
19: 4, 6, 8
21
Ruth 2:14, 14
14, 16[g]
3: 3, 7
1 Sa. 1: 9, 18
2:36
9:13, 13
19, 24
24
14:24, 28
30, 33
34+A
20: 5, 24
34
21: 4
28:20, 22
23, 25
30:11, 12
2 Sa. 9: 7, 10
11:11, 13
25[e]
12:20, 20
21
13: 5, 6, 9
10, 11
17:29
19:35, 42
1 Ki. 1:41
13: 8, 9, 15
16, 17
18, 19
22, 22
23, 28
17:12
18:41, 42
19: 5, 6, 7
8, 21
20: 4, 7
24[h], 24[e]
2 Ki. 4: 8, 8
40, 40
43, 44
6:22, 23
28, 28
29, 29
7: 2, 8, 19
9:34
18:27, 31
19:29, 29
23: 9
1 Ch. 29:22
2 Ch. 28:15
30:18
31:10
Ezra 2:63
6:21
9:12
10: 6
Neh. 4: 3
5: 2[h], 3
14
7:65
8:10, 12
9:25, 36
Est. 4:16
Job 21:25
31: 8, 17
39
42:11
Psa. 21:27, 30
26: 2
49:13
58:16
77:24, 25
29
101: 5, 10
105:28
127: 2
Pro. 9: 5
13: 2
23: 7
Pro. 24:13
25:16
27:18
29:45
Ecc. 2:24, 25
3:13
4: 5
5:11, 17
18
6: 2, 2[i]
8:15
9: 7
10:17
Cant. 5: 1, 1, 1
Isa. 1:19
3:10
4: 1
5:17
7:15, 22
9:20, 21
10:17
11: 7
21: 5
22:13, 13
23:18
29: 1—A
1
30:24
36:12, 16
37:30, 30
44:16, 19
49:26
55: 1[k], 2
56: 9
59: 5
60:16
62: 9
65:13, 21
22, 25
Jer. 2: 7
7:21
12: 9[e]
16: 8
22:15
27:17
36: 5, 28
38:29, 30
48: 1
Lam. 2:20
Eze. 2: 8
3: 3, 3
4: 9, 10
10+A
10, 12
13, 16
5:10, 10
12:18, 19
16:13
18: 2
4+A
6, 11
15 A[b]
19: 3, 6
24:17, 22
25: 4
33:25+A
34:28[m]
36: 8 A[f]
14
39:17, 18
19
42:13
44: 3, 29
31
47:22
Dan. 1:12
7: 5
10: 3
11:26
Hos. 4: 8, 10
8:13, 13
9: 3
10:13
11: 6
13: 8 A[f]
Joel 2:26
Amos 9:14
Mic. 6:14
7: 1
Hab. 1: 8
Hag. 1: 6
Zec. 7: 6

[a] pro συμφάγω.
[b] pro βιβρώσκω.
[c] A ἔδω.
[d] pro ἔδω.
[e] A καταφάγω.
[f] pro καταφάγω.
[g] A ἀφίημι.
[h] S[1] ἄγω.
[i] S[1] καταφάγω.
[k] AS πίνω.
[m] A ποιέω.

φαίνω.

Gen. 1:15, 17
21:11
30:37
35: 7[a], 21
38:10
42:15
45: 5
Exo. 25:37
Nu. 23: 3, 4
1 Sa. 18: 8
20:20
2 Sa. 11:27
1 Ki. 6(18)A
22:32
1 Ch. 21: 7+A
Ezra 7:20
Neh. 4: 1[b], 7
13: 8
Psa. 76:19
96: 4
Pro. 11:31
21: 2
23: 5[c]
24:49
26: 5, 16
27: 7[d]
Isa. 32: 2
47: 3
60: 2
Eze. 32: 7[e], 8

[a] A ἐπιφαίνω.
[b] AS εἰμί.
[c] BS[1] πίπτω.
[d] S[1] φέρω.
[e] A δίδωμι.

φαιός.

Genesis 30:32, 33 35

φακός.

Gen. 25:34
1 Sa. 10: 1
26:11, 12
16
2 Sa. 17:28
23:11
2 Ki. 9: 1, 3
Eze. 4: 9

φαλακρός.

Lev. 13:40
2 Ki. 2:23
2 Ki. 2:23+A
Eze. 29:18[a]

[a] A φαλάκρωμα.

φαλακρόω.

Ezekiel 27:31 A

φαλάκρωμα.

Lev. 13:42, 42
43
21: 5
Deu. 14: 1
Isa. 3:24
15: 2
Jer. 29: 5
Eze. 7:18
27:31 A
29:18 A[a]
Amos 8:10

[a] pro φαλακρός.

φαλάντωμα.

Leviticus 13:43[a]

[a] AB ἀναφαλάντωμα.

φανερός.

Gen. 42:16
Deu. 29:29
Pro. 14: 4
15:11
Pro. 16: 2
Isa. 8:16
33: 9
64: 2

φανερόω.

Jeremiah 40: 6

φαντασία.

Hab. 2:18, 19
3:10
Zec. 10: 1

φάντασμα.

Job 20: 8 A[a]
Isa. 28: 7 A[a]

[a] pro φάσμα.

φάραγξ.

Gen. 14: 3
26:17, 19
25—A
Nu. 13:24, 25
21:12
32: 9
Deu. 1:24
2:13
13+AB
14, 24
36
4:46
21: 4, 4, 6
Jos. 7:24
10:12
12: 1, 2, 2
13: 9, 16
16
15: 1, 7, 7
8, 8
17: 9, 9
19:11
2 Sa. 24: 5
2 Ki. 23:10
2 Ch. 14:10
26: 9
32: 6
Neh. 2:15
3:13
11:30+S[3]
Psa. 59: 2
103:10
Pro. 24:52
Isa. 7:19
Isa. 8: 7
10:29
11:15
15: 7
17: 5
22: 1, 5, 7
28:21
30:28, 33
33
34: 9
35: 6
40: 4
57: 5
65:10
Jer. 7:31, 32
32—S[1]
39:35
Eze. 6: 3
31:12
32: 6
34:13
35: 8
36: 4, 6
38:20
39:11
Mic. 6: 2
Zec. 14: 5, 5

φάρες.

Daniel 5:25, 28

φαρέτρα.

Gen. 27: 3
Job 30:11
Psa. 10: 2
Isa. 22: 6
Isa. 49: 2
Jer. 28:11, 12
Lam. 3:13
Eze. 27:11

φαρμακεία, -κία.

Exo. 7:11, 22
8: 7[a], 18
Isa. 47: 9, 12

[a] A ἐπαοιδή.

φαρμακεύω.

2 Ch. 33: 6
Psa. 57: 6

φάρμακον.

2 Ki. 9:22
Psa. 57: 6
Mic. 5:12
Nah. 3: 4, 4

φαρμακός.

Exo. 7:11
9:11, 11
22:18
Deu. 18:10
Jer. 34: 7
Dan. 2: 2
Mal. 3: 5

φάρυγξ.

1 Sa. 17:35
Pro. 5: 3
8: 7
24:13
Cant. 5:16
Jer. 2:25
Lam. 4: 4

φασέκ.

2 Ch. 30: 1, 2, 5
15, 17
18
35: 1, 1, 6
7, 8, 9
2 Ch. 35:11, 13
16, 17
18, 18
19—AB
Jer. 38: 8

φάσκω.

Genesis 26:20

φάσμα.

Nu. 16:30
Job 20: 8[a]
Job 33:15+A
Isa. 28: 7[b]

[a] A φάντασμα, S[1] θαῦμα.
[b] A φάντασμα.

φάτνη.

2 Ch. 32:28
Job 6: 5[a]
Job 39: 9
Pro. 14: 4
Isa. 1: 3
Joel 1:17
Hab. 3:17

[a] (S[1] πάθμης.)

φατνόω.

1 Ki. 7:40
Eze. 41:15

φατνώματα.

Cant. 1:17
Eze. 41:20
Amos 8: 3
Zeph. 2:14

φάτνωσις.

1 Kings 6:13+A

φαυλίζω.

Gen. 25:34
Nu. 15:31
2 Sa. 12: 9
Job 30: 4
31:13
42: 6
Pro. 21:12
22:12
Isa. 33:19
37:22
49: 7
Mal. 1: 6, 6

φαύλισμα.

Zephaniah 3:11

φαυλισμός.

Isa. 28:11
51: 7
Hos. 7:16

φαυλίστρια.

Zephaniah 3: 1

φαῦλος.

Job 6: 3, 25
9:23
Pro. 5: 3
13: 6 A
Pro. 16:21
22: 8
29: 9

φαῦσις.

Gen. 1:14, 15
Psa. 73:16+S[2]

φέγγος.

2 Sa. 22:13
23: 4
Job 3: 4[a]
10:21
22:28
38:12[a]
41: 9
Eze. 1: 4, 4, 13
Eze. 1:27, 28
10: 4
43: 2
Hos. 7: 6
Joel 2:10[b]
3:15
Amos 5:20[b]
Hab. 3: 4, 11

[a] C φθέγγος.
[b] A φθέγγος.

φείδομαι.

Gen. 19:16
20: 6
22:12, 16
45:20
Exo. 2: 6
Deu. 7:16
13: 8
19:13, 21
25:12
33: 3
1 Sa. 15: 3
24:11
2 Sa. 12: 4, 6
18: 5, 16
21: 7
2 Ki. 5:20
2 Ch. 36:15, 17
Neh. 13:22
Job 6:10
7:11
16: 5, 13
20:13
27:22[a]
30:10
33:18
42: 3
Psa. 18:14
71:13
Psa. 77:50
Pro. 6:34
10:19
13:24
16:17
17:27
21:14
24:11
Isa. 13:18
14: 6
54: 2
58: 1
63: 9
Jer. 13:14
14:10
15: 5
17:17
21: 7
27:14
28: 3
Lam. 2: 2, 1
21
3:42
Eze. 5:11
7: 9, 4
8:18
9: 5, 10
16: 5

Eze. 20:17
24:21
36:21
Joel 2:17, 18
Joel 3:16
Jon. 4:10, 11
Hab. 1:17
Zec. 11: 6

[a] C γινώσκω.

φελμουνι.

Daniel 8:13

φερνή.

Gen. 34:12
Exo. 22:16, 17
Jos. 16:10

φερνίζω.

Exodus 22:16

φέρω.

Gen. 4: 3, 4
27: 4, 7
13, 14
30:14
31:35, 39[a]
32:13
33:11
36: 7
43: 1, 21
23
23 A[b]
47:16
49: 3
Exo. 28:26
32: 2, 3
35: 5, 21[c]
21, 21
22 ter
23, 24
24, 25
27, 29
29
36: 3, 3, 5
39:14
Lev. 2: 2
4: 5 A[d]
28, 28
5: 6, 7, 8
11, 12
15, 18
6: 6, 21
7:19
14:20 A[2] [c]
15:14, 29
16.15 A[d]
17: 4, 4, 5
9
23:10, 12
26:36
Nu. 5:15 A[f]
6:10
7: 3
11:14, 17
15:25
18:13
Deu. 1: 9, 12
12: 6, 11
14:22
26:10
Jos. 6:13[g]
7:23
15: 2
18: 6, 9
Jud. 3:18[d]
6:18 A[b]
7:25
15: 1 + A
16:18 A [e]
18: 3[i]
21:12[i]
Ruth 3:15
1 Sa. 9: 7[k]
10:27
15:13, 15
17:54
18:27 A[e]
20:38
25:27, 35
31:12
2 Sa. 1:10
3:22
4: 8
6:17
8: 2, 6, 7
16:20
17:28
1 Ki. 1: 3
8: 1[a]
9:14, 28
10:11, 25
12 p24 l 38
17: 6
2 Ki. 2:20 — AB
4:21 A[e]
42
5: 6, 20
10: 6, 8
12: 4
17: 4
21:12
1 Ch. 10:12
11:19
12:40
16:29
18: 2, 6, 7
21: 2
22: 4
2 Ch. 1: 6[a], 6[b]
17
2: 6
9:10, 12
13, 14
14, 24
15:11
17:11, 11
24:11 A[d]
14
25:12, 14
27: 5
28: 8
29:31
31: 5, 6
10, 12[k]
32:23
35:16
Ezra 3: 7
4: 2
8:17, 30
Neh. 8: 1, 2
15, 16
10:31, 34
35, 36
37
39 B[d]
11: 1
12, 27
13:12, 15
15, 16
18
Est. 6: 8
Job 4: 2 C[m]
13:25
15:35 S[1] [m]
17: 1
22:12
40:26
Psa. 28: 1, 1, 1
2
Psa. 67:30
75:12
77:20[n]
95: 7, 7, 8
Pro. 6: 8 A[f]
16:26 C[o]
24:56
27: 7 S[1] [p]
Cant. 8:11 — A
Isa. 1:13
17:13[q], 13
21:14
28:15, 18
29: 5, 6
30: 6, 17
32: 2, 2
43:23 — ABS
52:11
53: 3, 4
60: 6, 6
17 ter
61: 6
Jer. 6:20
13:24
17:26, 26
18:14
Jer. 20: 9
30: 5, 10
42:17 — A
46:16
51:22
Eze. 17: 4, 8
19: 9 + A
27:24
34:29
36. 6
15 A[e]
37: 5
40:44
Dan. 1: 2
5: 2, 3[i]
23
6:17
11: 6, 8
Hos. 9:16
Joel 2:22
Amos 4: 4
5:22
Zeph. 3:10
Hag. 2:19
Mal. 1:13[r]

[a] A ἀναφέρω. [b] pro δίδωμι. [c] B[a] ἀναφέρω. [d] pro εἰσφέρω. [e] pro ἀναφέρω. [f] pro προσφέρω [g] A αἴρω. [h] pro ἐκφέρω. [i] A ἄγω. [k] A εἰσφέρω. [m] pro ὑποφέρω. [n] S[1] δίδωμι. [o] pro φορέω. [p] pro φαίνω. [q] A καταφέρω. [r] S[2] προσφέρω.

φεύγω.

Gen. 14:10, 10
39:12, 13
15, 18
Exo. 4: 3
14: 5, 25
27
21:13
Lev. 26:17 — A
36, 36
Nu. 10:35
16:34
24:11
35: 6, 11
15, 32
Deu. 4:42
19: 4, 11
28: 7, 25
Jos. 7: 4
8: 5, 6
20 — A
10:11, 16
20: 4 A
6 A
Jud. 1: 6
4:15, 17[a]
7:21, 22
8:12
9:21
40 — A
51
11: 3[b]
20:32, 42
45, 47
1 Sa. 4:10, 16
17
14:22
17:24 A
51
19: 8, 12
18
21:10
22:17, 20
23: 5, 6
27: 4
30:17
31: 1, 7, 7
2 Sa. 1: 4 — A
4: 4
10:13, 14
14, 18
13:29, 37
15:14
17: 2[c]
2 Sa. 18: 3, 17
19: 3, 8, 9
23:11
24:13
1 Ki. 2:28, 29
29, 29
11:43
12:18
21:20, 30
30
2 Ki. 3:24
7: 7
8:21
9: 3, 10
23, 27
27
14:12, 19
1 Ch. 10: 1, 7, 7
11:13
19:14, 15
15, 18
21:12
2 Ch. 10: 2, 18
13:16
14:12
21: 9
25:22, 27
Neh. 6:11 + AS[3]
13:10
Job 27:22
30: 3
Psa. 30:12
59: 5
67: 2
103: 7
113: 3, 5
138: 7
Pro. 28: 1
Cant. 8:14
Isa. 10:18, 18
29
13:14
16: 3
20: 6
21:14
15 AS[d]
22: 3, 3
24:18
27: 1
30:16, 16
17, 17
31: 8, 9
Isa. 43:14
48:20
Jer. 4: 6, 21
26: 5, 6
15, 21
27:16
24 S[e], 28
28: 6
30: 8
31: 6, 19
44
Jer. 44:13, 14
45:19
Dan. 10: 7
Amos 5:19[c]
6: 5
9: 1
Obad. 14
Jon. 1: 3, 10
4: 2
Nah. 2: 6, 8
Zec. 2: 6

[a] A ἀναχωρέω. [b] A ἀποδιδράσκω [c] A ἐκφεύγω. [d] pro φονεύω. [e] pro γινώσκω.

φήμη.

Proverbs 16: 1

φημί.

Gen. 24:47
Exo. 2: 6
Nu. 24: 3, 3, 4
15, 15
1 Sa. 2:30
2 Ki. 9:26, 26
2 Ch. 34:27
Ezra 4:17
Job 24:25
Psa. 35: 2
Pro. 24:55
Jer. 2: 3
9: 3 — ABS
6 — ABS
23:12 + A
25:12 + A
27:20 + A
30: 2, 15
31:12, 35
Jer. 31:38
34:12
36:23
37: 3, 17
21
38:20, 27
28, 31[a]
32, 33
37, 37
36
36 + A
38
41:22
44:18
49:11
Eze. 13: 7 + A
35:13 + A
Zec. 2: 5 A[b]

[a] AS λέγω. [b] pro λέγω.

φθάνω.

Jud. 20:34[a]
42[b]
2 Sa. 20:13
1 Ki. 12:18
2 Ch. 28: 9
Ezra 3: 1
Neh. 8: 1
1 + S[1]
Ecc. 8:14, 14
Ecc. 12: 1
Cant. 2:12
Dan. 4: 8, 17
19, 21
25
6:24
7:13, 22
8: 7
12:12

[a] A ἀφάπτω. [b] A καταφθάνω.

φθάρμα.

Leviticus 22:25[a]

[a] AB[1] φθαρτός.

φθαρτός.

Lev. 22:25 AB[1] [a], Isa. 54:17 AS[3] [b]

[a] pro φθάρμα.
[b] pro σκευαστός.

φθέγγομαι.

Jud. 5:11 A[a]
Job 13: 7
Psa. 77: 2
93: 4
118:172
Jer. 9:17
Jer. 28:14
Lam. 1:12
Amos 1: 2
Nah. 2: 7
Hab. 2:11

[a] pro διηγέομαι.

φθέγμα.

Job 6:26

φθειρίζω.

Jeremiah 50:12, 12

φθείρω.

Gen. 6:11
Exo. 10:15
Lev. 19:27
Deu. 34: 7
2 Sa. 20:20[a]
1 Ch. 20: 1
Job 15:32
Isa. 24: 3, 4
54:16
Jer. 13: 9
Eze. 16:32[a]
Hos. 9: 9
Zeph. 3: 7[b]

[a] A διαφθείρω. [b] AS[2] διαφθείρω.

φθίνω.

Job 31:26[a]

[a] (S[1] φθινύθουσαν.)

φθόγγος, φθέ–

Job 3: 4 C[a]
38:12 C[a]
Psa. 18: 5
Joel 2:10 A[a]
Amos 5:20 A[1] [a]

[a] φθέγγος pro φέγγος.

φθορά.

Exo. 18:18
Ps. 102: 4
Isa. 24: 3
Jon. 2: 7
Mic. 2:10

φιάλη.

Exo. 27: 3
38:23
Nu. 4:14
7:13, 19
25, 31
37, 43
49, 55
61, 67
73, 79
84 — A
85
86 + A[2]
1 Ki. 7:26, 31
1 Ki. 7:36
2 Ki. 12:13
25:14, 15
1 Ch. 28.17
2 Ch. 4: 8, 21
Neh. 7:70
Pro. 23:31
Cant. 5:13
6: 1
Jer. 52:18
Zec. 9:15
14:20

φιλαμαρτήμων.

Proverbs 17:19

φιλεχθρέω.

Proverbs 3:30

φιλέω.

Gen. 27: 4, 9, 14
26, 27
29:11, 13
33: 4 + A
37: 4
48:10
50: 1
Exo. 18: 7
1 Sa. 10: 1
Est. 10: 3
Job 31:27
Pro. 7:13
Pro. 8:17[a]
21:17
24:41
29: 3
Ecc. 3: 8
Cant. 1: 2
8: 1
Isa. 56:10
Jer. 22:22
Lam. 1: 2
Hos. 3: 1

[a] S ζητέω.

φίλημα.

Pro. 27: 6
Cant. 1: 2

φιλία.

Pro. 5:19, 19
7:18
10:12
15:17
Pro. 17: 9
19: 7
25:10
27: 5

φιλιάζω.

Jud. 5:30 + A
14:20[a]
2 Ch. 19: 2
20:37

[a] A ἑταῖρος.

φιλογεωργός.

2 Chronicles 26:10 A[a]

[a] pro γεωργός.

φιλογύναιος.

1 Kings 11: 1 A[a]

[a] pro φιλογύνης.

φιλογύνης.

1 Kings 11: 1[a]

[a] A φιλογύναιος.

φιλονεικέω.

Proverbs 10:12

φιλόνεικος.

Ezekiel 3: 7

φίλος.

Exo. 33:11
Deu. 13: 6
Jud. 5:30+A
14:20[a]
15: 2[b], 6[b]
1 Ch. 27:33
Est. 1: 3, 13
2:18
3: 1
5:10, 14
6: 9, 13
13
9:22
Job 2:11
6:27
19:13, 21
32: 1, 3
35: 4
36:33
42: 7, 10
p 18
Psa. 37:12
87:19
138:17
Pro. 3:29
6: 1, 3, 3
12:26
14:20 *ter*
15:28
16:28, 29
17: 9, 17
18
18: 1
19: 4, 4
22:24
25: 1, 8, 10
17, 18
26:19
27: 6, 10
10, 10
14
29: 5
Jer. 9: 4, 5
20: 4, 6, 10
37:14
Dan. 2:13, 17
18
Mic. 7: 5

[a] A νυμφαγωγός.
[b] A συνεταῖρος.

φιμός.

Job 30:28
Isa. 37:29

φιμόω.

Deuteronomy 25: 4

φλεγμαίνω.

Isa. 1: 6
Nah. 3:19

φλέγω.

Exo. 24:17
Deu. 32:22
Ps. 103: 4
Pro. 29: 1
Jer. 20: 9
23:29+A
Dan. 7: 9
Mal. 4: 1

φλέψ.

Hosea 13:15

φλιά.

Exo. 12: 7, 22
23
Deu. 6: 9
11:20
1 Sa. 1: 9
1 Ki. 6:29+A
30+A
Eze. 43: 8, 8
45:19, 19

φλογίζω.

Exo. 9:24
Nu. 21:14
Psa. 96: 3
Dan. 3:27

φλόγινος.

Genesis 3:24

φλόξ.

Gen. 15:17
19:28
Exo. 3: 2
Nu. 21:28
Jud. 13:20, 20
Job 18: 5
41:11 A[a]
12
Psa. 29: 7
82:15
105:18
Pro. 24:23
Cant. 8: 6
Isa. 5:24
10:18
13: 8
Isa. 29: 6
30:30
43: 2
47:14
50:11, 11
66:15
Lam. 2: 3
Eze. 20:47
Dan. 3:22+A
23
7: 9
11:33
Hos. 7: 4
Joel 1:19
2: 3, 5
Obad. 18

[a] *pro* πῦρ.

φλόξ.

Judges 3:22[a], 22[b]
([a] A φλεγός.) ([b] A φλεβός)

φλυκτίς.

Exodus 9: 9, 10

φοβερίζω.

Ezra 10: 3−S[a]
Neh. 6: 9[a], 14
Neh. 6:19
Dan. 4: 2

[a] (S[1] φοβερουσιν).

φοβερισμός.

Psalm 87:17

φοβερός.

Gen. 28:17
Deu. 1:19
2: 7
8:15
10:17
Jud. 13: 6[a]
1 Ch. 16:25
Neh. 1: 5
4:14
9:32
Psa. 46: 3
65: 3, 5
75: 8:13
Psa. 75:13
88: 8
95: 4
98: 3
105:22
110: 9
144: 6
Pro. 12:25
Isa. 21: 1
Dan. 2:31
7: 7, 19
Hab. 1: 7

[a] A ἐπιφανής.

φοβερῶς.

Psalm 138:14

φοβέω.

Gen. 3:10
15: 1
18:15
19:30
20: 2, 8
21:17
22:12
26: 7, 24
28:13, 17
31:31−A
32: 7, 11
42:18, 35
43:22
46: 3
50:19, 21
Exo. 1:17, 21
2:14
9:20, 30
14:10, 31
15:14 A[a]
20:18
34:30
Lev. 19: 3, 14
30, 32
25:17, 36
43
26: 2
Nu. 12: 8
14: 9, 9
21:34
22: 3
Deu. 1:21, 29
2: 4
3: 2, 22
4:10
5: 5, 29
6: 2, 13[b]
24
Deu. 7:18, 19
8: 6
10:12, 20[b]
13: 4, 11
14:22
17:13, 19
19:20
20: 1, 3, 8
21:21
25:18
28:10, 58
66, 67
31: 6, 8
12, 13
Jos. 1: 9
4:14
14+A
8: 1
9:30
10: 2, 8, 25
11: 6
24:14
Jud. 4:18
6:10, 23
27
31 8[c]
7: 3, 10
8:20
14:11+A
Ruth 3:11
1 Sa. 3:15
4: 7, 20
7: 7
12:14, 18
20, 24
14:26
15:24
17:11
1 Sa. 17:24 A
18:12
21:12
22:23
23: 3, 17
28: 5, 13
20
31: 4
2 Sa. 1:14
3:11
6: 9
9: 7
10:19
12:18
13:28
1 Ki. 1:50, 51
2:29
3:28
8:40, 43
12 p 24 l 13
18: 3, 12
19: 3
2 Ki. 1:15
4: 1
6:16
10: 4
17: 7, 25
28, 32
32 *to* 39
41
19: 6
25:24, 26
1 Ch. 10: 4
13:12
16:30
22:13
28:20
2 Ch. 5: 6
6:31, 33
20: 3, 15
17
32: 7−AB
Neh. 1:11
2: 2
4:14
6:13, 16
7: 2
Est. 2:20
9. 2
Job 3:25 S[2 d]
5:21
21+A
22
6:21
9:35
11:15
32: 7
37:23, 23
Psa. 3: 7
14: 4
21:24, 24
26
22: 4
24:12, 14
14+B
26: 1, 3
30:20
32: 8, 18
33: 8, 10
10
39: 4
45: 3
48: 6, 17
51: 8
52: 6
54:20
55: 4, 5, 12
59: 6
60: 6
63: 5, 10
64: 9
65:16
66: 8
75: 9
76:17
84:10
85:11
90: 5
101:16
102:11, 13
Ps. 102:17
110: 5
111: 1, 7, 8
113:19, 21
117: 4−S
6
118:63, 74
79, 120
127: 1, 4
134:20
144:19
146:11
Pro. 3: 7, 25
13:13
14: 2, 16
24:21, 24
29:25
Ecc. 3:14
5: 6
7:19
8:12, 12
13
9: 2
12:13
Isa. 7: 4, 16
8:12
10:24
12: 2
13: 2+AS
19:17
29:23
33: 7, 7
7 AS[3 e]
35: 4
37: 6
40: 9
41: 5, 10
13
43: 1, 5
44: 2
50:10
51: 7, 12
13
54: 4, 14
57:11, 11
59:19
60: 5
63:17
66:14[e]
Jer. 1: 8, 17
2:30
3: 8
5:22, 24
10: 2, 2, 5
17: 8, 8
23: 4
26:27, 28
29:22[f]
33:19
39:30
40: 9
46:17
47: 9
48:18
49:11, 11
11, 16
Lam. 3:56−A
Eze. 2: 6, 6
3: 9
11: 8
18:14
26:16, 18
27:28
Dan. 1:10
5.19
6:26
10:12, 19
Hos. 10: 3
Amos 3: 8
Jon. 1: 5
9 S[3 g]
10, 16
Mic. 6: 9
7:17
Hab. 3: 1
Zeph. 3: 7
Hag. 1:12
Zec. 9: 5
Mal. 1: 6+S[2]
2: 5
Mal. 3: 5, 16
16
Mal. 4: 2

[a] *pro* ὀργίζω.
[b] A προσκυνέω.
[c] *pro* βοάω.
[d] *pro* φροντίζω
[e] AS σιβομαι.
[f] A σείω.
[g] *pro* σιβομαι.

φόβητρον.

Isaiah 19:17

φόβος.

Gen. 9: 2
15:12
31:42, 54
35: 5
Exo. 15:16
20:20
23:27
Deu. 2:25
11:25
28:67
32:25
Jos. 2: 9
2 Sa. 23: 3
1 Ch. 14:17
2 Ch. 14: 7, 9
20: 5
Neh. 5: 9, 15
6:16
Est. 1 22
(9) 17
9: 3
Job 3:24, 25
4: 6, 13
13
7:11+S
9:34
13:11, 21
15: 4, 21
20:25
21: 9
25: 2
31:23
33: 7, 15
16
38:17
39: 3, 16
19
41: 5, 16
Psa. 2:11
5: 8
13: 3−A
5, 5
18:10
30:12
33:12
35: 2
43:17 S[1 a]
52: 6, 6
54: 6
Psa. 63: 2
89:11
90: 5
104:38
110:10
118:38, 120
Pro. 1: 7
29 C S[2 b]
2: 5
7: 1
8:13
9:10
10:27, 29
14:26
15.16, 27
16: 1
18: 8
19:23
22: 4
23:17
29:48
Isa. 2:10, 19
21
7:25
8:12, 13[c]
10:27, 29
11: 3
19:16
21: 4
24:17, 18
26:18
33: 3, 3, 7
8, 18
Jer. 30: 5
31:43, 44
37: 5, 5, 6
39:40
Lam. 3:16
Eze. 26:17
27:28−A
30:13+A
32:23, 24
26, 30
32
38:21
Dan. 10: 7
Jon. 1:10, 16
Mal. 1: 6
2: 5

[a] *pro* πρόσωπον.
[b] *pro* λόγος.
[c] S βοηθός.

φογώρ.

Nu. 23:28
25:18, 18
31:16
Deu. 3:29
Deu. 4:46
34: 6
Jos. 22:17

φοιβάω.

Deuteronomy 14: 1+AB[a]

φοινίκεος, –οῦς.

Isaiah 1:18

φοινικών.

Ezekiel 47:18, 19

φοῖνιξ.

Job 40:25

φοῖνιξ.

Exo. 15:27
Lev. 23:40

Nu. 33: 9
Deu. 34: 3
Jud. 1:16
3:13
4: 5
2 Sa. 16: 1, 2
1 Ki. 6:27
(32)A
(32)A
32
7:22
2 Ch. 3: 5
28:15
Neh. 8:15
Job 29:18
Psa. 91:13
Pro. 29:42+S²
Cant. 7: 7, 8
Eze. 40:16, 21
22, 26
31, 34
37
41:18
18+A
19, 19
20, 25
Joel 1:12

φονευτής.

Nu. 35:11, 16
16, 17
17, 18
18, 21
Deu. 4:42
19: 3, 4
Jos. 20: 3, 3
2 Ki. 6:32
9:31
Pro. 22:13
26:13
Isa. 1:21

φονεύω.

Exo. 20:15
21:13
Nu. 35: 6, 12
19, 21
21, 25
26, 27
27, 28
30, 30
31
Deu. 4:42
5:17
19: 6
22:26
Jos. 10:28, 30
32, 35
35
20: 5 A
6 A
21:13, 21
27, 32
Jos. 21:36, 38
Jud. 16: 2[a]
20: 4, 5[a]
1 Ki. 20:19
21:40
2 Ch. 25: 3
Neh. 4:11
6:10
10+S³
Est. 9:12+S³
Psa. 61: 4
93: 6
Pro. 1:32
7:26
Isa. 21:15[b]
Jer. 7: 9
Lam. 2:20
Eze. 11: 7 A[c]
Hos. 6: 9

[a] A ἀποκτείνω. [b] AS φεύγω.
[c] pro πατάσσω.

φονοκτονέω.

Nu. 35:33, 33
Psa. 105:38

φόνος.

Exo. 5: 3
17:13
22: 2
Lev. 26: 7
Nu. 21:24
Deu. 13:15
20:13
22: 8
Deu. 28:22+A
Job 21:22[a]
Pro. 1:18
28:17
Isa. 59: 7[b]
Jer. 22:17
Eze. 43: 7, 8, 9
Hos. 4: 2

[a] AC σοφός. [b] AS¹ ἄφρων.

φορβαία.

Job 40:20

φορεῖον.

Gen. 45:17[a]
Cant. 3: 9

[a] A πορεῖον.

φορεύς.

Exo. 27: 6AB¹ [a]
7AB¹ [a]
Exo. 27: 7AB¹ [a]

[a] pro ἀναφορεύς.

φορέω.

Pro. 3:16
Pro. 16:23, 26[a]

[a] C φέρω.

φορθομμίν.

Daniel 1: 3

φορολογέω.

2 Chronicles 36: 4−A

φορολόγητος.

Deuteronomy 20:11

φορολόγος.

Ezra 4: 7, 18
23
5: 5
Job 3:18
39: 7

φόρος.

Jos. 19:48
Jud. 1:28, 29
30, 31
33, 35
2 Sa. 20:24
1 Ki. 4: 6
5:13, 13
14
10:15
p 22
1 Ki. 12:18
2 Ch. 8: 8
10:18
36: 3
Ezra 4:13, 20
6: 8
7:24
Neh. 5: 4
Lam. 1: 1

φορτίζω.

Ezekiel 16:33

φορτίον.

Jud. 9:48 A[a]
49 A[a]
2 Sa. 19:35
Job 7:20
Psa. 37: 5
Isa. 46: 1

[a] pro κλαδος.

φραγμός.

Gen. 38:29
Nu. 22:24, 24
1 Ki. 10 p 22
11:27
Ezra 9: 9
Job 38:31
Psa. 61: 4
79:13
Psa. 88:41
143:14
Pro. 24:16
Ecc. 10: 8
Isa. 5: 2, 5
58:12
Nah. 3:17

φράζω.

Jud. 5: 7 A[a]
Job 6:24
Job 12: 8

[a] pro δυνατός.

φράσσω.

Job 38: 8
Pro. 21:13
25:26
Cant. 7: 2
Hos. 2: 6
Zec. 14: 5[a]

[a] A ἐμφρασσω.

φρέαρ.

Gen. 14:10
16:14, 14
21:14, 19
25, 30
31, 32
33
22:19, 19
24:11, 20
62
25:11
26:15, 18
19, 20
21, 22
23, 25
32, 33
28:10
29: 2, 2, 2
3, 3, 8
Gen. 29:10
46: 1, 5
Exo. 2:15
8: 3 A¹ [a]
Nu. 21:16, 16
17, 18
18, 22
1 Sa. 19:22
2 Sa. 3:26
Psa. 54:24
68:16
Pro. 5:15
23:27
Cant. 4:15
Isa. 15: 8
Jer. 14: 3
48: 7, 9, 9
Amos 5: 5

[a] pro φύραμα.

φρήν.

Pro. 6:32
7: 7
9: 4
11:12
12:11
Pro. 15:21
18: 2
24:45
Dan. 4:31, 33

φρίκη.

Job 4:14
Amos 1:11

φρικτός.

Jer. 5:30
18:13
Jer. 23:14

φρικώδης.

Hosea 6:10

φρίσσω.

Job 4:15
Jer. 2:12
Dan. 7:15

φρονέω.

Deu. 32:29
Psa. 93: 8
Isa. 44:18, 28
Isa. 56:10+AS
Zec. 9: 2

φρόνησις.

Jos. 5: 1
1 Sa. 2:10
1 Ki. 2:35
(3) 1, 1−AB
3:28
4:25, 26
10: 4, 7, 8
2, 24
11:41
Job 5:13
17: 4
Pro. 1: 2
3:13, 19
7: 4
8: 1, 14
Pro. 9: 6, 10
10:23
14:29
16:16
32+
AC² S²
19: 8, 8
24: 5, 25
Isa. 40:28
44:19
Jer. 10:12
Eze. 28: 4
Dan. 1: 4, 17
2:21
5:12

φρόνιμος.

Gen. 3: 1
41:33, 39
1 Sa. 2:10
1 Ki. (3) 1
p 1
p 46
3:12
4:26
5: 7
Job 34:34 A[a]
Pro. 3: 7
Pro. 10:24+A
11:12, 29
14: 6, 17
15: 1, 21
17:10, 21
27, 28
18:14, 15
19: 7, 25
20: 5
Isa. 44:25
Hos. 13:13

[a] pro σοφός.

φροντίζω.

1 Sa. 9: 5
Job 3:25[a]
23:14
Psa. 39:18
Pro. 29:39

[a] A εὐλαβέομαι, S² φοβέω.

φροντίς.

Job 11:18
15:20
Job (40: 45S¹ [a])

[a] pro βροντάω.

φρουρά.

2 Sa. 8: 6, 14
1 Ch. 18: 6, 13

φρουραί.

Esther 9:26, 26, 28, 29

φρύαγμα.

Jer. 12: 5
Eze. 7:24
24:21
Hos. 4:19
Zec. 11: 3

φρυάσσομαι.

Psalm 2: 1

φρύγανον.

Job 30: 7
Isa. 40:24
41: 2
Isa. 47:14
Jer. 13:24
Hos. 10: 7

φρύγιον.

Psalm 101: 4

φρύγω, φρύσσω.

Lev. 2:14
Lev. 23:14

φυγαδεία.

Ezra 4:15, 19
Eze. 17:21+A

φυγαδεῖον.

Numbers 35:15

φυγαδευτήριον.

Nu. 35: 6, 11
12, 13
15, 25
32
Jos. 20: 2, 3, 3
21:13, 21
36, 38
1 Ch. 6:57, 67

φυγαδεύω.

Psalm 54: 8

φυγάς.

Exo. 23:27
Pro. 28:17
Isa. 16: 4

φυγή.

2 Sa. 18: 3
Job 27:22
Ps. 141: 5
Isa. 52:12
Jer. 26: 5
Jer. 30:13
32:21
Amos 2:14
Nah. 3: 9

φυή.

Neh. 4: 7
Dan. 4:12, 20
Dan. 4:23

φύλαγμα.

Lev. 8:35
22: 9
Nu. 4:31
Deu. 11: 1
Zeph. 1:12
Mal. 3:14

φυλακή.

Gen. 40: 3, 4, 7
41:10
42:17, 19
30
Exo. 14:24
Lev. 24:12
Nu. 1:53
3: 7, 7, 8
25, 28
31, 32
36, 38
38
4:28, 32
8:26, 26
9:19, 23
15:34
18: 3, 3, 4
5, 5
31:30, 47
Jud. 7:19
16:21 A[a]
25, 25A[a]
1 Sa. 11:11
2 Sa. 20: 3
1 Ki. 2: 3
22.27
2 Ki. 11: 5, 6, 7
17: 4
25:27, 29
1 Ch. 9:19, 27
12:29[b]
23:32, 32
32−AS
26:16−A
16, 18
18
2 Ch. 7: 6
8:14
13:11
16:10
2 Ch. 18:26
23: 6
35: 2
Neh. 3:25
12:25+S³
40 S³
45, 45
13:14+S³
Job 7:12
35:10
Psa. 38: 2
76: 5
89: 4
129: 6, 6+A
140: 3
141: 8
Pro. 4:23
20:28
Isa. 42: 7
Jer. 17:21 A[c]
28:12
39: 2−S¹
8, 12
40: 1
44: 4, 15
18, 21
21
45: 6, 13
28
46:14, 15
52:33
Lam. 2:19
Eze. 19: 9
23:24[d]
40:45, 46
44: 8+A
8, 14
15, 16
48:11
Hab. 2: 1

[a] pro δεσμωτήριον. [b] A φυλή.
[c] pro ψυχή. [d] A προφυλακή.

φυλάκισσα.

Canticles 1: 6

φύλαξ.

Gen. 4: 9
1 Sa. 17:20 A
22 A
2 Sa. 22: 3, 47
47
23: 3
Neh. 2: 8[a]
3:29
Neh. 12:25 + S^3
Est. 2: 3, 8, 14
15 – A
Ecc. 12: 3
Cant. 5: 7, 7
Isa. 62: 6
Eze. 27:11

[a] S^3 φυλάσσω.

φύλαρχος.

Deuteronomy 31:28

φυλάσσω.

Gen. 2:15
3:24
18:19
26: 5
30:31
31:24, 29
41:35[a], 36
Exo. 12:17, 24
25
13:10
15:26
19: 5
20: 6
22: 7, 10
23:13, 15
20, 22
31:13, 14
16
34:18
Lev. 8:35
18: 4, 5
26, 30
19: 3, 19
30, 37
20: 8, 22
22: 9, 31
25:18
26: 2, 3
Nu. 1:53
3: 7, 8
10, 28
32, 38
6:24
8:26
9:19, 23
18: 3, 4, 5
22:35
38 + A
23:12
31:30, 47
Deu. 4: 2, 6, 9
15, 40
5: 1, 10
12, 15
29, 32
6: 2, 3, 17
17, 25
7: 9, 9
11, 12
8: 1, 2, 6
11
10:13
11: 1, 8, 32
12: 1, 28
32
13: 4 + A
18
15: 5
16: 1, 12
20 A[b]
17:10, 19
23: 9, 23
24:10, 10
26:16, 17
18
27: 1
28: 1, 13
15, 45
29: 9
30:10, 16
32:46
33: 9

Jos. 1: 7
6:18
10:18
22: 3, 5, 5
23: 6, 11
Jud. 1:24
2:22, 22
7:19
13: 4, 13
14
1 Sa. 1:12
7: 1
13:13, 14
19: 2, 11
21: 4
22:23
25:21
26:15, 16
29:11
30:23
2 Sa. 11:16
15:16
16:21
18:12
20: 3, 10
22:22, 44
23: 5
1 Ki. 2: 3, 3, 4
(3) 43
3: 6, 14
6(12) A
8:23, 24
25, 25
58, 61
9: 4, 6
11:10, 11
34 + A
38, 38
13:21
14: 8A, 27
21:39
2 Ki. 6: 9, 10
9:14
10:31
11: 5, 6, 7
12: 9
17: 9, 13
15 – B
19, 37
18: 6, 8
19:24 A[c]
21: 8
22: 4
23: 3, 4
25:18
1 Ch. 9:19, 19
23
10:13
22:12, 13
23:32
26:10
28: 7, 8 – B
29:18
2 Ch. 6:14, 15
16, 16
7:17
12:10, 11
13:11
19: 7
23: 6
33: 8
34: 9, 22

2 Ch. 34:31
Ezra 4:22
Neh. 1: 5, 5, 7
9
2: 8 S^3[d]
16
9:32
10:29
11:19 + S^3
12:45
13:22
Est. 6: 2
Job 10:12, 14
13:27
14:13
22:15
23:11
24:15
29: 2
33:11
36:21
39: 1
Psa. 11: 8
15: 1
16: 4, 8
17:22, 24
18:12, 12
24:20
30: 7 BS[e]
33:21
36:28, 34
37
38: 2
40: 3[f]
55: 7
58: 1, 10
70:10
77:10, 56
85: 2
88:29, 32
96:10
98: 7
102:18
104:45
105: 3
106:43
114: 6
118: 4, 5, 8
9, 17
34, 44
55, 57
60, 63
67, 88
101, 106
134, 136
146, 158
167, 168
120: 3, 4, 5
7, 7, 8
126: 1, 1
131:12
139: 5
140: 9
144:20
145: 6, 9
Pro. 2: 8, 11
4: 4, 13
21
5: 2
6:20, 22
24 S^1[e]
7: 1, 2
8:32 + AS^2
34
10:17

Pro. 13: 3, 6A
18
14: 3
15: 5
16: 4, 17
17
19: 8, 16
27
21:23, 28
22: 5
24:23
25:10
27:18
28: 7
29:18
Ecc. 3: 6
4:17
5: 7, 12
8: 2, 5
12:12, 13
Cant. 1: 6
Isa. 7: 4
21:11, 12
26: 2, 2, 3
27: 4
42:20
52: 8
56: 1, 2, 4
6
60:21
Jer. 3: 5[f]
4:17
5:24
8: 7
9: 4
16:11
17:21
38:10 – S^1
39: 2 – S^1
42: 4
43: 5, 20
52:24, 31
Eze. 11:20
17:14
18: 9, 21
27
20:13 + A
18, 19
21
33: 4, 5, 5
6, 8[g]
34:16
36:27
37:24
40:45, 46
43:11
44: 8 + A
8, 14
15, 16
24
48:11
Dan. 9: 4, 4
Hos. 4:10
12: 6, 12
Amos 1:11
2: 4
Jon. 2: 9
Mic. 6:16
7: 5
Hab. 3:16
Zec. 3: 7, 7 A[e]
11:11
Mal. 2: 7, 9
15, 16
3: 7, 14

[a] A συνάγω. [b] *pro* διώκω.
[c] *pro* ψυχω. [d] *pro* φύλαξ.
[e] *pro* διαφυλάσσω.
[f] AS διαφυλασσω. [g] A ἀφίστημι

φυλή.

Gen. 10: 5, 18
20, 31
32
12: 3
24: 4, 38
40, 41
28:14
36:40
Gen. 49:16
Exo. 2: 1
24: 4
28:21
31: 2, 6
35:30, 34
36:21
37:20, 21

Lev. 24:11
25:49
Nu. 1: 4, 16
21, 23
25, 27
29, 31
33, 35
37, 39
41, 43
44, 44
47 – A
49
2: 5, 7
9 A[a]
12, 14
20, 22
27, 29
3: 6
4:18
7: 2, 12
18
10:15, 16
19, 20
23, 24
26, 27
13: 3
5 *to* 16
17: 3
18: 2
24: 2
25: 5
26:55
27:11
30: 2
31: 4, 4, 4
5, 6, 6
32:28, 33
33:54, 54
34:13, 13
14 *ter*
15, 15
18 *to* 28
36: 1, 1, 3
3, 4, 4
5, 7, 7
7
8 – A
9, 9, 12
Deu. 1:13, 23
3:13
5:23
10: 8
12: 5 A[b]
14[c]
16:18
18: 1, 5
29: 8, 18
33: 5
Jos. 1:12
3:12
4: 2, 4, 5
12
7: 1, 14
14, 16
16
11:23
12: 6, 7
13: 7, 7, 8
8, 14
15, 29
31 A[2 d]
31 + A[2]
14: 1, 2, 2
4
15: 1, 20
21
16: 8
17: 1
18: 2, 4, 7
11
19: 8, 9
16, 23
31, 39
47, 51
20: 8
8 – A
8
21 *passim*
22: 1, 7, 9
10, 11

Jos. 22:13, 14
15, 21
30, 31
32, 33
34
23: 4
24: 1
Jud. 13: 2 + A
18: 1, 1, 19
30
19:29 A[e]
20: 2, 10
12, 12
21: 3, 5, 6
8, 15
17, 24
Ruth 3:11
4:10
1 Sa. 9:21, 21
10:19[f], 21
21, 21
15:17
20: 6, 29
29: 3 A[g]
2 Sa. 5: 1
7: 7
15: 2, 10
19: 9
20:14
24: 2
1 Ki. 7: 2
11:32
12 *p* 24 *l* 49
l 54
14:21
18:31
2 Ki. 17:18
21: 7
1 Ch. 5:18, 23
26
6:60 *to* 63
65, 65
65 – AB
66, 70
71, 72
74, 76
77, 78
80
12:2 A[h]
31, 37
17: 6
23:14
26: 1 B[i]
32
27:16, 20
21, 22
2 Ch. 5: 2
6: 5
11:16
12:13
33: 7
Ezra 6:17
Est. 2: 5
Psa. 71:17
77:55, 67
68
104:37
121: 4
4 – S^1
Pro. 14:34
Isa. 19:13
49: 6
63:17
Eze. 19:11, 14
20:32
21:13
37:19 *ter*
45: 8
47:13, 21
22[k], 23
48: 1, 19
23, 29
31
Dan. 3: 4
7 – A
29, 31
5:19
6:25
7:14
Hos. 5: 9

Amos 1: 5, 8
3: 1, 2, 12
Mic. 2: 3
5: 1[m]
6: 9
7:14 + A
Nah. 3: 4 AS^2[n]
Hag. 1: 1, 12
14
2: 2, 21
Zec. 9: 1
Zec. 12:12
12 – S
12
12 + A
12 + A
12, 13
13, 14
14
14 + S^3
14:17, 18

[a] *pro* παρεμβολή. [b] *pro* πόλις
[c] A πόλις. [d] *pro* υἱός.
[e] *pro* ὅριον. [f] A χιλιάς.
[g] *pro* βασιλεύς. [h] *pro* φυλακή.
[i] *pro* πυλη. [k] A υἱός.
[m] B πύλη. [n] *pro* λαός.

φύλλον.

Gen. 3: 7
8:11
Lev. 26:36
Neh. 8:15 *quq*
Job 13:25
Psa. 1: 3
Pro. 11:14
Isa. 1:30
34: 4, 4
64: 6
Jer. 8:13
Dan. 4: 9, 11
18
Hag. 2:19 S^1[a]

[a] *pro* ξύλον.

φύραμα.

Exo. 8: 3[a]
12:34
Nu. 15:20, 21

[a] A^1 φρέαρ.

φύρασις.

Hosea 7: 4

φυράω.

Gen. 18: 6
Exo. 29: 2, 40
Lev. 2: 4, 5
6:21
7: 2
9: 4
Lev. 14:10, 21
Nu. 15: 4 A[a]
1 Sa. 28:24
2 Sa. 13: 8
1 Ch. 23:29

[a] *pro* ἀναποιέω.

φυρμός.

Ezekiel 7:23

φύρω.

2 Sa. 20:12
Job 7: 5
30:14
Job 39:30
Isa. 14:19
Eze. 16: 6, 22

φυσάω.

Isaiah 54:16

φυσητήρ.

Job 32:19
Jer. 6:29

φυτεία.

2 Ki. 19:29
Eze. 17: 7
Mic. 1: 6

φύτευμα.

Isa. 17:10
60:21
Isa. 61: 3

φυτεύω.

Gen. 2: 8
9:20
21:33
Deu. 16:21
20: 6
28:30, 39
Jos. 24:13[a]
Psa. 1: 3
79:16
91:14
93: 9
103:16
106:37
Pro. 27:18
Ecc. 2: 4, 5
3: 2, 2
12:11[b]
Isa. 5: 2
17:10, 11
11 A[c]
37:30
40:24
44:14
65:22
Jer. 2:21
12: 2
36: 5[i], 28
38: 5

Jer. 38: 5 + AS[3]
5
39: 41
49: 10
51: 34
Eze. 19: 10, 13
28: 26
Amos 5: 11
9: 14[e]
14 B[f]

[a] A καταφυτεύω. [b] AOS πυρόω. [c] pro σπείρω. [d] S καταφυτεύω [e] AB καταφυτεύω. [f] pro ποιέω

φυτόν.

Gen. 22: 13
1 Ki. 19: 5
Job 24: 18
Eze. 31: 4, 4 + A
34: 29
Dan. 11: 20

φυτός.

Ezekiel 17: 5

φύω.

Exo. 10: 5
Deu. 29: 18
Pro. 11: 30
26: 9
Cant. 5: 13
Isa. 37: 31
Eze. 37: 8[a]

[a] A ἀναφύω.

φωνέω.

1 Ch. 15: 16
Ps. 113: 15
134: 17 + A
Isa. 8: 19, 19
19: 3
24: 14[a]
Isa. 29: 4
38: 14
Jer. 17: 11
Dan. 4: 11
Amos 3: 6
Zeph. 2: 14

[a] AS βοάω.

φωνή.

Gen. 3: 8, 10
17
4: 10, 23
11: 1, 7
15: 4
16: 2
21: 12, 17
17
22: 18
26: 5
27: 13, 22
22, 34
38 − A
43
29: 11
30: 6
39: 14, 15
18
45: 2, 16
Exo. 3: 18
4: 1, 8, 8
9
5: 2
9: 23, 28
29, 33
34
15: 26
18: 24
19: 5, 13
16, 16
19, 19
20: 18, 18
22: 23
23: 22, 22
24: 3
28: 31
32: 17, 17
18 *ter*
Lev. 5: 1
25: 9
26: 36
Nu. 3: 16, 30
51
4: 37, 41
45, 49
7: 89
9: 20
10: 13
13: 4
14: 1, 22
16: 34
20: 16
21: 3
Deu. 1: 34, 45
4: 11 + B
12, 12
30, 33
36
5: 22, 23
24, 25
26, 28
28
8: 20
9: 23
13: 4, 18
15: 5
18: 16
21: 18, 18
20
26: 7, 14
17
27: 10, 14
28: 1, 2, 9
13[a], 15
45, 49
62
30: 2, 8
10, 20
33: 7
Jos. 6: 10
20 + A
22: 2
24: 24
Jud. 2: 2, 4, 20
5: 11
6: 10
9: 7
13: 9
18: 3, 25
20: 13
24: 3
Ruth 1: 9, 14
1 Sa. 1: 13
2: 25
4: 5
6 + A
14, 14
15
7: 10
8: 7, 9, 22
11: 4
12: 1, 14
15, 17
18
15: 1, 14
14, 19
1 Sa. 15: 20, 22
24
19: 6
24: 17, 17
25: 35
26: 17, 17
28: 12, 18
21, 22
23
30: 4
2 Sa. 3: 32
5: 24
6: 15
12: 18
13: 14, 16
36
15: 10, 23
19: 4, 35
22: 7, 14
1 Ki. 1: 40, 41
41, 45
8: 30 A[b]
55
9: 3
14: 6 A
17: 22 + A
18: 26, 27
28
29 + A
41
19: 12, 13
21: 25, 36
2 Ki. 4: 31
6: 32
7: 6, 6
6 − A
10
10: 6
11: 13
18: 12
28 − B
19: 22
1 Ch. 14: 15
15: 16, 28
2 Ch. 5: 13 *ter*
15: 14
20: 19
23: 12
30: 27
32: 18
Ezra 1: 1
3: 11, 12
13, 13[c]
13
13 − B
10: 7
12 + S[3]
Neh. 4: 20
9: 4
Est. 4: 1
Job 2: 12
3: 18
4: 10, 16
6: 5
9: 16 − ABS
21: 12
28: 26
33: 8
34: 16
37: 3, 3, 3
4
38: 7, 34
40: 4
Psa. 3: 5
5: 3, 4
6: 9 − S[1]
9: 13 A[b]
17: 7, 14
18: 4
25: 7
26: 7
27: 2, 6
28: 3, 4, 4
5, 7, 8
9
30: 23
41: 5, 8
43: 17
45: 7
46: 2, 6
Psa. 54: 4, 18
57: 6
64: 2 S[d]
65: 8, 19
67: 34, 34
73: 23
76: 2, 2
18, 19
80: 12
85: 6
92: 3, 4
94: 8
97: 5, 6
101: 6
102: 20
103: 7, 12
105: 25
114: 1
117: 15
118: 149
129: 2[e], 2
139: 7
140: 1
141: 2, 2
Pro. 2: 3
3 +
AB*C[2]
5: 13
8: 4
26: 25
27: 14
Ecc. 5: 2, 5
7: 7
10: 20
12: 4, 4
Cant. 2: 8, 12
14, 14
5: 2
8: 13
Isa. 5: 30
6: 4, 8
13: 2, 4, 4
15: 4
18: 3
24: 8
14 + AS[f]
28: 23, 28
29: 4, 4, 6
30: 17, 17
19, 30
31
31: 4
32: 9
33: 3
36: 13
37: 23
38: 5 + AS
40: 3, 6, 9
42: 2
23 + S[1]
24 + S[1]
48: 20
50: 10
51: 3
52: 8, 8
54: 17
58: 1, 4
65: 19, 19
66: 6, 6, 6
Jer. 3: 15, 23
3: 13, 21
25
4: 15, 16
19, 21
29, 31
31
5: 15
6: 17, 23
7: 23, 28
34 *qtr*
8: 16, 16
19
9: 10, 13
19
10: 22
11: 3 S[g]
4, 16
12: 8
16: 9 *qtr*
18: 10, 19
Jer. 22: 20, 21
25: 10 *qtr*
26: 12, 22
27: 21, 28
42, 46
28: 16, 54
55, 55
29: 3, 22
31: 3, 34
32: 16, 22
33: 13
37: 5, 19
38: 15, 16
39: 23
40: 11 *qnq*
42: 8
47: 3
49: 6, 6, 13
14, 21
50: 4, 7
51: 23
Lam. 2: 7
3: 55 − A
Eze. 1: 24, 24
24 + A
24 + A
24 + A
25
2: 1
3: 12, 13
13, 13
9: 1
10: 3, 5
11: 13
19: 7, 9
Eze. 21: 22
23: 42
26: 10, 13
15
27: 28, 30
31: 16
33: 4, 5, 32
35: 12
37: 7 + A
43: 2, 2, 6
Dan. 3: 5, 7
10, 15
4: 28
6: 20
7: 11
8: 16
9: 10, 11
14
10: 6, 6, 9
9 + A
Joel 2: 5, 5, 11
3: 16 − S[1]
Amos 1: 2
2: 2
3: 4
6: 5
Jon. 2: 3, 10
Mic. 6: 1, 9
Nah. 3: 2, 2
Hab. 3: 10, 16
Zeph. 1: 10, 14
3: 2
Hag. 1: 12
Zec. 6: 15
11: 3, 3

[a] A ἐντολή. [b] pro δέησις. [c] A εὐφροσύνη. [d] pro προσευχή [e] A προσευχή. [f] pro βοή. [g] pro λόγος. [h] A κραυγή.

φωρίω.

Proverbs 26: 19 AS[2] [a]

[a] pro ὁράω.

φῶς.

Gen. 1: 3, 3, 4
4, 5, 18
Exo. 10: 23
27: 20
35: 16
39: 17
Lev. 24: 2
Nu. 4: 16
Jud. 16: 2 + A
1 Sa. 25: 34, 36
2 Sa. 17: 22
23: 4
2 Ki. 7: 9
2 Ch. 4: 20
Est. (9) 16
Job 3: 9 S[1] [a]
16, 20
12: 22, 25
17: 12
18: 5, 6, 18
22: 11
24: 16
26: 10
28: 11
29: 3, 24
33: 28, 30
31 + A
34: 32
37: 2, 10
11, 20
38: 15, 19
Psa. 4: 7
35: 10, 10
36: 6
37: 11
42: 3
48: 20
55: 14
77: 14 S[1] [b]
88: 16
96: 11
103: 2
Ps. 111: 4
118: 105
135: 7
138: 12
148: 3
Pro. 4: 18
6: 23
13: 9, 9
16: 15
20: 27
Ecc. 2: 13
11: 7
12: 2
Isa. 2: 5
4: 5
5: 20, 20
9: 2, 2
10: 17
13: 10, 10
18: 4
26: 9
30: 26 *ter*
42: 6, 16
45: 7
49: 6
8 + S[1]
50: 10, 11
51: 4
5 − A
53: 11
58: 8, 10
59: 9
60: 1, 3, 19
19, 20
62: 1
Jer. 4: 23
10: 13
13: 16
25: 10
28: 16
38: 35, 35
Lam. 3: 2
Eze. 32: 7, 8
41: 11
42: 7, 10
11, 12
Dan. 2: 22
6: 19
Hos. 6: 5
Hos. 10: 12
Amos 5: 18, 20
8: 9
Mic. 7: 9
Hab. 3: 4, 11
Zeph. 3: 5 − A
Zec. 14: 6, 7

[a] pro φωτισμός. [b] pro πῦρ.

φωστήρ.

Genesis 1: 14, 16, 16, 16

φωτίζω.

Exo. 38: 13
Nu. 4: 9
8: 2
Jud. 13: 8 A[a]
23 A[b]
1 Sa. 29: 10
2 Ki. 12: 2
17: 27, 28
Ezra 2: 63
9: 8
Neh. 7: 65
8: 3 S[1] [c]
9: 12, 19
Job 3: 9 A[d]
Job 33: 31 + A
Psa. 12: 4
17: 29, 29
18: 9
33: 6
75: 5
104: 39
118: 130
138: 12 − A
Pro. 4: 18
Ecc. 8: 1
Isa. 60: 1, 1, 19
Hos. 10: 12
Mic. 7: 8

[a] pro συμβιβάζω. [b] pro δείκνυμι. [c] pro διαφωτίζω. [d] pro φωτισμός.

φωτισμός.

Job 3: 9[a]
Psa. 26: 1
43: 4
Psa. 77: 14
89: 8
138: 11

[a] A φωτίζω, S[1] φῶς.

χαίνω.

Gen. 4: 11
Eze. 2: 8

χαίρω.

Gen. 45: 16
Exo. 4: 14, 31
1 Sa. 19: 5
1 Ki. 3 *p* 16
5: 7
8: 66
2 Ki. 11: 14, 20
20: 13
Est. (9) 15
Psa. 95: 12
Pro. 2: 14
6: 16
17: 19[a]
23: 25
24: 19
Isa. 13: 3
39: 2
Isa. 48: 22
57: 21
66: 10, 14
Jer. 7: 34
38: 13, 13
Lam. 1: 21
4: 21
Eze. 7: 12
Hos. 9: 1
Joel 2: 21, 23
Jon. 4: 6
Hab. 1: 16
3: 18
Zeph. 3: 14
Zec. 4: 10
9: 9
10: 7, 7

[a] A κείρω.

χαλαβώτης.

Leviticus 11: 30[a]

[a] AB καλαβώτης.

χάλαζα.

Exo. 9: 18, 19
22, 23
23, 24
24, 24
25, 25
25 − A[1]
26, 28
29, 33
34
10: 5, 12
15
Jos. 10: 11, 11
Job 38: 22[a]
Psa. 17: 13
77: 47, 48[b]
104: 32
148: 8
Isa. 28: 2
30: 30
32: 19
Eze. 38: 22
Hag. 2: 17

[a] S[1] θάλασσα. [b] S[1] αἰχμαλωσία.

χαλαστός.

2 Chronicles 3: 5, 16

χαλάω.

Exo. 36:29
Isa. 33:23
Isa. 57: 4
Jer. 45: 6

χαλβάνη.

Exodus 30:34

χαλεπός.

Isaiah 18: 2

χαλινός.

2 Ki.19:28
Job 30:11
Psa. 31: 9
Isa. 37:29
Hab. 3:14
Zec. 14:20

χάλιξ.

Job 8:17
Job 21:33

χαλκεῖον.

1 Sa. 2:14[a]
2 Ch.35:13
Job 41:22

[a] A χαλκός.

χάλκειος.

Jud. 16:21
Job 20:24
Job 40:13

χάλκεος.

Exo. 26:11, 37
27: 3, 4, 4
10, 11
17, 18
19
30:18, 18
37: 6
8+A
9+A²
15, 17
18
38:19, 20
21, 22
22, 23
24, 26
26
39:10
Lev. 6:28
26:19
Nu. 16:37, 39.
21: 9, 9
Deu. 28:23
1 Sa. 17: 6,6,38
2 Sa. 8: 8, 10
22:35
1 Ki. (3) p1
4:13
7: 4+A
13, 16
16, 24
31
8:64
14:27
2 Ki. 16:14, 15
17
2 Ki. 18: 4
25:13, 13
14, 17
17
1 Ch. 15:19
18: 8, 8
10-ABS
2 Ch. 1: 5, 6
4: 1
6:13
7: 7
12:10
26: 6
Job 6:12
41: 6
19−A
Psa. 17:35
106:16
Isa. 45: 2
48: 4
Jer. 1:18
15:12, 20
52:17
17−A
18, 20
22, 22
Eze. 9: 2
27:13
Dan. 2:32
4:12, 20
5: 4, 23
7:19
Mic. 4:13
Zec. 6: 1

χαλκεύς.

Gen. 4:22
2 Ch. 24:12−A
Neh. 3:32
Job 32:19
Isa. 41: 7
54:16

χαλκεύω.

1 Samuel 13:20

χαλκός.

Gen. 4:22
Exo. 25: 3
27: 2, 6
31: 4
35: 5, 24
32
39: 7
Nu. 31:22
Deu. 8: 9
33:25
Jos. 6:19, 24
1 Sa. 2:14 A[a]
17: 5
2 Sa. 8: 8
21:16
1 Ki. 7: 2, 2, 6
1 Ki. 7:32, 32
34+A
2 Ki. 25:13, 16
1 Ch. 18: 8
22: 3, 14
16
29: 2, 7
2 Ch. 2: 7, 14
4: 9, 16
18
24:12−A
Ezra 8:27
Job 28: 2
41:18
Isa. 36:16 B[b]
60:17, 17
Jer. 6:28
52:17, 20
Lam. 3: 7
Eze. 1: 7
16:36
22:18, 20
24:11
27:12+A
40: 3
Dan. 2:35, 39
45
10: 6

[a] pro χαλκεῖον. [b] pro λάκκος.

χαμαί.

Job 1:20
Dan. 8:12

χαμαιλέων.

Lev. 11:30
Zeph. 2:14

χαμανείμ.

Ezra 8:27+B

χάος.

Mic. 1: 6
Zec. 14: 4

χαρά.

1 Ch. 29:22
Est. (9)17−S¹
9:17, 18
22−S
Psa. 20: 7
29:12
125: 2
Pro. 14:13
29: 6
Isa. 39: 2+AS
55:12, 12
Isa. 66:10
Jer. 15: 2 S¹[a]
2 S¹[a]
16
16: 9
25:10
Lam. 5:15
Joel 1: 5, 12
16
Jon. 4: 6
Zec. 8:19

[a] pro μάχαιρα.

χαραδριός.

Lev. 11:19
Deu. 14:17

χαρακοβολία.

Ezekiel 17:17

χαρακόω.

Isa. 5: 2
Jer. 39: 2−S¹

χαρακτήρ.

Leviticus 13:28

χαράκωσις.

Deuteronomy 20:20

χάραξ.

Deu. 20:19
1 Ki. 12 p24l23
21:12, 12
Ecc. 9:14
Isa. 29: 3
31: 9
Isa. 37:33
Jer. 40: 4
Eze. 4: 2
21:22, 22
26: 8

χαράσσω.

1 Ki. 15:27[a]
2 Ki. 17:11

[a] A πατάσσω.

χαρίζομαι.

Esther 8: 7

χάρις.

Gen. 6: 8
18: 3
30:27
32: 5
33: 8, 10
15
Gen. 34:11
39: 4, 21
43:13
47:25, 29
50: 4
Exo. 3:21
Exo. 11: 3
12:36
33:12, 13
13, 16
17
34: 9
Nu. 11:11
32: 5
Deu. 24: 3
Jud. 6:17 A[a]
Ruth 2: 2, 10
13
1 Sa. 1:18
16:22
20: 3, 29
25: 8
27: 5
2 Sa. 14:22
15:25
16: 4
1 Ki. 11:19
14:16 A
2 Ch. 7:21
Est. 2: 9, 15
17
5: 8
6: 3
7: 3
8: 5
Psa. 44: 3
83:12
Pro. 1: 9
3: 3, 22
34
4: 9
5:19
7: 5
8:17+AS²
10:32
11:27
12: 2
13:15
15:17
17: 8, 17
18:22
22: 1
24:30
25:10
26:11
28:23
Ecc. 9:11
10:12
Cant. 8:10 S[b]
Eze. 12:24
Zec. 4: 7, 7
6:14
12:10

[a] pro ἔλεος. [b] pro εἰρήνη.

χαρμονή.

Job 3: 7
20: 5
40:15
Jer. 31:33 S³[a]
38:13[b]
40:11 A[a]

[a] pro χαρμοσύνη. [b] A εὐφροσύνη

χαρμοσύνη.

Lev. 22:29
1 Sa. 18: 6
Jer. 31:33[a]
40:11[b]

[a] S³ χαρμονή. [b] A χαρμονή.

χαροποιός.

Genesis 49:12

χάρτης.

Isa. 8: 1+A
Jer. 43: 2 A[a]
Jer. 43: 6 AS[a]
23

[a] pro χαρτίον.

χαρτίον.

Jer. 43: 2[a], 4
6[b]
14−S¹ [c]
14, 20[c]
Jer. 43:21, 25[c]
27, 28
28, 29[c]
32

[a] A χάρτης. [b] AS χάρτης.
[c] A βιβλίον.

χασελεῦ.

Neh. 1: 1
Zec. 7: 1

χάσμα.

2 Samuel 18:17

χαυών.

Jer. 7:18
Jer. 51:19

χαφουροί.

Ezra 8:27

χεῖλος.

Gen. 11: 1, 6, 9
22:17
41: 3, 17
Exo. 7:15
14:30
26: 4, 4
Exo. 26:10, 10
Lev. 5: 4
Nu. 30: 7, 13
Deu. 2:36
3:12
4:48
Deu. 23:23
Jos. 11: 4+A
13: 9
Jud. 5:15+A
7:12
22+AB
1 Sa. 1:13
1 Ki. 7:10[a], 10
11 *ter*
9:26
2 Ki. 2:13
10:33
18:20
19:28
2 Ch. 4: 5, 5
Job 1:22+A
2:10
8:21
9: 3 A[b]
11: 5
12:20
13: 6
15: 6
16: 5
27: 4[c]
32:20
33: 3
40:21
Psa. 11: 3, 4, 5
13: 3−A
15: 4
16: 1, 4
20: 3
21: 8
30:19
33:14
39:10
44: 3
50:17
58: 8, 13
62: 4, 6
65:14
70:23
88:35
105:33
118:13, 171
119: 2
139: 4
10−A¹
140: 3
Pro. 4:24
Pro. 5: 2, 3
6: 2, 2
7:21
8: 6, 7
10: 8
13−B
18, 19
21, 32
12:13, 14
19, 22
13: 3
14: 3, 7
15: 7
16:10, 13
23, 27
30
17: 4, 7
7−S
18: 6,7,20
22:11, 18
23:16, 16
24: 2, 41
43
26:23, 24
27: 2
29:49
Ecc. 10:12
Cant. 4: 3, 11
5:13
6: 5
7: 9
Isa. 6: 5, 5, 7
11: 4
28:11
29:13
30:27
36: 5
37:29
59: 3
Jer. 3:21
7:29
17:16
Lam. 3:61
Eze. 24:17
43:13
47: 6,7,12
Dan. 10:16
12: 5, 5
Hos. 14: 2
Hab. 3:16
Mal. 2: 6, 7

[a] B¹ τεῖχος. [b] pro χίλιοι.
[c] A στόμα.

χειμάζω.

Proverbs 26:10

χειμάρρος, −ρροος, −ρρους.

Gen. 32:23
Lev. 11: 9, 10
23:40
Nu. 21:14, 15
34: 5
Deu. 2:36, 37
3: 8, 12
16 *ter*
4:48
8: 7
9:21
10: 7
Jos. 13: 9
32 A[a]
15:47
16: 8+A
17: 9
Jud. 4: 7, 13
5:21 *ter*
15: 8 A[b]
16: 4+A
1 Sa. 15: 5
17:40
30: 9, 10
21
2 Sa. 15:23−A
23
17:13
2 Sa. 22: 5
23:37
1 Ki. (3)37
15:13
17: 3, 4, 5
6, 7
18: 5, 40
2 Ki. 3:16, 17
10:33
23: 6
6−A
12
24: 7
2 Ch. 7: 8
15:16
29:16
30:14
33:14
Neh. 2:15
Job 6:15
21:33
22:24
28: 4
Psa. 17: 5
35: 9
73:15
77:20
82:10

Ps. 109: 7
123: 4
125: 4
Ecc. 1: 7, 7
Cant. 6:10
Isa. 66:12
Jer. 29: 2
38:40+A

Lam. 2:18
Eze. 36: 4
47: 5+A
5
Joel 3:18
Amos 5:24
6:14

[a] pro Ἰορδάνης.
[b] pro τρυμαλιά.

χειμερινός.

Ezra 10:13
Pro. 27:15
Jer. 43:22
Zec. 10: 1

χειμών.

Ezra 10: 9
Job 37: 5-CS[2]
Job 37: 5
Cant. 2:11

χείρ.

Gen. 3:22
4:11
5:29
8: 9
9: 2, 5, 5
14:22
16: 6−A
9, 12
12
19:10, 16
16, 16
20: 5
21:18
22: 6, 10
12
24: 2, 9
22, 30
47
25:26
27:17, 22
22, 23
23
30:35
31:29, 42
32:11
11−A
16+A
33:10
35: 4
37:21, 22
22, 27
38:18, 20
28, 28
29, 30
39: 1, 3, 4
6, 8
12−A
13, 22
23, 23
40:11, 11
13, 21
41:35, 42
42, 44
42:37
43: 8, 11
14, 20[a]
25
46: 4
47:29
48:14, 14
17−B
17, 22
49: 8, 24
24
Exo. 3: 8, 19
20
4: 2, 4, 4
4, 6, 6
6, 6, 7
7, 17
20, 21
5:21
6: 1, 8
7: 4, 5
15, 17
19−A
19

Exo. 8: 5, 6
16, 17
9: 3, 8, 15
22, 23
29, 33
10:12, 21
22
12:11
13: 3, 9, 9
14, 16
16
14: 8, 16
21, 26
27, 30
31
15: 6, 9
17, 20
17: 5, 9
11, 11
12, 12
12, 16
18: 4, 8, 8
9, 9
10, 10
19:13
21:13, 20
24−A[1]
24−A[1]
22: 4
23:31
28:37
29: 9, 9, 10
15, 19
20, 20
24, 24
25, 29
33, 35
30:19, 21
32: 4, 15
19, 29
33:22, 23
34:29
35:25
38:27
Lev. 1: 4, 10
3: 2, 8, 13
4: 4, 5
15, 24
29, 33
5: 7, 11
7:20
8:14, 18
22, 23
24, 27
27, 28
33
9:17, 22
10:11
11:27
12: 8
14:14, 15
16, 17
17, 18
21, 22
25 to 30
15:11
16:12, 21

Lev. 16:21, 32
19:18
21:19
22:25
24:14
25:26, 28
35, 47
49
26:25, 46
27: 8
Nu. 3: 3
4:28, 33
37, 41
45, 49
5:18, 18
25
6:19, 21
7:88
8:10, 12
9:23
10:13
11:23
14:17 A[b]
30
15:23, 30
16:40
20:11, 20
21:34
22: 7, 23
29, 31
24:10, 24
25: 7
27:18, 23
31: 6
33: 1, 3
35:17, 18
21
36:12
Deu. 1:25, 27
2: 7, 15
24, 30
36
3: 2, 3, 8
24
4:28, 34
5:15
6: 8, 21
7: 2, 8, 8
19, 23
24
8:17
9:15, 17
26
29−A
10: 3
11: 2, 18
12: 7, 11
17, 18
13: 9, 9, 17
14:24
15: 7, 8
10, 11
16:10, 15
17
17: 7, 7
19: 5, 12
21, 21
20:13
21: 6, 7, 10
23:14 A[c]
24: 1, 3, 5
21
25:11, 11
12
26: 4, 8
27:15
28: 8, 12
20, 32
29:3+AB[e]
30: 9, 14
31:29
32:27, 39
40, 41
33: 3, 7, 11
34: 9, 12
Jos. 2:24
5:13
8: 1, 18
18, 18
18, 19

Jos. 9:32
10: 6, 8
19, 30
32, 35
14: 2−A
17: 4
19:48
20: 5 A, 9
21: 2, 44
22: 9, 31
24: 8, 10
11, 33
Jud. 1: 2, 4, 6
7, 35
2:14, 14
15, 16
18, 23
3: 4, 8, 10
10−A
15, 21
28, 30
4: 2, 7, 9
14, 21
24
5:26
6: 1, 2
9−A
9, 13
14, 21
36, 37
7: 2, 2
6[d], 7
8, 9, 11
14, 15
16, 19
20, 20
8: 3, 6, 6
7, 15
15, 22
34
9:16, 17
24, 29
33, 48
10: 7, 7, 12
11:21, 30
32
12: 2, 3, 3[e]
13: 1, 5, 23
14: 6, 9[f]
15:12, 13
14[g], 15
17, 18
18
16:18, 23
24, 26[h]
17: 3, 5, 12
18:10, 19
19:27
20:28
Ruth 1:13
4: 5, 9
1 Sa. 2:13
4: 3, 8
5: 3, 4, 4
6, 7, 9
6: 3, 5, 9
7: 3, 8
13, 14
9: 8, 16
10: 1, 4, 7
18
11: 7
12: 3, 4, 5
9, 9, 9
10, 11
15
13:22
14:10, 12
13, 19
26, 27
27, 34
37, 43
48
15:12, 28
16: 2, 20
23
17:22A, 37
37, 37
40, 40
46, 47

1 Sa. 17:49, 50A
57 A
18:10 A
17 A
17 A
21
25−A
19: 5, 9, 9
20:15+A
21: 3, 3, 4
8, 8, 13
22: 6, 17
17
23: 4, 6, 7
12A, 14
16, 17
20
24: 5, 7, 11
11, 12
12, 13
14, 16
19, 21
25: 8, 26
31, 33
35, 39
39
26: 8, 9, 11
23, 23
27: 1, 1
28:15, 17
17, 19
19, 21
30:15, 23
2 Sa. 1:14
2: 7, 16
3:12, 18
18, 18
34
4: 1, 11
12
5:19, 19
6: 6
8: 1, 3, 10
10: 2, 16
11:14
12: 7, 25
13: 5, 6
10, 19
14:16, 19
15: 2, 5, 18
18−A
36
16: 8, 21
17: 2
18: 2, 2, 2
4, 12
12, 14
18, 19
28, 31
19: 9+AB
9, 43
20: 9, 10
21
21: 9, 20
22, 22
22: 1, 1, 21
25, 35
23: 6, 10
10, 21
21
24:14, 14
16, 16
17
1 Ki. 2:25
(3)p 16+A
7:17, 19
21, 21
8:15, 22
24, 38
41+A
53, 54
56
10:13
19−B
19−A
11:11, 12
26
26+A
31, 34
35

1 Ki. 12:15
p 24 l 29
l 31
13: 4, 4, 6
6, 33
14: 3 A
18 A
26
15:18
29−A
16: 1, 7, 7
34
17:11, 16
18: 9, 46
20:28
21: 6, 13
28, 42
22: 3, 6, 12
15, 34
2 Ki. 3:10, 11
13, 15
18
4:29, 34
34
5: 5, 11
18, 20
24
6: 7
7: 2, 17
8: 8, 9
20, 22
9: 1−A
7, 8
23, 24
35, 36
10:10, 15
15, 24
11: 7, 8, 11
12, 16
12:11, 15
13: 3, 3, 5
16 qlr
25, 25
14: 5, 25
27
15:19
19+A
16: 7, 7
17: 7, 13
13, 20
23
18:21, 29
30, 33
34, 35
35
19:10, 14
18, 19
23, 26
20: 6
21:10, 14
22: 5, 9, 17
24: 2
1 Ch. 4:10
5:10, 20
6:15, 31
11: 3, 23
23
12:17
13: 9−S
10
14:10, 10
11
16: 7, 40
17:23+S
18: 1, 3
19:11
20: 8, 8
21:13, 13
15, 16
17
22:18
23:28
24:19
26:28
28:19
29: 5, 5, 8
12, 12
16
2 Ch. 1:17
6: 4, 12

2 Ch. 6:13, 15
29, 32
7: 6
8:18
10:15
12: 5
13: 8, 9, 16
15: 7
16: 7, 8
17: 5
18: 5, 11
14, 33
20: 6
21:10+A
10
23: 7, 18
18
24:11, 13
24
25: 3, 15
20
26:11, 11
19
28: 5, 5, 9
29:23, 25
31
30: 6, 12
16
31:15, 15
32:11, 13
14, 14
15, 15
15, 17
17, 19
22, 22
33: 8
34: 9, 10
14, 16
17
17−B
25
35: 4, 6, 11
36: 5, 15
17
Ezra 1: 6, 8
3:10
4: 4
5: 8, 12
6:12, 22
7: 6, 9, 14
25, 28
8:18, 22
26, 31
31, 33
9: 2, 5, 7
11
10:19
Neh. 1:10
2: 8, 18
18
3: 2, 2
4[i]
4−B
4−A
5
7-ABS
8, 9, 10
10, 12
17, 19
4:17
5: 5
6: 5, 9, 9
8: 6-BS[1]
9:14, 15
24, 27
27, 28
30, 30
10:29, 31
11:24
12: 8
13:13, 13
21
Est. 2: 8
3: 9+S[3]
10−S[1]
4: 8
6: 2
9+S[3]
8: 7
9:16+S[3]

Job 1:10, 11
12
2: 5, 10
4: 3
5:12, 15
18, 20
6:23+A
23
8: 4
9:24, 30
10: 3, 7, 8
11:13, 14
12: 9, 10
13:14, 21
14:15
15:22, 25
16:11, 17
17: 3, 9
19:21
20:10, 24
21: 5, 16
22:30
23: 2, 2
27:11, 22
23
28: 9
29:12, 20
30: 2, 21
31: 7, 21
25, 27
35
33: 7
35: 7
36:32
37: 6
39:34
40:27
Psa. 7: 4
8: 7
9:17, 33
35
16:14
17: 1, 1, 21
25, 35
18: 2
20: 9
21:17, 21
23: 4
25: 6, 10
27: 2, 4, 5
30: 6, 9, 16
16
31: 4
34:10−A
35:12
36:24, 33
37: 3
38:11
40: 3
43: 3, 21
46: 2
48:16
54:21−S[1]
57: 3, 11
62: 5
11−S[1]
67:32
70: 4, 4
71:12+BS[1]
72:13, 23
73: 3, 11
74: 9
75: 6
76: 3, 21
77:42, 42
61, 72
79:18
80: 7, 15
81: 4
87: 6, 10
88:14, 22
26, 49
89:17
17+AS
90:12
91: 5
94: 4, 5, 7
96:10
97: 8
101:26

Ps. 103:28
105:10, 10
26, 41
42
106: 2
108:27
110: 7
113:12, 15
118:48, 73
109,173
120: 5
122: 2, 2
124: 3
126: 4
128: 7
133: 2
134:15
17+A
135:12
24+S
137: 7, 8
138: 5, 10
139: 5
140: 2
142: 5, 6
143: 1, 7, 7
11
144:16
149: 6
150 p 6
Pro. 3:27
6: 1,3,10
17
7:20
9:12
10: 4, 11
11:21, 21
12:24
13: 4
14: 1
16: 5, 5
18:21
19:24
21: 1, 25
23: 2
24:33, 48
63, 67
26: 9,9,15
29:31, 34
37, 38
Ecc. 2:11, 24
4: 1—C
5
5: 5, 13
14
7:19, 27
9: 1, 10
10:18
11: 6
Cant. 5: 4, 5, 5
14
7: 1+A
Isa. 1:12, 15
15, 25
2: 8
3:11
5:12, 25
25
6: 6
8:11
9:12, 17
21
10: 4, 5
10+AS
14, 32
11: 8, 11
14, 15
13: 2[k], 7
14:26, 27
17: 8
19: 4, 16
22:21
23:11
24:21
25:11, 11
28: 2, 4
29:12
31: 3, 7[m]
33:15
34:17

Isa. 35: 3
36: 6, 15
18, 19
20, 20
37:10, 19
20, 27
38: 6
40: 2, 12
41:20
42: 6
43:13
44: 5—AS
45: 9, 11
12
47: 6
48:13
49: 2, 16
22
50: 2
51:16—A
17, 18
22, 23
56: 2—S[1]
59: 1, 3
60:21
62: 3, 3
64: 8
65: 2
66: 2, 14
Jer. 1: 9, 16
2:34, 36
3: 8
4:31
5:31
6: 3, 12
24
10: 9
11:21
12: 7
15: 6, 17
21, 21
16:21
18: 4,6,21
19: 7
20: 4,5,13
21: 5, 7
10, 12
22: 3, 24
25, 25
23:14
25: 6
26:13, 24
27:15, 43
28: 7, 25
29: 3, 10
11
31:26, 37
32: 1—S[1]
3, 14
33:14, 24
24
34: 2, 6
36: 3, 21
37: 6
38:11, 32
39: 3—S[1]
4—S[1]
4—S[1]
21, 24
25, 28
36, 43
40:13
41: 2, 3
3—A
21
43:14—S[1]
14+A
44: 2, 17
45: 3, 4, 4
5, 10
16 18
19, 23
46:17
47: 4
48: 5
49:11
50: 3
51: 8, 25
30 *ter*
Lam. 1: 7, 10

Lam. 1:14, 14
17
2: 7, 8
15, 19
3: 3, 40
63
4: 2,6,10
5: 6,8,12
Eze. 1: 3, 8
2: 9
3:14, 18
20, 22
6:11, 14
7:17, 21
27
8: 1,3,11
9: 1, 2
10: 2 A[a]
7, 7, 8
12, 21
11: 9
12: 7+A
13: 9, 18
21, 21
22, 23
14: 9, 13
16:11, 27
39, 49
17:18
18: 8, 17
20: 5, 6
15, 23
28, 33
34, 42
21: 7, 11
11, 12
14, 14
17, 17
20, 31
22:13+A
13, 14
23: 9,9,28
31, 37
42, 45
25: 6,7,13
14, 16
27:21
28:10
29: 7, 7
30:10, 12
12+A
22, 24
25
31:11
33: 6,8,22
34:10, 27
35: 3, 5
36: 7
37: 1, 17
19, 19
20
38:12, 17
39: 3, 3, 9
21, 23

Eze. 40: 1, 3
3+A
5
43:26
44:12
46: 5,7,11
47: 3, 14
Dan. 1: 2
2:32, 34
38, 45
3:15, 17
4:32
5: 5, 5
23, 24
6:27
7:25
8: 4, 7
25, 25
9:10, 15
10:10
10+A
11:11, 16
41, 42
Hos. 2:10
7: 5
11: 6
12: 7, 10
13: 4, 14
14: 3
Joel 3: 8
Amos 1: 8
5:19
7: 7
9: 2
Jon. 3: 8
Mic. 2: 1
4:10
5: 9, 12
13
7: 3, 16
Nah. 3:19
Hab. 2: 9
3: 4
Zeph. 1: 4
2:13
(2)15
3:15, 16
Hag. 1: 1,3,11
2: 1, 14
17
Zec. 1:21
2: 1, 9
4: 9, 9
10, 12
7: 7, 12
8: 4,9,13
11: 6, 6, 6
8 S[1 o]
13: 6, 7
14:13 *ter*
Mal. 1: 1, 9
10, 13
2:13

[a] A *μάρσιππος*. [b] *pro ἰσχύς*. [c] *pro πρόσωπον*. [d] A *γλῶσσα*. [e] A *ἐνώπιον*. [f] A *στόμα*. [g] A *βραχίων*. [h] *vide χειραγωγέω* [i] S[1] *θύρα*. [k] A *ψυχή*. [m] S[1] *δακτυλος*. [n] *pro δράξ* [o] *pro ψυχή*.

χειραγωγέω.

Judges 16:26 A[a]

[a] *pro κρατοῦντα τὴν χεῖρα*.

χειροπέδη.

Job 36: 8
Ps. 149: 8
Isa. 45:14
Jer. 47: 1, 4
Nah. 3:10

χειροποίητος.

Lev. 26: 1, 30
Isa. 2:18
10:11
16:12
19: 1
Isa. 21: 9
31: 7
7—AS
46: 6

χειροτονία.

Isaiah 58: 9

χειρόω.

Job 3: 8
13:15
Job 30:24

χείρων.

1 Samuel 17:43—A

χελιδών.

Isa. 38:14
Jer. 8: 7

χελώνη.

Hosea 12:11

χελώνιον.

Deuteronomy 34: 7—B

χερέθ.

Jeremiah 44:16

χεροκένως.

1 Chronicles 12:33

χερούβ, —βεῖμ, etc.

Gen. 3:24
Exo. 25:17, 18
18, 18
19, 19
21
26: 1, 31
37: 3, 5
6+A
38: 6, 7, 7
Nu. 7:89
1 Sa. 4: 4
2 Sa. 6: 2
22:11
1 Ki. 6:21
22—AB
23
23+A
24, 24
25
25—B
26, 27
30+A
30+A
32
7:15, 22
8: 6, 7, 7
2 Ki. 19:15
1 Ch. 13: 6
28:18
2 Ch. 3: 7,8,10
11, 11
12 A
12 A
13, 14
5: 7, 8, 8
Psa. 17:11
79: 2
98: 1
Isa. 37:16
Eze. 9: 3
10: 1, 2, 2
3, 4, 5
6
7+A
7, 8, 9
9, 14A
15, 16
16, 18
19, 20
11:22
28:14, 16
41:18 *q/r*
20, 25

χερσαῖος.

Leviticus 11:29

χερσόομαι.

Pro. 24:16
Jer. 2:31
Nah. 1:10—S[1]

χέρσος.

Isa. 5: 6
7:23, 24
25
Hos. 10: 4
12:11

χεττιίμ.

2 Kings 23: 7

χέω, χύω.

1 Ki. 7:11+A
16+A
Job 29: 6, 6
38:38
Jer. 7:20[a]
Eze. 20:33, 34
Hos. 4: 2
Joel 2: 2
Mal. 3: 3[b]

[a] A *ἐκχέω*. [b] S[2] *ἐκχέω*.

χηλή.

Lev. 11: 3
Deu. 14: 6

χήρα.

Gen. 38:11
Exo. 22:22, 24
Lev. 21:14
22:13
Nu. 30:10
Deu. 10:18
14:29
16:11, 14
24:19, 19
21, 22
23
26:12, 13
27:19
2 Sa. 14: 5
20: 3
1 Ki. 7: 2
11:26
17: 9, 10
20
Job 22: 9
24: 3
27:15
29:13
31:16
Psa. 67: 6
77:64
93: 6
108: 9
131:15AS[1a]
145: 9
Pro. 15:25
Isa. 1:17, 23
9:17
10: 2
47: 8
49:21
Jer. 5:28
7: 6
15: 8
18:21
22: 3
29:12
Lam. 1: 1
5: 3
Eze. 22: 7, 25
44:22, 22
Zec. 7:10
Mal. 3: 5

[a] *pro θήρα*.

χηρεία.

Isa. 47: 9
54: 4
Mic. 1:16

χήρευσις.

Genesis 38:14, 19

χηρεύω.

2 Sa. 13:20
Jer. 28: 5

χθές.

Gen. 19:34[a]
31: 2[a]
29[a], 42
Exo. 2:14[c]
4:10[b]
5: 7[b]
14[b]
Exo. 21:29[b]
36[b]
Deu. 4:42[b]
19: 4[b], 6[b]
Jos. 4:18[b]
2 Sa. 3:17[b]
15:20—A[c]

[a] A *ἐχθές*. [b] AB *ἐχθές*. [c] B *ἐχθές*.

χθιζός.

Job 8: 9

χθών.

1 Kings 14:15 A

χίδρον.

Lev. 2:14, 16
Lev. 23:14

χιλιαρχία.

Numbers 31:48

χιλίαρχος.

Exo. 18:21, 25
Nu. 1:16
31:14, 48
52, 54
Deu. 1:15
Jos. 22:14, 21
1 Sa. 8:12
17:18 A
18:13
22: 7
2 Sa. 18: 1
1 Ch. 13: 1
15 25
26:26
27: 1
29: 6
2 Ch. 1: 2
17:14
25: 5
Zec. 9: 7
12: 5, 6

χιλιάς.

Nu. 31:36+A
43+AB
1 Sa. 10:19 A[a]
1 Ki. (3) p 1[2]—A
3: 4—A
4(26)A

1 Ki. 4(26) A
8:63—B
21:15[b]
2 Ki. 3: 4[2]—A
1 Ch. 21: 5[3]—B
2 Ch. 7: 5[2]—B
9:25[1c]
Ezra 2:12[4], 31[e]
39—B

[a] pro φυλή. [b] B 60 pro 7000. [c] A μυριάς. [d] B τρεισχίλιοι. [e] B δισχίλιοι.

χίλιοι.

2 Sa. 8: 4[a]
1 Ch. 12:31+S
2 Ch. 14: 9—B
Neh. 7:34[b]
Job 9: 3[c]
Cant. 8:11—A

[a] A ἑπτά. [b] S δισχίλιοι. [c] A χεῖλος.

χιλιοπλασίως.

Deuteronomy 1:11

χίμαιρα.

Lev. 4:28, 29
Lev. 5: 6

χίμαρος, -ρρος.

Lev. 4:23, 24
9: 3, 15
10:16
16: 5, 7, 8
9, 10
15, 18
20, 21
21, 22
22, 26
27
23:19
Nu. 7:16, 22
28, 34
40, 46
52, 58
64, 70
76, 82
Nu. 7:87
15:24
28:15, 22
30
29: 5, 11
16, 19
22, 25
28, 31
34, 38
Deu. 14: 4
2 Ch. 29:21, 23
Ezra 6:17
8:35
Neh. 5:18
Psa. 49: 9
65:15
Mic. 6: 7[a]

[a] A ἀρνός.

χιονόω.

Psalm 67:15

χιτών.

Gen. 3:21
37: 3, 23
31, 31
32, 32
33
Exo. 28: 4, 35
36
29: 5, 8
35:19
36:35
40:12
Lev. 6:10
Lev. 8: 7, 13
10: 5
16: 4
2 Sa. 13:18, 19
15:32[a]
1 Ki. 20:27
Ezra 2:69 A[b]
Job 30:18
Cant. 5: 3
Isa. 3:16, 24
36:22
61:10

[a] A ἱμάτιον. [b] pro κόθωνος.

χιών.

Exo. 4: 6
Nu. 12:10
2 Sa. 23:20
2 Ki. 5:27
1 Ch. 11:22
Job 6:16
9:30
37: 5
38:22
Psa. 50: 9
147: 5
148: 8
Pro. 25:13—B
Isa. 1:18
55:10
Jer. 18:14
Lam. 4: 7
Dan. 7: 9

χλαῖνα.

Proverbs 29:40

χλεύασμα.

Job 12: 4

χλευασμός.

Psa. 43:14 AS[2 a]
78: 4
Jer. 20: 8

[a] pro κατάγελως.

χλιδών.

Nu. 31:50
2 Sa. 1:10
2 Sa. 8: 7
Isa. 3:20

χλόη.

2 Sa. 23: 4
2 Ki. 19:26
Job 24:24 A[a]
38:27
Psa. 22: 2
Psa. 36: 2
89: 5
103:14
146: 8—A
Dan. 4:12, 20

[a] pro μολόχη.

χλωρίζω.

Lev. 13:49
Lev. 14:37

χλωροβοτάνη.

2 Kings 19:26 A[a]

[a] pro χλωρὰ βοτάνη.

χλωρός.

Gen. 1:30
2: 5
30:37, 37
Exo. 10:15
Nu. 22: 4
Deu. 29:23
2 Ki. 19:26[a]
Job 39: 8
Pro. 27:24
Isa. 15: 6
19: 7
27:11
37:27 A[b]
Eze. 17:24
20:47

[a] vide χλωροβοτάνη. [b] pro ξηρός.

χλωρότης.

Psalm 67:14

χνόος, χνοῦς.

2 Sa. 22:43 AB[a]
2 Ch. 1: 9 B[a]
Psa. 1: 4
17:43 ABS[a]
34: 5 ABS[a]
77:27 S[a]
Isa. 5:24
17:13[b]
29: 5
41:15[b]
48:19 S[a]
Hos. 13: 3[b]

[a] pro χόος. [b] A χόος.

χοεύς.

1 Ki. 7:12+A, 24

χοῖνιξ.

Ezekiel 45:10, 11, 11

χοιρογρύλλιος.

Lev. 11: 6
Deu. 14: 7
Ps. 103:18[a]
Pro. 24:61

[a] AS[2] λαγωός.

χολέρα.

Numbers 11:20

χολή.

Deu. 29:18[a]
32:32
Job 16:13[b]
20:14
Psa. 68:22
Pro. 5: 4
Jer. 8:14
9:15
Lam. 3:15, 20

[a] AB[a] ἐνοχλέω. [b] AS[2] ζωή.

χόλος.

Pro. 16:28 S[a]
Ecc. 5:16

[a] pro δόλος.

χονδρίτης.

Genesis 40:16

χόος, χοῦς.

Lev. 19:36
Job 31:24

χόος, χοῦς.

Gen. 2: 7
Lev. 14:41, 42
45
Deu. 28:24
Jos. 7: 6
2 Sa. 16:13
22:43[a]
1 Ki. 18:38
21:10
2 Ki. 13: 7
23: 4, 6, 6
12, 15
2 Ch. 1: 9[b]
Neh. 4:10[c]
Job 39:14
Psa. 7: 6
17:43[d]
21:16
29:10
34: 5[d]
Psa. 43:26
71: 9
77:27[e]
101:15
102:14
103:29
Ecc. 3:20, 20
12: 7
Isa. 17:13 A[f]
41:15 A[f]
48:19[e]
49:23
52: 2
Lam. 2:10
Eze. 26: 4, 12
Hos. 13: 3 A[f]
Amos 2: 7
Mic. 7:17
Zeph. 1:17
Zec. 9: 3

[a] AB χνοῦς. [b] B χνοῦς. [c] BS[1] ὄχλος. [d] ABS χνοῦς. [e] S χνοῦς. [f] pro χνοῦς.

χορδή.

Psa. 150: 4
Nah. 3: 8

χορεύω.

Jud. 21:21, 23
1 Sa. 18: 6
6+A
1 Sa. 21:11
1 Ki. 1:40

χορηγέω.

1 Kings 4: 7, 7, 20

χορηγία.

Ezra 5: 3, 9

χόριον.

Deuteronomy 28:57 AB[a]

[a] pro κόριον.

χορός.

Exo. 15:20
32:19
Jud. 9:27 A[a]
11:34
21:21
1 Sa. 10: 5, 10
29: 5
2 Sa. 6:13
1 Ki. 1:40
1 Ki. 21:14 B[b]
15 B[b]
17 B[b]
19 B[b]
Ps. 149: 3
150: 4
Cant. 7: 1
Isa. 5:12+S
Lam. 5:15

[a] pro ἐλλουλίμ. [b] pro χώρα.

χορρί.

2 Kings 11: 4, 19

χορτάζω.

Job 38:27
Psa. 16:14, 15
36:19
58:16
80:17
Ps. 103:13, 16
106: 9
131:15
Jer. 5: 7
Lam. 3:15, 29

χορτασία.

Proverbs 24:15

χόρτασμα.

Gen. 24:25, 32
42:27
43:23
Deu. 11:15
Jud. 19:19

χορτομανέω.

Proverbs 24:46

χόρτος.

Gen. 1:11, 12
29, 30
Gen. 2: 5
3:18
Gen. 9: 3
Deu. 32: 2
2 Ki. 19:26
Job 13:25
40:10
41:19
Psa. 36: 2
71:16
91: 8
101: 5, 12
102:15
103:14
104:35
35 S[1 a]
105:20
128: 6
146: 8
Pro. 19:12
27:24
Isa. 10:17
15: 6, 6
32:13
37:27
40: 6, 6, 7
42:15—AS
44: 4
51:12
Jer. 9:22—S[1]
12: 4
14: 6
Dan. 4:12, 22
29, 30
5:21
Amos 7: 2

[a] pro καρπός.

χορχόρ.

Ezekiel 27:16

χράω, χράομαι.

Gen. 12:16
16: 6
19: 8
26:29
34:31
Exo. 11: 3
12:36
1 Sa. 2:20
2 Sa. 1:21 A[a]
Est. 1:19
2: 9
3:11
8:11, 11
9:12, 13
27
Job 10:17
Job 13:20[b]
15: 8—ABCS
16: 9
18: 4
19:11
23: 6
30:14
34:20
Pro. 5: 5
10: 5, 26
17: 8
24:44, 44
25:13
Isa. 28:21
Jer. 13: 7, 10

[a] pro χρίω. [b] A χρεία, C χρῆσις.

χρεία.

2 Ch. 2:16
Ezra 7:20
Job 9:33+A
13:20 A[a]
31:16
Psa. 15: 2—B
Pro. 18: 2
Isa. 13:17
Jer. 22:28
31:38
Dan. 3:16

[a] pro χράω.

χρεμετίζω.

Jer. 5: 8
Jer. 38: 7

χρεμετισμός.

Jer. 8: 6, 16
13:27
Amos 6: 7

χρέος.

Deu. 15: 2, 3
1 Sa. 2:20

χρεωφειλέτης.

Job 31:37
Pro. 29:13

χρή.

Proverbs 25:27

χρήζω.

Jud. 11: 7[a]
1 Sa. 17:18 A

[a] A θλίβω.

χρῆμα.

Jos. 22: 8
2 Ch. 1:11, 12
Neh. 11:24[a]
Job 6:20
Job 27:17
Pro. 17: 6, 16
28:16 S[2 b]

[a] S[3] ῥῆμα. [b] pro πρόσοδος.

χρηματίζω.

1 Ki. 18:27
Job 40: 3

Jer. 32:16, 16
33: 2, 2
36:23
Jer. 37: 2
43: 2 A[a]
4 A[a]

[a] pro λαλέω.

χρηματισμός.

Proverbs 24:69

χρήσιμος.

Gen. 37:26
Pro. 17:17
Eze. 15: 4
Zec. 6:10, 14

χρῆσις.

1 Sa. 1:28
Job 13:20 C[a]

[a] pro χράω.

χρησμολογέω.

Jeremiah 45: 4

χρηστός.

Job 31:31
Psa. 24: 8
33: 9
51:11
68:17
85: 5
99: 5
105: 1
106: 1
108:21
111: 5
118:30, 68
Ps. 135: 1 AS[1] [a]
144: 9
Pro. 2:21 + AS
Jer. 24: 2, 3, 3
5
40:11
51:17
52:32
Eze. 27:22[b]
28:13
Dan. 2:32[c]
Nah. 1: 7

[a] pro ἀγαθός. [b] A ἐκλεκτός.
[c] AB[2] καθαρός.

χρηστότης.

Psa. 13: 1, 3
20: 4
24: 7
30:20
36: 3
52: 4 S[1] [a]
64:12
Psa. 67:11
84:13
103:28[b]
105: 5
118:65, 66
68
144: 7

[a] pro ἀγαθός. [b] A πιότης.

χρῖσις.

Exo. 29:21
30:31
31:11
35:28
38:25[a]
39:16
40: 7 A[b]
Lev. 7:25, 25
8: 2, 10
12, 30
10: 7
Nu. 4:16
Ps. 150 p 6

[a] A χρῖσμα. [b] pro χρῖσμα.

χρῖσμα.

Exo. 29: 7
30:25, 25
35:14, 19
Exo. 38:25 A[a]
40: 7[b], 13
Dan. 9:26

[a] pro χρῖσις. [b] A χρῖσις.

χριστός.

Lev. 4: 5, 16
6:22
21:10, 12
1 Sa. 2:10, 35
12: 3, 5
16: 6
24: 7, 7, 11
26: 9, 11
16, 23
2 Sa. 1:14, 16
2: 5 − A
19:21
22:51
23: 1, 3[a]
1 Ch. 16:22
2 Ch. 6:42 − B
2 Ch. 23: 7
Psa. 2: 2
17:51
19: 7
27: 8
83:10
88:39, 52
104:15
131:10, 17
Isa. 45: 1
Lam. 4:20
Eze. 16: 4 + A
Dan. 9:25
Amos 4:13
Hab. 3:13

[a] A κύριος.

χρίω.

Exo. 28:37
29: 2 − A
7, 29
36
30:26, 30
32
40: 7, 8, 11
Lev. 4: 3
6:20
7:26
8:11, 11
12
16:32
Nu. 6:15
7: 1, 1, 10
84, 88
35:25
Deu. 28:40
Jud. 9: 8, 15
1 Sa. 9:16
10: 1, 2
11:15
15: 1, 17
16: 3, 12
13
2 Sa. 1:21[a]
2: 4, 7
5: 3, 17
2 Sa. 12: 7
19:10
1 Ki. 1:34, 39
45
5: 1
19:15
16 − A
16
2 Ki. 9: 3, 6, 12
11:12
23:30
1 Ch. 11: 3
14: 8
29:22
2 Ch. 23:11
36: 1
Psa. 26: 1
44: 8
88:21
150 p 6
Isa. 25: 7
61: 1
Jer. 22:14
Eze. 16: 9
43: 3
Dan. 9:24
Hos. 8:10
Amos 6: 6

[a] A χράω.

χρόα.

Exodus 4: 7

χρονίζω.

Gen. 32: 4
34:19
Exo. 32: 1
Deu. 4:25
23:21
Jud. 5:28
2 Sa. 20: 5
Psa. 39:18
Psa. 69: 6
Pro. 9:18[a]
29:39
Ecc. 5: 3
Isa. 14: a 1
51:14
Dan. 9:10
Hab. 2: 3

[a] A ἐγχρονίζω.

χρόνος.

Gen. 26: 1 A[a]
15
Exo. 14:13
Deu. 12:10
22:19, 29
32:29
Jos. 4:14
24 A[b]
24:29
Ezra 4:15 A[c]
Neh. 10:34
13:31
Est. 2:15
5:13 + S[3]
9:28
Job 2: 9, 9
6:11
10:20
12: 5, 12
14: 5, 11
13
29:18
32: 7, 8
Psa. 88:46 AS[4]
Pro. 1:22
7:12, 12
Pro. 9:11, 18
15:15
28:16
Ecc. 3: 1
Isa. 9: 7 + A
13.20
14:20
18: 7
23:15, 15
27:10, 11
30:27
33:20
34:10
10 − AS[3]
17
38: 5
49: 1
51: 8
54: 7, 9[e]
65:20
Jer. 29: 9
37: 7
38: 1
45:28
Dan. 2:16, 21

[a] pro καιρός. [b] pro ἔργον.
[c] pro ἡμέρα. [d] pro θρόνος.
[e] S[3] καιρός.

χρυσαυγέω.

Job 37:21

χρύσεος, −οῦς.

Gen. 24:22, 22
53
37:28
41:42
Gen. 45:22
Exo. 3:22
11: 2
12:35
Exo. 16:33
20:23
25:10 − A
11
17 AB[2] [a]
22 − A
23
24 + A
25
26: 6, 29
32, 37
28:29, 30
32
30: 3, 4
32: 2, 3, 31
35:22
36:23, 23
24, 27
28, 33
34, 38
37: 4
38: 3 + A
3, 6
10 + A
12, 13
16, 17
17, 17
18, 18
19
40: 5, 24
Lev. 8: 9
Nu. 4:11
7:14, 20
26, 32
38, 44
50, 56
62, 68
74, 80
84, 86
86
8: 4
31:50
Jos. 7:21
Jud. 8:24
25 + A
26, 26[b]
26 + A
1 Sa. 6: 4, 5, 8
11, 15
17
18 − A
2 Sa. 1:24[c]
8: 7, 10
1 Ki. 7:34, 34
35, 35
36, 36
10:16, 16
17 − A
1 Ki. 10:21, 21
25
12:28
14:26, 26
15:15
2 Ki. 5: 5
10:20
12:13
24:13
25:15
1 Ch. 18: 7, 10
28:14, 16
17, 17
29: 7
2 Ch. 4: 7, 8, 13
19, 22
9:15
15 + AB
15, 16
16 − B
24
12: 9
13: 8[d], 11
24:14
Ezra 1: 9, 10
5:14
6: 5
8:27
Neh. 7:70
Est. 1: 6, 6, 7
4:11
5: 2
8: 4
(9)15
Job 28:17
Psa. 44:14
Pro. 1: 9
11:22 + S[2]
25:11, 12
Cant. 3:10
5:14, 15
Isa. 2:20
31: 7
Jer. 4:30
28: 7
52:19, 19
Dan. 2:38
3: 1, 5 − A[1]
7, 11
12, 14
15 − B
18 + A
5: 2, 3, 4
7, 16
23, 29
Hos. 2: 8
Zec. 4: 2, 12
12

[a] vide χρυσοτορευτός.
[b] A χρυσός. [c] A χρυσίον.
[d] A[2] πολύς.

χρυσίον.

Gen. 2:11, 12
13: 2
24:35
44: 8
Exo. 25: 3, 10
12, 16
22, 27
28, 30
36, 38
39
26:29, 29
32, 37
28: 5, 8
13, 14
15, 20
20 − A[1]
22
30: 3, 5
31: 4
32:24
35: 5, 22
32
36: 9, 10
12, 13
15, 20
Exo. 36:20, 22
25, 38
37: 4, 6
38: 2, 5, 9
11, 18
18
39: 1, 1, 12
Nu. 7:86
22:18
24:13
31:22, 51
52, 54
Deu. 7:25
8:13
17:17
29:17
Jos. 6:19, 24
22: 8
2 Sa. 1:24 A[a]
8:11
12:30
21: 4
1 Ki. 6:19
19 + A
19 + A
1 Ki. 6:19, 20
20 + A
26, 28
(32) A
(32) A
32
7:37
9:11, 14
28
10: 2 A[b]
10, 11
14, 14
17 A[b]
18, 21
22, 27
15:18, 19
16 p 28 − A
21: 3, 5, 7
22:49 A
2 Ki. 7: 8
12:18[c]
14:14
16: 8
18:14
20:13
23:33, 35
35
1 Ch. 18:11
20: 2
21:25
22:14, 16
28:18
29: 2, 3, 4
5 − AB
5 − AB
7
2 Ch. 1:15
2: 7, 14
3: 4, 5, 6
6[d], 7
8, 9, 9
10
4:20, 21
5: 1
8:18
9: 1, 9, 10
13, 13
14, 17
18, 20
20, 21
27
15:18
16: 2, 3
21: 3
25:24
32:27
36: 3, 4, 4
Ezra 1: 4
2:69
7:15, 16
18
8:25, 26
Ezra 8:27, 28
30, 33
Neh. 7:71 ABS
71 − AB
Job 23:10
27:16
28: 1, 6, 16
17, 19
31:24
Psa. 18:11
67:14
71:15
104:37
113:12
118:72, 127
134:15
Pro. 3:14
8:10
10 + AB[a]
19
16:16
22: 1
27:21 AC[b]
Ecc. 2: 8
12: 6
Cant. 1:11
5:11
Isa. 2: 7
3:23 AS[b]
24
13:12, 17
39: 2
40:19
46: 6
60: 6, 17
Jer. 10: 4, 9
Lam. 4: 1, 2
Eze. 7:19
19 + A
16:13[1], 17
27:12
22 AB[b]
28: 4, 13
13
38:13
40:39 + A
Dan. 2:32
10: 5
11: 8
38 A[b]
43 A[b]
Hos. 8: 4
Joel 3: 5
Nah. 2: 9
Hab. 2:19
Zeph. 1:18
Hag. 2: 8
Zec. 6:11
9: 3
13: 9
14:14
Mal. 3: 3, 3

[a] pro χρύσεος. [b] pro χρυτός.
[c] A ἀργύριον. [d] A χρυσός.

χρυσόλιθος.

Exo. 28:20
36:20
Eze. 28:13

χρυσός.

Jud. 8:26 A[a]
1 Ki. 10: 2[b]
17[b]
2 Ch. 3: 6 A[c]
Ezra 1: 6, 11
Neh. 7:71[d]
Job 3:15
41:21
42:11
Pro. 17: 3
27:21[e]
Isa. 3:23[f]
60: 9
Eze. 16:13 A[c]
27:22[g]
Dan. 2:35, 45
11:38[a]
43[b]

[a] pro χρύσεος. [b] A χρυτίον.
[c] pro χρυσίον. [d] ABS χρυτίον.
[e] AC χρυσίον. [f] AS χρυσιον.
[g] AB χρυσίον.

χρυσοτορευτός.

Exodus 25:17[a]

[a] AB[2] χρυσᾶ τορευτά.

χρυσοχόος.
Isa. 40:19 | Jer. 10: 9, 14
46: 6 | 28:17

χρυσόω.
Exo. 25:10 | 2 Ch. 3: 6–AB
24:32, 37 | 7, 8[a]
38:18 | 9, 10
2 Ki.18:16

[a] A καταχρυσόω.

χρῶμα.
Exodus 34:29[a], 30[a]

[a] A χρώς.

χρώς.
Exo. 28:38 | Lev. 13:13, 14
34:29 A[a] | 15, 15
30 A[a] | 16, 21
Lev. 13: 2, 2, 3 | 15: 7
3, 4, 11 | 16: 4

[a] pro χρῶμα.

χυδαῖος.
Exodus 1: 7

χύμα.
1 Kings 4:25

χύσις.
1 Sa. 5: 6 A[a] | 1 Ki. 7:11+A

[a] pro σύγχυσις.

χυτός.
2 Ch. 4: 2 | Job 40:13

χύτρα.
Nu. 11: 8 | Joel 2: 6
Jud. 6:19 | Mic. 3: 3
1 Sa. 2:14 | Nah. 2:10

χυτρόκαυλος,
A χυτρόγαυλος.

1 Kings 7:24, 24, 24, 29

χυτρόπους.
Leviticus 11:35[a] [a] B κυθρ-

χύω vide χέω.

χωθάρ.
2 Kings 25:17, 17, 17

χωθαρέθ.
2 Chronicles 4:12, 12, 13

χωθωνώθ.
Nehemiah 7:70, 71

χωλαίνω.
2 Sa. 4: 4 | Psa. 17:46
1 Ki.18:21

χωλός.
Lev. 21:18 | Job 29:15
Deu. 15:21 | Isa. 33:23
2 Sa. 5: 6, 8, 8 | 35: 6
9:13 | Mal. 1: 8, 13
19:26

χῶμα.
Exo. 8:16, 17 | Jos. 8:28
17 | Neh. 4:2–ABS
Job 14:19 | Isa. 25: 2
17:16 | Eze. 21:22
20:11 | Dan.12: 2
22:24 | Hab. 1:10
28: 6

χωματίζομαι.
Joshua 11:13

χώνευμα.
Deu. 9:12 | Hos. 13: 2
2 Ki.17:16 | Hab. 2:18
Jer. 10: 3

χώνευσις.
Exo. 39: 4 | 2 Ch. 4: 3

χωνευτήριον.
1 Ki. 8:51 | Mal. 3: 2
Zec. 11:13, 13

χωνευτής.
Judges 17: 4 A[a]

[a] pro ἀργυροκόπος.

χωνευτός.
Exo. 32: 4 | Jud. 18:18, 20
34:17 | 1 Ki. 7: 4, 19
Lev. 19: 4 | 14: 9 A
Nu. 33:52 | 2 Ch.33: 7
Deu. 9:16 | 34: 3, 4
27:15 | Neh. 9:18
Jud. 17: 3–A | Isa. 42:17
4 | 48: 5
18:14 | Dan.11: 8
17+A | Nah. 1:14

χωνεύω.
Exo. 26:37 | Isa. 40:19
38: 3, 10 | Jer. 10:14
18, 20 | 28:17
1 Ki. 7: 3, 33 | Eze. 22:20, 20[a]
2 Ki.22: 9 | 21, 22
2 Ch. 4: 3, 17 | 22
34:17 | Mal. 3: 3

[a] A[1] ἐπαφίημι.

χώρα.
Gen. 10:20, 31 | Est. 3:12
11:28, 31 | 12+S[3]
15: 7 | 12, 14
32: 3 | 14+S[3]
36:40 | 4: 3
41:57 | 8: 9, 9
42: 9 | 11+S[3]
Exo. 14:27 | (9)17
Lev. 13:23, 28 | 9:12 A[d]
37 | 19, 27
Nu. 32: 1, 1 | Job 1: 1
Jos. 4:18 | 2:11[e]
5:12[a] | 32: 2
1 Sa. 6: 6 | 42 p 18
1 Ki. 7:15, 41 | Ps. 104:44
41, 42 | 105:27
18:10 | 106: 3
21:14[b] | 114: 9
15[c], 17[c] | Pro. 8:26
19[c] | 29: 4
2 Ki.18:33 | Ecc. 2: 8
1 Ch.20: 1 | 5: 7
2 Ch.15: 5 | Isa. 1: 7
32:13 | 2: 6, 7
Ezra 2: 1 | 7:18, 19
4:15 | 8: 8
5: 8 | 9: 1, 2
7:16 | 10: 9
Neh. 1: 3 | 10 AS[f]
7: 6 | 13:14
9: 7 | 18: 3, 3, 7
11: 3 | 19:17, 19
Est. 1: 1, 22 | 20
22+A | 21:14
2: 3 | 22:18
Isa. 27:13 | Eze. 28:25 A[g]
28: 2 | 29:12
36:10, 18 | 30: 7, 23
37: 7, 12 | 26
18 | 34:13
Jer. 3:18 | 35:10
4:29 | 36:19
16:15 | 38:13 A[h]
23: 8–S[1] | 39:27
Lam. 1: 1 | Dan. 2:48, 49
Eze. 5: 5, 6 | 3: 1, 2, 3
6: 8 | 12, 30
11:16, 17 | 8: 2
12:15 | 11:24
19: 8 | Amos 3: 9, 9
20:23, 34 | 10, 11
41 | 6: 8
21:20 | Jon. 1: 8
22: 4, 15 | Mic. 5: 5
25: 7

[a] B κουρά. [b] A πόλις, B χαρός·
[c] B χορός. [d] pro περίχωρος·
[e] A πόλις. [f] pro ἀρχή.
[g] pro ἔθνος. [h] pro κώμη.

χωρέω.
Gen. 13: 6, 6[a] | 1 Ki.18:32
1 Ki. 7:12+A | 2 Ch. 4: 5
24

[a] A δύναμαι.

χώρημα.
Ezekiel 32: 6 A[a]

[a] pro προχώρημα.

χωρίζω.
Lev. 13:46 | Ezra 9: 1
Jud. 4:11 | Neh. 9: 2
6:18[a] | 13: 3
1 Ch.12: 8[b] | Pro. 18: 1
Ezra 6:21 | Eze. 46:19

[a] A κινέω. [b] A διαχωρίζω.

χωρίον.
1 Chronicles 27:27, 27

χωρίς.
Gen. 26: 1 | Jud. 20:15 A[a]
46:26 | 17 A[a]
47:22, 26 | 1 Ki. 5:16
Lev. 9:17 | 10:15
Nu. 6:21 | Ezra 2:65
16:49

[a] pro ἐκτός.

χωρισμός.
Lev. 12: 2 | Zec. 13: 1[a]
18:19

[a] AS[2] ῥαντισμός.

χωροβατέω.
Joshua 18: 8, 8, 9

ψαλίς.
Exo. 27:10, 11 | Exo. 37: 6–8
30: 4

ψάλλω.
Jud. 5: 3 | Psa. 20:14
1 Sa. 16:16, 16 | 26: 6
17 | 29: 5, 13
18 A[a] | 32: 2, 3
23 | 46: 7, 7, 7
18:10 A | 7, 8
19: 9 | 56: 8, 10
2 Sa. 22:50 | 58:18
2 Ki. 3:15 ter | 60: 9
Psa. 7:18 | 65: 2, 4, 4
9: 3, 12 | 67: 5, 26
12: 6 | 33
17:50 | 34–S
Psa. 68:13 | Ps. 107: 2, 4
70:22, 23 | 134: 3
74:10 | 137: 1
91: 2 | 143: 9
97: 4, 5 | 145: 2
100: 2 | 146: 7
103:33–A[1] | 149: 3
104: 2

[a] pro ψαλμός.

ψαλμός.
1 Sa. 16:18[a] | Psa. 61: 1
2 Sa. 23: 1 | 62: 1
Job 21:12 | 63: 1
30:31 | 64: 1
Psa. 3: 1–A | 65: 1
4: 1 | 66: 1
5: 1 | 67: 1
6: 1 | 70: 1+S
7: 1 | 22–S[1]
8: 1 | 72: 1
9: 1 | 74: 1
10: 1 | 75: 1
11: 1 | 76: 1
12: 1 | 78: 1
13: 1 | 79: 1
14: 1 | 80: 1, 3
18: 1 | 81: 1
19: 1 | 82: 1
20: 1 | 83: 1
21: 1–A | 84: 1
22: 1 | 86: 1
23: 1 | 87: 1
24: 1 | 91: 1
28: 1 | 93: 1
29: 1 | 94: 2
30: 1 | 97: 1, 5
31: 1 A[b] | 98: 1
32: 1+A | 99: 1
34: 1+A | 100: 1–A
35: 1+A | 107: 1
36: 1+A | 108: 1
37: 1 | 109: 1
39: 1 | 137: 1
40: 1 | 138: 1
41: 1+A | 139: 1
42: 1 | 140: 1
43: 1–S | 142: 1
45: 1 | 146: 1
46: 1 | 150 p 6
47: 1 | Isa. 66:20
48: 1 | Lam. 3:14
49: 1 | 5:14
50: 1 | Amos 5:23
60: 1+S | Zec. 6:14

[a] A ψάλλω. [b] pro σύνεσις.

ψαλτήριον.
Gen. 4:21 | Ps. 149: 3
Neh.12:27 | 150: 3
Job 21:12 | p 6
Psa. 32: 2 | Isa. 5:12
48: 5 | 38:20
56: 9 | Eze. 26:13
80: 3 | 33:32
91: 4 | Dan. 3: 5, 7
107: 3 | 10, 15
143: 9

ψαλτός.
Psalm 118:54

ψαλτῳδέω.
2 Chronicles 5:13

ψαλτῳδός.
1 Ch. 6:33 | 2 Ch. 5:12
9:33 | 20:21
13: 8 | 29:28
15:16, 19 | 35:15
27

ψαρός.
Zec. 1: 8–S[3] | Zec. 6: 3, 7

ψέκας.

Job 24: 8
Cant. 5: 2

ψελλίζω.

Isa. 29:24
Isa. 32: 4

ψέλλιον, ψέλιον.

Gen. 24:22, 30
47
Nu. 31:50
Job 40:21
Isa. 3:20 − S[1]
Eze. 16:11
23:42

ψευδής.

Exo. 20:16
Deu. 5:20
Jud. 16:10, 13
1 Ki. 22:22, 23
2 Ch. 18:21, 22
Job 24:25
Psa. 32:17
39: 5
57: 4
61:10
Pro. 6:19
8: 7
12:22
14: 5, 25
17: 4, 7[a]
19: 5, 9
22[b]
21: 6, 28
23: 3
24: 2, 29
31, 32
43
25:14, 18
26:28
28: 6
29:48
Isa. 30: 9
Jer. 6: 6, 13
7: 4, 8
8: 8
Jer. 9: 5
10:14
14:14, 14
15
15:18
16:19
20: 6
23:25, 26
32
28:17
34: 8, 12
47:16
Eze. 12:24
13: 6, 7, 8
9, 23
21:29
22:28
Dan. 2: 9
11:27
Hos. 7: 1, 13
10: 4, 13
12:11
Amos 6: 3
Jon. 2: 9
Nah. 3: 1
Hab. 2:18
Zec. 5: 4
8:17
10: 2, 2
13: 3

[a] S² πιστός. [b] AS² ψεύστης.

ψεύδομαι.

Lev. 6: 2, 3
19:11
Deu. 33:29
Jos. 24:27
2 Sa. 22:45
1 Ki. 13:18
Neh. 6: 8
Job 6:10, 28
8:18
27:11
31:28
34: 6
Psa. 17:45
Psa. 26:12
65: 3
77:36
80:16
88:36
Pro. 14: 5
Isa. 57:11
59:13
Jer. 5:12
Hos. 9: 2
Hab. 3:17
Zec. 13: 4

ψευδομαρτυρέω.

Exo. 20:16
Deu. 5:20

ψευδοπροφήτης.

Jer. 6:13
33: 7, 8
11, 16
34: 7
Jer. 35: 1
36: 1, 8
Zec. 13: 2

ψεῦδος.

2 Ch. 30:14
Job 16: 8
Psa. 4: 3
5: 7
58:13
Pro. 9:12
24:23, 23
Isa. 28:15, 15
17
30:12
44:20
Jer. 3:10, 23
5: 2
Jer. 9: 3
13:25
23:14, 32
34:13 + A
44:14
50: 2
Eze. 33:31
Hos. 4: 2
7: 3
11:12
Mic. 2:11
6:12
Mal. 3: 5

ψεύστης.

Psa. 115: 2
Pro. 19:22 AS²[a]

[a] pro ψευδής.

ψηλαφάω.

Gen. 27:12, 21
22
Deu. 28:29, 29
Jud. 16:26
Job 5:14
12:25
20:10 A[a]
Ps. 113:15
134:17 + A
Isa. 59:10, 10
Nah. 3: 1
Zec. 3: 9
9:13

[a] pro πυρσεύω.

ψηλαφητός.

Exodus 10:21

ψηφίζω.

1 Ki. 3: 8 + A
1 Ki. 8: 5 + A

ψήφισμα.

Est. 3: 7
Est. 9:24

ψῆφος.

Exo. 4:25
2 Ki. 12: 4 + A
Ecc. 7:26
Lam. 3:16

ψιθυρίζω.

2 Sa. 12:19
Psa. 40: 8

ψιθυρισμός.

Ecclesiastes 10:11

ψιλή.

Joshua 7:21

ψιλόω.

Ezekiel 44:20

ψόα.

Lev. 3: 9
2 Sa. 2:23
3:27
2 Sa. 20:10
Psa. 37: 8 A[a]

[a] pro ψυχή.

ψόγος.

Gen. 37: 1
Psa. 30:14
Jer. 20:10

ψοφέω.

Eze. 6:11
Eze. 25: 6[a]

[a] AB ἐπιψοφέω.

ψόφος.

Micah 1:13

ψυγμός.

Nu. 11:32
Eze. 26: 5, 14
Eze. 47:10

ψυκτήρ.

Ezra 1: 9 − B
Ezra 1: 9 − B

ψύλλος.

1 Samuel 24:15

ψυχή.

Gen. 1:20, 21
24, 30
2: 7, 19
9: 4, 5, 5
10, 12
15, 16
12: 5, 13
17:14
Gen. 19:17, 19
20
23: 8
27: 4, 19
25, 31
32:30
34: 3, 8
35:18
Gen. 37:21
41: 8
42:21
44:30, 30
46:15, 18
22, 25
26, 26
27, 27
27 − A
49: 6
Exo. 1: 5
4:19
12: 4, 15
16, 19
15: 9
16:16
21:23, 23
30
23: 9
30:12, 15
16
31:14
35:21
Lev. 2: 1
4: 2, 27
5: 1, 2, 4
15, 17
6: 2
7: 8, 10
10, 11
11, 15
17, 17
11:10, 43
44, 46
46
16:29, 31
17: 4, 10
11 *ter*
12, 14
14, 15
18:29
19: 8, 28
20: 6, 6, 25
21: 1, 11
22: 3, 4, 6
11
23:27, 29
30, 30
32
24:17, 18
18
26:11, 15
16, 30
43
27: 2
Nu. 5: 2, 6
6: 6, 11
9: 6, 7
10, 13
11: 6
15:27, 28
30, 30
31
16:37
19:11, 13
13, 18
20, 22
21: 5
23:10, 10
29: 7
30: 3, 5, 5
6 *to* 13
14[a]
31:28, 35
35, 40
40, 46
35:11, 15
30, 30
31
Deu. 4: 9, 15
29
6: 5, 6
10:12, 22
11:13, 18
12:20, 20[b]
21, 23
23
13: 3, 6
14:25
25 − B
Deu. 16: 8
18: 6
19: 6, 11
21, 21
22:26
24: 2, 8, 9
26:16
27:25
28:65
30:2, 6, 10
Jos. 2:13, 14
9:30
20: 3, 9
22: 5
23:14
Jud. 5:18, 21
9:17
10:16[c]
12: 3
16:30
18:25 *ter*
Ruth 4:15
1 Sa. 1:10, 15
26
2:16, 33
35
17:55 A
18: 1 A, 1 A
1 A, 3 A
19: 5, 11
20: 1, 3, 4
17
22: 2, 22
23, 23
23:20
24:10, 12
25:26, 29
29, 29
26:20, 21
24, 24
28: 9, 21
30: 6
2 Sa. 1: 9
3:21
4: 8, 9
5: 8
11:11
14: 7, 14
19
16:11
17: 3, 8
18:13
19: 5, 5
5 + A
23:17
1 Ki. 1:12, 12
29
2: 4 + A
23[d]
3:11
8:48
11:37
16:33 − A
17:21
22 + A
19: 2, 2, 3
4, 4, 10
14
21:31, 32
39, 39
42, 42
2 Ki. 1:13, 13
14
2: 2, 4, 6
4:27, 30
6:11
7: 7
9:15
10:24, 24
12: 4 + A
23: 3, 25
1 Ch. 5:21
11:19, 19
12:38, 38
15:29
17: 2
22: 7, 19
28: 9
2 Ch. 1:11
6:38
2 Ch. 7:11
9: 1
15:12, 15
31:21
34:31
35:19
Est. 7: 3
7 + S³
9:16 + S³
Job 1: 5
2: 4, 6
3:20 + A
20
6: 7 AS²[e]
11
7:11, 15
9:21
10: 1 − S[1]
1
12:10
13:14
14:22
16: 4
4 + A
19: 2
21: 8, 25
24: 7, 12
27: 2, 4
30:16
31:39
33:18, 20
22, 28
30
30 AS²[f]
31 + A
36:14
38:39
41:12
Psa. 3: 3
6: 4, 5
7: 3, 6
9:24
10: 1, 5
12: 3
15:10
16: 9, 13
18: 8
20: 3[g]
21:21, 30
22: 3
23: 4
24: 1, 13
20
25: 9
26:12
27: 3 − S
29: 4
30: 8, 10
14
32:19, 20
33: 3, 23
34: 3, 4, 7
9, 12
13, 17
25
36:15 S[1 h]
37: 8[i], 13
38:12
39:15
40: 5
41: 2, 3, 5
6, 7, 12
42: 5
43:26
48: 9, 16
19
53: 5, 6
54:19
55: 7, 14
56: 2, 5
7 S[k], 7
58: 4
61: 2, 6
62: 2, 6, 9
10
63: 2
65: 9, 16
68: 2, 11
19, 21[m]
33 + S
Psa. 69: 3
70: 9 S[n]
10, 13
23
71:13, 14
73:19, 19
76: 3
77:18, 50
83: 3
85: 2, 4, 4
13, 14
87: 4
15 AS[o]
88:49
93:17, 19[m]
21
96:10
102: 1, 2, 22
103: 1, 35
104:18
105:15
106: 5, 9
9 + AS
18, 26
108:20, 31
114: 4, 7, 8
118:20, 25
28, 81
109, 129
167, 175
119: 2, 6
120: 7
122: 4
123: 4, 5, 7
129: 5, 6
130: 2, 2
137: 3
138:14
140: 8
141: 3, 8
142: 3, 6, 8
11, 12
145: 1
Pro. 1:19
2:10
3:22
6:16, 21
26, 30
32
7:23
8:36
10: 3
11:17, 25
30
12:10, 13
14
13: 2, 3, 8
9, 19
25, 25
14:10, 25
16: 1, 17
24
18: 7, 8
19:15, 16
18, 19
20: 2
21:10, 23
22: 5, 9
20 BS[h]
23 S[1 p]
23, 25
23:14, 24
24:14
25:13, 25
26:25
27: 7, 7, 9
23
28:17
29:10, 17
24
Ecc. 2:24
4: 8
6: 2, 3, 7
9
7:29
Cant. 1: 7
3: 1, 2, 3
4
5: 6
6:11

Isa. 1:14, 16
3: 9
5:14
7: 2, 2, 4
10: 7, 18
13: 2 A^r, 7
15: 4
19:10
21: 4
24: 7
26: 9
29: 8
32: 6, 6
33:18
38:14, 17
42: 1, 25
44:19, 20
47:14
49: 7
51:23
53:10, 10
12
55: 2, 3
56:11
58: 3, 5, 10
10, 11
61:10
66: 3
Jer. 2:24, 34
3:11
4:10
19 − S^1
19, 30
31
5: 9, 29
6: 8, 16
9: 9
11:21
12: 7
13:17
14:19
15: 1, 9
17:21[a]
18:20
19: 7
20:13
21: 7, 9
22:25, 27
25:16
27:19
28: 6
31: 6
33:19
38:12, 14
25, 25
39:41
41:16
44: 9
Jer. 45: 2, 16
17, 20
46:18
47:14, 15
49:20
50: 6
51: 7, 14
30, 30
35
Lam. 1: 6 + S^1
11, 16
19
2:12, 19
3:17, 20
24 − AB
26, 50
57
5: 9
Eze. 3:19, 21
4:14
7:19
13:18 *ter*
19, 19
20 *ter*
14:20
16: 5, 27
17:17
18: 4 *qtr*
20, 27
22:25
23:17, 18
18, 22
28
24:21, 25
25: 6, 15
27:13, 31A
33: 5
5 + A
6, 9
36: 5
44:25
47: 9
Hos. 4: 8
9: 4
Amos 2:14 − A
15
Jon. 1:14 − S^1
2: 6, 8
4: 3, 8
Mic. 6: 7
7: 1, 3
Hab. 2: 4, 5
10
3: 2
Hag. 2: 9, 13
13 + A
Zec. 11: 8, 8[t]
Psa. 79: 6
80:17
Pro. 25:21[s]
Isa. 58:14
Jer. 9:15
23:15
Lam. 3:16
Eze. 2:10
16:19
Dan. 4:22, 29
5:21

[a] A αὐτός. [b] A καρδία. [c] *vide* ὀλιγοψυχέω. [d] A εὐχή. [e] *pro* ὀργή. [f] *pro* ζωή. [g] S^2 καρδία. [h] *pro* καρδία. [i] A ψόα. [k] *pro* πούς. [m] S^1 καρδία. [n] *pro* ἰσχύς. [o] *pro* προσευχή. [p] *pro* κρίσις. [q] AC καρδία. [r] *pro* χείρ. [s] A φυλακή. [t] S^1 χείρ.

ψῦχος.

Gen. 8:22
Job 37: 8
Ps. 147: 6
Zec. 14: 6[a]

[a] B ψύχη, AS^2 ψῦχος.

ψυχρός.

Proverbs 25:25

ψύχω.

Nu. 11:32[a]
2 Sa. 17:19[b]
2 Ki. 19:24[c]
Jer. 6: 7, 7
8: 2

[a] B σφάττω. [b] A κύπτω. [c] A φυλασσω.

ψωμίζω.

Nu. 11: 4, 18
Deu. 8: 3, 16
Deu. 32:13
2 Sa. 13: 5

[a] AS τρέφω.

ψωμός.

Jud. 19: 5[a]
Ruth 2:14
1 Sa. 28:22
1 Ki. 17:11
Job 22: 7
24:10
Job 31:17
Ps. 147: 9
Pro. 9:13
17: 1
23: 7
28:21

[a] A κλάσμα.

ψώρα.

Lev. 21:20
26:16
Deu. 28:27

ψωραγριάω.

Leviticus 22:22

ὦ, ὤ.

Gen. 27:20
Nu. 24:23, 23
2 Ki. 3:10, 21
6: 5, 15
20: 3 + AB
Job 19:21
Isa. 6: 5
Jer. 4:10
6: 6
22:18[a]
23: 1
41: 5 A^b
Eze. 22: 3
24: 5
30: 2, 2
34: 2
Jon. 4: 2 + ABS^1
Nah. 3: 1
Hab. 2: 9, 15
Zeph. 3: 1
Zec. 2: 6, 6
11:17

[a] AS^3 οὐαί. [b] *pro* οὐαί.

ὤα.

Exo. 28:29
36:31
Psa. 132: 2

ὧδε.

Gen. 19:12
38:22[a]
40:15
Exo. 3: 5
Nu. 32:16
Deu. 12: 8
20:15, 15
Jos. 2: 2
4 + A
8:20 − A
20 − A
18: 8
Jud. 4:20[a]
16: 2[a]
18: 3, 3
19: 9 + A
9
Jud. 20: 7 A^b
Ruth 2:14
4: 1, 2
2 Sa. 18:30 − A
1 Ki. 2:30
22: 7
2 Ki. 3:11, 11
7: 3, 4
1 Ch. 29:17
2 Ch. 18: 6
Ezra 4: 2
Ps. 131:14
Isa. 22:16 *ter*
Eze. 8: 6, 9
15 + A
17
&c., &c.

[a] A ἐνταῦθα. [b] *pro* ἐκεῖ.

ᾠδή.

Exo. 15: 1
Deu. 31:19, 19
21, 22
32: 1, 44
Jud. 5: 1 + A
12
2 Sa. 6: 5
22: 1
2 − A
1 Ki. 4:28
8:53
1 Ch. 15:16 + A
22, 27
16: 8 − S
42
2 Ch. 5:13
7: 6
23:13, 18
34:12
Ezra 2:65 S^a
Ezra 3:12
10:24 S^{3a}
Neh. 12:27, 36
Job 36:30 BS^{1b}
Psa. 4: 1 − A
9:17
17: 1
29: 1
38: 1
41: 9 AS^{2c}
44: 1 − A
47: 1 − A
64: 1
65: 1
66: 1 + S
67: 1
68:31
71: 1
75: 1 − S
82: 1
Psa. 86: 1
87: 1
90: 1
91: 1, 4
92: 1
93: 1 + A
94: 1
95: 1
100: 2 B^d
107: 1 − A
119: 1
120: 1
121: 1
122: 1
123: 1
124: 1
125: 1
126: 1
Ps. 127: 1
128: 1
129: 1
130: 1
131: 1
132: 1
133: 1
136: 3, 3, 4
143: 9
Isa. 5: 1 + S^2
25: 1 + A
26: 1 + A
9 + A
38: 9 + A
Amos 5:23
8:10
Jon. 2: 3 + A
Hab. 3: 1, 19[e]

[a] *pro* ᾄδω. [b] *pro* ἠδῶ. [c] *pro* δηλόω. [d] *pro* ὁδός. [e] S^1 ὁδός.

ὠδίν, ὠδίς.

Exo. 15:14
Deu. 2:25
1 Sa. 4:19
2 Sa. 22: 6
2 Ki. 19: 3
Job 2: 9
21:17
39: 1, 2, 3
Psa. 17: 5, 6
47: 7
114: 3
Isa. 13: 8
21: 3
Isa. 26:17
37: 3
66: 7
Jer. 6:24
8:21
13:21
22:23 A^a
27:43
Eze. 7: 7
Hos. 9:11
13:13
Mic. 4: 9
Nah. 2:10

[a] *pro* ὀδύνη.

ὠδίνω.

Psa. 7:15
Cant. 8: 5, 5
Isa. 23: 4
26:17, 18
45:10
51: 2
Isa. 54: 1
66: 7, 8, 8
Jer. 4:31
29:23
Mic. 4:10
Hab. 3:10

ᾠδός.

1 Ki. 10:12
2 Ki. 11:14
2 Ch. 9:11
Neh. 11:23 + S^3

ὠθέω.

Nu. 35:20, 22
Job 14:20
Psa. 61: 4
Ps. 117:13
Isa. 30:22
Jer. 41:10

ὠμία.

1 Ki. 6:12
7:16
16 + A
20, 25
25 − B
1 Ki. 7:25, 39
2 Ki. 11:11
11 − A
2 Ch. 23:10, 10

ὤμιον.

Job 18:13 A^a

[a] *pro* ὡραῖος.

ὦμος.

Gen. 21:14
24:15, 45
49:15
Exo. 12:34
28:12, 12
25
36:14, 26
28
Nu. 7: 9
Deu. 33:12
Jos. 4: 5
9:10[a]
Jud. 9:48
16: 3
1 Sa. 10: 9
17: 6
1 Ki. 7:20
2 Ch. 35: 3
Job 31:20, 22
36
Isa. 9: 6
10:27, 27
14:25
22:22 − B
46: 7
49:22
60: 4
66:12
Jer. 38:21
Eze. 12: 6, 7, 12
24: 4
25: 9
29:18
34:21
Mal. 2: 3

[a] A ὅρος.

ὠμός.

Exodus 12: 9

ὠμοτοκέω.

Job 21:10

ᾠόν.

Deu. 22: 6, 6
Job 39:14[a]
Isa. 10:14
Isa. 59: 5, 5
Dan. 8:25

[a] AS οὖς.

ὥρα.

Gen. 18:10, 14
29: 7
Exo. 9:18
10: 4
13:10 − B
18:22, 26
Lev. 16: 2
Nu. 9: 2
Deu. 11:14
33:13[a], 14
16
Jos. 11: 6
Ruth 2:14
1 Sa. 25: 6
2 Sa. 24:15 − A
1 Ki. 19: 2
21: 6
2 Ki. 4:16, 17
7: 1, 18[b]
2 Ki. 10: 6
Neh. 8: 3
Est. 9: 2 S^{1c}
Job 5:26
15:32, 33
24: 1
5 + A
6 − A
36:28
37: 4 + C
38:23
Isa. 52: 7
Dan. 3: 5, 6, 15
4:16, 30
5: 5
9:21
12:13[d]
Hos. 2: 9
Zec. 10: 1

[a] A ὅρος. [b] A ἡμέρα. [c] *pro* ἡμέρα. [d] A εἰμί.

ὡραιόομαι.

2 Sa. 1:26
Cant. 1:10
Cant. 7: 1, 6

ὡραῖος.

Gen. 2: 9
3: 6
26: 7
29:17
39: 6
Lev. 23:40
1 Sa. 9:20
2 Sa. 1:23
1 Ki. 1: 6
2 Ch. 36:19
Est. 2: 7 + S^3
Job 18:13[a]
Psa. 44: 3
64:13 S^{2b}
Cant. 1:16
2:14
4: 3
6: 3, 5
Isa. 28: 1 + S
63: 1
Jer. 11:16
Lam. 2: 2
Dan. 4: 9
Joel 1:19, 20

[a] A ὤμιον. [b] *pro* ὅρος.

ὡραιότης.

Psa. 44: 4
49: 2, 11
67:13
Psa. 95: 6
Isa. 44:13
Eze. 16:14

ὡραϊσμός.

Jer. 4:30
Eze. 7:11 + A

ὥριμος.

Job 5:26
Jer. 28:33

ὠρίων.

Job 38:31
Isa. 13:10

ὠρύομαι.

Jud. 14: 5
Psa. 21:14
37: 9
103:21
Jer. 2:15
Eze. 22:25[a]
Hos. 11:10
Zeph. 3: 3
Zec. 11: 3

[a] A ἐρεύγομαι.

ὠρύωμαι.

Ezekiel 19: 7

ὡσαύτως.

Exo. 7:11, 22
Lev. 24:19
Deu. 12:22
Jos. 14:11
Jud. 8: 8[a]
Isa. 10:15 A[b]
Eze. 40:16
&c., &c.

[a] A κατὰ ταῦτα. [b] pro ὡς.

ὥσπερ.

Exo. 21: 7
Lev. 4:26
2 Sa. 24: 3 − A
Job 19:11 − S[1]
22:24 A[a]
40:12 A[a]
41:18 + AS[2]
Ecc. 5:15
Isa. 17:11 A[a]
Hos. 9: 7
&c., &c.

[a] pro ὡς.

ὠτίον.

Deu. 15:17[a]
1 Sa. 9:15
20: 2, 13
22: 8, 8, 17
2 Sa. 7:27
22:45
Job 29:11 C[b]
Psa. 17:45
Isa. 50: 4
55: 3 A[b]
Amos 3:12

[a] A οὖς. [b] pro οὖς.

ὠτότμητος.

Lev. 21:18
Lev. 22:23

ὠφέλεια.

2 Sa. 18:22
Job 21:15 − C
22: 3
Psa. 29:10
Isa. 30:5 + AS[3]
Jer. 23:32
26:11
37:13

ὠφελέω.

Psa. 88:23
Pro. 10: 2
11: 4 + A
25:13, 13
Isa. 30: 5, 6, 7
44: 9
47:12
57:12
Jer. 2:11
7: 4, 8
12:13
15:10, 10
23:32
Hab. 2:18

ὠφέλημα.

Jeremiah 16:19

ὤχρα.

Deuteronomy 28:22

ERRATA AND ADDENDA.

Page 3. *Omit* ἄγξις. Psa. 31 : 9 A, *pro* ἄγχω.

,, 18. *For* ἀνεπιείκεια *read* ἀνεπιεικής.

,, 42 βελόστασις. *For* Eze. 4 : 2 17,17 *read* Eze. 4 : 2 17 : 17

,, 93 ἐπικαλέω. *To* Jos. 21 : 9 *add* A ἐπικληρόω (not recorded by Tischendorf).

,, 96 ἐπιφυλλίζω. *To* Lam. 2 : 20 *add* A ἐπιφαυλίζω.

,, 103. *For* εὐοδιάζω *read* εὐωδιάζω.

,, 118 ἰάομαι. *Remove* Job 13 : 4, *and enter the same under* ἰατής.

,, 123 καθίζω. *Remove* Exo. 12 : 22, *and enter the same under* καθιγω.

,, 129 κατάκαρπος. *Remove* Zec. 2 : 4, *and enter the same under* κατακάρπως.

,, 132 κατατείνω. *To* Lev. 25 : 53 *add* A κατατενίζω.

,, 141 κρεμάω, -μάννυμι. *Add* -μάζω.

,, 145 κύπτω. *Remove* Job 22 : 29, *and enter the same under* κύφω.

,, 162 μηρυκάομαι. *To* Deu. 14 : 8 *add* B μαρυκάομαι.

,, 184 παραβιάζομαι. *To* Amos 6 : 10 *add* A παραβιώτης.

,, 234. *Enter* σῦς Psa. 79 : 14, A ὗς.

APPENDIX.

WORDS NOT INCLUDED IN THE FOREGOING.

UNCIAL CODICES.

(NUMBERED AS BY HOLMES AND PARSONS.)

I. Cottonianus.
II. Vaticanus.
III. Alexandrinus.
IV. Sarravianus.
V. Colbertinus.
VI. Caesareus.

VII. Ambrosianus.
VIII. Dublinensis.
X. Coislinianus.
XI. Basiliano-Vaticanus.
XII. Marchalianus.
m *margin* of any of the above.

MS, MSS. One or more CURSIVE Manuscripts (in text or margin).
LXX (in Daniel only). Readings of the Septuagint (Codex Chisianus).

ORIGEN'S HEXAPLA.

Aq, A Aquila.
Sy, S Symmachus.
Th, T Theodotion.

5th Fifth Translation, E′
6th Sixth Translation, S′
7th Seventh Translation, Z′

Su ὁ Σύρος.
Sa τὸ Σαμαρειτικόν.
Heb ὁ Ἑβραῖος.
δ γ Διπλῆ γραφή.

rel *(reliqui)* 'the rest.' οἱ λοιποί.
inc *(incertum)* 'uncertain.' Ἄλλος, sine nom. &c.

For further explanation of the above, see the Montfaucon or Oxford Edition of the Hexapla.

The Chapters and Verses have been conformed to those of Tischendorf's Edition of the LXX.

In this Appendix no attempt has been made to give *all* the references where a word occurs.

In some places two and even three variations are given by different authorities for the same translator.

APPENDIX.

ἀβασάνιστος.
Job 21:13 Sy

ἀβέβαιος.
Psa. 77: 8 Sy

ἀβεβαιότης.
Job 4:18 Sy

ἁβρός.
1 Sa. 15:32 Sy

ἀγαθότης.
Gen. 20: 5 Aq

ἀγαθώτατος.
Gen. 47: 6 *Heb*

ἀγανακτέω.
Jer. 23:11 (Aq)

ἀγαυριάω.
Psa. 27: 7 Aq
Isa. 13: 3 Aq
66:12 Aq

ἄγγιστρον.
1 Ki. 7:26(40) A S

ἀγγρίζειν.
Pro. 15:18 Sy

ἁγίως.
Psa. 133: 2 Sy

ἄγκυρα.
Jer. 52:18 Sy

ἀγλάϊσμα.
Psa. 47: 3 Sy
88:18 Sy
Pro. 19:11 Sy

ἀγλαϊσμός.
Job 39:13 Sy
Psa. 44: 8 Sy

ἀγμός.
Isa. 19:15 Th

ἀγνοηματίζω.
Psa. 118:10 Aq

ἀγνωμονέω.
1 Sa. 13:13 Aq

ἀγρίζω.
Pro. 15:18 Sy

ἀγριοβάλανος.
Isa. 44:14 Aq Th

ἀγριότης.
Job 39: 4 Sy

ἀγροτέκτων.
Lev. 11:19 Xm

ἀγύμναστος.
1 Sa. 17:39 *inc*

ἀγχόνη.
Job 7:15 Aq

ἀγωνιάω.
1 Sa. 4:13 MSS
Dan. 1:10 LXX

ἀδαμά.
Gen. 2: 7 Sy Th
3:17 Th
Lev. 20:25 Xm

ἀδάμαστος.
Jer. 38:18 Sy

ἀδεής.
Pro. 19:25 Sy

ἄδεια.
Isa. 61: 1 Aq
Jer. 11: 8 Aq

ἀδηλοποιέω.
Job 9: 5 Sy

ἀδημονέω.
Job 18:20 Aq
Psa. 60: 3 Sy
115: 2 Sy
Ecc. 7:17(16) Sy

ἀδημονία.
Eze. 7:27 Sy
12:19 Sy
23:33 Sy

ἀδιαλείπτως.
Job 16: 8 Sy
Psa. 73:23 Sy

ἀδιανόητος.
Jer. 5:21 Sy

ἀδιάπνευστος.
Job 32:19 Sy

ἀδικασία.
Psa. 54:10 Sy

ἄελλα.
Hab. 2:15 *inc*

ἀζυμίτης.
Lev. 7: 3(13) Xm

ἀηδής.
Gen. 48:17 Sy
1 Sa. 29: 7 Sy

ἀήττητος.
Psa. 88: 8, 14 Sy
18 Sy

ἀθανασία.
Psa. 47:15 Aq

ἀθεΐα.
Psa. 18:14 (Aq)
Hos. 4:15 Sy

ἀθέμιτος.
Hos. 6: 9 5th

ἀθεότης.
Psa. 18:14 (Aq)

ἄθικτος.
Lev. 8: 9 Sy
21:12 Sy

ἀθροισμός.
Psa. 29: 6 Aq
30:14 Sy
Isa. 24:22 Sy

ἀθρόος.
Job 20: 5 Aq
Psa. 31:20 Aq

ἀθρόως.
Psa. 6:11 Aq

ἄθυμος.
Job 30:28 Sy

ἀθυμότης.
Psa. 25: 6 Aq

αἴγαγρος.
Deu. 14: 5 Xm

αἰγίων.
Jud. 6:21 Sy

αἰδέσιμος.
Isa. 9:14 Sy

αἰθήρ.
Job 36:28 Sy
37:17, 20 Sy
Psa. 35: 6 Sy
76:18 Sy
Pro. 8:28 Sy

ἄϊν.
Exo. 29:40 MSS

αἰνίσσομαι.
Eze. 17: 2 Sy

αἰνοποιέω.
Deu. 32:43 Aq
Psa. 31:11 Aq
64: 9 Aq
80: 2 Aq

αἱρετισμός.
2 Ki. 12:16 MSS

αἰφνίδιος.
Job 7:18 Aq Sy
Psa. 63: 8 Sy
Eze. 26:16 Sy

αἰφνιδίως.
Psa. 54:16 Sy

αἰχμή.
Jud. 3:22 Sy
1 Sa. 17: 7 Sy

αἰωνίως.
Gen. 6: 3 Sy
Psa. 60: 7 Sy
88:38 Sy
148: 6 Sy
Amos 1:11 Sy

ἀκαθαίρετος.
Psa. 150: 1 Sy

ἀκαθαρτίζομαι.
Lev. 14:36 MSS

ἀκαμπής.
Job 27:13 Sy Th

ἄκανος.
Job 31:40 Sy
Cant. 2: 2 Aq
Isa. 34:13 MSS

ἄκαπνος.
Isa. 41:19 Sy

ἀκαταμάχητος.
Cant. 8: 6 Sy
Eze. 28: 7 Sy

ἀκαταστατέω.
Gen. 4:12 *Heb*
Hos. 8: 6 Sy

ἀκέραιος.
Pro. 18: 8 (Sy)

ἀκλινής.
Job 41:14(15) Sy

ἀκμάζω.
Eze. 16: 7 *Heb*
23: 3, 21 Sy
Zec. 11: 8 Sy

ἀκμή.
Gen. 18:12 Sy

ἀκμονευτής.
Isa. 41: 7 Sy

ἀκόλουθος.
Psa. 67:26 Sy

ἄκονις.
Psa. 126: 4 6th

ἀκόντιον.
1 Sa. 20:36 Sy

ἀκοντισμός.
Pro. 25:18 Th

ἀκρέμων.
Isa. 11: 1 Aq
60:21 Aq

ἀκριβάζω.
Gen. 49:10 Aq
2 Sa. 1:19 Aq
2 Ch. 4:18 MSS
Psa. 59: 9 Th
Pro. 8:27 Aq Th

ἀκρίβασμα.
Lev. 19:30 Xm
Deu. 6:17 Aq
Psa. 18: 9 Aq
118:23 5th

ἀκριβαστής.
Deu. 16:18 Aq
Jud. 5:14 Aq
Psa. 59: 9 Aq
Isa. 33:22 Aq Th

ἀκριβολογία.
Jud. 5:16 Aq

ἀκριβόω.
Lev. 18: 3 MSS
Isa. 30: 8 Aq
49:16 Aq

ἀκριτί (—τεί).
Jer. 17:11 Aq

ἀκρίτως.
Gen. 18:25 Sy
Eze. 22:29 Sy
Hab. 2:15 Sy

ἀκροβυστίζω.
Lev. 19:23 A S T

ἀκρόβυστος.
Exo. 6:12 Aq
Jos. 5: 7 VII
Isa. 52: 1 Aq

ἀκρώμιον.
Job 31:22 Sy

ἀκτή.
Gen. 2:15 Sy
14: 3, 8 Th

ἀκτίν.
Eze. 1:14 Sy

ἀκυρόω.
Nu. 30: 9, 13 Aq
Job 5:12 Aq
33:14 Sy

ἀκωλύτως.
Job 34:31 Sy

ἀλαζονεία.
Job 9:13 Sy
Isa. 37:29 Sy
51: 9 Sy
Jer. 31:29 XIIm

ἀλαζοσύνη.
Jer. 29:17 Aq

ἀλαίω.
Lam. 2:22 XIIm

ἀλαλαί.
Mic. 7: 1 Aq Sy

ἀλαλέω, —λόω.
Psa. 30:19 Aq
38: 3 Aq

ἀλεκτρυών.
Pro. 24:66 Aq Th

ἀλεωτός, ἀλιω—
Jud. 16: 7 Aq

ἀλικμητός.
Isa. 30:24 A S T

ἀλκή.
Dan. 11: 4 LXX

ἀλλαγή
Psa. 54:20 Aq

ἀλλόκοτος.
1 Sa. 26:19 Sy
Jer. 7: 6 Sy

ἀλλομορφόω.
Eze. 31:15 Sy

ἀλμυρόω.
Gen. 27: 1 Aq

ἀλόγιστος.
Nu. 6:12 MSS

ἀλόγως.
Amos 6:13 Sy

ἀλοιφάω, —όω.
Gen. 6:14 Aq

ἄλση.
Gen. 2:15 Sy

ἄλσωμα, —να.
2 Ki. 17:16 Aq
23: 4, 7 Aq

ἄλυσις.
Exo. 28:14 Aq Sy
22 Aq Sy
25 Th

ἀλύτρωτος.
Lev. 25:23 Sy

ἀμαθής.
Psa. 48:11 Sy

ἀμαθία.
Pro. 14:24 Sy
Ecc. 2:13 Sy

ἀμαύρωσις.
Amos 5:26 Th

ἀμείβω.
Gen. 50:17 Aq
Pro. 11:17 Aq Th
Eze. 27: 9 Sy

ἀμείνων.
Ecc. 4: 9 Sy

ἀμέλεια.
Psa. 89: 8 Sy
Eze. 39:26 (Sy)

ἀμεριμνέω.
Psa. 35: 8 Sy
61: 9 Aq Sy
90: 4 Sy

ἀμεριμνία.
Psa. 59:10 Sy
107:10 Sy
Isa. 32:18 MSS

ἀμέριμνος.
Psa. 111: 7 Sy

ἀμερίμνως.
Jud. 18: 7 Sy
Jer. 39:37 Sy

ἀμετάθετος.
Isa. 33:20 Sy Th

ἀμεταστρέπτως
Hos. 7: 8 5th

ἀμέτρως.
Pro. 16:26 Th

ἀμιλλάομαι.
Jer. 12: 5 Sy
22:15 Sy

ἀμοιβή.
1 Sa. 24, 20 Sy
Psa. 27: 4 Aq
Pro. 12:14 Aq Sy
Isa. 1:23 Sy

ἀμόρφωτος.
Psa. 138:16 Sy

ἀμυγδάλινος.
Gen. 30:37 Sy
Jer. 1:11 Th

ἀμύλιον.
Exo. 16:31 Aq

ἄμυλος.
Exo. 16:31 Sy

ἀμυρίτης.
2 Sa. 6:19 Aq Sy

ἀμύσσω.
Zec. 12: 3 Th

ἀμφήκης.
2 Sa. 20: 8 MSS
Isa. 41:15 Th

ἀμφιβληστρεύω.
Isa. 51:20 Aq

ἀμφιβόλως.
1 Ki. 18:21 Sy

ἀμφορεύς.
1 Sa. 1:24 Aq
10: 3 Aq
25:18 Aq

ἀμωμότης.
Psa. 25: 1 Sy
11 (Th)

ἀναβλύζω.
Psa. 77: 2 Sy
Pro. 1:23 Aq Th
18: 4 Aq Sy

ἀναβλύσσω.
Pro. 18: 4 Aq Sy

ἀναβλύω.
Pro. 15: 2 Aq Sy

ἀναβόλαιον.
Isa. 3:22 Sy

ἀναβολέομαι.
Isa. 59:17 Aq

ἀναγκασμός.
Lev. 6: 2 Xm

ἀναγράφω.
Psa. 21:31 Sy

ἀναδέχομαι.
Psa. 55: 13 Sy
118:122 Sy

ἀναδέω.
Eze. 23:15 Th

ἀνάδοσις.
Eze. 47:12 Mss

ἀναζάω.
Gen. 45:27 VIIm

ἀναζωόω.
Psa. 29: 4 Sy
118:149 Sy
Hos. 6: 2 Aq
Hab. 3: 2 Sy

ἀναθυμίασις.
Gen. 19:28 *Heb*
Cant. 3: 6 Sy

ἀναιδεύομαι.
Pro. 7:13 Th

ἀναίδην, ἀνέ-
Job 15: 4 Sy

ἀναίσθητος.
Job 35:16 Sy
Pro. 17:21 Th

ἀναιτίως.
Job 9:17 Sy
34: 6 Sy
Psa. 34: 7 Aq Sy

ἀνακεφαλαιόω.
Psa. 71:20 Th 5th

ἀνακλάω.
Lev. 1:15 *Sa* Xm
5: 8 Xm

ἀνακλίνω.
Pro. 2: 2 Aq

ἀνακόπτω.
Jud. 5:23 Th

ἀνακρεμάζω.
2 Sa. 18: 9 Mss

ἀνακροτέω.
Pro. 23:35 Th

ἀνακτάομαι.
1 Sa. 30:12 Sy
Psa. 22: 3 Sy
103:11 Sy
146: 6 Sy
Lam. 1:16 Sy

ἀνακτίζω.
Psa. 50:12 Aq

ἀνάκτορον.
Psa. 25: 8 Sy

ἀναλειψία.
Psa. 108:24 Sy

ἀναλεκτήριον.
1 Sa. 17:40 Aq

ἀναληπτήρ.
2 Ki. 25:14 Sy
Jer. 52:18 Aq Th

ἀναλογία.
Lev. 27:18 Xm

ἀναλογίζομαι
Job 21: 5 Sy
Isa. 38:15 Sy

ἀνάλογος.
Ecc. 7:15(14) Sy

ἄναλος.
Eze. 13:10,11,15 Aq
22:28 Aq

ἀναλύω.
Jos. 22: 8 Mss

ἀναμαρτησία.
Psa. 72:13 Sy

ἀναμονή.
Psa. 38: 8 Sy
70: 6 Sy

ἀνανεάζω.
Job 20:20 Sy

ἀνανεόω.
Psa. 29: 2 Aq

ἀνανέωσις.
Job 20:20 Sy

ἀναντίρρητος.
Job 11: 2 Sy
33:13 Sy

ἀναξαίνω.
Pro. 26:21 Aq Th

ἀναξυρίς.
Dan. 3:21 Sy

ἀναπέμπω.
Psa. 89: 3 (Sy)

ἀναπεπταμένος
Neh. 4:13 Mss

ἀναπετάω.
Eze. 13:20 Sy

ἀναπήγνυμι.
Nu. 25: 4 Aq
2 Sa. 21: 6,9 Aq

ἀναπίθω.
Amos 7:10 Sy

ἀναπίνω.
Isa. 19: 5 Aq

ἀναπλόω.
Isa. 23:11 Sy

ἀναπνεύμασις.
Gen. 19:28 *Heb*

ἀνάπνευσις.
Exo. 8:15 Aq

ἀναπνοή.
Gen. 2: 7 A S T
Job 6: 4 Sy
Ps. 137: 7 Sy

ἀναπολέω.
Psa. 38: 4 Sy
41: 5 Sy
76:12 Sy

ἀναπόστρεπτος
Job 9:13 Sy

ἀναρρέω.
Isa. 53: 2 Aq

ἀνάρρηξις.
Eze. 30:16 Sy

ἀναρροφέω.
Job 5: 5 Sy

ἀναρρύω.
Psa. 33: 5 Aq

ἀνάρτυτος.
Job 6: 6 Sy
Eze. 13:10,11,15 Sy
22:28 Sy

ἀνασαλεύω.
Mic. 2: 4 (Th)

ἀνασείω.
Job 2: 3 Aq
Isa. 36:18 Aq Sy

ἀνασκαφαί (-φε)
Gen. 49: 5 Aq

ἀνασκολοπίζω.
Isa. 36: 2 Aq Sy
40: 3 Aq

ἀνάστατος.
Gen. 4:12 Sy
16 Sy
Isa. 16: 3 Sy
Lam. 1: 8 Sy

ἀναστατόω.
Psa. 10: 1 Aq
58:12 Sy
Isa. 22: 3 Sy
37:13 Sy
Hab. 3:16 Mss

ἀνάστεμα.
1 Ki. 6:14(10) Aq
Isa. 37:24 Aq

ἀνασωσμός.
Gen. 45: 7 Aq

ἀνατυράσσω.
Psa. 38: 3 Aq Sy
Amos 7:10 Sy

ἀνατλάω.
Job 19:26 Mss

ἀνατμητικός.
Psa. 54:22 Sy

ἀνατολικός.
Gen. 15:19 Sy
Job 1: 3 Sy
Eze. 40:10 Sy

ἀναύξητος.
Jer. 22:30 Aq

ἀναφθέγγομαι.
Job 39:35 Sy

ἀνάφθησις.
Isa. 1:31 Aq Sy

ἀναφυή.
Zec. 6:12 Aq

ἀναφύρω.
Lev. 2: 4 A S T

ἀνάφυσις.
Job 14:14 Sy
38:27 Sy

ἀναχώρησις.
Psa. 54: 8 Sy

ἀνδραγάθημα.
Ecc. 5:10 Sy

ἀνδριάς.
Dan. 2:31,31 Sy

ἀνδρίς.
Gen. 2:23 Sy

ἀνδρύνομαι.
Exo. 2:10 X
Jud. 11: 2 Mss
Ruth 1:13 Mss

ἀνεγείρω.
Psa. 40:11 Sy
Isa. 49: 8 Sy
58:12 Sy
61: 4 Sy

ἀνέδην.
Job 15: 4 Sy

ἀνελκύω.
Jer. 45:13 Sy

ἀνενδεής.
1 Sa. 2: 5 Sy

ἀνέντροπος.
Eze. 7:24 Sy

ἀνεξερεύνητος.
Pro. 25: 3 Sy
Jer. 17: 9 (Sy)

ἀνεξέταστος.
Pro. 25: 3 Aq

ἀνεπίβατος.
Jer. 9:12 Sy
Mal. 1: 3 Sy Th

ἀνεπίγραφος.
Psa. 70: 1 Mss

ἀνεπιστημόνως
Job 21:34 Sy

ἀνεπιστήμων.
Psa. 72:22 Sy

ἀνερευνάω.
Psa. 76: 7 Sy

ἀνευλαβής.
Isa. 57:11 Aq

ἀνευόδωτος.
Jer. 22:30 Aq Sy

ἀνευφημέω.
Psa. 62: 8 Sy

ἀνηλειψία.
Psa. 108:24 Sy

ἀνθηρός.
Gen. 2: 8 Sy

ἄνθιμος.
Eze. 16:10,13 Aq

ἀνθρακία.
Psa. 119: 4 Aq

ἀνθρωπότης.
Psa. 48: 3 Sy

ἀνθυφαίρεσις.
1 Sa. 15:23 (Aq)

ἀνιάομαι.
Psa. 68:21 Sy

ἀνίασις.
Eze. 23:33 Sy

ἄνικμος.
Job 8:10 Aq

ἀνιμάω.
Psa. 29: 2 Sy

ἀνόδευτος.
Jer. 18:15 Aq

ἀνοδία.
Job 12:24 Sy

ἀνοησία.
Psa. 48:14 Aq
Pro. 11:14 Th

ἀνοητίζω.
Jer. 10: 8 Aq

ἀνοήτως.
Job 42: 3 Sy

ἀνομβρέω.
Pro. 18: 4 Th 5th

ἀνομοιογενής.
Lev. 19:19 Mss
Deu. 22: 9 Sy

ἀνομοιόφυλος.
Lev. 19:19 Sy

ἄνταρσις.
2 Ki. 11:14,14 Sy
Isa. 8:12 Sy

ἀντίβλησις.
Eze. 2:10 Aq

ἀντιδάκτυλος.
Exo. 29:20 Aq

ἀντιδιάκειμαι.
Deu. 22:11 Aq

ἀντιδικάζω.
Jud. 6:31 Mss

ἀντιδικασία.
Pro. 20: 3 Aq

ἀντιδικία.
Pro. 6:14 (Aq)
19:13 Aq
28:25 Aq

ἀντικαταλλάσσω
Job 28:17 Sy
Eze. 5: 6 Sy

ἀντιλαλέω.
Psa. 138:20 Sy

ἀντιπαρατίθημι
Psa. 88: 7 Sy

ἀντιπροσώπως.
Exo. 26: 5 *Sa*

ἀντισταθμάομαι.
Job 28:19 Sy

ἀντιστρέφω.
Gen. 48:14 (Sy)
Psa. 34:12 Sy

ἀντιφθέγγομαι
Job 39:32 Sy

ἀντιφωνέω.
Gen. 43: 8(9) VIIm

ἀντοφθαλμέω.
Hab. 3:10 Mss

ἀνυδρία.
Isa. 32: 2 Sy

ἀνύπαρκτος.
Job 24:17 Sy
Psa. 93: 5 Sy
Pro. 19: 7 Sy

ἀνυπαρξία.
Job 18:11,14 Aq
27:20 Aq Sy

ἀνυπερθεσία.
Psa. 7: 7 Aq
Hos. 5:10 Aq
Amos 1:11 Aq

ἀνυπερθετέω.
Psa. 77:21,59 Aq
88:39 Aq

ἀνυπότακτος.
1 Sa. 2:12 Sy
10:27 (Sy)

ἀνώνυμος.
Job 30: 8 Ms

ἀνωφέλεια.
Jer. 4:14 Aq

ἀξινάριον.
1 Sa. 13:20 Sy

ἀξιοπιστία.
Eze. 16:31 Sy

ἀξιοπρέπεια.
Lam. 1: 6 (Sy)

ἀξιοπρεπής.
Psa. 89:16 Sy

ἀόχλητος.
Job 3:18 Sy

ἀπαράκλητος.
Dan. 3:22 Sy

ἀπαραλλάκτως
Ezra 6: 9 Mss

ἀπαριθμέω.
Exo. 21: 1 Mss

ἀπαρτάω.
Lev. 26:30 Xm

ἀπάρτισμα.
1 Ki. 7:46(9) Sy

ἀπειρημένον.
Lev. 18:23 Aq

ἀπειρία.
Psa. 68: 6 Sy

ἀπελέγχω.
Psa. 118:118 Sy

ἀπεμέω.
Jon. 2:11 Sy

ἀπέννοια.
Psa. 138:20 Aq

ἀπερέω.
Lev. 20:12 (Aq)

ἀπερίτρεπτος.
Psa. 95:10 Sy
124: 1 Sy

ἀπεσχηκώς.
Isa. 42:19 Th

ἀπεψία.
Nu. 11:20 Sy

ἀπλάνητος.
Job 12:20 Sy

ἀπλάστως.
2 Sa. 15:11 MSS

ἀπληστεύομαι.
Jer. 28:34 Aq

ἀπληστία.
Pro. 15:16 (Th)

ἀποβδελύσσω.
Psa. 21:25 MS

ἀποβλέπτης.
1 Ki. 7:41(4) Aq

ἀπόβλημα.
Nu. 35: 3 Th

ἀπόβλητος.
Lev. 7: 8(18) Aq
Deu. 7:26 X
Jer. 22:28 (Sy)
Hos. 8: 5 5th
9: 3 Sy

ἀποβλύζω.
Psa. 58: 8 Sy

ἀπόβρεξις.
Nu. 6: 3 Aq Sy

ἀπογραφή.
2 Ch. 35: 4 MSS
Psa. 86: 6 5th
Dan. 10:21 LXX

ἀποδεκτός.
Cant. 1:13 Aq Sy

ἀποδέχομαι.
Psa. 24: 3 Sy

ἀποδιατηρέω.
Psa. 60: 8 Aq

ἀποδύω.
Est. 6:11 MSS

ἀπόζω.
Exo. 7:21 MSS

ἀποθαυμάζω.
Dan. 4:12 LXX

ἀπόθετος.
Deu. 33:19 Aq
Psa. 16:14 Sy
30:20 Aq Sy

ἀποθλιμμός.
Exo. 3: 9 Aq

ἀποκαλέω.
Gen. 4: 4 Aq

ἀποκαραδοκέω.
Psa. 36: 7 Aq

ἀπόκαυμα.
Psa. 101: 4 Sy

ἀποκηλέομαι.
Gen. 4: 4 Aq

ἀποκλάω.
2 Ki. 6: 6 5th
Psa. 140: 7 Aq

ἀποκλεισμός.
Psa. 141: 8 Aq

ἀποκληρόω.
Deu. 4:19 MS

ἀπόκομμα.
Eze. 20: 7 Aq

ἀποκοπή.
Deu. 24: 3 Aq

ἀποκρυβή.
Isa. 16: 4 Aq

ἀποκρύφως.
Hab. 3:14 Aq

ἀπόλαυσις.
Psa. 118:143 Aq

ἀπόλημμα.
Exo. 28:29(33) Aq

ἀπολήγω.
Dan. 5:27 LXX

ἀπολιμπάνω.
Job 20:21 Sy

ἀπόλυσις.
Psa. 67: 7 Sy
Isa. 61: 1 Sy

ἀπολύτρωσις.
Dan. 4:29 LXX

ἀπομαίνομαι.
Dan. 12: 4 LXX

ἀπομένω.
Jer. 47: 4 Sy

ἀπομερίζω.
Dan. 11:39 LXX

ἀπομηκυνίζω.
Lev. 26:11 Xm

ἀπομιτρόω.
Lev. 21:10 MSS

ἀπομοχθόω.
Isa. 7:13 Aq

ἀποναρκάω.
1 Sa. 30:10, 21 Th
Pro. 26:15 Sy

ἀπονεύω.
Psa. 138:19 Sy
Cant. 5: 6 Sy

ἀπονοέομαι.
Jud. 9: 4 Sy

ἀποξένωσις.
Obad. 12 (Aq)

ἀποπατέω.
1 Sa. 24: 4 Sy

ἀποπαύω.
Psa. 88:45 Sy

ἀποπετάζω.
Exo. 5: 4 Aq
32:25 Aq
Deu. 32:42 Aq

ἀπόπλεγμα.
Exo. 28:29(33) Aq

ἀπόρησις.
Job 11: 8 Sy

ἄπορος.
1 Sa. 18:23 Aq Sy
Pro. 28: 3 Aq Th
Ecc. 8:14, 14 Sy

ἀπόρρευσις.
Deu. 22:21 Aq
1 Sa. 25:25 Aq

ἀπορρήσσω.
Isa. 59: 5 Sy

ἀπόρρητος.
Job 11: 6 Aq Sy
Psa. 24:14 Aq
63: 3 Aq
Eze. 2: 6 Sy

ἀπόρροια.
1 Sa. 14:27 Sy
Eze. 1:14 Aq

ἀπορύσσω.
Psa. 70:24 Sy

ἀποσήρωτον.
1 Ch. 23:29 MSS

ἀποσιγάω.
Psa. 31: 3 Sy

ἀποσκεδάννυμι.
Pro. 29:18 Aq

ἀποσκολοπίζω.
Psa. 67: 5 Aq
118:118 Aq
Isa. 57: 14 Aq

ἀποσμήχω.
Pro. 20:30 Sy

ἀποστεγάζω.
Jer. 29:11(10) Sy

ἀπόστροφος.
Psa. 20:13 Sy

ἀποστρώννυμι.
Gen. 21:32 X

ἀποσύρω.
Isa. 30:14 MSS

ἀποτειχίζω.
Psa. 53: 7 Sy
58:11 Sy
91:12 Sy Th
Eze. 4: 3 Sy

ἀποτείχισμα.
Ecc. 9:14 Sy
Eze. 17:17 Sy
21:22 Sy
26: 8 Sy

ἀπότμημα.
Psa. 135:13 Aq

ἀποτομία.
Jer. 28:35 Sy
Nah. 3: 1 Sy

ἀποτρέπω.
Exo. 5: 4 Sy

ἀποτυμπανίζω.
Dan. 7:11 LXX

ἀπόφασις.
Ecc. 8:11 Sy

ἀποφορά.
Ezra 7:24 MSS

ἀποχυτήρ.
Jer. 52:19 MSS

ἀποψύχω.
Eze. 17: 9 Sy

ἀπραγία.
Pro. 12:11 Sy
28:19 (Sy)

ἄπραγος.
Jud. 9: 4 Sy

ἄπρακτος.
Jud. 5: 6 MSS

ἀπροαίρετος.
Psa. 77: 8 Sy

ἀπροσδόκητος.
Hab. 2:15 5th

ἄπωθεν.
Eze. 27:26 Sy

ἀπωκισμός.
2 Ki. 24:15 MSS

ἀπώτερος.
Dan. 9: 7 LXX

ἀραιός.
Psa. 81: 3 Aq
Pro. 10:15 Aq Th

ἀραιόω.
2 Sa. 3: 1 Aq
Isa. 38:14 Aq

ἀρατρόπους.
Jud. 3:31 Th

ἀρδεία.
Jud. 1:15 Sy

ἄρδω.
Job 21:24 Sy

ἀρεταλογία.
Psa. 29: 6 Sy

ἀρίθμησις.
Nu. 7: 2 Xm

ἀριστεία.
Jud. 4: 9 Sy

ἀριστερεύω.
1 Ch. 12: 2 MSS

ἀρκετός.
Deu. 25: 2 Aq

ἁρματηλάτης.
1 Sa. 8:11 XI

ἄρμενον.
Psa. 73: 5 Sy

ἄρνησις.
Job 16: 8 Aq

ἄρρητος.
Lev. 18:23 Sy

ἄρρυπος.
Job 25: 4 Sy

ἀρρώστημα.
Isa. 1: 5 Aq
Jer. 10:19 Aq Sy

ἄρτυσις.
Job 41:22 Sy

ἀρτύω.
Cant. 8: 2 Sy

ἀρύω.
Pro. 8:35 Sy

ἀρχῆθενδε.
Eze. 8:16 Aq

ἀρχιποίμην.
2 Ki. 3: 4 Sy

ἀρχοντικός.
Ecc. 10: 4 Sy
Isa. 32: 8 Sy

ἀρωματίζω.
Gen. 50:2,2,3,26 Aq

ἀσελγῶς.
Hos. 7:14 Aq Sy
Jer. 2:23 Aq Sy

ἄσθμα.
Eze. 8: 17 Sy

ἀσκέω.
Jud. 3: 1 Sy

ἄσκωμα.
Jos. 3:13, 16 Sy

ἀσπιδωτός.
1 Sa. 17: 5 Sy Th

ἄσπιλος.
Job 15:15 Sy

ἀσπλαγχνέω.
Job 41:1(2) Aq Th

ἄσπλαγχνος.
Deu. 32:33 Aq
Pro. 17:11 Sy
Eze. 31:12 Sy

ἀστραγάλειος.
Gen. 37: 3 Aq

ἀστραγαλωτός.
2 Sa. 13:18, 19 MSS

ἀσύμφωνος.
Psa. 54:10 Sy

ἀσυνετίζομαι.
Jer. 10: 8 Aq

ἀσχημόνησις.
Psa. 43:16 Sy
68: 8 Sy

ἀσχολέομαι.
Ecc. 1:13 Sy

ἀσχολία.
Ecc. 1:13 Sy
2:26 Sy
4: 8 Sy

ἀσωτεύομαι.
Isa. 28: 7 Th

ἄτακτος.
Deu. 32:10 Aq
Eze. 12:20 Sy

ἀτάκτως.
2 Ki. 9:20 Sy

ἀτειχίστως.
Zec. 2: 4 Sy

ἀτέκνωσις.
Psa. 34:12 Aq

ἀτελεσφόρητος.
Job 31:40 Sy

ἀτελής.
Isa. 5: 2 Sy

ἀτενίζω.
Job 7: 8 δ γ

ἄτη.
Exo. 10: 7 Sa
Zeph. 1:15 Aq

ἀτονέω.
1 Sa. 30:10, 21 Sy
Psa. 25: 1 Aq
30:11 Sy
78: 8 Sy
114: 6 Sy

ἄτονος.
Job 5:16 Aq
Psa. 81: 3 Sy

ἀτονόω.
Psa. 68:24 Aq

ἀτοπία.
Lev. 16:21 Xm

ἄτρεπτος.
Job 15:15 Sy

ἀττάκης.
Lev. 11:22 Xm

αὐθαίρετος.
Exo. 35: 5, 22 Sy

αὐθωρί.
Dan. 3:15 LXX

αὐλισμός.
Isa. 10:29 Sy
Jer. 9: 2 Sy

αὐλιστήριον.
Isa. 10:29 Aq

αὐξητικός.
Isa. 32:12 Aq

αὔξω.
Nu. 6: 5 Sy

αὖος.
Psa. 101: 4 Sy

αὐστηρός.
Deu. 32:14 Aq

αὐταρεσκία.
Ecc. 6: 9 Sy

αὐτεξούσιος.
Jer. 41:16 Sy

αὐτομάτως.
Isa. 37:30 A S T

αὐτοφυής.
Isa. 37.30 A S T

αὐτόφωρος.
Job 34:11 Sy

αὔχησις.
Pro. 4: 9 Aq
19:11 Aq
Isa. 52: 1 Aq

αὐχμόομαι.
Psa. 6: 8 Aq
30:10, 11 Aq

ἀφαγνισμός.
Nu. 8: 7 MSS

ἀφάνεια.
Eze. 23:33 Th

ἀφάρπαξ.
Lev. 11:19 Xm

ἀφέλκω.
Job 5: 5 Aq

ἀφελῶς.
1 Ki. 22:34 MSS

ἀφήμενος.
Isa. 53: 4 Aq

ἀφθαρσία.
Psa. 74: 1 Sy

ἀφθογγος.
Job 21: 5 Sy

ἀφθορία.
Hag. 2:17 III

ἀφόδευμα.
Isa. 36:12 Sy

ἀφοδευτήριον.
2 Ki. 10:27 (Sy)

ἀφοπλίζω.
Hos. 11: 8 Th

ἀφοσιόω.
Lev. 26:43 Xm

ἀφρονίζω.
2 Sa. 15:31 Aq

ἀφυπνόω.
Jud. 5:27 X, XI

ἀχλύς.
Job 3: 5 Sy
Eze. 12: 7 Aq

ἄχνη.
Dan. 2:35 (Aq)

ἀχορτασία.
Deu. 28:20 Sy

ἀχόρταστος.
Psa. 58:16 Sy

ἄχραντος.
Exo. 17:16 VIIm
Lam. 4: 7 Sy

ἀχώριστος.
Psa. 54:12 Sy

ἀψευδής.
Job 36: 4 Sy

ἀψίνθιον.
Pro. 5: 4 Aq
Jer. 9:15 Aq
23:15 Aq

βαϊνός.
Gen. 40:16 Sy

βάϊον.
Cant. 7: 8 Sy

βαλαύστιον.
Cant. 4: 3 (Sy)

βαναυσία.
Job 28: 8 Aq
41:25 Aq Th

βαρέω.
Gen. 18:20 Sy
Isa. 1: 4 Sy

βαρυκαρδιος.
κάρδιος.
Pro. 14:14 Sy

βαρύτης.
Exo. 14:25 VIIm

βασανιστήριον
Jer. 20: 2 Sy

βασταγμός.
Psa. 80: 7 Sy

βδέλλιον.
Gen. 2:12 *rel*
Nu. 11: 7 *rel*

βδελυρία.
Psa. 32: 2 Sy

βέβαιος.
Gen. 41:32 Sy
Exo. 6: 6 VII[a]
1 Sa. 23:23 Sy
Hos. 6: 3 5th

βεβαιότης.
Psa. 35: 6 Sy
59: 6 Aq
142: 1 Aq

βελτιόω.
Jer. 42:15 Aq

βελτύνω.
Jer. 42:15 Aq

βιότευσις.
Isa. 29: 1 Aq

βίωσις.
Psa. 38: 6 Sy

βλαισός.
Lev. 21:18 Xm

βλάστημα.
Gen. 1:11 Aq
Psa. 47: 3 Aq
Jer. 23: 5 Sy
31: 9 Sy

βλῆμα.
Exo. 30: 6 MSS

βοήθημα.
Pro. 14:15 Aq

βοηλάτης.
Isa. 61: 5 Sy
Jer. 28:23 Sy

βόησις.
Psa. 21: 2 Th 5th

βοθυνώτης.
2 Ki. 25:12 Aq

βοράς.
Amos 7: 1 Aq

βορατῖναι.
Cant. 1:17 Aq

βόρατον.
Ps. 103:17 Sy
Cant. 1:17 Sy
Isa. 60:13 Sy

βόσκησις.
Ecc. 1:14 Sy
4:16 Sy

βουκόλος.
Am. 7:14 A S T 5th

βούλευμα.
Psa. 80:13 Aq
Pro. 1:31 Aq

βούλησις.
Lev. 22:29 Xm

βράθυ.
Isa. 41:19 Th
55:13 Sy
60:13 Th

βρασμός.
Isa. 28:19 Aq

βραχιάλιον.
2 Sa. 1:10 Sy Th

βραχιόνιον.
2 Sa. 1:10 Aq
8: 7 Aq
Isa. 3:20 Th

βρέφος.
Psa. 8: 3 Aq
Isa. 65:20 Aq

βρόγχος.
Isa. 58: 1 A S T

βρομώδης.
Job 41:23 Sy

βροχθίζω.
Gen. 24:17 Aq

βροχωτός.
Exo. 28:14 Aq Sy
22 Sy

βρυχάομαι.
Psa. 21:14 Aq Sy

βρύχημα.
Job 3:24 (Aq)
Psa. 21: 2 Aq
31: 3 Aq
Eze. 19: 7 Sy

βρωματίζω.
Deu. 8: 3 Aq

βρωμέω.
Exo. 7:18 VIIm

βρωτήρ, βρωστήρ
Isa. 50: 9 Aq
Hos. 5:12 Aq

βωβός.
Exo. 4:11 VIIm

βωλοκοπέω.
Isa. 28:24 Sy

γαλήνη.
Psa. 106:29 Sy

γαλουχέω.
1 Sa. 6: 7 Sy
Isa. 49:23 Sy

γάνωσις.
Amos 7: 7 Aq

γειτνιάω.
Job 26: 5 Sy

γειτονία.
Gen. 49:14 Sy

γέλασμα.
Hab. 1:10 Aq

γενεαλογία.
1 Ch. 4:33 MSS
Ezra 8: 1 MSS

γενναῖος.
2 Sa. 2: 7 Sy

γεννηματίζω.
Psa. 91:15 Aq 5th

γήϊνος.
Job 4:19 Sy

γιγαρτώδης.
Isa. 1:25 Th
Eze. 22:18 Th

γνωσιμαχέω.
2 Ch. 12: 7 Sy

γόβα.
Lev. 11:22 Xm

γόγγυσος.
Pro. 16:28 Th

γογγυστής.
Pro. 26:20 Th
22 Sy
Isa. 29:24 Sy

γοητικός.
Pro. 26:22 Aq

γονατίζω.
Gen. 24:11 Aq
41:43 Aq
49: 9 VIIm

γονοποιέω.
Lev. 26: 9 Xm

γοργεύω.
Ecc. 10:10 Sy

γοργότης.
Ecc. 2:21 (Sy)
4: 4 Sy

γραφεύς.
Psa. 44: 2 Sy

γρόνθος.
Exo. 21:18 (Aq)
Jud. 3:16 Aq
Isa. 58: 4 Aq

γυναικοτραφής.
1 Sa. 20:30 MSS

γυρίζω.
Exo. 13:18 VIIm

γύψος.
Gen. 40:16 Aq

γύρωσις.
Isa. 19:17 Aq

Γώγ.
Amos 7: 1 II III

δαιμονίζω.
Psa. 90: 6 Aq

δαιμονιώδης.
Psa. 90: 6 Sy

δακτυλοδεικτέω.
Pro. 6:13 Sy

δαμάλαιος.
Psa. 21:13 Aq

δαμάλης.
1 Ki. 18:25 Aq
Psa. 21:13 Aq

δάμαλος.
Psa. 21:13 Aq

δειλιάω.
2 Ch. 20:17 MSS

δεῖνα
Ruth 4: 1 Aq
1 Sa. 21: 2 Aq Sy

δεινοποιέω, δειν-
Isa. 51: 9 Aq MSS

δεισαλία, δυσ-
Isa. 28: 8, 13, 13 Th
30:22 Th

δεκάκις.
Gen. 31: 7 Sy
41 Aq

δένδρωμα.
1 Sa. 22: 6 Aq

δενδρών.
Gen. 21:33 Aq
1 Sa. 31:13 Aq

δεξιάζω.
1 Ch. 12: 2 MSS

δεσμοφύλαξ.
Gen. 40: 3 I

δέσποινα.
Isa. 47: 5 Sy

δευτέριος.
Deu. 28:57 Aq

δευτερόγονος.
Gen. 30:42 Aq

δηγμός.
Psa. 90: 6 Aq

δημεύω.
Dan. 3:29 (96) LXX

δημιουργέω.
Job 38: 4 Sy

δημοκατάρατος
Pro. 11:26 Th

διαβαστάζω.
Exo. 15:13 Sy
Psa. 30: 4 Aq
41: 5 Sy

διαβηματίζω.
2 Sa. 6:13 Aq

διάβητος.
Isa. 28:17 Sy

διαβόλως.
Jer. 6:28 (Aq)

διαδειγματίζω.
Psa. 21:13 *ino*

διαδηματίζομαι
Psa. 21:13 Aq

διαδικάζω.
Job 23: 6 Sy
33:13 Sy

διαδικασία.
Psa. 54:10 Sy

διαδικασμός.
Eze. 48:28 Aq

διαδοχή.
Psa. 10: 3 6th

διαδράω.
Psa. 89: 9 Sy

διαζώνη.
Exo. 29: 9 Aq

διάζωσμα.
Exo. 28:27 Aq
Lev. 8: 7 Aq

διαθρέω.
Ecc. 1:13 (Sy)
7:26 (25) Sy

διακενῆς.
2 Sa. 1:22 Sy
Job 11:12 Sy

διακινέω.
2 Ki. 4:35 MSS
Job 26:11 Aq

διακοσμέω.
Deu. 4:19 Sy
2 Sa. 23: 8 MSS

διακόσμησις.
Psa. 32: 6 Sy
Cant. 7: 5 Sy

διαλακτίζω.
Psa. 67:31 Sy

διαλαλέω.
Psa. 50:16 Sy
76: 4 Sy
77:65 Sy

διάλειψις.
Lev. 25: 6 Xm

διάλεξις.
Psa. 103:34 Sy
Cant. 6: 5 Sy

διαλλαγή.
Psa. 29: 6 Sy
68:14 Sy

διαμάχομαι.
Exo. 2:13 Aq Sy
21:18 Aq Sy
Pro. 24:19 Aq Th
Cant. 1: 6 Sy
Dan. 10:20 LXX

διαμελετάω.
Psa. 76:13 Sy

διαμελίζω.
Dan. 3:29 (96) LXX

διαναβαίνω.
Deu. 1:21 MSS

διανεμέω.
Psa. 59: 8 Sy

διάνοιξις.
Isa. 61: 1 Th

διαπαλαίω.
Gen. 25:22 Sy

διαπαρακύπτω.
1 Ki. 6: 8 (4) MSS

διαπείρω.
Pro. 7:23 Th

διαπελάζω.
Psa. 89:10 Aq

διαπέτασμα.
Eze. 27: 7 Th

διάπηγμα.
2 Ki.16:17 Aq

διαπηδάω.
Cant. 2: 8 Sy

διαπλανάω.
Jud. 19: 8 XIm

διαπλοκή.
Psa. 124: 5 Aq

διαπόνημα.
2 Sa. 5:21 Aq
Psa. 15: 4 Aq
126: 2 Aq
Isa. 58: 3 Aq

διαπόνησις.
Isa. 50:11 Aq

διαπορέω.
Dan. 2: 1 Sy

διαπράσσω.
Psa. 45: 9 Sy
Ecc. 2:11 Sy

διαπρέπεια.
Psa. 28: 2,4 Aq
44: 4 Aq
Isa. 35: 2 Aq
53: 2 Aq

διαπρέπω.
Psa. 71:16 Sy

διαπρήθω.
Nu. 5:21 MSS

διάρμα.
2 Sa. 24: 7 Aq
Isa. 34:13 Aq

διάρπασμα.
Isa. 33:23 Aq

διαρρέω.
Jer. 30: 4 MSS

διαρτισμός.
Eze. 4:12 Sy

δίασις.
Isa. 28:20 Th

διασκέδασις.
Isa. 5: 7 (Aq)
24:19 Th

διασπαράσσω.
Lam. 3:11 MSS

διασταθμίζω.
Ps. 57:3 Aq Th 5th
Isa. 33:18 Sy Th

διάστασις.
Isa. 40:12 Th

διάστροφος.
Hos. 7:16 5th

διασύρω.
2 Sa. 12:14,14 Aq
Psa. 9:24 Aq
Pro. 1:30 Aq
Isa. 1: 4 Sy

διασωσμός.
Psa. 54: 9 Aq Th

διαταράσσω.
1 Ki.21:43 Sy

διατέμνω.
2 Sa. 18:23 AST

διατιμάω.
Lev. 27:14 *Sa*

διατίμησις.
Lev. 27: 2,8,13 Xm

διατινάσσω.
2 Sa. 6:16 Aq
Job 16:12 *Heb*

διατορεύω.
1 Ki. 6:18 Aq Th

διάτρητος.
Eze. 40:16 MSS

διατροφή.
1 Ki. 5:11 Aq

διαυγάζω.
2 Ki. 7: 5 MSS

διαύγασμα.
Hab. 3: 4 MSS

διαυγής.
Pro. 16: 2 Aq

διαυγίζομαι.
Job 25: 5 Aq

διάφευξις.
Isa. 37:31 MSS
Jer. 32:21 Sy

διαφθονέω.
Est. 6: 4 MSS

διαφόβημα.
Jer. 37:16 MSS

διαφόρως.
Dan. 7: 7 LXX

διαχαράσσω.
Isa. 49:16 Th

διαχειρόομαι.
Job 30:24 MSS

διαχώρησις.
Eze. 4:12 Sy

διάψευσμα.
Psa. 61: 5 Aq
115: 2 Aq

διαψηλαφάω.
Gen. 31:34 Aq
Isa. 59:10 Sy

διβαφές.
Exo. 25: 4 *rel*

δίβαφος.
Exo. 28: 5 Sy
35:23, 35 Sy

διδακτήρ.
Jud. 3:31 Aq

διδράσκω.
Gen. 31:20 MS

διδυμοτόκος.
Cant. 4: 2 Aq Sy

διεγείρω.
Psa. 77:38 Sy
Job 3: 8 Sy

διέγερσις.
Eze. 23:20 *Heb*

διειδής.
Eze. 1: 4 *Heb*

διευθύνω.
1 Sa. 24: 4 Aq

διηνεκής.
Lev. 6:20 Xm
Psa. 47:15 Sy
88:30 Sy

διηνεκῶς.
Psa. 30: 3 Sy
41: 6 Sy
44:18 AST
76: 3 Sy

δίιπταμαι.
Job 35:11 Aq Th

δικαιοκρισία.
Hos. 6: 5 5th

δικαιοπραγέω.
Gen. 18:25 Sy

δικασία.
Deu. 1:12 Aq
Jud. 12: 2 Aq
Psa. 17:44 Aq
Pro. 18: 6,19 Aq

δίκελλα.
1 Sa. 13:20 Sy

δίκρανος.
Psa. 73: 6 Sy

διμερής.
Dan. 2:41 LXX

διό.
Psa. 115: 1 II

διόλον.
Jer. 39:30 (Sy)

διομόομαι.
Psa. 109: 4 Sy

διπλασίασμα.
Lev. 25:36 MSS

δισσῶς.
2 Ki. 2: 9 MSS

δίστεγος.
Gen. 6:16 Sy

διφθέρωμα.
Isa. 8: 1 (Th)

διχάζω.
Lev. 1:17 Aq
Deu. 14: 6 Aq

διχασμός.
Deu. 14: 6 Aq

διψαλέος.
Isa. 32: 2 Aq

διψάς.
Psa. 62: 2 Sy

διώκται, —κεται.
Hos. 6: 8 Sy

δοκιμασία.
Deu. 33: 8 Sy

δοκιμή.
Psa. 67:31 Sy
Eze. 16:61 XII

δολιεύομαι.
Gen. 37:18 Aq Sy

δολοφονέω.
Hos. 6: 8 5th

δοματίζω.
Eze. 16:33 Sy

δοξασμός.
Isa. 13: 3 Sy

δόρυς.
1 Sa. 17: 7 Aq Th
19:10 MSS
2 Ki. 11:10 Sy
Psa. 56: 5 Sy

δορυφορέω.
Psa. 140: 6 *inc*

δορυφόρος.
Pro. 6:11 Th

δουλαγωγέω.
Gen. 43:17 Xm

δουλευτός.
Lev. 23: 7,8,21 MSS
25,36 MSS

δουλικός.
Exo. 21: 7 Sy
Lev. 25:39 Xm

δοχεῖον, δόχιον.
Lev. 8: 8 Sy

δρομάς.
Jer. 2:23 AST

δρομόω.
Psa. 67:32 Aq

δρομώδης.
Job 41:25 *inc*

δρυμών.
Jud. 1:35 Xm

δυσαλία *vide* δεισαλία.

δυσαρεστέομαι.
Psa. 94:10 Aq Sy
Eze. 6: 9 Aq
20:43 Aq

δυσειδής.
Lev. 14:37 Xm

δυσίατος.
Gen. 6: 4 (Aq Sy)

δυσοσμία.
Amos 4:10 Sy

δυσπάθεια.
Psa. 72: 4 Aq

δυσπραγέω.
Job 5:24 (Sy)

δυσχερής.
Exo. 18:26 Th

δυσωδία.
Isa. 34: 3 Sy

δυσωπέομαι.
Gen. 19:21 Sy
Job 13:10 Sy
Mal. 1: 8 Aq Sy

δωδεκάπηχυς.
Jer. 52:21 Sy

δωροδοτέω.
Eze. 16:33 Aq

δωροκοπία.
Deu. 10:17 Aq
Psa. 25:10 Aq Sy
Pro. 6:35 Aq

ἑβδομάζω.
Eze. 21:23 Th

ἑβδομαῖος.
Gen. 4:24 Sy

ἔβενος.
Eze. 27:15 Sy

ἐγγλύφω.
Jer. 17: 1 Sy

ἔγγονον.
Deu. 28: 4 XI
Job 21:24 MSS

ἐγγράφως.
2 Ch. 30:22 MS

ἐγγυμνάζω.
Jer. 26:14 Aq

ἐγκαθυφαίνω.
Exo. 28:17 MS

ἐγκαίω.
Psa. 38: 4 (Sy)

ἐγκακέω.
Gen. 27:46 Sy
Nu. 21: 5 Sy
Pro. 3:11 Sy
Isa. 7:16 Sy

ἐγκάκησις.
Psa. 118:143 Sy

ἐγκάρσιος.
Eze. 17: 3 Sy
31:10 Sy

ἐγκατάπληξις.
Ezra 3: 3 MS

ἐγκατάσκευος.
Eze. 27:24 Aq Sy

ἐγκεντρίζω.
Jer. 26:20 Aq Sy

ἐγκληρονομέω.
Deu. 3:28 MSS

ἐγκοιμάομαι.
Eze. 29: 3 Aq

ἐγκόμβωμα.
Isa. 3:20 Th

ἔγκομμα.
Exo. 34:12 MSS

ἐγκόπτω.
Dan. 9:26 MSS
Zec. 12:11 MSS

ἐγκότησις.
Hos. 9: 7 Aq

ἐγκράτεια.
Lev. 23:21, 28 Xm

ἐγκρατῶς.
Lev. 23:29 Xm

ἐγκύκλιος.
Dan. 4:33 LXX

ἐγκύμων.
Psa. 77:71 Sy

ἔγκυος.
Jer. 38: 8 XII'

ἐγχαράσσω.
Isa. 30: 8 MSS

ἔδνον.
Gen. 34:12 Sy
1 Sa. 18:25 MSS

ἑδραῖος.
Psa. 32:14 Sy
50: 8 Sy
88:38 Sy
Pro. 4:18 Sy

ἐθίζω.
Jer. 11:19 Aq

ἔθος.
1 Ki. 18:28 Sy Th

εἰδέα.
Lev. 14:37 Xm
Eze. 1:13 Sy

εἰδωλεῖον.
Dan. 1: 2 LXX

εἰδωλοποιΐα.
Hos. 6: 9 5th

εἰκαῖος.
2 Sa. 6:20 Sy

εἰκαιότης.
Pro. 24:31 Aq

εἰκασμός.
Gen. 26.12 Aq

εἴλημα.
Psa. 39: 8 Aq
Cant. 7: 5 Sy
Eze. 27:24 Aq Sy

εἰλητός.
Eze. 2: 9 Sy

εἰλικτός.
1 Ki. 6:12 III

εἰλίνδησις.
Psa. 54: 6 Aq

εἰργμός.
Deu. 22: 9 Aq

εἶργω.
Psa. 118:101 Aq

εἱρκτή.
Job 13:27 Sy
Jer. 36:26 *Sa*
44:15 Sy

εἴσαει.
Psa. 42: 5 Sy

εἰσακοή.
Gen. 16:11 Aq

εἰσεπιφέρω.
Exo. 16: 5 MS

εἰσηγέομαι.
Psa. 63: 6 Sy

εἴσλειψις.
Jer. 37:11 Th

εἰσπνέω.
Ecc. 1: 5 Aq

εἰσπράκτης.
Exo. 5:13 Aq
Job 39: 7 Aq

εἰσπράσσω.
Job 3:18 Aq
Zec. 10: 4 Aq

ἐκβεβηλόω.
Lev. 21: 7 MSS

ἐκβιαστής.
Pro. 6: 7 Aq Th

ἐκβιβασμός.
1 Sa. 15:23 Aq

ἐκβιβαστής.
Deu. 16:18 Aq

ἔκβλητος.
Job 3: 7 Sy

ἔκβρασμα.
Lev. 13: 6, 18 Sy

ἐκβράσσω.
Isa. 57:20 Sy

ἐκβυρσεύω.
Lev. 11:40 Xm

ἐκδικία.
Deu. 32:43 *Heb*

ἔκδικος.
Psa. 98: 8 Sy

ἐκδοκιμάζω.
Job 7:18 Aq Sy

ἔκδοσις.
Lam. 1:17 Sy

ἔκδοτος.
Isa. 46: 1 Sy
Jer. 51:30 Sy

ἐκδυναστεύω.
Jer. 27:17 Sy

ἐκθάλλω.
Hab. 3:17 MSS

ἐκθαμβέω.
2 Sa. 17:12 MSS
Job 33: 7 Aq
Isa. 52:12 Aq Sy

ἐκθερμαίνω.
Psa. 38: 4 Sy

ἔκθεσις.
Dan. 1: 5 LXX

ἔκθετος, ἐκθέτης.
1 Ki. 6: 8 Sy
Eze. 42: 3, 3 *inc*

ἐκκακέω.
Jer. 18:12 Sy

ἐκκαυλέω.
Psa. 128: 6 Sy

ἔκκαυσις.
Isa. 64: 2 Sy

ἔκκλισις.
Isa. 58: 6 Sy
Jer. 35:16 Th
Eze. 9: 9 A S T

ἐκκολάζω.
Lev. 22:24 Aq

ἐκκόλαμμα.
Exo. 36:13 V X
Eze. 40:16 MSS

ἐκκοπή.
Isa. 51: 1 Aq

ἐκκόπημα.
Jer. 31:39 MSS

ἔκκοπος.
Isa. 43:24 Th

ἔκλαμπρος.
Lev. 13: 4, 13 Sy

ἔκλαμψις.
Lev. 13:26 Sy

ἐκλανθάνω.
Psa. 12: 2 Sy

ἐκλεκτόω.
Isa. 52:11 Aq

ἐκλεκτῶς.
Psa. 2:12 Aq

ἐκλιμώσσω.
Deu. 28:65 Aq

ἐκλογή.
Isa. 22: 7 Aq
37:24 Sy Th

ἐκμάσσω.
Psa. 17:46 (6th)

ἐκμυζάω.
Isa. 66:11 Aq

ἐκμύζησις.
Pro. 24:68 Aq Th

ἐκνικάω.
Ecc. 1: 8 Sy

ἐκνίπτω.
Exo. 30:18 MS

ἔκνοια.
2 Sa. 6: 7 Aq

ἐκπαιδεύω.
Dan. 1: 5 LXX

ἐκπαλαίω.
Jud. 20:33 MS

ἐκπετασμός.
Job 36:20 Aq

ἔκπληξις.
1 Sa. 14:15 Aq
Job 4:13 Sy
Psa. 30:23 Sy
87:16 Sy

ἐκπονέω.
Psa. 67:10 Sy

ἐκπράκτης.
Job 39: 7 Aq

ἐκπρηστής.
Isa. 30: 6 Aq

ἐκπυρόω.
Hos. 7: 4 5th

ἐκρέω.
Job 14:11 Sy
Psa. 87:10 Sy

ἐκσμῆξις.
Lev. 6:28 MS

ἐκσποδιάζω.
Nu. 4:13 *inc*

ἐκστατικός.
Jer. 37: 5 Sy

ἐκστερεόω.
Psa. 128: 6 6th

ἐκσυρίζω.
Job 27:23 Sy

ἔκταξις.
2 Ki. 4:13 MSS

ἐκτιτρώσκω.
Job 21:10 Sy

ἐκτοκεύω.
Isa. 66: 9 Aq

ἐκτορνεύω.
Exo. 25:36 Sy

ἔκτοτε.
Isa. 16:13 Sy

ἐκτρυχόω.
Isa. 24: 6 Sy

ἐκυρός.
Gen. 38:25 Aq

ἐκφάγω.
Psa. 104:35 Sy

ἐκφαίνω.
Psa. 26:12 A S 6th
67:32 Sy
Pro. 14: 5 A S T
Dan. 2:19 LXX

ἐκφαυλίζω.
Pro. 15:20 Sy

ἔκφευξις, ἔκφυ-
Psa. 54: 9 Sy

ἐκφθείρω.
Isa. 54:16 A S T

ἐκφρύγω.
Job 27:20 A S T
Eze. 24:11 MSS

ἔκφυμα.
Lev. 13: 7 Sy

ἐκφύω.
Psa. 103:14 Sy

ἐκφωνέω.
Dan. 2:20, 27 LXX

ἐκχλευάζω.
Pro. 14: 9 Sy

ἐκχώννυμι.
Eze. 17:17 Aq

ἐκχωρίζω.
Amos 7:12 MSS

ἔλασις.
2 Ki. 9:20 Aq

ἐλαφίνης.
1 Sa. 24: 3 Aq

ἐλάφιον.
Pro. 5:19 Sy Th

ἐλαφρύνω.
Job 39:34 Aq

ἐλεεινός.
Dan. 9:23 LXX
10:11, 19 LXX

ἐλεϊσμός.
Jer. 43: 7 Aq
45:26 Aq

ἐλεφαντίασις.
Deu. 28:27 Sy

ἐλλαμβάνομαι
Pro. 24:63 Th

ἐμβόλισμα.
Eze. 16:16 Aq Th

ἐμβράσσω.
Gen. 40: 6 Aq

ἐμβριμάομαι.
Nu. 23: 8 VIIm
Psa. 7:12 Aq
Isa. 17:13 Sy
Dan. 11:30 LXX

ἐμβρίμησις.
Psa. 75: 7 Sy
Isa. 30:27 Th
Eze. 21:31 Sy
Hos. 7:16 Aq Sy

ἔμβρυον.
Exo. 21:22 MSS
Job 3:16 Th

ἔμμωμος.
Mal. 1:14 Sy Th

ἐμπαιγή.
Pro. 11:15 Sy

ἐμπαράσκευος.
Psa. 26: 3 Sy

ἐμπρηστής.
Deu. 8:15 Aq

ἐμπρόθεσμος.
Eze. 21:25 Sy
35: 5 *inc*

ἐμπτίσσομαι.
Pro. 27:22 Aq Th

ἐμφανισμός.
Nu. 5:18 MS

ἐμφιλονεικῶς.
Lev. 26:21 Xm
24 *Sa*

ἐμφύσημα.
Lev. 13: 7 (Aq Sy)
Job 37: 9 Sy

ἐναλαλάζω.
1 Sa. 31: 4 (Aq)

ἐναλλαγή.
Psa. 9:12 Aq
Isa. 66: 4 Aq

ἐνάλλαγμα.
Isa. 66: 4 Aq

ἐναλλάκτης.
Isa. 3: 4 Aq

ἐναλλακτικός.
Deu. 22:14 Aq

ἐναλλάσσω.
Gen. 48:14 I X
1 Sa. 21:13 Aq
31: 4 Aq

ἐναντίωσις.
Gen. 26:21 Sy
Lev. 26:28 Xm
Ezra 4: 6 MSS

ἐνασελγέω.
Jud. 19:25 Aq

ἐναυλίζω.
Jud. 14:19 Aq
1 Sa. 10:10 (Aq)
16:13 Aq

ἐνδεδωκός.
Lev. 14:56 X

ἐνδεσμέω.
Exo. 23:22 Aq
Psa. 6: 8 Aq
8: 3 Aq Th

ἐνδιαιτάομαι.
1 Sa. 19:19 Sy

ἐνδότερος.
Exo. 26:33 MS

ἐνδοξασμός.
Psa. 45: 4 Sy
46: 5 Sy

ἐνδύμιος.
Pro. 26:22 Th

ἐνδύτης.
1 Sa. 17:38 Aq

ἐνεδρευτής.
1 Sa. 22: 8 Sy

ἐνεκτόν.
Exo. 13:16 (Aq)

ἐνεχείρασμα.
Exo. 22:26 VII

ἐνθήκη.
Gen. 41:36 Sy
Isa. 23:18 MSS

ἐνθύμησις.
Job 21:27 Sy
Eze. 11:21 Sy

ἔνικμος.
Job 8:16 Aq

ἐνικός.
Eze. 37:17 MSS

ἐνιλατεύω.
Lev. 26: 9 MS

ἐνισχυρίζομαι.
Psa. 51: 9 Sy

ἐνίσχυσις.
Psa. 27: 8 Sy

ἐννεός.
Hos. 9: 7 Sy

ἐννόημα.
Pro. 12: 5 Th

ἐνοπλισμός.
2 Sa. 2:23 Aq
3:27 Aq

ἐνόχλησις.
Psa. 54: 4 Sy
Isa. 1:14 A S T

ἐνόω.
Lev. 17:14 Sy
Hos. 4:17 Sy 5th

ἐνσεισμός.
Eze. 26: 8 Th

ἐνσκιρρόω.
Isa. 27: 1 Th

ἐνστηλόω.
2 Sa. 8:14 MSS

ἐντίναγμα.
Isa. 28: 2 MS
32: 2 Aq

ἐντόπιος.
Exo. 12:48 VIIm

ἐντορνεύω.
Exo. 25:33 Sy

ἐντρίβω.
Gen. 19:13 MSS

ἔντριχος.
Psa. 67:22 Sy

ἐντυγχάνω.
Dan. 6:12 LXX

ἐντυφλόω.
Lev. 26:16 *inc*

ἐνυβρίζω.
Lev. 24:11 Xm

ἔνυδρος.
Hos. 10: 1 Aq

ἕνωσις.
1 Ch. 12:17 MSS

ἐξαιρέτως.
Deu. 32:12 Aq

ἐξάκουστος.
Psa. 65: 8 Sy

ἐξαμυγδαλίζω,
—λόω.
Exo. 25:33 Aq

ἐξανάδοσις.
Lev. 13: 6, 18 Aq

ἐξανάστασις.
Gen. 7: 4 MSS

ἐξανεγείρω.
Isa. 15: 5 (Aq)

ἐξανθίζω.
Lev. 13:42 X

ἐξαπλόω.
Pro. 26:22 Th
Isa. 25:11 Sy

ἐξαποστολή.
Isa. 27: 8 Th

ἐξαρθρόω.
Psa. 68:24 Sy

ἐξαυχενισμός.
Nah. 3: 1 Aq

ἐξεικάζω.
Hab. 3: 6 MSS

ἐξέναντι.
Eze. 40: 2 Aq

ἐξεράω.
Lev. 18:28 Aq

ἐξερμενίζω.
Psa. 105:30 Aq

ἐξευρίσκω.
Job 37:22 Sy
Ecc. 8:17 Sy

ἐξευτελίζω.
2 Sa. 6:16 Sy
Psa. 68:34 Sy
122: 4 Sy

ἐξευτελισμός.
Psa. 122: 3 Sy

ἐξέψω.
Eze. 24:11 XII

ἐξιλεόω.
Deu. 32:43 Aq
2 Sa. 21: 9 (Aq)

ἐξισάζω.
Psa. 88: 7 Sy

ἐξίσωσις.
Zec. 4: 7 Aq

ἐξίτηλος.
Hab. 3:17 MSS

ἐξοικίζω.
Jer. 34:17 Sy
47: 1 Sy

ἐξοικισμός.
Eze. 3:11 Sy

ἐξολισθάνω,
–θαίνω.
Psa. 35: 3 Sy
Pro. 12:13 MSS

ἐξορίζω.
Lev. 18:25, 28 Xm
2 Sa. 8: 4 Aq

ἐξορθρίζω.
Psa. 109: 3 Aq

ἐξουδενισμός.
Psa. 122: 4 Aq

ἐξουσιαστικός.
Ecc. 8: 4 Sy

ἐξυπνιάζω.
Pro. 23:35 AST

ἔξωμος.
Isa. 15: 4 Aq

ἐξωμοσία.
Lev. 22:18 Xm
23:38 Xm

ἐξώστρα.
2 Ki. 1: 2 Sy

ἑορταστήριον.
Isa. 33:20 Th

ἐπαγριόω.
Psa. 34:16 (Sy)

ἐπαινέτης.
Jer. 30:14 AST

ἐπαλείφω.
Eze. 13:10 MSS

ἐπάλληλος.
Hos. 8:12 Sy

ἐπαναβαίνω.
Job 36:20 Sy

ἐπαναγκαστής.
Job 3:18 Sy

ἐπανακάμπτω.
Isa. 35:10 AST

ἐπανακλίνω.
Cant. 2: 5 Sy

ἐπανάπαυσις.
Isa. 30:30 Sy

ἐπανάστημα.
Gen. 7: 4 MSS

ἐπαποστολή.
Psa. 77:49 Sy

ἐπαποτίνω.
Isa. 59:17 Th

ἐπαστής.
Psa. 57: 6 Sy

ἐπαυχένιος.
Eze. 13:18 Sy Th

ἐπαχθής.
Job 16: 2 Sy

ἐπείγω.
Isa. 59:19 Sy
Dan. 3:22 LXX
Hos. 6: 3 5th

ἔπειξις.
Exo. 12:11 Sy
Eze. 30: 9 Sy
Zeph. 1:18 Sy

ἐπειρωμένος.
Isa. 27: 1 Aq

ἐπεισπορεύομαι.
Lev. 26.33 MS

ἐπείτοιγε.
1 Sa. 25:34 Sy

ἐπεκκεντέω.
Zec. 12:10 Aq

ἐπεκλέγω.
Deu. 21: 5 MSS

ἐπένδυμα.
Exo. 25: 6 AST
Eze. 16:10 Sy
26:16 Sy

ἐπεξέρχομαι.
Jer. 27:34 Sy
Hab. 1: 7 Sy

ἐπευφημέω.
Neh. 12:42 MSS

ἐπηρεαστής.
Psa. 56: 2 Sy

ἐπήρεια.
Psa. 54:12 Sy
90: 3 Sy
98: 8 Sy

ἐπηχέω.
Dan. 6:21 LXX

ἔπηχος.
Eze. 8:17 Sy

ἐπιβαρύνω.
Exo. 21:30 MS

ἐπίβλητος.
Eze. 27:20 Sy

ἐπιβλυγμός,
–υσμός.
Gen. 2: 6 Aq
Job 30:12 Aq
Pro. 1:26 Aq

ἐπιβολή.
Hos. 5:14 Sy

ἐπιγαμβρευτής
Deu. 25: 7 Aq

ἐπιγνωρίζω.
Pro. 20:11 Sy

ἐπιγώνια.
Psa. 143:12 Aq

ἐπιδάκνω.
Pro. 16:30 MSS

ἐπιδεκτός.
Isa. 60: 7 Sy Th

ἐπιδέννομαι.
Isa. 1: 6 Sy

ἐπίδεσις.
Hos. 5:13 Aq

ἐπιδεσμεύω.
Isa. 3: 7 Th

ἐπιδεσμέω.
Psa. 146: 3 Sy

ἐπίδεσμος.
Eze. 30:21 Aq

ἐπιδευτέρωσις.
Psa. 76:11 Sy

ἐπιδέχομαι.
Pro. 19:20 Sy

ἐπίδομα.
Lev. 13: 7 Aq

ἐπιδοξότης.
Ps. 103: 1 Aq
Eze. 7: 7 Aq
Zec. 6:13 (Aq)

ἐπίδοσις.
Lev. 13: 7 Aq

ἐπιδοχή.
Pro. 16:23 Sy Th
Isa. 29:24 Th

ἐπιδύτης.
1 Sa. 2:19 Th

ἐπιεικαίως.
1 Sa. 12:22 X

ἐπιείκεια.
Dan. 4:20 LXX

ἐπίζεμα.
Hos. 10: 7 Sy

ἐπιζημιόω.
Exo. 21:22 MSS

ἐπιθεσία.
Psa. 34:20 Aq

ἐπιθέτης.
Psa. 1: 1 Sy

ἐπιθνήσκω.
Lev. 11:32 MSS

ἐπικαίρως.
Psa. 9:10 Sy

ἐπικαρπία.
Ecc. 9: 5 Sy

ἐπικατάρασις.
Jer. 29:13 MSS

ἐπικλείω.
Gen. 2.21 Aq

ἐπίκλησις.
Isa. 1:13 Sy

ἐπικοπή.
Deu. 28:25 MSS

ἐπικράτεια.
Hos. 11:12 Aq

ἐπικρίνω.
Lev. 24:12 Xm

ἐπίκρισις.
Lev. 24:12 Xm

ἐπικυλισμός.
Pro. 2: 9 Sy
15 Th
5: 6, 21 Sy

ἐπιλήπτομαι.
1 Sa. 21:15 MSS

ἐπιλογίζομαι.
Job 35:15 Sy

ἐπιλογισμός.
Cant. 7: 4 Aq

ἐπίλυσις.
Gen. 40: 8 Aq
Hos. 3: 4 Sy

ἐπιλύω.
Gen. 40: 8 Aq
41: 8, 12 Aq
Hos. 3: 4 Th

ἐπιμαρτυρία.
Jer. 11: 7 Th

ἐπιμελής.
Pro. 11: 2 Sy

ἐπιμιξία.
Eze. 27: 9, 13, 27 Sy

ἐπίμονος.
Deu. 28:59 Sy

ἐπινικάω.
Ezra 3: 8, 9 MSS

ἐπινίκιος, –ον.
Psa. 4: 1 Sy
5: 1 Sy
Isa. 63: 3 Sy

ἐπίπλαστος.
Job 13: 4 Sy
Psa. 93: 5 Aq
Isa. 31: 7 Aq

ἐπιπλέω.
Job 24:18 Sy

ἐπιπλησίον.
Jos. 9: 6(33) MSS

ἐπιπνίγω.
Nah. 2:12 MS

ἐπιπόθημα.
Psa. 139: 9 Aq

ἐπιπόθησις.
Eze. 23:11 Aq

ἐπιπόλαιος.
Eze. 17: 5 AST

ἐπιπωμάζω.
Psa. 43:20 Sy 5th
68:16 Sy

ἐπιρραίνω.
Eze. 46:14 Sy

ἐπίρρινον, –ίνιον
Job 42:11 Sy
Eze. 16:12 Sy

ἐπίρριψις.
Hab. 2:15 Aq

ἐπιρρυτής.
Zec. 4: 2 Aq

ἐπιρρώννυμι.
Job 16: 5 Sy

ἐπισήμως.
Psa. 73: 4 Sy

ἐπισκέπτης.
Eze. 23:23 Aq

ἐπισκέπω.
1 Ki. 6: 8(4) Sy

ἐπισκοπεύω.
Psa. 65: 7 Sy

ἐπιστάσεις.
Eze. 40:43 Aq

ἐπιστασία.
Nu. 26: 9 MSS

ἐπιστημονίζω.
Isa. 52:13 Aq

ἐπιστημόνως.
Gen. 48:14 inc
Psa. 46: 8 Aq 6th

ἐπιστημόω.
Psa. 2:10 Aq
31: 8 Aq
93: 8 Aq

ἐπιστρωννύω.
Eze. 27:30 MS

ἐπιστύλιον.
1 Ki. 7: 9(20) Sy

ἐπισυσκευάζω.
Exo. 3:22 MSS

ἐπισύσχεσις.
Lev. 23:36 MS

ἐπίσχεσις.
Lev. 23:36 Xm
Nu. 29:35 Sa
Deu. 16: 8 Aq

ἐπισωρεύω.
Job 14:17 Sy
Cant. 2: 4 Sy

ἐπιταγή.
Dan. 3:16 LXX
Mic. 7:11 Sy

ἐπίταγμα.
Job 25: 3 Sy

ἐπιτείχισμα.
Jer. 40: 4 Sy

ἐπίτηδες.
1 Sa. 9:24 Sy
Jer. 45: 4 Sy

ἐπιτηρέω.
Psa. 70:10 Sy

ἐπίτοκος.
1 Sa. 4:19 Sy

ἐπιτριμμός.
Deu. 23: 1 Aq

ἐπίτριπτος.
Psa. 9:10 Aq

ἐπιτροπή.
Jer. 10:17 Aq

ἐπιφθέγγομαι.
Psa. 2: 5 Aq
58: 9 Sy

ἐπιφλυγμός.
Gen. 2: 6 Aq

ἐπίφοβος.
2 Sa. 7:23 Aq
Psa. 88: 8 Aq Sy
129: 4 5th
Cant. 6: 3, 9 Sy

ἐπιφράσσω.
Gen. 8: 2 Aq

ἐπιφυλάσσω.
Eze. 41: 8 (Th)

ἐπιχρίω.
Eze. 13:10 Sy
22:28 Sy

ἐπιχύνω.
1 Ki. 22:35 MS

ἐπιχυτήρ.
Zec. 4: 2, 12 Sy

ἕπομαι.
Exo. 4: 8 Sy

ἐποπτεύω.
Psa. 9:35 Sy
32:13 Sy

ἐποργίζομαι.
Dan. 11:40 LXX

ἐπορθρίζω.
Job 24: 5 Sy

ἐποχέομαι.
Psa. 67: 5, 34 Sy

ἐποχή.
1 Sa. 14: 6 Sy
Pro. 24:51 Aq

ἐπῳάζω.
Gen. 1: 2 Sa

ἐπῳδή.
Psa. 57: 6 Sy
Ecc. 10:11 Sy
Isa. 3: 3 Th

ἐργάομαι.
Job 22:17 Th

ἐργαστήριον.
Jer. 44:16 Aq

ἐργάτης.
Psa. 93:10 Sy

ἐρείπιον.
Job 3:14 Sy
Psa. 9:7 Sy 6th
101:7 Sy
Eze. 13:4 Sy

ἐρεισμός.
Isa. 3:1 Aq

ἐρημάζω.
Jer. 26:19 Sy

ἔρημα.
Lev. 2:16 Xm

ἐριθεία.
Eze. 23:11 Sy

ἐριθεύομαι.
Eze. 23:5,12 Sy

ἐριστής.
Eze. 44:6 rel

ἑρμηνεία.
Pro. 1:6 Aq Th

ἑρμηνεύς.
Gen. 42:23 I, VI
Isa. 43:27 Aq Sy

ἐρυθρόω.
Isa. 63:1 Sy

ἐσθής.
Lam. 4:14 Sy

ἐσουβή.
1 Sa. 17:18 MSS

ἐσπευσμένως.
Psa. 67:32 Aq

ἑστίασις.
Gen. 26:30 Xm
Jer. 16:5 Aq

ἐσχατεύω.
Jud. 5:28 MSS

ἑταιρεία.
Amos 6:7 Sy

ἑταιρέω.
Psa. 59:10 Aq

ἑταιρία.
Pro. 18:24 MSS
Jer. 16:5 Sy

ἑταιρικός.
Pro. 21:9 Sy Th

ἑταιρίς.
Hos. 4:14 Sy

ἐταστής.
Psa. 7:10 Th

ἑτερογενής.
Deu. 22:11 Sy

ἑτερόγλωσσος.
Ps. 113:1 Aq
Isa. 28:11 Aq
33:19 Aq

ἑτεροκλινέω.
Psa. 16:11 Sy

ἑτερολογία.
Psa. 138:4 Sy

εὐαγγελισμός.
2 Sa. 18:20 MSS

εὐαρέστησις.
Exo. 29:18 A S T
Lev. 1:9 Th
Eze. 20:41 Sy

εὔγλωσσος.
Exo. 4:10 MSS

εὐδιανόητος.
1 Sa. 25:3 Sy

εὐδόκητος, –τη.
Psa. 67:31 Sy
Cant. 6:3 Sy

εὐδοξία.
Job 36:11 Sy
Ps. 103:1 Sy

εὐειδής.
Dan. 1:4 LXX

εὐζωΐα.
Gen. 30:11 Aq

εὐζωνίζω.
Gen. 49:19,19 Aq

εὐθαρσέω.
Psa. 60:5 Sy
90:2 Sy

εὐθαρσής.
Psa. 56:5 Sy

εὐθετέω.
Ecc. 11:6 Aq

εὐθυμέω.
Psa. 31:11 Sy
Pro. 15:15 Sy

εὐθυμία.
Psa. 42:4 Sy
50:10 Sy

εὔκαρπος.
Jer. 11:16 Aq

εὔκλαδος.
Psa. 47:3 5th

εὔλογος.
Exo. 4:10 VII, X

εὐμένεια.
Pro. 16:15 Sy

εὐνοέω.
Gen. 34:15 5th
Dan. 2:43 LXX

εὐνομία.
Pro. 8:14 Aq
Isa. 28:29 Aq

εὐπάθησις.
Jer. 37:10 Th

εὔπορος.
1 Sa. 31:12 Aq

εὐπραγέω.
Psa. 35:4 Sy
Hab. 2:5 Sy

εὐπραγία.
Job 36:11 MSS

εὐπρεπέω, –όω
Pro. 2:10 Aq

εὐπρεπίζω.
Psa. 140:6 Aq

εὐπρεπῶς.
Eze. 32:19 MS

εὕρεσις.
Psa. 31:6 Aq

εὐρυχωρέω.
Psa. 17:37 Sy

εὐρώς.
Psa. 38:12 Sy

εὐσήμως.
Dan. 2:19 LXX

εὐσθενής.
Job 10:16 Heb

εὔστροφος.
Eze. 10:13 Sy

εὐσχολία.
1 Ki. 6:17 Aq Th

εὐτελής.
1 Sa. 15:9 Sy
18:23 Aq
Psa. 11:9 Sy
Pro. 10:20 Sy

εὐτρεπίζω.
Isa. 40:3 Sy
Jer. 12:3 Su

εὐτροφία.
Psa. 67:16 Sy

εὔτροφος.
Amos 4:1 Sy

εὐτυχέω.
Gen. 30:11 MSS

εὐφημέω.
Psa. 31:11 Sy
32:1 Sy
66:5 Sy
144:7 Sy

εὐφημία.
Psa. 41:5 Sy
46:2 Sy
99:2 Sy
125:2 Sy

εὔφημος.
Psa. 62:6 Sy

εὔφορος.
1 Sa. 16:23 Sy

εὐφρόνησις.
Psa. 77:72 (Aq)

εὐχαριστία.
Psa. 41:5 Aq
68:31 Aq
Amos 4:5 Aq

εὐχέρεια.
Jer. 6:14 Sy

εὐχρηστέω.
Ecc. 10:19 Sy

εὐψυχέω.
Pro. 24:66 MS

εὐωνίζω.
Psa. 11:9 Aq

ἐφαπτίς.
Eze. 26:16 Aq

ἐφέδρευσις.
Job 37:2 Aq

ἐφεστρίς.
1 Sa. 2:19 Sy
24:12 Sy
Job 1:20 Sy

ἐφηβεία.
Psa. 126:4 Aq

ἐφικνέομαι.
Job 11:8 Sy
32:12 Sy
Ecc. 9:10 Sy

ἐφίπταμαι.
Jer. 29:23 MSS

ἐφοδευτής.
Gen. 42:9 Aq

ἔφοδος.
Jer. 10:18 Sy

ἐφόριος.
Jud. 6:4 MS

ἐφορμάω.
Jud. 5:22 Aq
14:6 Sy
1 Sa. 10:6,10 inc

ἔφορος.
Psa. 58:11 MS

ἐχέτλη.
Jud. 3:31 Sy

ἔχιδνα.
Isa. 59:5 Aq

ζεστός.
Lev. 6:21 inc
7:2(12) Xm

ζευγίζω.
Nu. 25:3 Aq Th

ζηλοτυπουμένη.
Nu. 5:29 XI

ζόφος.
Exo. 10:22 Sy
Job 28:3 Sy
Psa. 10:2 Sy
Isa. 59:9 Sy

ζυγαί.
Gen. 45:22 Su

ζύγιος.
Lev. 19:36 MS
Pro. 11:1 Aq Sy
16:11 Aq

ζωγραφία.
Pro. 7:16 Th

ζωγρεῖον, ζῶγρος
Jer. 5:27 Aq Sy

ζωογόνος.
Gen. 3:20 Sy

ζωτικός.
Gen. 1:2 Su

ζωωνή.
Psa. 7:12 Heb

ζώωσις.
Gen. 45:5 Aq

ἠγιασμένως.
Psa. 133:2 inc

ἥδιστος.
Psa. 140:6 Sy

ἥδομαι.
Eze. 23:7 Sy

ἠλόω.
Psa. 118:120 Aq

ἡμέρευσις.
Ps. 1:2 A S 5th 6th
31:4 Aq

ἡμερόδεκτον.
Lev. 25:29 Xm

ἡμερολεγδόν.
Lev. 25:29 IV

ἡμίκορος.
Hos. 3:2 rel

ἡμίνα.
Eze. 45:24 Su

ἥνυστρον.
Deu. 18:3 MSS

ἠρεμαῖος.
Exo. 7:11,22 Aq

ἠρεμέω.
Job 38:19 Sy
Psa. 34:15 Sy
82:2 Sy
121:6 Sy
Isa. 34:14 Sy

ἠρεμία.
Jud. 18:7 Sy
Job 4:16 Sy
34:29 Sy
Psa. 29:7 Sy

ἡσυχόομαι.
Amos 6:10 Aq

ἧττα.
Exo. 32:18 Sa

θάλαμος.
1 Ki. 14:28 Aq

θαλλός.
Gen. 8:11 Sy
Pro. 11:28 Sy
Eze. 31:3 Sy

θαμβευταί.
Zeph. 3:4 Aq

θαμβεύω.
Gen. 49:4 Aq

θάμβησις.
Deu. 16:3 Aq
Psa. 30:23 Aq

θαρυτόπος.
Eze. 6:13 Sy

θαρσύνω.
1 Sa. 23:16 Sy
Cant. 4:9,9 Sy

θέαμα.
Exo. 3:3 Sy

θεατής.
Deu. 18:11 Th

θέλγω.
Exo. 22:18 Aq
Job 31:27 Aq
Jer. 20:7,7 Aq
Hos. 7:11 Aq

θέναρον.
Pro. 24:27 Aq

θεομάχος.
Job 26:5 Sy
Pro. 9:18 Sy
21:16 Sy

θεραπαινίς.
Exo. 21:27 MS

θέρειος.
Psa. 31:4 Aq

θεριστήριον.
1 Sa. 13:20 X

θερμῶς.
Jud. 5:25 MSS

θεωρία.
Ecc. 5:10 Sy
Isa. 53:2 Sy
Eze. 10:10 MSS
Dan. 5:7 LXX

θήλασμα.
Psa. 31:4 6th

θημωνιάζω.
Exo. 15:8 VIIm

θήραμα.
Lev. 17:13 MSS
Ecc. 7:27 MSS

θηρευτής.
Psa. 21:17 Aq Sy

θηράω.
1 Sa. 24:12 Sy

θηριάλωσις.
Gen. 49:9 Sy

θηρόβρωτος.
Gen. 31:39 MSS

θιγγάνω.
Cant. 5:4 Sy

θλιβώδες.
Gen. 32:7 inc

θολόω.
Psa. 30:10 Sy
45:4 Sy
Jer. 32:24 Aq

θορυβώδης.
Ecc. 7:26 Sy

θρασύνω.
Exo. 4:21 Sy
1 Sa. 23:16 Sy
Job 11:12 Sy

θρησκεία.
Jer. 3:19 Sy
Eze. 20:6,15 Sy
Dan. 2:46 Sy

θρῖναξ.
Isa. 30:24 Sy

θρύπτω.
Psa. 57:8 Sy

θύϊνος.
1 Ki. 10:11 Sy

θυλάκιον.
Gen. 43:21 VIIm
2 Ki. 5:23 MSS

θύλαξ.
Hos. 3:2 Sy

θυμίαμα.
Exo. 23:18 MS

θυμεόω.
Isa. 31: 5 Aq
38: 6 Aq

θύτης.
Dan. 2:27 Sy

'ΙΑ' (Jah.)
Psa. 67: 5 Sy 5th

ἰά.
Jer. 31:33, 33 Su

ἰάνθινος.
Exo. 25: 5 rel
Eze. 16:10 Aq Sy

ἰασμός.
Jer. 32:16 inc

ἴξος.
Deu. 14:13 MSS

ἱερατικός.
Jud. 17: 5 Sy
Ezra 2:69 MSS
Neh. 7:70, 71 MSS

Ἰησοῦς.
Hab. 3:13 6th

ἱθαρατόπος.
Eze. 6:13 (Aq)

ἱκεσία.
Psa. 27: 2 Sy
6 Th
30:23 6th
118:170 Sy

ἱκετηρίς.
Job 40:22 MSS

ἱκετικός.
Pro. 27: 6 Aq

ἰκτίν.
Psa. 103:17 Sy

ἰλάζω.
Lev. 6:26 Th
37 Xm

ἱλαρεύομαι.
Psa. 30: 8 Sy
Cant. 1: 4 Sy
Isa. 49:13 Sy

ἱλαστής.
Psa. 85: 5 Aq Th

ἱλατεύω.
Lev. 8:15 Sa
26:43 Xm
Ps. 102: 3 Th
Dan. 9:18 LXX

ἰξός.
Deu. 14:13 Aq

ἱπποστάσιον.
Dan. 11:45 Sy

ἶρις.
Eze. 1: 4 Heb

ἰσχυροποιέω.
Eze. 27:27 Aq

ἰχθυακός.
Zeph. 1:10 rel

ἰχθυοφόρος.
Job 40:26 Sy

καγχάζω.
2 Sa. 6:16 Sy

καγχλάζω.
Job 41:22 Aq

καθάπτω.
Cant. 1: 6 Sy

καθάρισις.
Lev. 12: 4, 5 Aq

κάθαρμα.
Deu. 29:17 Aq
Eze. 6: 4 Aq

καθαρότης.
Exo. 24:10 MSS
Job 22:30 Sy
Psa. 88:45 Sy

καθαρῶς.
Psa. 2:12 Sy

καθήλωσις.
Eze. 7:23 (Sy Th)

καθημέραν.
Isa. 58: 2 Sy

καθησυχάζω.
Psa. 82: 2 Aq

καθικνέομαι.
Psa. 37: 3 Sy

καθίπταμαι.
Eze. 17:23 Aq

κάθισμα.
Lev. 15: 9 Xm

καθοδήγησις.
Isa. 38:15 Th

κάθυγρος.
Job 40:16 rel

καινοποιέω.
Isa. 61: 4 Sy

καίριμος.
Lev. 16:21 Xm

καίρινος.
Jer. 27: 8 Sy

καιρίως.
Deu. 32:35 Aq

κακίζω.
Exo. 21: 8 Aq

κακοβουλία.
Psa. 138:20 5th

κακογνωμονέω
Psa. 30:14 5th

κακογνωμοσύνη.
Psa. 25:10 Th

κακογνώμων.
1 Sa. 25: 3 Sy

κακοηθίζομαι.
Pro. 26:18 Aq

κακοποιΐα.
Pro. 22:16 Sy

κακουργέω.
2 Sa. 10: 6 Sy
Pro. 13:20 Sy
Ecc. 8:11 Sy

κακουχία.
Deu. 16: 3 Aq
Psa. 9:14 Aq
43:25 Sy
131: 1 Aq

κακοφρονέω.
2 Sa. 15:31 Aq

κακωνυμία.
Exo. 32:25 Sy

καλάμημα.
Jer. 29:10 MSS
Obad. 5 Th

καλαμώτης.
Pro. 24:63 MS

καλιά.
Gen. 6:14 Sy

καλλιεργέω.
Psa. 140: 7 5th

καλλίκαρπος.
Gen. 49:11 VIIm

καλλωπισμός.
Eze. 16: 7 Heb

καλοποιέω.
Lev. 5: 4 X

καλπάζω.
Jer. 8: 6 Aq

καλύκωσις.
Cant. 2: 1 Aq
Isa. 35: 1 Aq

καμπτός.
Pro. 2: 9 Aq

κάμψις.
2 Ki. 10:12 Aq

κανθαρίς.
Hos. 13: 3 Sy

κάπτω.
Dan. 1:12 LXX

καπυρός.
Jos. 9:11 Sy

καραδοκέω.
Psa. 129: 5 Aq
141: 8 Aq

καραδοκία.
Pro. 10:28 Aq
Psa. 38: 8 Aq

κάρος.
Gen. 2:21 Sy
15:12 Sy
1 Sa. 26:12 Sy

καροῦχα.
Isa. 60:20 Sy

καρπεύω.
Ecc. 12: 5 Aq

καρπέω.
Jos. 5:12 MS

καρτερός.
Amos 2:16 Aq
Zec. 6: 3 Aq

καρτερόω.
Pro. 29:35 Aq Th
Isa. 44:14 Aq Th

καρχαρούμενος
2 Sa. 6:16 Aq

κάρωσις.
Psa. 59: 5 Aq

καταβδελύσσομαι.
Eze. 34:27 MS

καταβόσκησις.
Isa. 6:13 Sy

καταβροχή.
Pro. 3: 8 Th

κάταγμα.
Psa. 146: 3 Sy

κατάγχω.
Jud. 11:35, 35 Th

καταδεέστερος.
Job 13: 2 Sy

καταδίκη.
Psa. 89: 3 Sy

κατάδυτον.
Psa. 87: 7 5th

καταιγίζω.
Psa. 49: 3 Th
Isa. 54:11 Sy
Eze. 1: 4 Sy

καταισχυμμός.
Psa. 43:16 Sy
Mic. 2: 6 Sy

κατακαλυπτήρ.
Exo. 27: 3 MS

κατάκαρος.
Gen. 19:12 inc

κατάκλειστος.
Isa. 3:23 MSS

κατάκλισις.
Hos. 7:14 Sy

κατάκλυσις.
Dan. 11:40 MSS

κατακνίζω.
Pro. 27: 4 Sy

κατάκορος.
Gen. 49:12 Aq
Pro. 23:29 Aq

κατάκρισις.
Nu. 13:33 inc

καταλαζονεύομαι.
Psa. 136: 3 Sy

καταλαλάζω.
Psa. 146: 7 Aq

καταλεαίνω.
Dan. 7:23 LXX

κατάλεγμα.
Jer. 32:16 Sy
Eze. 2:10 Sy

καταλογισμός.
1 Ch. 4:33 MSS
5: 7 XI

κατάλογος.
Gen. 47:12 Aq

καταμεγαλύνομαι.
Psa. 37:17 Sy
40:10 A S T

καταμέμφομαι.
Gen. 44: 4 MSS

καταμέτρησις.
Job 28:25 Aq

κατανίκημα.
Isa. 63: 3 Sy Th

καταξιόω.
Gen. 31:28 MS

καταπαιδεύω.
Lam. 1:13 Sy

καταπατάκτη, —τήκτη.
Jer. 36:26 Aq

καταπελτόω.
Jos. 9:11(5) MSS

καταπήξ.
Job 38: 6 Sy

καταπληκτικός.
Cant. 6: 9 6th

κατάπομα.
Jer. 28:44 Aq Sy

καταπονέω.
Job 39:16 inc
Lam. 3:48 MSS

καταπόνησις.
Exo. 3: 7 (Sy)
Psa. 31:10 Sy

κατάποσις.
Pro. 23: 2 Aq

καταπροφασίζομαι.
Jer. 45:19 Aq

καταπτύρω.
Gen. 41: 8 Aq

καταράκτης.
Hos. 13: 3 Aq

κατάργησις.
Lam. 1: 7 Sy

καταρεμβεύω.
Nu. 32:13 XI

κατάρροια.
Psa. 77:44 Aq
125: 4 Aq

καταρροφάω.
Job 39:30 Sy

καταρτισμός.
Isa. 38:12 Sy

κατασκέπασμα.
Exo. 26:36 VIIm

κατασκεπαστός
Nu. 7: 3 Aq

κατασκεύασμα.
Exo. 28: (27) Sy

κατασκευαστός.
Nu. 7: 3 inc

κατάσπευσις.
Pro. 1:27 Th

κατασπουδασμός
Zeph. 1:18 Aq

καταστάζω.
Psa. 118:28 Sy

καταστέλλω.
Psa. 64: 8 Aq

κατάστρωμα.
1 Ki. 6: 9 (5) Sy
14(10) Sy

κατασυρίζω.
Dan. 11:26 LXX

καταταπεινόω.
Exo. 1:14 MS

καταταχέω.
1 Ch. 21: 6 MSS

καταταχύνω.
1 Ch. 21: 6 MSS

κατατίλλω.
Eze. 23:34 A S T

κατατιτρώσκω.
Eze. 22:16 Sy

κατατομή.
Jer. 31:37 Sy

κατατυλόω.
Deu. 8: 4 MSS

κατατυραννέω.
Gen. 43:17 Xm
Nu. 16:13 Sy

καταφανής.
Gen. 22: 2 Aq
Deu. 11:30 rel

καταφλυαρέω.
Jer. 20: 7 Sy

καταφορά.
Gen. 2:21 Aq
1 Sa. 26:12 Aq
Pro. 19:15 Aq
Isa. 29:10 Aq

κατάφρακτος.
Job 39:22 Sy

καταφρόνησις.
Pro. 12: 8 Sy
Eze. 17:20 Sy

καταφρύγω.
Job 30:30 inc

καταχωνεύω.
Job 40: 8 Sy

καταψεύδομαι.
Job 16: 8 Sy

κατάψυξις.
Gen. 3: 8 Th

κατέαγμα.
Lev. 24:20 Xm

κατελαύνω.
Ps. 140: 5 Aq
Isa. 28: 1 Aq
41: 7 Aq

κατέμπροσθεν.
2 Ch. 3:15 MSS

κατεπαίρομαι.
Psa. 60: 3 Sy

κατεπίθεσις.
Psa. 31: 2 Aq
119: 2 Aq

κατεπιλαμβάνω.
2 Sa. 15: 5 Ms

κατέργασμα.
Pro. 8:22 Aq
Psa. 45: 9 Aq

κατερείπω.
Job 36:34 Th

κατηγορέω.
Job 7:13 Sy
2 Sa. 19:27 Mss

κατηγορία.
Gen. 43:17 Xm

κατισχυροῦμαι.
Job 15:25 Th
Psa. 85:14 Aq
88: 8 Aq

κατίσχω.
Pro. 12:25 Th

κατοικιστής.
Jer. 27: 7 Sy

κατόπιν.
Jos. 10:19 Sy
2 Sa. 5:23 Sy

κατούλωσις.
Isa. 58: 8 Aq

κατοχεύς.
Exo. 26:17 Sy

κατοχή.
Cant. 8:11 Sy

καῦσος.
Psa. 31: 4 Sy

καυστός.
Lev. 6:30 Th

καύστρα.
Isa. 30.14 Mss

κεκράγω.
Psa. 27: 2 5th 6th

κελαδέω.
Isa. 42:13 Aq
52: 9 Aq
54: 1 Aq
55:12 Aq

κελεύω.
Jer. 31:33 Sa
2 Ch.34: 8 Mss

κελλάριον.
Gen. 43:29 VIIm

κέντημα.
Pro. 12:18 Sy Th

κένωμα.
Gen. 1: 2 Aq
Deu. 32:10 Aq
Job 26: 7 Aq
Isa. 40:23 Aq

κέρασις.
Isa. 34:11 Th

κεραμικός.
Dan. 2:41 LXX

κεραμύλλιον.
Isa. 63: 3 Aq

κεραύνιος.
Exo. 28:17 Sy

κερδαίνω.
Job 22: 3 Sy

κέρδος.
Gen. 37:26 rel
Ecc. 4: 9 Sy
Mic. 4:13 Sy

κερεϊνός.
Psa. 49: 9 A S 5th

κέρκιον.
Lev. 6:33 rel
8:25 Sy Th

κηδίασις.
Isa. 28:20 Th

κιβώριον.
Amos 9: 1 Sy Th

κιγκλίς.
Eze. 40: 9 Sa

κιγχλιδωτός.
2 Ki. 1: 2 Aq

κικεών.
Jon. 4: 6 Aq Th

κίνημα.
Isa. 28:19 Th

κιρρός.
Pro. 8:19 Aq
Isa. 13:12 Aq

κισσός.
Jon. 4: 6 Sy

κλαγγή.
Job 39:19 Sy

κλάδευσις.
Cant. 2:12 Aq Sy

κλάνιον.
2 Sa. 1:10 Aq

κληματίζω.
Lev. 25: 4 Ms

κληρουργία.
Ruth 4: 7 Sy

κληρουχέω.
Psa. 81: 8 Sy

κλῆτος.
1 Sa. 14:38 Aq

κλονέω.
Exo. 15:14, 15 Aq
Jud. 9:13 Sy
Psa. 4: 5 Aq
Isa. 13:13 Aq
64: 2 Aq

κλόνησις.
Job 3:26 Aq
14: 1 Aq

κλόνος.
Eze. 12:18 Aq

κλύζω.
Isa. 28:15 Aq Sy
Psa. 31: 6 Aq

κνάω.
Job 2: 8 *Heb*

κνίς.
Isa. 31:13 A S T
55:13 Sy

κοιμήτρον.
Jud. 4:18 Sy

κοινολογέομαι.
Psa. 54:15 Sy

κοινομυΐα.
Exo. 8:21 Ms

κολάζω.
2 Sa. 8: 1 Aq
Pro. 22:23 Sy

κολαπτός.
1 Ki. 6:27(29) Mss

κολιάνδρον.
Exo. 16:31 Ms
Nu. 11: 7 Ms

κόλλησις.
Isa. 41: 7 Sy

κολλυρίτης.
1 Ch.16: 3 Mss

κολοβότης.
Exo. 6: 9 Aq

κολυμβάω.
Isa. 25:11 Sy

κόμβος.
Gen. 42:35,35 VIIm

κονδυκέρατος.
Lev. 22:23 Xm

κονδυποτήριον.
Isa. 51:17 Th

κόνις.
Job 40: 8 Sy
Psa. 21:30 Sy

κονία.
Gen. 32:24 Aq
2 Sa. 1: 2 Sy

κοντάριον.
Psa. 34: 2 Sy

κόπριος.
Psa. 82:11 Aq

κοπρών.
2 Ki.10:27 Mss

κοπώδης.
Ecc. 1: 8 Sy

κορμός.
Job 14: 7 Aq Th
Isa. 11: 1 *rel*

κορυφαῖος.
Eze. 23:23 Aq

κοσκινίζω.
Amos 9: 9 Aq Sy

κόσκινον.
Amos 9: 9 Aq Sy

κοσκίνωμα.
Exo. 27: 4 *rel*
35:16 Mss

κόσμημα.
Cant. 1:10 Sy

κόσμησις.
Psa. 31: 9 Aq

κόστος.
Exo. 30:24 Ms

κράββατος.
Amos 3:12 Aq

κράτειλος.
Psa. 28: 1 6th

κρατερός.
Psa. 48:15 Sy
Zec. 6: 3 Aq

κρατύνω.
Psa. 27: 7 5th
63: 6 Sy
Isa. 35: 3 Sy
Eze. 27:27 Th

κρηπίδωμα.
Eze. 43:14, 14 Aq

κρίωμα.
Eze. 40:14, 14 Aq

κροκύφαντος.
Isa. 3:19 Aq

κροκυφάντωτον
Jer. 52:22 Aq Sy
23 Aq

κρουνισμός.
2 Sa. 5: 8 Aq

κρουνός.
Psa. 41: 8 Sy

κροῦσμα.
Isa. 1: 6 Sy

κρύος.
Psa. 77:47 Aq

κρύφα.
Job 13:10 Sy
31:27 Sy

κρυφιαστής.
Gen. 41: 8, 24 Aq
Exo. 7:11 Aq
8: 7 Aq

κρυφίως.
Hab. 3:14 Sy

κτενιστός.
Isa. 19: 9 Sy

κτήτωρ.
Joel 1:11 Sy

κτύπος.
Job 28:26 Aq Sy
38:25 Aq

κυέω.
Job 3: 3 Sy
Psa. 7:15 Sy
50: 7 Sy
Isa. 33:11 Sy

κυθρόγαυλος.
1 Ki. 7:24(38) Mss

κυκάω.
Psa. 2: 1 Sy

κύκησις.
Psa. 64: 3 Sy

κυκλεύω.
2 Sa. 5:23 Sy

κυκληδόν.
Job 37:11 Sy

κυκλοτερῶς.
Eze. 24: 5 Sy

κύκλωσις.
Psa. 65:11 Sy

κύλισμα.
Eze. 10:13 Sy

κυλισμός.
Pro. 2:18 Th

κυνηγέτης.
Psa. 21:17 Aq Th

κυνοκέφαλος.
2 Sa. 3: 8 Sy

κύπρινος.
Cant. 1:14 5th

κωκυτός.
Psa. 143:14 Sy

κώρυκος.
2 Ki. 4:42 XI

λαγών.
Lev. 3: 4 Xm
Job 40:11 Sy Th
Psa. 37: 8 Aq
Isa. 11: 5 Sy
Jer. 37: 6 Sy

λαθραῖος.
Pro. 21:14 Mss

λαϊκός.
1 Sa. 21: 4 A S T
Eze. 22:26 Sy
48:15 Sy Th

λαϊκόω.
Deu. 20: 6 *rel*
28:30 Aq
Eze. 7:22 Aq

λαιλαπίζω, -πέω
Psa. 49: 3 Aq
57:10 Aq
Isa. 54:11 Aq

λαιλαπώδης.
Psa. 54: 9 Aq Th

λαιόπους.
Gen. 30:35 *inc*

λακκόω.
Ruth 1:12 X, XI

λάμια.
Isa. 34:14 Sy

λαμπηδών.
Isa. 58:11 Aq

λαμπρός.
Pro. 20:11 Th
Cant. 5:10 Sy
Lam. 4: 7 Sy

λαμπρύνω.
Ps. 118: 9 Sy
Pro. 20: 9 Sy

λαοκατάρατος.
Pro. 11:26 Sy

λαρνάκιον.
1 Sa. 6: 8 Sy

λάρναξ.
1 Sa. 6: 8 Aq

λαῦρος.
Psa. 56: 5 *inc*

λαφυρέω.
Isa. 59:15 Aq

λεαίνω.
Isa. 41: 7 Aq

λειόγλωσσος.
Pro. 6:24 Sy Th

λειόω.
Pro. 28:23 Aq

λειποψυχέω.
Gen. 45:26 Sy

λείψανον.
Jud. 5:13 Sy
•Psa. 16:14 Sy
75:11 Sy
Eze. 11:13 Sy

λεκτίς.
Isa. 66:20 Sy

λεπιδωτός.
1 Sa. 17: 5 Sy Th

λεπιστόν.
Lev. 23:14 Ms

λεπτοκοπέω.
Isa. 27: 9 Sy
28:28 A S T

Λευιαθάν.
Job 3: 8 Aq Sy
40:20 Aq Sy
Isa. 27: 1 A S T
Eze. 32: 2 Aq

λευκίζω.
Lev. 13:19 Mss

λευκόπους.
Gen. 30:35 Sy

λεύκωμα.
Lev. 21:20 A S T

λεωπετρίανδε,
λεο-
Psa. 67: 7 Aq

ληκύθιον, -θιά
1 Ki.17:12 Aq

ληνοβατέω.
Jer. 31:33 Sa
32:16 (Sy)

ληστεύω.
Hos. 7: 1 5th

ληστρικός.
Hos. 6: 9 5th

ληστρίς.
Psa. 136: 8 Sy

λιβάς.
Gen. 49:11 X

λιθέα.
Cant. 5:11 Aq

λιθοβολία.
Lev. 24.16 Mss

λιθολογέω.
Mic. 3:12 Aq

λιθολογία.
Psa. 78: 1 Aq

λιθόριον, λιθου-
Psa. 78: 1 Aq

λικμητήριον.
Isa. 30:24 Th
Jer. 15: 7 Sy

λικμητής.
Jer. 28: 2 Aq Sy

λικμίζω.
Amos 9: 9 Mss

λιμώδης.
Job 6: 5 Sy
30: 7 Sy

λιπαρία.
Isa. 28: 1 Aq

λιπαρότης.
Psa. 72: 7 Sy

λιποθυμέω, λει-
Gen. 45:26 Sy
Jud. 4:21 Sy
Psa. 76: 4 Sy

λίπος.
Nu. 11: 8 Sy
Jud. 9: 9 Sy
Psa. 72: 7 Sy

λῖς.
Job 4:11 Aq

λιχάς, λιχανός
Isa. 10:12 Aq

λογάς.
Jer. 28:27 Sy

λόγχη.
Lev. 14:10 Ms

λογοποιία.
Psa. 101: 1 Sy

λόφος.
Psa. 64:11 5th

λοχαγός.
2 Sa. 4: 2 Sy

λόχος.
Gen. 49:19 Sy
1 Sa. 30: 8, 15 Sy
2 Sa. 3:22 Sy
Hos. 6: 9 5th

λυγμός.
1 Sa. 25:31 Aq Th

λυδεόω.
Isa. 33: 9 Aq

λύρα.
1 Ch. 25: 3 Sy
Psa. 80: 3 Sy
150: 3 Aq Sy

λωποδύτης.
Hos. 7: 1 5th

λωφάω.
Gen. 8: 1 Sy

μαγκιπίσσα.
1 Sa. 8:13 Ms

μάγγωζον.
Eze. 27:24 Aq Sy

μάζα.
Hab. 2:11 Aq

μάθησις.
Pro. 2:17 Sy

μακρυσμός.
Psa. 55: 1 Aq
119: 5 Aq

μαλάβαθρον.
Cant. 2:17 inc

μαλαγματίζω.
Hos. 6: 1 Sy

μαλάσσω.
Eze. 23: 3 Sy

μάλη.
Pro. 19:24 Sy
26:15 A S T

μάλιστα.
Gen. 42:21 Aq

μαλλός.
Eze. 8: 3 Sy

μανδύα.
1 Sa. 4:12 Aq

μανιακός.
Jud. 8:21 Mss

μάρμαρος.
Lam. 3: 9 Mss

μασθός.
Isa. 60:16 A S T

μασχάλη.
Pro. 19:24 Aq

ματαιοπονέω.
Psa. 61: 4 Sy

μεγαλαύχημα.
Eze. 32:12 Sy

μεγαλείωμα.
Jer. 31:17 Ms

μεγαλόθυμος.
Pro. 19:19 Th

μεγεθύνω.
Nu. 6: 5 Aq
Cant. 6: 9 inc

μέθοδος.
Psa. 24: 4 6th

μειδιάω.
Psa. 38.11 Sy
Amos 5: 9 Aq

μειόω.
Isa. 51: 6 inc

μελαίνω.
Job 30:30 rel

μελανοδοχεῖον.
Eze. 9:11 Aq

μελετητικός.
Eze. 7:10 Th

μεληδόν.
Exo. 29:17 Ms

μελικήριον.
Exo. 16:31 Sy

μελλέω.
Gen. 19:16 Aq
Hab. 2: 3 Aq

μελοκοπία.
Nah. 3: 1 Sy

μελῳδέω.
Psa. 26: 6 Aq Sy
65: 4 Sy
70:22 Aq
137: 1 Aq 5th

μελῴδημα.
Psa. 4: 1 Aq
6: 1 Aq
8: 1 Aq
9:17 Th

μελῳδία.
Job 30: 9 Sy
35:10 Aq
Psa. 80: 3 Aq
91: 4 Sy
Isa. 24:16 Aq

μελῳδός.
Psa. 67:26 Sy

μέμφομαι.
Job 1:22 Heb

μέντοιγε.
Jer. 43:25 Sy

μεσάζω.
1 Sa. 17: 4 Aq

μέσακρον.
1 Sa. 17: 7 Mss

μεσάντιον.
1 Sa. 17: 7 Mss

μέσαυλον.
1 Sa. 17: 7 Mss

μεσῆλιξ.
1 Sa. 17:23 Mss

μεταβαίνω.
Psa. 23: 7 Sy

μεταβούλευμα.
Job 21: 2 Sy

μεταγενής.
Psa. 47:14 Sy

μεταγινώσκω.
Psa. 29:13 inc

μεταίχμιος.
Jud. 5:16 Sy

μετακίνημα.
Psa. 43:15 inc

μετακλάω.
Psa. 74:10 Sy

μετακλίνω.
1 Sa. 8: 3 Sy
Psa. 43:19 Sy

μεταλαμβάνω.
2 Sa. 3:35 Sy

μεταμανθάνω.
Job 39:35 Sy

μεταμορφόω.
Psa. 33: 1 Sy

μετανάστατος.
Isa. 58: 7 Th

μετανάστης.
Jer. 30: 5 Aq Th

μεταναστρέφω.
Zeph. 3: 9 Sy

μέταρσις.
1 Sa. 2: 3 inc
Isa. 23:13 Aq

μετασχηματίζω.
1 Sa. 25: 8 Sy

μετατρέπω.
Eze. 1: 8 Aq
10:11 Sy

μεταφορά.
Hos. 8:12 Th

μεταφυτεύω.
Psa. 1: 3 Aq
91:14 rel

μεταχρόω.
Lev. 13:13 Sy

μετεωρέω.
Ecc. 10: 9 Sy

μετεωρότης.
Job 11: 8 Aq
40: 5 inc
Eze. 1:18 Aq

μετοίκησις.
Zec. 13: 1 Mss

μήκιστος.
Eze. 17: 3 Aq

μηλέα.
Cant. 8: 5 Sy

μήνη.
Psa. 88:38 Sy

μήνυμα.
De. 14:20(21) VII m

μηνύω.
Nu. 25: 5 Sy
Job 12: 8 Sy

μηχάνημα.
Psa. 65: 5 Sy
76:13 Sy

μηχάνωμα.
Lev. 8: 7 Sy Th

μιαιφόνος.
Psa. 25: 9 Sy
54:24 Sy
138:19 Sy

μιασμός.
Deu. 26:14 Aq
2 Sa. 11: 4 Sy

μιμέομαι.
Eze. 16:61 Aq

μίμημα.
Eze. 23:14 Aq

μινυρίζω.
Psa. 48: 5 inc

μισθαρνέω.
1 Sa. 2: 5 inc
36 Sy

μισθοφορία.
1 Sa. 17:18 Sy

μίσθωσις.
Gen. 31: 7 Aq

μισοποιέω.
Psa. 80:16 Aq
82: 3 Aq

μισοποιός.
Psa. 80:16 Sy

μόλυβδος.
Exo. 15:10 Mss
Job 19:24 Mss

μοναχός.
Gen. 2:18 Sy
Psa. 21:21 Aq
34:17 Aq
67: 7 Sy Th

μοναχόω.
Psa. 85:11 Aq

μονόζωνος.
Psa. 67: 7 5th

μονομάχη.
Psa. 21:21 Aq
34:17 Aq

μονότης.
Psa. 21:21 Sy
34:17 Sy

μονόχειρ.
Lev. 21:20 Ms

μονόω.
Gen. 49: 6 Aq
Job 3: 7 Heb
30: 3 inc

μόριον.
Job 38:31 Sy

μορφόω.
Psa. 33: 1 Sy
Isa. 41:13 Aq

μόρφωμα.
Gen. 31:19 Aq
Jud. 17: 5 Aq
Hos. 3: 4 Aq

μοσχόταυρος.
Lev. 4: 3 Xm

μότωσις.
Isa. 1: 6 Aq

μοχθηρόομαι.
Job 6:25 Aq

μοχθόω.
Isa. 7:13 Aq

μοχλεύω.
Pro. 18:19 Mss

μυέω.
Nu. 25: 5 Sy

μυζέω.
Job 20:16 rel

μυζήτης.
Psa. 77:46 Sy

μυκάομαι.
1 Sa. 6:12 inc
Job 6: 5 Sy

μυρεψητήριον.
Job 41:22 Aq

μυρέψιον.
Isa. 57: 9 Sy

μυρσινεών.
Zec. 1: 8 Aq Sy

μυσάζω.
1 Sa. 25:26 Aq

μυσαρία.
Eze. 16:58 Sy
23:27 Sy

μυσερός.
Lev. 26:30 Xm

μύσος.
Lev. 18:17 Sy
Psa. 25:10 Aq
Eze. 22: 9 Sy

μυσόω.
1 Sa. 25:33 rel

μυστικός.
Isa. 3: 3 Sy

μυχθίζω, -θέω
Psa. 2: 4 Aq

μυχθισμός.
Ps. 122: 4 Aq
Hos. 7:16 Aq

μύω.
Isa. 6:10 Sy

μωλωπίζω.
Cant. 5: 7 Aq

μωρία.
Job 24:12 Sy

νάβλη.
Psa. 80: 3 Aq Sy

ναζιραία, ναζα-
Lev. 25: 5, 11 Xm

νακτός.
Exo. 13:16 Aq
Deu. 6: 8 Aq

νᾶνος.
Lev. 21:20 Xm

ναῦλα, -λη.
Psa. 32: 2 Aq
91: 4 Sy
150: 3 Sy

ναύτης.
Eze. 27: 9 Aq
29 Sy

νεανιότης,
-ικότης.
Psa. 9: 1 Aq 6th
109: 3 6th
126: 4 inc

νεαρά.
Exo. 13: 4 inc

νεοσσοτροφία.
Job 39:16 inc

νεφώδης.
Isa. 13: 2 inc

νέφωσις. Job 3: 5 Aq

νῆμα. Gen. 14:23 Sy

νήστης. Dan. 6:18 LXX

νικοποιέω. Ezra 3: 8 MSS

νικοποιός. Psa. 4: 1 Aq
5: 1 Aq
&c., &c.

νομεύς. 1 Ch. 4:41 MS
Amos 1: 2 Aq
Mic. 5: 5 Aq

νομίζω. Job 13: 5 Sy
Psa. 49:21 Sy

νομοδότης. Psa. 75:13 Sy

νοσέω. Gen. 48: 1 Sy
1 Sa. 30:13 Sy

νότιος. 1 Sa. 20:41 Aq
Hab. 3: 3 Th

νότονδε. Gen. 12: 9 Aq

νυκτερεύω. Psa. 90: 1 Sy

νυκτοπότιον. 1 Sa. 26:11 Sy

νυμφευτής. Exo. 3: 1 Aq
18: 1, 5 Aq

νυμφεύω. 1 Sa. 18:21 Aq

νυμφών. Joel 2:16 XII

νωθρεύομαι. Jud. 19: 8 Aq

νωτοκοπέω. Exo. 13:13 Th
Isa. 66: 3 Th

νωχελεύομαι. Pro. 18: 9 Aq
24: 9(10) Aq
Hab. 2: 4 Aq

ξένη. Pro. 23:27 Th

ξενίζω. Neh. 5:17 MSS

ξέστης. Lev. 14:10 Xm

ξηρότης. Psa. 67: 7 Sy

ξόανον. Eze. 6: 4 Aq

ξυλόκοκκον. Nu. 3:47 VIIm

ξυλοπέδη. Job 13:27 Aq
33:11 inc

ξυστής. 2 Ki. 12:12 MSS

ξυστρωτός. 1 Ki. 6:18 Aq Th

ὁδίτης. Jer. 14: 8 Sa

ὁδοιπορία. Job 6:19 inc

οἴ. Zeph. 3:18 Aq

οἰάκωσις. Job 37:11 Aq

οἰκετία. Job 1: 3 Sy

οἰκητήριον. Psa. 67: 6 Aq
90: 9 Aq
Jer. 32:16 MSS

οἰκοδόμημα. Amos 9: 1 Aq

οἴκονδε. Psa. 67: 7 Aq

οἰμωγή. Exo. 2:24 Aq Sy
Psa. 11: 6 Aq Sy
87:14 Sy
101: 2 Sy
Mal. 2:13 Aq

οἰμώζω. Psa. 71:12 Sy
Jer. 28:32 Sy

οἰμώσσω. Mal. 2:13 Sy

οἰνάνθη. Cant. 2: 5, 13 Sy

οἰνία. Isa. 62: 8 Aq
Zec. 9:17 Aq

οἰνών. Cant. 2: 4 Sy

ὀκνηρεύω. Nu. 32: 9 MS

ὀλίγιστος. Psa. 80:15 Sy

ὀλίγως. Isa. 10: 7 Aq

ὀλιόω. Jer. 14: 2 Aq

ὀλισθηρός. Pro. 2:16 Sy
7: 5 Th
Eze. 12:24 Sy

ὄλισθος. Psa. 72:18 Sy

ὅλμος. Jud. 15:19 rel
Pro. 27:22 Aq Th
Zeph. 1:11 Aq Sy

ὁλόξηρος. Psa. 57:10 Sy

ὁλοτελῶς. Deu. 13:16 Aq

ὁμαλή. Isa. 35: 1 Aq

ὁμαλός. Deu. 1: 1 Aq Sy
1 Sa. 23:24 Aq
Psa. 25:12 Sy

ὀμβρέω. Psa. 77: 2 Aq

ὅμιλος. 1 Sa. 19:20 Aq
Psa. 1: 5 (Sy)

ὀμιχλόω. Psa. 64:13 Sy

ὁμόγνωμος. Gen. 49: 5 VIIm

ὁμογνώμων. Psa. 118:24 Sy

ὁμοιότροπος. Psa. 54:14 (Sy)

ὁμότροπος. Psa. 54:14 Sy

ὅμως. 1 Sa. 21: 5 inc

ὀνάς. Gen. 45:23 VIIm
Nu. 22:23 Aq
Jud. 5:10 Sy
Zec. 9: 9 Aq Sy

ὄνειρος. Psa. 72:20 Sy
Ecc. 5: 2, 6 Sy

ὀνομασία. 2 Ch. 28:15 MSS
Psa. 48:12 Sy
67: 5 Sy

ὀξυντήρ. Job 41:21 Aq

ὀπισθοφανής. Gen. 9:23 I, X

ὁπλίζω. Jer. 52:25 Sy

ὁπουδήποτε. 1 Sa. 23:13 Sy

ὀπτάνιον. Hos. 7: 4 5th

ὀπωρισμός. Deu. 7:13 Aq
Isa. 65: 8 Aq

ὁραματίζομαι. Psa. 10: 4 Aq
57: 9 Aq
Cant. 7: 1 Aq
Isa. 30:10 Aq Th

ὁραματισμός. Job 4:13 Aq
Pro. 29:18 Aq
Dan. 9:24 Aq
Hab. 2: 2 Aq

ὁραματιστής. Isa. 56:10 Sy

ὀρέγω. Job 8:20 Sy
Eze. 16:49 Sy

ὀρθότης. Isa. 57: 2 Aq

ὀρθοτριχέω. Ps. 118:120 Sy
Isa. 13:21 Th
34:14 Th
Eze. 27:35 Sy

ὀρθρισμός. Pro. 11:27 Aq

ὀρίγανον. Nu. 19: 6 MSS

ὁριοθετέω. Exo. 19:12 rel
Deu. 19:14 Aq
Zec. 9: 2 Aq

ὀρνίζω. Isa. 38:14 Aq

ὀρόδαμνος. Job 40:17 MSS

ὁροθετέω. Exo. 19:12 VIIm

ὄρυγμα. Pro. 23:27 Sy

ὄρυζα. Exo. 16:31 Sa

ὀρυκτός. Isa. 2:29 Aq

ὄσπριον. Dan. 1:12, 16 LXX

ὀσπριώδης. Lev. 2:14 Aq

ὀστεΐνος. Gen. 18:18 Aq
Psa. 34:18 Aq

ὀστέωσις. Isa. 40:29 Aq
41:21 Aq

ὀστοΐνος. Exo. 1: 9 Aq
Deu. 7: 1 Aq
9: 1 inc

ὀστώδης. Gen. 49:14 Aq
2 Ki. 9:13 Aq

ὄσφρανσις. Hos. 14: 6 MS

ὀτρύνω. 1 Sa. 25:14 Aq

οὐδαμινός. Neh. 4: 2 MS

οὐδένωσις. Isa. 34:11 Th

οὐδός. Eze. 40: 6, 7 Sy
47: 1 inc

οὐλόκομος. Lev. 23:40 Xm

οὖλος. Deu. 24:21 Aq

οὐσία. Ecc. 2: 8 Aq

ὀφλέω. Jer. 15:10 Sa

ὄφλημα. Psa. 31: 1 (6th)
54:12 Aq

ὀφρυόομαι. Psa. 67:17 Aq

ὀχετός. Job 22:24 Sy
Psa. 64:10 Sy
125: 4 Sy
Eze. 34:13 Sy

ὄχησις. Psa. 67:18 Sy

ὄχθη. Gen. 41: 2 MSS

ὀχλάζω. Psa. 58: 7, 15 Aq
Pro. 7:11 Aq
Jer. 4:19 Aq

ὀχλέω. Ezra 4:13, 22 MSS
Hab. 2:15 inc

παγίδευμα. Ecc. 7:27(26) inc

παγκτησία Lev. 25:23 Aq

παιδιότης. Psa. 109: 3 Aq

παλαιστιαῖος. Jud. 3:16 Aq Sy

παλαίστωμα 1 Ki. 7:46(9) Aq

παλάμη. Nu. 6:19 Sy
Job 11:13 Sy
36:32 Sy

παλινδρομέω. Isa. 38: 8 Sy

παμμεγέθης. Psa. 67:31 Sy

πάμμικτος. Psa. 77:45 (Aq)
101:31 Aq

παμμυΐα. Exo. 8:21 Aq
Psa. 77:45 (Aq)

παμπληθής. Psa. 34:18 Sy
138:17 Sy

παμπληθύω. Job 36:31 Aq

πάμπολυς. Job 36:31 Sy
Psa. 30: 6 Sy

πάνδημος. 1 Sa. 20:29 Sy

πανούργημα. Nu. 5:12 MS

πανούργως. Psa. 82: 4 Sy

πανσέληνος. Pro. 7:20 Aq

πανσπερμία. Psa. 64:10 Sy

παντελής. Job 30: 3 Aq

παντοδαπία. Isa. 66:11 Aq

παντοῖος. 2 Sa. 6: 5 Sy
Eze. 23: 6, 12 Th
Dan. 2: 6 LXX

πάντως. 2 Sa. 14:14 Sy

παπυρεών, -ρών Exo. 2: 3, 5 Aq

παπύρινος. Isa. 18: 2 Sy

παραβάτης. Psa. 16: 4 Sy
138:19 Sy
Jer. 6:28 Sy

παραγραφίς. Isa. 44:13 Aq

παραγωνίσκος. Isa. 44:13 MSS

παραδειγματισμός. Psa. 30:21 Sy

παραδηλόω. Exo. 27: 8 MS

παραδοκάω. Psa. 32:20 Aq 6th

παραδοξασμός. Isa. 9: 6 Sy

παράδοξος. Psa. 89:10 Sy
117:23 Sy
138:14 Sy

παραδόξως. Psa. 89:10 Sy
Isa. 29:14 Sy

παραζήλωσις. Eze. 8: 3 Sy

παραζητέω. Lev. 27:33 Xm

παραίνεσις. Ps. 118:56, 100 Sy

παραινέω. Ecc. 8: 2 Sy

παρακάλυμμα.
Exo.26:36 *inc*

παράκειμαι.
Zec. 14: 5 Sy

παράκλητος.
Job 16: 2 Aq Th

παρακλίνω.
2 Sa. 14: 1 MS

παρακλύζω.
Psa. 123: 4 *inc*

παρακολουθέω
Ecc. 2:12 Aq Sy

παρακυρόω.
Job 40: 3 Sy

παράκυψις.
1 Ki. 7:41(4) Sy

παραλείπω.
Job 14:19 Sy
2 Ki.20:13 Mss

παραλογισμός.
2 Sa. 3:27 Mss
Job 13: 9 Aq

παράλογος.
Ezra 4:22 Mss

παραμυθέομαι.
2 Sa. 10: 2 Sy
Job 2:11 Sy
Isa. 40: 2 Sy
Jer. 38:13 Sy

παραμυθία.
Psa. 70:21 Sy
Isa. 66:11 Sy

παραπλαγιάζω
1 Sa. 23:26 Mss

παραπληκτεύομαι.
1 Sa. 21:14, 15 Aq

παραπλησίως.
Hos. 8: 6 5th

παραπρολέγω.
Jer. 36:26 Sy

παραρρυέω.
Pro. 4:21 Sy

παραστάς.
Jud. 3:22 Aq
Isa. 57: 8 Aq
Eze. 40:10, 12 Sy
16, 21 Sy

παράστασις.
Nu. 8:24 Sy
1 Ki.10: 5 Mss

παρασύρω.
Job 22:16 Sy

παρατάνυσμα.
Exo. 27:16 Aq Sy
37: 5 Aq
Nu. 4:25, 26 Aq

παρατανυσμός.
Exo. 26:36 Aq

παρατήρησις.
Exo. 12:42 Aq

παρατρέπω.
Job 12:24 Sy
21: 4 Sy
34: 5 Sy
Ps. 140: 4 Sy

παρατυγχάνω.
Ecc. 11: 3 Sy

παράφορος, -φερος.
Lev. 25:10 Aq
Deu. 28:34 Sy

παράφρων.
1 Sa. 21:14 Sy

παραφυλάσσω.
Jon. 2: 9 Sy

παρειά.
Cant. 4: 3 Sy

παρεκτός.
Lev. 23:38 Xm
Deu. 1:36 Aq

παρελαύνω.
2 Sa. 2:19 Sy

παρελκύω.
Ps. 119: 5 Sy

παρέλκω.
Eze. 32:18 Sy Th

παρεμβλέπω.
Cant. 1: 6 Sy

παρέμβλησις.
Isa. 29: 1 Aq

πάρεργος.
Pro. 26:22 Sy

παρερεθίζω.
Psa. 30: 1 Th
Pro. 24:19 Sy

παρηγορέω.
Gen. 24:67 Sy
Job 7:13 Sy
Psa. 68:21 Sy
Isa. 40: 1, 1 Sy
Eze. 16:54 Aq Sy

παροδίτης.
2 Sa. 12: 4 Aq

παροικίζω.
Eze. 12:25 Sy

παροιμιάζω.
Nu. 21:27 *inc*
Eze. 24: 3 Aq Sy

παροιμιαστής.
Ecc. 12:10 (Sy)

παρόμασις.
Psa. 89: 8 Aq

παρορμάω.
Pro. 6: 3 Sy Th

παρορμίζω.
Hos. 5:10 Sy

παρωρισμός.
Isa. 24: 7 Aq

παστάς.
Isa. 57: 8 Aq

παστόω.
Deu. 33:12 Aq

πεδιάς.
Nu. 31:12 Sy
2 Sa. 4: 7 Sy
15:28 Sy
Amos 6:14 Sy

πειθαρχέω.
Dan. 7:27 LXX

πεκούλιον.
Ecc. 2: 8 Sy

πεμπταΐζω.
Exo. 13:18 Th

πενθεινός.
Isa. 61: 2 Aq Th

πενθήρος.
Jer. 9:10 Sy

πενθίμος.
Jer. 9:19 Sy

πενθοποιέω.
Lev. 26:22 Xm

πεπιστωμένως.
Nu. 5:22, 22 Aq
Deu. 27:15 Aq
Psa. 40:14, 14 Aq
Isa. 25: 1 Aq

πέραθεν.
Isa. 18: 1 Sy

περαΐτης.
Gen. 14:13 Aq

περάω.
Jer. 12: 5 *Su*

περιαμαρτάνω, -τίζω.
Exo. 29:36 *rel*
Lev. 6:26 *inc*
8:15 *rel*
9:15 Aq
14:49 *rel*

περιαμαρτισμός.
Zec. 13: 1 Sy

περιγραφή.
Job 22:14 Sy

περιγράφω.
Job 26:10 Sy

περιγώνιον.
Isa. 44:13 Aq

περιγωνίσκος.
Isa. 44:13 Mss

περιδέρραιον.
Eze. 16:11 Sy

περιδιώκω.
Job 13:25 Aq

περιδρομή.
Eze. 28:16 XIIm
43:14 Sy

περιειλέω.
Job 38: 9 Aq Sy
Ps. 142: 4 Aq
Isa. 57:16 Aq

περιεργάζομαι
2 Sa. 11: 3 Sy
Ecc. 7:30 Sy

περιηχέω.
Jer. 18:18 Sy

περίθεσις.
Psa. 31: 9 Sy

περικαίω.
2 Ki.16: 3 *inc*

περικαμπής.
Isa. 40: 4 Aq
Hos. 6: 8 Aq

περίκαρπα.
1 Sa. 10: 3 Aq

περίκειμαι.
2 Sa. 20: 8 Mss
Isa. 61:10 Sy
Jer. 32: 9 *inc*

περικεντέω.
Pro. 19: 7 Mss

περικλάω.
Job 8:12 Aq
Eze. 17:22 Aq

περικλώθω.
Exo. 28:11 Mss

περικόπτω.
Psa. 74.10 Aq
Zec. 11:10 Aq

περικρατέω.
Jer. 20: 7 Sy

περικυλίω.
Cant. 2: 5 Sy

περιλύω.
1 Sa. 5: 9 Aq
Psa. 29:12 Aq
Isa. 52: 2 Aq

περινοέω.
Pro. 3: 4 AST

περίνοια.
Psa. 76:12 Sy

περιξυράω.
Lev. 19:27 Sy

περιορισμός.
Eze. 43:13, 17 Sy

περιουσία.
Psa. 16:14 Aq

περιουσιάζω.
Gen. 31:18 Xm

περιπάτημα.
Psa. 72: 9 Sy

περιπέδινος.
Gen. 14: 3, 8 Aq

περιπήγνυμι.
Lev. 15: 3 Sy

περιπνίγω.
2 Sa. 22: 5 Mss

περιρραντισμός
Zec. 13: 1 Sy

περισκέλιον.
Lev. 16: 4 Mss

περισκοπέω.
Psa. 36:32 Sy

περισπουδάζω.
Psa. 67:17 Sy

περιστεριδεύς.
Lev. 1:14 V

περιστερίδιον.
Gen. 15: 9 Aq

περιστεφανόω.
1 Sa. 23:26 *rel*

περιστοιχίζω.
Psa. 47:13 Sy
Hos. 8:10 5th

περιστρώμα.
Pro. 7:16 Aq Th

περιστρώννυμι
Pro. 7:16 Aq Th

περισφίγγω.
Cant. 8: 9 Sy

περισφραγίζομαι
Pro. 24:66 Sy

περιτείχισμα.
2 Sa. 20:15 Mss

περιτραχήλιος.
Gen. 38:25 Sy
Pro. 1: 9 Aq
Cant. 7: 1 Sy
Hos. 2:13 Sy

περιτρέπω.
Job 9: 6 *rel*
12:20 Sy
Psa. 25: 1 Sy
45: 7 Sy

περιφέγγω.
Eze. 1:27 Sy

περιφλευσμός.
Deu. 28:22 Aq

περιφλογισμός
Deu. 28:22 Sy Th

περίφραγμα.
Isa. 29: 1 Th
Eze. 16:23 Sy
Mic. 7:12 *inc*

περιφράκτης.
Isa. 58:12 Aq

περιφρύγω.
Cant. 1: 6 Th

περιφύομαι.
Job 30:13 Sy

περιχαράσσω.
Job 13:27 *Heb*

περιχωρίον.
Psa. 57: 9 Sy

περίψημα.
Jer. 22:28 (Sy)

περίψυκτος, -υχος.
Jud. 11:34 Mss

περκνός, -κος.
Gen. 30:22 Mss

περόνη.
Exo. 35:10 Sy Th
Job 40:19 Sy

πέτρος.
Exo. 4:25 Aq
Psa. 77:15 Aq

πηκτός.
Jer. 10: 5 Th

πήλιον.
Exo. 28: 4 *Su*
Lev. 8:13 *Su*

πήρα.
1 Sa. 18:40 Sy

πήρωσις.
Deu. 28:28 Aq

πηχίζω.
Eze. 43:13 XIIm

πηχισμός.
Eze. 43:13 XIIm

πῆχμα.
Eze. 43:15 Aq

πικραμμοί.
Job 3: 5 Aq

πιλέω.
Psa. 135: 6 *inc*

πιμελή.
Job 15:27 Aq Sy

πιμελής.
Jud. 3:17 Aq
Ps. 117:27 Aq

πιμελόομαι.
1 Sa. 2:29 *inc*

πινακίδιον.
Eze. 9: 2 Sy

πινακίς.
Eze. 9:11 Sy

πίνωσις.
Pro. 25:12 *inc*

ΠΙΠΙ.
Jehovah.
Nu. 16: 5 *rel*
Psa. 25: 1 Aq Sy
27: 1 Aq Sy

πίστωσις.
Lev. 6: 2 Xm

πλαγίως.
Lev. 26:24 IV

πλαδαρόομαι.
Isa. 19: 3 Aq

πλακώτης.
Jer. 31: 5 Sy

πλανητεύω.
Lev. 16:21 Xm

πλάστης.
2 Sa. 22: 3 Mss
23: 3 Mss
Isa. 61: 8 Aq Th
Zec. 11:13 Aq

πλατύψυχος.
Pro. 28:25 Sy

πλέγμα.
Isa. 28: 5 Aq Th

πλεκτός.
Exo. 27:11 Xm

πλεονέκτημα.
Gen. 37:26 Aq
Isa. 56:11 Mss

πλεονέκτης.
Psa. 9:24 Aq Sy

πληθύς.
Psa. 30:11 Sy

πλήκτης.
Psa. 34:15 Sy

πληκτικός.
Jer. 37: 5 Ms

πλημμυρέω.
Ecc. 1: 7 Sy
Jer. 12: 5 Sa

πλῆξις.
Pro. 17:10 Aq

πλησιόχωρος.
Dan. 11:24 Mss

πλινθάριον.
Exo. 5:16 VIIm

πλόκαμος.
Cant. 4: 9 Aq

πλύσις.
Psa. 59:10 Sa

ποδοκάκη.
Job 13:27 inc

πόθος.
Psa. 9:24 Aq

ποιμνιοτρόφος
2 Ki. 3: 4 Aq
Amos 1: 1 Aq

πολιόομαι.
1 Sa. 12: 2 Mss

πολιορκητής.
Isa. 30:19 Th
63: 9 Th

πολίχνη.
Isa. 26: 5 Aq
29: 1 Aq

πολλαπλασίως
2 Sa. 12: 8 Sy

πολύβουλος.
Pro. 11:14 Sy Th
24: 6 Sy Th

πολυκαρπία.
Psa. 64:10 Sy

πολύλαλος.
Job 11: 2 Sy

πολύμιτος.
Eze. 27:16 Sy

πολυπραγμοσύνη.
Ecc. 7:30 Sy

πολύστρεβλος.
Pro. 28:16 inc

πολυφόρος.
Isa. 32:12 Sy Th

πολυχειρία.
Hos. 6: 9 5th

πομπή.
Psa. 43:14 inc

πονηρόφθαλμος.
Pro. 23: 6 Ms

πονικός.
Pro. 15: 1 Th

πορθέω.
Deu. 2:34 Sy
Jer. 41:22 Sy
44: 8 Sy

πορίζω.
Ecc. 9:11 Sy

πορφυρόω.
Isa. 61: 6 Aq

ποσαχῶς.
Psa. 62: 2 Th

ποταμόω, –ίζω
Jer. 28:44 Aq

ποτισμός.
Pro. 3: 8 Aq

ποτιστής.
Gen. 40: 5 Aq

ποτίστρια.
Exo. 2:16 VIIm

πραέως.
Isa. 40:11 Th

πρᾶος.
2 Sa 22:28 Mss
Psa. 17:28 Sy
Zeph. 3:12 Mss

πρασιά.
Cant. 5:13 Aq Sy
6: 1 Aq Sy
Eze. 17: 7, 10 Aq

πρασιάομαι.
Psa. 41: 2 Aq 5th

πρασιόω.
Joel 1:20 Aq

πρέμνον.
Eze. 17: 7 Sy

πρέπω.
Pro. 26: 1 Sy Th

πρεσβευτής.
Isa. 18: 2 Aq

πρηστήρ.
Eze. 1: 4 Aq

πρινεών.
Gen. 14: 3, 8 Aq

πρίνινος.
Eze. 27: 5 Aq

πριστήρ.
1 Ki. 7:16(9) Aq

προαπολαμβάνω
1 Sa. 2:29 inc

πρόβολος.
Lev. 1:16 Mss

προγίνομαι.
Ecc. 10:14 Sy

πρόδομος.
1 Ki. 7:13(6) Aq
44(7) Aq
Joel 2:17 Aq

προεκπέμπω.
2 Sa. 19:31 Mss

προέλευσις.
Exo. 21: 8 Sy
Psa. 64: 9 Sy
120: 8 Sy

προθεσμία.
Job 28: 3 Sy
Dan. 9:26, 26 Sy

πρόθυμα.
Exo. 24: 6 Aq

προῖκα.
Exo. 18: 2 VIIm

προκαθίστημι.
Jud. 14:11 XI

προκαλέω.
Psa. 39: 2 Sy

προκατάρχω.
Psa. 116: 7 inc

προκρίνω.
Job 36:21 Sy

προμαχέω.
Psa. 73:22 Sy

πρόμετρος.
2 Sa. 21:20 Sy

προνεύω.
Amos 7:17 Sy Th

πρόνοια.
Jos. 20: 3 Mss
Psa. 70:12 Sy

προοδεύω.
Psa. 83: 7 Sy

προπάτωρ.
Psa. 29: 8 Sy

προπέμπω.
2 Sa. 19:31 XI

προπηλακίζω.
Psa. 54:13 Sy
73:10 Sy

προπηλακισμός.
Psa. 43:14 Sy

προπίπτω.
Psa. 72: 7 Sy

προποιέω.
Psa. 136: 8 inc

πρόποσις.
Est. 7: 2 Ms

προσβιβάζω.
Deu. 6: 7 Ms

προσβλέπω.
Psa. 83:10 Sy
Jon. 2: 5 Sy

προσβόλωσις.
1 Sa. 13:21 inc

προσγελάω.
Job 29:24 Sy

προσγράφω.
Dan. 3: 3 LXX

προσδόκιμος.
Job 17:12 Sy

πρόσειμι.
1 Sa. 17:16 Mss

προσέλευσις.
Ps. 120: 8 inc
Pro. 4:23 Sy

προσεμπυρίζω.
Exo. 22: 6 Ms

προσερίζω.
Deu. 1:26 Aq
9: 7 Aq Sy
1 Sa. 15:23 Sy
Psa. 5:11 Aq

προσεριθεύομαι
Eze. 23: 9 Sy

προσεριστής.
Isa. 30: 9 Aq
Eze. 2: 5 Aq Sy
12: 2 Aq Sy
17:12 Sy

προσηλύτευσις
Gen. 47: 9 Aq

προσηνεία, –νία
Ecc. 9:17 Sy

προσθήκη.
Pro. 1: 9 Aq
Eze. 27:33 Sy

πρόσθλιψις.
Psa. 42: 2 Aq

προσίημι.
Job 42: 9 Sy
Jer. 6:10 Sy

προσκινέω.
Job 31:27 Sy

προσκλίνω.
Psa. 39: 2 (Sy)

πρόσκλισις.
Eze. 7:11 Sy

προσκοπεύω.
Job 15:22 Sy

προσκοπέω.
Nu. 24:17 Aq

προσκόπησις.
Eze. 7: 7 Aq Sy

πρόσκρουσις.
Pro. 29: 6 Aq

πρόσκρουσμα
Eze. 26: 8 Th

προσπαίω.
Psa. 90:12 Sy

προσπλήρωμα.
2 Ch. 32: 5 Sy

προσπλοκή.
Exo. 28:28 Aq

πρόσπταισμα
Exo. 10: 7 Sy

προσρήγνυμι.
Psa. 2: 9 Aq
Isa. 27: 9 Aq

πρόσρηξις.
2 Sa. 5:24 (Sy)

προσταγή.
Dan. 3:28(95) LXX

προστατέω.
Est. 2: 9 Ms

προστρίβω.
Gen. 3:15 Aq
Pro. 6:13 Sy

προσφεύγω.
1 Sa. 29: 3 Sy
Eze. 29:16 Sy

προσφιλία.
Psa. 44: 1 Aq

προσφύγιον.
2 Sa. 19:42 Ms

προσφύω.
Dan. 7:20 LXX

προσφωνέω.
2 Ch. 29:28 Mss

προσωποποιΐα.
2 Sa. 14:20 Sy

προτάσσω.
Psa. 59: 9 Sy

προτιμάω.
1 Sa. 2:29 Sy

προφανῶς.
Lev. 26:43 Xm

προχωρέω.
2 Ki. 25:11 Mss

πρωτεία.
Cant. 5:13 Sy

πρωτεῖον.
Job 22:24 Sy
28:16 Sy
Psa. 44:10 Sy
77:51 Sy

πρώτιστος.
Deu. 21: 2 inc

πρωτογεννάω.
Eze. 47:12 inc

πτελέα
Isa. 41:19 Sy

πτηνός.
Job 5: 7 Aq 6th

πτῆξις.
Pro. 18: 7 A S T
Eze. 32:25 Aq rel

πτίλον, –ος.
Lev. 1:16 Sy Th
Job 39:13 Sy

πτισάνη.
2 Sa. 17:19 Aq Sy

πτύξ.
Isa. 30: 8 Sy

πτωματίζω.
Deu. 25: 2 Aq
1 Sa. 30:10, 21 Aq
Ps. 139:11 Aq

πτωχοφανής.
Pro. 13: 7 Th

πυγμαῖος.
Eze. 27:11 Aq

πύκασμα.
Ps. 117:27 Sy
Eze. 31:14 Sy

πυκνόω.
Cant. 1:16 inc

πυλωρέω.
1 Ch. 16:42 Mss

πύξινος.
Gen. 6:14 inc

πυριατός.
Exo. 25:38 rel

πυρίνιον.
Nu. 25: 8 Sy

πυρόν.
Exo. 29:18 Aq Th
Lev. 2: 3 Aq
9 Aq Th

πυρσός.
Jud. 20:38, 40 IV

πωμάζω.
Psa. 139:10 Sy

ῥεῖθρον.
Exo. 4: 9 VIIm
7:24 Aq
Job 20:17 Sy
Psa. 77:14 Sy
Isa. 27:12 Sy

ῥιγοπύρετος.
1 Sa. 21: 7 Mss

ῥιζοβολέω.
Psa. 79:10 Sy

ῥίζωσις.
Eze. 17: 5 Sy

ῥινητός.
Jer. 10: 5 Sy

ῥινόκερως.
Job 39: 9 Aq
Psa. 28: 6 Aq

ῥίξ.
1 Sa. 13:21 inc

ῥιπίζω.
Dan. 2:35 LXX

ῥῖπος.
2 Sa. 17:19 Mss

ῥιπτάζω.
Isa. 51:20 Aq

ῥοίζησις.
Exo. 19:13 Aq

ῥοίζομαι.
Isa. 29: 4 Sy

ῥοῦς.
Psa. 68: 3 Aq

ῥυθμόω.
Isa. 44:12 Sy

ῥυπόω.
Deu. 8: 4 XI

ῥύπτω.
Eze. 21:21 *Heb*

ῥώθων.
Gen. 7:22 Ms

σάγος.
Jud. 4:18 Th

σαλευτός.
Deu. 6: 8 Sy
11:18 IV

σαλπισμός.
Lev. 23:24 X*m*
Nu. 23:21 Th

σαπρός.
Lev. 27:14 *Sa*
33 X*m*

σαρδόνυξ.
Gen. 2:12 Aq

σαρκικός.
2 Ch. 32: 8 Mss

σάττω.
2 Sa. 16: 2 Mss

σαφής.
Deu. 13:14 Mss

σεβάζομαι.
Hos. 10: 5 Aq

σειρόω.
Jer. 31:12 Sy

σειρωτός.
Exo. 28:28 Sy Th

σεῖστρον.
2 Sa. 6: 5 Aq Sy

σήκωμα.
Isa. 28:17 Th

σημειοσκοπέω
Deu. 18:10 Sy
Mic. 5:12 Sy

σημειοσκόπος.
1 Sa. 28: 3, 9 *inc*

σητοβρώς.
Job 13:28 Sy

σήπη.
Job 17:14 Aq
21:26 Aq

σιγή.
Psa. 21: 3 *rel*
38: 3 Sy

σίδηρον.
2 Ki. 6: 5 Mss

σικχαίνω.
Gen. 27:46 Aq
Exo. 1:12 Aq
Pro. 3:11 *inc*
Isa. 7:16 Aq

σίκχος.
Lam. 1: 8 Sy
Eze. 7:19, 20 Sy
11:18 Sy
20: 7 Sy

σίλιγξ.
Job 28:10 Ms

σινδόνιον.
Ruth 3:15 Sy

σίρωνος.
Jud. 8:26 Mss

σιταρκισμός.
Gen. 43: 1 VII*m*

σίτησις.
Psa. 131:15 Sy

σιτίζω.
Lev. 1:16 Aq

σιτιστός.
Psa. 21:13 Sy
Jer. 26:21 Sy

σιτοδοχεῖον.
Joel 1:17 Sy

σιωπηλός.
Isa. 47: 2 Sy

σκάζω.
1 Sa. 17:39 Sy
Psa. 34:15 Sy
37:18 Sy

σκαλεύω.
1 Ki. 21:38 Aq
Psa. 63: 7 Aq
76: 7 Aq

σκάλιστρον.
Jer. 50:10 Aq Sy

σκαμβόω.
Isa. 59: 8 Aq Th

σκανδαλίζω,
—λόω.
Isa. 8:21 Sy
63:13 Aq
Dan. 11:41 LXX
Mal. 2: 8 A S T

σκασμός.
Psa. 34:15 Aq

σκαφίον.
1 Sa. 13:20 Sy

σκελισμός.
Jer. 14:14 Aq

σκέπασις.
Deu. 33:27 VII

σκεπαστός.
Nu. 7: 3 Aq
Isa. 66:20 Aq

σκέπαστρον.
Job 24:15 Sy

σκευάζω.
Exo. 23:19 Sy
Isa. 57:14 Th
62:10 Th

σκευή.
Gen. 31:25 Ms
Isa. 61:10 Sy

σκευοφύλαξ.
1 Sa. 17:22 Mss

σκέψις.
Psa. 63: 3 Sy

σκηνοποιέω.
Isa. 13:20 Sy
22:15 Sy

σκηνοποιΐα.
Deu. 31:10 Mss

σκήνωσις.
Psa. 25: 8 Sy
77:51, 60 Sy

σκιρρόω.
Isa. 27: 1 Aq

σκιρτοποιέω.
Psa. 28: 6 Th

σκιρτάω.
Psa. 28: 6 Aq

σκιώδης.
1 Sa. 10: 2 *inc*

σκληρία.
Ecc. 7:26 Mss

σκόπευσις.
Hos. 5: 1 Aq

σκοπευτής.
Isa. 56:10 Aq
Eze. 3:17 Aq

σκοπέω.
Psa. 5: 4 *inc*
Pro. 11:13 Sy

σκοπή.
Gen. 14:17 1
Deu. 3:27 Sy

σκόροδον.
Nu. 11: 5 X

σκορπισμός.
Jer. 32:20 A S T

σκοτασμός.
Psa. 87:19 Sy
Cant. 1: 5 Sy
Isa. 59: 9 Aq

σκοτομηνία.
Job 3: 6 Aq

σκοτώδης.
Mic. 4: 8 Aq

σκουτάριον.
Psa. 34: 2 *inc*

σκύβαλον.
Eze. 4:12, 15 Sy

σκύθης.
Gen. 14: 1 Sy

σκυθρώπως.
Psa. 34:14 *inc*

σκύλαξ.
Gen. 49: 9 Aq
Psa. 16:12 Ms

σκύλευσις.
Job 15:21 *Heb*

σκυλευτής.
Eze. 23:15, 23 Aq

σκύφος.
Gen. 44: 2 Aq
Exo. 25:30 Aq
Jer. 42: 5 Aq Sy

σκωληκίασις.
Job 17:14 Sy Th

σκωλόομαι.
Deu. 7:25 Ms
Hos. 9: 8 Aq

σκωρία.
Ps. 118:119 Sy
Isa. 1:25 Sy
Eze. 22:18, 19 Sy

σμήχω, σμί—
Lev. 6:28 X*m*

σμικρός.
1 Ki. 12:10 Sy

σμίλη.
Jer. 43:23 Sy

σούχινα.
1 Ki. 10:11 Aq

σπαθαρίσκος,
—ικόν.
Gen. 38:14 *inc*
Isa. 3:23 Sy

σπαίρω.
Job 26:11 Sy

σπάνις.
Deu. 28. 20 Aq
Pro. 14:28 Sy
Mal. 2: 2 Aq

σπάραγμα.
Lev. 19:28 Ms

σπαραγμός.
Isa. 51:17 Sy

σπάρτος.
Isa. 28:17 Sy

σπατάλη.
Ecc. 2: 8 Sy
Cant. 7: 6 *inc*
Isa. 13:22 Mss

σπαταλός.
Deu. 28:54 Sy

σπείρωμα.
Jer. 50:10 Aq

σπερμαίνω.
Gen. 1:29 Aq Th

σπερματία.
Psa. 64:10 Sy

σπιθαμιαῖος.
Psa. 38: 6 Sy

σπιλόω.
Lev. 15: 3 *Sa*

σπίλωμα.
Isa. 13:12 Aq

σπινθραξ.
Cant. 8: 6, 6 6th

σπόνδυλος.
1 Sa. 4:18 Sy

σπουδασμός.
Eze. 27:36 Th

σταγετός.
Pro. 19. 13 Aq

στάδιος.
Dan. 4: 4(9) LXX

σταθμίζω.
Exo. 22:17 VII*m*
Job 28:25 Aq
Pro. 24:12 Aq
Zec. 11:12 Sy

σταθμοῦχος.
Exo. 3:22 Sy

στασιάζω.
Psa. 74: 5, 5 Sy
Isa. 19: 2 Aq

στατήρ.
1 Sa. 17: 7 Aq
Eze. 4:10 Sy

στεάζω.
Psa. 19: 4 *inc*

στεῖρος.
Deu. 7:14 Aq

στενότης.
2 Ch. 15: 4 Mss

στενόω.
Pro. 4:12 Aq

στέργω.
Deu. 15: 7 Th

στερέμνιος.
Gen. 41: 2 Aq

στερεωματέω.
2 Sa. 22:43 Ms

στέφω.
Psa. 8: 6 Aq
Pro. 14:18 Th

στήλωμα.
Jud. 9: 6 Aq
Isa. 6:13 Th

στηριγμός.
Isa. 3: 1 Sy

στιβάς.
Eze. 46:23 Aq

στίζω.
Gen. 2: 8 *inc*

στιλβή.
Lev. 13:36 Sy

στιλβός.
Eze. 27:18 Sy

στιλπνότης.
Deu. 7:13 Aq
Zec. 4:14 Aq

στίμμις.
Isa. 54:11 Aq Sy

στῖφος.
Cant. 6: 9 Sy

στοίβασις.
Lev. 24: 6 Ms

στομίζομαι.
Job 39:30 Aq

στομόω.
Isa. 41:15 Sy

στόνος.
Job 4:10 Ms

στραγγεύω.
Gen. 19:16 Sy
Pro. 18: 9 Sy
24: 9 Sy
Hab. 2: 3 Sy

στράτευμα.
1 Sa. 13: 3 *inc*
Psa. 43:10 Sy

στράτευσις.
Psa. 59:12 Sy
107:12 Sy

στρέβλευμα.
Pro. 6:12 Sy

στρεβλοκάρδιος.
Pro. 17:20 Sy Th

στρεβλότης.
Pro. 4:24 Aq Th
6:14 Aq

στρεβλωτήριον
Jer. 20: 2 Sy

στρηνιάω
Isa. 61: 6 Sy

στρῆξις.
Lev. 26: 9 X*m*

στρογγύλωμα.
1 Sa. 19:13, 16 Mss

στρουθίζω.
Isa. 10:14 Th
38:14 Th

στρουθοκάμηλος.
Lev. 11:15 X*m*
Deu. 14:14 Aq
Isa. 13. 21 Aq Sy
Mic. 1: 8 Aq Sy

στρωτήρ.
Cant. 1:17 5th

στρώτης.
Jer. 31:12 Aq

στύραξ.
Gen. 37:25 Aq
43:10 Aq Sy

συγγράφω.
Ecc. 12:10 Aq Sy

συγκατάγω.
Psa. 28: 5 Sy
67:24 Sy
Eze. 6: 9 Sy

συγκατακαλύπτω
2 Ch. 4:12 Mss

συγκαταριθμέω.
Nu. 32:30 Mss

συγκεράννυμι.
Dan. 2:43 LXX

σύγκλασις.
Pro. 19:29 Th

συγκλειστής.
2 Ki. 24:16 Mss

συγκοιμάομαι.
Deu. 21:13 Mss
1 Sa. 2:22 Mss

συγκοιτάζομαι
Deu. 28:30 Aq

συγκολάπτω.
Lev. 22:24 Aq

συγκομιδή.
Exo. 23:16 Sy

συγκρατέω.
Psa. 16: 5 Sy

σύγκρουσις.
Eze. 3:13 Sy

συγκρούω.
Nu. 34:11 IV
Ps. 108:11 Sy
Isa. 29: 1 MSS

συγκρύπτω.
Psa. 82: 4 Aq
Pro. 10:14 Aq

συγκύρημα.
1 Sa. 20.26 Sy
Psa. 90: 6 Sy

συγκυρία.
1 Sa. 6: 9 Sy

συγκύφιον.
1 Sa. 6: 9 Sy

συγχρίομαι.
1 Sa. 30:19 *inc*

συγχωνεύω.
Nah. 1: 6 Aq

συγχώννυμι.
Exo. 8:14 Aq

συγχωρέω.
Est. 5:14 MSS

συγχώρησις.
Gen. 47:22 *inc*

συζυγία.
Eze. 23:17 Aq

σύζυγος.
Eze. 23:21 Aq

συκόμορον.
Psa. 77:47 Sy
Isa. 9:10 *rel*
Amos 7:14 Aq Sy

συλάω.
Exo. 3:22 Aq

συλεύω.
Exo. 3:22 Sy
Pro. 10:30 Sy Th

σύλλεγμα.
Lev. 23:22 X*m*

σύλλογος.
Psa. 1: 5 Th

συλλύω.
2 Sa. 14: 6 XI

σύμβαμα.
Ecc. 3:19 Sy

συμβολοκόπος
Pro. 23:21 AST
28: 7 Aq Th

συμβουλευτικός.
Pro. 14:17 Sy

συμβούλιον.
Pro. 15:22 Th

σύμμαχος.
Psa. 82: 9 Sy

συμμετρία.
Exo. 30:32 Aq

συμμολύνω.
Dan. 1: 8 LXX

συμπαθέω.
1 Sa. 22: 8 Sy
Job 2:11 Sy

συμπαίω.
Isa. 38:12 Aq Sy

συμπάσχω.
1 Sa. 22: 8 *inc*

συμπενθέω.
Jer. 31:17 Sy

συμπεριπλέκω.
Pro. 7:18 Aq Th

συμπλημμελέω
Hos. 4:15 AST 5th

συμπλήρωμα.
1 Ch. 16:32 MS

συμποιέω.
Isa. 37:11 AST

συμποσιάζω.
Deu. 21:20 Aq

συμπράσσω.
2 Sa. 3: 9 Sy

σύμπτωσις.
Gen. 44:29 VII*m*

συμφλογίζω.
Isa. 42:25 Th

σύμφοιτος.
Est. 7: 7 MS

συμφορά.
Eze. 7:26, 26 Sy
Zeph. 1:15 Aq

σύμφορος.
Ecc. 2: 3 Sy

συμφρυγμός.
Lev. 26:16 MSS

σύμφυλος.
Zec. 13: 7 Aq

συμφωτίζω.
Lev. 10:11 MS

συμψάω.
Jud. 5:21 MS

συνάδελφος.
Nu. 8:26 Aq

συναινέω.
Jer. 5:31 Th

συνακολουθέω.
Nu. 32:12 MS

συναλλαγή.
Ruth 4: 7 Sy
Eze. 16: 8 Aq

συναλοιάω.
Dan. 2:45 LXX

συναναλαμβάνω
Exo. 9:24 Aq

συναναπλέκω.
Job 39:13 Aq

συναντίζω.
Mic. 2: 8 Aq

συνάντισμα.
Deu. 23:10 Aq

συναπέρχομαι.
Ecc. 5:14 Sy

συναρπαγή.
Psa. 34:20 Sy

συνάφεια.
Gen. 3:16 Aq
Ps. 121: 3 Sy

συνδιαιτέομαι.
Psa. 54:15 Sy

συνεγγίζω.
Deu. 2:37 MS

συνείδω.
Lev. 5: 1 MSS
Dan. 3:14 LXX

συνειλέω.
Isa. 51:20 Th

συνεῖπον.
Dan. 2: 9 LXX

συνεισφορά.
Exo. 23:16 *Sa*

συνεκτικός.
Dan. 6: 3 Aq

συνεκτοκίζω.
Isa. 66: 9 Sy

συνεξαίρω.
Job 4:21 Th

συνεπαίρω.
Eze. 1:19, 20 Sy

συνεπιβάτης.
Isa. 22: 6 Th

συνεπίθεσις.
Ps. 118:118 Aq

συνεργός.
Isa. 38:12 Th

συνετάζω.
Psa. 15: 7 MSS

συνεταιρίζομαι
Psa. 107:10 Aq

συνευρίσκω.
1 Sa. 15: 6 Aq

συνεφίστημι.
Nu. 16: 3 MS

συνήθεια.
Pro. 17: 9 Sy

συνήθης.
Psa. 51:14 Sy
Pro. 17: 9 Sy

συνηχέω.
Psa. 58: 7 Sy
82: 3 Sy

συνθραύω.
Ecc. 12: 6 Sy

συνισόω.
Psa. 93:20 5th

συννέφεια.
Job 3: 5 Th

σύννους.
Dan. 4:16 Sy

σύνολος.
Deu. 32: 5 Sy

συνόμιλος.
Job 19:19 Sy

συνουσιάζω.
Gen. 26: 8 MS

συντέλεσις.
Ps. 118:96 Aq
Amos 1:14 MS

συντέλεσμα.
Ezra 4:13, 20 MSS

συντήκω.
2 Sa. 13: 4 MSS

συντομή.
Isa. 28:22 Aq

σύντομος.
Pro. 19:13 Aq

συντρέφω.
2 Sa. 12: 3 MSS
Isa. 33:18 MS
Dan. 1:10 LXX

συνυψόω.
Jer. 29:21 (20) MSS

συνωμοσία.
Eze. 22:25 Sy

συρράσσω.
Isa. 27:12 MSS

συρρέω.
Jer. 28:44 Sy

συσκέπτομαι.
Psa. 2: 2 Sy

σύσκεψις.
Psa. 63: 3 Sy

συσκιασμός.
Exo. 13:20 VII*m*
Psa. 26: 5 Aq
59: 8 Aq
Amos 5:26 Aq

συσσύρω.
1 Sa. 12:25 Aq
15: 6 Aq
26:10 Sy

συστάς.
Job 38:28 Aq

συστολή.
Eze. 7: 7 Aq

συσφιγκτήρ.
Psa. 44:14 Sy

σύσφιγκτος.
Ex. 28:4, 14 Aq Sy

σύσφιγμα.
Exo. 28:14 Aq Sy

σύσφιγξις.
Exo. 28:35 *rel*

συσφραγίζω.
Exo. 28:11 Th

συχνεών.
Gen. 22:13 Aq

σφαῖρα.
Isa. 29: 3 Aq Th

σφαλμός.
Ps. 120: 3 Aq
Eze. 9: 9 Aq

σφήξ.
Isa. 7:18 *Heb*, *Sa*

σφιγκτήρ.
Exo. 28:13 Aq Sy
2 Sa. 1: 9 Aq

σφίγξ.
2 Ch. 9:21 MSS

σφυρεύς.
1 Ki. 7: 2(14) MS

σφυροκοπία.
Pro. 19:29 Sy

σχετλιάζω.
Eze. 6:11 Sy

σωλήν.
Job 40:13 Sy

σώρευμα.
Gen. 31:47 *inc*

σωφρονίζω.
Isa. 38:16 Aq

σωφροσύνη.
Ecc. 10: 4 Sy

ταγή.
Jer. 52:34 MSS

ταλαιπωρίζω.
Isa. 21: 2 Sy
33: 1 Sy

ταχίζω.
Hab. 3:19 MSS

ταχυκάρδιος.
Isa. 35: 4 Th

ταῶς.
Lev. 11:18 X*m*

τέγος.
Nu. 25: 8 Aq

τεκνόω.
Gen. 16: 2 Sy
Exo. 21: 4 MS

τελείωμα.
Job 12: 2 Aq

τέλεον.
Psa. 12: 2 Aq

τέλεσμα.
Psa. 134: 7 *inc*

τελεσφορέω.
Psa. 64:10 Sy
Isa. 37:27 Sy

τέλμα.
Ps. 134: 7 *inc*
Jer. 45:22 Aq Sy

τέμαχος.
1 Sa. 17:18 *inc*

τέναγος.
Eze. 47:11 MSS

τένδα.
Nu. 25: 8 VII*m*

τενοντοκοπέω.
Exo. 34:20 Aq

τενοντόω.
Exo. 13:13 Aq
Deu. 21: 4 Aq
Isa. 66: 3 Aq

τένων.
Lev. 5: 8 X*m*
Deu. 9: 6 Aq
Job 16:12 *Heb*
Jer. 7:26 Sy

τερήστιος.
Nu. 13:34 Sy
Psa. 39: 6 Sy
76:12 Sy
118:18 Sy

τετραπρόσωπος.
Eze. 1:15, 17 MS

τέττιξ.
Jer. 8: 7 Sy

τεῦχος.
Psa. 39: 8 Sy
Isa. 8: 1 Sy
Eze. 2: 9 Sy

τέχνημα.
Lev. 8: 7 MS

τηγανιστόν.
1 Ch. 9:31 MSS
23:29 MSS

τηλαύγασμα.
Lev. 13:24 MSS

τημελέω.
Psa. 30: 4 Sy
Isa. 40:11 Sy

τιθασός.
Jer. 11:19 Sy

τιθηνίζω.
Isa. 53: 2 Aq

τιμουλκέω.
Pro. 11:26 *inc*

τιμιόω.
Psa. 71:14 Aq Sy

τίτθη.
Gen. 24:59 Aq

τιτθίζω, τιθι—
Isa. 53: 2 Aq

τιτθός.
Pro. 5:19 Aq
7:18 AST
Eze. 23: 3 Sy XII

τλάω.
Pro. 9:12 MSS

τμῆμα.
Psa. 74: 7 5th
135:13 *inc*

τονθορυστής.
Pro. 16:28 Aq
26:20, 22 Aq

τοπαρχία.
2 Ch.13:19 inc

τραγάκανθα.
Jud. 8: 7 Aq

τράγημα.
Deu.33:13,14,15 Aq

τραγωδός.
Gen. 31:27 VII

τρανῶς.
Isa. 32: 4 Sy

τραυματισμός.
Isa. 53:10 Sy

τραχηλοκοπέω
Exo. 34:20 Sy
Isa. 66: 3 Sy

τραχύτης.
Psa. 30:21 Aq

τριβανόω.
Psa. 6: 8 Sy

τριγχός.
1 Sa. 25:22 inc
Jer. 30: 3 Mss

τρίζω, –ζέω.
Isa. 38:14 Sy
Amos 2:13 Aq

τριήμερος.
1 Sa. 9:20 Sy

τριήρης.
Isa. 33:21 Aq

τρίμμα.
Gen.25:34 Ms

τρίοδος.
Jer. 45:14 Sa

τριπλόω.
Ecc. 4:12 Sy

τρισκελής, –λίς.
1 Sa. 13:21 inc

τρισμός.
Psa. 65:11 Aq

τρίστεγος.
Gen. 6:16 Sy
Eze. 42: 6 Sy

τρίσωμος.
Isa. 40:12 Aq

τριχιάω.
Lev. 17: 7 Aq
Deu. 32: 2, 17 Aq
Isa. 13:21 Aq
34:14 AST

τριχόω.
Gen.25:25 Sy

τρόπαιον.
2 Sa. 8: 3 Sy
Isa. 63: 3 Th

τροποφορέω.
Deu. 1:31 Mss

τρόπωσις.
1 Ki.22:35 Mss

τρυγάζω.
Jer. 29:20 Aq

τρυπανισμός.
Isa. 51:12 Aq

τρυπητήριον.
Exo. 21: 6 VIIm

τρυφαλίς.
1 Sa. 17:18 inc

τρυφερία.
Gen. 18:12 Aq
1 Sa. 15:32 Aq

τρυφερῶς.
Pro. 15: 1 Th

τρυφητής.
Deu.28:54 Aq
Amos 6: 7 Sy

τρῶσις.
Psa. 76:11 Sy
Cant. 7: 1 Sy
Eze. 30:11 Sy

τύφω.
Isa. 42: 3 Ms

τυφῶν.
Psa. 148: 8 inc

τύφων.
Isa. 13:21 Aq

ὑδραγώγιον.
2 Sa. 8: 1 Aq

ὕδρευμα.
Jer. 46:10 Th

ὑδροκηλία, –κε–
Hos. 5:10 Sy

ὑδροποτέω.
Dan. 1:12 LXX

ὑλομανέω.
Hos. 10: 1 Sy

ὑλοχαρέω.
Isa. 35: 2 Mss

ὑμνητός.
Psa. 47: 2 rel

ὑμνολογέω.
Psa. 55:11 Sy
64: 9 Sy

ὑμνολογία.
Job 33:26 Sy
Psa. 64: 9 Sy
149: 6 Sy

ὑμνοποιέω.
Psa. 55:11 Sy

ὗνις.
1 Sa. 13:20 Sy

ὑπαγκώνιον.
Eze. 13:18 Sy

ὑπαναχωρέω.
Gen. 16: 6 X

ὑπαντάω.
Dan.10:14 LXX

ὕπαρ.
Psa. 125: 1 inc

ὕπαρχος.
Psa. 2: 2 Sy
Dan. 6: 7 Mss

ὑπαυχένιος.
Eze. 13:18 Sy Th

ὑπενδίδωμι.
Eze. 3: 9 Sy

ὑπεραθετέω.
Psa. 88:39 Aq

ὑπεραπατάω.
Isa. 29: 9 Mss

ὑπεράποθνήσκω.
Jud. 9:17 Mss

ὑπερασπιστήρ.
Psa. 17:36 Sy

ὑπέρβασις.
Exo. 12:11 Aq

ὑπερβολή.
1 Sa. 2: 3 Sy
Jer. 14:14 Sy

ὑπερδικάζω.
Psa. 9: 5 inc

ὑπερδικέω.
Psa. 42: 1 Sy
67: 6 Sy
118:154 Sy

ὑπέρεισμα.
Psa. 53: 6 Sy

ὑπερεκβλύζω.
Pro. 3:10 inc

ὑπερέκχυσις.
Job 41: 6 Aq

ὑπερεπαίρω.
Ps. 106:41 Aq
138: 6 Aq

ὑπερέπαρσις.
Psa. 47: 4 Aq

ὑπερεπιθυμέω.
Psa. 118:173 Sy

ὑπερζέω.
Gen. 49: 4 Sy

ὑπερηφάνως.
Psa. 16:10 Sy
30:23 Sy

ὑπερκρίνω.
Psa. 50: 6 Aq

ὑπερλείπω.
1 Sa. 14:36 Mss

ὑπερμαχέω.
Deu.33: 7 Sy
1 Sa. 11: 3 Sy
Psa. 77:35 Sy
Isa. 63: 1 Sy

ὑπερμάχησις.
Exo.12:11 Sy

ὑπερμάχομαι.
Gen.15: 1 Sy

ὑπερνικάω.
Psa. 42: 1 inc

ὑπερόγκως.
Isa. 28: 7 Th

ὑπερόριος.
Jos. 15:33 Ms

ὑπερόχησις.
Eze. 40:21 Sy

ὑπερφέρεια.
Job 37: 3 Aq
40: 5 inc
Pro. 16:18 Aq

ὑπέρφοβος.
Dan. 7:19 LXX

ὑπερφρονέω.
Job 31:13 Sy
41: 6 Sy

ὑπηρετέω.
Gen. 49:15 Sa
Nu. 4:23 Ms

ὑπόγειος.
Psa. 118:85 Sy

ὑποδείκτης.
Psa. 83: 7 Sy

ὑποδιδάσκω.
Neh. 8: 7 Mss

ὑποδίπλωσις.
Job 41: 4 Sy

ὑποθάλπω.
Gen. 1: 2 Sa

ὑπόκρισις.
Psa. 34:16 Sy

ὑπόνοια.
Dan.4:12(16) LXX

ὑπορθόω.
Psa. 43:19 Sy
72: 2 Sy

ὑπορύσσω.
Psa. 34: 7 Sy
118:85 Sy

ὑποσπασμός.
Deu.15: 1 Aq

ὑποσπάω.
Psa. 140: 6 Aq

ὑποσταλάζω.
Psa. 32: 8 Aq

ὑπόστεμμα.
2 Sa. 17:28 Sy

ὑπόστρωμα.
2 Sa. 17:28 Sy
Isa. 28:20 Th
Eze. 13:18 Sy

ὑποσχίζω.
Isa. 28:24 Sy

ὑποτύφω.
Pro. 6:27 AST

ὑπούλως.
Lev. 19:16 Xm

ὑπουργέω.
Exo. 35:18 VIIm
Nu. 18: 2 Mss
2 Sa. 9:10 Aq

ὑπουργία.
Exo. 35:18 VIIm
Nu. 7: 3 Sy

ὑπόφορος.
Jos. 16:10 Mss

ὑπόχυμα.
Lev. 21:20 Aq

ὑποχώρησις.
Eze. 40:21 Sy

ὑπώρεια.
Jos. 15:33 Ms

ὑφή, ὕφος.
Lev. 8: 7 Xm
1 Sa. 6: 8 Aq

φαγέδαινα.
Deu.28:20 Aq
1 Sa. 5:11 Aq
14:20 Aq

φαγεδαινόω.
Deu. 7:23 Aq

φακωτός.
Lev. 21:20 VIIm

φαλάκρωσις.
Mic. 1:16 Aq Sy

φαντάζω.
Isa. 56:10 Aq

φαρμακόω.
Psa. 57: 6 inc

φάρος.
Lev. 6:11, 11 Xm
16:23 Xm

φατνεύω.
Pro. 14: 4 Th

φατνιάζομαι.
Pro. 14: 4 Aq

φαύσκω.
Gen. 44: 3 X

φεῖσις.
Lev. 20:17 Xm

φθείρ.
Exo. 8:16 inc

φθογγή.
Job 37: 1 Aq
Psa. 9:17 Th
Isa. 59:11 Aq

φθονερός.
Pro. 28:22 inc

φιλανθρωπία.
Psa. 111: 3 inc

φιλάς.
Exo. 26:24 inc

φίλη.
Cant. 1:15 Aq
2: 2 Aq

φιλίππειος.
Pro. 8:19 Th

φιλοπονία.
Ecc. 2:10 Sy

φιλόσοφος.
Dan. 1:20 LXX

φιλοτροφέω.
1 Sa. 28:24 Sy

φίλτρον.
Cant. 2: 5 Sy

φλοιός.
Job 30: 4 Sy

φλύαρος.
Pro. 16:28 inc

φόβημα.
Deu. 4:34 Aq
Psa. 9:21 Aq

φολιδωτός.
1 Sa. 17: 5 Aq

φολίς.
Lev. 11: 9 Ms
Deu. 14: 9 Aq
Job 41: 4 Sy

φονεύς.
2 Ki. 9:31 Mss

φορά.
Psa. 66: 7 Sy
Hab. 3:17 Mss

φορτικός.
Job 7:20 inc

φοσσατεύω.
Gen. 49:19 VIIm

φοσσάτον.
Gen. 49:19 VIIm
Exo. 14:24 VIIm

φουρκίζω.
Nu. 25: 4 VIIm

φράγμα.
2 Sa. 24: 7 Aq Sy

φρονίμως.
Ecc. 7:11 Sy

φρουρέω.
Psa. 87: 9 Sy

φρούρημα.
Job 38:16 Aq

φρούρησις.
2 Sa. 5:23 Ms
24 Aq Sy

φρούριον.
Jud. 6: 2 Sy
2 Ki.23:11 Sy
1 Ch.11: 5 Sy

φρουρός.
2 Sa. 8: 6 Sy
2 Ki.23:11 Sy

φρυκτός.
Jos. 5:11 Aq Sy
Ruth 2:14 inc
1 Sa. 25:18 Aq
2 Sa. 17:28 AS

φυλακτήριος.
Eze. 13:18 Heb

φύλαξις.
Exo. 12:42 Sa
Isa. 26: 3 Aq

φῦλον.
Psa. 2: 1 Aq
43: 3 Aq
148:11 Aq

φῦσα.
Lev. 1:16 Sy Th

φύσημα.
Deu. 8:15 Aq
Job 20:26 Sy
Psa. 26:12 Sy

φύσις.
Gen. 1: 2 *Sa*

φωλεός.
Jer. 17: 6 *Sa*

φωλεύω.
Job 38:10 MSS

φώνημα
Amos 4:13 Sy

φωτεινός.
Psa. 138:11 Sy

χαίτη.
Job 18:16 Sy
Psa. 79:12 Sy 6th

χαλκουργός.
Neh. 3:32 MSS

χαράκωμα.
Jer. 52: 4 Sy

χάρισμα.
Psa. 30:22 Th

χαριστικός.
Psa. 111: 5 Sy

χαριτόω.
Psa. 17:26, 26 Sy

χάρμα.
Psa. 47: 3 Aq

χαροποιέω.
Psa. 20: 7 Sy

χαροπός.
Gen. 49:12 MSS
Pro. 23:29 Sy

χαυνόω.
Psa. 64:11 Sy

χείλωμα.
Exo. 38: 2 Aq

χειράλυσις.
Jer. 47: 1 Sy

χειριδωτός.
Gen. 37: 3 Sy
2 Sa. 13:18 Sy

χειρονομέω.
1 Sa. 19: 9 MS

χελών.
Jer. 52:20 Aq

χερμαδιέω.
Deu. 21:21 Aq

χερσεία.
Jer. 29:14 (Aq)

χεῦμα.
Deu. 7:13 Aq

χιλιοπλασίων.
2 Sa. 18: 3 Sy

χιονίζω.
Psa. 67:15 Sy

χλαμύς.
1 Sa. 24: 5 Sy

χλευάζω.
Pro. 4:21 Th
14: 9 Aq Th
19:28 Aq Th
Isa. 28:22 Aq Th

χλευαστής.
Psa. 1: 1 Aq
Pro. 20: 1 Aq Th
22:10 A S T
Isa. 28:14 Sy Th

χοίρειος.
Isa. 66:17 Sy

χοῖρος.
Psa. 79:14 MS
Isa. 65: 4 Sy
66: 3 Sy

χολάω.
Psa. 77:21, 59 Sy
88:39 Sy

χορεία.
Psa. 52: 1 A T 5th
87: 1 Aq

χρειώδης.
Ecc. 12:10 Sy

χρεοδοσία.
Deu. 24:13(11) Aq

χρηματιστήριον.
1 Ki. 6: 9(5) Aq Sy
2 Ch. 5: 7 MSS
Psa. 27: 2 Aq Sy

χρύσινος.
Gen 45:22 *Sa*

χυδαιόω.
Isa. 33: 9 Aq

χωλεύω.
Gen. 33:13 MSS

χωνεύω.
1 Ki. 20:15 MSS

χωρογραφέω.
Jos. 18: 8 *inc*

χῶρος.
Jos. 1: 9 *rel*

ψαθυρόω.
Jos. 9:11(5) Aq
Ps. 101: 4 Aq

ψαλμῳδός.
1 Ch. 6:33 MSS

ψευδολογέω.
Dan. 11:27 LXX

ψεῦσμα.
Job 13: 4 Sy
34: 6 A S T
Psa. 61: 5 Sy
Pro. 23: 3 Aq Th

ψηφίον.
Amos 9: 9 Aq

ψηφίς.
Pro. 24:62 Sy

ψηφολογέω.
Cant. 3:10 5th

ψιθύρισμα.
Job 26:14 Sy

ψύα.
Lev. 3: 9 X*m*
2 Sa. 2:23 Xl
3:27 Xl
Psa. 37: 8 Sy Th

ὠράριον.
Gen. 38:18 *Sa*

ὡρολόγιον.
Isa. 38: 8 Sy

ὤρυγμα.
Isa. 5:29 Sy Th

ὡσανεί.
Gen. 37: 7 Sy

ὠχρίασις.
Amos 4: 9 Th

www.ingramcontent.com/pod-product-compliance
Lightning Source LLC
Chambersburg PA
CBHW020844020726
47497CB00005B/1241

* 9 7 8 3 3 3 7 2 3 5 8 1 9 *